TOUCHED

THE COMPLETE SERIES

BOOK ONE

TOUCHED

THE CARESS OF FATE

A novel by

Elisa S. Amore

Translated by

Leah Janeczko

Evan's first chapters translated by

Anne Crawford

Text AMORE to 77948 to get new release alerts!

Join the conversation about the *Touched* saga using the official hashtags:
#TouchedSaga or #Thecaressoffate.

Visit the official site to discover games, quizzes, book trailers, and much more at:
www.touchedsaga.com

Follow TOUCHED on:
Facebook.com/TheTouchedSaga
Twitter.com/TheTouchedSaga

If you have any questions or comments, please write us at
touchedsaga@gmail.com

For Foreign and Film/TV rights queries, please send an email to
elisa.amore@touchedsaga.com

PRAISE FOR THE *TOUCHED* SAGA
What readers are saying about *Touched*

"The most passionate saga of recent times."—Franci Cat

"The many emotions and plot twists plus the fast-paced dialogue make this story an absolutely brilliant first novel."—Sognando tra le righe blog

"These two are the new Romeo and Juliet."—Coffee and Books blog

"Enough with vampires, enough with werewolves, the new masters of fantasy are the Angels—and not just any Angels, but Angels of Death. A love story that takes hold of your mind, warms your heart, and touches your soul." —Valeria D.

"A really amazing fantasy novel where love is mixed with the supernatural in a superb way."—IlRecensore

"I felt like Gemma, I felt her joy and her pain along with her. I also felt Evan's anger, his love, gentleness, and fear, all along with him."
—Libri Per Passione blog

"From a paranormal point of view, what strikes me most, apart from the Norwegian legends about the Subterraneans, is the coexistence of two supernatural figures that are rarely seen together."—Sangue Blu

"A strong, passionate love that is able to defy any obstacle and any fate."—Bliss

"Beautiful, riveting, and damn romantic."—Tea, Amazon

"I was very intrigued by Evan's point of view: his inner battle between the desire to love Gemma and to do his duty."—Beatrice, Booklovers blog

"Evan, an Angel of Death fighting for the life of his love even though it is he who has been designated to be her executioner; and Gemma, a human being so courageous, so in love that she does not fear even death. It really touched me."—Elena, R. Fantasy blog

"It is a story that hits you straight in the heart. It really moves you, and not all stories can do that."—The Bookworm

"If you loved *Twilight, Hush, Hush, Fallen* and other sagas, you can't miss this book for anything in the world."—Angela, Amazon

To my husband Giuseppe and little Gabriel Santo
Thanks to you I'm a better person.
You mean everything to me.

What are you willing to sacrifice when the only person who can save you is the same one who has to kill you?

PROLOGUE

Lake Minnewanka, Canada

Long ago, people believed that when someone died, the Angel of Death was already there, ready and waiting to take his soul. Whispered legends heightened the fear of death. It's not death people should be afraid of, though; it's time. They say time is like a snowflake: if you try to catch it in your hand, it only melts faster. The truth is no one can stop time . . . nor can they know when their own will run out.

I held an ice crystal in my palm and watched it melt. It was beginning to snow. The mist had crept like a ghost over Lake Minnewanka, where Benson had moored his father's expensive boat. I snorted. It didn't matter how cocky the kid acted, he was just a little boy with a wallet as overstuffed as his ego.

Smoothing his thick black curls, Benson came up behind Harley. He grabbed her by the hips and ran a hand over her curves, accentuated by the wetsuit she wore. "Hey, you never told me how sexy you are with this outfit on," he murmured against her cheek.

Harley's fair skin was reddened by the cold, but she was not a girl to be easily intimidated—either by the cold or by unwanted advances. "Keep your hands where they belong, Ben. We didn't come here for this." She shook him off and moved away, pulling the neoprene hood over her blond hair and checking her oxygen tank to make sure it was full.

"Says who?" Ben said with a sneer.

"Says me," Tom cut in, exasperated by Ben's arrogance. He was a lanky redhead, considerably thinner than Ben. Like Harley, he'd put on his wetsuit while Benson had been guzzling yet another beer. I'd lost count of how many he'd downed.

We were at the lake because they wanted to try out their new diving gear—except for Benson, that is. He had no intention of diving himself and had only come along for the chance to impress Harley.

I turned and caught sight of my reflection in the window of the small stateroom. My unruly hair fell over my forehead. The mist made it look darker. In contrast, my silvery gray eyes flashed like lightning in an ice storm. Behind me, the others were arguing over nothing. I wasn't going to get involved. Not yet.

"Hey, Red, throw me those beers," Benson ordered. He began to snigger. "Fuck, you look ridiculous in that wetsuit! Like a shrimp that's gone bad."

"At least I can take it off. Too bad you can't do the same with your face, dickhead."

"Wanna try?" Benson shot back with a sneer.

Harley got up and placed herself between the two. "Knock it off, Ben! We're not here to fight, we're here to dive. And we'd better get a move on before the weather gets worse. I want to see the ghost city."

"Right, guys, go ahead and dive into the 'lake of the spirits,'" he replied derisively.

Harley snorted, hiding a smile. "Those are just superstitions. It was the sudden strong gusts of wind that made the indigenous people believe the lake was haunted. That's why they called it the 'lake of the spirits.' On the other hand, the submerged town *is* real, and I want to see it."

It was true. The icy waters of Lake Minnewanka concealed an entire town, submerged after the construction of a dam. Now the empty, ruined buildings lay at the bottom of the lake, a ghost town frozen in time.

"You'd better stay here, you might wet your pants," Tom taunted.

Benson shoved him roughly. "Since you're gonna be in the water anyway, why don't you just swim back to shore, little shrimp?"

"Ben, you're such an asshole when you're drunk," the girl scolded him.

Tom laughed. "Only when he's drunk?"

"Say that again, shrimp," Ben spat, giving him another shove.

"What the fuck? You two act like a couple of first-graders. I don't know what I was thinking of, inviting you along, Ben," Harley said, disgusted.

"My boat, maybe?" Benson answered her. "Or maybe you were interested in something else . . ." He smirked.

I approached them and leaned against the railing, continuing to ignore them. I preferred to focus my attention on the sepulchral wail of the wind as it announced the coming storm. The wind and I had a lot in common: no one could see us. Like a ghost, I watched these three young people as they frittered away the fleeting time their mortal lives allowed them on Earth.

I wasn't a ghost, though. I was something much worse, and all too soon they would realize it.

"Let me go, Ben!"

The girl's protests cut into my thoughts. Benson had moved close to her again and was embracing her against her will.

"I know why you came," he slurred.

"I told you to knock it off!" she insisted.

"Come on, I'll show you." He pushed her against the cabin wall and kissed her, ignoring her protests.

"Hey!" Tom grabbed Benson by the shoulder. "Did you pour beer into your ears too? She just told you to leave her alone."

"You'd better watch out. Don't you know sharks eat shrimp for breakfast?" Benson gave him another rough shove and tried to hit him, but Tom easily evaded his lurching attack, returning it with a right hook to the other boy's nose.

The sudden searing pain made Benson cover his face. Pulling his fingers away, he saw they were stained with blood. He lunged forward and tackled the other boy around the waist, hurling him to the ground and raining blows on him.

"Ben, stop it!" Harley implored him. "You'll kill him!" She tried to pull him off, but he sent her flying with a shove, cracking her head against the wall.

Rage boiled up in Tom. Throwing the other boy off him, he got up, wiping the blood from his nose with the back of his hand. "That's enough now, buddy," he said, trying to reason with Benson. "You're sloppy drunk. It's time to lay off the booze."

"And I'm telling you it's time to take a cold bath. Isn't that what you came here for?" With a drunken laugh, Benson lunged at Tom, who stepped nimbly out of the way. The other boy toppled over the railing into the water.

With a satisfied smile, Tom hurried to Harley and helped her up. "Are you okay?"

She nodded, dazed. "Fine. I'm sorry I dragged you out here."

"I told you it was a bad idea. And now we have to fish that idiot out of the water."

"A cold dip is just what he needed," Harley said. They looked over the bow of the boat, scornful expressions on their faces.

"Hey, shark boy, who's gonna be swimming to shore now?" Tom called down. He and Harley scanned the lake, but saw no sign of Benson.

"Where did he go?" she wondered, the beginnings of concern in her voice.

Tom leaned over the bow, his eyes on the water. "Shit," he muttered, his expression grim.

"Ben!" cried the girl. A spectral silence seemed to creep into her bones. Her panic mounting, she called again, "Benson! Come on out! This isn't funny! Why isn't he responding? He said he knew how to swim."

"He was too drunk. Let's check the stern. Maybe he passed out and he's floating somewhere around here."

They made the rounds of the boat, squinting over the edge at the dark water, but there was no trace of Benson.

"He isn't anywhere!" Harley cried in dismay. "We have to look for him."

"You stay here in case he appears," Tom said, beginning to get ready. "If he's down there, I'll find him. He can't have just vanished. I'd better hurry, though. He's not wearing a wetsuit and hypothermia comes on quickly." He strapped on his oxygen tank and ran to the swim platform. Harley watched as he submerged himself in the water, disappearing from view in a few seconds.

The snowflakes were falling faster now, as if they too wanted to join the search for Benson. I approached Harley, who was anxiously scanning the lake, waiting for her missing friend to reemerge. As I rested my hand on hers, I felt the shiver run through her body. Agitated, she turned toward me. She was so close I could feel her breath against my chest. To her, though, I was invisible. She couldn't see me. No one could.

She looked over my shoulder at her diving gear. "Oh, to hell with it," she muttered. She couldn't sit there waiting with her arms folded. Pulling on her fins and her oxygen tank, Harley plunged into the freezing waters of Lake Minnewanka. I watched as she disappeared beneath the surface.

The mist crept over the lake as if wanting to hide any trace of the three teens. I saw them, though. All three of them. I could hear the beating of their hearts, the chattering of Benson's teeth, the sinister sound of the water as it flowed around them . . .

It was Tom who found him first, lying at the bottom of the lake. He had gotten caught on something. Harley saw them and rushed to help, sharing her mouthpiece with him so he could breathe while Tom freed him. It only took a second. They knew there wasn't much time.

I could hear their hearts beating nearer and faster as fatigue overtook them. I stepped onto the swim platform and bent to touch the water. Reflected in the surface, my gray eyes shone, reminding me of who I was . . . and what I had come to do.

It was time.

My reflection contorted as the water froze under my fingers. Beneath the mist, the layer of ice raced toward the borders of the lake, forming an impenetrable barrier. I watched as Tom, Harley and Ben rose from the bottom of the lake only to find a slab of ice blocking their way. The three teens swam desperately in the direction of the shore, trying to find the edges of the ice, but without success. They looked at each other, the incomprehension on their faces turning to terror.

They were trapped.

I could read in their terrified eyes the thoughts crowding their minds as the adrenaline surged frantically through their veins. They beat their fists impotently against the ice, but there was nothing that could free them from their frozen prison . . . because I was there for them. As I closed my fist the air remaining in their tanks vanished. They thrashed in the water, desperately seeking oxygen, tearing off their now useless mouthpieces. The more they struggled, though, the more their lungs filled with icy water.

Three heartbeats slowed and stopped.

They say the true meaning of life can only be understood when one is face to face with death. I got to my feet and looked Harley in the eyes just as the spark of life was extinguished in her. The exact instant when she surrendered to time, mourning the snowflakes she would never catch in her hand.

A freezing wind gusted over the waters of the Minnewanka as three souls left their bodies. I was still gazing into Harley's lifeless eyes when I heard her voice behind me.

"Who are you?"

Clenching my fists, I turned to face her. The souls of the three teens stared at me, awaiting my answer. *Now* they could see me.

"My name is Evan James." I lifted my silver-gray eyes to theirs. "I am Death."

My somber words lost themselves in the mist as the ice imprisoning the lake receded. Three lifeless bodies floated on the surface.

Their time on Earth had run out.

Angels are not what you think they are. Nor are their duties.

1

WHEN EVERYTHING CHANGED

Lake Placid, NY

I materialized in the garage, the motion detector switching on the lights as I appeared. It was where I spent a large part of my time when I wasn't busy taking the lives of mortals. Pulling the cover off my motorcycle, I climbed into the saddle and the engine rumbled. It was an MV Agusta F4 CC—a true collector's item, seeing as only a hundred of them had ever been made. There was nothing more satisfying than a good race after a mission, especially because it helped fill the time until the next one. I twisted the accelerator and an aggressive roar rebounded off the walls of the garage. The door rose at my command and I rode out, ready to speed along the deserted mountain roads under cover of the morning mist.

My rides were the only times I materialized, allowing myself to be seen by mortals. I rose up onto my back wheel, overtaking a solitary car. The driver leaned on the horn.

I smiled to myself. He wouldn't be so quick to react that way if he knew who he was dealing with. In my human form, my eyes were a normal chocolate brown. No one would have suspected that beneath the mask was a Soldier of Death with eyes of ice. With a single touch I could kill him instantly. I hadn't received an execution order for that particular human, however. His soul was safe for now.

The bike's engine rumbled underneath me as I sped away from him. Every day I felt the lives of dozens of people flowing through my fingers, yet the only time I felt truly alive was when I was on my bike.

A shiver of excitement ran up my spine. The time I spent tinkering with my bike and polishing it in the garage relaxed me, but riding it was a whole different ball game. I felt the adrenaline coursing through my veins like a tormented soul trapped inside me. I closed my eyes, savoring the moment. When I opened them, my inner executioner had awakened again.

It was time. My new mission awaited me. I could feel it in every part of me. I halted my motorcycle at the edge of the forest and dematerialized. It would be a quick one.

I found myself in the midst of the forest, helplessly attracted by the soul I'd been assigned to. I heard his heartbeat before I saw him. A heart that would soon cease to beat. Adam Lussi was walking briskly through the trees. He was bald, but robust and strongly built. Though not yet fifty, a heart attack would suddenly cut his life short.

I stopped some distance from him. I had no need to come any closer in order to carry out my mission. I clenched my fist and his heart rate accelerated. He leaned against the trunk of a tree, short of breath, and brought a hand to his chest as the pain increased. Pearls of perspiration beaded his forehead.

Suddenly a shout broke the silence of the forest. "Iron! Irony, come out of there! Where are you?" It was a girl. She was so upset she didn't even realize Adam was there. I watched as he approached her, coming up behind her. Her arrival had distracted me, allowing him to catch his breath again. "Hey! You lost?" Adam asked her. "Need help? I could give you a ride home."

The girl backed away from him, on her guard. I felt her heartbeat accelerate. "I'm looking for my dog."

"Sorry. I haven't seen him."

"Thanks. I'll keep looking." She scanned the forest around her, a worried look on her face. No doubt she thought it was wiser not to be too trusting.

She had no idea what the real danger hiding in the forest was.

"All right then, but be careful. It'll be getting dark soon and the forest isn't a safe place to be at night."

The girl nodded and quickly vanished among the trees.

"You don't know just how dangerous it can be," I muttered to myself, returning my attention to my mission. I needed to hurry. Adam's time was just about to run out, and I needed to secure his soul. I dematerialized, reappearing in the prearranged place I would wait for the man. The moment had arrived.

I heard a heartbeat approaching, and prepared myself to finish my mission, but all at once I realized that the sound I sensed wasn't coming from Adam's heart. It was the girl again. She was looking around her with a worried expression, peering into the trees as if she were afraid of something. As if she knew what they were hiding. What had brought her into the heart of the forest?

All at once, a small animal emerged from behind a bush. It was her dog. The girl ran to scoop it up.

"Irony, finally I found you!" she exclaimed, her voice breaking.

I felt Adam's soul calling to me. He was coming. "Damn it," I muttered. The girl had better leave, or I would have to find a way to make her go. Suddenly, I felt her heart skip a beat. Wondering what had happened, I turned to look at her. Her long dark hair hung over her shoulders, but couldn't hide her tension. Her body stiffened. She tilted her head slightly in my direction as if perceiving some danger behind her.

Just then she turned abruptly and her eyes bored into mine.

A shudder ran through my body and I held my breath. For one absurd instant I was afraid I had materialized involuntarily, but that wasn't the case. I was still in my ethereal body. My eyes were as gray as molten silver. I was invisible to mortals. Even so, she continued to gaze at me—as if she could actually see me.

I furrowed my brow and looked deep into her eyes, huge dark eyes that held a power unknown to me. Her heartbeat accelerated, but without fear this time. *I* was the one to feel fear, trapped as I was by her spell.

"Gemma!" A distant shout abruptly severed the connection between us. She turned toward the voice. I took advantage of the distraction to leap into a tree, from where I continued to watch her.

"Peter! I'm here," she called back.

A boy joined her, breathing heavily from exertion. "You scared the shit out of me! Are you crazy, taking off like that? I've looked everywhere for you!"

She said nothing, her expression unsettled. It was her heart that gave me the answer. It beat ever faster as she surreptitiously looked around her, searching for me. I remained hidden, like a fugitive ghost, as the breeze stirred the leaves on the trees.

"Where did he go?" she murmured uneasily.

"Where did who go?" Her friend was confused.

"There was a boy . . . " the girl said, more to herself than to her friend. She seemed disappointed that I'd vanished.

I peered down from the tree so I could see her better. Who was she? And why did she have such power over me? Suddenly I almost wanted to show myself, to see if I would still be visible to her. I shook my head at the insane thought. I couldn't show myself. No matter who she was.

The two of them left the clearing, the girl scanning the trees as she went, forcing me to remain hidden. It was as if she sensed my presence. The very thought was absurd, though. Absurd and incredible.

Someone else appeared on the path beneath me. It was Adam, the mortal I'd come to kill. I clenched my jaw, mentally scolding myself for allowing my attention to be distracted from my mission. It was the only thing that mattered. I had to stay focused.

I leapt down from the tree, landing on him and breaking his neck with one brutal blow. Adam didn't feel a thing. He collapsed on the ground, lifeless.

When I saw what I'd done, I slammed my fist into the trunk of a tree. "Fuck!" I muttered, furious with myself. I'd made a mistake. The deaths we brought about were always supposed to look like natural ones. Instead, I'd made it look like a homicide for which the culprit would never be found.

I vanished and materialized in the spot I'd left my bike. I climbed on, started the engine, and took off like a missile. The aggressive roar of my bike echoed through the trees, but no matter how fast I went, I couldn't outrun the feelings tormenting me. I was angry with myself. Not because I'd made a mistake, but because I didn't care. All I could think about were that girl's eyes, deep as an abyss that had swallowed me up. They filled my mind and there was an unfamiliar feeling in my chest, an excitement I hadn't felt before.

How was it possible that she'd seen me?

I had to find out. I had to see her again.

2

A REAPER'S DUTIES

Hidden by the darkness, I watched the girl and her friend entering their houses, which were across the street from each other. I felt torn, as if I were betraying a part of myself. I was used to studying souls; the difference was that this time I wasn't studying hers for a mission. I was doing it only for myself.

I shook my head. What the hell was I doing? I should just go home. But then, she was different from anyone else I'd ever met. No one had ever seen me while I was in my ethereal form. I had to find out more.

I materialized in her room. I knew she wasn't there, because there was no trace of her soul. It was easy to figure out the personalities of mortals based on the objects they accumulated. Maybe I could find the answers I sought in her possessions. Her shelves were crammed with books whose titles I scrutinized. Some were classics, others contemporary. She seemed to be attracted to paranormal themes, based on the number of books she had about ghosts, vampires, and witches. I hid a smile; she would never expect an Angel of Death to be rummaging through her things.

One volume, tossed carelessly on the bed, caught my eye: *Jane Eyre*, by Charlotte Brontë. I ran my fingers over the cover, fascinated. I knew the story well, and it seemed she also had read it more than once, judging by its well-worn cover. I opened it, increasingly intrigued by the girl I'd seen—Gemma, I suddenly remembered. She had filled the margins with notes, thoughts, and opinions about the story. I smiled. In some places she'd even gone so far as to disagree with the author. The depths of her soul must be profound.

I put the book back where I'd found it and turned my attention to the photos tacked to the walls. There were dozens of her and her neighbor Peter. A thought flashed through my mind: were they in a relationship? I searched the walls for a photo that might confirm my suspicion, but it remained unclear.

On her shelves were a collection of cameras and rolls of film. So she liked books and photography. There was also a typewriter on her desk. I pressed one of the keys and my mind filled with memories of the past, of when I'd been a mortal myself. I had loved writing and drawing.

All at once the doorknob turned, filling me with panic. It was Gemma. I could sense her soul. I materialized near the door, terrified by the idea that I might not be able to hide myself from her. I did have another choice, of course—I could leave before she saw me. I didn't even consider the possibility.

"Who turned the lights on?" she murmured to herself. She closed the door and turned toward me. I held my breath, but she just hung up her backpack and turned away again. I frowned, confused. Could she not see me any more? Had I just imagined it all?

Nonetheless, I made the most of my new opportunity, excited by the chance to observe her more closely. I stood beside her. She was reviewing the photos she'd taken that day. I peered at the camera screen, fascinated. What was she looking at that was so interesting? Without realizing it, I brushed against her. She stiffened and I saw a shiver run through her. Gooseflesh rose on her arms. She glanced around the room with the same curious look on her face I'd seen in the forest, as if she knew I was still there. I studied her closely, more and more amazed.

Not only had she seen me, *she could perceive my presence.* The irrational impulse to brush against her again rose in me.

I shook my head, trying to banish my ridiculous thoughts. What was happening to me? I had to remember who I was . . . and what my duties were. For some reason, the girl held a strange power over me, the power to make me forget those basic facts. I must be careful. It wasn't impossible that I could lose control at a moment's notice and materialize against my will, as had happened in the forest. Even though warning thoughts flooded my brain, I couldn't force myself to leave. I wanted more.

I wondered if she could feel my touch as well. If just her eyes could paralyze me, how would it feel to touch her? I was reaching my hand toward hers in order to find out when she suddenly recoiled. I flinched, afraid she'd seen me, but she turned away from me. She appeared to be searching for something, a spirit presence she perceived but couldn't see. Her heart beat fast, but not in the same way it had the first time we'd encountered each other. This time it was fear. I was frightening her.

"Who's there?" she murmured to the empty room. She gazed cautiously around. All at once her dog woke up and began to bark frantically. Gemma jumped, then hurried to calm him, sitting down on the bed next to him. "I need to stop reading so many paranormal books, wouldn't you agree?" She exhaled nervously.

Gemma wore a black hair tie around her upper arm. She took it off and used it to tie her long dark hair up into a messy bun. Putting on a pair of black-framed reading glasses, she opened *Jane Eyre* and began to read aloud. I watched her, overwhelmed by the impulse to stay there listening to her.

No. I couldn't give in to that impulse. I had duties and I had to focus on them. I ran a hand over my face. What was I doing? I was behaving in a way that was totally contrary to who I was. Was I so reckless I was willing to risk everything? I had to leave.

I sighed in frustration. Not only had I not found the answer to the question of why she was so different, things had gotten worse rather than better. A new question had etched a path in my brain: Why did she make *me* feel so different?

I took a step back and vanished, tormented by that new doubt.

I went home, resolved to leave Gemma in peace. Cleaning and polishing my motorcycle was just what I needed to clear my mind. Hidden like a thief in Gemma's room, I'd held my breath when she'd turned toward me—but this time she hadn't seen me. I should have considered that a good thing, a sign that perhaps I'd been mistaken and could return to my former life. For some reason, though, the idea depressed me. I longed to feel again the electrifying sensation her eyes had ignited in me when they'd met mine.

Why hadn't she been able to see me this time? Did it depend on her, or had I just been more successful this time in controlling my powers?

"Hey, bro." Drake materialized, appearing in the garage next to me. The most mischievous of my brothers leaned against my bike and grinned at me. "I looked everywhere for you. Where were you hiding? When you can't find *me,* it's usually because I'm with at least one chick."

Normally I would have responded to Drake's humor in kind, but this time I remained silent.

"What's with the frown?" Simon had appeared behind Drake, holding on to the two ends of the nunchaku he had draped around his neck. He was shirtless and his body gleamed with sweat. He'd obviously just finished a workout.

I concentrated on polishing the fuel tank of my bike. However, I could only hold out against the insistent looks on my brothers' faces so long. I put down the polishing cloth.

"You're acting weird. What's up with you?" Simon demanded. He was the wisest of us; I was pretty sure he could help me solve my problem.

"I fucked up on my last mission. I left evidence," I admitted, the image of the man I'd killed so brutally suddenly filling my mind.

"That's not like you," Simon chided me. Like me, my brothers were Death Angels, sent to collect the souls of those whose time had run out. The tattoo gripping Simon's left forearm like a claw showed his station. The same one I had on my arm. The same curse. "You know our duties better than that," he continued. "No one can ever suspect what we do. It must always be part of the natural order of things."

Drake snorted. "What does it matter? He carried out his mission, right?"

"No," I retorted brusquely. "Simon's right."

Drake was the only one of us who took our duties lightly. We Death Angels had only one rule: orders came first. Nothing in the world would ever impede us from respecting that supreme commandment.

"Chill, Evan. So the perfect toy soldier made a mistake. So what? I do that on purpose."

Simon and I looked at Drake reprovingly. He shrugged, unrepentant. He'd always been an undisciplined Executioner, not like the two of us, who were dead serious about our missions. Consequences had never mattered to Drake—much less Simon's and my disapproving looks.

"Why did you screw up?" Simon persisted. "I know you. There had to be a good reason. You never make mistakes."

Taking a deep breath, I confessed. "It was a girl."

"Oho! Now this is getting more interesting," Drake said.

"It's not what you're thinking." I hastened to correct his impression. If he'd seen me spying on Gemma, I would have become the butt of his jokes for all eternity. A Soldier of Death hidden like a thief in a mortal girl's bedroom. That was most definitely not who I was.

"Yeah, right. You wanted to have a little fun with her. I knew this moment would come sooner or later," he shot back, undaunted.

"A mortal?" asked Simon.

I nodded, remembering the reason I'd done what I'd done. Only Souls could see us. The fact that she was a mortal made her powers of perception extraordinary. "I've got to see her again," I said instinctively. The mere thought of it electrified me. But another desire was fighting its way to the fore within me. It wouldn't be enough for me to see her again, I wanted her to see *me*.

"No. You can't," Simon stated firmly.

"Of course he can," Drake contradicted him. "What's more, he *must*. It's 'part of the natural order of things.'"

"Evan, you can't jeopardize your duty for a girl. You're an Executioner. We don't interact with mortals."

"I don't want to interact with her . . . I don't think. I only want to observe her."

"Observe her? That's a bit disturbing, even for me." Drake grimaced.

"Says the Grim Reaper." I snorted.

"C'mon, I can show you something better than that, bro." A smug smile curved his lips.

"I'm not a teenager, Drake. And I'm not you either. I don't want what you're thinking from her."

"So what *do* you want, Evan?" demanded Simon. "What's so special about this girl that she even caused you to make a mistake?"

I turned toward my brother, feeling the excitement mounting in me. "She can see me."

My revelation left Simon wordless. Drake, on the other hand, let out a long whistle. "Wow, that *is* a big deal."

"What do you mean, she can see you?" Simon asked once he'd recovered the power of speech.

I ran a hand over my face, preparing to tell all. They were my brothers, after all. "I was on a mission when she suddenly showed up out of nowhere and looked right into my eyes."

"Maybe you were in your human form and you just hadn't realized it."

I shook my head, though it really wasn't necessary. Simon knew as well as I did that it wouldn't be possible for us to be confused in that way. In our ethereal form, everything felt different. Everything was far more intense than when we were in human form. Every heartbeat, every breath, every soul that came within range became part of us. "I was in my ethereal form," I affirmed. Generally, we didn't assume human form unless it was absolutely necessary. Drake was the exception to the rule, obviously. He often went out in human form to pick up girls.

"Have you told Ginevra?"

"No. She would only try to interfere and end up complicating things even more."

"I heard that." My sister appeared out of nowhere. She grabbed the rag I'd been using to polish my bike and snapped me on the back of the neck with it.

She was part of our group, though she wasn't exactly like the rest of us. She was different. Her green eyes lengthened like a serpent's as she approached Simon and kissed him.

"Why don't you two get a room?" teased Drake.

"We've got one: the garage," she shot back, her smile mocking. "You two can leave—or stay and watch, if it turns you on. It's all the same to me."

Simon laughed at her audacity and kissed her back. "By the way, Drake," he said as if suddenly recalling something. "Didn't you say you had a mission?"

"His mission has red hair. And she happens to be waiting for him upstairs, naked," Ginevra added sardonically.

"Shit!" Drake swore. "I can't believe I forgot! Hasta la vista, baby!"

Ginevra threw the polishing rag at him, but Drake vanished in a split second and it fell to the floor.

"Typical Drake," I murmured, shaking my head. My brother was incorrigible. For him it wasn't enough to take the lives of his prey, he always had to go further. The girls were convinced they'd made a conquest of him; they never suspected his true intentions. The redhead upstairs would never even see it coming, the moment Drake took her soul like a hungry wolf. He enjoyed toying with his prey before bringing out his grim scythe.

With Drake gone, Simon turned serious. "What are you going to do? You can't allow a mortal to distract you from your mission. I know how important your work is to you. You've devoted your whole life to it."

He was right. I knew it, but some new and unfamiliar instinct within me rebelled against his words. I tried to hide my feelings. All I could think about was getting back to Gemma as soon as I could. I longed to feel her eyes on mine again.

"I need to find out how she does it," I confessed.

"You need to leave her alone."

Was he right again? I knew he was, and yet I couldn't stop thinking about her and that magnetic gaze of hers that reached deep inside me. I'd experienced a strange sensation when Gemma had looked at me. A hollow feeling in my chest. I'd felt paralyzed, like a deer in the headlights. Our encounter had left me in a daze, even after she'd faded into the forest. What sort of strange creature was she to be able to have that effect on me? I ran a hand over my face. An Angel of Death, helpless before a mortal. I felt ridiculous . . . and electrified at the same time. I couldn't hide it any more.

I couldn't escape the truth. It would be better to leave her alone. The problem was I didn't want to.

"I can't back out now," I said with decision.

"Why not?"

"Because that's not all," I admitted.

"What are you talking about, Evan? Is there something else you haven't told us about this girl?"

I lifted my eyes to meet Simon and Ginevra's. I'd pushed the knowledge to the back of my mind, pretending it wasn't important, but I couldn't ignore the facts any more.

"I've received an execution order for her. Her time is about to run out."

I had to find the answers to my questions before it was too late.

GEMMA

Death, if it comes unexpectedly, may be cruel, but it isn't frightening, because you don't have the chance to realize what's about to happen.

Knowing your own fate in advance, on the other hand, is a terrifying form of torture, maybe even worse than death itself. A prelude to madness.

Fearing the shadow of death with each breath is an agonizing countdown that leaves you exhausted and saps your will to fight until its echoing whisper fades into an icy silence that deprives you of everything. It's like a deadly poison that takes effect silently, draining your energy, battering your mind's defenses until you ultimately want to give in to its comfort, letting it shroud you in its dark mantle so the fear itself won't kill you . . . slowly.

The Angel of Death was there for me and soon he would come to take me, because one way or the other I had to die. It was my fate, and who was I to defy it?

3

THE SHADOW OF A GHOST

Four weeks later

The days fly by like the pages of a book ruffled by the breeze. It's been weeks since my encounter in the forest with the mysterious boy, but his silver-gray eyes are seared into my brain like a brand.

How can ice burn like fire?

No one has seen him or heard of him. It's as if I encountered a ghost. A ghost that stalks me. I'm obsessed with him. I see him everywhere, I perceive his presence everywhere, as if he's following me. Not even at night can I banish him—he haunts my dreams. At times I'm so frightened I want to cry—or scream. Other times I feel drawn to him, as if having his presence near reassures me. I know all these thoughts are ridiculous. There's no such thing as ghosts. Even so, there are days when I feel his presence so acutely I think I must be going mad.

However, I'm NOT mad. I know that now, because I saw him again today. And for the first time, I wasn't the only one to see him. He came to our school play. At first I thought he was just in my imagination, but then my friends Faith and Jeneane became aware of the confident-looking boy leaning against the wall as well.

He's real. The boy from the forest really exists.

When our eyes met, my heart nearly stopped beating. In the darkness of the auditorium, his eyes on me almost made me afraid. Light and shadow battled it out on his face. He looked like an angel, yes, but one of darkness. His body was toned and buff, just the way I remembered it. His dark, tousled hair fell over his forehead, giving him a bit of a dangerous look. He was wearing jeans, and the sleeves of his dark-colored T-shirt were pushed up, revealing the tattoo on his left arm, an indistinct tangle of inked lines that snaked up from his forearm toward his shoulder, giving him the air of a warrior. Knowing that he exists has brought all my old fears back. I keep thinking of our first encounter, of his eyes . . . of that man who was killed in the forest that same day. They haven't been able to find out anything about what happened, but the police suspect he was murdered.

~~*What if he killed Mr. Lussi?*~~

There's something sinister about him that I can't explain. So why am I not afraid of him?

I should want to stay away from him, now that I know he's real, that he really was in the forest that day and might even be involved somehow in the homicide. Instead, I can't wait to see him again. My heart leaps to my throat just to think of the way he smiled at me today. Our eyes were locked on each other's, just as they were the first time, and we couldn't stop smiling. It almost seemed as if we were long-lost lovers finding each other again. Why did he come to the play? Could he have come for my sake? I feel my stomach twisting into a knot every time I think of him and . . .

I lifted my eyes from the notebook I was writing in and pulled my earbuds out, distracted by a faint ticking sound. Running my eyes around the walls of my room, I shook my head. He wasn't a ghost. I needed to convince myself of that once and for all.

Another tick. It was coming from the window. Someone was tossing pebbles against the glass. My heart skipped a beat. Could it be him? I was almost afraid to find out. I got up and slowly approached the window while Lana Del Rey's melancholy voice continued to whisper through the earbuds hanging over my shoulder.

My hopes of seeing him again were speedily replaced by disillusionment. It was only my neighbor and best friend, Peter Turner.

"Hey! What on earth are you doing here?" I asked, opening the window. Only after I'd said d I realize how rude I'd sounded.

You invited me over, remember? I sent you a text," he said, being [illegible] not to talk too loud.

I checked my phone and read his message.

I'M OUTSIDE. COME DOWN.

"Sorry, I didn't see it," I whispered. "My parents are still awake. You know I can't go out this late! What are you thinking?"

"I just wanted to see you." He seemed embarrassed, but only for a second. "Well, make way! I'm coming up!"

When we were little, Peter used to climb the ivy-covered trellis all the time to sneak into my room. He hadn't done it for years, and for a moment, seeing the top of his head from my window took me back to the past. My parents had never allowed Pet to be up in my room with me after curfew, not even when we were little. We'd solved that problem with the trellis, and he'd often snuck into my room through the window to talk and watch movies or reruns of *Dawson's Creek*. Sometimes, just for fun, he told me I was his Joey, but up until then I'd never actually realized that maybe he would never be my Dawson.

"Careful," I whispered, trying not to let my parents hear me. "It might not support your weight any more!" His stubbornness made me smile.

"What are you trying to say? I don't weigh that m—" Before he could react, gravity pulled him down to the ground mid-sentence. I couldn't hold back a laugh. A sound from downstairs put us on guard and Peter pressed his back against the wall to avoid being discovered. I stifled another laugh and he looked up at me. "Think it's funny, do you? Well, I'm not giving up," he whispered.

"Are you trying to hurt yourself? You're too big, it'll never hold!" I whispered. My words didn't dissuade him. I didn't know anyone more stubborn than him. Except myself, of course. "Hang on a second." I went back to find my camera and slung it around my neck. "Okay, get out of the way. I'm coming down." I crawled over the windowsill, grabbed onto the trellis, and slowly climbed down. Peter came over and held me by the hips to make sure I wouldn't fall. "There we go. That wasn't so hard, was it?"

"Says the squirrel."

"Hey!" I punched his shoulder and he laughed. Deep dimples appeared in his warm smile as his brown eyes teased me. I'd always been a good climber. Peter got onto his bike and waited for me to get mine. "Where are we going?" I asked.

His dark curls stuck out every which way from under his bike helmet, like a messy nest. "The field. The guys are waiting for me. We're going to practice for the lacrosse game day after tomorrow."

I got on my bike and pedaled after him down the dark, silent streets.

Peter had always been athletic, like most of the boys in Lake Placid. I couldn't imagine life without burgers, candy bars, and French fries, but Peter took good care of his body; he worked out hard every day and was a real health nut. I was the only one who called him Pet. It was a sort of nickname I'd used ever since I was a little girl and had spelled his name wrong.

When we reached the field, Peter threw his bike to the ground with a clatter that rang through the night. Our friends Jake and Brandon were already there along with the other teammates. "Root for me!" he shouted as he walked over to join them.

"I'll bet on the other team like I always do," I joked.

The bleachers were empty; there was no sign of Jeneane and Faith. Climbing to the top where there was a better view, I snapped a few shots of the guys. I needed to take pictures of the team for the yearbook. I'd always loved photography, maybe because of my longing to capture and immortalize every little detail I could. I zoomed in on Peter and was trying to get him in focus when a shadow passed over my lens. Lowering the camera as a shiver slowly ran through me, I looked around. Someone was there with me. I could feel it.

Suddenly I couldn't hear the guys' voices any more. All my senses were trained on a single sensation: someone was watching me. On my guard, I went down the steps. No one was there—only a gloomy aura that shrouded the night. Yet I had the feeling the darkness was deceptive . . . A noise made me freeze. I whirled around toward the back of the stands, but there wasn't enough light to see and I moved closer. Something on the ground stirred. I held my breath and crept nearer. A scream escaped my throat when I saw them: the feet of a corpse.

All at once someone grabbed me by the shoulder. I spun around, terror gripping me, but a shaft of light pointed at my face paralyzed me. "Hey, haven't I told you kids you're not allowed to go crawling around here at night?" The man lowered his flashlight and I finally exhaled. It was Jake's dad, the chief of police.

"What's with all the ruckus this late at night?!" another voice nearby grumbled. We both turned. An old homeless man muttered something and went back to sleep. It wasn't a corpse, I realized with relief.

"Well? What are you doing out here so late?" the policeman asked, turning back to me.

"Mr. Wallace, we weren't doing anything wrong."

"Maybe you weren't, but the streets haven't been so safe lately. Go home. That stubborn son of mine is going to hear me loud and clear this time," he said to himself. The police siren rang out just once, as a warning. "Jake! Move your ass and get in the car now!"

"Sir, yes, sir," he answered, annoyed, as Brandon hurried off in the opposite direction.

I got onto my bike and waited for Peter.

"Let's get out of here before he changes his mind and escorts us back," he said.

I began to follow him toward home, but a sudden gust of wind penetrated my bones, forcing me to stop. As I looked around, still shaken, a headlight blinked on nearby, the bike hidden somewhere in the darkness. The sound of its engine coming to life broke the silence of the night.

"Gemma, are you coming or aren't you?" Peter called out.

I watched the motorcycle as it drove off. "Yeah, let's get out of here," I murmured as another shiver ran through me. Maybe the police chief was right: it was no longer safe to be out on the streets.

4

DREAMING

It isn't written . . . I can't fight it . . . I can't prevent it. I'm sorry . . .

The words were still echoing through my head as I opened my eyes, feeling groggy and lightheaded. I lay in bed for a few minutes, staring at the ceiling as day broke, letting myself remember his features before they completely vanished. Under my skin I had the strange conviction I'd just been with him again. But it had only been a dream.

Outside, thick fog filled the streets with a gloomy light, but I was too ecstatic to even notice. As I walked to school, the atmosphere took me back into last night's dream. I'd been in the woods, surrounded by trees, just like I had been that day. I was alone, but I sensed a hostile presence around me, as if someone was watching me. As if *he* was watching me. I felt his eyes on me, like a hunter's on his prey. The thought both excited and frightened me. Because this time I was the prey.

I tilted my head back and peered around, squinting as I searched the branches, driven by the strange awareness that I'd find him, but no one was there. The sun suddenly blinded me. I was mesmerized by the way the light touched the leaves, its delicate rays filtering through the interwoven branches.

Something moved. Right there, in the middle of the light. I tried to focus on the strange shape surrounded by golden reflections. Was it an animal? I moved closer.

It was certainly bigger than me. Maybe I should run. It might kill me, and yet that likelihood didn't frighten me. It was perfectly still, watching me from atop the lowest, largest branch. Whatever it was, it must have been more frightened than I was, because it seemed to be holding its breath and waiting for me to leave, like a chameleon trying to make itself invisible to the eyes of a predator.

I moved closer still and recognized him from the beating of my heart. Like a wave crashing onto a rocky shore, a wild emotion washed over me, drowning me.

There was something about his features that bewitched me. The blue shirt he wore brought out the icy shade of his eyes. Its long sleeves were rolled up to his elbows, the tattoo branching out on his arm, his facial features perfect, his skin firm and supple. I imagined his soft touch on me. I reached out, but then pulled back my hand, frightened by the powerful emotion that I knew would devastate me if I dared touch him. And his eyes . . . It was as if I held the memory of them within my deepest self.

He was studying my every movement as though he'd never seen another human being in his whole life.

For a second I couldn't breathe. As he stared at me from under his dark, unruly hair, I saw thin, imperceptible streaks of amber sparkle in his eyes like diamonds, like liquid silver glinting in the light. The color was so unnatural and yet so perfect . . . Eyes of ice.

Our gazes locked, entwined like they had the first time we'd seen each other. I stepped forward, unable to control myself. In response, he crouched and leapt down to the ground. He reached out to touch me and paused warily, inches from my face. I trembled because I yearned for his touch, if only for a moment. I held out my hand, seeking his, my palm facing him. My breath caught as the emotion that contact with him would trigger overwhelmed me. I'd never touched him before. He studied my hand for a second and gently rested his palm against mine.

It was like a star bursting inside me. His eyes locked onto mine and an electric shock ran from him to me, connecting us. Eye to eye. Palm to palm. He looked astonished at the power of our contact, and closed his hand, interlacing his fingers with mine as though he never wanted to let me go. His eyes pierced deep, deep into my own. A shiver caressed my back at the extraordinary warmth of his skin. I half closed my eyes and at that instant heard the sound of his voice for the first time.

I won't hurt you. His sweet whisper crept into my mind, penetrated my soul, reaching places hidden and unknown even to me. It was so deep and intense it left me dazed and trembling. I felt he'd whispered directly into my heart. The world around us disappeared as I, at the mercy of some enchantment, saw nothing but him. A dark spell that enveloped my heart. Only when a puff of wind caressed my face did I re-emerge, realizing the forest around us had vanished.

I gasped. Now I was standing at the very edge of a cliff overlooking the sea. Frightened by the sudden height, I instinctively clung to him. Embarrassed by the stolen contact, I tried to pull back, but before I could he drew me to him with endless tenderness. For a moment I forgot how to breathe. His deep, hypnotic gaze was like a lasso around my heart. Powerful and dark.

Don't be afraid, a whisper replied to my thoughts. *Trust me, just this once.*

I looked at him, spellbound. His sensual voice enveloped me like black velvet, but his lips hadn't moved. The sweet sound had filled me from within, making its way to my heart. How could it be?

Every qualm instantly disappeared, banished by a strange, unexpected feeling of trust. I peered down at the empty space below us and held back a shudder. The endless sea crashed against the rock as though it were trying to seize us. Although the wind lashed at my skin, taking my breath away, I wasn't cold because he was with me. Or was I breathless because his face was so close to mine? A comforting, tingling sensation spread through my whole body.

I closed my eyes and let the emotion fill me. "I'll never forget this moment," I murmured. I felt a longing in my heart to gaze into his eyes, but when I looked up his expression had turned grim. Was he already regretting this?

"Did I say something wrong?" I asked shyly.

He seemed lost in a world all his own, but a second later his lips parted. "*All of this* is wrong. What am I doing? I shouldn't even be here." He said this as though trying to convince himself, but something was stopping him. I didn't dare hope it was me. "I, I *need* to understand. I need to," he whispered in a dull voice as he stared down at the waves crashing against the rocky cliff.

I felt a pang in my stomach. "What's so wrong about this? Why do you think you shouldn't be here?"

His face darkened. "Bewitched are the eyes of those who are not allowed to understand. My eyes, my soul, prisoners of a fire that consumes my essence."

"What do you mean? I don't understand." Was he bewitched by me? Was that what he meant? No, he was talking to himself.

"It doesn't matter," he murmured, lost in thought.

"It matters to me. Tell me what's going on."

"You wouldn't understand."

"I could try."

"I can't," he said through clenched teeth. "I'm not permitted to."

I stood stock still, mystified. I had the impression that inside him a battle raged. He seemed angry with himself. What could be making him so upset?

Suddenly, his expression grew serious and every last hint of indecision vanished. Impetuously, he cupped my face in both hands. His piercing gaze, so intense, so close to mine, hit me like a wave of pure emotion. For a second I found that glimmer of authority disorienting. "Listen to me," he said. "I made a mistake by coming here. You must never think about me again. It's wrong—for you, for me, for everyone. Forget my face. Forget you met me. You never saw me in the woods, it was just your mind playing tricks on you. You must erase me completely from your memory," he ordered, as if he expected me to do exactly what he'd just said.

I was staggered. The coldness of his words went through me like a sword of ice and I shook my head, my face still cupped in his hands. "Wha—why? What you're saying doesn't make any sense. Why should I forget we met? Everything about you is unforgettable," I said all in one breath, staring into his eyes.

My objections produced absolute confusion on his face, as if he'd expected total acquiescence on my part. "What the hell? Damn it, I've ruined everything! It's all my fault! I keep coming back. I keep coming to see you, to touch your mind in the hopes of finding the key."

"The key to what?" I asked, exasperated.

"The key to you," he whispered.

I stared at him, dazed.

He focused again, his voice determined. "I have to stop coming to see you. I must pull back. I, I have to let you go. I've already broken too many rules. Things should never have gone this far. I lost control. Forgive me. I've only made things harder for you. What the hell's gotten into me? You *have* to forget about me!"

"I don't want to forget you," I said, my heart trembling from this unexpected confession.

"You don't understand, damn it!" he snapped, making me start. But then his gaze became tender. "Gemma." For a second my heart lost its steady rhythm. Hearing my name on his lips sent a wave of heat from my belly to my chest. "We . . ." He stopped, weighing his words. I couldn't take my eyes off the curve of his lips. "We're bound by destiny, but not in the way you think. You've got the wrong idea about me. You don't know who I really am. Why I came here. You don't know what I'm being forced to . . ." His voice trailed off and he let his arms drop to his sides, trying to compose himself. "Everything would be a lot easier if you had no recollection of me."

"Why?" I asked, gripped by desperation. Suddenly I wanted him, I wanted nothing but him. I wasn't ready to lose him so soon.

His eyes narrowed to slits. "There are things we can't control. We can't fight them," he declared firmly, closing his eyes, clearly overcome by a feeling not even he understood. Resignation, maybe. "*I* can't fight it. I have my duty. I can't prevent it. I'm sorry," he whispered brokenly. I wasn't entirely sure whether he was talking to me or trying to convince himself.

I frowned. Why was he insisting I forget him? What had I done wrong? I didn't want to accept it, and the look of defeat on his face pained me. "What duty are you talking about, and what does it have to do with me?"

His eyes lingered on mine, his expression tormented, as if he was looking for the answers as well. "I only wish I could have more time." He gazed at me for a long, long while, seeming devastated. "It's my mission. I can't help it. It's all I know."

"More time for what? Here we are, just us. Right now. We've got all the time we need."

"You're wrong. There's no time, not for us. It isn't written. I can't fight it. I can't prevent it. I'm sorry." His voice whispered in my head until it faded away, cradling me in the stillness between sleep and wakefulness.

I was so lost in the memory of that dream that I realized I'd reached school only when Peter's familiar voice snapped me back to reality, the dream vanishing into the mist of the gray morning.

"Gemma!" he shouted, running up to me. "Hey, I saved you a seat on the bus. Why didn't you take it? Your mom drop you off?"

"I walked," I explained, a little evasive.

"In this fog?"

I pressed my lips together in confirmation and walked along, staring down at the sidewalk, still damp from the morning dew. For a while neither of us opened our mouths.

Two beeps broke the silence. We'd received texts at the same moment. We pulled our phones out to check.

"It's Jake."

"It's Faith."

Peter and I grinned at each other because we'd spoken at the same time. Our friends had met up at what we called Grassy Knoll and were waiting for us there. We had a little time before first period. Peter casually took my hand and we rushed off. We'd always held hands, ever since we were kids. And yet, after everything that had changed lately, I suddenly had a funny feeling. *Everything that had changed inside me.*

We found them there at the lakeside. I heard Taylor Swift's voice blasting from Jeneane's headphones. Her head was resting on Brandon's knees and his visor was lowered over his eyes. Was he sleeping? Probably. Faith was lying face down on the grass, engrossed in a magazine article about One Direction. In her locker she even had a poster of Louis Tomlinson, her idol. All three of them wore Blue Bomber lacrosse sweatshirts.

At first glance, our group might have looked like a clique in which everyone had found their other half. Jeneane Whitney and Faith Nichols often flirted with Brandon Rice, a blond guy with brown eyes, and Jake Wallace, dark-haired with piercing eyes. They were both jocks and had athletic physiques. The four of them weren't really *couples*, actually, but saying they were just friends would be the understatement of the century. For years now the two boys had hung on the two girls' every last word—not that that kept them from looking around.

Jeneane had a devastating effect on every male who looked her way. She was well aware of her attractiveness and had an incomparable power that she wielded as if it were an extra sense. Fair-skinned, with blond hair, a penetrating gaze, and a gorgeous body, she was very self-confident.

Faith had an entirely different kind of beauty: a head of fiery red hair, which she almost always wore up in a ponytail, pale skin, and stunning green eyes. She was a horsewoman, both in life and in spirit, although the shyness she tried hard to conceal sometimes tamed the fire that burned within her. Her parents owned a farm and horses were her greatest passion.

Faith and Jeneane even painted their nails the same color. They were like inseparable siblings. Pretty much the same thing went for Peter and me—minus the nail polish.

I'd never cared for the way Faith and Jeneane treated boys, but we'd been friends since we were in our cribs, so hanging out with them came naturally to me. "Hey!" I said, sitting down beside Jake. He held up his hand in reply and went back to focusing on his math book. I pulled out my notes and handed them to him. "Here, use these."

"You rock!" he cheered.

"Don't mention it."

"Any news on Mr. Lussi's death?" I asked point-blank.

"He was murdered," Jeneane replied. "Nobody's been talking about anything else."

"I hate this place—it's like living in an aquarium!" Brandon said.

Jeneane raised his visor and looked him in the eye. "That's the best thing about small towns."

"The best thing or the worst thing, depending on your point of view," I muttered.

"An aquarium?" Peter perked up. "What kind of fish would you be, Brandon? Oh, I know: ever hear of a species called the donkey fish?"

"You learn that in one of your comic books?" Brandon jeered. Peter *lived* on comic books.

"There's nothing funny about it. Stop kidding around, guys," Faith said, a scared look on her face. "I saw the man's photograph in the *Lake Placid News*. My God, I can't get the picture out of my head!"

"You're right, they shouldn't have published it," Jake said, as thoughtful as always when it came to Faith. "It really is gory."

I couldn't get past the thought that I'd met the old man just before his death. I heard his voice echo through my head: *I could give you a ride home-ome-ome…*

"Do they have any idea who might have done it?" I insisted.

"Right now they're clueless," Jake replied.

"C'mon. Maybe something scared him, made him trip and hit his head, like a bear—or something scarier," Peter suggested.

"What's scarier than a bear?" Faith asked, shuddering.

"Who knows, maybe there are werewolves in the forest," Brandon said, trying to frighten her. Jake stared at him hard and then smiled at Faith to calm her.

"It's unlikely, Pete," Jake said. "The position the body was found in was too unnatural for him to have just tripped."

I gulped, a tingling filling my head.

"Everything okay?" Peter's concerned voice reached me right after I felt the gentle touch of his hand on my back. For once I wished he didn't know me so well that he noticed whenever I was the least bit upset.

"Why shouldn't it be?" I said.

"Gemma, you've been acting so *strange* lately. I'm starting to worry. What's up with you?" Peter insisted.

"Hey! Maybe *she* killed Mr. Lussi!" Brandon exclaimed.

Peter scowled at him. "Shut up, you moron!" He moved his lips to my ear. "If something's bothering you, you can tell me about it, you know that," he whispered, looking into my eyes.

I noticed that the conversation had suddenly stopped. The others were stealing glances in our direction while pretending not to be interested. Embarrassment washing over me, I pulled back. "Don't worry, really, it's nothing." The truth was I couldn't help but shudder at the thought that I'd been in the very spot where in all likelihood a murder had been committed. I'd seen that man and right afterwards, maybe just minutes later, he was dead.

Was I actually upset about the man's murder? Or was it more that I was scared of finding out *who* might have killed him?

I pulled my old iPod out of my backpack. My friends made fun of me because I refused to change with the times and listen to music on my phone the way everyone else did. My iPod might have been a prehistoric artifact, but it was special to me, because my grandma had given it to me before she died.

I chose the Lana Del Rey folder and turned the volume all the way up. Her voice could carry me far away, delving into my soul and revealing things I didn't know about myself.

In a few minutes, I calmed down. Music was my life, along with books. It was almost surreal how whenever I walked into Bookstore Plus it seemed to be the book that chose me. A perception, almost a mutual desire.

Peter sank down beside me and stole one of my earbuds. Together, we listened to *Born to Die*, one of my favorites by Lana. Maybe I'd never even noticed him doing that before. Peter was my best friend. We'd grown up together and he would always be a part of me. Yet something between us had changed since I'd met the guy in the forest. The thought made me sad. I smiled at him and pretended for a moment that everything was still the way it used to be.

I abandoned myself to Lana's melodious voice, thinking of *him*. The whole world, *my* whole world, seemed to revolve around those eyes. His face haunted me, his eyes stalked me.

Faith pulled the earbud out of my ear as I sang beneath my breath. "Hey, you guys already figured out where you're going to college?" she asked.

"It's not like we have to make up our minds now. There's still time to think it over," Peter said.

The others nodded. But I'd made clear plans all the way back in grade school: I wanted to be a journalist or a reporter that worked on documentaries. I liked being in contact with nature and animals. "You guys haven't thought about what you want to do after high school? Seriously?" I asked. How could they not care?

Faith thought it over a moment. "I'd like to be a veterinarian . . . I think."

"Good idea, you'd be great with animals," I assured her.

"You'll probably end up being a writer, Gemma," she said, making me smile. I read lots of books, but it had never crossed my mind to write one, although I didn't dislike the idea.

"I want to work in fashion," Jeneane chimed in, sitting down on the grass between Faith and me. I would have guessed she'd want to be a singer or maybe an actress, given her passion for putting on a show. "Wait, guys, let's capture the moment." Jeneane pulled out her phone and adjusted her hat. Faith and I crowded into the shot. I kept my knees pressed up against my chest while Faith was practically lying on top of us. "We'll call this one *What Will Become of Us?*"

"Or how about *Happy Times Before Getting Our Math Test Results?*" Jake said, smiling.

"Haha." Jeneane shot him a not-so-amused look. "I'll post it on my Facebook page."

"Jake, what are you going to do after graduating?" Faith asked, clearly more interested in Jake than she wanted to let on.

"Enlist," he said, as if his mind was already made up. Faith went silent, stunned by his decision. Jake was the son of the chief of police, so it wasn't really a surprise that he would follow in his father's footsteps and choose a military career, but the very thought of it saddened Faith.

"I don't need to think about what I'm going to do after graduation," Brandon said with his usual arrogance. "I'm already what I want to be."

"What, a poser? I didn't know that was a paying job," Peter said, making us all laugh.

"I mean a *sports legend*, if you know what that is."

"You'll see for yourself when I outscore you during the game," his friend shot back.

Brandon, Peter, and Jake had played lacrosse together since they were little. They were very close, a team within the team, but they liked to compete and poke fun at each other too.

"What about you, Pete?" Faith asked. "What are your plans for the future?"

Peter thought it over a moment, although there was no need. I knew what his plans were. "I want to draw comics for Marvel. After college, of course." He shrugged in reply to the others' skeptical glances. I believed in him and he was so good that if he committed himself he would definitely reach his goal. "Doesn't cost anything to dream. Meanwhile, I'm going to work at my dad's smithy. That is, if he decides not to drag us all to Europe."

Even though we'd been a bit distant over the last few weeks, that possibility kept coming back to scare me. With a twinge of melancholy, I got up and walked over to the shore. I peered down into the water. Despite the fog, the surface was as clear as a mirror.

A strange flashback filled my mind as I stared at my reflection. It had happened a year ago, at Split Rock Falls. I'd strayed away from my friends, drawn by some obscure force into the thick of the forest, to the bank of a small pond. I'd gone up to the water's edge and seen something beneath the surface. Against my instinct, I'd dipped my fingers into the water, curious to find out what it was. That was when I'd seen it. My own dead body, staring back at me with its eyes open wide. The reflection of a nightmare. I'd almost died of fright. Hearing my screams, Peter had run to help me, but when he got there, there was nothing in the pond any more. He was the only person I'd told about what I'd seen, but he thought it had all been in my mind.

I shuddered now, because despite everything it was still vivid to me. I'd had nightmares for days, tormented by the fear of seeing the reflection of my fate. The strange occurrences of the last few weeks had made the blood-chilling memory resurface. Even now I felt like I was being watched.

I thought back to the mysterious boy and the dream I'd had the night before. His presence was so strong in my mind that I thought he was everywhere. It felt as if he were constantly lurking somewhere nearby, watching me. Since I didn't know his name, my brain insisted on calling him Wild Thing. Wild was the power with which he drew me to him, into him. Wild was the emotion that had crept into me and was growing uncontrollably.

I crossed my legs and rummaged through my backpack, looking for a book. I always brought at least two with me. I'd sought the company of books ever since I was a little girl. I pulled out *Divergent* by Veronica Roth in an attempt to distract myself from those unsettling thoughts. I had a not-so-secret crush on Four, the main male character. Resting the open book on my lap, I took a picture with my phone, including the book, the tops of my shoes and the lake in the background. The water was enchanting at that time of morning. I chose a rosy filter and posted the picture on my Instagram account with a few of the hashtags I always used: #homesweethome #bookstagram #booknerd.

Lying down on the cool grass, I thought back on the dream again and those incredible eyes of ice. It had split my heart in two, making it tremble with an emotion I'd never felt before. No one had ever told me a gaze could have such power over someone.

The nameless boy had entered my mind, never to leave it again.

Jeneane's shout shook me out of my thoughts. "You stupid moron! That's freezing!" Brandon must have splashed water on her.

"Gemma, c'mon!" Faith said, waving me over.

I laughed to myself and slid my things into my backpack. Peter and Jake were up ahead, probably talking over their attack strategies for the lacrosse game.

Just as I ran into the street to catch up with them, a huge black motorcycle appeared out of nowhere and came to a halt inches from me.

Breathless with fright, I looked at its rider. His eyes were directed straight at me. I saw them through the dark visor of his helmet. He continued to gun the engine, waiting, but the girl sitting behind him squeezed him tighter and he zoomed off, leaving me standing in the middle of the street.

I'd never seen that motorcycle before. Was it the same one I'd seen last night? Could it be . . . I shook my head to drive off the thoughts of the mysterious boy and ran after my friends so I wouldn't be late for class.

Peter and I were crossing the schoolyard when his face suddenly darkened. "He's still here." He clenched his fists at his sides.

My head shot up and my eyes darted everywhere, searching for Wild Thing like water in the desert. A second later I swallowed, my throat parched with disappointment. "W-who do you mean?" I asked.

Peter glared at me. "Don't pretend you don't know, Gemma!" The bitterness in his voice left me astonished. Peter was always so sunny, I'd never seen him this furious. "You know who I mean," he said through gritted teeth. "I saw how you were looking at him at the Spring musical last night—and, more importantly, how he was looking at you." He lowered his voice, almost hissing. "I don't like him. There's something strange about him, something *sinister*."

Why had he said that? Could he be jealous? My mom seemed to be convinced Peter had a crush on me, but it was ridiculous. I couldn't imagine Peter and me together, not in *that* way. I had no experience with boys. I mean, sure, I'd had dozens of 'book boyfriends,' crushes on characters in novels, but he was real and besides, he was Peter. To me, he was like a brother. "You're overreacting, Pet. He's just some guy. I don't even know his name! No reason for you to be jealous." I blinked rapidly, embarrassed by what I'd just let slip out of my mouth.

"I'm not jealous. I just don't like the way he looks at you. Last night after the show, before you left, I followed him to see where he was going."

"But why would—" I started to say, but Peter cut me off.

"He hid behind a tree, thinking no one saw him, but I did. And I don't like what I found out, not one bit. He kept staring in the same direction and when I looked, it was you, Gemma! He was totally spying on you."

"That's enough. You've crossed the line, Pet," I warned him, losing my patience.

"Why won't you believe me?! Anyway, I don't want him getting near you. Haven't you heard what people are saying?"

"Since when do you care about gossip?" I snapped accusingly.

"Rumor has it he's a strange guy. I don't trust him. For all we know he could even be a murderer. And again, why was he spying on you like that? Besides, I haven't told you the strangest part: I looked away from him for a second and he vanished. *Vanished*, you hear me?! It was like he vaporized or something. It was so weird, for a second I thought I'd imagined it. One minute he's there and the next he's gone, like a ghost. Look, I got goosebumps just thinking about it."

"You read too many comic books," I said, trying to laugh it off. Inside I was turning pale, thinking of the first time I'd met him in the woods and the harrowing pictures of the man with the broken neck that Jake had taken a picture of in his dad's office. Worse than the ones published in the paper. "You're being paranoid."

Peter was right. There was something dark and mysterious about that boy, I could sense it. It was my heart that was refusing to consider it seriously. Even the way he'd silently slipped into Lake Placid made me question him. No one knew anything about him—in our small town, of all places, where it was impossible to keep anything a secret.

And then there was that bizarre sensation that paralyzed me every time our eyes met. I didn't even know his name, so why was I so overwhelmed with emotion? It was like some obscure, disturbing, inescapable force had bound me to him. I realized I didn't care whether or not I knew his name or where he came from. The longing to be near him was too strong. And even if a part of me thought it was crazy, the intensity of those eyes whenever they met mine was enough to ignite a flame of hope in my heart. Could he be feeling the same longing?

5

DISAPPOINTMENT

I walked into the school, my pulse accelerated at the thought of seeing him again after my dream. We'd been together last night, he just didn't know it. The same emotion that pounded in my ears with every step kept my eyes glued to the floor, depriving me of the courage to face him.

I turned down the hallway, my head lowered, as the sound of students passing me mixed with the thumping of my heart. Everything around me suddenly seemed to slow down. I looked up to avoid losing my balance and instantly saw his face.

Some dark spell was summoning me to him. He was at the end of the corridor, looking cocky, leaning against the wall with one hand, his black sleeves pushed up to his flexed forearms, facing me.

Though the throng of students heading into the classrooms formed a wall separating us, the connection that bound me to him grew stronger and stronger as I made my way toward him, trembling with every step. My heart seemed to know him, my body seemed to be waiting for me to reach him and take his hand, letting him hold me tight, like in my dream. But this was the real world and I didn't even know his name. When a group of students moved aside, giving me a clear view of him, something pierced my heart, stopping it.

He wasn't alone.

There was a girl with him. No, not a girl, a goddess. The mere sight of them smiling and looking at each other was enough to paralyze me. I felt as though someone had ripped my heart out of its warm home only to toss it into an icy puddle. She was looking at him with a self-confident air, her shoulder pressed against the doorframe, while he leaned toward her. Their bodies were almost touching.

The image erased everything else. Students, teachers, the talking, the muffled laughter. The hallway was empty and silent like my heart, deprived of its beating, my lungs deprived of air. I saw every last hope drift away like a ghost, disappearing before my eyes.

The low murmur in the hallway returned and only then did I notice the whispering of all the boys, floored by the goddess's extraordinary beauty. She paid no attention; she must have been used to it. Or more likely, *he* was the only thing she wanted to focus on.

Even I could barely believe that so much grace and beauty could be concentrated in just one girl. Naturally Wild Thing would surround himself with girls like her. I reluctantly forced myself to admit it was crazy to have thought anything different. Her long blond hair caressed her back, curling at the ends. It looked so soft. Though it wasn't very warm inside, she wore a silky, sleeveless, white top, opened in the front. A pair of close-fitting jeans clung to her breathtakingly long legs. On her feet she wore open shoes that matched her shirt.

My heart started pounding in my chest again as the distance between us gradually lessened. The scent of delicate floral perfume wafted over me as I was about to pass them. Hers, no doubt. My legs struggled to keep moving. I stared at my feet, trying to pass unnoticed. While discomfort battled with disappointment inside me, from the corner of my eye I noticed her turn to look at me. I couldn't keep myself from pausing to look back at her—as if an ancient instinct were forcing me to establish that connection.

Intimidated, I turned to face the girl and unexpectedly looked deep into her fierce, sensual eyes, which stared back at me intensely. It made me feel naked, like she was reading what was inside me. Her piercing jade-green irises looked like they were being lit up from the inside. Sunlight shone through them, giving them a hint of aquamarine. An incredible color.

My breath caught in my chest as an uncontrollable instinct induced me to shift my gaze to Wild Thing. My heart skipped a beat when I found his eyes waiting for mine. I *had* to look at him, even if only for a second, no matter how wrong it might be. But now that girl was beside him, watching me, so I looked back down at the floor as the chatter in the hallway returned to its normal volume. Approximately three seconds had gone by.

I caught sight of Peter's triumphant expression. I knew he'd come to the same conclusion I had, and I was surprised to find myself horrified by the smug satisfaction I saw on his face.

I dragged myself to class, numb with disappointment. The boys' excitement about the new girl was almost tangible. They were all in a buzz about her, like bees around their queen. Even the girls, gathered together in a huddle, were talking about the news, although it was the boy that absorbed most of their attention.

Not being the least bit interested in joining their little group, I opened my notebook and started doodling as I waited for class to begin. I just wanted the day to be over.

"Hey, Gemma, seen the new girl yet?" Faith's voice distracted me, forcing me to look up at her. "Looks like they're a couple. Her and the new boy, I mean."

"You still haven't found out his name," I deduced. I had to admit I was curious despite myself.

"Can you believe it?"

"Exciting, don't you think?" Jeneane said, appearing behind her, drawn by our whispering. "He looks so *dark* . . . and nobody knows anything about him. And on top of that, today he shows up with the goddess of the nymphs! This is crazy. I never thought I'd say it, but the guy's a total mystery, even to me."

Mr. Butler walked in and everyone sat down at their desks, dropping their conversations. I looked down at my page of doodles, knowing that not even the most interesting class would inspire me to pay attention.

A sudden murmur made me look up. Every muscle in my body froze, leaving me breathless. Just like me, the whole class sat there spellbound by the mysterious allure emanating from the two new students standing beside the teacher. My heart was beating out of control.

"We have two new students," the teacher said. "As you know, the school year is almost over, so it would be considerate on your part if you helped them orient themselves." Mr. Butler paused. Even he seemed bewildered by their presence. "Very well, kids, introduce yourselves to the class."

"Thank you, Mr. Butler. My name is Evan James." His voice, velvety and sensual, mesmerized the entire class. His eyes darted to mine as a sudden shiver ran down my arms.

Evan James. Enchanted, I found myself whispering his name in my mind. His voice had an overwhelming impact on every girl in class, almost as if he had the power to control our minds. I tried to resist the fascinating effect of his half-closed eyes with their dangerous mix of aloofness and sweetness, but I couldn't keep my body from trembling.

There was something familiar about the timbre of his voice. *Trust me, just this once . . .* No. It couldn't be. It was ridiculous. That voice was *the same one I'd dreamed. Impossible!* I shook my head. I couldn't have heard his voice. And yet—

"And this is Ginevra—" he managed to add before the teacher cut him off.

"Very well, find a seat. I have a rather important topic to explain."

Ginevra. Her name whirled in my head. It had such a majestic ring to it. Suddenly my brain stopped. I lowered my head, panicking, pretending to study the mustard-colored paint of my desk. They were heading toward the two empty desks immediately to my right.

My heart in my throat, I waited to see if he would sit down in the one farther away, leaving her with the desk next to mine, but he sat down to the girl's left, leaving only the narrow aisle between us. A tingling sensation ran up my arms. My body was betraying me.

Mr. Butler's voice was reduced to a low murmur in my ears, completely buried under my thoughts and the frantic beating of my heart. He was too close for me to concentrate on anything else. I could even perceive his scent. Wild Thing almost smelled like the woods. *Evan,* I corrected myself.

From time to time, I would imperceptibly tilt my head in his direction, hoping he wouldn't notice. And every time I did, he would gaze straight at me, as if expecting my look. From that distance, I clearly saw the color of his eyes. They were *dark.* A warm, reassuring color, nothing at all like those icy colors my mind had changed them into during my dream. They perfectly matched the color of his hair, which was pure dark chocolate. And yet, I thought I could still make out those golden flecks in his irises, like fine strands of caramel. But then again, mine had only been a dream, inspired by my memory of what he looked like, which I'd probably confused because of the sunlight in the woods.

It bothered me to think how rude the teacher had been to cut his introduction short. If it had been up to me, I'd have let him talk nonstop for hours. I was sure I would never have tired of the sensual sound of his voice. A little embarrassed from feeling his deep, deep eyes on me, I reached up and, trying to act naturally, swept all my hair to one side, to feel less exposed.

I glanced at the other end of the classroom, where the kids continued to turn and squirm in their seats, trying to get a better look at the newcomers. Jeneane's conceited voice rose up over all the others, saying snidely, "You can all take a number. I saw him first."

My jaw dropped. Had she seriously not seen the queen of the goddesses sitting right there next to him? It was hard to believe anyone could have not noticed her. I smiled instinctively, because that accomplishment, though small, was actually mine: I'd been the first to see him. Still, it didn't matter which of us had looked into his eyes first. He had *Ginevra.* That was all that mattered.

"C'mon, he hasn't even noticed you exist! Just once, would you give the rest of us a chance?" one of the girls grumbled.

"You'd like that, wouldn't you? Well, I don't feel like being so generous! He'll notice me, wait and see."

If Jeneane wanted someone she went out and got him, no apologies. And now she wanted *him.* For the first time since I'd known her, I wished I had even one ounce of her self-confidence. This time, though, I doubted her strategies would get her anywhere. No boy could resist the disarming blue of Jeneane's eyes, but not even she could compete with Ginevra. No one could.

In reality, I knew it was just a game to Jeneane. Lots of times I'd heard her talking about her escapades. I could never figure out how she could always be so cold, how she never ended up in a real relationship with anyone. In her twisted mind, she probably saw it as a challenge, a sick sort of diversion no boy could resist. Sooner or later they all fell into her trap. Like a skilled, graceful spider, Jeneane wove a web no one could escape from. But once she'd caught them, she would cast them aside as though she were afraid to establish a deeper bond with them.

Not him, I growled in my mind, as though he somehow belonged to me. *Not him*, I thought, with a tremble of fear deep in my heart, hoping that just this once someone wouldn't succumb to her charms.

The hours flew by despite my desperate longing for time to stand still at school since *he* was there. "You're wasting your time, guys." I set down my tray full of food, feigning disinterest while actually using the lunch hour as an excuse to pry into the other girls' conversation. My comment made them all turn their heads toward me.

"Why? Did you dig up some news?" Faith asked, looking as disappointed as she was curious.

"Isn't *Ginevra* news enough for you?" I reminded her.

"You give up so easily," Jeneane was quick to say.

"What do you mean?" I was anxious to hear her answer, hoping it might rekindle my hopes even the slightest bit.

"For all we know she could totally be his sister!" she said matter-of-factly.

My heart lit up again. Because of my insecurity, I hadn't considered the possibility that Evan and Ginevra weren't a couple. Thinking about it, I realized he'd introduced her as Ginevra, and the teacher had interrupted him before he could say her last name. Maybe Jeneane's idea wasn't so crazy after all. They both had the same hypnotic charm. That tiny hope, nourished by my heart, began to unfurl through my doubts as I looked over at the two of them, eager to spot some kind of resemblance in their features.

Evan was staring down at the table, which meant I could steal glances at him without his noticing. From the tilt of his head, it looked like he didn't want to be listening to Ginevra. Maybe she was accusing him of something. She talked and talked, but he didn't open his mouth once.

Like déjà-vu, Evan unexpectedly looked up at me, closing the distance between us, and my heart leapt to my throat. I saw a hint of curiosity against a backdrop of disconsolate bitterness that hardened the features of his face. I was certain it was the same bitterness I'd sensed the night before, as though it hadn't been just a dream, but an actual memory. Our eyes remained locked for a long moment as I tried to understand why he was so troubled. Had Ginevra noticed him constantly staring at me?

The bell rang shrilly, once again severing that invisible cord connecting us.

The repressed ardor in his gaze had struck me with such devastating emotion that I couldn't focus on my classes. My brain had shut down as it tried to grasp what lay behind his agony.

Peter was practically begging for my company when the bell rang, finally freeing me from what had become a prison. The crowd of students leaving the school headed off in two different directions: a small, elite group, to which I didn't belong, walked down the hill to get their cars from the parking lot behind the school; those who didn't have that privilege, like Peter and me, trudged over to wait for the school bus.

I watched Evan and Ginevra as they left the school, curious to see which way they would go. Evan headed straight toward the parking lot and I let out a self-deprecating sigh for having foolishly hoped to have his company on the way home. I expected to see them pass by in their car, but a high-pitched roar in the distance filled the street, making the hairs on my arms stand up. I'd heard the noise before, that morning. It was the same motorcycle that had almost hit me. We all gaped when we saw Wild Thing riding the aggressive-looking black motorcycle. It had to be really expensive, judging from the reaction of all the boys around me. The sound was high-pitched but subtle, making me think of an angry feline's growl.

"Hey, Kyle," a boy behind me whispered, "you see that bike?! So awesome! I think it's an MV Agusta. Frame's totally carbon fiber. I've never seen such a *monster* before!"

"You definitely haven't. That's an F4 CC. Not even I've seen one so close up before. Check out those racing exhausts! Nothing but sweet music coming out of those four titanium organ pipes. I hear it can go up to 195 miles an hour. Shh, quiet! Listen to that. I've heard it on YouTube before, but hearing it live, it's sick! Look, I've got goosebumps," Kyle said, his voice breaking, almost beside himself.

"A CC?" the first boy asked his friend, who seemed to be an expert on the topic. I perked up my ears to overhear all the information I could.

"Don't you know anything? A Claudio Castiglioni! Two hundred horsepower of pure adrenaline! See the double C's on its fairing? There are only a hundred of those bikes in the whole world. That's all they made."

"Only a hundred?" his friend said. "Man, when I saw him with the hottie I thought there was no way I could be more jealous, but now? That guy's one lucky dude to have gotten his hands on one of those babies." His voice was tinged with envy.

"Lucky?! You mean loaded! Those few 'lucky dudes,' as you call them, shelled out a hundred thirty grand each. You can't find them anywhere any more. And if one of them ever happened to fall into your hands, man, I can't even imagine how much you'd have to cough up now," he said reverently.

Evan revved his bike as he impatiently waited for Ginevra to climb on behind him. They had their helmets tucked under their arms. I couldn't help but stare at them, feeling a pang in my gut. Still, despite the distance, I saw that his eyes were like headlights pointed straight at me.

He slid his foot onto the pedal, putting the bike in gear as Ginevra wrapped her arms around his chest and my heart started to tremble again. A sharp pain made my stomach burn. I wasn't very familiar with the feeling, but I managed to give it a name anyway.

Jealousy. Seeing them together made my whole chest burn. Unlike most other girls, I didn't envy Ginevra her beauty, grace, or elegance, but I would have given anything to be where she was just then.

They headed in our direction, both of them looking at me steadily. I couldn't figure out if it was just a coincidence or if they were actually staring back at me, but I couldn't bring myself to find out by looking away. That would mean giving up the ecstatic sensation of having Wild Thing's eyes on me. It was strange how such a strong, proud expression could seem both authoritative and puzzled at the same time. Pushing down my discomfort, I forced myself to hold Evan's gaze the whole time, even as the distance between us continued to lessen. My heart was pounding in my chest.

I watched him disappear around the corner, his scent lingering in the air behind him, the scent of a waterfall hidden in the depths of some mysterious forest.

6

DREAD

Captivated by the memory of his gaze, I distractedly watched the bus pull away without me. A moment later there were no more students in the schoolyard and everything was silent. A gloomy layer of fog covered the streets. I was perfectly accustomed to the grim, gray mist, but the feeling lurking at the bottom of my chest made it feel less familiar. I found myself unconsciously picking up my pace.

Suddenly the creepy feeling that someone was watching me from close by left me short of breath. I stopped and looked around, but there was no one on the streets. I stole glances over my shoulder, not brave enough to stop again and check, but as soon as I focused on the street again, the bone-chilling sensation came back to torment me.

I mentally calculated the distance between me and the comfort of home and put one foot in front of the other faster and faster, in unison with my heartbeat. Turning the corner nervously, I at last spotted our front gate in the distance, and sped up until I found myself running the last exasperating yards. I jammed my hand into my pocket and grabbed my keys in a desperate attempt to save time before I reached home.

Grabbing the bars of the gate, I tried to put the key into the lock, but my hands were shaking so hard I barely managed to keep it from slipping out of my fingers. Finally, it unlocked with a click. I anxiously threw the gate open wide and shut it behind me, whirling around, short of breath, to see who'd been following me.

I was astonished when I saw no one on the other side of the gate. Studying the street warily, I hurried to lock myself indoors, but not even within the walls of my own home did the feeling that a ghost was walking right through me over and over again completely disappear.

I walked down the hall, turning on all the lights, confused by the unusual silence that hung in the air. Only when I spotted a slip of paper on the table did I understand why. Casting a quick glance behind me, I leaned over the table to read what it said.

Squirrelicue,

Unexpectedly busy. I whipped up a little something in case you got hungry. It's in the fridge.

I'll make it up to you.

Love you,
Mom

I let out the air I'd been holding in my lungs and forced myself to stop trembling. They'd just ended up working longer than expected—nothing unusual. And yet, the feeling I was being watched continued to torture me. The house being empty did nothing but increase my panic. I rushed to my room, hoping to find some comfort in the company of Iron Dog, the plump, tawny pug I'd had for ten years. One look at his huge dark eyes always made me forget all my sorrows. But when I walked through the door, I went deathly pale.

Iron Dog was awake, on his feet, his image reflected in the mirror behind him. He turned and moved toward it cautiously, his ears low, in guard position, flicking his tail, not even noticing me there. Was it possible I wasn't crazy, that the ghost really existed and Irony could sense its presence? I felt a pit in my stomach as I watched him move his tongue in empty space, slowly, like he was licking the air. No, like someone was in front of him, someone invisible to me. I stood there in the doorway, petrified.

I tried calling him, hesitantly at first, finally getting his attention. As though I'd woken him from a dream, he trotted over to me.

I'd had a big lunch at school, but my stomach twisted with hunger. I went down to the kitchen, but despite Irony's reassuring company, not even entering that comfortable, familiar room gave me the solace I was hoping for. Disturbing things kept happening.

I'd once read that animals have an extra sense that can detect the presence of spirits. But if that were true, I wouldn't have perceived it as well. Or maybe humans also had some kind of sensory perception, just a less developed one? A sixth sense that made you shudder when a ghost was near. Given all the paranormal novels I devoured, I couldn't even be sure whether the source of the information was fictitious.

And yet, Irony's uneasiness made my stomach churn. I tried to calm him down, but he kept scampering all around the kitchen. I'd never seen him so on edge before.

Then I remembered. It had happened once before, just before he'd disappeared into the misty forest. I grabbed the phone, almost yanking it off the wall, and dialed automatically, hoping Peter would hurry over to keep me company. I was sure he'd find my fear laughable, but I didn't care. I needed him there. My knees were shaking at the thought of spending all afternoon alone.

Every ring reverberated in my spine, but there was no answer. Under my skin I still had the creepy feeling I was being watched.

In the silence of the nerve-racking wait, Iron Dog's low growl made me flinch. My heart in my throat, I turned toward the guttural sound. Trembling attacked my knees and then every other part of my body.

There was no one in front of him. Irony was growling at the empty wall. Scared out of my wits, I lunged for him, leaving the receiver dangling on its cord, and took the stairs three at a time. Inside my room, I locked the door and stood with my forehead pressed against it. I wasn't sure why I was so convinced I was safe in my room, but for some reason, my agitation began to lessen.

Sitting at the window, I started to reread my tattered copy of *Jane Eyre*, but the words eluded me as I watched the sun make its way across the sky, hiding behind occasional gray clouds, until my eyelids grew heavy and I gave in to the comfort of the darkness behind them.

Torn from sleep by a noise, I jolted awake. The old Charlotte Brontë novel lay on the linoleum floor, but I doubted its worn leather binding could have made a noise loud enough to wake me up. Looking out the window, I saw that the moon had already found its place in the sky, though it felt like I'd only dozed off for a few minutes.

There was a strange metallic clang. I walked cautiously to the door and opened it, straining my ears, trying not to make a sound. The hall was darker than night, but I forced myself to grope along it, following the dim shaft of light coming from the living room. At the stairs I paled. The noise was coming from the front door.

Someone was trying to break in. The phone rang, shattering the silence and sending my heart racing into my throat as I held my breath. The sound echoed through the darkness of the hall. Now a completely different concern turned my blood to ice: how could the phone be ringing if I hadn't hung it up? Could someone have come inside while I was asleep? And what about the lights? Who'd turned off the lights? I was sure I'd left them all on.

The lock groaned as if it were being forced. The knob began to rattle convulsively. Suddenly, there was another click and the knob froze, as did my heart. Breathless, I grabbed something off a shelf and drew closer. I couldn't see clearly what I was holding, but it felt heavy enough to hurt someone if I used it right. I watched the door open slowly. In the darkness I could make out a hand reaching inside and feeling around on the wall for the light switch.

"Gemma, what are you doing there with that doughnut?"

Light flooded the room, revealing my dad's reassuring face. I dropped my arms. "It's you!" I said, heaving a sigh of relief.

"Who did you think it was?" Mom asked, surprised.

"You almost gave me a heart attack!" I said bitterly. "What were you thinking, breaking into your own home?" My voice was still full of fear.

"You're a real scaredy-cat, you know?" my dad chuckled. "Did you mean to hit us with that?" A laugh escaped him as he pointed at the doughnut-shaped paperweight I was still holding.

"Sorry, Squirrelicue, your dad left the house keys at the diner and we had to force the lock. I tried calling but you didn't answer."

Just then, my stomach growled, reminding me that I'd skipped more than one meal today. Deciding to reheat my second lunch in the microwave, I followed them into the kitchen, pausing in the doorway to look at the phone receiver. It was in its place on the hook.

And yet I was perfectly sure I'd left it dangling. In any case, with my parents at home, everything seemed so unreal. Looking back, I realized I'd spent all afternoon terrified for no reason at all and that I'd conjured up creatures that existed only in my head. I really had to stop reading all those paranormal novels.

But later, when I was lying in bed, part of me was afraid to fall asleep. After the day's strange events, I was sure the night would bring nightmares that were even worse. I closed my eyes and, to my amazement, finally dozed off.

I turned to stare at the deserted street behind me. The fog seemed to want to hide it. I had the funny feeling I'd already lived through this experience before. My heart accelerated with every passing moment, hoping I would understand the warning it was sending me.

My footsteps pounded on the pavement like a hammer banging on an anvil and my senses were strangely alert, but my instinct to stay on guard took precedence over everything else. Someone was there with me. I couldn't see him, but I was sure he was there. I could sense him, like water running across my skin or a sound caressing my ears.

Someone was following me.

I picked up my pace, terrified, hurrying to reach our front gate as a battle raged in my body. My instinct was telling me to run while something else was forcing me to stay. I felt a pain in my heart but didn't give in until I found myself inside the gate, panting.

I whirled around. My heart stopped beating.

Evan.

His icy gray eyes were fixed on me with fiery intensity, narrowly assessing me. How was it possible for ice to melt as if it were fire?

Our surroundings suddenly changed and the metal bars between us faded away. My front walk disappeared, leaving behind it a place that was just as familiar to me: the woods. My mind continued to take me back there, as if it wanted to reveal something to me.

The fog drifted though the trees and floated past us like ghosts as our eyes locked. We were so close I felt the warmth of his body on my skin. My eyes were lost in his and his in mine, exploring unknown places, and I feared I wouldn't be able to contain the emotion that flooded through me. My heart was pounding so hard I could distinguish every upbeat and downbeat. It was like a concert of emotion—the most beautiful melody I'd ever heard.

An uncontrollable instinct—the deep, unstoppable desire to put my hand on him to see if he was real—made me reach out, but before I could touch him, Evan vanished into thin air as though he'd guessed my intentions and wanted to elude me, though I couldn't imagine why.

He silently reappeared behind me. An indecipherable shiver ran through me and I sighed, waiting for my breathing to slow. I whirled around, but he vanished again, reappearing among the trees, leaving a conspicuous distance between us. I stepped forward, trying to lessen that distance while keeping my eye on him so he wouldn't vanish again.

His gaze was fixed on me, intense and fiery. His clenched fists and jaw reminded me of the first time I'd seen him. Was he studying me? A chill seeped through my skin, going so deep it brushed my bones, and Evan's shadowy, handsome face was right in front of me, so close to mine.

I hesitated a second, holding my breath. The intensity of his gaze almost hurt. He smiled, his lips bewitching me, his wild eyes fixed on me as I melted, surrendering to him. As if he'd finally won the battle that had been forcing him to keep his distance, Evan raised his hand to my face, pausing only for an instant. I half closed my eyes, longing for contact with his skin.

Savoring every second, I shuddered at the warmth of his ardent hand as it set the skin of my neck on fire and slid down my arm. I watched it descend until it slowly reached my hand. His fingers moved lightly, searching for mine. He stroked my palm with his thumb, gently. I did the same and Evan passionately grabbed my hand.

With that warm, reassuring touch, every fear vanished, replaced by a deep feeling of peace that filled every particle of my being. Part of me was still mystified by his presence, his coming to Lake Placid, everything about him, but time and time again, all he had to do was reach out to me, even if only with his gaze, for every concern to be banished like fog dispersed by the sun.

"What is this power of yours?" His voice rose into the silence like a melody. "I try to fight it, but every time I can't help but surrender."

"Why do you want to resist?" My instinct tried to stop the words, but my heart wouldn't let them be silenced. Why was he struggling to fight that inexplicable connection that bound us? It was clear he felt it too.

"I didn't say I *wanted* to," he said firmly. His eyes on mine made my heart tremble.

"What power? Surrender to what?"

"Surrender to you," he blurted. He went back to studying my hand in his, as if I were a creature from another planet. "I shouldn't be here. I shouldn't interfere. It's just that . . . I don't know what's happening to me. I can't help it, I . . ." He paused. "I can't do without something inside you, something it triggers *inside of me.*" He pronounced the words clearly, one by one, seemingly realizing the truth of what he was saying as he said it.

But what could be so different about me? Why did he seem so fascinated by me? Every time our hands touched, his gray eyes flickered with surprise. Surprise mixed with something else. Something that mystified him.

Evan's face was a mask of uncertainty and confusion, but I sensed the euphoria he was trying to hide. It was as if he wasn't allowed to feel what he was feeling. He was mad at himself because he couldn't help it. I would have driven those feelings away if only I could. Instead, knowing there was nothing I could do, I watched him silently struggle with his ordeal.

"You don't understand." His face darkened for a moment and then cleared. "How could you—" He half smiled, his gaze growing misty. "It's always come so easily and instinctively to me. Why should it be any different with you?" He turned back to study me again, as if he could find the answer to his question there. He stared at our hands, still joined, and his eyes shot up to mine. "I can't control myself when you're around. Nothing works like it should. Why?" He was troubled. "Why don't I know who I am any more?"

Did he really hope to find the answer in my eyes? I could tell he didn't actually want me to understand what he was saying, but I didn't care. All I needed was to be there with him. I laced my fingers with his and squeezed them. "You don't need to control yourself around me," I reassured him. "Let yourself go."

"I can't. I'm . . . afraid I'll lose myself," he said, his voice suddenly resolute, his face growing sterner. "I need to abort the mission. I can't do it. I . . . I'm not the right one. Not this time," he sighed, letting go of my hand and clenching his fists. I looked him in the eyes and the bitterness I saw there told me he'd just made a decision. "I'll have someone else do it in my place," he whispered, turning his back on me to leave.

It sounded like gibberish, but I realized it was something important. "Abort the mission? Why are you talking like a soldier?"

Evan stopped in his tracks, his back still to me. I stared at his tattoo as the muscles in his arm flexed. "Orders come first."

What did he mean? My questions—and even the doubts arising in my mind—seemed to be pushing him away from me. I decided it wasn't important. Whatever it meant, no matter what it cost, I didn't want to lose him.

"It doesn't matter if you can't explain what's going on. I won't ask you any more questions." He stood up straighter, as though what I'd said had struck him. "I promise."

I needed to do something because I had the feeling I was about to lose him forever, and it made my heart ache. I walked up behind him and took his hand, just as he'd done to me. He hung his head, studying our fingers as they interlaced, then turned to look into my eyes. For a second the burden seemed to lift from his shoulders, as though the touch of my hand had regenerated him. But in his struggle against whatever was tormenting him, the relief was short-lived.

"I can't." His words drifted in the wind as he disappeared. Powerless and terrified, I watched him dissolve with the fog.

"Wait!" My shout echoed through my bedroom. I rolled over and sat up in bed, shaking my head when I realized it had only been a dream.

It was all so crazy . . . The dream had felt so *real*, I couldn't believe it hadn't been. All the mystery surrounding Evan had doubtless fed my imagination. I couldn't think of any other reason for my strange dreams, which by now were recurring, with Evan in the leading role.

I crawled out of bed, still dazed, and got ready for school. If nothing else, I knew what to expect from the day ahead.

7

ALCHEMY

The strange occurrences didn't disappear with the night. School was relatively deserted and silent when I showed up. The first bell hadn't rung yet and students were just starting to unenthusiastically fill the halls.

I used the time to organize my locker. The blue paint on its door was as shiny as ever, but a tornado seemed to have passed through the inside.

How can I resist you?

Evan. My heart skipped a beat and I closed my eyes. The lingering traces of his voice, as light as words whispered softly in my ear, drifted away, to my regret. I savored the last sweet echo, surrendering to the sound before it vanished entirely.

I turned around slowly, expecting to see Evan right there behind me, and gave a start when I saw him standing at the far end of the hall. But I was so sure I'd heard his voice . . .

"Hey, Gemma!" Brandon hurried over to me. "You seen Pete around? The game's tomorrow and we need to work on our attack strategy."

"Sorry, I haven't seen him yet today," I mumbled, still dazed.

"Hey, you feeling all right?" Brandon stared at me, worried. "Well, if you see him, tell him not to be late to practice. Speaking of which, why don't you come watch us?"

A shiver ran down my spine as my eyes lost themselves in the sight of Evan's face. Something was worrying him.

"Gemma, did you hear me?" Brandon asked.

"Huh? Yeah, sure, I'll tell him you're looking for him," I said.

I couldn't explain what was happening. I was starting to worry something might actually be wrong with me. I'd heard Evan's voice inside my head.

I was obsessed with him.

Embarrassed, I turned back and tried to watch him without his noticing. He was leaning against his locker, looking worried. As Ginevra continued to chatter to him, his expression grew more and more serious, almost shocked. What I would have given to know what she was saying to him! I forced myself to look away and walked into the classroom, disoriented by the paranormal experience.

In class I felt Evan's eyes on me even more than yesterday. Part of me kept telling myself it was wrong to feel the way I did. I wasn't even sure if he and Ginevra were related, after all. What if Jeneane was wrong? Evan's boldness did nothing but embarrass me, especially with her sitting right there next to him. But then again, Ginevra hadn't even bothered to notice that he kept looking at me. Confused by my conflicting feelings, I ignored the lesson. If I kept this up, my GPA would suffer, but for the first time in my life I didn't care.

What is it about you?

The sound of Evan's voice snapped me out of my trance and my eyes shot to him, my skin tingling. It had happened again: I'd heard his voice in my mind, like the sweetest of melodies.

I looked away, worried about what was happening to me. Evan was leaning over his notebook, drawing incomprehensible symbols like the ones in his tattoo. And yet I could swear I'd heard a trace of frustration in his voice, an equal mix of curiosity and irritation. I looked over at him again. He was fully focused on the crumpled paper which he continued to cover with ink.

His rolled-up sleeves revealed the veins in his firm arms every time he moved his pen. From time to time I caught a glimpse of the tattoo on his left forearm. It consisted of small, black, stylized symbols. Maybe it was a message written in some ancient language. I wished I could decipher the strange writing. The ink seemed to encircle his arm like poisonous roots branching out, trying to penetrate his flesh. A shiver ran through me as I stared at their ends: they almost looked like claws trapping him in their grip. At one point, he caught me with my eyes glued to his tattoo and his expression darkened. He looked down at it and then back up at me, a flicker of surprise in his eyes.

Now he wore an intense expression, as though he were concentrating on something more than just the page. A mix of desire and hesitation. I read the apprehension in those deep brown eyes that were as dark as chocolate. What was tormenting him?

It was impossible that I'd actually heard his voice. It was probably just another of my fantasies rooted in my uncontrollable desire for him.

The most frustrating thing was that I couldn't tell anyone about it.

Peter never cut class, but today I hadn't seen him at school.

After my last class of the day, photography, I felt too shaken to go home so I figured I'd take Brandon up on his invitation and watch the lacrosse team. They practiced every day from three to four, and I was sure Peter wouldn't miss it for anything in the world. At Lake Placid High they took sports very seriously.

The whole team wasn't there yet, but a few players were doing knee bends and jogging around the track, the yellow logo standing out on their Blue Bombers jerseys. I sat down on the lowest bench of the bleachers. It was still a good half hour until practice, so I decided to spend the time eating something and reading a bit of *Jane Eyre.*

I sat down cross-legged, opened my book, hung my head over it, and distractedly nibbled on a sandwich. It wasn't nearly enough, given how empty my stomach still felt once I'd finished it. I'd always been like that when I was stressed—I could never eat enough to feel full. Luckily, knowing I'd still be hungry, I'd stocked up in the cafeteria. My parents wouldn't be going home for a late lunch today so I'd gotten two helpings of everything.

I bit into a snack-size pizza without looking up from the page I was on, pulled out two chocolate bars from my backpack, and set them down close to me.

You're eating all that by yourself? Evan's voice came back to haunt me. I froze in confusion, then shook my head, deciding to ignore it. I distractedly cracked open a can of soda and took a sip, but it almost fell out of my hands when I heard his voice echo in my mind again. *I mean it, I think it's a bit much for just one person.*

I sighed, exasperated. I had to be on the verge of a nervous breakdown. I focused on my book but couldn't stop thinking about Evan.

Aren't you leaving some for your friends, at least? he said, laughing. Keeping my head bowed over my book, I continued to ignore the voice. By now it was clear something was wrong with my head. Years of lack of interest in boys were mutating into an insane longing for Evan that was overwhelming me to the point of obsession.

I'm bothering you. Sorry. There was a hint of sadness in his voice. *I didn't mean to be rude. We haven't even been introduced. I'm Evan James.*

My heart skipped a beat, sending a desperate signal to my brain. He was there. And he was talking to *me.* I tilted my head and raised my eyes.

Evan smiled. He was sitting just behind me, amused by the shock and embarrassment my face must have revealed. He stared at me in silence, waiting for me to say something.

I smiled meekly and for a second all I could think of was how relaxed his face was. I'd never seen it without a dark veil of confusion. "I'm really hungry," I stammered, still dazed.

"So do you always refuse to talk to strangers, or does that rule apply only to me?" he asked, teasing.

I blinked. I'd been so absorbed in Jane's mad reasoning as she rejected her beloved Rochester in my book that I hadn't noticed the bleachers weren't completely empty any more. The players on the field, on the other hand, had noticed the two of us talking and were looking our way, grinning. I must have been the only girl Evan had said a word to since he'd shown up in Lake Placid. Except for Ginevra, of course.

"I was just wondering where you put all that food. There's no way you should be in such good shape if you eat like that," he added, smiling.

"I only do it when I'm nervous," I said, my cheeks flushing from the hidden compliment.

"And are you nervous *now*?" he asked sweetly, leaning his face in toward mine. His voice was sensual, persuasive. My heart skipped a beat, crushed by the weight of those dark eyes so close to mine.

Of course I was, but I certainly couldn't tell him why. He'd think I was crazy if I admitted to being obsessed with him. I myself could barely believe what was happening to me. Dreaming about a total stranger every night and then hearing his voice in my head? It was insane. I forced myself to look away, afraid my body would betray me.

"I'm just . . . stressed out," was all I said, turning one of the chocolate bars over in my fingers. "I guess studying too hard really isn't good for you." I broke off a square and put it in my mouth. "Anyway, my name's Gemma Bloom," I mumbled, as the chocolate slowly melted on my tongue.

"I know your name," he replied in a self-assured tone, a seductive smile on his lips. I looked at him in surprise. *That* was certainly nice to hear. Or was he just teasing me?

Evan smiled, looking directly into my eyes, as if on the verge of revealing a mystical truth for my ears only. "It's written on your necklace." He reached out his hand to examine my pendant and an electric tingle ran up my spine the instant his fingers touched my skin.

Evan pulled his hand back, hiding his uneasiness behind a look of embarrassment. *No*, it wasn't simple embarrassment. Worry was more like it. It seemed I wasn't the only one who'd felt that energy flow through our bodies, and it had left him baffled.

"Sorry," he whispered shyly. His expression grew more confused.

I reached up and grasped the butterfly-shaped pendant that hung from its chain, bracing myself for the pang of nostalgia I always felt when I thought about it.

"It must be important to you." His hypnotic gaze searched mine, his curiosity probably roused by the sudden look of sadness on my face. His comment left me so astonished I couldn't speak. No one had ever asked me about it before. Not even Peter—but on the other hand Pet knew the whole story behind the heirloom.

"In a way. I've had it since I was a little girl. I never go anywhere without it."

Evan didn't respond. Sliding onto the bench beside me, he looked down at the pendant and back up at my face, encouraging me to go on. My heart did a somersault, having him so close for the first time.

I doubted he was actually interested in my past, but even though we were strangers, I felt a deep sense of intimacy with him. "It belonged to my grandmother," I stated simply.

"You were really close," he said intuitively.

For some strange reason, the words started to pour out of me like a swollen river before my brain could even approve them. For an even stranger reason, I didn't *want* to stop the flow of emotions. It was as if I'd known Evan forever. Not like Peter, but like a part of myself.

I told him how Grandma had been like a second mother to me. An example, a role model. I barely noticed how much time went by as I sat there in the stands talking to him. Part of me still believed it was just another dream. It was so easy to talk to Evan, so *natural*. He listened, fascinated, eager to know everything about me.

"When I was little, I couldn't understand why my parents kept leaving me with her. Inside, I resented them for neglecting me because of their work. But Grandma was happy to help raise me and for years she was my mentor. We were really close," I admitted, filled with sweet nostalgia. "The name engraved on my pendant is hers, actually. I was named after her. In Latin, Gemma means—"

"'A flower ready to blossom,'" Evan said, staring at me intensely as he finished my sentence. For a moment I was lost in his eyes. "But it also means 'precious gem.'"

I gulped, spellbound by his voice. I'd never known anyone so mysterious and fascinating. "This is so weird, *I'm* usually the know-it-all of the group," I joked, making him laugh. "Anyway, this pendant belonged to my grandmother. She died suddenly, unexpectedly." I struggled to hold back the sadness that the thought of her always caused me.

"Life is a dream, death an awakening," he whispered, his face close to mine.

"You're quoting Tolstoy," I replied, impressed.

"I may be the know-it-all of *my* group," he shot back with a grin.

"Yeah, right, and now you're going to say she'll be here with me as long as I keep her in my heart." I was trying to be sarcastic but my listless tone betrayed me.

"Actually, I was about to say as long as you wear her necklace, but your version sounds a lot better." He looked into my eyes with exasperating sweetness and I couldn't help smiling back at him. His fingers moved slightly across the bench and touched mine. I found myself copying his gesture, resting my own against his. This light, light touch triggered a storm of emotions inside me: suddenly my chest felt heavier, my breathing slowed, and my lips parted as I watched our fingers barely brush against each other on the wooden surface, my mind in a fever. I raised my eyes and looked into his, swallowing hard because my throat was suddenly parched.

"I . . . I'm not so sure any more."

Evan cast me a reassuring glance and my eyes began to water. "You're tearing up," he said. A furrow of regret formed on his forehead. "I'm sorry, it's my fault. I shouldn't have opened old wounds. It's just . . ." He paused, meeting my gaze. "This is going to sound crazy, but I feel like I've always known you. I feel so *close* to you," he admitted, his eyes searching mine. "If I didn't know it was impossible, I would swear I've met you before."

I blinked several times, floored by his revelation. How was it we both felt the same thing? As though a powerful connection united us. As though our souls had known each other in past lives. A mystical, supernatural bond. "Hey! Are you reading my mind?" I asked, keeping my tone light.

"Now *that* would be interesting," he said, making me blush.

"What is it you want to know, exactly?" I asked, confused and embarrassed.

His expression grew deeper and more intense. He seemed quite serious. "I'd like to find the answers. Have more time. Understand what happens to me when I'm with you." The confession left me speechless. *When I'm with you?* It was the first time we'd ever been alone, so why did I also have the feeling it wasn't?

Ginevra's face popped into my mind. For a moment I'd almost forgotten she might be his girlfriend. Jeneane seemed pretty convinced she wasn't, but the possibility was still out there. At the thought of her, I quickly withdrew my hand from his touch, instantly missing it.

"I don't see Ginevra anywhere," I said, hoping he'd take the hint.

Evan answered without taking his eyes off mine. "She's . . . somewhere, I don't know where. I wanted some time to myself."

I'd never been so confused in my life. "Why are you here?" I whispered loudly, almost insolently. Evan didn't say a thing. His expression spoke for him: not even he knew the answer to that. He smiled at me, taking my breath away, and stood up without a word.

How rude, I thought. He wasn't even going to bother to say goodbye? After I'd opened up to him? I was puzzled by his ambiguous behavior.

Then his hand clasped mine. The warmth ran up my arm and spread all the way to my heart as his grip, at first impetuous and full of yearning, gave way to an endless tenderness. It was as if he knew what I'd dreamed last night and was giving in to the urge to relive it. He brushed his thumb against my palm, making my stomach flutter, and put his face next to mine, his voice caressing my ear: "You're forgetting your promise."

I closed my eyes as I felt his lips moving slowly, whispering against my skin. Swallowing as warm shivers ran down my body, I opened my eyes in a dazed, feverish state only to realize Evan had disappeared, leaving me to decipher his enigmatic message.

Lost in my fantasies, I heard someone call my name. One of the players was running toward me, taking out his mouthguard. I looked out at the field for the first time. Practice must already be over.

"Hey, Gemma!" Jake was holding his lacrosse stick and wore the required protective gear, along with a helmet, which was what had kept me from recognizing him.

"Hey, Jake! Faith's not here, if it's her you're looking for. She had a riding lesson. I heard Raul say he was taking her."

I bit my lip as Jake clenched his jaw. Raul was a dark-skinned boy with blue eyes who'd had a crush on Faith ever since grade school. His family lived on a ranch where his dad gave riding lessons and organized excursions on horseback for tourists. The summer before they'd dated a little and although they'd broken up, he was nuts about her.

Jake muttered something and swore through his teeth. Faith and Raul's closeness infuriated him. You could see from a mile away that he was crazy about her. "Actually, I came to make sure you were all right." He nodded over my shoulder, in a clear attempt to indicate my encounter with Evan. He was always such a protective guy, even toward me.

"Oh, you saw us . . ." My agitation grew. He must have noticed the intimacy of Evan's gesture when he took my hand and whispered in my ear. What if he told Peter?

"What was James doing, sitting here? You looked so shocked when he got up and left like that. Did he insult you or something? I can take care of him if you want."

"No, Jake, everything's fine. After he got up I thought he'd left without saying goodbye, that's why I was upset. I didn't realize he was right behind me, and when he took my hand I—"

"Took your hand?" The look on Jake's face made me freeze. "No one was behind you. I saw it clear as day, he stood up and walked off without even looking back."

I paled as doubt struck me: Had I only imagined it?

8

A FLEETING HOPE

All that afternoon I tried to decipher the last thing Evan had said to me, but it was no use. I didn't remember ever promising him anything. In fact, that was the first time I'd ever spoken to him, apart from the conversations we'd had every night in my dreams. Not that those counted, of course. And then there was the strange thing Jake had said. A mystery, an unsolvable riddle I couldn't make heads or tails of no matter how hard I tried.

My desk chair squeaked against the linoleum floor of my room as I got up to go out for some fresh air. Outside our front door, I glanced over at Peter's house. I was sure he would have been happy to keep me company, but not so sure I could give him the attention he deserved. And so, setting aside the idea of seeking refuge in the forest, I ran down my alternatives and realized it would be best to go to my parents' diner for a while. Leaving my sweatshirt hood down, I let the light rain caress my hair. As I walked, I read the names, one by one, of the high peaks in the Adirondacks that were carved into forty-six gray stones dotting the red brick sidewalk that skirted the two-plus-mile-long shore of Mirror Lake.

Main Street ran alongside the lake, surrounded by neighborhoods full of shops and restaurants on both sides. In the center, right on the shore, Bandshell Park was used as the venue for lakeside weddings and concerts, while across from it, on a rise, stood the beautiful Adirondack Community Church.

The houses downtown were smaller than the ones in the residential areas but they were charming and colorful. Some were painted white, others brown, blue, or green. Just outside the village, the shore was lined with beautiful wooden houses, farms, and even log cabins. The main attraction was the antique Victorian movie theater.

My mom was surprised to see me walk in. During the winter I usually spent my afternoons reading novels or my textbooks, so my parents were used to seeing me at work only over summer vacation.

"Hey, Alex!" I said to a young woman with dark blond hair who was waiting tables.

"Gemma!" A warm, engaging smile lit up her face. Alexandra McFaddin worked at our diner three times a week so she could set aside some money to go to Nazareth College in Rochester. When we were little, she, Peter, and I used to play together a lot, even though she was a few years older than us. But then her family moved into a bigger house in another part of town. Although we rarely saw each other any more, time hadn't changed our friendship and my affection for her was still the same. "Sick of studying, huh?"

I took the dark red apron out of Alex's hands and she offered to tie it behind my back. "Something like that." I smoothed down the front of the apron and smiled at her. She went to wait tables while I served the clients sitting at the counter, although I doubted I'd be able to concentrate.

I hadn't heard voices in my head at all that afternoon, which was reassuring. It took my mind off the idea of turning to a shrink for help.

Until that moment.

Hmm . . . muffins, doughnuts, or peanut-butter fritters? But then again, the blueberry crumble looks awfully good.

My heart skipped a beat. "Stupid voice," I hissed, hanging my head low over the counter and carefully arranging the fritters more neatly on their trays.

"So you don't like my voice?"

I looked up and froze, mortally embarrassed when I realized who was right there in front of me. "N-no," I stammered, unsure how to cover for myself.

"Ah," Evan said, surprised.

"No! It's just . . . I didn't see you there," I said, a burst of heat rushing to my face. I wondered what color my cheeks had turned. "I thought it was—"

"You thought it was . . . ?" Evan said, a grin on his face.

I couldn't string my words together in any sensible order. I bit my tongue and glanced over his shoulder at Alex, who was gesticulating at me to cheer me on, a surprised smile on her face. "I thought you were someone else, that's all," I lied, using the first excuse that my stunned brain managed to come up with. "Sorry about that."

Confusion spread over his face, as if my words had somehow put him on guard. I had the nagging suspicion he knew exactly what was happening to me, but I pushed the thought out of my mind.

"Anyway, I, I like your bike." What a stupid thing had just come out of my mouth, bypassing my brain!

"So, you like my bike," he repeated, cocking his head as a flash of satisfaction appeared on his face and his half smile turned into a grin.

"Yeah, I mean, I like the sound . . . I mean, it's nice, the sound, it . . . you know," I stammered, so embarrassed I wanted to run and hide. "It sounds like a lion growling," I went on, wrapping it up all in one breath. My eyes had grown wide from the shame. My God! What was happening to me? Was I possessed? Could I rewind the scene and take every word back?!

Evan smiled, half amused, half flattered, but before I could sink into the pit of awkwardness I'd dug, he leaned his face toward mine, his voice deep and caressing. "You should hear her when she's angry," he joked, his shadowed gaze fixed on mine.

"What brings you to this part of town?" I asked in an attempt to guide the conversation to safer ground.

He raised his eyebrows and looked from one end of the room to the other. "Well, this a diner, isn't it?"

Right. Was it my imagination or was he teasing me again? But then again, making a fool of myself in his presence came so naturally to me. I frowned and Evan let out a gorgeous laugh. I was starting to think there was nothing about him that wasn't attractive, but, like a moth drawn to a flame, I was sure that following my instincts would inevitably mean my own death sentence. When he sensed my embarrassed silence, he cleared his throat. "Sorry, I didn't mean to be rude. Let me start over." He squared his shoulders and put one hand to his chest, making a slight bow. His gaze was so powerful, so penetrating, so wonderful, all at the same time. "Would you be so kind, milady, as to permit me to indulge in your blueberry crumble? I'm certain it will be delectable and . . . sweet." He weighed each word as my body wobbled, lost in his gaze. "And my lips are anxious to receive it from your hands, to relish its flavor." I struggled to keep my heart from stopping.

"Gemma!" my dad shouted from the back, breaking the magic spell that bound us while Alex, pretending to be busy wiping off the tables, let out a little laugh that she immediately hid behind a coughing fit.

"Coming!" I called over my shoulder after a moment of hesitation as I tried to summon up my self-control from wherever it was hiding inside of me. I cut Evan a wedge of crumble, slid it onto a napkin and held it out over the counter. Suddenly I teetered, realizing I might touch him again. Why on earth hadn't I grabbed a plate like I always did? Evan reached out and my heart trembled.

I kept holding on to the napkin as he took it in his hand, sweetly brushing his fingers against mine as his eyes locked on mine. The contact with his skin inebriated my senses and electric tingles spread out all over me.

"Gemma, are you coming or aren't you?!" my dad insisted testily.

I pulled back my hand, noticing in Evan's eyes that the emotion had shaken him too. It was as though what happened when we made physical contact was a mystery for him as well and he wanted to touch me again to try to re-experience it.

Against my will I looked away, and with butterflies in my stomach, went through the doorway behind the counter. As I did, out of the corner of my eye I saw Evan sit down at a table by the window.

"What's all the fuss, Dad?" I asked, annoyed that he'd interrupted us.

"You need to . . . There are trays to be washed," he replied, choosing his answer carefully. He grumbled something I couldn't make out, though I think I heard the words "lips" and "relish."

"Why don't you run them through the dishwasher?" I asked, confused and exasperated.

"Joshua! Leave her alone," my mom said, coming to my rescue. She shot me a sidelong glance and lowered her voice. "*Who* is that boy?" Pleased, she opened her eyes wide and nodded toward the dining room. It was starting to dawn on me why Dad had called me into the back.

"Nobody," I said, hoping she wouldn't notice my cheeks flushing. "He's just a guy from my class."

My mom studied me carefully. "Nobody? You didn't look so indifferent a minute ago."

"Huh? Were you guys spying on me?" I said in a low voice, still embarrassed at the thought that my dad had heard me flirting with Evan.

"I'm just curious," she said with a shrug, looking almost hurt. "Aren't I allowed to be? You've never seemed interested in anyone before. I was starting to think something was wrong with you."

"Oh, thanks, Mom!" I groaned, not even trying to conceal my sarcasm.

"Well, what?! This is the first boy you've liked in *seventeen years*! You're so beautiful, sweetie, but you never notice the way they look at you."

"But you do?" I tilted my head, surprised.

"Oh please, you're the only one who never notices! Last summer the diner was full of boys, and I don't think it was because of your dad's strawberry malts. Not to mention Peter. Are you still convinced you're just a friend in his eyes?"

I blushed, embarrassed by how confidently my mom always told me what I could never figure out on my own.

"All I'm saying is, it was about time you finally took your eyes off your books and looked around. So, tell me everything! I want all the details!" she said enthusiastically. She'd clearly been waiting a long time for this moment.

"Shh! Not so loud. I told you, there's nothing going on between us," I insisted. But then, saddened by her obvious disappointment, I forced myself to give her some glimmer of hope. I was sorry to make her think I didn't want to share things with her. "Not that I haven't thought about it."

Her face lit up again like a little girl who's just been given candy. "Well? Tell me about him!" she insisted, touching my heart with those big, bright eyes of hers that sometimes reminded me of my own.

I shrugged, not knowing which details to expand on. "He moved here not long ago and I don't even know if he's available."

"What do you mean? How could you not know?" She took me by the arm, leading me away from the vigilant ears of my dad, who was pretending to work.

In a way, I was relieved to finally be able to talk about it with someone. Of course, I never would have imagined Mom as a confidante. On the other hand, she was probably the only one who wouldn't have ulterior motives. Before talking, I switched on the coffee grinder so the deafening noise of the beans would help cover our voices. "There's a new girl at school too. She's *gorgeous*," I admitted, grimacing. "And the two of them seem inseparable." I felt a pit in my stomach.

"Have you ever seen them acting intimate?"

"No, but they're always together."

"So what? That doesn't mean anything. You and Peter are always together too. What makes you think she isn't his sister, for instance?"

"Jeneane said the same thing," I replied, my tone lighting up again.

"I never thought I'd say this, but for the first time I agree with her," she said. In Mom's opinion, Jeneane had never exactly been "good company." "Why don't you go ask him?"

"What?! Mom, no!" I exclaimed, shocked. What made her think I'd be brave enough to ask Evan about Ginevra? Didn't she know her own daughter?

"Why not? He's right here, just yards away! What's holding you back!?"

"I'd be too embarrassed."

"You need to learn to seize the day. Shyness is a lasso that binds the wings each of us has. Only if you untie it can you fly. Don't give up on something if you might regret it later. Sometimes all you need to do is reach out and take what's in front of you. Someone else might beat you to it and you'll miss your chance. Spread your wings, Squirrelicue, and go talk to him."

I couldn't say she was wrong, but I just couldn't follow her advice.

"Does he look at her the same way he looks at you?" she whispered in my ear, then quietly stepped back and disappeared.

The instant my eyes darted to Evan's, so deep and warm, I found them waiting for me. Like two perfectly fitting halves of some mechanism, our gazes remained enmeshed for a seemingly endless moment, exchanging information words couldn't express.

My emotions left me dazed every time. I doubted the same thing happened to everybody. Such a devastating sensation couldn't be common. Every moment was leading me into a comforting, embracing abyss. A mysterious one. A dangerous one. But one from which I would choose never to return if only I could stay there forever.

Part of me sensed that path would lead me to my end, but I didn't care as long as he walked down it with me. It was too late for me to turn back now.

I'd begun to lose myself in him.

With each moment that passed, unconsciously and uncontrollably, I was beginning to fall in love with Evan.

9

FIRE

Although he'd long since finished his crumble, Evan lingered at the table, staring out the diner window at the rain. From time to time, I gave in to the temptation to steal glances at him, and I was reassured when I caught him doing the same with me. It made me happy. Finding comfort in my mom's advice for the first time, I pushed the image of Evan and Ginevra as a couple completely out of my mind.

I looked out the window and finally glimpsed the sun peeking timidly through the blanket of clouds. On another occasion it would have cheered me up, but now I was sure—no, I was *afraid*—Evan was about to leave.

Soon, the screech of his chair against the floor told me I was right. My heart in my throat, I watched him stride over to the cash register where my mom was waiting, eager to get a closer look. I tried hard to ignore the embarrassing looks of approval she kept sending my way. I was afraid Evan might notice.

Worried that after he paid he might leave without saying goodbye, I gestured to her from behind the counter, hoping she'd understand and get lost. To my surprise, she understood instantly and walked away, leaving us alone.

Evan shyly made his way over to me and my knees started to tremble again. "I hadn't tasted anything so delicious in centuries," he said, breaking the silence.

"Yeah, well, um, it's all thanks to Dad," I blathered. *All thanks to Dad?* What the heck kind of a reply was that?

"He's quite an overachiever then," he said softly. I didn't understand what he meant by that. "Pastries aren't the only sweet thing he's good at making," he whispered boldly, flashing the most seductive of smiles.

Trembling, my heart grasped the allusion, but I nervously talked around it. "Yeah, actually, his fritters aren't bad either. I think they're great. You should try one next time."

Next time. I so hoped there would be a next time.

My answer got a laugh out of him. Even his smile was perfect, like every other thing about him. His white teeth gleamed behind his full lips. I imagined the sensation of feeling them on mine and instantly shook my head, realizing I was standing there staring at them.

"Right, his fritters." He stifled a smile as he walked to the door. "Well, see you at school . . . sweet thing," he added, winking at me. His attitude was so disarming I couldn't even reply. My heart was beating like crazy as I watched Evan walk through the glass vestibule and out the diner door.

Was it just my imagination or was he getting bolder?

The sun was ready to retire after its long journey through the sky and darkness prepared to descend on the little town of Lake Placid. "I'm going to get going," I told my mom. I walked over to the table where Evan had been sitting and ran my hand over its surface. The wood beneath my fingers was rough, covered with graffiti left by tourists. Dedications, initials, engravings. But one stood out; it was carved deeper than all the others. I leaned over and looked at it.

Rise up
and gather
the brightest stars

My heart started pounding and I began to tremble.

"Why don't you wait for us? We can all go home together for a change." I looked toward the doorway leading to the back. Mom was standing there, her eyes on me.

"I'd rather go now," I said, walking off before she'd finished talking. "See you at home." I was riddled with doubt: could he have carved those words for me? I had a lot to think about, a whole afternoon to re-examine in my mind, word by word. My stomach was aflutter and I was walking three feet above the ground. My feet knew the way home all on their own, so I was able to take my mind off that.

Someone yanked me backwards, almost making me fall. From the force used I could tell a man had done it, but only after a moment did I catch sight of his uniform.

"You can't go down there, miss," the policeman said firmly.

"What do you mean? I have to go home."

"I'll repeat that: You can't go that way!"

The idea of taking another street bothered me. I didn't want to have to pay attention to where I was going. "Why not?" I asked.

"There's a fire. Now step aside and let me do my job. I need to clear the street."

"Moron," I grumbled. Only when I saw what was happening not far in the distance did I understand how serious the situation was. How could I not have noticed the chaos?

All of Lake Placid had gathered there. I nervously hurried past the policeman, ignoring his protests, and dove into the crowd, trying to make my way through.

They were all staring in the same direction. Trying to get a better view, I took a few more steps forward, the heat of the flames beginning to scorch my face. I glimpsed an apartment building, its walls engulfed in flames. People's cries of dismay grew louder and more intense with every step I took. Then sirens drowned them out, announcing the arrival of the firefighters. There was little they would be able to salvage from the inferno by now, though.

The flames rose from the blackened windows, blazing overhead and whipping back and forth like red and yellow ribbons. I was close enough to see the firefighters outside the building assisting men, women, and children, their faces covered with soot, their clothing torn. The less fortunate—those who'd lost consciousness from smoke inhalation or had more serious cuts and burns—were being taken to the hospital in ambulances. It was a terrifying sight.

A woman's shrieks rose up over all the other troubled shouts. A shiver ran down my spine when I heard her and instinctively I pushed my way through the crowd. I discovered it was a woman of around thirty, her face aged by pain as the flames burned in her eyes. She was sobbing and screaming desperately to the rescuers, who were trying to calm her down without effect.

"Amy!!! My baaaby! Please! Save my baaaby! You have to save her! She's only four!" she continued to shriek, overcome with desperation. A murmur of compassion mixed with dismay spread through the entire crowd.

"AMYYY!!!"

The deafening, agonizing scream wrenched the hearts of the people in the crowd, silencing them. From where I stood, I could barely overhear the firefighters, but by the serious looks on their faces I guessed the authorities were trying to inform the woman that it was too late: the flames had completely engulfed the building and nothing more could be done for the little girl.

"We didn't find anyone else alive. I'm sorry, ma'am." The unlucky policeman who had been given the painful task spoke with cold detachment, forcing himself to hide his grief from the young woman. It made no difference. No matter how he said it, nothing could change it: her daughter was dead. No words could relieve her suffering.

"No. No. No. Nooo!!! Saaave her! Please! You've got to save her! She's still alive!" the woman shrieked through her tears, making me shiver with every desperate sob. "Why? Why didn't it take me instead?!"

I longed to run to her and hold her close. But no comfort would ever be enough. She kicked and thrashed while the authorities tried to hold her down.

I was on the verge of bursting into tears but forced myself to gulp them down, looking up at one of the windows of the building in flames. Something inside caught my eye. I frowned, trying to make out the confused images, and jumped when I saw a shadow partly hidden behind the blanket of smoke.

I focused on the vague shape and for a moment everything around me suddenly fell silent as if someone had switched off the volume. I peered at the strange figure, trying to make it out. It was definitely a man, probably a firefighter. But all the smoke kept blurring and distorting the image. I wanted to shout out to everyone but was afraid it was just another one of my visions. I focused more intensely and was relieved to see he wasn't alone.

Another smaller form was next to him, holding his hand.

I gaped. *The little girl!* My heart trembled and I stumbled over myself trying to get a fireman's attention. "Quick! He found her! Get them out!" I shouted with a mix of elation and dismay.

"Calm down, young lady, what are you talking about?" The man tried to catch my eye, but I continued to stare up at the shadow in the building, afraid I'd lose sight of them.

"The little girl! He's got the little girl!" The fireman stared at the building blackened by flames, a puzzled look on his face. "There's a man up there with her, can't you see him?!" I insisted, seeing his skepticism. "You've got to hurry!"

He took me by the arm and said in a low voice, "If this is a joke, it's not one bit funny. That woman is devastated, for Christ's sake! Have a heart!"

Bewildered, I looked back and forth between him and the window. Was he blind? "But he's *right there* on the third floor!" I said desperately, fighting back tears. "How can you not see him?! It might be one of your men!"

The fireman swore beneath his breath and glared at me. "The third floor completely collapsed. There's nobody left in the building, damn it! Do I have to draw you a picture?" He composed himself and studied me carefully. "You didn't happen to inhale any smoke, did you? You feel okay?" I blinked, dazed, his voice fading away in my mind. "Miss, do you need a doctor? Why don't you go have them check you out? You look pale," the fireman was saying, but the sound seemed to be coming from far away.

Couldn't he see them too? How could he not? "I'm fine," I finally managed to say, hoping he wouldn't try to force me onto a stretcher. "I just want to go home." I raised my eyes one last time. The shadows twisted with the flames and became clear again: it was a man and a little girl. Or was it? I couldn't trust my own eyes any more. The shadows disappeared in a cloud of smoke.

I nervously scanned the building's front doors in the hopes the man would walk out, carrying the girl to safety, but no one else came out of the building. The flames died down, the smoke blackened the sky, and the crowd dispersed.

Was I having hallucinations too now? Wasn't hearing voices in my head enough already? If I'd had to bet on how reliable my perceptions were lately, I'd definitely bet against myself.

A thought crossed my mind. There was something about the man's form that . . . No. If my obsession with Evan could make me this irrational, I was going to have to admit there was something seriously wrong with me. But the more I thought about it, the clearer the image became in my mind. It was suddenly joined by a second one: the man found dead in the woods. Two incidents. Two deaths. And Evan was there on both occasions. Could he possibly be involved somehow? It couldn't be a coincidence. How could my feelings for him be enough to exonerate him from the cold, impartial eyes of logic? No matter how hard my heart struggled against it, there was something sinister about Evan.

But this time I couldn't be so sure I'd actually seen him . . . could I? I shook my head, exasperated by my own paranoia. I wasn't sure I could take any more of the pain that my suspicions had instilled in my heart. I forced back the urge to cry and headed home.

The woman's anguish continued to haunt me as I hurried down the sidewalk. Losing a daughter after having raised and loved her for four years was a pain someone could never learn to live with. Ever. Because losing someone you love is always unbearably painful.

I walked along, my head down, tormented by the screams that continued to echo in my mind. I'd never witnessed such desperation before. The only thing I could compare it to was scenes from books or movies, but in those a superhero always brought the little girl back to her mom's arms. This was real life. There would be no happy ending for the devastated mother.

Disoriented by the crowds filling the sidewalks, I'd been walking distractedly, paying no attention to where I was going. Only when it was too late did I realize I'd turned down the wrong street. The houses grew smaller and smaller behind me as I made my way toward the forest. I knew it wasn't the right direction, but something I couldn't put my finger on was driving me on. Not even my instinct. Quite the opposite, in fact: my instinct was urging me to get away from there, and fast. It was some kind of ancestral, mystical attraction, a beckoning I could neither ignore nor resist. It felt *dangerous*. But I didn't care. I sensed the path before me would lead me through my own inner labyrinth.

I came to a sudden halt, baffled. Thick stone walls towered overhead at the end of the path, an inaccessible fortress. What was hiding behind those mighty, majestic walls? Was it abandoned, maybe? The white rock was so ancient, it looked like it had been there forever.

I looked around, trying to figure out where I was. The path had led me out of Lake Placid and into an area I'd been to on occasion. Still, I was sure I'd never seen any piece of property like this before. Cautiously, I ran my palm over the wall and energy suddenly raced through my body. I flinched and jumped back. It was the same energy that had led me there.

I touched it again, but this time I didn't feel anything. Hoping to find a gate, a door, or some other way inside, I walked along the wall, running my hand along a huge crack in its surface. Curiosity consumed me. I had to discover what was hiding inside the fortress walls. Just as I began to think they were impenetrable, I saw the crack widen into a gap a few yards ahead of me, big enough for a slim person to squeeze through.

I hesitated, frightened by the foreboding appearance of the walls. The gap looked like it might lead directly to hell. But before I could heed my instinct to turn and flee, the impulse that had led me there forced me on. I squeezed through the gap and was almost overcome with emotion. I had no idea what heaven looked like, but if there was one on earth it had to be the place I'd discovered behind those walls. It seemed as if all the world's flora might have originated from that enchanting setting, a breathtaking sight to behold. Towering trees, guardians of the earthly paradise, lined curved paths.

As if coming to life in my presence, the green mantle covering the ground swayed, dancing in the gentle breeze. Springtime ruled supreme, painting everything with a thousand colors. Vines crept up the trees, spreading over the boughs, and flowers blossomed everywhere, filling the air with their delicate fragrance. Infinite droplets of water beaded the needles on the pine trees like little diamonds, sparkling in the last rays of sunlight.

I looked more carefully. Farther back, hidden behind lush hedges, I saw a roof. Although I couldn't be sure from where I was standing, I guessed it was the back of a house. If this was just somebody's back yard, I didn't dare imagine what wonders lay indoors.

Not far from where I was standing, something moved. I froze.

Someone was there, in the garden.

10

FATAL KISS

I felt as if someone had stabbed me in the heart. The foolish hope I'd been nurturing winked out like a candle in the wind. Entranced by the garden, I hadn't noticed the little wooden bench partially concealed behind some shrubs. Not until someone sitting there moved. Facing her, his back to me, Evan leaned in closer toward Ginevra, and my heart raged inside my chest.

What up until then had been only a suspicion was finally confirmed, shattering all my illusions. Although Evan was facing the other way, it was impossible not to recognize those soft curls that caressed the back of his neck, tinged with red by the warm rays of sunset.

He was wearing the same dark shirt he'd worn that day at school, and Ginevra was sensually running her hand up his back beneath it. Even the enchanted garden paled before Ginevra's beauty, fading as it willingly offered all its colors to her. Her long golden hair flowed over one shoulder and her skin had no need to be kissed by the sun; it glowed with its own light.

Their faces drew nearer until they were almost touching. A lump formed in my throat. Seeing them kiss would make my heart wither. I'd waited so long to find out what there was between them, I thought I'd be prepared for the worst. Instead, I felt like I'd fallen into a deep, dark pit.

There was no way they were brother and sister. My chest felt empty, as if an ice-cold hand had torn everything out of it as I stood there watching.

Anger. Disappointment. Frustration. Conflicting feelings battled it out. Above them all was a jealousy I hadn't realized I was capable of that suddenly rose up inside me like lava in an erupting volcano. I felt as if Ginevra was trespassing on some part of me, because for some utterly incomprehensible reason, deep in my heart I felt that Evan already belonged to me and me alone.

Seeing his hands on her, their mouths so close together, filled me with devastating rage. I felt like grabbing Ginevra by the hair, but then the thought of the afternoon with Evan came back, making my heart ache. Only a few hours before, he'd caressed my hand. I remembered the powerful jolt of electricity I'd felt when he touched me.

Now I was standing there watching those same hands cup another girl's face and draw it closer to his own. I wished I could know what it felt like to have his lips on mine. I felt betrayed. Fooled. Empty.

Could I really have misunderstood everything? His boldness, all his attention, had put a glimmer of hope into my heart that had grown stronger every time we met, but now it was being violently uprooted. Could I really mean nothing at all to him? My heart refused to accept the possibility.

"We have company." Still looking into his eyes, Ginevra informed Evan of my presence, not even glancing my way. I looked at her just in time to see her lock her razor-sharp eyes on me. Her opalescent irises were as intense as the sea where it touches the horizon. They didn't seem hostile, only curious.

For an instant we stared at each other. I tried to resist the hypnotic power that kept me glued to my spot, but even the air seemed to be working against me. And while all I could do was think about how I wished I could hit her with all the hatred I felt, her expression continued to reveal not a trace of hostility or even jealousy. There was just . . . frustration. The same shadow that often haunted Evan's eyes.

I desperately hoped it wasn't pity too. I'd rather she hated me.

Ginevra rose to her feet, snapping me out of my trance and making me step back cautiously, not taking my eyes off her face. She seemed to want to stop me, but now, freed from the invisible grip that had kept me standing there, I turned and ran.

"Hey! Wait!" Her voice reached me in a faded echo, but since it lacked the power of her gaze, it couldn't hold me back. I wanted to run as far away as possible. More than anything else, I *had* to avoid letting Evan see me. Being spotted by Ginevra was already humiliating enough. Having to hold back my tears in front of him, showing him my feelings, would have been too much to bear.

I stopped running to catch my breath and make sure no one was following me. My throat was dry and my eyes were brimming with tears. The path was deserted, and since it was far from the city, I was sure no one could see me. The knot in my throat dissolved, releasing an endless stream of tears that left pale streaks on my skin, ashen with misery.

I'd never cried over a boy before. I had no idea disappointment could cause such a reaction. I breathed in deeply, painfully filling my lungs with air, and started running again, hoping the wind would extinguish the fire burning in my chest. I wanted to go home and hide in the comfort in my room. That afternoon, so full of conflicting emotions, had been too much for me.

It was so strange how fast you could go from walking on a cloud to sinking into the deepest despair. But life doesn't always ask you what you think is fair. Moods change, like the seasons; the only difference is how quickly everything transforms.

Just a few hours ago I'd felt I was living a dream, but then it had turned into a nightmare. I'd been so stupid. Were a few moments of happiness really worth experiencing such excruciating pain? Was it better to be ignorant, to nurture false hope? Or to face the hard, painful truth?

I wasn't sure I knew the answer.

Even now, who could say I'd be able to turn the page and forget Evan just like that? Some irreversible mechanism had been triggered. Evan had gotten under my skin. But I'd discovered that it was truly agonizing to mean nothing to someone who meant everything to you. I could only rely on the healing power of time, hoping it would help me forget him.

Meanwhile, I kept seeing that petrifying, heart-rending image in my mind. Part of me had already considered the possibility that Evan and Ginevra were a couple, but actually seeing them together, so close, had changed everything. Nothing would ever be the same again.

The streetlights flickered on as I splashed nonstop across the wet asphalt. There were still lots of people on the streets, their anonymous features blurred to my eyes. The sky had cleared, revealing its stars. No clouds darkened the horizon. They'd all come together to darken my heart.

I didn't care what people might think, seeing me in that state. The only reaction I was worried about was my family's. Once I got home, I'd have to make sure my parents didn't see me this way.

A breeze blew gently on my face, drying my tears and tousling my hair like a comforting caress. I breathed in the fresh spring air avidly, then flinched when I suddenly banged into something solid. The impact threw me completely off balance and I fell, my nostrils filled with a scent that made my heart beat faster.

A scent as fresh as a waterfall in the depths of the forest. *Evan.*

"Ow! That hurts! Hey! Where are you running off to?" How was it that his voice could wipe away all my pain, physical and emotional? Or was it simply his presence that did it?

I pressed my lips together, fearful they would betray me by pouring out my anger at him. Like a vile traitor, my brain projected before my eyes the image of his lips on Ginevra's, but my heart, more loyal, erased it instantly, rebelling at its attempt to overpower me. It was strange, but I wanted to bask in the illusion that his kindness to me actually meant something. Just for a little while longer.

"Well? Care to tell me where you're off to in such a hurry, sweet thing?" A grin formed on his lips and my heart surrendered to him. I couldn't believe everything had changed since just a couple hours before, when we'd soared together between heaven and earth. But how had Evan managed to change clothes so quickly? He was wearing the red shirt he'd been wearing in the diner, not the dark one I'd seen him in back in the garden. And why was he acting like nothing had happened? Was it possible that Ginevra hadn't told him she'd seen me? If so, why? To spare me the embarrassment? Just the idea seemed ridiculous. Why should she cover for me when all I could do was think of the soft curve of Evan's lips? After all, he was her boyfriend.

The cold, damp surface beneath me reminded me that I was still on the sidewalk, unable to raise my eyes, which were puffy from crying. I must have looked like an idiot, but all my conflicting emotions were overwhelming me. I didn't know how to act naturally.

I wished Evan would go away and leave me alone, but instead he knelt down on the pavement, not worrying about getting his jeans wet. From that distance, there was no way I could hide my tears from him. His fingers tenderly lifted my chin. Like every other time, the physical contact generated an electric current, a light, comforting tingle that spread through my body and down to my stomach.

"You're crying."

I looked away. I didn't want him to feel sorry for me. But he gently grasped my chin, forcing me to look at him. I stared into his eyes that were misted with concern. They were too close for me not to yield to their spell. Almost in a daze, I felt his hand brush the hair away from my forehead and a sense of peace filled my head. It must be his gaze that had that healing effect on me.

His lips curved into the most seductive of smiles, taking away my newly regained breath. Evan was so handsome it almost hurt. I knew he was expecting an answer, but I also knew I wasn't about to give him one. He ran his thumb gently down my cheek, as if to wipe away the streaks left by my tears, and my heart quivered. "Well? Want to tell me what happened?" When I didn't answer, he offered me his hand to help me up. "You look so upset."

The thought of taking his hand made me tremble with desire. Even just brushing my fingers against his that afternoon had triggered such intense emotions. I shivered when my skin touched his and for a moment, erased the name Ginevra from my vocabulary. All that existed now were Evan and me and his hand in mine.

I noticed a mark on his skin I hadn't seen before, a scar on the back of his hand that looked a lot like a burn. Was it possible he really had been inside that building? I stood up, my eyes lingering on his hand before I let it go. "You're hurt."

Evan quickly pulled back his hand and hid it in his jeans pocket. "It's nothing." His face had suddenly darkened.

"Thanks for the help," I murmured, quickly changing the subject.

"So you didn't lose it, then." He stared at me, smiling again.

I frowned, confused.

"The power of speech. I was starting to think you bit your tongue off when you bumped into me."

I raised an eyebrow at his childish joke and he tapped the tip of my nose with his finger. Why did he keep touching me? Couldn't he see how confused it made me?

It wasn't my fault his attitude disoriented me. Part of me still felt betrayed and blinded by jealousy. Why was he being so nice? Was toying with my emotions really so much fun?

"I had a long afternoon, that's all," I said as my wounded pride tried to wrestle free of his deep, intense gaze. But my heart got the better of me and I stood there, longing to lose myself in the depths of his eyes.

For one single instant, I had the impression the same was true for him. Reason kept telling me to run, but every heartbeat was crying out his name. Was I mistaking his kindness for something else? Had I really been misreading the way he looked at me? I still sensed that invisible cord that connected me to him so strongly it made my heart ache.

"I'll take you home." The firmness with which he said it made it clear he wasn't going to take no for an answer. "I don't live far from here. Let's go get my motorcycle and—"

"No!" I blurted.

Evan stared at me, surprised by my vehemence. "I'm not letting you wander the streets in this condition. Follow me," he ordered, grabbing my hand.

No matter how much I longed for his company, going back there was out of the question. I didn't want to see Ginevra again. Now that I stopped to think about it, how could he have been coming from the opposite direction when we ran into each other?

More calmly, I said, "That's really nice of you." I reluctantly slid my hand out of his firm grip. "I'm almost there," I lied.

Evan leaned forward, forcing me to back up until I was pressed against the wall, and rested his hands on either side of my head, his eyes locked onto mine. My heart broke into a gallop.

"Don't be silly." His voice was persuasive, but it wasn't enough to change my mind. "I'm taking you home." There was something dark in his eyes, some kind of energy I couldn't fathom. Both sensual and wild.

"I told you I'm okay. Really," I insisted.

Evan seemed astonished by my stubbornness and dropped one arm to his side. "But your house is on the other side of town!" he added with exasperation, narrowing his eyes.

"How—" I stammered, confused. Why would he know that? "Never mind." Evan made no reply, skillfully letting the conversation drop. "Seriously," I reassured him, trying to act natural, "it's really nice of you to offer me a ride, but it won't take me long to get home. I walk really fast. Besides, the fresh air will do me good."

Evan frowned, uncertain, and then gave in, flashing a big grin at me. He leaned in to speak in my ear. "That means I'll miss out on the chance to have you with me on my bike," he whispered with a mix of sensuality and tenderness. A shot straight to the heart.

Wasn't he worried Ginevra might see us together? My head had caught fire again, ignited by his ambiguous behavior. "Yeah, um, some other time, maybe," I said, deciding he was just teasing me. A pang of reproach gripped my chest; my heart was screaming at me to accept. I forced myself to ignore it and pulled my hood up over my head. "See you at school," I mumbled, making sure not to look him in the eye, and started running again.

11

VISIONS

It was strange to have to deal with all these new, conflicting emotions. Usually logic guided me, but I'd heard that when it came to affairs of the heart, the voice of reason faded away and disappeared. I, too, had discovered that my instincts took charge when it came to Evan.

More than anything, I wanted to throw myself on the bed, bury my head under the pillow, and leave the long, grueling day behind me. But I knew that despite myself I would go back over that nerve-racking afternoon a thousand times.

No one had ever taught me to handle certain emotions, and I had the scars to prove it. When it came to others, giving advice had always been easy. Following it, not at all. And now that I was the one who needed help, I felt terribly alone. When I was little, my parents and teachers had encouraged me to socialize, but I'd spent more and more time in my shell, cut off from everyone. I'd always preferred the peace and quiet of a good story to the noisy company of other kids. Only now did I realize why they had tried for years to encourage me to let my friends in. But I never followed their advice, and now I was paying the consequences.

Still, I wasn't entirely sure it was due only to my loner personality. The truth was, I felt different from the other girls. And I couldn't even figure out if solitude was pursuing me or if I was the one seeking it out.

The only person I'd ever established a strong connection with was Peter. A boy. I'd never seriously imagined not being able to turn to him for help one day. For the first time I regretted not having a close girlfriend in my life.

I started to wish I'd accepted that ride from Evan. I was exhausted, drained not only emotionally but also physically, having run so hard, and my throat was parched.

Steps away from my front walk, I noticed the gate was ajar. I grumbled at myself for forgetting to close it, entered the yard, and clicked it shut behind me. The lights were off. My parents hadn't come home yet.

I hurried to the front door. I didn't like the idea of being in the dark, and the disturbing things I'd seen that afternoon still haunted me, along with older yet just as disturbing memories. The fire. The woods. The screams. The broken neck. I tensely searched my pockets for my keys. Right. Left.

Empty. I shrugged my backpack off, looking around nervously. I flipped through my two novels, checked the zipper flaps, and even looked in my camera case, but I couldn't find my keys anywhere, and it was so dark I could barely see. The longer I looked, the more panic overtook me. It was getting darker by the minute, the sky lit only by a pale quarter moon.

I had no intention of sitting outside and waiting for my parents to get home. I'd always had a problem with the dark. My mind went back to Evan over and over again, nagging at me for not accepting a ride from him. If only I had his number, I could call him and beg him to come get me.

I looked around nervously, trying to make out details of the yard, which in the dim light looked eerie. I could tell that Peter's family wasn't at home either because their shutters were all closed and their yard was pitch dark. High in the sky, the quarter moon mocked me, grinning, while an ominous half-light shrouded everything, reawakening my biggest fears.

Something moved behind me. My heart lurched and started racing. I whirled around, panting, but the yard was cloaked in silence.

Squinting from the corner of my eye, I glimpsed a shadow dart behind me. Fear paralyzed me. "Who's there?" I shouted into the night. My trembling voice faded into the darkness.

Hadn't I already had enough for one day? To the list of disturbing emotions, did I really have to add terror? Without moving a muscle, I peered in fright at the area around our front walk. Even the wind was still, holding the air hostage. The silence was so oppressive I couldn't tell if the thumping noise I heard was echoing through the darkness or coming from inside my chest.

"Looking for these?"

Evan's hushed, sensual voice sounded near the back of my neck. I froze without turning around and gulped, overwhelmed by unexpected emotion. Instead of startling me, his presence was like a soothing balm, triggering an immediate sense of relief. Recovering control of my body, I slowly turned to look at him. I couldn't be sure, but his eyes almost looked lighter, like I remembered them in my dreams. They seemed to reflect the moonlight. He held out the bunch of keys I thought I'd lost.

"Evan . . ." When I finally managed to speak, my voice was unsteady from surprise. "How, how did you . . . ?" I wasn't really sure what I was asking.

"I took my bike." Evan skillfully dodged the question.

"Okay, but how did you get in? I locked the gate." Suddenly I wasn't sure I wanted to hear the answer any more.

He smiled at me, his gaze captivating. "So what? I climbed over it. A damsel in distress needed me," he teased, shrugging.

"But I didn't see you climb over it. In fact, I didn't see you at all. I didn't even hear your motorcycle."

"Are you saying I'm a ghost rider?" Evan laughed at his own joke and I felt my cheeks burn. What was I insinuating, that he'd slipped into my yard like a phantom?

He noticed my embarrassment. "What can I say, sweet thing? I'm the silent type and you seem like a girl who's easily distracted." He hid a grin. "Besides, it's so dark out, you'd have to have eyes like a falcon to see me coming over the gate at the end of your walk, wouldn't you?" He moved his face closer to mine and pulled the hood of my red sweatshirt up over my head, lowering his voice. "But then again, what big eyes you have . . ."

I was caught off guard by how close he was. "Careful," I said, "I might mistake you for the big, bad wolf." *If you weren't so damn sexy, I thought.*

But it wasn't true. With him I didn't feel I was in danger. I felt safe. Irresistibly, dangerously safe.

Evan laughed. "You like fairy tales, Little Red Riding Hood?"

"Only the ones with happy endings," I shot back.

His face grew sad and he retreated a pace. "Not all fairy tales have happy endings."

I studied him silently. "Anyway, it's illegal to ride a motorcycle without a helmet."

"Huh?"

"Your helmet. Where is it?"

"I like to feel the wind in my hair," he replied, grinning, "and the thrill of speed." He raised an eyebrow, a mischievous glimmer in his eyes. I shut my mouth. I had the impression that arguing with him would be a waste of time. He always found a way to brush things off.

"For the record, you could have used the keys to let yourself in," I said, resigned, and he shrugged as if it hadn't even occurred to him. "Besides, how did you know where I live? Have you been spying on me by chance?" I asked, half annoyed and half worried. I was totally attracted, but I still wasn't sure who Evan was or how involved he was in the mysterious incidents that had begun to happen in Lake Placid.

A deep, melodious laugh rose up from his chest. "I had no choice but to follow you, sweet thing." Why on earth did he keep calling me that silly, childish . . . *adorable* nickname? "I ended up with your keys, Gemma," he explained, focusing the full force of his seductive gaze on me, despite the skeptical look on my face. He almost seemed to be trying to control my mind. "You dropped them when we bumped into each other. I thought I'd bring them back to you, but if you don't need them—" He pulled back the hand in which he'd been holding out my keys and turned to leave. "Well, I'll be off."

"Wait!"

Evan promptly froze. I couldn't be sure, since his back was to me, but I guessed he had a little smile on his face.

"Please," I forced myself to add, hoping to make up for the harsh tone I'd just used. I couldn't help it; hostility kept unexpectedly rising up in me. I didn't know if my rejection of Evan's attentions was because I knew he belonged to someone else or if my instinct distrusted him. It looked like I'd found out for myself why people say love is blind, because no matter how much my instinct insisted, my heart remained untarnished by doubt. "That was rude of me. You just wanted to help and I keep pushing you away."

My apology didn't have the effect I'd expected. My words seemed to awaken within him a slumbering agony. His expression darkened. He slumped his shoulders and hung his head so low I couldn't see his face. His silence almost convinced me he was on the verge of leaving, but then he unexpectedly turned.

The look on his face went straight to my heart. Evan stepped slowly toward me. From his grin, I could tell he was aware of the effect he had on me whenever he looked my way.

I let myself blush, comforted by the reassurance that the complicit night would hide the heat that rose to my cheeks. Moving with studied slowness, Evan reached out and took my hand as I watched him, mesmerized. He rested the keys on my palm and closed my fingers with his, cautiously moving his lips to my ear. The warmth of his breath left me in a daze.

What was he doing? And how was he depriving me of all control over my own body? My eyes half closed, lulled by the barely perceptible sound of his lips parting beside my ear.

"You have *nothing* to apologize for."

I swallowed, trembling at the hypnotic sound of his whisper. The meaning of his message eluded me. The heat of his breath penetrated my skin, spreading from my ear through my entire body until it softened into a tender warmth that filled my heart.

When I opened my eyes, Evan was disappearing around the corner.

Trying to shake off the emotion still gripping my stomach, I slid the key into the lock. Once inside, I leaned back against the front door as another shiver ran up my arms. I forced myself to walk down the hall and dumped my backpack on the floor. From the stairs, I could hear Iron Dog snoring noisily. I shook my head, smiling. The world had been filled with colors and I couldn't stop thinking about Evan's voice, the magnetic attraction his skin had on me when he came near, the power of his gaze. I headed distractedly to the bathroom, butterflies in my stomach. Could my brain be selecting which bits of information it retained? My face was still streaked with tears, but all I could think of was my hand clasped in his.

I turned on the tap and water flowed into the sink. While it was getting warm, I brushed my hair and put it up in a bun so it wouldn't get wet. I had the habit of wearing a black scrunchie around my upper arm. In winter, the long sleeves of my sweatshirts would push it down to my forearm. I couldn't even remember when I'd started doing it, but I never took it off, not even at night.

After brushing my teeth carefully, I leaned down, filled my cupped hands with water and splashed it on my face. The warmth on my skin was instant relief, rinsing away every last remaining trace of the day. Lingering there a few seconds, enjoying the sensation, I stuck my face under the tap. When my eyes had also been refreshed, I reached out my right hand, groped for a towel, and patted my face dry, especially around my eyes, which were still puffy and numb from the tears. I didn't want my parents to notice my mood when they came home. Wanting to check how red my eyes were, I looked into the mirror and saw Evan's piercing gaze fixed on me. Trembling with pure terror, I spun around, but the doorway to the hall was empty. A shudder ran over me.

Seized by panic, I slammed the door shut. With clenched fists, I wrapped my arms around my body, leaned against the wall and slid down to the floor. Even at that moment I sensed a dark presence hovering in the air, making me shiver. It was like someone was there watching me from close up, like they were *touching* me. I felt I was losing my mind. I was alone in the room, there was no such thing as ghosts, and people didn't come back from the dead . . . right? So why did it feel possible? Could my obsession with Evan be driving me insane? How could my head be coming up with the dark fantasies you only read about in novels?

I sighed. That afternoon had probably been a lot harder on me than I'd wanted to admit, that was all. Still, the idea of opening the door and going out into the hallway made me shudder. How I wished I had gleaned a little courage from my books instead of absorbing only the creepiest, scariest parts. But I wasn't a heroine in a book. When it came to real life, I couldn't help being scared about hearing voices in my head, sensing presences, and seeing shadows no one else could see. But why did it all lead back to Evan?

The light flickered and went out. I jumped up and threw open the door. There was something wrong in the air. I had to get out of there and fast. I ran into my room and slammed the door shut with all my weight, almost knocking it down. Trying to catch my breath, I locked it and scanned the room. Pulling my iPod out of a drawer in my walnut desk, I fell onto the bed, exhausted and drained. The music penetrated the barrier of tension that had built up inside me and slowly melted it as I stared at my light-green walls and my breathing returned to normal. I turned the volume up full blast, hoping to pull the plug on the world and let myself drift away with the mesmerizing voice of James Blunt. *Tears and Rain* lulled me until I nodded off.

12

WARNING

I was lost in the pitch dark. The cold had penetrated my bones. At least, I hoped the shivers running through my body were caused by the temperature.

It seemed the worst sensations I'd experienced by day had come back to torment me by night. I couldn't see where I was, but the idea of standing still terrified me, so I inched my way forward, feeling around on the floor with my foot before shifting my weight onto it. The wood creaked with each step, making a sinister sound that echoed through the room.

A window swung open with a groan. I jumped, but then was grateful for the beam of moonglow it let in, even though it drenched everything in a spectral half-light. The unmistakable smell of old wood and damp earth reached my nostrils, taking me back to when I was a little girl.

All the other children had avoided going near the big old house that was said to be haunted. Peter and I, on the other hand, made it our secret hideaway. To get there, we'd sneak through the woods to make sure some superstitious adult wouldn't try to stop us. From the eastern side of the house you could see Lake Placid partially hidden behind a tangle of branches and gnarled tree trunks. We would close the doors on the world and hide inside, letting our imaginations take us places no one else could go, where stories came to life and ghosts danced in the parlor, played the mahogany grand piano, took us by the hand. The house was full of secret places, as though specifically designed for people to hide in. It had lots of passageways that connected the various rooms or led down to the cellar. Still others led outdoors, to spots among the trees in the woods. Peter would spend ages searching for me until I got tired of waiting and would devise some way to let him find me.

The dusty, worn furniture, which was as old as it was majestic, reminded me of the huge manors I'd read about in nineteenth-century novels. Back when I was little I'd believed the portraits hanging on the walls were constantly staring at us.

I walked toward the window, guided only by the pale shaft of light, but something moved before I could reach it. A whimper escaped me. Someone was there, hidden in the darkness, in the farthest corner of the room. With unusual courage, I cautiously moved toward it as the floorboards creaked beneath my feet.

"Is someone there?" My voice came out tinged with fear that I tried to stifle. In reply, I heard a low groan as my eyes grew accustomed to the darkness. I made out the shape of a figure huddled on the floor, hidden in the shadows. The eerie rocking motion it was making, its body racked with sobs, made the blood in my veins run ice-cold. Was it the murderer, who'd come to hide in the house? I froze, terrified.

Suddenly, the window shutter flew open, banging against the outside wall. The noise made me jump as another shaft of moonglow poured in, illuminating the person's face. She stared at me fiercely, her eyes brimming with pain, bloodshot. I leaned closer, dismayed to see it was the mother of the little girl who'd perished in the fire. She continued to stare at me, her knees clasped to her chest, as if imagining she was cradling her daughter. Her dull, blank, exhausted eyes lingered on mine for a few seconds before she stared down at the floor again, rocking back and forth.

I was full of anguish, like I had been during that terrible fire. Her screams came back, echoing through my head. All at once they stopped. I reached out and rested my hand on the woman's shoulder. When she felt my touch, she slowly raised her eyes and stared into mine, but only for a moment—she was distracted by something behind me. "Amy . . ." she whispered in a frail voice.

I went deathly pale and slowly followed her gaze over my shoulder, my eyes open wide in a horrible presentiment. Terror trapped the air in my lungs. A little girl with golden hair stared at me from a few steps away.

Every muscle in my body was trembling. A strange perception made me absolutely certain that life had abandoned her little body. Her face was ashen and there were rings around her eyes, yet she wore an unusual look of serenity that prevented the shadows of death from showing through her skin. There was no hint of pain, suffering, or terror in the girl's eyes. Quite the opposite. She looked pleased, satisfied. Fulfilled. As if death had completed her, made her happy, even.

Her lips were upturned in a graceful smile. She raised her hand and slowly waved it from side to side, saying goodbye. I watched the scene, stunned. Amy reached out into the darkness, as if searching for the hand of someone hidden there.

I squinted and spotted a shadowy form. I wasn't sure if it had been there the whole time or appeared only later, like a ghost. Whoever it was seemed reluctant to come out into the open. Amy looked up at the person holding her hand as I stared at them, petrified and bewildered.

A scream pierced the silence. The mother's shrieks grew stronger, shriller, as she shouted her daughter's name through her sobs, afraid the person would take her little girl away. I turned back to the woman to comfort her, but she was gone. She'd disappeared, leaving behind only the echo of her grief-stricken voice and a bare, damp wall covered with mildew. Suddenly, a burst of heat lashed at my face, blinding me with its intense light. I whirled around and discovered the whole room had caught fire. The flames were consuming the wood.

No. Taking a closer look, I found I wasn't in the lake house any more. I was inside that building where little Amy's life had been cut short. Her fiery prison. I made my way through the flames; maybe if I got to her in time I could carry her to safety. The fire continued to throw up sheets of flame, separating us. Amy stared at me, not even blinking, surrounded by the flames.

"Run!" I shouted to her, but no sound came from my lips. I felt that the smoke was crushing my lungs. The shifting flames revealed what I hadn't been able to see before: the person hidden in the darkness.

"Evan," I whispered, my eyes going wide. My gaze locked onto his. He stared back at me, distraught, guilty. Breaking the spell, he turned his back to me, his hand clasping little Amy's as he led her away. I wanted to stop them, but Evan came to a halt, as though he'd guessed my intentions.

"There's nothing you can do," he warned me without turning around, sorrow in his voice. "There's nothing anyone can do." He sounded resigned.

Why was he so upset? The little girl was with him now. He could save her.

"I can't," he whispered through clenched teeth, replying to my thoughts. "I can't deny who I am." He raised his eyes to mine and his expression grew serious. "Time's almost up."

My body reacted to his words with a shudder. My instinct seemed to have grasped the meaning behind them. Something ominous that my heart refused to understand. The look Evan was giving me seemed more like a *warning*. He closed his eyes and when he opened them again something glimmered. It looked like a tear, but it vanished in the heat of the fire before I could be sure. His gaze suddenly pierced mine. "I won't be able to avoid it. I'm sorry," he said.

Something was tormenting him. From this close up, it looked unbearable. I felt it coming straight from him to me, through my skin. I wished I could wipe it from his face, it was so hard for me to bear. Why was he suffering? And why was his sadness having such a contagious effect on me?

"What? What won't you be able to avoid?" I asked, unsteadily finding my voice again.

Evan looked torn, as though struggling to decide whether or not to answer me. "You'll be next." His words sliced through me like a sword of ice. Helpless, my eyes wide, I watched him begin to fade away into the flames, taking the little girl with him. His voice echoed through the depths of my mind, repeating the words endlessly, like a boomerang coming back over and over again. I watched in astonishment as they vanished, hand in hand.

13

SUSPICION

I opened my eyes, panting, my forehead beaded with sweat, and realized I was in my bed. The light was peeking through the crack between the curtains. The alarm clock on my nightstand read six a.m. School started at seven-thirty. At least I wouldn't be late, for a change.

Lying in bed, I stretched, noticing I was still wearing the same clothes I'd worn the day before. A cold shiver ran over me as my mind recalled the long day I'd left behind. It was no surprise I'd had another of those strange dreams. I was getting used to them, in fact.

I still had my shoes on and in my hand was the cord to my iPod, which I'd fallen asleep listening to. I found it lying upside down on the linoleum floor. Sitting up, I was surprised to discover it still had some power left. A somber melody was coming through the earbuds. I raised them to my ears and a shiver ran through me as Amy Lee's hypnotic voice sang *Before the Dawn.*

Not a sound was coming from the rest of the house except for my dad's snoring. Barefoot, I tiptoed to the bathroom, trying not to wake my parents. I carefully closed the door, turned around and started at the sight of my own reflection; the eerie memory of what I'd seen in the mirror the night before still made me tremble.

As the water in the shower was heating up, I let my sweaty clothes slide to the floor: worn jeans, a green military top and a dark red sweatshirt. I waited for steam to fill the room, tested the temperature of the water and stepped inside. Pointing the jet of water onto my neck, I slowly pushed my hair to one side, letting the boiling hot water run down my body. The comfortable sensation of the water on my skin melted the tension in my muscles and relaxed me, body and soul.

I didn't know what to expect today. I just hoped it would be less intense than yesterday. Despite myself, I couldn't banish the confused images that haunted me like malicious ghosts. Reality mingled with my dreams, blurring the line between the two. I attempted to assemble the memories connected to Evan into a logical pattern, but no matter how hard I tried, my heart kept me from putting the insane puzzle together.

For a second, I was tempted to crawl back under the covers and skip school to avoid seeing Evan. I wasn't sure I could face the confused emotions he was triggering in me. Even less did I want to see him with Ginevra, now that I knew they were a couple. She'd had all the time she needed to tell Evan about the embarrassing episode of the previous afternoon. It was too humiliating.

Then again, I couldn't hide forever, and I knew for a fact that unless you faced problems head-on, you risked failing. It was better to keep moving forward and overcoming obstacles than to just stand there doubting myself. That was what my grandmother always used to say.

Deep down in my heart, I had the feeling my sudden boldness stemmed from something completely different. The truth was, I was dying to see him again. I stepped out of the shower, steam rising from my skin and filling the room. I opened the window a crack to let it out, rubbed my wet hair with a hand towel, and wrapped my body in a large white bath towel. I went to the mirror but couldn't see my reflection, so I raised a corner of the towel to wipe it clean, then stopped, baffled.

There was something written on the mirror. I squinted, trying to make out what it said before the steam vanished and it disappeared. Stunned and shocked, I read:

Gemma
∞

Who could have left my name on the mirror in that graceful writing? And why interlace it with the infinity symbol?

Only when the steam had completely vanished did I realize I'd been standing there stock-still. I peered into my own eyes with the strange sensation that they didn't belong to me, watching as my pupils dilated at the memory of the face reflected there the day before. Could Evan actually have been there? My whole body trembled, but I drove away the thought as quickly as it had appeared. The very idea was ridiculous.

"Gemma, is that you?" My mom's groggy voice came from the hall. "Who are you talking to?"

Worried, my eyes darted back to my reflection. Had I been speaking out loud? What was happening to me? I felt more and more like my body was slipping out of my control. Or was my mind disconnecting from my body?

"Are you on the phone? Who is it, this early?" she insisted, raising her voice so I'd hear her.

"Nobody, Mom, I was just singing, that's all." The moment I said it, I felt a burden being lifted: no doubt the writing on the mirror was a message from my mom. She'd just been moved when she saw I'd fallen asleep still wearing my clothes. An unusual way to remind me that she loved me.

I shook my head and ran my fingers through my hair. Had I really thought Evan had come into my bathroom to leave me a coded message on the mirror? I felt like an idiot for even considering it.

I bounded down the steps three at a time and grabbed a chocolate doughnut from the kitchen table.

"Take your umbrella!" my mom shouted from upstairs. "The forecast says rain."

I opened the door, stopping on the threshold before leaving. "I love you too, Mom!" I shouted up the stairwell.

Cold drizzle fell on my head and ran down my hair as I hurried to the bus stop. Watching the rain through the bus window relaxed me. I leaned my head against the glass and closed my eyes, listening to the comforting sound of the raindrops splashing onto the leaves.

A loud noise made me open them again. My eyes darted to the road. I had no doubt it was Evan's motorcycle. I sat up straighter so my breath wouldn't condense on the cold windowpane, blurring my view. The motorcycle pulled up alongside the bus and slowly began to pass it.

Ginevra's eyes shot to mine without a trace of hesitation. Like she'd known exactly where I was sitting. Evan stared at the road ahead of him as locks of his wet hair, darkened from the rain, flopped over his forehead. Ginevra's golden hair streamed out behind her, carried by the wind. They both had their helmets tucked under their arms.

I felt a pang of uneasiness in the pit of my stomach. There was no denying they were perfect for each other. I was nothing in comparison with Evan, let alone Ginevra. Next to them, I was a puny, flickering candle beside a gigantic lighthouse.

Ginevra watched me until Evan sped up and they disappeared from sight. Had she told him? My heart was pounding in my throat at the thought that once I got off the bus I'd have to face the situation.

I glanced around the school parking lot, hiding behind my umbrella, sadly discovering that Evan's motorcycle wasn't there. In the English classroom, I sat down at my desk and looked out at the stream of students rushing inside to get out of the rain.

The room slowly filled up. I shifted my chair to make room for Jeneane, who showed up last, right before the teacher. My eyes darted back and forth distractedly. Evan's desk was empty. As though washed away by the rain, every last trace of anxiety about seeing Evan disappeared, eclipsed by the fear that I wouldn't see him again. Slumped dejectedly in my chair, I started to wonder what could have kept him from coming. Ginevra hadn't come either. If they hadn't been heading to school, where had they gone? I was consumed with curiosity. The thought of the two of them together, who knows where, made my stomach burn.

Now that I had to go without it, I realized Evan's presence had a soothing effect on my mind. Like a drug, it could make the outside world and all its problems disappear. The lesson felt endless, stifling. I couldn't stop glancing at his empty desk. Trig went by more quickly, probably because he wasn't in that class with me. During lunch I chewed slowly, staring silently at my tray, resigned to Evan's absence. The only thing people at school were talking about was the fire and the little girl who'd died in it. Hearing that the rain had stopped pounding on the roof, I turned to check the sky and my heart skipped a beat when I saw Ginevra sitting at the table by the window.

I held my breath and looked for Evan, but he wasn't there with her. She was looking blankly out the window. From time to time she squinted slightly, as though trying to follow a conversation. A crazy thought, since no one was sitting near her. She was so distracted that I stared at her for a little longer than I should have. Just then, she raised her eyes and looked straight at me like she had that morning. Unable to hold her gaze, I immediately looked down at my tray and felt the blood rush to my cheeks. Part of me felt guilty about the pang of desire that struck me whenever I thought of Evan, even though I knew he was with someone else.

The fact that Ginevra didn't glare at me with anger or jealousy like she should have just made me feel worse. Overcome with guilt, I shyly got up from my chair, said goodbye to the others, and left the cafeteria, feeling her cold gaze on me the whole time.

The newfound hope of seeing him during Spanish class wiped away the guilt the moment I escaped the weight of Ginevra's eyes. My instinct seemed to be behind it, not my heart. Or more likely, it was just a selfish side of myself I'd never known I had. Breathing in Evan's presence was becoming more and more of a necessity. It was strange how my desire had completely eclipsed the embarrassment that had made me want to avoid him. My blood longed for the emotions he aroused in me, like a junkie desperate for his next fix, well aware of how harmful it was. Who knew why?

I knew.

He can't live without it. Just like I couldn't go without Evan any more. When he wasn't there, I felt I couldn't breathe, even though I realized how crazy the feeling was. *Supernatural.* Could some dark magic have indissolubly connected me to him?

"Encantado de tenerla entre nosotros," Mr. Wilson welcomed me to class with a hint of sarcasm as I walked to my desk, hanging my head.

"Siento llegar tarde," I apologized sheepishly.

I considered Mr. Wilson an excellent teacher. He had the rare ability to keep us constantly interested, one way or another, and gladly interrupted his lesson to laugh with us students and speak openly, often touching on topics that weren't strictly scholastic.

Today, though, not even Mr. Wilson's Spanish class would be enough to take my mind off Evan. His absence filled the whole classroom. There was no reason for me to keep hoping he'd show up. Evan simply wasn't coming today. I forced my brain not to think about him any more, but my heart was screaming its dissent.

My last class of the day was photography, and the darkroom was located right off the school lobby. It was one of my favorite courses because it relaxed me. I'd always loved it, and in the half-light of the darkroom I could focus on my thoughts.

Before the teacher turned off the lights, I smiled and said hello to my friend Rhiannon Patterson, a sweet girl I'd known for a few years whose passion for the subject I shared. She was very pretty, blond, and had a captivating smile. Rhiannon had a knack for photography and was one of the most promising students in our class, even if my pictures weren't bad. The first time we'd seen each other was through the lenses of our cameras when we were thirteen. I'd been at the lake with Peter and he asked why I'd started laughing for no clear reason and, on top of that, why the girl with braided hair walking over to us was laughing too. She took us to her house and showed us her collection of shots in the darkroom in her basement. My parents had promised we would set up our own darkroom, but I was starting to suspect it would never happen. It was too expensive, and at home there were always more important things we needed to buy.

In the pitch dark, I handed Faith her camera. For the course, the school lent us film cameras. Once I'd sealed my film reel inside the lightproof canister in front of me, the teacher switched on the red light, making my classmates look like anonymous, sinister shadows. One by one, I added and removed the developer, stop bath and fixer. Each of us had taken pictures of animals. Mr. Madison was going to award extra credit to the most evocative one. My photo was of a squirrel on a tree branch that hung over the lake. Faith, instead, had shot a close-up of her beautiful horse, Hope. I'd always liked how their names sounded together. Faith and Hope.

The smell of the chemicals was so strong it was going to my head. I gave my canister to Mr. Madison, who was rinsing them for us in the sink, took a strip of negatives I'd developed the week before, and began to enlarge one of the shots on a sheet of photo paper.

I kept thinking about Evan, wondering when I'd see him again. I shivered, my skin tickled by a puff of cool air, though the door was closed. I went back to focusing on my project. *To focusing on Evan.* Why did I keep thinking about him so incessantly? Like a poison, he'd gotten into my mind and I couldn't think straight any more. Just then, I felt him right there beside me. Instinctively, I turned to check, even though the very thought was ridicu—.

I froze. My senses hadn't been fooling me. Evan really *was* there beside me. My heart raced. Why was he there? Was he taking photography too now? Even more, how had he gotten in? I was sure he hadn't been there when the teacher switched off the lights. I stared at him, incredulous, and he stared back at me insistently. With unexpected boldness, he stroked my arm, making me tremble. My heart was pounding in my chest. He took my hand in his and studied our entwined fingers. He moved so close to me it left me dazed.

Overcome with emotion, I tried to control my breathing. As I bathed the paper in the chemicals and hung it to dry, he followed my movements, accompanying my hands. I looked at the negatives but couldn't concentrate. His fingers continued to caress my arm and then slid down to clasp mine. He was slow, as if studying every tremble caused by the touch of our hands. He brushed the tip of his nose against my neck and I felt him draw a deep breath, right behind me, sending a shiver down my spine.

I closed my eyes and surrendered to emotion. "What are you doing here?" I murmured softly.

He was silent for a moment but finally answered, "I can't resist you."

I trembled at the sound of his whisper in my ear.

"Did you say something?" Faith's voice snapped me out of my spell.

"Huh?" I said, embarrassed. "No, I—" I spun around, shocked. Evan was gone. *How was it possible?*

"Hand me the photo paper, would you? Hey, what's wrong? You see a ghost?" she joked, but I didn't hear her.

My heart beat wildly. I took a breath, but the smell of the chemicals made me dizzy, as did the red light and my classmates' shadows. On the verge of fainting, I ran out into the hallway, into the light. The other students' protests about my having opened the darkroom door followed me, but I didn't care. I ran into the bathroom and leaned against a sink, gripping the gray plastic, my head down.

It was like I'd experienced a waking dream. But I couldn't tell if the genre was horror or romance. Evan's presence was everywhere. He was like a ghost who'd come to haunt me, to hound me.

I turned on the faucet and splashed water on my face. It was all so crazy. Evan hadn't even come to school today. Was my desire for him actually so strong it was causing hallucinations? My mind refused to accept that he'd really been there, but my body was my witness. He'd touched me. His touch had been real. Every part of me had sensed it.

I can't resist you.

And his voice? Had it all been in my head again? Ever since Evan had come into my life, everything had become bizarre and irrational . . . but full of amazing emotions.

I stared at my reflection, the blue doors of the stalls in the background. I'd just lived through that scene with a perfect stranger from the movie *Ghost.* And it had been so beautiful and magical. I was going crazy. It was official. And yet, why should it matter if an event was real or dreamed, if you really experienced it? No matter what you called it, it existed. It was an emotion you felt. A memory you kept.

No matter what had happened, I'd *felt* those sensations.

"Gemma!" Jeneane called out, catching up to me in the rain.

"Hey," I replied, raising a hand, totally lacking in enthusiasm.

"So what's up with you anyway?" The bitterness in her voice took me completely by surprise. "You're getting weirder and weirder," she scoffed, looking at me almost like she didn't recognize me any more. I hadn't thought about how the change in my behavior might come across to the others. "I'm not the only one who thinks so, you know. Pete and the others have noticed too. You come to school, but it's like your mind's a million miles away. Just make sure the teachers don't notice or your GPA is going to nosedive," she warned me, not troubling to hide the hint of sarcasm in her voice.

"I'm a little tired, that's all," I said.

"Faith told me you ran out of photography class. What happened?"

"Nothing. Nothing happened. I'm just a little stressed. I haven't been sleeping very well lately." Deep down, it wasn't a total lie.

Unlike Jeneane, I'd never been very talkative. My replies bothered people because they were too monosyllabic. Her vocal cords, on the other hand, were like an electronic device that worked nonstop. One word activated her voice, and it just kept going until you were desperate to figure out how to switch it off. And most of the time her brain didn't seem to be connected to it. Sometimes it was so hard for me to follow what she was saying that I'd just nod my head without even trying to understand the gist of the conversation. If there was one, that was. Instead, I'd often focus on her breathing, wondering when she would stop to take a breath. It was fascinating, her extraordinary ability to fill her lungs with such an incredible amount of air.

"So are you coming or not? Hello?!" Still blathering, Jeneane was waving her hand in front of my face. I realized I'd done it again.

"Where?" I asked, re-entering my body.

"There! This is exactly what I'm talking about. I bet you didn't hear one word of what I just said," she complained, exasperated. I looked at her guiltily. "We're going to the lacrosse game tonight," she explained. "Everybody's going to be there. Are you coming or not?" she asked, probably for the hundredth time. "It means a lot to Pete," she added. Where was Peter, anyway? "I bet you didn't even notice he's picked up the habit of cutting class." Jeneane said it almost reproachfully.

Pet. I was suddenly overcome with guilt. I hadn't been thinking about him at all lately. Evan had gotten into my head, driving out everything else. Regretfully, I realized Pet had begun to keep his distance from me too. Now that I thought about it, he hadn't called me for days. I tried hard to remember our last conversation, but my mind drew a blank. Was Jeneane right? Did I really seem so distant on the outside? Peter meant too much to me to risk losing his friendship. I had to call him and clear things up as soon as I could.

"Thanks for the invitation," I told Jeneane, "but I don't feel very well. I think I'm going to stay home." I said goodbye with a little wave and hurried off. I was certain the rain would be much more comforting than Jeneane if she was set on nagging me all the way home.

"Whatever!" Her exasperated voice reached me as she lined up with the other students to board the bus.

"What happened at school today, Squirrelicue? Your photography teacher, Mr. Madison, called right before you got home."

I rested my fork on my plate. "Nothing. I just got dizzy, that's all. The chemicals we use in the darkroom must have gone to my head. What did he tell you?" Did he know I'd had an imaginary love story right there in his darkroom?

"He just said you ran out of his class and didn't come back."

"Oh. Okay." That was a little reassuring. I'd hate to have to drop his course out of embarrassment.

"Now that I think about it, he didn't just call because of that. He said you'd forgotten to hand something in to him. His number's on the fridge if you want to call him back."

Shit. I was supposed to turn in the photographs I'd taken of the students during the school year. Rhiannon and I were in the Yearbook Club. In addition to the professional portraits of the students, the yearbook included shots we'd taken. The club was far from popular, since it meant a lot of work, which I didn't mind at all. I found it relaxing snapping pictures, choosing them, grouping them . . . So many emotions captured forever on paper. I'd secretly immortalized moments of my classmates' lives. Candid shots were the best kind, because they showed the subjects' souls. Today had been the deadline for turning in our pictures to the teacher and I'd completely forgotten. I had to remember to call him. And I still had to think of a quote to include beneath my portrait.

After late lunch with my parents, I grabbed my backpack in search of my phone and holed up in my room. Sitting on the bed, I hugged my knees to my chest as I dialed Peter's number. The line began to ring as I drummed my fingers on my shoe, waiting for him to pick up. I'd been treating Pet so appallingly. How could I not have noticed his absence? I couldn't forgive myself.

My impatience grew with every ring. Peter had never taken so long to answer before. Was he mad at me? I couldn't blame him. I dialed the number again to make sure I hadn't gotten it wrong. The phone continued to emit its bleak tone but no one on the other end decided to take the call. That wasn't like him. On my third try, the sound of his voice calmed my anxiety. I realized how much I'd missed him, even though I'd seen him at school only the day before. Or had it been longer than that? "Hey, Pet!" I cheered, letting my excitement show.

"Oh, it's you." His voice, on the other hand, went dull when he heard mine. It hit me right in the heart. I knew it was entirely my fault. I shouldn't be giving Evan all that attention if it was going to cost me my friendship with Peter. To Evan I didn't exist. He had Ginevra. And I risked losing Peter too unless I managed to sort things out with him.

"You're not very happy to hear from me," I said sadly, hoping it wasn't too late to fix things.

"No . . . Gemma, sorry, it's not you," he replied vaguely. "I'm just wrapped up in something I've been working on." He clearly didn't want to tell me what he was talking about.

"You didn't come to school."

"Is that why you called?" He seemed to be in a hurry to hang up. "Everything's fine, thanks for asking," he said indifferently. Hearing the coldness in his voice tortured me. He'd put up a wall between us. Or maybe I'd been the one who'd done it.

"Come on, tell me about whatever it is you've been doing," I said, begging for his attention.

"Um . . . I'm not sure I should talk about it. It'd be better if I didn't get anyone else involved. Sorry, Gemma."

Anyone. The word echoed in my head. I'd become *anyone* to him. "Not even me? We've never kept secrets from each other." My tone had become almost imploring, but the words actually sounded fake to my ears. I'd been the first one to keep a secret from him. I wasn't sure now exactly what the secret was or why I'd kept it from him. Suddenly, I couldn't remember any of the stupid reasons I'd stopped confiding in Peter to such a point that I'd actually pushed him out of my life.

"You know you can trust me," I said, judging from his silence that he only needed a little coaxing.

"Okay! Okay, I'll tell you." His enthusiasm rose suddenly. "But don't think I'm crazy—and don't get angry. After all, you asked."

Get angry? Why would I get angry? "I'll remember," I reassured him. Still he hesitated. It was starting to get on my nerves. "Well? Don't keep me in suspense, Pet. What's it all about?"

"That James guy."

I almost dropped the phone. I was torn between curiosity about what Peter would tell me and anger at his contemptuous tone. "What's Evan got to do with anything?" I snapped, almost growling. It sounded more like a retort than a question.

Peter let out a groan of disgust because of the protective tone I'd taken. "Whose side are you on, anyway? Gemma, there's something about him and the others. I don't trust them. I know they're hiding something."

"What do you mean, they're hiding something? That's ridiculous!"

"I tried to look into his past, to find out what school he transferred from, but I couldn't find anything at all. It's like he doesn't even exist! The same thing goes for his girlfriend. Who are they? What are they hiding?"

I flinched. Of everything he'd just said, what bothered me most was the word "girlfriend." But there was something I was missing. "Wait, back up a second. You said 'the others.' What others? Are you talking about Ginevra?"

"There are four of them," he told me, sounding like a proud, satisfied detective who'd discovered an important lead.

"Peter, what are you talking about?"

"Evan and Ginevra aren't the only ones! There are two other guys. They're not much older than we are, I think," he explained, getting more and more excited.

"How do you know that?"

"I saw them! Gemma, I know where they live and—"

"What? You went to their house?" I said, appalled. Actually, I had no right to yell at him for something I'd done myself.

"This morning I went to school early to go running and I saw him ride by with the blond chick. I noticed they didn't stop, so I followed them in my dad's car and saw where they live. Man, you should see the place! It's this massive ancient manor. I'd never seen it there before."

I'd seen for myself how vast the estate was. "So what? What's so strange about that? I don't get it." I was trying hard to seem nonchalant, but a strange instinct was compelling me to defend Evan and his friends despite the fact that I didn't even know them.

"What's so strange about it? Gemma! Did you hear what I just said? I've definitely never seen a house there before. And you can't build such a huge place overnight."

"How can you be so sure? Maybe you'd just never noticed it. After all, you never go that far outside Lake Placid. You don't even like the forest."

"How did you know it's outside of town?" he asked quickly, catching me off guard.

I bit my lower lip so hard it almost started to bleed. "You . . . said so a minute ago," I lied.

"Gemma, I'm sure I'm right. There's something strange about them. I don't trust them. We don't know them. Who's to say it wasn't one of them who killed Mr. Lussi? Who else would have done it?"

The thought made my blood run cold. I should be trusting my best friend—I mean, this was Peter. But I couldn't ignore how upset I was that he'd accused Evan. I felt the need to flat out defend him, but I didn't dare. That would jeopardize everything. "Are you actually accusing them of murder? Don't you think you're overreacting? They're kids, like us. We don't know them, true, but that's not reason enough."

"Yeah it is, if somebody's dead. I saw something. I'm not sure of it, but—" Peter seemed to be on the verge of letting me in on something, but changed his mind. "I'm not going to pretend like it's nothing. I still haven't told you that this morning Evan went into the house with Ginevra. After a few hours, she rode out on his motorcycle. I watched the place all day long and nobody else left the house."

"So what? Ginevra turned up at school today. What's so strange about it?"

"Nothing, except that Evan just came home a moment ago."

From the silence that fell, I knew he was waiting for me to put two and two together, but I just couldn't follow him. "I don't get it," I admitted, exasperated.

"I told you nobody left the house! How'd he end up *coming back* later on?"

"Didn't it cross your mind that there might be some kind of back entrance?" As I was saying it, I realized how wrong that sounded. I'd seen the fortress wall for myself and there were no secondary exits. I hadn't even seen a main entrance. And if Peter had gotten in through that opening in the wall, there weren't many alternatives.

"I've never been more serious in my life. I'm going to find out what they're hiding. Nothing's going to stop me." Hearing how solemnly he spoke, I rolled my eyes, relieved that he couldn't see me. "And don't roll your eyes at me!" he snapped, making my jaw drop.

Thinking about it, I liked this supernatural-detective version of Peter more than his quiet, shy version. Maybe this was his way of avoiding the monotony of his peaceful little hometown life. Or, even more likely, he read way too many comic books.

"Did anyone see you?"

"Not only did they see me, one of them threatened me. Take my word for it, they're dangerous. Especially the girl. There's something creepy about her."

"Someone threatened you?"

"One of them was in the middle of an actual fistfight with Blondie when I noticed there was this other one crouching on the roof watching them. I hear a thud and I see that Ginevra's hurled the first kid against a tree trunk. The earth literally shook under my feet. Seconds later, the guy from the roof? He's right there next to me. Saw me spying on them. Asks if I'm looking for something. I'm so spooked by his reappearing act I can't say a thing, and then he mutters something that sounds like a threat."

"Well, don't forget, you were spying on them at their own home. He had every right," I retorted.

Peter ignored me. "I pretended to leave but I just hid nearby. That's how I saw Evan coming back."

"You're so stubborn!"

"I'm not afraid of them. And you might not believe me, Gemma, but I wouldn't trust them if I were you. Listen, I didn't want to say this and make the police suspicious, but the last time we were down by the lake, when you got lost, I saw Mr. Lussi in the woods. Right before I found you."

"Are you saying *I* killed him?" I asked sarcastically. I knew where he was going with this. "Peter, you shouldn't have kept it a secret!"

"Neither should you, then. He told me he'd talked to you." My heart leapt to my throat. "I kept quiet to protect you." I felt like a total hypocrite. Peter knew I'd lied to him, but he was still taking care of me, while I was stubbornly protecting some guy I barely even knew. "At first I didn't believe you'd seen someone in that spot in the woods where I finally found you, but then James showed up at school. I saw the look on your face. You recognized him! *He* was the guy you saw. A little while later, we heard Mr. Lussi had died. You don't have to be Sherlock Holmes to figure out what happened. Don't act like it didn't cross your mind. And after what I saw today, I'm even more sure they aren't who they say. Stay away from James," he said sternly. His voice softened. "At least do it for me."

I gulped. What if Peter was right? *No. What he's saying is ridiculous,* I told myself. Something in his voice as he said those last words told me I was wrong to think it was all because of his comic-book imagination. His suspicion of Evan was simply the result of his jealousy. He was just trying to prove that Evan was wrong for me. Like I didn't know that already.

"Peter, you don't have to prove anything to anyone. Just drop it, please," I begged him.

"Do you really not feel it? There's something evil about him. How can you not realize it?"

Yeah, I thought, *her name's Ginevra.* "You don't even know him," I sighed, my patience used up.

"I don't need to know him. It's something I can sense."

"And I sense you're getting paranoid. Come on, Pet, you can't be serious!"

"Goddamn it, Gemma, open your eyes! Have you seriously not noticed anything strange about those two? At school Ginevra does nothing but talk, and he never even answers her. It's like she's reading his mind. I've watched them. Even their showing up all of a sudden made me suspicious, but strangely, nobody except me seems to care."

I didn't want to admit it, but he wasn't all wrong. Lots of things had happened since I first saw Evan in the woods. Strange things that Peter didn't know about. Unlike Pet, though, I'd never really seriously considered they might have to do with him. "You're being paranoid. There's nothing strange about them!" I snapped, exasperated. And yet I couldn't completely shake the apprehension that had wormed its way into my mind.

"You're wrong, Gemma, and I'm going to prove it," he promised, not a trace of doubt in his voice.

"If you say so," I said, shrugging. There was no point in contradicting him any more.

"Gotta go. See you at the game?"

I would rather have stayed home, like I'd told Jeneane that afternoon, but I knew how much me being there meant to Peter. I owed it to him. "Of course, I wouldn't miss it for the world."

"Should I swing by to get you after practice?"

"I'll bike. See you there," I said, although it was nice of him to offer to walk me there right in the middle of his pregame concentration.

"See you later, then."

"Don't forg—" I began, but Peter had already hung up.

The conversation with Peter had taken a completely unexpected turn. A new wave of concerns had joined the ones already lapping at the shores of my mind. I began to suspect Evan really was hiding some dark secret. After all, from the very start I'd sensed something sinister about him. I'd followed some kind of primordial call all the way to his house. And then the voices, the visions. The nightmares. And Evan was connected to all of it.

Could Peter actually be right? I fell back onto my bed, my eyelids growing heavy. Could Evan really have something to hide?

EVAN

14

UNEASINESS

"Evan, finally you're back! It took you ages!" Ginevra came up to me as I forced myself to walk through the door. "Well? Don't keep me waiting, how did it go?" she asked apprehensively.

"They said no," I replied, furious. My jaw muscles ached from gritting my teeth for so long.

"I'm so sorry," she whispered, moving closer.

I looked at her, clenching my fists, overcome by frustration. I still didn't know how I'd ever manage to finish what I'd come here to do. They'd refused to pass my assignment on to someone else like I'd hoped.

"Don't worry," Ginevra reassured me, resting her hands on my shoulders. "I'll help you see this through. It'll be over soon."

"I hope so, but meanwhile we've got another problem to worry about. That guy Peter, he's suspicious."

Ginevra held back a laugh and went on, her voice filled with serious sweetness. "Yeah, I sensed that. Everyone except him stopped wondering about us. He must be immune to your thought control. In any case, he's harmless, Evan. I'm keeping an eye on him. Just remember to move your lips more at school, okay?"

"He's getting too curious. If he keeps it up I'll have to do something about it. This morning I saw him spying on the house through that hole Simon and Drake made in the perimeter wall," I told her, shooting a reproachful glance at my brothers.

"Hey, what? Can I help it if I'm a force of nature?" Drake said, flashing me a sardonic smile.

"I'll show you who's a force of nature! Bring it, you ape! I can take you anytime, anywhere!" Simon said, taking Drake's remark as a challenge and rushing at him.

"Stop it!" I yelled. I'd never been so on edge before.

"Whoa, at *ease*, soldier! Calm down! We're just having a little fun. What's up with you? Not long ago you used to have fun too. Don't you like boxing any more?" Drake said, trying to provoke me with a feint.

"At least try to be more careful. You knocked a hole in the wall, damn it! Somebody might have seen you!" I snarled, grabbing Drake's fist mid-swing and glaring at him.

"I'll seal it up personally if it'll make you feel better," he said, hearing how serious I was.

"You've wasted enough time already. Don't forget," I warned him sternly, "we can't attract attention. Things are already complicated enough as they are."

"You should tell Ginevra that. She almost uprooted a tree right in front of the kid."

"You what?!" I fumed.

"Since you're in the mood for confessions, why don't you tell him about your little chat with him?" she shot back.

Drake shrugged. "I just told the kid that if he kept holding his breath like that he might croak."

I clenched my fists. I was beside myself, but my brother seemed to think the whole thing was funny.

"You're forgetting the part where you said you could help him do it. Scared him half to death," Ginevra admonished him.

"I was really nice about it! I added 'if you want me to'!"

Simon, the wisest among us, sensed how on edge I was and shot a look at Drake to shut him up.

"Evan, relax. We noticed he was spying on us and had some fun putting on a little show for him. Who's he going to tell? Nobody would believe him. The whole town is under our influence. They barely notice us at all."

"That's not what I'm worried about," I admitted, filled with a strange anger. I fell silent for a moment, unsure whether to admit to them what I was feeling. "More than once I've had the urge to kill him."

"Be serious," said Simon reproachfully. "He's just a kid."

"Why, Evan? Because he's nosy? Or is it something else?" Drake raised an eyebrow and I shot him an icy glare. I wasn't in the mood to let him provoke me. "You know what your problem is?" he asked. "You do your duty, but deep down you've never realized how much fun it can be!" He grinned.

"There's *nothing* fun about what we do, Drake."

"There, exactly. This is where you mess up. Why can't you see? It's not a question of what we do, it's *who we are*. You refuse to look at things from the right perspective."

"And what's the right perspective? Why don't you illuminate us, Drake?" I growled, totally dejected.

"There is no Redemption. We are what we are and nobody can do anything about it. Their life flowing through you, the death you leave in its place—don't you find our power exhilarating? You're the one complicating your own existence, bro. Once you accept that, you'll start enjoying it!"

"Drop it, Drake," Ginevra warned.

"No, Drake's right," Simon interjected, "except for what he said about Redemption, of course." He panted as he dodged the occasional punches Drake continued to throw at him. "Evan, there's nothing different about the girl, and in any case it shouldn't matter to you. You've always seen our situation more clearly than the rest of us. Don't start doubting it now. You've always said one day all this will make sense. Hell, what happened to your Spartan nature, soldier? What's keeping you from seeing things objectively? Follow orders and don't think about it. Nothing simpler than that."

Having a serious conversation with my brothers when they felt like kidding around was far from easy. Their behavior usually didn't annoy me, but today I couldn't take it. I was nervous, irritable. I felt the weight of the world on my shoulders.

Honestly, I didn't have an answer to Simon's questions, and handling the situation had never seemed harder. "Not this time," I sighed, exhausted, staring at the floor. "Not with her."

Ginevra cleared her throat. "Speaking of which, Evan, there's something you should know." Her tone captured my attention. It even made Simon and Drake stop fooling around. "Peter isn't the only one who showed up here," she admitted, looking guilty. "I was in the garden," she said with unusual slowness, "on the bench out in back . . ."

"Get to the point, Gin," snapped Drake, not known for his patience.

"I was with Simon. I mean . . . we were *together*. And Gemma saw us." She lowered her eyes, feeling the weight of mine on her. "Simon had his back to her and she thought—she thought it was you, Evan. She mistook Simon for you. She's convinced you and I are a couple," she concluded, her voice full of remorse.

"Why didn't you tell me before?" I shouted.

"Why should I have? Her feelings aren't important, Evan. They shouldn't matter to you at all!"

I knew Ginevra was right. So why did it upset me to know Gemma was suffering? Her soul was so sensitive and incredibly deep. Was it the innocence in her eyes that made me worry about her, or was it something else?

"But that's not all," Ginevra continued. "For her it was only confirmation of a suspicion she'd had for a while. But don't be angry at me for not telling you before, Evan. I did it for your own good."

I held back the urge to punch a hole in the wall, then buried my face in my hands and cursed under my breath, unable to stop the flow of thoughts rushing through my brain. I didn't say anything, knowing I'd regret whatever came out of my mouth. All I could come up with were curses.

"I'm sorry," she said, sensing the anger I was bottling up. "I didn't want to make things even more complicated than they already are. You think I can't tell what mood you're in? I just wanted to protect you."

"It's my right to decide what's best for me, don't you think?" I growled, unable to hold back my resentment.

"I tried to stop her, but she ran off," she said regretfully.

"Now I get why . . ." My voice trailed off as I finally understood. "That must have been right before we ran into each other yesterday. She was so upset." I glared at Ginevra.

"Well, since we're on the subject, what were *you* thinking, Evan? What did you want to do, take her for a little spin on your bike?"

"I offered her a ride, that's all," I said, frustrated. *She'd been crying over me.* "If only I'd known it then. Fuck! Doesn't she already have enough pain in store for her?"

I felt a pang of sadness for her. I didn't want her to suffer any more than she already had to. Not because of me. If only I could prevent it, just this once. She'd given me so much. But the tears I'd seen in her eyes had been for me. I was the cause of her suffering. Yet again.

For some strange reason, I couldn't stand it. Her delicate face sprang to my mind, streaked with bitter tears. I thought she was still beautiful, even like that.

I felt the instinct to protect her, although I couldn't explain why. There was no denying I was actually here for a completely different purpose.

"Evan, by tomorrow it won't matter any more. Stop torturing yourself," Ginevra insisted, her eyes full of concern.

Tomorrow.

Was that all the time there was left? Just one more day and it would all be over. Everything would go back to normal and I'd go back to that semblance of an existence I insisted on calling "life."

"How could I not have noticed anything last night? I don't know what the hell's happening to me! I don't recognize myself any more." I buried my face in my hands wearily.

"Evan, this whole thing is insane. You can see that for yourself! You're going too far. You enroll in school, you act like you're one of them—you're living a life that doesn't belong to you! We shouldn't even have stayed in this place for so long."

"There wasn't time!" I retorted, my emotions leaving me helpless. "The most convenient solution was for all of us to stay in the same area since our assignments were all concentrated here," I said, trying to convince her. Or more likely, myself.

"No, Evan. Lie to me if you want, but don't lie to yourself. We all know why you wanted to stay here. It was because of Gemma."

Hearing her name made me flinch.

"It's hopeless, get it through your head. Snap out of it, Evan! We're what we are, each of us has responsibilities to bear. You've got to finish what you came here to do. It's not up to you to decide."

"You think I don't realize that?" I snapped, furious. I couldn't help it. Still, I wasn't mad at Ginevra, not any more. I was mad at myself, at my own nature.

"There's nothing you can do for her. We've already talked about it," she reminded me. Nothing she could say was going to get me out of the mood I was in. "It won't be much longer, time's almost up. *It's her time.* You can't change that. It's her destiny."

It was true, and we'd already talked about it over and over, but all our talk hadn't done anything to make me feel better. Less than a month had gone by since our arrival in Lake Placid. Meeting Gemma had made it the most difficult, most painful period of my entire existence. I couldn't understand why having to carry out this particular mission was so hard for me. For the first time in my life, I felt sorry. More than anything else, I couldn't figure out why I felt the need to protect her from the fate in store for her.

I sank down onto the sofa, planting my elbows on my knees, and buried my head in my hands, hiding my face, tormented.

A moment later, Ginevra came up behind me and gripped my shoulders gently. "Evan," she whispered, sounding concerned, "I'm sorry for you, honestly, but I've never seen you like this. This whole thing is destroying you."

I couldn't agree more. I was in pieces. The past month had been an interminable countdown that would soon reach its end. Just one more day, and then it would all be over. When we left Lake Placid, no one would have any memory of us. Simon would make sure of that.

And for us, everything would go back to normal.

But was that really what I wanted? Would the pain that was tearing me apart, the pain none of us could understand, would it vanish along with her in the space of a day's time?

It seemed impossible. I would never forget her face. Or her heart.

I'd never listened to my instincts, to my desires. Or maybe I'd never had any before. I'd never allowed myself to act entirely in my own self-interest.

Carrying out the missions assigned to me had always been what I'd done. Like a soldier, I followed orders. It was mechanical, nothing personal about it. But not this time, not if *she* was the target. I still couldn't figure out what was different about her.

"You're wasting your time. You'll never understand it. Stop torturing yourself," Ginevra said. Sometimes I forgot she could hear me even when no one else could.

My face still buried in my hands, I called to her in silence. *I don't know who I am any more. Please, help me,* I begged her in my thoughts. No one else in the room could hear it. *I don't know what to do,* I admitted in anguish.

I heard the guys' heavy footsteps as they left the room. Ginevra must have asked them to go with a gesture or a look, which sometimes accomplished even more than my powers could.

"Want the truth?" she asked cautiously.

Please. I looked up, miserable.

"I think you made a mistake in getting so close to her. You should have dropped it when you had the chance. Instead, you insisted on trying to find out why Gemma was different. You need to stop following her everywhere. Okay, she can see you and sense your presence, so what?"

It was unbelievable. I was leading my family to the brink of exasperation. But I couldn't help it. For the first time in a long, long time, I was finally *feeling* something, whatever it was. "I just wanted a little more time so I could figure it out. Gemma's different from anyone else I've ever met. No one else can see me when I'm in my ethereal form. There must be some explanation. I've always been good at controlling people's minds, but she won't do what I say, even when I straight out order her. And when I enter her mind to visit her in her dreams, she *sees* me even though she shouldn't be able to, and *she comes up to me*, wants to touch me. I try to resist her, to ward off the urge to experience it all, but I end up losing control every single time and giving in to the desire to feel her touch. I'm being driven by who knows what remote instinct I thought I'd buried over all these centuries. When I'm with her I just can't control myself. You wouldn't understand. I know I should stay away from her, but I can't. No one has ever touched me before." I grabbed my hair, frantic. "God, it feels amazing." I squeezed my eyes shut, overcome by foreign, totally incomprehensible emotions.

"I wonder if she would have the same effect on the others, too," Ginevra whispered to herself. "We could ask Drake to—"

"No!" A fire suddenly flared up in my chest. "No one goes near her."

I was surprised by my own tone. It had been a warning.

My mind was out of control, passing through the gates of time, moving backwards to the day we'd first met in the woods. The four of us had just arrived in Lake Placid. I'd been watching Gemma pet her dog, thinking I was invisible to her. But then she'd turned toward me like she could see me. The idea seemed ridiculous—there was no way she could possibly see me in my true nature—but she kept looking in my direction. She'd kept looking *right at me*, her eyes locked onto mine.

If Gemma had shown up only minutes later, she might have discovered my dark side. The predator. The Executioner.

The man's heart was supposed to give out—a natural death, like many—but I'd made a mistake. Gemma had left me so confused that I'd ended up taking it out on him. I'd broken his neck. It was brutal. And because of it, his death had seemed suspicious.

How was it that I'd become so desperate?

At first I was only confused; the mystery made me curious and awakened my most deeply buried instincts. I'd never felt so electrified over anything. *She could see me.* I was fascinated and scared at the same time. For four whole weeks I'd limited myself to watching her from afar, trying to figure out what made her different from anyone else I'd ever encountered.

Why was she able to see me? The question haunted me.

I'd followed her everywhere from a distance but learned nothing. Only in dreams had I let myself get close to her. Even then, she shouldn't have been able to sense my presence, but she did, and each time I'd felt something new, something different. Deep down, there was a part of her that was afraid of me, although she fought it. I'd realized it that night on the cliff, the first time I'd entered her dreams.

Ever since then, I'd been irremediably connected to her. She fascinated me—I couldn't stay away. I had to find out what was different about her. I had to get close, to try. Before it was too late. Over time, the feeling had changed until it slowly consumed me. Confusion, astonishment, and curiosity were soon replaced by guilt, suffering . . . and pain, when I realized I wasn't ready to be separated from her yet. Without realizing it, I'd removed the mask of the black knight I'd always worn, while allowing strange, soothing sensations to take me over. Like a lost child, I'd wandered into those big, dark eyes that looked at *me* like no one ever had before. It couldn't end like this.

"There's nothing you can do to prevent it. Don't you realize how crazy this all is? You even dragged me into it by forcing me to enroll at her school," Ginevra said, interrupting my train of thought.

Since Ginevra could read my mind, keeping secrets from her was virtually impossible. Though I'd practiced shutting off my thoughts to her a few times, I'd never worried about sharing them with her. No one could have asked for a more loyal, more reliable confidante. She was more than a sister to me. Blood bonds weren't always indestructible, whereas ours was. Ginevra was my whole family, along with Simon and Drake. I owed everything to them.

"I wanted to understand," I told her, "to figure out what's different about her. After the first day, I realized I couldn't do it without your help. You know that."

"During the day, maybe, but not at night. Thoughts can lie, they can hide the truth even from the person thinking them if they aren't fully aware of what's going on. The unconscious mind, on the other hand, doesn't lie—and only *you* have the power to interpret it. You can read *inside* her. When it comes to that, your power's stronger than mine."

I clenched my jaw, thinking about how spending a whole night with Gemma was never enough for me. I wanted more time so I could understand her—so I could understand myself. So I could discover the reason for my longing to be near her. I found myself spending all day long anxiously waiting for night so I could be with her without reservation, even if her dreams were so turbulent. And I was always disappointed when the first light of day caressed her face and I realized our time together was about to end.

"For the millionth time, what can it possibly matter?" Ginevra said, responding to my thoughts again.

I sighed, inconsolable. "It matters to me." During one of our nights together I had realized how wrong it was, but Gemma's promise that she wouldn't ask me anything as long as I stayed there with her had changed my mind. I would inevitably have to give her up; I might as well enjoy the emotions until the moment came. But the more time I spent with Gemma, the more I realized how hard it was going to be to let her go and give up all these new sensations.

"Plus, you've got to stop staring at her all the time. It confuses her."

"It's just that I can't understand her power."

"She hasn't got any powers! Can't you get that through your head?" Ginevra groaned, exasperated.

"She has power over me. You were the one who noticed she could hear my voice in her head. Even my thoughts are so drawn to her I have no power over them. Don't you see how weird that is? When I'm with her I lose all control. Yesterday I even followed her into her house," I admitted wearily.

"Evan!" Ginevra gasped in disapproval.

"There was nothing I could do. I couldn't help it. I tried to control myself, but it was no use. Then she saw me in the mirror and it scared her. I had to blow a fuse in her bathroom so it wouldn't happen again."

In the next room, Drake let out a snicker, which quickly turned into a stifled gasp. Simon must have punched him to shut him up.

"I did something even worse," I admitted. "This afternoon I visited her at school, but this time I let her see me. I lowered my guard, and on purpose."

"In front of everybody?" Ginevra snapped. "Have you completely lost your mind?"

"I couldn't resist. It was going to be the last time. I thought I would never see her again, after my request to the Màsala. But they wouldn't let me abort the mission." The game had already begun. Maybe that was what was driving me out of my mind. I couldn't bear it. All I'd had to make sure of was that she didn't turn in her photographs, but I'd chosen the self-centered way to do it. I'd wanted to have a little more of her before letting her go.

"For her own good, you should make her forget you. You've got to stay away from her, Evan."

"I *don't want* to stay away from her." I gulped, suddenly realizing what I'd said. What was happening to me?

"Do you know the consequences she's going to suffer if you keep this up? She's going to wait for you. Her soul's going to keep searching for you but it'll never find you. She'll have no peace, and for all eternity. Is that what you want for her?"

No, it wasn't, but even so, I couldn't control myself. Was I really so selfish? I ran my fingers through my hair as though it might wipe away the pain. "I need to understand why Gemma has this power over me. I know she's different, but it's not just that. Something's happening to both of us. It's been that way right from the start, like some sort of chemical reaction. It draws us together no matter how hard I try to resist. It's so intense it's almost unbearable sometimes. I thought I'd eventually manage to control it, but it's only gotten worse. My body, my powers, my mind . . . nothing belongs to me any more when I'm with her. It's like everything is shifting toward Gemma, like my spirit's surrendering to her, surrendering to this overwhelming power. It's like I'm not the one guiding it any more. Maybe my instinct is."

"Or your heart," Ginevra said in a barely audible whisper.

A shudder ran down my spine.

What was she trying to say? I didn't even remember having a heart. For centuries it had been crushed, buried beneath an empty existence. I'd forgotten myself, like ruins grayed with time, oblivious to the power of certain emotions. I didn't think I was still capable of experiencing them. Maybe I never had been, even before.

I'd seen countless eyes fill with desperation, pain, resignation, even love at times, but had always observed them as a detached spectator. They were distant feelings that never reached me. I'd always felt like a blade of steel that could reflect emotions but not absorb them, like metal does with light. Then along had come Gemma, throwing everything into confusion.

"I remember the first time she touched me," I murmured, losing myself in the memory of that dream. She'd been able to see me, but could she have physical contact with me too? The question had soon turned into a longing to know the answer, so I'd tried, and my world had changed the instant our palms touched. I never would have believed such intense emotions existed if the touch of her hand hadn't pierced my heart.

"She was sorry for me, can you believe it? She didn't even know who I was. She had no idea what I was capable of or what I might do to her. But she was worried about me anyway. She could read the confusion on my face, and I hadn't even said a word to her. How could she have known? The more I fought that connection, the harder I tried to escape it, the faster I went back to her. I followed the impulse against my will. I couldn't resist. For centuries, all that's mattered are orders. But now I'm taking orders only from her. It's like I *have* to be near her, to feel the warmth of her touch. I can't describe the feeling that runs through me when she's near. When she touches me. Why? What's happening to me? Is this my punishment? Or maybe it's some test that God is putting me through. Do you think this is my apple? Do you think Gemma is my forbidden fruit?"

I looked up at Ginevra in search of answers no one could give me.

"I don't know," she said without the slightest hesitation, her voice hard. "But you can't afford to give in to the temptation. Evan, you've got to come back to your senses. This whole thing has gone way too far. I'd be the first one to suggest a solution *if only there were one*. You're losing sight of who you really are and you can't afford to do that. You're an Executioner, remember? You need to focus on yourself and the mission you've been given."

I stared at the floor, overcome with frustration and the longing to live in another world. A world where I wouldn't have to hide my true nature. A world where I wouldn't be forced to carry out that damned execution order. Not my world. Not this one. But a place like that didn't exist. I felt trapped in a maze with no way out, where all paths led back to her.

"Face it, Evan: in a few hours Gemma's going to be just a memory. Accept the inevitable," she insisted, leaving no room for hope. "I want to make sure one thing's clear, Evan." Ginevra looked me in the eye. "It's not *you* that's going to kill her."

I shuddered when I heard her say it out loud. "Yes it is," I said. I was exhausted from the agony that hounded me. "I just wish it weren't true."

"You can't protect the person you have to kill. You can't deny who you are," she said, walking out of the room, her words echoing behind her.

The silence was short-lived. My brothers instantly strode in from the next room.

"The problem is that you're thinking about it too much." Drake plopped down onto the sofa beside me. "What do you care? She's just a mortal, and after tomorrow you'll never see her again. You just need to find a way to pass the time between now and then."

"You can't jeopardize everything because you feel guilty, no matter how unusual the situation is," Simon added.

"You know the name of the game: blood spilt, no guilt," Drake insisted, as though his words could change how I felt. "We can't afford to pity them, and up until now you've never had any problem with that. You've always been a perfectly emotionless Executioner."

"I don't need you to run through a list of my finer points, okay, Drake?" I snapped in frustration.

"All I'm saying is that even if the girl's making you feel something now, it doesn't mean anything. You always take things too seriously. You should learn to love it. Just enjoy the moment and get rid of her anyway!"

"*Enjoy the moment?* So I should act like you and go around seducing doomed souls right before taking their lives?"

"Can I help it if I'm irresistible?" he said, raising an arrogant eyebrow.

"Drake, we're more than that. We're their fate."

"That's not true! Their fates have already been written. In a sense, we're a gift. Is it so wrong to help them have some good clean fun before they die? Think of it as their last wish."

I forced a smile, masking my frustration. "And you'd be that wish?" I asked him.

Drake grinned, a cocky look on his face. "Most times I am."

"Would you cut it out already?" Ginevra groaned. "This conversation's going nowhere. I've already heard it a million times."

"She's right. Enough with the chitchat. I know what'll help. You need to remember who you are," Drake said, standing up and gesturing for me to follow him. His smile said more than his words.

I was feeling more and more nervous. I'd dragged my entire family into my own personal hell. I followed him without even thinking. Wherever he meant to take me, I decided it didn't matter. I just wanted to take my mind off the thoughts that had been gnawing at me for a month now.

"I'm coming with you," Ginevra said, having read his mind.

"Forget it. Guys' night out, so unless you know some magic spell to grow yourself a new toy between your legs . . . I mean, unless you've done that already."

"You're disgusting!"

"True, but that's what you like most about me." He winked at her and Simon glared at him. "What'd I say?!"

"Believe me, she's just fine without a toy," our brother shot back.

"No doubt about that. The two of you could wake the dead when you're at it."

"Careful," Ginevra said, slapping Drake on the shoulder. "I could always decide to make *your* toy disappear."

"You wouldn't dare," he said, but his laugh didn't completely mask the fear in his voice that she might actually be able to do it.

"I wouldn't provoke her if I were you," I told him.

Seconds later we were downstairs, our motorcycles roaring beneath us and our headlights shining on the garage door as it slowly opened.

15

GUYS' NIGHT OUT

The club was packed. The music we'd begun to hear five blocks away was nothing compared to what hit us when my brothers and I walked through the door. In his hopeless attempt to distract me, Drake had taken us to a nightclub in downtown Plattsburgh.

It wasn't the first time I'd seen Drake carry out his orders, but I was pretty sure he'd actually taken us out just so he could show off.

We pushed through the crowd, making our way to the bar. I had no idea who Drake's prey was, but judging from his watchful expression, they couldn't be far away.

I pushed my sleeves up to my elbows and waved the bartender over. "Something strong." I looked around the room: hundreds of bodies dancing frenetically under psychedelic lights.

"Hey, Evan," Drake said, pointing at the photographs on the wall behind the bar. "Didn't you take care of that guy?"

I took a closer look and recognized him. Jasper Mason. Most times we didn't talk about our assignments, but the soccer player's death had been big news all over the world, monopolizing the sports stations' newscasts.

"You could have taken that one a bit slower." Simon smiled. He'd been partly fascinated, partly amused by my encounter with the scumbag. I'd never liked rapists.

"He deserved it." I threw my head back and downed my shot, then gestured to the bartender, who refilled my glass. I'd chosen a gruesome death for Mason, but he'd definitely asked for it.

We knew the exact place and time when our orders were to be carried out. As for the means, however, I sometimes gave myself some wiggle room. "Someone had to make him atone for his sins." His mind had been dark. Sometimes I wondered how filthy souls like Mason's could deserve redemption. If it had been up to me, I'd have let him suffer for his sins. Evil wouldn't have spared him for long. But then I told myself that, all things considered, it was for the best: a soul had been reclaimed rather than lost.

And at the end of the day, forgiveness had nothing to do with me.

"Your idea of a good time," said Simon.

"Definitely," I replied, smiling as I remembered the terrified look on Mason's face.

Drake had been quiet this whole time. I turned toward him and noticed his concentrated expression. He was listening. He turned to face me, looking determined.

Whoever his prey was, they must have arrived.

A shrewd smile on his lips, my brother nodded in his target's direction. It only took a second for me to spot her: a spirited blond who was going wild on the dance floor. She wore a gray see-through top with a plunging neckline and tight pants that showed off her toned legs. Her lipstick was a very bright shade of red, probably an attempt to draw attention to the rest of the package.

Despite the distance, I perked up my ears to hear her conversation, isolating her voice. All the other noises in the club went silent. The girl sounded anxious. "You got it? C'mon! Don't tell me you didn't bring it," she groaned. I'd seen a lot of girls like her. Most of the time it didn't end well for them.

"Would you chill, Selina? My buddy's not here yet. Which means you still have time to reconsider. You sure it won't be too much for you? There's always coke. What kind of friend would I be if I didn't warn you?"

"Since when did you ever worry about me?" she shot back, annoyed. "First you say it's like heaven on earth and then you refuse to show me the way there?"

Selina should have felt a shock run through her when she pronounced those words, but she had no idea her wish would soon come true, and in the most terrible of ways.

"All right, if you really want to. Just don't blame me when you're going through hell tomorrow morning." The boy was still reluctant. "If your brother finds out I was the one who got it for you, I'm dead," he grumbled.

"Don't be paranoid, he's not gonna find out! Axel, take the money and focus on having a good time!"

"Okay, Selina, but just this once. And don't forget: I warned you."

Axel walked away from his friend.

Simon, Drake, and I exchanged knowing glances. Having warned her wouldn't be enough to spare him the remorse. Guilt would consume him for the rest of his life.

Selina had started dancing again, sandwiched between two guys, probably total strangers, who were grinding against her to the music. Once in a while she'd look around for her friend, who was keeping a low profile, leaning against the wall in the darkest corner of the room.

I had Axel pegged in no time: he was the type who surrounds himself with beautiful girls just for the fun of entertaining them. He wasn't very tall or particularly good-looking, but his dark complexion and the scar running along his eyebrow made him look like a damned soul in search of atonement. Meanwhile, Selina's girlfriends had bought beers, which they drank straight from the bottle as they made their way through the crowd, their hips swaying.

Suddenly I froze, sensing a hostile presence. My eyes darted to my brothers and saw they'd sensed it too. We weren't the only ones out looking for fun tonight. I glanced back at the dark corner and a shudder ran through my body.

Evil was preparing to attack.

No one except my brothers and I could see it as it tried to corrupt the boy's soul. Would Axel resist Temptation?

"This is the second time this week." Another guy, taller and more muscular than Axel, had walked up to him. Despite all the noise, I heard them clearly, as though no one else were in the club.

"It's not for me, it's for a friend."

"Who, the hottie you were talking to? If you think you're going to tap that after giving her this, you're kidding yourself."

"I've already tapped that. Besides, it's none of your business, Chad. You gonna sell it to me or not?"

"I don't know, how old is she? At least tell me she's not a minor."

"What, you got a conscience all of a sudden? She's twenty-three. Or maybe you're just asking because you want to tap that yourself."

Chad looked like a bouncer. The two of them must have been pretty tight, because Axel didn't seem intimidated by his muscles.

"What would I want with a bitch like that? I'm just sorry for you, man, 'cause you're gonna have to take her home all messed up."

"Fuck! If her brother catches me he'll kill me."

Chad rested his hands on Axel's shoulders. "What are you doing, man?" he said, sounding almost fraternal. "Don't get yourself into trouble for a bored little slut who just wants to party and screw. This is strong stuff and she's just a kid, for fuck's sake!"

The dealer had managed to get through to the boy's conscience; Axel seemed to be on the verge of changing his mind. But he didn't, because a stronger voice was whispering its dissent inside him. The voice of evil was laying claim to him. Though Axel was unaware of it, heaven and hell were contending for his soul at that very moment. Only his decision could save him.

"It *is* a lot of money," he said, reconsidering. Suddenly he seemed to lose all his qualms; evil had whispered its promises to him. "Sorry, man, she paid me up front."

I gritted my teeth. Axel had made his decision. The wrong one. He'd given in to his personal temptation.

The Màsala held people's lives in their hands, but not their souls. They decided how long humans would be on earth, but their destinations depended on the people's own decisions, a fact they were less and less aware of.

When Axel's time came, it was more than likely he wouldn't find one of us waiting for him.

"I'm up." Drake threw back another shot and strode toward Axel, who was hurrying back to Selina. Drake collided with him and the boy tumbled to the ground.

"Hey! Watch where you're going!" Axel shouted, groping around on the floor in search of the baggie containing the yellow tablet that had slipped out of his hand. He took one look at Drake's build and instantly fell silent, shooting to his feet and holding his hands up defensively. Drake flashed a cunning smile and looked him in the eye. His voice was low and persuasive, his words commanding: "I'm not really here. You never saw me. You gave Selina the ecstasy, but you're tired, you overdid it with the stuff, and you can barely stay on your feet. Take a taxi home and sleep until tomorrow. When you wake up, you'll have a lot to feel bad about."

Axel nodded, hypnotized by Drake's voice as he continued to look him in the eye. Controlling humans' minds was one of the things Drake enjoyed most. Axel turned and disappeared into the crowd.

Drake leaned down and picked up the pill from the floor. When he straightened up again, his appearance had changed. He pulled the hood up over his head and strode over to Selina in his new body.

"Axel, finally!" she shouted.

"Good things take time." It was Axel's voice that had spoken, but I knew it was my brother in the guise of the boy. An Executioner. Just like me. Drake's ability to change his appearance was useful for his missions, but he often used it just to have fun.

Axel held the tablet out to Selina.

"Can I trust it?" She looked confident, but I heard a slight tremor in her voice, almost like she'd recognized the shadow of death lurking beneath his hood.

"Quality stuff." He winked at her reassuringly.

She popped it into her mouth and swallowed. "Outta my way! I'm gonna take over the world!" She let out a yell and grabbed a bottle of beer from her girlfriend, who was shaking her thing on the dance floor.

Axel turned around and Drake's face reappeared as he walked back to me, grinning. "Kids today! They just don't know how to have fun." He leaned against the bar and drained the contents of my glass, the hood still over his shaved head.

"But it seems you do," I shot back. He grinned again, a familiar glimmer in his eyes. The predator inside him was preparing for the hunt. He'd laid his trap; the dirty work was yet to come.

"Feel free to take notes, bro," he said, grinning even more broadly.

I'd always considered my missions an unavoidable duty. They'd never caused any reaction in me other than indifference or a sense of obligation. For some strange reason, though, Drake found them fascinating. A dangerous game in which others always paid the price.

"My idea of fun is a little different from yours," I said.

"Give it up, Drake." Simon, who'd been elsewhere, walked up behind us. "You'll never convince him."

"You're telling me! You two are both hopeless. Still, I felt it was my responsibility to try."

I shook my head and Simon laughed. We saw things very differently from Drake, who would never understand our faith in Redemption.

"For the last time, there's nothing fun about bringing a human being's life to an end," I said.

"Wanna bet?" Drake smirked, knocking back another shot and slamming the glass down on the bar. He walked off, suddenly looking ravenous as headed toward his victim.

"He's still convinced there's no salvation for our kind."

"It's a lost cause." Simon shook his head, half amused, half worried, about how lightly our brother took his responsibilities as a Subterranean. "One day he's going to wind up in trouble."

"It's just his perverted tastes. Just because we're not crazy about killing people doesn't mean we don't know how to have a good time," I said.

Simon raised his glass in a toast. "*I* can't complain." He tried to conceal a smirk, but it was obvious he was referring to Ginevra and the overwhelming passion they shared.

"Low blow." I clinked the rim of my glass against his. "My idea of a good time can't compete with yours, but if you ask me, no execution order could be as thrilling as a late-night race." I'd had more fun on our ride there than I'd had since we'd set foot in the club.

"That a challenge?"

I shrugged, tempted by the idea. "Unless you're backing down—"

"I never back down, you should know that by now."

"No handicaps."

Simon thought it over: we wouldn't be able to use our powers during the race and he knew I was unbeatable on the road, but he couldn't refuse.

No rules. No limits. Only the road, the wind, and the roar of our engines. I couldn't have asked for anything more.

"I'm in. Let's wait for Drake and see if you can beat not one but two of us," he said. "That is, unless he gets carried away with something else." Simon nodded over my shoulder in our brother's direction.

I turned to look. Drake was in the middle of the dance floor, surrounded by Selina and her girlfriends. "He's going for it, for sure," I said, shaking my head.

Selina was sensually grinding her body against his, clearly trying to seduce Drake, who was holding her by the hips.

"If I didn't know how this was going to end, I'd leave him here to enjoy the evening," Simon remarked.

"Doesn't matter," I said, shrugging. "I'm sure he'd find a way to have fun even without Selina."

I watched them dancing in the crowd. Drake seemed so at ease among humans, almost like he was one of them. But then again, he was used to putting on whatever mask would work most to his advantage. It was just another disguise, even when his appearance didn't change.

Even so, Drake hadn't forgotten the role he was there to play in the girl's life. He'd just decided to take advantage of it. When the time came, the Soldier would carry out his mission without fail, because for our kind, no matter what your mood was when duty called, orders were all that mattered.

I smiled. For the first time I was fascinated by my brother's way of doing things. He was running his lips down her neck, his hands exploring her bottom.

Confusion was still churning inside me, but watching Drake took my mind off it for a while. I knew my respite wouldn't last long, though. Gemma's time was drawing nearer and nearer, and soon I'd have to reckon with the ghosts haunting me. The thought made my heart stop.

For centuries I hadn't felt the slightest emotion when obeying orders. Why did the only feeling I'd finally managed to experience have to be so grim? My emotions had reawakened, but in the worst possible way.

I drove the thought from my mind and focused on Drake again, hoping his upbeat spirit would be contagious. Selina was stroking his forearm. "You never told me your name. I don't think I've seen you around here before."

Drake lifted one corner of his mouth in a half smile, because she'd brushed her hand right over his tattoo, even though she couldn't see it. That was our curse, and soon it would be hers too. "You don't need to know my name." He began to kiss her again, this time more passionately, as she moved against him rhythmically.

Suddenly, his expression changed, and his face took on a look of determination, unnoticed by the girl.

"Why don't we go someplace quieter?" Selina asked, bolder than ever. It was the drug kicking in, lowering her inhibitions. "It's so hot in here." Her speech was slightly slurred from the mix of ecstasy and alcohol. Her body lurched in a desperate attempt to resist before surrendering, but she was too wrapped up in Drake to notice.

"Sorry, babe." Drake looked at her for the first time with his eyes of ice. His grin revealed his amusement. "Time's up."

He nodded over Selina's shoulder and she turned to look. The crowd, too, had stopped moving, frozen between confusion and terror. The girl's eyes bulged as she saw the empty shell of her body lying on the dance floor.

16

PRISONER

At the club exit, Drake slapped me on the shoulder, pleased with our night out. "Tell me you learned the lesson."

"If there's one thing I learned, it's that you've got even more cheek than I imagined. I didn't think that was even possible." We left the crowd gathered around Selina's body behind. All attempts to reanimate her would be useless; Drake had already completed his assignment and helped her transition. She hadn't even noticed when her body had begun to jerk harder and harder until, no longer able to withstand the lethal dose she'd taken, it had surrendered. Had Drake actually made her death more peaceful by fooling around with her? Maybe I was wrong after all and my brother's approach offered his victim one last moment of pleasure, just like he'd always said. I knew Drake, and his main goal had definitely been his own pleasure, but was it so wrong if, in the process, he ultimately made her transition less traumatic? I couldn't answer these questions, and in the end it didn't matter to me anyway. Now that the doors of the club had muffled the music, deafening confusion had filled my head once more.

My brothers and I walked toward our motorcycles, parked at the curb, but a whistle not far away caught my attention. I looked over and recognized him. It was Chad, the dealer who'd sold the drugs to Axel. He was leaning against a car with a girl smoking a cigarette who must have been Selina's age. Without thinking, I rushed at him, grabbed him by the shirt, and hurled him into the windshield. The girl screamed as the glass shattered beneath Chad's weight.

"Hey! Are you crazy?! You wanna kill him?!" she shrieked at me over the shrill squeal of the car alarm that filled the night.

"No." I smiled to myself and stepped toward her. "It's not his time yet."

The girl stared at me, unsure whether to be afraid or fascinated. Unnerved by what I'd done—or maybe just trying to seem older—she raised her cigarette to her lips and took a drag. Without taking my eyes off her, I snatched it away. The girl coughed, surprised.

"Open your purse and take out the powder," I ordered her, and she did exactly as I said. "Dump out every last speck." My voice was deep and persuasive. Again, she obeyed without hesitation. She opened the packet, her eyes locked onto mine, and the drug scattered on a gust of wind that I'd raised myself.

"You should take better care of your health." I threw the cigarette on the ground as she continued to stare at me, hypnotized by the darkness concealed in my voice.

I turned away and a moment later she snapped out of her trance, finally free from my spell. "Asshole!" she yelled after me, rushing to help her friend, who was sprawled on the hood, unconscious. What I'd said hadn't been a suggestion but an order, and she would have no choice but to follow it.

I had no idea why I'd acted like that. I usually didn't pay much attention to what humans did. Maybe I'd just wanted to take out my frustration on the guy . . . or maybe something inside me was changing. Whatever it was, I sensed that the new emotion was *human.* At least Chad would stop doing his dirty job for a little while.

We kicked our bikes into gear and the roar of the three engines filled the street. Adrenaline coursed through my veins. I turned to Simon, ready to race, but immediately recognized the focused look on his face: he'd just received an order. "You'll have to take a rain check, right?" I groaned.

Instead, Simon smiled at me. "*Au contraire.* It's just what we needed." He accelerated and powered away, tires squealing, challenging us to follow him.

The stakes would be different, but this time we'd be having my kind of fun.

We roared down the wet streets in a heart-stopping race.

Speed always made me feel alive. I was hoping the wind would wipe away the disorienting confusion I'd been feeling. I was a Subterranean. Following orders was all that mattered. That's how it had to be. I impulsively sped up, as though to underline the conviction inside me.

Simon passed me on the curve. His Desmosedici had instantly proved its horsepower and pulled him out into the lead. He and Drake had warmed their back tires by peeling out, leaving behind a huge cloud of white smoke, but that wouldn't help them shake me off their tails. I was determined to win—not only the race against my brothers but also the battle raging inside me. I overtook Drake and with a flick of my wrist popped a wheelie. I reveled in the determination I was pursuing, but it continued to elude me.

We tended to keep a low profile when we were around other people, but when we got on our bikes that good intention went straight to hell and we usually put on quite a show, competing to see who was the most daring rider on the back roads. I let my brothers pass me and lagged behind as they tried to put more distance between us, teaming up to block my way, a clear sign of how much I intimidated them.

Drake was pushing his bike to its very limits, on the verge of losing control. Instead of using his powers to avoid crashing into the guardrail, he leaned to the right, oversteered and accelerated to top speed. Realizing he wouldn't be able to avoid impact, he dragged his hand against the ground to slow down, then cranked the accelerator to the max and shot off, howling in victory when he righted his bike.

I planned to overtake them on the straight stretch.

Simon had taken the lead and Drake, in an attempt to pass him, sped up too quickly and found himself unintentionally rising up on his back wheel. He released the accelerator and the bike slammed back down, shearing off Simon's mirror, which shattered against the asphalt. I instinctively accelerated and veered to avoid it, my back tire skidding.

I smiled because it was my turn now. Approaching a curve to the right, I sped up and passed them, taking advantage of their deceleration as they headed into the turn. I hit the brakes so hard I popped a wheelie. The second the bike touched down again, I accelerated, and Simon and Drake lost any chance of catching up with me. At each curve, my bike sideslipped beneath me. It was incredible how exhilarated it made me feel.

The roar of the engine filled my head. Right then, on that stretch of road, there wasn't room in my mind for anything else. I concentrated on the sound, how it made me feel. I swerved sharply and the bike reared up, roaring through the night. My engine was so powerful that all it took was a slight flick of my wrist to make it rise up on its back wheel. I carved such a deep turn in the curve that my elbow brushed the asphalt.

Racing made me feel powerful. Invincible. Fulfilled.

I shifted my weight forward to lighten the rear and make it skid into the curve. Oversteering, I left a cloud of white smoke behind me for my brothers as a sign of victory.

Knowing I'd soon have to face reality, I tried to escape it a little longer: I shifted down a gear and, accelerating, popped my front wheel up, driven by the powerful engine. I continued like this for quite a while, playing my wrist to keep the front wheel raised. But the faster I went, the faster that grim, tortured reality pursued me. I couldn't outrun it; it was inside me. It had taken me prisoner. I was a Soldier, but just then I felt like a hostage.

Drake pulled up alongside me, also on one wheel, and we both lowered our bikes at the same time, as if in some mysterious choreographed dance.

We pulled up even with a minivan, one of the few vehicles we'd encountered over the last half hour. In the back seat, a little boy was watching our wild race, fascinated, his hands pressed up against the window. I wondered what he was thinking, at his innocent age of five at most, without the weight of the world on his shoulders.

Simon nodded to me and I understood instantly.

The minivan was his target.

Drake pulled up in front of the van while Simon and I positioned ourselves to each side. The man driving looked confused by our maneuvers, but probably thought we were a group of thugs.

He had no idea he was about to have a blowout and that because of the wet pavement he'd lose control of his vehicle . . . and his family.

The sound of our engines echoed through the silent night. It was Simon's assignment, but I needed to feel back in my place again. I needed to remember what my duty was. What it always had been. Heartless. Merciless.

I pulled in closer to the van and delivered a sharp kick to the back tire. The impact was so strong that the minivan skidded, screeching across the wet asphalt with a flat.

The man tried to regain control, but Simon jumped up onto the seat of his motorcycle and leapt onto the hood, crouching down to look the driver straight in the eye. The van crashed to a halt, marking the end of its wild ride—and the lives of its passengers.

A trail of smoke rose from under the hood, the back tire still spinning. Drake and I pulled over as Simon finished what we'd started. I should have stayed out of it, but I couldn't help it. Tonight, desperate to change my feelings, desperate not to feel that heavy weight on my chest, I wanted to bend the world to my will.

I knew taking it out on strangers would do nothing to relieve that burden or make me go back to being what I'd always been: a Soldier, the black shadow of destiny that takes away your last breath. Devoid of emotion. Just like I was right then. I didn't feel anything. So why should it be different with Gemma?

The little boy stared straight at me, pulling me out of my thoughts. When I looked back at him, he partially buried his face in his mom's lap, still peeking at me.

She held him tight. Though she realized what had just happened, her instinct to protect her child kept her from showing her shock at the sight of her mangled body lying in the wreckage. A body she no longer inhabited.

We could sense every one of their emotions. "Come here, Logan," said Simon, but the little boy shook his head, scared.

"Mommy, why does that man know my name?" he asked after a pause.

She stroked his head reassuringly.

"I'm afraid, Mommy. Don't leave me."

The mother held him even tighter. "I'm right here, honey. I'll never leave you again," she said softly.

Simon knelt down to look the little boy in the face and stroked his temple, washing away his fear.

"Where are you taking us?" the boy asked, instantly confident.

Simon smiled. The parents looked at him, holding each other close. "To a beautiful place."

Logan smiled back at him. They disappeared, leaving the minivan on the road. Inside the wreckage lay three bodies, but not a single soul.

17

VENTING

I punched the thick leather over and over. The bag filled with cement rocked under my pounding, jerking on its chain. The skin on my knuckles was cracking from my brutal blows.

After Simon's execution order I'd gone home, pushing my bike to its very limits, and when the engine had reached maximum performance I'd used my powers to make it go even faster, challenging the air itself. I was like a bolt of lightning escaping the storm. The only problem was that the storm was inside me.

Strangely, the race hadn't satisfied my need to vent. Once home, I'd shut myself up in the workout room, the only place where not even Ginevra's mind could follow me. I'd taken off my shirt, wound black gauze around my palms and begun to punch. And punch.

I could have vented my frustration in my ethereal form but I decided not to. I wanted to feel the violence of each blow on my flesh in the hope of smothering another kind of emotion—a stronger, more uncontrollable one. But, as I'd feared, not even physical wounds could take my mind off the pain deep in my chest. The cuts on my hands were bleeding, but they'd disappear in a minute or two. Would I be able to recover in the same way once Gemma was dead? The question haunted me.

The answer came to me from places unknown: those wounds would never heal.

I was about to deliver another right jab when a puff of air brushed my ear. I dodged the blow, raised my hand and blocked the fist that Simon had just swung from behind me. In a second, I had him pinned against the wall. He wrenched himself free and tried to hit me again. I blocked his punches, faster and faster, until it was my turn. The workout room had suddenly become our battlefield. It wasn't the first time. My brothers and Ginevra and I often sparred for fun, but today I was driven by a completely different emotion. I wasn't sure how to define it: aggravation, rage . . . powerlessness. It was a feeling that, no matter how fast I'd ridden earlier, I hadn't been able to shake. Even the punches I was throwing had a different energy because they were coming from some part of me that I couldn't identify. Simon was attacking me more ferociously than normal, sensing my need for it.

We moved through the massive room in a dark dance, a hand-to-hand battle in which our brutal blows would have killed the strongest of humans.

Even the walls became part of our battlefield. We used them to elude each other with backflips and a range of acrobatics. Using my powers, I sent the punching bags that hung from the ceiling hurtling around with lethal precision. Simon attacked me over and over with a long fighting stick, but I dodged his blows. It was a ferocious, grueling battle that I had no intention of losing. In the challenge against the Màsala I was powerless, but in the one against my brother nothing could stop me. I felt like a swollen river confined by a levee that was ready to burst. The walls were cracking open and I was prepared to destroy everything in my way. I tried to catch Simon in a series of different holds, but he skillfully broke free and counterattacked.

"You can always say uncle when you've had enough," I sneered.

Simon ran up the wall to avoid my attack. "What, now that I'm starting to enjoy myself?" He smiled and swiftly spun me around, managing to push me down to the floor. "You upstaged me in battle earlier," he told me, still smiling. True, back on the road I'd struck the minivan instead of leaving it to him.

I swung my legs around, freed myself from his grip, and trapped him under my body. "I couldn't help it. I'm doing it right now too, in case you hadn't noticed." I leapt to my feet and pinned him against the wall. "Besides, you should change. You're a mess." His shirt was torn to shreds. He hadn't taken it off before our fight.

The door burst open, distracting me, and Simon seized his chance to reverse our positions. "I'll add it to the list of things you owe me. Right below the new mirror for my motorcycle that Drake's going to be getting me," he said, looking at our brother standing in the doorway.

"I take you guys out for a night on the town and then you don't invite me to your little party down here?" Drake said sarcastically. "Well? Who won? I'll take him. Right here. Right now."

"I accept," I answered firmly. "But let's make it two against one. I haven't finished with Simon yet."

The two of them fist-bumped in a show of brotherhood.

"Haven't you had enough?" Simon slapped me on the shoulder.

"I'm just warming up."

Simon smiled at my persistence, or maybe it was because he'd actually believed I'd vented all my rage. "Unfortunately, it'll have to be for another time. I just got an assignment. Half an hour tops and I'll be back."

"Busy day," I said, smiling to myself.

Simon had been assigned two missions in a matter of hours, but it was a pace we knew well. We were all accustomed to giving Death a hand whenever it ordered us to deliver its icy breath to the life of a mortal. The frequency of the executions varied from day to day for each of us.

"Same as usual," he replied sardonically.

We were almost always summoned to duty several times a day, but none of us saw it as a sacrifice. To a Subterranean, following orders was a badge of honor. It was a way to atone. Even so, periods of intense activity might also be followed by days—at times even weeks—of total calm. None of us could know for sure when our next assignment would turn up, although we normally didn't have to wait very long.

We received some orders months in advance, others with just a few moments' notice. Natural deaths were easier. For accidents, on the other hand, we had to plan everything, checking every little detail that would help bring the victim to their end.

"That's better," Drake said. "It'll give you guys the chance to clean up. I mean, look at you two. Christ! Were you in an arena full of lions? Go change, Simon, or your victim will think you're a zombie straight out of hell."

Simon looked down at his clothes and laughed, because for once Drake was right. I joined him, and our laughter filled the workout room. "I didn't expect such a quick surrender, but in that case I'll go take a shower."

"Not a surrender," Drake said. "Once you're back in shape we can talk."

"More in shape than this`?" I spread my arms to show off my well-trained body and make it clear he wasn't intimidating me. I was sweaty, my jeans had been torn here and there during the fight, and the cuts on my chest were already healing, but I could have beaten him with both hands tied behind my back.

"Meanwhile, I'll go check on Blondie," Drake said, just to provoke our brother. Simon pulled off his shirt and threw it at him. With a sly smile on his lips, Drake vanished from the room.

In the ensuing silence, Simon slapped me on the shoulder. "Better?" he asked. It was clear now that by fighting me he'd been trying to help me battle my demons. He'd understood my need to vent.

"Yeah, thanks." I bumped my fist against his.

It was a lie, but he had no way of knowing that. I didn't want my brothers to see me so vulnerable. I'd never been weak, but these new emotions were wearing me out.

"Evan." Simon looked me straight in the eye. "I know this mission is going to be more difficult than usual for you, but don't forget what we're fighting for. *Na svargo narakam vina.*"

Without hell, there is no heaven.

I nodded, lost in thought, and he disappeared, summoned to duty. Redemption was our promised land. Why did I have to face such a difficult trial to prove I was worthy?

Tossing a white towel over my shoulder, I walked out of the room, reaching the bathroom in my human form. I didn't want to shed my physical body, even though I was sure that was where the sensations I was feeling were coming from. They were human, even though they'd put down roots within me. Or maybe I was afraid that in my angelic form, in which everything was amplified, I wouldn't be able to bear it.

I turned on the water in the shower and pulled off my jeans. In moments, the room was filled with steam. I leaned my palms against the wall and let the water run down my back.

The image of Gemma in the shower came into my mind. I thought about how she'd closed her eyes, the way she'd pushed her hair to one side as the water flowed down her skin . . . and the longing I'd felt.

Spying on her was wrong. I knew that, but I couldn't help it.

I closed my eyes and my vision seemed to become reality. Suddenly she was there in the shower with me. I ran my nose down her shoulder, breathing in the scent of her wet skin. It was so intoxicating. I slid my hand down her side and clasped her flesh, overcome by an unknown desire. Overcome by the longing to draw her to me. I was shaken by the madness of my own thoughts.

She lifted her chin and I looked into her big, dark eyes. A shiver washed over me. I was breathless.

A knock on the door snapped me back to reality. I clenched my fist and slammed my palm against the stone wall, cursing. The wall cracked under the blow.

I shook my head, my hair dripping wet, and ran my hands down my face. I felt like I was losing my mind. I had to stop torturing myself. That new part of me trying to emerge had to be held back.

I was a Soldier. And Gemma was my target.

18

TORMENT

I sank down onto the sofa and closed my eyes, overcome with frustration. The night out with my brothers had helped clear my head, and I'd realized the soldier in me was still strong, even if he was crushed by confusion. I just had to give him space so he could fight it off. Or maybe I was just kidding myself and the confusion was stronger than the soldier.

I was alone. On the verge of collapse.

Ginevra was right. I knew it. I knew I had no choice. Destiny had drawn Gemma's name and bound it to mine in death.

What was I questioning, then? It was just a waste of time. I would do what I had to, no matter what. It wasn't up to me to decide. No one cared what I wanted. Someone else had already decided for me, for her, *for us*.

No, I had to force myself to accept that there would never be an "us." Her destiny was already written, her path chosen, and I had nothing to do with it. Now that I'd finally found something worth living for, I had to give it up. Could fate be any more merciless?

There was only one day left. Gemma had to die.

I would lose her forever, and along with her I would lose the feelings I'd rediscovered. I would go back to living in an empty, unfeeling, lifeless shell.

I lay there on the sofa in the dark until my eyes closed and I forgot about the inexorable passing of time.

I had no idea how long I'd been lying there. It could have been minutes, hours maybe. It felt like days. And I would have stayed there if an unexpected mission hadn't called me to duty. Another execution order to carry out before dealing with Gemma's life. Before saying goodbye to the emotions that only she triggered in me.

Maybe it was better that way, being able to distract myself, force the soldier in me to re-emerge so I could face Gemma's mission with more conviction. *With more detachment*, like Drake said.

My new victim was a boy in Kentucky. I focused on his soul and a moment later materialized where he was: a large field right in the middle of a football game. The players were all running from one side to the other but I had no doubts about who my target was. His soul was summoning me, as though it recognized me. In those few moments that preceded the passing, a mortal's soul was inexorably linked to that of the Subterranean who'd come to take it, although the person couldn't see him yet.

Except for Gemma.

I clenched my fists to drive away the thought. I had to concentrate.

The boy passed me, rushing after the player with the ball. I focused my attention on him, taking away all the oxygen around him. A few steps later, he stopped, rested his hands on his knees and gasped for air. No one took any notice of him, thinking he was tired from running.

He ripped off his helmet and threw it to the ground. I stepped over to his side to study him more carefully.

There comes a moment during every execution when the victim's fear transforms into awareness. The very instant right before dying, when the target realizes his time is about to end, that I'm there beside him . . . that Death has come to take him. It had always been an exhilarating sensation because for that brief moment it felt like his soul could sense me. For a long time, that fleeting sensation of power had been enough for me. Until Gemma had looked deep into my eyes.

I focused on him again. There wasn't a trace of oxygen in his lungs. He seemed desperate.

Without hesitating, I rested a hand on his heart and felt it beat for the last time. His eyes opened wide. He clutched his chest, crumpled to his knees and fell to the ground.

Seconds later, chaos erupted all around him.

Drake was right, feeling a mortal's life flow through you was exciting, like an adrenaline rush.

I stepped back, making way for the paramedics who'd rushed out onto the field to try to revive him. The team had gathered around the boy's body, the crowd had fallen silent . . . but he was gone.

Something caught my attention.

I scanned the crowd and my eyes locked onto Gemma's. She was staring at me, perfectly still in the stands.

A shiver ran through me. *It was her.* I couldn't be wrong. What was she doing there? Had her power led her to me? Had she seen me as I took the boy's life?

The thought scared me. It was crazy. Pretty soon I'd be taking Gemma's life too, but I still didn't want her to see the darkness that lurked inside me, Death.

"Where am I? What happened?" The boy's voice distracted me from my thoughts. His soul had definitively left his body.

I glanced at him but then turned back to search for Gemma. She was gone. I stared at the empty stands, stunned. I felt crazy. My soul had never been in such agony before. Gemma wasn't dead yet, but my thoughts about her were already haunting me like she was a ghost. What would I do once she passed on?

"Ryan! Scott! I'm right here! Coach? Help me, please! Why isn't anyone helping me?"

The boy's desperation recalled me to my duty.

"They can't," I said softly, knowing his soul would hear me loud and clear.

"I'm dead?! What happened?"

He was kneeling beside his body, but moved aside when they loaded it onto a stretcher. The thoughts of Gemma had distracted me, and I'd let him see his own lifeless body in the worst possible way. *Damn it.* How many more mistakes would I make because of her? No, it wasn't Gemma's fault. I was the one who'd lost control of myself because of her.

"I'm here to help you," I reassured him, forcing myself to concentrate.

His face lit up. "You mean you can heal me? You can make me go back into my body?" he asked, full of hope. A hope I would have to deprive him of, just as I'd deprived him of air.

"No one can do that. Life on Earth is only borrowed time. We need to appreciate the time that's given to us, because ultimately we have to give it back. And your time is up, Jimmy."

"But it's too soon!" he cried. "I'm just a kid!"

"We're not the ones who choose how long our journey lasts. But we can choose our destination. I was sent for you, to take you to a place without time. Come with me."

"Do I have a choice?" He looked around, searching for a way out.

"Every mortal soul has the right to choose. But you wouldn't like the alternative. Trust me and you'll be fine."

Jimmy peered into my eyes, drawn by the comforting spell of my voice. In my angelic form, I sensed every emotion emanating from his soul.

I held out my hand. He took it, and I felt all his fear vanish instantly. A second later, he disappeared before my eyes. His soul was safe. Nothing counted more for a Subterranean. Like every other time, I was pleased that I'd completed my mission, but it only lasted a second. A darker sensation had gripped my heart.

It was Gemma's turn. Her time was up too and I was the one who'd been sent to do it.

Gemma ran, earbuds in her ears, almost like she was in a hurry to meet her fate. *To meet me*, Death. The grim reaper that would cut her life short.

I materialized on the street in front of her and she stopped, sensing I was near. It was strange, her managing to do that. She looked behind her hesitantly and took out her earbuds, from which came a melancholy song about death and destiny. Funny how she'd picked that particular song.

Time was up.

I had to act fast or I risked going insane. The nightmare had to end. It was the only way I could find myself.

Gemma started running again and I turned my back on her. I would have liked to take her hand and accompany her on that last stretch of road, to feel the power of her touch one last time. But I lacked the courage. I decided I wouldn't watch.

I clenched my fists as Gemma's foot landed on a circular wooden platform. On my command, the wood broke into pieces and Gemma tumbled into the darkness.

There was a scream, and then silence.

I gulped. I was almost afraid to move closer, but I had no choice. I had to see my orders through to the end and have her soul pass on.

I stopped on the edge of the hole that had swallowed her up and searched the darkness.

It was a stone well and she was at the bottom of it. She stirred and I held my breath, cursing myself for making everything so difficult. She was unconscious, her face streaked with blood. I couldn't turn away. I'd made a huge mistake. Gemma was supposed to have died on the spot. Bleeding to death would be much more painful for her.

But this way we can spend a little more time together.

I instantly banished the selfish thought.

Gemma opened her eyes and looked around, frightened. Totally oblivious to the fact that Death was looming over her—in my guise. She tried to get up, but the pain in her head had left her in a daze. The impact had been brutal.

She looked up. I was petrified. I felt like a vulture staring down at its prey, waiting for it to die.

"Help! Is anyone there?" she cried. "I'm down here! Somebody help me!"

I clenched my fists at my sides, confused. Why didn't she see me? Had she lost her power? She was injured, as frightened as a caged animal. Though she continued to call out, no one was going to pass by. I'd hidden her traces; she wouldn't be found in time.

"Peter! Pet! I'm down here!!"

Hearing that name turned my insides to ice and made my muscles tremble. Once again, I felt the senseless urge to take the boy's life. All it would take was one touch . . . Why was I thinking that? It was a question with no answer.

It was strange. Gemma couldn't see me in my ethereal form, just as should have been the case from the start. But this was the first time it had happened, and I couldn't resist the urge to look at her from closer up, now that she might not have her power any more.

I materialized at the bottom of the well, hiding in the darkness. I still wasn't sure she couldn't see me, even though I'd transformed.

I stopped, staggered by intense emotion. She was crying. I clenched my fists, forcing myself not to move closer. I knew being next to her would make things worse, but maybe I could touch her one last time, to commit to memory the power of the sensations she made me feel . . .

No, that would be crazy. Ginevra was right, I was self-centered. I had to stop now and get it over with. She was right there, just steps away from me. I'd waited too long.

"Who's there?"

Her voice was so confident I almost jumped. I stepped back, hiding in the shadows. But she huddled up and turned away. She couldn't see me.

I cautiously drew closer and sat down beside her, so close I could feel her fear resonate in the air. I studied her carefully: her big dark eyes, the pale freckles left by the sun. She raised her eyes and looked at me. Or more accurately, she looked *through* me. I'd fooled myself into thinking she could see me, that her deep eyes were searching mine . . . one last time.

Instead, she rested her head against the wall and began to talk as if she were delirious, her breath halting.

I closed my eyes. I couldn't wait any longer.

"Are you here to kill me?"

I flinched and turned to look at her. I wasn't sure if she was talking to me; she seemed to have lost contact with reality. I decided I could give her one last moment of comfort before taking her away. Or maybe it was just another self-serving gesture on my part.

I wrapped my arm around her shoulders and she rested her head on my chest.

"Am I going to be okay?" she murmured in a frail voice.

I took her hand and stroked it. "Yes. You'll be fine."

Gemma smiled, reassured. "And you? Are you going to be okay?" she asked, leaving me defenseless.

I didn't know the answer to that question. It might have been the one that agonized me the most. Maybe not, maybe I wouldn't be okay. But the time for being self-centered was over.

I laid a hand over Gemma's heart.

"Evan . . ." she whispered.

My eyes opened wide.

But I'd already followed the impulse to kill her.

I woke with a start and looked around, utterly confused. *I'd been dreaming?* How deeply rooted inside me was this agony? Deep enough to shake me to the core? I was a master of dreams, but I myself dreamed only on rare occasions. I ran my hands down my face. It had all seemed so real. I'd felt Gemma's life flow inside me, but this time I hadn't felt that shiver of exhilaration from the death I'd brought her. I'd felt devastated.

The answer to the question she'd asked me; I had to accept it. Meeting Gemma had changed me. Losing her would condemn me. That's what my subconscious was trying to tell me. I'd always been so focused on the subconscious of others that I'd never listened to my own.

Even so, there was nothing I could do to change her fate. Gemma would die by my hand. Despite everything.

It was so quiet I heard every tick of the clock on the wall in the next room. It marked the time, each second more oppressive than the last.

Tick-tock-tick—tock—tick——tock.

Even the sound was mocking me by seemingly slowing its pace.

I would gladly have gone unconscious if only I could have, and eluded time entirely. But even my dreams were tortured. Trapped in an ethereal form I no longer recognized, I would have to bear every minute between now and the end. An end that, I began to hope, would come to us quickly.

"Come to *us*," I whispered, surprised by how naturally I had included myself in that inevitable end which would cut Gemma's life short. Hers—not my own. So why did it feel like I would be dying too?

I couldn't stand the idea of losing her, but if I couldn't prevent it, I might as well spare myself the agony right away. I sat there, perfectly still, for what felt an eternity before footsteps snapped me out of my trance.

I didn't need to look up to know who it was. I was well acquainted with the sound of each of my family members' footsteps. From the soft, graceful touch with which the shoes caressed the marble floor, I recognized her instantly.

Gin, you're still here?

"Sorry, I can't stand seeing you like this. You're still thinking about her." There wasn't a shadow of doubt in her voice.

"Did you read that in my mind?"

"I read it in your eyes."

I looked up at her questioningly.

"Every woman would love to see that look on her man's face. It's so clear you're thinking of her there's no need to read your mind."

"I can't do without her. I've tried to stop thinking about her but I can't, not even for a minute."

"You guys just killed off an entire family and now you're grieving over one girl?"

Ginevra was right. I didn't feel the slightest bit guilty about those people, about that little boy. Why didn't I feel anything? I'd never wondered about that before. Gemma had made me question everything. Drake had fun with it, at least, and Simon had Ginevra. What did I have? I'd never felt anything, and now I was being forced to give up the one person who'd managed to reawaken my emotions.

Maybe I was just being selfish. After all, I knew her soul would be fine. But what would become of me? I couldn't bear the thought of giving up the euphoria Gemma made me feel.

"You dreamed," she said, searching my thoughts.

"Crazy, isn't it?"

"It's human."

That's exactly why it was crazy. "What sense is there in being able to control others' dreams when you have no power over your own desires?"

"Desires often lead to perdition, don't forget that."

"I already feel lost."

"No. You aren't. And I'll always be here with you to remind you of that. Did you receive your instructions?" Ginevra's voice was cold, icy, emotionless again. A clear attempt to declare the case closed.

There was nothing I could do for Gemma. They hadn't even relieved me of the assignment so I wouldn't have her blood on my hands. They'd left me with no choice. The Màsala had been adamant. No one dared speak their name out loud. The earth had even shaken in their presence when I met with them.

Reluctantly, I forced myself to nod. None of us ever knew what the others' instructions were, but Ginevra could read them directly in our thoughts.

"Good. Gemma will leave the house to go to the school, but South Main Street will be closed off, so she'll have to take Station Street until she reaches Mill Pond Drive from the other side tomor—um, in a while," she corrected herself, looking out the window at the veil of night. I followed her gaze to the garden, filled with a darkness as grim and relentless as the wild beast lurking inside me. The monster who would take Gemma's life.

I looked at the clock for the hundredth time. Anxiety gripped me. It was two in the morning. Just five hours until the end.

My chest grew tighter and tighter as the minutes passed.

"First, you make sure she turns down that road and then you make sure the truck loses control. You know what has to happen next: Gemma will never show up at the school," she said coldly, as if the whole thing had nothing to do with us.

I was unexpectedly struck by mental images of that imminent future. They burst into my mind, stunning me, flashing before my eyes as though I'd already experienced them. Instead of sleeping in, like she would do on a normal Saturday, Gemma would leave her house early to go to the school. Destiny had wanted her to forget to turn in a project the day before. And I'd made it happen. I'd had no choice. She would take her bike, as she often did, only to find that that whole area was blocked off, closed to traffic due to a problem with the gas pipes, which I would see to myself. By manipulating the air, I would make her lose control of her bike.

I'd gone over everything countless times, something I'd never done before. Gemma wouldn't miss her appointment with Death. Her appointment *with me.*

With a wave of my hand I would seal her fate.

I visualized the truck barreling out of control from her perspective. I could almost sense the terror she would feel the second before it hit her. At exactly seven o'clock.

I saw it, her green backpack lying on the pavement, her light-colored clothes splattered with blood, her bike reduced to a twisted tangle of metal . . . and her lifeless body crumpled on the pavement.

She was so beautiful, even like that, like a precious necklace cast into the sea, sparkling as it slowly descends amid the silvery reflections of the water streaked with rays of sunlight, growing fainter and fainter until, making way for darkness, the chain settles on the sea floor for all eternity. In my mental image, her eyes were closed like they were when I watched her sleep, but her heart had stopped beating.

I looked at Ginevra. In her eyes shone the same coldness that had always shone in mine.

We can't choose what we are. But when it came to Gemma, every last trace of that coldness disappeared.

So many lives cut short, one after the other. Men, women, children. I'd never hesitated to carry out orders before. I'd never questioned my duties. I knew I was just a pawn in the hands of the Brotherhood.

Why did it have to be so difficult with her? Why had I grown attached to someone I couldn't keep? What did Gemma have that I hadn't already seen thousands of times? It was so strong it made me feel a guilt I'd never known before. And then, that yearning for her, that uncontrollable urge to surrender to the emotions she and she alone conjured up in me.

The thought filled me with a sudden longing. I had to see her again.

I wanted to be with her one last time. Wasn't I allowed to say goodbye? Wasn't I permitted to spend one last night together with her? That was a decision—the only one—that I could make for myself.

I closed my eyes and concentrated on Gemma's face in my mind. When I opened them again, I was in her room. I stood there at the foot of her bed for a while, making sure I didn't wake her.

Her dog let out a low growl from his cushion. He could sense my presence, even though he was asleep, but my scent didn't alarm him any more, not enough to wake him. I smiled. It hadn't been easy, but in the end he and I had become friends.

Gemma stirred in bed. From the way her body was tangled up in the sheets, it seemed her sleep had been restless. Her reading glasses had fallen to the floor, along with her copy of *Jane Eyre*. That book must be special to her. Judging from how worn the cover was, she'd probably read it many times. I wished I could show her my original 1847 edition of it, just to see her eyes light up with amazement.

She was so adorable. She must have nodded off while reading. I was tempted to pick up her glasses, but then I remembered how I'd frightened her that night by turning off the lights and hanging up the phone. I had no idea what made me want to take care of her like that, even in those little things. The urge was almost uncontrollable.

The walls were covered with pictures. Curious, I stepped over to look at them. There were photographs of her as a little girl, and other, more recent ones. In almost all the snapshots, Gemma was with her friend, that guy. In a few close-ups she was alone, a smile lighting up her face tanned by the summer sun. *He must have taken those.* I grunted, thinking about how Peter was always hovering around her.

When I'd seen him climbing up to her window, a strange emotion had boiled up inside me. Not even thinking, I'd clenched my fists and made the wooden slats give under his weight. I had no idea what drove me to react that way, but suddenly I hadn't wanted him to go into her room. Gemma had smiled at him and he'd tried again. I'd had to force myself to leave. If I hadn't, I might have broken his neck.

Gemma continued to toss and turn under her powder-blue sheets. With every movement, the scent of her skin rose into the air, inundating my supernatural senses. A corner of the sheet was pulled back at her waist, as was the bottom of her shirt, revealing a glimpse of the sensual dimples of Venus on her back. My breathing went almost perfectly still, as though my lungs had a will of their own.

Thin lines creased her forehead. For a second, I hoped it was because I wasn't in her dream. In any case, I decided to wait a little longer before joining her there, wanting to savor that special moment when she couldn't see me.

I took another step toward her so I could watch her from closer up. Once I was beside her, I reached out to caress her face, unable to control myself, longing for the sensation that only her skin could make me feel. It was as though it were imbued with a stimulating substance, some sweet, intoxicating poison. But her skin beneath my fingertips was so soft . . . Supple and warm.

I slowly leaned down until my lips almost brushed her ear.

"I'm here," I whispered, closing my eyes, to soothe whatever was upsetting her in her dream. I knew she could hear me, only she was capable of that.

Gemma reacted instantly, relaxing at the sound of my voice. The crease on her forehead disappeared and she began to breathe evenly, comforted by my presence.

I couldn't take my eyes off her. Despite how long I'd lived, I'd never seen such a wonderful creature before. Her dark hair was spread out on the pillow in disarray, flowing down to her shoulder. From time to time a soft lock caressed her face and I found myself gazing at it ravenously, as captivated as a thief staring at treasure. A shaft of silvery light illuminated her skin from nape to cheek. Her skin glowed like a diamond.

It took all my self-control to resist the urge to touch my lips to hers, run them along the curve of her face and taste her skin, my warm breath on her, moving down to her chin, her throat, then her shoulder, her breast that rose shyly beneath the shirt that was too insubstantial to curb my need. For a moment I was lost in that desire, that delirium, that prelude to madness.

I found it adorable, that stubborn, intense look that would fill her big eyes, as dark as black diamonds, when she searched my face, struggling to understand what was causing me such agony.

It felt like some mysterious power stirred within her when I was near. A power not even she could hold back, one that struck both of us, carrying us away to some distant place inhabited by only the two of us, our gazes forever locked. A power that deprived me of the strength to escape her.

Deep eyes full of life, as bright as stars, twinkling like fireflies in the night. Was it too much to ask that this light not be taken from them?

Gemma . . .

Whatever it was that had been troubling her faded away, leaving behind peaceful, rejuvenating sleep. For a second, I felt a pang of disappointment that I'd wiped away the uneasiness she'd felt because of my absence. Her longing for me probably wasn't as deeply rooted as mine for her.

Gemma parted her lips, shaking her head as if she'd perceived my thought, and a wave of emotion washed over my body.

God, my heart is pounding.

I winced at my own thought; I didn't have a heart, not any more. Then why did I feel the way I did? It felt like it was still there in its place, beating to the rhythm of Gemma's breathing. Like it wanted to burst out of my chest and scream with rage.

It was as though I were chin-deep in water, consumed by the knowledge that I wouldn't be able to breathe much longer. Overwhelmed by this feeling, I gasped a deep breath as though it would be my last before sinking into the abyss and losing my senses. There were still a few hours left before I would drown in pain, forever extinguishing the spark that had brought me back to life.

All my self-control was gone. My thoughts wandered aimlessly as I stared at her face, at the pure innocence of the creature before me. The creature I had to kill. Confused, incoherent thoughts dominated by savage emotions I couldn't comprehend, that I couldn't stop.

No matter how difficult it was to face the harsh reality of the unlucky star under which I'd been born, I couldn't put my emotions before fate.

After all, who was I to challenge destiny? No one.

Who was Gemma to cause me such pain?

Everything.

The answer came to me from places unknown. No matter how darkened I was by my emotions, I *had* to find the strength to battle the hidden enemy haunting me like some spiteful ghost, dissuading me from my duty. A duty I couldn't question. A duty I couldn't disregard.

Who, then, did I need to fight to drive away the pain? Myself? Unlikely. It must be coming from a stronger entity, and I no longer felt strong. I couldn't even control my own thoughts. It was definitely a powerful energy, an uncontrollable one. But if I didn't know its nature, how could I fight it and keep it from clouding my mind?

I felt like I'd gone insane.

It was getting harder and harder to resist that uncontrollable force I couldn't name. It continued to grow. Torment, desire, yearning for her. An enemy as powerful as it was obscure. It made my chest ache.

God, she takes my breath away. I felt like a madman, consumed by incomprehensible emotion. *Why do I feel this way? Where is this power, this pain coming from? I don't understand it, I can't control it. Yet I feel that it's part of me. It's inside me, silently devouring me. It put down roots without my noticing it, and there's nothing I can do to stop it. I can feel it growing every day.* My mind was reeling, overwhelmed by the growing wave of desperation, as I brushed the back of my hand over Gemma's fingers, barely touching her so I wouldn't wake her.

I can't name it, but it hurts. Could it be regret? No. It's stronger than that. Is it pain, then? No, it's deeper, fiercer. Is it the other side of pain, as wild and ardent as fire? Could this be the love *everyone talks about? Would I be able to recognize it if it pierced my heart with its arrows?*

There was no way I could be sure; I'd never felt it for myself. Not during my mortal life, let alone during the empty shell of the existence in which I'd been trapped for hundreds of years since.

Could love strike so suddenly, like a train barreling down the tracks, unable to stop? Could an emotion be so devastating that it burns like lava, clouding your thoughts, leaving you utterly unable to choose? Like a stealthy, greedy thief who steals your heart and every part of you while you stand there and watch it happen, a helpless spectator, with no way out?

A wave of pure emotion washed over me, and all at once, everything became clearer.

That heartbeat I felt was her, growing in the deepest corner of my heart like a flower pushing its way up through the ice and snow.

My apprehension cleared away like mist as I realized I loved her. I loved this sweet creature. And I would love her forever.

It was a brutal twist of fate: now that I had finally managed to give a name to my torment, now that I knew I loved Gemma more than myself, I was about to lose her forever.

Could destiny be any crueler?

And could a man, having seen the light, return to the darkness? Maybe a man could, but I wasn't a man. She would never leave my mind.

I would be hers forever.

How could I go on without her? Forgetting her would be impossible—it would be like forgetting myself. Gemma was a part of me now, an essential piece of my own spirit. Torn away from me, she would leave behind a wound that would never heal.

What sense did living forever make if I couldn't see her, touch her . . . love her. I would give up eternity to live as a mortal with her if only they would let me. But my wishes didn't matter. I was a predator sent out by Death, and I wasn't allowed to choose my prey. I just had to carry out orders.

Anguished by that awareness, I understood that everything I'd always fought for, everything I'd always believed in and defended, didn't matter any more. The new emotion was like a volcano that after centuries of lying dormant suddenly erupts, destroying everything in its path, everything I'd once been.

Nothing was worth anything any more if I couldn't have her. The only thing that mattered was contained in the little body lying there in front of me. Gemma.

Looking at her, for the first time I felt I wasn't alone. But that fleeting sensation wasn't destined to last. I drew a deep breath and filled my senses with her scent. I held that breath inside me until my soul was satiated.

I felt like I'd known her forever, but only a few weeks had gone by since we'd first met. Like a bolt of lightning, her gaze had pierced my heart, opening a permanent laceration there.

I let the memories flood in. Thinking back on the anger in her voice made me smile, now that I knew the reason behind it. She thought I was involved with Ginevra when instead I only wanted her. I hadn't known it then, but I was already hers and would be forever. I'd thought I'd been suffering because I had to give up all the emotions I was finally experiencing, but I was wrong. It was *her* I didn't want to give up. The memory of the brief moments we'd shared warmed my heart. Those nights, in her dreams, they were all ours, although she would never know it. Those were the moments when I'd felt for the first time that I could be myself, fully and without reserve.

I took another deep breath.Would I ever feel like that again, as only she could make me feel? Free. Satisfied. Complete.

Impossible. How could I feel complete if half of me had been torn away? Because that's what Gemma was to me: my other half, my Eve. Without her, part of me would die forever.

All at once a ray of hope appeared in my thoughts, lighting them up like a comet and driving away the darkness into which I'd been slipping.

It was then that, for the first time, I glimpsed another path. I would come up with an alternative plan.

There was no way I'd be able to bear the empty existence that awaited me once Gemma's light had been extinguished. There would no longer be any existence left to live. Death, cruel witness, was mocking us. Fate had allowed me to fall in love with her. Maybe this had been written too. It was inevitable, and Death would be doubly satisfied. If I couldn't prevent her death, I would seek my own. After carrying out my orders and sealing Gemma's fate, I would bring my own existence to an end. My mind was made up.

I looked at the clock on her nightstand. Only two more hours and a tragedy would take place. Two lives would be cut short: that of a human and that of an Angel who was desperately in love with her.

I didn't have much time. It would have been easier to leave the room rather than force myself to suffer through a farewell, but the longing to look into her eyes again, to feel her gaze burning into mine, overpowered me.

I would have one final memory of her to treasure, to bury in some inaccessible corner of my heart where I would take refuge before disappearing forever.

I stroked the back of her hand. At my caress, her lips parted. The almost imperceptible words she whispered would have been incomprehensible to a human ear, but they weren't to mine; I grasped their true essence, what her unconscious was trying to tell me.

My eyes opened wide as I deciphered her soft, tormented murmur.

Where are you? Where are you and why can't I see you? I can feel you're here, but I can't see you.

My heart trembled. She was waiting for me. Knowing that Gemma felt the same yearning I did filled my spirit. But why should that matter now? Soon it would all be over. So why was my heart brimming with happiness?

Too late, I'd discovered in love a humble emotion that could thrive on fleeting moments of joy despite the awareness that they couldn't last.

"*Evan . . .*"

Gemma's anxious whisper made me even more impatient. I wanted to be with her one last time. I wanted to say farewell.

Farewell forever.

19

FAREWELL

Once inside Gemma's mind, I found myself in the darkness—pitch-dark even to my eyes—in which Gemma often hid. In it, I sensed the uneasiness her soul harbored. Something was troubling her, but she wasn't afraid, which meant she suspected nothing of her imminent death. She hadn't read my mind like I'd feared.

I groped along, seeking her in the gloom. The sound of water led me to her. She was kneeling on a rocky shore, the waves flowing toward her gently as if to comfort her, lapping against the very edge of her black gown's organza frills. I wanted to embrace her, I wanted to protect her, but my embrace would be nothing but a deception, because I was there to take her away.

"Evan."

Her voice rang gently through the cool night air. The sweetness with which she uttered my name made me burn with guilt. She should hate me but instead she was happy to see me. She had no idea who she was dealing with, no idea that the person who loved her more than any other was the same person who would soon take her life. How would I find the courage to kill her? I clenched my fists, forcing myself to repress those thoughts, to lock them up in a remote corner of my mind that Gemma could never explore. Tonight would be our last chance ever to be together.

The instant she turned to look at me, I understood why darkness had fallen: her glowing beauty had lit up the night and the jealous stars had run to hide.

She smiled, motioning me over. Like a ghost mingling with the air, I vanished like mist and reappeared next to her. Without asking permission, I sat down next to her and took her hand. Lacing my fingers with hers, I lifted them to brush them against my lips, still holding her gaze. Like a dark spell, the emotion that swept over me made me forget, if only for an instant, the cruel destiny we were heading toward, lurking behind the first light of day.

In that endless moment, it was only her and me, Evan and Gemma. No one could ever take tonight away from us.

"I was afraid you wouldn't come." Gemma moistened her lips, watching mine as they slowly slid down her hand, brushing her palm, her wrist and her fingers again.

I forced myself to look away from her as the ocean beneath us transformed into a chasm that grew ever deeper. "Nothing in the world could have kept me away," I reassured her.

"Tell me what's worrying you."

I flinched, gripped by a sense of foreboding as the ocean sank lower and lower. Was I reading inside of her, or vice versa?

At times Gemma's insight amazed me. She could interpret emotions in me that were inaccessible even to me, but since I wanted tonight to be magical for both of us I had to struggle to conceal them, to seem calm, to hide the anguish consuming me.

I didn't want Gemma to share my agony. I wanted to give her a part of me tonight so she could remember me forever, even after her soul had left her body.

I stroked her cheek, trying to reassure her, and brushed my thumb along that little line of concern on her forehead, hoping it would disappear.

"I'm better now that you're here with me," I whispered. I was lying, naturally. Having her there in front of me and being able to read her soul through her eyes was making me suffer all the more.

We moved closer together, so close our bodies risked touching with each breath. A magnetic energy pulsed all around us at the mere possibility of physical contact. It exploded when her elbow brushed mine, sending a quiver through my ethereal body as it spread out, a dark, irresistible energy that overwhelmed me.

The air grew cooler as the plain on which we were now sitting continued to levitate imperceptibly, carrying us higher and higher.

I suddenly realized our height was reflecting Gemma's mood. Her elation was making her walk on clouds, but in the meantime, the emptiness below was growing deeper and gloomier. There was an abyss beneath us, the ocean no longer visible. I couldn't make sense of that gaping chasm. What was worrying her? No matter how hard I tried, reading Gemma proved to be more difficult than it had ever been before.

There was no way she could have sensed the truth in my mind; I'd been careful not to reveal my emotions. Then I understood: the abyss was reflecting *my* worries, not hers. Gemma could read me, no matter how hard I tried to keep my anguish hidden from her. She could sense my uneasiness and it was sounding alarm bells inside her.

She wasn't worried about herself. She was concerned for me, for the assassin who was going to take her life.

Touched by her incredible selflessness, for a second I was tempted to tell her everything, to explain what was torturing me. I barely resisted the urge, realizing what a mistake it would be to give her the key to her own death.

I looked away and scanned our surroundings in search of something that might take Gemma's mind off my mood. There was little I could do for her, but I wanted to at least offer her a memory of us that she could cherish deep in her heart. As she did in all her dreams, Gemma had conjured up a place of extraordinary beauty and I let it inspire me.

I stroked the back of her hand until her fingers returned the caress and let myself slowly sink back onto the carpet of grass, inviting her with my eyes to join me. Overhead, the sky was dark, black.

"Think a storm's coming?" I asked, folding my arms under my head.

Gemma bit her lip, thinking. "I hope not. It really is a shame it's cloudy tonight."

I smiled. She didn't realize she was an artist. In that little world of ours she could paint the night with sparkling diamonds, using the sky as her canvas.

"Are you so sure it is?" I asked, seeking her eyes. Gemma looked at me for a moment and stared back up at the sky, puzzled, as my eyes studied her features.

"I don't see a single star," she replied after careful examination.

"Look," I whispered, pointing my finger at the sky above us.

"There's nothing there," she insisted, shaking her head.

"It just seems that way. Sometimes you need to dig deeper to see what you're looking for. Just because you can't see something doesn't mean it's not there. *Look closer*," I whispered, my head brushing hers.

"I think I've heard that somewhere before." She smiled slightly, her voice hushed, but the shiver that ran over her spoke louder than her words.

I caressed the air, stroking the mantle of black above us as if to erase the darkness. As my hand swept across it, the darkness slid from the sky, pulled away like a cloth, revealing the infinite stars behind it. Gemma gasped and the smile disappeared from her face, leaving only astonishment. A silver glimmer sparkled in her eye, reflecting the starlight. "Evan, what— Did you do that?" she stammered.

Actually, she could have done it herself, she just didn't realize it. I hid a smile. "It's a beautiful night, isn't it?" *Our last one*, I thought, but forced myself to push it from my mind.

"It's *amazing*! I've never seen anything so wonderful in my whole life."

"That's only because you've never seen yourself through my eyes," I whispered.

Gemma stared at me for a moment and looked away, embarrassed by my boldness. I could read her every emotion, her every heartbeat, so I knew it was making her uneasy, but I couldn't help it. I couldn't be next to her without constantly wanting to touch her. At times I tried to sublimate my desire through compliments, to subdue it through words.

Despite the darkness of the night, the starlight illuminated her face enough to reveal the soft blush on her cheeks. I couldn't get enough of the breathtaking sight. While Gemma was admiring the firmament, I was contemplating her, utterly spellbound. Like two endless mirrors, her deep eyes reflected her soul, showing me its inner splendor.

A myriad of stars covered the night like the vault of a diamond-studded cave. A myriad of emotions passed through my ethereal body like an incandescent meteor shower.

She sighed. "I feel so small in the presence of all this immensity."

"You shouldn't," I said, the words coming out on their own. "All this is nothing compared to what's inside of you, Gemma. There's something in you, something I can't do without any more. I don't know why, but your light shines brighter than any other. Don't feel small, because there's no star more precious in all the firmament," I whispered, holding her gaze. "This night belongs to you. Rise up and gather the brightest stars." I'd carved those words into the table at the diner, hoping it would encourage her to follow her mother's advice. Gemma had tried to avoid being overheard, but I'd heard them all the same.

I was aware that the things I was saying were throwing her emotions into turmoil, but no matter how hard I tried I couldn't hold back. Like every other time I'd been with her, I'd lost control. How could I master myself now that I knew I loved her?

"Ever wonder what might be up there?" she asked. "The universe is so immense, so full of secrets." Embarrassed, Gemma avoided my eyes and instead stared intensely at the sky, a fascinated expression on her face as she waited for her discomfort to pass. "Isn't that Ursa Major?" she asked, pointing to a spot among the stars.

"You know the constellations?" I said, surprised. It meant I'd chosen the right topic.

"Not really. But I think they're fascinating, *mysterious*, even." She stole a glance at me and went back to staring at the night.

"Don't mysterious things scare you?" I asked despite myself.

Gemma looked down, grasping my allusion.

"You should hear some of the myths behind the constellations," I said, returning to the topic to make her feel more at ease. "I'm sure you'd like them. I like learning about mythology."

"Oh, so there's something you don't know already?" She grinned.

A smile escaped me. "I know a few stories, if you'd like to hear them."

"Why not?" she said, trying to sound casual. She didn't realize I sensed the curiosity building up inside her, and the excitement she was trying to hide made me smile. Was she trying to seem more mature in my eyes? Didn't she realize I found it adorable?

"The one you just pointed to is Ursa Major. Callisto," I added.

"Callisto?" she asked, shaking her head.

I nodded and smiled at her. To my surprise it was enough to make her blush again. "She was one of Zeus's countless lovers," I continued, as more and more interest appeared on her face. "Legend has it that when Zeus's wife Hera found out about his betrayal, she took revenge on Callisto, first by turning her into a bear and then by having her almost killed by Arcas, Callisto's son by Zeus and an expert hunter. But Zeus intervened just in time and placed the bear in the sky along with her son, who became Ursa Minor, keeping both of them safe from harm."

Lying at my side, Gemma stared at the sky, engrossed in my story, while every breath she took intensified my attraction to her. I longed to touch her, even just for a second. I desired her with my whole being, with every fragment of my tortured self.

"It's fascinating. I'd never heard it before," she said.

"That's just one of the hundreds of stories I know. Greek mythology has always interested me. Look," I whispered, pointing over our heads. "See that V-shaped line? That's Perseus, son of Zeus. To prove his valor, Perseus was sent out to slay Medusa the Gorgon, a monster who could turn anyone who looked her in the eye into stone. The night before his departure, Athena appeared to him in a dream and gave him a magic sword to cut off Medusa's head and a shield to use as a mirror. Hermes, on the other hand, gave him winged sandals to reach the island where Medusa dwelled.

"During his journey, Perseus encountered the three Nymphs of the North who gave him a magic helmet that would make him invisible and a magic sack to hide the monster's head in. Armed with these gifts, Perseus easily accomplished his mission. Pegasus, the winged horse that he rode on his journey back, was created from the blood that dripped out of the sack, mixed with seawater. See, he's the four-sided shape over there," I said, pointing out its stars.

"The boxy one?" Gemma asked.

I lowered my head in a nod.

"That's called Pegasus's Great Square. One of its four stars is also part of the constellation Andromeda."

"Andromeda. I think I've heard that name before."

My gaze lingered on hers a moment before I continued the story, happy it was having the effect I'd hoped for; there was no trace of worry on her face. "During the journey, Perseus saw a beautiful princess off the Greek coast—"

"Andromeda," Gemma said.

"She was chained to some rocks on the shore of a tiny island, terrified by the horrible monster that was creeping toward her, about to devour her. Perseus swooped in, pulled Medusa's head out of the sack and faced it toward the monster, instantly turning it to stone. As a reward for saving Andromeda, he was offered her hand in marriage. So, what else do you want to know? Ask away," I said, seeing her eyes full of questions.

"What was Andromeda doing on the shore? I mean, who chained her up there?"

I looked at the sky in the direction opposite Ursa Major. "See that W-shaped constellation?" I asked, indicating its exact spot. Gemma moved closer to me to have a clearer view of where I was pointing. I held my breath. As soon as she noticed, she sat up, embarrassed, and hugged her knees to her chest. I sat up too, and leaned in toward her, unable to resist my longing another second. A longing I felt under my skin that was growing wilder and wilder.

I moved my face near hers, almost brushing against her cheek. She didn't move. We'd never been so close before. I could even hear her heartbeat accelerating.

Slowly, I turned to look into her eyes. Our lips were just inches apart, yearning to be closer. Her warm breath came faster and faster against my skin.

I couldn't resist any longer. My body escaped my control as my gaze lost itself in her parted lips. I tilted my head and drew closer. One kiss . . . What could possibly happen with just one kiss? With my lips I barely brushed the corner of her mouth, delicately, almost imperceptibly. An overwhelming emotion took my breath away.

I'd never felt so elated before.

I was anticipating the taste of a stolen kiss, and I could feel Gemma's warm lips trembling in expectation, but she suddenly pulled back, breaking the magic of the moment. It wasn't a refusal, though; I could read her emotions and knew she longed for that contact too.

"Um, yeah . . . I see it," she stammered as I stole a glance at her, a half smile on my face.

Breathless from the emotion of that brief, forbidden contact, I made myself pick up my story where I'd left off. "That's Cassiopeia," I said, peering up at the sky. "She's Andromeda's mother."

"Her mother?" she asked, frowning. I knew exactly what she wanted to ask.

"Cassiopeia was proud of her daughter's beauty and her own. She was so vain she boasted that they were even more beautiful than the sea nymphs. That enraged Poseidon, the god of the sea, who sent the terrible monster Cetus to destroy their city."

"The monster Perseus killed," Gemma said, following the story closely. "But I still don't understand. Why was Andromeda chained to the rocks?"

"The only way to appease Poseidon and save the kingdom was to sacrifice her daughter to the monster," I explained, smiling.

In contrast, her face instantly grew darker. "What a horrifying story!"

I was surprised to see how suddenly her mood changed. I still wasn't used to it. "But Perseus saves her in the end," I reminded her.

"It doesn't matter! It's so sad. She was her mother. I can't imagine how anyone could sacrifice someone they love."

Her words ran me through like a blade of ice, leaving a chill inside me, a chill that crept into my soul.

Isn't that exactly what I was about to do myself? My heart sank. I was overwhelmed.

"Sometimes a person has no choice," I said through clenched teeth. "Sometimes we're forced to do something against our will," I said, staring at the ground, filled with self-loathing.

"There's always a choice," she said sternly, looking into my eyes. "*Always.*"

I would have given anything to be able to believe her. But I knew it just wasn't so.

Devastating silence filled the night, a witness to our sadness, until Gemma looked up at the stars again. "Is that Orion?" she asked, breaking the silence.

I nodded, still unable to pull myself out of it. "It might be the most beautiful of all the constellations," I whispered from the void into which I had sunk, my voice stifled with pain. "It's the easiest one to spot. He's shaped like a hunter holding a club and a shield. At waist height, you can clearly make out the sword in his belt."

"Orion's Belt." Gemma was surprised to recognize the name. "What's his story?" she asked, fascinated.

She'd shaken her sadness again and for a moment I forced myself to forget my own. "Orion was the greatest hunter of his time and he would often go hunting with Diana, the goddess of the hunt. But one day Diana's brother Apollo noticed that she was neglecting her duties because of Orion, so he decided he had to die. And so, while Orion was swimming in the open sea, far from shore, Apollo, the sun god, shone a bright sunbeam on him and challenged his sister to hit the shiny speck with one of her arrows." I shuddered, realizing how much the story resembled my own. Suddenly, I felt incredibly sorry for Diana, forced to kill the person she loved most in the world. "Oblivious to the trick, Diana accepted the challenge and shot her beloved, slaying him."

Images of the imminent tragedy burst back into my mind, silencing me. For a moment I was lost in those visions, as vivid as photographs: my own love lying on the ground, lifeless, as blood seeped from her body, drenching her sweatshirt, which had once been as candid and pure as her fragile human heart. The sight of the blood sickened me, as did my contempt for myself and my nature. I could almost feel the hot liquid on my fingers, see it on my hands that would be guilty of committing the involuntary crime. I could have ripped open my own chest from the excruciating pain I felt inside.

Suddenly her delicate hand touched mine, bringing me back to the present, to my spot beside her, the only place I wanted to be. She lay back on the grass, the better to see the sky, and I followed her example.

I noticed her expression had saddened and quickly tried to repair the damage. Hoping to avoid giving her worries the chance to return, I continued my story.

"When Diana found Orion's body, she put it in her celestial chariot and took him up into the sky, attaching him there with brilliant stars. She placed his most trusted dogs at his feet to stand guard, but that's another story."

"Where did you learn all these myths? At the school you went to before moving here?"

I smiled. "Not really. Let's just say I've had a lot of time to cultivate my interests."

"You could write a book," she said with admiration.

After a moment of excruciating silence, I found my smiling mask in my mind and put it on. Deep in my heart I was racked with pain. I'd always known those stories but strangely enough it was like I was hearing them for the first time. Only now did I seem to grasp their meaning. After all, they weren't so different from my predicament. I'd never thought much about the tragic theme common to all the stories: the main characters finding themselves killing their beloved. It had happened with Diana and Orion, with Callisto and Arcas, and even Cassiopeia and her daughter.

Now it was our turn. Evan and Gemma.

I was going to end her life forever and it was eating away at my conscience. If only I could place her among the stars to protect her. Her light would outshine all the others and the whole world would fall in love with her. Fate would realize what a mistake her death would be and revoke its cruel sentence.

Gemma was about to die. I felt like I already had. When you know you have to give up the person you love, you die inside. How could I even think of spending eternity without her?

Mine was a fate worse than death. I could never accept the empty existence that awaited me without Gemma. I'd made up my mind, and it was an irrevocable decision: this night would be the last one for both of us.

The silence was deafening. I didn't speak, Gemma didn't speak, but inside we were both screaming, though for different reasons.

I shifted my weight onto one arm, leaning on my elbow, my torso turned toward her. Gemma continued to lie there on her back on the grass. The longing to remove the distance between us came back to overwhelm me. I struggled to overcome the almost irrepressible urge to touch her. Her skin must be so hot compared to the cool night air . . . For a moment I let it control me, I let myself be driven by the emotion.

I delicately brushed back a wisp of hair that had fallen over Gemma's face, the back of my finger lingering on her skin as it followed the soft curve of her cheek, her skin silver in the diamond starlight. For the first time, she didn't move away from my touch. In fact, she seemed to enjoy the contact.

She studied me with a focused yet calm look. The immensity of the night paled before the infinite reflection in her eyes.

I gazed at her steadily as she peered up at the sky, her mind wandering among the stars, following the heroes I'd told her about. She turned on the grass, rolling onto her side to face me. Our bodies were so close, lying one in front of the other. Gemma clearly hadn't come so near intentionally; she wanted to move away a little but at the same time she didn't want to show me how embarrassed she was, so in the end she didn't move.

In the silence of the night, our desires rose and intertwined in gazes full of promises. Our souls spoke voicelessly, harmoniously, as we listened to their silence, holding back the desire to touch each other. Like an unstoppable energy, my repressed desire caused a tremor that spread through my entire body.

I looked down at the narrow space that separated us and, in a bare patch between the blades of grass, I smoothed down the sandy earth and slowly moved my finger, writing on that makeshift page what my soul was crying out.

θαῦμα, -ατος, τό

I looked up into her eyes, which brimmed with curiosity. "What did you write?" she asked.

"*Thauma*," I whispered, gazing at her. "It means 'thing of wonder.' The ancient Greeks used it to describe something unique. Like you are to me."

Gemma looked down, probably to hide the blush on her cheeks that was returning at regular intervals. She stretched her hand out toward mine and began to draw imaginary lines on my palm. Unable to hold back my desire any longer, overcome by a passion more intense than I'd ever known, I grasped her fingers in mine, wanting never to let her go. I forced myself to breathe deeply, hoping to drive away the emotion that had clouded my mind.

"I haven't finished telling you about the stars," I said, trying to regain control.

She shook her head slightly and looked at me with curiosity .

"See that star up there?" I asked, pointing.

"Which one?"

I leaned in toward her, my cheek almost touching hers. "The brightest one," I said, pausing to look at her as she scanned the sky. I brushed back the locks of hair that cascaded over her shoulder, revealing her delicate skin. She continued to stare upward as my breath drew invisible symbols on her neck.

"I see it now. That's the morning star," she whispered uncertainly.

I shook my head slowly.

"Oh, I thought it was. What's it called?"

"Its name is Gemma," I whispered in her ear, "because it lights up the night all on its own. Just like you. Can't you see? It's shining brighter than all the others, Gem." I ran the tip of my nose along her skin and she trembled. "It's your star now," I said in a hushed voice.

The star must have heard my whisper; it began to shine more brightly in the sky.

"Nobody can own a star."

"But you can connect it indissolubly to the memory of someone. That way, deep down in your heart, a part of the star becomes yours forever. Every time you feel alone, no matter where you are, every time you miss me, look for it in the sky. It will help you remember me," I whispered, holding back the emotions that threatened to overwhelm me. In the place where she would go, there was a spot where she'd be able to see it whenever she wanted to think of me.

"Memories are for people who aren't together any more. What are you trying to tell me, Evan? I don't want memories. I want you."

For a moment I almost suspected she'd guessed the destiny that would soon separate us. "All things considered, I'm happy," I said, dodging her question. I didn't want to lie to her.

"You don't look the least bit happy." She was repressing the anguish she'd felt when I said that, but I sensed it all the same.

"Gemma, I can't regret the destiny in store for me. Can anyone blame the spark that lights a candle, even though it means condemning it to slowly burn up? For a little while, the candle sees the light. In the same way, I've been blessed to have had you in my life."

"What do you mean 'for a little while'?" she asked, her voice filled with tormented anger.

I looked down, holding back a curse for letting that slip, for venturing into a conversation I wasn't sure I could handle.

"Stop talking as if all this were about to end. What are you planning? I can't lose you now that we've found each other. I need you. *My soul* needs you, and yours needs mine, I can feel it. We have to stay together, Evan," she whispered, imploring me with the sweetest eyes I'd ever seen. Like I had a choice. Hearing my name on her lips was salt rubbed into an open wound.

I'd have done anything for her. Everything. But despite myself, that was the one wish it was impossible to grant her.

Stroking her cheek with my fingertips, I gazed directly into her eyes, trying to reassure her, although it was no easy task given how distracted I was by her full lips drawing me nearer .

Our bodies were very close: two fires that burned with the desire to fuse together and blaze. Every single cell within us yearned for that contact.

I moved my face toward hers, slowly, to give her the chance to pull away if she wanted to. She didn't, and my desire flared even higher, setting me on fire as my mouth lingered a fraction of an inch from hers, our foreheads touching with each breath. I lifted my chin and felt her lips brush against mine, soft and warm like I'd imagined them. I closed my eyes, surrendering to the emotion, and touched her lips again at their very corners as Gemma stayed perfectly still, almost without breathing.

Her lips parted to match mine, making my heart leap. Their consent made my chest burn. I raised my eyes imperceptibly and looked into hers, eager and full of desire. Our lips remained perfectly still, suspended against each other for what seemed like an eternity. As if we both wanted to capture the moment forever.

I touched her mouth lightly, caressing it. Savoring that anticipation was like chasing the stars yet never reaching them. I burned with desire, a desire I knew was reciprocated, a desire I had no intention of denying. I pressed my lips against hers, tenderly coaxing them apart as the emotion grew with each breath.

Gemma parted her lips and her warmth merged with mine as my tongue gently brushed hers, guided by the movement of our lips. Emotion swept me, exploding in a tumult of passion. My hands moved with a will all their own, my fingers sinking into her hair as I tried to control my breathing. I was a slave to my desire. All my resistance vanished like fog in the sunlight. My body pressed against hers, longing for contact, and pinned it under my own as our lips moved and locked at the mercy of some unknown delirium. I could no longer subdue the whirlwind of passion that had overwhelmed me, the heat that throbbed in my chest. Feeling her body beneath mine made me shudder. I separated my mouth from hers for just a second and rested my forehead against hers, glimpsing her desire for me in her eyes.

Holding her gaze, I let my hand slip down her body, barely touching her, until it reached her back. Her formal black gown had disappeared and she now wore everyday clothes. I slid my fingertips under her top. Gemma ran her hand up my arm to my neck. I leaned down and kissed her palm, closing my eyes, trapped in a whirl of heat. When my lips parted, her finger slid slowly down my face, pulling my lower lip down.

She caressed my neck, running her fingers along the contours of my muscles. I couldn't take my eyes off her as her fingers continued down my shoulder and arm. She slowly stroked my chest, utterly thrilling me. Never before had I felt such powerful emotions. My eyes closed at the shudder her sensual touch caused in me.

When I opened them again, Gemma was clasping the military dog tag I wore around my neck. She turned it over in her fingers, puzzled, and pulled me back toward her, inviting me to press my lips against hers again.

Her gaze was so sensual, my reaction utterly indescribable. There was something in her eyes that roused a part of me I couldn't control, making me feel like a wild man at the mercy of his desire.

She was so tiny beneath my body, so defenseless. I felt the need to protect her, wrap my arms around her and hold her tight against my chest where she'd be safe.

Her delicate touch enthralled me as our eyes exchanged silent vows only our hearts could hear. Until my lips slowly pressed hers yet again.

I wished I could stop time and make this moment infinite. Eternal. Indelible. I would stay with her forever in our little world. Nothing would separate us ever again.

Suddenly, the sky took on a faint golden hue, drawing my attention. There was a change in the air. A glimmer.

I took my eyes off Gemma's and my heart stopped. A pale, soft light glowed on the horizon over the sea. Lighting up the sky, darkening every part of me. Bringing me back to reality, wretched and cruel.

Dawn.

The sun was about to rise. Inside, I felt it setting forever as an emptiness deep in my heart reminded me of the cruelty of our imminent fate.

Time had run out.

I stood up, avoiding her gaze. I didn't have the courage to look her in the eye. I was afraid the lump in my throat that was keeping me from breathing might dissolve into tears.

I held out my hand. Gemma took it and when she was standing in front of me she took the other. Only then did I finally look into her eyes and see how worried she was.

I squeezed her hands and drew her toward me, almost pulling her. "Hold me tight," I begged her. I wanted to keep her close to me, hide her in my arms until our bodies melted into one so no one would come looking for her.

I locked her in my strong, desperate embrace. There was no reason for me to control my reactions. Nothing mattered to me any more. Gemma was my whole life and cruel destiny was about to take her from me.

I cupped her face in my hands, sinking my fingers into her soft hair, breathing in her intoxicating scent so I'd be able to remember it when I took the poison. That way, when I closed my eyes, I could imagine her still there with me. I was drunk on her and our impossible love.

I gazed at her intently, still amazed at how beautiful she was in the warm colors of the first light of day. I rested my forehead against hers so she wouldn't see the torment in my eyes, unable to shed those forbidden tears, and kissed her fiercely.

Gemma returned my kiss with the same intensity. An intensity that cried out in desperation. Mine . . . hers . . . By now I couldn't tell where I ended and Gemma began. Like two halves, our hearts had become one.

It was pure anguish to know that our first kiss would also be our last. And that Gemma would never realize it. I held her against me, moving my lips on hers, longing desperately to cling to her forever. I knew that once our lips parted, the light would take her from me.

In the distance, the sun rose insistently, mercilessly, growing stronger as it imperceptibly lit up the sky and Gemma's face. I tried to separate my lips from hers but instantly felt lost without her warmth and pulled her back to kiss her again . . . and again.

I wanted to rule that moment. I wanted time to stop. Right there, right then. By now I was desperate, on the brink of insanity, of inconsolable madness. I didn't want the light to take my Gemma away from me.

Night, wrap us in your starry mantle, hide us, please! I cried silently, hoping the night would grant me a few moments more, lingering before surrendering to the day. *Or at least hide my Gemma, my blossom, hide my precious gem within your dark folds. I offer you all of myself in exchange for her protection. I beg you, Night, silent accomplice of all lovers, don't let the cruel judge that is the light take her away from me, depriving you of all your stars.* But the sunlight was deaf to my final cry of desperation. It advanced quickly, threatening to steal my Gemma from me.

When the first sunbeam touched her skin, the heart I'd found again after all those centuries shattered.

In utter agony, I kissed her forehead. "Remember . . ." I whispered, my eyes searching hers. The tips of our noses touched. Desperation filled me. My hands gripped her face more tightly. I never wanted to let her go. "Don't forget me. Promise. Look up at the sky every chance you get and you'll know I'm there with you." I pressed my lips against hers, utterly resigned. "Don't forget us, Gemma." I felt defeated in a battle I hadn't even been allowed to fight.

"Evan . . ." Hot tears fell from her eyes, bathing my hands. I dried her cheeks with my fingers. "Don't leave me. Please," she begged, sobbing. "You can't leave me now that I love you."

I was awestruck by the effect of those three simple words. Simple, yet all-important. So painful I felt a tear run down my face and for the first time I discovered my body was capable of crying.

My elation from her unexpected confession dueled with the incredible desperation her words had also triggered within me. "*Samam*," I whispered. *So do I.* This time it wasn't Ancient Greek, but the world's oldest language, the one I knew best. I couldn't find a better way to say it to her.

I was sure she would understand. I tried to remember how to breathe, but the pain was suffocating. I held her tightly against my chest and moved my lips to her ear. "You've been the only one for me," I whispered tenderly. "Farewell."

I felt her body trembling, and vanished before her eyes.

I found myself back in her room. Infinite pain was wound tightly around my heart like barbed wire. Gemma was so *perfect* lying there in bed. Even with that little frown, her face was so beautiful. Unique, extraordinary. No one could have imagined that soon her body would stop breathing, her heart cease to beat. I would gladly die in her place if that would be enough to save her. The thought of taking her life revolted me, precipitating within me a savage loathing of the world, of the Màsala. Of myself.

I gazed at her one last time, stopping to stroke her hand before making way for those cruel rays of sunrise streaming in through the window uninvited, heralding the dawn. The morning. The end.

My heart had shattered into a thousand pieces. And with it, every fiber of my being disintegrated, like a vampire exposed to the light. Full of bitterness, I prepared to say goodbye.

GEMMA

20

REAWAKENING

I muttered incoherently, bothered by the light. Shooting pains ran through my head and I was dazed. As I tossed and turned, half conscious, I had a strange feeling of loss like a gaping hole in my stomach.

I wasn't sure where I was. Still groggy, I forced my eyes open and cut the cord connecting me to another world. I touched my pillow, overcome by sadness, my eyes brimming with stifled tears.

No. Not this time, I thought, desperate. I couldn't have dreamt it, not this time. I felt I was sinking into a bottomless pit, into the void, into darkness.

Alone.

What kind of trick was my mind playing on me?

I couldn't accept that it had only been a dream. I could still feel Evan's hand clasped in mine. I'd felt his skin against mine. I was sure I'd felt the warmth of his body. And his lips . . . I brushed my fingers against my own with a whimper. I could still taste him.

Was it possible none of it was true? The magic of last night together couldn't have been only a mirage, a product of my imagination, a secret desire hidden in my unconscious. It had all been so real!

Overwhelmed with grief, I sat up but couldn't drag myself out of bed, as though staying there would allow me to keep my memories, prevent them from fading away with the morning. I rested my elbows on my raised knees and buried my face in my palms.

Unwelcome light was coming in through the window, insolently robbing me of that night, that magic . . . robbing me of my Evan.

I had the terrible feeling nothing would be as it had been.

Unable to hold them in any longer, I let the tears stream down my face. They took me back to that memory, that desperate farewell. What was my unconscious trying to tell me with such a somber dream? Then I remembered: I'd seen Evan and Ginevra together. Was it because of that?

In a flash, my disappointment was replaced by the fear that the dream might vanish at any second. I wanted to keep the memory intact, not forgetting even one detail of last night, preserving it like a precious treasure. I clung to the pictures in my mind with all my might, but for some strange reason I found I didn't need to; they didn't seem to be fading. They were as vivid as if I'd actually experienced those moments and those emotions. They seemed more like a memory than a dream.

Relieved, I trudged to the bathroom to take a shower. I realized I was guilty of ingratitude. I should have been overjoyed at the gift the night had given me. So why did I feel so heartbroken? Why did I continue to despise the morning, the sunlight, which, like thieves, had taken him from me, coming between us and tearing me away from his embrace?

I couldn't remember ever having such powerful emotions before. Why should I be feeling them now?

Evan's farewell had been so intense. When he'd disappeared before my eyes, pain had washed over me, crushing me, and although the light continued to grow stronger, I felt darkness envelop my heart. I was alone. The cold had seeped into my bones, depriving me of Evan's protection that had warmed my heart.

How could those sensations not be real? I could swear they were.

If I hadn't woken up in my bed, I would have leapt into a fire just to prove I'd actually experienced those moments with Evan. And yet—no matter how ridiculous it might seem—I couldn't completely shake that nagging doubt, as if there were some remote chance I hadn't made it all up.

I distractedly went back to my room and rifled through my disorganized closet. I wanted to wear something dark today, to fit my mood, but instinct made me choose a white sweatshirt, probably hoping it might lift my spirits somehow. I slipped on the first pair of jeans I found plus a pair of dark boots, which in summer I replaced only with Nikes. I pulled open the curtains to let in a little more light and was about to open the windows so the room could air out while I was gone, but the minute I touched the handle I stopped, filled with a sense of foreboding. Although I'd grown accustomed to it, the feeling I was being watched had never been so strong before. The curtains stirred, as though from a puff of wind, but the windows were still closed.

I slowly searched the room, scrutinizing the air as if it would reveal something. The room was empty, and yet the sensation didn't fade. It felt like a dark presence lurking beneath a mantle of invisibility, studying me from close up. This morning, fear had given way to curiosity. I was beginning to be fascinated by all those strange sensations that had been bubbling up inside me for some time now. If I couldn't avoid them, I might as well learn to tame them.

Before leaving, I scratched Iron Dog's head, but today I felt the unusual need to stay and pet him, watching his muscles relax at my touch.

"Hey, lazybones," I whispered. "I'll take you for a walk when I get back," I promised, smiling. "I'd love to know how you manage to sleep all day." I shook my head as he opened his round, dark eyes in reply and closed them again after a moment.

I walked to the door, pausing as I grabbed the doorknob. Another sensation. Stronger. Harder to ignore.

I was suddenly struck by an uncontrollable need to turn around and engrave every detail of my room in my mind. I studied the shelves filled with mementos, looked at each of the objects that, like pieces in a jigsaw puzzle, formed my life.

Grandma's clock, the giant stuffed bear Peter had won at Great Escape in Lake George a few years ago, the stacks of books in the bookcase. Each volume a part of my life. One glance at the spine and I could remember exactly when I'd devoured the story. Every page brought back a different emotion.

The paint on the walls was flaking slightly in some patches, but I'd never felt ready to paint over it, as if the very color were a part of my life. Photos covered the walls, evidence of the slow work of time that had silently changed my appearance. Memories of my childhood spent with Peter. Fishing with Peter. Camping with Peter. Going to school with Peter. A carefree life that felt more and more distant.

How many times we'd played together in that room. The memories came to life for a moment, as though my mind had rewound a tape. While my body remained perfectly still, I watched two children chasing each other, jumping on the bed, trying to frighten each other with horror stories, and the girl, when she grew frightened, starting a pillow fight to make the boy stop.

Like a ghost in my mind's eye I watched Peter come in through the window and pull out a movie he'd tucked into his hood so he could use both hands to climb up the trellis to my room. I would never forget those memories. Peter was a part of me. That was clear from the pictures on the walls; he was in so many of them, always sunny and smiling, even when I was pouting.

My heart leapt as it made a wish. Evan. Maybe one day, on one of those walls, I could add a photo of the two of us together.

Maybe I was still just dreaming.

I took a deep breath and forced myself to open the door. Before leaving, I grabbed my iPod from the desk and put it in my pocket, casting one last look around the room. I had the funny feeling I'd never see it again, like I was about to set off on a journey.

From the comforting murmur of their voices, I knew my parents were already awake. I found them in the kitchen, lounging at the table over piping-hot cups of coffee.

"Morning, sleepyhead!" my dad chimed, half-closing one eye. He'd never been good at winking and his contorted face was amusing.

"For the record, I woke up at dawn with a terrible headache. What's for breakfast?"

My mom nodded toward the oven. "It's still hot—don't burn yourself."

I pulled out the blueberry crumble and cut a slice for each of us. With the first bite I thought of Evan sitting at the table in the diner. I couldn't believe that had been only yesterday. So many things had happened since then. Imaginary or real—my mind could no longer tell the difference between what was true and what wasn't. The thought of him and Ginevra together didn't upset me as much as it had the day before when I'd seen them. I couldn't be mad at either of them, because in the meantime something inside me had changed. The overwhelming emotions I'd felt last night, the pain in Evan's eyes, the warmth of his mouth had wiped away all the rest. It didn't matter if my brain said it wasn't real; my heart had *experienced* those sensations. And that was enough for me.

After breakfast, which lasted longer than usual, I got up to leave.

"Where you off to in such a rush? Today's not a school day," my dad asked, curious.

"I need to turn in my yearbook pictures. Mr. Madison gave me an extra day since he's going to be at the school for a couple hours this morning." Yesterday afternoon I'd called him to apologize and luckily he'd given me this second chance.

"Sick!" my dad exclaimed.

I glowered at him. Once in a while he tried to imitate teenagers' slang to sound younger, but it just made him sound ridiculous. Not that he was old. He was just, well, Dad. I got my backpack ready, making sure to remember my flash drive with the school photos.

"Stopping by the diner afterwards?"

"I don't think so. I'm meeting up with Peter and the guys at Mirror Lake later on."

"How'd the lacrosse game go last night?"

"It wasn't anything special. The Blue Bombers lost by a hair."

"What bad luck," my dad said.

It wasn't luck, I thought to myself. I'd known Peter my whole life and I'd never seen him so distracted before. And that's what had cost us the game. Before we went home, we'd agreed to meet out at the lake in the morning. No, I was the one with bad luck; because I'd been so scatterbrained I had to go to school on Saturday.

"Want a ride?" my mom asked.

I considered her offer for a split second. "Thanks, but I feel like taking my bike." I wanted to spend some time reliving the dream in my mind on my way there. I leaned over my dad's shoulder and grabbed a doughnut from the middle of the table.

"My little girl nervous about something?" Dad was familiar with my habit of turning to calories when something was upsetting me. Actually, I had a funny feeling in the pit of my stomach.

"Nothing in particular," I reassured him. "And don't call me your little girl, you know I can't stand it." I instantly regretted the bitter tone I'd let slip out of my mouth.

"You're still my little girl. Don't you forget it," he insisted, mischievously tousling my hair.

I forced myself not to reply and opened the door, my backpack slung over my shoulder. Acting on some strange impulse, I looked back and stared at my parents, still immersed in conversation at the kitchen table. I felt the urge to run and hug them like I used to when I was a child. Maybe it was because Evan's farewell had upset me, but suddenly I wanted to tell them how much I loved them. I held back the impulse and shut the door behind me.

21

THE END

In the front yard, I still had the strong feeling I was being watched. I looked around, an act that had recently become automatic. This morning, the feeling was stronger than ever.

I raised the garage door and pulled out my old mountain bike. My dad had wanted to get me a "girlie" bike but I'd asked for a more rugged model that would be better for going on trips with Peter in the Adirondacks.

I put in my earbuds and chose a Lana Del Rey album: a mix of melancholy and sweetness. Exactly what I felt in my heart. Leaving Cherry Street, I turned down Hurley Avenue, pedaling with my head bowed, totally lost in thought as the cars passed me by.

The memory of my dream was a sweet blanket totally enveloping me, protecting me from the cold. I barely noticed the cars racing past, swerving to avoid hitting me. I couldn't concentrate on where I was going. Realizing all my distraction was putting me at risk for not showing up at the school, I forced myself to slow down and pay more attention.

I turned right on Station Street and crossed the intersection of Sentinel and South Main like I did every morning, already forgetting to pay attention to where I was pedaling. I almost rode straight into a fireman. Was it starting to become a habit? The road was closed. I took out one of my earbuds and overheard a man complaining about a gas leak in the neighborhood pipes, and the fireman telling him to move away.

I sighed, grumbling over my distractedness. The whole neighborhood had been closed off but I hadn't noticed the barriers they'd put up. Since I couldn't go through there, I took a longer route so I'd have time to relish the memory of my dream. I turned back, passed the train station, and headed down Station Street to reach Mill Pond Drive from the other side. After a few yards I slowed down, almost frightened by how strongly I felt that invisible presence hovering around me.

It was intense. I felt like I could reach out and touch it. I inhaled deeply, my nostrils tickled by a fragrance I knew well. I stood there, perfectly still, as my eyes dilated from the scent.

Evan.

I sniffed my shirt to see whether it was coming from me and checked the road, almost as if I expected to find Evan hidden there behind one of the maple trees.

No one was following me, and yet the familiar scent lingered.

I shook my head to drive the ridiculous notion out of my twisted mind and pedaled faster. Meanwhile, *Bel Air* had begun. I loved that song. Melancholy and so magical. The soft touch of fingers on a piano carried me off, back into my dream. I remembered Evan's kiss, which sent electrifying tingles under my skin. I reached out my hand and brushed it against the leaves of the trees lining the road, letting them tickle my fingers. To my right, the lake shimmered as I sped past it. I'd never had such an intense feeling before. It wasn't like butterflies in my stomach—it was more like an Evan-shaped hole in my heart that burned whenever I thought of his absence. I closed my eyes and let the fresh morning air caress my skin, singing in a whisper.

Evan's eyes, shadowed and gray, hounded me. I couldn't get them out of my head. I distractedly slipped a hand into my sweatshirt pocket, took out my phone, and punched in the code. The screen lit up, showing the time: 6:55. I crossed the tracks and went straight on toward Mill Pond Drive. The street skirted the woods.

Lana Del Rey's voice was like a soothing balm.

As I passed, a flock of birds rose up from the trees, casting a broad shadow on the pavement. I looked up, following their flight, drifting away with the notes of the piano. Uplifted. To another world. Into Evan's arms. The moment had been magical, mesmerizing. Because it wasn't a dream, it was a *memory*. I didn't care if my brain opposed it. I'd never felt as good as I had last night.

I stretched out my arm again toward the leaves. They brushed against my fingers. This time I sat up straighter and let go of the handlebars, surrendering to the melody, the cool morning breeze caressing my skin.

I wished I could close my eyes and relive the thrill of his kisses. My lips remembered their taste, as though even my body could take part in that imaginary journey. Evan had worked his way under my skin.

The beating of my heart accelerated impulsively at the thought of his chest pressed against mine, pinning me to the grassy lawn, his lips brushing against mine, the flames growing stronger and stronger. The way he'd held me tightly in his arms had made me tremble.

The wind blew harder, distracting me from the memory. My skin shivered in response, almost as if it sensed a veiled threat as the aura of that invisible presence grew more and more powerful.

I regained control of the bike and pulled the phone out of my pocket to check the time again. 6:59. I lowered my hand to put it back but caught my iPod cord by mistake, pulling an earbud out of my ear. As I instinctively hunched my shoulder to try to hold it in place, a shrill blare turned the blood in my veins to ice. Without the music in my ears, I heard it loud and clear for the first time.

My heart froze, shrouded by a black cloud of terror, and the phone slipped from my fingers as I saw a looming shape as red as blood racing toward me. Time, the air, my breath, every single thing was trapped in that frozen instant.

A bone-chilling sound, shrill and insistent, reverberated throughout my body. The deafening blast of an air horn. Too loud. Too close.

Terror petrified me. I couldn't breathe and my muscles refused to move. I felt a pain in my chest. The screeching squeal of tires grated on my ears, drowning out the sound of the cell phone clattering to the street. Everything else turned dull and colorless as that single red flame whooshed straight at me. I couldn't get out of the way, I'd lost control of the bike. I was frozen, but the wheels continued to carry me toward my fate.

A horrifying realization shook me to my core: it was a semi, and it was too close to avoid me.

It was going to hit me. My journey would end here, on this street.

Like the last remaining bowling pin, unable to move as the ball comes barreling down the lane straight at it, I too was perfectly still, awaiting death, as my mind raced back to the faces of those I loved, the last gift given to me by time. Peter. Mom. Dad. *Evan.*

For a second, my heart stopped at the intensity of his silvery gaze. I couldn't tell whether it was just a memory, a mirage projected by my heart, of if he was really there, hidden behind a tree, his crystal eyes staring straight at me like they had in my dreams, now filled with more torment and anguish than ever before.

The last grain of sand was poised to slip through the hourglass of my life. I closed my eyes, imagined it falling inexorably. When it touched the bottom, it would all be over. The truck would hit me.

I sensed the exact instant when that last grain of sand fell into empty space, propelled by the powerful wall of air that washed over me an instant before impact, lashing at my face so fiercely it took my breath away. The whole world grew muffled, the blare of the horn reduced to a hum as I surrendered to panic, the beat of my heart pulsing deafeningly in my ears, pounding in slow motion as I took my last breath.

Another, stronger gust of air struck me and then, impact. In my heart, the memory of Evan's kiss.

Game over.

22

GHOST OF ICE

I had no idea what to expect from death, if I'd live on in another form or another body. My only certainty, so strong it was almost palpable, was the feeling of calm that enveloped me like a protective shell as I slid through an icy tunnel that caught at my body and face, hindering my breathing.

The last thing my eyes had seen before everything went dark was my bike, reduced to a tangled heap of metal. And yet the impact hadn't been so overwhelming. Maybe the darkness had eclipsed the pain.

A loud rustling noise like dry leaves stirring grated on my ears. I wanted to cover them but it was no use. I couldn't move. Something was pinning my limbs. Something hard.

Dazed, I tried to open my eyes. My eyelids were heavy, but I wanted to escape from the darkness pressing down on me before it was too late. A glimmer appeared in the darkness, then a blinding flash of light struck my pupils, forcing me to shut my eyes again. I kept trying, although I was so confused my brain wouldn't let me focus on my surroundings.

Walls of splintered colors raced past me dizzyingly. The speed blurred the colors, though I could occasionally make out patches of blue and splotches of green and brown.

My head was spinning. I felt as if I'd woken up on a runaway merry-go-round. The icy air took my breath away. I had the strange feeling my body wasn't moving, that everything else was speeding by, as if I were suspended in midair. Or was I drowning, at the mercy of the current maybe? No, I couldn't feel water on my skin. I felt like a ghost made of ice. If my surroundings hadn't been so confused, if that whirlwind of cold air weren't taking my breath away, I would have sworn I wasn't moving. Instead I was slicing through the air like a particle of wind, protected by a firm grip that enveloped me like a warm shell. Overcome by sensations too overwhelming for me to work through the confusion clouding my mind, I closed my eyes again, allowing myself to be gently rocked.

Wherever I was going.

Was this death? A frenzied journey through a tunnel?

The earth stopped spinning and the whirlwind died away. I felt myself falling backward but with a comforting feeling of security. My back touched a cold, damp surface, while something warm brushed my temple. A gentle, familiar touch.

I forced my eyes open. Like liquid silver, eyes of ice, caring and intense, shone through the darkness that had trapped me.

Evan.

"Shh . . . Everything's fine. You're safe now."

The protective sound of his voice lulled me in another world.

"Do you realize what you've done?"

"I couldn't help it. It all happened so fast . . . just a second before it hit her . . . I think it grazed her ankle."

The distant, hushed sound of voices infiltrated the fortress in which my mind had sought refuge.

My ankle. Only then did I sense the point from which the pain radiated up to my knee. A blaze raged in my head. I reached down and felt the surface beneath my back, finding it cold and damp. After a few seconds, I realized it was earth.

Disoriented and still dazed, I struggled to understand the low, agitated murmurs. A shaft of light struck my pupils, forcing me to squeeze my eyes shut, but slowly I managed to open them again. Emerging from the darkness, I recognized the silhouettes in front of me. Evan and Ginevra were arguing, unaware that I'd regained consciousness. I tried to shake off the grogginess that wouldn't allow me to focus on their faces. I still couldn't move any part of my body without excruciating pain.

Evan was speaking to her in a tone I'd never heard him use before. Powerful, authoritative, determined. I barely recognized him. I squinted, trying to focus, fascinated by the new tone in his voice. I studied his features, his clenched jaw and piercing gaze as he looked at Ginevra and, for the first time, I didn't detect a trace of the confusion that often afflicted him. It was as if he'd cast off one mask and was wearing a different one, illuminated by the new light that shone in his eyes. He was laying down the law for Ginevra, his face stern and determined, free from shadows. I stopped caring about whether or not I was still alive as long as Evan had that new light within him. I was probably dead, and they didn't notice my presence simply because they couldn't see me. I wasn't sure I wasn't a ghost, and I was too weak to find out. Everything seemed so strange and surreal.

"Relax, Ginevra." Evan's voice was calm now, with a hint of satisfaction. The exact opposite was true of Ginevra's. She was spouting a stream of curse words. "And don't swear, it doesn't become you." With effort, I managed to see a dimple form in Evan's cheek as he smiled, perfectly relaxed.

"Relax?!" Ginevra was absolutely hysterical, and though she was trying hard to keep her voice down, she sounded like an enraged tiger. "Oh, right, you tell me to relax! Do you have the faintest idea what's going to happen now?! To all of us?"

"You're not involved, Ginevra."

"Well, Simon is going to be, you know he is. What on earth were you thinking?" she hissed contemptuously, her voice filled with bitter reproach. "We're all in trouble now. *You're* in trouble, Evan," she corrected herself.

"Are you saying I can't count on you?"

Ginevra's pride kept her from answering right away. "I didn't say that," she said after a moment of silence, still frowning. "What you did is *extremely serious.* How are we going to fix it?"

Evan's relaxed expression turned into a threatening sneer. "*Fix it?*" he repeated, disgusted, and shot her a fiery glare that made her flinch. "I'd do it a thousand more times if I had to!" His expression suddenly softened, verging on sadness. "Don't you see? I'd given up. I thought I was ready. I did everything I had to, right up to the end. But then she turned toward me and *looked at me.* I saw the fear in her eyes and felt the most excruciating pain I'd ever experienced. Right at that moment, everything became clear. I knew what I had to do, without a shadow of doubt. I knew I couldn't let it happen."

"You threw away your only chance for Redemption. This is *not* going to end well. They'll come looking for her, you know that, and your sacrifice will have been pointless. You can't prevent it!"

"Yes I can. It's not going to happen. I'm going to protect her." Evan's voice was filled with pride.

"And how are you going to do that? The Brotherhood is going to find out about it soon enough."

"We have a little time before they do. I need to think." Evan rubbed his temples, agitated by Ginevra's warning.

"You can't be sure."

"Fuck it, I don't care about them! The Màsala could never—"

"No!" Ginevra cut him off and lowered her voice. "Are you crazy? Don't say the name out loud," she warned, looking around, as if worried someone might have heard. "Christ! Have you gone completely insane?" she snapped, pacing back and forth until a furrow formed on the ground. Suddenly, she stopped and glared at him. "Don't even think it, Evan. You can't be with her, not like that. It'll never happen!"

"I realize that." Evan's voice, filled with resignation, was lower now.

I had no idea what was going on between them. Was it a lover's quarrel? My ears were taking in the words, but my mind couldn't hold onto them. They were disappearing before I could process them. In any case, I was getting fed up with Ginevra's attitude. It was like she was trying to lead Evan back down the difficult path he'd been on when I met him.

I didn't care if he was hers. I wished I could shut her up, scream at her to stop yelling at him, but I didn't have the strength to open my lips. An involuntary groan escaped me, making them turn in my direction.

Evan shot Ginevra a reproachful look, as if it were her fault they hadn't noticed I'd woken up. I shook my head, trying to drive off the last trace of confusion. I didn't perceive any movement, but I instantly found them both leaning over me. I must have hit my head.

"How do you feel?" Evan's whisper reached me like a gentle caress as he ran his hand over my hair.

I managed to focus on his face, but there was something strange, something I couldn't put my finger on.

His eyes . . . Was I dreaming, maybe? Evan's eyes shone with a silvery light, shadowy and gray, almost as if they belonged to some supernatural creature. Like the day we'd first met. Like in the secret world where I saw him every night in my dreams. Evan stared at me intensely, allowing me to study him. I'd never seen his eyes from so close up before. Amber streaks ran through them like gilded lightning in an icy sky. From that distance, they emitted such power I wasn't sure I could keep looking into them without them piercing my heart and making me faint.

"I can't, I can't say, exactly," I made myself answer. "My head hurts."

Evan and Ginevra exchanged a look.

"What happened?" I asked, tripping over my words.

To my surprise, it was Ginevra who spoke up. "You should learn how to ride a bike. That truck was about to kill you. Evan pushed you out of the way a second before it ran you over." Her voice was so bitter cold it could have done the impossible and frozen fire. For a moment I almost felt guilty for still being alive. "You were lucky," she told me, crossing her arms and turning her back on me. "This time," she added in a low voice. It almost sounded like a threat.

Evan shot her a piercing glare. If looks could kill, Ginevra would have dropped dead on the spot.

Her contempt for me was clear from her voice. Why did she hate me so intensely? I couldn't believe it was because she was jealous. She couldn't actually want me dead because of that. In a moment of lucidity, her words echoed in my head: *We're all in trouble now.* Could it be my fault?

Even then, I sensed her hostility in the way she looked at me.

"Come on, I'll take you home." Despite the irritation in Evan's voice, there was no longer any trace of confusion, and he drew me back into his spell. "Can you walk?" he asked, helping me to my feet.

I would have liked to seem fearless to him, but the movement made me moan with pain. "My ankle hurts," I admitted, rotating my foot gently.

"We should take her to the hospital," Ginevra said, but Evan scowled.

"No need. I'll take care of her. It'll heal," he snapped. I watched them exchange challenging looks, as if they were communicating in secret.

"You wouldn't dare." Ginevra narrowed her eyes to slits. "Don't complicate things, Evan," she hissed.

"I know what I'm doing," he said, finishing the conversation. He turned to look at me. "Put your arm around my neck. I'll carry you."

It was incredible how tender his voice became when he spoke to me. I did as he said, feeling my heart warm at his offer. The blood rushed to my face and I found myself blushing at the thought of being close to him.

He and I had done far more than that in my imagination, but he didn't know that. A wave of images filled my head, melting me. Memories of Evan and me, his mouth on mine, his hot body on top of mine. No, not *memories*, I forced myself to admit. None of it had ever really happened. How could I act casual? How could I look him in the eye and forget his deep, passionate kiss as though I'd never experienced it? Because this was real life. None of what had happened in my dreams was real.

He lifted me from the damp ground with a single fluid movement, effortlessly, as my lucidity returned. Looking around for the first time at the trees towering overhead, blocking the sunlight, I understood where I was, although I didn't recognize that exact spot.

What were we doing in the woods?

"Hold on tight."

His voice was so close to my ear. I tried hard to hold back a shiver but it didn't work. I rested my head on his shoulder, studying the way his neck muscles flexed with every movement.

"Cold?"

My heart trembled when I saw a half smile appear on his lips, so close it almost left me breathless. He'd noticed the effect the sound of his voice had on me. "N-no, I'm fine," I stammered, blushing. Actually, I was burning up as I clung to his warm, muscular body.

Around Evan's neck was a dog tag, the same one he'd worn in my dream. I must have seen him wear it at some point but forgotten I had. It was resting against his sleeveless dark-green T-shirt, over which he wore a matching shirt that was completely unbuttoned. My hand brushed against the metal and I blushed again, remembering how shamelessly I'd pulled him to me, yearning for his lips. The memory was so vivid I was tempted to do it again, almost like it was a habit.

My fingers moved on their own, clasping the chain, and Evan smiled at me as though he recognized the gesture and knew my intentions.

I forced myself to drive off that insane thought, because nothing like that had ever happened between us in real life. Because there was no "us" and there never would be. There was just me, him . . . and Ginevra.

"Something the matter?" He'd clearly noticed the change in my mood.

"I'm just a little . . . shaken," I lied, hiding my face in the fabric of his shirt. His cheek was so close I had to fight the urge to surrender to the magnetic pull drawing me to him. In his arms I felt incredibly light. Taking a deep breath, I filled my nostrils with his scent, the smell of the dew-swept forest on an April morning, delicate, fresh, able to reach inaccessible places inside me, to pluck unknown strings and make them vibrate with warmth.

Now that I could breathe him in from so close up, I was more and more convinced I'd smelled his scent in the air that morning.

What a crazy thought. And yet, there was a small part of me, one completely devoid of reason, that continued to go against all logic by confirming my suspicion. Evan looked at me as though attracted by that reflection, and I lost myself in his eyes. I let his gaze explore mine as I realized that . . . *Impossible.* I started, confused, distrusting my own senses. There was no longer any trace of the silver that had been shining in his eyes a moment ago.

They were dark.

What kind of trick was my mind playing on me this time? I didn't say anything, afraid he'd think I was crazy. But I knew what I'd seen. I was sure I'd seen his eyes clearly in the forest. Or had I? But then again, it wouldn't be the first time my senses had betrayed me.

"What now?"

I couldn't see Ginevra's face behind Evan's shoulder, but her voice was unmistakable. I hadn't even noticed she'd been following us.

Evan leaned down and set me on the ground, looking around cautiously. "I'll secure the perimeter. Keep an eye on her," he ordered Ginevra in an authoritative tone before striding off.

Secure the perimeter? What on earth was he talking about? I'd probably hit my head harder than I thought. I'd learned to deal with ambiguity when it came to Evan, but right now I was too drained to think about it.

I wasn't sure if I was more baffled by the fact that I had to rely on Ginevra's support as she helped me reach my front door or the way Evan was scanning the street with concerned eyes, checking every corner as if expecting to catch a thief lurking somewhere. My instinct objected. Not a thief; an *assassin.*

"Your parents aren't home," Evan said. It clearly wasn't a question, so I just nodded. My parents would be working the breakfast shift, so there was no need for me to check. "Lock yourself inside, Gemma. I'll be back in a minute."

I was confused by Evan's serious tone. His eyes darted around the street, but instead of being scared by his behavior, I couldn't help but think how fascinating it was to see him acting like that first day I'd seen him in the woods, like a warrior. Fierce. Wild.

I followed Ginevra's suggestion to hide inside the house, but looked at both of them one last time before closing the door. They both seemed concerned, though for different reasons.

After I'd locked the door, I limped over to the couch. Without Evan's comforting presence to take my mind off my ankle, the throbbing pain returned to center stage. I dumped my backpack on the floor and collapsed onto the cushions, covering my eyes with the back of my hand.

As I thought about it in the silence, what had happened seemed even more insane. How could I still be alive? My mind rewound the tape and relived the entire sequence of those terrifying seconds. I had been sure the semi was about to hit me. What had Evan been doing there in the middle of the woods? In my mind's eye I clearly saw my final glimpse of him standing there in the trees, staring at me with a devastated look on his face. I'd thought it was just a mirage, a last wish hidden deep in my heart. And yet, he really had been there and he'd pushed me out of harm's way. But how had he managed to get to me in time and then end up unscathed? I'd seen what had happened to my bicycle. A fate for which I too had been destined. My aching head told me this was no time to think it all through.

I was still alive. Like the heroes in the novels I read, Evan had come to save me, rescuing me from a fate that had already been ordained.

Evan.

Knowing that was enough to push the whole experience from my mind, like a puff of breath on a dusty surface, in spite of how terrifying it had been. I remembered the feeling of being clasped in Evan's arms and my breathing spiraled out of control. I buried my head in the cushions and lost all sense of time, keeping my hand over my eyes to block the light as I steadied my breath and tried to relax. I let myself be lulled by the half-light, finding it comforting.

In the darkness and silence, fear began to creep over me. Evan's warning gradually returned to my mind, making me realize only then that up to that point I hadn't been afraid. As though my brain had stored it all up in a drawer to be opened later. The tension I'd heard in his voice began to sound alarm bells, making my anxiety flare up again.

Why had he seemed so worried? After all, he'd pushed me to safety, so why was he talking as if it weren't over? As if I weren't completely out of danger? Did he think it hadn't been just an accident? The thought that the truck driver might have tried to run me over on purpose was ridiculous. It had just been a terrible mishap, a brush with disaster. Evan had saved me from certain death, so why all the concern over my wellbeing now? What else could happen to me?

The air stirred, giving me goosebumps and making me wish I'd closed the windows. When I smelled Evan's scent I got up from the couch but was surprised to find the living room completely empty. The windows behind the couch were both closed. I took a deep breath, filling my nostrils with the aroma. I had no doubt it was his, not after I'd smelled him from so close up. It was so strong now I doubted my own senses. It was like Evan was there and my eyes were playing tricks on me, keeping me from seeing him. I instinctively grabbed the hem of my top and sniffed it, wondering if my clothes had absorbed his scent. But the smell wasn't coming from me. It filled the air, it was everywhere.

"Feeling better?"

I jumped at the sound of Evan's voice. Whirling around, I found him standing behind me.

"Evan . . ." The fear made me let out a groan and I sank down onto the couch. "You scared me half to death!"

"Sorry, I didn't mean to. You've already had a big enough scare for today." He walked over to the couch.

"H-how did you get in?" I asked, stunned.

"Through the door." His eyes wavered, as though he'd given himself away. "I told you I'd be back," he added.

I swallowed, panicking. "The door was locked, Evan," I said, my voice breaking as a new feeling arose inside me: the survival instinct, which had been hidden who knows where and for how long.

"Don't be silly," he said, trying to sound convincing. "I mean, I told you to lock it but you were pretty shaken up. You probably forgot." He stared at me, trying to get me to believe it, but I knew what had happened.

"I clearly remember locking it," I insisted, looking hard at him.

"Come on." Evan sat down beside me on the couch. "How else could I have gotten in? The windows are closed and you would have noticed if I'd knocked the door down, don't you think? Listen, you just came face to face with death. You were still shaking when I set you down. I know you *think* you locked it, but you can't be sure." His eyes stared steadily into mine and he was strangely concentrated, as if trying to brainwash me. He cracked a smile, but I sensed his hesitation. "Gemma . . ."

My heart began to beat irregularly. For a moment his black-velvet voice had gotten past my defenses.

"You've been through a traumatic experience," `he continued, stroking my forehead sweetly. An uncontrollable impulse made me pull back from his touch. I was surprised to discover that the shooting pain in my head was coming from that very spot. "Does it hurt?" His voice had grown tender.

"Only a little," I lied, tightening my lips. Actually, the pain was coming from my forehead and shooting out in a circle around my skull, leaving it aflame. Evan clearly wanted to drop the subject of how he'd gotten in, and not for the first time, but I didn't want to insist. It might make me come across as ungrateful. After all, he had saved my life.

"You need to rest. You've had a traumatic morning. It must have been rough, finding yourself facing death."

"Can I ask you something?"

Evan seemed surprised that I'd ignored his comment and had been so blunt, and he was probably nervous about my question. Or maybe about the answer he'd have to refuse to give me. There was clearly something about Evan I wasn't allowed to know. And instinct told me I was better off not knowing it.

"Why is Ginevra so mad at me?"

The simplicity of the question took him by surprise.

"No one's mad at you, Gemma," he said, clearly relieved. What had he been afraid I might ask him?

"Then why was she so angry back in the woods?" I insisted. I was sure it was because of jealousy. Ginevra had doubtless caught me staring at her boyfriend now and then. Not to mention all the attention he gave me or the way his voice became so sweet just for me. Ginevra must have noticed, but did I actually intimidate her enough to trigger a homicidal instinct in her? The very idea made me smile. I was so insignificant compared to her.

"She's mad at *me*, not you," Evan reassured me, a touch of sadness crossing his face. "You haven't done anything wrong, Gemma."

My heart leapt every time he said my name, enveloping it in the spell that was his voice. "She wishes you'd left me to my fate," I said.

Evan hesitated, as if I'd hit the nail on the head, but I couldn't believe Ginevra could actually be so cruel. Could she really want me dead, literally? Did I really pose such a threat to her?

"It's not what you think." For a second, it seemed like Evan was replying to what I'd been thinking. "It's complicated. You can't understand. And I can't explain it to you."

"Try," I said encouragingly.

"Out of the question." His tone was peremptory. "I can't."

Discouraged by the authority in his voice, I closed my mouth and let the silence separate us.

23

CLOSENESS

More than ever now, I felt like I'd known Evan my whole life. The accident had brought us closer. We were alone in my house, sitting side by side on the couch, and yet I felt strangely comfortable. There was a level of harmony I'd never reached before, not even with Peter. Reluctantly, I forced myself to remember that what I felt was mine and mine alone. Evan was with Ginevra.

"Try to get some rest," he suggested, stroking my hair, his tone thoughtful. I wasn't sure whether the room was spinning because I'd hit my head or if his hand left me in a daze whenever he touched me. "I have to take care of some things. I'll come back to check on you later." He stood up.

"Evan—" My voice came out in a broken sob. I couldn't resist the urge to try and stop him. I didn't want him to go, but I had no idea how to make him stay. "Do you really have to leave?" I asked sincerely, surprising myself with my assertiveness.

"Yeah, I do." He stared at the floor as though something were upsetting him. When he raised his eyes again, he found mine waiting for them. "Don't be afraid. You won't be alone. Now you need to rest." As he said these last words his eyes bored into mine, almost as if in a last-ditch effort to control my mind. I suddenly felt so sleepy that when the door closed behind Evan my eyelids grew heavy and I found my way back to unconsciousness.

I felt a deep sense of peace, like I was swimming in a sea of languid serenity or cradled in a bed of harmony. And yet sleep hadn't entirely stolen me away from the real world. I was in a strange limbo halfway between the two. I was perfectly aware I was lying on the couch. I could feel the sunbeams growing brighter and more penetrating as they streamed through the window and warmed my skin. Though my whole body was bathed in warm sunlight that filled me with lassitude, I felt it especially on my head and aching ankle. It was probably just the pain that gave me that impression. I'd never felt such an incredible sensation of wellbeing in my whole life

Unfortunately, the sound of a door slamming tore me out of that languor. I recognized my mother's hurried footsteps in the hallway. "Mom, you're back!" I raised my torso just in time to see her start at the sound of my voice.

"Honey, what are you doing home so early? Weren't you supposed to meet your friends at the lake?" she asked, looking concerned. "Did everything go okay with your teacher?"

"Um . . . It's a long story, Mom. I'm sure it would only bore you," I stammered, not sure what to say. I didn't know how presentable I was—there hadn't been time for me to look in a mirror. It suddenly dawned on me that I'd have to explain the gash on my forehead. I raised my hand to the spot to check how deep the cut was, but before my fingers touched it, I noticed the pain in my head was gone and I now felt an amazing sense of lightness.

There was no more ache, no more soreness. The burning sensation had vanished entirely. I ran my fingers over my forehead, puzzled to find the skin smooth. There was no cut. In any case, I wouldn't be able to hide the fact that I'd sprained my ankle because of my limp, and I certainly couldn't stay there on the couch all day long. I'd have to make up an excuse.

"What time is Peter coming to pick you up?" she asked from the kitchen.

Peter? I didn't remember making plans with Pet.

"I stopped by the dry cleaner and picked up your dress. You're going to look beautiful tonight, Squirrelicue."

My eyes grew wide with alarm. I grabbed my backpack and pulled out my assignment book to check what day it was.

April 20th. Prom.

My jaw dropped. I was shocked by how disconnected I was from the world.

Prom? How could I have forgotten?

At our school, prom was always in mid-May, but this year it was being held early. Was that why it had slipped my mind? Or was Jeneane right? Had I totally shut myself off from everything and everyone around me? Even worse, how could I go to the prom in my condition? I couldn't bail on Peter at the last minute and disappoint him, but then again I didn't want to make him spend the night sitting in a corner with me while everyone else was having fun. I certainly wouldn't be good company with a twisted ankle.

I searched my pockets and backpack for my phone and, with horror, remembered what had happened to it. My fingers snagged in my iPod cord. I stared at it, astonished. I didn't remember still having my earbuds in. The sensation of the earbud being pulled out of my ear filled my mind and I couldn't stop the flashback. The deafening squeal of brakes, the red blur rushing at me— I closed my eyes to shut out the terrible memory. Death had come to take me but for some unknown reason, I had escaped it. My heart skipped a beat, contradicting me. I knew the reason. Evan had saved me from my fate, risking his own life in the process. I could never repay him for the gift he'd given me.

I got up from the couch and strode over to the wall phone, then stopped, staring at the receiver, when I realized how quickly I'd reached it. I raised my foot and rotated it slowly, more and more confused.

The pain was gone.

"Everything okay?" My mom stared at me, puzzled.

"More than okay," I said, astonished. How had I healed so quickly? I bore no trace of the horrible accident. Not a single trace. Could it all have been a dream?

Great. I couldn't even trust my memory any more.

Still stunned, I dialed Peter's number to confirm our plans. Although going to the prom together had been a foregone conclusion, we hadn't talked about it recently.

The phone rang only twice before he picked up.

"Pet!" I said when I heard his voice.

"Hey, Gemma! Where the heck have you been? We were all supposed to hang out at the lake this morning. I tried calling you a million times. We need to make plans for tonight. Did you forget?"

"I, um . . . Right. Yeah." I stole a glance over my shoulder at my mom, who was fiddling around, pretending not to be interested in the conversation. "It's kind of a long story. I'll explain later. The invitation still stands, then, right?" I asked, suddenly unsure whether the recent events might have changed something.

"Of course it does. Why wouldn't it?" He sounded so calm, all my fears drifted away.

Peter and I always went to the school dances together. We'd decided it back when we were little kids and had always stuck to the agreement. By now, everyone at school was so sure they'd see us show up together that for years no one had even wasted their breath inviting one of us.

"I'll swing by your place at seven." It sounded like he was in a rush.

"Okay, see you then," I said, ending the conversation. I wondered if he still had his suspicions about Evan.

Evan.

For a minute I let myself wonder what it would be like if I'd made an exception, if for the first time I'd gotten an invitation from someone other than Peter. A *real* invitation. But deep down I knew it would never happen.

I wasn't even sure Evan was going to the prom, and in any case Ginevra would definitely be his date. I had to face the facts. She was his girlfriend. Not me. Why couldn't I get it through my head? Was I really still jealous of her?

As I helped my mom make lunch, I gradually realized how fit I felt, as if I were wearing a new skin. Like when I was a little girl, always scampering through the trees as spry as a squirrel, my long ponytail flying behind me. It was back then that I'd earned the nickname Squirrelicue. I couldn't remember the last time I'd felt so in shape physically, although mentally I was still a bit exhausted from the intense morning I'd had.

After all, I'd looked death straight in the eye. I pushed the bone-chilling thought out of my mind before my mom could notice how upset I was.

"Well? What time is Peter coming?" She was ecstatic.

"Seven," I said distractedly. "And when's Dad getting back? I can't eat too late, I have a lot to do before I get ready," I lied. Actually, I just wanted to go to my room and be alone for a while to reflect on the bizarre day.

"Well, put your bike in the garage first. You know your dad hates it when you leave it in the driveway."

I froze. What was she talking about? A vague suspicion spread over me. I rushed down the hall and opened the front door, my heart in my throat.

"Gemma, everything okay?" my mom called from the kitchen.

But I didn't answer. I was gaping at the sight of my bicycle. It was leaning against the garage door. It was really mine. And it didn't have a scratch on it.

The oven timer rang, announcing that the meatloaf and potatoes were ready just as my dad came through the front door.

"Perfect timing," I said. I looked at their faces and was struck by the sudden awareness of what I'd almost lost today.

"How come you're home? Weren't you going out with your friends? And did you turn in your—what was it again?" he asked.

"Yearbook photos. Actually, I didn't even end up going," I admitted. At least that part of the story was true. "My headache was so bad that halfway to the school I turned around and came home to bed." I hated lying—it was natural to feel an aversion to something you couldn't do well. I was rarely able to come up with believable stories and I normally ended up giving myself away one way or the other. I wasn't cut out for secrets. And yet, I had no choice.

"Have a seat, you two," Mom said. "Gemma, try to finish it all. There's no telling when you'll have the chance to eat something tonight," she added, knowing how much I disliked meatloaf.

"Don't worry, the school's serving refreshments. And if there's food anywhere within a ten-mile radius, rest assured I'll track it down," I replied. After all, I was bound to be pretty nervous tonight.

Besides, the unusual energy flowing through my veins this afternoon was making me insatiably hungry. My mother was amazed to see me clean my plate even before my father had.

After a hot shower, I fell onto my bed, earbuds in, shutting off the outside world. I closed my eyes and surrendered to the notes of James Blunt. Suddenly I sensed a presence in the room. I opened my eyes and jumped, surprised to see Jeneane standing by the bed.

"Jeneane!"

"Hey! I knocked but you didn't answer, so I figured I'd come on in."

"What are you doing here?" I blurted, realizing only a second later how rude it sounded.

"Hello to you too!" she said, shrugging. "I hope you don't mind me stopping by. Where were you this morning? I wanted to talk to you down at the lake, but you never showed. Are you sick? Did you catch something contagious?" She backed up, looking me up and down to check the state of my health.

"No, I'm just . . . just a little tired, that's all. What did you want to talk to me about?"

My question made her eyes sparkle and her face light up in a breathtaking smile. "Listen, I've got an awesome idea! And you absolutely can't say no!" A makeup bag appeared in her hands. She'd clearly been hiding it behind her back.

I shot her a reluctant look, but Jeneane ignored it completely and sat down on the bed as I crossed my legs. "So here's the plan."

"I'm all ears," I said, letting a hint of sarcasm slip out.

"Tonight's prom, right?" She looked me straight in the eye to make sure I was following every word.

"Right," I said with a nod.

"Well, you've *got* to look gorgeous. I'm going to take care of that!"

"Jeneane," I began, hoping to dissuade her.

"Don't say anything. Just leave it to me."

"Wait—wait! What are you doing? What's the plan?" I asked, terrified by her expression.

Jeneane flashed one of her perfect smiles and sat me down at my desk, pulling back my hair even though I hadn't agreed to anything yet.

"No time for questions. First I have to put this on you. Don't move."

As she smoothed a creamy foundation onto my face I let out a groan. "Jeneane, what are you doing?" I tried to ask, but her hands on my cheeks made me smoosh the words together.

"Girl, I'm going to turn you into a princess!" For some strange reason, it sounded more like a threat than a promise.

"Aren't you going to the prom too?" I asked as she skillfully applied makeup to my face.

"Are you kidding?" My question was so ridiculous it made her stop and look me in the eye "You think I'd skip it? I wouldn't miss it for anything in the world!"

"Who's your date?"

I instantly regretted asking. I was sure Jeneane must have told me a hundred times and I simply hadn't been listening. I also knew I must be the only person in school who would let such an important piece of information slip. My mind had been only on Evan lately.

"I know what you're thinking, but don't worry, I never mentioned it to you," she said, smiling smugly for catching me red-handed. "I asked Brandon to go with me."

She asked Brandon. Yeah, I bet.

"And you . . . are going with Pete," she said matter-of-factly. "But you'd rather be going with somebody else." She looked at me out of the corner of her eye as I started, surprised she knew. I stared at her, as stunned as if I'd caught her reading my diary. I had to admit, Jeneane was pretty sharp. "Don't gape at me like that!" she said. "I'm an expert when it comes to that kind of thing. Besides, I just put two and two together, that's all." She shrugged, looking pleased.

"Is it really so obvious?" I asked, annoyed that I'd been so easy to read.

"Only to me, don't worry. So what's up with Pete?"

"I don't know how to handle things any more. He's never been so jealous before," I forced myself to admit.

"Only because you've never really been interested in anyone before. Why do you think I'm here? Gemma, I've known you literally since we were born and I've never seen you interested in *anybody*. I've been waiting years for this to happen and there's no way I'd let you mess it up. Tonight you're going to be beautiful. You'll turn every head, believe me." She looked me in the eye, one eyebrow raised.

"It's just a shame the only boy I've ever been interested in already has someone. You're forgetting *Ginevra*." I said her name with reverential contempt.

"I already told you you're wrong. Trust me. I've seen the way he looks at you. It's through our eyes that we decide what kind of connection we want to have with another person. If you let them look into your eyes for longer than a few seconds, you're letting them see inside you, bond with you. It's like you're opening your heart to them. I have to admit I'm a little jealous of you."

"You? Jealous? *Of me*?" I couldn't believe my ears. "But you're, like, the queen of the whole school! *I'm* the one who's jealous of *you*. I've always envied your self-confidence."

"You see? That's exactly what makes you irresistible. You're *beautiful*, Gemma. How can you not realize that?"

A sound escaped me, a mix of surprise and disapproval. "Yeah, sure! And to think I've never had a boyfriend. Well, except Derek McCullagan, but he doesn't really count."

"That's only because you never wanted one in the first place. Guys need to be encouraged, even with just a look, otherwise they'll never make a move. Do you honestly think no boy has ever been interested in you? How can you not notice them checking you out all the time? You're so pretty, I think it intimidates them."

"What?! Are you kidding? Listen, stop teasing me, it's not funny—"

"Pete's crazy about you! You must have at least noticed that, seeing how tight you guys are."

Okay, maybe I wouldn't have noticed what was going on with Peter if my mom hadn't pointed it out. Could she be right? I couldn't believe she was being serious. I felt like I'd been living on another planet this whole time.

"It's easy for you," I told her. "You're so self-confident. When you want someone all you have to do is reach out and grab them. Well, not literally, of course."

"That's exactly my point. The interest the boys at school take in me is totally superficial. You think I don't realize that? No one's ever honestly interested in *me*, in who I am on the inside. But if *you* decided to show a guy you liked him, you'd totally steal his heart. That's why I never let anyone get really close to me. I can't risk falling in love because I know what guys want from me. I know what they see when they look at my body. On the other hand, the way Evan looks at you . . ." Her happiness for me was tinged with sadness. It showed in her eyes, although she was clearly trying to hide it.

"Then why do you go out with them all?" I asked, shocked that she was aware of the situation.

"At least that way I can convince myself I'm the one using them. That's why I never really commit, so I can avoid being let down when I find out they weren't really interested in me after all. Which is inevitable."

"Jeneane, you can't say that! They're all crazy about you. Maybe one of them is right for you and you just don't realize it because you're too scared to get hurt. Don't ruin your own chances! I mean, Brandon's been crazy about you since grade school. And not for the reason you think. Okay, maybe a little," I admitted, biting my lip. "All I'm saying is you'll never know unless you give it a chance."

"Don't feel sorry for me, it's not that bad. It gives me a sense of satisfaction and I'm fine with it, at least for now. Maybe when the right guy comes around I'll realize it. Meanwhile, nobody else is going to have me."

"I thought you liked Evan too," I admitted, glancing at her, curious.

She pursed her lips, trying to hide a smile that was both sly and sweet. "I'll admit, he's *fascinating*, but I would never try to compete with you."

My jaw dropped. I was floored. "You can't be serious." I raised an eyebrow, unable to believe she really felt that way.

"Besides, to be honest, he kind of scares me. There's something different about him, something mysterious. He's got this allure to him, like there's a Prince of Darkness lurking behind his sexy smile. Sometimes it actually gives me the creeps. And you should see the way he glares at Pete! A couple times I even got the impression he'd kill him, if looks could, but is just holding back."

I gulped. I'd sensed the same thing, but part of me stubbornly refused to acknowledge it.

Jeneane's voice softened and I realized she was staring at me. "But then I see how he looks at you and I confess I've never been so envious of anybody in my whole life." Warmth slowly spread over my cheeks. "I'm totally convinced nobody's ever looked at me like Evan looks at you. He wants you, Gemma. I'm sure of it. It's *you* he wants."

After everything she'd said, I discovered there was a little corner hidden deep down in my heart that still had hope. But I knew what I'd seen in Evan's garden. Jeneane didn't know about it, which is why she kept pushing me toward him. Strangely, I let her go on believing it. Maybe I wanted to leave room for that tiny hope that she continued to nurture in me.

"Well, I hope you're right," I added as she passed a blush brush over my cheeks.

"*Et voilà*!" Jeneane straightened up and stepped back to admire her work, looking satisfied. "Perfect! Even better than I imagined!"

"Let me see." I tried to get up from my chair, but she held me down by the shoulders.

"Slow down. I'm not done yet. You expect an artist to present her work before it's finished?" She grinned.

Hanging out with Jeneane wasn't so bad after all. It had been such a long time since we had.

"Here, take your dress," she said. "Put it on so we can start working on your hair." I felt like a doll being handled by an impertinent little girl. "And no peeking in the mirror!" she warned me.

I did what she said with resignation. I put on the purplish-red dress, making sure I didn't muss the makeup—I wasn't used to wearing stuff on my face—and went back to her. She stared at me in silence.

"Jen, is something wrong? Did I smudge my lipstick?" I raised a hand to my mouth, seeing her enigmatic expression.

"Oh my God. Your dress is . . . perfect. I'm speechless."

"Now *that's* hard to believe," I said, looking at her out of the corner of my eye with a smirk.

I loved that dress. I'd seen it in a shop window and instantly knew I wanted it. As it so happened, it perfectly fit the occasion, because later on they announced that the theme for that year's prom was *Red Carpet: A Night Out in Hollywood.*

The shade of red flattered my dark hair and fair complexion, although I tanned quickly in summertime. The neckline was woven into a sort of bow and the fabric flowed gently down my sides, flaring just above the knee.

"Ugh!" Jeneane groaned, "what is that, a nest on your head? You waiting for squirrels to move in or something?"

I laughed, although I wasn't so sure to what extent she was kidding. "My hair isn't so bad, it's just a little messy."

Her parents were hair stylists. They had a salon downtown and Jeneane's hair always looked perfect, unlike mine, which was a little wavy, curled at the ends, but nothing disastrous.

"Good thing I showed up. I don't know what you would have done without me."

"Yeah, it was a real stroke of luck," I said, a hint of sarcasm in my voice.

Jeneane helped me sit down, making sure the dress wouldn't get creased. For a minute, given the intimacy we'd suddenly rediscovered after all this time, I considered telling her what was going on with me. It felt like if I didn't get some of it off my chest I'd end up losing my mind.

As her hands sank into my hair, my lips parted against my will. "Listen, something . . . something strange happened to me today. It's got to do with the reason why I didn't meet you guys," I continued, still hesitant.

"Are you trying to drive me crazy? Don't keep me guessing. You know how impatient I get! Spit it out!" she said excitedly, not even trying to hold back her curiosity.

"I was biking to the school to drop off my yearbook photos and a semi almost ran me over."

Her hands stopped, still in my hair. I tilted my head a little to look at her and saw the blood drain from her face, leaving her incredibly pale. "Evan saved me," I told her, suddenly overcome with emotion. For some reason, an unknown instinct warned me not to continue.

"Shut up! You're joking, right?"

"How could anybody joke about something like that?" My skin went ice cold at the memory of the death that had passed me by.

"Wow! That is so *romantic*!"

"Romantic? I almost ended up under a truck!" I shot back, aghast. "Besides, Ginevra was there with him."

"Still getting in the way?" she grunted.

I repressed a laugh. "She's his girlfriend, Jen." Why was it Jeneane always seemed to forget that?

"Ooh, you're jealous! You're in love!" She'd probably noticed how red my cheeks had become.

"What? No! It's just that . . . well, I've felt this incredible *attraction* ever since I first saw him. I can't think about anything else, it's like an obsession. Something inside me has changed. I don't feel like the same person any more."

"It's called *love*." Jeneane was sure of herself, but I was talking about something completely different, and maybe I was realizing it for the first time. It was a new sensation, but at the same time, familiar. It was like Evan had reawakened some part of me that was buried deep, deep inside.

"Hey, have you seen that strange tattoo on his arm?" I asked. "I wonder what it means. I'm pretty sure it's some foreign language. Maybe it's Ginevra's name or something." I actually just wanted Jeneane to say it wasn't so. She'd ogled him so thoroughly that by now she must have deciphered whatever it was that was written on his arm.

"What tattoo? Evan doesn't have a tattoo on his arm. If he did I'd have noticed it. You mean you're even seeing things now? You really are messed up," she teased me.

I sat there, stunned. How could she be so convinced? I'd seen it clearly enough.

"Don't be so tense. Tonight Evan will only have eyes for you. Trust me, you're irresistible. Speaking of which, make sure you stay away from my Brandon," she warned with a hint of sarcasm. "One more curl and . . . done. That's it, you're ready!" She spun my chair around so I was facing her and fell silent.

"How do I look?"

Jeneane took me by the hand and pulled me over to the mirror. "See for yourself."

I looked at my reflection and gasped.

"My God, you really do look like a princess, Gemma."

I raised a hand and ran it over my cheekbone, surprised by what Jeneane had managed to do with my skin.

The makeup was so light it was barely noticeable, but it was enough to bring out my eyes like never before. My lips had just a hint of color while my hair fell down my back in soft curls, a few locks pinned up to frame my face.

"I'm speechless, Jeneane. You've worked a miracle," I admitted, still amazed at how different the reflection in the mirror was from how I normally looked.

"What miracle? I just enhanced what was already there. You'd already done the lion's share of the work. Don't be so modest," she said affectionately.

"I don't know how to thank you, really."

"I do—let me run, or I'll never be ready in time!" she called from the door after hurriedly collecting her things.

"Thanks!" I shouted as she left.

Jeneane popped back into the doorway and winked. "I've done my part, the rest is up to you. Good luck."

"Jeneane!" I impulsively grabbed her arm before she could shut the door behind her. "Please don't tell anyone what I just told you, okay?"

Jeneane smiled at me with a conspiratorial look. I had no idea why I felt the need to hide what had happened, but something was telling me that not even I knew all the answers.

24

INTIMIDATION

About an hour had gone by since Jeneane had left my room. The clock read 6:45, reminding me that Peter would be there any minute. For the Spring Dance they usually rented an outdoor venue somewhere in town like the Crown Plaza Resort, the Lake Placid Golf Club, or the Whiteface Lodge. But this time the teachers had decided to hold the event at school.

The doorbell rang sooner than I expected, so I slipped on my ballet flats and rushed downstairs. Peter was already standing there at the front door.

I saw how surprised he was by the sight of me. My mom watched his reaction out of the corner of her eye, pleased. Peter wasn't used to seeing me dressed up. Or, more likely, something had changed in him since the last time he had.

"Wow," he exclaimed, not trying to hide his surprise, "I'm speechless. What'd you do with my Gemma?"

My mom's eyes darted to me and a hint of embarrassment hung in the air. Peter's cheeks flushed the instant he realized he'd affectionately insinuated that I belonged to him.

I nudged his shoulder in an attempt to ease the tension while my mom snapped pictures of us. "It might seem crazy, but even I can be feminine once in a while. Let's go," I said, grabbing the lapel of his black tux and pulling him forward, "or we'll be late."

If I hadn't been obsessed with Evan, tonight I would have found Peter attractive. I wasn't used to seeing him dressed up for a black-tie event either, although he was wearing gym shoes and his shirt was a bit too untucked to actually consider him formally dressed. But despite everything, the bar was set too high now for me to be attracted to him.

"Bye, Mrs. Bloom!" Peter gripped the doorway with one hand before letting me drag him away.

"Have a good time!" my mom called across our front walk as Peter started the car he'd rented.

The ride to school felt endless. From time to time I glanced out the window to make sure Peter hadn't taken a longer route. It wasn't the first time I was going to a school dance with him, but it was definitely the first time I'd found myself worried about his expectations. I was terribly uncomfortable inside the cramped car, and my discomfort made it feel even smaller than it actually was—almost too small to contain all the tension our bodies were emanating.

I could clearly read Peter's hopes for that evening in his eyes and was almost overwhelmed by the awareness that I couldn't make it happen.

I felt like I'd lost my best friend.

"You didn't have to . . . I mean . . . you could have taken your dad's car," I said, trying to ease the tension, "like last year."

"Not tonight," he said. "You look really, really good."

I bit my lower lip but stopped the moment I noticed the strange taste of the lip gloss. "You too," I said, embarrassed. "But, what, no bow tie?"

Peter cast me a sidelong glance. "I refuse to wear ties!" he exclaimed, laughing at himself.

"I thought this year would be different. I mean, we're growing up."

Peter grinned at me and snapped the elastic band I wore on my arm as always. "Some things never change."

He was right. I hadn't given up my habits just to satisfy a social convention either. Being true to myself felt good, no matter what the circumstances were.

I silently thanked heaven when we pulled up in the school parking lot. I felt unable to handle this new relationship which, against my will, was starting to go beyond the limits of friendship.

Peter hurried to open the passenger-side door for me and offered me his hand to help me out. No matter how comforting and familiar his touch was, I could think only of Evan as we walked up to the gym, which had been turned into a ballroom for the occasion.

The doors were opened by brawny boys in tuxes who were in charge of checking the tickets. The warm light coming from inside made me look up from the red carpet that led from the entrance into the main part of the gym. Suddenly anxiety gripped me. I forced myself to hold my breath as my heartbeat wavered at the thought of seeing Evan again. He was the only thing on my mind and I was dying to be near him.

After a few deep breaths, I walked through the door. The space was so elegantly decorated I could barely believe it was actually the gym. Our very familiar school colors—blue and yellow, which covered the walls every day—were barely visible, as the whole gym was draped in velvet. From the ceiling hung a massive chandelier laden with crystal prism drops that sparkled, reflecting the light on the floor and walls. Regal and majestic, the long red carpet crossed the entire room, forming a perfect walkway to stroll down for professional photos.

Peter took my hand and held me back. As I turned to look at him, he pulled out the corsage he'd ordered.

"I asked your mom what color your dress was." He slipped it onto my wrist, looking into my eyes as he did so, while our picture was taken. I held his gaze. Peter was so sweet and I loved him so much. Not the way he wanted, though. There was nothing I could do about that. I wanted to be swept away, I wanted a love that consumed me.

I looked down at the corsage sheepishly.

"Thanks," I murmured. It really was beautiful: a small cluster of white carnations interwoven with a black lace bracelet. Only then did I notice that Peter had pinned a matching boutonnière onto his lapel. That particular flower symbolized eternal faithfulness. I wondered if he knew that.

I looked around in an effort to relax. It was still early, but the room was already pretty packed. My first instinct was to look for Evan's face among the crowd. I peered around, scanning the entire room.

"Looking for someone?" Peter didn't even try to hide the reproach in his voice.

"Don't start, Pet."

"I could tell you the same thing. You're here with me—try not to forget it. I'm going to go look for the others. I have the funny feeling I'm going to need something stronger than punch tonight. Maybe I'll get a little drunk before I come back. That way it'll be easier to pretend you care anything about me."

"Peter, please, don't ruin everything!"

"I don't have to, you're already taking care of that yourself."

Peter stormed off, leaving me stunned. I almost didn't recognize him any more. I watched him walk away and my eyes met Ginevra's. She was on the other side of the gym.

It was impossible not to notice her. She shone like a beacon in the dark of night. A star in full Hollywood style. Everyone's eyes were glued to her. Even the girls couldn't help but stare at her and her radiance. Who could blame them? Ginevra left everyone breathless. Her fringed pearl-white gown, so fine and elegant, made her look like an angel who'd descended from heaven. Among the crowd she sparkled, shining like a comet amid simple stars. The flounces of her gown draped her body softly, clinging to her until right above the knee, baring her long, sensual legs, while the back ended in a sheer train, like a phoenix rising from silver flames. Her golden hair hung over her shoulders in a myriad of shiny curls, while around her neck she wore a thin, eye-catching necklace in the shape of a dangerous-looking serpent that wound down to her neckline.

No matter how elegant I felt tonight, seeing Ginevra shattered any fantasies I'd had.

Unable to crawl back out of the deep pit of inadequacy into which I'd fallen, I walked over to the refreshments table to drown my disappointment—along with the hope that Evan would "only have eyes for me," as Jeneane had sworn—in punch.

Discouraged, I began to seriously consider whether I should reassess Peter's interest in me. He was more in my league. Evan was definitely too good for me. Actually, he was too good for any girl other than Ginevra.

When the cluster of students beside her moved away, I finally saw Evan and suddenly Ginevra's light faded, eclipsed by the powerful dark magnetism that drew me to him.

It would have been difficult not to notice Evan tonight. First of all, he was the only one not wearing the traditional tuxedo. Over casual slacks, which did nothing but make him even more attractive, he wore a dark gray top, the sleeves pulled back to the elbows. His black tattoo stood out on his arm. But it certainly wasn't his clothes that monopolized my attention.

I had to admit it: they were perfect together, he and Ginevra. The classic couple everyone envied.

Someone must have spiked the punch, because I suddenly felt dizzy. Or maybe the thought of the two of them together was addling my brain. I couldn't accept it, even though I felt ridiculous for thinking Evan might be interested in a run-of-the-mill girl like me. I was the naïve nerd that kids at school would borrow notes from, while Evan was as beautiful as an angel.

I hid among the crowd so I could stare at him undisturbed, confident that having all those people around would keep him from noticing me. Ginevra moved her lips nonstop while Evan listened to her, not even opening his mouth. Judging from his expression, somehow what she was saying both bothered and amused him. I couldn't take my eyes off the sensual curve of his lips as he smiled and his eyes as they narrowed, making him so irresistible and sexy.

All at once Evan whipped his head around and looked at me, catching me staring. My heart leapt. He'd moved so quickly I hadn't had time to look away.

His eyes locked onto mine instantly, as if he'd known exactly where to find me, but he hadn't noticed me standing there before, I was sure of it. Was Ginevra talking to him about me, maybe?

Involuntarily, my lips twisted into an awkward greeting. In reply, Evan cocked his head, staring at me intently, one corner of his mouth raised in the most seductive smile I'd ever seen.

His gaze was attentive, like I remembered it, but the sensuality in his smile was entirely new. My heart threatened to escape my control.

Despite the distance between us, our eyes were glued to each other. It felt like everyone around us had disappeared and that invisible cord had returned to connect my heart to his.

But Ginevra's presence was strong enough to distract me from Evan's gaze. Out of the corner of my eye I saw her looking back and forth between him and me, irritated, until her cold, razor-sharp eyes slashed the cord that united us, bringing Evan's attention back to her.

When he took his eyes off me, I returned to the punchbowl and filled the still-empty paper cup I'd been clutching. Or maybe I'd already filled it up and finished it all. I couldn't remember.

I didn't feel like being at the prom any more. My expectations for the evening had already gone up in smoke at the sight of Ginevra's intimidating glare. And I'd ruined Peter's hopes too. Speaking of Peter, I wondered where he'd gone. I'd completely lost sight of him. Neither one of us would be getting what we wanted tonight. Deep in my heart, I hoped he'd at least found company. The room was full of dolled-up girls who would have given anything to be his date tonight. Not that any of them deserved him. Maybe such a girl didn't even exist. Even I felt I didn't deserve his attention.

"Hey, hot stuff!"

A loud, arrogant, masculine voice distracted me from my thoughts. It was close. Too close, actually. It had come from right behind me but, slurred as it was from whatever they'd used to spike the punch, it didn't sound very familiar. Judging from his breath, which reeked of alcohol, he must have finished the rest of the bottle himself. I looked up from the table and cocked my head to listen without turning around, afraid of bumping into him.

From the corner of my eye I recognized him. A swimmer's shoulders, ash-blond hair, beady blue eyes. Daryl Donovan. King of the Winter Carnival that was held every February at our school, not to mention the hockey team champion.

And he was talking to me.

Anyone else would have been flattered by his attention, but I was torn between contempt for his arrogance and fear that Evan might see me with him and get the wrong idea.

I ignored him, looking down at the table, hoping my indifference would make him go away. Instead, his presence grew stronger. He was looming over me like a bear towering over its prey.

"You look sexy tonight," he whispered directly into my ear.

He'd tried to make his voice sound sensual, but it had the exact opposite effect, sending a disgusted shiver down my arms. When I caught a whiff of his breath, a wave of nausea rose up from my stomach.

To my horror, I discovered that my indifference was doing nothing but amusing and exciting him even more. It was very likely he wasn't accustomed to being turned down. "So where've you been hiding? Pretty lil' flower like you's just waiting to be plucked," he whispered, leaning forward until his chest touched my back.

Overcome with disgust from the brief contact, I turned around and tried to push him away, but he was too heavy and didn't budge an inch. Though he was having a hard time staying on his feet because of all the alcohol, he still completely overpowered me.

"Get away," I warned him, horrified.

"Aw, c'mon!" he insisted with a grin, continuing to edge closer. "I just wanna have a lil' fun, just for tonight."

I found him repugnant. He was getting more arrogant and insolent with every passing second. I began to worry I wouldn't be able to stop him.

I looked around for help, but no one seemed to notice us at all. Screaming would have been useless—the music was too loud for anyone to hear me. And he was way bigger than me. If he'd felt like it, he could have dragged me out of the room and no one would have tried to stop him. Nobody would dare stand up to Daryl. He was a big shot at school, as well as a troublemaker, and my rejection was only arousing him more. He'd taken it as a personal challenge, I could tell from the gleam in his eye.

Panic washed over me. I tried to hide my terror, but doubted it was working.

"You know how many girls would love to be in your shoes?" he said, irritated. He was seriously turned on, I could feel it. And he was starting to lose control.

"I told you, leave me alone!" I shouted, my fear growing and my eyes brimming with tears. Where was Peter? With his build, he wouldn't have any problem getting Daryl off my case.

"C'mon, chill, I know you want it too. I promise you won't regret it," he said breathlessly, his voice hoarse with excitement.

This was getting serious. Daryl was moving closer and closer, and my attempts to push him away were futile. I was already backed up against the table and he was blocking my way with his muscle-bound body.

"Don't be such a prude," he panted, his breath hitting my face.

Tired of waiting for my consent, he reached out, but his reflexes were slow and his hand wavered in midair, giving me the chance to realize that he intended to grab me by the neck and press his slobbery lips against mine.

Unable to push him away, I squeezed my eyes shut in disgust, bracing for the worst, but nothing happened.

I opened my eyes again and my heart skipped a beat when I recognized the tattoo wound around the arm that had gripped Daryl's hand a second before it made contact with my skin.

"Don't touch her," Evan growled, taking my breath away as he squeezed the boy's wrist. Daryl was confused by his presence. Judging from his fiery glare, Evan seemed ready to reduce the guy to ashes.

"So who are you, her boyfriend?" Daryl asked, irritated. The threatening tone in Evan's voice hadn't registered, probably because of how wasted he was.

For a moment, Daryl's question eased the tension in Evan's angry expression as his gaze went to my face. Our eyes met for a single moment in the acknowledgement of a deep, unspoken desire. For a second, the warmth it conveyed to me almost nourished my hope that he felt the same way I did.

And for one fleeting moment—maybe because of how he protected me whenever I needed him, maybe because I longed for him with my entire being—I felt like he was mine. I was already his forever, but he would never know it.

Evan's expression grew bloodthirsty again, as if he were fighting the urge to kill the guy. "Believe me." He flashed a captivating half smile, his eyes still burning into Daryl's. "I'm somebody you do not want to mess with. Stay away from her." Evan's authoritative growl rang out like a command, but Daryl would have been wise to take it as a warning.

Despite his own order, Evan continued to grip Daryl's wrist so tightly he couldn't move it. I was sure that if he didn't let go soon he'd snap it in two. I could almost hear bones creaking, though Daryl wasn't letting any pain show on his proud face. His expression was bewildered, as if he couldn't figure out where he was. He was probably stunned that someone had not only stood up to him, but had no intention of relaxing his grip. Evan continued to glare at him, ready to act at any second, like a puma staring at its prey before pouncing on it and slaughtering it.

I shot him a look, trying to tell him it was enough. His dark, narrowed eyes were still locked onto Daryl's, and I was overwhelmed by the feeling that I was sinking into a dark well, hypnotized, as a strange glint, golden and almost imperceptible, flashed across them.

Daryl's expression changed radically, as if awakening from a drunken slumber. Finally lucid, he grasped the threat in Evan's eyes. Suddenly he looked terrified, as though frightened by a private conversation between them, one I hadn't heard.

"Okay, dude, let go."

I couldn't believe how much fear edged Daryl's trembling voice as he begged Evan to leave him alone. I mean, this was *Daryl Donovan.*

Only then did Evan brusquely unclench his hand. Daryl backed away, gaping at him, only turning around when he was sure he was far enough away to have a head start if he needed one.

Seeing him disappear into the crowd, I heaved a sigh of relief. Evan's face relaxed into a reassuring smile. "Everything all right?" he asked, his voice incredibly caring.

"I think so," I said, still shaken by his presence.

Not even the terrifying experience I'd just been through had made my heart race like his smile did. I'd seen two different, totally opposite sides of Evan today. Tough and authoritative with others, sweet and caring only with me.

His expression completely changed when he was dealing with me. Not even with Ginevra was he so… *protective.* The thought warmed my heart.

Suddenly, the wild, booming music, which up until a moment ago had echoed against the walls, softened into a sweeter melody, one I'd never heard before.

"I don't see your date anywhere." Evan's seductive gaze locked onto mine, making me wobble as I stood there. "I got you away from that thug—don't I deserve at least one favor in return?"

His question left me baffled. I couldn't imagine what he might want from me, but before I could ask him, the answer came and my heart stopped.

"May I have this dance?" he said softly, offering me his hand without taking his eyes off me even for a second. A dark, seductive look in which I read the promise of forbidden places inaccessible to all others. A gaze in which I knew I risked losing myself.

My brain was still trying to come up with a reply when my hand moved, guided by a surge of pure emotion, and rested gently in his palm. A jolt spread through my body with the intensity of a flaming arrow the instant my skin touched his.

Still fixed on me, his eyes sparkled. He raised my hand to his lips and hesitated a second. My heart raced at the thought that he would press them against the back of my hand, but instead he turned it over and tenderly kissed my palm as my heart trembled from my intense emotions. Why had he done that? Shivers ran through my body. I was suddenly struck with déjà vu: he'd done that in one of my dreams. How was it possible?

Evan's charm was like moonglow in the forest. It drew me closer, yet frightened me at the same time. Even so, I couldn't do without it. We made our way to the dance floor, hand in hand.

Who knew how long and how intensely I'd longed for, dreamed of, this moment, but I was frozen stiff with embarrassment, and it kept me from moving closer to him.

The air was electrified, as if my body were being magnetically drawn to his, but every time I tried to move closer, a shock raced through me like a lightning bolt. The attraction between us was so strong it could have caused a city-wide blackout.

The lights were dim, a glowing amber color as soft as candlelight. Evan clasped my hand as our bodies swayed to the rhythm of the soft music. The notes of a violin trembled in the air, a sad, intense, desperate, yet incredibly sweet motif.

"I've never heard this song before," I said between the harmonious notes, breaking a silence in which I actually felt perfectly comfortable. It was as if the song were delving into me. As if he himself were the song. Fascinating, dark, and mysterious all at once. It was inside me, I could feel it.

"Do you really like it?" His narrowed eyes smiled at me enigmatically.

"I think it's beautiful. Do you know what it is?"

"It's ours," Evan replied softly. "This is our song," he repeated, wearing the sweetest look I'd ever seen. Shaken by his remark, I rested my other hand on his chest to steady myself. I had the impression he was staring at me more intently than usual. Unable to hold his gaze, I looked at his dog tag, which made me blush every time I found myself staring at it. It must be important to him if he never took it off.

Evan cradled my back gently, moving like a gentleman from a bygone age. I felt his eyes on me, but I couldn't find the courage to look directly into them. Not from that distance—he was so close. I felt I might lose myself forever in him, in his eyes as deep and dark as the universe. Suddenly, the soft touch of his hand grew stronger, and smoothly yet firmly he drew me to him, making me gasp with emotion. The blood rushed to my head and I looked up into his eyes, dizzy. His whole body was touching mine and his eyes were making me melt like honey over a fire. It was as if he also felt the need to cancel every trace of distance between us, to allow our bodies to fuse together in a dance guided by our heartbeats. Evan squeezed my hand firmly. It seemed that he too had fallen prey to the same sensations.

I was intoxicated by my emotions, totally deprived of self-control, utterly at the mercy of the sweetness in his gaze, afflicted by a fever I didn't want to recover from. Every heartbeat drew me to him. Every cell in my body belonged to him. I felt his warmth through our clothes. *No.* It was me who was burning up.

I lowered my eyes, resting them on his full, enticing lips. The blood in my veins boiled with the longing to feel them on my own.

You've taken my breath away tonight.

His hushed voice filled my head, enveloping me like black velvet. Dazed, I looked into his smiling eyes, trying to understand how he'd spoken to me. I'd heard his whisper, but his lips hadn't moved. I was sure because I'd been looking right at them. Was my obsession with him really confusing me that much? Was it simply my longing to hear those words that had made them appear in my mind? In response to my troubled expression, a reassuring smile appeared on his face.

I felt the compelling need to say something, if for no other reason than to take my mind off the thought of biting his lips. I wasn't sure I could control myself any more.

"I still haven't thanked you for today. This is the second time you've saved my life."

"You're dancing with me. That's all the thanks I need," he said promptly, wielding a seductive smile. "Are you all right?" He stroked the spot on my forehead where I thought I'd been injured. His eyes were tinged with sadness. "Just the thought that you were about to die—"

"Evan, why didn't you take me to the hospital?"

He smiled at me sweetly. "Because there was no need to."

Had nothing happened to me? Really? That's not how it had seemed at first. I'd clearly seen my bicycle lying on the street in a mangled heap. But then later, I'd found it intact in our driveway. Then my wound had vanished after Evan had left. Everything had disappeared as though the accident had never happened. I was on the verge of pointing this out to Evan, but he squeezed my hand even harder and stared at me insistently, making me forget all about it.

"Please don't look at me that way," I begged, my heart in my throat because his warm gaze was constantly on me.

"Why?" he asked with a sly smile. The dimple in his cheek melted me even more than his voice had. What could I tell him, that it threatened to drive me crazy?

"Because I risk losing myself in you." The words escaped my control.

"*Samam*," he whispered, making my heart tremble. I had no idea how I knew, but I was certain the word meant *me too.*

Some self-destructive impulse made me look away. Not far off, Peter was watching us, looking both resigned and furious. He gulped down what was left in his paper cup without taking his eyes off me, then clenched his fist, crushing the cup in his hand. He stared at me for one last minute, as if saying goodbye, and disappeared into the crowd. I wanted to stop him, but my place was there with Evan. Then I looked over and my eyes met Ginevra's. She was watching us from a distance, looking incensed.

Unfortunately, Evan's place wasn't with me.

I regretted allowing myself to be distracted by the two of them, leaving room for my feelings of guilt to re-emerge. From the magical little world in which we'd hidden away, we'd returned to reality, and it was all my fault. I was overcome with sadness. "Ginevra's waiting for you," I murmured dejectedly, nodding in her direction.

Evan's lips curved upwards, as if he were mocking me about something only he understood. It was the most sensual smile I'd ever seen and for a moment it mesmerized me. It had me nailed to my spot, keeping me from running off. He brushed his fingertips over my shoulder, following the movement with his eyes, and with unbearable sweetness swept my hair back from my neck. His mouth moved to my ear until his lips were brushing against it. "I don't care at all about Ginevra, haven't you figured that out yet?" he whispered sweetly.

I swallowed, trembling at the sensation of his hot breath on my skin, while a dreamy lassitude filled me until I melted. This time I was sure he'd actually said it. That gentle puff of air was proof. I couldn't remember how many times I'd longed to hear those words from his lips.

Our foreheads were so near they brushed together with every breath. Feeling our bodies touch made me tremble, pulling me back into the dream.

"I enrolled at this school just for you."

"But you didn't even know me," I murmured shyly.

"I know you. I know you like no other. Because I know your soul."

The confession pierced my heart. What did it mean? A shiver ran through me.

As though in answer to a summons, I stroked his forearm, mesmerized by the symbols covering it. It was the most mysterious thing I'd ever seen.

He watched me, letting me touch him, but his expression slowly darkened, as if my gesture had awakened something inside him. Melancholy glimmered in his eyes as he looked at me. "It's you I want to be with," he whispered in a barely audible voice. "If only it were up to me to choose . . ."

Like a beautiful spell transformed into a terrible curse, I felt my heart shatter deep in my chest. Searching for answers, I sought his gaze, but the sadness I found there took my breath away.

"You can't?" I asked, disillusioned. Following an impulse I couldn't hold back, I said, "Is it because of Ginevra?"

Evan rested his forehead against mine and squeezed his eyes shut, overcome by this new emotion. I couldn't understand: why the sudden change of mood? What was worrying him now?

"Ginevra has nothing to do with it. A world where you and I can be together doesn't exist, Gemma."

His rejection ran me through like a blade of ice. Coupled with the words I'd so longed for him to say were the only ones I would never have wanted to hear.

"But why?" I asked him, caught between confusion and misery. If Ginevra wasn't a problem, what was keeping him from being with me?

"I don't . . . I can't, I'm sorry," he said in a broken voice, suddenly unable to look me in the eye. "It's complicated." He leaned his forehead against mine again, his expression torn by the painful denial. "God only knows how much I wish I could be with you, but I can't."

His emotions were so powerful they brought back the memory of my dream. As Evan squeezed his eyes shut, not wanting to look at me, I felt like I'd already been through this whole thing. And I didn't like the way this was turning out at all.

"You can't tell me you want me and then leave me like this," I whispered desperately, my forehead still resting against his. I struggled to gulp down the knot in my throat, trying to keep the tears from coming. I'd yearned for that confession for too long to give him up right after discovering that he wanted me as much as I wanted him.

Suddenly his jaw clenched and something in his expression radically changed. His gaze petrified me like cement as his eyes, so intense just a second before, filled with dark poison. It was as if he was caught between two worlds. He stared into space, seeming to be concentrating on something completely different, heeding some kind of signal I couldn't perceive. He cocked his head as if listening for something.

Ginevra abruptly appeared at his side, looking worried. "He's here." She said it so gravely it made me start.

"I know," he replied firmly, looking down. His stony gaze revealed overwhelming concern. I'd never seen him so intense and grim, not even when I was about to be run over. For the first time, something entirely new tinged his expression. *Fear.*

"What do we do?" Ginevra asked nervously, staring at him.

Evan clenched his fists and set his jaw. "I'm not letting him near her," he said in a resolute tone.

"What's going on?" I spoke up anxiously, having been totally excluded from their conversation. Neither of them paid any attention to me, as if I'd become invisible.

"I'll be back in a minute," Evan said, his shadowed gaze scanning the room, worried. "I'll deal with him. You take care of her. *Don't lose sight of her,*" he commanded. Ginevra nodded unquestioningly.

I was completely lost. I couldn't understand what all this meant. Why did everything always have to be so confusing and complicated when it came to Evan?

Suddenly he grabbed my face and looked straight into my eyes with matchless intensity, as though on the verge of kissing me. "You have to trust me," he whispered in response to all my fears. .

My body turned to stone as I watched him stride off through the crowd.

25

THE RECKONING

Evan was gone, leaving me alone with Ginevra, which was enough to make me shudder. The tension between us was palpable. I'd never been alone with her before and the particular circumstances tonight made everything even more bizarre.

"There's no time to explain." Her cold warning left me speechless, as though she were reproaching my thoughts. "You need to come with me," she ordered, grabbing my hand before I could protest. When her fingers touched mine, a strange jolt ran through me. A powerful, *familiar* connection. As if with that touch my blood had mixed with hers. It was such a strong sensation that I impulsively jerked back my hand. Ginevra turned to stare at me as if she'd felt the same energy.

"*There's no time,*" she snapped.

I was in danger of being overcome by panic. What the hell was going on? Why was *Ginevra* dragging me across the ballroom? And why was I letting her? Deep down I knew the answer: Evan had asked me to trust him and in order to do that I had to follow her.

As we silently slipped through the crowd like fish swimming upstream, a loud, sharp noise that sounded like the crackling of electrical cables made my heart race. I whipped my head around, trying to spot the source of the noise, but Ginevra continued to tug on my arm to keep me from slowing down.

A shower of blue and red sparks burst from the enormous amps like fireworks. It must have been a short circuit. Everyone panicked. The lights flickered and went out, plunging the room into total darkness. There was a crescendo of alarmed voices.

Invisible in the gloom, Ginevra came to a halt, my hand clutched in hers. The students' shouts disoriented me.

"Look out!" she screamed.

Everything happened very fast. Before I could react, she let go of my hand and something rammed into me hard, as if a football player had suddenly tackled me. For a moment I couldn't feel the floor beneath my feet. There was a crash. A deafening one. The terrifying sound of thousands of glasses being shattered against the wall.

At first I thought the impact hadn't been so brutal, but acute pain shot through my arm as I realized the floor was too close. In fact, I was lying on it.

The blue emergency lights blinked on, dimly illuminating the room. A murmur spread through the crowd. Dazed by the confusion that had filled the gym, I looked around for Ginevra and was shocked to see she was on the opposite end of the room. How had she managed to push me so incredibly far? And why?

Frightened and confused, I looked around and my blood ran cold. An ocean of broken glass covered the gym floor. I was shocked to see some of my classmates stanching the blood that ran from their arms while others clutched wounds on their legs, their trousers and gowns torn by the shards. My heart skipped a beat when my eyes crossed the room and saw, at Ginevra's feet, the skeleton of the massive chandelier that, until a moment ago, had illuminated the room. It lay on the ground, shattered. My corsage had been crushed by its crystals, the white petals scattered everywhere. It must have fallen from my wrist when Ginevra pushed me away. I went deathly pale. Tremors ran down my arms at the realization that she'd just saved my life.

Though I still couldn't figure out how she'd done it, she'd pushed me far enough out of the chandelier's way to prevent the shards of broken glass from hitting me.

In spite of the distance between us, my terrified gaze was locked onto hers, cancelling out everything else. Ginevra strode across the room and forced me to my feet, though my knees shook, threatening to give way beneath my weight. Her face was devoid of emotion—she looked like she was wearing a wax mask. "There's no time for thank yous," she said, paying no attention to how shaken I was. "We've got to go, Gemma!" She pulled me along again as I struggled not to fall into a catatonic state.

My dry mouth and parched throat felt like I'd swallowed some of the pieces of glass. I couldn't explain what was happening, but it seemed to be something far more frightening than a short circuit. It was something that had alarmed Evan and Ginevra—something that had to do with *me.* But I could tell I wouldn't be getting any answers out of Ginevra. I'd have to save my questions for Evan. He *had* to give me an explanation.

Instead of leaving through the main doors of the gym, Ginevra pulled me into the corridor, which looked more ominous and foreboding than it ever had. The flickering of the fluorescent lights overhead did nothing but increase my tension. I had the bone-chilling sensation I was in one of those horror movies Peter often made me watch. Evan and Ginevra's confusing behavior, the alarmed looks on their faces, and most importantly, my complete incomprehension of what was going on all increased my terror as we hurried down the corridor.

"Okay, you've got to tell me what's happening," I insisted, but my voice trembled, revealing how upset I was.

"No, we've got to get out of here. Evan won't be able to hold him off for long." The fact that Ginevra didn't bother to hide her concern increased the panic gripping my chest. The eerie moonlight crept in through the windows of the side doors, filling the hallway with a ghastly glow. I forced myself to hasten my steps, aware that those doors were our only means of escape, even though I had absolutely no idea who or *what* we were trying to escape from. As we neared the doors, panic hit me so hard that I broke free from Ginevra's iron grip, rushed to the exit, and threw myself against the door, pressing down with all my might on the push bar, my panic at stellar levels. As I raced through the door, I whirled back toward Ginevra, who'd almost caught up with me, but her face turned to a stony mask of terror.

"NO!!!" Her shriek sliced through the silence of the corridor, her eyes locked on something behind me.

I spun around, but the door slammed shut on its own, trapping Ginevra inside. I shook the handle violently, trying to open it, but it was jammed, leaving me abandoned outside. In the dark. Alone.

I stared at her through the window, terrified, as she uselessly banged on the push bar, trying to unjam it.

"Run!" Her dismayed shout came through the door. But what frightened me even more than her voice was her icy gaze, fixed on something behind me. I turned around, terrified, and saw nothing but ominous darkness awaiting me.

If this was a joke, I didn't find it the least bit funny. I would have believed I was actually in an episode of *Scare Tactics* if my instinct hadn't told me Ginevra's terror was definitely real.

"Go, Gemma! Run!"

Her voice bewildered me. Panic seized me. I forced myself to move away from the door, but my paralyzing fear had atrophied my legs, leaving my feet glued to the sidewalk. I couldn't figure out why there was so little light. The short circuit must have affected the whole block. I didn't know what to do, but an archaic instinct tingled beneath my skin, telling me to follow Ginevra's orders.

Something stirred in the trees. Something eerie and sinister.

I continued to tell myself it was all too crazy to be true as my eyes slowly grew more accustomed to the pitch dark of the night.

A blur shot from one side of the street to the other and claws of icy fear gripped my heart. Even my breath refused to make a sound, threatening to suffocate me.

With a sharp pang of terror, I forced my limbs to move and walked away from the building as Ginevra stared at me through the window. She looked more and more frightened, devastated that she couldn't help me.

I began to run aimlessly, my heavy breathing in my ears as the sound of my footsteps against the asphalt filled the street with a lugubrious, hair-raising echo. I just wanted to get far away, to escape from the nightmare.

Almost all my energy drained, I stopped to catch my breath, resting my hands on my trembling knees. Suddenly, just when I thought I was safely alone, headlights flashed on in the silence, blinding me. I instinctively shielded my eyes with my hand. Who on earth was in the car? And what did they want from me?

The engine roared to life, slicing through the deathly silence.

Whoever was in there seemed set on scaring me to death. As if I weren't already frightened enough as it was. The driver revved the engine over and over, each time more aggressively, and each time they did, the sound hit me straight in the heart. I hoped I would wake up from this nightmare any second now.

Only when I heard the squeal of tires did I understand the driver's true intentions.

Whoever it was didn't want to scare me. They wanted to kill me. Again, and on the same day? I was starting to think death was pursuing me.

The tires spun faster and faster. The smell of burnt rubber reached my nostrils. The car was on the verge of hurtling toward me, but just before the driver's foot left the clutch, the squeal of the tires was drowned out by a fiercer roar coming from another direction. I spun around as a black motorcycle thundered onto the street. My heart leapt in my chest when I recognized it. It skidded to a halt an inch away from me.

I looked up, breathless.

"Get on!" Evan ordered.

Without hesitating I grabbed his arm and leapt onto the seat behind him just as the car raced toward us like an arrow shot by a skilled archer.

Evan gunned the throttle. The bike reared and we shot off. I tightened my arms around him as we flew down the road at an inhuman speed in an attempt to lose the car. I should have been terrified, but every ounce of my fear had been eclipsed the moment Evan appeared, replaced by a deep feeling of safety and protection.

As we passed under a streetlight, I looked back at the car and recognized it: a bright-red Viper I'd often seen in the school parking lot. I'd heard kids mention it, but I'd never been interested enough to find out who it belonged to. I tried to see who was driving but couldn't make out their face through the windshield.

In seconds, Lake Placid disappeared behind us. The lights of the town cast our shadows on the pavement before us as we zoomed down Old Military Road in the direction of Saranac Lake, the berserk car close behind us. My heart leapt when it came close to ramming the back of the bike, but Evan noticed in time and twisted the accelerator. "Hold on!" he roared into the wind.

I squeezed my knees around him and clung to him with all my might. Evan sped up even more, raising the front wheel off the ground and leaving the car behind. My adrenaline shot to levels I'd never felt before, a mix of terror and thrill.

The sense of security Evan instilled in me curbed my fear enough for me to realize that the speed was going to my head, filling my veins with a rush of energy that ran throughout my body. I felt like an arrow slicing through the wind. The air lashed at my face, whipping my hair around wildly behind my shoulders. But even more exciting was feeling Evan's chest under my hands, flexing at every curve. I could feel every muscle through the light fabric of his shirt.

Driven by an irresistible urge, I stroked his chiseled abs, as hard as marble. Desire threatened to overwhelm me. For an instant, I forgot what was happening, as if nothing else existed. Evan wanted me and I was on his motorcycle, clinging to him, engulfed in the heat of his body.

He said something, and the vibration in his chest distracted me from the thought. I couldn't make out the words, but I knew he was cursing the relentless car. From my position, I could see his jaw was clenched and he seemed more and more furious. Something told me he was beside himself with anger.

The icy wind lashed at my fingers. As if he'd read my mind, Evan took his left hand off the handlebar and a second later I felt its heat on my own. His hands were more exposed to the wind than mine, but his skin was far warmer. I trembled at the contrast. He laced his fingers with mine and squeezed them, silently comforting me. The gesture made me giddy, a tremble running from my heart down to my stomach and back up again.

A second later, Evan tensed and gripped the handlebars firmly with both hands again.

We roared along through the lights of Saranac Lake. Before I knew it we'd left the town behind us. I leaned to the side slightly to look at the road in front of us, but the wind took my breath away. I wondered how Evan could breathe while going so fast without a helmet, but he didn't seem to be having trouble. As for me, I could barely keep my eyes open.

The road in front of us branched into two forks: the first continued in the same direction we were traveling, skirting the woods; the other led downhill and away from town. Evan sped along without giving any indication which way he meant to go.

Almost imperceptibly loosening his grip on the accelerator, he allowed the car to approach until it had almost caught up with us. I guessed from the determined look on his face that he was doing it intentionally, but instinct made me squeeze my eyes shut and brace myself when the fork in the road was dangerously close.

Only at the last second did Evan veer hard to the right, accelerating as he did so, the back wheel skidding. We managed to shake the car, which was caught off guard and ended up going the other way. My heart leapt when I turned and saw that the road behind us was empty.

Something was wrong, though, because Evan was still tense and didn't release his grip on the throttle. Why wouldn't he relax, now that the car was no longer behind us? The wind hindered my movements, but something made me look to our right.

The blood ran cold in my veins.

There was a black shadow racing through the trees beside us. A shudder ran through me. I had no idea what the thing was, but it definitely wasn't human.

The howl of Evan's motorcycle was joined by another deafening noise. I was shocked to discover it was the car again, racing through the trees on a dirt road to our left, heading toward us.

My entire body shuddered with terror. Who could want me dead so desperately? I quickly ran down a mental list of the people I'd dealt with recently, everyone who might have something against me, but nothing made me think any of them would be homicidal. None of them would be capable of that. Except…

My eyes opened wide. *Daryl Donovan.*

Was it possible his pride had been wounded so badly? To the point that he wanted to kill me? Evan's reaction must have enraged him, or maybe he was simply too drunk to realize what he was doing.

Evan accelerated again, making us fishtail. The car gave no sign of giving up. It raced through the trees on the rocky terrain. I ventured to glance at our speedometer and gasped when I saw how fast we were going, slicing through the wind like a fiery arrow—191 miles an hour.

How was I even managing to breathe at that speed? And how could the car actually be keeping up with us?

Just as I turned to look at the dirt road, the car, going at top speed, swerved brusquely in our direction. In front of it were two trees so close together they formed what looked like an impenetrable obstacle. Instead of slowing down, the car sped up. Its side mirrors smashed against the trees, the pieces flying into the air before crashing to the ground. Tires squealing, the car skidded onto our road without losing speed and resumed its wild pursuit.

I heard Evan curse again. I could feel his tension in his tight chest muscles. The bike fishtailed as he accelerated hard, skidding onto a hidden back road.

But not even that sudden maneuver was enough to shake the car behind us. I hoped Evan had a backup plan.

I leaned over his shoulder to see where the road led and uncontrollable panic left me breathless. I was so shocked I inadvertently relaxed my grip on Evan, but he quickly grabbed my hand before I could slide off the seat, clasping it to his chest to encourage me to hold on tighter. I obeyed and closed my eyes, wondering what he intended to do, given that the road in front of us ended in a heap of rubble that was drawing closer and closer—huge blocks of cement that we were zooming straight toward. I held my breath. At the very last moment the bike spun around, coming to a dead stop a handspan away from the wall of cement, so close that the gravel scattered in the process sprayed back onto me.

I tried to catch my breath, but the car was barreling toward us and I was horrified to realize we had our backs to the wall. We were completely trapped. He was going to crash right into us! What on earth was Evan thinking?

"Evan!" Panicking, I looked up at him in terror, but saw that he wasn't at all scared or even the least bit concerned. Quite the opposite. A strange fervor glimmered in his eyes, as though he was excited by the challenge.

He cursed and I finally managed to make out what he was saying.

"C'mon. Come and get her. Just a little closer." His gaze grew keener as his mouth spread into a crafty smile. "Hold on tight," he told me. The low whisper came directly from his chest, filling me with apprehension. It wasn't a suggestion. It was a *warning*.

What did he mean to do? My instinct told me I didn't want to know. In any case, he didn't give me the chance to ask, but jammed his foot onto the left pedal, putting the bike in gear. With a flick of his right wrist he gunned the accelerator and the bike shot forward, jerking me back.

The bike headed straight for the car, instantly gaining incredible speed as the distance between the two vehicles shortened inexorably.

No matter how much I trusted Evan, he was putting me through a test that was too grueling to ignore. Had he decided to kill us? I held on to him tightly, adrenaline preventing me from closing my eyes. The car came toward us like a missile. I held my breath and tensed every muscle in my body, bracing for the crash, but at the last second Evan squeezed the clutch hard and, before releasing it, accelerated to the max. The motorcycle rose up onto one wheel a moment before impact, leaping up onto the Viper's low hood with a deafening crash. The tire skidded over the windshield, leaving a dent all the way up to the car's roof.

I heard the hair-raising sound of shatterproof glass being crushed beneath the back wheel. An instant later, the bike landed on the road in perfect balance and skidded to a halt, raising a huge cloud of dust. I gasped for air as we watched the car continue its crazed course, too late to stop. It swerved to avoid the wall in front of it, but it was no use; it crashed into the thick cement barrier.

The driver's door burst open on impact, revealing the inside of the car.

My heart stopped. It was empty. The driver's-side airbag had deployed, but no one was behind the wheel.

"Evan." I tried to speak, but only a confused gasp came out. What on earth was going on? How had the car been driving all on its own? I had the impression Evan knew more than he was letting on. At that point I was absolutely certain he was hiding something from me.

Even though I didn't trust my senses any more, I couldn't deny what I'd just seen with my own two eyes: the car was empty. Ever since Evan had burst into my life, bizarre things had been happening. Things that were impossible to explain, at times things I wanted to believe didn't matter. There was one thing I could no longer deny, though: there was something about Evan, something disturbing and sinister, that my instinct had detected from the moment I first laid eyes on him. Something my heart had refused to accept.

A dark, ominous secret.

Part of me, the more instinctive part, recommended caution. As for the other part—the one blinded by love for Evan—all it took was one look from him to silence my instinct.

And yet, I could no longer ignore what was going on around me. I couldn't pretend I didn't see the sinister glimmer in his eyes. A shudder of terror ran through my bones.

Evan glanced at me as I stared at the empty driver's seat, struggling to steady my nerves that were threatening to go to pieces from all the tension I'd stored up inside me tonight.

Something dark had crept into my life. And I didn't intend to ignore it any longer. Evan owed me an explanation.

As though he'd heard my silent demand, he jammed his foot down onto the gear lever, putting the bike into first. We roared off, rearing up and leaving the crumpled wreckage behind us.

26

DISTURBING SUSPICIONS

On our way back to Lake Placid, Evan took it easy on the road for the first time since I'd climbed onto his motorcycle. I eased my grip on his chest, finally reassured, but he immediately twisted the gas, forcing me to cling to him again. I looked at the road, my heart in my throat, worried about his sudden acceleration, but there was a twinkle in his eye and a sly smile on his lips, showing it had been his silent protest. A smile warmed my heart and my fingers moved up his abdomen, sliding onto his chest.

The sensation of holding him so close made my head spin, and with the fear of being chased now gone, the physical contact made my blood boil, eclipsing everything else. I couldn't believe I was really there. I rested my temple on his back, overwhelmed by emotion, and Evan unexpectedly grabbed my hand, sending an electric charge racing up to my head and back down to our interlocked hands.

I realized I was probably being too stubborn about ignoring what I should be paying attention to: my instinct, which demanded I distrust him. I also knew I should feel something entirely different from that overwhelming emotion that blotted out everything else, like ocean waves washing away a message written in the sand. Just like those ocean waves, Evan's warmth could smooth the sharpest shards of glass, wipe away the confused tracks of passing footsteps, dispel my every concern. Pervaded by the comfort of his protection, my heart wasn't capable of containing the slightest trace of fear.

I had no idea where his bike was taking us—to the moon, the stars, or a universe all our own. But it didn't matter to me, as long as he was there by my side. The sky had cast off its dark mantle and was studded with stars.

The moon, almost full and curved like a shell, shone high above, illuminating the road. Its soft, silvery light reflected off the surface of the lake, casting moonbeams that streamed behind us like the train of a shimmering gown.

The night didn't seem so ominous to me now. The wind had softened, greeting us with a tender caress before gently flowing away. Even the trees that had looked so daunting in the darkness now seemed to offer us their protection, diffusing the night's scent through the air. I took a deep breath of the spring breeze, tasting the musk and pine that filled the air. I loved the smell of the woods.

Something caught my eye. It was a bright dot that shone more brilliantly than any other star in the infinite darkness above us. Filled with tender emotion, I found myself smiling. Only when he returned the gesture, sending another tingle through me, did I realize I'd squeezed Evan's hand tighter. I couldn't believe I was there with him, after all the times I'd longed with bitter envy to take Ginevra's place on that seat.

Instead he wanted me. Not her. Yet something was forcing him to deny himself what he longed for.

A world where you and I can be together doesn't exist.

His words had frozen my heart like icy water, leaving it brimming with piercing pain. Even so, learning his true feelings had given me the strength to hope, and nothing in the world could make me accept a conclusion different from the one my heart believed in.

Evan's expression revealed no emotion, but there was something about the way his eyes scanned the road that made him seem apprehensive. His body was tense, his back muscles stiff, his gaze watchful.

What was worrying him now?

The answer came to me in a spine-chilling recollection, destroying my sense of calm. I'd pushed it into a dark corner of my mind, far from my attention.

What was that thing that had chased us?

Evan definitely knew something about it and was keeping me in the dark—that was why he was so worried.

Like a million moths fluttering around in my head, his strange conversations with Ginevra clouded my brain. Incoherent memories began to take shape in my mind, fitting together like pieces in a jigsaw puzzle until they formed a picture, albeit an incomplete one.

There was something about Evan. Something dark. Peter had sensed it before I had. An avalanche of memories surfaced in my mind. Unintelligible, senseless pieces of information, but they all had a common denominator: Evan. I knew that to get to the bottom of everything I had to crack the code. Many strange things had happened since he'd moved to town, things that, up until then, I had to admit I hadn't really thought much about. The constant feeling I was being watched, the mysterious shadow I'd seen in the fire, Evan's voice echoing in my head, the way he'd rescued me from certain death, saving me from being hit by that semi—

The memory sent a wave of tiny shivers all over my skin.

What was the mysterious secret he was trying to hide from me?

The motorcycle's engine softened to a purr. I looked up to discover we weren't at my house. My heart skipped a beat, giving me a clue as to where we were. I'd already seen those majestic, impregnable walls. He'd taken me to his place.

Without giving me the chance to object, Evan sped up, passing through a massive wrought-iron gate. The bike slowly wound its way down a path lined with pines and cypresses that looked like they were centuries old.

The moonlight seemed to be shining more brightly here on his estate, lighting up the fortress hidden among the trees. He turned the engine off, but its roar continued to echo in my head.

"Did you enjoy that?" Evan climbed off, smirking. Irresistible. God, he was utterly devastating when he looked at me that way.

"Oh, sure! I can't wait to do it again," I forced myself to say, matching his sarcasm. I looked down at the motorcycle, finding I was stroking its black leather seat. "Actually, I have to admit it was really nice," I said softly. "A boy at school said they only made a hundred of these. I guess I should feel lucky to have had the chance to ride on one. Maybe I should go back and thank that guy!" I joked, trying hard to seem relaxed and laugh off all the tension weighing on my chest.

Evan smiled openly, clearly pleased by the interest people had shown in his precious toy. "Not a hundred. Not if you start counting from zero." He looked at me with satisfaction. "They made a hundred and one of them, to be exact." His smile made me imagine there was a memorable story behind this as his fingers stroked a little platinum plate attached to the steering column, on which his name was elegantly engraved alongside a small zero. "Let's just say it was a somewhat *special favor*," he admitted, his smile curving into a grin. "Anyway . . ." Unexpectedly, he leaned his face closer to mine, his look turning seductive. "You would have come for a ride with me sooner or later."

I began to tremble as he stared at me with the smile of a wolf hidden in the thick of the forest. I still felt a strange uneasiness, as if behind that smile lurked a threat.

Avoiding his seductive gaze so he wouldn't see the wave of emotion that had washed over me, I peered around the garden, a disoriented look on my face. "Where are we?" I stammered, my voice transparently fake as I pretended I'd never been there before.

Evan glanced at me, hiding another smile. "You sure you don't know?"

I couldn't help but look down, unable to meet his eyes. I wished the ground would swallow me up. It was obvious Ginevra had told him.

I looked up at the sky again and my star shone more brightly, catching my attention. I stopped to stare at it, lost in a world all my own, a world where Evan and I could be together.

I felt his gaze on me.

"What's so interesting up there?" His mouth was close to my ear again.

I made myself look away from the sky, suddenly embarrassed. "Nothing . . . nothing important," I stammered, uncomfortable now for a totally different reason as I examined the ends of my hair before pushing it all to one side, nervously smoothing it down with my hands. Looking down, I didn't realize how close he'd come until I felt the warmth of his breath on my bare neck.

"I bet you were looking at your star, Gem," he whispered, wrapping my heart in a cozy shell.

My knees began to shake and I struggled to stay standing. "What did you call me?"

Gem. He'd called me Gem, I was sure of it. No one else had ever called me that, with the sole exception of Evan in the dream I'd had last night. The memory was still crystal clear in my mind. "Wait, how did—how did you . . ." I couldn't find the words. How did he know about the star?

Evan smiled, enjoying my reaction. "Everyone has a star, Gemma," he replied, as if he'd read my mind.

"Even you?" The question escaped my lips. "Which one is your star, Evan?"

He smiled to himself, as if amused by something I didn't know about. More and more frequently I had the impression he enjoyed teasing me. He leaned in closer to my cheek, never losing his impertinent smile. "I can't tell you." The warmth of his reply tickled my skin.

I shook my head, steeling myself against the charms he boldly continued to use on me. He was enjoying himself as he observed my reactions.

"You owe me an explanation," I stated firmly.

"For what?" He feigned confusion, his eyes darting to the side. Evan knew perfectly well what I was talking about.

"I want to know what happened tonight. I'm sure you and Ginevra know exactly what's going on. You've got to explain it to me, Evan."

"Gemma, there's nothing to explain." The hesitation in his voice betrayed his uneasiness. "That guy at the prom, the one who was all over you. I'm pretty sure it was him following us."

"Don't lie to me, Evan. I'm not stupid—you can't fool me. Daryl wasn't in that car. *No one* was in that car. It was empty! Cars don't drive themselves. How do you explain that there was no one behind the wheel?"

I tried hard to hold his gaze, but I had the impression he was trying to get inside my mind again, like he wanted to force me to give up. "And what was that thing that was following us? I saw it, Evan." I looked at him hard, almost accusingly. My lips were trembling again at the thought of that creature chasing us and how scared I'd been that it might have grabbed me from the moving motorcycle. Whatever it was, it certainly had an evil, hostile aura. A dark, malign presence I'd sensed under my skin.

"I don't know what you're talking about." No matter how hard he tried to act cool, Evan seemed more and more nervous.

"Yes you do, and you owe me an explanation." My voice grew harsher as I insisted yet again. "I'm not staying one minute longer unless you tell me what's going on!"

Evan looked down and clenched his fists, staring at the gravel path beneath his feet, but his lips didn't move. In that silent refusal he admitted he had the answers but wasn't willing to tell me what they were.

"Okay, whatever." I looked him in the eye and turned my back on him.

"Where do you think you're going?" His voice conveyed an equal mix of anger and concern.

"Home," I snapped. "It's late."

"You can't go!" More than a suggestion, his growl was an order.

"You can't stop me," I said stubbornly, setting out down the path.

"You don't understand!" His furious, frustrated hiss stopped me in my tracks. "You have to stay. It's dangerous."

Evan imbued those last words with such sweetness that I began to change my mind.

"Please," he went on, "you're only safe here. Stay with me."

My heart wavered as Evan wore down my defenses. I wasn't willing to give in, though. I wouldn't let the mysterious power concealed in his voice soften me up. I wanted the truth. "Safe from *what*?"

Although my back was turned to him, his sigh of exasperation overwhelmed me. "I can't, Gemma. I can't tell you anything. *Why won't you understand*? Fuck!" he shouted, enraged.

"Safe from *who*, Evan?" I wasn't about to drop it. He had to tell me everything. "Who's keeping you from telling me who you are?" I shouted. "Who's keeping you from being with me?"

I wanted to shout a thousand other questions, but of all the things tormenting me, this was the answer that meant the most to me. I stared at the bars in the gate, waiting, still amazed at how bold I'd just been.

Judging by Evan's sigh, the answer wasn't easy for him to say. "Gemma, we—I'm not like you."

A piece of my heart disintegrated. Of course we were different. *I* was too different from him. He deserved better and he'd realized it himself.

"I wasn't prepared to hear that," I replied stiffly.

For a brief moment a painful silence divided us like a cement wall.

"Damn it, it's not what you think! You wouldn't want me any more if I told you who I am." His voice, at first hesitant, became charged with disarming frustration.

The lump in my throat suddenly eased, taking with it all the bitterness that had gripped my heart. I'd misunderstood him. Evan didn't think I wasn't right for him; he thought he was wrong for me.

I couldn't imagine anything more absurd, more ridiculous. What did he have to confess that could possibly be so terrible? He'd already stolen my heart. The rest didn't matter, just as long as he stayed with me.

"It can't be that bad." I shook my head, a little smile on my face revealing the relief I felt in my heart.

"You don't know what you're talking about. You'd run away from me," he said, half frustrated, half regretful.

"Then why wait?" His hesitation made my voice harden again. "I'm leaving anyway."

"All right. Okay! Go, if you believe it's best for you. But think carefully," he warned, and from the nearness of his voice I knew he was right behind me. "Are you sure you want to go out this late at night? All alone? It's a long way back to your place." His voice took on a tinge of gloom that made my body go tense in spite of myself. "Aren't you afraid that shadow might catch you?"

The blood in my veins ran ice cold. I gulped before turning to face him. "So you admit something's out there!" I said accusingly, looking him in the eye. "Evan, on more than one occasion I've found myself just a step away from death. And all in one day. Do you want me to believe it's just a coincidence?"

Something in Evan's gaze made me think he was about to give in. His voice suddenly became gruff and hesitant. "There's no such thing as coincidence," he replied, articulating each word carefully. "I need you to trust me, Gemma."

"Then give me a reason to. Tell me who you are, Evan," I insisted.

He shot me a piercing look that was so fierce it made me wobble. "You sure you're strong enough to bear the burden?" he asked, his jaw clenched, trying to intimidate me. His question opened unknown doors inside me, reaching obscure places I'd never been allowed into before. Trapping me inside them. "Think it over carefully, Gemma. Some things are better left unknown," he continued, noting the glimmer of fear that appeared in my eyes. "There'll be no turning back."

I forced myself to nod, lowering my head slightly, unable to persuade my lips to open and utter the words, keeping my eyes locked onto his the whole time.

"Then it's decided. I'll explain everything." Although he'd given in, the tortured look on his face showed no sign of lessening. Evan looked around, suddenly on the alert. "But first let's go inside where it's safer."

The concern he was trying so hard to keep out of his voice was devastating. That thing must still be out there. And it was after me. I followed him up the path as my heart struggled between the satisfaction I felt over winning our argument and the fear his warning had reawakened in me.

Was I really sure I wanted to know? Maybe I wasn't ready, but it was too late to change my mind now.

27

CONFESSIONS

The path led to an ample courtyard with an imposing structure behind it. It wasn't a house, but a magnificent, ancient mansion, consisting of two floors topped with a massive yet graceful roof supported by majestic wooden beams that matched the dark window frames.

In the upper part of the façade, half of which was decorated with bas-reliefs in rough stone, were patches of light-colored plaster. Each carefully designed detail was in perfect harmony with the unspoiled natural beauty that ruled in the immense garden.

In the right-hand wing, the linear structure was interrupted by a giant, hexagonal picture window that disappeared around the back, above which ran a splendid terrace with an ornate wrought-iron railing.

I paused to admire it, forgetting for a brief moment the circumstances that had brought me there. Hesitating for a moment, I took a deep breath before beginning to climb the circular stone stairway that led up to the front door. Sensing my agitation, Evan took my hand, encouraging me with a warmhearted smile.

The large door of dark wood slowly opened. I stopped on the threshold, peering inside in search of Ginevra or whoever had opened it for us. My confusion grew when I discovered that the immense, marble-floored, grand salon was empty. Moving cautiously, I glanced at Evan, both curious and a little frightened by what I might discover.

"Please, come in," he said gallantly with a flourish of his hand as I continued to look back and forth between his face and the regal salon in front of us. "Welcome to my home. I mean, *our* home," he corrected himself after a brief hesitation.

"You mean . . . yours and Ginevra's?" I realized only after asking the question that I was afraid to hear the answer. I still wasn't sure what kind of relationship they had and the thought of the two of them living together felt like pins pressed into the palms of my hands.

"Actually there are four of us," Evan said, smiling, almost as if he sensed my jealousy.

Despite everything, I couldn't keep a bit of relief from appearing on my face. But then again, he hadn't shown any particular romantic interest in Ginevra, except for . . . I realized my emotions had completely erased the memory of their kiss from my mind. Evan definitely owed me more than one explanation in that regard. "Me and my family," he continued, weighing the last word before pausing to study my somewhat bewildered expression.

"You're *all* related?" I asked shyly, hoping he'd grasp my allusion.

"We're more like comrades, actually. War buddies, soldiers." He laughed, but I didn't see anything funny about it. Was he teasing me again? He noticed my confusion and winked at me. "We don't have a blood relationship. At least not in the way that you mean," he explained, looking me in the eye. "It's not just that. It's something even stronger." His expression had suddenly grown proud.

Knowing that Evan was beginning to trust me instilled a sense of security in me, making me feel closer to him—even though deep in my heart I felt I'd always known him. I couldn't see Evan as someone who'd come into my world to be a part of it. I saw him as a part of me.

"We watch each other's backs, at the cost of our lives," he continued while I stood there staring at him, fascinated by the fervor with which he described the sentiment that united them, jealous that Ginevra was also a part of it. "I used to think it was the strongest bond there could be between people."

"Used to?" I asked instinctively, surprised and embarrassed by my bouts of boldness, which were becoming more and more frequent.

"Before I met you," he stated simply. His dazzling smile and warm gaze searched my eyes. "Happy? I'm answering your questions." He grinned mockingly.

"Oh, you're not getting off the hook that easy!" I shot back, playing along, surprised to notice how easily I was growing accustomed to being so close to Evan. Just a few hours earlier I'd been talking to Jeneane about him when we were up in my room. I had to remember to thank her one day for that.

"Come with me," he whispered sweetly, taking my hand and gently pulling me to the center of the grand salon.

Once we were inside, the door closed behind us with a gentle click, making me spin around. I glanced at Evan, but his expression didn't betray any emotion at all.

It must have had a sophisticated sensor system. And yet a tiny voice in my head contradicted me, scoffing at me for the ease with which I tricked myself into driving away the apprehension that continued to creep up inside me like a worm inching its way through the soil.

Deep in my heart, I was afraid it was another one of the mysteries Evan would have to explain.

The white marble floor reflected the light of an immense chandelier whose fine steel branches alternated with tiny crystal spheres, forming a giant ball that hung over a low table, also of crystal, in front of a couch.

The rustic stone interior was combined with luxurious, elegant, modern decor. Narrow panels of purplish-red stone graced the walls, perfectly matching the giant couch in the same color in front of which a massive, ultrathin, plasma TV hung on a stone panel a shade darker than the walls. Soft, warm light issued from behind the panel.

To the left of the couch was a rectangular fireplace set into the wall in which a pile of cinders and ash could be seen. The upper part, which protruded slightly, was chocolate-colored, while the cherry-red plaster within was varied at intervals by small stone protrusions.

To the right, the massive hexagonal window reached almost to the entryway, offering a heavenly view of the garden, which was illuminated by small spotlights that sparkled on the ground like tiny stars.

On the opposite side of the room I glimpsed the kitchen, separated from the living room by a series of closely positioned chocolate-colored walls, set at a diagonal to each other and almost overlapping. It was huge, in light oak, raised a step higher than the room we were now in, with another giant picture window overlooking the garden.

My mouth was dry with astonishment. I'd never seen anything like it.

"This is all Ginevra's work," Evan explained, noticing how amazed I was. "She's more attached to material possessions than we are. She likes everything to be glamorous, elegant. Actually, it reflects her personality. I'd be just fine with a smaller house, but when she gets something into her head, who can stop her?" He laughed at something I didn't understand. "I wouldn't dare stand in her way!"

"Come on, let's go upstairs." He clasped my hand, looking pleased at my reaction to his home, and led me across the living room to a long, wooden, floating staircase. The steps zigzagged their way up a stone wall with a thin layer of water sliding down it like artificial rain. I couldn't help myself—I reached out to touch the silvery trickles in the miniature waterfall, giving a start when the water dampened my fingertips, almost as if I'd thought it wasn't real.

Everything was so incredibly luxurious it left me gaping. Evan grinned as he studied my expression.

"I guess you must be used to seeing the amazed expressions girls have when they first see this place," I said. *Who knows how many of them he's brought here?* I added in my mind.

He laughed, leaving me in suspense. "The girls who come here are usually too drunk to look around."

"Oh," I sighed, my heart sinking. The smile didn't leave his face. He must be used to this too, to breaking the hearts of foolish girls who fell for him, thinking they were special. After all, what did I expect? It was hard to imagine an Evan who didn't take girls up to his room, with that gorgeous smile and dark, penetrating gaze of his. Maybe it was his obvious aloofness towards others that made me think so. Even the attention he paid me at school had come as a surprise to everyone. I'd always had the impression there was some sort of mysterious relationship between us, a mystical, intense one, as if we had belonged to each other in another life. Or maybe I was just imagining it all.

"I wonder what time it is," I blurted out of embarrassment, instantly regretting the words. I'd gladly stay there with him forever.

"Must be pretty late," he said, grinning. It was as if time didn't matter to them. If Evan had said his family told the time by looking at the stars I could easily have believed him.

"My parents know I went to the prom, but they'll worry if I don't get home soon," I reflected aloud, growing nervous.

"Don't worry," Evan said softly. "I got in touch with Drake. He's already taking care of it."

"You did what? And when?" I asked, puzzled. "And who's Drake?" My agitation grew and my heartrate accelerated.

"Don't worry, Drake's one of my brothers. And you can relax, your parents won't even notice you're gone." Evan seemed to enjoy keeping me in suspense.

"How can you say that? Not long from now, my dad is going to check my room. Believe me, you have no idea how worried he gets. He'll stay up until I get home."

"Drake knows what he's doing. Your folks aren't going to notice the difference." He laughed. "You'll see for yourself soon enough."

I climbed the last step, trying to understand what he meant, but it was no use.

The upper floor was more dimly lit, with recessed lighting shining softly on a broad, unusually shaped corridor paneled in warm colors ranging from purple to brown to gold. The hallway wound its way past the different rooms, each of which had a door in dark wood that stood out against the light parquet. The hallway was so long I had the impression I was looking at an infinite reflection in a mirror. The wall opposite the stairway, in contrast, was a single pane of glass overlooking the garden.

"What's in there?" I asked, seeing a door that was far larger than all the others.

"Ginevra's room." He smiled to himself as I stared at it uneasily. "She loves to overdo it."

I was suddenly eager to go out and see how the amazing estate looked from above. Driven by that impulse, I caught up with Evan and followed him through a French door and out onto the terrace.

As he shut the door behind us, I admired the railing in wrought iron, twisted into exquisite interwoven motifs resembling a tangle of branches and flowers with snakes slithering through them here and there.

From that height we could see the entire front section of the estate and a good part of the side. A large oak tree had gracefully overgrown the terrace, its branches brushing the floor. Below, the stone path wound through the trees, illuminated by the small spotlights positioned on the ground. In the distance I glimpsed a little wooden footbridge by an enchanting pond partially hidden by the foliage.

Paradise.

The sky was intense. I'd often seen it at that hour but there was something different about it tonight. I closed my eyes, stopping to breathe in the cool, moist air.

Suddenly a gentle breeze ruffled my hair, bringing with it a scent that was even fresher and more delightful. I opened my eyes and Evan was there in front of me, though I hadn't heard his footsteps.

"Like it?" he asked.

"It's absolutely amazing," I said softly, looking for just the right words. "But where are the others? I haven't seen anyone." The thought of meeting them made me nervous.

"Simon and Ginevra must be down in the workout room. They'll turn up soon. For now, we're all alone." The sinister glimmer that flashed in his eyes made me start, but then I remembered it was Evan. I didn't know what had sent that shiver through me—the emotion of being alone with him, or *fear* caused by the very same thing. It was probably both. For some bizarre reason, I was torn between the two. I couldn't help but notice it, although my heart continued to rebel.

"I wish I had the keys to enter your world," I admitted in a small voice.

"You don't need keys. My world is your world. You just need to learn to see it through my eyes."

I wasn't sure what he meant by that. A part of me, albeit an insignificant one, was afraid of him and continued to shout that I should run away, challenging the voice of my heart that was overpowering it. Suddenly I wasn't sure I wanted to delve into conversations I might not understand, but by now I was too far in to turn back. I swallowed hard.

"My throat's a little dry," I said, my voice hoarse.

"Wait here, I'll get you some water."

Before I could say anything Evan was through the door. Two seconds later he appeared behind me, making me jump. Gaping, I stared at the crystal glass full of water he held in his hand. I hadn't even had time to step over to the railing.

"How did you do that?" I gasped, not sure whether to be amazed or terrified.

Evan didn't lower his gaze but held my eyes, moving closer cautiously. "That's what I am," he replied, his forced smile not quite masking his uneasiness.

Perplexed by his remark, I raised the glass to my lips and took a large gulp of water. I turned to look at the trees beyond the terrace, but actually stared into empty space as I tried to organize my thoughts and decide what questions to ask him. I wasn't sure I wanted to know the answers any more.

Evan had moved away, confused by my ambiguous reaction. I glanced at him as he leaned against the railing on the other side of the terrace, his fists clenching the wrought iron, his arm muscles tensed. For a moment, I was hypnotized by his tattoo. Something told me it played an important part in all this.

I forced myself to look away from him, turning back to stare at the shapes formed by the entwined tree branches. Something darted behind me at warp speed, stopping right behind my back, preceded only by a little gust of wind. I held my breath, a shiver of terror rushing over my skin.

"Sorry, I didn't mean to scare you."

His gentle whisper made the hairs on my arms stand on end. Out of the corner of my eye I looked at the spot where I'd just seen him a split second before. He wasn't there. The glass slipped from my hands and I flinched, expecting to hear the crystal shatter against the floor, but the sound never came. Evan grabbed it a second before it made impact, looking at me the whole time, as if studying my every reaction.

Confused emotion clouded my mind, preventing me from using my vocal cords. All I could do was mumble something incomprehensible as his focused gaze tried to decipher mine.

"T-thanks."

Evan handed me the glass, intact and still full. "Don't mention it." His gaze had never been so penetrating as it was just then.

"I suppose this is one of the things you need to explain to me," I managed to say.

"Yeah," he admitted.

The silence of the night covered us with its mantle as I stroked the glass with my fingers, waiting for the explanation. Evan's face sweetened, sexy little creases appearing under his eyes.

"It's you," he whispered tenderly.

"It's me what? What do you mean? I don't understand."

"I'm answering your question." He smiled and my expression darkened. "You asked me which star was mine. It's you."

His unexpected statement took my breath away but I made myself ignore it. "You know I'm not going to take that as an answer," I shot back in a vain attempt to cover up how self-conscious his remark made me.

Clearly discouraged, Evan grew serious again and stared blankly at the floor. "I don't know where to begin," he admitted, looking uneasy for the first time. "What do *you* think?" he asked with exasperating sweetness, but on his face I saw a look of fear as he waited for my answer.

Why was he asking me? No matter how hard I tried, I couldn't think of a logical explanation for anything that had to do with him—that was the whole point. Maybe I would have to set aside all logic. "Evan, there's *something* about you, something different. I can't explain what it is, but I can sense it beneath my skin and I have to admit it scares me sometimes. What I know for sure," I said, trying to keep my voice steady, "is that you have the strange habit of saving people." I was certain this would brighten his mood.

His reaction took me by surprise. "That's what you think? That I *save* people? Nothing could be further from the truth. You have no idea how wrong you are," he whispered bitterly.

"Wha—how can you say that? Look at me, I'm alive thanks to you! You've saved my life more than once. Plus . . ." I paused, debating whether it was really a good idea to give in to my ridiculous, relentless longing for answers. "Plus there was the girl in the fire," I blurted before I had the chance to regret it. I'd kept the suspicion bottled up for far too long.

"Amy," Evan whispered, looking regretful and visibly shaken by what I'd said.

"You were there," I whispered in a tiny voice, unsure if I should tremble or let the hope that he'd saved the girl light up my face. "You saved her."

"Only in part," he said, keeping his gaze low to avoid looking me in the eye.

"I was sure I recognized you in the flames! So it's true, you *did* manage to save her!"

"That's not what I said," he replied coldly. "This isn't what normally happens. You . . ." His voice broke with frustration and his face grew grim. "You shouldn't have been able to see that," he admitted all in one breath. "What else did you see?"

On the one hand Evan was plainly upset by the unexpected turn in our conversation, but on the other he seemed to need answers himself.

"I saw you there with her. She was alive. You were holding her hand, but the flames were getting higher and higher," I said, sorting through my jumbled memories. "A cloud of smoke covered you. I couldn't see past it and you both disappeared. I *tried* to get them to pull you out of there, but nobody would lis—" I had to stop. Evan's face had become a dark mask torn by remorse. If I'd reached out my hand I was sure I could have touched his suffering with my fingertips.

"It's not like you think," he said coldly, his gaze lost in a memory all his own.

I'd never seen Evan so serious. I was shocked to notice that the iron railing he had clasped was now twisted.

"You mean you didn't manage to save Amy?" I made myself look away from his hands, afraid the door that had opened between us would suddenly close.

He was consumed by the guilt and remorse that had appeared on his face the moment I reminded him of what he'd done. My glimmer of hope that the little girl was alive slipped away like a ghost.

"Don't blame yourself, Evan." My hand obeyed the impulse to rest on his arm. "You were brave enough to rush into the flames to try to rescue her. You risked your life for someone you didn't even know."

Evan raised his eyes and looked into mine. When they met, I knew something was wrong. Suddenly I remembered how quickly he'd moved a moment ago and my instinct reawakened, warning me not to go down this path.

"Weren't you afraid of dying?" I whispered.

Evan didn't move a muscle. The weight of the silence that fell threatened to crush me. It was so deep I could hear his lips part. "I couldn't have," he gulped, looking almost frightened.

"What do you mean, Evan? You have to be clearer; I'm still not getting what you're saying," I insisted. There was no turning back now.

Evan frowned as if holding back tears, in the grip of an uncontrollable emotion. I wondered what could be so traumatic and so important as to make him this frustrated. He looked away and narrowed his eyes before turning back to me, as though he needed a second to summon his courage.

"I could never be afraid of dying, Gemma," he admitted.

My heart trembled. "Why not?" I asked cautiously, filled with apprehension. Evan looked straight into my eyes, making my whole body shiver.

"Because I'm already dead."

I gave another shudder and my blood ran ice cold.

28

INSTINCT AND DESIRE

"Gemma, say something, please."

I couldn't. I couldn't feel a single muscle in my body. I was frozen. Trapped in a slab of ice. For some time I'd suspected Evan was hiding a dark side from me, but no matter how afraid of his secret a part of me had been, I could never have imagined anything like this. It was too much for me.

It would have been too much for anyone.

His words were still whirling in my head, trapping me inside a limbo from which I felt I would never return, my gaze lost in the distance over his shoulder as I tried to avoid looking into his eyes. I could see he was anxiously waiting for me to respond.

As soon as my brain had processed the information, the cloud of confusion fogging my mind dissolved, replaced by the rush of adrenaline that immediately followed. Without warning, the little part of me that had always been afraid of him came to the fore in my mind, taking control and yelling at me for not listening to its repeated warnings. As fear gripped me, I bolted for the door, guided by an irresistible instinct, but before I could reach it, it slammed shut. I stopped, petrified. Anxiety flooded me and I could feel my chest heaving spasmodically, but it was as if my body no longer belonged to me. Before I could look for another way out Evan appeared in front of me, barring the way. My legs threatened to give way under my weight. My heart was pounding so hard it throbbed in my ears as if it, too, were searching for a way out. My head began to spin, warning me it was about to surrender. Never before had I felt so powerfully the emotion that filled me at that moment: pure terror. Black. Ominous. Sinister.

Hands rested on my arms in a gentle embrace. I felt their warmth but my mind was somewhere else, lost in darkness, while my body was paralyzed, nothing more than an empty shell.

"Calm down. Everything's fine."

I looked at him but could barely see.

"Gemma."

Evan's voice was very close to my face, as if he were trying to come in through my gaze and join me in whatever place I'd lost myself in. My body trembled, warning me not to return.

"Look at me, Gemma. Look me in the eye. It's still me, it's Evan. Nothing's changed."

I couldn't snap out of it. Since my body wasn't able to escape from him, my mind had sought shelter somewhere far away. I was trapped in a dark cell with no way out.

"Don't be afraid of me. I would never hurt you. Please, stay with me."

My mind clearing for a fleeting moment, I understood what he was saying and fought with all my might to silence the voice in my head that continued to scream at me to run away.

The love I felt for him that had been buried by his confession was trying hard to crawl up out of the darkness into which it had descended, making its way past the almost uncontrollable urge to flee. And while that part of me wanted to escape him, the other part, which was larger but being suffocated by the former, was screaming that I should stay.

"Here, drink some water," he said, concerned, handing me the glass, which was still full.

My lips trembled as they parted and I took a swallow, trying hard not to let my teeth chatter against the glass. "I need to sit down," I admitted hesitantly, resting my hand on his arm to steady myself.

I'd barely perceived a break in our physical contact—as if he hadn't moved at all—when I was astonished to discover he was holding a giant cushion in his hands.

He'd done it again.

I cast him a sidelong glance.

"Sorry," he said in a soft, tender voice before looking at me. "I'd better take this more slowly, huh?"

"Sounds like a good idea," I admitted, embarrassed to realize he'd been right all along when he warned me I wouldn't be able to handle it. Still, he couldn't blame me; his terrible secret weighed more than I could bear. I wasn't sure yet whether or not I could deal with such a shocking confession.

"It's just that with you it's so easy to lose control." He smiled and helped me put the cushion, which was big enough for both of us, on the floor and sit down. "It's been like that from day one," he admitted, gently sweeping my hair back over my shoulder.

I forced myself to look him in the eye, trying to repress the little patch of fear nestled in the back of my brain that stubbornly refused to go away. By now the worst was over, and knowing it comforted me.

"Nothing like this has ever happened to me before," he said as I looked at him in silence. "It's like I go into tilt when you're around." He stifled a laugh. "Completely haywire." His face brightened, though cautiously. "It feels so good to be getting this off my chest."

I struggled to understand the logic behind what he was saying, adamantly refusing to acknowledge the fact that I was going to need to set aside all logic if I was to be on his wavelength.

"From day one?" I repeated, suddenly overcome with emotion. Did Evan also feel that strange connection between us?

"Ever since I came to Lake Placid. Since the first time I saw you, in the woods." Evan leaned closer, his face an inch from my lips as he studied my expression, clearly interested in something I didn't know was in me. "I have no idea how you do it. I've wondered a hundred times. My body reacts strangely to your presence. I can't control it when I'm with you. Maybe that's why you can see me when you shouldn't be able to. I shouldn't have gotten so close, but I couldn't help it. I was so fascinated by you. The urge to see you—to *touch* you—was so hard to resist that I gave in to the temptation each and every time. I lost myself. You led me to madness and then brought me back again.

"I can't resist you. I *don't want* to resist you. It's like I can breathe only when you're with me, only when you're near. The rest of the time is an eternity of suffocating breathlessness. I've battled myself, I've battled everyone, but I haven't been able to hold back what I feel. I've discovered I *need* you, Gemma." His intense gaze and black-velvet voice left me dazed. It felt like a powerful poison that dulled my senses and clouded my mind. His words intoxicated me, his whole self, his sensual voice. I was on the verge of passing out, with his scent so close and so strong it made my head spin.

"Wait," I said, having taken a moment to process what he'd said. "What do you mean I can see you when I shouldn't be able to?"

Evan looked down and smiled to himself, his voice as low and penetrating as a sinister shudder. "Have you ever found yourself, when you're all alone, detecting a *presence* in the silence? You can't see it, but you know it's there."

A wave of emotion washed over me and my eyes opened wide. I was petrified. "It was you," I said in a tiny voice, thinking back on the feeling I was being watched that had become so familiar to me. "It was you all along," I repeated, struggling not to fall into a state of shock.

Evan nodded cautiously and smiled, looking almost pleased.

"And was it you who wrote my name on the mirror?" The question came out all on its own as I tried to get a grip. Embarrassment colored my cheeks at the thought of Evan in my bathroom and me naked in the shower. "Why did you do that?"

Evan shrugged. Maybe he wasn't really sure himself. "I don't know what got into me. I thought it was crazy but I couldn't help it. My fingers moved all on their own. I felt insane. I wanted to understand, no matter what. I probably thought I'd find the key to understanding who you are." He looked at me out of the corner of his eye, his lips suddenly enchanting. "Or maybe it was only to distract myself." He winked and my face flushed instantly. I opened my mouth, unable to find anything to say, and Evan raised his hands defensively. "I only took one little peek!"

"You creep!"

"Okay, okay, I deserve that." He laughed, but this time I wasn't sure he was kidding. I punched his arm and his laughter instantly died down, his eyes locked tenderly onto mine. He'd felt the same sensation I had.

"Why do you think I feel energy running through me every time you touch me?" I'd tried to ignore it, but instead of fading away it continued to tingle under my skin, as though there was a part of me, deep down, that wanted to understand its message.

Meanwhile, Evan had lost himself in a world all his own. "I don't know. You're my demon and my angel on earth," he said, deep in thought. There was tenderness in his words, tenderness mixed with melancholy.

"It's so *bizarre!* Part of me is still waiting for you to tell me this is all a big joke."

"And the rest of you?" he asked, almost as if afraid to hear my answer.

"The rest of me," I confessed, looking into his eyes, "knew it all along." As the words came out, I realized along with Evan that it was true. "I didn't know how it was possible—I thought it was just an obsession—but I kept *sensing* you, even when you weren't there."

"An obsession, huh?" he said, a grin appearing on his face. "You thought you were obsessed with me." He raised an eyebrow, looking pleased.

"I couldn't help it, I didn't know what to think!" I stammered. I made myself change the subject. "So what else can you do, read people's minds?" I asked, holding my breath as I waited for the answer, suddenly afraid. His scrutinizing my most intimate thoughts would be more terrible than his seeing me naked.

Evan, on the other hand, seemed amused. "No, I can't do that. Although—" he laughed to himself—"I have to admit I wish I could. It's a pain having to turn to Ginevra every time I can't figure out what you're thinking."

"Hold on—Ginevra? What's she got to do with me?" I asked, both confused and annoyed because he'd brought her up. Then came a glimmer of clarity. "You mean . . ."

Evan continued to nod, his lips curved sensually upward. His expression was finally free of his past agony.

Ginevra could read people's minds. What on earth could possibly be worse than that? *My God . . .*

"Don't worry." Evan broke the thread that my brain was mechanically weaving into a tapestry of awareness as it worked backwards through my memories. "Some things stay between the two of you. She'd never tell me anything you wouldn't tell me yourself. She considers it a sort of woman's code of honor. We've even argued about it a few times."

I exhaled, unable to keep my heart from racing. I should remember to thank Ginevra if I got the chance.

"In any case, I'd never ask her for any information that's too personal. In compensation," he said, his smile growing crafty, "I have my own way of communicating with you. Let's just say it's like *you* can read *my* mind." He laughed out loud.

My eyes opened wide as I suddenly understood. "I've heard you! I've heard you in my mind!" I exclaimed, at the mercy of conflicting emotions. The pieces of this insane puzzle were starting to come together. There was nothing wrong with me after all. I should have just listened to my instinct. I wasn't crazy, I'd actually heard his thoughts. The relief of knowing this cleared the way for curiosity.

I looked into his eyes as his voice echoed gently inside my head. Deep inside, as though it were coming from my heart. *"It's called epis-numa. It's a tiny region of the brain that mortals don't even know they have. My mind can link to it, forming a unilateral connection. I can send my thoughts to you, even from miles away. It's the exact opposite of Ginevra's power, which works in the opposite direction by connecting to the epis-mantra."* He smiled, enjoying my astonished expression.

"Normally it only happens if I'm the one who decides to establish that connection, but with you it's different. You make me lose control," he said, frowning, still confused by the situation. "Once the connection's made, the mind of anyone I want is completely under my control," he said, and a part of me trembled at this confession.

"Have you ever forced me to do something?" I asked, disconcerted.

Evan smiled. "I've never been able to." I didn't have to read his mind to see how frustrated it made him. "Although I have to admit I've tried lots of times."

"Well, if it's any consolation, my dad always says I'm the most obstinate person on the planet," I joked.

Evan laughed, turning back to look at me. "I have the power to bend anyone to my will. *Any mortal soul.* But when I'm with you, I don't even have power over my own thoughts. I can't maintain my ethereal form very long and I materialize unexpectedly. My mind connects to yours without my permission. It's like you unmask every spell I'm capable of. My powers seem stronger in your presence, but I can't control them. They elude me. My body and mind respond to you and not to me any more. How do you explain that?" He seemed to find the mystery irritating and fascinating in equal parts. His eyes had lit up and were studying mine, as though he expected to find the answer there.

"If it hadn't been for Ginevra, I never would have found out about it. The first time it happened was at school, when you were sorting out your locker. She was listening to you and all of a sudden she heard my voice in your thoughts. Both of us were floored. We couldn't explain how it had happened. I already knew you could see me, but nothing like that had ever happened to me before."

I searched my mind for that hazy memory and blushed, remembering the emotion I'd experienced at the time. It felt like months had gone by since that day. So much had happened since then, culminating in his confession that finally explained the mystery. Everything was taking shape and coloring in the picture I'd slowly pieced together bit by bit. "You did it at the prom too, didn't you?"

"I did it intentionally that time," he said, grinning. "Speaking of which, you're a great dancer," he whispered. "Really good rhythm."

I blushed. Was it a real compliment or was he just teasing me? "That's because I used to climb trees a lot," I blathered. Huh? What on earth had made me tell him something like that? I could already imagine him trying to hold back a smile. "In any case, you're not so bad yourself. Dancing, I mean. You didn't step on my toes even once."

Evan laughed out loud. My attempt to downplay things had failed miserably.

"You think I'm silly, don't you?"

"Very," he said, a sparkle in his eye, "but I like it." He looked at me insistently and I hurried to change the topic.

"What about my bike? Are you the one who fixed it?" The question came out spontaneously and, given the circumstances, "fixed" sounded like the wrong word. But it was a mystery I couldn't stop thinking about.

"Ginevra again."

"What else can she do?" This conversation was surreal.

Evan laughed. "It'd be quicker to tell you what she *can't* do."

"And the others? Do they have superpowers too?" I didn't know how else to phrase it.

Evan threw his head back and laughed again. I frowned. What was so funny? No one had ever made me feel so dumb before.

Unexpectedly, he brushed his thumb across my lips, staring at me intensely. Emotion washed over me. Why on earth did he always have to do that to me?

"I'm sorry. We're not used to hearing them called that. We're not characters out of some Disney movie, you know." He winked at me, a smile hiding behind his reply.

At least he knew Disney movies. That was already something.

"So do I need to be careful about what I think when I'm around your brothers?" I insisted, determined to finally pull down all the veils shrouding the truth about them.

"No. We Descendants can't read minds. Not the three of us, at least. That's Ginevra's special ability," he said, looking at the railing in front of him as though choosing his words carefully. He looked at me for a moment, reading my expression, and blurted, "Hers and her Sisters'. Witches can read minds."

"Wha—What?! Back up. Ginevra's . . . a *witch*?!"

I could barely say the word. Part of me was still expecting someone to pop out at any moment and point at the hidden cameras. I couldn't believe this was really happening, that it wasn't a joke or a dream or one of those stories I loved reading. This was *my* world. The world I'd grown up in, where there was a clear boundary between what was real and what couldn't possibly be real. Now that wall was crumbling and everything was blending together—though this wasn't some new world I'd been dragged into. Evan was just helping me to decipher my own world in a different way, to see things with new eyes, eyes that could see past that boundary. *All of this was so insane.*

Evan looked more and more amused by my reaction. "She used to be a Witch, but take my advice: never bring it up around her. She doesn't like to talk about it. It puts her in a bad mood."

"Not a problem," I said, shaking my head. "Thanks for the warning."

The silence that followed seeped into my bones like snake venom. We both knew where the conversation was taking us. The wait for that moment had felt endless, and now that the time had finally come, I was afraid the words wouldn't find a way past the lump in my throat. And yet somehow I had to find the strength to ask him the question. *I had* to force myself at all costs, because I sensed the answer was important, even if deep down in my heart I was afraid it would change everything.

"Evan." I swallowed, avoiding his gaze and trying to keep my voice steady. He sensed how serious I was and looked straight at me, taking my breath away. I managed to continue. "You said 'Descendants.' What are you?" Freed from the burden of those words, I finally looked into his eyes, just in time to see something flash across them.

"I knew you would ask that." His low voice was filled with bitterness again.

For an infinite moment, neither of us opened our mouths. The silence was so oppressive I suddenly wished I hadn't asked. If I'd been able to, I would have rewound time like a tape recorder and erased it. Evan locked his eyes onto mine and stared at me with matchless intensity. "I'm an Angel, Gemma." His voice caressed my name so sweetly that my heart prevented my reason from fully grasping his solemn confession.

Evan stroked the back of my hand, encouraging me to respond. He was probably afraid my mind would get lost in the darkness again, but for the first time I wasn't upset by his confession. Part of me, as though it had always suspected it, told me it couldn't be any other way.

"Does it shock you?" he asked gently, concerned by my silence.

"I don't think so," I said, unsure. "It's just, why are all of you here?" I had no idea why my brain had come up with that question, but my voice had obeyed its command before my lips had the chance to hold it back.

Evan's gaze wavered, as if, of all my questions, this one perturbed him the most. His face filled with sadness. "Well, you see, we're rather special Angels." It was as if an insurmountable wall had risen up, breaking the connection we'd established. I sensed how hard he was trying to get around it, and I couldn't understand why he didn't just knock it down.

"Special? What do you mean, exactly?"

"The race we belong to is a bit unusual. It's our lineage that makes us different, our bloodline."

"I still don't understand."

Evan filled his lungs and looked directly into my eyes, making sure he had my full attention. "I know what I'm about to tell you might sound crazy, but my brothers and I are descended from the children that Eve once hid from God, ashamed that she hadn't yet purified them by bathing them in the sacred river."

As Evan studied my expression I tried to pretend the bizarre story wasn't fazing me. I suspected my irregular heartbeat was giving me away, though.

"When God discovered those children, He decreed that, as punishment, that which had been hidden then would remain hidden for all eternity. That's probably why some people call us Subterranean Angels—they think creatures like us live underground, but actually the name came from our curse. In any case, over the last few centuries no one's talked about us any more, with the exception of a few Norwegian legends that stood the test of time."

"Why on earth should anyone be punished like that? Isn't God supposed to forgive everyone?" I blurted. Then I realized how ridiculous I sounded. Me, talking about God. I still couldn't delve into this new world without the suspicion I was being made fun of.

"Of course," he said sternly, "but even He has His laws. A world, a society, a family without rules would descend into chaos. It would be hell."

"What did you mean by 'hidden'?"

"We didn't fall from grace, we merely . . . descended," he murmured, a grim look on his face.

"What does that mean for you? Is your soul lost?"

Evan laughed to himself, seeing the effect his confession was having on me. "My soul isn't lost. It's just hovering between heaven and hell."

I stared at him, bewildered.

"Here, on *earth*," he explained, smiling. No matter how hard he tried to hide it, I still detected a touch of sadness in his eyes. "All things considered, it's not so bad. We're just halfway between the terrestrial world and Eden."

The look on his face snapped me out of my daze and made me seriously consider what he was saying. Hadn't I already seen proof of his powers? Why should I think he was only kidding?

Like a raging river, the explanations I'd cautiously dammed up burst free and washed over me.

Eden? What was he talking about? Could it all be true?

Angels, heaven, hell . . . *My God.*

I froze, thinking back to our escape on his motorcycle. If he really was an Angel, his opposite must also exist: fearsome demons and who knew what other monstrous creatures. A shudder ran down my spine, making the hairs on my arms stand on end. I began to feel the burden of all that information. It was threatening to overwhelm me.

"Everything okay?" Evan asked, concerned. I hadn't managed to hide how shaken I was and my face must have turned incredibly pale.

"It's not fair, it's not your fault. Millennia have gone by. It's unfair that you should pay for someone else's mistake."

"I like to think it won't last forever," he admitted. "I've always lived with the hope of Redemption." I couldn't tell from the tone of his voice if he was trying to convince me or only himself. "After all, it's not so different for you mortals. You inhabit the earth to atone for someone else's sins too. It's a purgatory for you just like it is for us. You were denied Eden, and that's why you're made to experience suffering and difficulties every day. It's a test, don't you see? God could have cast Eve and her companion into hell like He did with those who were punished for betraying Him, but He gave you another chance. The chance to *choose.* That's why mankind has free will. God doesn't want to force you to love Him, He wants each and every person to freely choose to do so. Only by proving they're worthy, by following His laws, can humans return to Eden, from whence they came. Why shouldn't the same thing be true for me? Why shouldn't I be able to prove I'm worthy too?"

It was the longest, most sincere statement Evan had ever made to me. His voice had grown passionate. In his tone I heard intense hope, but the hint of sadness that lingered in his gaze suggested that wasn't all. Something else was eluding me.

"I'm sure you can do it, Evan," I said encouragingly yet cautiously as I felt doubt rise inside me, pushing to break free. "And when you . . . Um, I mean . . ."

"What do you want to know?" Evan asked, hearing the hesitation in my voice.

"I've seen you in your angelic form. Sometimes I only sensed your presence, but other times *I saw you*, Evan. And you didn't look like a ghost or a spirit. You were flesh and blood. So, well, I was wondering, is your ethereal body somehow *tangible*?"

"Not to mortals," he answered quickly, as if accustomed to answering that particular question, "but you, Gemma, have the power to change that." He looked into my eyes to underline how important that detail was to him. Glancing away, he stared at the floor, as though in some way he felt overwhelmed. "No one had ever touched me before, and the emotion I felt the first time you did was so powerful it made me want to learn more about you."

A gust of wind ran over my skin, ominous yet familiar, making me shiver. Evan looked up cautiously, as if afraid of frightening me. I swallowed with difficulty, my throat dry from emotion. My breathing grew irregular as his eyes, suddenly as gray as molten silver, searched mine inexorably. He'd transformed. The emotion paralyzed me, taking my breath away.

"*Can you see me?*" Evan's voice enveloped me like a warm mantle as our gazes remained silently entwined, exploring the mystery.

"Shouldn't I?" I said hesitantly, almost under my breath.

"You're the only person who's ever looked me straight in the eye."

I sighed, my heart trembling in my chest. "Can I . . . can I touch you?"

Evan slowly raised his hand, palm toward me. Driven by a deep desire, I extended my hand toward his, barely grazing his fingers. He swallowed, and after a moment closed the space between us, resting his hand against mine, palm to palm. "My God." His eyes wavered, as if moved by ecstatic emotion, while a tingle ran over me, a hot shiver that moved from my skin to my heart.

"It's an incredible sensation," I whispered, staring at our hands pressed together.

"Incredible and extraordinary."

My eyes returned to Evan's and found them waiting for me.

"Isn't it?" He smiled and for a moment the complicity of that shared smile united me to him more than a thousand words ever could.

"I have another question," I said, after a moment of silence.

"I'm listening."

"Only if you promise you won't laugh," I warned, embarrassed by what I was about to ask.

"Promise," he said, holding back a grin.

I shifted awkwardly on the cushion and crossed my legs. "This is going to sound stupid—but aren't angels supposed to have wings?"

Evan burst out laughing, making me feel ridiculous.

"You love making fun of me! You promised you wouldn't laugh!" I said, frowning. "I'd like to see you in my shoes." I nudged his arm. The instant I touched him, his face grew serious, as if a violent emotion had struck him.

"Why don't you see for yourself?" he dared me, leaning his back slightly in my direction, a teasing, challenging look on his face.

I blushed, staring at his back, and for a second my heart beat faster.

"Go on, it's okay," he said, looking me in the eye. Touching his hand hadn't been enough to bring down the reserve between us, but then again I'd never been so bold before. And yet I suddenly felt a strange emotion beneath my skin, a mysterious instinctual knowledge that touching him again would carry me into a new world. I knew he was only teasing me, but the temptation was too powerful to ignore.

I reached out hesitantly, seeking his gaze, and in his eyes—suddenly filled with desire—I saw a glimmer of impatience to feel that contact burn on his skin. I swallowed and gently rested my palm on his back.

My hand moved cautiously, searching for anything unusual, as Evan's muscles flexed beneath my fingers. Even his shirt couldn't block the electricity produced by the connection between our bodies.

I felt the overwhelming urge to touch his skin without the obstacle of fabric. Responding to my longing, Evan suddenly turned around, grabbed the hand I'd touched him with and in an instant was on top of me, my body beneath his, pressed down into the cushion as if swept away by an unstoppable wave of pure emotion, an impulse he'd been unable to control. I breathed rapidly against his mouth as my warmth combined with his, his hair brushed my forehead, his fiery gaze locked onto mine as our fingers laced together over my head. My heart skipped a beat and for a second I thought it had stopped forever. His dog tag brushed against my chin and I reached out to grab it, but, like a furious whirlwind dragging me away, I was stunned to discover Evan still sitting in his spot on the cushion beside me, my hand resting on his back. I gulped, utterly bewildered, my breathing still accelerated because of the scene that had dazzled me like a movie shown only in my head; a crisp, clear view of reality that had swept me away. Still stunned by the intense emotion, I couldn't tell whether my mind had been catapulted into the memory of my dream when I touched his body, or if it was just the reflection of my desire for him guiding me.

"Well? Find anything?"

I shook my head, his melodious yet slightly sarcastic voice snapping me out of my daze. Suddenly, doubt gripped me. "Did you do that?" I asked him point-blank.

"Do what?" he said, confused.

"I saw . . . Oh, never mind." I stopped myself from telling Evan about my vision; he definitely would have teased me about it.

Evan shot around and squeezed my arm. "What did you see, Gemma? No, wait, don't tell me." He was shaken, fascinated, his eyes growing wider. "You saw the two of us. I grabbed you and pinned you down to the floor, didn't I?"

My heart lurched. He'd seen the same thing? How was it possible? I'd felt powerful sensations on my skin as if I'd actually experienced it. Could it be that the same was true for Evan? My God. What was happening between us? Neither of us seemed able to understand it.

"You saw it too?" I asked, stunned by our powerful connection.

"It's incredible. It's like we're in symbiosis. Sometimes I feel struck by a strange power when I'm around you. It's a bond between us, some inexplicable alchemy. Can't you feel it too? It's impossible to resist. Or *control*."

That particular detail seemed to disturb him the most.

"But what happened, exactly? Did you project those images into my mind?"

"I didn't do anything. It's like our minds joined together for a moment, connected in some parallel world where we followed our instincts, our desires, despite the fact that our bodies were here. When you touched me, I felt an irresistible desire to touch you and I imagined doing it."

"I imagined it too. But it felt like we actually did." I blushed; I hadn't meant to say that.

"Yeah." Evan was frowning, absorbed in the new mystery, as if nothing so fascinating had happened to him for a long, long time. "It's incredible, it's like my powers get stronger when you're around, but I'm not even sure it depends on me." He studied me for a few seconds, amazed, and smiled with that hint of mockery I was starting to get used to. "So, what about those wings? Manage to find them?" he asked, grinning.

"Very funny."

"You can always try again." He raised an eyebrow and his smile grew sly. "I don't mind. Why don't you take a closer look? Maybe you'll be luckier this time."

I gave him a push, making him turn back around. "Don't make me feel any dumber than I already did asking you!"

"You're never dumb," he said, his face unbearably sweet, before smiling to himself and adding, "Okay, I admit it: all that stuff about the wings, just kidding. It's only a legend. We don't need wings to move from one dimension to the other. They're parallel worlds and we're souls, essences as pure as air, so we can cross through them. If it weren't like that, even mortals would need them to be able to cross to the other side after they die."

I had to admit his explanation made sense. "Are there many others like you? How can you be recognized?"

"We can't. And there are millions of us around the world. We blend in with people and nobody ever notices us. No one knows who we really are. There's just one difference that manifests in our natural form compared to our human form, but no one even sees it because we're invisible to mortals in our natural form."

"Your eyes," I said, beating him to it.

Evan nodded. I was shaken by the recent memory of his silvery gaze lost in mine. But now his eyes were darker than the night.

"In our physical form, they go back to the color they were during our mortal existence. But when there's no physical body to mask them, our eyes are gray, like liquid silver. The soul casts off the body, revealing its colors: pure and transparent, like ether. But when that happens no one can see us."

"No one but me," I reminded him.

"Yeah. It's so strange."

I ran a hand down his arm where the tattoo wrapped around it. He followed my movements with his eyes.

"And then there's that," he said, a touch of melancholy in his voice. "You can see it, can't you?"

"I shouldn't be able to, should I?" I said.

Evan smiled. "That's the sign of the children of Eve, a constant reminder of who we are. We each get one right after we die. It's our curse."

"Does it hurt?" I asked.

"Not as much as the burden of having it," he admitted. Seeing that it saddened me, he smiled. "Any more questions?" he asked eagerly. He seemed to be teasing me again. Or, more likely, he was just happy to finally be getting it all out in the open.

It didn't take me very long to think it over; an endless list had already formed in my mind, but one question stood out against all the rest, driven by a frightened, trembling, little voice in some dark corner of my mind. I couldn't silence it. "You said I was in danger. Why?"

Evan tensed. He clenched his jaw, his hands balled into fists on the cushion beneath us. I seemed to have asked him the one question I shouldn't have. The only one he would never have wanted to answer.

And yet he had to. I had the *right* to know. "Evan, you've got to tell me." I stared directly into his eyes with a determination

I didn't even know I had. "What was that shadow? I *saw* it as it was chasing us."

Something was keeping him from answering, something inside him. He'd already told me who he was. What else could he say that was so shocking? What was he hiding?

"Evan, answer me!"

"What you saw—" He hesitated.

"What was it?" I insisted.

"An Angel of Death," he blurted. "An Executioner."

The whole world fell apart at my feet. *An Angel of Death.*

What did it want from me? The answer came in the form of a shiver that ran down my spine.

Angels, heaven, hell . . . What was really going on? As I stared into space I felt Evan's gaze seeking mine. Unable to react, I'd done the only thing I could do: detach myself from everything and hide away in a warm, cozy shell behind the inaccessible doors of my mind. I could barely hear Evan's voice lingering in the air, as inarticulate and muffled as an echo.

"He's come for you. You shouldn't still be here, Gemma. I'm sorry," he said, confirming the terrible suspicion that had left me frozen in its icy grip. My heart skipped a beat when I heard him say it aloud.

"You mean—" I stammered.

"Your time was up the minute that semi came at you. Death was waiting for you."

I shuddered like never before. "You saved me," I said, finally understanding the importance of those words. *My time was up.* "So it was you who healed my head and my ankle? You hadn't really gone away. That warmth came from *you*!"

Evan nodded.

"Amazing," I whispered to myself. "You changed my fate."

"I only got in its way, I'm afraid."

I looked up at him. "Where is he now?" I forced myself to ask, gripped by a terrifying new fear.

"He'll come back looking for you, but don't worry, he won't come close as long as you're with us. I won't let him."

"Are you here to protect me?" I asked, caught between gratitude and uncertainty. "Is that your mission?"

His eyes darted around, as if my question had made him uncomfortable. He bowed his head and hesitated a moment before answering. "*Tvaddhetunā sarvaṃ saṃçayasthaṃ karomi sarvaṃ tu sahasrakṛtvaḥ punar akariṣyam.*" His voice was grim yet mesmerizing, sending a shiver through me.

"What does that mean?" I whispered.

"That I'm risking everything for you, but I'd do it again a thousand times." Another smile spread over his face. "You're safe here with us, don't worry," he whispered, gently touching the tip of my nose. I had the impression he'd put on a mask, that he wasn't being completely honest.

The deep feeling of protection only Evan could provide flooded through me. Even so, that frightened little voice was making its way through my thoughts, trying to resurface. I tried to push it down.

He turned toward me, an intense look on his face. "Don't struggle against your fear. It's normal. It isn't wrong to feel it. You'd be wrong *not* to feel it."

What he said hit me like a blast of air. How could he know my exact emotions? "How— You said you couldn't read minds. How can you know what I'm feeling?"

He smiled. "I've learned to recognize your body language, Gemma. I can decipher the look on your face." For some reason his expression turned sly. "Your unconscious can reveal secrets that you yourself aren't even aware of. It goes where thoughts can't, plucks inaccessible strings. It's hard for me to interpret at times, especially when it comes to you."

"You can read people's unconscious?" I asked, stunned.

Evan nodded and looked at me, very focused. "I can see inside you, Gemma. I can read your most hidden emotions through—"

"—dreams," we both said at the same time.

"My God! So . . ." Suddenly everything was clear. It hadn't been a coincidence that I remembered those dreams so vividly I couldn't tell them apart from real life. There was a reason, even if I hadn't been able to understand where the dream ended and the real world began. "It was real. It was all real! I didn't just imagine it, you were *actually* there."

"It was all real," Evan said, stifling a smile, one eyebrow slightly raised.

My heart reacted by flooding me with heat and sending an alarm signal to my brain. Agitation rose in me as I realized what it meant. My cheeks instantly grew flushed and my heart throbbed violently in my temples. Instinctively I raised my fingers to my lips and felt them tremble, exulting.

Evan and I had kissed.

The weight of his gaze was on me, impatient to meet my own, but I was sure he had an impertinent little smile on his face and I didn't know if I could handle it. Meanwhile, my heart wanted to leap out of my chest for joy. For some time now I'd suspected my emotions had been too intense for the dream to have been simply a figment of my imagination.

Evan and I had kissed. The clear image of that kiss rose up in my mind again, coloring my cheeks.

A memory.

With a mix of embarrassment and euphoria, I made myself break the silence. "So you like the constellations."

Evan laughed at my awkward attempt to change the subject. "The origins of the constellations are ancient, you know. Since the dawn of time, man has observed the sky and drawn imaginary lines connecting one luminous spot to the other. Each culture composed its figures using its own imagination. What to the Greeks was a bear was a wagon to the Romans, a hippopotamus to the Egyptians, and a dipper to the Chinese. Like it is here, can you imagine?" His explanation made me smile. "But I've always found it interesting how the Greeks, in particular, turned the sky into a stage on which heroes and gods performed, led by the imagination. In my mind, the stories make the sky a sort of giant picture book, and every night for thousands of years its characters have come to life before our eyes. All you need to do is look at them." His voice had softened to a hush as a whirlwind of emotion filled his eyes, which had rested on me the whole time.

"Can you . . . can you make me dream whatever you want?" I whispered, embarrassed and tripping over my words.

"It's your mind, Gemma. Dreams are mirrors that reflect your soul, your true essence. They reveal your fears, your anguish, your *desires*." With this last word, he stopped and stared at me. "It's your unconscious that comes out, I can only try to interpret it."

"And are you able to?" I asked, suddenly filled with the fear of what Evan might be able to read inside of me.

"Not always," he admitted regretfully. "With you it's harder. That's another way things don't work like they should with you."

"Don't work? What do you mean?" I found the courage to meet his gaze.

"I've never come across a soul like yours before. It's complex, different. Almost indecipherable. When I'm in your dreams, it's like your mind creates interference and won't let me hide from you. It feels like there's an irresistible power between us, a giant magnet that pulls me towards you."

I gulped, amazed that his feelings were so similar to mine.

"My powers are complementary. Through the unconscious, I can fully read anyone I want. It's kind of like having the key to a complex secret code. I can interpret the symbols, limitations, and weaknesses, and bend a person's will as I please when I'm connected to them. I'd never been in someone's dreams more than once; generally all I need is one night to create a detailed map of the person. But then I met you. You shouldn't be able to hear my voice. That is, the conscious part of you shouldn't, only your soul should. See why I'm so fascinated by you?" His expression turned into a grin. "Drake says I'm drawn to you like a bear to honey." He smiled at the joke and then grew serious again. "Looks like I just can't resist you."

"Ah, so you're . . . a bear?" I said, raising an eyebrow before I could keep the question from leaving my lips. Only from his warm breath on my neck did I realize Evan had moved closer to me. My heart trembled in my chest as his lips grazed my skin, resting gently on the curve of my neck. "You can't be meaning to pounce on me."

"Why not?" His whisper filled me with heat.

I half closed my eyes and instinctively parted my lips, savoring the memory of his mouth on mine. Evan brushed his lips over my neck, moving slowly up toward my chin. I felt a hot shiver every time his mouth touched me.

"Do you feel what I feel?" he whispered as his lips moved sweetly toward my ear.

"What do you feel?" I whispered back, entranced by this hypnotic enchantment.

Evan ran his lips up the curve of my chin, moving them in a slow search for my mouth as my heart raced like never before. He delicately brushed the corner of my lips, leaving me burning with desire, consumed with anticipation. Without moving away he raised his eyes slightly to meet mine, hesitating as if seeking my consent in them, permission I'd already given him even before he'd asked for it.

"This," he whispered, his voice enveloping me like warm silk. Slowly his mouth touched mine, ever so slightly, with endless tenderness, as my lips moved imperceptibly to follow his. "You are my dark paradise," he murmured to himself. My breathing seemed to have abandoned me. Languid heat spread over my eyes, forcing me to close them as I let myself be borne away on a wave of emotions, longing for Evan to finally kiss me.

"*A-hem.*" Someone nearby cleared their throat a second before Evan could fully press his lips against mine. "Am I interrupting something?"

Ginevra.

Evan's irresistible scent lingered on me like a mysterious spell from which I couldn't awaken. I was so bewitched by the warmth of his lips so close to mine that for a second I considered ignoring Ginevra, grabbing him by the shirt and pulling him back toward me. There was nothing in the world that could make me want to stop. As I forced myself to hold back the urge, Ginevra let out a little laugh.

I felt my face go pale as I realized what she found so funny. *I'd forgotten she could read my mind.* How I wished the earth would swallow me up then and there. But Ginevra intervened before I could say anything stupid. "Hello, lovebirds." She smiled to herself.

"What's so funny, sis?" Evan asked, puzzled by the look on her face.

Perfect. I stole a glance at Ginevra, wondering if she was planning to betray me. What a ridiculous turn of events: I was going to end up taking care of my fate myself by jumping off the terrace out of shame.

Ginevra looked at me out of the corner of her eye, a crafty smile on her face as she walked up to us. She leaned down next to Evan until her mouth was right by his ear. I trembled.

"It's a secret," she whispered, gazing steadily at me as she did so.

Evan studied my expression as I heaved a sigh of relief, trying hard not to show how nervous I was. Puzzled, he turned to look first at me and then at Ginevra. "What's up, you two?" he said, narrowing his eyes, a little smile on his face.

I looked at Ginevra, who winked at me before standing up again. Reassured, I shrugged and raised my eyebrows, pretending not to understand. It seemed to be Ginevra's little way of making up for interrupting us right when Evan was about to kiss me.

She turned to him. "That was fast. I knew there was no way to stop you—you were bound to do it sooner or later."

"She had the right to know," Evan replied.

"This whole thing is getting more and more complicated. I still don't know if we'll be able to handle it," she said, worried.

"We'll find a way. There's always a solution." Evan glanced at me, alluding to what I'd said to him that night under the stars. "We just need a plan. And we need it fast, before—" He stopped mid-sentence, looking at me. "We have to be one step ahead of him, no matter what."

I shuddered at the words he hadn't been able to say. I was still trying to process all the information I'd received, and I felt shaken and unsure what effect this new world was actually having on me.

Ginevra's eyes on me distracted me from my thoughts. "Don't worry," she said in a low voice, stroking my elbow, "we're not going to hurt you." She'd read my fear through my thoughts.

"You're trembling," Evan said, surprised and frustrated that he hadn't noticed my state of agitation as Ginevra had. "Are you afraid?" he asked, worried.

"No," I blurted.

Ginevra stole a glance in my direction and was about to contradict me. I still wasn't used to watching what I thought when she was around. I would have to learn to.

"I wish I weren't but I can't help it," I was forced to admit.

Evan stroked my cheek and stared at me intensely. "Trust me," he whispered, "nothing's going to happen to you. You just need to trust me."

I couldn't bring myself to answer him. I nodded, still shaken.

The embarrassing growling of my empty stomach broke the silence. Once again, I considered throwing myself off the terrace.

"Sorry," I said, embarrassed, biting my lip.

"Evan! This isn't like you!" Ginevra snapped. "Have you forgotten Gemma needs food to survive?"

"Forgive me, I'm not used to thinking about things like this," he said, mortified.

"Don't apologize, I'm not hungry," I lied, but my stomach betrayed me again by growling as I said it.

Ginevra took me by the hand and led me inside. "Come with me, we'll get you something to eat," she insisted as she pulled me down the hallway.

My mouth watered at the thought of food and at a faint aroma I thought I smelled in the air, as if there were a home-cooked meal somewhere nearby. I couldn't remember the last time I'd eaten anything.

Thanks, I thought, speaking to her through my mind. Ginevra turned toward the stairs, casting me a friendly look to show she'd heard me. *For everything.* I hadn't yet had the chance to thank her for saving me at the prom. If it hadn't been for her, the chandelier would have crushed me. Nevertheless, knowing that the monster would come back looking for me left a lump in my throat.

What else would I have to go through to escape my fate? I wasn't sure I could hold out for very long. Maybe I wasn't strong enough. Was I really sure Evan would manage to save me every time?

No one could answer that question for me.

Without turning around, Ginevra squeezed my hand tighter to reassure me. I looked back, but Evan wasn't with us any more, even though he hadn't passed us. I hurried to follow Ginevra down the stairs, driven by the longing to see him again.

29

REFLECTION IN THE MIRROR

Walking into the kitchen from the living room, I immediately found Evan on the other side of the table, smiling at me encouragingly. *Handsome as a god.* He escorted me to the table, gallantly pulling out a chair for me, then, with a flourish, showed me the table piled high with all kinds of food.

I gaped. "Evan . . ."

"I wanted to make it up to you," he said, smiling.

"Don't take all the credit," Ginevra retorted scornfully.

"Thanks." I looked at them. "To both of you, but it's too much, really! I could never eat all this, not even if I hadn't touched food for a whole week."

"Don't worry about that," Evan reassured me. "Go ahead and eat whatever you want. Ginevra will polish off the rest." He hid a smile as Ginevra shot him an angry look.

I stared at the table, amazed at the incredible amount of food. "How did you manage to come up with all this in only ten seconds?" I exclaimed.

"Magic," Ginevra said, winking at me. She'd meant it as a joke, but it didn't come across that way. She looked amused at my expression. I touched a piece of bread to make sure it was real and Evan laughed, making me glare at him.

"It all looks great. Thanks," I said quickly, downplaying my reaction.

"Ginevra tends to overdo it sometimes," he said.

"I didn't know what she liked to eat," she said in her defense. "She loves all kinds of food!"

I blushed, embarrassed. She'd clearly read my mind during some of my more "passionate" flirtations with food. I became a bottomless pit when I was nervous.

"You two have a lot in common then," Evan said.

"Shut up," she warned. "Gemma, you skipped dinner, and it's almost time for breakfast now."

"I'll make up for it," I said, feeling hunger pangs. The aroma of the food wafted through the air and tickled my nose. Unable to wait any longer, I sank my teeth into a slice of pizza topped with French fries and washed it down with ice-cold orange soda.

When the meal was over, I felt my belly would burst. I couldn't remember the last time I'd gorged myself like that. Though the first few bites had curbed my hunger, I'd eaten a lot to avoid disappointing Ginevra, who watched me enthusiastically every time I took a taste of something different. I looked around at the kitchen for the first time. "Don't you guys eat?" I blurted, realizing only then there wasn't a stove.

Evan and Ginevra exchanged brief glances before answering.

"My brothers and I don't need food," Evan said, studying my reaction.

"But you can eat," I said. "You ate blueberry crumble when you came to the diner."

He smiled. "That was an excuse to see you, Gemma," he admitted with a sensual smile. "Besides," he said, grinning at Ginevra, "she eats enough for all of us."

She shot him a withering look and a sharp knife rose into the air, hovering over the table and pointing at Evan threateningly. My chair screeched against the floor as I jumped in my seat, terrified.

Evan's expression, however, seemed more amused than scared. "Don't tell me you mean to eat me now!"

"Yes, but first I'm going to carve you up," she said, a fierce look on her face, and the knife zoomed toward him on its own at the speed of light. I jumped in my chair again, frightened, only to see the blade stop inches from his face.

Evan let out a laugh, reaching up to grab the knife handle as I stared at them, stunned. "Where are your manners? We have company," he scolded her. A smile on his lips, he leaned over to whisper in my ear. "I told you it was best to avoid irritating her."

"Um, I'm right here?" Ginevra reminded him, laughing. "Don't worry, Gemma. We're just kidding around."

I looked at Evan, dazed and still terrified, and he winked at me. Would he ever stop teasing me?

"Don't count on it," Ginevra said in response to my thought.

"You'd better get used to it."

I tried to smile, but the effort it took me was plain to see.

"You look tired," she said.

Now that she'd pointed it out, I could barely keep my eyes open. How long had it been since I'd last slept? It felt like days.

"You should get some rest," Evan said. I heard his melodious voice, but suddenly I couldn't see his face any more. I was on the verge of collapsing. "You've been through a rough day and we don't know what's in store for us tomorrow. I'll take you upstairs."

"No!" I replied quickly.

"I'll give you my room," Evan assured me sweetly.

"Gemma, there's nothing to be afraid of," Ginevra said, sensing my concern.

"Nothing's going to happen to you here with us," Evan added.

"Okay, but I'd rather stay down here. The couch is fine. It looked comfortable. Besides, all I need is to lie down and close my eyes for a few minutes and I'll be as good as new."

"Sure, of course you will!" Ginevra said with a sarcastic grin.

"What time is it, anyway?" I asked, suddenly worried by how much light was already filling the garden.

"Quarter past seven. And in any case, there's a clock right over there. It's that round thing with the big moving hands." Poking fun at how tired I was, Ginevra pointed at the wall behind her, on which was a large clock I hadn't noticed before. The hands moved slowly as my eyelids drooped, and I thought about how my parents would already be at the diner, working the Sunday brunch shift.

I noticed Evan and Ginevra exchanging silent glances. They seemed to have heard something that had put them on guard. The thought that the evil being might have found me woke me up, leaving me not the least bit sleepy.

"What's wrong?" I asked, panicked.

"Don't worry," Evan said, trying to calm me. "It's one of ours."

Ginevra's eyes opened wide as she spotted something behind me. "Drake, wait!" As I turned around, she groaned, "Too late."

Utter shock left me breathless, speechless, devoid of thought. My mind was suddenly blank, wiped clean by the image my eyes were sending my brain. "What the—"

In front of me stood an exact replica of me, staring back at me like my reflection in a mirror. For the first time, I had the horrifying suspicion I was dead and on the outside now, looking at the body I'd just abandoned.

I touched my chest impulsively to make sure I was there. Everything was in its place. I wasn't dead, I was still in my body, alive and well. I stepped closer, drawn by the urge to touch it and make sure it was real, that it wasn't a figment of my imagination. But I hesitated and stepped back again as my brain struggled to choose between running away and passing out. In the end I found myself halfway between the two, gaping as Ginevra and Evan looked at me apologetically.

"I tried to warn you," she said to my twin ruefully.

"Everything okay?" Evan asked with concern, stroking my arm as I started to feel I'd permanently lost my power of speech.

"Sorry, Gemma," Ginevra said. "This really is too much," she added in a low voice to Evan before turning back to me. "We should have warned you. This is Drake," she explained, pointing at the other Gemma, who in the meantime had been carefully studying my every movement.

"Hey!" my double chimed, flashing a funny-looking smile that wasn't very flattering to my face.

Hearing that voice, identical to my own, made me shudder. I felt like my body didn't belong to me any more, like I was seeing it from a distance. It was a surreal, utterly illogical sensation. I had the urgent need to look at myself in a mirror. I glanced down at my hands and was relieved to recognize them as mine.

Ginevra went over to her, her footsteps silent. "Drake, would you mind?" she whispered in my double's ear, nodding in my direction.

"Oh. Right! Sorry, babe," the girl replied in my voice. "I'll give you your body back."

Suddenly her candid, innocent face changed shape and became rugged . . . and *handsome.* Even more dangerous than Evan's. He smiled at me with a slightly ominous gleam in his eyes and his face relaxed.

I stammered something unintelligible as I tried to process what I'd just seen. What parallel world had I ended up in? What had happened to the peaceful, monotonous life I was accustomed to?

"It was hit by a truck," Ginevra quipped in response to my thought. "A red one, in fact, just like the car." She glanced at the dress I was wearing. "I'd pick a new outfit if I were you. Red is *definitely* not your lucky color." She grinned at me as I tried to smile back at her, but couldn't.

I looked over at Drake again. Instead of my small, frail body, now his physique was vigorous, trim, and muscular. Very muscular. He looked even brawnier than Evan and seemed a few years older than we were.

"*This* is Drake," Ginevra said, walking to his side.

"The fun one," he added, raising his hand.

Evan had been right when he'd said my parents wouldn't notice the difference. So I had to thank him as well, and I would have if I hadn't been left speechless. Drake had turned into an exact copy of me and taken my place at home so my parents wouldn't notice I was gone. Such a kind thing to do. It warmed my heart.

"Is he an Angel too?" I asked hesitantly, finding my voice again.

Evan and Drake glanced at each other.

"He's one of us," Evan said. "He'll take your place whenever we need him to. I told you there was nothing to worry about."

It was comforting to think someone would replace me if anything happened to me. My family being spared the grief was at least a partial consolation.

"That's not an alternative," Ginevra said, reading my mind. "Not any more. Nothing's going to happen to you, that's a promise." I wasn't so convinced.

"Man, my ears are still ringing," Drake groaned, rubbing them as Ginevra started laughing. "That pain in the neck of a dog of yours wouldn't quit yapping all night long. Your dad came to check on you four times because of it. I wanted to strangle it."

My eyes went wide with concern. "You didn't hurt him, did you?"

"Relax," Evan reassured me softly, "he'd never do anything like that."

Hard to believe. Judging from his build, he probably could have crushed Irony with one hand.

I couldn't stop staring at them all. I felt like a fly in a room full of butterflies. I was definitely the only one there suffering from an inferiority complex. Ginevra was radiant and Drake looked like a Greek god, although Evan was even handsomer.

Drake's head was shaved, but his hair was definitely dark, judging from his complexion. His eyes were also dark; at that moment they were as black as coal, but I knew they wouldn't be the same color if I saw him in his true essence. He stared at me steadily, his gaze piercing. I'd felt a shiver of terror when I looked into them for the first time, but I knew the feeling was totally unjustified. The three of them weren't the bad guys, though I wasn't even sure why they were continuing to protect me.

Drake looked like a military type. Everything about him made me think he was a soldier. His prominent cheekbones framed his face, as did his slightly square jaw. The Subterranean tattoo stood out on his muscles. There was something about him—I couldn't explain what it was, but it made me uneasy. An instinctive reaction.

"Believe me," Drake said lightheartedly, "I came pretty close to doing it." There was a hint of sarcasm in his voice.

They all laughed at his joke, which only I didn't understand. Evan leaned over and whispered in my ear. "For the record, Drake's the one who brings all the girls here. You're my first."

My heart skipped a beat. He took my hand and gazed into my eyes as I looked back into his. He was so close it made me dizzy.

"Wasn't someone here about to get some sleep?" Ginevra asked, glancing my way.

"Actually, I've never felt so awake in my life," I admitted. There was no longer the slightest trace of the sleepiness I'd felt up until a minute ago. "Is there anyone else I should meet?" I asked Evan. "I thought you said there were four of you."

"Simon," Ginevra replied, her expression turning sweet. "We were in the workout room, but he got a . . ." Her voice trailed off. I looked at Evan just in time to glimpse the odd look he was shooting at his sister.

"He had some things to sort through, I think," she corrected herself, still staring at her brother with a strangely reproachful look.

"Try calling him, Evan," Drake said. "It's meet-and-greet time."

"Drake's right," Ginevra added. "He should be finished by now. We need him here. There's a lot for us to talk about and we need to come up with a plan."

Evan nodded before turning to me. "But after that you'll get some rest," he ordered me firmly. "I'll try to contact Simon." He closed his eyes and concentrated for a moment as we watched him in silence. He was calling his brother mentally.

"Simon's my boyfriend," Ginevra whispered in my ear pointedly, hiding a half smile.

"Oh, I didn't know," I replied, although what she said didn't really sink in. I was still too stunned and confused by the whole bizarre situation.

I suddenly heard Evan's entrancing voice in my mind. I looked up and discovered that his eyes were still closed and his lips sealed.

Simon, where are you? You have to join us. We need you, he whispered mentally. I stared at him, too bewitched by the sight of him to look away. When he noticed, he smiled at me and winked.

This time he hadn't lost control, he'd wanted me to hear him. He'd given me permission. I felt a warm glow of gratification.

"What's up, guys?" The timbre of a stranger's voice broke the silence.

"Finally! Where you been, dude?" Drake said impatiently. He was the only one of us who'd been entirely excluded from the conversation, so he'd been waiting in silence. Not only I but also Ginevra seemed to have heard Evan through his thoughts.

Simon, the only family member I hadn't met, had materialized right in front of Drake, his back turned to me. I was surprised to see how much he looked like Evan, seen from behind. His hair was a lighter shade, but their hairstyles and the cut of their shoulders were incredibly similar; anyone could easily have mistaken them.

"It wouldn't be the first time," Ginevra whispered in my ear.

"I was wrong!" I exclaimed, stunned, as I remembered the kiss I'd seen. Ginevra nodded, a little smile on her face. "So he's—"

"My boyfriend," Ginevra said, finishing my sentence as she slid her arm around Simon's waist.

I finally connected the dots. I hadn't seen Ginevra kissing Evan in the garden, she'd been kissing Simon. And to think I would have been spared a world of grief if only I'd known!

"Well, there's one thing you should always remember to do before jumping to conclusions," she told me.

"What's that?" I said, curious.

"*Ask.*" She grinned. "I tried to stop you." She winked at me and pulled Simon closer to her. "I would have told you sooner or later," she said, throwing her arms around her boyfriend's neck. Now that he was standing beside her, he didn't look so tall any more.

A few moments had passed since Simon had appeared in the room and only then did he turn to look at me, a puzzled expression on his face.

"If Drake's over there," he said, pointing at his brother, "then you must be Gemma. Were you guys going to introduce me or do I have to do everything myself? Hi, I'm Simon." He smiled, holding out his hand, his voice velvety and kind.

"Nice to meet you, Simon," I replied, trying to hide my amazement. Looking him in the face, it was ridiculous to have thought he resembled Evan. They were like night and day, although both were gorgeous.

Simon had a more angelic face than the others. It inspired trust. His features were soft and his hair a very light brown, almost blond, while his eyes were closer to sky blue. I wondered if all Angels were so irresistibly fascinating. It couldn't have been otherwise.

"Where on earth have you been so long? You know I don't like to wait. It makes me foul-tempered," Ginevra said, teasing.

"More than usual, you mean?" he shot back with a smile.

She threw a piece of food at him but Simon dodged it and pinned his girlfriend to the wall.

"Hey! No fair," she purred.

I looked away.

"Just trying to make up for it," Simon replied, grinning. Ginevra let herself go in a passionate kiss that made me a little uncomfortable, probably because Evan was standing next to me and I had the almost irrepressible longing to do the same thing with him. He was so close his arm was brushing against mine.

He looked at me out of the corner of his eye before leaning over and whispering in my ear. "They do this all the time," he said, sounding apologetic, though a smile danced on his lips.

"Don't mind them. You'll see a whole lot worse around here," Drake said, smirking.

"No problem, it's okay," I replied, my voice hesitant from embarrassment. "How long have they been together?"

"Practically an eternity!" Evan exclaimed, smiling, skillfully dodging the question. I quickly looked away from him, confused. I didn't know what he meant by that, or how old all of them actually were.

"An Angel's heart is difficult to penetrate, but once you're inside it, there's no way out," he whispered, seeking my gaze.

I started at his allusion, the sweetness in his voice making me melt. Then I turned to look at Simon and Ginevra. I felt an overwhelming desire to have the same kind of relationship with Evan that they had. I wanted Evan more than anything else in the world.

"Gemma, I really think you should get some sleep," he suggested, a touch of regret in his voice. "I'm afraid things are going to be difficult when you wake up."

His words made my fear resurface. I had no idea what was in store for me and I was terrified by the thought of facing that infernal creature. That Angel of Death was there for me and soon he would come to take me, because one way or the other I had to die. It was my fate, and who was I to defy it?

Death, if it came unexpectedly, might be cruel but it wasn't frightening, because you didn't have the chance to realize what was about to happen. Knowing your own fate in advance, on the other hand, was a terrifying form of torture, maybe even worse than death itself. A prelude to madness.

Fearing the shadow of death with each breath was an agonizing countdown that left you exhausted and sapped your will to fight, until its echoing whisper faded into an icy silence that deprived you of everything. It was like a deadly poison that took effect silently, draining your energy, battering your mind's defenses until you ultimately wanted to give in to its comfort, letting it shroud you in its dark mantle so the fear itself wouldn't kill you . . . slowly.

"Gemma, did you hear me?" Evan insisted, stroking my shoulder.

"Yeah, you're right," I said, holding back tears. I couldn't accept it. Why me? Why me, of all people? I wasn't ready to let everything go. I wasn't ready to give up Evan. Not so soon.

"Is this all right?" he asked me, leading me to the couch, which he'd made up with a pillow and a quilt.

"It's fine," I replied numbly, the listless tone of my voice betraying my fatalistic thoughts. "Evan!" I said, calling him back before he left the room. "Don't leave me . . . please," I whispered in a tiny voice, almost pleading.

He smiled. "I'll be right here in the next room, I promise," he reassured me, walking back into the kitchen.

I seriously doubted I'd manage to get any sleep. It was already late morning and sunlight was pouring in through the picture window, keeping me from closing my eyes.

At that instant, the room went completely dark. Alarmed, I raised my head to check the windows and found the heavy drapes had closed, as if they'd obeyed my command. Ginevra peeked into the room from the kitchen. "Need anything else?"

"N-no, thanks," I managed to say, still shaken.

But with the darkness, my fear returned, even stronger than before. Evan was right. I hadn't been given the keys to enter another world; I'd just learned to see the one I'd always inhabited with new eyes. And everything that lurked within it.

I peered at the perimeter of the room, nervously scanning every corner. It was so dark I couldn't even see my own body, but I hoped I'd be able to detect any kind of movement, even the tiniest one, so I'd have the chance to call for help if I needed to.

There was no hope of my falling asleep. I started to feel neurotic, a step away from hysteria. I struggled to keep my eyelids from closing but, realizing I really needed to get some rest, I grabbed a corner of the blanket and pulled it up over my head. Hidden beneath the cozy fabric, I felt safe for the first time. I took a deep breath of the air trapped under the heavy quilt and a delicate scent filled my nostrils. I could still smell Evan on my skin. I closed my eyes and imagined he was there with me.

Only then, overcome with exhaustion, did I surrender to sleep.

EVAN

30

DANGEROUS STRATEGY

"She asleep?" I asked Ginevra, trying to get over my concern. As my brothers left the room, Ginevra cocked her head, listening for Gemma's thoughts.

"I can't hear her any more," she said after a moment.

"Good. All this has been really hard on her. I don't know if she's wrapped her brain around it yet—or if she ever will," I said, fear rising up from the bottom of the heart I'd rediscovered not long ago.

"There's no denying she's in shock," Ginevra said, "but can we blame her? Who wouldn't be?"

I looked at her sadly as we moved closer to Gemma, lowering our voices to a hush so she wouldn't wake up.

"Let's give her time to reflect. She'll understand, she'll accept you, you'll see," she said, trying to be reassuring.

"Look at her," I whispered, being careful not to wake the little angel I'd fallen desperately in love with. "Isn't she *beautiful*?" I stroked her warm, rosy cheek. "I could spend eternity watching her sleep. I can't take my eyes off her. It's a like a spell. It paralyzes me."

A few locks of hair were strewn over her face. I reached out to brush them back but froze when she stirred at my touch.

"She's restless," Ginevra confirmed, saying aloud what I was thinking. "She can't relax. Look how tense she is. Why don't you visit her in her dream, Evan?" she asked.

"No. I want to give her room to breathe," I said, although it gave me pain not to be near her.

Ginevra was surprised by my hesitation. "Well, I think you should try to ease her mind."

"She needs time, like you said. If I went to her now, I'd just risk confusing her." I paused, filled with a deep sadness. "If she decides to accept me for who I am and wants me at her side, it'll have to be her own decision, hers and her heart's. I don't want it to be because I pressured her."

Gemma abruptly turned under the blanket, making me lower my voice.

"Shh. Let's let her sleep," Ginevra whispered, leaving my side. "She's going to need it."

"I'll be right there," I said softly, wanting to stay another moment longer. When Ginevra had left the room, I stroked Gemma's neck with the back of my hand. "I'm not going to let anyone hurt you, I promise," I whispered, brushing my lips against hers upside down. I looked at her one more time and joined Ginevra in the kitchen, leaving behind a piece of my heart.

"It's so liberating to finally be myself around her instead of being forced to wear the mask we put on day after day. But I still can't stand the thought that she might not accept me or might even be *scared* of me. It's frustrating to have to live with the possibility."

"You have to accept it, Evan. It's the flip side of the coin. She'll get through this, I know she will. What she feels for you is very powerful. She just needs time, trust me."

I hoped she was right, but the reason I was so upset went a lot deeper than that, and I couldn't hide it from Ginevra, no matter how much I wanted to.

"Evan."

I looked up, knowing exactly what she was going to say before she even opened her mouth.

"Why didn't you tell her?"

I didn't reply. I didn't know the answer.

"Don't you see it's only going to complicate things?"

"Why? It doesn't matter any more." I glanced into the salon, worried Gemma might overhear us.

"Of course it matters! What's she going to think when she finds out that *you* were supposed to be her Executioner? That *you* were the one sent to kill her?"

Deep in my heart, I shuddered at the thought. "She doesn't need to find out," I said quietly, overcome with guilt.

"Well, it's a risk you're going to have to take if you want to be with her. She's bound to find out, and it would be better for her to find out the whole truth all at once, no more secrets. It would be better for everyone."

"You think I don't know that? Or that I haven't tried?" I hissed. "I planned on telling her, but then she asked about Amy."

"The little girl you killed in the fire," Ginevra said.

I glared at her for saying it out loud. My sadness grew as Ginevra silently listened to the thoughts she'd already read in my mind before I voiced them. Still, I felt like if I didn't get it all out it would crush me.

"I didn't expect Gemma to ask. It floored me. You should have seen the look in her eyes when she thought I'd saved that little girl. She thought I was upset because I hadn't been able to take Amy to safety. How could I admit I was actually there to *kill* her? It wasn't the guilt consuming me, it was the mask I had to put on in front of her. Ginevra, I couldn't tell her what I was."

"You should have tried, Evan," she insisted, ignoring my frustration.

"No," I said with conviction. "I couldn't. It would have been too much for her. She was so scared. I wanted to hug her, hold her tight against me and tell her I wouldn't let anything happen to her, not for anything in the world." I stared blankly at the floor, drawn back in by the memory of the desolate existence I'd been trapped in before meeting Gemma. "My life used to be empty and I didn't know it. I'm not going to let anyone take her away from me. If anybody even dares come close to Gemma I'll send them straight to hell," I swore, an unfamiliar rage filling me at the thought that anyone would try to hurt her. "She's my heaven," I murmured.

Nobody would touch her. Not as long as I was there to protect her.

"You can count on us, Evan. We'll help you keep her safe."

"No. You guys have risked enough already. I still don't know what price I'll have to pay, but the Brotherhood is going to summon us. I'm amazed they haven't done it already."

"We're a team. One for all. If Gemma's the girl you want, she's one of us now. We'll protect her no matter what."

Thank you, I thought.

"Don't thank me yet. There's something else we need to take care of: our strategy," Ginevra stated firmly. Suddenly she stiffened and peered around.

"What's wrong?" I asked, worried.

"He's here, nearby. I can feel him," she barely whispered, all her senses on high alert.

I was enraged. "He wouldn't dare confront us in our own home," I snarled, clenching my teeth as I scanned the room. Sensing a presence, I spun around, but was surprised to find Drake and Simon, who'd silently appeared behind me. "Oh! It's you." I took a deep breath, trying to quell the blood boiling in my veins.

Meanwhile, Ginevra's eyes remained vigilant. My brothers' appearance hadn't calmed her. Since she was a Witch, she was more skilled than any of us at sensing the presence of an Angel.

"Hey, take it easy, Evan," Simon said, resting a hand on my shoulder. "You're tense. We need perfect focus. Or have you already come up with a plan?"

"You think we could convince him to stand down?" Ginevra asked.

"Impossible," I said. "He's not going to give up until he's killed her. Orders come first. Nothing else matters to him."

"Then how can we keep him from doing it without killing *him*?"

I shot Ginevra a look brimming with rage, almost like she'd insulted me.

"You can't be thinking—" Simon was horrified. "Evan, don't tell me you mean to kill him! He's a Descendant! He's one of us!"

I clenched my fists until they ached. "I'll do it if I have to. *Anything*, to keep from losing her."

"But this isn't his fault!" Simon insisted. "He's just a pawn in the hands of the Brotherhood. He's only carrying out orders, you know that. He's innocent, he'd never do anything to hurt us."

"He wants to hurt *her*, and that's reason enough for me," I snapped. "He's not going to take her away from me, even if I'm forced to sacrifice his life. If it's my last resort, I'll kill him. I need you guys to know that up front." I stared silently at Drake, hoping he'd back me up.

"Evan," he said, "you know it's impossible to kill an Executioner, unless—"

I nodded. "There's only one way to do it. I've already thought about that," I told them, glancing at Ginevra. She seemed shocked by my idea.

"My poison," she whispered, appalled.

"It's the only weapon that can kill a Soldier of Death: a Witch's poison. And we have that to our advantage," I said.

My strategy left my family speechless. They stared at me, horrified, wondering how I could plot anything remotely similar against a member of my own race, united by blood over centuries of successions, sacrifices, and deaths. Their accusing looks filled me with self-loathing.

Under any other circumstances it would have been insane to even think of doing anything like it. But Gemma changed everything, and I had no choice but to consider it. Why didn't any of them seem to understand? I wasn't going to let him lay a finger on her. To protect her I'd kill that Angel and anyone else who came after him. Nothing would stop me.

In Gemma I'd found my Eve, my other half. Though some didn't know it, somewhere out there in the world there was a kindred spirit that completed each of us, and not everybody was lucky enough to recognize that person. It had taken centuries, but I'd found her and nobody was going to take her away from me, much less Death, the coward that had made us its keepers. Sooner or later, I'd come up with a solution. Gemma was mine, all mine. Forever mine.

I turned toward Ginevra. *Do you still have any?* I asked her telepathically.

The look on her face gave her away—she didn't want to answer me. "Evan, you can't really be thinking of using my poison—"

"I have to," I said through clenched teeth.

"It would never work, Evan. Consider the consequences, damn it all!" Drake warned me.

"*I don't care about the consequences*," I snarled, precisely articulating each word. "Gemma's all that matters." My voice sounded cold and hard, even to my own ears. I was desperate, willing to do anything. My love for her overshadowed everything else.

"Calm down, Evan, there must be another solution," Simon pleaded. I'd never seen him so concerned.

"You don't understand!" I howled in frustration. "We've got to stop him, damn it!"

"Evan, Evan, listen to me," Ginevra interjected, her voice calmer as she looked me in the eye. "After him, others would come. This kind of war would never end! Do you really want to force her to live in hiding forever? Think carefully: Drake would have to take her place, and she'd never be able to go back to her life. She'd never see her family again or her friends. Is that really what you want for her? She'd end up killing herself. I mean, the thought's already crossed her mind! What kind of life could she ever have if she's constantly being chased by Death? Living in terror would slowly kill her. No one would be able to bear it."

Somehow, Ginevra's words got through to me in the midst of my wild rage, forcing me to reflect.

"You're right," I admitted, resigned. I couldn't let Gemma be the one to pay the consequences. None of this was her fault.

"There must be another way to keep him from finding her," Ginevra suggested.

I fell silent. Her words echoed in my head, almost hinting at the solution. "Of course," I whispered. "Ginevra, you're a genius!" I narrowed my eyes as my brain rapidly formulated a plan.

"It's perfect!" Ginevra gasped euphorically as she studied the strategy taking shape in my mind.

"What's up?" Drake asked anxiously.

"Evan's found a solution," Ginevra replied, letting me be the one to explain the plan we would implement.

"Which would be . . . ?" Simon sounded impatient but also plainly relieved there was an alternative.

"We hide her," I announced, my heart filled with hope. Simon and Drake stared at me quizzically .

"Hear him out. It might work," Ginevra said before they could criticize me. Meanwhile, her eyes continued to scan the room with unnerving suspicion.

"Gemma's fate is sealed," I explained to my brothers. "She has to die. Fine. So she'll die. We can't change what's written."

Their disapproving murmurs rose up and filled the room, but I smiled, more and more convinced the plan would work.

"You don't want to kill the Angel any more? You want to kill Gemma instead?" Simon asked, bewildered. My new plan clearly horrified him more than the first one. "I don't understand."

I felt like I was radiating a new light, a glimmer of hope that my crazy plan might work and the nightmare would be over forever.

"Well?" Drake snapped impatiently. "Have you gone nuts or what?"

"No, I haven't," I said, vaguely distracted by Ginevra, who continued to look around uneasily.

"Gemma takes the lethal poison, not the Angel. Gemma has to die. It's inevitable, right? No one can change their destiny. No one can fight it. What's written must come to pass."

"Tell them how you would convince her to poison herself," Ginevra said, urging me to explain the details she'd already read in my mind.

"Wha—What? You mean you're going along with this?" Simon asked, horrified. Neither of us paid any attention to him.

"I'll force her if it comes to that," I said, utterly resolved.

No matter how hard and cold my voice might have sounded, there was a new warmth rising up inside me, kindled by the hope of a future with Gemma. I was willing to do anything to get us out of our predicament, even something this extreme. I was becoming more and more convinced that everything would turn out fine, that Gemma and I could have a future together.

"It would be better if you gave it to her without telling her, Evan," Ginevra suggested. "It'd be easier on all of us. Just put a drop of it in her glass and her body will be dead in an instant. We wait for her to wake up, and it's all over. We'll take care of the rest. Believe me, knowing would only scare her. She doesn't have to know about it."

"C'mon, you two! Could you explain to the rest of us what the hell you're talking about?" Drake shouted impatiently.

"Listen, guys. We can't fight destiny, no matter how incomprehensible or wrong it might seem to us. It takes precedence over everything else and it's beyond our control. We can run, but it'll come back each and every time to take whatever it wants, unless . . ."

"Unless what? Cut to the chase!" Drake said, exasperated.

"Unless we turn the tables on it," I said, my heart in turmoil.

"Is this some kind of riddle or are you going to explain the plan?" Drake groaned.

"Don't you get it? The answer was right there under our noses all along! What we needed wasn't an escape plan but a loophole. Gemma needs to meet her fate. Okay, she *has* to die, but that doesn't mean we can't bring her back."

I looked at them impatiently, trying to decipher the expressions on their faces, but it seemed as if they'd gotten lost along the way.

"Are you out of your mind?" Simon bellowed.

Not the reaction I'd hoped for.

"Why not? It might work," Ginevra pointed out.

"It *might.* And what if it doesn't? You thought about that, Evan?" Drake spoke up.

"Why so cautious all of a sudden, Drake? Haven't you always been the one who loves a challenge? I hoped at least *you* would react differently, for God's sake!"

"This decision isn't about me, Evan. I just don't want to see you make a huge mistake. You could lose her forever. Nobody knows better than me what . . ." Drake's voice trailed off and dropped to a hush. "Are you willing to run that risk?"

"I have no choice," I roared.

"It's too dangerous, Evan," Simon interjected, worried. "Besides, what makes you think Gemma's going to agree to your plan? You think she's willing to defy Death? You think she's that brave?"

"I know she is," I answered.

"No one is!" he insisted, more upset than before. "Evan, think about it: this has never happened before. We don't know what we'd be up against. The situation could get out of hand."

"You're wrong. It happens all the time and you know it. There's a halfway point between life and death. People come and go without even realizing it. Lots of people wake up miraculously."

"You're talking about being in a coma! This is different, Evan. Some coma patients wake up again because it isn't written that they're supposed to die yet. Their souls wander until they find their way back, their bodies kept alive by machines in the meantime, but it's only because there's nobody there to usher them to the other side. No Subterranean is there waiting for them. Even if Gemma agreed to run the risk, he'd be there waiting for her."

"That's not a problem. I've already thought everything through. I'll pretend to realize I made a mistake and want to make up for it by killing her. I'll find a way to be sure he sees me when Gemma takes the poison. He doesn't have anything against *us*, Simon. He doesn't want to hurt us. I can reason with him. Once he's seen her lifeless body, he'll let me stay with her one last time. I'll tell him I want to accompany her myself. I'm sure he'll understand. I just hope he can't read minds," I murmured, forcing a smile to ease the tension. Actually, the possibility that he might have that power worried me more than anything else. It would ruin everything.

My brothers looked like they were starting to understand my plan. It would be risky, there was no denying that. If I couldn't convince the Dark Angel to leave quickly, I'd lose her forever. I'd only have a few minutes before she was jeopardized by the lack of oxygen to her brain.

In my heart I knew I could do it, but desperation about that small risk of failure pierced my heart like a flaming arrow. I had to risk it, though. For her. For *us*.

"What if the Angel doesn't trust you? If he's not willing to let you be the one to help her cross over? You'd lose her in that case too. If he insists on doing it himself you'll never see her again, Evan."

The thought turned me into a slab of ice. Wasn't that the very reason I hadn't let the semi kill her when her time had come? I grabbed my hair, overwhelmed with consternation. The cruel destiny our race had been condemned to had never felt so heavy as it did right now. Forced into exile, halfway between life and death, unable to see other souls once they'd crossed over and unable to show ourselves to them. *Hidden*. Forgotten. Abandoned to ourselves, to oblivion. For eternity. I would never see her again.

I took a deep breath, filling my lungs to ward off my frustration. "We'll follow my plan and if something goes wrong I'll pay the consequences," I made myself say with confidence, trying to hide my agitation. My chest ached at the thought of that possibility. "I need to know: can I count on you?"

The guys' expressions were half skeptical, half convinced. Only Ginevra seemed fully convinced the desperate plan might work, probably because she'd sensed the fervor that inflamed my thoughts. I hoped that was the reason—otherwise I'd have to consider another possibility, the doubt that continued to burn in my mind, wearing down my resolve: Ginevra wasn't one of us. Maybe my brothers were right. Maybe I should listen to them more instead of letting my emotions drag me into a decision supported by a Witch who couldn't possibly understand the dedication with which a Soldier of Death carries out his orders. With no reservations. No exceptions. Canceling out all else.

I needed to reflect, but suddenly I couldn't. My mind was drawing a blank. The minute hand on the clock was moving quickly, keeping me from thinking, as if time had decided to put me under pressure. Anxiety crept up again, filling every gap, sneaking into every free space, feeding on my uncertainty.

"Don't torture yourself," Ginevra said in a low voice, resting her hand affectionately on my shoulder. "It'll work. I'm not a Soldier of Death, but I believe in you. I've always believed in you, Evan. Don't let doubts creep into your mind to cloud what you saw so clearly a moment ago. Doubts are like mischievous demons, Evan. You have to drive them out of your head."

"You're right. It's just panic messing with me."

"You shouldn't doubt your plan. It'll be easier if we all really believe in it. If you hesitate, you risk being discovered."

I nodded, regaining control of my thoughts.

Time slipped by quickly. Outside, the sun prepared to disappear over the horizon, as though it too were being chased by demons.

Gemma was still sleeping and as yet, there was no sign of our enemy. Before waking her up, I ran over in my mind what I would say to convince her to follow my plan, but no matter how hard I tried, none of the alternatives I came up with seemed right. Anything I told her would end up terrifying her.

I'd immediately rejected Ginevra's suggestion. I could never poison her without her knowledge. Gemma didn't deserve to be tricked and I was sure she'd be strong enough to face reality.

I was *tired* of lying to her. I wanted her to be a part of my world and that couldn't happen unless I was totally honest. Gemma had to see me for what I actually was. She had to know my dark side. I would surrender to her completely, explain everything, hope that she would understand and trust me. Hope that her heart would choose the real me without reserve. Without secrets.

I'd made up my mind. There was no turning back. Even though I had no need for air, I took another deep breath and got ready to talk to her. She'd had enough sleep. It was time to wake her.

It would all be over soon. Another breath, and I hurried toward the salon. Suddenly impatient, my heart throbbed at the thought of seeing her face again, her sweet, penetrating gaze, her shy smile. I couldn't stand this endless, exhausting wait to hear her voice again. I was *obsessed* with Gemma. Like my entire existence had been one long wait until the moment I met her.

I went through the doorway. My heart, ecstatic only a moment ago, instantly withered.

Gemma was gone.

The whole world came crashing down at my feet. An icy claw gripped my chest, preventing me from breathing as I stared at the empty sofa, my eyes burning violently, my body frozen with terror, unable to react. I felt the energy draining from me and crumpled to my knees, utterly desperate. The light in my heart had gone out.

With everything left in me, I thought of her face and screamed out her name in my head, as though I could somehow bring her back to me, wherever she was. As hopeless as a man sentenced to death, I stared, petrified, at the empty sofa, the covers dumped on the floor. How could I have let it happen? Where was my star? Had that dog found a way to take her?

An obscure impulse like a dark, ominous wave brought me to my feet. Rage and evil took possession of me, banishing everything I'd been before.

I had to find him. I had to *kill* him. I would scour the planet if that was what it took. The fiend didn't deserve to exist. I would hunt him down and slaughter him just for taking her away from me. And if the dirtbag had harmed even a hair on her head, he'd end up begging me to kill him just to end the merciless torture I would subject him to. I was devastated, caught between oblivion and reason. Gemma was my light; without her I'd be lost to darkness. I'd never felt such powerful, uncontrollable hatred before, not for anyone.

I forgot my plan—which had already failed—forgot what mercy was, forgot myself. It was personal now, between me and him. The bastard's days were numbered.

31

FATAL DROP

"What's wrong?" Ginevra rushed into the salon, her voice edged with anxiety from having sensed the desperation in my thoughts.

I stared at the empty sofa, devastated.

"Gemma!" she gasped.

"He took her," I hissed in rage and desperation.

"But how? It can't be, Evan! How could he have?"

"I haven't been able to come up with an explanation yet."

"How did he do it? Evan, how could he have slipped into our house without my sensing his presence? No, wait. I did. I sensed something unusual, but it seemed too ridiculous to believe. I detected a presence, but it wasn't here! I checked! That's why I didn't bother telling you. How do you explain something like this?"

"Not a clue. We don't even know what to expect because we don't know what powers he has, damn it!" We both found it inconceivable that he could have come in and taken her away without our noticing.

"He couldn't have been here, it's impossible. I rule that out. So how'd he do it?" Her expression darkened as she thought aloud. Something crossed my mind.

"Yeah, you may be right. If he wasn't here, he must have convinced her to leave! I am such an idiot. Why didn't I think of it before? He's like me," I exclaimed. "He can read inside her. He must have gotten into her head while she was sleeping and convinced her to run away from us."

"But why didn't I hear her thoughts when she woke up?" Ginevra wondered, stricken with guilt.

"He must have blocked you. He wanted to get her out of here. If only I'd listened to you. Fuck!" A furious roar escaped me. I'd gladly burn in hell for the chance to go back and visit her in her dream.

"You wanted her to rest, Evan. You didn't want to disturb her. Don't feel bad."

Deep in my heart, I knew Ginevra was right. Then why did it hurt so horribly? It was all my fault. If I'd gone to her in her dreams I would have kept him from touching her. Instead I'd left her all alone with him. With that *monster*.

The pain grew sharper at the thought of how terrified Gemma must have felt when she found herself facing that demon all alone. And all because of me, because I wasn't there to protect her.

An unstoppable surge of rage boiled deep down in my gut, exploding with devastating power. I smashed my fist onto the crystal coffee table, shattering it before Ginevra's astonished eyes. As I ran my hand through my hair, something hot trickled down my face and dripped onto my forearm.

Ginevra's arms gently encircled my shoulders.

"It's all my fault, don't you see? I was supposed to protect her!" I snarled, overcome by a desperation I'd never known before. "I don't know what I'll do if I don't find her in time."

Actually, I knew perfectly well what I would do if I lost Gemma. Without her, nothing would mean anything any more. Gemma had become my light. I wasn't willing to go back into the darkness. What sense would there be in existing for all eternity as an empty shell? It was sheer agony.

"You know I would never let you." Ginevra had found her way into my thoughts, no matter how hard I'd been trying to hide them from her.

"It's my decision," I said firmly. "Besides, you won't be able to stop me. Sooner or later I'll get exactly what I want."

Silence fell. A gray, devastating silence as grim as death.

"You haven't answered my question," I reminded her as my eyes lit up with the fire burning behind my pupils. "Do you still have some?" My teeth were clenched as I pronounced those bitter words. It was almost as if the poison I was talking about had slipped into my mouth.

"Not if you have any intention of using it on yourself."

"I won't lie to you: that's beyond my control. But I still have one more chance, if we act fast."

Ginevra scrutinized me.

"My guess is you kept a little back in case you needed it one day." I raised an eyebrow and looked her in the eyes, encouraging her to admit it. I was sure Ginevra had saved a little poison, given her natural propensity to be always in control.

Her body suddenly vanished in a puff of mist, like fog dispersed by the wind. I stared at the spot she'd disappeared from, confirming my theory, and my eyes narrowed as I realized I was right. Filled with new determination, I went upstairs to join her.

Strange as it was, I'd never gone into her room before. I'd never stopped to wonder why none of us were allowed to walk through her doorway for any reason. Except Simon, naturally. Ginevra had been very clear about that rule. Despite the powerful connection between her and me, she was the only female among three males, so I'd always deemed it proper to respect her privacy.

But even under these extreme circumstances Ginevra was clearly reluctant to let me in. I began to suspect she was hiding something.

At first sight, the room looked like it had been arranged with maniacal attention to detail. There was a disturbing number of mirrors on the walls. Stacks and stacks of books filled the bookshelves. They emitted the same ominous aura that always surrounded Ginevra. To my surprise, the walls were painted in bright, even brilliant, colors, and the light was multiplied by the mirrors. Set into one of the cream-colored walls was a massive vault door in elegant dark gray.

What was a vault doing inside her bedroom? And why didn't I know anything about it?

"Don't be mad at me for keeping this hidden from you, Evan." Ginevra suddenly seemed worried, almost like she was afraid of how I would react.

"What are you talking about, Gin?" I asked cautiously, trying to curb my suspicions. What the hell was Ginevra hiding behind that door? My mind was riddled with confusion.

"I did it for all of you. It was too dangerous. I had to keep it as far away as possible."

Why did she suddenly seem guilty? And about what? "Ginevra, what's going on? Whatever you've been hiding isn't important, not right now," I assured her, my voice firm. "If what's in there can save Gemma, open it up, for God's sake! We haven't got much time."

She hesitated a second, checking my thoughts to make sure I was being honest, but I hadn't lied to her. Her secret didn't matter to me at all. I wouldn't even have bothered wondering about it if it hadn't been necessary. But it was.

"Ginevra, what are you waiting for?" I said, frustrated.

She glanced at me one last time, a look of weary resignation on her face, and raised her arm, her palm pointed at the sealed door. A moment later, a shiver spread through my bones, as cold as a last breath escaping death's lips, as a light shone in Ginevra's eyes, turning them a stronger shade of green. Her irises narrowed into vertical slits, like a snake's. It had been a long, long time since I'd last seen her like that, and the memory of that time made me shudder. She rotated her wrist counterclockwise. There was a click and the vault door swung open with an ominous groan.

"Follow me." Her voice had grown colder, as though dominated by some dark force.

I crossed through the doorway immediately after Ginevra, feeling a disturbing sensation of cold that seemed to be coming directly from my bones. Semidarkness enveloped us inside the tiny room. Even my sharp senses struggled to penetrate it and send information to my brain. Something wasn't right. Dark, evil energy swirled around me, withdrew and advanced again. It was a blood-chilling sensation I couldn't explain, but inside me it triggered remote yet familiar instincts buried by time. I'd felt that sensation on my skin before.

As if to ward off the agitation that had struck me, Ginevra lit up the room with a sudden wave of her hand. And I realized I'd been wrong.

It wasn't a cramped room. We were in a garden, a lush, narrow glade where branches and plants swayed over the verdant terrain. A little corner of paradise. Amazed, I stifled a gasp and wondered what else Ginevra was hiding from us. The voice of my instinct insisted I pay attention to the chill that had washed over me, but I ignored it, dismissing the ridiculous notion. Ginevra would never go so far.

Seconds later she stopped in her tracks and gestured for me not to move. The mysterious anxiety within me fought harder to emerge, overwhelming me, freezing every muscle, as I discovered what Ginevra had carefully hidden from us for so long. The focal point, the origin of all that dark energy.

I'd been wrong again, it wasn't a corner of paradise. It was a corner of hell.

I stared at the glass case in front of me, feeling like I was trapped in a slab of black ice. *Ginevra*! I wanted to scream at her, but even my thoughts were frozen. It was like every part of me, subjugated by primitive terror, suddenly refused to obey my command.

There was no need for an explanation. I already knew what the glass prison contained. Inside it Ginevra had hidden her serpent. The only adversary an Angel of Death ever had to fear. The only creature capable of annihilating us.

The moment it sensed my presence, the serpent writhed and shot from one corner of the case to the other, gripped by the relentless instinct to sink its fangs into my flesh and corrode my blood with its lethal poison.

"Shh," Ginevra said, trying to calm it down, but the hatred its very nature harbored for my race wouldn't let it. "Everything's okay. Easy, now. I'm here with you."

Like a mysterious spell, Ginevra's voice somehow soothed the animal's instinct. I forced myself to look into its eyes, losing myself in the darkness lurking there, and for the first time I understood the earlier instinct that had tried to warn me. In that creature dwelled pure evil, and my essence was interfering, clashing with it.

"You kept it," I whispered, my voice brimming with contempt.

"You were never supposed to find out," she said, her expression a mix of shame and determination.

"We thought you'd killed it! Damn it, Ginevra! How could you?" I shouted.

"I couldn't do it, Evan! He's a part of me. You can't understand. A Witch forms a special, inseparable bond with her serpent. My thoughts are his thoughts. My flesh is his flesh. Could you ever kill a part of yourself, no matter how evil its nature might be?"

"Does Simon know about this?" I asked, absolutely infuriated, ignoring her excuses.

Ginevra nodded, hanging her head guiltily. "I made him promise not to tell you. Please don't be mad at him. It was too dangerous to get you and Drake involved. Nothing was going to happen as long as you weren't allowed into my room," she said, trying to reassure me. She failed.

I froze at the thought of what *could* happen. It wouldn't affect me because I'd already chosen my fate, but I was worried about my brothers. The unspoken war that since the dawn of time had been waged between the two mortal enemies, Witches and Angels, had never subsided. The evil nature intrinsic to each Witch drove her to hunt down mortals who'd inherited the gene of the Subterraneans—in whose veins ran the blood of our race—to prevent them from becoming Angels of Death and carrying out the mission of ushering souls to heaven. That way, humanity would eventually lose itself in hell, the Witches' realm.

It was a battle for souls. When a new Subterranean appeared on earth for the first time, a Witch was already there, ready to try to corrupt his soul. By reading his mind, she could know whether he was close to surrendering or if he had no intention of being seduced. In the latter case, she would disappear before the Angel had the chance to slay her. But if he wasn't strong enough to resist the temptations she laid before him, if the Witch managed to beguile him with her bewitching, sexy, irresistible beauty, she would kill him with her poison. Witches were the most enchanting creatures in existence, and also the most dangerous. All it took was one drop of their poison to annihilate a Subterranean for all eternity. No one knew what happened to his soul. Everyone assumed it wound up in hell. But not even that worried me. To me, no hell could be worse than having to bear an existence without Gemma.

We'd all thought Ginevra had gotten rid of her serpent when she'd renounced her Sisters to be with Simon. She told us she had. She'd betrayed them for him, and because of it they wanted to annihilate her. She was prepared to make that sacrifice, but she was saved thanks to her close relationship with the eldest Sister, who'd spared her. Since then, the Witches had kept a constant eye on her, and the forces of darkness had returned from time to time, trying to tempt her, but they always failed. Her love for Simon was too powerful for her to give in to evil ever again.

I could understand the bond Ginevra had with her serpent, but I couldn't get over the fact that she'd exposed Simon to such a risk.

"Simon is safe," she told me now, following my train of thought.

"How could you not see how dangerous this is? You were supposed to get rid of it, like you've made us believe all this time. Only you can kill it, Gin. If any of us tried, even if we avoided its venomous fangs, it would end up killing you in the process."

"Forgive me. I couldn't bring myself to kill him. I was on the verge of doing it. Simon stopped me when he saw how agonized I was, how much pain it caused me to even think of giving him up. Simon forgave me for not finding the strength to end it."

"But why aren't you thinking of Simon?" I accused her angrily.

"Simon runs the least risk of all of you, you know that. I would never let anything happen to him. He means more to me than anything else," she insisted.

"Well, what if the door was accidentally left open and that thing slithered out into your room? Ever imagine that?"

"He'd know what to do," she replied coldly. "I've ordered Simon to kill him."

I knew Simon was capable of doing it. Like all Angels, he could control the elements, and while a Witch's poison was the one effective weapon against a Subterranean, an Angel's fire was the same against a Witch.

Cruel fate had amused itself by bringing their two enemy souls together, not to battle, but to fall helplessly in love, forcing them to live on the razor's edge day after day.

"You know he would never do that to you," I said, looking her in the eye.

"He swore he would. An Angel's promise must mean something, I suppose."

"What difference does that make? He would never kill your serpent, because he knows it would kill you too! He'd rather die."

"No! I'd never allow him to," she said, her voice tinged with the tears that the notion had brought to her eyes. "Our bond is a lot stronger than that. I'd sense the danger and be there to help him. Simon never runs risks—none of you do. Trust me, Evan. I've kept the situation under control for a long time and will continue to do so. My serpent won't hurt any of you. A Witch's word means something. Besides, Evan, we should talk about this some other time. Don't forget why we came here: *Gemma*."

Hearing her name made everything else disappear.

"Do it," I ordered, clenching my jaw.

Ginevra stepped inside the case, closing the door behind her, and looked down at her serpent. Its small size didn't convey how lethal it was. She lifted it from the tree trunk it was coiled around. I could tell from the way they were staring so intently at each other that they were communicating.

Ginevra raised her free hand toward a panel that opened up in the wall on the far side of her room, outside the door of the vault. Not wanting to break the connection between them, she opened it with a flick of her wrist without taking her gaze off the creature. Holding my breath, I watched a tiny vial dart toward her like a nail drawn to a magnet. The vial went right through the glass wall of the case, so strong was her magic. Ginevra showed it to the serpent who in the meantime had wrapped itself around her arm, hissing every time it met my gaze. She stared straight into its eyes and the creature suddenly relaxed its grip and slithered down to her hand so swiftly it made me back up, even though the glass pane between us assured my safety. But the beast wasn't interested in me, it was under Ginevra's control now. It scared me to think my sister had such a powerful bond with such an evil creature.

The serpent reached the vial that Ginevra was holding in her hand and pierced the cap with its fang, as sharp and pointed as a needle. A sparkling droplet, crystal clear and fatal, fell to the bottom of the vial.

One drop was enough.

Ginevra whispered something to the serpent that, despite all the languages I spoke, was incomprehensible to me. She pulled it away from the vial and put it back on the branch.

"We can go now. We're done here," she told me, her voice cold. It seemed like a part of the creature had seeped into her when they'd established their connection, just as Ginevra had controlled it a moment before.

I followed her out of the room, looking over my shoulder at the case. Free from her control, the serpent wouldn't stop hissing, infuriated by my presence.

Ginevra sealed the vault door carefully and walked straight to her desk as though she'd done this many times before. I watched as her eyes returned to normal, ridding themselves of the darkness. She opened the drawer and pulled out a dagger. "You're sure you want to do this?"

"Never been so sure of anything in my life."

She nodded, never taking her eyes off me. "There's no way you can get him to drink the poison. You'll have to stab him," she warned, her voice grim, as though the idea of killing the scumbag might scare me.

"I can't wait," I hissed, a growing rage lashing at my heart. I was burning with the longing to face the damned Angel. Ginevra opened the little vial and tipped it, making the poison slowly slide down the glass wall. She held the dagger underneath it and the droplet fell onto the sharp blade.

"Be very careful not to cut yourself, Evan." She slid the dagger into a leather sheath and handed it to me.

I tied it firmly to my belt and stared at her, on my face the look of someone ready to kill. "That's not going to happen. At least not accidentally," I confessed. I knew what I'd do if it turned out I was too late to save Gemma.

Ginevra nodded again, grief-stricken. She realized that in that case neither she nor anyone else would be able to stop me. "So how do we find her?" she asked sadly, her voice weary. She seemed sure the Executioner was somehow hiding Gemma from us, just like he'd managed to lure her away from our protection.

"I don't know." Frustration seeped into my voice. "I've been trying to reach her with my thoughts, but I can't find her." We didn't know exactly how long ago she'd disappeared. We didn't know where he'd hidden her or why Ginevra and I weren't able to perceive her.

Usually all I had to do was focus on her, the same as with anyone else, to materialize at her side. So why couldn't I sense *anything* now? An impenetrable void surrounded her, concealing her behind absolute silence. No matter how hard I tried, I couldn't perceive the aura emanating from her soul. It was like she was dead. I instantly shoved the thought from my mind, angry at myself for even thinking it.

"Try again," Ginevra said encouragingly, reading my frustration. "Call to her, Evan. Keep on calling to her. I'm sure she'll hear you."

I concentrated on Gemma again. No results. All I sensed was silence. Again and again. It was like an insurmountable wall was keeping me from going to her. I tried to get past it, as desperate as an insect banging against a window to reach the light, but every attempt failed. Anguish closed in on me as the seconds went by until I felt suffocated.

"I can't find her," I admitted, devastated. "Search for her thoughts, Gin!" I begged, a slave to desperation. "You've got to find her! Listen for her voice. Please."

"You think I haven't been trying? I can't hear her. I'm sorry. There's silence all around her, it's like—"

"Focus!" I barked. "You've *got* to hear her. Focus!" I screamed, unable to bear the weight of the words I'd kept her from saying. "Please," I implored her, agonized. I couldn't stand the idea that the silence might be the icy halo of death that had already descended on her.

Ginevra closed her eyes and her face instantly tensed. I waited a few moments, even holding my breath so I wouldn't break her concentration.

"I sense something. *It's him.*"

The air left my nostrils in a snort of rage.

"He's very powerful."

"Where is he? Tell me where he's keeping her!" I snarled, blinded by the longing to kill him.

"I can't—I can't reach them. I'm sorry. He can sense me too, and he's blocking me."

Hatred for that worm burned my very soul. I clenched my fists, ready to pour out all my fury on the first thing I could take a swing at, but Ginevra stopped me before I could vent my anger. "Calm down, Evan, we need to concentrate!"

"I swear he's going to pay for this." My eyes felt like they were burning in some mysterious pyre. "He can't keep me from her. I'm going to find her and I'm going to show him no mercy." Anger consumed me, seared me like fire. "I'm going to plunge this dagger into his chest and send him straight to hell! And if it turns out I'm too late, I'll follow him there. I hope the poison's enough for both of us."

"That's not going to happen," Ginevra reassured me as I sat down on her bed, my eyes hidden behind my fists. "We'll get there in time. Focus, Evan, think of Gemma. Think of her like you've never thought of her before."

I closed my eyes as Ginevra's voice dispelled the rage clouding my mind.

"There's an inexplicable connection between the two of you. I can sense its power. It's intense, indissoluble, it's something not even death can break." Her voice was growing more and more persuasive, like a spell, drawing me inside it, calming even my breathing. "Follow it, Evan. Follow that cord that connects you to Gemma. Reach her through that connection. Only you can sense the soul inside her. Somehow it's connected to your own. Look for her inside yourself."

Her voice had softened to a hush that led all the way to Gemma, to the infinite love I felt for her, to the alchemy that united us. *Gemma, where are you?* I shouted in my mind, my voice breaking with desperation, hoping my words would find their way to her. *Where is he hiding you? I can't find you! Gemma. My angel . . . Gem.*

For a split second, like a lightning bolt piercing the sky, she was there.

"I found her!" I shot to my feet, filled with new hope. The hope that it wasn't too late.

GEMMA

FOUR HOURS EARLIER

32

THE ANGELUS

The light illuminated the room softly, like candlelight. A sweet melody filled the air, and although everything around me was calm and peaceful, my heart was racing wildly.

I looked at my feet, noticing that my body was moving to the rhythm of that sweet sound, swaying in someone's arms. Peter smiled at me as I raised my eyes, holding me tighter as though he wanted to keep me there. I looked around, confused. Why was he here at the prom? What had happened to Evan?

The room was full of people dancing as the band on stage played our song. "I bet you're thinking of him." Peter's voice sounded almost threatening.

"No, no. I . . . Pet, where were you? You disappeared."

To my surprise, a hint of sadness suddenly darkened his face. "I didn't disappear, Gemma. *You're* the one who can't see me. You only have eyes for him and you never notice me. I wish he would disappear!"

His accusation, though true, left me puzzled. "Where is he?" I blurted, unable to escape the anxiety weighing on me.

His expression instantly hardened into a bitter glare. "Him! Him! Him! Enough! I can't take it any more! Is Evan the only person who exists for you?" Despite his tone, it hadn't been a question but another accusation.

I let out a dejected groan. Peter had never lost his temper with me like this before. He seemed blinded by anger. Deep-rooted anger toward Evan. "What's gotten into you, Pet? Stop it, you're scaring me."

"*I'm* scaring you? It's not me you should be scared of, and you know it."

"W-what do you mean?" I stammered, following my instinct to defend Evan at all costs. "Who told you that? What do you know?" I said accusingly, my voice growing firmer.

Peter stopped dancing and grabbed me by the shoulders. "Gemma, listen carefully. There's something *evil* about that guy. You can't trust him," he warned, the look on his face so intense it left me breathless. There was something different in his eyes, as if they weren't really his. "*You can't trust him,*" he repeated slowly, so I'd take in his message.

I stared at him for a minute. His echoing words pierced my protective shell, reawakening fears I thought I'd buried. By now I knew what Evan was hiding from everyone. I knew the mask he was forced to wear, so why did I still feel agitated, as if a voice were continuing to whisper into my ear, hinting that there was even more to know?

Peter's face became more and more blurred. I tried hard to focus on his features, but he slowly disappeared, fading like a ghost as the echo of his voice grew fainter, repeating that I couldn't trust Evan.

He vanished completely, and everything around me seemed to turn gray. The light grew cold and dull, like in a black-and-white picture. I could just barely make out a few details surrounding me.

I looked around, suddenly shocked. There was no one else in the room. I was alone.

A sinister shudder of anxiety gripped my body. Piles of streamers and empty paper cups littered the floor. Even the music had stopped and all I could hear was my own breathing. I couldn't explain what had happened or where all the others had gone.

In the bone-chilling silence, a gust of freezing-cold air suddenly hit me, rushing through my hair. The blood in my veins turned to ice. Not because of the cold air, but because of my absolute certainty that someone *was* there, after all, lurking in the shadows. Terror had come back to torment me.

It had to be him. The Reaper Angel. *He'd found me.*

I looked around desperately. Where was Evan? Why wasn't he there to protect me like he promised he would? The thought of having to face that infernal creature all on my own made me shudder. How could I defend myself? Me, a useless, insignificant mortal, how could I battle an Executioner? How could I keep him from killing me without mercy?

My heart lurched, answering my question: there was no way I could.

It was the end.

I took a deep breath and prepared to face him. "I know you're here!" My trembling voice echoed through the empty room. "Don't hide!" I shouted, forcing myself to steady my voice this time.

Like a bolt of lightning, a dark figure shot across the room from one patch of shadow to another. I started with fright, trying to follow it with my eyes so it wouldn't sneak up on me from behind. Again and again it moved, finally stopping beside the dark wall in front of me.

My breathing stopped. I panted, gasping for air, struggling against the panic that threatened to overwhelm me.

The shadow remained hidden, shrouded in darkness, watching me until my brain finally regained control over my body. My panic subsided and I narrowed my eyes, trying to penetrate the darkness in which the figure was hiding. A whimper escaped my lips. He looked so *human.*

"I know who you are," I hesitantly made myself say.

An unexpectedly alluring voice issued from the gloom. It was low, penetrating. "You think you know all there is to know, but you're wrong."

His voice.

Astonished, I struggled to resist the effect it was having on me, destabilizing me to the point that it kept me from grasping the meaning of his words. It was as if I were momentarily bewitched. A leg appeared, moving slowly out of the shadows. Taken by surprise, I flinched and took a step back to maintain the distance between us, but the second my foot touched the ground, a stabbing pain shot through my heel. I stifled a shriek and looked down. Not far from me, the giant chandelier lay on the ground, destroyed. Thousands of pieces of broken glass covered the ground. The sharp crystal shards threatened my every move.

"Careful, wouldn't want to hurt yourself." His voice rose up, hypnotic and entrancing. I could just make out his grin through the darkness. It told me he was enjoying witnessing my desperation.

Meanwhile, the pain in my foot grew stronger, making me wonder how deep and how serious the wound was. I stole a glance at it and found that a large shard was embedded in my heel. Blood was gushing out and forming a pool on the floor. The blood-spattered prisms sparkled as they reflected my image like a dark omen.

I forced myself to ignore the lacerating pain, forgoing the chance to pull the glass from my flesh, and darted my eyes around, searching for my assassin. I couldn't afford to lose sight of him.

"Does it hurt?" he asked, pleased. It was hard to believe such a cruel monster could be lurking behind such a deep, alluring voice. It was clear from his chuckle that the suffering I was undergoing now would be nothing compared to what I would soon have to endure. Containing a rush of frustration, I struggled to keep silent and hide the grimace of pain on my face.

The monster took another step forward, coming into the light.

While my voice had threatened to abandon me when I'd first heard him speak, now that I saw his face, I was paralyzed. He wasn't a shadow, he was a man, a young and incredibly attractive man. No scythe in his hand, no black hood over his head. His appearance wasn't the way I'd imagined it in my worst nightmares. Just the opposite: this Reaper Angel was *gorgeous.*

He wasn't very tall. His hair was short, but his sideburns narrowed into a thin line that framed his face, joining with a dark goatee. And his gray, gray eyes . . . Eyes of ice. They glimmered, bewitching me, glowing in the dim light. They were strangely familiar . . . No. It couldn't be. Was it possible Death could take on an angelic appearance? For a moment I let myself be mesmerized by his fascinating aura, so terrified and enchanted I forgot why he'd come.

"You look surprised." My body tensed. I had to keep my emotions from showing. "What were you expecting? Did you think I'd be a monster? Is that how they described me?" He smiled, his voice as soft as black velvet.

"I know who you are," I repeated, finally able to speak again. "Evan told me about you." Like an antidote, the sound of my own voice snapped me out of the spell he'd poisoned me with. And when I remembered who I was actually facing, I couldn't hold back a cold shiver.

"You're trembling," he said. His voice became darker, with a sharp edge. "Are you afraid?"

"No," I was quick to reply, aware that my expression was giving me away. It was a lie: I'd never been so terrified in my life. Actually, I was *frozen* with terror, hibernating beneath a slab of ice that kept me even from breathing.

"Hmm." He shook his head, drawing closer. "You'll learn soon enough that you can't lie to me."

I flinched, suddenly afraid he could read my mind.

"I can sense it, you know," he whispered, pacing in slow, ever-diminishing circles around me like a vulture. "Your fear." I squeezed my eyes shut and swallowed, trying not to make a sound. "I don't blame you for that—you should be scared," he whispered directly into my ear. "But I see that's not everything."

He smiled as if something had surprised him. "Well, I wasn't expecting *this*," he added, grinning like a wolf with its jaws locked around its prey. "I don't know if I should be offended or amused. I'm not the only one you're afraid of."

"You're wrong!" I lied again, amazed at how quickly I'd reacted. Deep in my heart, I knew I was the one who was wrong. The little voice in my head that I thought I'd buried had suddenly reappeared, feeding on his words, growing so strong it escaped my control. Peter's voice echoed in my ears: *Evan. You can't trust him. He's dangerous.* I shook my head to drive it away, but every attempt just made it stronger.

With sorrow, I realized it wasn't Peter's voice that was tormenting me. It must have been my conscience, the survival instinct that had always urged me to run away from Evan, the voice my heart had always prevented me from obeying.

I tried with all my might to suppress my suspicions of Evan. He'd been honest with me, revealing his deepest secrets, so why should I still have any doubts about him?

"If that were true," the Angel went on, responding to my suspicion, "where's your hero now? Why doesn't he come save you? Wait—wait. Let me rephrase that." He smiled, a strange, evil gleam in his eyes. "Are you still sure he wants to save you?"

"Stop it!" I shouted. "I'm not afraid of Evan." But my voice inevitably grew faint, belying my words.

"Wrong. I've already told you, you can't lie to me. You need to know that."

"Why would I be afraid of him?" As I voiced the question, I realized I wanted to know the answer myself. "I know who he is. And I know who *you* are," I said accusingly, my voice firm. "Evan told me everything."

"Hmm. Wrong again." Like a mischievous ghost, this Angel of Death was having fun torturing me.

I couldn't figure out why I was growing more and more confused with every word he spoke. My head felt foggy, as if I were slowly losing control of myself. He had bewitched me. His words were slowly poisoning me, hiding behind that mesmerizing voice like an evil spell.

"Are you really sure Evan told you everything?" he insisted, his eyes narrowed in a wicked smile.

I recoiled. What was he insinuating?

"As I imagined," he said, smirking when he noticed the surprise painted on my face. "I'm willing to bet he didn't mention he was sent here to kill you."

His blood-chilling words struck me like a bolt of lightning, piercing my chest, killing something inside me. I wanted to deny it, refute it, refuse to accept what he'd said, but my brain instantly registered it as absolute, unquestionable truth. For some bizarre reason, I felt it really was a fact. Maybe part of me had always suspected it. I couldn't even open my mouth to speak.

"He tried to kill you," he said, mocking my expression, which had been reduced to a blank gaze.

"That's not true," I forced out in a stubborn attempt to contradict him, my voice trembling as I stared into empty space.

"Are you sure? When the semi was about to run you over on your bike, how do you think Evan managed to show up at the right place at the right time? Why do you think he was there, Gemma?"

Like an earthworm, his voice dug its way toward the very last part of me that stubbornly resisted. My heart ached.

"He was there for you, he'd come to take your life."

His words corroded my skin like acid. And yet, on the razor's edge between reason and madness, the thumping of my heart gave courage to that little part of me that was still trying to fight back. "But he didn't," I heard myself say, as if in the voice of another. I felt like I'd lost contact with myself, connected to reason only by a fragile bond that continued to struggle, desperate to survive. I tried to bolster it, but it was no use.

"Not yet, but he will soon. You're kidding yourself, thinking you can live a life that no longer belongs to you. He can't change his nature. What you need to realize, Gemma, is that none of this depends on him. Or on me. Your fate is sealed. There's a time for everything. A time for each of us. Death has sent its Soldiers to claim your soul, and it will continue to do so until it's taken you. Imagine this as a game of chess where we're just pawns being moved by someone else. And you're his target. I'm sorry. Evan simply went through a period of distraction. Of weakness. It happens to all of us sooner or later, but loyalty to what we are is deeply rooted in each of us. I bet he's already had a change of heart and at this very moment, while you and I are here talking, he's deciding how to kill you, Gemma. He wants you dead so he can redeem himself."

"That's impossible," I whimpered, holding back tears. I refused to believe his cruel words, but my awareness that he wasn't lying was increasing exponentially. "What does his redemption have to do with me?" I asked, devastated, fearing the answer.

The Executioner raised his left hand, revealing his forearm. My eyes widened as a grin spread over his face. "Because he's like me! What did you think he was? He's an Angel of Death, Gemma—and he came for you."

A shiver ran down my spine, my eyes glued to the mark of the Children of Eve. I shook my head. No. No. No! It couldn't be true, he was tricking me! And yet, his eyes . . . They were identical to Evan's.

"Death wants you at its side, and we're its reapers. We're shadows of fate. Ferrymen of souls. Accept it."

"Enough!" I shouted through my tears. "Why should I believe you?"

"Oh, you already believe me. I can sense it. Evan's the one who killed the man they found in the woods."

"No!" I screamed, begging him to stop.

"Evan started the fire and took the little girl too. He killed her, Gemma, let her burn to death. Mercilessly. You never wanted to accept it, but a part of you has always known. Unconsciously, you even avoided asking yourself the right questions—because you're mortal, weak, and in love with Evan. Whereas he *betrayed* you, Gemma. He only wants to kill you."

"Stop it! Enough!" I shrieked, covering my ears with my hands so I wouldn't hear anything else. Tears continued to stream from my eyes, which were now puffy, keeping me from seeing where my legs were suddenly carrying me as my mind desperately attempted to deny his words. How did he know exactly what I felt? How had he managed to dig deep inside me, uncovering the things I'd been trying to hide even from myself?

I tried to make it to the door across the room but the Angel blocked my way. "It's hard to accept, I know," he said in a low voice, flashing an entirely false look of sympathy.

"Why don't you just kill me now and get it over with?" I groaned, giving up.

The Angel considered my suggestion before speaking, as though choosing his words carefully. "I have something to confess to you— a *secret*," he whispered, putting his face close to mine. "I was sent in only to kill you, but I don't know if I'm going to follow orders this time, because that would be doing you a favor. Maybe I'll let your Evan be the one to do it while I sit back and enjoy the show. In fact, I should be grateful to you. This little game is amusing me even more than I'd hoped.

"Poor little Gemma, the only person you've ever loved betrays you, deceives you. All this passion of yours, all this suffering . . . they've relit a fuse inside me that went out long ago. They've reawakened the Angelus in me, liberating the pain I'd repressed. Fortunately I can take all of it out on *you*.

"For far too long I carried out orders without experiencing any emotion. Now I feel alive for the first time in many, many years. Once my name was Faustian. Then that part of me died, leaving behind only the demon. Now I'm simply Faust," he said, his lips twisted in a sadistic grin.

"You're a monster!" I shrieked with all the voice I had left.

"A monster?" he hissed, cocking his head, his expression pure evil. "Why's that? You've never been anyone to me. Why should I spare you? Or feel compassion for you? Can't you see who the real monster is?" He studied my face. "Evan lied to you, tricked you, and is ready to turn his back on you. Well? Which one of us is the monster? Him or me? Answer me!" he bellowed. "Who's the monster?"

I was shattered, devastated. I wasn't sure my body could contain so much desperation and frustration. *Faustian*: such a sweet-sounding name for such a cruel creature. Faust was definitely more appropriate.

He scrutinized me. "You must love him a lot if part of you is still fighting for him." His statement left me even more stunned. Could he read my feelings? "But it's weak; I can feel it fading. It's about to surrender."

I hoped with all my being that it wouldn't. Inside of me, I still wanted to believe there was hope—even just a glimmer—that Evan didn't really want to kill me.

I grabbed hold of this dream and clung to it tightly, but it slipped through my fingers. I couldn't get it back. I felt mired, as if my mind didn't belong to me any more. I tried to make myself think clearly, but I just couldn't reason.

"You're stubborn. I wasn't expecting that," he said, still studying me. Suddenly, something caught his attention and he cocked his head, as if listening. His face twisted into a smirk of evil satisfaction.

"I'm curious to see how far your stubbornness will go. Let's see if you still have your doubts after what I'm about to show you," he said, a wicked smile on his lips.

I stared at Faust, puzzled, wondering what he meant, but before I could ask, he answered my question. "You'll see it with your own two eyes."

Could he really prove it to me? But the worry that frightened me the most was: if Faust was right, was I really prepared to face it? Deep down in my heart I knew the answer.

No. I never would be.

33

BETRAYAL

Before I could understand what the Reaper Angel was talking about, our cold, eerie surroundings were replaced by a warm, reassuring light. I looked up, quickly recognizing the unusual hazel- and chocolate-colored walls.

We were in Evan's kitchen. Just then, someone talking caught my attention.

"Oh! It's you," Evan said, his voice agitated. For a second, I thought he was talking about us appearing, but realized I was wrong when Simon responded.

Simon. Drake. Ginevra. They were all there. I studied their faces, bewildered. None of them seemed even to care about our presence. But most importantly, why wasn't anyone alarmed by the sight of the Executioner next to me?

Evan finally seemed to notice me and headed straight toward me. But something was wrong. The look in his eye was strange. Absent, detached. He looked so grim it left me confused—and scared. I found myself panting from the sudden fear that gripped me. A strange sensation stirred in my chest. A hostile, dangerous one.

Was he really about to kill me? Was it really time for me to die? As Evan strode toward me, I decided I wouldn't put up a fight. I didn't care about dying any more if it was Evan who wanted me dead. I didn't care about living any more either, for the same terrible reason.

My heart pounded with his every step as he came toward me quickly, without slowing his pace. There wasn't a hint of hesitation in his face. I filled my lungs with a long, agonized breath, thinking it was my last.

When Evan was inches from me, I shut my eyes, resigned to dying for him. At the same instant, a strange energy suddenly washed over me, taking my breath away. It was like a train coming at me full speed or a cascade of ice-cold water, as violent as a hurricane, as painful as a punch.

For a split second, I had the strangest sensation: I felt drained and filled at the same time. Something wasn't letting me breathe. It was as though a waterfall were pouring down onto me.

When I emerged, I whirled around, gasping for air, unable to believe what had just happened.

Evan was behind me. My body hadn't stopped him. He'd passed through me as if I didn't exist, as if I were . . . a *ghost.* An icy shudder gripped me. I peered down at my body, still trembling, wondering what was happening to me. Doubt entered my mind: was I already dead?

A cruel, familiar snicker tore me out of my delirium.

"Faust, what's going on?" I asked, bewildered. "Why aren't they noticing me? Am I dead?" Had it really been that easy? For a second I almost felt relieved.

But Faust's malicious laughter told me I was wrong, mocking me yet again. "You're not dead," he said, chuckling, "not yet."

I looked down at my body again, more confused than I'd ever been. My hands, my feet—nothing seemed to have changed. Everything was in its place. So what was going on?

"Why can't they see us?" I asked him, exasperated. I walked over to Evan and stared straight at him, but his silver eyes looked right through me. He couldn't see me. I heard his voice as though in the background, the sound too low for me to make out what he was saying. It was as if someone had picked up a remote control and hit the mute button.

"They can't see us because we're not really here," Faust said, answering the question burning in my mind. But for every answer, more doubts and more questions arose. What did he mean? I was there, standing right in front of Evan, but he couldn't see me.

Simon, Drake—neither of them sensed my presence. Only Ginevra looked somehow anxious. She had a wary look on her face and kept nervously scanning the room, but couldn't see us.

"If we're not here, where are we?" I asked, confused.

Faustian smiled. "Try to concentrate, Gemma. What's the last thing you remember?"

At first, I didn't understand what the ridiculous question meant, but there was no point in stubbornly trying to follow his logic. By now, my life had been turned upside down and there was no logic to it any more.

I tried hard to remember, but it was all so confused and distant, as though months or years had gone by since my last memory. It was all so *faded.*

"I was here, with Evan and Ginevra. Then the others arrived."

"Keep going," Faust encouraged me, enjoying this new game. "What else do you remember?"

"I was sleepy, exhausted. It was dark and I was afraid to close my eyes." That terrible sensation was a clear memory. It was vivid in my thoughts and still terrified me. "I was trembling," I admitted. "I was afraid, and then—"

"And then you fell asleep," Faust said, adding the words I wasn't able to find myself. At the mercy of the befuddlement clouding my mind, I still didn't understand. "Come," he ordered me, a trace of kindness in his voice.

I stepped toward him. When I looked into his eyes, searching for answers, he nodded toward the salon, prompting me to look.

The room was shrouded in a ghastly darkness. I couldn't see my hand in front of my face. Only after a moment did my eyes begin to grow accustomed to it. I noticed a movement at an unusual height a bit farther into the room.

Someone was there, hidden in the dark. My eyes narrowed to slits. Suddenly, like a revelation, I remembered that was where the couch was.

Evan, Drake, Simon, and Ginevra were all in the kitchen, so who could it be? Whoever it was, their troubled breathing made it clear they were sleeping, if restlessly.

I moved closer. Just then, the blanket covering the person slid to the floor, revealing a face.

I started. It was me on the couch. *And I was asleep.* Drops of perspiration beaded my forehead as my eyes darted nervously behind my closed lids.

I couldn't believe it was all true. I had no choice but to accept it, but it was *too much.*

"It's me," I whimpered, my voice breaking with emotion.

"It's you," Faust confirmed. "We're inside your mind."

"Am I dreaming, then?"

The Angel nodded, though through the darkness I could barely see it. "Let's say it's more of a nightmare than a sweet dream," he said, snickering.

"I don't need you to tell me that, I already know it's a nightmare. The worst one I've ever had, if it makes you happy!" I shot back bitterly, surprised I could still find a sense of humor.

Faust burst out laughing, apparently reassured by the fact that no one except me could hear him. "Ah . . . it certainly will be soon. Don't forget what we came here to do. I still have to show you something." His words sounded more like a warning than a reminder.

Just then, the others' voices reached us from the kitchen, echoing against the walls of the salon as though someone had pointed the remote at them and turned the volume back up.

Judging from their animated voices, they seemed to be arguing. I walked back toward the kitchen to find out what they were talking about. Evan was speaking. I quickened my pace, impatient to feel comforted by the sound of his voice, but his words froze me in the doorway: "Gemma's fate is sealed. She has to die. Fine. So she'll die. We can't change what's written."

Excruciating pain pierced my heart as my soul slowly died. I didn't know words strong enough or tears bitter enough to express the intensity of the emotion ripping through me: a massive wave that pushed me underwater as I thrashed, unable to breathe. The walls closed in around me, suffocating me. I could never have imagined a death worse than the one I was feeling now deep in my heart. I was anguished, devastated, racked with unbearable torment. I felt I would stay there forever, motionless, frozen in my tracks, paralyzed by the pain. I couldn't accept the truth even though I'd heard it with my own two ears.

It was too painful. Far too painful.

A voice replied to Evan's, though I couldn't tell for sure who it belonged to, deafened as I was by my suffering. "You don't want to kill the Angel any more? You want to kill Gemma instead? I don't get it."

My gaze lingered on Evan's face for a moment. He seemed so determined, so proud of his plan. He wanted to kill me. I couldn't believe it. Faust hadn't lied. Even more terrifying than what Evan was saying was the gleam in his eyes. It was as though they were sparkling.

He wasn't being forced. No, he'd decided to do it, and actually seemed excited about the idea.

If only death would take me then and there, cradling me in its comforting silence. Living and bearing such pain was intolerable. It hurt too much. Thousands of needles lanced my heart, threatening to kill me with every breath.

I wished I could hate him for the pain he was inflicting on me, hate him for deceiving and betraying me. But I couldn't. I loved him. I loved him more than anything in the world, more than myself. But I had to give him up.

Racked with pain, I grasped only snippets of what he was saying: "Gemma will be the one to take the lethal poison. Not the Angel. Gemma has to die. That's inevitable, don't you see? No one can change their destiny. No one can fight it. What's written must come to pass."

It was all so absurd, so impossible.

"Tell them how you would convince her to poison herself." Ginevra's calm voice rose up in the silence.

Her too, I thought, horrified. How could she be so cruel after pretending she and I were friends? Had she been faking it all along? I felt doubly betrayed as I listened to Evan and Ginevra plotting to kill me.

"I'll force her, if it comes to that," Evan stated, clearly resolved.

His every word was a knife thrust mercilessly through my heart. I had heard love couldn't kill you but right then I felt it was on the verge of doing just that. His voice was hard and cold, detached, as if he couldn't wait to get it over with.

I shuddered, thinking of what Faust had said: *Which one of us is the monster?* My instinct hadn't betrayed me, it had been right all along. But no matter how incredible it might seem, no matter how hard I tried, I couldn't see Evan as a monster, even though I'd heard him condemning me to death.

Simon tried hard to make Evan see reason. I would need to thank him for his mercy if I had the chance, though by now I doubted I would. There seemed to be no way out for me. I was done for. One way or another, I had to die. If Evan didn't kill me, Faust would. In any case, my minutes were numbered.

I looked wearily at the couch I was lying on, perfectly still, and stared at my fragile, defenseless body awaiting its demise.

Faust's voice echoed in my head, mocking and cruel: *What are you willing to sacrifice when the only person who can save you is the same one who has to kill you?*

An uncontrollable impulse to rebel rose up inside me. I couldn't, I *didn't want* to give up just because they'd made that decision. Not at that price. I wasn't going to sacrifice my life. I had to resist. I had to fight back. I had to at least try. They would wait until I woke up, so I had a small advantage. Maybe if I got a good head start they wouldn't find me. Was there really a place where I could hide from Evan?

An incredible rush of energy washed over me, giving me the answer. It was my survival instinct pushing me to react. There was no time to waste. Faust had disappeared. His presence probably wasn't necessary any more, given that Evan had changed his mind and decided to kill me. I could still barely stand to think of it. Accepting it would be impossible, but I had to do something.

I had to wake up. I rushed over to my unconscious body, unsure how to awaken it.

A new feeling arose amid the previous ones: *power*. I'd never felt anything like it in my whole life. For the first time I realized I was in a dream and could access powers that the real world couldn't offer me. I tried to focus on how to put an end to the nightmare and escape from the house where they were plotting to kill me. I had to run away, as far away as possible, in the hope that no one would find me.

Suddenly, like a bolt of lightning illuminating my mind, I remembered the times I'd woken up in a cold sweat, breathless, feeling like I'd been drowning, unable to swim back up to the surface. Or when I was falling into empty space and would wake up a second before hitting the ground. I looked around the room, dismayed to discover there wasn't any water nearby. Was the thin trickle of the water wall beside the staircase enough? I couldn't risk it. Dismissing the first solution left me with no choice but the second one. I at least had to try.

My first and most immediate instinct told me to hurl myself through the picture window that was covered by heavy drapes. I was on the ground floor, but the impact just might work to wake me up. After all, I was inside my head; the actual height should be irrelevant. I took a deep breath and got ready to run, certain that neither the drapes nor the glass would be enough to stop me. Just like what had happened with Evan's body, I would pass through the window and find myself outside, unharmed. The feeling of falling would wake me up, I was sure of it. I was already breathless at the thought of the terrible sensation I would experience.

Closing my eyes, I tensed my muscles and rushed toward the window with total confidence. A second before my body touched the cloth, though, my surroundings suddenly changed. In the blink of an eye the drapes disappeared, leaving in their place the dusty glass of an old window, and beyond it, empty space. I wasn't in Evan's house any more. Something in my dream had changed, transporting me to the old house on the lake. I felt a pang of terror as a dark force hurled me outside. The impact was far more violent than I was prepared for.

My brain was instantly obscured by the deafening crash of the window shattering into thousands of pieces, and a second later the void swallowed me up, along with hundreds of shards that rained down in a shower of glass. I tried to scream, but the ground below me raced inexorably closer and I couldn't make a single sound.

I knew it was all in my imagination, no matter how real it might seem, and yet I couldn't repress a wave of panic that left me breathless. The air lashed at my face. But the sharpest ache came from my heart. For a second, I wanted to slam into the ground and put an end to that unbearable pain that pierced my heart like poisoned thorns.

I surrendered to that desire, and my body hit the ground with brutal impact.

I opened my eyes, gasping desperately for air, my body drenched in sweat. A second later, my mind cleared and began to assemble the pieces of the puzzle that had led me there. Had I only dreamed it all or was it really happening? The pang in my heart gave me the answer, crushing any hope that the nightmare hadn't been real.

From the next room came the family's low voices, making my heart bleed. For a moment, I almost wanted to pretend nothing had happened and go back to sleep, abandoning myself to whatever it was fate had in store for me. But my body ignored my heart and reacted, rejecting the idea of giving up my fight for survival.

I had to run away before they noticed I'd woken up.

34

THE ESCAPE

I looked around quickly in a desperate search for a way out. The only doors I knew of were too exposed; I could never go through the front door without their noticing, and the kitchen, naturally, was out of the question. I assessed my alternatives, trying to do it quickly so Ginevra wouldn't have time to pick up on my thoughts.

Stumbling through the darkness, I tripped and bit my lip in self-reproach as I groped along. To my relief, I soon recognized the staircase leading up and climbed it one step at a time, trying not to make any noise.

The terrace was my only hope, the only way out I knew of. Maybe I could find a way to climb down without being noticed and reach the ground floor unharmed, or at least without any major injuries. It would be ridiculous if, while everyone was out to kill me, I accidentally killed myself.

When I opened the French door and saw the soft light of sunset, I found the solution. The branches of the big oak tree sprawled over the terrace, offering me their protection like strong arms ready to hold me. I certainly wouldn't find anything better.

I took a deep breath, convincing myself I could do it. It wouldn't be difficult. Quickening my pace, I grabbed hold of the largest branch, but a flashback paralyzed me. The intense emotion I'd felt when Evan had brushed his lips over my neck in that very spot on the terrace filled me as if it had just happened and he was still there, smiling at me and whispering into my ear. Whenever Evan touched me, whenever his eyes looked into mine, I didn't want to be anywhere else except with him. But it hadn't been anything but vile deceit, and now, with bitterness in my heart, I was forcing myself to run away from him, of all people. The thought that Evan actually wanted to kill me was still so impossible, so surreal.

The only thing I felt right now was the unalloyed instinct to survive. There wasn't a trace of resentment in my heart that he'd decided to give up on us for his own redemption. I only felt betrayed, deceived. It would have been better if Evan had let me die on the day I'd been destined to instead of tricking me and giving me the fleeting hope of a future with him. Fate had led us back to our roles: the doomed mortal and the Angel of Death. Prey and predator. One against the other in a battle in which I felt I'd already lost everything.

No matter how much my heart refused to give up the love that bound me to him, my only choice was to hide and hope he'd never find me. I awkwardly climbed up onto the branch, clinging to the rough bark. It felt like my entire body was pierced by pins and needles that drove in deeper with every step, but the desperate desire to live made me ignore the pain. Or, more probably, the bottomless chasm of pain devouring me from inside made everything else seem bearable.

I reached the ground with only a few scrapes on my legs. My dress was torn here and there, the oak's final attempt to hold me back. The last rays of sunset lit up the path as if offering me their guidance. I smoothed down my crumpled red dress. Less than a day had elapsed since the prom, but it felt like an eternity since I'd danced with Evan as he held me tight. I banished the thought and broke into a run without allowing myself time to look back. Probably because I wasn't sure the lump in my throat would ever go away if I did.

I reached the gate, banging against its impenetrable bars. Had I really imagined I'd find it open? Desperation threatened to overwhelm me. I couldn't climb over it without their noticing me. The stone wall was too high for me to scale.

I had a flash of inspiration. I knew another way out. The gap in the wall. A self-mocking smile came to my lips when I thought back on how much pain I'd felt that afternoon. A trifle compared to the sharp blades slicing into my heart now.

I tried to get my bearings and remember where the spot in the wall was. The garden was huge and I didn't want to risk wasting too much time looking for it. Then I remembered that from the gap I'd seen the back of the house, which meant I was on the opposite side. Without giving myself time to think, I ran as fast as I could in that direction.

The cool air was fragrant with the scent of the flowers that filled the garden. It whipped at my face, keeping my tears from falling.

I was about to give up when the wooden bench I'd seen from the gap in the wall appeared, bathed in the soft light of sunset. But I still must have been far away, because I couldn't see anything that looked like an opening. Had they repaired it? Advancing cautiously so no one would notice me, I moved closer, taking shelter among the large tree trunks, until I saw the hole in the wall. Hope filled my heart again. I was free.

Only then, when I'd regained my courage, did I let myself cast a fleeting glance behind me. I couldn't fathom how Ginevra could possibly not have heard my thoughts in her mind this whole time.

With difficulty, I began to crawl through the narrow gap. Just as I finally emerged on the other side, someone behind me grabbed the hem of my dress. I froze, breathless.

They'd found me.

A lump in my throat, I spun around to see who it was. Evan? Ginevra? Someone else, there to take me back to my fate?

I exhaled when I realized I was alone and my hem had gotten caught on the rough stone. By now the dress was in tatters. I didn't care if it got any worse, so I yanked it free, leaving a strip of fabric dangling from the wall. I didn't have time to do anything about it because I didn't feel safe. I had to get out of there fast.

I put one foot in front of the other and started running, completely oblivious to where my desperation was leading me. They wanted me dead and I wasn't sure I'd be able to stop them.

The streetlights flickered on as I listened to my brisk footfalls on the asphalt. Only the beating of my heart was louder, and in the background, Lana Del Rey's voice filled my head. My breathing grew labored and I looked back for a second without slowing down. Suddenly, the lyrics of *Born To Die* seemed to have been written for me. It was a relief to see that Evan's house had disappeared behind me. The surge of adrenaline in my blood eased.

Only then did the bottomless pit in my stomach come back to torture me. I slowed down, spotting a thick cluster of trees and shrubs in which I could hide. I'd reached the wood that rose up on the shore of Lake Placid. Without hesitating, I started running again and plunged into it, not caring about the dangers that might be lurking there after sunset. Nothing could frighten me more than the idea that I'd lost Evan forever.

I continued to cling to the idea of the two of us together, even though he didn't want me any more. He wanted me to die, he'd stopped fighting for us. *He didn't want me any more.* I couldn't get the thought out of my mind. How could he do something like that to me? Sobs choked me as tears rolled down my grief-stricken face and vanished in the wind.

Evan wanted to poison me. And that's exactly what he was doing. The pain spread, coursing through my veins like an unbearable venom, killing me slowly. Every part of me was in anguish. *Then why couldn't I hate him? How could I still love him so intensely, ignoring the fate he was condemning me to? Why couldn't I be mad at him?*

I tried to stifle the question that my heart continued to scream, burying it deep inside myself because it was too much to bear. *Why hadn't his love for me been strong enough to keep him from wanting to kill me?*

I knew the answer. He was an Angel of Death. I was just a soul with a sealed fate. It seemed he'd finally realized that. It was my fault if I'd foolishly believed I could have a future with him.

There were no magnanimous Angels of Death. I'd read enough books about myths and legends to realize that. I'd naively hoped I could write a new story, our story, but it was just an illusion. I was the victim and Evan my Executioner.

Although I'd managed to hide, how would I be able to bear the idea of living without Evan and depriving myself of the emotions only he could trigger in me? How could I give him up, his lips, after I'd tasted them? The lump in my throat grew so tight I could barely breathe. Pain flooded every part of me.

The sun was setting behind the horizon. The trees overhead filtered the last faint rays of light as I ran as fast as I could, leaves crunching beneath my feet. I ran toward the darkness, a mysterious darkness that had nothing to do with nightfall, toward a dark, unknown destiny. Who would come to save me now?

35

THE HUNT

The further the sun sank behind the mountains, the eerier and more lugubrious the atmosphere became. It felt like thousands of eyes were hidden in the forest, watching me. But I didn't care. I'd lost the most important thing of all; what could my life be worth now, in comparison?

The silence of the forest steadied my breathing and my mind lost itself in a thousand conjectures. Memories of times spent with Evan crowded my brain unbidden, as if part of me was still making them resurface. I wasn't sure if my mind was just being cruel or attempting to make me see something I hadn't noticed before. I'd met Evan for the first time right here in these woods. Back then I'd had no idea what that encounter would end up meaning to me. I'd had no idea how it would change my life. My heart had been chained in steel shackles, and yet I sensed that hiding myself in those memories took the edge off the pain.

Faust was right. Death wouldn't be so horrid if I had Evan by my side. Instinctively, I raised my fingers to my lips, summoning the memory of the taste of his, and a tear slid down beside them, reminding me how bitter real life was. Evan had saved me from my fate, but he must have regretted it and decided to do Death's bidding after all. He'd rescued me from the semi, from Daryl's aggression, and from the crazed car, which I now knew had been under Faust's control.

I couldn't figure out *when* exactly Evan had given up fighting for us. After all, he'd always been so protective of me. The thought that he wanted to kill me began to seem more and more ridiculous—*too* ridiculous—despite the fact that I'd had substantial proof of his betrayal.

Suddenly my head felt lighter on my shoulders as though a sense of oppression were beginning to ease. I realized only then that an impenetrable layer of fog had been clouding my mind; it was as if a gentle breeze had come to drive it away.

Could anything have driven Evan to regret what he'd done to the point that he actually *wanted* me to die—so intensely I could see it in his eyes? It suddenly seemed absurd, insane, illogical. I stopped, unsure whether the forest was spinning around me or if it was all in my head.

Could Evan actually have given up the struggle for us? I'd heard him with my own ears as he sentenced me to death—but could there be some hidden explanation?

My heart grabbed hold of the possibility with both hands and clung to it tightly so it wouldn't get away. I regretted now how impulsively I'd run off. Could it all have been a fleeting illusion that my mind had come up with just to drive away the pain?

I needed to sort through my thoughts, so I continued to run, refreshed by the breeze. I was torn. My temples throbbed to the rhythm of my heartbeat.

Which one should I listen to: my body, which had helplessly witnessed the pronouncement of my death sentence; or my heart, which kept crying out his name? Could my own senses have tricked me? Or were my feelings for Evan clouding reality?

GEMMMAAAAA!!!

The heartrending scream exploded in my head, stopping me in my tracks.

"Evan," I whispered, devastated by the anguish in his voice.

Not anger or bitterness because I'd escaped, but *desperation.* Only intense, overwhelming desperation. I blinked and a stream of sweet tears streaked my face, washing away all my uncertainty.

He loved me.

Evan had never stopped loving me. What had driven me to doubt him after everything he'd done for me? I couldn't remember any more. My heart had tried to warn me, but something had prevented me from listening to it. A conviction that I now found ridiculous, because it didn't even belong to me. It was as though someone else had instilled it directly in my mind. Now Evan's voice had uprooted it, dissolving the fog that had been clouding my judgment.

Gemma . . .

I jumped, terrified. The silence had given way to a whisper, as bone-chilling as the hiss of a demon. It wasn't Evan's voice. When I recognized it, I was gripped with pure terror.

It was Faust. He was back.

Gemma . . .

The voice tunneled through my terror and burst into my mind, which began to spin again.

Gemma . . .

The whisper seemed to be coming straight from hell, or maybe it was lurking in my head, or even in the trees. Or everywhere.

I waited for my breathing to slow, trying to reach Evan with my mind and push away the mantle of terror that was closing in around me, distancing me from him. The silence had become so ominous that every breath of wind and every rustling leaf made me jump.

Exhausted by sheer terror, I cried out his name in my head in a desperate attempt to make a connection between my thoughts and Ginevra's mind, but I failed, time and time again. It was like I'd been sucked down into a dark pit, so deep it hid me from the world.

I was alone again. With Faust. But this time it wasn't a nightmare, it was real life. To my shock, I suddenly realized he had been the one who'd led me there. He was a puppeteer pulling the strings that controlled me, his marionette, so I would run away from Evan's protection.

Something moved in the trees. Frightened, I whipped my head to the left. A black shadow leapt out, making my blood run cold, and then disappeared into the foliage before the shudder it had caused could make its way down my spine. Even the leaves seemed to be holding their breath.

A massive rush of adrenaline made me break into a run. The trees took on a ghostly appearance as I rushed past them at a speed I wasn't sure I could keep up for much longer. Still, it didn't matter how fast I ran or how far I got. There was nowhere I could hide from the Executioner whom Death had sent to kill me. His ghastly voice pursued me, whispering my name among the trees, reminding me I couldn't escape.

Nevertheless, I had newfound hope. No matter how my knees were trembling, I knew I could hold out until Evan came to save me. Because he *would* come, I was sure of it. I just had to play for time.

Like a wish granted, the trees opened up, revealing the old lake house. In a last grueling effort, I focused on my legs, trying to channel all the energy I had left into their muscles so I could seek refuge inside.

Although I was aware its walls wouldn't prevent the Angel of Death from reaching me, my heart still hoped I could survive long enough to be rescued. Why wasn't Evan there to protect me? How could I dream of surviving that terrible monster with eyes of ice for long? I couldn't understand why I wasn't getting through to Evan or Ginevra. Why couldn't he sense my soul? Why couldn't she hear my thoughts? Was I wrong after all?

I raced through the rusty gate and threw open the front door, slamming it behind me. Inside, I pressed my back against the wall and slid down to the floor, panting, in the silence and the darkness.

I trembled.

36

HIDE AND SEEK

I couldn't tell how long I sat there, still short of breath from the run and my terror. It felt like hours. It was so dark outside I lost the notion of time.

Just when my body had stopped trembling and I thought Faust might have given up the hunt, the unmistakable creak of rusty iron stopped my breath.

Someone was trying to get in. What reason did Faust have to come in through the door when he could hide from me by using the darkness as his accomplice?

My heart in my throat, I slowly got up from the floor, trying not to make a noise, and cautiously peeked through the window. The gate continued to make that unsettling creak, swinging back and forth as if someone was having fun moving it. It was a ghostly movement that had nothing to do with the wind.

And yet no one was there.

Why hadn't Faust taken my life yet? He could have done away with me in the blink of an eye. What sort of morbid amusement did he hope to derive from scaring me to death? Could he be that evil? Was it possible there weren't laws in their world to keep him from acting like this?

Without giving myself a chance to reflect, I opened the door to the cellar stairs. I knew any attempt to cling to life would be useless, but part of me still refused to stop fighting.

I knew every nook and cranny in the lake house, every dusty old passageway. And I knew that somewhere in the wall downstairs was a door to an underground passageway that led outside. I just had to find it. When I was little I had often hid inside it, just for fun, to keep Peter from finding me.

Out of habit, I groped on the wall for the light switch, but the moment my fingers brushed it, it dawned on me that naturally it wouldn't work.

The worn wood groaned beneath my feet, forcing me to move with extreme caution. An intense smell of mildew impregnated the walls, leaving the air acrid and almost unbreathable. I stopped in the doorway for a second, but a sinister groan from outside convinced me to keep moving, testing each dusty stair with my foot before putting my full weight onto it as I climbed down into the darkness of the dank cellar. Just as I reached the bottom stair, the door slammed shut behind me, trapping me in the cellar, which wasn't as I remembered it. Several years had gone by, but I was sure the place had never seemed as daunting, forbidding, and eerie as it did right now, barely illuminated by a ghostly moonbeam that crept through the tiny barred window. As anxiety gripped me, I threw caution to the wind and quickly left the stairway behind me. With each step I ran into cobwebs, sending a shiver over my skin.

I was utterly discouraged; no matter how carefully I searched the dusty old shelves, I couldn't find the door that would free me from that ghastly trap. All at once, with a glimmer of hope, I recognized the tattered canvas that covered the way out, but a sudden noise behind me made me spin around. My body reacted instantly, leaping to the side a scant second before a huge crash raised a cloud of dust that filled the cellar. I covered my mouth with my hands, coughing and gasping for air. As the dust began to settle, the moonlight mocked me by revealing the massive bookcase that had almost crushed me and now lay on its side at my feet like a sleeping giant. My heart leapt to my throat, ready to surrender, while my knees trembled, threatening to buckle under my weight. I began to be convinced it was impossible to run away from Death.

Like the hissing of a poisonous snake, Faust's blood-curdling whisper came back to torment me, joining me on that sinister stage. *Gemma . . .*

I was horrified to see that the fallen bookshelf was completely blocking the passageway. It hadn't crushed me, but it had buried my last hope. Climbing the steps three at a time, I arrived at the stairway door, where I grappled desperately with the knob. Panic washed over me when it wouldn't open. I was trapped. And Faust was there with me, I could sense his presence. He must have tired of the chase.

A lump rose in my throat as I realized I was about to die. I cried out for help, my voice rising uncontrollably as I pounded on the wooden door. But it was pointless. No one would hear me because no one ever came near the old house. This cellar would be my tomb.

Relaxing my grip on the knob, resigned and defeated, I took a step back and stared blankly at it, my tears ready to flow.

Fate had touched me with its icy fingers, wrapped me in its dark wings, its plumes as corrosive as poison on my skin, as heavy as chains, imprisoning me in a body that was no longer my own. It was only a matter of time. There was nowhere to hide, nowhere to run. Like a hungry falcon, its shadow loomed over me watchfully. I felt the weight of its wings upon me. The wings of death.

I blinked. I was so frightened I could have sworn the knob had slowly moved. With a sinister sound, the door began to open, confirming my suspicion. I stared at the knob, paralyzed with fear, bewildered and terrified beyond all measure.

No one stood in the doorway. Faust was playing with me like a cat with a mouse. I wondered what difference it could possibly make to keep fighting him.

Repressing my fear, I walked through the doorway, my heart in my throat. I ran through the parlor, throwing everything I could get my hands on behind me, driven by the panic his blood-chilling voice produced in me. As if anything could prevent an Angel sent by Death from catching me.

Gemma . . . Where are you running? The whisper filled my mind. He was toying with me. *I'll find you wherever you go. You can't hide from me.*

A shiver ran over me. He was right.

You can't run from me forever.

"You're insane!" I screamed into the empty room.

I reached the long, steep staircase that led to the second floor and began to rush up it. In the silence, a loud creak warned me not to trust the worn stairs, but before I could think to slow down, my foot broke through the rotten wood. A sharp, shooting pain made me dizzy.

I tried to pull my foot out, but it was lodged in the splintered wood that had lacerated my flesh. My panic grew greater when I sensed Faust's presence, though I couldn't see him. Casting a terrified glance around, I used both hands to try to yank my leg out as a blast of freezing air hit me. I struggled with all my might, fumbling in terror, until I finally managed to pull it free.

Unbearable pain paralyzed my leg. I slipped off my shoe to check the wound and was astonished. That gash on my heel—it was so familiar. I had the impression I'd already lived through all this.

I slid off my other shoe and dragged myself up the stairs, limping badly, as a deafening silence filled the house. There was no sign of Faust.

When I'd almost reached the landing I turned around, afraid he might be right behind me. I faced forward again as I placed my foot on the top step and my heart almost stopped cold. Faust stood there, staring at me with paralyzing heartlessness. I lurched back in fright, the empty space behind me making my every movement perilous. I peered up at him, trying to understand his intentions. If he made the slightest move I would tumble backwards down the steep staircase. Death would soon follow the fall. My chest rose and fell rapidly and pure terror gripped me, but I silently held his cold gaze as Death observed me with its eyes of ice. Without warning, Faust's expression turned more intense and furious.

Everything happened in a blur. From the corner of my eye I saw his arm flash out toward me. The next thing I knew I was flying through the air backwards. I made myself keep my eyes locked onto his face, darkened with evil, every instant of my fall.

Then, impact.

The pain was excruciating, paralyzing. I instinctively raised a hand to the back of my head and stared at my shaking fingers, smeared with warm blood.

I couldn't understand the reason for his rage. Was it just that he enjoyed seeing me suffer? Wasn't taking my life enough? Why torture me? Was Faust really so sadistic? I couldn't believe that was all it was. There had to be something more driving him to act so brutally.

I tried to get up, but my body, traumatized by the violent fall, refused to cooperate. Awkwardly, I rolled onto my side. When I looked up again, my vision blurred, Faust was standing in front of me. I raised my head with difficulty, dimly glimpsing an evil smile on his lips. Suddenly, he vanished.

I seized the chance to get up, channeling all the energy I could muster into my arms. On my feet again, frightened by how difficult it was to keep from staggering, I leaned against the banister.

My vision faded in and out and a lacerating pain shot all the way up the back of my neck. I couldn't tell if the room was spinning or if I was just imagining it. When I tried to lift my foot a tremor ran up my leg, keeping me from continuing, as my eyes struggled to focus on the wavering image of my lacerated heel. I attempted to rest my other foot on the first step of the staircase but before I knew it, a devastating force hurled me forward. I was shocked to find myself hurtling through the air and crashing down on the second-floor landing.

I gasped for breath, my cheek against the floor, and tried painfully to open my eyes. Was life about to abandon me?

A monster. Faust was a monster. Like an icy echo, his laughter swept over my soul, grim as the voice of death.

Crumpled on the floor, I felt my heart beating. I wasn't dead yet. Dazed and battered, my teeth clenched, I searched inside myself and found the strength to get up.

I hobbled down the hallway, barefoot, trying to ignore the atrocious pain I felt in every inch of my body. I wasn't sure nothing was broken.

Gemma . . .

My body shuddered every time I heard his cruel, infernal whisper. "Why are you doing this to me?" I screamed, my tears overflowing. "Kill me if you have to!"

I could knock your head off with a single blow, if it weren't forbidden, but that way I'd miss out on all the fun. Faust's wickedness echoed through the room in a sinister laugh.

"What kind of a monster are you?"

I'm sorry. His voice suddenly grew serious and resolute, without a trace of pity or remorse. *But it's a debt that must be paid.*

"Why?" I screamed, dragging myself along. "Tell me why!" I tried to stifle my desperation, but an even more blood-chilling silence filled the old house.

Why kill me slowly? Was he trying to shed my very last drop of blood? What was the point of my sacrifice?

Like a pearl, the moon shone through the window at the far end of the hallway. As I passed them, the ceiling lamps broke free and crashed down, barely missing me. Guided by the soft moonlight, almost as if it were a fairy who had come to rescue me, I focused on the window in a desperate attempt to reach it and put an end to all my suffering.

Maybe that's where I was actually supposed to go. Faust must have slowly led me to the very spot where I was fated to die.

Driven by a last flicker of desperate opposition, I banged on the glass, hoping the window would open. It didn't, so I peered through it, looking for anything outside I could cling to to avoid falling, but there was only empty space below. And the window was so high up.

To my horror, I realized the end had come. I thought of my parents, how they would grieve when my body was one day found there in the old house in the woods where they'd never allowed me to go.

"End of the line." For the first time, Faust's voice reached me loud and clear, free from the ghastly echo that had shrouded it before. He was behind me.

I turned slowly, a defeated look on my face, realizing there were just a few steps between us.

"Tell me why!" I screamed, caught between resignation and desperation. "You're about to kill me—you could at least offer me an explanation." This time it was a demand. "Why didn't you kill me right away? Why all this hatred toward me?" I shouted, my eyes narrowed to slits as I struggled to hold back my tears.

Faust's face turned unexpectedly serious and his expression grew so sad I suspected he was trying hard to drive a memory from his mind. Despite the atrocities I'd undergone at his hands, I was still amazed by how handsome he was. It was almost as if that somehow absolved him in my mind of all the torture he'd put me through. I shook my head to free myself from his mind control as he stared into space and relived aloud in a hoarse, empty voice the memory that was haunting him.

"Nineteen fifty-three. We were in the car, Penny and I . . ."

He paused, lost in a memory that was clearly devastating for him. "It was pouring down rain, the water crashing against the windshield. I couldn't see a thing," he muttered, making me shiver. "Suddenly, I saw something in the middle of the road—an animal, maybe." Anger was in his voice, his eyes still blank as he lost himself in the moment, reliving the scene as though there were still new details to discover. "I swerved, I *tried* to avoid it, but the road was slick." His features hardened, verging on desperation. "The car skidded out of control. Then there was silence." He closed his eyes as I held my breath. "I don't remember the impact. We were out of the car. I couldn't understand what that boy was doing with us. I was sure I'd never seen him before, but he kept calling me by my name. I took my girlfriend's hand, afraid he was going to hurt us, but his face seemed kind. I remember every second of it. He nodded over my shoulder and I looked behind me. I was shocked.

"The car we'd been in had crashed into a tree.

"I tried to keep Penny from seeing the horrific sight as I peered inside the crumpled wreckage. I couldn't take my eyes off the two bodies caught inside it—mangled, unrecognizable."

A shiver ran down my arms. In the midst of my terror, I felt a touch of pity when I heard the disarming sorrow in his voice. Still, I forced myself to remember that I would be paying dearly for his pain. "I'm sorry. What happened to you is absolutely horrible, but what does all this have to do with *me*?"

When he looked up, his bloodshot eyes brimming with rage and torment wiped away any trace of pity inside me, making me shudder with pure terror. His pupils glimmered with a hatred I couldn't fathom. "*He* was there," he said, gritting his teeth. "I tried to convince him, to persuade him not to separate us, but he took her, he took her! He took her away from me!" His snarling voice broke with emotion and I froze, finally understanding. "We were supposed to be together forever, even after death," he whispered, his face devastated by the memory.

"Evan," I murmured weakly.

"*Him*," he confirmed, rage overtaking him again. "For decades I've waited for this moment, fearing it might never come." He glared at me, determined and ready to kill me. "And now the hour of reckoning has arrived."

I'd been wrong all along. This was a personal vendetta. Nothing would stop him.

"At first I didn't know who you were. You were with the Witch and he wasn't around. When he came to protect you and I sensed how much he cared for you, and you for him, I finally found a reason to fight. Don't you see? This is the greatest challenge of my life. I finally have the chance to repay him the favor. I couldn't stop Evan from taking Penny away and now he can't stop me from doing the same to him. Today Evan settles his debt."

"Evan is going to save me." The words escaped my lips, my voice almost pleading.

Faust stared at me with a shrewd smile, shaking his head. "Is that what you think? Are you really still hoping he'll come to your rescue? Why do you think he hasn't done it yet? I'm sorry—the answer might disappoint you—but your Evan isn't coming."

The assurance with which he said it left me breathless, as if he'd destroyed the very last hope I'd been clinging to.

"He's desperately searching for you, you know." Perversion gleamed in his eye as he stared at me, relishing my pain. "But he can't find you—and I'm not going to let him until it's too late."

"You're underestimating the bond between us," I said heatedly.

"Hmm." He paused, pretending to be taking my threat seriously. "I wouldn't get my hopes up if I were you." A demonic smile appeared on his face. "I've done a good job so far, wouldn't you say? You followed my plan to perfection. You fell into my trap, accept it. You're all alone now. Evan will get here too late. And when he does I'll be able to delight in the agony, the rage in his eyes when he realizes he's lost you forever. That *I* made your soul pass on, just like he did to my beloved Penny's. After that, I won't care what happens to me any more."

Despite all the torture I'd undergone, the look on his face at that moment terrified me more than anything else. He didn't even care about his own fate as long as he could take his revenge. Nothing could save me from him.

"I'm happy the difficult part is over. All that's left is the final act in this tragic story. I must confess I was afraid I'd never have my chance, but everything's gone according to plan. Deep down I should have expected this. After all, you're just a mortal. Vulnerable and fragile, like the rest of them, and too easily manipulated. You're moved by emotions, worked up so easily, ignoring all logic. You let yourselves be carried away by feelings, by *passion*, running around like chickens with your heads cut off when all you really need to do is stop a moment and think."

In silence, I took in his every word as the suspicion I'd had in the forest became a certainty.

"But what would you know about that?" he said with a sneer, sounding vaguely accusatory. "He challenged everyone and everything to keep you alive. He was willing to give up his soul, though his punishment would be never-ending, because by choosing not to kill you, he lost the chance to redeem himself. He even stood up to the Màsala, for which he's going to pay dearly, I can assure you. And all because you were more important to him than everything else. I know the feeling, I know it well. You, on the other hand, fell into my trap so easily! You think you love him more than your own life, and yet it took so little to convince you not to trust him."

"You brainwashed me," I gasped, a tremble in my voice. "It was *you* who made me run away from Evan," I whispered, shocked and overcome with guilt. I'd already realized my mind had been poisoned by Faust, I just hadn't understood how, exactly.

He peered at me, smiling. "Did you really not understand? I was toying with you, Gemma, from the very start. When I entered your dream, I still didn't know how I'd be able to convince you to leave their house. You were safe as long as you were there. I couldn't have touched a hair on your head. Can you believe it? But you cooperated with everything so nicely."

His words withered me. What a fool I'd been; I'd fallen for his story hook, line, and sinker.

"I have to admit, at first I didn't think it would be so easy. Then I looked inside you and discovered your most deeply buried fears. They were insignificant trifles hidden in the innermost corners of your unconscious, safe and sound, but I fanned the flames of your fears without your noticing. I fanned them until they were unbearable. You felt betrayed, didn't you? The pain was intolerable. You struggled against it, but you couldn't resist, because I was there blocking your mind, keeping you from reasoning freely." He poured out his confession, smug satisfaction on his face.

A myriad of emotions filled me. I was furious with Faust for using mind control to manipulate me, but part of me was happy to finally know for a fact that my suspicions about Evan were groundless. Why hadn't it dawned on me that Faust might have the same powers Evan did?

He'd read my unconscious, uncovering every secret, reading my soul and detecting each emotion before it surfaced. He'd taken control, prevented me from reasoning, and instilled suspicion in my mind, all so he'd have me in the palm of his hand. My heart, feeling it had lost everything, lashed out at him in a scream of frustration. "You used mind control on me! How dare you?"

"It was necessary," he said mockingly, his voice almost soft and caring. "Besides, soon enough you'll have far more horrible things to blame me for." His mouth twisted into a malicious smile.

I smiled to myself, repressing my rage, because I knew how wrong he was. Having given up hope, I was convinced death would be silent, drab, empty. Black. Where pain doesn't hurt any more. Nothing at all like the red of the bitter emotion that had made my heart ache so when Faust convinced me I'd lost everything. But death couldn't steal everything from me as long as I had Evan's love. The only thing I held against Faust was what he'd tricked me into doing. The rest didn't matter any more.

When Evan told me about his power I hadn't fully understood what it meant. To understand it, I'd had to experience for myself how powerfully your own mind can be torn out of your control, driven by your doubts and insecurities. And yet my heart had tried to warn me. Instead, I'd made a mess of everything. I'd let Faust bend my will. But then again, I really had heard Evan plotting my death. Or was that just another of Faust's lies?

"What about what I heard them say?" I asked, instinctively giving in to the longing to understand.

"Actually I'd already had the opportunity to make you suspicious of him. I just took you there to increase your suspicion even further. I'd intended to trick you into thinking he was betraying you, but then I heard what they were talking about and thought you should hear them too. Everything fell into place quite nicely, don't you think? Not even if I'd whispered the words into Evan's ear could it have gone better! At that point all I had to do was shuffle the cards a little.

"He had a plan. An *excellent* plan," he said, his voice filled with satisfaction. "Actually, your Evan never wanted to kill you at all. I just found a way to make you think he did."

"How is that possible? I heard him say it," I insisted, still confused.

"What you heard was only part of their conversation. The truth is he was trying to save you. He had no intention of harming you. How could he? He loves you more than anything in the world. But I made sure you didn't know that. He loves you with all his heart and at this very moment he's going completely out of his mind because he can't sense your soul." An evil grin spread over Faust's face. He closed his eyes and took a deep breath, concentrating. "I can sense his agony. The Witch is searching for your thoughts too," he whispered, a smug look on his face.

"Why can't they sense me?" I asked, gripped with panic.

Was Evan really trying to track me down? My heart ached at the thought of the anguish and frustration he must be feeling.

Faust smiled again before opening his eyes. "Because I'm blocking them. I've spent the last several decades preparing for this moment. Do you really think it would have been so easy for you to escape from three Subterraneans and a Witch? I concealed your escape and I'm shielding our presence right now, generating a protective barrier no one can penetrate. Not even the Witch can scratch it, despite all her power.

"I still haven't figured out what she's doing with them. You probably don't know this, but Angels and Witches have always been mortal enemies, and she's very powerful. It was hard to keep her at bay, especially when we were so close to her there in the kitchen." He stared into space. "That Witch makes me shudder," he murmured to himself, shivering.

His face lit up again. "But that only helped spice up my plan. In any case, you need to face facts. None of them has managed to locate you. It's just you and me. No one's going to find you in time," he assured me.

The proud expression he wore as he stared at me did nothing but drain me of every emotion except guilt. Evan had found a way to protect me, but I'd ruined everything. Now I would pay the price.

"Well, then!" Faust boomed, shattering the silence, his voice tinged with smug satisfaction. I looked up at him and saw he was studying me carefully. "You're right where I wanted you." He twisted his lips into a malicious grin, his eyes dark and foreboding.

My heart leapt into my throat, sensing the danger in his eyes as I peered through the window at the empty space behind me. I had a flash of déjà vu and my heart lurched. I'd already been here before.

Someone had tried to warn me in my dream, like a premonition.

"No, please . . . Wait!" My voice broke with emotion as desperation gripped my throat, because I'd already seen the shattering glass and knew how this was going to end. I wished I could have held on to a little courage, but the words had come out before I could help it.

Had I really thought I could defy fate? My destiny was already written. Putting it off would only make everything harder. No one could escape death.

Faust's face looked momentarily saddened, as if, despite everything, part of him suffered from my agony. Then, swiftly, he flung out his arm and a devastating force burst out at me as violently as a tornado, hurling me backwards before I had time for a last breath.

I smashed through the window, shoulders first.

As though my senses had sharpened, I felt every inch of the glass as it shattered against my back. The deafening crash swallowed up every other sound, cutting me off from the rest of the world and I found myself drowning in a wild explosion of shards. I imagined the pain Evan would suffer for not having arrived in time to save me.

I tried to breathe, but the glass was dancing in front of my face, threatening to cut my throat. The ice-cold air stung my skin. I gasped and my vision grew blurred. I suddenly felt emptied, as if my body no longer weighed anything. Sound ceased, and everything around me went into slow motion. I wasn't afraid of death any more. Sweet oblivion lulled my senses as I plunged toward the ground. I was so tired of running away.

My only regret was a single name: *Evan.* I couldn't bear to lose him so soon. My mind filled with memories of him as the sharp air stole my breath. I should have felt gratitude for those few moments life had given us, but I couldn't find any trace of that emotion in my body. Mocking destiny had brought us together only to separate us forever.

I closed my eyes, cradled by the wind, and my heart sought refuge in one last thought of him. *Goodbye, Evan,* I whispered in my mind. A tear ran down my cheek.

Gemma, my angel . . . Gem!

A sweet tingle spread over me. My longing to hear his voice again, even for a second, was so intense that I almost thought I'd heard him whisper my name in my mind.

I opened my eyes again, on the verge of losing consciousness, and they met Faust's. He was staring down at me from above, his lips moving, mouthing something slowly so I could make out the words: *You can't escape fate. Death always wins.*

My body turned over as it plummeted down, and suddenly all I could see was the ground right below me.

It was over.

The impact knocked the breath out of me.

"Not if you have an Angel to protect you."

I blinked, stunned by the sound of Evan's voice. Struggling through the fog that clouded my vision, I managed to focus on his face. He was staring at me with a deep, loving look.

"Are you all right?" he asked tenderly.

My eyes filled with tears. "You're here," I murmured, releasing the anguish I'd been holding in. I wasn't sure if I was all right. My body slowly began to feel again and I discovered I was in his arms.

Evan had caught me a second before I hit the ground. He was holding me tightly, like he never wanted to let me go. He caressed my forehead with tremendous tenderness, brushing the hair back from my face, his gaze never leaving mine. In his eyes I could still see how worried he'd been, but I also saw relief for having shown up just in time.

His expression suddenly changed, growing dark, reminding me that it wasn't over. Evan tensed, his body as hard as stone. He clenched his fists and ground his teeth. His face twisted into a black mask, the look in his eyes thirsting for revenge. The earth beneath his feet trembled from the roar of rage that exploded from his chest. I'd never seen him so furious before. His head shot up, finding Faust's embittered eyes waiting for him. Evan set his jaw and leaned down to gently lay me on the ground, his fiery eyes locked onto Faust's. "Stay here," he ordered, his voice suddenly inexpressive. Before I could reply, Evan was gone, leaving a cloud of dust behind him.

Suddenly everything happened very fast.

I looked up at Faust's face, which now seemed nervous and worried. All at once, a deafening explosion made me cringe and cover my ears as the house's windows all blew out at once, hit by a furious tornado, a black hurricane that screamed for revenge. I covered my head to protect myself from the broken glass that came showering down over my bloodstained hair.

Everything went deathly silent, throwing me into a panic. My heart started pounding again in spite of the stabbing pain that gripped my chest with every breath. I painfully forced myself to my feet, shifting my weight from one leg to the other, my eyes darting nervously from one empty window to the next, looking for a sign of Evan. Despite his order to stay where I was, my heart was up there with him and I couldn't keep my body from following it.

I started toward the door, immediately feeling my leg protesting the decision. The pain in my foot flamed up every time it touched the ground. The contact stung like salt in an open wound.

Overwhelmed with anxiety, I dragged myself to the door and turned the knob over and over again, but it wouldn't budge. In a flash, I understood the immensity of my love for Evan. Only a moment ago, when Faust had hurled me through the window, I'd been resigned to death. But at the thought of losing Evan, every single part of me had instantly rebelled, refusing to give up. I had to reach him at all costs.

By delivering myself to death, Faust would have his revenge and Evan would be safe.

I went over to a boarded-up trapdoor hidden in the ground. I knew the tunnel behind it would lead me directly into the parlor. Dropping to my knees, I pushed away the layer of damp earth that covered it, grabbed hold of the wooden boards, and pried them free. The rusty nails gave way, as did the rotten wood, offering me a way in. I lowered myself into the underground passageway, gritting my teeth against the pain that washed over me again and again, threatening to plunge my mind into darkness. The tunnel grew narrower and pitch black. As the walls closed in around me, I was hit with the powerful stench of rotting flesh, causing waves of nausea I wasn't sure I'd be able to hold down.

Suddenly I was struck by the terrifying sensation that my body was about to abandon me there. I would lose consciousness in that underground tomb where no one would ever find me. The air seemed to be running out.

A clap of thunder brought me back to my senses. No, it hadn't been thunder. I scrambled to reach the end of the passageway as the sound grew louder and louder. Somewhere above me a battle was raging. I instinctively ducked when something banged against the floor above my head. It was like the house was falling to pieces under the blows. I pushed cautiously, again and again, trying to raise the trapdoor that was imprisoning me in the underground tunnel, but failed with every attempt. I could barely breathe. The suspicion that this pit would become my grave started to verge on certainty. I made myself hold back a stream of tears, oppressed by the darkness.

The wooden boards above my head rattled, and a tremor of joy ran from my stomach to my chest. A puff of fresh air caressed my face as the hatch was flung open from above. It must be Evan. Then my heart trembled and stopped.

It was Faust.

He stared at me contemptuously, his lips twisted into an evil grin. An atrocious fear cast me into the blackest panic. If Faust was there waiting for me . . . where was Evan?

"No. It can't be," I whispered, brokenhearted, and sealed my lips tight so my teeth wouldn't chatter. I couldn't believe Faust had defeated Evan. I couldn't accept it. Not when it was my turn to protect him.

"Your dear Evan said to tell you goodbye."

"*No!*" I shrieked.

Suddenly his body was violently flung away, becoming a blur to my eyes. I jumped at the sheer speed with which it had been done. My heart started beating again. Evan was still alive. I was still in time to save him.

Driven by that desire, I forced my body to support me as I pulled myself out through the trapdoor, gritting my teeth. The pain in my foot had irremediably spread to my knee, and my lungs pumped painfully as though my ribs were broken, every breath leaving me in anguish. The fire burning in the back of my head threatened to overwhelm me.

"Gemmaaa!" Two bolts of lightning shot past me, pulling the wall panels behind them in the fury of the battle, moving at such speed that I couldn't make out their bodies.

I flattened myself against the wall, concentrating on their shapes, trying to understand which of the two was winning. After a moment, my eyes managed to make out the punches they threw. They moved in sync in a dark, violent dance, dodging the blows one after the other.

I tried to reach Ginevra with my mind, projecting my thoughts to her as panic consumed me and my tortured body flinched at the violence of each blow.

My heart skipped a beat when Evan grabbed Faust and hurled him against a ceiling beam on the other side of the room. The ceiling collapsed, burying Faust's body beneath a pile of rubble. Evan and I looked each other in the eye for a second, his expression tormented.

"Hide!" he shouted at me, his voice broken with frustration. "Gemma, you have to hide!"

But I no longer had the strength to move my legs. Pain had paralyzed me. A huge crash drew our attention, and a searing pain in my shoulder made me gasp. My fingers quickly closed around the wound and a stream of blood gushed through them as I discovered that, like a fiery arrow shot by an able archer, a large, spike-shaped fragment of wood had torn through my flesh and lodged deep inside my shoulder. I crumpled to my knees, gasping.

Hundreds of these spikes had burst through the air, filling the room with a huge cloud of dust and debris. There was no sign of Faust.

My senses slowed by the pain, I was distraught to see the two Angels fighting again, whirling like ghosts in a battle whose prize was my life.

I couldn't bear the idea that Evan might die in order to save me. My heart belonged to him now and it would die along with his. Besides, Death wouldn't be satisfied with only his life; it would continue to send out its demons to hunt me down, making his sacrifice pointless. There was only one outcome that could quench its dark thirst: my surrender.

The floor shuddered every time their bodies collided.

"Enough!!! Stop it!!!"

The scream came directly from my heart, which trembled an instant later when I realized it had distracted Evan for a split second, long enough for Faust to grab him. My desperation verged on madness.

"No! Let him go, please!"

But Faust's evil heart thrived on my anguish, and he hurled Evan brutally onto the old grand piano, which collapsed beneath his weight. Unharmed, Evan shot back to his feet and the battle resumed, raging nonstop.

Their bodies emanated an energy that pushed everything out of their paths. It was as though the power of the earth was supporting them, as if the elements had come together to help them, a single invisible ally.

From time to time, through all the noise, I heard Evan cursing at Faust. As if the furious roar that rose from his chest increased his power, Evan struck him with brutal force, flinging him to the top of the stairs. I held my breath as Evan rushed over to me, looking anxious.

"Are you okay?" His eyes lingered with concern on the wound in my shoulder, which seemed to be the most gruesome of all my injuries. The wooden spike was still sticking out of my flesh like a stake driven into a vampire's heart. "I have to get you out of here." Without taking even a moment to think, he picked me up and shot forward, but Faust materialized in front of us, blocking our way, and hurled us each to opposite sides of the parlor.

"Gemmaaaa!" Evan's desperate cry filled the room.

I looked up and was shocked to discover Faust behind me, glaring at me with a fierce, twisted grin. "It's true what they say, you know," he said as Evan's enraged glare locked onto him from the other side of the room. "Revenge is a dish best served cold."

Evan turned to look into my terror-filled eyes, clearly not understanding what Faust meant. "I presume you don't even remember me." Faust smiled, seeing the lost look on Evan's face.

Evan weighed his words before answering. "Should I?"

Faust hid the bitterness in his smile by lowering his eyes as he shook his head slowly. "You see, Evan, fate plays nasty tricks on us at times. Because you took my beloved from me, and now at last I have the chance to repay you the favor. The irony of fate: the tables have been turned."

Evan's expression wavered as he realized what was going on. "Faustian!" he suddenly remembered. "There was nothing I could do for her. You know that!"

Faust's chest shook in a silent chuckle. "Then why should it be any different for me?" he asked, his voice edged with sarcasm.

Before I could even tremble, a ferocious roar burst from Evan's chest. "Because I'm not letting you near her!" he snarled, baring his teeth.

But Faust was too close to my battered, defenseless body. He pointed his hand at my head as though he wanted to suck the life out of me from that very spot. I squeezed my eyes shut to avoid his merciless gaze that left me breathless with terror.

"DON'T TOUUUCH HEEER!" A bellow of sheer ferocity swept the room as Evan charged at Faust. At that very instant, Ginevra, Simon, and Drake appeared on the opposite side of the parlor and rushed to my side.

"You okay?" Simon asked, helping me up and looking at me with concern.

"Doesn't look like it." Drake examined my wounds, a horrified expression on his face—although I wasn't completely sure there wasn't a hint of sarcasm in his voice.

"Evan! The dagger!" Ginevra shouted as the two Angels struggled on the floor. I turned around as Evan whipped a knife out of his belt. Suddenly I felt a strange tingle under my skin. Some mysterious impulse made my eyes lock onto the blade. I stared at it, perplexed, as a powerful aroma filled my nostrils, making my head spin.

Evan pinned Faust to the floor and tried numerous times to stab him, but his adversary parried every thrust. Struck by a dark force, the knife flew out of his hand, landing far from them.

"No!" Evan shouted, stopping his brothers, who were rushing to help him. "It's either me or him," he said, his voice reduced to an angry hiss.

He turned toward the dagger. Obeying the Angel's command, it slid back across the floor with a blood-curdling screech. Evan gripped it firmly, skillfully flipped the weapon over in his fingers and plunged it into Faust's chest. The other Angel let out a groan of astonishment and Evan's eyes wavered an instant, suddenly veiled with bitterness. From his remorseful expression, it was clear he'd never killed another Angel before. They held each other's gaze as their silent conversation filled my head.

You killed me. But you're a Subterranean. I didn't think you'd go so far. I just wanted her . . . Meanwhile, the veins on Faust's face began to swell like serpents slithering beneath his skin. *What will become of your Redemption?*

I don't care.

Why not? Faust asked, his voice frail and hoarse.

Evan stared at him intensely before answering: *Because I love her more than anything.*

Then don't let anyone take her from you. The pain is eternal. Faust gasped a last breath before vanishing into thin air.

My eyes lingered, hypnotized, on Evan's tormented face as he stared at the empty floor where Faust had been a second ago, and a sudden burst of heat washed over me. My nostrils filled with a bitter, intense smell—the same one that had risen up and reached my mouth, filling it with the taste of metal. I looked down at my dress. Scarlet splatters drenched the fabric. The floor beneath me bowed, threatening to collapse under my weight. Something hot trickled down my neck and as it dripped onto the floor I watched it with a blank stare.

Blood.

Nausea pervaded me. I reached up and felt the back of my skull, discovering that warmth was once again flowing from the deep wound, spreading languidly through my hair, already matted with congealing blood.

I tried to breathe, but something was obstructing my lungs. I sought the others' eyes, but no one seemed to notice me, not even Ginevra. It was as though time had stopped. Evan was frozen to the spot, bent over the empty floor.

Pins and needles crept up my legs and spread upward through my body. My energy drained away as my knees shook. My heartbeat thumped in my ears, drowning out all else, as if I were hidden away in some parallel world. I heard it falter, pulsing slower and slower.

Boom-boom.

Boom—boom.

Boom————boom.

A cold shiver enveloped my body. *Boom.* One last thump sounded in my chest. Then, silence.

When the pins and needles reached my head, darkness shrouded my eyes. I parted my lips, bothered by the taste of metal, and felt blood trickle out of the corner of my mouth and down my chin.

I glimpsed the blurry floor drawing inexorably closer and felt one last, heavy breath escape me.

"EVAN!!!"

Ginevra's desperate scream reached me on the floor, the last thing I heard before life left me.

37

OBLIVION

I found myself suspended in a dark, impenetrable void, as black as night. I sensed presences but couldn't reach them, as though the darkness had arms that could push me down. It felt like I'd always been wandering in that oblivion, with no thought, completely adrift, swept up in a cloud of peace. I was *certain* I didn't belong to the world any more. The pain had subsided. I felt light, in harmony with everything, filled with a strong sense of wellbeing. Yet the darkness was pulling me further and further down as I surrendered to the silence, sinking into an abyss from which I couldn't resurface, a well without light.

So this was the end.

I looked for a glimmer of light to guide me, but everything was shrouded in darkness and silence. All at once, the buzzing of a thousand insects penetrated that barrier, trying to reach me. I withdrew, wanting to avoid them, but the sound turned into a more comforting hum. I tried to reach out for it, to cling to the familiar sensation it produced in me, to move closer to the sound, but I couldn't emerge from the darkness that had me trapped in its mantle and refused to let me go.

The hum grew stronger and stronger.

Voices.

I tried to recognize them, but my effort made them grow muffled. So I waited, allowing them to guide me through the oblivion in which I wandered.

"She's lost a lot of blood."

Whoever had spoken had tried hard to hide their concern behind a veil of confidence, but somehow I noticed it.

"Think it's too late?"

The concerned voice was definitely Ginevra's.

"Her heart's stopped!" the first voice exclaimed, edged with an anxiety that this time came through.

"I can't find her! Fuck!"

Evan.

I would have recognized his voice even if I'd been buried at the bottom of a frozen ocean. Why had it broken with such frustration? I couldn't bear it. His desperation filled me with the longing to break the icy barrier separating us. It was like he'd cast me a line so I could emerge from the darkness. And finally I was drawn back in by the light.

I found myself at the foot of what remained of the piano. Evan and the others were a bit farther away, their backs to me. I stared at them, puzzled because they were being so indifferent and acting so strangely. I couldn't understand why they were all huddled over the floor.

"This is my fault! Goddamn it!" Evan's voice held a desperation I'd never heard before. He cursed angrily, as if consumed by deep, unbearable pain.

Why was he still suffering like this? Couldn't he see I was safe now?

"Evan . . ." From my lips, the thread of my voice followed his dismay until it reached him. As though I'd screamed it, Evan, Simon, Drake, and Ginevra all turned around at the same time and looked at me. The weight of the world came crashing down on me as their movement revealed what their hunched figures had been blocking from my view.

My body. It was lying on the floor in a scarlet pool, lifeless. The spark of life had abandoned it, rendering it useless. The sight catapulted me into a cold, inaccessible world of shock.

"Gemma—"

Evan's cautious voice tried to penetrate the apathetic state that had petrified me as I stared blankly at the empty, lifeless body. A useless shell that no longer moved. Not a breath. Not a heartbeat.

Death had settled the score.

"Gemma."

I looked up at Evan. His expression confused me. His eyes said he was *relieved* to see me. I studied the others' faces one by one; they all gave me the same impression. It was like my presence had suddenly cheered them up. Didn't they realize I was dead?

Evan tried to come closer, but the look of shock on my face convinced him to do so very cautiously. "Everything's fine, Gemma," he whispered, his eyes locked onto mine, as if he was trying to keep me from looking elsewhere.

I tried to inhale and my eyes wavered when I discovered it wasn't my state of shock that had taken my breath away. My new body couldn't breathe, it didn't need to any more.

"Everything's fine. We feared the worst," he said, taking another step closer, his voice broken by the echo of the agony that had afflicted him. "But you're here now," he said, visibly relieved.

"But I'm . . . *dead*," I whispered, petrified.

"We're still in time," he said in a vain attempt to reassure me.

"In time," I murmured to myself, staring into space.

"I'll bring you back. Come with me. Take my hand," he whispered, still advancing cautiously. He extended his arm. "The others are already healing your body." Evan moved forward, trying to prevent me from looking over his shoulder where his brothers were leaning over the tortured body that lay on the floor, deprived of its essence. The body that until a moment ago had been my own. "There's no need for you to see it," he said considerately.

Ignoring his advice, I stared at Simon and Drake who were kneeling with their palms turned toward my ravaged body as Ginevra paced back and forth, looking nervous.

I reached out to Evan, but a little voice rose up from the bottom of my heart, telling me what I had to do. The time had come for me to save him.

"No. Wait." My hand froze halfway to Evan, before he could take it. I stared at it for a second and then, finding the words, I looked up into his eyes. "You're an Angel of Death."

Evan's eyes darted back and forth in surprise as I studied his reaction. As though he couldn't bear its weight, he hung his head to avoid my gaze. So Faust had been telling the truth.

"I didn't want to lie to you," he said, his voice breaking. "I—I didn't want to scare you," he admitted, his tone trapped in a cage of bitterness. "I couldn't stand the thought that you might be afraid of me."

I wavered, overwhelmed, but forced myself to go on, staring him steadily in the eye so he couldn't avoid my gaze again. "Did you want to kill me?" I asked, my voice breaking from the terror of hearing what Evan might say.

"Gemma . . ." His gaze burned into mine with an intensity I'd never seen before. "I can't change what I am or what I do. Yet I've done it. For you. I never, ever wanted to kill you, not for a second, but I had to. Those were my orders. I'm Death. And I came for you. I can't hide any more," he confessed, racked with desperation, as though afraid of my reaction to his secret.

"But you didn't do it." My heart had sent the whisper to my lips to let the truth sink in for both of us. Evan stared at the floor, shaking his head.

"You should have told me! I would have understood. It doesn't matter to me what you are." I made sure he was looking me in the eye as I said it.

"If there's anything I'm more afraid of than your indifference, it's that you might be scared of me."

"I'm not scared of you," I said firmly, "but I don't want you to pay this dearly for my life. Faust told me you were risking everything for me. You won't be able to save yourself any more because of me. You won't be able to redeem yourself, will you?"

His silence confirmed my deduction.

"Evan," I insisted, trying to make him see reason, "you'll be damned forever."

"Don't say that! Don't even think it!" he said, pulling me closer. "It's not *your* fault. *I* was the one who decided. I'd only be damned if I didn't have you with me any more." His forehead brushed my own, his fiery silver eyes on mine. "I'm not even sure it's possible. No one can even prove there really is a Redemption."

"I don't want to ruin your chances," I insisted.

Redemption was the only purpose of his existence and nothing in the world would make me want to stand in his way. The time had come for *me* to save *him*, to protect him from a mistake that in all likelihood he would end up regretting. My life wasn't worth so much; when would he finally realize that?

As if he'd heard my thought, Evan cupped my cheeks in his hands. A new sensation gripped me as I felt the warmth of his skin light up my face in a flame of pleasure, as if—the physical body no longer in our way—the energy that connected us could spread more intensely, bursting with every contact. I half closed my eyes, letting the warmth fill me.

"Gemma." Evan sank his fingers into my hair, overwhelming me with an intensity I'd never felt before as a wave of ecstasy spread from him to me and back to him, the flow of energy that had always united us now almost tangible in this ethereal form. "It's too late. My world would be meaningless without you. I'd be nothing but a lost soul. *You're* my Redemption. Nothing else matters. Nothing would matter any more if I lost you now," he whispered, resting his forehead against mine again. I was lost, at the mercy of his touch.

"Evan, no." Broken-hearted, gulping down the lump in my throat, I forced myself to try to persuade him. I wanted to cry, but I'd run out of tears. "Take me to the other side, please. You, you'll lose everything because of me. I don't want that to happen. I can't let you do it."

Evan stroked my cheek with his thumb, as if he could see the invisible track of the tears I wished I could shed. Our gazes locked for a long, long moment. "You're my world, Gemma. The only way I can lose everything is if I lose you. I'd rather be damned forever than live an eternity without you," he whispered, slowly moving his cheek closer to mine without touching it, until his lips were brushing my ear. He spoke in a low voice. "Stay with me, Gemma, please. I *need* you."

Half closing my eyes at the infinite sweetness of his whisper, I moved my head back an inch, astonished by the new sensations running through me. I opened my mouth to speak, but at the sight of his tortured gaze I closed it and nodded. He'd changed my mind.

Evan smiled at me with new hope and squeezed my hand in his, leading me to my body, over which Simon and Drake were still leaning.

"We're ready," Simon told him confidently. "It's up to you now."

Evan nodded and let go of my hand to join them. As he knelt down, he looked up at me and smiled. "They did a good job." His gaze softened as he invited me to look at their handiwork.

I peeked over their shoulders with the feeling in my chest that if I'd still had a heart, its beating would have deafened me. My body lay on the ground, intact and unharmed, as if it had never been lifeless. Simon and Drake really had done a fine job healing it.

Without taking his eyes from mine, Evan leaned over the still-empty shell, his hand poised over my heart. For a moment his gray eyes searched mine before closing and surrendering to perfect concentration.

An electric current bore me away. A single heartbeat jolted me. I opened my eyes as a wave of heat pervaded me and found myself lying on the cold, damp floor.

Once again in my body.

EPILOGUE

"It's nice to breathe again." I smiled at Evan as I walked slowly toward him. He'd been waiting for me to join him at the lakeshore and greeted me with a radiant smile.

"To me it's no big deal, just an acquired habit."

I shuddered as I recalled the feeling of stasis I'd experienced. It was a very big deal to me. "Thanks. For the clothes and . . . everything else."

"Thank Ginevra for that." He smiled.

"Honestly, I feel brand new!" I said, enjoying the sensation of freshness that filled me. I felt strangely cleansed, and my prom dress was clean and as good as new. Ginevra must have taken care of that for me before I woke up.

"Oh, I don't think *that's* because of your dress," he said, amused. "After all, it's not every day someone undergoes an experience like yours."

"Yeah," is all I said, biting my lip, still too shaken by what I'd gone through to see the humor in it like he did.

I stepped past Evan to the water's edge, letting my thoughts ripple on its surface. The sun would rise soon. The first rays were already turning the dark horizon to a purplish glow that merged with the mirror of water. Despite the faint light, a pinpoint of brightness had escaped the night and continued to shine: my star. I smiled at the memory that flashed through my mind.

My eyes had never seen anything more radiant and full of hope than that morning. I'd known that place my whole life, but it felt like I was seeing it for the first time.

It was a new day. A new dawn. A new life, together with Evan.

I closed my eyes and breathed in the cool air still heavy with dew, hoping the memory would remain engraved in my mind.

I'd felt the caress of fate. Death had sought me out. I hadn't escaped it, but I'd been given a second chance and I wasn't going to waste a single minute of the new life I had ahead of me. I smiled, my heart suffused with warmth, thinking that Evan would live it by my side.

My eyes still closed, I felt his body touch mine, his hot breath on my neck. He slowly wrapped his arms around me in a firm yet gentle embrace, as if to confirm my thoughts and tell me he would be there for me, that he was there now and would never leave me again.

He sensually swept my hair back, baring my neck, and slowly, delicately, brushed his cheek against it, sending a tingle through me. His chest moved slowly against my back, letting me feel his every breath.

"Evan . . ." An instinct I knew I couldn't control made me ask the question that haunted me. I stared at the rippling water dancing to the melody of the breeze. "Why didn't you let me die the first time?" I was distracted by the warmth of his body against mine. It left me dazed. "I mean, you barely knew me."

His chest rose as he took a deep breath, weighing his words. "I can't lie to you. I spent a long time fighting what I felt. Carrying out orders was all I'd ever known. I'm an Angel of Death, even though I know that scares you. It's true, I should have killed you, but I just couldn't. I couldn't bear the thought of never seeing you again. I'd been watching you, spending time with you, although you didn't know it. All those moments gave me the chance to understand what was changing me. What I felt for you, Gemma. And for no one else. Your gestures, your eyes that could see me, against all logic, the way it made me feel when I touched you and you were so shy you pulled away, the sensations that touching you gave me . . . I realized I couldn't live without them any more." Evan rested his chin on my shoulder, pulling me closer. "No, Gemma. I could never have killed you and given up your smile or that funny face you make when you're trying hard to seem angry and you wrinkle your nose and you don't realize that all it does is make you look adorable." He stroked my shoulder. "Or the way you twirl your hair around your finger when you're nervous and walk with your head down, caught up in thoughts that carry you so far away no one could ever reach you." His lips brushed my earlobe, making my heart tremble. "Watching you sleep drives me out of my mind," he whispered. "What do I care about heaven when I can have an even purer angel?"

My eyes filled with unexpected tears. I was an angel with broken wings whom he'd taught to fly.

"I couldn't let it happen," he went on. "It was like feeling the wind for the first time, seeing colors like I'd never seen them before. I felt *alive.* It would have meant killing a part of me. Before I met you, I thought I had everything, but then I realized I had nothing. I'd never felt the need to be close to anyone. Just the opposite, in fact, I was so sure I'd be alone for all eternity. The thought never even fazed me. Not until I met you and was on the verge of losing you. I'd always been a Soldier, but you took me prisoner. I knew I couldn't lose you and give up my heart that I'd just found again. The heart that you stole. If you had died, it would have disappeared along with you. You're my mate, Gemma. My Eve," he whispered tenderly into my ear.

"Your Eve? You mean I'm your temptation?" I said in a low voice, teasing, as his hands slowly slid down my arms, making me tremble.

"I mean that when I look at you, I see my other half."

I closed my eyes as he laced his fingers with mine. I knew exactly what he meant. I felt the very same way. We completed each other. We were like two parts of a mechanism designed to fit together.

His chin was resting on my shoulder. I slowly turned toward him and looked him in the eye. From so close up, his scent was intoxicating. "Evan." He looked at me so intently that for a moment I paused. "Wouldn't it have been easier for us if I'd just died right from the start?" I made myself ask.

"Not at all. Nothing would be left of us but a memory, and there's no way I could have lived with that. I knew I'd be tormented by regret forever if I lost you."

"Does it have to do with your lineage? I mean, the reason you would have lost me." I vaguely recalled what Evan had said on the terrace, but I hadn't completely understood.

Evan nodded, looking down, and prepared to explain. "Dying is always a shock." I flinched. His words triggered the vivid memory in my mind. "It's always traumatic to see your own lifeless body. Our mission isn't over once we've put an end to someone's life. We have to make sure the soul accepts the loss. Reassure it, so it will let us accompany it beyond this world. Each of us has powers to help us carry out the assignment smoothly. Some are needed to bring people to their deaths, others to guide them to eternal life, showing the souls how to pass on. Plus, in our ethereal form, we can perceive every sensation, so we can read someone's soul without the body getting in the way—a little like in dreams, but more intensely." An almost imperceptible sorrow shadowed Evan's face. "But then, once our duty is done, we're not allowed to see any of them again. That's our punishment. For a Subterranean it's inconceivable that anything could be more important than our mission, and that was true for me too. You changed me, Gemma, and I'm not willing to go back to what I was before. If you die, I'll die too. I'll die inside. That's why I didn't kill you the first time. Even then I couldn't stand the thought of losing you."

"You're not allowed into Eden? Is that what you're trying to tell me?" I struggled to put the puzzle together, but it felt like a piece was still missing.

"I can go in, but to my eyes it's deserted. It's heaven—don't get me wrong—but it's still deserted. I can't see anyone and no one can see me."

I stared at the ripples on the windswept lake, filled with a deep feeling of guilt for depriving him of that hope.

"I tried to explain it to you, remember? That's why we're called Subterraneans. God banished us, exiled us. It's like a layer of ether is hiding us from the others, making us invisible. We can interact with mortals, though." He forced a smile.

"I shouldn't have let it happen," I whispered, torn by remorse for the hint of regret I glimpsed in his eyes despite his efforts to hide it.

"It's with you that I want to be, Gemma," he said, his voice as determined as the look on his face as he stared at me. "Even if I have to go to hell to do it."

His conviction overwhelmed me. It was so comforting to have him at my side, to feel the warmth of his body so close to mine. I breathed deeply and Evan's hands squeezed mine even tighter.

"Any other questions?" he asked, finding a smile again. It was irresistible, the way his smile sweetened his face.

"Just a hundred or so," I shot back, looking at him out of the corner of my eye. "Actually, there's something I still don't understand."

"Ask away."

"When you were in the kitchen, you said I would have to take the poison. I heard you say it. What was your plan, exactly?" I teased, a touch of reproach in my voice. It made him laugh.

"I thought that if I killed you, Death would be satisfied and stop hunting you down. At that point I'd bring you back to life. It was a desperate plan, risky, but the only one that came to mind. I really couldn't be sure it would solve things, but I had to give it a shot, even if it didn't turn out the way I'd planned."

"In any case, everything worked out like you'd hoped."

"Not exactly. I gladly would have avoided killing another Subterranean, but I was forced to. He thought all I would do was fight him, trying to prevent your death. Luckily we had the poison."

"The poison? Didn't you need to use that on me?"

"An ordinary dagger alone wouldn't have been enough to get rid of Faustian, so we tipped it with a special, extremely powerful venom," he explained, following my gaze as I sat down on the shore. "That's the only weapon that can kill one of us."

I shivered at the thought of the bone-chilling sensation I'd felt when the glimmer of the blade had hit my eyes. I'd felt like I'd fallen prey to an evil spell, as though some unexpected force had reawakened from the earth and lunged at me.

"Do you think it's possible I smelled it?" I asked hesitantly.

Evan started with surprise and turned to stare at me, an amused look on his face. "Allow me to remind you what state you were in! No, I don't think what you're saying is possible. Ginevra's poison is odorless. Otherwise I would have been the first one to smell it. Our senses are sharper." He let out the laugh he'd been holding back. "You lost a lot of blood—your brain must have been oxygen deprived," he said, making me shiver again. In fact, I found myself shivering at regular intervals. I hoped my brain would soon let me forget the whole thing.

"Did I hear you right? Did you say it was Ginevra's poison? Are you telling me Ginevra's *venomous*?" I asked, gripped with anxiety.

Evan threw his head back and burst out laughing. I'd clearly misunderstood. "Well, you're not all wrong. I'm not sure she isn't. Anyway, the poison we used came from her serpent."

"Her serpent?" I cringed with fright. I'd never liked snakes, ever since the time one had scared the horse Peter was riding. It had reared and thrown him from the saddle.

"Every Witch has one. Together they form a single being, like body and soul."

"And they use the venom against Angels because they consider you their enemies, right?" I asked.

I'd seen for myself how powerful the Subterraneans were and I found it incredible that a tiny animal could be capable of defeating such powerful creatures.

"Hey, you know a lot more than I thought."

"It was Faust. He explained that you were enemies."

"You mean he found time to strike up a conversation while he was torturing you?" His eyes wavered, filling with hatred. I could see him driving away the thought and focusing on my question. "Witches are the highest, most powerful incarnation of evil in existence. Since Creation, leading souls into perdition has been their sole interest, and we're always getting in their way. They did it to Eve, hoping to initiate her into evil, but God spared her; instead of sending her to hell for her transgression, He condemned her to earth and granted her and her mate a second chance. It was a Witch who sent a serpent to tempt Eve. God cursed the evildoing creatures forevermore, decreeing 'On your belly you will go and dust will you eat.'"

"What does that have to do with Subterraneans, exactly?"

"When they discovered that Eve's banished children had been condemned to taking souls back to heaven, the Witches began to slay them to prevent them from doing it. They're very powerful, but we completely outnumber them. Only one Witch is born every five hundred years, and each one is considered invaluable to her Sisters. We, on the other hand, number in the millions. Still, if they declared war on us, no one would be able to stop them. For now, they're having fun slowly corroding the world."

"So they tempt people and lead them into evil?"

Evan's expression darkened slightly. "They *are* evil."

He said it so solemnly it made me shudder. "What about Ginevra?" I made myself bring up this concern, although I wasn't entirely sure I wanted to face the subject. "She doesn't seem wicked."

"That's because she's learned to control that part of herself. Ginevra isn't one of them any more. She's still a Witch, naturally, but she lives with us now. And that makes her one of us."

"Faust mentioned something about rules," I said, hoping he could tell me about that aspect of his life.

"He couldn't use his powers directly on you. Ultimately it needed to seem like a natural death or an accident, a heart attack, an act of aggression—anything, as long as it didn't raise suspicion. But I think it's my turn to ask questions now, don't you?" Evan's expression grew hard. "What was it Faust told you that managed to lure you away from me?"

I avoided his gaze, gripped with guilt. "I struggled against his mind control," I said, feeling miserable. "Part of me resisted up to the end, refusing to believe what he told me, what he accused you of. But then he took me into your kitchen and I heard what you were all saying. I only heard snippets of your conversation, though, so I had no idea you planned to bring me back to life after giving me the poison."

"So that was why you ran away!" Evan gasped, lost in some memory I wasn't aware of. I could see how devastated he'd been when he found out I'd run away.

"Forgive me, Evan. It was all my fault. I ruined everything. Faust made me believe you wanted to kill me. I don't know how he did it, but I really thought it was true. I wasn't myself, you have to believe me!" I begged him. "When I regained control of my mind, I instantly realized I'd been crazy to doubt you, but by then it was too late."

"Don't worry. I know well the power that took you over. Faust was controlling you, brainwashing you. It's not your fault," he reassured me.

I shuddered, realizing what he'd chosen not to say: Evan had that same terrifying power. I'd discovered firsthand that nothing is more frightening than helplessly losing control of your own mind.

"I'm sorry I didn't keep it from happening." His eyes filled with bitterness, his mind clearly moving backwards, trapped in the memory. "Just the thought of not being able to find you," he said in a hushed voice. "It was unbearable. I felt empty and useless. It was a horrifying sensation. I knew you were in danger and with every passing second I felt like I was dying because I couldn't do anything to help you. I was desperate, afraid each minute might be your last, and the very thought that I wouldn't be there beside you to bring you back made me shudder," he confessed in frustration.

"Then what happened? How did you find me?" I asked, still unclear on that detail.

"I was out of my mind with desperation. I'd never known what real fear was. Never," he stressed, looking me in the eye. "I focused all my energy on you, but I couldn't make a connection. I kept calling to you, but I was blocked, groping in total darkness. Right when I was on the verge of giving up all hope, a connection opened up between us, just for a split second, but it was enough for me to find you. I'm sure it was our alchemy that connected us. I know you can feel it too. The emotion is incredibly powerful."

"I heard you! I heard your voice! That must have been the instant you managed to find me," I said. "And here we are now," I added, trying to calm him and drive away the look of melancholy clouding his face.

"Let's not think about it any more," Evan agreed, following me as I headed toward a big maple tree.

"It's strange," he said to my surprise, smiling to himself. "There's one thing you haven't asked me yet."

"What?"

Evan glanced at me uncertainly, like he found it unbelievable that I still hadn't asked him the question he'd expected me to. "Aren't you curious to know how old I am?"

Because of the tension I saw on his face as he waited for me to answer, I teased him, looking down, biting my lip, keeping him on pins and needles a little while longer. I cast him a sidelong glance, sensing his concern, then looked deep into his eyes, making it clear from my expression what I thought about it. "It doesn't matter to me."

"Aren't you afraid I'm too old for you?" he said, laughing, turning forward again to look at the maple tree we were heading toward.

"At this point, I'm not afraid of anything any more!" I said sardonically.

"Oh-ho! So we've become fearless, have we?" Evan said, smiling. As he waited for me to reply, he glanced my way, assessing my silence before saying: "I'm three hundred and nine."

My heart skipped a beat. I tried to hide my shock, but my eyes wouldn't keep still, blinking spasmodically. "I . . . I s-swear you don't look a day over two hundred and ninety!" I said with a grin, trying to steady the quiver in my voice.

He flashed a smile before growing serious again. "I wanted you to know," he said solemnly, "before you decide."

Leaning back against the maple, I turned to look at him. "Decide what?" I asked uncertainly. In the freshness of the early morning, I could smell the bark's mossy scent.

Evan reached out and rested his arms against the tree trunk on either side of my head, trapping me with his body as a tremble rose up from my middle and made its way to my heart.

"If you want to be with me," he replied, and my heart skipped another beat. With resolute tenderness, he locked his eyes on mine, silently waiting for a reply which, inside of me, I'd already given him the first time I'd ever seen him. And yet, hearing his proposal voiced left me in a daze, flooding me with an indescribable emotion.

"I already told you it doesn't matter to me," I said softly.

"Careful—it'll be forever, you know," he warned me gently, stroking my cheek with his thumb.

I couldn't speak. His touch had deprived me of all control. My emotions were in a frantic whirl, making my whole body tremble.

"Every day . . ." he whispered, slowly leaning forward until his cheek tenderly caressed mine. His movements measured, he sank his fingers into my hair, melting me in a delicious lassitude. " . . . and every night," he whispered in my ear, brushing his lips against it, "for as long as you want."

I longed desperately to shout out my consent, but I couldn't speak. My intense emotions had left me in a trance.

His lips moved down my neck, brushing against my skin with boundless sweetness as his hand cupped my head, immersing me in sweet languor. "You said a world where we could be together didn't exist," I whispered, my skin trembling at his every breath.

"So we'll fight for one. I'll defy the entire universe if you'll fight with me."

My voice broke with emotion that threatened to overwhelm me. "Count on it," I managed to say in a barely audible whisper, utterly under the power of his spell.

My heart fluttered when Evan withdrew his mouth from my neck and looked at me intently, melting me like warm honey. His presence, his voice, his touch—so gentle, so real—everything about him mesmerized me. I felt like I'd been bewitched by some dark spell.

"Then you'll be mine," he whispered, "forever and ever." Slowly, he pressed his lips to mine. I rested my hand on his chest, so firm beneath my fingers, and surrendered to him, losing myself in his soft, luscious kiss as a wave of emotion swept me away, flooding me with a warmth I'd never known before.

Every last part of me was his. I felt I belonged to Evan unconditionally. As if I'd been born for him and he for me.

When our lips parted, he gently rested his forehead against mine, his hot breath on my mouth. I opened my eyes and my gaze fell on the dog tag that glimmered against his gray shirt. I stroked it, turning it over in my fingers, still under the spell of his kiss. Infinite emotion pierced my heart when I saw the writing on its flat surface. Engraved on the steel, our names were combined in elegant lettering.

"Gevan," he whispered, taking my breath away.

"Evan, how—when did you have this done?" I managed to ask, overwhelmed by emotion. He smiled at me, narrowing his eyes, the sexy little creases under them deepening adorably.

"The first time I saved you, when I realized I'd be yours forever. You're part of me, Gemma."

How could my body ever contain such powerful emotion? I felt like my heart was on the verge of betraying me.

"I have something for you," he said, slipping his hand into his back pocket. The moment he pulled it out, the thin silver chain sparkled, capturing a sunbeam from the dawn light.

I started when I recognized it and instinctively raised my hand to my neckline, finding the skin beneath my fingers bare. It was the pendant I never went without.

"You lost it in the woods," he explained, holding it out on his palm. "May I?" He looked me in the eye, seeking my approval, but without waiting for my answer, he opened my palm and rested the pendant on it, brushing the thumb of his other hand against my skin. The white gold suddenly glowed with an almost imperceptible light.

"What . . ." I tilted my head as I stared at it, perplexed.

"The engraving." He smiled tenderly.

With the fingertips of my other hand, I clasped the butterfly-shaped pendant and brought it close to my eyes. A lump rose in my throat because the engraving on my pendant had changed; it wasn't my name glittering on the white gold any more. Instead, our two names had become one. The unspoken promise that I would never be alone again.

"Are you angry?" Evan asked, searching my eyes, looking guilty.

"Evan, it's . . . I'm speechless. It's so *beautiful*," I sighed. The concern vanished from his face instantly.

"I know you never take it off. This way I'm sure you'll always have a part of me with you. May I?" He took the chain from my hands and swept my hair to one side, inviting me to hold it up.

I did, turning around and baring my neck. His fingers brushed against my skin, lingering for a few seconds on my nape. Another shiver ran through me at his touch, and I knew for certain I'd never grow used to that contact.

"There's something I need to ask of you."

I let down my hair and turned to face him again, concerned by how serious he'd sounded. "What?" His charm left me dazed every time, trapping me in some unknown world. Looking him in the eye as I waited for his question, I knew he could ask me for anything and I would gladly give it to him.

"You need to promise me something," he said solemnly.

I nodded, waiting.

"I don't want there to be any more secrets between us, no matter what. Secrets are dangerous. Look at where the smallest one led us. I want you to be mine, mine and mine alone. And I'll be completely yours, without reserve." His gaze pierced me as he waited to hear my reply.

"I promise," I vowed.

Evan caressed my face and I trembled again, emotion washing over me. I couldn't believe it was really happening, that he was really there, so close I felt the warmth of his breath on my face. He ran his thumb over my lip, his eyes following the movement. I felt I might go mad with desire.

"How intensely can you fall in love with someone in such a short time?" I whispered, my eyes locked on his lips.

"To the point of madness," he replied in a hushed voice, swallowing. Then he kissed me with dark tenderness.

"Evan." I closed my eyes as a new fear rose up to torment me. "Do you think they'll come back looking for me?" I suddenly feared someone might take me away from him.

Evan looked away for a moment, reflecting. "I roamed the earth for centuries in search of something that would bring me back to life. Now that I've found it, I won't let anyone take it from me. I'll protect you at all costs." Despite the firmness in his voice, his eyes betrayed his concern. "I won't lie to you; I can't be sure it's really over, but I won't let anything happen to you, Gemma. We'll be together. And it will be forever."

"My *forever* is a little different from yours." I smiled to myself, because with Evan's gaze on me, every trace of fear disappeared. "But even if Death does eventually find a way to separate us, until that moment, I'll be satisfied with every second offered to me."

Evan lifted my chin sweetly, resting his eyes steadily on mine so I could read the promise there. "Not even time will separate us. If I have to defy the entire universe, I'll find a solution to that too."

His lips touched my forehead, sealing his vow.

BOOK TWO

UNFAITHFUL

THE DECEPTION OF NIGHT

A novel by

Elisa S. Amore

Translated by

Leah Janeczko

PROLOGUE

Lake Placid, NY

"Faster! Faster!!!" Adrenaline pumped wildly through my veins as I shouted to Evan, my heart pounding like crazy.

The car swerved dangerously onto the highway, racing at an inhuman speed with a roar so fierce it made the hairs on my arms stand up. Lake Placid was far behind us. My breath coming fast, I stole a glance at Evan's face. It was twisted into an expression I'd learned to decipher: a mix of excitement, determination, and defiance—a combination I liked.

Clinging to the dashboard, I turned back to check out the car we were trying to shake: a smoke-gray Lamborghini Reventón with tinted windows. It was right on our tail, ripping the asphalt off the road. "It's gaining on us!" I cried, trying to control my heartbeat.

"They won't catch us that easily," Evan growled. His eyes narrowed to slits as he gripped the steering wheel, shooting me a captivating smile. "We're faster." He raised his eyebrows, the soft curve of his parted lips mesmerizing me, and jammed his foot down on the accelerator. The engine howled.

The Ferrari 458 Italia we were in shot across the scorching hot asphalt like a missile and I hung on for dear life. The speed took my breath away, pushing me back hard into the leather seat. The upholstery was red and contrasted elegantly with the car's sporty silverstone-gray exterior. I adored the color because it remin

ded me of Evan's eyes when the somber sky over Lake Placid darkened them.

Although speed wasn't a problem for him, I still hadn't gotten used to it even though being chased on cars and motorcycles had become an integral part of my second life over the last few months, almost a constant. Despite everything, beneath the thin layer of fear there was a stronger, more deeply rooted sensation under my skin: excitement. The emotions Evan had introduced me to were vivid and precious, especially because they were mine alone: no other mortal experienced them. I couldn't live without them any more. Just a few months ago, death had touched me with its icy fingertips, but I'd never felt this alive before.

"Oh my God! Evan! Look out!!!" I shrieked. A huge semi had suddenly pulled onto the road. My heart lurched. It would be impossible to swerve around it and we were going too fast to stop in time. Instead of slowing down though, at the last second Evan boldly downshifted into fifth, making the rear wheels skid. He jammed his foot onto the accelerator, pushing us into the opposite lane as the semi zoomed by like a blurry rocket.

"That wasn't on the agenda!" he exclaimed with a smug smile.

Terror and excitement washed over me. I took a deep breath and let out a whoop, almost shivering. Evan laughed at my enthusiasm and shook his head.

"You're crazy." I smiled, my heart still trembling.

"What can I say?" he shot back, shrugging. His gaze was shrewd, his smile beguiling.

I glanced out the rear window. "We lost them!"

Evan narrowed his eyes, his gaze locked on the road, his proud smile set in an expression as steely as it was dangerous. The car was gone, but he didn't seem at all convinced it was over.

Proving me wrong, we heard the aggressive roar of an engine and a second later the Lamborghini swerved into view behind us. Evan showed no sign of agitation. The car's engine rumbled again challengingly and my heart leapt to my throat when I saw the gray front end of the Lamborghini nosing at our rear wheels. The two cars gripped the asphalt, their engines growling over the tar set aflame by their tires. The roar behind us persisted, more and more aggressive, making my stomach quiver.

"They're too close, Evan! Speed up! They're right behind us!" I shouted, panic gripping me. My excitement was even stronger, though. It raced through my body like electricity, enhancing every sensation.

The sly half smile on Evan's lips spread, his gaze piercing and seductive. "Time to get serious," he murmured with that tough expression that always drove me wild. "Hold on tight."

I instantly understood it wasn't a suggestion. It was a warning.

Before I could take a breath, Evan jammed his foot on the brake and the car abruptly slowed, eluding our pursuer who shot past us like a bullet. Next, he grabbed the emergency brake and yanked it back while turning the steering wheel with his left hand.

I felt a pit in my stomach that spread to my head as the car spun out. I would have liked to catch my breath, but Evan didn't give me the chance. The tires squealed against the asphalt, still damp with early-morning dew, and raced off in the opposite direction, pressing me back into my seat. My chest rose and fell convulsively as I tried to position myself in some way that might keep me from shaking.

Over my shoulder I glimpsed the Lamborghini coming toward us like a missile homing in on its target as our Ferrari zoomed onto Old Military Road at two hundred miles an hour. "Evan!!!" My voice was shrill, almost desperate.

"Brace yourself!" he ordered me through clenched teeth without giving me time to react. The words were still trapped in my throat when he swerved brusquely onto Mill Pond Drive so fast the landscape became a distorted blur of color as the car skidded into the school parking lot, squealing across the asphalt and shoving me against the window. Only seconds later did I anxiously turn and see the Lamborghini behind us copy Evan's maneuver and skid to a halt just yards from us.

I sank into my seat, still shaking, and took a deep breath. At last, everything was still. A car door clicked open, breaking the stunned silence of the students who'd been left wordless by our arrival. My heart was still pounding, my head spinning. My eyes shot to the side-view mirror as the Lamborghini's door swung up like an eagle preparing to take wing. The driver stepped deliberately out of the gray leather and Alcantara suede seat. A shiver ran over my skin, adrenaline still pumping through my veins. As I tried to regain control of my breathing, regular footsteps approached.

"Not bad, little brother!"

Ginevra's long, sensual legs halted next to the driver's door, her voice muffled by the glass. Evan tilted his head toward me and smiled with satisfaction before lowering the window. Ginevra leaned down, gracefully rested her elbows on his door, and winked at me, a smile on her lips. A soft cascade of blond hair hung over her shoulder, hiding part of the neckline of her dress, which was gray with black stripes around the bodice. Its skirt bared her breathtaking legs that, as always, ended in sky-high heels. For some strange reason, her poised, elegant bearing never made her seem inappropriate, no matter what she wore. Quite the opposite: one look and the rest of the world felt out of place and awkward when she passed.

I gave her a little wave, barely raising my fingers, and smiled to myself. My throat was still dry from the race. Although I was dazed and shaken, the thrill won out every time. It was an amazing sensation: pure adrenaline churned out by sheer excitement, totally devoid of fear. It flowed beneath my skin, enhanced by the awareness that at Evan's side I ran no risk. Racing at two hundred miles an hour at the crack of dawn sent an incomparable surge of electricity through me. It was a feeling I'd known for only a short time but one I'd had to get used to quickly. And I would never give it up. Once I'd tasted it, I'd discovered that certain emotions were hard to forget. My body craved it; adrenaline quenched its thirst. I'd lived my life on standby, waiting for Evan to arrive so I could live every moment to the fullest.

Evan hadn't answered Ginevra yet. He just smiled to himself, looking amused. I'd seen this a million times before.

"Don't make that face. I can beat you whenever I want," she insisted with a pout. "You'd better stay warmed up because I want a rematch." Ginevra was totally incapable of admitting defeat.

"Wasn't *this* the rematch?" I put in timidly, imagining that the exact same scene must have played out between them before they stopped by my place this morning.

A sharp look from Ginevra made me bite my lip. Evan let out a laugh, even more amused by his sister's stubbornness. "I'm all yours," he promised, raising his eyebrows.

We got out of the car and Evan walked around the Ferrari to me, but Ginevra was quick to link her arm in mine. "That means I'll keep her hostage until then."

"In your dreams." He grabbed my hand and pulled me toward him, his smile slow and studied. I stifled a laugh, seeing Ginevra frown as we walked off. Turning back toward her, I mouthed *Sorry*. Evan stepped behind me to block me from Ginevra's view. It was incredible how the two siblings competed with each other.

"Once in a while we could show up like normal people, don't you think?" I teased, still trying to recover from the last curve.

He glanced at me, his expression sly. "We could." He squeezed my waist from behind and whispered into my ear: "But that wouldn't be as much fun—don't *you* think?"

The warmth of his breath in my hair sent a quiver through me. He'd found a way to distract me from Ginevra. I shook my head as a murmur spread among the students of Lake Placid High. They cast curious glances at Evan and Ginevra's cars that stood out among all the others in the parking lot. In general I tried not to be bothered by the interest they raised wherever we went in them—unlike Ginevra, I wasn't exactly comfortable being in the spotlight—but cars aside, our spectacular entrance had definitely drawn attention.

"I told you the Ferrari would be overdoing it on the first day of school," I murmured in embarrassment.

Evan tried to object but before he could open his mouth Ginevra swooped in from behind. "This is an important day! We needed to celebrate!" She turned to her brother. "You owe me one."

"Celebrate what, exactly?" I said, though I wasn't sure if I would be better off not asking.

"Today's the first day of your last year of school, Gemma!" she said with surprise, as though the answer were obvious.

I rolled my eyes and decided to humor her. There was no need for Ginevra to keep coming to school, but she'd decided to attend classes anyway. I wasn't totally convinced it was to keep up appearances like she'd said or whether it was so she could continue to keep an eye on me, as my instinct suggested.

In any case, no matter how frustrating it was, Evan was enough to draw attention even without his Ferrari. Their underground garage was packed with flashy, expensive cars they'd gotten who knew where. To Ginevra, money was certainly no issue.

Evan and I usually took his motorcycle. Common sense made him save the Ferrari for nighttime rides when he'd swing by my place and I would sneak out the window at the first light of dawn when Lake Placid was still sleeping. The same thing definitely couldn't be said of Ginevra. Sometimes it was hard to dissuade her once she'd made up her mind. This was probably one of those mornings when Evan hadn't managed to ignore his sister's out-of-control competitive spirit. Ginevra couldn't get enough of standing out.

I spotted some of my friends in the distance: Brandon, walking with his arms around the shoulders of two new girls; Jake, who was getting out of his dad's police car; Faith and Jeneane, hopping off the school bus; and Peter, just arriving on his bike, wearing a Blue Bombers sweatshirt, ready to begin a new lacrosse season. Everything was so familiar and yet so different.

The shrill sound of the bell welcomed us as we walked through the school doors. I forced myself to take deep breaths until the adrenaline had subsided and the annoying hum in my ears was gone. I squeezed Evan's hand and his fingers returned the gesture. That sound announced the beginning of a new year. A new year together with him.

"O true apothecary!
Thy drugs are quick.
Thus with a kiss I die."

William Shakespeare, *Romeo and Juliet*
Act V, Scene III

GHOSTS FROM THE PAST

A few hours earlier

"The year was 1720. A September night, just like this one." Evan's gaze was distant, his voice deep and melancholy, as if the memory of his past might carry him away at any moment. He struggled to voice the words, as though afraid the events would come back to life in his head. I didn't want to pressure him. I'd never insisted he give me details about his past but he went on, his tone dull. "I was seventeen." He lay down next to me on the grassy lawn on the shore of Mirror Lake, gently resting his head on my lap, and closed his eyes as I looked down at him. "I remember every minute." A twitch under his eyelids told me his mind had taken him back to that distant 1720, but only for a fleeting moment. A second later he opened his eyes again, escaping the memory that was probably too painful for him to experience a second time.

In silence, I waited for him to speak.

"Every single moment of that miserable night is engraved on my memory." He stared at the cloudless sky. His eyes were focused but his blank expression made me doubt he was really there with me. Despite himself, he was lost in the memory.

"Evan, you don't need to tell me if you don't feel ready. What happened to you in the past doesn't matter. All that counts is that you're with me right here, right now," I assured him—though it wasn't true.

A trace of a smile appeared on Evan's face as if he could tell I'd lied. Then he looked me straight in the eye. "I want you to know everything about me. No more secrets, remember?"

"In this case I don't think it counts as a secret," I said. Instinctively, I sank my fingers into his soft, wavy hair, the color of coffee beans.

"I want to tell you anyway."

I waited patiently, continuing to stroke his head during the silence that followed.

"Passing on is a traumatic experience for all of us. Every Subterranean remembers it with sorrow and bitterness, as if we'd hoped for a . . . a better death." He grimaced. "Or a different fate. But we soon learn, one way or another, that if the blood of the Children of Eve flows through our veins it doesn't matter how we pass on. All that counts is our punishment, the sentence we have to serve. That is, if we're even allowed the hope of atonement."

"You aren't damned," I said instantly.

He looked at me. "I know that now. Otherwise I wouldn't have you. I can't imagine any worse damnation than never having met you—or losing you. In any case, those of us who manage to survive never forget."

"Survive?" I gasped, as surprised as I was alarmed. "You mean you risk dying again right after you've just . . . died?" The word sent a shiver down my spine. I tried not to think about the fact that Evan wasn't alive any more. He was so warm, so . . . human.

He smiled, but it was an empty smile. There was no sparkle in his eyes.

More silence.

"My father was a middle-class London merchant. We weren't rich but we weren't poor either. By day he earned a respectable income, but his nights were spent reinvesting the family money in far-from-reputable activities. Alcohol and women were his sole interests and, for my mother and me, our heaviest burden. She meant more to me than anything else in the world. I remember that I saw her through my childish eyes as an angel, and myself as her little warrior. I wanted to protect her from him but that wasn't always possible. You can save someone from any danger, but no matter how important that person is to you, you can't save them from their own feelings. Those are hard to change. In only a few years Father had disgraced our family name."

From time to time Evan stopped, losing himself in long pauses, his breathing deep and labored. Anguished, even. "As a young boy, night after night, my mother's silent weeping was deafening to my little heart. It was as loud as a scream, an unbearable pain that tore me up inside. I would slip into her room to comfort her. She would hold me tight and our embrace seemed to soothe her. It wasn't until later that I realized she was pretending so I wouldn't be upset. I was just a boy, but I felt like the only man in our house.

"I grew older and started to stand up to him. Our arguments became more frequent and uglier, especially when he would come home in the mornings drunk and half dressed. He was my father but I hated him. I couldn't understand why my mother still hoped to see him change, but I gave in to her wishes and instead of making him leave all I did was argue with him. Her happiness was all that mattered to me. Father was handsome, charming, trim, quite tall, with a wisp of a beard as blond as his hair, but his behavior made him unworthy of my mother's good graces."

"What was she like?" I asked, even though I had carefully studied the family portrait that hung in Evan's room. I was curious to know more about the woman Evan had loved so much, but I regretted the question the moment I saw a glimmer in his eyes.

"There wasn't a woman who didn't envy her fair complexion and soft dark curls."

"Like yours," I was quick to point out.

He smiled. "Yes. Like mine," he said, clearly pleased he'd inherited his mother's looks and not his father's. He seemed relieved there was no strong resemblance to the man he despised.

"Her manners were kind and graceful, though her true beauty was in her soul. Her porcelain skin was the envy of all the ladies. Until she met my father, that is. Then their envy quickly turned to compassion. He'd won her heart by hiding love letters in loaves of bread he would send her, but once they were married his attitude changed. It was probably my father's behavior that kept me from returning the attentions of the girls in our neighborhood," he admitted, apparently realizing it only now.

"What *kind* of attentions did they pay you, exactly?" I said, feeling irritated, as if the girls from his past could even matter. None of them had been alive for centuries, but in spite of myself a twinge of jealousy gripped my stomach.

Evan didn't bother to hide a smile. "Nothing that mattered," he reassured me. Looking me straight in the eye, his head still resting on my lap, he reached up and swept a lock of hair from my face, holding my gaze as he did so. "There's never been another girl for me. Back then I had to take care of my mother. I didn't have time for another woman. You've been my one and only, Gemma."

The pause that followed lasted even longer than the others, as if Evan were preparing to reveal the most difficult, painful part. It was so obvious I could almost see the tangle of thorns trapping his words; every time he tried to free them, the thorns pierced his heart before he could open his mouth.

I waited in silence until he was ready to relive the memory. "It was a peaceful September night—but not at our house. In my heart there wasn't a trace of the stillness that filled the streets. Inside I was screaming with rage and frustration. With hatred. I could feel my mother's pain echoing everywhere. In my head, my chest. Every part of me suffered for her. Father had gone out for the millionth time but that night was different from the others. Looking into my mother's eyes, grown dull and weary, I saw something different in the dim light of the candle she kept on the windowsill where she was waiting up for him as she did every night. The look she had on her face is seared into my memory as though with a branding iron. It still burns whenever I remember it. I'll never forgive my father for making my last memory of my mother be that exhausted, empty look in her eyes.

"I decided enough was enough. I went out to find him. I'd never done it before but that night I was determined to bring him home, by force if necessary. I was young, strong, and brawnier than he was. But my good intentions quickly vanished. It took me less than a minute to realize it wasn't worth it; he was in the doorway of a tavern, too drunk to stand, his arms around two bawdily dressed girls. They must have been more or less your age. They staggered down the street, laughing provocatively and behaving scandalously for ladies of that era. When he saw me, my father didn't even take his hands off them. Utterly shameless. I was ashamed for him. I was ashamed *of* him.

"'William!' he chortled as I walked toward him. He was too drunk to notice the disgust and scorn in my eyes. 'Hey! I'm talking to you, lad. Come here. Look what lovely pullets I found in the henhouse. I got one for you too!' He squeezed the girls closer, like a trophy to be shared, and I realized I'd never known true hatred and contempt until then. 'Come! What are you waiting for?'

"Rage boiled inside me as he spoke. 'Come on, laddie! You can do it!' Then he turned to the girls, laughing, not even bothering to lower his voice. 'You must forgive the boy. He's never had a woman before.'

"That's when I got close enough for him to focus on my face. 'And he still clings to his mother's skirts.' He lowered his voice and made a theatrical gesture. 'What's wrong with you? You aren't afraid to know what a real woman is, I hope!' he said in a mocking tone.

"The two girls snickered without taking their eyes off me, as if they were interested in his proposal. But all I could see was that man. I glared at him with disgust as I neared him, trying not to think of the look in my mother's eyes that still set the blood in my veins on fire.

"Suddenly his voice became animated. 'My ladies!' he cried with the enthusiasm of someone about to do someone else a favor. 'Voila! I present to you my son, Evan William James!' He introduced me with a bow that knocked him off balance. The two girls tried to hold him up.

"I didn't lift a finger to help him. With a drunken laugh, he straightened up. 'He came all the way here for one of you two. Who'll volunteer? Or do you want to choose for yourself, William?' he asked before the sneering girls could decide. 'What is it, son? What's wrong? Come now!' he said when I didn't answer. 'These two lassies aren't to your liking?' he said testily, lifting their chins toward the dim light of the only lantern. 'For tonight you'll have to make do.'

"They must have seen the fury in my eyes because the two girls' expressions changed the instant I got close enough. They were so scared they broke away from him and backed up. If looks could kill, my father would have dropped dead on the spot.

"As I stood there, he leaned over and whispered in my ear, 'Choose one so tonight you can finally become a real man.' Then he sneered at me. Wrong move. His words were like gasoline on a fire. I rushed at him, shoved him, and struck him across the face so violently that he landed on the ground yards away from the girls, who were shocked by my brutality.

"'You're no man,' I hissed in disgust. 'You never have been.' Then I walked off, not feeling the least bit guilty about his bloody jaw. I never saw him again."

I shared Evan's silence for a long moment.

"It must have been terrible," I finally said, horrified by his story.

"Not at all," he said. "It was the most liberating, most gratifying thing I'd ever done. The thought of having to leave my mother in his hands was what worried me when I realized I'd never see her again."

Knowing he hadn't finished, I didn't break the silence that followed.

"I went back the way I'd come, running down the cobblestone streets. The places where Father amused himself were in the most squalid neighborhoods, fitting only for the likes of him. It hadn't taken me long to find him. I'd known he would be on the outskirts of town in the most disreputable dens of vice. Now that the burden had been lifted from my chest, the silence inside me was so intense that my footsteps echoed off the buildings in the dark, deserted alleys.

Suddenly the silence was broken by a shriek of terror that sliced through the night like lightning. I was instantly on guard, trying to figure out where the desperate voice was coming from. A woman, at that hour of the night. Imagining she needed help, I rushed in her direction. Although people today think modern society is violent and dangerous, it's actually a lot safer than it used to be, believe me. There were a lot more robbers on the streets of London in the eighteenth century than there are today in New York City. Anyway, I immediately suspected it was a criminal. When I saw them I was surprised. I had just run around the corner and my breath caught in my throat, not from fear—I didn't feel a trace of it—but from outrage.

"There were four of them, all more or less my age or maybe a few years older. They were dressed well, even better than I was, so they must have been from upper-class families. They were all drunk as skunks. Back then noblemen amused themselves by terrorizing people, and the focus of their amusement that night was a young lady. From her clothing, I guessed she was a noblewoman. She wore a full-skirted white lace gown that matched her long gloves and around her neck was a string of pearls. Her face was so innocent, and the terror I read in her eyes when one of the boys slid his hand under her skirt made me run to her rescue. It wasn't unusual for spoiled noblemen like them to rape girls, even dragging them out of their carriages. Their crimes often went unpunished."

"How terrible." Appalled, I could find nothing else to say.

"It was rare for a nobleman to be punished. The art of violence was part of their education. They had the right to carry weapons and they never went without them. I was petrified by the spine-chilling scene I was witnessing in that alley. I was just a boy and it took me a few seconds to react. My presence hadn't disturbed them in the least, or maybe they hadn't even noticed me there, blinded as they were by excitement. I remember one of them covering her mouth with one hand while unbuttoning his trousers with the other.

"It was at that point that the girl looked in my direction. In her eyes I glimpsed the same look I'd seen in my mother's, filled with resignation. Without thinking, I tackled the boy who was forcing the girl against the wall and we fell to the ground. A gun went off and I froze. The boy beneath me wrenched himself free from my grip. I heard the echo of their footsteps, but when I turned around it was too late. The four boys had run off down the alley and the darkness had swallowed them up. I looked down at the hand I'd instinctively raised to my aching chest and realized I wouldn't be going home that night."

I sat there in shock as uncontrollable shivers ran through my entire body. "It's a terrifying story," I finally said, attempting to bring his attention back to me. But Evan was still there in the alley, lost in his memories. In his eyes I could see he'd just relived the tragedy, and I'd done it with him.

"It's just one of many. There were worse crimes in London's deserted alleys in the dead of night. The streets weren't safe. It was what happened afterwards that was unusual."

His words startled me. I hadn't known he had more to tell.

"I didn't have time to realize what was happening. After a moment I fell to the ground and lost consciousness." Evan stopped, lost in thought, reflecting on the distant past. "I felt a profound stillness coming from inside me. It was everywhere, surrounding me, engulfing me. Suddenly a harmonious sound broke the stillness, like music from a harp, but more . . . human. The sound pulled me out of the darkness, back to the surface. All at once I was on my feet again. Confused, I shook my head. The sound came again. I stood still, trying to understand where it was coming from. I wanted it. I longed to reach it with every fiber of my being. I followed it unresistingly. The voice began to whisper my name over and over, like the sweetest of melodies. I couldn't resist it. It was a girl's voice, calling to me with excited giggles like a child playing hide-and-seek. I was irresistibly attracted, like I'd been hypnotized and had no control over my own body or mind. That's when I received the mark."

"Your tattoo," I murmured, stroking the symbols that wound around his left forearm.

Evan nodded. "For a few seconds the burning sensation drove her out of my head. Then I turned the corner and saw her. It was the girl in the white gown. Blinded by my earlier rage, I hadn't noticed how beautiful she was. She wore her red hair up and a few locks hung over her delicate neck. Her voice continued to beckon me until I went to her and instinctively stroked her rosy cheek. I couldn't take my eyes off her full red lips."

I went rigid, not prepared to hear more. A stab of pain had pierced my heart and I wanted him to stop, but Evan went on before I could protest.

"I wanted her and yet I had this strange feeling that I wasn't really in my right mind, like I was falling under some evil spell. Seeing me hesitate, the girl tried to encourage me with her eyes. She lifted her hand and ran it along the curve of her bosom. I thought she might be trying to repay me for chasing off the boys, but I wasn't interested in that kind of reward. Still shaken from having stood up to my father, I wanted to rush home to tell my mother everything. I didn't want the girl and yet I had the strange urge to touch her. She seemed to sense it and, taking my hand, she slid it under her skirt. The contact with her warm skin made me shiver."

A deep ache throbbed in my heart when I heard Evan say these last words. I knew it made no sense to feel such resentment—so much time had passed—but I couldn't help it. The mental images his description was conjuring up were unbearable. No matter how distant they were, Evan's emotions pierced my heart like a dagger.

"A cold shiver," he continued. His eyes locked onto mine as if he'd perceived my thoughts and wanted to reassure me. We were sitting close together, almost facing each other. "An evil chill I'd never felt before, so cold it permeated my bones. It was almost painful, as though someone had trapped me under a thick layer of ice and I couldn't reach the surface. The more I struggled internally, the more it overwhelmed me; I was totally at the mercy of that pain. I couldn't breathe but, against my will, my lips continued to move closer to hers. Shards of ice ran me through every time I tried to resist. My body, in contrast, wasn't offering any resistance. It was attracted to her; it wanted her, but I'd never been that kind of guy. It wasn't that I was indifferent to her beauty, but normally I would have made the decision not to give in to her. I'd always been strong-willed, and my intolerance of those who lacked a sense of decency was probably due to Father's behavior.

"It was only when I looked her in the eye that everything changed, as if I'd unexpectedly found the key to escaping her control. Not caring about appearing rude, I grabbed the hand that was holding mine, doing with it as she pleased, and shoved it against her chest so hard she winced. I had only a second to stare into her sensual, pouting gaze. I saw defiance in her eyes as if, despite my rejection she was still trying to make me change my mind. Then she vanished before my eyes."

As Evan said this it dawned on me. "She was a Witch." I was so stunned by everything he was saying that it came out as a whisper.

He lowered his head in confirmation. "It was a trap. The boys had just been bait. By giving in to evil they'd sealed their fates, but I was her actual target."

"So she wanted them to kill you? But why?" I asked, confused.

"To claim my soul through seduction. That's how they do it. They fog your brain."

"They use sex to steal souls?"

"They use *desire.* Lust is one of the most underestimated sins and the one most often committed. The seductive power of a Witch is so strong it's hard to resist."

"But you did," I pointed out, relieved.

Evan nodded. "It's as though each of us has to atone in our own personal way for original sin by resisting temptation like Adam couldn't."

"Then what happened?" I asked, curious.

"Actually, I still hadn't realized what was going on. I saw the girl vanish and thought I'd taken a nasty blow to the head. I started walking home, thinking about my mother. In my mind, I relived what had happened with my father. I was anxious to tell her about how I'd stood up to him. I wanted to reassure her that from that moment on I'd take care of everything, we'd move away, she'd never be subjected to his humiliations again. Circumstances had forced me to grow up quickly, taking care of the family and the shop when I was still little more than a child. I felt ready.

"Then something caught my eye, something hidden in the dim light at the end of the alley. I moved toward it and began to make out a shape lying on the ground. A body. I ran to help, but when I neared it I saw a pool of blood around the body. There was nothing I could do. Whoever he was, it was too late.

"I was just about to leave when a strange instinct compelled me to move closer. I reached out, turned the body over and saw his face. It hit me like a bolt of lightning right in the chest. It was me. And I was dead.

"I knelt there staring at my corpse, paralyzed, powerless to react and unable to find the courage to leave it and walk away. The bullet had passed through my heart. The shot must have been fired from close range, but it hadn't been the boy beneath me who pulled the trigger."

I cringed at the thought of such cruelty.

"And yet I was too horrified to stay there either. My body was a piece of dead meat lying on the ground. I got up and ran away as fast as I could. I had a strange knot in my throat I couldn't ease. It was as if all my tears had suddenly dried up: tears not for myself, but for my mother. A single thought hounded me: who would take care of her? I had no choice but to leave her to her sad fate, living out her life with that good-for-nothing worm of a husband.

"I was amazed when the following months proved me wrong. My aggressive reaction taught Father a lesson and that was the last time he ever stayed out until dawn. My passing helped bring them together again and their marriage was saved. I couldn't have been happier. They couldn't see me but I watched them whenever possible. They were united in their grief over losing me, but at least they were *united.* If I had to die, I can't imagine a better reason. The happiness in my mother's eyes cancelled out everything else. For years that was all I'd wanted. My wish had come true." Despite Evan's words, his face was stony.

"I think it's best not to think about the past any more," I said, hoping it would improve his mood, and added with a wink, "Let's focus on the future." I was resolved to break down the walls of reserve he'd just talked about. Actually, since I'd known him I'd found his attitude to be anything but reserved.

He laughed, almost as if he'd read my mind.

"What ever happened to that good boy?"

He drew closer, his gaze turning sly. "I'm more of a good boy than you imagine. It's not easy being around you and not . . ."

"And not what?" I asked provocatively.

"And not allowing myself to be consumed by the fire."

"After three centuries, you should have learned to keep that fire under control."

"For three centuries I was surrounded by shadows and ice. *You're* my fire. And whenever I'm near you I risk being consumed."

"Then I might get burned too. I'd better keep my distance."

"Who says I'll let you? We're not in the seventeen hundreds any more. If we'd met back then, you certainly would have had to keep your distance, and only after I'd seen approval in your eyes could I have asked for your hand."

"Right, sure. I just can't see you acting like a fine young gentleman!"

"That's how I would have acted by day," he said, a wolfish look on his face as he sensually drew nearer. "But then I would have tapped on your window every night." He whispered the words directly against my mouth and then kissed me. A long, warm, deep kiss. "No. I don't think I could have managed to stay away from you even by day."

I smiled and rested my forehead on his. "Weren't we supposed to focus on the future?" I asked, still provocative, biting my lip to subdue the fire that burned inside me whenever our bodies touched.

"I'm thinking about the future right now," he murmured, moving his lips closer.

"And what do you see, pray tell?" I whispered, enchanted by his seductive gaze so close to mine.

Evan looked me straight in the eye. "It's right in front of me. You're my future. Nothing else matters." He brushed his lips against my chin, light, tiny kisses that slowly moved to my mouth. "Gemma Naiad Bloom, you're like the sun to me," he whispered.

"You mean you can't look at me for more than a few seconds without your eyes hurting?" I teased.

Evan smiled, his lips so close they tickled mine. "I mean your light is so bright it eclipses everything else." Another kiss, longer and more delicate, at the corner of my mouth. "Not even the stars, no matter how dazzling, how radiant, can shine in the presence of the sun, so they hide, fearing comparison. My sun is you. Your light blinds me and I see nothing—" he whispered under his breath, touching my lips ever so lightly, teasingly, "—but you." Every part of my body trembled from the stolen contact. "You are my sun and my fire. Being near you warms my soul. Without you, I would be relegated to the cold, the dark. I would lose myself forever."

As I was still melting in Evan's warmth, he unexpectedly pulled back and looked me in the eye, smiling like the cat that ate the canary. "Time's up," he whispered, puzzling me.

A loud noise woke me with a jolt.

I opened my eyes groggily. Sadness crept over me as I gradually made out the ceiling overhead. My alarm clock was still blaring, announcing that the day had begun, when I turned and met Evan's dark eyes. He was leaning against my bedroom window, looking vaguely amused. "Good morning," he whispered sweetly, not even trying to hide the smile on his face. Before I could say a word he was lying at my side, his hand brushing a lock of hair from my cheek. My eyes were immediately drawn to the dog tag that glinted on the dark-red, long-sleeved shirt he wore. *Gevan.* My heart still skipped a beat every time I read our names engraved together on the metal.

"You're such a liar!" I punched him on the shoulder, frowning and trying unsuccessfully to sound annoyed. "Why do you keep messing with me? You should warn me when we're inside my head. But then again, why would you, since you've realized that teasing me is more fun than anything else in the world?"

"I didn't just 'realize' it. I've always known it," he said with a grin. All at once his expression grew more serious, verging on sadness. "I'm sorry. It's the only way I can read inside you, Gemma. Plus it saves you the embarrassment of having to hide your feelings. You know it's useless. When you're aware we're in your dreams you're never completely comfortable because you know I can detect all your emotions."

"You should tell me anyway."

"I'll try to remember that. But this time it really was necessary. I needed to sense your feelings while I told you about my past. I didn't want to upset you too much."

Evan's explanation stopped me from replying and I accepted his apology with a simple glance. He grinned at me cheerfully. "You'd better get ready. You wouldn't want to make me late for my first day back at school, would you?"

I couldn't believe time had flown so fast. Five months had already gone by since the beginning of my second life, the night I'd called a truce with death. But a dark feeling inside me made me suspect it wouldn't last forever, that my covenant with fate was destined to be broken. Although the last few months had been the most intense period of my entire life, I'd never stopped jumping at every sound and wondering when Death would come to take me. I'd never lowered my guard and I knew Evan hadn't either, though he tried hard to hide it. Wherever we were, I could sense the concern in his watchful glances. I'd always been good at that, as if Evan were part of my body. And so I drank in every moment, savored every sensation, every breath, afraid it might be my last. I forgot my fears only when I sought refuge in my books, hiding away in other worlds. But then I had to return to reality—a reality where, despite all my fears, there was Evan. I couldn't have wished for better.

"Right." I gave a resigned sigh. "Here we go again!" I pressed my lips together and tried to summon up a little enthusiasm. It was annoying to have to concentrate on anything that distracted me from Evan. We'd become inseparable. We were together all day and at night he would sneak into my dreams. I'd sensed the strength of my connection to him when we'd first met on that March afternoon that was destined to change my fate. It felt so long ago and yet whenever I looked back I found the past following me like a ghost.

"You know, at first no one understood me," I confessed out of the blue, "but I could feel it. I felt deep down that something in my life was about to change, that pretty soon something was going to turn it upside down." I looked him in the eye. "No, not something. *Someone.* I always knew, from the moment I saw that strange light—and then you appeared."

Evan studied my face, puzzled. "What light?"

"The burst of light that lit up the sky just before I met you in the woods," I said, recollecting the memory that I'd thought he shared.

"I have no idea what you're talking about," he said, almost amused.

I blinked in confusion. I hadn't expected Evan to contradict me. He threw his head back and his spirited laughter rang out. "Gemma, there are millions of us and we're constantly moving around. There's no strange flash of light heralding our arrival. If there were, the sky would be an endless fireworks show." His reply threw me so off guard it left me wordless. I'd always been convinced the light was somehow connected to their arrival in Lake Placid.

Evan laughed again, probably amused by my expression. "Don't be silly. It must have been a UFO. Besides, Angels can't fly, didn't you know that?"

Disoriented, I decided to drop it. Footsteps outside my door put me on alert. We exchanged a fleeting glance and he vanished the second my mom came into the room.

"Morning!" she chimed. "Awake already? I came to check. Just wanted to make sure you didn't oversleep on the first day of school."

"Thanks for reminding me," I mumbled, throwing myself back onto the bed and pulling the covers over my face. Actually, I was hoping she wouldn't notice my cheeks were still aflame. Feeling the mattress sag beneath her weight, I uncovered my head. She was sitting beside me, looking at me with a doting expression that made me cringe. My God, Evan was somewhere in the room. I hoped she wouldn't say anything embarrassing.

"Eighteen years old! I still can't believe you've grown up so fast," she said with a sigh.

"Mom, it's not my birthday yet!" I protested, blushing with embarrassment.

"But you're already so *different*," she insisted, almost with regret. "You'll be graduating this year and you already have a boyfriend . . ."

I stiffened. My face must have been crimson. Evan was probably getting a kick out of my expression. Unexpectedly, he reappeared behind my mom. I cringed and shot him a disapproving look, but he continued to move closer, forcing me to make a face that would stop him in his tracks.

"Gemma, are you all right?" Frowning, Mom glanced over her shoulder and turned back to look at me. Instead of worrying about Evan's presence, I should have been watching my reactions.

Evan continued to shake his head, clearly finding the situation hilarious. Then I noticed his eyes glowing like a diamond of ice. For some strange reason neither of us understood I was the only person capable of seeing him in his ethereal form.

The situation at home had gotten simpler since Evan's endless requests to meet my folks had finally worn me down and I'd introduced him to them, albeit reluctantly. He was used to following a different etiquette. Since then his brother Drake had had to take on my physical appearance and replace me a lot less often but, given his willingness to help, we frequently took advantage of this power of his, especially at night.

Before meeting Evan and his family I'd never seen a bond as strong as the one they all shared. It was a deep, unconditional affection that had instantly extended to me. I could feel it under my skin. For the first time in my life I felt I was part of something. They treated me like I was a member of their family too.

Ginevra in particular had turned out to be the sister I'd never had, probably because she was the most aware of how intense my feelings for Evan were and his for me, which in some way made them her own. Whenever I remembered how convinced I'd been that she was my rival I felt stupid and hoped she wasn't around, otherwise she'd have managed to read it in my mind. It was a relief not to have to compete with Ginevra's exasperating beauty, even though she was always trying to boost my self-esteem. Out of kindness, of course.

"You'd better get ready," Mom said, leaving the room.

"What on earth were you thinking?" I hissed at Evan, shaking, the moment the door clicked shut.

"Did you say something?" She opened the door a crack and peered in.

I instantly froze and stole a glance at Evan's eyes. They were still gray, meaning she couldn't see him. "No, Mom. I'll hurry and get dressed," I stammered with embarrassment.

She shut the door again and I sighed, my heartbeat gradually slowing.

"Are you trying to give me a heart attack?" I whispered, being careful not to speak loud enough to be overheard. I raised my hands in frustration. He gently took me by the wrists, breaking down all my defenses. I tried to free myself but it was no use. Evan was too strong.

"Relax, she can't see me," he murmured, pulling me against him. I melted into his embrace as he stared at me from under his long eyelashes, his gray eyes flecked with gold. "You're so beautiful it almost scares me," he whispered.

"Scares you? Why?" I asked, bewildered.

"Because for the first time I have something to lose."

I pressed my lips against his, parting them gently.

"Give me a few minutes to go home and get my motorcycle. I didn't need it last night. Meanwhile, get ready," he whispered between one light kiss and the next.

"Okay, but come back soon."

Every time Evan had to leave me, even for a little while, I panicked. A strange anxiety filled me, as though I were underwater and someone had taken away my snorkel. I couldn't breathe.

Sometimes Evan had to go away on a mission, the nature of which I didn't want to know. On those occasions—which had been more frequent lately—I avoided thinking about what was going on in who knew what part of the world Evan had been called to to intervene. In general he was never gone for longer than a few hours, but it was long enough to agitate me and reawaken the ghosts that I tried to lock up in the farthest reaches of my subconscious. And yet there they were. They always came back.

When he returned I never asked him for an explanation. I didn't have the strength—or probably the courage—to handle the answers. I preferred not to know.

"I'll ride like a madman to get back to you as fast as I can," he promised. I abandoned myself to the warmth of his lips and he vanished, leaving me with the memory of his kiss.

I sighed, my heart full of butterflies. "You *always* ride like a madman," I murmured. Smiling, I shook my head. My ears were burning and my breathing was rapid, as if I needed more air. Why did Evan always have this effect on me?

I hurried to the closet, took out an old pair of jeans faded at the knees and put them on along with my gray-and-red Nikes and a hooded sweatshirt in the same colors.

Ten minutes later an aggressive roar from outside told me Evan had arrived, but it didn't sound like his motorcycle. I glanced out the window, though my mind had conjured the image even before my eyes could.

Evan beamed at me, leaning against the hood of his Ferrari, and waved for me to join him as another car right behind him—Ginevra's Lamborghini—revved its engine. He shrugged, amused, and I shook my head in resignation.

I took the stairs two at a time and opened the door before Mom could try to make us stay for breakfast, but Evan was right there in front of me, blocking the way.

"Mr. Bloom," Evan said, nodding at my dad, who nodded back. Then he turned to my mom. "Mrs. Bloom."

"Good morning, Evan," she said with her customary enthusiasm. She had no idea we'd just spent the night together. "Care to join us for breakfast? Go on, help yourself to whatever you want."

Evan cordially held up his hands. "Thanks, but I already ate at home," he lied.

I'd never been enthused by the thought of Dad and Evan in the same room. Anxious to get out of the kitchen, I grabbed something from the table and slid it into my army-green backpack. Evan watched me steadily as I zipped it up, a strange look on his face.

"What?! I'll eat it when we get to school!" I said.

"She'll eat it when we get to school," he repeated, resigned, turning to my parents.

I walked out the door and closed it behind us. It was going to be a long day, I was sure of it.

The September morning promised to be hot; the sky was clear and the air still. "You changed your mind?" I asked Evan, nodding at the car. "I thought you were going to get your bike." I tried not to show my embarrassment as I imagined the looks we were bound to attract at school.

Wearing a sly smile that obviously masked something else, he glanced at the tinted windshield of the car behind us. "We have something else planned before going to school."

Behind us, Ginevra rolled down her window. The gleam in her jade-green eyes said it all. There was going to be a race. A shiver ran through my body.

"Don't forget to buckle up," Ginevra said with a hint of sarcasm.

"Good thing I didn't eat," I grumbled.

"Shall we go?" Evan said.

"Do we really have to?" I asked, although I already knew the answer. But my reluctance was probably due more to having to start school again than to the attention we'd draw with their sports cars. I would never forget our summer vacation together, not for the rest of my life. It was hard to face the fact it was over.

Evan opened the passenger door for me and strode back to his side. I sank into the low seat as he and Ginevra exchanged challenging looks in the rearview mirror. Things were looking bad. *Very bad.* I wasn't sure he wasn't communicating telepathically with his sister. His eyes sparked with impatience, as did Ginevra's. I could see her face reflected in the sun visor mirror.

"Hold on tight," Evan told me before zooming off.

2

THE WALLS OF THE SOUL

Despite my initial reluctance, the first hours flew by in a flash. The thought that I would have Evan sitting next to me during most of my classes was comforting, though his presence did absorb a lot of my attention.

"You busy this afternoon?" he asked as I opened my locker.

What a strange question, I thought, searching for my Spanish book.

Evan peeked inside my locker. "*Forbidden.*" He picked up a novel half-buried under pages of calculus notes and cast me a sly glance, leaning in toward my ear. "I see you've started to enjoy breaking the rules. You don't need to read manuals, though. If you want, I can show you a couple things that aren't exactly allowed." He grinned.

I took the book from his hands and bopped him on the head with it. "Dummy. It's not a manual! It's a beautiful love story between a brother and sister."

"Love story? Where I come from that's called incest. And I thought I'd heard everything!"

"Well, it's wonderful," I said, contradicting him. He laughed.

"Sure it is." He raised an eyebrow and looked at me slyly again. "You didn't answer my question." He banged the locker shut to grab my attention, his biceps taut.

"Hmm . . . Just a sec, let me see . . . Oh, right! There's this boy, you know. I've got to introduce you to him sometime. I think I'm going to hang out with him. If you don't mind, that is," I teased, assessing his face.

"Bad idea," Evan grunted. He leaned in and whispered directly against my skin, "If you did, I would have to kill him." He rested his forearm on my locker, trapping me against it.

I shook my head. "I don't think you'd be able to." His breath on my face was leaving me dazed. "For your own good, you shouldn't try to fight him," I whispered, my voice breaking with emotion as Evan stroked my skin with the tip of his nose.

"And why not?" he asked softly, moving his lips closer to my throat.

The warmth of his breath gave me goosebumps. I swallowed, forgetting where we were. "Well, he's . . . pretty strong. *Incredibly strong*," I whispered, trapped in the thrill caused by the heat of his body so close to mine. Over the last few weeks it was as if a fuse had been lit between us that could trigger an explosion at any moment.

"Oh, really? What else is he like?" he whispered, stroking my neck with his nose.

My eyes fluttered nervously. "This might shock you, but I'm beginning to suspect he's an Angel."

"An Angel?" he replied, shaking his head. "Then I don't stand a chance."

"And he's gorgeous too," I added.

Evan smiled. "Definitely not as gorgeous as you," he quickly said, his gaze both sweet and firm. "Still, I'm afraid you'll have to decline his invitation."

"Why on earth should I?" I asked, bewitched by him, utterly at the mercy of my emotions.

"Because," he whispered, resting his lips below my ear, "I have a surprise for you."

"A surprise? What kind of surprise?"

His face lit up. When he smiled like this, little creases formed under his eyes, driving me wild. "I'm afraid you'll have to wait to find out. That is, if you're willing to run the risk."

"What risk?"

Evan stepped even closer, his breath caressing my skin. "The risk of being alone with me." I swallowed, waiting to feel his lips on mine, but instead he moved them to my ear. "But then," he whispered, "your Angel might get jealous and, again, I would have to kill him."

"No danger of that," I said, shaking myself out of the dreamy state he'd put me in. "I don't think he's the jealous type."

"You don't—you don't think that I—that *he's* the jealous type?"

"*I'm* the one who should be," I said confidently.

He drew a long breath against my neck, wound his hand in my hair and pressed his lips against mine. "You don't know how wrong you are about that." He moved back just far enough to look me in the eye, his hand still in my hair, his tone suddenly serious. "I'd rip the heart out of anyone who dared to even touch you." He caressed my earlobe with his lips tenderly as his voice enraptured me. "You're mine," he whispered. "All mine."

"Definitely," I agreed. I sought his lips but before I could touch them I noticed the silence that ruled in the now-empty hallway. It shook me out of my trance.

"We'd better get to class," I said, tucking my hair behind my ear. Actually, I was afraid I wouldn't be able to control myself any more. "So what can you tell me about the surprise?"

Evan laughed at my curiosity without offering me an answer.

In the hours that followed I didn't manage to get even a scrap of information out of him. But then again, patience wasn't my virtue and he knew it. It wasn't fair of him to lead me on like this. Whenever I asked him about it, he looked at me with a strange smile on his face. My curiosity grew with each passing minute.

"Can't you tell m—"

Evan rested a finger on my lips to cut me off. He looked down at my hand and clasped it in his. Then he slid his thumb through the elastic band around my wrist and slowly slid it back up to my forearm where I always wore it in winter. During the summer, instead, I kept it around my upper arm. I'd had it so long I felt naked without it, but once in a while, when Evan was gone for longer than a few hours, he would take it as a keepsake.

"I think you're ready now," he said, leaving me even more puzzled. "But you'll have to be patient enough to wait a few more hours to find out," he warned, more and more amused by the look on my face.

Classes flew by with the predictable lightness of the first days of school. The classrooms were just as I remembered them, our blue-and-yellow school colors lining the walls, and even in the cafeteria our little group was still the same, with just one enjoyable difference: Evan sat beside me now. It made me happy, but it made someone else unhappy, I was sure of it. Peter feigned indifference, but sometimes when Evan kissed me or held my hand I became aware of his furtive glances and the bitterness hidden in his eyes felt like a punch in the chest. My best friend was suffering because of me and although I was sorry about it, there was nothing I could do.

Giving in to my impatience, the afternoon arrived at last, heralded by Evan's BMW X6, a black shark on the gray asphalt.

"Finally," I exclaimed. After school I'd eaten a late lunch with my parents and eagerly waited for Evan to pick me up.

"Your surprise wasn't ready yet," he apologized, though I was sure he was intentionally being vague just to pique my curiosity. He'd always enjoyed teasing me.

"I imagine you're not going to tell me what that means," I said, resigned.

Evan laughed and tapped me under the chin. "What is it exactly that you don't get about the word 'surprise'?"

I shot him a sidelong glance as I buckled my seatbelt. Evan lowered his head and looked at me. "I wanted everything to be perfect."

With this, another silence fell. Only one thing was clear at this point: his idea of a surprise allowed for no hints or clues of any kind, so I promised myself I wouldn't bother begging for them. His driving was aggressive but I was perfectly at ease sunk back in my seat. All of a sudden Evan laughed and I wondered why.

"Stop chewing on your shirt," he said, grinning.

"I wasn't!" Embarrassed, I hid my fists inside my sleeves.

"Now you need to close your eyes," he ordered after a moment, his tone gentle. "It's part of the surprise." I made a wary face and he shrugged in response. "And no peeking," he warned before I even had the chance to try. In the darkness behind my closed eyelids, I heard his engine being switched off.

"We're there."

"So can I open my eyes?" I asked eagerly.

Evan chuckled. "Your impatience is equaled only by your stubbornness."

"Look who's talking!" I shot back, my eyes still closed.

His door slammed shut, cutting off the last half of my remark. Almost instantly, I heard my door open and felt a wave of fresh air that smelled like the woods.

"Here, I'll help you out." Evan took my hand and I entrusted myself to him. "But don't open your eyes," he insisted.

The seat of the SUV was pretty high up and I held on tight to Evan until I heard the crackle of dry leaves beneath my feet. We had to be in the forest, I was sure of it. I could recognize its scent with my eyes shut. I took a deep breath of the cool, fragrant air, letting Evan guide me for a few yards. Then he stopped and I did the same.

"Now you can open them," he whispered, his tone cautious, as if he wasn't entirely certain what effect the surprise might have on me. I froze, not sure I wanted to open them. I didn't know if my hesitation was a reflection of Evan's or if it was caused by something else. A sense of foreboding. I took a deep breath and, when I felt ready, banished the feeling and raised my eyelids.

What I saw left me petrified, trapped in a body too heavy to drag away even as my mind screamed at me to run.

"You weren't ready yet. I knew it!" Evan cursed under his breath. "Ginevra warned me I should wait."

I shook my head to recover from the shock. "N-no, everything's fine," I said, hoping to wipe the disappointment off his face. My reaction had clearly ruined the surprise for him—and his good mood.

Silently I thanked God Evan couldn't read my mind and realize I was actually fighting back tears. Still, it was something I would have had to face sooner or later. I swallowed and stared at it again: the old lake house. I couldn't take my eyes off the worn walls covered with red ivy. Not a day went by that I didn't think about what had happened that night and not a day went by that I didn't try to suppress the memory and bury it in the deepest reaches of my mind.

Staring at the house that looked so comforting now by the light of day, it was almost impossible to believe it was the place where I'd experienced my worst nightmare. The place I'd been tortured. The place I'd died. A shiver turned my back ice cold. Why had Evan brought me back there? Why inflict such cruelty?

"Gemma, I'm sure you're wondering why I'm making you face the issue, but I'm also sure you already know the answer. At night I can sense your fears and I want to help you overcome them. You said yourself once that you can't go on climbing over all the walls you find in your way—you need to destroy them to be able to say you've overcome the fears—or you'll always end up expecting them whenever you turn around." He paused. "Think you're ready?"

I nodded, worried that if I tried to speak the words might catch in my throat.

"Come on," he whispered, cautiously holding out his hand.

After a moment of uncertainty, I took it. My knees shook with the same intense terror I'd experienced months ago and thought I'd left behind. Reliving it was harder than I would have expected.

I climbed the first step and the contact with the wood triggered a chaotic stream of images that raced through my mind too quickly for me to grasp them. All I could see was blood, shards of glass, terror. And then that face . . . Faust's eyes blinded by hatred, corroded by his thirst for revenge.

I thought I might faint.

Evan urged me forward, climbing the wooden steps to the front door with me. "The surprise isn't over yet," he whispered to reassure me, my hand clasped in his.

It was hard to breathe; I took deep gulps of air as if I were about to go underwater. The door opened by itself.

Inside, however, I didn't find what I'd expected. What my eyes registered had no connection whatsoever to the difficult, painful memory I'd kept hidden in the darkest recesses of my mind. Everything was spick and span, as if that hellish night had never happened. There was no trace of the stage on which the violent battle had been enacted, first featuring me—tortured to a bloody pulp—and then Evan, who'd struggled to defend me and save my life until the curtain had finally fallen and I'd died.

I'd been given a second chance and I owed it all to Evan and his family.

Finding myself in that place again, reliving the memory, was the last thing I'd expected. But the light that shone inside the house gave it a new look, new possibilities. For a moment it didn't even seem like the same abandoned structure I remembered with such bitterness. It was so different.

The dust had been swept away and the walls were no longer gray with age. The coral curtains seemed to glow in the light that filtered through them. Amazed, I let go of Evan's hand and stepped forward, looking around. My action finally seemed to relax him; he smiled with relief and a glimmer of satisfaction.

Anything that might have reminded me of that night had been repaired. The floor was intact and the stair my foot had plunged through, leaving a gash in my flesh, had been fixed. Everything looked shiny and new. The windowpanes had been replaced, the roof mended, even the ceiling beam had been reinstalled. Everything was so perfect and orderly that for a second I almost thought I might have dreamed it all. It was just a comforting lie—I knew it—but it was comforting all the same.

"Thank you," I whispered to Evan.

"I did my best. Actually, we all pitched in so you'd forget, Gemma—in the normal sense of the word, just to be clear. I know you'll probably never be able to erase the memory completely, but I was hoping this might help."

"It does," I reassured him, holding back a pang of emotion, because it was the truth. "It's like nothing ever happened in this house. Thank you, Evan. You've done something I thought was impossible."

"We'll make new memories here. Memories of *us*." He smiled, lost in a thought all his own. "But don't forget to thank Ginevra too!"

"I'll remember. And thanks for helping me get over everything in the more traditional way too. You know what I mean."

"You mean Simon. He would never have done that without your consent."

"I think they're two sides of the same coin. On the one hand, his power to summon any memory and read it through the eyes of the person who's experienced it is fascinating, but I find the other aspect terrible."

"Deleting memories is a painful process, but its effect is even worse. I agree with you that it's terrible. Eliminating a part of your past is like leaving a hole in your mind, a gap that threatens to make you stumble eventually. Memories, even distant or seemingly inaccessible ones, are always there, just waiting for a scent, a gesture, a look, to unearth them from your subconscious. But when you delete them, the process is irreversible and, no matter how crazy it might seem, a part of you, a part of your personality, is wiped away forever. Every instant helps make us who we are. Our minds never stop and every thought is another step toward who we'll become. Simon is very careful with his power. He only uses it in extreme cases, to erase a traumatic experience."

"Like dying," I said.

"Like dying," he confirmed somberly.

"The grand piano!" I exclaimed, walking over to the instrument that my mind remembered as a crumpled heap. It was now intact.

Evan followed me, looking pleased. Feeling like a little girl looking at presents ready to be unwrapped, I ran my hand over its mahogany curves. A shaft of golden light reflected off its surface, making it glow. I rested my hand on the ivory keys, pressing one of them with my finger. The note that played was faint and echoed softly through the room, nothing at all like the out-of-tune senseless series of notes Peter and I would bang out when we were little kids.

"Do you play?" he asked, his voice more melodious than the piano note.

"No, but something tells me you do," I said, looking at him skeptically.

Evan bowed his head, smiling at the veiled compliment, then raised the piano top and searched inside. Just as I was craning my neck to see what he was looking for he pulled out a violin. I stared at him, puzzled, but he didn't give me the chance to speak. "It's part of the surprise," he said, looking amused at my expression of amazement. It was the same violin depicted in the family portrait in Evan's room. I recognized it by the beautiful flower carved into its scroll. He saw me staring at it and stroked it with his fingertips.

"It's an orchid. It was my mother's favorite flower. Our housekeeper Edina would always place a fresh one on our piano. My mother had this violin crafted just for me so I would always remember her. For many years after my death she always kept it with her, and when she died I went back for it."

"It's beautiful," I murmured.

He beamed. "I have an electric one too, but it gets on Ginevra's nerves."

"The one with the hole in the middle!" I exclaimed, remembering an unusually shaped instrument I'd seen beside the piano in their house. The wood was wine-colored and looked solid, but there was actually a hole in the middle of it.

"I like to keep up with the times," he said with a wink, his smile softening. His eyes grew intense as he rested the violin on his shoulder.

I watched him in silence, fascinated. Evan tucked the violin under his chin, his gaze penetrating mine. For a moment I felt naked, as if he'd torn down every barrier between us and was reading me, reaching places not even I knew about. Our eyes, our minds, our souls were irremediably intertwined. He clasped the bow in his right hand and the whole room filled with sound, transporting me beyond the confines of reality.

3

BEYOND THE LIMITS OF REALITY

The melancholy conveyed by Evan's music was so intense it was almost tangible, a melodious testament to the pain he bore inside—pain he was revealing for the first time. He had closed his eyes with the first notes, drawn in by the stream of emotion, and as my skin quivered to the sweet, sad strains, my heart bled to see the suffering on his face. He was lost in a memory. His fingers moved quickly, striking the bow against the strings almost angrily in pursuit of that dark emotion. Seeing him vulnerable like that disoriented me. For the first time Evan looked defenseless, unprotected by the tough, impenetrable armor I was so accustomed to seeing him wear. He'd taken it off, inviting me closer. I'd relived with him the memory that most tormented him, and now that memory was taking shape, coming alive under his fingertips. Every tiny vibration that rose into the air seemed to return, striking him straight in the heart.

Then the music softened into a slower theme brimming with sadness and nostalgia. Evan knit his brow, lost in the shadows of his past and, slowly, the melody gave way to silence. He opened his eyes, his gaze lost, and I smiled at him because I'd understood the meaning behind his gesture: he'd wanted to give me a part of himself.

"I hadn't played that for centuries," he whispered, the same sadness in his eyes I'd seen when he'd lost himself in the memory of his mother. The sadness of nostalgia, the regret of knowing you'd lost someone forever. "It was my mother's song."

"Danielle." I said her name in a whisper. "It's lovely. Did she compose it?" I asked hesitantly.

Evan nodded, struggling to re-emerge from the devastating memory. "She always used to play it when I was a boy sitting beside her at the piano. When I was too anxious to fall asleep, I would often doze off to the sound of her voice humming that melody."

The melancholy notes mirrored the sadness Evan's mother must have felt night after night as she waited for her husband to come home, playing her song time and time again, pouring her pain into the ivory keys and forcing herself to hide her feelings from her son.

When Evan turned to look at me, a hint of a smile appeared on his lips and I was ashamed of the fleeting emotion I'd just felt. My face had betrayed me, only for a moment, but long enough for him to detect my mild disappointment. It wasn't like me to be so self-centered but I hadn't been able to keep a thought from forcing its way into my head. Evan had glimpsed a glimmer of hope fading inside me—the hope that he'd improvised those notes right then and there for me. I forced a smile, embarrassed by how easily he'd managed to probe my feelings. He rested the violin on his shoulder again, his gaze locked onto mine.

Seconds later, notes returned to fill the silence as his fingers moved quickly on the ebony fingerboard and the bow being drawn over the strings conveyed the intensity of a different emotion: frustration. Almost as if the notes could talk, nostalgia had been replaced by dismay.

I recognized the piece instantly. I'd heard it only once before but my brain had jealously guarded the memory, bringing it to the forefront of my mind a thousand times, conjuring the magic of our first dance together when Evan had confessed his feelings and our bodies had touched for the first time.

I looked at him, surprised, but Evan smiled at me calmly. "Remind you of anything?" he whispered, a sly look on his face.

"You said it was our song," I murmured, blinking. "You mean you composed it yourself?" I stared at him, amazed by the revelation.

"Just for you," he whispered, his eyes focused on me. The melody rose into the air, intense and full of harmonic nuances. A motif that I now knew was all mine—all ours.

"I often played this back when I thought I had no choice," he explained as a light tingle swept over my body. "I felt oppressed, but I still hadn't figured out why. I couldn't understand why it hurt so much to think about you," he went on as the intense, heart-rending music yielded to a sweeter, calmer melody, releasing a river of emotions inside me, hot and cold at the same time. I could never forget how that night had changed my life—the night that should have been my last. "I added this part only after I'd saved you. It sprang from my fingers without my realizing it, like it had always belonged here. It showed me that my decision was the only one I could possibly have made." His hands came to rest, finishing the song.

"Why didn't you ever tell me you could play so well?" I asked after a few seconds.

"Bragging isn't one of my virtues. But that night at the dance I dedicated it to you, remember?"

"Yes, but I could never have imagined you'd written it for me."

"It all seemed so complicated back then," he murmured, stifling a bitter laugh. "When actually"—he brushed a lock of hair from my face and tucked it behind my ear—"it's so easy to love you, Gemma. It's like breathing, something so automatic, so natural, that you can't survive without it unless you're searching for death."

I half closed my eyes at the warmth of his lips on mine. He barely touched them, withdrew slightly, then kissed me again in a sensual game that threatened to drive me crazy. His dark eyes probed mine, hiding another, deeper desire. Physical contact with Evan had always triggered strong emotions in me, but over the last few weeks the invisible cord that connected me to him had caught fire and I was in danger of losing my way. My longing for him was becoming harder and harder to contain, especially when his gaze met mine and I could see his desire for me in his eyes. I felt a primitive yearning whenever he touched me, whenever he kissed me. I longed to feel his hands on me, his body against mine. I was afraid I'd catch fire every time his kisses intensified, expressing what we weren't able to reveal aloud.

Evan leaned his head over my shoulder and caressed it with his nose, barely touching my skin, then kissed it tenderly as I melted in his warmth.

"Y-you should teach me sometime," I stammered, desperately trying to control myself.

"To do what?" he whispered as his lips continued their slow exploration of my neck.

"To play. I'd like to learn how to play."

My eyelashes trembled as his mouth slowly curved into a smile. He slid behind me and, still holding the violin firmly, raised my arms. "Why not right now?"

His voice caressed my ear, making me quiver. "Not a bad idea," I replied, dizzy.

"Hold it like this." He gave me the violin and positioned it on my shoulder. As I leaned toward the instrument the back of my head brushed against his chest, making my heart flutter. I closed my eyes and Evan swallowed, standing behind me in silence for a moment. "You need to rest your chin here. It'll feel awkward at first, but later on you won't even think about it." He clasped my right hand in his, holding the bow, and drew it across the strings. "Now close your eyes and let the music guide you."

I did as he said and another slow melody filled the silence. Evan's hand guided mine, moving it slowly as his hot breath tickled my ear. I couldn't think of anything but his body behind mine. I could feel his every breath, every muscle, every movement.

"You're pretty good," he whispered, a sly smile painted on his face.

"I am—unless we consider that you're the one who's playing; you're only using me. Your hands are moving the strings," I said sardonically. As usual, he was teasing me.

"Then maybe I should move them somewhere else . . . Onto you, for example," he said provocatively, tracing a line across my neck with his nose.

My eyelids fluttered as his meaning sank in. Evan laughed out loud and moved away from me. Without him to lean on, I felt dizzy for a second. Or maybe it was my untamable longing for him. "I'd better sit down," I said as I lowered myself, straddling the piano bench.

Evan laughed again, no doubt aware of how he was making me feel. He sat down on the bench facing me, one leg on each side. "All this music must be having a strange effect on you," he said, his smile turning into a grin. Before I could breathe he grabbed my rear with both hands and pulled me toward him. "Or maybe it's me," he whispered against my lips, his wild gaze locked onto mine as I melted, burning with desire. Resting his forehead against mine, he attempted to control himself, but his unsteady breathing betrayed him, faithful testimony of his emotions.

I was dazed, trapped in a dreamlike state. His lips were so close, his body so hot. The heat between us had grown so intense it left me feverish. I stared at his mouth and he at mine as our tormented breaths merged. His lips brushed a corner of mine, and again, igniting my longing for him as our tongues touched ever so slightly. The touch of him on my lips was paradise.

"I could faint from pleasure at the touch of your mouth," I whispered, utterly under his spell.

Evan's hands clasped my waist and his thumb slowly slid beneath my top. My skin burned beneath his fingers. Our mouths wavered a millimeter from each other, exploring a new desire, almost as if they'd never touched before. We stared at each other's lips, intoxicated by the same thought. "Maybe we need some fresh air," I suggested, trying to calm my heartbeat. The electrical connection stretching from him to me threatened to electrocute us with each breath.

Evan smiled, leaning back slightly. Although he never pressured me in these situations, he always made me be the one to stop us. "As you wish," he replied, sounding resigned, his gaze on mine. He took my hand, led me to the door, and paused on the threshold. "And so he took her hand and clasped it in his own because she knew he would never leave her," he said, his breath uneven, running his thumb over my lip. Sometimes we had fun speaking in the third person like we were characters in a book.

"And she felt as though her heart would burst," I said, my head spinning.

Evan sought my mouth again, unable to subdue his desire. "We risk setting the house on fire," he whispered with a smile.

"That would be a shame." I shook my head, trying to recover from the surge of emotion he'd triggered in me.

Evan noticed and smiled again, seeming proud of the effect he'd had on me. "Ginevra would never forgive us," he exclaimed, amused. "She worked so hard to make everything perfect."

"Well, I know how we can avoid it."

"Interesting," he said with a sly smile. "What do you suggest?"

I bit my lip, shot him a look that dared him to follow and pulled him through the trees toward the lake.

"Where are you taking me?" he asked, curious.

"I want to show you something," I said, intentionally vague. It was my turn to surprise him. Something had crossed my mind: a place Peter and I used to go to a lot when we were children breaking the rules. It wasn't far from the old lake house. Evan followed me without protesting until the calm waters of Lake Placid were spread out before us. I stopped, satisfied.

"Are we there?" he asked, letting slip a hint of impatience. Unsure of my intentions, he looked at his car, parked nearby.

"Not yet," I said, keeping him in suspense to get back at him. With a smile, I jerked my chin over our heads at the cable that stretched across the mirror of water.

"You can't mean—" Evan shot me a glance and I confirmed his suspicion with a nod, looking him in the eye. He laughed, understanding the crazy idea I had in mind. To reach the uppermost point of the cable, we had to climb to the top of a rugged slope where it was tied to a big tree. Although I hadn't been there for years the old wooden steps were just like I remembered them. Hanging from the zip line were thick handles that would slide down the cable all the way to the small clearing on the opposite shore. It was an experience I'd always found electrifying.

I grabbed one of the two handles and turned to face Evan.

"Looks like fun!" he exclaimed without a trace of hesitation.

"Follow me," I dared him, my gaze sensual, and leapt into the void.

I plunged downward. When I was close enough to the water, I stretched out my legs so my feet grazed its surface. Evan leapt after me, catching up in no time. We twirled through the air, one beside the other, as Evan pulled my cord closer to him, hanging on with only one hand.

Moments later we'd reached the opposite shore. I barely felt my feet touch the ground. Evan was holding me gently in his arms, almost like we were levitating. He relaxed his grip and for a moment I lost my balance.

"Well?" I asked him, studying his expression. "Fun?"

Evan shot me a strange look and grabbed my hand. "I know a way that's even more fun." He reached over his head, grabbed his red T-shirt, and pulled it off. His dog tag jingled against his white undershirt that was so tight every muscle showed. He smiled at me, his eyes locked onto mine for a moment with that penetrating look that made my head spin. My heart skipped a beat as I thought of us back on the piano bench just minutes ago, but before I could ask him for an explanation he grabbed me, cradled me in his arms, and carried me up to the top.

I was about to take hold of one of the handles but Evan stopped me. "Wait." He moved closer. "I want to try something first." He grabbed both handles in one hand and opened his other arm to guide me over. "After you," he whispered, holding my gaze.

"What do you have in mind?" I asked warily, casting a sidelong glance at his teasing smile. I grabbed the first handle and after a moment felt Evan's body against mine.

"Ready?" Evan whispered, his lips behind my ear.

I tilted my head and my cheek brushed his, right behind me. The light contact between us rendering words impossible, I half closed my eyes as his breath on my neck made my heart tremble. He took firm hold of the handles supporting us both and leapt into the void.

Considering the combined weight of our bodies, I prepared to hold my breath, certain that the wind would make the crossing more difficult and we would end up in the lake. I expected the descent to happen quickly like last time, but instead we seemed to be moving slower. I heard Evan's low laugh vibrate through our bodies and guessed why, basking in the pleasant sensation the thought triggered in me: Evan was controlling the air to make us move slower, to prolong the interval when our bodies were pressed together. Almost in slow motion, the surface of the water came nearer until our feet were inches above it. Evan's warm voice caressed my neck. "Now let go."

"W-What?!" I exclaimed, shocked. What was he thinking?

"I'll hold you." Evan let go with one hand, encircling my body from behind with his arm as he held on tighter with the other to support us both. "Trust me, Gem," he insisted in a tender voice.

An uncontrollable impulse made me obey him. I cautiously relaxed my grip and let go. Evan held me up with one arm without any apparent difficulty. I squeezed his hand as the surface of the water slowly ran beneath our feet. He let go of the handle with his other hand and I froze in panic, my breath caught in my throat, but his arms held me tenderly. The breeze softened as we gradually slowed down in a way that defied the laws of physics and then stopped halfway across. My foot was touching the liquid surface but I wasn't sinking.

"Evan!" I exclaimed, frightened and amazed.

We were floating, suspended on the mirror of water. "What's—How is this possible?" I clung harder to his arm, which was rock solid, his muscles flexed, as my eyes shot nervously to the lake beneath our feet. Evan raised me slightly, turning me to face him. Though I knew I wasn't running any risk, my body refused to relax and continued to move cautiously.

"Well? Fun?" he said, echoing my question.

I slowly raised my eyes and found his smiling ones waiting for me.

"Evan! We're suspended on top of the water!!!" I cried, my fingers clutching his arm.

"Yes." He smiled as if it were the most natural thing in the world. "Isn't it electrifying?"

I looked for the right words but it was no use. It all seemed so bizarre yet it was real. "It's incredible," I said in a barely audible whisper.

It was as though Evan's coming into my life had brought down all the barriers between the real and the imaginary. There was no border between them any more; the two worlds had merged, bound together by a gossamer thread of magic—the same thread that had bound me to him since the very first day.

Evan pulled me closer to him and held me tighter.

"We're hovering on top of the water," I stammered, still unable to wrap my head around it. "It's illogical, *impossible*. How did you—?"

His laughter interrupted my babbling. "I'm an Angel, Gemma. Once in a while I like to remind you of that. I want you to be part of my world."

I leaned in to kiss him and his fingers tenderly stroked my back. Sometimes it was so natural—so *human*—to be with him that I forgot about the power intrinsic to all Subterraneans like Evan: the ability to control the elements. Fire, water, earth, air—they all obeyed his commands so he could carry out his orders.

Suddenly doubt gripped me. No, it wasn't doubt. It was a sense of foreboding. My eyes shot to Evan's. "How do we get back to shore?" I said, worried, looking for the two handles. They were long gone.

The mocking smile that spread across his face gave me the answer. All at once I realized why Evan had taken off his shirt. He'd planned this. Before I had the chance to object, the support under my feet vanished and I plunged into the cool water, still in Evan's arms that didn't let go of me for a second.

4

DANGEROUS EMOTIONS

"Woohoo!" Evan shouted, whipping back the dripping-wet hair that fell over his forehead. God, was he a sight to behold.

"It's freezing!" I shrieked as we treaded water in the lake.

Evan grabbed my hips and pulled me to him. "I can always warm you up," he whispered, his tone sensual. A laugh escaped him.

"You think this is funny?" I said indignantly, pretending to pout. The water wasn't actually so cold. "I can do it on my own." I pushed him away.

Evan raised his eyebrows and stared at me with a sly expression. "I never doubted you could swim." He pulled me against him harder and my heart leapt to my throat at the rough contact with his body, his face a fraction of an inch from mine. His moist lips rested softly on my mouth and the warmth they filled me with penetrated all the way to my bones. He kissed me again and again, twining his fingers in my wet hair. My hands slid up his shoulder blades, squeezed his hard shoulders, stroked the skin left bare by his undershirt.

The minutes ticked away, heedless of our longing for time to stand still, until the sunlight began to fade behind the dark mantle of forest. The sunset was our backdrop as we came out of the water. My fingers were wrinkly and my sopping-wet clothes clung to my skin as I shivered in the cool September air.

"You're cold," Evan said, thoughtfully warming my arms with his hands.

"Just a little," I stammered, forcing my teeth not to chatter.

"Take this." He leaned down, grabbed the red shirt he'd left on the grass, and offered it to me. "What are you waiting for?" he said, his eyes on me as I hesitated. "Take off your clothes and put this on. It's dry."

I took it, embarrassed. "What about you?" I asked shyly, pointing at his clothes that were as soaked as mine.

He grabbed his white undershirt by the neck and pulled it over his head. My heart skipped a beat as I stared at his bare chest as though seeing it for the first time. The reason for the quiver deep in my heart became clear to me: desire. The fierce desire to touch him, to stroke his smooth, tanned skin without the hindrance of clothing.

"I won't catch a cold if that's what's worrying you," he assured me.

From his smile, I guessed my dazed expression must have given me away. I instinctively looked away and made myself turn around, but Evan took my wrist firmly in his hand.

"Come on." He pulled me against him roughly, his gaze sensual. His voice took on the warm tone that made me melt every time I heard it. "Don't tell me you're still embarrassed to see me undressed."

I babbled something incomprehensible and lost all control as Evan held me close. His body was so warm. I tried hard to find my voice, trapped in the flow of my emotion, and opened my mouth only to close it again, powerless.

Evan's grin broadened at my awkwardness. "I was only kidding! Come on, Gemma!" he said, relaxing his grip. "I'll wait for you here. Go change or *you'll* be the one who catches a cold."

I must have been a statue of embarrassment because Evan touched his fingertip to my nose to snap me out of my daze. I blinked and stared at the red shirt. "Yeah, I guess I should," I murmured, heading toward the car.

"Everything okay back there?" Evan's voice reached me behind the door of the BMW as I took off my wet clothes, dropping them to the ground. I wasn't sure whether the trembling in my chest was because I was afraid he might take a peek in the mirror—or because I was afraid he might not.

"I'm naked and wet and going home wearing only your shirt. Is that 'okay' enough for you?"

"Hmm . . . an interesting prospect. I'd say it's okay enough." He smothered a snicker.

I got into the car and shot him a look brimming with sarcasm. "I'm really happy you're having so much fun teasing me today."

Evan leaned toward me, his face inches from mine, taking my breath away. He reached across my body and shut the door, then sat back and started the car. "Who says I was teasing?" he said with a grin, looking at me out of the corner of his eye. He stared at my mouth for a second and then, clearly unable to resist the impulse, slid his eyes down my body in a slow exploration of my legs, barely covered by his shirt. He began to move closer, his face growing serious, uncontrollable desire in his gaze, and I understood that the game threatened to become dangerous.

For the first time, his movements seemed hesitant, cautious, almost embarrassed. He slowly swept back my wet hair on one side, baring my neck, and gently caressed my skin, his face inches from mine. Tenderly, he drew his lips to the curve of my neck and rubbed his temple against my cheek. After a moment he sought my gaze, a tortured look on his face, and his forehead came to rest on mine. With a deep breath he closed his eyes, his chest trembling, revealing his desire. Was it possible he was experiencing the same emotions I felt in my heart?

"God, you're so beautiful," he whispered against my lips as his hand hesitantly slid down my skin to where the shirt didn't cover it. I half closed my eyes, pervaded by a quiver of uncontrollable heat.

"It's your shirt," I murmured, lacing my fingers with his. "You should lend it to me once in a while."

Evan smiled, his forehead resting on mine. "But then I'd have to kill anybody who saw you," he whispered, stifling a smile before growing serious again. "Do you realize you risk driving me crazy?" he murmured, narrowing his eyes.

I sought his lips with mine and ran my fingers down his bare chest, letting myself be swept away by my uncontrollable desire for him, to feel his hands on my body. I felt feverish as my mouth melded with his, my heart ready to burst. My skin wanted him. Driven by the need to eliminate the distance between us, I moved closer, lifting myself a little without taking my lips off his. My body brushed his and my need for him overwhelmed me.

In the middle of the blaze of passion that enveloped us, a glimmer of lucidity made me pull my lips away from Evan's and rest my forehead against his, forcing myself to regain control of my breathing.

We'd never spoken about it openly but I could sense how intensely Evan wanted me. At times I had the feeling his human body couldn't contain the passion that set his blood on fire. And yet he always managed to control himself, leaving the decision about when to stop to me.

Forehead to forehead, our eyes expressed our desire, locking for a long moment as our breathing grew steady again.

"We'd better go back so you can dry off," he said, my hesitation checking his impulses. I nodded without saying a word as my heart rebelled, continuing to race.

"Where are we going?" I asked as we drove, breaking the silence. Probably neither of us had ever experienced such feelings before.

"My place. That way you can put on something"—he cleared his throat and I thought he was about to say *dry*—"less dangerous." He shot me a glance.

"Less dangerous . . . " Interesting choice of words.

Contact with him had lit a fire inside me that burned silently day after day, blazing up whenever his body was close to mine. Sometimes all it took was one look from him to set it aflame, like gasoline.

A few minutes later the car stopped in Evan's driveway. I dried my hair in the bathroom and went to join him in his room but unexpectedly found it empty. I fell onto his bed. On the ivory-colored walls, the old family portrait caught my eye. It had always been there and I'd studied it down to the last detail, but his parents' faces, gazing at me from the canvas yellowed by time, had taken on a new meaning now that I knew their story. In the portrait Danielle was seated beside a piano in blond wood. Soft dark curls cascaded to her shoulders, partially obscuring Evan's hand as he stood behind her. On her lap she held a pair of long gloves in white lace. Her face looked strained, her smile dictated by circumstances. I studied her more carefully, looking into her eyes, and was startled by the depths I saw in them. It was almost as if they were actually looking at me.

The elder James stood on the other side of the grand piano, his haughty posture effectively conveying the clear-cut division between him and his family.

Evan had one arm hanging at his side, his shirtsleeve rolled up, holding his violin, of which I could see only the flower carved into the scroll. I stopped to examine it and thought how bizarre it was that this was actually him in the centuries-old painting. He hadn't changed at all except that his hair was bit shorter and less rebellious. The defiant look in his eye was the same. His dark, austere, fearless gaze stared at me from the canvas, taking my breath away. I would have loved him back then too, I was sure of it.

"Does it frighten you?" Evan's cautious tone startled me. Who knew how long he'd been watching me from the doorway.

"Not at all," I reassured him. "I wish I'd known you then," I admitted.

Unexpectedly, my answer made him laugh. "I brought you some dry clothes." He came into the room and laid them on the bed.

"I imagine I have Ginevra to thank for these."

"I'll wait for you outside so you can change."

The gallantry of his words, no matter how forced, reminded me that this was the same Evan who'd posed for that portrait three centuries ago.

"Evan," I said, causing him to pause in the doorway. "After your—" I searched for an alternative to the word *death*. "After your transformation, your appearance didn't change. I was wondering if the rest stayed the same too," I mumbled, awkwardly trying to make myself understood—though at the same time I wasn't entirely sure I wanted him to realize what I was getting at.

"That depends. What do you mean, exactly? What is it you want to know?"

Why the hell did he always have to be so direct?

"Um, well, I was wondering if—compared to when you were human—I mean, if an Angel can—" Could I manage to make him understand? I wasn't so sure.

"If he can . . . ?" he prompted, though the smile he was trying to hide spoke volumes.

"If he can still feel the same emotions, act like a human. I was wondering if your sensations have stayed the same like your body."

He came over and sat down beside me, never moving his eyes from mine. "I can't feel human emotions any more, Gemma."

The disappointment on my face made him smile. I'd felt his desire growing along with mine day after day, but maybe I'd been completely wrong. Maybe it had just been a reflection of my desire for him, a delusion. Was that what he was trying to tell me? "I thought—so you'll never feel what I feel when I'm with you," I murmured sadly. There was no point in asking him. A bitterness that I tried unsuccessfully to hide rose in my throat. I'd been fooling myself.

"I can't feel the same emotions I did when I was human," he continued, looking at me intently, "but only because the ones I feel now are much stronger."

My heart skipped a beat, allowing me to breathe again.

"They're feelings a human body isn't capable of containing. My perception no longer depends on imperfect human senses. But you should know that, Gemma. You've experienced it yourself."

I flinched at the memory Evan was evoking. Although I kept it deeply buried, it only took a moment for it to re-emerge: the sensation I'd felt when I'd left my body. I had felt freed of an enormous burden; all my perceptions—even the simple touch of Evan's hand—were amplified hundreds of times. Every impact was stronger, more vivid, more intense. So that was what Evan must feel.

I nodded in silence, shaken by the revelation.

"When there's no body to contain them, feelings expand infinitely, like they're exploding, and they're a thousand times more intense. It's like the body's an obstacle that muffles every sensation, every emotion, every desire."

I looked into his dark eyes and a new worry made its way to my lips. "How does it work when you're in human form, like now?" I asked, puzzled.

"For me it's almost the same. It doesn't matter what form I'm in. By now I've lost my original human body. In *this* body the spirit prevails over the flesh. I can materialize when I want to, but it's like I no longer belong to this world. I'm made of different matter, as if the spirit can take on corporeal form. It's hard to explain."

"No, I get it. That's why you can be injured but not killed."

"Exactly. My wounds heal in no time. I think our bodies are made of some supernatural substance that's more similar to the soul. It looks and feels like flesh but its structure is different—it's a stronger, indestructible alloy." He smiled to himself before going on. "So you don't have to worry about my not feeling the same sensations you do, Gemma." He moved his face so close to mine it touched my forehead. "Because what I feel is even stronger," he murmured against my lips before brushing his over them. "Sometimes I'm not even sure I can control it," he whispered and then swallowed, his Adam's apple rising and falling.

"What if you decided not to control it? Could you . . . *behave* like a human too? You're still an Angel," I insisted, trapped between hesitation and the need to know. I hoped he could see what I was getting at because I really didn't know how else to ask.

Evan's lips smiled on mine and the exasperating sensuality of his gaze suddenly became more decisive. He grabbed my hips and pulled me to him, taking my breath away. In a split second my back was flat against the bed, my legs—still bare—trapped beneath him. "Didn't I make myself clear?" he whispered in a smothered sigh of repressed desire. With one hand he held my wrists and pinned them to the pillow while with the other he pulled me against him so I wouldn't try to escape the contact to which the only thing stubbornly offering resistance were his jeans.

All control abandoned me as the whirl of arousal I sank further into with each breath swept me away. It was too strong to resist or ignore. I closed my eyes and surrendered as Evan's soft lips explored my neck. My hands slid under his shirt and he muffled a groan. "You want to send me to hell."

"You've discovered my plan," I replied, dizzy with desire.

"He wanted to resist, but by that time he'd lost all control."

"You want to play that game again?" I smiled against his lips. For a moment he fell silent and stroked my belly. My heart exploded in my chest.

"He looked at her with the eyes of one who had never loved before. His hand trembled as it slowly slid under her shirt. Not because he was afraid, but because he feared he wouldn't be able to stop himself this time."

"Then don't stop."

"*Ahem . . .*"

From the door came the noise of a throat being cleared and we froze. Ginevra.

"Get lost," Evan growled in exasperation. "We're kind of busy here in case you hadn't noticed."

Ginevra smiled. "Didn't it cross your mind to close the door? I tried knocking, but evidently you were too busy to hear me." I could have died from embarrassment. "I'll leave when I've gotten what I want, Evan," she said, determined, crossing her arms over her chest like a little girl.

"She wants to race," Evan explained under his breath.

"Well? You promised!" she retorted. Ginevra simply couldn't handle losing.

Evan shot her a furious look, trying to make her give up the idea. "We're not going to have a rematch right now, G. Maybe you haven't realized it, but you're not the center of the world. I've got other things on my mind right now," he snapped, glaring at her.

"I can see that," she said, looking at me as Evan shot her a look, begging her to leave. Or, more likely, telepathically ordering her to leave.

The door slammed shut behind Ginevra.

"You shouldn't have," I told him, feeling guilty about how he'd treated her. "We can go, if you want." I hoped he wouldn't take me seriously.

"You're more important than a stupid race," he whispered, moving closer again. "Besides, unless I'm mistaken, we started a conversation, and I don't like to leave things half-finished."

I smiled, ready to pick up where we'd left off. "You're right," I whispered as his mouth touched my neck, "one should never leave things half-finished."

"So did you get the answer you wanted?" he murmured against my skin, a sly smile forming on his lips.

"I *think* so," I began, pretending uncertainty, "but I'm not entirely sure."

Evan raised my thigh and pinned me against the bed with his body. A shudder surged through me as he kissed me passionately. Suddenly he stopped, still on top of me, and looked me in the eye. "Not a second goes by that I don't want you, Gemma."

I nodded, dizzy, my heart thumping against his chest.

"I don't want to rush you," he whispered, his hand gently caressing my bare thigh. "Although it feels like I might go insane whenever I touch you." A frustrated sigh escaped him as he rested his forehead against mine, trying to regain control of his breathing.

I closed my eyes, stunned by what he'd said because I felt the same exact thing. "Then I'd better get dressed now before I risk making you give in to temptation," I said, teasing.

He shot me an irresistible smile. "People of my bloodline aren't exactly known for being able to resist temptation. You know, with Eve and all that."

"God, no! I don't want to condemn the world to catastrophic reprisals," I said, laughing with him.

Evan raised himself on his palms, his body suspended over mine, his hands framing my head. His hair hung down and his gaze softened on mine. "Condemn me, then, with a kiss," he whispered against my lips, "and I'll be forever damned, if you wish it so, in exchange for that one kiss."

He touched his lips to mine but I pulled back. "Never would I wish you damned—not for my sake nor any other reason in the world," I said, playing along, my eyes locked onto his.

"Alas, you condemn me to a far worse torment by denying me your lips," he went on as I tried to elude him. "Seal our pact with a kiss, my lady, and I'll willingly accept damnation," he whispered in the sweetest tones I'd ever heard.

"How could I not indulge such a heartfelt request? Then I condemn you, Evan William James, with this my kiss." Gently, I rested my lips on his.

Evan looked at me for a long moment, his expression uncertain. "If I'm damned now, can you explain why I feel like I'm in heaven?"

His irresistibly tender gaze made me smile. "I don't know. I think that kiss condemned both of us because I feel like I'm there too." I bit my lip, the longing for him to kiss me again making my head spin.

"Did I condemn you?" He withdrew, tormented. "Forgive me, my love, and give me back my damnation." He kissed me again to take back his pledge, a groan escaping him. "Damn me again, I beg you. The desire for your kisses is too great a pain to bear."

"And so, just as I damned you, with this kiss I absolve you of your sins. Here." I kissed him delicately. "Now you are free."

"Cruel deception! I don't want to be free!" He grabbed me by the hips and swiftly rolled beneath me, inverting our positions. "I entrust to you my freedom, my queen. Bind me with the chains of love. Kiss me again, I implore you, and I will be your slave," he whispered, raising his head to kiss me.

I smiled against his lips, considering his offer. "Hmm . . . my slave, huh?" I bit my lower lip, still smiling. "That's an interesting prospect. But watch out—if you keep saying it I might take you up on it."

"Romeo, I'm still waiting!" Ginevra reprimanded him from behind the door, making fun of the game he and I often played, improvising reinterpretations of scenes from books.

Evan fell back onto the bed, exasperated. "Unbelievable!" he grumbled. "She never gives up! Can't a guy have any privacy in this house?" he shouted through the wooden door as I held back a laugh.

"I think you should go," I said, encouraging him in spite of myself.

"Giving in to her will only make her more stubborn. She needs to learn she's not the only person here."

"Come on, Ginevra isn't that demanding." Evan shot me a skeptical look. "Okay, maybe a little," I admitted.

"The problem is she can't think of anything but herself and her own interests."

"Guys, I'm right here!" Ginevra exclaimed from behind the door.

"Come on in, Gin," I called to her, amused.

"Can I? Are you sure? You aren't naked or anything, are you?" she asked, making me blush, then walked in without giving us the chance to reply because her mind had already read the answer. "Please oh please oh please," she wheedled, trying to persuade him, her voice theatrical and her big green eyes disarming.

Evan smiled and shook his head, his answer the same. "You know I love you but I can't, really, G. It's already nine o'clock."

I glanced nervously at the clock, surprised it was already so late. "You'd better take me home. My mom and dad will be back soon and you know how my dad gets when I come home too late."

Ignoring Ginevra, Evan inched closer to my lips, resuming the tormented mask he'd worn a moment ago. "What affliction you cause me by depriving me of your presence," he whispered, stroking my cheek.

"Oh God!" Ginevra groaned, rolling her eyes. "Who are you and what have you done with my brother? I'd better leave you two alone." She turned her back on us.

"You'll have to go through three centuries of PDAs before we're even. I've had to put up with a whole lot worse. In case you've never realized it, you and Simon are as inseparable as doughnuts and icing."

"Ha ha, very funny!" she responded sarcastically. "I hope I'm the icing! Or do I seem more like the doughnut to you?"

Trying not to laugh, I decided to intervene before the room caught fire. "Believe me, you look nothing like a doughnut."

"Thank you, sister." She winked at me and left the room.

"She's hopeless," Evan said, a smile on his face, resting his hands on my waist.

"Yeah, but it's impossible not to love her."

"That's true too," he said, still lying underneath me.

"Can't you stop time?" I whined, refusing to let him go. "You're an Angel, you should be able to do that."

Evan smiled and squeezed his eyes shut. "Here, let me try." He screwed up his face, tightening every muscle as I watched with bated breath. Then he opened one eye and peeked at me. "Did it stop?"

He raised an eyebrow and I hit him with the pillow. "You're a clown, you know that? When are you ever going to stop teasing me?"

Evan let out a laugh and pinned me beneath him again, his gaze becoming tender as he kissed me. "I really *did* try," he said, hiding a grin.

"Yeah, right. Well, we'd better go before my dad comes to take me home by force."

"I'll take you, though it'll be hard to be away from you tonight." He locked eyes with me, serious again.

I instantly knew what he meant. "So you were being serious. You have to—"

Evan tightened his lips, confirming my fears. "I can't get out of it."

"Okay, don't say any more." I didn't want him to go into detail. That dark aspect of his life gave me the shivers. Evan wouldn't be spending the night with me. He wouldn't be joining me in my dreams because while I was sleeping, somewhere out there—who knew where or how far away—someone else would lose their life. By Evan's hand.

Another shiver, cold and unexpected, froze my heart. All it took was a wave of Evan's hand to extinguish a life—and yet it wasn't his fault at all. Fate moved the strings in our lives while he carried out orders like a soldier. So why did that aspect of him still scare me so much? Why couldn't I accept that it was life taking its natural course? I knew the answer, no matter how hard I tried not to think about it. Deep in my heart, I was still afraid of the moment when someone would come for me. Another Reaper Angel like Faust. Or like Evan. Sometimes it seemed impossible that the shadow of death lurked in the depths of his gaze and the warmth of his touch. And yet neither he nor any other Subterranean decided whose time had come. The fact that I'd survived certainly didn't give me the right to judge them. I owed my life to Evan; he was the one who'd forged a path that diverged from the fate I'd had in store for me. I had no right to judge his dark side just because it scared me.

"Hey." Evan snapped me out of my thoughts. "Everything okay?"

"It's just— Will you be gone all night?"

Evan slowly slid his hand up my sleeve and pulled off the elastic band I wore around my forearm, claiming it as his own. He held it tightly in his hand and looked at me. "Yes, unfortunately, but you'll find me when you wake up. I'll stop by and take you to school. Now get dressed." A light kiss on the lips. "I'll go down and get the bike ready."

I nodded regretfully as I watched him walk out the door.

I'd had no idea how quickly time had flown until I felt how cool the air had become that September night. I looked at the dark sky hidden behind a leaden veil of clouds that promised a storm and tried not to think of it as an ill omen since Evan wouldn't be with me that night. I was safe now—I just had to find a way to convince myself.

I walked over to the black MV Agusta, squeezing my eyes shut at the wild roar that filled the courtyard as Evan gunned the accelerator with a smug expression on his face. Stroking the leather seat before climbing on, I experienced the thrill I always felt before we went out on his bike. I readied myself for the charge of pure adrenaline waiting for me, sitting behind a wild, totally out-of-control Evan. The adrenaline went to his head too.

"Shall we?" He flashed his foxiest smile. I slid forward on the seat and wrapped my arms around his chest. "Hold on tight," he said, tilting his head, but I already knew what to expect.

I rested my chin on his shoulder, giving in to my insane, never-ending desire for his body. "Sooner or later we should buy helmets."

Evan grinned as if this were a joke. "We don't need helmets," he said. His laughter shook his chest.

"That might be true for you, but in case it's slipped your mind, I'm still delicate and fragile!" I teased, and his expression softened.

He lowered his hand and stroked my calf while perceptibly slowing down. His touch was so gentle it made me tremble. "If you were alone, I would *insist* you wear one. No one knows better than me how dangerous the roads can be for a mortal. But when you're with me you don't need one, Gemma." He flashed a smile, tilting his head back until it touched mine. "Nothing could ever happen to you. I wouldn't allow it. I'm an Angel. You're safe with me," he said comfortingly. His tone made me melt. "We could take a spill at two hundred miles an hour and nothing would happen to you," he added with a smirk.

"Don't you dare!" I warned, instinctively holding him tighter.

"That I can't promise you," he murmured with a grin, giving me a sly glance. His hand left my calf and I had only a split second to register his warning before he gripped the handlebars. "Hold on tight, babe," he said. The instant Evan felt my arms tighten around him, he twisted the throttle, hauling the bike up onto its back wheel.

There was no denying the excitement that ran through me whenever he did a power wheelie like that. His wild riding style thrilled me and I surrendered to the exhilaration that filled my head, the adrenaline that flowed through my veins. The sensations left me dizzy. At times like this I could sense every detail with incredible precision. It was as if my vision became sharper, triggering a sort of super high-res optical zoom in my brain.

The air was chillier outside Lake Placid, far from the glow of the streetlights that made the roads seem warmer, but I didn't care. As long as I was holding Evan tight I was in heaven.

Unfortunately, reality always returned to tear me away from him and there was never enough time. To my regret, Evan pulled into my driveway and turned off the engine. The knowledge that he would be gone that night returned to frustrate me. I climbed off the seat, pushing my hair to one side. It had gotten tangled in the wind and I tried to comb it out with my fingers, but it was futile. "Well, good night, then." I raised my lips to his in a shy kiss.

"That's what I wish you. As for myself, I already know it won't be good, not without you." He kissed me back.

"So don't go." The words escaped me even though I knew it was impossible.

"I'll stay if you ask me to," he said tenderly.

"Don't get my hopes up. You know you can't," I reminded him in a whisper.

Evan sought my lips, smiling. "True. Still, I'll be back soon. I promise," he murmured, his face inches from mine.

"I'll be waiting on pins and needles."

"Dream of me." He kissed me again and started the engine.

"That's like wishing me good night."

He winked at me and rode off, trailed by the sound of his engine. When the echoing roar faded, the darkness sank into my bones.

I was outside, all alone and in the dark.

EVAN

5

THE HUNT

"No way! Young Casanova, back already? Aren't you spending the night with your babe?"

I smiled, switched off my motorcycle in the driveway, and turned toward Drake. He was bare chested, hanging upside down from the branch of an oak tree.

"Trying to turn into a bat?" I asked—jokingly, because my brother had the power to change his human appearance but couldn't transform himself into an animal.

Drake laughed and flipped off the branch onto his knees. He looked up at me, his icy Subterranean eyes glimmering in the darkness. "Did you mistake me for a vampire?"

"Same difference, isn't it?"

"You need to keep up with the times, bro. Vampires aren't the same as they used to be. Speaking of which, I hope you didn't come to ask me to fill in for Gemma. I've been spending more time with that mutt of hers than with you guys lately."

"He isn't a mutt, he's a pug."

"He's a rat with a pig's tail. If that's not a mutt I don't know what is."

I laughed. "Gemma loves him. You'd better not go calling him that in front of her or she might sic him on you."

"Can't promise you that. I don't get it. How can she love the thing? It's a monster. The other night it tried to bite my finger off! I can barely keep myself from throwing it out the window when it growls at me. Stupid dog, don't you see I've got your owner's face?"

"If he recognizes you he's not so stupid after all. When you take on Gemma's appearance, not even I can tell the difference."

"Where is she, anyway?"

"It's midnight. Where do you think she is? I dropped her off at home. I'd still be with her if it were up to me. But no, I get to spend the night with a bunch of drunk teenagers instead."

Drake threw his hands up, annoyed. "I knew it! They always give you the fun missions."

"What on earth could be fun about a group of sixteen-year-olds?"

"Don't ask him that." Simon had appeared, leaning against the doorway, his hair wet. "You'd be shocked by all the answers he'd manage to come up with."

"Look who's back. Finally risen from the ashes, I see," Drake said.

"Did I miss something?" I asked, looking at Simon who had a smug smile on his face.

"I went for a little swim with Ginevra, that's all," he said.

"Yeah, right. A little swim in a fiery pool of passion. Why do you think I was training outside?"

"If you didn't want to hear us you could've used the workout room. The walls are soundproof," Simon pointed out.

"Not when the two of you are around."

Simon laughed out loud just as Ginevra sprang up behind him. "I finally found you! Were you hiding from me?" She bit his earlobe and whispered something I tried hard not to hear.

Simon grinned and took her hand. Turning to Drake he said, "Maybe you should stay out here a little longer." He winked as Ginevra led him away, shutting the door behind them.

"I'd better take his advice," Drake grumbled. "C'mon, bro, *please* let me come with you."

"Forget it. I already know what you're thinking. I'll do a nice clean job and be back before dawn."

"Come on, you want to leave me here with those two? Don't forget I always cover for you while you're out having fun with your girlfriend."

"You bastard—you thinking of bailing on me?"

Drake flashed a crafty smile. "Not if we have a little fun tonight like back in the old days."

"Sounds like extortion."

"Seems more like negotiation to me."

I sighed. Drake could be stubborn. "Okay, as long as you don't overdo it."

Allen County, Kansas
12:15 a.m.

"Shit! I think I stepped in something," Drake cursed, making me laugh. The mission had taken us to the fields of Kansas. Nearby we could hear the excited voices of a group of teens. Drake and I drew closer and watched them for a while.

"No fair! Layla pushed me out into the open!" said a blond with dark eyes.

"It's not my fault you got caught, Audrey! Now you're it," said another girl. Her hair was raven-black hair with a silver streak on one side. She wore black eye makeup and her neck was tattooed.

"Forget it, Layla. I'm afraid to go around looking for everybody," Audrey said. She grabbed the hand of a guy who must have been her boyfriend, instinctively seeking his protection, but he just smiled.

"What are you scared of, possums? You can always use your claws on them," he said, grinning. "Sometimes you leave me with some pretty nasty scratches."

"Whoa!" chorused the other kids.

"Asshole." Audrey dropped his hand, annoyed. "It's dark out and this place gives me the creeps. I'd rather hide. Is there a problem with that?"

"What did I say? I just wanted to reassure you. No ghosts around here."

"I'll be it," another boy told her. He was tall and lean and had just been staring at her hand as she'd reached for her boyfriend's.

I looked him in the eye and instantly understood what he felt for her: he was jealous. It made me think of Peter, the way he stared at Gemma and how his face changed when she looked at me instead of him. I decided I might have a little fun tonight after all.

"You can't, Adam. We have to follow the rules," said a black boy with cornrows.

"What do you care, Jarret? Mind your own business. You heard Audrey—she's afraid of the dark. You want to force a girl to wander around the fields in the middle of the night? I said I'd take her place, so you all go hide."

"I'll do it, then," Audrey's boyfriend said. "It's not your job to protect my girlfriend, McGrent."

"You could have thought of that before, Ron. Or maybe you're afraid of the dark too," Adam sneered.

Ron grabbed him by the shirt. "This is my place and I make the rules. You want to look all brave in front of the girls? I'm not afraid of anything," he snarled. His eyes were glazed over. Judging from the smell in the air some of them had been drinking.

"Okay, chill. Whatever," Adam said, holding up his hands. Ron let go of him.

Drake laughed as he watched the scene. "I've always loved hide-and-seek!"

Five guys and three girls had gathered in the clearing in front of the house. Two of them had snuck off to one side, their intentions evident on their faces, while a third was fiddling with his iPhone.

"Aren't they a little old for this game?" I said.

"They're teenagers, Evan. Most of these guys have more testosterone in their systems than gray matter in their skulls. I bet none of them can wait to find a spot to hide with one of the girls—two, if they're lucky."

Drake reached down and took a brownie from a plate resting on a low stone wall. He inhaled its aroma deeply and closed his eyes before slipping it into his pocket.

"Did you really just put a pot brownie in your pocket?" I scoffed.

"You're right. I'll grab one for you and Simon too. Think little Gemma would want one?"

"Forget it. I'm not giving her one of those things."

"Why not? You two could really get down with one of these."

"Gemma and I don't need to get high for that."

"Your loss." He tucked another one into his pocket.

"You're unbelievable," I said, shaking my head. Meanwhile, the yard had grown silent. The kids had gone into hiding. "Anyway, let's focus on the mission now. Let the hunt begin."

"I'm ready to play."

I smiled. Our eyes were gray as molten silver.

When we walked by the kids, some of them shuddered and peered around uneasily, but none of them could see us. Drake followed Ron, who was wandering through the tall grass in search of his hidden friends, unaware that he was being hunted as well. The boy moved slowly, trying not to make a sound, but now and then something—a sinister shiver—make him look over his shoulder.

A wooden swing hanging from a maple branch moved. He flinched and whirled around. "Who's there?" Taking a few steps toward the swing, he stared as it swung steadily back and forth as if someone were gently pushing it, though there was no wind. The boy gulped and grabbed the chains to stop the ominous creaking that filled the night. He walked away, but after a few steps the noise began again, freezing him in his tracks. When he turned around he saw the swing moving back and forth even faster than before. Smothering a scream, he raced to the house, threw open the door, and slammed it shut after him. Drake was already inside, hidden in the shadows, with no intention of cutting the poor boy any slack.

I could hear Ron's heart beating wildly in the silence. It seemed he'd perceived something sinister. What he didn't know was that it was Death, passing right by him.

Drake knocked over a pot and the boy stifled a scream, his eyes shut tight. He curled up on the floor, panting, his knees clasped to his chest. A chair passed in front of him, scraping against the floorboards with a menacing sound. Next, a wooden spoon flew across the room, followed by another and yet another, almost hitting Ron, whose eyes bulged as they whizzed past him, colliding with the walls. He covered his ears with his hands, doubtless more terrified than he'd ever been in his life.

A sudden silence fell. Drake materialized but remained hidden in the shadows. Though the room was shrouded in darkness, the boy could sense something. "Who's there?" He drew closer, one slow step after the other. From out of nowhere a cat leapt at him, making him jump. He whirled around to run away but found himself face to face with Drake. With a shriek, he ran in the opposite direction, but in the darkness hit a wooden beam head-on and fell to the floor, unconscious.

Drake's laughter filled the room. "God! I haven't had this much fun in days!"

"You were pretty rough on him. He's going to have nightmares for the rest of his life."

"You're saying I scared him? And I thought he wasn't afraid of anything! Shame he doesn't have claws like Audrey," Drake laughed, his gray eyes glittering. "There are four of them left. Want to find out who's bravest?"

"Drake, we agreed we wouldn't overdo it."

"What do you care? Let's let them have a little fun!"

"Let *them*? I don't think *he* was having any."

"Relax! I'm just trying to make their night more interesting. Look on the bright side: after all those brownies they ate, they'll figure they were hallucinating and will never eat them again. So in a way I'm doing this for their own good."

"Yeah, right. Go ahead and kid yourself."

Drake grinned sheepishly. "In a few years they'll look back on this and laugh," he assured me.

I grew serious. "I doubt they'll remember any of this after I do what I came here to do."

"Yeah, so there you go. I'm not the bad guy. You're the one who's going to spoil their party."

He was right. Years would pass but only one memory of that night would haunt them. Drake had had some fun, but in the meantime I'd made sure all the kids were where they were supposed to be.

The time had come for me to play. Only mine wouldn't be just a game.

"Hey, keep those hands where they belong!"

A guy and a girl had hidden in the hayloft, but I had the impression they were more interested in another kind of game. They were the two who'd been ogling each other the whole time. I recognized them from his black ponytail and her red hair.

"Shh, quiet or they'll find us!" he whispered, pulling her against him.

She laughed and pretended to fight him off while actually guiding his hands onto her, her breath coming fast as he kissed her neck.

"Oho! I knew you were a killjoy! Him or her?" Drake asked, watching them with a gleam in his eye.

"Neither. They can have a little more fun. At least for now."

"Then if you don't mind I think I'll join them."

"What do you mea—No, wait. I don't want to know."

Drake had already transformed. He looked like a younger version of himself. "The more the merrier in this kind of game." He winked at me and went to lie down behind the girl.

She gave a start and turned toward him. "Who are you?" Her eyes were still misty with desire and the brownies were no doubt taking effect.

"Shh," Drake whispered, sweeping her hair back behind her ear. "I'm only a figment of your imagination." Believing him, she relaxed and let herself be kissed on the mouth while the other boy touched her all over.

"What a bastard!" I shook my head and chuckled. I went out of the hayloft, leaving Drake with the couple. Outside the night was silent. I listened, sensing every hidden sound, every heartbeat, every breath. None of the kids could hide from me; I could track down even the most cunning. Only one was keeping my senses alert, however. I concentrated on him and his soul led me to the place he'd hidden—to the place *I'd* made sure he'd hidden.

Standing on the roof of the little wooden house, I stared at Adam, sitting on its edge, his back to me. He was smoking weed and watching a few of the others hidden below. He seemed older than the rest of them. Maybe he was in a higher grade at school or, more likely, he'd been held back a few times. In some way the guy reminded me of Peter and this made something boil inside me, something I had to struggle to push down. Maybe it was his curly hair or his lacrosse jersey. Or more probably it was the way he'd been staring at that girl. Yeah, that must have been it. But I had to focus on my mission and carry out orders.

A creaking noise broke the silence and Adam spun in my direction. "What was that?"

I turned the rooster-shaped weathervane slowly as he watched, frightened not just because there wasn't any wind but because I was turning it first in one direction and then the other. When I abruptly stopped, he peered around and listened to the renewed silence. He sighed and stared at the half-smoked joint in his hand, shaking his head, then stubbed it out next to his foot. I flicked it away with my invisible touch, making it bounce. His eyes darted around again and another creak interrupted the sound of his rapid breathing.

"What's going on? You're playing a joke on me, aren't you, guys? C'mon, it's not funny!"

He couldn't see me, but I let him hear the wood creak as I moved toward him. Adam heard the sound coming closer and looked around like a cornered animal. I could hear his heart beating like a drum.

His wasn't the only heartbeat on the roof, though.

I clenched my fist and the beam beneath Adam's hands snapped in two, leaving him without support. He instantly lost his balance, but someone hidden in the darkness leapt out and grabbed him by the leg just in time. With incredible strength he pulled Adam back up but slipped and fell in the process. Adam lunged over the edge in a useless attempt to grab him.

The thought ran through my mind that I would have preferred it if Adam had been my target.

"Connor!" Adam screamed, clutching his hair.

I walked to the edge of the roof and looked down at the boy lying motionless below us. Drake appeared beside him, looked up at me, and smiled. "We done already?"

I smiled back. "We've only just begun."

6

DANGEROUS GAMES

"Connor!!! Oh my God! Is he dead?"

The girls rushed to him, shrieking. Adam knelt beside his friend as the others watched, frozen with terror.

"Adam, what happened?"

"Do something!" Audrey screamed. "We can't leave him there like that!"

"I, I w-was falling off the roof. He caught me but then he fell instead."

"What were you guys doing on the roof?" asked the pony-tailed guy I'd seen in the hayloft.

"What do you think we were doing, Preston? We were hiding!"

"Nice fucking hiding place! Can't you see the house is ready to collapse?"

"You saying it's my fault? I didn't tell him to hide up there. I didn't even know he was there."

"Guys, cut it out! Stop fighting!" Layla said.

The redheaded girl fell to her knees beside Connor and began to sob.

"Paige, get up! Let's go," Layla said to her anxiously.

"Connor! I've always been such a bitch to you and now you're dead." Paige took him by the shoulders and started to shake him. "Forgive me, Connor! Forgive me!" she sobbed.

Connor opened his eyes wide and let out a whoop, making everyone jump. He propped himself on his elbows and started laughing as his friends stared at him in shock.

"You freaking moron!" The girl punched him on the shoulder and he fell back, still laughing.

"Fuck, man! You scared us half to death!" Adam said. "What were you doing hiding there?"

"Saving your ass." Connor shot out a hand and the others helped him up.

"So you didn't die. It was all a joke," Audrey blurted as Connor put his glasses on.

"No shit, Sherlock."

"We thought you were dead! How could you play a prank like that on us?"

"I just wanted to see how much you guys love me!"

"Five more minutes and we would have buried you," one of the guys said, chuckling. "In fact, what do you all say we bury him anyway? C'mon, grab him!"

"Whoa, whoa! Hold on! What are you doing?" Connor said, but the guys grabbed him by the wrists and ankles. "C'mon! It was just a stupid joke! Put me down!"

"On three, we dump him in the water," said Jarret, the boy with the cornrows. "One, two—"

"Wait!" Layla stopped the boys before they could throw Connor into the water tank. "I've got a better idea. Why don't we play Truth or Dare? It's more fun! Each of us gets asked a question, and whoever refuses to answer it honestly has to do a dare."

"I'm down!"

Connor protested as the guys dumped him on the ground. He touched his head, stifling a groan of pain. "Somebody bring the brownies. Looks like we're going to need them. Hey! What happened to Ron? Anybody seen him?"

"Hey, you're right. I haven't seen him for a while now. He was supposed to come find us."

"He's in here!" There was a splash followed by a shout.

"Hey! Are you crazy?" Ron shook his wet hair as he came out of the house. One of the guys had dumped a bucket of water on him to bring him to his senses—or maybe just for fun.

"What happened, Ron? You decide to take a nap right in the middle of the party?" Adam said, grinning.

"I passed out, moron. I don't even remember what happened."

"Have a brownie. It'll help you remember," Jarret suggested. Everyone laughed.

"If I eat another one of those things I think I'll puke."

"Then we need to find a different punishment for you," Layla said. "You go first. Truth or dare?"

"Hey, why me? I don't even want to play!"

"You said it yourself: this is your place, so you go first," Adam said.

"Okay then. Truth."

"Brave! Let's see . . . Confess: when was your first time and who was it with?" Layla asked.

"What, you don't remember?" Ron said, winking at her with a sly smile.

"You lying asshole! It's not true! Don't listen to him. I'm still a virgin!" In the silence someone whistled while someone else faked a coughing fit to hide their laughter. "Time to pay, smartass. It'll teach you a lesson." Meanwhile, Audrey was glaring at Layla as if she didn't believe her.

"What, do I have to eat another brownie?" he asked with a sneer.

"You'd like that, wouldn't you? I've got a better idea," Layla said. "You'll do sit-ups, dunking into the water tank. You're already wet anyway."

"What? Are you crazy? You must have eaten too many edibles."

"You can't say no. Those are the rules. Or aren't you sure you can do it?" She shot Ron a challenging look, but he was already grabbing the back of his shirt. The whole group cheered as he pulled it off without taking his eyes off Layla's. He sat on the edge of the tank and Jarret and Preston held his legs down.

Drake appeared at my side, watching them. "That Ron guy reminds me a lot of myself when I was his age."

"Yeah, you seem barely older than him."

"I wasn't talking about my appearance," he said.

"I wasn't either."

Drake laughed and slapped me on the stomach.

"GO! GO! GO! GO! GO!" The whole group cheered Ron on as he dunked his torso into the water and resurfaced. One, two, three . . . ten times. When he was done he popped up, shook his wet hair, and let out a battle cry as the other boys pulled him out and the girls cheered.

From time to time Connor raised a hand to his head. Though he hadn't admitted it to his friends, the impact had been brutal.

The girls all opted for the dare, refusing to bare their sins. One was told to do a belly dance on the edge of the tank. Another had to kiss everyone present. When she tried to refuse, the others threatened to throw her into the water, so she had no choice but to agree to the long round of kisses.

Then it was Connor's turn. He chose truth but then refused to answer the question. When Ron complained that his dare had been the hardest, they decided to force Connor to do it too. He stumbled to the edge of the tank and took off his glasses, determined to look brave, but when he saw his reflection in the black mirror of water he tried to get out of it.

The others barred his way. "Don't be a wuss! Just do five!"

All at once a sinister shudder ran over me. I looked at Drake and we exchanged a long look. He'd felt it too. We turned around. Behind us stood a Witch.

"Kreeshna," Drake murmured, a flame in his eyes.

The Witch had dark skin and long hair in a braid that hung over her right shoulder. A smaller braid wound around her forehead like a diadem. Her black eyes glittered like a cobra's and for a second her pupils narrowed to slits, strengthening the impression. She vanished and reappeared behind the kids.

I heard Drake snort and gripped his arm. He seemed on the verge of attacking. An eerie whisper drifted to us on the wind; the Witch was murmuring her dark litany into the kids' ears, planting the seed of evil in those willing to listen to her.

She stopped behind Layla. "Come on, what are you waiting for? Push him down!" the girl was saying.

"What? No! What the hell do you think you're doing?" Connor protested, but it was no use. "Wait! I'm not feeling so good."

"Don't listen to him, it's just another trick," Layla shot back.

"Down! Down! Down! *Down! Down! Down*!" The kids cheered as they dunked him.

"One!"

Connor struggled, panicking. He re-emerged and attempted to take a deep breath but before he could they pushed him back in, counting the dunks.

"Two!"

"Down! Down! Down!"

"Three!"

"Down! Down! Down!"

"Wait, guys! Stop!" Adam shouted in alarm.

Everyone froze. Connor had stopped struggling. I glanced at Drake and was worried to see he couldn't take his eyes off the Witch.

"Fuck! Get him out of there, quick!" Jarret ordered.

"Connor! Connor, can you hear me?" Adam ran to him.

"He's just kidding again," Layla said.

"Shut up!" Adam snapped. "He's not breathing! Maybe he hit his head when he fell from the roof. Why didn't I think of that?"

"Oh my God! You mean he's really dead?" Audrey whimpered. No one replied. They all stood there, petrified, staring as Adam tried to resuscitate Connor.

He gave up and looked at his friends. "He's dead."

A wail of dismay rose from the group.

"What have we done?" Paige grabbed her hair.

Audrey covered her mouth and stared at her friend's corpse in shock. "It can't be. He can't be dead."

"But he is. And now we've got to decide what to do."

Behind Layla, the Witch smiled and continued to whisper into the girl's ear, her eyes on Drake's face the whole time.

A sudden warmth rose in me. I took a deep breath and closed my eyes. When I opened them again I was at the center of the group. Connor was standing at my side and his motionless body lay on the ground.

7

THE ALLURE OF DARKNESS

Connor looked around in fright. His friends were panicking. When he saw his body he froze, backed up, and looked at me. "Go away," he whispered.

"Connor, listen—" I said in an effort to reassure him, but he took off across the fields. Drake materialized in front of him. The boy jumped and changed direction but Drake foresaw his every move. He took on Connor's appearance and when Connor saw him he let out a scream and tumbled backwards. I approached him as he scrambled away across the ground.

"I don't want to hurt you," I said, trying to put him at ease.

"You sure the same goes for him?" Connor asked, lifting his chin at Drake. My brother's shaved head gave him a threatening air.

Drake snorted, finding it funny. "You should be more worried about your friends."

"What do you mean?" Connor shot to his feet and ran to the middle of the group where they were having a heated debate.

"We've got to hide him," Layla was saying. "Let's bury him somewhere."

"No!" Connor was shocked. "What are they doing? Are they out of their minds?" He walked around them, shouting to get their attention, but it was no use—they couldn't see or hear him.

Everyone froze. "Did you guys hear that?" They'd heard him. How was that possible? The Witch smiled. She must have let Connor's voice reach his friends. To scare them, maybe, or—more likely—to defy me, after reading my mind, as all Witches were capable of doing.

"It was Connor! I'm sure of it!" Layla exclaimed. "He's going to curse us. He's going to curse all of us! We've got to burn the body!"

"Are you insane?" Adam said. "We've got to call the police. Maybe there's still time to help him."

"No!" Ron said. "No police. They'd find my brother's weed. I can't bring the cops here. I'd be fucked. He's dead. There's nothing more they can do for him now. Layla's right—we've got to hide him."

Evil breathed more of its poison into the girl's soul. *You'll go to jail because of what you've done. No one will ever talk to you again . . .*

"I don't want to go to jail," Layla murmured in a tiny voice.

You're better off hiding him. You can just say he disappeared. No one will ever find him . . .

"We'll say he disappeared," the girl repeated, under the Witch's sway. "It'll work as long as we all tell the exact same story."

"That bitch!" Unaware that she was under the influence of evil, Connor could barely keep himself from rushing at her.

"Connor." I rested a hand on his shoulder and used my powers to calm him. "It doesn't matter. It's not your problem any more. Don't worry about it."

"How can I not worry? They're talking about my *body*!"

"It's not your body any more. All that matters now is your soul, your essence. That's all you'll need in the place I'm taking you. I'm here to guide you to the other side."

Connor swallowed, curious. "It's just that—I thought she was my friend. How can she be saying this stuff?"

"She's scared and weak. There are times in life when you need to make decisions. Those who are strong can make them on their own and resist the temptation placed before them. Those who are weaker, on the other hand, decide to give in to it. You made the right choice. You should be happy because you're coming with me."

"But Layla won't?"

I clenched my jaw. The girl's soul had already been poisoned. "No. She won't belong to our world."

"Hold on." Connor shuddered. "Who's that woman?"

In his current form, I could sense how strong his emotions were. He felt fear, but also fascination. The Witch gazed at him and smiled.

"She's here for the girl, not for you."

"Is she going to kill her?" he asked, worried.

"No, but she'll slowly take her soul. When Layla's time comes, no one like me will be there for her."

"So could she take mine too?" he asked, frightened.

"No, I wouldn't allow it. The fate of your soul has already been determined. Layla could still resist—there's always time to redeem oneself until the soul leaves the body. At that point, nothing more can be done. If her soul is corrupt, evil will claim it."

"We've got to warn her! Layla, don't listen to her!"

"It's too late. Only she can decide whether to listen to evil or renounce it. Each of us is fully in command of our choices, just like you were. It's called free will."

"But that woman's influencing her! She's *making* her say all those things!" he protested.

"Not exactly. She's putting options in front of her, sowing the seeds of doubt, pushing her to follow the path of least resistance. It's called temptation. Layla could resist but she's choosing not to. Temptation is an evil that humans don't often recognize."

Connor looked at his friend and sighed in resignation.

"Now we need to go."

"What if I don't want to?"

"You have no choice. I'm here for you, to show you the way. I need to carry out my mission. Not even I have a choice. Besides, if I left, sooner or later darkness would come to claim your soul—and you wouldn't want that to happen. I don't want it to either. I need to help you pass on. That way you'll be safe."

"What about my parents? I don't want to leave them. I'm not ready yet." Connor was distraught. I could sense it.

"You don't belong to this world any more. You feel confused right now because you're trapped between two worlds. Where you're going, your soul will be at peace."

"But . . . will I see them again?"

I flinched. That question was the one that worried me more than any other: not seeing Gemma again once she died. But Connor wasn't condemned to solitude like I was. He wasn't a Subterranean but a mortal soul that would soon have life eternal. I swallowed and looked him in the eye to reassure him. "Yes. One day, when the time comes, you'll see them again."

He smiled at me, turned to look at his friends one last time, and then took the hand I was holding out to him. "Goodbye," he whispered, and disappeared.

His soul was at peace.

I sighed and looked around for Drake, but my smile soon vanished because he wasn't there—and neither was *she*. In the distance, a bolt of lightning lit up the sky.

"Damn it!" Drake was under the Witch's influence.

I materialized behind them, clenching my fists. I had to move with extreme caution or it would be the end of Drake. She had pushed him against a tree and demolished his defenses, and was now using his own power against him by taking on the guise of another woman. Drake seemed so entranced by her that I instantly realized what had happened: the Witch had taken on the appearance of the fiancée Drake had lost and he'd surrendered control of his mind to her.

I stared in alarm at the sight of the Witch's serpent. It had slithered up to its mistress's neck and was hissing into Drake's face, poised to attack.

"Drake!" I shouted. The Witch turned toward me, her eyes two black pools, her face a mask of rage. She raised a hand to the sky and brought it down. A bolt of lightning shot toward me, but I deflected it onto a nearby tree that exploded in a million sparks.

The explosion snapped Drake out of his trance. Freed from the Witch's spell, he struck her just as she was hurling another bolt of lightning. The movement distracted me and I didn't see it in time. It zoomed straight toward me, blinding me, but Drake instantly appeared at my side, held out his hand, and raised a shield. The thunderbolt crashed against it, dispersing its energy. We were safe behind the barrier, but blue and white beams of electrical energy darted back and forth over it like anxiously pacing animals ready to pounce.

I joined my powers with Drake's and together we hurled the thunderbolt back at the Witch, who disappeared and reappeared right in front of us a split second later. We exchanged defiant looks. Everything—nature itself—went still in the presence of two Subterraneans and a Witch. She couldn't defeat us on her own, just her against the two of us. Her serpent hissed a threat and the Witch smiled, training her black eyes on Drake. Blowing him a kiss, she vanished.

I grabbed Drake by the shoulders and shoved him against the tree. "What were you thinking?!"

"I've got a score to settle with her," he said, looking grim.

"Yeah, I realize who that Witch was. I was there too, remember?" Of course I remembered her: Kreeshna, a woman of Amazonian proportions with dark skin and a lethal gaze. She'd killed a lot of Subterraneans the day I first met Drake, but I'd managed at least to save him. "Christ, Drake! She could have killed us both!"

Drake sighed and rested his hand on my shoulder. "I know. I'm sorry, man."

We gave each other a rough hug, easing the tension in the air.

"No problem. You're my best friend. You okay?"

"I was so stupid!" he said. "I'm sorry. I don't know what got into me. I put your life in jeopardy. If it hadn't been for you, that Witch would have taken mine. She came on to me. I was sure I had it all under control. I pretended to play along but then she clouded my mind and . . . that's all I remember."

"She used your power. She turned into someone else," I said.

Drake's eyes wavered and it was like the Witch's thunderbolt had returned from out of nowhere and struck him. My hunch had been right: it was the girl Drake had lost, the one he never stopped grieving for, no matter how hard he tried to hide it. I knew he didn't like to talk about her. He pushed that part of him deep down so no one would see it, withdrawing into himself. He looked at the world from behind a tough outer shell and let everything else roll off his back. Sometimes I envied him; other times I thought it must be terrible.

"Thanks, bro. You saved me," he said.

"Once again," I reminded him with a laugh. Slapping him on the shoulder, I said, "That's what we do, though, isn't it? We've got each other's backs."

"I'm not risking my life when I cover for you with Gemma's parents."

"I wouldn't be too sure about that. Iron Dog is bound to attack you one of these days."

"Let's hope not or we'll find out what the little rodent tastes like roasted."

"That's disgusting!"

"What did I say? Everybody knows I can't stand the thing. If it were up to me, I'd already have gotten rid of it. You don't know how hard it is for me not to smother it in its sleep!"

"Poor Irony," I murmured. For a long moment neither of us said anything, then I took my phone out of my pocket and punched in Gemma's number.

"She awake already?"

"No. I just let it ring once. She'll find the missed call when she wakes up. That way she'll know I was thinking about her."

Drake didn't reply. For a moment he seemed lost in thought . . . or in his memories, maybe. "Ever wonder what things would be like if you'd decided differently?" he finally asked.

"I don't know how I would feel if I'd decided not to save Gemma," I admitted. It was impossible to imagine my world without her in it. I looked at the sky. The clouds were gathering, churning and brimming with energy, ready to unleash a downpour. "To me, Gemma is the storm, the thunder, the lightning . . . but she's also the sun and the stillness of the moon. She's all those things and without her I would be an empty sky. No sounds, no colors. I'd be lost in a black universe. She's my energy."

"I know the feeling."

I turned to look at Drake, then lowered my head and stared at my shoes. He probably beat himself up every day about the choices he'd made. The wrong ones, the ones he would never stop regretting. No, I had no doubts. If I had chosen not to save Gemma that day in spring, I would have regretted it forever.

"I—I'm in love with her. I love her with all my being," I confessed.

"She's so beautiful it would be hard not to love her," he said, teasing me.

"Hey, stay away from her!" I punched his shoulder, laughing.

Drake raised his hands. "I meant for *you* not to!"

"Drake, you think one day you might find another girl to make you forget your bad memories?"

"Nope," he replied without hesitation, " . . . but I never get tired of trying." He wiggled his eyebrows and we both burst out laughing.

For a Subterranean, love went beyond mere mortal emotion. Once our spirit had united with someone else's, it was impossible to sever the bond. But Drake had bonded with his fiancée when he was still alive, so maybe there was still hope for him, though I wasn't totally convinced.

We talked for a long time, sitting at the foot of the pine tree. I liked hanging out with Drake. Everything seemed simpler when he was around.

A glimmer appeared in the sky, heralding the dawn. I looked at my brother, absorbed in his thoughts, and rested my head quietly against the tree to watch the rising sun.

GEMMA

ANCESTRAL CALL

Blue. I was surrounded by nothing but an intense, unvarying, infinite cobalt blue. It seemed to dominate everything, extend everywhere, as far as I could see. I had no idea where I was nor did I care. I felt the soft, grassy, slightly damp ground beneath my back. The sound of lapping water in the distance filled me with a feeling of tranquility. The blades of grass rustled softly as they danced in the light breeze. They caressed my hands as I moved them over the soft mantle, feeling its consistency.

I heard every sound around me, even the remotest. Every whisper drifted through me as if I were part of it. My mind lost itself in the infinite cobalt that hung over me, protected from the outside world by the melody that lulled me into a pleasantly peaceful state. Lying there, the feeling that I needed nothing else became more and more of a certainty, as though the sky were a void that absorbed all my thoughts, carrying them farther and farther away to a place where nothing else existed.

All at once a whisper, so delicate and hypnotic I was sure it must belong to some enchanting creature, entered my consciousness. I closed my eyes and focused on the sweetness of the sound, forgetting everything else. The breeze lightly brushed my skin as if a ghost were passing over me, and the sound resolved into a voice.

"Naiad . . ."

No one ever called me by my middle name. Confused, I propped myself up on my elbows. The voice vanished, carried away on a breath of air. I lay down again, filled with a sense of peace too profound to worry about it, and it returned, whispering my name, lulling me with its tender melody. I half closed my eyes, almost as if the voice had trapped me in an enchantment in which oblivion summoned me, forcing me to forget the world. I was sure I'd never heard a sound so imbued with power, and deep in my mind I heard the promise that if I managed to reach it, that power would become mine. Driven by the desire for it, I opened my eyes and listened closely without moving a muscle for fear of losing it again.

Who could such a soft, enchanting voice belong to? And how did they know my middle name? The desire to know spread through my mind until it became unbearable. My body rose impulsively, guided by the sound of my name whispered in the wind.

"Naiad . . ."

Like a siren's hypnotic song, the enchanting call was impossible to resist. I barely noticed my body drifting toward the lake. Cool water wet the tips of my toes and awakened me from the trance that had led me to its edge. I looked down and frowned to see my bare feet lapped by the waves that danced on the lakeshore. Raising a hand to my head, I experienced the strange feeling that someone had crept into my mind, leaving behind the mark of their trespass. My eyes wandered over the clearing, confused about how I'd reached the shore without realizing it.

"Naiad . . ."

I shivered as the call insinuated itself into my brain. As if I were under a spell, all hesitation suddenly seemed illogical. I forgot everything except the visceral desire to reach that voice. It was as if some instinct buried deep inside had taken hold of me. Nothing in the world was more important.

I lifted my bare foot, expecting it to sink into the water, but it stopped short of the lake's surface. I raised the other foot and then the first one again, moving forward without wondering why my body was suspended on an unmoving pane of glass.

A flurry of cool air shook me out of my dazed state. It was as though part of me were struggling against the desire that had gripped me. Confused, I stared at the mirror of water offering me its support. The shore was far behind me and my body was completely dry.

"Naiad . . ."

Like a deadly poison, the voice unexpectedly took on a sinister edge that eroded my will to resist its call. It was more somber now and seemed to be coming from the depths of the lake. I didn't care what I had to go through to reach it. I took a step and this time my foot entered the water, which wet it up to the ankle. Another step. And then another. The farther I went, the stronger the voice became, seeming to come now from within, like a part of me. It was a breeze that blew gently on my worries, clouding them. I had the vague sensation the place had changed, almost as though the shores of the lake had been replaced by a grotto in which I was being held prisoner, but I couldn't perceive it clearly. The surface of the lake glowed with strange, pearly reflections.

The cold water wet my wrists . . . my arms . . .

"Naiad . . . let yourself go . . . Don't resist us . . ."

The whisper filled my head, trapping me in its melody until the water reached my chin, jarring me out of the enchantment. The veil that had led me to that place dissolved. Then why did I *long* to go further? Why did I covet the promises hidden in the voice? The yearning to reach it had grown so powerful I wasn't even frightened of the darkness drawing me into the depths of the lake—I even forgot to grant my body one last breath. What could a breath be worth compared to what awaited me under the water?

My nose, cheeks, eyes disappeared beneath the surface of the lake as the water underneath solidified into a crystal staircase that guided me ever deeper. The water engulfed me to the ends of my hair and the cold penetrated my flesh as darkness enveloped me.

Sporadic air bubbles floated up from my body toward the surface and I watched them helplessly, feeling emptied of breath. Even so, I continued to descend, driven by the dark force possessing me. The voice was ever present in my head, urging me on. I couldn't give up, not now that it had become so intense, so *close*. It was so kind and comforting, full of a promise I couldn't relinquish.

Suddenly I felt I was sinking, my body too heavy to hold up. The water was crushing me, the pressure squeezing my chest, preventing me from going further. I felt suddenly weak, wanting nothing more than to surrender to the arms of darkness and let myself be cradled by the water caressing my skin.

All at once, a gleam of light illuminated the shadows that clouded my mind and the abyss into which I was sinking, deprived of all strength. I found myself staring at it, forgetting all else except the desire to reach it. It was so radiant. If only I could find the strength to attain it I would be saved, I knew it.

"Naiad . . . You'll be safe here . . . Don't resist and no one will be able to harm you any more."

The voice bound me to it. I blinked and another puff of air escaped my mouth when I saw its source, close enough for me to reach out and touch. It was a breathtakingly beautiful woman with long dark hair that flowed and drifted in the currents. She wore a long white gown that swayed around her, enveloping her pearly skin.

"Come to me." She held out her hand.

I tried to bring her into focus but the image split into two and then merged back into one. Her lips curved in a sweet smile, her features so harmonious that the only thing that prevented me from taking her hand was my weakness. I suddenly felt on the verge of fainting.

I tried to extend my arm but a sharp, baffling pain gripped my chest before I could touch her fingers. Seeing my hesitation, her face instantly metamorphosed into the most evil expression of power and mastery my eyes had ever beheld. I flailed in the water, trying to get away, but a jolt of terror forced the last bit of air from my lungs and I lost myself to utter darkness.

"Gemma! Gemma!"

"Evan!" I woke with a start, crying out his name.

"Everything's fine," he said, drawing me to him. "I'm here now."

I hid my face in his chest, shaken and breathing convulsively. I could still feel the need for oxygen and my forehead was beaded with sweat as the memory faded little by little. No—it wasn't a memory. It had only been a nightmare.

"You really scared me," Evan said, brushing the hair from my forehead. He looked concerned. "You were tossing and turning like crazy when I got here. I was just about to join you in your dream when you woke up." The torment hidden in his eyes told me he hadn't forgiven himself for the time Faust entered my dream and convinced me to run away from him.

"I dreamed I was drowning." Although I wanted to reassure him, I could still feel the sensation of the water closing in around my throat.

"I'm sorry I wasn't there to prevent it," he said regretfully, stroking my hair.

"What a strange dream," I murmured, still dazed.

"It's not so strange. We went to the lake yesterday. Your mind must have combined that information with your fears, your emotions. That's how it happens. The brain never stops working. While you sleep, logical thinking gets broken up and memories get confused with things that have never happened."

"I saw a woman," I said, clinging to the memory that was rapidly vanishing as if it had just occurred to me that the information might be important. "She was waiting for me at the bottom of a lake, or maybe it was a spring inside a cave, I'm not sure. She wore a white gown. She wanted me to follow her."

For some reason the worried look on my face made him smile. "Calm down, Gemma. It was just another nightmare. It has nothing to do with the real world. I bet it's already fading."

I made a face that confirmed his assumption.

"Good," he said with a satisfied nod.

The fact that Evan was right relieved me a little. It was different when he visited me in my dreams. His being there blurred the line between the dream world and the real world and in the morning I woke up with a new memory—not a faded image created through mere imagination, but an actual memory, crisp and indelible. A real circumstance experienced in my mind together with him.

"You know dreams don't fade when a Subterranean establishes contact with you."

The words "Are you sure of that?" escaped me. I was more worried than I'd thought, and still not entirely convinced. For some ridiculous reason, my instinct continued to contradict him. "You're right," I said, capitulating to the look on his face before he could answer. "I'm just afraid they—"

"Don't even say it. They're not going to find you, Gemma. It's not going to happen." I hid my face in his chest and he hugged me tightly, as if by doing so he could hide me inside him. "It's over now. If they wanted to find you they would have done it already. No one is coming to look for you."

I heaved a deep sigh at his words, remembering the fear I'd felt day after day, so gut-wrenching I hadn't been able to breathe. "I hope you're right," I said uneasily. A whimper escaped me, revealing the anxiety that gripped my stomach.

Sensing my dismay, Evan cupped my face in his hands and rested his forehead on mine. "I'm not going to let them hurt you," he whispered against my lips. "I'll always be at your side to prevent it. Trust me." He looked at me as though he could enter my very essence. I nodded and buried my face in his chest again.

9

DANGEROUS REVELATIONS

"I was still thinking about yesterday," I told Evan as we walked through the school doors.

"About what, exactly?" he asked, curious.

"I can't figure out why you never told me you were such a good musician."

He smiled. "I already said I don't like to brag. You'd seen the piano before in the music room by the garage. The violin's always been there too. It's not my fault the only time we went in there you didn't ask any questions. If I remember correctly, you didn't feel much like looking around."

I blushed, remembering his hands on me and how he'd distracted me from everything else. So actually, it *had* been all his fault. Besides, that day was the first time I'd seen Drake, Simon, and Ginevra training in the workout room next door and it had left me shocked. Evan had told me several times that it was the only place they could truly let it all out without all of Lake Placid thinking there was an earthquake, but deep down I knew the real reason: they were keeping themselves prepared.

"Only because you never mentioned you liked playing it. How could I have known?" I shot back, trying not to show how much the memory had shaken me.

"Um, by asking?" He raised an ironic eyebrow.

"After all the insane things I saw you do over the summer, you didn't seem like that kind of boy," I said, grinning.

Evan opened his mouth in astonishment. "Well, they weren't insane enough to make you talk me out of them. In fact, you seem to like all the excitement," he said teasingly. He stopped and wrapped his arms around my waist, a sly smile on his lips.

"Only in those extreme cases when I don't know if I'm going to come out of it dead or alive," I said, entertained.

"Hmm, I have one in mind right now." He leaned in and kissed me lightly.

"Have I ever told you you're crazy?" I kissed him back just as tenderly.

"Only a couple times."

"Clearly not often enough. At first I thought you were trying to kill me, you know. That you regretted saving me and wanted to get rid of me. Confess!" I said with a grin.

"Okay, you got me." He laughed, but a trace of seriousness flickered in his eyes. "I don't know what sense it would make to keep you in a glass case when I know nothing can happen to you when you're with me. Emotions should be lived to the fullest, Gemma, or you run the risk of them fading away. And there are some sensations you can never experience unless go you out and look for them. The important thing is to be in control of them instead of letting them overwhelm you."

"Fading away?" I asked, amused, casting a sidelong glance at him.

"I mean the spark. That charge that makes little kids throw themselves headlong into things before fear puts the brakes on their impulses. Few people still have that spark by the time they're adults."

"Oh, you mean irresponsibility," I teased, even more entertained by the conversation.

"I mean courage."

"You're forgetting that my time is up."

Evan squeezed me against him more tightly. "And you're forgetting that you have an Angel to protect you."

I freed myself from his embrace and looked at him. "No. I never forget that." Rising onto my tiptoes, I rested my head against his for a moment.

"Feel like going to my place?" he asked me point-blank.

"Now? But what—"

"Don't worry, I'll ask Drake to fill in for you at lunch with your folks." He smiled. "He owes me a favor."

I glanced at him, curious. "What did he do to deserve such a punishment?"

"Him? Nothing! I saved him from Simon and Ginevra. And then, let's just say something that wasn't on the program came up."

"What sort of something?"

"Something that'll keep him in our debt for a long, long time."

"Hmm, that doesn't sound bad. But poor Drake! I feel a little sorry for him. I wonder if Irony will ever get used to him."

"He'd better!" Evan laughed at what seemed like a private joke.

I chuckled and nudged him with my shoulder.

"I think I'm about to explode," I told them. The food was always sublime when Ginevra was the one taking care of it.

"At least warn us first, sunshine, and give us a chance to duck for cover," Drake joked from the living room where he was lounging on the couch watching a documentary about arachnids.

"I thought I just had," I shot back.

"You'd better get to Gemma's," Evan told him. "You're already late. Make yourself useful instead of loafing around."

"Sir, yes sir!" Drake winked at me. "I definitely like this Evan better than the gloomy version of him back when he had to—Well, you know."

"Shut up, Drake!" Ginevra threw some food at him, smiling. "Pass me another slice of pizza, hon," she said to me. We all turned to stare at her in disbelief. "What?" she retorted, a puzzled look on her face.

"How many have you had already?" Evan asked, aghast.

His sister shrugged and glared at him. "It's authentic! It came all the way from Italy!"

"You're disgusting."

"I've always said so but nobody ever believes me," Drake said.

Among all of Ginevra's abilities, being able to pig out on anything without gaining an ounce was the most incredible of her magic powers—not that I'd ever worried about my weight, but who wouldn't love to be in her shoes?

"You're just saying that because you have such a jaded palate," Ginevra told Evan, making me curious.

"Wish you did?" he shot back.

Something in their exchange must have gone over my head because Ginevra cast Evan a far-from-reassuring look. "I guess my palate will just have to settle for this delicious, flavorful, piping hot slice of pizza," she teased him, biting into it with a theatrical gesture. I couldn't really tell whether their usual kidding had actually been replaced by veiled insults.

"What does she mean, 'jaded palate'?" I asked Evan under my breath. "So you *do* eat, after all?" He'd never mentioned it to me.

His expression softened as he looked into my eyes. "It's based more on need than pleasure, although the two aren't mutually exclusive."

"You never told me you *needed* to eat," I said, still surprised.

"I don't need food as you know it. What I eat is—Well, it's a pretty thorny topic, to be honest. We've never really discussed it."

I started to wonder how many other unexpected details would crop up. "You can't always use that as an excuse!" I said acidly. I was suddenly shocked by the tone I'd taken with him.

Evan turned to me and lowered his voice reassuringly. "We've never talked about where I come from."

His answer caught me off guard. "I thought you were forbidden to talk about it," I said, almost accusingly.

"No, it's because you're discreet. You never asked me about it and I didn't want to force you. I thought you didn't feel ready to know more yet. You've already had so much to handle."

Evan's explanation made me decide to drop it because I honestly couldn't blame him. He'd always been one step ahead of me. By reading my emotions he could perceive with perfect timing what I needed even before I realized it myself. Sometimes I had the impression my subconscious revealed as much to him as it hid from me.

For seventeen years I'd known a world that now seemed so distant. It felt like it had totally disappeared, eclipsed by Evan's world. Angels, Witches, heaven, hell . . . If I stopped to think about it, it all seemed so insane that part of me was still terrified—the part that Evan had access to whether I liked it or not.

Lost in these thoughts, my eyes shifted to Ginevra's hand and glimpsed it reaching for the last slice of pizza. Suddenly I felt dragged into another dimension, struck by a devastating, uncontrollable emotion. A violent one.

Rage.

Rage that rushed up from deep inside me. Furious. Unexpected. Unstoppable. "What the fuck do you think you're doing?!" I had no control over the words that spewed from my mouth. As if it had a life of its own, my hand snatched the food from hers and flung it across the room. It was like someone had taken over my body. Something dark and evil was stirring inside me. I could feel its strength. "You think you're entitled to everything just because you think you're *better* than the rest of us?" I screamed, horrified by the ungovernable impulse that was driving me to say these things. A little voice hidden in a corner of my brain begged me to stop.

Icy silence descended on the room. My insides mirrored the frozen faces of the others. I rubbed my arms, ashamed of my reaction. Simon and Drake stared at me in shock. I wished the earth would open under my feet and swallow me up.

"Everything's fine," Ginevra whispered cautiously, probably reading in my mind how ashamed I was. But nothing was fine, not at all. What the hell had just happened to me? I stared at the floor. Emptiness filled me. None of it seemed real.

"I . . ." I stammered, my voice lifeless. "I don't know what got into me." I was disgusted with myself. "I'm not even hungry. I have no idea why I reacted like that." I looked up at Ginevra. "Forgive me, Gin," I begged, mortified. I hid my face in my hands and found they were trembling, as if some violent energy were surging through them.

"It's no big deal, Gemma," Evan said to dispel my obvious embarrassment. "Everybody loses their temper once in a while. Besides, we all know Ginevra's a total glutton. It does her good to be reminded of it once in a while." He said it lightheartedly enough to clear the tension in the air, but in my heart the fog hadn't budged an inch. Still, I forced a smile, masking the agitation that still threatened to consume me.

With a jerk of his head, Evan invited me to follow him upstairs. Unable to look Ginevra in the eye, I barely glanced at her and followed him to his room.

"What do you think got into me?" I asked Evan, leaning against the desk in his room.

"What do you think?" he echoed, slowly moving closer.

"Honestly, I don't know how to explain it. All this anger flared up inside me and I couldn't keep it from exploding. It was overwhelming, Evan. I've never felt anything like it."

He reached for my hands and pulled me to him. "It's nothing you should worry about. You're making too much of it."

As soon as Evan's lips rested on mine I felt relieved and the last remaining traces of the terrible memory instantly vanished. I pulled back to look at him, filled with the suspicion that he'd caused the soothing sensation. "Was that you?" I raised an eyebrow, even more convinced he'd used his powers to guide my thoughts elsewhere and ease the tension.

Evan moved his lips closer to mine. "Don't know what you're talking about." But the smile he tried to hide gave him away.

He watched me as I slipped out of his embrace and went to the built-in bookcase that took up an entire wall. Rows of well-worn books were lined up side by side like little soldiers. Their pages were yellowed by the centuries, their smell comforting. The first time Evan had showed it to me, he'd had to drag me away by force. I scanned it, studying the titles on their spines. "So many books," I said aloud.

Evan shrugged. "They were the only things that gave my life meaning before I met you."

"Not counting your car," I teased. "And your motorcycle."

He laughed and hung his head, probably because I always replied with something sarcastic when receiving a compliment. I realized it but couldn't do anything about it. "Not counting those," he agreed.

I grinned and turned back to look at the books more carefully. With an affectionate smile, I remembered when Evan had given me his 1847 edition of *Jane Eyre*. I hadn't been able to sleep for a whole week after that. Lost in this memory, I didn't notice that in the meantime I'd begun to trail my finger over the meticulously organized books. I'd almost reached Shakespeare when I stopped, curious, on a dusty book that looked older than the others.

"*Tristan and Iseult*," I murmured as I carefully took it out, my eyes filled with fascination. I blew across its top edge, raising a cloud of dust. The leather cover was worn. "I've always loved this story," I told him eagerly, resting one knee on the mattress and sliding down onto my belly facing the foot of the bed.

"That makes the list of things we have in common even longer," Evan said, clicking on a playlist on his laptop that was sitting open on the desk. "Actually, it's a legend of Celtic origin that dates back to the Middle Ages." He lay down beside me on the bed, staring at the ceiling as the soft notes of Hans Zimmer's *And Then I Kissed Him* filled the room.

I leafed through the book, my fingers brushing the fragile, yellowed paper. Evan gently took it out of my hands and turned the pages, a confident look in his eye. He was clearly searching for something. I could tell he'd found it when he stopped, rolled onto his side, and gazed at me. Then he looked down at the old yellowed page.

They were like the honeysuckle vine,
Which around a hazel tree will twine,
Holding the trunk as in a fist
And climbing until its tendrils twist
Around the top and hold it fast.
Together tree and vine will last.
But then, if anyone should pry
The vine away, they both will die.
My love, we're like that vine and tree;
I'll die without you, you without me.

He recited the verses with a sad awareness in his voice, as if they were his own. When he was finished I lay there in silence listening as the echo of his words faded inside me.

"The verse reminds me of a couple I know," he said softly, a bitter smile on his lips. "Constantly hounded by a fate that tries to divide them, forcing them to repress their love. But not even death manages to separate them." His gaze lingered on mine. "It's the two of us, Gem. Together," he whispered in a low voice, touching my lips. "Like the hazel and the honeysuckle. Like Tristan and Iseult."

"No!" I protested, realizing his meaning.

"I couldn't go on living without you," he said, closing the book with a little puff of dust.

"But you *have to*," I said, a pleading look on my face. "You can't—you can't even *think* of something like that, Evan!" My fate was uncertain and Evan had already planned his if worse came to worst. My life could end at any minute, but his couldn't come to an end because of me; I would never allow it.

"I've already made up my mind."

"Change it," I ordered him with a determination I didn't know I had.

"I can lie to you if you want, but I'm not going to change my mind. I can't even stand the thought of losing you. *I'll die without you*," he said slowly, looking me in the eye.

A shiver ran down my spine and I looked around, sensing something.

Evan looked at me, frowning. "Something the matter?"

"I have a bad feeling. A sense of foreboding." He stared at me and the serious look on my face caused concern to appear on his own. "Something's wrong, Evan. Their strange lack of interest in me and especially in *you*. Why weren't you ever held accountable for what you did?"

"I don't know. I imagined I would be denied entrance to Eden, but there must be some reason behind their apparent disinterest. I'll pay for my decisions, you can be sure of that. The Elders never go about things directly. They're far more subtle."

"I don't know. It's like I can feel something brewing. The uncanny silence that comes before a storm. Doesn't it seem odd to you too?"

He put his arm around my shoulders and rested his forehead against mine, driving off the anxiety threatening us both. "We'll face it together," he whispered tenderly.

"All right," I made myself reply even though I wasn't convinced. I got up from the bed, his eyes still on me, and went to the bookcase to put the book back. Another book fell off the shelf but I caught it before it hit the floor. "*Paradise Lost.* The irony of fate." I chuckled and looked at the book for a long moment, lost in a silly thought. "You think Milton's vision of heaven did it justice?" I asked casually, hoping his answer might reveal to me what mankind had always been forbidden to know.

Evan looked at me with a strange smile. I frowned. "What did I say?" I asked, at a loss.

"You can ask me . . . or you can see for yourself."

"See for myse— What are you talking about, Evan?" I asked, stunned.

From the way he laughed out loud, I guessed this particular book hadn't ended up in my hands by coincidence. "Actually I've been considering it for a while now and I think you're ready."

I began to worry that I'd actually understood what he was saying, but the thought that flashed through my mind was too ridiculous to take seriously.

"I want to show you my world," he said matter-of-factly.

Another shiver spread all over my body, giving me goosebumps.

"I want you to be part of it."

My thoughts blurred and I tripped over my words. "You—No, wait, y-you want—oh, no! You can't be serious. This is another one of your jokes. You're talking about—" I stared at him in shock as Evan nodded with a little grin on his face.

"We're living in *your* world. It only seems fair for you to know the place I come from too."

I sank onto the bed. Evan took my hands as his enthusiasm grew. "You don't know how long I've waited for you to be ready, Gemma. You've got to see it!"

"Do you think it's really possible?"

"Why shouldn't it be? It's like home to me. It's hard enough not being able to see the other souls there. I want at least to show it to the one person who matters to me."

"It could be dangerous," I said. The idea was as tempting as it was frightening.

"It won't be. Trust me, no one will see us." He knelt down in front of me and made me look at him. "It'll be just you and me, in heaven." I rested my forehead against his. "The two of us against the world," he added. "What do you say?"

Sometimes it was impossible to talk him out of his recklessness and just as impossible to resist that look in his eye, as wild as it was tender. "I feel like I'm already in heaven," I whispered, my eyes closed and my forehead against his. Even so, the idea made me tremble and I couldn't refuse. I bit my lip, my unspoken acceptance sending a tremor of excitement through my heart. A glance at the clock told me it was already five in the afternoon.

Evan squeezed my hands and pulled me to my feet. His lips brushed my ear. "Close your eyes," he whispered. "Empty your mind of all thought and let me guide you. Trust me completely."

A strange tingle filled my head. Instinctively, my lips sought his to dispel the fear that, in spite of myself, was mixed with excitement. Evan held me in his arms and the tingle spread all over my skin. It was a pleasant sensation that made me dizzy. When he relaxed his grip on my arms, I wasn't completely sure I was ready to open my eyes, so I hesitated. A sweetly scented, intoxicating breeze caressed my skin and I understood at once that we weren't in his room any more. A fresh delicate fragrance filled my nostrils, arousing my curiosity.

I opened my eyes and everything I had known up to a moment ago ceased to exist. The sight was so astonishing I realized nothing would ever be the same—because *I* wouldn't be the same any more. Everything I'd feared, everything I'd always believed no longer made sense; but then again nothing had ever made sense until this moment. It was a new reality that my spirit drank in thirstily. No, not new. A part of me trembled under my skin, as if this world were all I knew. It belonged to me, I could feel it deep in my soul. I belonged to this place. *I wanted it.* At all costs.

I inhaled deeply. The air had a different aroma, new to my still-human earthly senses. Still, part of me recognized it as familiar. It must have been my soul. This was where it had come from and where it wanted to return. I could feel it.

The reward . . . Eden.

"My God," I murmured, looking around, astonished by the landscape that exploded in a myriad of colors, shapes, scents beyond my wildest imagination.

"Well?" Evan's pleased voice snapped me out of my daze. "What do you say about Milton's description?"

My mouth opened and closed convulsively before I finally found my voice. "This is even better than Pandora!" I exclaimed, unable to believe it was real. My eyes widened, trying to take it all in.

"The first woman created by Zeus to punish mankind?" Evan asked, looking confused.

I made a face at him. "The film created by James Cameron at a price tag of two billion dollars!" From his expression I guessed he had no idea what I was talking about. "Come on, haven't you ever seen *Avatar*?" His eyebrows rose higher. "You must at least have heard of it!" I insisted. He shook his head, a bewildered look on his face.

I continued to get waves of goosebumps. Clearly my body wasn't used to being in that place and handling the intense emotions it triggered in me. Or more likely, my soul was struggling, begging to be allowed to return there where it felt it belonged. The sensation was both electrifying and frightening.

The air had a strange, almost tangible consistency. I found myself moving my hand through it, studying it. It was hard to perceive colors as I knew them; brilliant silver particles filled the air, flowing over every surface. Everything shone like a diamond struck by moonlight or the harmonious shimmer of a mirror of water at sunset.

"This is why people on earth are so attracted to everything that sparkles." I looked at Evan. He'd just answered my thoughts. "A part of them still remembers," he whispered. I drank in his explanation, too entranced by my surroundings to wonder how he seemed to be reading my mind.

The light was warm, like the moment just before sunset or just after dawn. It must still have been daytime there in paradise and yet there was no sun in the sky. In its place, a warm moon watched us from above with its silvery rays reflecting a delicate shimmering light. It was so close and so immense it felt like I could reach out and touch it.

It was as if day and night, sun and moon, darkness and light had agreed to coexist in perfect harmony. A happy medium between the golden rays of day and the pale diamond reflections of night. It occurred to me that on earth our sun and moon were also being punished, forced to chase each other without ever meeting, while here they could unite, melting together in their love.

The particles in the air reflected the moonglow, filling the sky with incredible colors like the northern lights. I couldn't take my eyes off the sky: a warm, delicate mantle of red and golden shades that glowed above us like stardust, flowing like a silk scarf stirred by the wind. This place seemed to have been carved out of the inside of a diamond with light shining through it.

"Come with me." Evan took my hand. "I want to show you something."

"Where are we going?" I asked, following him without protest.

"You'll see." Evan was bursting with enthusiasm and I was drowning in my emotions.

The vegetation around us was lush, an infinity of harmonious colors. Evan led me through a thick patch of woods full of massive flowers. I stopped to study one from close up, too fascinated to resist. There were hundreds of them, all as tall as me, lined up one behind the other like sentinels, forming rows of contrasting colors from deep purple with pink streaks to cherry red sprayed with golden reflections to night blue with silvery speckles.

Evan watched me silently, pleased by my enthusiasm. I couldn't imagine how he must be feeling. This was the first time he'd ever shared the emotions this place instilled with anyone.

I stroked a silky flower bud for a few seconds and something seemed to stir inside it in response, making me pull back instinctively in alarm. To my amazement the flower slowly opened before my eyes with a graceful movement. The next moment, the other buds opened as well, forming a fan of colors that extended as far as my eye could see. I stared with fascination at the rainbow that had come to life at my touch. In a matter of seconds the entire host of flowers had awakened, releasing shimmering specks of stardust that sparkled on my skin.

Something glowed inside one of the blossoms, catching my attention. I frowned, repressing my urge to touch the silvery light.

"Those are Sephires," Evan whispered at my side. I could feel him looking at me, enjoying my wonder.

"They're amazing." My voice was only slightly louder than his.

Evan seemed to hold his breath as I said this. Had I done something wrong? Before I could ask him what, the light glimmered and moved. Then, as if each flower could communicate with its neighbor, they all lit up in unison, trembling. Countless luminous points rose into the air like a silent swarm of bees, whirling around us without making a sound.

My mind was lost in the dazzling display. Tiny, beautiful creatures danced around us like fireflies in the night. I couldn't remember seeing anything more spectacular in my whole life. My skin tingled as the tiny stars drifted past and it felt like the sky was at my fingertips. Evan and I exchanged a look that said more than a thousand words. His eyes glowed like moonstones.

"Tell me I'm not dreaming," I whispered in a tiny voice.

"You're not dreaming," he replied, smiling.

"It's all so incredible. And magical. How can a place like this exist?"

"It always has," he whispered, reluctantly leading me away. "Deep in their hearts, everyone keeps a memory of it. They've simply forgotten to believe in it."

"I feel like I could stay here forever," I confessed.

"I can sense that," he said, looking at me out of the corner of his eye, seeming slightly worried that I felt that way. After a few steps he chuckled and I looked at him suspiciously.

"What's so funny?" I asked.

"You are," he said, earning himself a sharp look from me. "Don't get me wrong, it's just that here I can read you more clearly than anywhere else, even more than in your dreams." His lips brushed my ear. "Here, your soul is completely naked to my eyes," he whispered with a hint of mischievousness. "The energy your spirit draws from this place is so strong it keeps your body from hiding what you're feeling. Every single emotion is revealed to me like a reflection in a mirror."

"And reading my emotions is that amusing?" I asked, embarrassed.

"I can't deny it." He laughed. "Don't get mad. To me this world is as real as yours is to you, and I love sharing in your excitement, Gemma. I'm happy I can read your emotions just now. Couldn't be happier, in fact."

I opened my mouth but closed it again. "Is this what you wanted to show me?" I asked after a while.

"No, but we're almost there," he said.

The path we were on grew steeper. Although I felt an explosion of emotion, something suddenly worried me—an unusual sense of uneasiness. "Evan!" I noticed my voice trembling. "Are you sure there won't be consequences for this?" After all, who was I? Why should I be granted such a privilege? "Don't you think we're overdoing it? Maybe we shouldn't be transgressing in this way," I murmured as my uneasiness rose. I held my breath in the silence preceding his reply.

"I can't lie to you." I paled. "I'm not entirely sure there won't be consequences for me for bringing you here. But I'm willing to run the risk. Let them punish me. It's worth it," he said solemnly.

"You're crazy," I said, shaking my head.

"Love has made me crazy but it's the sweetest form of madness and I accept it willingly." He winked at me, his smile tender.

I tried to take in as much information as possible, hoping to remember this place forever. Even the colors glowed with hues that didn't look natural to me—or more likely the ones I was used to were the unnatural ones.

Everything suddenly made sense in my life. Who I was, why I existed . . . what was in store for me. No matter what happened, this was my fate.

I would have remained in this state of unconscious exaltation if meeting Evan's gaze hadn't pulled me into his melancholy. As long as I was human and mortal, I could never be part of his world, but once my fate had made this place my home, Evan would be the one who couldn't be part of it. Death would separate us forever because Evan had been banished and would never be able to see me again. The sadness of this reality overwhelmed me. Within moments his pain had become mine and together we slid into the dark pit of that awareness.

"It's not fair," I whispered bitterly. Something that had eluded me, obscured by my excitement, now crashed down onto me like a deadly wave: we were all alone.

"It's so quiet. No one's here." I listened carefully. All I could hear was the sound of flowing water somewhere not far away. The breeze drew my attention, caressing my skin with its rich scent. I saw a moose raise its head, interrupting its grazing. "Can't you Subterraneans even see each other?"

"It's no problem for me. I'm used to it," he said, but his tone of voice belied his words.

"It can't be forever," I protested, as if my opinion mattered. "It can't, really." My frustration was replaced by guilt. My presence in Evan's life had led him to give up everything that was dear to him, to give up hope. "What you did was done out of love. That should make some kind of difference."

"No one can know for sure," he murmured, sounding defeated, his tone as distant as his gaze.

"But they give you missions, orders to carry out. All this must have some kind of purpose!"

"I've been telling myself that for centuries," he said.

"That can't be *it.* It can't. Every flame eventually dies out. It's inevitable. And my life won't last forever," I reluctantly reminded him. For the first time, the words took on new meaning in my mind. If dying meant belonging to this world, death per se didn't frighten me any more. What terrified me was the thought of what it would inevitably take from me: *Evan.* Although my soul longed to return to this place, I would give it all up without a second's hesitation if only it meant having the chance to stay with Evan. And wasn't that exactly what he'd done for me? Until now I probably hadn't fully understood what his sacrifice meant.

"You'll manage to redeem your soul. I'm sure of it," I promised him, resolute. No one deserved it more than he did.

"It's not so important—not as long as you're still alive." For a moment I thought I heard a quiver in his voice. "And maybe I'll find a solution for this too." He forced a laugh, then stopped abruptly as if he wasn't really convinced.

"It's not so important?" I replied, annoyed. "How can you say something like that? I don't need to read your subconscious! You think I don't know you well enough to understand what you're feeling?" His eyes narrowed to slits. "I know perfectly well how much you want to atone and see your mother again." His gaze wavered as if he hadn't been expecting that. I tried hard to hold his eyes. "You've never told me that but I know it's true."

"No." He looked away. "It seems you don't know me well enough. Otherwise you'd know that you're the only thing that matters to me now. Maybe there was a time when my soul being damned was a burden, a time when I felt lonely, useless, empty, and my only goal was to cling to the thought of the one person I had ever really loved. But then you arrived." His hand slid into my hair and his eyes on mine grew tender. We were forehead to forehead. "What sense is there in living without a heart, Gemma? Because my heart beats with yours," he whispered. "My very breath is bound to yours." Holding my gaze, he laid his hand on my chest over my heart. I felt it beat under his fingers. "If your heart stopped it would silence mine forever too. I couldn't live even one minute knowing you were gone. I wouldn't be able to stand it—not in this world or any other."

"Don't say that! Don't even think it!" I cried, devastated. Now I was sure he was telling the truth. "You would be the one to break my heart. I wouldn't be able to bear it. I need to know you exist and that you're alive somewhere in the world or it would be like losing you all over again." I realized how self-centered it sounded only when I'd shared the thought with him. It was strange how the prospect of spending my whole life with him—if I was allowed to live it—wasn't enough any more in view of his immortality.

Evan wrapped his arms around me and his voice caressed my ear tenderly. "All these centuries spent without you have been so meaningless," he whispered. "If I'd known I would find you one day, I'd have lived just to see you breathe, Gemma. I can't lose you now that I've found you. I won't let it happen. No one will ever separate us without killing us both. Not even death. That's a promise." He held me close and I breathed in his scent.

We were alone, he and I, lost in this paradise all our own.

10

DIAMOND NIGHT

Evan led me through an area dotted with trees of all different sizes. Their branches spread out, weaving harmonious motifs along the path as if playing together. The leaves reflected the silvery light of the moon, and the strange heat it emitted warmed me to my bones. My senses were intoxicated by the trail of aromas and the smell of fruit that filled the air. The flowing water wasn't far away any more; the sound was louder now.

"You still haven't told me where we're going," I reminded him.

"It's a surprise," he said with a smile. He ducked his head under a large oak branch and turned back to make sure I didn't run into it.

The forest was full of fragrances. I could already smell the scent of water, fresh and heady. A cool, invigorating breeze caressed my skin and I closed my eyes. When I opened them again Evan was standing in front of me, his hand resting on a long branch that hung down from what I guessed was a willow tree. "Ready?" he asked. I looked at him, full of anticipation. There was no need for me to answer. Evan pulled the willow back as if it had been a natural curtain and the sound of water became deafening. I moved forward, pushing the branches aside, and stopped short, stunned.

Spread out in front of me like a treasure guarded by the forest was a majestic crescent-shaped waterfall that plunged into a river stretching as far as the eye could see. The rock ledge over which the water flowed—a jagged semicircle edged with white foam—was far, far overhead. I cast an incredulous glance at Evan, who took my hand.

"Come with me." He squeezed my fingers, almost as if afraid to lose me as he moved toward the cascade.

The cool breeze left my skin damp. "What are you doing?" I shouted, puzzled.

Facing the rock wall, Evan pointed at its top and smiled. "Time to climb." It sounded like a warning.

"What?!"

"Don't worry. I'll hold you."

I could barely hear his voice over the deafening roar of the waterfall. No matter how dangerous his suggestion seemed, my trust in Evan moved my feet forward. When we reached the slippery wall he stood behind me, pointing out handholds in the rock. I doubted anyone else ever climbed it to reach the top—there must have been a different, less dangerous way—but knowing Evan, I was sure he wouldn't even consider it.

My fingers slipped on the wet rock, but Evan acted as a safety net behind me, pressing me against the wall as if we were one being.

"This way," he shouted when we were halfway up.

I did a double take when he pointed not up but over at the center, right in the middle of the white inferno. Resisting the urge to look down, I tried to focus on the mossy wall instead.

"You can't fall," his voice whispered in my head. *"I'm right behind you. If you slip, I'll catch you."* He held me from behind, accentuating the contact with his body to let me feel he was there. I nodded and began to move cautiously toward the center. The horizontal climb turned out to be harder than the vertical one. I began to worry after few yards when the rocky surface became even slicker and the water splashed onto me from every which way.

"You sure this is the right direction?" I shouted, unable to restrain my anxiety. The sound of the water was too loud for Evan to hear me, but his body shook as if he was laughing.

A few steps farther ahead, my heart in my throat, I found a broader ledge to rest my feet on. I was almost afraid to look but Evan stepped in front of me and held out his hand. When I grabbed it he pulled me to him and held me tight. I let myself take a deep breath and stared at the darkness behind him, puzzled. "Where are we?" I asked.

The sound of the water had grown fainter and my voice echoed with unexpected volume against the walls. I glanced behind me and saw a thick layer of water, as transparent as a glass wall, separating us from the outside, enclosing us in a rocky cavern.

"Why didn't you carry me here on your shoulders? I wouldn't have slowed you down—or risked having a heart attack," I grumbled with a hint of sarcasm.

"The only thing you would have risked would be missing out on all the excitement. Don't deny it—I could sense it," he shot back confidently. "You can't separate powerful excitement from the fear generated by the risk involved. That's what pumps the adrenaline into your system. You have to take the whole package," he said, a mocking look on his face.

"What is this place?" I whispered, still shaken. Giving in to the urge to touch the crystal curtain, I reached out my hand, wanting to feel the water flow through my fingers.

"No!" Evan grabbed my wrist before I could. "The current's too strong. It could drag you down." His firm voice echoed against the rocks.

I looked over his shoulder. It was totally dark. Dense shadows seemed to be crowding forward to swallow us up. A shiver drew my thoughts to the ominous darkness and he smiled as the water thundered behind me, forming a barrier as invisible as it was impassable. Looking me in the eye, Evan cupped his hands together. I frowned, not understanding, but in the blink of an eye, a silvery light came to life in his palms, glowing like a firefly in the night. Amazed, I stood there staring at the little speck in Evan's hand as it grew into a sphere of soft white light about the size of an apple.

"This is angel fire," he explained, watching my reaction.

"It's white," I whispered, fascinated. Although I'd heard about it, I'd never seen it with my own eyes.

"That's because it's pure," he said.

Inexplicably drawn to its light, I stared at it for a moment and reached out to touch it, but something distracted me. Another light, a sparkle coming from another direction. I instantly sensed its power. The hazy, silvery light from the fire that burned on Evan's palm—as delicate as a will-o'-the-wisp—had lit up the darkness of the grotto and reflected against its walls, taking my breath away.

"Oh my God," I exclaimed, turning around and around to study the rocky ceiling. The universe seemed to have sprung into life above us. A multitude of stars twinkled in the darkness of the cave. Night sparkled with its silver mantle in this tiny corner of heaven.

"Are they . . . *stars*?" I murmured, my gaze lost in this night with no firmament. I pivoted slowly, fascinated by the twinkling specks that completely covered the rock walls. A mantle of stars that sparkled within reach, shining with their own light. "It's impossible . . ."

"They're not stars." The second Evan finished speaking, the fire he held in his hand glowed brighter. Its rays bathed the walls, revealing their secret.

"Diamonds," I whispered, fascinated, as the white light was refracted off the crystals in the rock, casting silvery prisms that chased each other across the walls.

Evan nodded, happy to have surprised me. "I used to come to this place a lot when—" He stopped, trapped in a memory that still seemed painful for him. "When I thought I had no choice. I've never been so happy to be wrong," he sighed, his gaze melancholy.

"You would come here," I murmured, studying the sparkling walls. I imagined him all alone in that twinkling grotto, reflecting on our secret encounters in my dreams—reflecting on my death.

"I didn't understand what I was feeling. The emotions were too strong for me to ignore and I couldn't explain why I was suffering at the thought of having to—" He looked away, his fist clenched at his side. "I just wanted the pain to go away. Not understanding it made me desperate."

"Evan—"

"So I would come here, listen to the water, watch the gems sparkle, and try not to think about it, try to forget. But every time my light struck one of the diamonds, I would see your eyes reflected in it. It was torment. I was obsessed with you." There was anger in his face. For a moment I thought I saw his eyes glitter with unshed tears, as though the memory was still too painful for him. "I already loved you, I just needed to realize it," Evan said, smiling now to himself.

I slid my hand into his. He lifted his other hand, the one holding the flame, and the light rose into the air, floating above our heads and illuminating the cave. I resisted the urge to press my lips to his; I felt uncomfortable expressing my feelings in that place, as though it were forbidden, but Evan sensed my desire and came closer. I raised my chin, moving just in time to avoid his mouth as it sought mine.

"Don't go there. We'd better not attract too much attention," I said, sealing his lips with my finger. Although I was the one who'd done it, the refusal drove me wild and I couldn't tear my thoughts away from Evan's lips. All I wanted was to enjoy their soft fullness, their delicious fruity flavor as he moved them against mine and the whole world revolved around us.

He took another step toward me and our bodies touched. His tone became velvety, challenging my self-control. "You can't reject me like this," he whispered, stroking my lip with his thumb. "Come on, just one kiss," he whispered directly onto my mouth.

I stood there, paralyzed by his hot breath as the need to kiss him trembled under my skin. He moved toward me slowly but I pulled away at the last minute. "This is no place to sin. It's like being in church!" I stammered, dazed. "I would never kiss you in a church!"

I composed myself as Evan straightened up, unsatisfied but smiling. "At least let me give you a present." He raised his arm.

"What kind of present?" I asked, worried.

He drew a semicircle in the air over his head and lowered his closed hand. When he opened it, a speck of light sparkled on his palm. A diamond. An instant later I saw another sparkle appear on the rocky crust as a new diamond silently formed in its place as though created by the rock itself.

"Don't worry," Evan whispered, sensing my fear that someone would discover us. The diamond rose from his palm, dancing in the air, and floated toward me before my eyes. With a wave of his hand he guided it to my neck, from which hung the butterfly pendant on which he had engraved our names. I looked down to follow the diamond's movement and watched as it incrusted itself in the white gold.

"Evan—"

"Shh." He rested his finger on my lips and winked at me. "It'll be our secret."

I touched the cold, sharp-edged jewel that sparkled under my fingers. "I'm speechless, Evan. It's really too much."

"You could always find a way to show me your gratitude," he said provocatively, raising an eyebrow.

"You're so stubborn!" I tilted my head, holding his gaze. His face was right in front of mine.

"I've heard that before," he whispered, drawing his lips closer for a few electrifying seconds.

"It's a shame I'm even more stubborn than you," I said, stepping back and leaving him hanging. "Does Ginevra know about this place?"

His face turned unexpectedly serious. "She's a Witch. There's absolutely no way she could ever set foot in here. They would detect her presence immediately. All hell would break loose."

"That's too bad." I shrugged and moved toward the way out. "I'm sure she'd love it. She's crazy about sparkly things."

Evan snickered. "Yeah, she'd love it, all right. But instead of admiring the diamonds, I think Ginevra would spend hours staring at her reflection in them."

I laughed at his joke, but doubt gripped me as I glanced at the transparent curtain a few steps from us. "I know that at this point you're probably going to consider this a rhetorical question, but how do we get down from here?"

Evan looked at me with a raised eyebrow, hiding a grin that instantly struck panic into my heart.

"Oh . . . no," I whispered. My eyes widened. "You can't mean—" I stammered. I looked down, refusing to believe what I suspected he meant.

"Scared?" His challenging tone triggered a rebellious reaction inside me. "You're excited about the idea of jumping. I can feel it," he added, his tone even more mocking, his cunning gaze fixed on mine.

His remark triggered a vortex of confusion in my brain. Conflicting, indecipherable feelings rebelled in me, evolving and changing an instant before I could control them.

"You need to decide what to listen to, Gemma." Suddenly his voice sounded far away. "What's stronger?" A strange impulse tickled my skin. "Fear? Or—"

The impulse was stronger now and it drove me to react. Before Evan had finished his question, I succumbed to it and rushed past him.

"—excitement?"

My body hit the cold, crystal-clear wall of water as Evan's last word reached me. It hung in the air, conveying an equal mix of amazement and admiration. And then the void. The cool breeze caressed my skin as I fell through the air, surrendering to its comforting embrace.

Right behind me, Evan whooped with excitement.

"It's like flying!" I shouted, trying to make myself heard over the roar of the waterfall as we plunged down, almost gliding through the air. A surge of adrenaline shook me from within, its intensity matched only by the force of the water as it thundered down into the pool. We were so high up!

I felt light, free, as if the whole universe belonged to us.

Then, impact. The water enveloped me and carried my body up to the surface. It was pleasantly cool, slightly below room temperature, and my skin instantly adjusted to it.

I was still trembling from excitement as another sensation rose up inside me: wellbeing. A deep sense of peace spread over me as I floated just below the surface, drifting in the current. I bobbed up just a second before Evan resurfaced, shaking his wet hair. "Woohoo, was that awesome!" he shouted, swimming toward me.

The water was calm except for the spot, marked by churning white foam, where the waterfall plunged into it. Frightened by something moving below us, I flinched and jerked my feet up. I squinted through the water but couldn't make out what it was. "Are those fish?" I asked Evan, amazed. They didn't look at all like fish—I couldn't tell where one began and the other ended.

Evan laughed. "No, those are more diamonds." I admired them, fascinated by the kaleidoscope of color that wavered beneath us as Evan trod water next to me. "Here they're worth about as much as a flower. The lakebed is full of them and when light hits them they emit shafts of colored luminescence that blend together in the current." He stopped at my back, barely touching me. "Just like when you came into my colorless life." He breathed the words against my neck and I turned around, floating in front of him.

"They're beautiful," I whispered, looking down at them again.

The lights darted around in the water and I tried to follow them, fascinated. Streaks of cobalt blue merged with iridescent currents ranging from pink to purple to light green to orange. Shafts of pearly light that moved toward me, pushed by the current as though alive. I instinctively dodged to the side but Evan grabbed me from behind and held me tightly against him.

"Don't worry," he whispered into my ear. For a moment the water felt warmer. Then I noticed where the heat was coming from: me. I began to burn up whenever Evan held me against his body. He clasped my waist. "You're out of your mind, you know that?" he said, amused. "You jumped out of that cave. I didn't think you'd actually do it." My reaction had been so instinctive even Evan hadn't expected it.

"I made up my mind, like you told me to," I replied, extricating myself from his embrace to grin at him. I floated in the water, moving myself with one hand around his body, as if he were the fulcrum of some imaginary circle I was tracing.

"Looks like you made the right choice, then," he murmured, turning slowly to follow me. His eyes rested on mine. "Never let fear or insecurity make decisions for you." Something in his tone suggested he was talking about an entirely different subject. Darting toward me, he abruptly pulled me toward him, his hand against my back so I couldn't escape, and spoke softly, a fraction of an inch from my mouth, enunciating every word. *"Always follow your instinct."*

"That can be risky sometimes, don't you think?" I murmured, letting him hold me up in the water. I realized my voice had dropped to a low whisper, driven by the sensations the contact with his body was causing. It was a dangerous game. I stared at his mouth as it drew closer almost imperceptibly.

I swallowed, so spellbound I couldn't move, and he pressed his lips to mine.

"Risk is part of the game," he whispered. "You need to be willing to run risks or you'll never be able to say you're in command of your choices. Fear will take control of them instead. Never let it stop you." For a long moment his eyes lingered on my mouth and then he looked me in the eye again. "Never let your fear stand between you"—he brushed his lips against mine and I felt a world of emotion—"and what you want." His gaze was a mix of sweetness and naughtiness.

"I see you know exactly what I want." The words trembled in my throat. "You're pretty convincing."

Evan brushed his cheek against mine, claiming permission for what I'd denied him so long: a slow, sensual, incredibly tender kiss. I parted my lips and let his soft tongue gently touch mine as his full lips, wet from the water, enveloped my mouth.

My head spun. I loved him. I loved him with every fiber of my being. I could feel it even there, in that corner of heaven where my soul was more exposed than anywhere on earth. It didn't matter where I was—to me, Evan was the only world that existed.

11

MOON MAIDENS

"Why you—" I opened my mouth to protest, but then decided to bop Evan on the head instead. He laughed. We'd explored the lakebed, touched the diamonds lodged in the rocks and chased the shafts of light they emanated. We'd had splash fights. At first I'd only defended myself from Evan's attacks, but then a real battle had broken out. Now Evan had swum down in search of something. While I was waiting for him to return, listening to the stillness all around me, he suddenly popped up in front of me, giving me a start.

"Find what you were looking for?"

"I made sure everything was all right. Let's go."

"Where?"

Evan smiled. "To the most beautiful place you'll ever see."

"*This* is the most beautiful place I've ever seen!"

He held out his hand, his eyes alight with enthusiasm. "I'm going to change your mind."

"Why do I have the funny feeling I should say no?" I asked, recognizing the impish tone he used when teasing me.

Evan threw his head back and laughed. "I wasn't sure about showing it to you, but after that leap you took a little while ago I decided you might be brave enough," he said to provoke me, raising his eyebrow.

"Brave enough for *what*?"

"To cross the rocks beneath the waterfall. There's an underwater tunnel connecting the river to a little—"

My eyes opened wide. "What?! Forget it. I'm claustrophobic!"

Evan took my hand, a smile on his face, ignoring my concerns. I knew why: he could tell how much I longed to see the place.

"It's the only way to get there. It's not so narrow. It'll be worth it. Besides, I'll be there with you."

It was a good thing Peter and I had grown up playing in and around the lake. "Okay. But only if you stay close."

Evan ducked under the water, my hand still clasped in his, and pulled me down with him. *"Of course I'll stay close to you. You'll need air,"* he told me with his mind.

I came to an abrupt halt, releasing air from my lungs as I made sounds of protest. Evan grinned. He'd waited until we were underwater, when it was too late for me to turn back, to mention that detail.

"Don't waste your breath," he warned me telepathically. *"You need to ration it. Let out little puffs through your nose once in a while. That will make it last longer. I'll give you more when you need it. I'll be your personal air supply."*

Even though I could only hear his voice in my mind, I could still perceive his mocking tone. *How long do you plan to keep me underwater?* I wanted to ask, but couldn't. Evan laughed again at the funny expression I must have had on my face.

He motioned for me to follow him, diving so deep that the light above us disappeared and darkness swallowed us up. Before I had the chance to feel afraid, though, Evan's hand began to emit a soft glow. The sphere of light illuminated the way for us like a beacon. Suddenly I stopped, afraid I would run out of air.

Evan sensed what I was feeling and was instantly by my side. *"I'll give you some air,"* he told me with his mind. Stroking my neck, he sank his fingers into my hair and pulled me to him. *"When I exhale, take a deep breath and hold it in tight."*

I nodded. He put his lips to mine and blew. When he thought he'd given me enough air, he turned to move away, but I pulled him back against me, pointing to my mouth and putting my hands around my neck as if I were suffocating.

"You want more." He guessed what I was doing and smiled. *"All right, if it'll make you happy."* He came closer and this time kissed me passionately before giving me more air. *"How's that?"* Evan looked at me through the darkness illuminated only by the sphere of light and I smiled. Sensing my anxiety, he grabbed my hand and led me through the tunnel in the rocks. The walls seemed to be moving, as if they wanted to close in around me and crush me. I stifled the thought and closed my eyes. Having a panic attack without being able to breathe was something I wouldn't wish on anyone. But then Evan stroked my palm, making me feel safe.

"Hang in a little longer, babe. We're almost there."

I screwed up my courage as a glow in the distance lit up the darkness and the rocky passageway gradually widened. Fascinated, I admired the walls in the new light. They were studded with crystals, fused with multicolored rock and strange, glittering stalagmites.

A moment later we left the tunnel and emerged into a small lagoon. Even though we were still underwater it felt like I could breathe again. When we finally resurfaced, I couldn't believe my senses. I took a deep breath and quivered with pleasure. The water was hot. I dunked my head, smiling at the pleasurable warmth.

"You never told me there were hot springs in heaven," I said. Something occurred to me and my eyes shot open wide. "There isn't a volcano around here, is there?"

Evan laughed. "Nope, no volcano."

"Then why is the water so hot?"

"That's exactly what I want to show you. Come with me."

We swam to shore. The delightful little lagoon was ringed by waterfalls and slabs of pink limestone. The water was so clear I could see the rocky floor, composed almost entirely of diamonds except for some strange, spherical, red stones that glowed softly.

"Come on," Evan said, coaxing me out of the water. I followed him, laughing in excitement like a little girl. Onshore, I turned in a circle, fascinated by everything there was to see. The lagoon was a pearly shell set amid an expanse of gorgeous ruby-red flowers that extended in all directions like a mantle. No. They weren't flowers. They were strange stemless mushrooms that swayed gently, the same ones I'd seen underwater.

"Save a little enthusiasm for later," Evan said, grinning. I closed my mouth, only realizing just now that I'd been gaping. He guided me through giant rock archways hung with red vines into what appeared to be a forest. For a moment it felt like we were back in the woods in Lake Placid, but then something up in a tree sparkled, bringing me back to reality—or better said, back to the dream.

Evan had stopped and was looking at me, waiting to see my reaction. We were in the center of a circle of trees. I was left speechless. This had to be the surprise he had mentioned before we crossed from one world into the other.

"Like it?" he asked, his eyes as excited as a child's.

Ruby-colored mushrooms grew upward in a spiral around each tree trunk, forming an artificial stairway. From time to time they glowed, pulsing with their own light. Then a melody broke the silence, a gentle *oooh . . . oooh* followed by a breath of warm air.

The sudden change in temperature made me shiver. "What was that?" I asked.

"It was them, the moon maidens."

"I thought they were mushrooms."

Evan laughed. "No. They're spirits of fire and air. They're heavenly creatures."

"Oh! Sorry," I murmured to them, embarrassed, and in reply they glowed one after the other.

"Moon maidens." I stepped over and touched one. It moved, let out a melodious sound and sent a puff of warm air onto my face. Meanwhile, Evan had leaned down to pick some flowers. "What are you doing?" I asked, watching as flowers grew back in the spot where he'd picked them.

"Watch." He opened his palm, showing me the little red blossoms, and stood there, listening.

"What—"

He rested his finger on my lips and the air filled with the melodious sound again: *Oooh . . . oooh . . .*

A current of warm air wafted the flowers from Evan's open palm and the petals scattered, whirling higher and higher overhead until they disappeared. For a moment I had the impression the sky above us rippled, drawing the petals into it.

"How beautiful," I whispered. "So *they're* what's doing it. It was them in the lagoon, too. That's why the water was so warm. It's the mushrooms emitting the heat!"

"Moon maidens," he said, correcting me.

"Oh, right. It's such a funny name. Why are they called that?"

"Because they emit minute pink and silver particles that sparkle, just like the ones given off by the moon."

I turned to look at the huge moon. It dominated the sky, lighting up the air with its colors.

"They say God was so entranced by the moon that she offered Him the gift of her handmaidens, celestial creatures that populated her, on the condition that He allow her to watch over them. That's why the moon is so much bigger here than she is from earth. But that's just a legend." Evan took my hand and led me to the center of the circle of trees. "I've got an idea." He walked away and came back with a moon maiden that pulsed in his hands with soft light.

"Evan—"

He stood behind me and let me be the one to hold it as he swept my hair behind my ear and I shivered at the touch of his breath.

"Make a wish," he whispered.

I closed my eyes as the echo of his words reached my heart. Together we held up the moon maiden, waiting for the fascinating creatures to make the sound that announced the puff of warm air. When we heard it, we let it go. The maiden lit up, floated into the air and disappeared, carrying my wish with it.

"That was incredible," I exclaimed softly.

Behind me, Evan moved his lips to my ear. "Now it's our turn," he murmured.

I frowned and he slowly raised my arms. "Ready?" He grabbed me around the waist and before I knew it our feet were a handspan above the ground. Another breath and the maidens sent forth their melody, blowing one after the other, as we rose higher, twirling in a circle. The long chains of maidens in the trees and their puffs of warm air created a vortex that pushed us ever higher until we were twenty feet above the ground.

I looked up, hoping to discover how the flowers had disappeared. Overhead, above the perfect ring of trees, there was a layer of water instead of sky. When I reached up to touch it, its surface rippled.

"It's a wishing well," Evan murmured behind me.

"Seriously?" I asked, excited.

Evan laughed. "No, but it might be for us."

All of a sudden the current of warm air keeping us aloft ceased and we plummeted to the ground. I landed in Evan's arms. He stared at me for a long moment before setting me down.

"And he continued to gaze at her, enchanted," he whispered. "Of all the creatures in heaven, she was the most extraordinary."

"Only because he was looking at her through his heart," I said.

"It was his eyes that looked at her and not his heart. He no longer had a heart, because she'd taken it from him as a keepsake, making him her prisoner."

"And you will continue to be my prisoner," I murmured, biting his lip, "because I have no intention of letting you go." I rubbed my nose against his and gazed at him intently. He could read inside me, but I didn't need to probe his soul to know how excited he was to be showing me all these wonders.

"Let's go," he said. "I can't wait for you to see some of the other places."

12

PROMISES

We reached a cave from the mouth of which a waterfall tumbled hundreds of feet through rings of rock located at different heights. We walked along a rocky path, climbing toward the top of what looked like a natural skyscraper. Fascinated, I stared at red-leafed trees that grew upside down, their branches reaching toward us. As we made our way along the path I heard the sound of falling water that gradually became closer and more deafening. When we finally reached the small summit I teetered and clung to Evan for support. The rocky ledge we were on broke off abruptly, plunging into the void as if we'd reached the limit of the world. Curiosity drove me on to the edge and I discovered where the sound of falling water was coming from. I held my breath as I saw below us a vast city all of alabaster. An infinite series of waterfalls flowed from the mountain into the river surrounding the city.

Evan looked at me, curious to see my reaction. The giant alabaster palaces towered over everything, streams of water flowing through them and small waterfalls pouring from their windows.

"What is this place?" I murmured, amazed.

"Come with me. I'll show you."

I stared at the waterfalls thundering down. "How do we get there?" I asked, afraid to hear the answer.

Evan nodded at a large tree trunk that lay among the rocks. "We'll ride down on that, but you'll have to hold on tight." My eyes went wide with terror and he laughed out loud. "Just kidding! There's a path." He winked at me and led me by the hand down a stairway carved into the rock that passed behind the waterfalls. For the first time I was grateful he'd only been teasing me; Evan was capable of anything.

We reached the bottom and I realized I'd been wrong. It wasn't alabaster. The city that rose from the water was made of unrefined diamond, so opaque it looked white. From below, the buildings looked even more majestic. Surreal waterfalls flowed here and there, reflecting the glow from the enormous moon above. A light mist cast a mysterious halo on everything, making the atmosphere gothic. I recognized features from different eras. Bridges with spires and pinnacles stood on rocks protruding from the water. Overhead was a statue of a dragon with its wings spread. I remembered seeing something vaguely like it when we'd studied French gothic cathedrals at school. In the distance atop tall, tall pillars were two more giant statues of lions that seemed to be guarding something. The buildings were of different sizes. The larger ones looked like sixteenth-century baptisteries complete with surrounding colonnades and Michelangelo-style cupolas, while the smaller ones had more Asian-looking domes. One in particular caught my eye. It was smaller than all the others and looked like a wedding gazebo, ivy-covered with carved floral motifs.

"We call this place Diamantea, the Celestial City," Evan explained. "Some simply call it the City. We don't really know what it's for. It's not small, but it can't be home to many souls, and it's the only building complex in all heaven. We think it's a place where souls meet, go for walks, or spend time together. This is where we appear when we cross over for the first time."

"Does the same thing go for mortal souls?"

"I think so but I'm not sure. No Subterranean knows. We can only guess. We help souls cross over, but once we get here our senses can't perceive them any more. There. That's the spot where I appeared." He pointed to his right at a roofless colonnade that reminded me of an arena.

I tried to imagine Evan in this place, lost and alone, but I couldn't visualize him any way other than the way I knew him: fearless and confident. Suddenly I started and spun around, alarmed. "Did you see that too?" A shiver lingered in my spine; for a second I thought I'd seen a shadow.

"There's nothing here, Gemma. Relax," Evan reassured me, sensing how nervous I was.

The city was both enchanting and eerie to me, knowing as I did that at this very moment hundreds, maybe thousands, of other souls filled the palaces that to our eyes appeared empty. Knowing that this was probably the spot souls from all over the world went after death.

"It's not a good idea to stay here," I murmured grimly. "Let's go."

"Okay," Evan said. "Let's go."

I took his hand and followed him. Not far away I glimpsed what looked like a cave covered with purple ivy suspended over the river at the edge of Diamantea. It turned out to be a natural passageway made of plants and artistically interwoven vines, a tunnel of lavender flowers.

I let go of Evan's hand and hurried to it, laughing. The scent was intoxicating. I turned toward him and opened my arms wide. "God, this place is enchanting!" My voice echoed with a strange melodic effect and I clapped my hand over my mouth. Evan held a finger to his lips. I crouched down, peering through the branches at the water that flowed beneath the tunnel. The world all around us was lilac-colored.

Delightful interlaced flowers covered everything, their shape like nothing I'd ever seen on earth. They were round and so full they looked like they were about to burst, but one end had a sort of doubled-over neck. I breathed in their scent and stood up. "I would love to lie down here and read for hours on end," I told him dreamily.

"Read me instead," Evan dared me, a roguish glint in his eyes.

I clasped the pendant I always wore and touched the stone Evan had given me, my diamond. It was still unfamiliar to my touch, but knowing it was there warmed my heart. Evan sensed this thought and held me close, pressing me back against the wall of flowers. He nuzzled my neck as if the scent were coming from me, then brushed his nose against my ear, sending a shiver down my back. "Did you know," he asked, "that when a male penguin chooses a mate, he scours the whole beach in search of the perfect stone to offer her? If she accepts it, they stay together for life."

"Are you saying you're a penguin?" I joked, even though he was so close it left me dazed, but he remained serious and kissed me right below the ear.

"I'm saying I've chosen you," he whispered.

I stroked the gem as a shiver spread his warmth through me. "Then I accept your stone." Suspecting that Evan was on the verge of forgetting where we were, I rested my hand on his upper arm to remind him.

"Don't stop me," he protested. "This is the tunnel of love."

"How would you know?" A smile escaped me.

"But it's true! Enamored souls come here and swear their eternal love for each other."

"You can't know that," I reminded him. He was teasing me, but it was a game I didn't dislike in the least.

Evan rested his hands on either side of my head, blocking my way. "Look, I'm the expert here," he insisted. He leaned in to kiss me, but I slipped under his arm and ran down the tunnel, unable to hold back the laughter that produced a strange echo.

"Where are you going?" he scolded, laughing as he chased me. I kept running. "Come back here! I still have to show you the surprise."

I stopped in my tracks and turned to look at him as a sly smile spread across his face.

13

SECRETS REVEALED

"What, do you mean that wasn't the surprise? But you said—" I was confused.

Evan led the way, quickly climbing a steep promontory. "I never said it was." He cast me a sidelong glance, grinning.

My wet clothes clung to my skin, but the warm air lessened the discomfort. My legs seemed to be holding out well though we'd been walking for hours now. How many, I couldn't say. I'd completely lost track of time, among other things, and the fact that the moonlight hadn't changed since we'd arrived didn't help me gain my bearings.

We'd walked across bridges of intertwined branches and crossed the river below them inside a giant water lily, blue streaked with silver, that had immediately closed over our heads. Evan had seized the opportunity to try to kiss me, but I'd dodged his every attempt, jostling the flower, which had begun to emit a soft glow, as if ticklish. We'd climbed rocks so high I had the urge to fly. Finally I glimpsed a pinkish sky beyond us, revealing that the peak was near. A rich floral scent filled my nostrils at all times. A breath of air caressed my hair and when I looked up, a shiver ran down my arms. I wasn't sure whether it had been caused by the gentle breeze or the breathtaking view that had opened up in front of me. I held my breath as the entire valley revealed itself to my eyes in all its glory.

An incredible, primeval glory.

Nature bloomed in splendid profusion, painting a surreal landscape whose colors and shapes formed a harmonious whole. Yet the valley contained something even more magnificent that held sway over everything else and riveted my attention. Despite the distance I grasped its vital essence as it stood tall, challenging the sky, towering over all the rest, ruling all that surrounded it. Majestic. Eternal. Ancient.

"The tree of life," I whispered, almost without realizing it.

"And of the knowledge of good and evil," Evan said.

Still mesmerized, I sensed a movement to my right and jumped when I saw two beautiful, tawny-furred creatures grazing on the red grass. They had thick lion's manes and two thin horns that curved back toward their long tails. They looked like big, prehistoric dogs. Then I remembered: these were the same creatures depicted in some of the statues in the celestial city. Evan went over to the two animals and one of them bowed before him, allowing him to stroke its fur.

"Tyadons are shy but loyal creatures that are always found in pairs. It's said that God placed the breath of life of one of them in the other so nothing could separate them and then sent them to earth to protect mankind. But then it was discovered that if one of them died, the other lost its *prana*, the spirit that dwelled within it. The battle for survival led to their extinction so God—seeing man's cruelty—decided to keep them for Himself," Evan explained. He laughed and leapt onto the tyadon's back.

I opened my eyes wide. "Oh no . . ."

Evan looked at me as if he'd just climbed onto a scooter instead of a giant prehistoric dog-lion. "We need a ride," he said, shrugging and smiling to himself. Before I could reply, he nudged the animal with his heel. It took off at a gallop, but he stopped it a few yards away. "You going to take much longer?" he joked, turning back to look at me.

I pressed my lips together, not about to give in, and quickly climbed onto the other animal. Once I'd mounted it I wasn't sure how to ride it. I grabbed its horns, which were spread out like handlebars on a motorcycle, but the tyadon shook its head, seeming annoyed, so I wound my hands in its thick mane, hoping I wasn't hurting it.

"I'd hang on tight if I were you," Evan warned me a second before the air was sucked from my lungs. The landscape became a blur and my brain finally caught up: my animal had shot off behind the one Evan was riding and we were racing like the wind. Their steps alternated rapidly, barely touching the ground, and at times they leapt so far forward I wasn't sure they couldn't fly. It was an electrifying, otherworldly experience. Racing at two hundred miles an hour on Evan's motorcycle had never left me as breathless as I was now, even though Evan controlled the air around us so I wouldn't suffocate. It was an indescribable thrill I knew I could never get used to.

I opened my eyes again when the air stopped lashing my skin. My animal had come to a halt right behind Evan's. I dismounted carefully, not because I was afraid I'd fall but because all my attention was riveted on what my eyes beheld. The colors were so intense they dazzled me. I looked up but couldn't see the sky. The tree towered over everything.

A mighty network of interlaced trunks rose majestically into the sky. The branches swooped down in dense and impenetrable arrangements, snaking across the ground. It was almost impossible to believe that the tree was a single living organism.

I looked at the opalescent, unusually colored leaves that clothed its branches. My neck craned, I swiveled and peered toward the sky. Silvery light winked through the sparse gaps among the leaves.

"It's so . . ." No matter how hard I tried, it was impossible to find words.

"Ancient?" Evan suggested.

"Magnificent. I feel its energy," I told him. A steady tingling coursed through me from head to toe.

"Is this how you imagined it?" Evan already knew my answer. There in that place, I was an open book to him.

"Not with all these colors," I admitted, fascinated by the incredible hues that covered it. Evan chuckled and for some reason I had the impression he was laughing at me again. A moment later, he pursed his lips. A soft melodious sound like a gentle whistle issued from his mouth and I started when a dense shadow moved over our heads. I looked up in alarm and my breath caught in my throat.

Butterflies.

His whistle had stirred them. Countless butterflies, as big as my hand, had risen into the air, leaving the trunks on which they'd been resting. The sky was filled with their incredible colors: red, purple, deepest blue, amber, even bright pink; opalescent shades that blended together to create new ones. The sight left me breathless.

Watching their colorful wings flutter around us, I tried not to make a sound that might scare them away. As they passed, a delicate floral fragrance lingered in the air, the same one I'd perceived in the distance. It was an irresistible scent.

Now that the leaves were uncovered and the tree stood before my eyes in its true form, I glimpsed the round shapes that grew from its branches like golden flowers.

"Is that . . ." My voice trailed off. I was awestruck.

"The fruit." Evan looked at me. "The one Eve ate despite being forbidden to do so." A shadow of sadness clouded his face, taking me by surprise. "The same one I'm forced to eat in order to survive," he added, trying to hide his bitterness.

Fascinated, I moved closer to the amber fruit. It was streaked with red, the color of pomegranates. I reached out but Evan's shoulders instantly stiffened and his face tensed. The message was clear: I wasn't allowed to touch them. I suppressed the urge though the yearning to give in to the temptation writhed under my skin.

An intricate network of veins ran along the branches, extending into the fruit as if they were one and the same. Though I knew it was impossible, it almost seemed to be pulsing, beckoning to me like a beating heart. The longing to touch the fruit washed over me and suddenly, holding it in my hands became the only thing that mattered. It smelled so good . . . It dawned on me that it wasn't the butterflies. The scent was emanating from the tree itself. The power it held over me was fascinating and frightening in equal parts.

"Gemma." Evan snapped me out of my trance, concern in his voice.

"It seems alive." As if hypnotized, I moved closer, feeling I could lose myself in this desire.

"Don't touch it." His tone was cautious and he was clearly trying to hide his nervousness.

I shook my head to dispel the urge clouding my mind and tried to focus on something else. "How is it you're 'forced' to eat it? What do you mean?" I asked.

"It might seem paradoxical to you, but it's one of the punishments my race has to endure."

"I wouldn't call it a punishment." I smiled. "I mean, it can't be so terrible. It looks scrumptious." I couldn't take my eyes off the fruit, as if it were absorbing my essence. It was almost like it could control me.

"It is. We only feed off its juice: ambrosia. Its taste is soft to the palate, creamy, rich, and intense on the tongue, an explosion of flavors that makes everything else taste bland. Its juice strengthens us and nourishes our souls and our powers. But without it—" His gaze grew hard, his tone grave. "No Subterranean would live for long. And death is a long, painful process. First it drains you of your powers." His eyes were unfocused, trained on some distant spot as if reliving a memory. "Then your strength, until you disappear entirely."

"That doesn't sound fun." I bit my lip.

"It isn't. Other souls, pure ones without the curse in their blood, are immortal and don't need anything to preserve their immortality. But for us it's a constant struggle for survival. Eve's transgression left us with a high price to pay, a burden for anyone who has the blood of the Subterraneans running through their veins. That's why we receive her mark, so none of us forget it."

"It's not so terrible," I repeated in an attempt to cheer him up. My throat was dry and I was consumed with the desire to taste the flavor of ambrosia.

"You don't know what you're talking about," he said severely. "In the beginning it is. It's beyond terrible, in fact." His gaze turned inward, lost in the distant memory. "We're put to the test from the start." A veil of painful memories descended over his eyes.

"Try to describe it," I said.

"You already know what happens when a mortal's life ends: a Subterranean comes to save them and bring their soul here so it won't get lost and no one else can claim it. But there's no one waiting for my kind. We're left alone, adrift, helpless. Forgotten. Hidden." His gaze darkened as he struggled against the bitter memory.

"'That which has been hidden from me will be hidden from the world,'" I murmured, thinking of the story Evan had told me—the punishment God had given Eve for hiding the children she hadn't yet bathed in the river. Water represented purification and, fearful of God and His power, she hadn't wanted to show him the children who hadn't been purified yet.

The same water I swam in. A shiver ran through me.

"No one comes to help a Subterranean when his mortal life ends, but a Witch is there to try to tempt and kill him. If he manages to survive that first trial, his soul wanders aimlessly, ignorant of the fact that he needs to eat of the tree to survive, for months, until his strength begins to diminish. And while his soul is growing weaker, the Witch is waiting for a second chance. She watches the Angel from afar, ready to steal his soul in exchange for promises which at that point the Angel can't refuse."

"But why do Witches long so intensely for your souls? What sense does it make?"

"We're not their real objective. *You* are." I shivered as he fixed me with a piercing gaze. "Imagine if they managed to get rid of us. Imagine if they killed all of us. There wouldn't be anyone left to help mortals travel here and their souls would be lost to evil. They would belong to it. It would be the end," he murmured, staring into space. "The end of everything."

Another shiver, colder and sharper. "You were right. It is terrible," I whispered, my voice trembling.

Evan smiled. "But that will never happen. They kill a lot of us, but they'll never manage to exterminate us all."

"Why bother killing you if you disappear anyway for lack of nourishment?"

"Killing a new Subterranean right away lowers the risk that he'll be found and helped to grow stronger. But that's just one of the reasons. Witches are capricious creatures and the Children of Eve are tempting prey."

"How do you find out what it is you need to survive?" I asked, more and more curious.

"Chance. Pure chance. If you're lucky, you run across another Subterranean to guide you before it's too late. No one else cares about us. It's only when an Angel eats the supreme fruit for the first time that he's officially recognized by the members of the Brotherhood and begins to receive orders in his mind. It's a sort of natural selection process. Learning to break down the barriers between the two worlds is too complex an operation for someone to do on their own. That's why your souls need us. Moving from one dimension to the other is a delicate undertaking. You need to know how to breach certain barriers without disturbing the balance."

"From the way you describe it, becoming a Subterranean must have been a painful experience for you."

"You can't imagine how painful." His voice was a murmur of sadness.

"But if it's all a question of descent, shouldn't your parents have been like you?" I asked.

"That's what I thought too, but evidently not. There's no handbook that explains the secrets that connect us to each other, and no Subterranean realizes what he is until his mortal existence comes to an end. My parents were mortal; I saw them grow old and die. I expected them to join me, but it didn't happen. It's like the gene is active only in some of us. Actually, I only saw their lifeless bodies. I was even deprived of my chance to say a final farewell because when it happened I was on a mission and didn't get back until they'd passed away."

"How terrible! But why didn't you ignore the orders? It meant so much to you."

"I've never broken the rules," he replied, his expression solemn.

"For me you did." Evan locked his gaze on mine, a tender smile hiding behind his eyes. "You said you had to come across another Subterranean to survive. Who was it that found you? Who saved you?"

Evan smiled as he sat down on a large branch that reached almost all the way down to the grassy ground and invited me to join him. Casting me a sidelong glance through his long eyelashes, he said, "It doesn't always happen like that. At least it didn't for me. In fact, it *should* have, but let's say my case was the exception that proves the rule."

I stared at him uneasily, waiting for him to go on.

"I didn't know who I was any more, what I'd become. It was like I'd been returned to the primordial human condition. I was famished but my instinct wasn't strong enough to help me find food. I went weeks without eating and had no strength left. Ginevra's the one I owe everything to. She's the one who found me. She saved my soul and that's why I'll always be in her debt."

"Ginevra? You were saved by a Witch?! I thought Witches were out to kill you! Wasn't she supposed to?"

He smiled at all the questions I'd bombarded him with. "Fortunately she'd already met Simon, though at that point she hadn't betrayed her Sisters yet. Simon and Ginevra would meet secretly and she was making a huge effort to keep the others from finding out about their relationship. She had to learn to control her thoughts so she wouldn't be discovered because all Witches have telepathic powers, including her Sisters. They communicate with each other through their minds. You have no idea how powerful the bond among them is—it's almost impossible to break."

"But she broke hers for Simon," I contradicted, searching for answers.

"That's true, but it wasn't easy for her, and there's no saying it's permanent. She managed because there's only one thing stronger than the power of evil and the bond that unites Witches: love. True, pure love . . . like ours," he whispered, squeezing my hand. "When Ginevra found me, I was close to death, on the point of vanishing entirely. Ginevra's relationship with Simon had made her more compassionate." For a moment I had the impression he was lost in that memory which almost didn't belong to him. "When she discovered that her Sisters were keeping their eye on me, preparing to attack me, it was a difficult decision for her but in the end she took me to Simon, who immediately had me eat of the tree. It took weeks for me to recover. Since then, we've all been together. We've become inseparable, a family. Although," he said, smiling to himself, "living with Ginevra can be pretty weird sometimes. All that pomp and luxury!"

"Yeah, right, sheer torture!" I said, nudging him with my shoulder.

"We don't need all that, actually, but for her it's fundamental. Just because she broke the bond with her Sisters doesn't mean she's less of a Witch. She uses her powers now to satisfy her whims. She can manipulate any material object simply by controlling it with her mind. Her power," he said, pointing at his temple, "is all right here, in her head. Ginevra can have anything she wants."

"Is this where I say I feel sorry for you? Forgive me, but I can't."

Evan laughed. "No, you don't have to. I never said I dislike it—I just said we don't need all that. Not that it's not nice."

"Nice?" I teased him again. *Nice* seemed like an understatement.

"All right, I can't complain. I must admit I got used to it pretty quick," he added, chuckling. "Living with a Witch has its advantages in the end. I know she seems tough, but she's actually really thoughtful toward us."

"And what can you tell me about Drake?" I asked.

"He showed up a lot later on."

"And your trio became a quartet."

He looked me straight in the eye and his expression softened. "But only now, since you've arrived, can we consider our family complete." Hearing those words filled me with warmth. It was nice to feel like an integral part of their family. "You are," Evan said, replying to my thoughts. "We all think so, you know. You're one of us. You always were for them, from the moment they realized how much you meant to me. Especially Ginevra. I didn't expect her to bond with you so strongly. You'd be amazed to know how much. She probably sees in you the reflection of the Sisters she had to abandon."

The bittersweet thought made me frown. I felt deeply connected to Ginevra too, as if we were sisters, and for the first time I realized everyone could see our bond.

Evan jumped off the branch, startling me.

"Is it time to go?" I asked, almost regretfully. A primitive instinct made me breathe in the fragrant air, to engrave its scent in my mind. Not far from the tree the river I'd first seen at the base of the waterfall flowed slowly, filling me with nostalgia.

Evan stopped and faced me while I was still sitting on the branch. He rested his hands on my knees and I took them in mine. His voice filled my head, soft and velvety. *"I want to make you my promise here,"* he told me, his lips perfectly still and his eyes locked on mine.

"What promise?" I asked, my voice coming out in a squeak.

"This tree is sacred. I can't imagine a better witness," he went on without answering my question.

"Evan, what—"

"Don't worry. I just want you to know what I feel for you."

"I already know what you feel for me, and I feel the same."

"No, let me finish," he insisted, his eyes probing mine as he took my hand and turned it over gently, as if afraid to break it. He stroked my palm and raised it to his chest. "You can't feel my heart."

I looked at him, confused.

"But I can. I feel it pulsing inside me whenever you look my way, whenever you breathe." His tone was so intense and tender I couldn't say anything. His expression tuned serious, his eyes filling with awareness. "I know that what I do scares you. I'm not perfect, Gemma, even if you think I am. But when I'm with you I feel like I am because I don't need anything else." His eyes burned into mine, filling me with emotions I'd never felt before. "I would be nothing if I lost you. I've known that since I realized the love I feel for you. You can't know you're incomplete until you find your other half. Alone I'm worthless. I'm just a broken soul, an unfinished painting, a starless sky. And what's the sky without its stars?"

"Evan—"

"It's a giant black hole. Like I would be without you," he said, cutting me off. "I don't want to tell you I love you—the word is so overused it's lost its meaning in your century and I'm afraid you wouldn't understand the magnitude of the feeling I'm trying to describe to you. No, it wouldn't express enough. What you need to believe is that I'm a part of you as much as you are of me. You're here inside me. Always remember that," he whispered, squeezing my hand on his chest.

I smiled at his tenderness and leaned against him. "And you're inside me," I agreed.

"Kiss me," he ordered me in his mind, his gaze sensual and commanding.

I widened my legs, allowing Evan to move in closer. He slid his hands around my waist, rested his hips against mine and kissed me. I forgot everything but his lips on mine, even where we were. His kiss made heaven and earth move for me and I was swept up into an infinite sky studded with stars.

"Hold me close," he whispered in my mind. I felt an urgent need to look him in the eye. I didn't want it to end, I didn't want to go back. "We can't stay here forever. It's risky," he said, trying to convince me.

"If we must." I resigned myself to the idea of leaving.

The tingle filled me again, and again it felt as if the world were revolving around us, as if Evan and I were at the center of a vortex that would have pulled me in if I'd opened my eyes. In a matter of seconds everything became stable again.

I opened my eyes, squinting cautiously at the walls of Evan's room as a frightening feeling of anxiety rose in my stomach. Now that heaven was far away again, only the memory of a waking dream, the seriousness of what we'd just done burst on me in all its gravity. After all, who was I to have a secret like that revealed to me?

"Maybe we overdid it this time," I whispered to Evan, but the sound of the door opening drowned out my words, startling me.

Standing in the doorway, Ginevra and Simon stared at us, puzzled.

"Why are you guys all wet?" Simon asked, frowning.

Evan tried to hide a smile. Ginevra raised an eyebrow. "Don't get too used to breaking the rules, you guys," she warned us, making Evan and me exchange a complicit look. He still couldn't wipe the grin off his face.

"It's really frustrating to always be the last one to know what's going on," Simon grumbled.

My eye distractedly fell on the alarm clock. It read 5:01. How was that possible? "Evan, there's something wrong with your clock," I pointed out.

He laughed, looking amused. "It works fine," he whispered into my ear. "It's just that where we were, time doesn't exist. I'll explain later." I blinked nervously as I took in what he'd just said.

The impatience in Ginevra's voice brought me back to the room. "You owe me something and I've come to demand it," she told Evan. "If you win, I'll give you an R8," she said persuasively.

"Thanks, but cars are like girls: once you find the right one, having lots of them doesn't matter." Evan winked at me with a little laugh.

"Speak for yourself!" Simon said. "I want an R8!"

I smiled, but Evan wasn't giving in. He spoke in a mock-threatening tone. "If you want victory, you'll have to earn it." He sought approval in my eyes.

"You can't put it off any longer," I encouraged him, despite myself.

"Okay, okay." He waved his hand in resignation.

Ginevra's face lit up with a satisfied look. "Careful you don't catch fire. I've heard that under extreme conditions your little toy tends to overheat," she warned him in a seductive tone, referring to his Ferrari but poorly concealing a clear double entendre. "Seems to be a pretty sticky problem."

"I've already modified the fastening of the bulkhead that protects the wheel well from the heat of the exhaust manifolds, but thanks for the heads-up." Evan exchanged looks with Ginevra and then focused his attention on me, his gaze softening. "Coming with me?"

"Or you could come with me," Ginevra said, raising a superior eyebrow. "Waiting for the others at the finish line is always more fun."

I shook my head with a smile. "I'd rather wait here if you don't mind," I replied, still in a daze.

Evan nodded and turned to Simon. "Drake?"

"I just left him in the workout room. We were going to fight but Ginevra insisted."

"Only because I want a witness there when I make him eat my dust." She narrowed her eyes at Evan and then cast a sly glance at me. "Don't worry. I'll bring him back to you in no time," she assured me, her smile captivating.

"Make sure he's still in one piece when you do!" I admonished her as they all walked out the door.

"Can't promise you that!" she shouted from the hall.

Once silence reigned in the room again I lay down on Evan's bed and realized I was hungry. All that adrenaline had whetted my appetite, leaving me with the urgent need to munch on something. I went down to the kitchen, explored every compartment of the fridge, and pulled out some strawberry ice cream. I spread it on a slice of bread I'd already covered with Nutella. Thick and thin. Hot and cold. The combination had an explosive flavor that Evan thought was as interesting as it was bizarre. I called it *Strawtella.* Ginevra loved it.

Grabbing an apple from the fruit basket on the table, I sank my teeth into its shiny, crunchy surface. For some strange reason I felt like I hadn't eaten in days. When I was done I opened one of the upper cabinets, still looking for food.

All at once I felt a tingle beneath my skin. A cold shiver. Someone was there with me, I could sense it. I whirled around and my heart skipped a beat when I saw him right in front of me.

"Drake!" I gasped, breathless from fright. Evan's brother had appeared behind me so unexpectedly. "You almost gave me a heart attack. What are you doing here?" I asked, still uneasy but happy it was only Drake.

He had a serious look on his face, his expression unusually wary. "You alone?" he asked, no expression in his voice, tilting his head to the side.

"Yeah," I said, confused. "Evan went out with Simon and Ginevra. I don't think they'll be long. In fact, they're probably already on their way back." I blinked nervously, unable to figure out why he was staring at me so steadily. He seemed to be studying me. I'd never seen this look in Drake's eyes before. I felt my cheeks flush and looked away, uncomfortable. "Um . . . Sh-shouldn't you be at my place? Evan said you owed him a favor."

My question seemed to confuse him and he hesitated before answering. "My presence wasn't needed any more," he said coldly, reminding me that my parents must have gone back to work. He stared straight into my eyes, making me feel even more embarrassed, then looked up at something behind me.

Puzzled, I turned around, but nothing was there. "Drake, what—" I stopped dead and the words hung in the air in the empty room.

Drake had vanished.

I shook my head, bewildered, as the sound of voices came from the front door. "You're back," I murmured, trying to overcome my embarrassment. Finding myself alone with Drake had never made me uncomfortable before. It must have been something in the way he'd looked at me. With Simon it was different—he had Ginevra. Drake, on the other hand, was the only one of the three brothers who didn't have a girlfriend. I was aware of this, of course, but it had never bothered me until I'd seen it in his eyes.

"Were you talking to someone?" Evan asked, curious.

"Wasn't Drake supposed to take your place?" Ginevra had already read the thoughts crowding my mind.

"I asked him that myself. Seems he had something else to do, I guess." I glanced shyly at Evan who was leaning his arm against the doorframe, a victorious look on his face. "He came looking for you," I explained. "He probably needed to tell you something."

"So why didn't he wait?" he asked, looking perplexed.

"Maybe it wasn't so important," I stammered.

"Mmm, delicious!" Ginevra groaned with pleasure. She'd sunk her teeth into my slice of bread spread with Strawtella. She opened her eyes again as we stared at her. "What?!"

I laughed and took the bread out of her hands, earning an aggrieved look from her. "Well? How'd it go? The race, I mean."

"How do you think it went?" Ginevra sounded satisfied, but her tone of voice clashed with the triumphant gleam in Evan's eyes. I shot him a sidelong glance and he winked at me with a sly little smile he didn't even try to hide.

Ginevra went over to him and whispered in his ear: "What did I tell you?" He stared at her steadily, the grin still painted on his face. "What does dust taste like, little brother?" She shot me a glance, looking pleased. "He's all yours now," she said, walking out of the kitchen.

I followed Evan up to his room. "You let her win," I said in a low voice when he closed the door and I was sure we couldn't be heard.

"I had to, otherwise she never would have left me alone. She was starting to get on my nerves. She's good, I'll admit it, but the road is my domain." He raised an eyebrow, a proud look on his face.

"Let's hear it for modesty!" I cheered sardonically.

"There's a subtle difference between arrogance and self-confidence," he said with conviction.

"If you say so. Anyway, how'd you manage to hide your intentions from her?" I asked, curious.

"You underestimate me. I can influence her thoughts with my powers. All I had to do was convince her of my sincerity."

"Shrewd."

"Pushing it, you mean! But she gave me no choice. At least for a while she'll stop trying to compete with me constantly."

"I wouldn't be so sure about that." I glanced at him and his expression turned mysterious.

"I think the winner deserves a prize," he whispered, approaching me. "Don't you?"

"Are you sure? Because in that case I'll have to call Ginevra. Technically *she* won the race," I teased, stepping back as Evan inched toward me, seeking contact. I took another step back and came into contact with the desk. Helpless, I stood there, trapped, as Evan kept moving toward me until our bodies touched.

"Technically," he whispered, his gaze locked onto mine. He brushed his nose against my cheek, grabbed me firmly by the hips and thrust me against the desk. "That means I'll just have to take what I deserve," he whispered in my ear.

The heat of his words ignited the fire inside me. The flames rose under his dark, seductive gaze until they consumed every inch of me. Evan lingered, his hot breath tickling my skin as he pushed me up against the desk in an attempt to intensify our contact, forcing my legs open wider. His hands pulled me against him, closing the distance between us. The contact was so passionate and intense it shook me, igniting my desire. A shiver swept down my back and fire filled my head. Every part of me was begging for him not to stop.

Evan grabbed the back of my head with primal urgency and raised his mouth from my neck to my lips. His ragged breathing mingled with mine, impatient and tormented.

"So," I gasped, caught up in his spell, "does this mean my lips are a prize worth fighting for?" I was at the mercy of my emotions.

"Your very breath is reward enough," he whispered without hesitation, his mouth moving down the curve of my neck.

"You settle for so little," I said provocatively. He pulled my hips against him again, lifting me impetuously, his hot breath on my mouth. Impulsively, I followed his movements, wrapping my legs around him as he pushed me down onto the bed, his hot body on top of mine as his mouth touched me below my ear, causing electric tingles with every breath.

"Do you think it'll always be like this?" I whispered as his hands moved over me.

"Like what?" he said without missing a beat.

"Will I always feel like I lose myself when your hands are on me?"

"As long as I live, we'll lose ourselves together." He stopped for a moment, seeking my gaze. "Far from everything and everyone. I'll challenge anyone for you. I'll take on the whole world." He rested his forehead against mine and his cold chain brushed my chin. "You're safe with me," he murmured, slowly kissing the curve of my neck again. "Here, just you and me against the world," he whispered against my skin.

A quiver ran through me all the way to the tips of my toes.

14

SOUL SISTERS

Light streamed rudely through the window, waking me from a long, dreamless night. "Ow," I groaned, lifting my head from the pillow and instinctively touching my temple. My head felt like it was being squeezed in a steel vise while a giant jackhammer tried to pierce my skull. There was no sign of Evan in the room. If this was how my day was starting out, the best course of action would be to climb under the covers and go back to sleep.

The beep of a horn nipped that idea in the bud and made me get up. My head throbbing, I staggered to the window. The roar of an engine reached me before I could look outside, and when I did, I quickly recognized the gray fairing and sleek shape of a motorcycle. It wasn't Evan's.

"Need a ride?" With a jerk of her head, Ginevra invited me to join her.

I fought down my disappointment and got ready as fast as I could, wondering where Evan was. Clattering down the stairs, I found Ginevra in the kitchen chatting with my parents, who were crazy about her and her charismatic personality. Like everyone was, for that matter. If she'd asked them to, they would have let me blast off in a rocket to help colonize Mars.

Over tight-fitting jeans tucked into tall, black high-heeled boots she wore a white shirt that hugged her generous curves. A black silk foulard scarf was draped around her neck and tied in a knot on her chest, making it look like a tie. *Or a snake*, I thought instinctively.

Outside, Ginevra put on a figure-flattering leather jacket in the same shade as her boots. She shook her voluminous hair that was always perfectly coiffed, emanating a cloud of floral perfume.

I climbed onto the rear seat. "Don't you have a helmet for me?" I asked, my nervousness showing in my failed attempt to take the edge off my voice.

"What's with the fixation on helmets?" she chided me before gunning the throttle. I grabbed hold of the gas tank, my fingers gripping the steel just in time.

"Where's Evan?" I tried to ask, but the fierce roar of her Aprilia RSV4 drowned out my voice.

"His intervention was needed," she said promptly, showing how superfluous words were with her since she could read anyone's mind. "His and many others', actually. Simon's with him."

I trembled at Ginevra's unexpected confession and at how easily she could talk about the subject.

"What's going on?" I asked, as surprised as she seemed to be that I'd been brave enough to ask.

"I don't know, but I think it's something big. An emergency in the Middle East."

"The Middle East?! But there's a war going on there!" I said, alarmed.

Ginevra looked at me in the mirror. "Exactly."

I opened my mouth, shaking off a shudder, and sorrowfully closed it again, staring blankly at the streaked asphalt that raced by beneath us. I couldn't come up with anything else to say, but Ginevra still gave me the answer I was looking for.

"He said he wouldn't be back before tonight."

"He'll be gone all day?!" I groaned.

Ginevra nodded and parked the bike in the school lot. Time wasn't as important to her as it was to me and I doubted she could understand my resentment. I didn't know how much time I had left before death returned to claim me. Because it would, I was sure of it.

"You'll have to settle for me." She yanked me by the shoulder and we made our way down the school corridors.

I was so used to Evan's company that the thought of him being gone all day long made me queasy. In a flash, the suspicion I'd had months ago became a certainty: Ginevra had enrolled at my school specifically for situations like this. My instinct had been right.

"C'mon, it won't be so bad," she teased, probing my thoughts.

I threw her a disapproving look but actually she was right. Her being there made Evan's absence less bitter. It was surprising how the bond between her and me had grown so strong in such a short time. Sometimes I actually missed her when I hadn't seen her for more than a few hours. Not even for Peter had I ever felt anything like it, and it was an extraordinary sensation. It wiped away the loneliness I'd grown up with. Evan's love, my connection with his brothers and Ginevra . . . I'd never hoped to find everything that had unexpectedly filled my life. Sometimes it seemed like too much.

In the past, I'd often felt like I was searching for something, as if, even with everything I accomplished, it was never enough. And now the tiresome dissatisfaction I'd always felt inside had finally been completely eclipsed. For the first time I didn't need anything else.

"Well? What do you want to do this afternoon?" Ginevra asked, her voice hopeful.

She'd already decided everything, I was sure of it, but still I tried to talk my way out of her plans. "No offense, but I think I'm going to stay home and read."

"No offense? Of course I'm offended!" she said in an annoyed voice, loud enough that people in the hallway turned to stare at us. "You want to leave me alone all day long? Forget it!"

"Really, I wouldn't be good company. I'm in a terrible mood this morning and have a splitting headache," I insisted though I knew it was useless.

"I don't think your bad mood is because of your head," she grumbled, shooting me a glance.

"You know everything," I said with a sigh, shrugging. "I couldn't lie to you even if I wanted to. Evan's never been away for so long before," I said sadly.

"Oh, come on, you won't die from going one day without Evan. You'll be too busy having fun with me!" she exclaimed, carried away with enthusiasm about her plans.

As we walked down the corridor, a freshman was so dazzled by Ginevra's very presence that he walked straight into the lockers, making us wince. I held back a laugh as he picked up his books and looked at her sheepishly.

"Hello to you too," she said, giving him a come-on look as she strode by, moving her long legs with feline grace. The boy continued to stare at her, babbling something incomprehensible, but Ginevra didn't slacken her pace. I shot her a disapproving look.

"What? I was just being nice!" she said.

I couldn't keep from laughing. "And you're going to end up in his fantasies for the rest of his life."

"Who says I'm not there already?" She stifled a laugh at what only she knew for certain.

In the cafeteria the only empty chair at our usual table did nothing but remind me how much I missed Evan. I took a seat next to Peter. Seeing that Evan wasn't there, he moved his chair closer to mine. "Hey Gemma! You alone?" he asked, a little surprised.

"Hey Peter! Do I look transparent to you?" Ginevra said sourly.

"N-no," he stammered. Ginevra's allure had an effect on everyone, especially when she decided to flaunt it. "Come on, you know what I meant," Peter said, turning back to me. "I'm talking about your boyfriend. Is Prince Charming off repairing the carriage?" he asked, unable to contain his sarcasm, which was actually directed at Ginevra.

I wished I could warn him to keep quiet because I was a little afraid of how this might turn out. Ginevra was sweet with me, but with other people you never knew what she might do.

"Watch what you say. He's not crazy about you as it is," she told him.

"Whoa, I'm not gonna be able to sleep, I'm so scared. So is the white knight off feeding his stallion?" Peter was really pushing it.

"I wouldn't call him that." Ginevra stared at him, an evil smile on her lips. "Black is definitely more his color."

A black knight. That's what Evan was. Deep down, Ginevra was right. Everybody around the table had fallen silent, tension spreading from one face to the next.

"There was something he needed to do," I said, hoping to make them stop.

"Will he be gone long?" Peter asked as though for a specific reason.

"Kind of," I said, crestfallen. "He'll be gone all day."

Peter's eyes lit up. I knew him well enough to understand that look, though I was sure I was the only one to notice it—except for Ginevra, of course. "We were just talking about going for a walk in the woods this afternoon. If you don't have plans you could come with us, Gemma."

I couldn't read minds like Ginevra could, but I didn't need to. Peter's hopefulness couldn't have been more obvious if it had been written on his forehead. Ginevra glared at him. "The two of you could come with us," he quickly corrected himself. "Of course I meant both of you," he stammered as Ginevra's expression became even haughtier.

"What walk in the woods?" Faith asked, surprised.

Someone cleared their throat to cover a laugh and Faith jumped in her chair. "Ow!" she exclaimed, shooting an angry look at Peter. Then she blinked nervously. "I meant 'Oh! The walk in the woods!' We were just talking about it a second before you guys showed up," she said awkwardly.

Ginevra and I exchanged a look of understanding as someone else stifled a laugh. "Sounds like fun," Ginevra said, looking at me to see if I liked the idea.

"I don't know," I grumbled reluctantly. "I don't feel so good today."

"Come on, just say yes!" Jeneane said. "When's the last time we all spent an afternoon together?"

"I can't even remember," Faith agreed, hoping to put her gaffe behind her.

"You guys went camping together all summer long!" I said accusingly, weighing their expressions.

"Yeah, but you weren't there. This is our chance to finally have you all to ourselves! Come on, Gemma, I know you don't have anything better to do," Jeneane said.

Their silent faces were hopeful. I'd had no idea they'd missed me. I hadn't really missed them. Was it all my fault? Evan absorbed all my attention, along with my new family. All of a sudden I felt horribly guilty for having neglected them.

"All right." The answer slipped out. After all, what could happen to me while spending an afternoon with my old friends?

"Great!" exclaimed Peter, who'd been holding his breath.

"Then it's decided," Brandon said.

"Okay if we meet at my place?" Faith suggested. "We can reach the woods easily from there. Shall we say three o'clock?"

"Sounds perfect," I said, resigned.

Ginevra was there to pick me up with the punctuality of a Swiss watch. Sitting behind the wheel of Evan's BMW X6, she was bubbling with enthusiasm about our spending a few hours together, since I usually spent most of my time with Evan. And yet it was so weird how she and I felt a need for each other. An invisible bond drew us together like the two poles of a magnet, me tending to underdo things and her to overdo them.

As always, she was impeccably dressed: casual boots laced up to the calf, tight jeans, and a brown vest that matched her boots and revealed the sleeves of her beige top. I climbed into the car, put my dark-red sweatshirt in my backpack, and pulled the white-gold butterfly pendant out from under the green, short-sleeved top that I wore with jeans and dark hiking boots.

"Still have a headache?" she asked me considerately.

"It *had* gone away, but thanks for reminding me," I replied sarcastically. My mood hadn't improved much since that morning, though my headache had relented, disappearing almost completely.

The sun was warm, though temperatures had dropped quite a bit compared to summer. The car's tinted windows muted the light.

"Hi, Mrs. Nichols!" I said, rolling down my window when we reached Faith's house. Her mom was bent over some bushes with red blossoms, holding a big, dangerous-looking pair of hedge clippers. Short, with dark hair, she didn't resemble her daughter at all. Today she wore a big straw hat to protect herself from the sun and green rubber knee-high boots.

"Hi, kids," she said warmly, raising her head slightly. She looked tired.

"We came to pick up Faith," I said.

"Oh, right! I think she's with Jeneane. I saw them heading toward the stable." The woman pointed at the large wooden construction a few hundred yards away.

"Horses give me the creeps," came a whisper from the back seat. I didn't have to turn around to know who it was or the reason horses scared him so much. "What?!" Peter protested, noticing the guys' raised eyebrows as they looked at him, surprised. "They're huge! They could kill you with a single kick, you know."

"Wuss," Ginevra teased.

I rolled my eyes, a faint smile on my lips. This was going to be an interesting outing. "I'll go get them," I said, pushing open the heavy door.

"I'll come with you," Ginevra said instantly.

"I don't need a bodyguard!" I said scathingly, immediately feeling guilty when I saw the looks everyone gave me. All Ginevra's concern about my safety was doing nothing but making me even more anxious.

"All right, sorry. I just wanted to keep you company," Ginevra said.

Some strange instinct made me slam the car door and stride off in irritation without even turning around. I headed toward the stable, as shocked by my own reaction as the others no doubt were.

The stable was clean, although stray wisps of hay covered the wooden floor. I inhaled the smell of the hay with pleasure.

Freedom. There were few situations my mind associated with this feeling, but among them was the image of a herd of pure-white wild horses, their manes flowing as they galloped across an infinite landscape chasing the wind.

Then I saw the horse in the stall Mr. Nichols was standing next to and the image instantly vanished, replaced by a stronger feeling: uneasiness. It was black, as black as pitch. And from the way its hostile eyes fixed themselves on me when I walked into the stable, it didn't seem to like me.

"Gemma!" Faith welcomed me with a giant smile. "You guys are here already?" She and Jeneane wore impeccable hiking outfits, Jeneane's in pink and Faith's in dark green.

"We didn't hear you drive up," Jeneane said, standing next to Mr. Nichols who was busy stroking the horse's huge black head over the top of its stall.

"Mr. Nichols," I said, nodding at Faith's dad who returned my nod. "The others are waiting in the car," I told her, hoping she would get the hint without my seeming rude to her dad. I had a bad feeling and suddenly all I wanted was to get out of there.

"I haven't seen Mr. Bloom in quite a while. How is your dad?" Mr. Nichols asked me politely.

The horse snorted nervously through its big nostrils, making me jump. "He's just fine, thanks for asking. It's because of work. He's always really busy. More than usual lately. I barely see him myself," I replied, trying to suppress my anxiety.

"Tell him I said hi."

"Will do. Nice horse you've got there. It's, um, *huge*," I said, as fascinated as I was frightened by the massive beast's black eyes. They riveted me like a black hole dragging me into its depths.

Jeneane coughed awkwardly. Had I said something wrong?

"His name's Mustang. He's my champion." A proud twinkle in his eye, Mr. Nichols stroked the animal's nose.

"Oh no, here we go again!" Faith groaned under her breath.

"Now you've done it," Jeneane whispered in my ear, biting her lip. She'd probably put up with Mr. Nichols's obsession with his horse long enough already.

"He's a stallion," he continued, oblivious to the looks on our faces. "He's won more races than Casey Stoner!"

"Who?" Jeneane whispered, making me smother a laugh.

"He's a champion MotoGP motorcycle racer," I explained, still smiling at Faith's dad who proceeded to rattle off the technical and aesthetic qualities that made his precious horse a champion. Mustang didn't seem interested in all the praise; he didn't take his eyes off me.

"I'm telling you, young ladies, in all my years I've never seen any horse run like Mustang. He's a force of nature!" he exclaimed proudly as Faith rolled her eyes.

"I bet he is," I mumbled, pursing my lips.

"Dad's fanatical about that horse," Faith whispered in my ear. "Sorry."

"No problem," I reassured her. "I think it's nice."

The horse snorted again and tossed his head, jerking Mr. Nichols's hand as it held the reins. Mustang seemed spooked. Like me.

"Wow! He's a real brute," I said, my voice edged with anxiety.

Mr. Nichols tugged on the reins, trying to hold him still, but Mustang didn't seem willing to obey his owner's commands. He kept snorting with his big, black, damp nostrils and skittishly pawing the hay-covered floor, his black eyes fixed on me with what looked like a malevolent expression. My heart skipped a beat as I gazed into their depths. I instinctively stepped back, trying to make it seem casual. For some strange reason the horse seemed to have it in for me.

"Easy," Mr. Nichols said softly. "Mustang! Easy! What's wrong?" He stroked the horse's nose as if expecting him to answer. "He's usually so gentle. I don't know what's gotten into him today," he said, clearly uneasy.

My eyes didn't leave Mustang's. The horse neighed and I backed up even farther, a terrible feeling flooding through me.

"Easy," Mr. Nichols continued to whisper as the animal moved in his stall, agitated, snorting through his giant nostrils.

It was like he hated me. His dilated eyes made me shudder, but no one was paying attention to me. Jeneane, Faith, and Mr. Nichols were all focused on the animal's strange behavior.

"Girls, maybe you should go and have fun," Mr. Nichols said. "He's probably just nervous because there are so many of us here. How odd. He's never acted this way before."

His words pulled me out of the pit of agitation into which I'd sunk. I nodded and waved goodbye, more anxious than ever to get outside and away from Mustang. The moment I walked out of the stable I took a breath of fresh air and noticed my hands were trembling.

Faith stopped in her tracks. "I left the flashlight in the kitchen!" she said.

"Flashlight?" I said, surprised. "You're planning to stay out that late?" More than a question, it was a protest.

"What, didn't they tell you?" Jeneane said, always eager to supply information to people who didn't know everything she did. "The guys are going to make a campfire when it gets dark."

"I'm bringing marshmallows!" Faith cried eagerly, gesturing at her pink backpack as I tried hard not to let my jaw drop.

"I wonder why they forgot to tell me," I said sardonically. Actually I knew perfectly well why. Peter had been the one to plan everything and I was sure deep down he was still hoping something might happen between us. It would have been harder for me to turn down spending a couple hours with my friends, which was what he'd told me, than going on an outing that lasted until late at night.

I mechanically reached for my elastic band to put my hair up in a ponytail but it wasn't around my arm. Then I remembered Evan had taken it as a keepsake and a hot shiver ran through my heart. At least he'd taken a piece of me with him.

"I'll go with you!" Jeneane caught up with Faith who was walking to the house. "I have to go to the bathroom before we leave. The bushes irritate my skin."

"I'll wait in the car," I called after them, unsure if they'd heard me. I began to walk quickly away from the stable but Mustang's furious screams startled me. My heart contracted in my chest and I began to shiver, totally in the grip of an unexpected anxiety. Although I was already a hundred yards away, the noise of his hooves resounded in my ears: the horse was out of control and, judging from the nervous reaction of his owner who was trying uselessly to hold him, not even he knew why.

The earth beneath me began to tremble and my heart raced: Mr. Nichols had let Mustang out of his stall. I was glued to my spot, my eyes locked onto the horse's as he neighed and snorted furiously. All at once I had a glimmer of lucidity: Mr. Nichols was leading Mustang into the paddock, so I had no reason to be afraid. The fence was newly constructed, its posts and bars thick and sturdy. The possibility that the horse might escape was all in my head.

Then something made me tremble: the tension in Ginevra's voice. "Gemma!" she called, leaning out of the car door. My alarmed gaze shot to hers just as a neigh far louder than the others put my instincts on high alert. I spun around and froze, registering only confused scraps of information.

Mr. Nichols was on the ground and Mustang was up on his hind legs, out of control. He kicked at the fence so violently that the sound of his hooves striking the hard wood echoed through the yard, making me shudder.

A primitive fear shook me to my core. Panic clouded my mind and suddenly everything happened so fast I didn't even have time to breathe. A ferocious black mass raced toward me like a raging bull in an arena. It would trample me in a matter of seconds. Everything around me became muffled and confused. My friends' terrified voices faded into the background as my mind focused on one sound: the thundering of hooves against the ground as Mustang's wild eyes bored into mine. No one else was around. It was just me and him.

"GEMMA!!!"

Ginevra's scream was like a sledgehammer breaking me free from the block of ice in which my body had been encased. Mustang was only a few feet away by the time my brain gave the order for me to duck. He was too close for me to elude him and it was too late for me to run.

I curled up on the ground, closed my eyes, and held my breath, bracing for the impact. A blast of sandy earth struck me and I heard the deafening silence of the others holding their breath. The echo of wild galloping grew fainter as, numb with terror, panting and trembling, I slowly raised my head and saw Mustang racing into the trees. Mr. Nichols, on Faith's small brown horse, galloped after the stallion in a desperate attempt to catch him.

I shuddered, the hairs on my arms standing on end as the sandy earth settled to the ground around me. In the moment of silence that followed, I looked at my friends. Motionless, they stared at me, pale and speechless.

Ginevra was the first to run to me. The look in her eye told me how difficult it was for her to limit herself to a human pace in this bizarre circumstance. The others followed her as if waking from a nightmare, and an instant later the silence was replaced by a frantic jumble of worried voices.

"Are you okay?" Ginevra rested her hand on my arm, her tone apprehensive and her expression more worried than anyone else's.

I wasn't sure I could speak. "I—I think s-so," I stammered, my eyelids fluttering. I raised a hand to my temple, which throbbed beneath my fingers. Everybody surrounded me, staring as if I'd just survived a shark attack. If Mustang had trampled me, it probably would have been even worse than a shark attack.

"What did I tell you guys?!" Peter exclaimed. "Horses are dangerous." He shot me a glance, looking almost reproachful, and in his eyes I could see how worried he was. No one else paid any attention to him.

"I'm taking you home," Ginevra said matter-of-factly.

"No!" I said quickly in a determined voice.

For a moment my tone made everyone fall silent. They were all studying my face, their own still full of concern. Unjustified concern, because the worst had passed.

"I don't want to ruin the outing for everybody," I insisted.

"But Gemma!" Ginevra shot me a pleading look.

"Everything's fine, all right?" I hissed. "Let's go."

Faith was still as pale as a wax statue. She seemed to want me to go home more than anyone else. "It could have been a tragedy," she murmured dully as she stared at nothing. As she lifted her face to mine I saw tears shining in her eyes. She probably felt guilty because the horse belonged to her dad.

"But it wasn't," I reassured her, looking at Ginevra.

Was it you who stopped him? The thought sprang spontaneously from my mind. Ginevra looked at me, nodding almost imperceptibly, replying in a conversation no one else could take part in. *Thank you*, I thought, so only she could hear.

"You sure you're okay?" she asked me out loud.

"It was an accident. It could have happened to anyone," I reassured them all, forcing myself to speak convincingly. The truth was I wasn't sure. Something inside me continued to say it wasn't true: the memory of how ferociously Mustang had looked at me. He'd wanted *me* and nobody else, I could feel it in my gut. "I just happened to be standing in his way, that's all," I added, trying to persuade myself as well as the others. "If it had been Peter instead of me, I'm sure it wouldn't have gone any differently," I lied. Peter shuddered at the thought.

The others were already convinced: the one I needed to reassure was Ginevra.

"Except he would have had to go home and change!" Ginevra taunted him in an effort to relieve the tension. Peter shot her a withering look and she took it back. "You're right. It's more likely you would have fainted," she added. She'd probably read this in his mind, because when Peter heard her say it his eyes went wide. "Come on! No need for you to get mad."

She rested her hand on Peter's shoulder but he continued to glare at her. He didn't realize Ginevra could hear all the insults he was keeping to himself out of politeness.

"I was only kidding!" she said, amused.

"Wow. You're hilarious," he shot back sourly.

Faith still couldn't get over it. "It's so weird! Nothing like this has ever happened with Mustang. He was calm before you showed up and he's usually gentle with everyone. My little sister rides him without any problems," she said, mortified. I stopped listening to her and focused on the strange uneasiness stirring in my gut.

"The important thing is that it's over," Jake said, "and nobody got hurt." He walked toward the car with the others. I started to follow him, but Faith held me back, still visibly shaken. She slowed her pace and we fell behind the rest of the group.

"You shouldn't feel guilty!" I insisted, already assuming that was what she wanted to say. "I'm fine, really. Don't worry about it."

"I wanted to ask you something," she said point-blank. I slowed down even more, surprised. "It's not your time of the month by any chance, is it?" she whispered, almost embarrassed.

"Am I having my period? No. Why?"

"I don't know if it's actually possible. I'm no expert. My horse is female." She hesitated a moment before going on, encouraged by how curious I looked. "It's the only explanation that comes to my mind. Mustang's reaction was so unusual because, well, I mean, I think the smell of blood might have set him off." She rolled her eyes and imitated her dad's voice. "He's a stallion."

"I'm sorry to prove your theory wrong but I'm not on my period. Besides, honestly, I don't think it's possible. I mean, come on!" I exclaimed. Her idea was crazy. "Mustang must have just been in a bad mood," I said, trying to reassure her. "It happens to everybody, doesn't it? Or maybe it *was* something about the way I smell." I pulled the edge of my collar to my nose and sniffed it. "Stop torturing yourself and let's go. Nothing happened. That's all that matters."

"Right," she said, still shaken.

"Ready to have some fun?" I cheered to the group as I strode over to them.

"Well, at least you're in a good mood again," one of the guys said from the back seat.

Ginevra and I exchanged glances. Only she knew the truth.

15

REAWAKENED INSTINCT

"You sure we're not going too far?" Peter asked Ginevra, who was leading the group along a rambling path none of us knew well.

"Afraid of the big bad wolf?" she teased, a feral look on her face. Her lips twisted into a sardonic smile. "Or witches, maybe?"

I shot her a disapproving look. I didn't know exactly what Peter had done to end up being the butt of all her sadistic jokes, but it wasn't hard to guess.

"Witches!" Peter snorted. "Aren't you a little big to believe in stuff like that?"

Ginevra leaned in close to his face. "Aren't you?" she said in a sinister whisper. Something about the look in her eye made Peter fall silent, almost as if he'd grasped the veiled truth behind her words.

"It was your idea to go for a walk," Brandon said. "At least we'll see something new."

"Yeah, sure we will!" Jeneane shot back, annoyed. "New trees, new rocks. And look down there! A new stream, all our own!" she said sarcastically. "So is it going to take much longer? My feet are starting to ache," she whined, panting like someone who's just scaled Mt. Everest.

"Exactly five minutes less than the last time you asked," Ginevra said.

"Hey, chill! Did you just get stung by a wasp or what?" Jeneane stared at her almost defiantly.

Behind them, Peter laughed. "I don't think so. I don't see any dead wasps lying around," he said. "I doubt there's anything that could survive after stinging her." Ginevra glared at him, a challenging look in her eye, surprising the rest of us who had expected a more elaborate answer.

"We're almost there," she said, responding more to my thoughts than Jeneane's grumbling. Her lips curved into a sly smile. "There's just one last push," she told us, looking amused, her eyes on a steep slope to our right that led away from the path.

"You can't mean—" Jeneane's incredulous voice trailed off.

Ginevra looked her up and down. "You can always stay here and wait for us," she suggested spitefully, not leaving Jeneane much choice.

"Or," Peter whispered in her ear as he passed her, "you can come with us and follow the queen of the witches."

Ginevra turned to look at him. "Thanks. You finally said something nice about me." Peter didn't realize he'd just paid her a compliment. I bit my lip to keep from laughing.

"Can't we follow the path?" Faith asked cautiously as if Ginevra made her nervous.

Surprisingly, Ginevra answered nicely. "That would take a good two hours. I'm offering you guys the chance to get there in fifteen minutes, tops. If that's okay with you."

"Hang in there just a little longer," Jake said to Faith considerately, resting a hand on her shoulder. Looking resigned, she nodded at the tenderness on his face.

As we made our way up, the slope grew even steeper. The ground was covered with leaves, dry pine needles, and gravel. An occasional rock lodged in the ground or a tree trunk jutting out of the sandy soil offered us a foothold.

Peter led the group, followed by Jeneane and Faith who were being helped by Brandon and Jake, while Ginevra and I brought up the rear.

"It's been over twenty minutes, Ginevra!" Jeneane groaned, looking tired and fed up.

Ginevra smiled and looked at me, shrugging. "It's not my fault she's a slowpoke!" I shot her a reproving look. "Fifteen minutes would have been enough time for me," she said in a low, amused voice.

I stared at her, open-mouthed. "I thought you meant fifteen *human* minutes!" I said reproachfully.

"Nobody asked."

"You're unbelievable," I teased her affectionately. I didn't mind climbing uphill through the trees at all. I could have kept going for hours. The strong smell of moss in the air relaxed me. My girlfriends, on the other hand, seemed exhausted.

"We're almost there!" Peter called. He was standing on a large trunk half-buried beneath layers of earth. Faith joined him on top of it and so did Jeneane.

As I trudged uphill, absently staring at the ground beneath my feet, my heart unexpectedly leapt to my throat for no reason at all. Instinctively, I raised my eyes to the trunk that Jake was now climbing onto, then looked back at my feet, moving forward, then again at the trunk, as if something were beckoning me. My instincts were strangely on alert, and yet the tree trunk was a perfectly sturdy foothold. It had been lying there on the ground for who knew how long.

A strange cracking sound rent the air. I looked up, alarmed, but no one else seemed to have heard it.

It was Brandon's turn to climb onto the trunk, a dozen yards up the slope from me. My eyes darted to his foot as he rested it on the trunk and the blood suddenly drained from my face. Before I could open my mouth, the trunk tore itself violently from the earth and began to roll downhill, dragging Brandon with it. He clutched at the ground, his fingers sinking into the earth. Shouts came from above but they were lost among the trees.

The blood froze in my veins as I watched the trunk barreling toward me, out of control. Panicking, I stepped back and lost my balance. The trunk bounced off the ground and came flying at me. As I fell someone yanked me out of its trajectory. It crashed against a tree and rolled down the hill. I suspected Ginevra had diverted it from its path and I hoped the others were still too much in shock to have noticed. Shaking from head to toe, I forced myself to take a breath. Ginevra had saved me again. Our eyes met, mine still filled with terror, and I saw she was petrified too. The others raced down the hill toward us as the trunk hit the bottom and smashed into a thousand pieces.

"Are you okay?" Peter shouted, breathless with worry as he rushed past the others. The question was starting to become a constant part of my life. Before I could answer him, he smothered me in a desperate hug as Ginevra looked on uneasily. "I thought you were done for," he whispered into my hair. Peter couldn't imagine I'd already survived far worse situations.

"Gemma!" the girls cried in concern when they finally reached us.

"It's okay, I'm fine," I reassured them, still looking at Peter. Of all of them, he looked the most shaken. I locked eyes with Ginevra in an attempt to let her know how thankful I was. "Well?" I exclaimed, trying to appear nonchalant though my heart was about to burst out of my chest. "Are we planning to put down roots here?"

Jake surprised me by resting a hand on my shoulder. "Girl, either you're jinxed or this is totally not your lucky day!" he kidded as my brain processed what he'd just said. My instinct had tried to warn me. I forced a smile and said something in reply.

Meanwhile Jeneane had stopped to stare at Ginevra, who looked back at her out of the corner of her eye. "Nice move. I didn't know you were so strong," she said, almost accusingly.

"Just lucky, that's all." From her tone, Ginevra seemed to have lost her sense of humor.

The minute the others turned around we exchanged a knowing look. Ginevra had to be careful not to attract attention like that.

After a few more minutes a small clearing surrounded by trees opened up before us. It didn't look much different from the one I was used to, but Ginevra insisted that the trees around it formed a perfect circle. No one seemed convinced it was a good enough reason to have dragged us all the way here.

I rummaged in my backpack for *Forbidden*, a novel by Tabitha Suzuma that I hadn't been able to put down for days now. "Book!" Brandon's warning cry made me flinch and I looked up. "Hey, hey, hey! No books allowed! Confiscate that book from Gemma!" I felt like a cornered animal. Before I knew it, Peter had pounced on me.

"All right, all right, I'll put it away!" I protested cautiously, a little alarmed by his impulsive behavior.

Peter fixed his eyes on me and said in a mock-threatening voice, holding back a grin, "We don't need some you-might-see-me-but-I'm-on-another-planet zombie version of Gemma!"

"It's bad enough having to put up with that at school," Jake chimed in sardonically.

I'd planned to finish the novel but had no choice but to hide it before my friends actually took it away from me. Instead, I pulled out my camera and took snapshots of them. Then we tossed our backpacks on the ground, split up, and went into the woods to gather firewood.

"Hey, Gemma!" Peter walked toward me.

At my side, Ginevra rolled her eyes. "Such a pain in the neck," she murmured in exasperation. "He needs to *talk* to you."

Do you mind? I asked her with my eyes so Peter, who hadn't reached us yet, couldn't hear.

It was clear from the look on Ginevra's face how irritated she was. "But he wants to be *alone* with you!" she exclaimed, surprised by my openness toward him.

"He's my friend," I reminded her.

Ginevra clenched her jaw and quickened her pace. Catching up to the rest of the group, she strode past the boys with a toss of her head, her wavy hair cascading over her shoulders like molten gold.

"Close your mouth, Brandon," Jeneane warned, seeing his expression. "You've got all day long to drool." Ginevra smiled to herself and I shook my head.

"So she finally gave you some room to breathe." Peter walked up to me. "I was starting to think your boyfriend had appointed her as your bodyguard. She never leaves you alone for a second!"

"We're really close," I said, bothered by his sarcasm.

"Like you and I used to be?" he asked bluntly.

His question hit me straight in the heart. I searched his gaze, feeling a pang in my stomach I couldn't express, then looked away, focusing on the path we were following. "It's different," I said in a small voice.

"Right." His tone was resentful. "But what we had was special too." I said nothing, but Peter wouldn't take my silence for an answer. "You think so yourself, don't you? Tell me you do."

"Pet . . ." I couldn't find the words. "You're a big part of my life. An important part, and that's never going to change."

He pressed his lips together in a bitter smile and said, "But I'm part of the past. That's what you're trying to tell me."

Since when had he become so straightforward? I hesitated. "I'm with Evan now. Don't be upset about it. That's just how things turned out. I don't want to lose your friendship, but I'll understand if you don't want me around any more. Don't misunderstand me: you'll always be a part of my life. I want you to be, even in the future," I reassured him. I felt guilty for being so direct, but I needed to be clear with him. "But only as a brother—like it's always been for me."

The look on his face finally expressed what he'd never managed to say in words: Peter didn't feel the same way about me. My confession seemed to have crushed his heart. I took comfort in the knowledge that the flame of false hope was more devastating—because it burned stronger and longer—than the flame of cold, hard truth, which flared up initially, but was soon extinguished by resignation.

"You're wrong." The sudden change in his expression confirmed it. "I'll *always* want you around." Peter tried hard to keep his disillusionment off his face, understanding how pointless it was to insist. Then he smiled at me as if the conversation had never happened. But a person's smile can be called sincere only when it's their eyes doing the smiling—and his were dull. "So what did you do over the summer, you and . . . your boyfriend?"

I looked at him sadly, unsure whether I should follow his lead. He'd changed the subject so abruptly it worried me. Rubbing salt in the wound I'd just inflicted didn't seem like a good idea, so I dodged his question. "No, tell me about you. I mean, you guys spent three whole months camping while I was stuck back here. Tell me everything! Was it fun?"

"It would have been more fun if you'd been there."

"Aw, I bet it wasn't all that bad."

His smile broadened as he tousled my hair. He knew I hated it when he did that. "Don't let it go to your head! We had a blast even without you." He grinned.

I gasped, feigning shock. For a moment I was glad of how easy it was to talk to Peter, just as if nothing had changed between us. But then he turned serious again. "It was just what I needed, to get away from . . . Lake Placid," he murmured, casting me a sidelong glance. *To get away from the sight of you and Evan together all the time* was what I read on his face, which was more honest than he was.

"Oh, man!" I shook his arm. "I leave you alone for one summer and you turn so serious! Where's the Peter I used to know? He would be dying to tell me every detail. What have you done with him?" It was my desperate attempt to get through to my friend, hidden somewhere behind this new Peter I barely recognized.

Unexpectedly, it seemed to work. He laughed at some memory that crossed his mind. "Would you believe it if I told you Jake managed to shoot spaghetti out of his nose?"

"Oh my God, how disgusting!" I exclaimed, grossed out.

"The guy would do anything to get Faith's attention."

"I doubt it worked. They should offer courses for guys like him who don't know how to pick up girls."

"Well, he *did* manage to make her laugh. In fact, she was laughing so hard she could barely breathe," he said.

"Good thing Brandon didn't have a brilliant idea like that. I don't think Jeneane would have reacted quite so well."

"You're probably right." For a moment I recognized my old friend, the one I missed so much, in his carefree expression. "But then again, Brandon got a laugh out of Jeneane too," he said.

"Oh, I've got to hear this."

"You'd better sit down first," he warned. "I'm not sure you'll be able to stay standing." He doubled over in laughter. "One night there was a party at the campground and Brandon picked up a girl." Peter was laughing so hard there were tears in his eyes. It was contagious; my lips curled into a smile. "She was gorgeous, no doubt about it, and he was strutting around because she even seemed older than us. They . . . they started dancing . . . and he found out . . ." Peter gasped out the words between laughs, "he found out it was a dude!"

"Brandon picked up a transvestite?!" I asked, astonished.

Peter nodded, unable to speak for hilarity. "He wanted to make Jeneane jealous but instead he made her pee herself laughing!"

"I won't ask how he found out it wasn't a girl."

"That's the funniest part!" he said, throwing his head back. "They danced all night long and then went off behind a tree and he tou—"

"Okay, okay, no need to go into detail!" I said quickly. "I wish I'd seen his face."

"He couldn't look us in the eye for two whole days."

"Poor Brandon. I'll try to go easier on him," I said, happy I'd erased the sadness from Peter's eyes. Unfortunately, it wouldn't begin to erase the sorrow he carried in his heart, I was sure of that. His hand accidentally brushed mine and our eyes met awkwardly. We both stopped laughing. Embarrassed, I nudged him. "Sounds like you had a good time."

"Yeah, it was fun."

I felt a sudden flicker of selfishness in my heart. Who was I to keep Pet from getting on with his life? I'd spent the most wonderful time in my life while he was off camping, so why did the idea that Peter was pulling away bother me? It wasn't like me. What was happening to me?

A jingle in my pocket startled me. My phone. I didn't need to check it to know I'd gotten a text. My stomach in turmoil, I slid my fingers into the back pocket of my jeans and pulled it out.

Evan. My heart skipped a beat and the expression on my face didn't escape Peter. "That him?" he asked, his tone flat.

I stared at the ground as guilt gripped my throat. "We'd better get back to the others," I said, hoping we could drop the subject. Deep in my heart, I was bursting with impatience to find some isolated spot where I could read the message from Evan, on the other side of the world.

"We haven't gotten enough firewood yet," he said.

I could see in his face how much he wished to keep me there with him and by extension, keep me away from Evan as well, just this once, but it was a wish I refused to grant. "The others have probably found enough for all of us," I said, prodding him to go back.

We walked back into the clearing just as the rest of the group emerged from the trees on the opposite side. Jake and Brandon carried logs for us to sit on and arranged them in a big circle. Jeneane held a handful of twigs, careful not to ruin the decorations on her nails. Faith and Ginevra's faces, on the other hand, were barely visible behind the huge armfuls of firewood they carried. They dumped them into the center of the circle and brushed off their clothes.

"Nice work," Ginevra told Faith, high-fiving her. Faith had also collected dry pine needles to use as tinder. She'd once explained that her grandfather, a beekeeper, used them as a natural fuel in the smoker. They emitted a thick, white, sweetly scented smoke that helped placate the bees when he was working with the hive. Their fear of fire made them fill up on honey until they were sated, which calmed them down.

"Who's got a lighter?" Faith turned to Brandon, who searched his pockets. "I thought you smoked."

"I was sure I brought one. It must have fallen out along the way," he apologized, looking around.

"Do I have to do everything myself?" Ginevra complained, making the whole group look at her.

"What are you going to do about it?" Peter said. More than a question, it was a provocation. He smiled at her sardonically and Ginevra gave him a crafty smile.

"I never reveal my secrets," she said, shutting him up. Peter turned his back to her.

I watched silently as Ginevra patiently waited for Jake to stack the wood, leaving a space in the center for air and scattering clumps of dry pine needles that would instantly catch fire.

"Gin, what are you—"

She winked at me and I left the question unfinished. Leaning over the pile of wood with a haughty little smile on her lips, she grabbed a small stick and pretended to rub it between her palms while the others waited, full of curiosity.

"You've got to be kidding!" Peter scoffed immediately. "There's no way you'll ever light a fire with that!"

Ginevra ignored him and shot me a fleeting glance, her lips moving quickly. "Distract them," she murmured, her tone firm, so fast I was amazed I'd been able to understand what she'd said.

I obeyed without hesitation. "Brandon, isn't that your lighter down there?" I signaled vaguely with my finger. Like marionettes, they all turned their heads to look where I was pointing. Everybody except Ginevra, who was concentrating on the fire. I watched her, fascinated, as the green of her eyes lit up, producing a spark.

"That's just a rock," someone said. By the time they turned back, the fire was burning.

"Wow! How the hell—" Brandon stammered, the first one to feel the warmth spread over his face.

"Oh. My. God!" Peter said, his tone caught between amazement and disbelief.

"No. Just me," Ginevra replied, grinning.

"Great job!" Faith said, as astonished as the others.

"*Magic*," Ginevra exclaimed in response to the incredulous looks on their faces. Behind her wild, provocative expression hid a smile only I could decipher. She was telling the truth, but no one would ever have guessed it.

The flames rose higher, coming close to Ginevra's face. Something Evan had once said crossed my mind as if he were whispering it in my ear right now: *Fire is the only weapon capable of annihilating a Witch.* Panic washed over me. "Gin, look out!" I shouted, shoving her away and crashing to the rocky ground as the fire crackled behind us.

"Hey! What's wrong?" she whispered, not a trace of resentment in her voice.

"Evan told me that—"

Words weren't necessary. Ginevra burst out laughing before I could finish my sentence. "Thanks for the thought, but there's no need to worry about me. Don't you think I can take care of myself?" she said with an affectionate grin.

Softly, so the others couldn't hear, I whispered in a tone that was almost reproachful, "Aren't you afraid of burning to death?"

"I certainly can't be killed by *your* fire!" she reassured me in a low voice.

"But I thought—"

"The fire that can kill a Witch is no different from yours, actually," she explained, "but it's only effective if an Angel is using it to purify evil. That's the only way it can keep its purity."

Embarrassed by my reaction, I lay back and spread my arms out on the ground. "Evan didn't mention that!" I said with a smile.

Ginevra lay down beside me and we both stared at the sky, neither of us worrying about dirt on our clothes or hair. Although the sun hadn't set, a few brighter stars were already shining in the twilight. The air smelled good. The scent of the forest was gradually replaced by the aroma of the campfire.

"I'll go sit with the others," Ginevra said unexpectedly, getting up. "That way you can read your message," she added, shooting me a little smile.

Sometimes her ability to read minds was an incredible advantage. I could never have come straight out and told her to leave me alone even though my eagerness to read Evan's text tingled beneath my skin, but she'd sensed my wish all the same. I smiled to myself, still impatient. I wanted to wait until I was alone.

"Gin?" I called after her.

She turned gracefully and waited patiently for me to ask the question she'd already read in my mind.

"Was it hard for you to leave your Sisters?" Given the closeness I felt between us tonight I thought it was safe to ask.

"The bond among Witches is ancestral," she said solemnly, "but love is stronger than everything else." She gave me a sweet smile, turned, and left.

I took the phone out of my pocket and my heart skipped a beat as I read Evan's name on the display. I unlocked the screen and it came to life, lighting up the night that was encroaching on the forest. My chest rose and fell with the agitation of my heart.

I miss you to death. I'm on the other side of the world, but my thoughts are captive back there where I left my heart. All I have to do is close my eyes to feel you're with me. Wherever I am, you're inside me, my love. See you tonight. Evan.

I closed my eyes and took a deep breath, filling my heart with his words. Then, opening it to him again, I typed a reply, my fingers flying over the keys.

Holding my breath for a whole day would hurt less than being away from you for this long. But all I have to do is lift my eyes to the heavens and look at my star to know that you're in my heart. Come back soon. Gem

"Where's Gemma?" A distant murmur of concern reached me as I realized night had fallen, surrounding me with darkness without my noticing. In my heart, the sun was shining. When I sat up, dazed by the brightness of the fire I'd been staring at, Ginevra was sitting on a log just far enough away to keep an eye on me. I got up and joined them as the light from the flames flickered on their faces.

"Good news?" Ginevra asked as I sat down beside her.

"You mean there's something you don't already know?" I said in a low voice.

"No, you're right. I tried to mind my own business, I really did. It's not that I want to listen to your thoughts, but I can't help it. It's what I am. Sometimes it's hard to block them out."

"Yeah, right. In any case, no one asked you to." I smiled at her affectionately.

"Well, what now?" Brandon's voice rose over the crackling flames. "Come on, guys! We're in the woods, sitting around a campfire. Don't you think something's missing?" he said, studying our expressions. "Like ghost stories?"

"Any better ideas?" Faith was quick to say.

"Faith, don't tell me they scare you," Peter teased.

"What if they do?" Jake spoke up in her defense. "You're afraid of snakes, after all."

Ginevra stiffened, though no one noticed but me. My relationship with her probably wasn't the only reason Peter instinctively felt so negative toward her.

"What the hell? It's not true! Who told you that?" he shot back uncomfortably.

"Come on, everybody knows it," Jeneane said.

"Well, now you know it's not true! I'm not afraid of anything," he said in a low voice, almost to himself. Everyone could see the embarrassment on his face.

Ginevra looked at me out of the corner of her eye, a strange little smile on her lips. There was no need to read her mind to understand what she was thinking. I started to shake my head in protest, but she didn't stop to consider my objection; she seemed to have already made up her mind. Unable to stop her, I buried my face in my hands. A second later, Jeneane, sitting across from us, let out an ear-piercing shriek. "A snake!" she screamed. Peter burst out laughing.

Poor Pet, I thought.

"You think I'm stupid? We were just talking about it a second ago, Jeneane. You could at least let a few minutes go by before pulling a prank like that. Awesome performance, though, I'll give you that!" he said, annoyed.

"There really *is* a snake!" Faith burst out, looking horrified. "And it's moving straight towards you, Peter! Get away from there! It's a poisonous one!"

"Don't be stu—" Peter heard the hiss and paled violently before he even looked at the ground. The snake was inches from him.

"This isn't funny," I whispered to Ginevra. The smirk she was trying to hide made me nervous.

"It is to me!" she said under her breath.

Peter sat like a statue, careful not to move a muscle. Frozen with terror, the others watched the snake slithering across the ground in Peter's direction. None of them knew he actually had nothing to fear, but how could I explain that it was just a sadistic practical joke Ginevra was playing on him?

"What do we do?" Brandon whispered between clenched teeth, as if afraid to draw the snake's attention onto himself.

"Somebody do something!" Jeneane cried, tears in her eyes.

I saw the fear on their faces and didn't know what to do. Why did Ginevra have to be so vicious?

Peter was petrified. The fire flared, lighting up his face, and I could see he'd broken out in a cold sweat. Seeing him so powerless and panic-stricken triggered something violent inside me. I couldn't bear to see the terror in his eyes. Ginevra was going too far. I had to do something. I switched off my brain, followed my instinct, and rose to my feet, but Ginevra immediately grabbed my wrist so tightly it hurt.

"That's enough, Gin!" I ordered her with all the authority I could force into my voice.

A corner of her mouth rose, her expression sly. "I'll take care of it," she said aloud so everyone could hear her. She could have made the snake slither away with her powers, but she chose not to. Instead, she moved gracefully toward it as the anxious group stared at her, looking as amazed as they were worried.

"Ginevra, are you crazy?" Jake shouted from the other side of the fire. "It's poisonous! Stay away!"

She continued to move toward the snake, completely unaffected by his remark, amused by her little game. The flames writhed in the air and her long eyelashes cast shadows on her face.

"Stop, damn it!" Peter shouted, furious because he'd been unable to do anything himself. All of them were powerless, but Ginevra continued to smile as she crouched down until she was face to face with the snake.

Paralyzed in an unearthly silence, we watched Ginevra lock eyes with it as if she were communicating with it telepathically. Actually, she was just showing off. The others watched her with bated breath. The snake responded by interrupting its hostile hiss. The silence was eerie; all we could hear was the ominous crackling of the fire. All at once she snatched the snake up, holding it behind its head and lifting it into the air as a murmur of surprise and admiration rose around the flames.

"He's just a little creature," she said proudly. "He's more afraid of us than we are of him."

"Funny, none of us are poisonous," Brandon said, his pride wounded.

"He doesn't know that," Ginevra said, raising an eyebrow. "He would never attack except in self-defense," she added, moving the snake from side to side to show us.

I stole a glance at Peter. He was still frozen with fright, his eyes locked on the snake in Ginevra's hand. As if she wanted to twist the knife in his open wound, she held it toward his face to show him, then walked to the edge of the woods and let it slither into the darkness. "He's gone," she told us smugly.

"You are fucking awesome!" Jake exclaimed as Ginevra returned.

"You sure it won't come back?" Jeneane asked, her face still pale.

"Don't worry, he won't," she said. "Sorry," she whispered to Pete as she passed him, "but we all need to overcome our fears. They're limitations we impose on ourselves."

"What a coincidence," Brandon said. "We were talking about your fear of snakes and then one showed up right next to you."

"Good thing you're not afraid of bears!" Jake said, breaking the tension. Everyone laughed and began to relax.

Ginevra sat down next to me as the rest of the group murmured admiringly about her. "Congratulations," I said acidly, watching Peter's face, still slack with shock. "You got what you wanted."

"It's not like you think. I did it for him," she said.

"For him?!" I retorted bitterly, feeling a wildness hidden deep inside me come to life and burst out at Ginevra. "What were you thinking? Look at him! He's terrified!" I said, shocked by the anger in my voice. Ginevra stared at me as if she didn't know me, as stunned as I by how I'd blurted out the thoughts I'd been holding back. *But I couldn't stop them.*

"All right," she admitted. "Maybe I overdid it a little, but now you're the one overdoing it. What's gotten into you? It was just a stupid joke! Would you chill?" she hissed.

Like a slap in the face, her words snapped me out of it, awakening my conscience. For a moment I found myself watching the scene from a distance. I'd felt it again: the uncontrollable impulse that drove me to react this way. *It was inside me.* I opened my mouth to speak but closed it before my thoughts took shape. Ginevra studied my bewildered expression and rested her warm hand on my leg.

"Sorry," I whispered. "I don't know why I reacted like that. You're right. Deep down I knew Peter wasn't in any danger, right?"

"Of course not," she said. "I was in complete control of the situation. I knew exactly what Peter was feeling. I could hear his thoughts. I wanted to help him overcome the trauma that's haunted him since he was little, when his horse got spooked by a snake and threw him from the saddle."

My mind filled with memories. "You're right," I said in a low voice, shaken. I well remembered the episode with the horse and the snake. "I thought he'd gotten over it."

"No, but tonight he was on the verge of doing it. He was about to face that snake, you know."

"I had no idea. I'm sorry," I whispered, mortified.

"That's okay. There was no way you could have known."

"Why don't you just use your powers of persuasion instead? I've seen what you can make people do."

"My power, like Evan's, can only make people act against their will. I can't eliminate a deeply rooted fear inside them. It would just keep resurfacing. Only Simon can work on such a deep level."

"I'm such an idiot! I ruined everything!" I groaned, burying my head in my hands.

"Don't worry," she reassured me, stroking my knee.

"You wanted to do him a favor and I thought you were just being a bitch! I'm such a mess. Forgive me! I've been losing control so easily lately and—" I covered my mouth with my hand and silence fell, a silence all our own. Meanwhile the voices of the others in the background faded into the distance.

"Speaking of which . . ." I looked up at her. "You know how much you mean to me," Ginevra said, "and I know you're the nicest person in the world, but lately there's something about you I can't figure out. It's like you've got a split personality. Your thoughts stop dead, you have mood swings, even the smallest things totally set you off. Maybe there's something worrying you that's making you react like this. We can talk about it if you want." She looked at me thoughtfully. It was so strange for her to ask me to talk to her about something she didn't already know.

"Believe me, I have no idea what's going on. You're probably right. Maybe I haven't totally overcome the whole death thing. Maybe I just hid it somewhere inside and when I get too emotional I can't handle it any more—I feel overwhelmed and lose control," I confessed regretfully. "It's like I'm constantly afraid an Executioner is out there waiting for his chance to attack me, and the feeling is wrecking my nervous system."

"I don't think you have anything to worry about. Months have gone by and nobody's come looking for you," she said, trying to reassure me.

"It would be great to believe that, but I can't control it. There's this tingling sensation under my skin like my instinct has reawakened, and I keep getting a terrible feeling in my stomach. It's cold, creepy."

Ginevra wrapped her arm around my shoulders affectionately. The others weren't paying any attention to us. "Sooner or later you'll put the whole thing behind you, you'll see. No Subterranean who isn't one of us will ever manage to get near you."

When I rested my head on Ginevra's shoulder she lowered her voice. "You're safe with us, Gemma. Take my word for it, no one's going to hurt you."

I felt sleepy and her words became fainter. My eyelids grew heavy and I could barely keep them open. I finally surrendered, closing them.

"You're not going to die . . ."

The words echoed in my head, sweet and soft, as my eyes opened, dazzled by the blinding sunlight reflected off the lake—a perfectly still mirror of water that stretched to the horizon like a pane of glass.

I rubbed my eyes, filled with an unusual feeling of lightness. It soon vanished, overpowered by a stronger emotion—a strange and now familiar sense of uneasiness. It gripped my mind as soon as my gaze landed on a distant figure veiled in white. It was a woman. She had her back to me and was clad in a pearly gown. Her hair flowed down her back like molten gold with a strange hint of copper that made it gleam with an unusual light. As if she'd sensed my presence, she turned her head and met my gaze, startling me. Her honey-colored eyes summoned me like an ancestral call. I felt something deep within me awaken, something new and intriguing. It battled the instinct that was warning me not to give in to the primitive need I felt to draw closer to the enchanting woman. But the need was stronger than the instinct and it prevailed.

The closer I came, the clearer the woman's outline appeared. When I was quite near her I discovered she wasn't alone. Another figure, hidden by her gown, was facing her, perfectly still. A shiver ran over my skin like a premonition.

"Evan," I whispered, bewildered, barely moving my lips. He didn't look at me or even acknowledge my presence, but focused all his attention on the woman. "Evan, what are you—"

The words died on my lips when the woman closed her eyelids, fringed with long lashes, and opened them again gracefully, fixing her gaze on mine. She rested her hand on Evan's neck and walked around him slowly, almost as if they were dancing. Her long legs made the white silk flow with each step until she stood behind him. She peered at him with a strange light in her eyes. *Desire.* With a satisfied expression she raised her amber eyes to mine. I couldn't move a muscle. Her hand moved slowly over Evan's skin and he tilted his head, following the movement as though it gave him pleasure, still paying no heed to me. I frowned, disconcerted. The woman smiled at me again and moved her lips to him, slowly sliding her finger down his neck and touching her mouth to his ear as if whispering something to him. Evan half closed his eyes with pleasure.

"No!" I screamed at the top of my lungs. I tried to reach them but couldn't move. Something was keeping me glued to my spot. My heart skipped a beat, then shrank back as Evan took the woman's hand, lifted it to his lips, and kissed her palm like he always did mine. "Evan . . ." I could barely breathe.

They gazed at each other for a long moment while I—powerless, trapped in my body—watched the woman rest her lips on his neck again. Evan encouraged her with his eyes. Desperation flooded me. Overhead, the clouds slid by quickly and the sun sank beyond the lake, dragging my heart with it into the darkest depths.

"Evan!" I shouted, but he couldn't hear me. My muffled voice echoed against the walls of my brain as if I were sealed in a crystal sphere. "Don't do it!" I shouted with all the desperation I felt.

She heard my cry and her eyes sought mine. A shudder ran through me and I squinted at her. Something about her looked familiar, almost as if I were staring at my own distorted reflection in a pool of water. I had the feeling that part of me had always known her. Suddenly my surroundings blurred and a stabbing pain in my head doubled me over. Confused images began to revolve around me as I writhed in pain. They suddenly stopped, showing me a serpent with yellow eyes, two narrow slits that stared at me. I flinched.

The image vanished, replaced by another that was even more dangerous: the woman's sharp, seductive gaze locked on mine. Eyes closed, I pressed my fingers to my temples to banish her cunning smile from my mind and the image of the serpent took its place only to disappear again, alternating with that of the woman. Now Evan's dark eyes filled my head and gripped my heart and again, the serpent. I covered my ears with my hands, unable to stop the rapid sequence of frozen images tormenting me; it was as if my brain had gone haywire and no longer responded to my commands. I felt like I was going insane as the flashes alternated faster and faster. The woman. The serpent. Evan. The serpent again. *Enoooough!* My screams pounded against the walls of my mind, blowing them up, but not a sound came from my lips. Again the woman. Evan. Again the serpent. *Stop it!*

The flashes suddenly focused on Evan's face. His eyes went wide as if someone had just struck him in the chest. He looked at me and I knew he could finally see me. "Evan," I murmured, but his eyes of ice were frozen in dull pain. "Evan," I whispered again.

The picture in my head blurred and disappeared, replaced by an image of Evan's arm as it fell heavily to the ground. Unbearable pain gripped my chest and the blackest darkness swallowed me up.

"Evan!" I screamed, panting, as a knot in my throat choked me and tears burned my eyes.

"Easy, Gemma," Ginevra whispered, brushing back the hair that clung to my damp face.

"Ginevra," I whispered in a daze. Neither the burning sensation in my eyes nor the pain in my chest had faded.

"Everything's fine. Evan will be here soon, you'll see," she said, trying to calm me down, but the feeling in my heart was stronger.

"He's dead! Evan's dead! Don't you see?" I hissed, confused, as tears continued to stream down my face. I clung to her comforting gaze in an attempt to climb out of the pit into which I'd fallen.

"Evan isn't dead. You had a bad dream, that's all."

My lips were trembling. I had a terrible presentiment. "Do you—do you think it's possible I can see things before they happen?" I asked, still shaken.

Ginevra looked at me with compassion. "Evan can't die," she said softly. "Gemma, you're just a little stressed. Try to relax." For a moment she fell silent and stared back at me, matching the intensity of my gaze. "I'll admit that at first I didn't think you'd be able to handle all this, but then I found out how strong you were, Gemma. You're stronger than you think. It's perfectly understandable for you to be so stressed. In fact, it's the least we expected. And I know you're shaken because Evan brought you into his world and shared things you thought were forbidden, and you're right. Sometimes my brother just doesn't think things through. Still, you have no reason to be so worried. It's just fear awakening your instinct and it seems my prank shook you up more than I thought it would."

Her words crept into my mind like a cloud of fog as my gaze, lost in the darkness of the woods, spotted something moving. My heart leapt to my throat and I cringed. A shadow. Ginevra read my thoughts and followed my gaze to the trees, then looked back at me, her expression calm, and squeezed my hand. Maybe she was right. I was starting to get paranoid.

I forced myself to take a deep breath and glanced at the clear sky. My star smiled at me, twinkling. Evan was fine and in a few hours I'd see him again.

"That was my mom." Faith's voice shook me out of my thoughts as I put my phone into my backpack. "Seems something horrible has happened in Iraq. She said there were massive casualties, including a lot of our soldiers. My brother called to say he's okay."

I shuddered so violently Ginevra sensed it through my skin. We exchanged a glance and a chill descended on us. "We'd better go," Ginevra told the group, squeezing my hand. "It's late."

16

SUBTLE JEALOUSY

When I woke up, I had a hard time remembering how I'd made it to bed. The light streaming through the window told me it was daytime, but that meant Evan should be there with me. I looked around, frustrated. No one was in the room with me except Irony, snoring on his cushion.

I dragged myself out of bed to get ready for school. My head was a heavy mass that weighed on my neck and my thoughts wandered, fleeting and muddled, leaving me in a daze. When I was ready I opened the door to leave, my stomach in a knot, ignoring the table laid for breakfast. The ice-cold air lashed at my face. It was strange no one had come to pick me up. There was no sign of Evan or Ginevra on the deserted street. What could have kept them?

I started to chew on the inside of my cheek as a multitude of questions filled my head. It had been so long since I'd walked to school that I had a terrible sense of foreboding.

Something caught my attention: a butterfly. I'd never seen such a pretty one before. It was big and black. *Completely black.* Its wings looked like velvet. I had the impression it was frightened, but it didn't fly off. Instead it came closer as if it knew me. I obeyed my urge to touch it and it moved its wings. Cautiously, I pulled my camera out of my backpack and took a few snapshots for the photography assignment Mr. Madison had given us a few days ago.

The sound of a car horn made me jump. I spun around, but saw no one on the street, so I turned back. The butterfly was gone—I looked around, but there was no trace of it. I set out again for school and another blare of a horn, closer this time, made me start again.

I shook my head, not recognizing the green pickup truck that had honked at me, and kept walking. The horn blared again insistently. I stared at the truck, but the light reflecting off the window kept me from seeing the driver. As if in response, the window slid down with a hiss.

"Need a ride?"

"Peter?" I squinted, frowning. "Pet!" I crossed the street with long strides. Peter rested his hand on the steering wheel, a satisfied smile on his face. "You've got a pickup?!" I exclaimed, amazed. "Since when do you have a pickup?"

"Get in," he invited with a jerk of his head. "I'm going your way." He shot me a glance as I sank into the low seat of the Ford Ranger. I still remember how excited I'd been the day we got our driver's licenses, but neither of us had ever had a car all our own before.

"Wow, this is awesome!" I said, stroking the black dashboard.

"It's not much—it's already a few decades old," he said, "but it's something—and it's mine." His lips curved into a proud smile.

"Are you kidding?" I asked, happy for him. "Remember how we used to play inside cardboard boxes, pretending they were cars?"

"You always wanted to drive but I never let you," Peter said, making me laugh.

"You said you were the *man* and that one day you'd take me for a drive in a real car."

"Yeah." Peter looked down and gripped the steering wheel. Looking at his fingers made me think of yesterday when our hands had accidentally touched. I didn't want Peter to suffer. He was a part of me—an important part. "That was a long time ago. We were just little kids. What we said back then doesn't matter." His tone was dull. Silence filled the truck as Peter pulled into the school parking lot.

"Hey! We're here now, right? You kept your promise."

"True," he said. We both laughed out loud just as my eye fell on Evan's BMW, parked almost directly in front of us. My heart raced. Evan was glaring threateningly through the windshield at Peter. I tensed. I'd never seen his eyes so dark before. He seemed to be trying hard to keep himself from killing Peter.

Evan got out of the car, slammed the door, and canceled the distance between us with long strides. His face wore a caustic expression that was far from reassuring. "What are you doing with him?" he asked me, cutting to the chase. His tone was cold, his gaze dark.

"He offered me a ride, that's all," I stammered.

"You could have waited for me. Do you have any idea what went through my mind when I found you weren't home?" he admonished me, a note of desperation only I could understand in his voice.

"Thanks for the ride, Peter," I mumbled quickly before walking off with Evan in an attempt to keep the two of them apart.

"See you in class!" Peter called after me.

"And do *you*," I shot back once I was sure no one could hear us, "have any idea what went through *my* mind when you didn't come to my house after telling me you would?"

Evan's face relaxed and his expression turned sly. "You missed me." He raised an eyebrow and lifted one corner of his mouth in a smile. "I thought you wouldn't even notice I was gone," he said, satisfied. But it was a challenge, I was sure of it.

"You can't—how can you even think something like that?" My eyelids fluttered nervously. I couldn't believe he'd just said that. "Maybe that's true for *you*," I said, throwing the insinuation back in his face.

"Sorry, but I had no choice. I should have gotten back last night, but I was delayed."

"Delayed?"

"It was more difficult than we'd expected," he said.

"Okay, okay. That's all I need to hear," I murmured. A strange tic had begun to pulse in my eyelid.

Evan looked away, a brooding expression on his face. "I know it's hard for you, but I can't change what I am," he said regretfully.

"All those people—" The words caught in my throat as I stared straight ahead.

"Each of them will have what they've earned, so you shouldn't feel sorry for them. You've seen with your own eyes what's on the other side. Those who went with us were lucky. We weren't the only ones recruiting souls in the trenches."

"W-what? You mean there were Witches too?"

Evan's face darkened. "When there are so many deaths all at once, they're almost bound to show up. Not all mortals have a Subterranean waiting to help them cross over. It's a privilege that has to be earned by resisting evil during their lifetimes. Otherwise they sign an unspoken agreement with the Witches who can't wait to claim the souls of mortal sinners. A lot of people lost their lives last night, but it was something that had to happen," he said, trying to convince me. "It was their fate. No one can do anything about it. You know what happens when you try to elude death."

"It always comes back looking for you," I said.

Evan squeezed my hand. "I didn't mean that. That's not always how it goes. And it's not our problem any more," he stressed reassuringly. "Anyway, you haven't answered my question."

"What ques—"

"I asked if you missed me," he said.

I shot him a glance. "What do you think?" I raised a flirtatious eyebrow. "And what about you? Am I mistaken or did I just witness a jealousy scene?"

He mimicked my expression. "What do you think?"

"Oho!" My jaw dropped and my eyes opened wide. I couldn't believe he was actually worried about Peter. "*You?* Jealous? Of *Pet*?"

"Why not? You were in his truck."

"Come on, it's only *Peter*. He's like a brother to me! You can read my emotions so you should know that already. Besides, he was just giving me a ride," I said, my cheeks pleasantly aflame because of his unexpected admission.

"That doesn't mean I can't be jealous of him."

"Why should you be?"

"Ginevra told me what he feels for you."

I opened my mouth and then quickly closed it, embarrassed. "I don't feel the same way about him," I said reassuringly.

"But he's still important to you. He's a part of your life—the life I had no part in—and that makes me crazy."

"Evan, I only want to be with you," I said as I stopped at my locker. "You have no reason to be jealous. Of Peter or anyone else."

Evan raised an eyebrow and took a slow step in my direction, forcing me back until I felt the metal pressed against my shoulders. "I can't help it if I'm jealous when it comes to you," he whispered. "I want you all to myself." He rested a hand beside my head.

"But I'm already yours," I said slowly, gazing into his dark eyes.

He pressed his lips together as if he didn't completely agree. "If that's true," he whispered tenderly, breathing the words a fraction of an inch from my skin, "explain why you haven't given me a kiss yet." He stared at my lips as if he wanted nothing more in the world.

"Do you mean to say you're asking me to kiss you?" I asked provocatively.

Evan smiled, just as provocative. *"I don't need to ask,"* he whispered in my mind, his mouth on mine. He coaxed my lips apart and suddenly my head was spinning. I wasn't sure if it was because of the deep, sensual tone of his voice inside my mind or my repressed desire for him. Being away from Evan for so long had been harder than I'd expected, especially because his absence had caught me unprepared.

"Next time remember to warn me when you'll be gone for so long," I whispered. I took my lips off his, but immediately pulled him back toward me by the shirt and kissed him again.

"Sounds like you weren't bored without me. Ginevra said you had a pretty lively evening." He smiled and I pretended I didn't understand what he was talking about.

"Nothing out of the ordinary, actually," I said, holding back a smile.

"I can't leave you alone for a single day! Tell me, are you trying to get my attention? Is that what you're trying to do?" he asked under his breath, his elbow resting on the locker and his body close to mine.

"Now that you mention it," I said, biting my lip sensually, "I can't rule out that possibility. You know, I have to say you made a big mistake, getting me used to all those strong emotions. Hasn't anyone ever told you bad habits die hard? You weren't here and I had to find some way to kill time," I teased, my voice low.

Evan brushed his lips against my neck, making me tremble. "The important thing is for you not to end up killing yourself."

"I'm not so sure I wouldn't be doing you a favor." I slipped away from him and grabbed his hand. We headed down the hall to class. "Or are you saying you'd miss me?" I cast him a glance, but his eyes were already on me and he smiled.

"Which brings us back to where we started," he said. In a flash he was in front of me. Grabbing me, he lifted me up, pressing my body against his. Our faces were at the same height, almost touching. "I would miss your every breath," he whispered, looking into my eyes.

My mouth sought his as I slid down against his body until my feet touched the floor.

"Let's skip school," Evan proposed under his breath.

"What?"

"Let's leave!" he said excitedly.

"And go where? Are you out of your mind?" I said in astonishment.

"We have a whole day to make up for," he said, assuming a seductive look to convince me. It was hard to ignore.

"Evan William James!" I said, pretending to be scandalized. "What kind of Angel are you?"

He moved his mouth close to mine, one corner curved in a sensual smile, and shot me a look that made my head spin again. "A dark one." He raised an eyebrow. "Be careful; I might even be dangerous."

"And crazy too," I purred.

"You're right. Guilty as charged."

"Oh, really?" Our voices were whispers murmured on each other's mouths. "Then you admit it."

"You should know. You're the one who made me lose my mind." He kissed me tenderly.

"You're saying *I* made you crazy?" I asked.

"Completely. I'm a slave who is mad with love, and you're my queen," he whispered, ensnaring me in his dark spell.

"No one should know how to kiss like this," I murmured, amazed by the softness of his lips.

"What do you say to my proposal now? Want to run away with me?"

"Slaves shouldn't be allowed to make proposals."

"Not unless they're dying with longing for their queen." He grew serious again and looked me in the eye. "Let's go to our hideaway, Gemma," he whispered. "I want to spend some time alone with you."

A warm sensation trembled deep in my chest and filled my head. The lake house had become our refuge. I began to consider the proposal but continued to toy with him. "You know, I'm not sure that's a good idea. If you're as dangerous as you say, maybe I should run away from you instead," I replied, challenging him with my eyes.

A corner of his mouth curled into a smile. "I don't think you could." He tightened his grip around my waist. "I'm too strong."

"And I'm not so sure I want to run away." The words escaped me, my mind clouded by his scent. "The truth is, you're my demon. You should let me get to class," I said, my breathing irregular. I wasn't very convincing.

"I could do as you say, or"—his lips were right next to mine—"I could ignore what you want and follow my instinct."

"What does your instinct say? I've gotten the impression your intentions aren't exactly honorable," I said accusingly, my voice seductive.

"Honorable intentions are for good boys."

"And you're not a good boy?"

"Not at all." He shook his head and looked at me through his narrowed, long-lashed eyes.

"You should have told me that before, don't you think?" I said as his hands tightened on my back.

"I thought you knew," he whispered. "You're still in time to escape," he warned, his smile sly.

"I think I'll run the risk."

"Careful . . . I might take advantage." He raised an eyebrow as his hand sensually made its way toward my rear. There was something irresistible in his manner and tone, a spell that made my head spin.

"I might even enjoy it," I whispered, biting my lip to provoke him. I raised my mouth to Evan's to seal the deal just as the last bell sounded, throwing a bucket of cold water on our bodies that were burning with desire.

"Too late," I whispered. "Someone else has decided for us."

"What makes you think I'm willing to give up so easily?" he warned, looking at me stealthily. Smiling, he took me by the hand and headed toward the Spanish classroom.

What are you doing? I mouthed. Evan had taken my hand and rested the tip of a black felt-tip pen on my skin. The teacher was explaining something, his back turned to us. Evan moved the pen across my palm, drawing a little heart.

"You're the only subject I can focus on." He smiled.

I raised my pencil to my lips and nibbled on it. "That's because languages are easier for you. You know more than the teacher does," I said, trying to follow the class.

Evan smiled at me with his eyes.

"So tell me, how many do you know, exactly?"

He laughed under his breath, counting on his fingers. "Hmm . . . Let's see . . . There's English, Italian, German, Nahuatl and—"

"Nah*what*?"

Evan shot me a sidelong grin.

"You're just making fun of me," I said resignedly, nudging his shoulder.

"You said it, not me." He laughed again and then tried hard to be serious. "I know *all* languages, even the extinct ones. We need to in order to communicate with the souls entrusted to us," he explained softly. "We acquire all knowledge with our first bite of—"

"A-*hem*." The teacher cleared his throat and shot us a threatening glance.

Evan craned his neck toward me and I looked at him warningly. "I can always help you study . . . on the condition that you accept my proposal." He batted his eyes at me, his face inches from mine.

"What proposal?" I whispered, puzzled.

"That we skip school. We still can."

"You know, you were right about that business of being crazy," I said, grinning, "but I'm afraid you'll have to wait until after school to be alone with me." I shot him an alluring look.

He leaned toward my ear and breathed words through my hair, giving me goosebumps: "I'll hold my breath until then." His tone was sensual and provocative.

My eyelids fluttered and it took me a few moments to regain the power of speech. Evan seemed to enjoy causing difficulties for me; he was well aware of the effect he had on me. "Ooh, what a sacrifice," I stammered, trying to come across as sarcastic. "You don't need to breathe." We both smiled as the teacher began to write letters with strange symbols on the board. During the silence that followed, Evan sought my hand under the desk and squeezed it. I returned the gesture, feeling a shiver run down my spine.

17

ADDING FUEL TO THE FIRE

Empty.

How was this possible? I was stunned. "Gin! Remember to restock the fridge after you empty it!" I yelled from the kitchen, smiling to myself. Ginevra had finished all the food again.

"Order whatever you want, hon," she replied affectionately from her place on the red leather couch as I continued to smile. "Home delivery!" she exclaimed, amused, as she abstractedly stroked Iron's wrinkly head. Ginevra had been bringing him home with her ever since I started spending most of my time with them and now she couldn't live without him.

"A cheese pizza wouldn't be bad, actually." I peeked around the three overlapping walls that separated the kitchen from the living room to look at Ginevra. Simon was lying on one end of the couch, his leg thrown over the back of it, and Evan was sunk into the cushions.

"One cheese pizza coming up!" she chimed.

I opened the fridge again and jumped back as a package of chocolate muffins tumbled from the top shelf, pushed forward by the mountain of food that had appeared. I blinked in surprise. "Don't you think you overdid it a little? I'm not *that* hungry!" I said teasingly.

"Oh! Don't worry, some of it's for me."

I shook my head and chose a carton of pineapple juice from the second shelf along with two candy bars and a slice of pizza. I shut the refrigerator door but heard Ginevra grumbling from the next room. "Hey!" she complained. I got the hint and opened the fridge again, taking out a second helping of everything, then awkwardly nudged the door shut, trying not to drop the food I was holding.

"While you're at it, get some popcorn too! It's in the top cabinet," Simon called. "Oh, and don't forget the soda! Hurry up! The movie's about to start!"

"I've only got two hands!" I protested, joining them in the living room, my arms full of food. "You could help, you know." Juggling the various containers, I shot a look at Ginevra.

"All you have to do is ask," she murmured with a laugh. They all got a kick out of my human awkwardness. Sometimes I wondered if they asked me to do things just to have fun watching me do them. Relaxed, she continued to stare at the screen in front of her as the food floated out of my hands. Alarmed, I tried to grab it, but then saw it drifting through the air toward her and realized it hadn't fallen—she'd taken it from me. I still wasn't completely used to her magic and often felt like I was in a Disney movie.

Ginevra's food moved straight toward her and she plucked it out of the air as the rest of the things continued to hover, waiting for someone to claim them. With a tinge of uneasiness, I reached out, took the slice of cheese pizza, and sank my teeth into it. "French fries would be good on this." I sat down next to Evan and watched the food arrange itself on the crystal coffee table in front of us. Although it was all so unusual, I'd come to feel I was part of the family. Our closeness reassured me.

"Oh, I forgot to turn off the light," I said. "Gin, would you mind?"

Ginevra gracefully flicked her pointer and middle fingers as if shooing away a pesky insect. It was an automatic gesture she didn't need to make—she could exercise her powers using nothing but her mind—but sometimes she liked to be a little theatrical. The room instantly went dark though we were all still in our seats.

The movie was almost over but I'd only managed to pay attention to a few scenes. Having Evan's body so close to mine distracted me from everything else. The way he stroked my hair and never took his eyes off me spoke volumes. A sort of static electricity surrounded us and in his eyes I saw the desire to leave the others in the living room and shut ourselves up in his room to break the rules a little.

That afternoon I'd turned down a trip to our hideaway so I could dedicate myself to a nobler pursuit: studying. I'd soon abandoned that, however, in favor of Ginevra's far more enticing proposal that we all watch *Vampires Suck*.

"Anybody know what happened to Drake?" Simon asked as the credits filled the screen.

"I haven't seen him since yesterday," Ginevra said. "To tell you the truth I have the funny feeling he's avoiding me. Is it the same with you guys?"

"I saw him a few hours ago. Why would he avoid you, G?" Simon asked.

"Feel like going out for some air?" I whispered to Evan, taking advantage of their conversation.

He had one foot on the floor and the rest of his body on the couch, his other leg draped over mine. "Where do you want to go?" he asked, the gleam of desire in his eyes mirroring his thoughts.

"I don't care. You choose. Anywhere's fine," I said in a low voice.

An unspoken proposal glinted in his gaze. "Don't tempt me," he whispered, tilting his head. "If you do, I'll have to take you up to my room." He raised an eyebrow, his expression provocative.

"I was thinking more of getting some ice cream at Ben & Jerry's."

"Do you ever think about anything but food?" Simon looked at me, amazed.

"Yeah, Gemma, what's been going on with your appetite lately?" asked Ginevra, who was sitting next to us.

"She's been spending too much time with you," Simon told her, grinning.

"This was actually supposed to be a private conversation," I said in a mock-threatening tone.

"What a witch you are!" Ginevra accused me, pinching my side.

I opened my mouth, taken aback but smiling. "Look who's talking."

"Want to come with us?" Evan asked them, but only to be polite.

"Spare me the pleasantries—I'm not buying it." Ginevra rolled her eyes. "I know what you're thinking. In fact, please spare me that too!" she said sardonically. "Just, when you get back, can you take a look at my car? There's something wrong with it."

"What's wrong with it?" Evan asked.

"If I knew that, I wouldn't be asking you, would I?"

"Very funny! You might as well admit you like the idea of me being the one to take care of it," her brother scoffed. Ginevra threw a piece of popcorn at his back. "I'm sure I'll have to change the brake pads too," he said. "Last time you literally burned up the brakes. Again."

"Make sure not to add too much pressure to the back tires to try to destabilize me or I'll burn the tires again too."

"I don't need to sabotage you when I can beat you fair and square."

"Don't be so sure about that. The drifting brakes I had you install will help me beat you around the curves, little brother."

"I've told you a thousand times you've got to downshift before entering a turn. When are you finally going to start heeding the advice of an expert?" he asked with a grin of satisfaction.

"Just as soon as an expert gives me advice," she shot back.

Evan laughed out loud. Ginevra would never give in.

"Were you really serious about going to Ben and Jerry's?" Evan whispered as if hoping to hear a completely different proposal.

I nodded as we left the house. "Why not? Let's go for a drive, soldier," I replied, making my way down the walk.

"As you wish," he murmured, holding back a smile as he opened the door of the BMW for me.

I looked out the window as we drove back from Mirror Lake a couple of hours later. It was strange how the place I was born and raised appeared in a new light now that I was sharing it with someone important. What was even odder was how everything appeared normal and unchanged. The shop windows, the people walking down Main Street . . . nothing seemed to have altered in the Lake Placid I'd always known. And yet nothing about the way I perceived the world was the same, as if Evan had lifted the veil from my eyes that had prevented me from seeing the reality hidden behind the appearances. Evan was an Angel, Ginevra a Witch, and I knew the true purpose of human life. I knew the answers mankind had sought for millennia. I'd seen Eden; I knew what awaited us. I'd been given a gift. If only I could share it with others, spread the incredible awareness. How would it change the lives of every other person on earth? The world would never be the same again.

"What are you thinking about?" Evan's voice pulled me out of my thoughts. His expression was serious, his hands gripping the black leather-covered steering wheel. Not knowing what was going on in my mind frustrated him.

"Just people-watching." I paused, staring through the closed window, my eyes unfocused. "They have no idea what's actually happening."

"Just like you not so long ago." He smiled, but I remained serious.

"What's so special about me? I don't deserve to know more than anyone else does," I acknowledged, my tone pensive.

Evan smiled again in satisfaction. "You deserve it because of what you just said." There was a long silence. "Hungry?" he asked, tilting his head and deliberately changing the subject as he turned onto Main Street.

"A little," I said, shrugging.

"What do you want to eat?"

"I wouldn't say no to a cheese pizza," I said. This was confirmed by a low grumble in my stomach even though I'd just inhaled a double scoop of Ben and Jerry's two hours ago. What could I do? I wanted more.

"Of course you wouldn't," he said, amused. "You would never turn down a cheese pizza."

"How could anyone turn down a cheese pizza?" I said.

A laugh escaped Evan as he parked outside Bazzi's Pizza on Main Street and turned off the engine. In the silence that followed, he propped his left elbow against the steering wheel, leaned toward me, and stroked my cheek with his right hand. His eyes turned serious again as he returned to our discussion of a moment ago. "Never underestimate yourself, Gemma." I shook my head, ready to contradict him, but he rested a finger on my lips, preventing me from speaking. "There's something special about you. I think I understood that the first time I saw you," he whispered, staring at my lips. "Something extraordinary that makes me lose control. I'd never met anyone with such power over me," he whispered.

"The only thing I have that's extraordinary is you. There's nothing special about me," I mumbled, looking at the dashboard.

"If you could see yourself through my eyes, you'd realize you're like a diamond in a pile of broken glass. The fact that you don't realize it makes you sparkle even brighter in comparison."

I continued to shake my head in disagreement. Evan sought my gaze and drew closer. "You have so many things inside you; you just need to let them out." He stroked my chin.

"Don't expect so much from me, Evan. I'm afraid you may end up disappointed," I warned. His eyes narrowed on me as if I'd just said something unacceptable. "No one can know better than me what's inside you. Not even you," he replied confidently.

I blushed. "Okay," I said, embarrassed. "Too many compliments make me dizzy."

"I think it's just hunger," he said, getting out of the car. A moment later he was looking in through my window, his hands resting on the roof. "Was it me or did I hear your stomach grumble a minute ago?" he said, grinning. Instinctively I rested my hand on my belly. I'd hoped he hadn't heard it. "What's it been, two hours since you last ate? How on earth do you stay in such good shape?"

"I don't eat *that* much," I said sheepishly.

"Wha—You don't eat that much?" he repeated, looking astonished.

"It's just—I eat often and my metabolism is fast," I stammered, to Evan's amusement. Still smiling, he walked away from the car. Through the rearview mirror I watched him head toward the pizzeria, a white stone building on the corner, until he disappeared behind the big red awnings. I switched on the radio and sank back into my seat while from the street came the chatter of people dining on the balcony of Generations, the restaurant across from Bazzi's. The melodious voice of Evanescence's Amy Lee filled the car. The CD was still in the player from the last time we'd gone camping.

I was just beginning to lose myself in the notes of *Hello* when an uneasy shiver crept across my skin. A frightful sensation. Cold.

Again.

Alarmed, I scanned the street. The sensation came again and I recognized it as it ran over my neck. It was an old feeling, as familiar as it was bone chilling: someone was watching me.

I peered around nervously, leaning over to get a better look around the Northwoods Inn sign and the tree-lined parking lot. Everything looked normal. As I checked out the cars my heart began to pump at an accelerated rate. The blood throbbed in my veins, agitating my breathing as my panic mounted.

"You okay?"

Evan's voice made me jump in my seat. Consumed by the fear that had returned to torture me over the last few days, I hadn't even noticed he'd walked back to the car. As he closed the door, I sank back in my seat and forced myself to breathe, my skin still cold and clammy. "That was fast," I said, not answering his question.

Evan flashed me a smile and pulled a French fry from the pizza box. "I can be convincing," he said with his sensual grin. "I had them put fries on it, just the way you like it." He raised an eyebrow.

"You trying to bribe me?" I said accusingly, returning his gaze. My panic had subsided.

Evan laughed. "If I wanted to do that I'd definitely be on the right track."

I lowered my eyes, embarrassed. What was he insinuating? "Yeah," I admitted, "pizza with fries works wonders with me—can't deny that." I lifted the lid and inhaled the aroma that instantly filled the car. The pizza box warmed my lap as I took out a big, piping-hot slice dripping with cheese. "Where are we going?" I asked, checking the clock on the dashboard. "It's almost seven."

"I promised Ginevra I'd take a look at her car." Evan raised a finger to his temple and twirled it. "If I don't she'll go out of her mind, and who can stand her when that happens?"

"Why doesn't she fix it herself? She's a Witch, she should be able to do it."

"Who said she couldn't?" he asked, glancing at me. "She likes having me as her mechanic, and deep down I don't mind being the only one who puts his hands on her engine."

"Your hands are amazing on anything."

"Is that so?" he whispered, a big grin on his face.

Oh my God. I thought I'd only said it in my mind! I felt the blood rush to my cheeks.

He tilted his head to look at me with his hands resting on the steering wheel, his smile seductive. "On anything in particular?" His voice had softened.

I decided to play along. "On me, for example."

"This is getting interesting."

"On my neck in particular, if you really want to know." It was the truth and I hadn't been able to hold it back. Feeling his hand on my neck always made me tremble.

Evan stopped the car in his driveway and immediately leaned toward me. He extended his hand, slowly drawing lines of fire on my skin. "Like this?" he whispered, slipping his fingers through my hair to my nape. A shiver of pure energy spread down my back, giving me goosebumps. God, the feeling made my head spin. I half closed my eyes, my body quivering, his face close to mine. "Exactly," I whispered, swallowing. His hot breath tickled my ear.

"And what do you say"—he gently slid his fingers across my skin—"if I move my hand like this?" He brought his fingers to the base of my neck.

"Perfect," I murmured.

He slowly brushed his thumb across my lips, igniting in me the yearning for his mouth, barely an inch away. Evan's cheek moved over mine, brushing my skin, and I let myself be swept away by the sensations. He raised his chin slightly and our lips touched. I parted mine, seeking contact, but Evan lingered, keeping his a fraction of an inch from me, limiting himself to light, fleeting touches.

I took a deep breath and lifted my own chin higher. His kiss was sweet, his lips full and soft as his fingers moved again to my neck, seeking shelter in my hair, filling my body with shivers.

"Now it's your turn," I whispered, not completely sure I'd regained control of myself. "You have to tell me something you like," I said to arouse him.

"That's easy." He took my hand and rested it on his chest over his heart. "I like it when you put your hand here." His voice was a low murmur as if someone might hear us.

"I do that all the time," I said, realizing it only then.

"True. And whenever you do it takes me back—back to when I kissed you for the first time, thinking it would be the last," he confessed. "I was desperate at the thought of giving you up. Feeling your hand on me devastated me. It made something explode inside me, an untamable fire." Evan squeezed my hand against his chest.

"Has that changed?" I asked under my breath.

"Never," he said firmly. "I feel the same emotion every time." I rested my forehead against his and touched his lips with my own. "We'd better go before your pizza gets cold," he said. He vanished and reappeared a second later, opening my door and holding out a hand to help me down, since the seats of the SUV were quite a bit higher than those of the other cars.

"Wait for me in the garage. I'll be right back." Evan headed toward the front door, leaving me outside. I nodded and walked around the corner, my eyes on the dark path.

The garage was in the left wing next to the kitchen's huge picture window and had two massive doors in dark wood. On the opposite side, another picture window revealed the vast room downstairs that housed the swimming pool.

Something made me look up, a fleeting movement behind the thick patch of trees beyond the path. It was too fast for me to see what it was. My heart constricted as a dark figure darted toward me and halted a few steps away. I gasped and dropped the pizza box from my trembling fingers.

"Mmm . . . pizza!" someone exclaimed, catching the box an instant before it hit the ground, opening it, and taking out a slice.

"Drake! You think it's funny, scaring me like that? Do you want to give me a heart attack?" I scolded him, my voice shaking. "Can't you show up like everyone else?" I said scornfully as my voice grew steadier and my knees stopped knocking.

"Hey, it's not my fault you're out here in the dark all alone," he shot back, arching an eyebrow. His dark gaze sharpened on mine, almost as if he wanted to probe my thoughts. It was the first time his eyes had studied me like this and part of me felt seriously uncomfortable.

My instinct told me there was something different about him though I couldn't put my finger on it—it was something beyond my understanding. "Are you letting your hair grow out?" I asked bluntly.

The question seemed to confuse him. "Nope, it's the same as always," he said. On closer inspection I realized he was right. It must have been something else.

"Evan's not around?" he asked, avoiding my searching look. I suddenly got a feeling of déjà vu.

"I'm right here," Evan said behind me. "Where've you been, Drake?"

"Here and there. Slaughtering souls as always." Drake winked at me and I shuddered. "Where else would I be?" He shrugged as if we were chatting about the weather.

"Watch how you talk in front of her," Evan warned.

"Hey, chill. I've had a lot on my plate recently. That better?" He threw me a surly look and then looked back at Evan. "Were you looking for me or something?"

"No. I didn't want to interrupt you in your—um, interrupt what you were doing." Evan also cast me a grim glance. It was clear what he meant and he was trying to talk his way around the subject to avoid upsetting me.

Drake shrugged again. "Just carrying out orders. We have no choice," he said, his eyes fixed on his brother's.

"Yeah, as if I didn't you know better than that."

Drake spread his arms. "Have you been drinking?" I asked him, smelling Scotch on his breath.

He narrowed his eyes and held up his hand, the thumb and forefinger an inch apart. Looking at me through the space between them, he said, "Just a little."

"You'd better go freshen up," Evan told him, grinning. "You're always a mess when you drink." Drake burst out laughing as he turned to go, his hands clasped behind his head, while Evan and I headed to the garage, following the path that skirted the house. Something made me turn around. I saw that Drake was still looking at me, his face more serious than I'd ever seen it. I stared back for a second and squeezed Evan's hand, suddenly uncomfortable. Seemingly without effort, Evan raised one of the two garage doors and lowered it again behind us.

"Has Drake always been alone?" I asked point-blank, a thread of bitterness running through my voice.

Evan frowned at me, surprised by my question. "Why do you ask?"

I struggled to find a more acceptable word than the one that had come to mind: *excluded.* "I think he might feel a little . . . lonely."

"What makes you say that?" Evan didn't sound convinced.

"Come on, don't tell me you haven't noticed. I get the impression he's changed a little lately too. Haven't you realized it?"

"What do you mean, exactly?" he asked with a puzzled look as he laid out his tools on the workbench.

"It's like all the life's gone out of him. He barely ever hangs out with us and when he does it's almost like he's not really there. I don't recognize him any more, he's like a different person." Evan listened carefully, a surprised look on his face. "So yeah, I think he might feel lonely. I mean, you and Simon both have someone, but he's all alone."

"He has us," Evan said innocently.

"It's not the same. You had them too before you found me."

Finally he seemed to understand. "I'd never thought of that. So you think he's jealous?"

"Hmm. Jealous might be overdoing it, but yeah, I think being constantly surrounded by couples might make him feel left out. It's just a theory," I was quick to add.

"Ginevra would have realized it," he said, thinking aloud.

"If I'm right, that might be why Drake's been avoiding her, like she said. Maybe he doesn't want her to know how he feels."

"What's made you think all this?" Evan asked thoughtfully.

"His face," I said. "The way he was looking at me tonight was odd."

"What do you mean?" I didn't know if it was a good idea to tell Evan everything Drake's look had made me feel. "What kind of look did he give you?" he insisted, as if sensing my hesitation to explain further.

"Well, if I didn't know Drake was your brother, I would have said there was a bit of slyness in his eyes. Like he was, kind of . . . coming on to me." It had sounded better in my head. Saying it out loud made me feel like such an idiot.

Evan burst out laughing. "That's crazy! Drake would never think of you that way." Then his expression changed as if he were considering the idea seriously for the first time. "He's my brother. It's ridiculous." He shook his head to drive off the suspicion.

"You're right. I don't know how I could have thought something like that," I admitted sheepishly. "It really is ridiculous." *Please God, let the earth open and swallow me up.* If only I could go back in time and erase that last embarrassing moment.

"I'll talk to him about it," Evan said, his tone serious.

"No!" I said quickly. "You can't. He would realize I'd said something to you. I already feel like such an idiot. Please, Evan. What I said was crazy—I misread everything. That's at least as clear as the fact that you're my boyfriend!"

"Hmm . . ." He drew closer. "That sounds so good. Say it again."

"Don't tell me I've never said it before," I teased, relieved I'd managed to change the subject.

"Not recently, you haven't." He held me close.

"Then I'd better fix that," I whispered, my face a handspan from his. "You, Evan William James, are my boyfriend."

"Say it again." His eyes were locked onto mine, his tone firm, almost commanding.

"You're. My. *Boyfriend.*"

He squeezed me tighter and rested his lips on mine. "I like hearing you say it." His voice softened to a sigh.

"I like saying it," I said, abandoning myself to him.

"Sounds like we're agreed, then."

"Sounds like we are." Another gentle kiss. "You know, I'm starting to think you're jealous," I teased him. The provocation worked.

"Jealous? Who of, this time?" He frowned, surprised, and I bit my lower lip.

"Of my pizza, of course! You keep putting yourself between us!" I exclaimed, pulling away from him and grabbing the pizza box.

Evan smiled and shook his head. "You got me. Want me to leave you two alone?" he said, grinning.

"It's the least you could do."

"If that's really what you want," he shot back, tucking his foot under the workbench and pulling out the dark-gray creeper, his gaze never leaving mine. Lying down on it, he rolled himself under Ginevra's car.

Still smiling, I stood on tiptoe and hoisted myself onto the metal workbench where Evan had laid out his tools. I gave myself a few minutes of silence to chew on the now-cold pizza and study the garage, which looked like a cross between a well designed, well organized auto repair shop and a racecar showroom.

Suspended from the ceiling was a fluorescent tube that ran around the entire perimeter of the garage and also branched off toward the center. The result was a bright white light that illuminated everything, dazzling my eyes whenever I looked at it.

The light-colored walls were accented by a row of black pillars that also ran down the center of the garage. Lining the walls were dark-gray panels hung with all kinds of tools. Evan was the one who took care of all the cars and motorcycles in the house. Although he'd never told me so, I'd realized right from the start that engines were his passion. It was easy to see from the twinkle of satisfaction in his eyes.

The BMW was parked outside, but its absence was barely noticeable in the huge garage filled with vehicles. Parked right in the center, the gray Ferrari shone like a starlet in the spotlight. The other cars followed it, lined up in an orderly, well-spaced row.

At first I'd been able to tell them apart only by their color but over time I'd learned their names. By the end of summer I'd spent so much time in the garage with Evan that I'd become a bit of an expert myself. The Bugatti Veyron Super Sport with its elegant carbon-blue trim was Simon's, and I'd learned that its 1200 horsepower allowed it to reach a top speed of 267 miles per hour, going from zero to sixty in 2.4 seconds. Drake, on the other hand, preferred Italian cars to French and had opted for a black Maserati GranTurismo S.

Despite Simon's ability to erase people's memories and Evan's power to control the mind of anyone who might be too interested in them, they rarely went out with all three cars at once in order to avoid drawing too much attention. They were safe to a certain extent—that is, except for Ginevra's obsessive tendency to put herself in the spotlight. She didn't at all mind being the center of attention.

Lined up on the far left of the garage were four motorcycles that confronted me menacingly, perfectly representing the sporty, aggressive riding styles of the four family members, as if even they knew no other way to express themselves.

Evan's MV Agusta CC seemed to be trained on me like a black panther ready to pounce. At first I'd been surprised to learn that the ferocious-looking gray Aprilia RSV4 belonged to Ginevra; no one had warned me the first time I'd seen her on it at dawn in a clandestine race where I'd been on the back of Evan's bike, clinging to him. Drake, instead, had a Yamaha R1 Laguna Seca, parked next to Simon's Ducati Desmosedici with its unusual black and white design.

To the right, just in front of the workbench I was sitting on now, on top of the retractable platform car lift was Ginevra's gray Lamborghini. Its elegant lines were reflected in the glass wall opposite it that held tires in all sizes. The futuristic design of its carbon fiber and steel body had been inspired by a fighter plane's fuselage and perfectly expressed Ginevra's sensual, provocative nature. Flowing lines and angular surfaces created a fascinating play of color further enhanced by sunlight. There were only twenty of these custom-built sports cars in the whole world, and it was worth over a million dollars.

Lying on the flat, four-wheeled creeper, Evan was working under the rear of the car where the engine was. From where I was sitting, I could see only his legs, as if the car had swallowed up the rest of him.

"Everything okay down there?" I asked, gulping down the last bite of pizza. Until now, the clink of his tools had been the only sound in the garage.

"Sounds like you're done." Evan's muffled voice stifled by laughter echoed between the car's wheels.

I loved the smell in the air—a mix of gasoline, new tires, and motor oil. I hopped down and went over to him. His knees were raised. I pulled off my burgundy sweatshirt, my necklace jingling against my army-green tank top, and sank down cross-legged beside the back wheel of the Lamborghini. It was elevated a foot or so off the black quartz floor that glittered as if studded with rhinestones.

"Okay if I sit here?" I asked.

"Sit wherever you like."

"Find the problem?" I added, peeking under the wheels.

"It was the alternator drive belt," he said as if I had any idea of what he was talking about. "The spring was almost broken and that was making the car vibrate. I replaced it. There, almost done."

A few minutes later Evan planted his foot on the floor and rolled himself out from under the car until he was lying next to me. Just above his right cheekbone was an oily black streak that gave him an even tougher look. The position I was in relative to him made the temptation to kiss him irresistible. Surrendering to my instinct, I rested my palms on the black floor and lowered myself to his mouth, but Evan pulled me roughly against him and held me tight. He smiled, lying beneath me, and pressed his lips to mine.

I opened my eyes only at the sound of his suave voice. "Careful," he whispered, "there's gasoline nearby." He raised an eyebrow and fixed his gaze on mine, leaving me defenseless.

"We'd better not play with fire," I said breathlessly.

"I could always try to control"—his eyes went to my mouth as if it had summoned them—"the fire." He swallowed. Then a sparkle appeared in his eye and a proposition in his sly smile. He slowly drew closer.

"Think you could manage it?" I asked as he tenderly kissed my chin.

"I'm not sure. Things might get out of hand . . ." Another kiss, just below my jaw.

"You know, someone once told me that sometimes you need to run risks," I murmured with pleasure, my skin pulsating beneath his hot lips.

"Whoever told you something like that must be crazy."

"I think so too, but maybe I should give him the benefit of the doubt."

Evan's eyes lingered on mine as he searched my words for implied permission. He began to kiss me again even more passionately, lifting his torso off the creeper without taking his mouth off mine. Before I knew it we were on our feet, our lips glued together, his hands on my hips as he thrust me against the car door, kissing me again and again.

My head was spinning. Our bodies sought each other, the awareness that I wouldn't be able to control myself much longer growing more intense by the second. I stopped to catch my breath without moving my face away from his. The air in the garage seemed scorching hot. Evan closed his eyes and rested his forehead against mine, drawing a deep breath.

After a minute, his hands found mine again and he swallowed. I watched his Adam's apple rise and fall, his eyes half closed as he struggled to control his overwhelming desire. He reached behind me, the silence between us alive with unspoken passion, and I heard the car door click and swing up. My heart beat wildly as his eyes probed mine, seeking my consent.

I followed him with my gaze as he slid down into the Lamborghini's upright leather and suede seat, still holding my hand. I leaned in under the scissor door and raised my knee to rest it on the seat next to Evan's leg, but he grasped it in a firm yet delicate movement, his eyes fixed on mine. Sliding his hand up my thigh, he guided it until I was straddling him.

Our fingers entwined and I felt feverish at the touch. Every movement, even the tiniest breath, seemed slowed down by a delicious tension. His body heat was intense against my thighs and I tried to keep myself raised slightly above him to avoid direct contact, but Evan had other ideas. My heartbeat accelerated as his hands slid down my back, making my skin tingle. He gripped my waist and fervently pulled me down onto him, his body trembling with yearning. The contact made me dizzy, melting me like warm honey as my legs spread open on top of him. His mouth touched my shoulder, opening and closing again, his tongue lightly brushing my skin.

I was aflame. The small space we were in emphasized the intimacy our bodies were claiming. The car was filled with Evan's hypnotic scent that made me even dizzier. He and I were a ticking time bomb that threatened to explode whenever we were alone. The detonator had been set and there was no way back. I felt it inside me whenever Evan touched me or his lips caressed my skin.

His hands held the backs of my thighs firmly so I couldn't move away from him, and every so often they pulled me closer in an attempt to erase even the distance created by our clothes. Responding to a primitive instinct, he ground his pelvis against mine. My body was on fire, the flames licking up from my belly, igniting every part of me.

"Evan . . ." I panted as our breathing merged. His desire shut out my voice as his firm, full lips moved down my throat, his hot breath warming my skin.

"I think . . ." Pleasure, hesitation, and yearning combined in my murmur. "I think you should stop." I took a deep breath.

His breath tickled my skin. "Do you?" he whispered, his tone sly. He didn't sound very willing to believe me.

"I thi—I think you should."

"Uh-uh." He shook his head. "I don't agree in the least," he murmured.

"Then I'm afraid I'll have to insist," I whispered back, my tone far from convincing.

"Since you put it that way," he replied, his voice barely audible, "where would you like me to stop?" His full lips parted against my shoulder, sending an electric charge surging through me. "Here?" He lightly sucked my skin. "Or"—his mouth moved to the curve of my neck, making me tremble—"here?" It slowly slid down to my collarbone. "Personally," he whispered, caressing my shoulder with his hand, "I think it would be better"—his fingers pushed aside my bra strap, which fell over my arm, baring the skin right above my breast as he followed it with his eyes—"if I stopped right . . ."—his hot lips moved down my chest, following the curves of my top—"here," he finished, hovering his mouth over my breast without touching it.

A jolt shot up from my back, rose to my neck, and filled my head. "Evan," I stammered, closing my eyes, my body longing to surrender to the sensations.

"Gemma . . ." His voice was an exasperated murmur that enveloped my name like black velvet as his hands returned to my hair and his mouth, tired of waiting, sought mine. Putting out this fire was going to be both impossible and painful—I might as well burn with him. I abandoned myself to the heat of his lips, losing myself in another dimension, when a cheerful melody suddenly vibrated in my pocket, reverberating inside the car and breaking the spell, a bucket of ice water on our fiery bodies.

I buried my head in Evan's shoulder, groaned, and pulled out the phone. "It's my dad," I told him, panicking when I read the time on the display. "Shit! How did it get so late?" Evan hid a satisfied smile. I pressed the call button. "Dad?"

My father's furious voice shot through my head from one eardrum to the other, booming inside the car. *"Gemma! Where the hell are you? It's midnight!"*

Feeling my face turn bright red, I lowered the volume on the phone as if that would help. "Dad," I said, but he didn't give me the chance to speak. I shot Evan a look. *Where's Drake?* I mouthed. For some reason I always took it for granted that he was filling in for me, but it wasn't like he was my babysitter. Besides, it was my own fault I lost all track of time when I was with Evan.

"I—I didn't realize it had gotten so late," I blathered. "I'm with *Evan,* Dad," I added, hoping he would hear the discomfort in my voice and lower his own. Dying with embarrassment, I looked at Evan. "He wants to talk to you," I whispered, cringing as I handed him the phone.

Judging from his expression Evan didn't seem the least bit concerned. I stared anxiously at his face, but saw no trace of nervousness as he spoke in monosyllables, nodding. "Yes. Right. Fine."

Silence. Evan handed the phone back to me.

"Well? What did he say?" I asked, worried. There were times when my wish for super hearing was as pressing as my need for air.

"I'm taking you home," he said calmly.

"What did he say to you?" I insisted nervously as Evan moved into the driver's seat and the car lift silently lowered the wheels to the floor.

"I don't think you want to know." He fell silent, his expression still relaxed as he turned the steering wheel. I sank into my seat, turning bright red with shame. Evan smiled at me as the Lamborghini's headlights flashed on, casting their light on the wall. The door began to rise and the car came to life with a roar that filled the garage. Aggressive, elegant, fierce. Like Ginevra.

"Won't she get mad if we use her car?" I asked, turning toward him as he continued to stare straight ahead. The last time we had, she hadn't taken it well.

He revved the engine, impatiently waiting until the garage door had slid all the way into the ceiling. With a tilt of his head he shot me a complicit, sensual look. "We need to take it for a road test." He winked at me and the Lamborghini let out a low, ferocious purr, then leapt into action with an even more aggressive roar, its wheels squealing against the shiny floor that was as black as the darkest night.

18

UNSCHEDULED ADVENTURE

"Good morning." Evan's velvety voice greeted me the moment I opened my eyes.

"What time is it?" I mumbled, groggy. The light coming in through the curtains was already too bright compared to what I was used to since school had started.

"I turned off your alarm. Don't worry, it's Saturday," he reassured me when I sat bolt upright in bed.

Taking a deep breath to release my tension, I slid down again and rolled onto my side, resting my head on my palm. Evan was in front of me, lying in exactly the same position. His hand stroked the edge of my army-green cotton top, moving sensually from side to side. His gaze told me what he was thinking.

"Meaning no school," I sighed blissfully.

"Meaning you and I can—"

The door abruptly opened.

"Gemma, what are—"

"Mom!" I bolted upright in bed, panicking. She looked at me, puzzled. My heart thumped as my thoughts chased each other desperately through my brain in search of some plausible explanation for Evan being in my bed so early in the morning.

She stood there in the doorway. "Who were you talking to?"

Her question surprised me and I spun around. Evan wasn't there. I heaved a sigh of relief, babbling something incomprehensible as my eyelids fluttered. Whatever came out of my mouth now, the only thing she could possibly accuse me of was talking to myself. Explaining how my boyfriend had managed to sneak into my room would have been far more complicated and embarrassing. Seeing that she wasn't really paying attention anyway, I caught my breath and relaxed. "You're still here?" I asked, trying to distract her.

"We were just about to leave. I came to say goodbye." Her expression changed. "And to make sure you won't come home so late again. Your father was furious last night. I'm surprised at you—you're behaving like you don't know him." She lowered her voice, not wanting him to hear us from downstairs. "I ran out of excuses trying to calm him down."

"Thanks," I stammered sheepishly. "Really, it was the first time I—"

"Just make sure it's the last time too," she said in a low voice, winking at me.

As the door closed behind her I anxiously turned to look for Evan. He was exactly where I'd left him. I saw his eyes were gray. If my mom had come back in, he would have been invisible to her. I sighed with relief.

"You knew," I accused him, narrowing my eyes. He was trying hard to keep a grin off his face. "You knew my mom was coming, you knew it!" I was annoyed.

At this point he couldn't help but laugh. "I have to admit, it was hilarious."

"You want me to be sent off to the loony bin? My mom thought I was talking to myself." Evan's lips quivered as he tried to hide how funny he thought it was. "Would you mind warning me next time? I'd like to avoid my parents having me locked up." His mocking grin was putting me on edge.

"In that case, I couldn't blame them, could I? It's not normal for someone to talk to themselves." Evan's voice faded as he disappeared before my eyes. Teasing me was one of his favorite pastimes. He reappeared a second later, smiling. "Or you could always tell her your boyfriend's an Angel, that he's here watching over you even when no one can see him." He spoke in a whisper in spite of the fact that we were alone in the house now and moved his face very close to mine.

"I'm not sure how she would take it." I stifled a smile, playing along. "Plus, I'm starting to think the word 'Angel' is used inappropriately where you come from."

"You think?" He lowered his head and tickled my ear with the tip of his nose.

"I'm more convinced by the day."

"You've never exactly seemed to mind my trespasses," he shot back boldly.

"I never said I did," I retorted.

"Because if you're complaining I can always force myself to keep my distance," he said, brushing his cheek against mine.

"I think I'm capable of resisting your sinful behavior."

He nibbled my earlobe as his voice caressed me. "Get dressed. I'll take you out to breakfast."

"I can just eat here. The house is empty now," I said, though he knew it even better than I did.

"That's not what I had in mind," he admitted, one corner of his mouth raised slightly.

"And what did you have in mind, exactly?" I eyed him suspiciously.

"There's something you've absolutely got to see," he said, a glint in his eyes as they turned dark.

Knowing Evan, I was sure I wouldn't be able to pry any information out of him. It was clear from the grin on his face. Resigned, I held his gaze for a second and then let it drop. There was one thing I was certain of: whatever Evan had in mind, it had to be dangerous. It always was, when he had that glint in his eyes.

"You still haven't told me where we're going." I tried to get an answer out of him again but my attempts went nowhere.

"And I have no intention of telling you." Evan smiled, his eyes fixed on the road ahead.

"I figured," I murmured.

He cast me a sidelong glance, the smile never leaving his lips. He seemed pretty pleased with whatever was on his mind. I wasn't entirely sure it would have the same effect on me. At least not immediately. We were riding in his Ferrari—that was enough to alarm me. Usually Evan only used this car for the clandestine nighttime races in which he almost always beat his siblings. Only in rare instances did the car's gray body gleam in the daylight. There had to be something special about this morning. I could tell from his occasional glances my way, brimming with excitement. I guessed he had high hopes about my reaction to his mysterious surprise.

When the car gradually slowed down I looked around curiously but didn't see anything particularly interesting. We seemed to be at an ordinary travel-service plaza.

"Are we there?" I asked eagerly.

"If you're talking about breakfast, then yes, your stomach will be grateful." He looked at me. "But if you're talking about our final destination, then no, not yet." He stifled a smile.

It was ridiculous how much he teased me.

The Ferrari pulled into a small parking lot, its metallic gray body reflected in the picture window of a café as we passed it. I wasn't completely sure where we were. We'd left my house about twenty minutes ago, but with Evan driving I could never judge distances based on the time it took us to get anywhere.

Through the window I glimpsed rustic wooden tables. Evan parked in a spot where he could keep an eye on the Ferrari from inside. He hadn't actually given me his reasons for parking where he did, but by now I was used to deciphering the look on his face, almost as if I could read his mind. It was pretty comforting that more and more often I was able to guess what he was thinking.

The bell by the café door jingled as we walked in. The interior was welcoming, done in warm, cozy hues. The cream-colored floor contrasted with the dark wood of the ceiling and furniture. Hanging from the windows were thick, soft curtains gathered to the sides, offering a view of the outside. The fabric was rust-colored, as were some of the walls.

The window at the far right looked out onto the parking lot with the road behind it. Not far beyond, next to the on-ramp, stood a gas pump.

"What do you want?" Evan studied the pastry case in front of us. It was small but had a good selection.

My stomach growled at the sight of it. "I can't decide." I bit my lip, the inviting aromas confusing me. I'd always loved food, but lately something in my metabolism seemed to be changing.

"Want me to get you one of everything?" he asked considerately.

"No, no!" I quickly replied as he gestured to the waiter behind the counter. "A chocolate doughnut will be just fine, thanks." Before I could stop him he ordered three of them and then pointed to a free table by the window.

"Worried about the car?" I teased, drawing a look of surprise from him.

"Just habit," he said. Despite the look of perplexity on his face, his eyes went to the Ferrari. "It's because I need it to take you to where we're going, that's all," he added with an air of mystery.

I looked at him out of the corner of my eye as the waiter came to our table. "Yeah, right! That's all," I echoed with a grin, leaning back in my chair so the waiter could place our order on the table. He was young, with skin as dark as his hair, an athletic build, and dimples in his cheeks that reminded me of Peter. Smiling at me politely, he handed me a tall glass of piping-hot steamed milk with a shot of espresso and a sprinkle of cocoa on the thick layer of froth. Just how I liked it, though I hadn't even noticed Evan ordering it. I shook my head and took a sip. With Evan there was no point trying to follow any form of logic.

He was sitting to my right, straddling his chair, his elbows resting on the back of it. "Is it good?" he asked, studying me as I dunked one of the doughnuts into the warm milk and chewed with relish. "There's no rush," he reassured me. "We've got all day."

"No way—I don't believe it! It's filled with strawberry ice cream!"

My enthusiasm made Evan laugh. "And covered with chocolate," he said. "I heard some kids talking about this place and these special doughnuts of theirs. It made me think of that stuff you make with Nutella."

"Strawtella!"

"Right, Strawtella. So I thought you should try them."

"These are the best doughnuts I've ever had in my life," I said, my mouth full, and swallowed another bite. "Oh! Don't tell my dad I said that." I bit into another, shooting Evan a glance. He laughed at the look on my face. "Seriously," I insisted, picking the crumbs from the plate and eating them. "Mmm, I definitely have to convince him to make these at the diner. Strawtella doughnuts. They're amazing! People will be lining up around the block!" The doughnut was warm and the ice cream melted on my tongue with every bite. It was an intense, delicious taste.

"I'll go order you some more," he said.

I stopped him before he could. "No, no! That's enough for today, but we have to remember to come here more often."

Evan smiled and stood up. "I'll go pay so we can get back on the road. We've still got a ways to go." He walked off before I could reply. For Evan the idea of me even taking out my wallet was inconceivable. In five months he hadn't let me pay for so much as a piece of gum.

Turning my head to the left, I looked at the Ferrari outside in the parking lot. The yellow logo with the black horse on its wheel caps sparkled in the sunlight against the anthracite-gray body. The café had only a handful of clients and their murmurs of admiration hadn't ceased for a second since we'd walked through the door. On top of that, a group of girls sitting in the corner kept looking in our general direction, though it wasn't entirely clear whether they were staring at the Ferrari or at Evan. From where I was sitting I could occasionally make out their low whispers and was pretty sure their admiration wasn't limited to the car.

A twinge of jealousy tied my stomach in a knot and my gaze instinctively went to Evan, casually leaning against the counter, wallet in hand. As if I'd called his name, his eyes met mine. It had been hard to resist the urge to glare at the girls at the table to intimidate them, but when my eyes locked with Evan's all my insecurity slipped away. I could tell he hadn't even noticed them. As this realization warmed my heart, he smiled at me, triggering the same reaction in me, and our gazes remained entwined.

Only a couple of seconds later his face altered radically, becoming a mask of horror. Though his eyes were still on mine, a veil of darkness dropped over them and I could tell he was no longer seeing me. All at once, a loud screech grated on my ears. My eyes shot to the parking lot and a shudder of terror seized me, trapping the breath in my lungs. I felt my heart bursting from my chest as my brain registered a blurry blue-and-white shape spinning through the air like a Frisbee or an enormous, out-of-control top hurtling directly toward the window.

It was a huge sport motorcycle, and I was its target.

"Gemmaaaa!!!" A roar of desperation drowned out the customers' cries of alarm. Evan tackled me with all his strength, knocking me to the floor and holding me tight. Despite my disorientation, I looked over his shoulder as, shielding me with his body, he raised his arm toward the window. A massive burst of energy shot from the palm of his hand and hit the glass like a tornado. There was a deafening explosion inside the café and the window shattered before the motorcycle could make impact. The deafening noise of the thousands of shards falling to the ground pierced my eardrums.

Trembling like a leaf, I felt Evan's hand rest gently on my hair. The explosion had thrown the bike abruptly off course, sending it hurtling in the opposite direction toward the gas pump. Inside, a murmur rose among the customers but Evan didn't seem to notice anything but me. "You okay?" he asked, stroking my forehead with his thumb, clearly shaken.

My heart was in my throat and I could barely breathe, but my first thought was of him. "Evan, you shouldn't have. Everybody saw you!" Concerned, I peered around at the looks on everyone's faces.

"I don't give a damn!" he growled. "Are you okay?" There was desperation in his voice and his eyes burned into mine as he caressed my cheek. I nodded. Taking a deep breath, he held me against him and kissed my forehead. "I wasn't expecting that. If I hadn't seen it in time—" He was so upset the words caught in his throat.

"Evan—" I stopped, suffocated by a bone-chilling foreboding.

He gritted his teeth and clenched his fists. I was sure my fear had communicated itself to him. One look was enough for Evan to grasp it. Neither of us paid any attention to the other customers who had gathered around the window, murmuring in shocked concern. Only Evan and I existed.

I saw a flash of hesitation in his eyes before he looked at me decisively. "No," he said firmly, answering my unspoken question. "It was just a coincidence." Fire rose in his gaze. "An accident."

Although there wasn't a trace of doubt in Evan's voice, a nagging thought throbbed at my temples until my head ached: *There was no such thing as coincidence.* He'd told me that himself.

"Incredible!" someone in the crowd said.

"Did you see that?!"

"It was that guy, I'm sure it was," someone else whispered, gesturing in our direction.

"How on earth did he do it?" another person wondered aloud.

I looked at Evan with concern but he instantly reassured me, whispering in my mind: *"Don't worry. I'll take care of them. I'll convince them they never saw us. They'll think there was a gas leak."*

I nodded and his hand squeezed mine as he helped me to my feet. All at once, there was a deafening roar. The gas pump the motorcycle had crashed into burst into flames, sending a violent wave of heat our way.

Everyone ducked and backed away, covering their faces with their arms. Evan wrapped his around me, shielding me with his body. "Come on. We've got to get out of here," he ordered me, pulling some hundred-dollar bills out of his wallet. He left them on the table and led me toward the door without sparking the least interest in the crowd who suddenly seemed to be looking through our bodies. He hadn't even needed to glance at them to convince them we weren't there. We'd become ghosts, invisible to their eyes.

"Evan." I stopped him and pointed at the security camera.

He stared at it and in less than two seconds the metal melted. Only when we reached the car did he let go of my hand. My heart was still pounding. I looked toward the road and caught my breath. The lifeless body of the motorcycle rider lay on the asphalt. Everything had happened so unexpectedly no one had noticed him.

All at once an unnaturally fast movement froze me in my tracks.

"Evan." I stifled a whimper, my gaze riveted on the other side of the street. "Someone's there." A shudder of terror slowly spread through me.

Evan's eyes shot to where I was looking. He frowned and turned back to look at me. My human sight couldn't make out the details of the figure across the street—not like Evan's could. Or had all the confusion just clouded my senses?

When he spoke, his voice betrayed anger rather than concern. "It's Drake." He pressed his lips together, his face full of fury. "He came for the rider."

Another shudder shook me, more violent than the last. I'd never seen any of them in these circumstances. Unable to look away, I swallowed, trying to moisten my parched throat.

"Christ, Drake! You should have been more careful!" Evan growled in his brother's mind, allowing me to listen in.

The blood froze in my veins and I couldn't take my eyes off Drake. Although he'd become like a brother to me over the last few months, right now it felt like I was seeing him for the first time. He wasn't alone any more in the middle of the empty road. A less attentive glance would have told me there were three people there, but I knew there weren't. Until a moment ago, the lifeless body lying on the asphalt and the young man beside Drake kneeling over it had been the same person. But then again, a less conscious glance would never have been able to fathom the ghastly sight.

I felt Evan's eyes on me. He was frowning and studying me carefully. "You can *see* them?" he asked. From the look on his face I couldn't tell if he was more stunned or upset. "Both of them? You *can see them?*" he whispered, not taking his eyes off mine.

"Is that bad?" I asked timidly. My hands were trembling.

"No. But it's not normal." Evan looked at me as if he were looking through me. I would have given anything at that moment to know what he was thinking. He licked his lips and came back to reality just in time to realize how much his answer had shaken me.

The Ferrari drove onto the on-ramp as unspoken words filled the space around us. Neither of us could find the courage to break the profound silence. Though I was confused, one thing stood out in my mind: Evan's remark and the look on his face had upset me more than everything else that had happened.

Before I could torture myself again with the memory of his expression, his voice pulled me out of my torment. "It's not bad," he assured me, as though I'd just repeated my question. His fingers caressed the red leather of the steering wheel. "At least I don't think it is. It's just strange—and incredible." He sought my gaze. "But there's nothing wrong with you," he repeated to make sure the message had gotten through.

I looked at him, pressing my lips together, and then gazed out the window. Silence returned.

Miles later, as the car roared along at such a speed it would have been virtually invisible to anyone we passed, I began to realize how ridiculous it was for me to be so uneasy. I couldn't blame Evan for being shaken up by something he'd never seen before in his whole life. Especially since it had something to do with me.

"Do you think we should be worried," I asked timidly, "if I can see all of you sometimes?"

His comforting smile broke the tension tingling under my skin. "No, not at all. I've always told you you're special, Gemma. Besides, if it hadn't been this way, if you hadn't noticed me that time in the woods, who knows? Right now we probably wouldn't be here talking about it. This *strangeness* of yours changed my life." He turned to look at me. "Because it let me fall in love with you."

I tried to convince myself. "You're right, it's stupid to get all worried about nothing."

Evan nodded confidently. "I agree." His words ushered in another moment of silence, this one calmer. His hand slid off the gearshift and touched mine, resting on my seat.

A corner of his lips curved seductively upward, forming a crease on the right side of his mouth. "Well." He drew my hand to his mouth and kissed my palm, then rested it on the gearshift. "Ready for your surprise?" He winked at me and his half smile broadened, wiping away every last trace of concern from my mind. Sometimes I wondered if Evan occasionally used his powers on me.

I waited a moment before replying. "You mean we're there?"

"I mean we're *almost* there," he said.

In the silence that followed I tried to interpret his answer. I decided it was best to pick up the conversation where I'd left off. "When you say 'almost,' what do you mean, exactly?" I said, starting to blather. "Because, you know, the meaning of the word can be totally subjective. You can interpret it in different ways depending on your point of view, so do you mean in ten minutes or half an hour or an hour or what?" I raised an eyebrow.

Evan held back a smile as we turned onto a small, steep road. I had absolutely no idea where we were. He tilted his head and looked at me as the car came to a halt. "I mean *now*."

Impatient, I freed myself from his gaze and looked out the windshield, surprised and confused when I saw where we were. Confused, mostly. There was nothing around us except an arid, sandy stretch of uninspiring land. I honestly didn't know what to think, but I tried hard not to let Evan's attentive eyes see my bewilderment. I studied the desolate landscape, still not understanding why he would bring me there. Out of the corner of my eye I noticed that in the meantime he was studying *me*. There was a mocking grin on his lips that was starting to exasperate me. Clearly something had escaped my notice.

We got out of the car. All at once Evan disappeared, reappearing at my side so fast the dirt beneath our feet didn't even stir. It was like when someone yanks a tablecloth off a table without disturbing the objects on top of it. He nodded at something behind me. "That way," he said, pleased, his eyes fixed on mine. At least the nerve-racking wait for the mystery to be revealed had finally come to an end—whatever the surprise was.

I looked over my shoulder and started, not sure whether I was amazed by the size of the building behind me or the fact that I hadn't noticed it before. Still, it was nothing that really enthused me. Was this the surprise? The structure seemed to be constructed of metal and looked a lot like an old abandoned warehouse. I honestly couldn't imagine why Evan had been so enigmatic about bringing me to a place like this. In any case, it seemed best to wait before telling him how puzzled I was.

He held out his hand to me. I took it and followed him toward the building. Something in the façade started to move and a low rumble grew stronger the closer we came. In seconds the entire façade broke into two equal halves from top to bottom as the two giant doors opened toward us without anyone touching them, revealing the entrance. The sunlight at my back prevented me from distinguishing the dark shapes I glimpsed in the vast interior. From the distance they looked like embalmed giants.

"Evan, what's in there?" I asked, curiosity getting the better of me.

"Your surprise." His tone was finally serious.

I stared at the huge building, wondering what might be hiding behind all those layers of dust. The air was damp, despite the desert-like surroundings, and billowy clouds had built up overhead, almost obscuring the amber-colored sky. The scant rays of sunlight that peeked through them didn't follow me as I crossed the threshold and the darkness swallowed me up. It took my eyes a minute to adjust and I realized that what Evan meant to show me was something enormous hidden beneath a thick canvas tarp that was covered with so much dust I could barely tell what color it was. I opened my mouth to speak, but my voice was drowned out by a different noise. Evan had grabbed the green tarp with both hands and yanked it off with a single jerk, a cloud of white dust rising from the fabric and filling the air. When it cleared I saw what it had been concealing.

The words died in my throat and I swallowed.

19

THE TERROR OF THE SKIES

"What on earth—What is it?" I asked, bewildered.

Evan smiled, finally satisfied. "I didn't think I would need to explain," he said, a sly, amused look on his face as I squinted at it.

"No, I, I mean, what—" All I could do was stammer. "Evan, that's a *plane*! Where on earth did you get a plane?" I asked, still confused.

"It's a fighter plane, to be exact," he said, smiling.

I stared at it, totally at a loss, then walked over and touched the fuselage, studying the details, running my hand across the gray paint faded by time. There was no denying it was magnificent. I flinched when I felt deep holes as big as nickels in its front end. My blood ran cold. They must be bullet holes. I tried not to imagine why they were there and instead focused on the picture on its side, by its left wing: the words *KILROY WAS HERE* and the doodle of a man peeking over a wall, his big nose sticking out. I smiled faintly as Evan studied my face with a pleased expression. Beneath the wing, "*U.S. ARMY*," stenciled in white letters, still stood out against the dark background. I had no idea how the plane had gotten all the way there or how long it had been hidden under the thick military tarp. It almost looked like it had always been there.

"What do you think?" Evan's voice rose in a whisper like the cloud of dust that had settled on the floor.

"It looks really old," I said after a moment of hesitation as I looked for the right words.

"Older than you think," Evan said. He joined me by the plane and silently stroked its painted surface, deep in reflection. "It's a P-51 Mustang. The terror of the skies during World War Two," he went on, serious, as he patted the side of the plane with his hand almost affectionately. His gaze seemed lost in memory. "It was Drake's," he said before I could ask. "Once in a while I like to come here and polish it the old-fashioned way, even though he doesn't like it. The others don't even know it exists, of course—otherwise Ginevra would have fixed it up her own way. But I like to use more normal methods just to relax from time to time. Or maybe, without realizing it, it was a way for me to try to feel more human before I met you."

"You *are* human," I replied instinctively. "Your emotions are human."

"No, they're not." He lifted my chin and kissed it softly, then looked me in the eye again. "And I've never been happier about it."

The electric charge his mouth sent through me when he whispered those words against my skin left me so dazed I couldn't reply. My eyelids fluttered as I tried to regain control. "How did you manage to block your thoughts about it from Ginevra?" I asked, fascinated by his ability to control his own mind as well as others'.

"I learned over time." Evan hid a sardonic smile, clearly understanding from the twinkle in my eye what I was about to ask him.

"Think you could teach me?"

He laughed. "Ginevra would go nuts! But"—he glanced at me, a sly smile on his face—"I guess I could. Anyway, we're not here to talk about that right now." The eagerness in his voice was evident.

"What are we here for, then?" The look on his face made me uneasy and a wave of emotion rose up in my throat, making it difficult to breathe. Still, I wasn't entirely sure it wasn't because of something else. Worry, maybe. "Evan, you can't be thinking of—" I blinked and steadied my voice. "You can't be thinking of going up in that thing?" I couldn't see his face, but I was more than sure he was smiling. I watched with alarm as he grabbed hold of the wing and nimbly swung himself up onto it. He climbed into the cockpit and looked down at me. "Why do you think I brought you all the way here?"

A mix of emotions churned inside me, rising to my throat. I stared at him for a moment and his sexy, enthusiastic smile made something tremble inside me, something in my chest that quivered with each breath. The sight of him behind the controls of a fighter plane was something I never would have expected to see, and yet for some reason he perfectly fit the role of a soldier. The clothes he wore—a black military-style jacket with patches and an army-green sweater—strengthened the impression even more. It was as if we'd gone back in time and Evan was there in that warrior eagle, ready to take off and soar through the skies to do battle like a soldier. An Angel of the skies.

"You think it's capable of flying?" I asked as the sputter of the engine drowned out my voice. The propeller on its nose came to life, more dust rising in a cloud from its whirring blades. A delicate wind blew on my skin and stirred my hair as Evan jumped out of the tiny cockpit and looked at me with satisfaction. He walked across the wing to where I was standing, knelt, and held out his hand.

My heart skipped a beat and pounded in my ears, challenging the roar of the airplane. It was *really* about to happen. Part of me was already aware of it, even if my brain was having a hard time ordering my hand to take hold of Evan's. I wasn't sure which was making me hesitate: fear or excitement. Evan always said that in certain situations one couldn't exist without the other. This must have been one of those times. And yet I wanted with all my might to take his hand, so why was I hesitating? I had nothing to be afraid of when I was with him—I knew that perfectly well—so it must have been because of my emotional reaction that was so powerful it paralyzed me when I saw this Angel hold out his hand to take me into the sky with him.

His voice resonated inside my head as he answered. *"Want to find out with me?"* It enveloped me like the rays of sunset. *"Fly with me, Gemma,"* he whispered in my mind.

I grabbed his hand and squeezed it with all my strength. A second later I was standing on the wing, wrapped in Evan's arms. Releasing me from his embrace, he took off his jacket and draped it over my shoulders. The dog tag he wore around his neck glinted against his green short-sleeved shirt. "So you won't get chilled," he whispered to me, forehead to forehead. He wouldn't need it.

Evan's arm muscles flexed as he grabbed hold of the metal rim overhead and slid down into the single-seat cockpit.

"It doesn't look big enough for more than one person," I pointed out warily.

Evan didn't respond, but sat me down in front of him so we could share the cramped space. In the end, being so close to him wasn't uncomfortable. He tucked his chin over my shoulder. "That just means we'll have to stay closer together," he whispered sensually in reply to my thoughts. He carefully shut the glass canopy above us.

Fascinated, I stared at the control panel without recognizing any of the levers that Evan was moving confidently. "This is the throttle," he explained, his voice calm, resting his hand on a lever to our left. He gripped it in his fist and smoothly pushed it forward. "This gives the plane power. Think of it like the accelerator in a car."

I watched him in silence as he used his other hand to grab a larger lever that looked kind of like a car's stick shift. I couldn't find words to express the emotions that filled me when the plane began to move and the hangar disappeared behind us. In spite of my excitement, though, all I could focus on was the heat emanating from Evan's body, snug against mine. I leaned to the side slightly to give him a better view of the controls as the landscape beyond the canopy raced by ever faster. Only my heart, maybe, was keeping up with its pace. I held my breath and his smile tickled my neck, his arm muscles flexing as he pulled one of the controls toward him.

"And this is the control stick," he said, speaking close to my ear. "If I pull it back like this, it brings the nose of the plane up." The craft gradually tilted up until the ground disappeared from view. We were so close together I was sure Evan could feel every heartbeat. "Or you can push it forward for a nosedive." He glanced at me, his expression sly.

"Don't even think about it," I warned, looking him straight in the eye. He laughed.

A moment later the barren field disappeared, replaced by the thick tangles of trees of the Adirondacks. Evan kept the plane at low altitude, flying just above the forest's majestic canopy.

"What's this for?" I asked, looking curiously at a straight line that scrolled continuously across a screen.

"That's the artificial horizon. It's used to check the plane's orientation relative to the horizon." Evan veered right and the line tilted, imitating his position in the sky. Just when I was almost sure I'd regained control of my breathing, a strange rumble rose from the propeller, making me flinch.

"Evan, are you sure this thing isn't too old?" I blurted, gripped by a feeling of alarm I tried hard to hide. My heart was in my throat and Evan's silence made me panic even more. But it wasn't his hesitation that worried me—it was his hands, jumping frenetically from one control to the other as the treetops grew sparser, revealing a mirror of water ready to swallow us up into its abyss. "Evan!" My voice held a hint of stifled desperation. At this point, there was no doubt about it: something was wrong.

He clenched his jaw and cursed.

"Evan, what's wrong?" I cried.

"Brace yourself!" he shouted between gritted teeth, his muscles tensed. "Oh, shit!" he snarled, clutching the control stick as his arms squeezed me in an iron grip.

"Evan!" I cried again, my voice suffocated with panic, but the plane quickly lost altitude, drowning out the rest of my sentence. My heart leapt violently in my chest as the lake below rushed toward us. Every part of me trembled with terror as I stared at the rippled water and dug my nails into whatever was beneath them. A scant few yards from the surface, I held my breath and closed my eyes, waiting for the impact.

Just then Evan's laughter resounded against my back, muffled by my hair. He confidently pulled the control stick toward him an instant before hitting the water and the plane righted itself, its wheels skimming the lake, tickling it, raising silver splashes against the windshield as we flew over the surface in perfect balance. I took a deep breath, my heart still doing somersaults, and turned to look at the gentle wake stretched out behind us. Evan was still laughing. I sighed, held my breath, and forced myself to laugh with him, my hands still shaking.

"Idiot!" I slugged his shoulder. "I hate it when you do stuff like that." I rolled my eyes, my breath still coming in gasps.

"That was fun, don't you think?" he said, grinning.

"You have a weird sense of humor," I shot back, glaring at him.

Evan nudged me with his shoulder affectionately. "C'mon, I was just kidding around. A harmless little dose of adrenaline certainly won't kill you."

"Right. As if I didn't have enough in my system already," I said, trying hard not to let him feel how much I was trembling. I took another deep breath and calmed down, letting myself smile with him. With that breath the scent that wafted up from his jacket and filled my nose distracted me from everything else. It was *his* scent.

Evan slowly pulled the control stick toward him and the fighter plane nosed up again, this time more smoothly, flying over the green treetops that disappeared below us.

20

PEARL OF FIRE

Whenever I'd chanced to look up at the sky when I was growing up, no matter how different it looked, I'd made the mistake of assuming it was always the same sky. But now it was like I was seeing it for the first time. I was sure that from that moment on I would never see it with the same eyes again.

Every second in the air with Evan seared itself into my memory. Once we were back on the ground it would stop burning, but it would leave a permanent mark on my heart. The ground had completely disappeared beneath us. The plane flew along through soft patches of clouds, gradually rising above a thick, continuous, reddish blanket of them. Although it was hours until sunset, the sky was a palette of intense shades, from red to orange to blue.

"Evan, we're flying!" I said, full of wonder.

"Yes." Evan smiled behind me. "We're flying," he repeated, pleased. His breath tickled my ear.

"My God. It's amazing," I whispered, enchanted. As I gazed through the glass canopy, my vision lost itself in the contrast between the orange and the pale blue. Hidden behind a fluffy cluster of clouds, the sun looked like a black pearl rimmed with fire. All around us the clouds scattered to the horizon, pierced by shafts of golden light that illuminated the dust particles in the air, making them sparkle like diamonds. Something about the sky's reddish hues reminded me of the place we'd been a few days before. It was still hard for me to conjure the thought in my mind, but I had to, because that's where I felt I was right now—in heaven.

"You don't need to tremble," Evan whispered behind my ear. "You're safe up here with me." His mouth grazed my skin.

"I'm not afraid." It was the truth. "I'm trembling because it brings up so many emotions in me."

"Give me your hands." His hot breath, as light as a caress, stirred the tiny hairs on my neck. It hadn't been a request; before I could reply, he'd already taken them in his own and wrapped them around the control stick. "If I could enfold all the love I feel for you the same way I'm holding your hands right now, I would transfer it from me to you."

I closed my eyes at the sound of his velvety voice, tilting my head back to touch his, intoxicated by his words. "You already are," I whispered.

"Hold it tighter, like this." When he squeezed his hands over mine I realized his intentions.

"Evan, don't be crazy!" I exclaimed.

"I trust you," he whispered. He smiled and cautiously relaxed his grip.

"My God," I murmured, releasing the tangle of emotions gripping my chest. "Evan, look!" I cried excitedly, but his hands were already moving slowly up my arms, caressing me. He stopped at my shoulders and squeezed them.

My heart skipped a beat. He breathed deeply into my hair and I sensed the power of his emotions: love, desire, hesitation . . . and something else I couldn't decipher. Fear? Maybe I didn't want to know. I tried to concentrate as Evan gently swept my hair back from my shoulder, almost as if it were the first time. I wasn't sure I could contain all these emotions. The heat in my chest was so intense it almost hurt.

"Bravo!" he whispered in my ear, making me tremble. The next moment, a light pressure tickled my neck as Evan rested his head behind mine, burying his face in my hair. The contact was as gentle as a caress. He exhaled deeply, his breath hot, and I shuddered again. He was still for a moment and I half closed my eyes, surrendering to the rhythm of his breathing.

A moment later, he returned his hands to mine, which I carefully slid off the control stick so he could take over. "How do you feel?" he asked.

"I don't think I've ever felt anything so thrilling before," I admitted.

Evan stole a glance at me and a tiny crease appeared at the corner of his mouth. Mischievousness sparkled in his eye just as a glimmer of alarm appeared in mine.

"You shouldn't have said that." His wolfish smile confirmed that he'd just given me a warning.

"What—"

Before I could finish, Evan pushed the control stick. The plane tilted to the right and rolled on its axis. I shrieked, my entire body tingling, and held on to Evan with all my might. A second later, the plane leveled out and we both burst out laughing with exhilaration.

"Are you sure this thing can fly so high up?" I teased, a smile still on my lips, trying to make myself heard over the sound of the engine.

"I can take you to the moon if you want." His voice filled my head with endless tenderness, reaching my heart with a warm quiver that made me half close my eyes. I'd never been this happy. Not until I'd met Evan.

"Evan," I murmured, caught between sadness and ecstasy. His laughter died away at my tone and his gaze rested on mine, listening. "Promise me you'll never leave me." I couldn't look him in the eye; the fear of losing him left me breathless.

"I promise," he whispered, his tone soothing but determined. "I'm not crazy, after all." He hid a smile in my hair.

"I'm not so sure about that," I said with a grin that faded before the serious look on his face.

"I wouldn't leave you for anything in the world." His eyes, deep and dark, were fixed on mine. "If you could read my heart, Gemma, you'd know how important you are to me," he whispered tenderly, his lips brushing my cheek.

I closed my eyes, losing all control. "I don't need to read your heart, I already know it."

For a moment, we looked at each other wordlessly.

"I'll stay with you as long as you want me."

"Forever, then," I replied with a little sigh.

"You don't know how many times I've come up here alone." His voice was tinged with pain. "You can't imagine how many times I've felt this same sunlight on my skin. But this is the first time I've felt its warmth," he said softly.

"That's because you're not wearing your jacket," I whispered, my eyes still closed because of the thrill his voice was sending through me, threatening to melt me any second.

Evan looked at me, his expression serious, and brushed his cheek against mine. "It's because you're here."

An unexpected shiver ran through me again.

As the plane taxied across the arid field I now realized was a runway, I felt emptied out, as though I'd just lost something or awakened from a fast-fading dream. And yet inside me I knew it wasn't true. I was still living my dream and would continue to as long as Evan was by my side. As long as *I* stayed by *his* side. Because sooner or later, death would return to hunt me down. I was sure of it. The thought was like a punch to the stomach.

Evan switched off the engine and I looked around. The plane had come to a halt in front of the old hangar. "You're not taking it inside?" I asked.

"You want to leave already?" he asked with a mix of surprise and disappointment.

"No," I was quick to say. "I want to stay if it's okay with you."

"That's what I had in mind," he admitted, opening the glass hood imprisoning us and climbing out onto the wing. For a second I thought it was so he could reach the ground more easily, but then he motioned for me to join him. I squatted on the metal and took a seat beside him, my legs dangling.

"This place looks abandoned," I said, glancing around.

His face darkened. "No one's come here for years," he said grimly.

"Not even Drake?" I asked impulsively.

"Especially not Drake. The memory's too painful for him. He doesn't even want to come near it." He paused. "Drake enlisted. He was a pilot." His expression grew serious as he stared into space, answering the questions I wasn't able to ask out loud. "He was eighteen when he got his orders, a volunteer fighting alongside the British in a war that wasn't his." There was something in his voice, a trace of bitterness, as if he were talking about himself, experiencing firsthand the pain he was describing. "He left everything behind, even the girl he was supposed to marry." He hid a bitter smile and I could see the disapproval on his face; he would never have done it. "Thought he could save the world. He didn't know he'd never see her again."

I shuddered, thinking of the deep holes in the side of the plane. "Drake died in the war?" I whispered, shaken.

"World War Two. He'd been fighting the Nazis for a year and regretted leaving everything to risk his life. But by then it was too late. He couldn't go back."

The revelation made my blood run cold. I'd never heard such personal details about Drake before. I'd had no idea how he had died, had never even wondered. Would I ever be able to look at him the same way again? After the last time I'd seen him, outside Evan's house, I didn't know if I would.

"After his . . . his death," I began, finding it hard to say the last word out loud. It wasn't an easy word to use when referring to people I interacted with every day. "Didn't he go looking for his fiancée, like you did with your family?"

"Yeah, but nobody was there." He looked me in the eye, his expression grave. "Later on he found out she'd enlisted as a Red Cross nurse so she could follow him, but she was sent to Normandy and died during the terrible battles there. The forces were parachuted in to support the disembarkation of hundreds of Allies, but not all of them reached the ground. The German counterattack machine-gunned them down as they were landing and she met the same fate."

"How horrible," I whispered, terror in my eyes.

"Yes. He never saw her again," he repeated, pausing on the last words. The glimmer in Evan's eye told me why he felt the pain as his own. It was the tragedy that most frightened him: losing me and never seeing me again.

I was afraid of the same thing, more intensely than I feared death itself.

"That's not going to happen," I assured him, touching his knee. I knew I was replying to what he was thinking. "You won't let it," I insisted, trying to convince myself.

His eyes wavered for a second, then his lips touched mine in a gentle kiss. "I'll never let it."

I stroked Evan's chest and clasped his dog tag in my fingers. He looked down at my hand. "That belonged to Drake too," he said, taking me by surprise.

"I didn't imagine it was Drake's. I know you never take it off."

"Because it's really important to me. He gave it to me himself, although I wish he hadn't."

"I don't get it. That doesn't make sense."

"It would have been better if it had gone to the person who was supposed to get it." He looked at me again and went on. "Drake has one identical to it. Most of the time he keeps it hidden under his shirt."

"You're right, now I remember seeing it. I didn't know they had the same story," I said, searching my mind for a picture of Drake.

"It hurts him to see it but he's never taken it off. It's like somehow he just can't let it go." He studied my reaction. "One of the tags was for him and the other was supposed to go to his fiancée Stella—I think that was her name. We never met. Drake was saving it to give to her when he returned from the war. He couldn't afford anything more."

"But he never made it back," I said in a tiny voice.

"Exactly," he sighed.

"So why do you have it?"

Meanwhile, Evan had lain down on the wing on his back, his knees raised. I lay down too, head to head with him, and we rested our heads on each other's shoulders.

"I was the one to find Drake."

His comment startled me. I hadn't thought of that. I couldn't imagine Evan during wartime or in any era other than our own. It still seemed so crazy.

"In those days evil spread quickly. A lot of people were dying and we were really needed. We worked nonstop, wandering the battlefields to help those in need, those who couldn't let go of their bodies—and we carried out orders too, naturally."

I shivered, hoping Evan wouldn't notice.

"And then I spotted Drake. He was alone and in a state of shock. It was hard for me to make him leave his bullet-riddled body. Before dying he'd managed to bring the plane down without crashing it. He's never talked to any of us about what happened."

"You were the one who read it inside of him," I said, anticipating his words.

"I was the first, and then Ginevra read his pain through his thoughts. He was tormenting himself about leaving Stella of his own volition when he could have protected her, for having lost the chance to say goodbye to her, and for not having been able to give her this." He turned the chain over in his fingers.

I tilted my head to look at him, then rested it on his shoulder again, brushing his cheek with mine.

"I bonded with Drake right away. I didn't know why. Maybe it was because I'd been the one to save him. Maybe Simon felt the same way about me. When you take someone under your wing you end up bound to them forever, I guess. Drake felt the same way about me and after a few days, when he started to recover, he decided to give me the dog tag that should have gone to her. He erased his name and engraved mine on it. When he gave it to me he told me I was the only person he had left in the world. I remember it like it was yesterday. His eyes were empty, but grateful at the same time, and what he said . . . It's all still crystal clear in my mind. I haven't taken it off since and neither has he."

"Maybe I shouldn't say this, but if it's something so important to you and Drake, why did you decide to put our names on it?" I asked, puzzled, my eyes fixed on the sky.

Evan laughed. "I knew you'd ask that. He gave it to me instead of the woman he loved because I was the only person who mattered to him. I wrote your name on it because *you're* the only person who matters to *me*. It seemed right that you be a part of it."

"Now that I know, what you did means even more to me," I told him, struck by the story. I rolled onto my side and rested my head on my elbow.

All Evan had to do was tilt his face to bring his lips close to mine. I wanted to kiss him but before I could he was already kissing me.

"It must be terrible to lose the person you love," I whispered, heartbroken.

"I can't imagine anything more painful." He looked deep into my eyes and fell silent.

21

ICE IN THE HEART

Evan and I had been driving back for some time now. The sun hadn't set but the cloud cover had thickened as if to make up for our absence in the sky. The upholstery was covered with crumbs. At first I'd refused the sandwiches Evan had taken out of the glove box because I was afraid I'd get his car dirty, but he'd deliberately sprinkled breadcrumbs on the red floor mats, leaving me with no excuse.

"Planning to hold me hostage much longer?" I said, grinning as I waited for his reaction.

"Something like that," he said, a cunning look on his face. "You don't seem to mind."

I shot him a glance and found him doing the same. "At this rate I'm afraid all the time you have left with me today is going to be wasted here in the car," I said jokingly. Evan looked at me and raised an eyebrow. "You're driving at a snail's pace!" I pointed at the speedometer, which read seventy-five miles an hour. A normal speed for anyone else, but not for Evan.

"Oho!" He seemed struck by the provocation. "*I'm* as slow as a snail?" he repeated deliberately.

"It's not my fault you got me hooked on excitement." I looked at him, emphasizing the last word provocatively.

He cocked his head and returned my look. "Think you can do better?" There was a note of challenge in his voice.

I held his gaze until I found my voice. "You don't need to ask twice," I warned, my eyes fixed on his in search of confirmation. What did he expect me to do, drive his Ferrari? Had he seriously lost his mind? It was crazy . . . and yet the idea stirred something in my blood. I couldn't wait to do it.

"I let you fly a fighter plane. I don't see why you shouldn't drive this," he said encouragingly, raising his thumbs from the steering wheel to indicate the car. Maybe he didn't think I was actually up to accepting the challenge, because the subtle note of mockery in his voice persisted. But then again, Evan knew me well enough to know I wouldn't back down.

He pulled over and took his hands off the steering wheel. "It's all yours," he told me, the grin never leaving his face. At that point I really couldn't say no. He walked around the car, watching me steadily through the windshield. I climbed over the gearshift—Evan preferred a stick to an automatic—and settled into his seat. By now my excitement had eclipsed my bewilderment.

"Whenever you're ready," he said with mischief in his voice once he'd slid into the passenger seat. Stunned, I looked at the leather steering wheel and stroked it. Driving Dad's old Audi was definitely nothing in comparison.

"You sure you can do better?" he said in the same challenging tone. Was there encouragement behind his mocking expression? I doubted it. "You're still in time to change your mind."

But I'd already pressed the ENGINE START button on the steering wheel and the Ferrari's aggressive roar drowned out half his sentence. I turned and shot him a defiant look, my answer to his question. "Whatever you say," I replied with a smile.

I pulled casually out onto the road, my fingers clutching the wheel because they were trembling and I didn't want Evan to notice. Excitement gripped my chest, adrenaline rushed through my veins, and my stomach was upside down, but I forced myself to appear calm to Evan's eyes.

The road was empty. Fate was on my side—or on the side of whoever might have been driving in front of me, depending on your point of view.

Once we were on a straight stretch I jammed my foot down on the accelerator, attacking the asphalt like a wild beast. The car lunged forward, pressing me back into the driver's seat and leaving me breathless.

"Whoa, whoa, whoa! Take it easy!" Evan warned me with a little smile as the arrow on the speedometer shot to sixty miles an hour. The wind whipped his words away. I couldn't slow down; it was too much of a thrill. I felt like an arrow shot from a bow. I accelerated more, reassured by the fact that Evan was there to protect me. Every inch of my skin tingled, vibrant and alive. It was like I had the world in my hands, like I could do anything, go anywhere. *I felt safe.*

"Well?" I asked Evan, keeping my eyes glued to the road. "Still think I can't do better than you?"

We were already going a hundred and twenty miles an hour. Evan was used to far greater speeds, but I'd already beaten my own record in the first five seconds of driving. Evan pressed his lips together and shook his head, almost as if he still weren't entirely convinced. His reaction compelled me to press my foot down even harder on the accelerator. I wouldn't have done it—I knew I'd already reached my limit—but I was beyond being able to resist the voracious urge that drove me on.

A hundred and thirty an hour. The road was a blur, but I was determined not to let my anxiety show. I camouflaged it with a mocking tone. "You're lucky, Evan." My eyes narrowed on the asphalt, razor-sharp as an arrowhead, while the landscape raced by in a river of hazy color. Deep in my heart, a feeling of uneasiness began to shout its dissent.

"Why lucky?" Evan asked, his voice calm.

"Now we'll be getting home sooner," I said roguishly. "You should be thanking me." Evan frowned, apparently unsure of what I meant. "This way we'll have more time to ourselves," I explained. From the corner of my eye I noticed that his lips had instinctively curved upwards in approval. I couldn't resist the urge to turn to him and smile. Evan smiled back, raising the corners of his mouth at the same time I did.

Suddenly all hell broke loose. The steering wheel jerked under my hands and spun out of control. I was hurled against the car door as though hit by an invisible train. I tried to speak but the air seemed to have been sucked out of my lungs and the car too. I tried to turn the steering wheel but the force with which it was spinning was too great to control.

"Evan!" I shrieked.

I heard him curse as terror flooded through me. "Damn it!!!" he shouted, attempting to grab the wheel. His voice also filled with panic as the car spun out of control, forcing us back in our seats. I didn't understand why he couldn't use his powers to make it stop.

A bridge was coming toward us at incredible speed.

"Evan!!!" I let out a desperate scream and met his terrified eyes. There was a sudden, brutal impact.

Then, darkness.

"Ge . . . "

His voice sounded far away, as if he were talking on a cell phone that kept cutting out.

"Hang . . . "

I tried to open my eyes but it was too difficult. Like sound, images faded in and out: flashes of light alternating with moments of total darkness. Another brutally harsh noise tore me out of the darkness and I glimpsed Evan beside me. He'd torn off the Ferrari's door with one hand.

"I'm here . . . here . . . here . . . "

At times the sounds repeated themselves in an endless echo. Again, darkness.

"Ge . . . "

I felt Evan's arms beneath me and my limbs felt heavy, as if they were dangling.

" . . . with me."

Another flash: Evan leaning over me. I felt at the mercy of the forces around me, dragged like a seashell on the shore: at times light, when the current was carrying me away from the beach; at times heavy, when the water receded, leaving me stranded on the sand. Then the pain arrived from every direction. It inundated me, making me long for the water to return and carry me off, leaving the pain behind. I tried to follow it and abandon myself to its current, but something continued to bring me back.

I could no longer see anything. Oblivion was claiming me. I wanted the pain to stop. It was too much.

Enough! Enough!

" . . . your eyes . . . eyes . . . eyes . . . ook at me!"

The desperate sound made me hurt even more. I felt a light pressure on my head, where the strongest pain was coming from. A strange heat filled my temples, burning like fire. I clenched my teeth.

The heat grew stronger, driving out the pain. Another burst of light crossed my eyes. Evan again. There was an unfamiliar edge to his voice: desperation.

Now I could see them, between the darkness and the flashes of light: his hands. Yes, now I could feel them. The warm touch of his hands on my head. It felt so nice.

Again, I felt myself slipping away. Again, darkness.

" . . . Please . . . ease . . . ease . . . " His voice shook. " . . . eave me."

His face appeared to me for a brief second, his expression tormented, agonized, almost in tears. I couldn't stand the pain. Not mine, his. Not any more. I couldn't bear to hear the anguish in his voice.

The darkness pulled me down again but I clung to his voice with all my strength.

"Ge . . . you hear . . . *Look at me.*"

I felt a whirl of energy bearing me up. The light arrived violently. I wasn't in the darkness any more. I'd re-emerged.

"Evan . . ." It was the first thing I managed to murmur, the only one I could think of. I finally saw him clearly. I was lying on the asphalt. He was leaning over me, his hands on either side of my body. When my lips whispered his name, he dropped his head toward my chest and his hair tumbled over his brow. Neither of us said a word for a long moment. I wasn't sure where we were or what had happened. I was too dazed to speak.

Evan gently brushed his forehead against my chin and looked at me, his eyes filled with a desperation I'd never seen before, his sooty skin streaked with tears. He took my face in both hands and rested his forehead against mine, closing his eyes, then let out a long breath, blowing warm air on my face. "I just died for the third time," he whispered, so softly I could barely hear him.

Bizarre as it might sound, I couldn't help but smile as his forehead continued to press gently against mine. "When was the second?"

Evan gave a deep sigh and smiled. "When I walked into the living room looking for you and you were gone."

The memory flashed through my mind like a fiery bolt of lightning. The thought of Faustian and the way he'd tricked me into running away from Evan still made me shudder. "You should reconsider being in a relationship with me," I said with a grin. "It doesn't seem to be very good for your health."

He smiled, our foreheads still touching, and kissed me cautiously, as if afraid he'd break me. "The fact that you're already kidding around is a good sign."

I blinked, still confused, dazed. "What happened?" I asked, unable to remember.

Evan didn't answer, just moved aside so I could see behind him. The whole world froze before my eyes.

"Evan!" I whispered, filled with terror.

Steps away, crumpled against a torn guardrail, Evan's Ferrari was totaled, its body twisted, its windows shattered, a tangle of scrap metal left unrecognizable by the violence of the impact. The front end had broken through the guardrail and the back end dangled over the edge, teetering between the asphalt and the water below the bridge.

"Your car . . . " I whispered, my voice full of regret.

The door lay some distance away. I remembered glimpsing Evan as he'd ripped it off its hinges.

"I don't care about the car!" he growled. "Your life is the only thing that matters." He stood up and put his hands to his head, looking nervous, as if the nightmare he'd just lived through was still tormenting him. His bloodstained hands left a smear on his forehead.

"I'm sorry," I murmured in a tiny voice, moving closer to him. A devouring sense of guilt rose from my stomach. *I* had been driving. It was all my fault. I'd totaled his car.

"Don't feel bad." His expression hardened. He turned and looked into my eyes. "It wasn't you."

Although the meaning of his words eluded me, something inside me trembled as Evan grabbed his hair in his fists. Something was tormenting him but I couldn't tell what, exactly. From the look on his face, it seemed to be a mix of emotions, with anger and shock struggling to outdo each other.

"Damn it!" he growled furiously. He slammed his fist violently against the roof of the car, crumpling the metal. The brutality of the blow made me flinch.

Worried, I stared silently at Evan as he rested both hands on what remained of the roof and lowered his head, his hair falling over his face. He turned slowly and looked at me with a distraught expression. Something in the way his eyes looked right through me made me shudder.

"They've found you."

The blood in my veins turned to ice.

22

GUILTY FEELINGS

"What? You, you mean—" I stared. My lips trembled convulsively and I felt I'd lost all control over my body.

"Damn it to hell! It's all my fault!" he cursed himself, his voice breaking with remorse. "I've been such an idiot!"

I still couldn't speak.

"Come on." Evan strode over. "I have to get you out of here." He picked me up from the ground gently as though I were made of crystal.

A metallic groan caught his attention, but his angry expression didn't alter. He turned toward the noise just in time for another loud creak from the Ferrari, which appeared to be teetering. A second later, it slid over the edge of the bridge and crashed into the water, sending a spray of droplets as brilliant as diamonds into the air.

The wind lashed at my face, leaving me breathless, and I buried my head in Evan's chest. He was already running, a silent missile darting through the trees like a ghost. I inhaled his scent and forgot everything else for a long moment—a single, comforting moment of relief before my body began to shake uncontrollably again at the memory of Evan's devastating remark.

They've found you.

I could think of nothing else. Someone was after me again, someone who wanted to kill me. I was on the run again. I was being hunted down again. Though I attempted again and again to drive it away, one thought filled my head incessantly: *would I survive this time?*

The wind stopped. I'd been so lost in my obsession I hadn't even wondered where we were headed. What could it matter now? No matter where I went, no matter where I hid, they would find me. I couldn't escape death. Evan couldn't protect me forever.

The air was cool and I was sure the sky would soon be shedding tears for me. I wished I could cry, but terror had paralyzed my senses and not even my tears could find a way out to help ease the pain.

Evan knelt down and laid me on the damp ground, then turned his back to me, his fists clenched at his sides. I reached out and stroked his arm. For some reason, it felt like I was the one who needed to comfort him. Guilt emanated from every inch of his body.

"Evan," I said, my voice barely audible and my eyes brimming with tears.

"How could I have let this happen?" His voice was a whisper of pain. "It's all my fault." His expression made me cringe with terror. I'd already seen that look in his eye. It only took a second for me to realize I'd seen it just once before: when Evan was leaning over my lifeless body, mangled from Faust's torture. When he thought he'd failed. *When I was dead.*

Was that what he saw in me now—a body already dead? Was there really no hope for me?

I wanted to squeeze his hand but my strength was gone. Unexpectedly, he took mine and looked up. "Come with me," he murmured.

I looked around for the first time and instantly recognized our hideaway, the lake house, a few yards ahead. Evan led me through the trees to the shore. Letting go of my hand, he walked out onto the strip of land at the water's edge and sat down on a rock covered with large roots that snaked all around it. Without a word, I did the same and sat down at his side on the rock. Neither of us said anything for a long while.

I focused on the harmonious movement of the water stirred by the breeze and tried to overcome my fear. Evan stared into space as I looked absently at a dry leaf floating on the water. It rocked gently like a feather borne along by the wind.

The lake was a mirror that reflected everything upside down: the sky, the clouds, the trees, almost as if another world existed under the water, a parallel dimension beyond its surface. I wished I could hide there. A raindrop rippled the surface right before my eyes, distorting that perfect image and reminding me there was no reality other than this one. Concentric circles formed around the place the raindrop had landed, growing wider and wider until the water returned to its former mirror-like state.

A second raindrop stirred the water. All around us, silence reigned. A third hit the surface, followed by a fourth, until the surface of the lake was dimpled by countless raindrops, making the upside-down image tremble.

I felt frozen inside, as if something had emptied my body and filled it with ice that stung painfully. The tree branches hung low, right over our heads, their dense leaves forming a canopy over us as the rain came down even harder, seemingly wishing to wash away the pain afflicting us both in that desperate silence that paralyzed my soul.

I opened my mouth for a second and then closed it. Choosing silence, I reached over and rested my hand on Evan's. He squeezed it, then raised it to his cheek and closed his eyes. He appeared to be devastated—so devastated that my desire to console him made me forget the reason for his torment.

Unexpectedly he exhaled in a barely perceptible sigh. "I've failed miserably."

"You haven't failed, Evan. I'm still here with you. You saved me," I said quietly, hoping to convince him.

He squeezed my hand even tighter as if afraid I would slip away from him. "No. That's not true. It's all my fault. I shouldn't have let it happen!" he hissed.

"I was the one driving the car, Evan. Why do you want to take the blame?"

He snorted as if I'd said something ridiculous. "The car has nothing to do with it. It could have happened any other way." Finally his eyes rested on me. "Don't you see? It's my fault they came back for you. I should have been more careful and instead I lowered my guard. I let myself get carried away by my feelings for you." He seemed to be struggling with himself. "I was too reckless."

"What are you talking about, Evan?" I asked, confused.

His face grew grave. "I shouldn't have broken the rules. I should have protected you and instead I took you into my world." He looked miserable. "I put you in danger. It was a mistake. Forgive me."

His words left me astonished. I finally realized why he felt so guilty. A series of images flashed before my eyes: the crazed horse, the falling tree trunk, the out-of-control motorcycle. They hadn't been coincidences. The events had begun right after that afternoon. And the shadow I'd seen . . .

I went ice-cold. So I hadn't imagined it. Was this the price I was going to have to pay for visiting his world: my life? My instinct had been right. It had been risky to challenge fate like that.

"They tried before too," I whispered, still caught in my memories.

"Huh?"

"They tried before." The faint voice that issued from my mouth was as cold as the blood in my veins. "This morning, and also before, when I was out in the woods with the others. Luckily I was with Ginevra. My God . . ."

Evan clenched his jaw as if that hadn't occurred to him yet. "When I think of what might have happened to you—" He looked away, beside himself with anger.

"You said they wouldn't notice my presence."

"They shouldn't have, but something went wrong. I don't understand. No one should've noticed, damn it! How could I have been so stupid?" he growled, raising his fists to his forehead. "We could have gone on living our lives without any problems, but I went and complicated everything. I shouldn't have run the risk."

"Evan, it wasn't your fault," I said, but my attempt to reassure him failed utterly. He barely seemed to have heard my voice.

"I put your life at risk on an idle whim!" He clenched his jaw, furious with himself.

"That isn't all it was for me, Evan." I took his hands and moved in front of him. Finally he looked at me. "I wanted to do it and it was worth it, because now . . ." I closed my eyes, struggling to voice my thoughts. "Now I know what's waiting for me. You gave me a gift." A tear slid down my face. Soon I would be dead. I would lose Evan forever.

"Don't even say it," he hissed. What I'd just said almost seemed to have made him angry. Then his tone softened. "If I lost you, I'd—"

"Evan, you think there's still hope that—"

"Hope is for people with no certainty." His eyes burned into mine, his tone adamant.

"How do we stop them?" I asked warily.

No matter how hard Evan tried to lie to me, no matter how hard he tried to lie to himself, I could sense his torment and it wasn't difficult to interpret it: he was afraid of losing me. "I don't care how," he snarled. "I'm going to exterminate them all. No one is getting close to you. What happened today caught me off guard, but it's not going to happen again. He's alone, but we've got Ginevra on our side. That's a huge advantage. It won't be hard." His eyes glittered as he laid his plans, his tone ominous.

I wasn't so sure it would be that easy. Given what had happened the first time, they were bound to send someone more skilled, more cunning, and more powerful than Faust. Now they knew who they were dealing with and to what lengths Evan was willing to go to protect me. It was stupid to think they wouldn't have an ace up their sleeves this time.

After a moment of silence, I turned to Evan and asked in a tiny voice, "Was it really about to happen?" He frowned and avoided my eyes. He already knew what I meant, but I had to say it aloud before it exploded in my head. "Back there, I—I was about to die." Unable to phrase it as a question, I let the statement hang in the air. Evan didn't reply. "It was you that brought me back." It was a confession, but he didn't know it.

"I know. I healed you. You'd smashed your head against the glass."

I gulped.

"No one else could have done it."

His words skimmed my consciousness, leaving a shiver on my skin, but that wasn't what I'd been referring to. "No. I wasn't talking about that."

Evan looked at me, puzzled.

"It was your voice. I held on for you. In a sense, it's like I *chose* to. I could have let myself go, let myself slide into the darkness that had enveloped me, taking away the pain. For a split second I almost wanted to. But then I heard your voice." I sought his gaze. "*You* brought me back, Evan."

He laced his fingers with mine, squeezing my hand as his face darkened into a mask of torment. "You have no idea what I went through in those five minutes. I was deathly afraid of losing you. You have no idea how much I suffered, Gemma."

Now it was me who squeezed his fingers. All at once a doubt surfaced in my mind, clouding my certainty. I sat down again next to him. "There's something I don't understand.

The last time it happened, when I died, you were afraid you wouldn't be able to bring me back in time because you weren't there to protect me. This time you were with me, so you could have saved me no matter what, right?" I studied his expression.

"I wasn't sure I could heal you all on my own. Your condition was too serious." My stomach lurched. How was that possible, if I was there now without even a scratch? "I only succeeded because you didn't give up. As long as your heart continued to beat I had a hope of healing you." Evan swallowed, his gaze empty. "But if you had died . . . I don't think I could have managed to bring you back all on my own."

I shuddered. "You didn't sense his presence?" I made myself ask in a steady voice.

"No," he said, frustrated. "My guard was down. I was too focused on you, on protecting you from the other dangers, the normal ones. There was no way for me to know he was there until it was too late."

"I shouldn't have gotten behind the wheel," I said guiltily.

"It would have happened anyway. I tried to keep the car from crashing, to stop it by controlling the air, but I couldn't. Under normal circumstances I would have been able to take control of the car before it even risked going off the road. You weren't in any danger. I didn't expect to meet with resistance. That's when I realized what was going on, but it was already too late."

"What do we do now?" Fear had gripped my stomach.

"Gemma, listen carefully. From now on it's important that you always stay near one of us. You need to be under our constant supervision, otherwise we can't protect you. If I can't be there, someone else has to stay with you—Simon, Ginevra, or Drake, it doesn't matter who. You'll be safe with us. But you can *never* be alone. Is that clear? *Never.*"

"Okay," was the only word I could utter.

"Let him try now." Defiance glimmered in his eyes. "I'll be here waiting for him."

I looked at Evan for a moment, digging my fingers into the earth. The rain fell slowly in a steady rhythm. From time to time a raindrop slid off the leaves near me, almost in slow motion, and sparkled through the air.

Our absent gazes were lost beyond the lake. Evan reached for my hand and smiled, as if for a moment he'd banished every thought, as if he wanted to forget everything and move forward, pretending it had never happened. But the problem wasn't what we'd been able to overcome or what I'd managed to survive. The problem was what we had in store for us.

What should I expect from that moment on? I decided it didn't matter. Whatever it was I had to face, Evan would be there at my side, every minute. Even if it was my last one.

That was enough for me.

23

HIDDEN SIGNS

"What's your favorite season?"

Evan's question surprised me. We'd never talked about the weather before. I looked at the foliage above us. The trees were still green but in a few weeks they would turn into bouquets of warm colors. I wondered if I'd survive long enough to see them again. As early as October, the leaves of the sugar maples in the forest turned to an array of red, orange, and yellow, framing Lake Placid and painting a stunningly colorful picture around the lakeshore. I closed my eyes and inhaled deeply, trying to engrave the image in my mind forever.

"All of them," I replied when I opened my eyes again.

"All of them?" Evan asked, curious.

"Does it surprise you?"

"I thought you'd say summer, or winter," he said, "like anyone else would."

"But I'm not anyone else." I watched the raindrops fall onto the lake.

"You definitely aren't," he answered with a smile.

"I think nature is perfect. Winter lasts just long enough for me to want summer to arrive and vice versa. I couldn't live in a world with only springs or summers. Each season has its scents, its colors, its charms."

Evan laughed. He seemed fascinated by my explanation. "So you really don't have a preference?"

I thought it over. "This," I told him, jutting my chin at the landscape around us. Evan frowned. It felt like a century had passed since I'd barely avoided death, but it had only been a matter of hours. The sun was about to set behind the clouds and only a few strong beams shone through.

"What do you mean?" he asked, puzzled.

"This. The summer rain. When the seasons combine. I like the strong smell of the damp earth." I breathed in the cool air. "The thunder sounds different, more comforting. Do you think I'm weird?"

Evan smiled to himself, but I wasn't lying. I'd always had a strange connection with nature, as if it were a part of me and I of it. When I was a little girl and got mad at my parents I would run off into the woods. After a couple of hours I would forget everything and go home. It was as if the forest spoke to me.

"You're adorable." He leaned in to kiss my forehead as I continued to stir the earth with my fingers.

We sat in silence for a few minutes, giving ourselves time to put our ideas in order. I continued to draw meaningless figures in the dirt as Evan stared at some vague point across the lake. Despite the distant, blank look on his face, it wasn't hard to imagine what he was thinking about.

My fingers mechanically clasped a little stone. I picked it up and studied its gray, angular details, then drew my arm back and threw it into the lake. It hit the surface with a soft, harmonious *plop*, raising a tiny splash. Spying another stone—a flatter, smoother one—beside my foot, I reached down to grab it, but Evan snatched it up first, our hands touching for a second. He gave me a sweet smile and stood up. "Want to see something?"

The rain was falling more gently now. It dripped onto his dark hair as I watched him pull back his hand with a studied movement and skip the stone across the water.

One. Two. Three. Four. Five. *Plop.*

A gasp of admiration escaped me. I'd never seen anyone skip a stone so many times before. In any case, if there was a rock-skipping record, I knew Evan could beat it with his eyes closed. He turned to look at me with a smug expression.

"Beginner's luck," I teased. My sense of competition wouldn't allow me to let him see how much he'd impressed me. Or more likely, it was my pride. I could never match that. Chances were my stone would sink without skipping even once. "Bet you can't do it again," I said. He looked so handsome with his damp hair clinging to his forehead.

"How many do you want?" he asked calmly, accepting the challenge.

I ventured an impossible number: "How about twenty-five?"

He smiled as if nothing could be easier. God, his smile was gorgeous. I wasn't ready to lose it forever. For a moment it had made me forget how sneaky he could be. By controlling the elements he could keep the stone from sinking into the water and make it skip across the surface forever if he wanted to. He continued to smile at me as I realized I'd lost before the challenge had even begun. Turning his back to me, he held a stone between his fingers and threw it confidently. I felt a tickle on my neck and shrugged my shoulder without taking my eyes off the skipping stone.

"Check it out," he told me, sounding pleased, a little smile on his lips.

I didn't reply, distracted by the annoying tickle on my back.

" . . . Seven . . . eight . . . nine . . ." Evan said. "Do you want to count or should I? Twelve . . . thirteen . . . fourteen . . ."

Out of the corner of my eye I noticed a strange blur on my shoulder and realized the tickling sensation was coming from right there.

" . . . Seventeen . . . eighteen . . ."

Evan's voice faded to a confused murmur. Focused on the tingling sensation, I wasn't paying attention to him any more. I tilted my head back and the blur moved into my field of vision. The tingle instantly spread throughout my body, galvanized by an internal shudder that triggered a wave of bone-chilling terror that ran through me from head to toe. The blur had suddenly taken shape and become clear.

A tarantula. I shuddered again. There was a tarantula on my shoulder.

"Evan." My voice was a mere thread. Or maybe I'd only imagined I'd said his name. I wanted to scream but couldn't produce any sound. I was paralyzed. Spiders had always been one of the things that terrified me most, and the knowledge that such a huge, hairy one was on my shoulder froze every muscle in my body.

". . . Twenty-four . . . twenty-five!" Completely unaware of what was happening, Evan turned around with a giant smile, but his face instantly blanched when he saw my imploring gaze. He stood without moving for a second, his eyes glued to the creature.

"I—I have a tarantula on my shoulder." My voice trembled, my head filled with racing thoughts. Old memories suddenly resurfaced.

"Don't move," Evan said cautiously as if to avoid scaring the creature. The thought of its hairy legs on my skin made me itch all over, but I found the strength not to move a fraction of an inch.

My pleading gaze was locked onto Evan's. I swallowed slowly, afraid even that tiny movement might set it off. Though fear clouded my mind, I tried to make a mental list of everything I knew about tarantulas. From what I could remember, they weren't poisonous. Also, they were black, whereas this one was brown. Then again, I'd never seen one with my own eyes before so I couldn't know for sure. Still, I was certain their venom wasn't deadly. So why did Evan have that look on his face, as if a mountain lion were about to pounce on me?

"Don't move." His voice was ice cold. "That's not a tarantula."

I stiffened. Something in his tone told me it was even worse than I'd imagined. I began to have trouble breathing. "Evan . . ."

"It's a Brazilian wandering spider," he said matter-of-factly as if I should know what that was. "It's very fast, very aggressive, and—most importantly—very poisonous."

My heart was caught in an iron vise and an uncontrollable trembling threatened to overwhelm me, but I forced myself not to move even a muscle. I saw the spider raise its front legs and panic left me breathless. It was preparing to attack.

"Evan!" My voice broke in a desperate plea, my eyes brimming with tears.

Evan's expression hardened, his eyes trained on the spider. He rushed at me at warp speed, snatched up the creature, and flung it across the lake into the distant treetops on the opposite shore.

My heart trembled with terror. I still couldn't breathe. When I looked at my hands I saw they were shaking.

Evan turned back to me, looking worried. "Did it bite you?"

I shook my head but instinctively looked back to check.

"That kind of spider has the natural ability to control the amount of venom it injects into a victim. It regulates the dose based on the circumstances. A Death Angel could make it inject a fatal dose." He sighed and hung his head, then looked up again, his gaze fiery. "It lives in the jungles of South America," he explained grimly as if the information might be useful. Right now, its origins seemed totally irrelevant to me. "It wasn't here by chance," he explained, his gaze resting on mine.

The more alert part of my brain grasped his meaning and I shuddered. Neither of us wanted to believe it. For my part, I hadn't wanted to see reality. Fear is like a boomerang: no matter how far you throw it, it always comes back at you. Sometimes it feels like the best thing to do is ignore what frightens you, but all that does is make the blow even more devastating. It's not a choice, though, but rather, a defense mechanism our brain automatically activates to try to protect us. I was being hunted again. Neither of us wanted to accept it.

Evan didn't move a muscle. His eyes narrowed to slits, scanning the trees, carefully observing every last inch of the forest surrounding us. All at once he seemed to hone in on one spot in particular, too far away for me to make out. His eyes still fixed on the forest, a corner of his mouth rose and his expression turned sharp, threatening. *Lethal.*

"Gotcha," he hissed. Before I could open my mouth he disappeared into the forest, leaving behind a cloud of dust and cold air that sank into my bones.

A suffocating ache in my heart, I stared at the spot where Evan had disappeared. There was no sign of him, as if he'd vanished into thin air. Somewhere inside me I shuddered violently. Right now Evan was with another Soldier of Death. Not just any Executioner, not like Faust, but one who was more prepared, more aware, *more dangerous.*

I couldn't bear the idea that something might happen to Evan. Faust hadn't known what he'd been up against, but this other Subterranean certainly wouldn't be caught unprepared. He would have taken precautions, and the awareness that Evan was running this risk for my sake hurt me all the way down to my bones. I would gladly have surrendered to my hitman rather than put Evan in danger. His life mattered more than mine.

I shifted awkwardly in my spot, my eyes wandering nervously around, looking for some sign of him—any movement among the trees would be enough—but everything was still. Evan seemed to have disappeared. The forest had swallowed him up. The woods were silent, listening to my desperation. Tears welled up in my eyes in spite of my efforts to hold them back. I couldn't see anything any more. Forcing down the lump in my throat, I continued to focus on trying to spot him.

Deep in the forest, a sudden movement made my heart leap. I wasn't sure whether I had actually seen him or just imagined it, because when I looked closer everything was perfectly still. My anxiety rose by the second, preventing me from thinking straight. I didn't know what to do. My impulse was to set out and search for Evan as long as I had air in my lungs, but it was possible that might just complicate things. One way or the other I always managed to do that.

There was nothing to do but wait. Yes, I would wait for him, heart in hand, until he reappeared safe and sound. He was destined to come back, I was sure of it.

Another movement distracted me. This time I was faster and caught sight of it before it disappeared among the trees. Two dark figures that shot back and forth across the forest like bolts of black lightning. The movements were blurry and confused.

I squinted but they were too far away and the light was too faint for me to make them out clearly. It looked like one of them was chasing the other, but I couldn't tell who was who. The rain plastered my hair to my face. Finally I heaved a sigh of relief. Evan wasn't the one being pursued—he was chasing the other Subterranean. I couldn't explain how exactly I managed to figure that out, but I knew I wasn't wrong. I could feel it inside. They were too fast for my human eyes to follow their movements. At times I saw them disappear and then reappear in another spot farther off in the forest.

Evan was always on the verge of catching his adversary, who always managed to elude him. He was fast, faster than Evan, but he seemed afraid to stop and fight. Every time Evan popped out in front of him, the other Angel disappeared and the endless chase resumed. It got harder and harder for me to tell them apart. Sometimes their shapes seemed to merge together.

Gusts of cold air shook the trees, reaching me as they rustled the leaves on the branches. What the hell was going on? Suddenly I couldn't see them any more.

The terrifying silence made me shudder down to my bones. I trembled like the leaves on the trees had a moment ago. Shifting my weight from one leg to the other, my body began to move forward on its own, driven by instinct—or, more likely, my heart. Another step, and another, as my gaze darted through the trees in search of any sign of them, no matter how small. Only when my breathing accelerated did I realize I was running. I couldn't feel my muscles at all any more. My mind was honed in on a single thought and my body had reacted to that thought, desperately seeking Evan.

A flash of light caught my attention and my eyes shot in that direction. At that precise instant, an explosion hit me in the chest and hurled me into the air, knocking the breath from my lungs. I collided with a tree and crumpled to the ground. I felt disoriented, as if my brain had momentarily been switched off.

Moving my head slowly from side to side, I felt a sudden pain in my chest that didn't feel like a normal physiological response. This pain was tearing me up from the inside, crushing my heart as if someone had it in his hands and was squeezing it, suffocating me. Where was Evan? What had happened to him? I sank my fingers into the earth and clenched my fists so tightly they throbbed as the first tears streaked my skin and the rain coursed down my bloodstained hair.

I couldn't have said how long I lay there on the ground. I had no idea where Evan was, what had happened to him, or what the blinding light had been. Something had exploded. It had been too far away for me to make out what it was, but it had sent out a shock wave powerful enough to send me flying.

My palms and knees sank into the damp earth as tears silently slid down my face and spattered the ground like raindrops. I snuffled and forced myself to reason. No explosion, no matter how powerful, could have killed Evan. Only a Witch's poison had the power to do that. So why was my heart in tatters?

"Gemma."

His voice sounded gently beside me as the rain continued to course down my hair. My eyes went to his face. "Evan!" A wave of relief hit me more powerfully than the explosion had, filling my whole body and wiping away every trace of pain. I pulled myself up and threw my arms around his neck, almost afraid he was only a mirage, a projection of my anxious mind. "Evan," I sobbed into his chest, the word muffled.

He stroked my hair as if I were a little girl in need of comforting. "Everything's okay," he whispered. For a second I almost hoped he'd killed the other Executioner. I wouldn't be able to bear another moment like this.

"He got away."

His words sent a tremor down my spine. So it wasn't over. This wouldn't be the last time Evan put himself in harm's way for my sake. I held him tighter, knowing he sensed my apprehension. "I was afraid you weren't coming back to me any more," I murmured, desperation in my voice.

"Hey." Evan lifted my chin to make me look him in the eye. "I will always come back to you."

I buried my face in his chest again. His muscles stiffened and a groan escaped his clenched teeth. Worried, I instantly relaxed my grip and leaned back to look at his face. His lips were pressed together, though he was trying hard to smile. When he saw my alarmed expression, which instantly told him more than any words could, he gave a slight shake of his head and was quick to reassure me. "It's nothing."

"Evan!" I whispered, lowering my eyes to his abdomen. "You're hurt!" Looking closer, I noticed a rip in his green shirt at the level of his ribs. Through it, I glimpsed an ugly burn mark, as if something had torn first through the fabric and then through his skin. When I reached out toward it, Evan pulled away from my touch, unsuccessfully concealing a grimace of pain.

"What happened? I thought nothing could injure you," I gasped.

"We were just playing around a little." He forced a faint mocking smile, then took me by the hand. "Come on. Let's go somewhere safer."

I followed him through the trees along the same course I'd taken. Earlier the distance had seemed longer, but I'd been so disoriented by fear I'd probably run in circles. The trees parted, revealing our hideaway just yards from us. I continued to steal glances at Evan's pain-stricken face. I'd never seen him look like that before and it seemed to transmit a part of his suffering to me. Although he was trying hard not to let it show, his eyes filled with pain from time to time.

The wooden front door opened wide before us. Evan continued to look around him in all directions. When the door closed behind us I felt a strange sensation, as if a bubble of bulletproof glass had suddenly surrounded me, a protective sphere that kept out panic, pain, worry. All at once I wasn't afraid of anything any more—even the terror of dying had disappeared. Evan had banished my fears from my mind, I was sure of it. Just like I was sure he'd tried, without success, to ease the one concern filling my mind right now, the only thing that really mattered to me: the bleeding wound on his abdomen.

I'd seen other marks on Evan's body before—small cuts, burns, scratches. They generally healed even before I could get more than a glimpse of them. This injury, on the other hand, seemed pretty deep and didn't show the least sign of improving. I wondered how it was possible.

I looked away from it and stole a glance at Evan's face when he wasn't looking at me. Dark and rebellious, his drenched hair hung over his forehead and his clothes were sopping wet—no less than my own, of course. My heart beat harder just looking at him.

"He's sneaky." Evan's voice shook me out of my thoughts. "He wants to make it look like an accident, even to us. It's like he doesn't want to come out into the open."

"Maybe he's just afraid of you," I said.

Evan shook his head, unconvinced. "It has to be something else. He must have a plan—otherwise I can't explain it." He stared into space, thinking aloud. "He always keeps his distance, just far enough away that I can't detect his presence and intercept him." His face went rigid and fire glimmered in his eyes. There was something he wasn't telling me, I could feel it. "But I'll be more careful from now on."

"What happened, exactly?" I asked cautiously.

"I tried to catch him." His tone went dull again, making me instantly regret my question. "But I couldn't." He looked away.

"It doesn't matter, Evan. How are *you*?" I reached toward the wound without touching it.

"It's nothing," he said reassuringly.

"Evan, why haven't you healed yet? I thought your wounds always went away quickly."

"Only the common ones. Things get complicated if the person to injure you isn't human. The bastard threw a fireball at me, a totally extreme measure." Evan's eyes seemed to grow more pensive, but his face was set. "He didn't want to fight and he wasn't trying to kill me."

I started. "But he couldn't have done that, right?"

Evan was silent for a moment. "No, but death isn't always the worst outcome. He only grazed me and I'm sure he did it on purpose."

Another silence.

"Then why did he attack you?" I asked. "Evan, why didn't he try to hit you full on?"

"He wanted to get away." Again that pensive look. "And that's what I don't get," he reflected aloud. "It's really strange. Too strange. I had the impression he didn't want to confront me. He kept running away and wouldn't let me see his face." Evan shook his head. "No, it can't be . . ." he murmured, barely moving his lips.

"Maybe he doesn't want you to know who he is," I suggested timidly, "so he can—I don't know—operate undisturbed."

"Maybe." His gaze was still distant, lost in thought, as if he'd come up with an explanation but wasn't convinced. "Or maybe not."

29

THE SKY IN A ROOM

"Does it hurt?" I asked, lightly touching the wound. His sopping-wet shirt clung to his body, outlining his chest, and the burn lacerating his skin showed through.

"Only a little," he murmured at my touch. From the look on his face I could tell he was lying. An icy shiver ran down my back, reminding me I was still wet too. My clothes felt frozen to my skin.

"You're cold," Evan said, his voice low, gently rubbing my arms to warm them. He released them and went over to the fireplace. When he raised his palms toward the blackened stone hearth, a spark flickered amid the stacked firewood. Soon a fire softly illuminated the room. Outside, the sun had already set. In moments the fire was blazing, emitting a wave of hot air that startled me. Shivering again, I eased into the pleasant sensation of warmth against my skin.

I looked at Evan, captivated by the golden glow the fire was casting on his face. He opened his palm and before I could ask what he was doing something took my breath away: another spark, rising from his hand. Taking the form of a tiny crystal sphere, like a will-o'-the-wisp, its white light glimmered silver before my enchanted eyes as he raised it to his mouth and blew it off his hand. The luminescent sphere exploded in a myriad of tiny, diamond-like sparkles that looked like little stars. They floated through the room, finally coming to rest above us, twinkling just below the ceiling.

I looked up to contemplate the mantle of stars, then looked back down at Evan. No one could take this moment away from us. It was just him and me, with a microcosm of the universe shining down on us from above. I wouldn't have given up this moment for anything in the world. There was nowhere else I would have wished to be but there with Evan in our private little universe.

It wasn't the first time I'd seen him create a sphere of light, but seeing so many tiny fragments of it all gathered together made me feel I was a part of something infinitely large.

Evan gazed at me as though I too were a star. *His* star. He smiled, his face illuminated by the warm glow, and I lost the power of speech. In the silence he gripped the bottom of his shirt, pulled it off over his head, and shook his wet hair. At this unexpected action my heart leapt to my throat. His dog tag jingled against his sleeveless white undershirt, which was wet and clung to his chest. His firm muscles rippled in his arms.

I moved closer to examine his wound, challenging my self-control as the flames in the fireplace burned on my cheeks, concealing my blush. "Does it still hurt?" I asked softly, touching the gash from which blood had trickled onto the white fabric. Evan pulled back slightly, stifling a grimace. "Can't you heal yourself?" I asked, unused to seeing him this vulnerable.

"Not on my own," he said, his voice unsteady from the pain he was trying to repress. "It's not a human wound."

"Let's go to the others, then!" I said, looking at him sharply.

"No!" His wild dark eyes mesmerized me, putting an end to my attempts to take him to his brothers. Then his expression softened. "I want to stay here with you." His eyes probed mine intensely, promising to take me places I'd never been before. "It's almost healed," he reassured me in a low voice. "I just need to bind it."

Without giving me a chance to breathe, Evan reached behind his head and pulled off his undershirt with a groan, baring his pecs. An electric charge surged from my heart to my throat and stomach, his golden skin taking my breath away. With a single swift movement of his well-defined muscular arms, he tore the white fabric into strips as easily as if it had been a sheet of paper.

"Here, let me," I murmured, looking at him encouragingly and taking the bandage from his hands.

Without a word Evan gave it to me and raised his elbows slightly so I could dress his wound. Though I was focusing on his side, I felt the heat of his gaze on me the whole time. My heart was beating so hard I was afraid he might hear it. I wrapped the bandage around his middle with careful movements, wondering why I couldn't stop shivering. It felt like something was on the verge of changing forever. My movements grew slower as I felt his breath moving closer. A delicious warmth filled my head, but I knew it wasn't coming from the fire. I tied the bandage in place and swallowed, unable to look him in the eye.

I couldn't stop trembling. Not because of the cold, I was sure of that, but because Evan was there with me. Of their own volition my hands began to move over his ribs, rising with extreme slowness until they were caressing his chest. Evan's eyes were on me all the while. His skin was incredibly warm. He tucked a lock of hair behind my ear as he lightly stroked my cheek. I looked at him with a strange shyness. When my eyes met his intense gaze I felt as if I were seeing him for the first time.

"God, you're beautiful," Evan whispered. My heart skipped a beat. I felt it tremble and half closed my eyes as he rested his forehead against mine. "Everything's going to be fine."

I nodded slightly without replying. He gently clasped both my hands in one of his. "Come nearer the fire." His tone was even gentler than his touch. "You should dry off."

With a hint of embarrassment I took off my shirt. Evan looked away until I'd straightened my camisole that had gotten pulled up in the process. I sat down on the big red rug in front of the fireplace. He came over, sat behind me, and wrapped his arms around me protectively. The silence in the room, a comforting silence full of promises, was broken only by our breathing. I stared at the flames that rose higher than our heads as I listened to the crackle of the burning firewood.

"I'm sorry for everything you've been through," he said.

"It's not your fault, Evan," I told him firmly.

"It is. I shouldn't have taken you to my world. You're seventeen. These should be the best years of your life, and—"

"They are," I interrupted quickly. "*This* year," I stressed, "has been the best year of my life. *Meeting you.* Evan, over the last few months I've experienced more with you than anyone else could in an entire lifetime."

Evan's gaze was lost beyond the flames. "When I saved you, you were given a second chance. It's my fault they're hunting you again." There was pain in his voice. "Maybe we shouldn't have gotten involved."

I suddenly felt my heart freeze as if the fire had been replaced by an iceberg. The bitter chill penetrated my bones. "Are you saying you should have left me?"

Evan smiled. "I wasn't talking about *me.* I could never do that, ever. I could kill myself, but I could never think of leaving you. It's just that—you shouldn't have to be going through all this. I'm so sorry. I don't know how you can stand it."

His words took me by surprise. Did he really not know I would run a thousand risks if it meant I could stay with him? I turned slowly to face him. "I would go through it all over again,

Evan, because all of it led me to you. Meeting you turned my whole life upside down, but being part of your world, being with you, has been the most wonderful thing life could offer me," I confessed, hoping he could read the emotion in my heart.

"I'll never leave your side, Gemma." His gaze melted me with its bold tenderness.

"I know. You gave me your promise." I let myself linger in the memory of that moment. It was so recent but felt so distant—he and I soaring through the sky, touching the clouds, forgetting the rest of the world.

"I mean I'll never let them hurt you," he said. I rested my chin on his upper arm as he held me closer and added, "I'll be there to protect you."

It was strange to be there with him after everything that had happened. Experiencing this magical moment with Evan banished all my worries, all my pain. This morning I'd left the house not knowing what was in store for me, not knowing death would return to track me down. Yet for some inexplicable reason, right here, right now, it didn't matter. It had been a long day full of conflicting emotions, but oddly enough all I could remember were the unforgettable moments I'd experienced with Evan. His warm body holding me close was the only sensation I wanted to focus on.

Those moments of panic had taught me one thing I would never forget: even if it's raining outside, the sun is always behind the clouds, even if you can't see it. You can never tell exactly when it will come out and shine again, but no storm can eclipse the sun forever. Not even the ones that rage in our hearts. You just need to wait for a gust of wind to blow away the clouds and allow the sun to shine again, even inside yourself. And that was what Evan was for me: my gust of wind.

I was staring at the flames in front of me when I felt his lips touch my shoulder, sending a tingle all the way down my spine. He delicately swept my hair back and his touch made me quiver again. His lips brushed my skin tenderly, moving from my shoulder to my neck. Tiny hot shivers spread through my body with each kiss. I closed my eyes as the emotion trembled all the way to my heart.

"You know . . ." The words were barely audible but I was sure Evan could hear them. I turned to look him in the eye. "Despite everything, this has been the most romantic afternoon I've ever spent." He pushed a lock of hair off my forehead and, without leaving my gaze, gently tucked it behind my ear, caressing my cheek. I half closed my eyes, letting the feelings wash over me. "I wish it would never end," I whispered even more softly.

His eyes half closed too, Evan leaned forward and brushed my cheek with his. "It doesn't have to," he whispered, his lips on my ear. The warmth of his voice tickled my skin, sending an uncontrollable tingle surging through my body. God, I was so happy. I wished I could stop time and stay there with him in our little hideaway, our little world where I would be safe forever.

I inhaled deeply, his scent enveloping me as if for the first time. His mouth slowly reached my face, touching my cheek and moving on to my lips with incredible sweetness. I closed my eyes and followed his movements as my body melted like warm honey and his mouth burned against mine. He gazed at me and I lost myself in those intense eyes that were as dark as night while inside me the sun rose, a sun that would never set. I was at war with the world outside, but I didn't care. As long as I was with Evan, I knew nothing could hurt me.

He kissed me with incredible tenderness. As if it had a life of its own, my hand stroked his skin. I trembled at every movement of his lips on mine, every breath, every heartbeat, as the two of us melted together into one.

I watched Evan's hand slowly caress my shoulder and gently move the strap of my camisole aside, leaving it dangling against my arm. I held my breath as his mouth moved to where his hand had just been, burning my skin. When he slowly pressed his lips to my neck, I closed my eyes and tilted my head, surrendering to him, savoring his sweet fruity taste that lingered on my lips.

I knew what was about to happen. We both did.

My skin knew it from how it quivered at his touch. My eyes knew it from the moment they'd met his in the brief silence full of meaning that had left me dazed. And so did my heart, which longed more than anything to melt into his. Every inch of me longed for this moment and I could sense that Evan wanted it just as intensely.

"This, above all else, flouts every rule," I whispered slowly.

"There's no rule that isn't worth breaking for you. I don't care about the rules." His tone was gentle and his gaze burned into mine as his hand sank into my hair and his mouth sought mine again, this time more fervently.

I rested my palms on the rug that was as soft as down to the touch. Our lips brushed playfully as I slowly slid backwards, almost unconsciously, guided by Evan's body as it pressed ever closer to mine. Once I was lying on the rug Evan looked into my eyes, accelerating my breathing. He was suspended over me, his hands resting on either side of my head and his dog tag hanging down between us. I stared at his body and the full, firm muscles lining his arms and torso. Stroking his chest, I felt my gaze return to his as if drawn by an irresistible summons. His velvety voice filled my brain. "There's something in your eyes that drives me out of my mind," he whispered with infinite sweetness.

I knew perfectly well what he meant because I felt the exact same thing. There was something in the special way he looked into my eyes, his hard gaze that softened only for me—it drove me wild. Against all logic, it made me lose myself.

Evan continued to kiss me as he delicately unbuttoned my jeans. I longed only for him. The clothes gently slid off our bodies and at last his bare skin was against mine. He swept my hair back and I felt safe.

His voice whispered inside my head, sweeter than ever before: *"If only you could see inside me, you'd know what I feel right now."* The thought echoed intensely in my mind, his voice tinged with torment, his gaze chained to mine.

"I feel the same," I whispered onto his mouth. It felt like I'd just told him a secret. My love for him was uncontainable; I was afraid my heart would swell so much my chest wouldn't be able to hold it any more.

I put my hands over my head, abandoning them on the rug. Evan's powerful arm reached up and clasped them in his right hand with boundless tenderness as his left caressed my body, barely brushing my neck and then my breasts, slowly. He stroked my belly and his hand slipped under my back.

An invisible cord bound my heart to his. Sensation overwhelmed me. His smell, the feel of his skin against my body, the delicate touch of his lips on mine. My skin burned beneath Evan's hand, consumed by a fire that could never be extinguished.

He pressed his lips against my neck and clasped my hands against the rug more firmly as a soft breath of air blew out the fire next to us and an overwhelming emotion swept me with unexpected intensity, an internal explosion that filled my heart and shattered every tiny fragment of my being only to reunite it with Evan's in a single, inseparable entity.

Evan was inside me.

I closed my eyes and let the sensations spread through me. Fire, earth, heaven, hell whirled inside me in a tumult of emotions. The universe had swallowed me up in its infinitude and I wandered within it together with him, entwined in our forbidden love. Hidden from everyone, sheltered in our own little corner of paradise where no one could reach us. Forever connected, softly crying out our love for each other.

No one could take me away from Evan. My flesh was his flesh and my spirit had merged with his like two metals forged by the flames of love into a single indissoluble element. I was his and would be forever.

Evan, Gemma, me, him: tonight all of that had been wiped away, becoming *us*, just us. Two worlds that had combined to become one reality, all our own, where no one could hunt down our love. Two perfectly fitting halves that formed an indivisible whole, so closely united it was seamless, so deep we could forget where one ended and the other began.

Evan moved above me with infinite tenderness, treating me like a delicate piece of crystal. My lips followed his and his mine, brushing together gently at one moment, locking together ardently at another. I'd never known my heart could withstand the intensity of such powerful emotions.

I felt the delicate touch of his hand beneath my back. Never before had he been so tender. His gaze lingered on mine as he swept a stray lock of hair from my face. He spoke, and the tenderness of his voice as it issued from his lips was entirely new. "If my heart could beat, right now it would be out of control," he whispered.

The soft curve of his full lips mesmerized me as they came closer. Tilting my head to offer him my neck, I realized that the pale light that barely illuminated the room was coming from the sparkling spheres, which were no longer fixed points of light below the ceiling. Now they were swirling, moved by the energy that united us, gliding slowly around our bodies like fireflies in the darkness.

I no longer felt like a single particle in the universe; the entire universe was inside me, locked in my heart that had swelled large enough to contain it. I felt a river of emotion flowing from me to him and back, connecting us eternally. It was as if we'd waited forever for this moment.

Making love with Evan was so intense, so incredible. He was so confident in everything he did, yet every movement, every caress was so gentle. Now, like never before, I felt I could see inside him. It was as if we had each walked a separate path that had brought our souls together and now the two paths had merged into a single one.

The more time passed, the more intense the feeling inside me grew, plucking strings I didn't even know I had as Evan ran his lips over my breasts, burning my skin with every touch. His mouth stroked my ear and his voice was a warm, velvety whisper that tickled my skin, making me tremble: "I love you to death."

I half closed my eyes and allowed the emotion to sweep me away.

25

CONNECTIONS BENEATH THE SKIN

I'd never experienced such intense emotion in my whole life and I knew nothing could ever match it. My heart was ready to burst. Evan was lying at my side, contemplating me. The fire in the hearth had returned to warm us. The dancing firelight played over our bodies.

"It was then that the Angel saw heaven for the first time," he whispered, stroking my neck.

I looked into his eyes and bit my lip to conceal a smile. "A reckless Angel."

"I would die for you," he said, his eyes probing mine.

"Don't even try it," I warned, and he smiled at me, the sexy little creases that drove me wild appearing under his eyes.

"My God, your eyes are so enchanting." He sighed. "When I look at you all my defenses fall away. I feel like you could ask anything of me and I would grant it."

My gaze had strayed to his mouth but I returned it to his eyes, resisting the urge to kiss him. "I thought there were certain transgressions forbidden to Angels," I teased, whispering against his lips, my gaze chained to his. "Shouldn't your moral code keep you from giving in to this particular kind of temptation?"

Evan stifled a laugh. "I thought a lot of things before I met you, but you turned my whole world upside down. When you're near me I don't even know who I am any longer." He leaned closer and whispered the words onto my lips: "I lost my mind and nothing makes sense any more." He kissed my bare shoulder and his soft voice caressed my neck under my ear. "My moral code tells me I shouldn't feel what I feel and that I should resist certain urges, but my instinct tells me I might die if I don't give in to them." I rested my forehead on his, his velvety voice putting me into a trance. "If all I had was you, I would still have everything."

I closed my eyes and swallowed, lost in the spell of his warm, penetrating gaze. Making love with Evan had been an otherworldly experience, not because he was an Angel but because of the boundless love that united us. The energy was still flowing through my body. I was in heaven. Suddenly I remembered when Evan had explained that his body perceived emotions more powerfully than a mortal's. I couldn't imagine how it was possible to experience a sensation more intense than the one still stirring in my bones. My body wouldn't have been able to bear it.

Evan sank his hand into my hair, demanding my attention, as I struggled to find my way back from the dimension I was in. I turned my head so my face was close to his and gazed at him as he continued to stroke my hair.

"Before, you said you loved me." My eyes locked onto his.

Evan smiled. "What, hadn't you figured that out already?" he whispered, playfully brushing a lock of my hair back and forth on my face.

"Of course." I smiled. "It's just—you once told me you weren't going to use that word. You thought it was—how did you describe it? Superficial," I teased. Instantly, though, the memory of the intensity with which he'd said those words banished all the mockery from my face, making my heart skip another beat.

"There's nothing superficial about us or what I feel for you, Gemma." His mouth moved to my ear. "We were made to be together," he whispered, "and no one can ever separate us. Not even Death." He gently slid his hand down my belly, his eyes following the lines traced by his fingers, back and forth, reaching the edge of my panties. Unable to tear my eyes from his face, I studied its outline, observing the way his wavy hair hung over his forehead, grazing his eyebrows that were as dark as his eyes, as deep as night.

"How did you get this scar?" he asked, pushing aside the edge of the fabric and stroking the silvery streaks on my lower belly.

"It's not a scar, it's a birthmark. Huh—" I took a closer look. "It usually looks paler." It was strange to see how it glowed in the warm firelight. "I could have your name tattooed there to cover it." I shot Evan a challenging look. "But then you'd have to do the same for me," I teased, trying hard to sound serious.

"Your name is already branded on my heart," he whispered tenderly. He stroked my palm with his thumb and I returned the gesture. I loved it when he did that. The simple touch drove me wild.

My fingers slid to his wrist and began a slow exploration of his forearm as I studied his tattoo. I'd never seen anything so fascinating and frightening at the same time. The letters were so small one could barely be distinguished from the next. They seemed to form a single design. Actually, there were different lines consisting of strange symbols that wound up to the inside of his upper arm. From a distance they looked like scratches made by sharp claws or roots that branched out as if to imprison his arm.

"What are these symbols?" I swallowed, studying them carefully as though I could decipher them.

"It's Devanagari, a very ancient alphabet," he said. "Some say it's the language of the gods."

"They're tiny." I continued to stroke his arm, following the lines on his skin as he turned gradually toward me, letting me examine them. For a moment, we both watched my fingers as they moved on him.

Evan looked into my eyes, his own intense. "It's a map of what we are."

I stroked the symbols in the center from which all the others seemed to emerge.

यमराज

"That one appeared first," he explained, seeming to recall the moment. "From there it spread out all over my arm."

I touched his skin, imagining the pain he must have suffered when he was branded with the mark of the Children of Eve.

"*Yama*," he murmured in a barely audible whisper. "He who irremediably draws souls to himself and to whom is entrusted their guidance and passage from one world to the other."

Looking into his eyes, I saw them light up as if he'd been looking forward for some time now to revealing to me what was written there. "At first I didn't know what it was. It all happened so fast. The mark appeared, then the Witch, and then I saw my lifeless body. I thought I'd been cursed—and I wasn't altogether wrong. When Simon found me and made me eat of the tree, I looked at my arm and everything was instantly clear: I could read it." He frowned, pulled into the memory despite himself. "Some of the marks are the same for all Subterraneans, while others define who we are and what our individual powers are."

After a long moment, he pointed out one of the words:

कमदशभत

"*Karmadeshabhuta.* It means 'spirit that determines fate.'"

I touched the symbol, fascinated. Branching out from it were five small lines. I slowly traced the first one.

"*Jala*, water," Evan said. He looked at me and I moved my finger again, stopping on the next line. "*Teyas*, fire," he whispered, staring at my mouth, in his eyes the memory of the fire that had just consumed us. "*Vayu*, air. And this one here is the power of earth, *Bhumi*. We're spirits of nature and can control its elements." He turned his arm until my fingers were touching another word. "Life, *Ayus*." He moved it again, focusing on another. "Death, *Mrty*. They're all part of nature."

"What about this one?"

"That's pronounced *Mantra*. It means 'free the mind.'"

The fire danced in the hearth, illuminating his tanned skin, his muscles flexing with each movement. I touched a symbol that looked more threatening than the others and Evan hesitated.

अमृत

"*Amrit*," he murmured grimly. "Deathless."

"Evan," I whispered, but he smiled at me, calm again.

"You'll like this one. *Svapna*. It indicates my special power to enter others' dreams."

"*Svapna* . . . You're right. I like it."

"It's different for each Subterranean. Drake has the symbol for transformation, shapeshifting. Simon has the one for deepest memories." He pointed at other symbols. "These, on the other hand, appear on all Subterraneans. *Guhya*, hidden. *Tamas*, darkness. *Pranama*, obedience. *Amrta*, ambrosia. *Jyotis*, light. *Naitya*, eternity. *Atmanas*, souls. *Moksha*, salvation."

I stroked his arm slowly, tracing the lines on the inside of his elbow.

With a shiver he closed his eyes and took a deep breath. "*Bhoga*," he whispered, pointing at one of the symbols. "Sensual pleasure." His dark eyes probed mine, holding me captive.

I gave him a smile and went back to studying the symbols, fascinated. "What does this one mean?"

Evan fell silent, looking troubled. "*Vyaya*, loss."

"*Vyaya*," I repeated, touching it again, my heart heavy. It represented what we most feared. Tracing the mark with my finger, I noticed that the symbols forming it were interwoven with another word. He explained before I could ask about it.

"*Abhaya*, fearlessness."

"You mean you've never been afraid?"

"Never. Not until I met you." He looked at me intently and I held his gaze.

A smile escaped me. "Are you saying you're afraid of me?" I teased, grinning.

He pulled me on top of him, only our underwear separating us. "I'm saying the thought of losing you is the only thing that's ever terrified me," he murmured onto my mouth. He touched my leg, slowly sliding his hand up my thigh, then clasped my rear and pulled me against him, sending a shiver through me.

"*Kama*," he whispered, looking me in the eye. "Desire."

I raised an eyebrow, mischief in my eyes. The heat of his erection pressing against me left me in a trance. "Desire? Is that what's written there?"

With a laugh, Evan raised my hand to his neck and slid it down to his bare chest. "No. That's what's written *here*."

It made me smile. "I think it's written a bit farther down," I teased. My eyes were drawn to the last word, which ran up his bicep. "And this one?"

Evan smiled and touched it, his finger brushing mine.

आनन्द

"*Ananda*, bliss. It's what makes all Subterraneans hope for a reward and for Redemption," he said.

I stared at his tattoo, realizing for the first time that some of them weren't simple words, but sentences interconnected in a single design. I lay down on my side next to Evan. His face filled with intensity as he recited the words like a prayer.

Devānāṃ bhadrā sumatirṛjūyatāṃ devānāṃ rātirabhi noni vartatām devānāṃ sakhyamupa sedimā vayaṃ devā na āyuḥ pra tirantu jīvase.

"Ah, of course. It's all so clear now." I smiled to myself.

He laughed, easing the gravity of the moment, and proceeded to translate the quote: "May the auspicious favor of the gods be ours, on us descend the bounty of the righteous Gods. The friendship of the gods have we devoutly sought: so may the gods extend our life that we may live."

"Amazing. It's basically the path to Redemption!" I exclaimed.

Evan remained calm. "That's what they say."

For a moment he seemed lost in thought while another question arose in my mind. "When did you realize I could see your tattoo?" I asked. When a Subterranean manifested himself, mortals couldn't see the mark. Only I could, for some reason neither of us understood.

"It was at school, when you were stealing glances at me from your desk. You looked at me and then at my tattoo. I couldn't believe it." Evan shook his head, still bewildered by my ability. "It's amazing." He laced his fingers with mine and guided our hands up, looking into my eyes. We lay there facing each other, palm to palm.

"Did you know the palm is full of nerve endings that connect to the entire body?" He moved his fingers and a tingle ran up my arm. "From here I can feel all your energy."

An image crossed my mind: Drake claiming the soul of the boy on the street. I'd only been able to make myself look away for a moment, so I'd seen it happen. Drake had touched the spirit of the boy, who had then vanished. Did that mean their power to guide souls across worlds lay in their hands?

"There's—there's something I've always wanted to ask you," I said.

"I'm listening."

"How do you . . . take people's lives?"

Evan paused before answering. He probably hadn't expected this question, given that I'd always avoided talking about it. "It's an impulse I feel inside."

"Could you end up killing me by accident? Do I run that risk?"

"Peter has run that risk lots of times," he admitted, laughing. I punched him on the shoulder for not taking me seriously. "So did Daryl Donovan. I definitely would have liked to kill him."

"Daryl I can understand. I mean, he tried to molest me at the prom. And then he provoked you at the party Jeneane threw at the end of the school year. But *Peter!* When?"

"Whenever I see you with him," he admitted, leaning in to kiss me. "I can't stand it when he's around you."

"You can't feel the urge to kill him just for that!"

"Sure I can. It doesn't mean I'll act on it—unless he really makes me mad." He laughed and looked at me again, his eyes roguish. "You, on the other hand, make me feel another kind of urge."

"Mmm, what kind would that be?" His provocation took my mind off his threats toward Peter.

"Let me show you." He arched an eyebrow and pinned me beneath him, his mouth touching me below the ear. A shiver ran down my neck and then another one, little tingles that tickled my heart. I laughed and pushed him back by the shoulders, but he continued to kiss me.

"Evan, how do you say 'You're inside me'?" I asked, remembering the words he'd said to me at the foot of the sacred tree.

He looked into my eyes, probing them. *"Antar mayy as."*

"Antar mayy as," I whispered, enchanted.

"Yatha tvam mayy asi . . . Just as you are inside me," he replied, holding my gaze. He raised my hand to his chest and his chain dangled between us. *"Mama hrdi* . . . In my heart." He laced his fingers with mine and squeezed my hand as the throb of my heartbeat melted me. *"Mamatmani* . . . In my soul."

I half closed my eyes because Evan had expressed exactly what I felt: he was inside me. In my heart. In my soul.

Unnoticed, time flew by like a silent thief who with every minute that passed stole another fragment of our incredible afternoon. I was happy, and when the thought that I'd had a brush with death crossed my mind, all I had to do was meet Evan's gaze and everything else vanished.

God, how I loved him. His deep, dark eyes touched my soul every time they rested on me. Lying on the rug, I followed my instinct to stroke his hair. He circled my waist with his arm and my skin burned beneath his hand.

"Think we can spend the night here?" he said, his eyes never leaving mine. His unexpected suggestion left me wordless. I wished I could say yes—God knew how much I wanted to—but I couldn't.

"My dad would kill me," I said, smiling.

He touched his lips to my throat with incredible sweetness, trying to persuade me. "We can always find a solution," he said between one light kiss and the next.

"I don't think Drake is going to like being our pimp."

He kissed me again. "I'm sure he would understand. I want to stay here alone with you." I propped myself up on my side and Evan tucked my hair behind my ear. "I want to kiss you until you fall asleep and hold you all night even if you can't feel it."

"Is that all?" I cast him a sidelong glance and a sly smile escaped him. "You can always come to my house tonight," I said.

Regret flashed across his eyes as if I'd made him remember something he didn't want to recall. "That's why I wish I didn't have to leave you tonight. Because I'm going to have to face reality again and be apart from you."

"Tonight too?" I didn't even bother to hide the dismay in my voice.

"You'll find me at your side when you wake up," he promised. "You won't even notice I'm gone." Holding back my disappointment, I tightened my lips. It was hard to believe his absence could go unnoticed. Whenever Evan left me alone the nightmares returned to haunt me. Everything I was living, everything I forced myself to repress during the day, came crashing down on me with full force. Still, I couldn't blame that on him.

"I don't want you to be alone, though. Things have changed and we can't afford to run any risks. You'll sleep at my place. Ginevra will stay with you and Drake will fill in for you." I nodded, relieved. "Nothing is going to happen to you," he whispered, stroking my hair. "You're under our protection."

"How are we going to get home?" I asked, concerned by the steady ticking of the rain against the walls of the hideaway.

"Don't worry. I've already contacted Simon telepathically. He's on his way. I tried to contact Drake too, but couldn't find him. He must be . . . out somewhere. Let's hope he gets back soon."

Trying not to think of the words Evan had decided not to say, I started to get up but he pushed me down onto my back and held me tight. "Where do you think you're going?" he whispered, a sly look on his face as he barred my way.

"I should get dressed, shouldn't I?" I asked.

"Uh-uh," he said. "Why should you? You look so good like this." He kissed my neck and then my shoulder as his muscled arms flexed at my sides, holding me captive.

"Your scent drives me wild," I said with a moan.

Evan smiled against my lips. "I never wear cologne."

I shook my head, brushing my nose against his to challenge his statement. "It was the first thing I sensed when you used to sneak up on me." His chain dangled between our bodies. I grasped it in my fingers and slowly drew his face closer to mine until my mouth was brushing his earlobe. "Do you want Simon to see me naked?" I whispered provocatively in his ear. Simon would be there any minute and all I had on were my panties.

Evan shook his head slightly and tightened his lips. "You know how to persuade me. I would hate to have to kill one of my brothers," he said, breathing the words onto my skin. He kissed me again and fell silent, his eyes suddenly serious. "But there's no limit to what I would do for you."

I rested my forehead on his and we both smiled, our lips a breath away from each other. "I don't think Ginevra would ever forgive you," I warned.

Evan looked away, pretending to consider it. "You're right, she wouldn't. I have no choice but to give in." Reluctantly, he lifted his hand from the floor and propped himself up on one arm, leaving me free. "You win."

A smile still on my lips, I finished dressing just as the now-familiar hum of the BMW broke the steady sound of the pounding rain. Evan held me tight by the front door as if he wanted to keep me there with him. I kissed him and all of a sudden a terrible feeling gripped my stomach: once outside, I would have to face reality. I didn't know what might happen after crossing that threshold, and as if that weren't enough, Evan wouldn't be with me tonight. I would have to face my demons on my own. Death was right around the corner, waiting for me. How much longer could I avoid a collision with destiny? No one could say—not even Evan.

The wooden door opened, admitting a gust of cool air that struck my still-warm face. I took a deep breath and crossed the threshold, taking shelter under the jacket Evan held over our heads. I could barely see where I was putting my feet until the sound of the rain was muffled by the stillness of the BMW's interior.

"Gemma." As Simon greeted me he glanced at my bloodstained clothes.

"Simon," I replied, looking down, a bit embarrassed. For some strange reason I blushed, as if he could see in my face what had happened between me and Evan, though I knew it was impossible. Simon was always the last to know things. It was Ginevra I was worried about. While I was relieved Evan hadn't asked her to pick us up, I couldn't avoid her forever and wasn't sure I could block my thoughts from her. No, I could never manage to do that. She would know everything the minute she saw us.

Simon and Evan fist-bumped and Simon shot him a sidelong glance. "Something go wrong? Where's your car?" he asked his brother, his face serious.

From the back seat I saw Evan's jaw tighten. "We have a bigger problem than the car," he said somberly.

Simon laughed. "What could be more important to you than your car?"

Evan turned to look at him and Simon's expression altered drastically. His eyes went wide. "They found her?" he whispered, looking horrified, still staring at Evan. He turned his eyes back to the road, his expression blank as Evan clenched his fists so hard his knuckles turned white.

Silence fell. The whole way home, the only sound was the tapping of the rain on the windshield. When Simon switched off the engine in the garage, nobody moved for a moment, all of us sunk into our seats in utter silence.

Simon was the first to speak. "Do you already have a plan?"

"Not yet," Evan muttered.

"We need to tell the others."

Evan nodded. "Gemma can't be left alone." His eyes sought Simon's. The tone of his voice left no room for doubt: it was an order. Their eyes remained locked for another moment, making me guess that their conversation was continuing.

Simon quickly confirmed my suspicion, replying to a question I hadn't heard, his tone firm. "It's not going to happen."

It wasn't hard to imagine what he was referring to. After he'd left the garage, I couldn't resist the urge to ask Evan. Climbing out of the car, I leaned against the door, knitting my brow. "What did you say to him?" I asked timidly, instantly feeling embarrassed for prying. My eyes wandered nervously around the garage, but my discomfort disappeared as soon as Evan cupped my face in his hands and leaned against me, pressing me against the car door.

"Just that they have to protect you. *At all costs.*"

Something in his eyes told me it wasn't the whole truth, just like I knew he'd excluded me from their secret conversation to avoid upsetting me. I accepted his explanation, even though no matter how hard he'd tried to hide it from me I already knew the real answer. The words echoed inside me as if I'd heard them for myself: *I don't want to lose her.*

As Evan and I walked to the door hand in hand a single thought filled my mind: Ginevra. I could practically sense her champing at the bit in the room next to the garage, as if she were waiting for me just behind the door, anxious to hear the details. I knew her by now. Or maybe it was just my fear putting me on edge.

Evan seemed to notice and squeezed my hand as a little smile spread across his face, suggesting he realized the reason for my nervousness. "Don't worry. It won't be so bad," he said, unsuccessfully trying to reassure me. The closer we got to the door, the faster my heart pulsed in my temples. He took the handle and opened the door. "After you," he whispered.

Warily, I peered around the living room, but it was empty. Just as I began to breathe normally, a cascade of golden hair flowed down the stairs. Ginevra. She stopped on the last step, her hand still on the railing. My heart sank when her eyes rested on me and I had the feeling I was under scrutiny, like when the teacher asks you a question the one time you didn't study. Why the hell did I always have to be so emotional? Ginevra's mouth fell open slightly and the indecipherable expression on her face made me wish the earth would open beneath my feet and swallow me up. Her eyes shifted to Evan and back to me as I tried hard to act casual and block my thoughts, but it was no use.

About three seconds had gone by.

"Oh." She closed her mouth, looking pleased. "So there's been a change of plans." Her eyes were glued to mine. I felt completely naked.

Evan let out a low laugh and his face hardened. "Gin, there's no need for me to explain anything to you. Unfortunately I've been summoned." He turned toward me as if to apologize. "I'm leaving her in your hands," he said sternly, his eyes burning into his sister's.

Ginevra nodded but Evan didn't seem convinced that she understood how important this was. *"She can't be left alone."*

"Don't worry," Ginevra said in a carefree tone, her eyes darting to mine. "We'll have loads of fun."

Evan's expression relaxed. He cupped my face in his hands and kissed me lightly on the lips. "I'll be back soon," he murmured. I nodded and he turned to take one last look at Ginevra. "Don't torture her, okay?" he said with a wink.

A broad smile spread across his sister's face. "Can't promise you that," she said to the now-empty wall. Evan had already vanished.

I nervously ran my fingers through my hair and looked down, another rush of embarrassment rising in me. Ginevra pounced on me and grabbed my hands. In the blink of an eye she'd pulled me up the stairs and into her room, looking like she was about to explode with enthusiasm. "For Lilith's sake! What are you waiting for?! Tell me everything!" she exclaimed impatiently. For a second, the innocent, enthusiastic look on her face made me think of Peter. Her bedroom door closed behind us.

"Shh!" I warned, scanning the room.

"Sorry! How did it happen? I want to know *every last detail!*"

I wasn't used to talking about myself. I'd never liked doing it. Her eager face was waiting for me to answer. But why? Wasn't probing my thoughts enough for her? "Why should I tell you what you already know?" I said awkwardly.

"Come on," she pleaded. "Nothing like this has ever happened! Imagine being the only girl in an all-boys club for such a long time!"

I opened my mouth to speak but quickly closed it, unable to reply. Her eyes lit up expectantly as she sat down beside me on the bed. What could I tell her? I looked down, wondering exactly how red my cheeks were right then.

"You're right, I always know everything," she admitted, coaxing me with an angelic expression. "More than people want me to know. But sometimes it's nice to hear someone simply *tell* me things. It's nice to have someone decide of their own free will to share what's on their mind with me."

I shot her a reproachful glance. "In this case it's not like I'm exactly *deciding* to tell you. You're not giving me much choice," I pointed out.

"A negligible detail! C'mon, please?" she said, taking my hands and growing serious. "What did you feel?" She waited, staring at me intently. She wasn't being nosy, only conspiratorial. How could I explain to her what I'd felt? I couldn't even conceive it myself. How could words express something so intense, so deep?

That afternoon with Evan had been all our own, and part of me didn't want to give up even a little piece of it or share it with anyone else, but right now I felt a strange pressure in my chest. My bond with Ginevra was pushing me to indulge her. At long last, I had a girlfriend—no, Ginevra was more than that to me. I had a sister.

"It's hard to explain what I felt," I confessed. "It was like exploding and melting at the same time. And he—" My cheeks burned and I felt flushed again. "Evan was incredibly tender."

Ginevra shot me a smile brimming with pride. "I'm so happy you're part of our family. Evan is so different from how he used to be and it's all thanks to you," she said, piquing my curiosity.

"Really?"

"You can't even imagine. Think of a soldier, a proud warrior, a merciless executioner, and you'll have the exact picture of what Evan was like before he met you. You put a new light in his eyes. You brought him back to life. I've never seen him like this before." Her voice was pensive, as though something she'd said had summoned a memory. "When I found Evan and looked him in the eye for the first time, his face held an emptiness I'll never forget. It was like he'd lost everything, even himself. Over time that look was replaced by a tough, impenetrable mask, but occasionally that original part of him would resurface from behind his armor. You wiped that empty expression off his face forever. It's like he's finally found the place he belongs. When he met you I could see how desperate he was because he couldn't understand what was going on. Deep down, right from the start I knew what would happen, because I recognized the storm of emotions in him that had hit me when I met Simon." She snorted, amused by her own thoughts. "Honestly, I never imagined there could be one speck of romanticism in him. My God!" she exclaimed with a grin.

"Are we talking about the same Evan? He's the sweetest person I could ever hope to meet."

"Only with you," she was quick to say. "He was always a tough guy, a fighter. Nothing could ever stop him, but with you it's different. The way he looks at you, it's . . ."

"Special?" I guessed.

"Unique," Ginevra said.

"That's what I feel for him too," I admitted. Strangely, I wasn't embarrassed any more; having this conversation with Ginevra seemed perfectly normal—comforting even. When she leaned forward to hug me, it was natural and instinctive for me to return the gesture. At the contact I felt the oddest sensation, like the tingle under your skin when you get an electric shock.

I had it all, everything I could ever have wanted. Why did fate want to take it away from me? What had I done to deserve that? Maybe it was the price I had to pay—my life in exchange for everything I'd been granted. I couldn't complain. Wasn't it a fair trade?

"Evan couldn't have chosen better," Ginevra said, releasing me from her hug.

"Gwen—" The unfamiliar name popped out of my mouth.

Ginevra's eyes opened wide, stopping me short. She looked as mystified as I felt. Where had that name come from? And why had Ginevra reacted that way? "Did I say something wrong?" I stammered.

"No, it's just that—one of my Sisters always used to call me that. No one's done it since.

"I'm sorry . . ." I said hesitantly.

"No, that's all right, I'm happy. You can call me that whenever you want. Anyway, what were you going to tell me?"

"I just wanted to say thanks—for everything. This is the first time I finally feel part of something."

Ginevra smiled mischievously. "For the first time, I'd say you've done pretty well. An Angel who's hopelessly in love with you and a Witch and two Executioners who are prepared to do anything to protect you. Can you think of a better team?"

I smiled, running my hand through my hair distractedly. "Definitely not. But what do you say we continue this conversation later on? I could use a shower." All of a sudden I was exhausted. I wanted to feel hot water on my skin, on my neck muscles, my back. I wanted to focus only on my thoughts and be alone to reminisce about this incredible afternoon. The unforgettable memories brought a smile to my lips the instant they reappeared in my mind: Evan's hands on my body, his mouth pressed against mine, his heat against me . . . inside me.

"Oookay!" Ginevra said, interrupting my train of thought. "I think I've heard enough."

I blushed, realizing I'd abandoned myself to more memories than I should have in her presence.

"You deserve five minutes of privacy." She smiled regretfully.

Privacy? Did she even know what the word meant? I smiled to myself and shook my head. "Five minutes? How about twenty?" I said rebelliously, hoping to convince her.

"You know where the spa is." She got up and walked toward the door. "I've already prepared everything."

I blinked in surprise. "Um, when, exactly?"

Ginevra smiled and rested her hand on the doorknob. "Now." She shot me a sly glance and disappeared, leaving the door ajar behind her.

Whenever Ginevra smiled and narrowed her eyes like that, it was incredibly sexy. I wished I had even half her allure. She was gorgeous and you could feel her charisma a mile away—it was so strong it was almost tangible.

I got up from the bed and went down the hall to the spa. The room was built to resemble a cave. The walls were tiled in slabs of sand-colored rock in varying thicknesses while the floor was Rainforest Green, an exquisite green marble from India shot through with brown- and ivory-colored veins that created the impression of being in a forest. At the back of the spa, three steps led into the Jacuzzi built into the rock that sparkled under the recessed lighting. The wall behind the Jacuzzi was also stone, but slanted. Water flowed over the irregular surface like a waterfall. With the exception of the recessed spots above the Jacuzzi, the room was candlelit. Spicy-smelling steam filled the air.

For a moment I considered not sinking into the tub and instead using the glass-stalled shower in the center of the room that was more practical and familiar, but the gentle sound of the flowing water was too inviting for me to ignore. Besides, Ginevra had been so thoughtful to prepare it for me.

I moved into the cloud of steam, dropped my clothes to the floor, and tested the water with one foot. It was scalding hot. Bubbles rose continually to its surface, wafting a delicate floral aroma through the room. I immersed myself completely and found instant relief. The warmth filled me, penetrating my bones.

What a delicious sensation. I lay back and closed my eyes, abandoning myself to my memories. Memories of me and Evan.

26

VIOLATED EMOTIONS

The Jacuzzi kept the water at a constant temperature, and the heat felt too good on my skin to get out. I'd lost all track of time. Still, it wasn't fair to make Drake replace me just so I could soak in their hot tub all night. I was already taking advantage of him enough. I reluctantly climbed out. There was a red bath towel lying beside the tub; Ginevra had thought of everything. I rubbed my hair dry and wrapped it around my body.

I was bending down to pick up my clothes when a gust of cool air made me shiver. My head shot up and I noticed steam billowing by the door. Someone must have opened it.

"Gin, is that you?" I asked warily, putting on my shoes.

The room seemed empty.

"Didn't anyone ever teach you to lock the door?"

I cringed with embarrassment. "Drake!" I wasn't sure what color my face had turned. He was definitely the last person I'd expected to see there.

"Sorry," he said, his tone solicitous as he came closer, "I shouldn't have barged in like that. Sometimes Ginevra leaves the door open. You know what she's like. I didn't think anyone was in here, and I couldn't have imagined it would be you."

Nervously, I smoothed my hair behind my ear. "No, no," I stammered, "no need to apologize. This is your house. It's my fault I didn't lock the door." *Had I really forgotten to?*

Drake stepped in front of me. I looked away, unable to meet his eyes. Now that I knew about his past, it was as if I were seeing him for the first time. I'd always thought of Drake as the fun one—the carefree, swaggering brother who never took anything seriously. But now, after hearing what had happened to him and knowing what he'd lost, I saw him in a new light. In a way, I felt closer to him than before, as if the feelings that bonded him to Evan were now bonding him to me a little too.

Somewhere inside me I found the courage to look straight at him, and flinched. There was something different in his eyes—a glimmer I'd never seen before—something totally undecipherable. Had he found out that I'd learned about his past?

The heavy wooden door thumped closed.

I tried to say something, but all that came out was an incomprehensible stammer. Regaining control after a few attempts, I said, "I—I . . . I think I'd better go now." The remark hung in the air as I walked around him with my head lowered.

Suddenly he shot out his arm, grabbed my wrist, and jerked me against him. My heart sent me a desperate warning, but it was too late—his mouth was already on mine, soft and parted against my sealed lips. I shoved him away, bewildered when he let go without protesting.

"What the hell is wrong with you?" I shouted. My heart was beating wildly. How could something like this happen? One minute I was lost in the memory of the magical afternoon I'd spent with Evan and the next Drake was kissing me?

His expression turned sly and a flash of cunning appeared in his eyes. "I thought you wanted it too."

My rage boiled up until it burnt my skin. "What? My God, no!" I put both hands to my forehead and pushed back my hair. "Drake, do you realize what you've done? For God's sake, don't you care about Evan?" My eyes suddenly fell to his neck. His dog tag was gone. Was it possible he'd misinterpreted my looks of compassion? Was it possible that what he felt for me could be that different from what I felt for him? "Don't you care about Evan?" I repeated, articulating each word. *Had he even forgotten about his Stella?* I thought, without daring to say it. The strangest thing was the look in Drake's eye. He didn't seem the least bit worried. In fact, he seemed more amused than anything else. His expression irritated me, feeding my anger. How could he thrust his affection for his brother aside so heartlessly? Was it possible he didn't love Evan back? Or even worse, that Evan had never realized it?

"I don't care about anybody."

Drake's cold, merciless voice made my hairs stand on end as his gaze burned into mine. Something behind me near the door caught his attention. I turned around to check but no one was there. Puzzled, I frowned. "Drake, if you think—"

When I turned around again Drake was gone. My words hung in the empty room. He'd disappeared, leaving me alone with my pounding heart. I knew well the nature of what I was feeling and could think of only one word to define it: guilt.

"Gemma, you done?" Ginevra called from the stairs, making me jump. "I heard noises. Everything okay?" I stared into space, petrified, not knowing what to say.

"Gemma?" Ginevra slowly came through the door as I looked blankly at the floor. When I felt her in front of me, I looked up into her eyes.

It took her only a moment to understand everything, to know every detail. We stood there in frozen silence. She continued to stare at me without a word, her eyes bulging. Meanwhile, my heart hadn't stopped galloping.

"No. It's impossible," she hissed, shocked. She wasn't the only one in the room in that state.

I stared at her, anguished, confirming everything. No matter how insane, inconceivable, or unexpected it was, no matter how hard it was for me to believe, it had actually happened. Drake had kissed me.

"It's—it's not so serious," I said, hoping to downplay it. I didn't want a relationship to be ruined because of me.

"Evan's not going to see it that way." Ginevra said it so assuredly it sent me into a panic. My alarmed gaze shot to hers. "You have to tell him," she stated, her tone cold.

The words poured from my mouth at lightning speed. "No! I can't tell him. Neither can you. He would be crushed!"

"But you *have to* tell him." Ginevra articulated each word as if realizing my brain couldn't handle them all at once right now.

"I don't want to ruin what they feel for each other." In my voice, regret, indecision, and frustration battled to prevail.

"You're not the one who ruined it. Drake did, a moment ago."

"Don't you see?" I whispered, feeling devastated. How could I tell Evan without destroying their relationship? I remembered the look in Drake's eye when he'd told me he didn't care about anybody, and shock burned my stomach. For some time now I'd noticed a change in Drake, in the way he stole glances at us. Evan's meeting me must have reopened past wounds and brought back painful memories for him. I couldn't find any better explanation. Everybody makes mistakes. Drake's kiss meant nothing to me and I was sure he'd just acted on impulse, that he already regretted it.

"That doesn't change the seriousness of what he did, and Evan needs to know. If you don't tell him, I will," Ginevra warned without a trace of hesitation in her voice.

"No—all right, but let me be the one to tell him," I said hesitantly, still not sure it was the best thing to do. I just hoped Evan would be able to understand and forgive his brother for doing something so foolish. There was no other way to describe it.

I thought of tonight's plans and a shiver ran through me. At this point, staying there at their house was impossible. I couldn't get Drake to take my place any more, so I had no choice but to go home where I would be in danger.

"Don't worry," Ginevra was quick to say, replying to my thoughts. "Do you think I'd ever leave you all alone?"

"Where is he now?" I asked, thinking of Drake.

"I don't know. I can't sense him or even detect his thoughts. Actually, he's been avoiding me for a while now. It's like he's a ghost," she said, thinking aloud.

"Why didn't you sense him before? When he was here in the spa with me. Before it happened, I mean. Why didn't you stop him?"

"I was downstairs with Simon. We were busy in the workout room. It's soundproofed, remember? Unfortunately it also has an effect on my mind. Somehow it blocks the sound of people's thoughts and"—she smiled to herself—"we were making a lot of noise, if you know what I mean. When I heard something strange I came straight up here to you. In any case, you can relax. He's not here any more."

"Will you stay with me tonight?" I asked, though I already knew the answer.

But Ginevra surprised me. "I can't," she said regretfully.

"What? Why not?" I asked, desperately hoping to make her change her mind.

"If something happened to you, I wouldn't be able to heal you. Trust me, it will be better for Simon to be there instead. If I sense a problem I'll be there in a flash. I can hear his thoughts even from here if I concentrate, whereas he wouldn't be able to hear mine."

"But I'll feel horribly uneasy!" I whimpered just as Simon called to us from the stairs.

Ginevra put her mouth to my ear. "Don't worry. You won't even notice he's there. He won't make you uncomfortable. He'll only be there to protect you."

Standing in the doorway, Simon stared at us with a bewildered look on his face.

Ginevra instantly noticed his reaction to our expressions. "I'll explain later. There's been a change of plans for tonight," she said.

"You mean you don't want a rematch any more?" he said, grinning.

"You're obsessed!" I said to her, amazed.

Ginevra shot me a glance and spoke under her breath, as if that would be enough for Simon not to hear her. "He's lying. He knows perfectly well I outdid him."

My bedroom ceiling looked so unfamiliar, a million miles away from what in a few months had become my new world. Evan's house had become a hideaway even more comforting than my own home. Or maybe it was his absence that made my room seem so cold and empty.

Gripped with anxiety, I tossed and turned under the covers, unable to fall asleep. I recalled Drake's face so close to mine, how ardently he'd pulled me against him, like I belonged to him. During that brief moment, I'd gotten the impression I'd never known him, that I didn't even know who he was. And yet he was still Drake, Evan's fun-loving brother, the only one who never worried about anything. How on earth had it even occurred to him? Why had he kissed me? Maybe what made me angriest was that tonight all I should have been thinking about was the incredible afternoon I'd spent with Evan. I should have been losing myself in the memory of the two of us locked in an embrace amid a thousand fireflies of light, making love as if we were in a dream. Instead, all I could think of was Drake and the fierce look on his face when he pressed his lips against mine. For a moment I was relieved Ginevra wasn't there listening to my thoughts.

I couldn't believe Drake had kissed me. As if that wasn't enough, I couldn't think of a good way to break it to Evan—because there *was* no good way. Still, I had no choice. I knew I wasn't to blame for what had happened, so why did I feel so responsible about their relationship possibly being ruined forever?

Where would I find the courage to tell Evan his best friend had betrayed him? How could I avoid the irreparable damage? It takes two to tango—I was aware of that—but inside me I didn't feel at all complicit in what Drake had done. From that perspective I hadn't betrayed Evan. When you truly love someone you can't imagine desiring anyone except that person.

My eyelids grew heavy and relief washed over me. Falling asleep would finally hush the deafening echo of those exhausting thoughts.

Another blink of my eyelashes, this one softer and slower. I couldn't see Simon but I knew he was there and his presence made me feel safe. The light from my bedside lamp dimmed and went out and the darkness swallowed up my thoughts. "Good night, Simon," I murmured, my lips barely moving.

"Good night." The whisper floated through the dark room, but I was already asleep.

27

PREMONITIONS

The ice-cold air slashed my skin like a blade. I felt it on my cheeks while my hot breath hid my mouth in puffs of white vapor. I didn't know what I was running from or where I was headed, but I ran and ran, dodging the trees. I was tired, my body was about to give up, and yet a little voice in my head kept me from stopping. I knew if I did it would be the end of me. Someone was chasing me—I sensed their presence, heard their breathing among the trees.

Without slowing my pace, I looked over my shoulder. No one was there, but I *knew* he had come to kill me. When I looked forward again the sky had grown brighter. A moment later I noticed that the thick treetops were no longer blocking it. I'd left the forest behind.

I slowed down, realizing I'd been in this place before. I frowned at the sight of Evan's car on the side of the road. Filled with the sensation that something wasn't right, I continued to run toward it. When I was quite near, my heart turned over; the front end of the car was crumpled around the broken guardrail. I put my hands to my mouth. The Ferrari was totaled.

Desperate, I ran up to it, a burning ache in my chest. My heart beat fast, outstripping the tempo of my footsteps on the asphalt. The closer I got, the more tightly terror clenched my stomach.

I stopped and walked toward the driver's window. Shards of glass were everywhere. They crunched beneath my feet. Someone was in the car. I drew closer, stunned, and my heart throbbed in my temples with a wild, unsteady beat. When I recognized the head that lay motionless on the steering wheel, all the blood drained from my face.

It was Evan.

Unable to breathe, I tried to keep myself from fainting as I saw the streaks of blood on Evan's face dripping onto the road in a scarlet puddle. I felt all my muscles trembling—small, uncontrollable spasms that turned my blood to ice. It couldn't be true. I was horrified by the pain—so devastated, so drained that not even my tears could find their way out, lost in my endless torment.

I reached out a trembling hand and gently pushed him back into the driver's seat. His head fell back, revealing his face, and an onslaught of emotions shot through me. But when I took a closer look at the bloodstained face, the most powerful emotion I felt was relief.

It wasn't Evan—it was Drake.

The pain vanished as quickly as it had come, replaced by confusion. A whisper drifted through the air and brushed my ear—a sweet sound, like a deep sigh. I let myself be distracted, distanced from everything else. It filled me. I felt as if it could carry me away from there.

Then I remembered Drake and shook my head, but something strange bothered me when I turned around to look at him again. I took a step back, confused by the old, dark-gray conveyance that had taken the place of the Ferrari.

His burned and blackened body was in his warplane. Blood covered his face and what was left of the shattered windshield. Gripped in his hand were the two dog tags he wore around his neck.

No. He wasn't dead. His body was still quivering, his lips barely moving.

"Ste—Stella," he gasped. My heart went ice cold. His body slumped over the controls, lifeless. The entire side of the plane was riddled with bullet holes, more than I'd seen before.

A pungent, metallic smell filled my nostrils. I looked around, disoriented, and heard the sigh once again. It felt like it was inside me; I sensed it in every fiber of my being, like it belonged to me. Some part of me recognized it. I could feel the breath on me almost tangibly. It was so intense I turned my head to follow it.

My eyes met the gaze of a woman who stood there perfectly still, staring at me.

I heard the sound again and flinched: it was my name, shrouded in a soothing murmur. It was coming from inside me, in my head, my thoughts, my gut. The sound was everywhere.

For a moment I looked into the woman's electric-blue eyes as the wind made her long hair billow behind her. It was black, with white tips. The energy she emanated was so intense and hypnotic that it took me a moment to notice the hundreds of dead bodies piled one atop the other on the dry earth beneath our feet. Everywhere I looked were lifeless bodies.

"*Naiad . . .*" My name echoed through my thoughts again like a melody wafted on the wind. The woman stood there, her eyes fixed on me. Her eyes were ice, yet so comforting at the same time.

A moan caught my attention. My thoughts flew to Drake and I instinctively turned to look for him, but immediately felt as if someone had stabbed me in the heart. The plane had disappeared, as had Drake. In their place once again was the twisted wreckage of Evan's car, but this time it was me behind the wheel, lying in a pool of blood.

I tried to breathe but the air was trapped in my throat. I began to sob. Trembling like a leaf, I moved closer to see if maybe it wasn't true, it wasn't really me. As I looked at the body, spasms of terror gripped me and the voice whispered my name again. Horrified, I couldn't tear my eyes away from the face in front of me: my own, splattered with blood.

Suddenly its eyes opened wide, making me jump.

I tried to scream, but suddenly found myself in my bedroom, gasping for air. Remembering all the blood, I touched my forehead. It was wet. I checked my fingers that trembled before my terrified eyes, afraid I would find them tinged with scarlet, but my fingertips were only beaded with sweat. Then why was my heart still pounding? Why had I had to dream not only of my own death but the deaths of the others as well?

I took a deep breath and told myself it had just been another nightmare. I always had them when Evan left me on my own.

It was dark outside the window. I nervously checked my alarm clock and saw it was only four in the morning. Under other circumstances that would have been a relief because it meant I had more time to sleep. That night, however, the thought of closing my eyes again terrified me; another nightmare awaited me, I was sure of it. But still, I was so tired.

I tossed and turned under the covers but couldn't fall asleep. I noticed a faint light just above my bedside table and remembered Simon must be somewhere in the room, watching over me. The thought calmed me a little.

His voice echoed from the ceiling as if he'd heard me. "Everything okay?"

"I've had better nights." I heard him chuckle in the darkness.

"I'm sorry Evan isn't here in my place," he admitted, sounding sincerely regretful.

"No, it's all right," I was quick to reply. "It's not your fault he's not here."

No matter how much I missed Evan, I was happy his family was so protective of me. From the bottom of my heart I appreciated that Simon was here, willing to confront my enemy in order to protect me.

"You were tossing and turning the whole night." Simon fell silent for a long moment, making me think he'd finished speaking, but then he continued. "I can protect you, but there's nothing I can do about your nightmares. I can't help you with those."

Judging from his rueful tone, I must have been seriously restless.

"Those aren't your fault either. Don't worry about it," I said, not wanting him to feel bad.

His reply took me by surprise. "He would rather be here instead of me too, and it's not his fault that he isn't."

"I know."

"No, maybe you don't, actually. I know Evan really well. I was there when we found him and we've been together ever since." He paused for a few seconds. "What we do—" He hesitated again. A movement in the half-light caught my attention and my eyes darted to the window. Simon was standing there, staring outside. He seemed to be searching for words as I watched his silhouette shrouded in darkness. "I understand it might seem frightening, but if you look at it from the right perspective it actually isn't so terrible." He turned toward me. "Our task is to free the spirit from the body in which it's trapped so it can return to where it belongs. Humans see death as the end of everything—I was human once and well remember the feeling—but it's not. Not for you. For you mortals, it's only the beginning."

He stared out the window again as I listened in silence. I'd never thought about the fact that Evan's brothers were going through the same kind of suffering he was. They had been condemned to the same fate, but neither Evan nor even Simon had reason to complain. At least not as much as their brother. Drake was alone, condemned to Earth forever, forced to give up Stella, the woman he loved. It must be terrible for him.

The thought made me remember the night before and a shiver ran down my spine. How could I take away the only thing he had left—his family's love? I shook my head to banish the thought. I was about to pick up our conversation where we'd left off, but Simon spoke first. "In any case, it's not up to us. We must act against our will. We're not the ones who decide."

"Who does, then?" I asked uneasily.

"Orders are imposed on us." His tone was hard, as if intentionally avoiding an unspeakable secret.

"By *whom?*" I insisted firmly. I'd never broached the subject with Evan, having always had the impression it was something better left unsaid. Or maybe I simply hadn't been brave enough. With Simon, on the other hand, it all seemed much simpler.

"By the Elders," he replied, looking me in the eye.

"You guys always seem afraid to talk about them, but who are the Elders, anyway? What do they have to do with all this? And above all, how do you know what they want you to do?" The intimacy created by the dim light made me brave and I finally gave my curiosity free rein.

"We just know, that's all. We feel it inside, like intrinsic knowledge, a thought coming from our own minds. They communicate with us even if we can't hear them. It's as though they insert the information directly into our heads."

"Is it the same for everyone?"

"From the first time we eat of the tree. Many of us don't survive, but those who do are acknowledged—it's as if a connection is created—and we begin to serve them. The Elders never intervene personally. They send us out instead to make sure each person on Earth meets the destiny that's been ordained for him or her. No one has ever seen them—or more accurately, those who have didn't survive long enough to tell the tale."

My heart pounded harder as I realized I'd paved the way to finally asking the question I'd been harboring for some time, too terrified to hear the answer. "Simon?" My voice trembled as I said his name. "Why do you think I have to die?"

His eyes wavered, avoiding mine. "I can't answer that." For a moment, the silence drowned out every sound. "But there's a reason for it. Nothing happens by chance."

I stared at the floor, thinking about what he'd said. I honestly couldn't imagine what good my death might do.

Simon interrupted my thoughts. "The Elders were chosen to maintain order, to determine who is to return. They're the ones who make the decisions, but none of us know the reasons behind their choices."

"What happens to the people who don't redeem themselves, the ones who can't return?"

I'd never seen Simon so serious before. The dim light cast a grim, mysterious halo on his face. "We don't receive orders for them."

"What happens to them?" I insisted.

"They become slaves."

The darkness in his eyes made me shudder. A bitter instinct warned me not to travel further down that path because it led through a minefield. And yet there was another part of me, hidden somewhere deep inside and thirsty for more knowledge, that made me go on. "Why didn't they find me before? All these months, what kept the Elders from finding out I wasn't dead yet? Can't they see everything?"

"No, they're not omniscient. They send us out to make sure destiny has been fulfilled. We're the arm of Death, the shadow of fate."

"But who are *they*, exactly?" I hoped Simon would stop dodging the question and finally tell me.

Seeming to summon his courage, he looked at me. "They're the Màsala," he explained, his tone so serious it sent a shiver down my spine. "No one dares speak their name. It's as if it's forbidden among us: an unwritten rule. They're the purest angels, members of the Order, a dark, secret brotherhood as old as the world itself. It might seem paradoxical, but they're the messengers God uses as instruments to implement His plan, celestial creatures appointed by the Supreme Being to maintain order in the universe. Long ago they were called devas. Some call them *those first to come* and for others they're the ancients or the elders. You humans call them archangels."

I shivered. After all the bizarre experiences I'd been through over the last few months, it was strange to feel all this emotion at just one word. It was easy to pretend nothing existed, that the spiritual realm wasn't real but just a figment of the human imagination built up over the centuries and handed down as law. God, archangels . . . Eden. But then, when reality finally hit you, no matter how insane or shocking it might seem, there was no denying it—all you could do was accept it and tremble.

Simon's silhouette began to fade before I had the chance to figure out if it was him or if I was starting to fall asleep again. I lay down face up on the mattress. As my eyelids struggled to stay open I heard Simon's smooth, gentle voice in my ears: "Now get some rest."

28

A BURDENED HEART

My legs tangled in the sheets as I rolled over and a moan of pain escaped me. It felt like something was forcing my head down into the pillow.

"Finally!" Evan's cheerful voice brought me back to reality, but all I could do was let out another moan. I glanced out the window, my eyes still half closed, but couldn't understand if it was too early or too late.

"What time is it?" I grumbled, raising my torso slightly.

"Five in the afternoon."

I shot bolt upright as if someone had thrown a bucket of ice water on me. Evan's sweet eyes met mine and the walls of the room closed in around me, crushing me.

Suddenly I remembered everything. Evan noticed the change in my expression and misunderstood. "Did you have another nightmare?" he asked with concern.

I took a moment to answer. "I think so, but I'm not really sure any more." Last night's terrible dream—so distant now—had lost all importance in comparison with the real world, which would definitely be far more grueling.

"Gemma, is something the matter?"

His eyes probed mine again and I looked away. The devastating memory of yesterday throbbed in my temples. It felt as if the secret had taken shape inside me and was trying to get out with every heartbeat as I struggled to force it back down. It was a massive boulder between us, one that couldn't elude Evan's notice for much longer. I couldn't hide the truth from him. I had to find a way to tell him everything.

He looked at me, puzzled, and I tried to pick up the conversation where we'd left off. "I must have dreamed something terrible." Deep down it wasn't a lie. I tightened my lips and stared down at my bare knees. I couldn't even bring myself to look him in the eye.

"I'm sorry." He caressed my cheek. When I felt his touch, I closed my eyes, tears stinging beneath my eyelids. After taking a deep breath I tried to speak but my voice trembled. Evan noticed and seemed to misunderstand yet again.

"This always happens when you're gone," I explained, referring to the nightmares. Actually, I couldn't remember my dream any more except for a few fragments that were already fading. The real world was what frightened me the most now. The thought of Drake's lips on mine and how Evan would react to the news was worse than any nightmare I could imagine.

When you love someone, you open up to them completely—you give them your heart and your entire being. You think you can tell them everything, no matter what, but it's only when you discover how much the truth can hurt them that you realize how difficult it is to face it. But you have to do it all the same, because lies are huge boulders blocking the path that unites you—boulders destined to grow larger and which you're bound to trip over. The larger they are, the smaller your chances of getting up and moving forward.

"How long have you been here?" I asked to distract him from the conclusions he must have been drawing. From the way he'd narrowed his eyes I could tell he realized something was wrong.

"A while." He smiled again, boosting my spirits. "I took over for Simon at dawn."

"Why didn't you wake me up?" I protested, embarrassed about having slept so late.

"I wanted to," he admitted. "There were times when I couldn't resist and came over to wake you, but then I went back and sat down again. You looked so tired," he whispered, sitting on the bed and leaning toward me. His mouth brushed mine. "I missed you."

I tensed, self-loathing filling me. The last lips on mine had been Drake's.

No! I couldn't react like this! I couldn't let this thing come between us. Not now, right when everything was going so well, not after making love with Evan.

"Everything's going to be fine," he whispered, resting his forehead on mine, again misunderstanding my tension.

"I have a headache, that's all." I forced a smile as my heart pounded in anticipation of confessing everything. "Where are my parents? How come they didn't wake me up for lunch?" I asked, so confused I couldn't even remember what day it was.

"We convinced them you were eating at my place. They didn't even notice you were still here."

"*We* convinced them?" I asked with alarm.

Evan smiled. "Drake gave me a hand. Sometimes I can barely—"

My heart lurched. "Drake was here?" Aghast, I felt the blood drain from my face.

Evan frowned, disconcerted by my reaction.

"You should have woken me up," I said sternly.

So they'd seen each other.

"You needed to rest," he replied. "Yesterday was a tough day for you, Gemma. Too much happened."

More than he could imagine, actually.

"Simon told me you'd had nightmares so I made sure you slept in soundly."

I couldn't object. My last few hours of sleep had been deep and dreamless. Forcing another smile, I tried to banish the thought of Drake from my mind, at least for a while. "So how many did you kill off last night?" I asked bluntly in an awkward attempt to normalize things, but even I was shocked by the bitterness of my sarcasm.

Evan frowned and I struggled to decipher his expression. He was right—this wasn't like me. "S-sorry, it sounded funny in my mind and obviously it wasn't." Grimacing with regret, I nervously ran my hand through my hair. What was happening to me? Why was it so hard to utter the simple words that continued to scream inside my head?

"Feel like going for a drive?" I asked out of the blue. "I could use some fresh air." Evan nodded, still bewildered.

I went to the bathroom, turned on the tap, and splashed scalding-hot water on my face. Still trembling, I clutched the rim of the sink. For a minute I stood there staring at my reflection, almost not recognizing myself. Then, resigned, I continued to wash up.

I had to find a way to make the weight in my stomach go away. I couldn't bear to see the worried look on Evan's face. Who knew what was going through his mind. I hated myself for never having learned to hide my emotions. If something made me happy or upset, trying to hide it was hopeless. Anyone could see it.

When I walked back into the bedroom, Evan's expression relaxed and a roguish smile appeared on his face. All it took was one glimpse of his eyes to understand his intentions. I hadn't gotten dressed yet. I raised an eyebrow and let the towel I was holding fall to the floor. My camisole matched my scarlet panties. Their lace edging was similar to the lace on the black panties I'd had on yesterday at the hideaway and aroused a dangerous look of interest in Evan's eye. I'd never worn these before, but last night I'd almost instinctively searched for them in my underwear drawer, knowing Evan would be there when I woke up.

He watched me as though he'd forgotten the rest of the world, as though only I existed. Taking my hand, he pulled me gently against him, brushing a lock of hair from my face. "Sure you want to go for a drive?" he whispered, his dark eyes on mine.

I looked down again, unable to hold his gaze for more than a few seconds. "I—I think we'd better." I pulled away, leaving him with his hand in midair at the height of my cheek. Out of the corner of my eye I saw his arm drop to his side and his expression turn blank. Our eyes met and I forced a smile.

"Does this have something to do with what happened between us yesterday?" His disappointed, hesitant tone floored me, hitting me straight in the heart. I blinked nervously. This couldn't be happening. Evan had misunderstood in the worst possible way.

"No!" I exclaimed instantly. "What are you thinking?" I went and took his hand. What on earth was I doing? How could I let this terrible secret ruin this moment?

"What's wrong, then?" he asked, exasperation in his voice. "You're so strange today and—"

"You were right. Too much happened to me yesterday." My voice broke on the last words. "More than you realize. You have no idea how I feel."

"Shh," Evan said, cutting me off and pulling me to him. He wrapped his arms around me again in an intimate embrace and I let myself be enveloped in his warmth. I could do it. I had to tell him. I'd finally found an opening to release the poison. I looked into his eyes . . . and sank back down into the pit. Why did this have to be so difficult?

"You can tell me about it later if you feel like it. Let's get out of here."

Part of me had yearned to hear him say just that. Somehow, putting it off was the most tempting solution, though I knew it would only prolong my torment.

"Feel like seeing what the others are up to?" Evan asked, behind the wheel of the BMW. Scenes from the nightmare suddenly reappeared distinctly in my mind, jumbled with images of reality. I shuddered at the thought of his Ferrari at the bottom of the lake.

"Or we could spend some time alone," I put in, instantly alarmed by his suggestion. I wanted to stay as far from their place as possible. What was even more important was to make sure Drake was far enough away when I told Evan. I honestly couldn't imagine how he would take it. Deep in my heart, I hoped to find a way to make the confession less bitter. I didn't want Evan to be mad at his brother forever, and Drake's presence wouldn't help the situation.

Evan smiled at my proposal, once again misunderstanding my intentions. This time, though, I went along with it.

Immersed in my private nightmare, I hadn't realized Evan had already pulled into his driveway. I squirmed in my seat. "I thought we'd decided to be alone." I tried to hide my nervousness but there was a hint of reproach in my voice.

Evan leaned toward me, his lips curved in a pleased smile. "I just need to get a few things," he whispered, kissing me before I could reply. "If you can hold out." He got out of the car and opened my door.

"I'll—I'll wait here," I stammered sheepishly. I didn't want reality to come crashing down on me because I'd probably end up crushed. I wasn't ready yet.

"Don't be silly," he said.

I got out of the car and immediately went into panic mode. My breath grew short as we walked, my heartbeat accelerating as the distance to the front door lessened. I heaved a sigh of relief when I found the living room empty and silent. Still, with them you could never tell when they'd turn up. I hoped Evan would be quick. I tapped my foot, enduring the nerve-racking wait. Drake might appear at any moment—or maybe he was already there and I didn't know it. I waited for Evan in the kitchen, anxiously peering around the empty room.

Ginevra came up behind me with feline stealth, making me jump out of my shoes. "Hey! You scared me half to death!" I accused her.

"Or maybe you're just a little on edge?" she asked, her glacial eyes trained on mine. I half closed my eyes under her searching gaze. Aware that she was probing me, I desperately tried to raise a wall between our minds. "What?! You haven't told him yet?"

"Told me what?" Evan appeared behind her, looking puzzled.

My heart skipped a beat. My eyelids fluttered from the strain and I felt myself being dragged down into a dark vortex from which there would be no escape. I felt Evan's impatient gaze on me but didn't have the courage to face him.

"What's she supposed to tell me?" Evan repeated.

Ginevra sensed my hesitation and looked him straight in the eye. "That Drake kissed her."

The words struck me in the chest like an arrow shot straight at my heart.

Evan's eyes, as gray as a stormy sky, sliced through me. For a moment I felt like a ghost of ice, invisible to his gaze. A shudder ran down my spine.

"Evan," I murmured. He stood paralyzed in front of me.

Ginevra clearly hadn't expected this reaction from him because she suddenly looked alarmed. "Evan, calm down," she whispered.

His expression was indecipherable to me but she knew exactly what was going through his mind. I would have given anything to be in her place right now. No—actually, I wasn't sure I really wanted to know.

"There's no need for that, Evan!" his sister said, her voice turning loud and harsh. My heart beat wildly. Without saying a word, Evan rolled his hands into fists and clenched his jaw, his eyes narrowing to menacing slits.

The only one privy to his intentions, Ginevra continued to beg him to calm down but her voice had grown faint in my ears, drowned out by the deafening panic that threatened to crush me. Abruptly, she fell silent.

Evan was furious. His implacable rage frightened me. He seemed as hard as ice and ready to kill. All at once he vanished, leaving us in the silence of the kitchen. Ginevra and I looked at each other and for a moment I thought I saw my panic reflected in her eyes.

"What's going on?!" I cried in alarm.

"Simon!" she shouted into the empty room.

A second later Simon appeared beside us. "You told him," he guessed, looking nervous.

"It's worse than I imagined," she said.

"Would you mind telling me what's going on?" I wanted to shout, but all that came out of my mouth was a hysterical noise. *It's worse than you imagined?* What the hell did that mean?

Ginevra's gaze sliced through me and she said the last thing I wanted to hear: "He went to find Drake." My body froze from head to toe.

"We've got to hurry," Simon spoke up, heading for the door.

Moments later the wheels of his car were skidding through the gravel. I was terrified and in shock. I wanted to be mad at Ginevra for telling Evan the truth so abruptly, because I hadn't been ready to face his reaction, but deep down I was relieved she'd lifted the burden from my heart.

"How do we find them?" I asked, torn with anxiety.

"He went to Roomer's," Simon replied.

"The night club? How do you know?" I asked, my nervousness growing.

"That's where Drake is."

"But I can't go in there!" I said in alarm. "I'm underage."

Simon's eyes narrowed in the rearview mirror. "Consider it one of the advantages of being with us," he said, flashing me a charming smile.

The car sideslipped on the asphalt, cutting the curves in half, as I chewed the inside of my cheek.

"He's there," Ginevra said, clearly picking up on Evan's thoughts through the distance.

Simon slammed on the brakes. "He's angry. My God, he's absolutely enraged. But I don't sense Drake."

"What do we do?" I said timidly, my nerves on edge.

Once again, it was Simon who answered. "Gemma, come with me. Maybe you can talk some sense into him." His face was grave.

When Ginevra opened the passenger door, Simon turned and glowered at her. "Stay here," he ordered, his face set. I'd never heard him speak to her so sternly before.

"Simon, the place is full of people. He's not going to do anything stupid," she said.

"He's dangerous. I can feel his energy and I don't know if he'll be able to control it. You need to stay here," he growled.

Following my impulse to rush toward the door, I left them behind. A bouncer stood there staring at me. I was afraid he was about to stop me, but he unexpectedly stepped aside and let me through. I turned around. Simon was a few steps behind me, his eyes locked on the bouncer's. The door opened just in time for me to see Drake standing by the pool tables and Evan charging him with unrestrained violence.

I shouted Evan's name, but he seemed to see nothing except Drake. My shout did, however, draw the attention of everyone else in the club. They turned to watch the scene as Evan shoved Drake against the wall, which cracked beneath the blow. A murmur spread through the room.

I sensed Simon's tension. He stood at my side as still as a statue. His hopes that Evan might stop if I was there had gone up in smoke and he clearly didn't know what to do. There were too many people there to intervene. Suddenly he stepped between the two, struggling to hold Evan back. "Evan!" he shouted, attempting to get his attention, but he was entirely focused on Drake. "Evan, you've got to calm down. Now!" he ordered firmly. "Look around you." Simon's eyes burned into his brother's. "We're not alone," he whispered. At this point Evan's gaze shifted to Simon's and he seemed to see him for the first time.

I was still trembling. For a moment no one in the club moved, as if they were all holding their breath. Drake stood there, his back pressed against the wall as Evan's eyes shot back to him. He was still irate, but he seemed to have snapped out of it. Evan leaned in and Simon moved his shoulder aside to let him. Drake's eyes were glued to Evan's, their faces inches apart. "I never want to see you again," Evan said between clenched teeth, his expression murderous.

His brother tilted his head in an unspoken challenge, never taking his eyes off Evan, who turned and walked out without even looking at me. It hit me straight in the heart.

He was mad at me too.

Simon and I exchanged worried glances. He slipped his hand into his pocket, pulled out a big wad of bills, and rested it on the bar before the owner's surprised face. "For the damages," he added, looking him steadily in the eye. "This should cover it."

The man reached over and picked up the money without saying a word. I was sure that soon no one in the club would remember anything of what had happened.

I came out of the club just in time to see Evan get behind the wheel of the BMW. I walked up to the car and he glanced at me through the window, then nodded for me to get in. I searched Simon and Ginevra's faces for their approval.

"He wants to be alone with you," Ginevra said encouragingly. "See you later." I hesitated a moment, staring at Evan in the driver's seat waiting for me, then opened the car door and got in, fearing the worst. The BMW left Lake Placid as the failing light around us magnified our silence. For a while, neither of us so much as breathed.

"So that's why," Evan said, his tone grave and his eyes on the road.

I looked down to gather my thoughts. "I didn't know how to tell you. I didn't want to ruin what you two have between you."

"Ruin what we have between us?" he said bitterly, turning my words around on me. My heartbeat faltered when I heard the resentment in his tone. "I thought we had a deal: no secrets," he growled, his anger superseded now by disappointment.

It was more than I could bear. "Evan, I wanted to tell you and I would have! It was just so difficult. You've got to believe me!" He shot me a glance. "It all happened so unexpectedly. He caught me off guard." I stopped short, realizing that if I kept defending myself like this I would only be making things worse for Drake. "You saw how nervous I was. I could never have kept it a secret from you. And I didn't intend to."

Again, silence. It was even harder to bear.

"Say something, please?" I begged.

His expression was stony. It was dark out now, but as I looked out the window I recognized the small, steep road Evan turned onto. A moment later, the car stopped.

"Why are we here?" I looked around, confused. Now that darkness had fallen, the long, arid field where we'd been the day before made me shiver. As I got out of the car, Evan, who was already at my side, sensed my tension and squeezed my hand. The warmth of his skin eased my nerves.

"Don't worry," he whispered, his face serious.

I'd missed his sweet, protective tone of voice. For a second tears of relief filled my eyes. I'd been worried this would go miserably, but maybe he wasn't so mad at me after all.

I followed him into the hangar. A faint light flickered on as we entered. We passed the plane and I lingered by its tail, looking straight into Evan's eyes. "You need to tell me what you're thinking," I said. It was an order, but it came out as a plea.

Evan stifled a humorless chuckle. Disappointment was plain on his face, and no matter how self-centered the thought was, I hoped his resentment was directed only at Drake. "What do you imagine I'm thinking?" he said bitterly.

"Still angry?" I asked warily.

"Angry? I'm beyond angry." His eyes burned. "But not with you," he added. His tone softened, as did his face.

"I'm sorry. I would never have wanted something like this to happen, but I'm sure you'll manage to forgive Drake and everything will go back to normal," I promised, but it was only my hope talking.

"Nothing will ever go back to normal. Drake is out for good," he said sternly.

"You can't be serious," I said, though in his eyes I could see the reflection of the proud warrior Ginevra had talked about.

"Why can't I?" he shot back.

"He did something stupid, that's true, but try to imagine what he's going through. You have me, and Simon has Ginevra. Drake, on the other hand, lost the person he loved forever! Don't you think that's a lot for him to deal with? Besides, everyone deserves a second chance," I said decisively.

"You're too good a person, Gemma." His tone made it sound almost like a rebuke, but then his voice softened. He came up and wrapped his arms around my waist. "But I don't care about anyone but you."

"Not even your brother?"

Evan tensed. "No. Not even him. He made his decision. And every decision entails a sacrifice." His tone was cold.

I couldn't stand to see this rupture separate them forever, not if I was the cause. And yet, no matter how hard Evan tried to appear stoic, I could see a glimmer of pain in his eyes that he was clearly struggling to force down. Yes, with time Evan would forgive Drake. I would do everything in my power to make that happen.

"There's just one thing I need to ask you." His eyes studied me intensely as he stroked my cheek with his thumb. I looked at him, puzzled by his afflicted expression. "I already know what you're going to say but I need to hear you say it," he whispered warily.

"What?" I lowered my head at the touch of his fingers so he would caress me a second time. It was good to feel him so close again. Actually, he always had been—I was the one who'd raised a wall between us.

"When Drake—when he kissed you," he began, forcing out the words, "what did you feel?"

I exhaled all the air I'd been holding in my lungs. *Evan was jealous.* Was he actually worried I'd felt even the slightest thing for Drake? I found the very thought ridiculous. Of course, he couldn't know that. He couldn't read what I had in my head or my heart. He couldn't know he would always be the only one to make it beat. The sight of him right now, his eyes glued to mine, anxious to hear my answer, filled my heart with tenderness.

As he waited for my answer, perfectly still, I leaned in and brushed my lips against his. I couldn't think of a better reply. I rubbed his nose gently with my own and shot him a mischievous glance. "Let me get this straight," I whispered slowly, a fraction of an inch from his mouth. "You want to know if I felt the same heat that burns my skin when *you're* near me?" I stared at his mouth and looked into his eyes again. "If I felt the electricity that runs through my body when your mouth"—I stroked his lip with my finger—"is on mine?" I kissed him.

Evan stood there, under my spell. When I moved to one side his mouth followed me, wanting more. This time I was directing the game. "Or"—as I looked him in the eyes I slowly took his hands and slid them down my body to my hips—"when your hands touch me . . ." Evan gripped my waist, slipping his fingers under the hem of my shirt. ". . . and it makes me lose my mind?" I whispered as he half closed his eyes, breathing deeply, holding back.

I'd created an electrical current between us that tingled on the surface of our bodies. I felt his desire for me and wanted him just as intensely. Slowly moving my mouth to his without touching it, I allowed our lips to linger a fraction of an inch apart. The longer I delayed, as if contact were forbidden, the wilder its lack made me feel. My heart pounded in my throat with impatience. My instinct was urging me to kiss him like never before, but I made myself repress the primitive impulse, bend it to my will—and the tension grew even greater.

Our lips touched, just barely. The accumulated energy surged through my body, igniting everything inside me. I brushed my mouth against his again, this time a little longer, but when I pulled away his lips followed me avidly and his hands grasped me firmly by the hips, refusing to let me go.

Something exploded inside me. I wouldn't be able to control myself much longer, but Evan couldn't resist another second. His mouth was on mine, hastening my loss of control. He swept me up off the floor. I instinctively wrapped my legs around his waist, my lips on his the whole time. My head was spinning.

"I wasn't joking when I said it: you're all mine," he breathed directly onto my mouth. He buried his face in my neck and the contact sent another electrical charge—wilder and more powerful—racing through me, melting me. Evan locked his fierce gaze on me. "No one else is allowed to touch you," he whispered, tender and commanding at the same time, as if his words were law. His tone made me even dizzier. It was still hard for me to believe Evan could be jealous on my account, and the sensation sent a delicious tingle through every fiber of my body. I was his. Inside, I knew it couldn't be otherwise, but it was exciting to hear him say what he'd just said.

I surrendered to his arms as he slowly laid me down, one hand under the small of my back and the other caressing my hip. I sank into something soft. It felt strange, and I realized it wasn't the floor, but I was too wrapped up in Evan to care.

"I want to be with you and no one else," I whispered against his lips, my breathing ragged.

His mouth slid down my neck and I glimpsed the military fabric beneath us, piled into a fleecy cloud of green cloth. His lips didn't stop moving against mine for a second and I let myself be guided, giving in to all their decisions. As his hands moved over my body, unfastening my clothing, I grabbed his shirt and pulled it off him. My body was in flames. The only thing left between us was a single thin layer of fabric.

As Evan prolonged his kiss, his hand continued to roam over me. For a moment his fingers fastened on the lace of my scarlet panties as though he wanted to rip them off me and was trying to restrain himself.

I burned with a fire that couldn't be quenched—not as long as Evan was there on top of me, fanning the flames. Not as long as he continued to press me against him with a sensual single-mindedness that drove me out of my mind. My lips were warm from his breath.

His hand slipped down my back and into my panties, clasping my rear as he kissed me passionately. He pulled down the silky fabric and I felt his knee press against my thigh in a gentle but firm movement that brought down the last of my defenses. And then he was inside me, triggering a hot shiver that swept me into a world of pure sensation. Fire burned beneath my skin—a fire that consumed me. My body trembled, exploding in a wave of pleasure that filled me all the way down to my toes. The flames invaded every part of me. I was burning, consumed in a blaze of passion.

"Gem," Evan whispered. No one except him had ever called me that.

I let myself drift away on the current of electricity and his voice enveloped me like warm velvet as his mouth set my neck on fire.

"Marry me."

A tingle ran over my skin, taking me to heaven again.

They say your first time is the one you never forget. I couldn't figure out why no one ever mentioned the second or the third because from what I'd already experienced, forgetting such a powerful emotion would be inconceivable. I was also sure that making love with Evan would be just as unforgettable every single time. Forever. There was no way I could touch the moon and return to earth without remembering it. Sometimes, afraid someone up there might notice and decide that so much happiness was too much for just one person, I tried to make myself repress the emotions and keep them locked up inside. But then my eyes would meet Evan's and I would betray myself.

"I wasn't kidding, you know." His voice sent a tingle straight to my heart. Had I really not just imagined his words? Had he actually asked me what I thought he had? "I want you to be my wife, Gemma. I want it more than anything else in the world," he whispered, stroking my ear with the tip of his nose.

"Evan—" My throat was tight with emotion as I looked into his tender gaze.

"We'll do it in secret. Simon will marry us and when you're eighteen we can tell everyone. I don't care who else knows it; I just want to exchange vows with you before God," he murmured as the intensity in his eyes made me melt. "Wait—I don't want you to answer right away. I've had time enough to realize that my life used to be meaningless. Now that I've found you I don't need any more time. Still, I know it might be different for you. I'm just asking you to consid—"

I passionately sealed his lips with my own as tears filled my eyes. "I don't need time to realize you're the most important thing to me, Evan," I sighed, resting my forehead on his. "If I had only one day left to live, I would want to spend it with you."

Evan pulled my hip and rolled me on top of him. My hair hung down, forming a curtain around us that shut out the rest of the world. We both smiled, our lips still touching. The feeling in my chest was so intense it almost hurt.

"I've been thinking about it for a while now. I wish I could have done things right—with a ring and everything. I wasn't planning on what happened with Drake last night."

"It's already perfect," I whispered. "I don't need a ring. I already have you—I don't need anything else."

"No, I want to give you my mother's ring." Evan looked into my eyes. "It's belonged to my family for a long time. It would mean a lot to me if you wore it from that day on, forever."

"Evan, I—" His words and penetrating gaze were so intense that for a moment they left me speechless. "It's really too much."

"You mean the ring or my proposal? You still haven't given me an answer, you know." He smiled.

I returned his smile and let my weight fall on him, burrowing into his body. His warmth was so wonderful, it made me feel like the cold didn't exist. "You're wrong. I gave you my answer before you even proposed." I kissed him on the lips and rested my head on his chest, forgetting the outside world.

29

STRANGE ENCOUNTER

Late October

I got out of bed and a shiver ran down my back. The temperature had dropped drastically over the last few weeks, but this morning my body was particularly sensitive to the cold. I guess I'd been more sensitive in general lately.

When I looked out the window I saw Evan already waiting for me, leaning against the hood of the BMW. I smiled at him and my breath left a mark on the glass, a white halo that lingered even when I walked away. Minutes later I was outside, my green backpack slung over my shoulder.

"Good morning," I said, kissing him lightly on the mouth.

His lips smiled against mine. "It is now," he whispered sweetly before opening the passenger door. It was a habit he'd never lost.

The recent weeks had been easier to bear. Though I could never forget Death's icy breath on my neck, the connection between Evan and me took my mind off everything else. Thinking of him—*being* with him—was like having a hideaway somewhere far from the rest of the world, far from danger, a place where I could be safe because the very thought of Evan made me feel that way.

We knew that the Angel of Death, whoever it was, was not going to give up the hunt and we were all waiting for him to make his next move. Sooner or later he would strike again and we would be ready. That's what everyone kept telling me.

In a little corner of my mind I harbored the hope that there really was a chance everything would work out in the end. But maybe it was just wishful thinking; there was another part that wasn't entirely sure.

Almost a month had gone by since we'd seen Drake. There had been no message, no phone call, no unexpected appearance. As far as I knew, he'd disappeared from our lives. The thought that it was my fault left me with a bitter taste in my mouth and a strange churning sensation in my stomach. All my attempts to persuade Evan to forgive his brother had failed. Each time, though, the regret I glimpsed in his eyes persuaded me to keep trying and so I did, with the feeble hope that one day I might be able to set things right.

When I got out of the car something cold touched my neck. I looked up and saw snowflakes drifting down from the sky like soft feathers cradled by the air. I held out my hand and stared at the flakes, enchanted. The first snowfall of the season, when the wind blew away the remaining leaves, always had this effect on me. Every time felt like the first time, despite the fact that Lake Placid was almost always covered with snow as soon as the weather turned cold.

"You like the snow?" To Evan I must have looked like a silly little girl, my hand held out to catch the flakes, my chin raised toward the sky. His mocking smile confirmed my suspicion.

I lowered my damp hand and wiped it on my jeans. "You don't?"

He laughed. "Now I know I do."

"Why?" I asked, my breath freezing in a cloud in front of my mouth. "You don't have to like everything I like, you know."

Evan smiled as if I'd just said something nonsensical. "Actually, that's not why. You know I don't like Strawtella," he shot back teasingly.

"Then why?" I asked, puzzled.

His smile softened and he looked at me tenderly, the sexy little creases under his eyes making an appearance. "The cold air brings out your eyes. It's stunning. I didn't know that before," he whispered in my ear. "But I do now."

Although my face was freezing cold, I felt warmth spread over my cheeks. Evan smiled. It was bizarre how he still managed to make me blush. There had to be something in his tone of voice that caused this instinctive, uncontrollable reaction in my blood.

Snowflakes continued to drift down, increasing in number as the morning progressed. From time to time I would stop to watch them through the school windows, mesmerized when a few crystals landed on the glass and let me admire them.

By the time classes were over, a blanket of white covered the whole campus and every surface. I hurried to the car, dodging the snowballs the students were throwing every which way across the parking lot. One of them was heading straight for Evan. I tried to warn him but he'd already noticed it. His arm shot out to grab it, but the snow melted a split second before it hit his hand. Incredible. Attempting to figure out where it had come from, I noticed a grin on his face and followed his gaze. Ginevra was across the street.

"Just wanted to cool you down a bit, little brother," his sister teased.

Her subtle innuendo—unless I'd misunderstood—made me blush again. I hoped neither of them noticed. Damn it, with all this snow it was even easier to see the color rise in my cheeks.

"It's a shame you didn't hit me then!" Evan was quick to reply, bending down. I blinked as I watched a snowball form without his even touching it. He threw it at Ginevra who in the meantime had whipped up an arsenal. The white spheres began to fly toward us at a speed I could barely follow, but none of them hit me—they all melted inches from my body, so close I could feel their chill. I didn't understand what the two of them found so amusing, since neither of them managed to hit their target even once, though one time, while Evan was protecting me, an unexpected snowball hit him right in the head. All three of us burst out laughing as he shook his damp hair.

The snow continued to fall all day long, becoming a blizzard in the afternoon. I ate a late lunch at home with my parents. Ever since my life had been under siege I'd tried to spend time with them too, though work at the diner took up most of their waking hours, especially since Dad had started baking cakes and doughnuts for the neighboring towns. Orders kept pouring in.

At three, Evan pretended to stop by to take me to his place—although actually he'd never left me. Every day he secretly stayed with me to protect me from anyone who might try to get close. This afternoon he would be gone, something he'd already warned me about yesterday morning before leaving calculus. I'd sat there at my desk, a little shaken like I always was when Evan brought up what he did. But then I'd opened my notebook and found a message from him, written in Devanagari.

अन्तर्मय्यसि मम हृदि ममात्मनि

I recognized the words at once because he'd said them to me after our first time together and the memory warmed my heart. *You're inside me—in my heart, in my soul.* I stroked the symbols, imagining Evan writing it there. He knew I liked to know in advance when he had to leave me. He'd been so sweet it made me forget everything else. Besides, I didn't mind spending a little time with Ginevra. The hours I spent with her flew by, a bit like they had when I used to hang out with Peter.

Peter. Although I saw him at school every morning I sometimes missed his constant presence in my life. We'd been inseparable for too long for me to feel otherwise. I still called him to see how he was doing, but nothing was the same any more, not even his tone of voice. The delicate balance had been upset and the change seemed irreversible.

"Will you be gone long?" I whined, sitting cross-legged on Evan's bed.

"A couple hours. I'm not going far."

"I haven't seen Ginevra yet," I said.

Evan smiled, no doubt privy to something I didn't know. "She's downstairs with Simon."

From his expression I instantly grasped what he was talking about. "I bet she's leaving him black and blue."

"Simon knows how to defend himself," he said, grinning.

"It would be fun to watch you sometime," I blurted, hoping he'd agree to my millionth request, but I already knew how he felt about it: the workout room was off limits for me when they were training.

"It's too dangerous for you," he said, his tone serious.

"From the looks of him I can't believe Simon is as dangerous as you say," I joked.

"Actually, he's always very careful with Ginevra. One mistake, one second of distraction, and he could kill her. You should have seen him fight Dra—" Evan stopped in mid-name as if he'd just remembered it was no longer part of his vocabulary.

And it was all my fault. Guilt was devouring me.

Evan's face had hardened. I knew him well enough to realize how much he was suffering though he would never have admitted it. I tried to get him to look me in the eye but it was no use.

"I let Ginevra know you'd be here before they started. She won't be much longer," he said, changing the subject. "Meanwhile, go downstairs if you want. The water in the pool is hot. You're safe here in the house."

"Don't worry, I'll find a way to keep myself occupied. You just try to get back fast," I threatened, pulling him onto the bed by his shirt.

Evan fell on top of me, his arms outstretched, and kissed me for a moment, then pulled back and rested his forehead against mine. "I have to go. Try not to drown in the pool while I'm gone."

"I'll do my best, but I can't promise anything." I smiled.

"Then I'll come back as soon as I can." He kissed me again.

"That was all part of my plan," I whispered onto his lips.

He disappeared and the room was instantly filled with his absence. I sat there a few minutes, contemplating the empty wall, then fell back onto the bed and closed my eyes, taking a deep breath. Without Evan, the silence was oppressive.

I got up from the bed, uneasy. Maybe going for a swim wasn't such a bad idea.

I tested the water with my foot before immersing the rest of my body. It was hotter than I remembered it being last time. Not even in the swimming pool, though, could I shake my uneasiness. The room was too large for me to lose myself in my thoughts—the sound of the water slapping against the sides of the pool echoed off the walls.

I swam for a few minutes, watching the snow fall on the other side of the huge picture window that overlooked the garden, but the silence soon made me antsy. I climbed out of the pool and wrapped a towel around my black swimsuit, a monokini that left my back bare.

"Don't do that. You totally look better without it," a sensual voice rang out behind me.

I jumped and spun around. "Evan!" I sighed with relief, breathless from the surprise. "What are you doing here?"

"You don't seem too happy to see me. If you want, I can leave," he said, raising an eyebrow, but his hands were already on my hips.

"N-no," I stammered. "I just—I thought it would take you longer than that. I was expecting to have to spend a couple of hours without you." Evan took a step toward me, looking hesitant. "You're back sooner than I'd hoped." A half hour at most had gone by since he'd left me.

"Really? Seems like days to me. I just couldn't stay away from you," he whispered onto my neck. "Actually, I can't stay long. I just thought I'd stop in and see how you were doing. You know, with one thing and the other."

"Good thinking," I said, pleased.

"Well? Mind telling me what you're doing with *that* on?" he asked, nodding at the towel wrapped around my body.

I looked down at it, a bit puzzled. "I took your advice. The water's great."

"M-hmm." Evan shook his head, amused by my remark. "But I meant what are you *still* doing with it on," he said, his voice low as he undid the towel and dropped it to the floor. His evocative gaze brimming with desire, he stepped forward and I moved back until my bare shoulder blades were pressed against the ice-cold wall. The chill made me flinch.

"Uh-oh," Evan whispered, resting both hands against the wall on either side of my head, blocking my way. "Now you're trapped," he whispered, his gaze as sensual as his tone.

"I'll let myself be tortured, if that's what you're getting at," I shot back, raising an eyebrow.

"You read my mind." His hand rested on my bare waist and he kissed me passionately. The cold returned, giving me goosebumps. No—not the cold. Something else. Evan's hands began to roam over my body in an unexpected manner as his lips explored my neck and descended to my breast. I looked around, strangely uncomfortable. "Evan," I murmured, but he was too absorbed to listen to me. "Evan, stop it," I whispered, not very convincingly.

"I have no intention of stopping," he said firmly, pulling me against him. I'd never seen him this aroused and unrelenting before.

"Someone might come in," I insisted. "Simon and Ginevra are in the next room."

"I don't care," he said, his breathing ragged as he continued to kiss me.

Pressing my hands against his chest to make him stop, I looked him straight in the eye, my face serious. "Well, I *do*. What's gotten into you?" I asked, puzzled.

"You're so surprised I want you?" he asked, arching his eyebrow.

My eyes wandered, checking the room. I kept feeling a strange sensation on my skin, as if there were a foreign or hostile presence somewhere in the vicinity. But it was impossible—Evan would have detected it.

I happened to glance at his neck. "Where's your dog tag?" I asked in alarm, pulling his shirt open slightly. Evan's eyes wavered.

He never took off his dog tag. For a moment I was afraid he'd lost it in who knew what part of the world. All at once an even worse thought crossed my mind, but I banished it instantly; it was unlikely Evan would have taken it off because of his falling-out with Drake.

He felt around on his chest. "I must have left it in my room."

"But you never take it off," I said.

"Yeah. Well, don't worry, I'll put it on again as soon as I get back," he whispered, pressing me against the wall. "I can't stay much longer," he warned before kissing me passionately again. I kissed him back and he disappeared without warning, his lingering voice echoing through the empty room with a hint of mischief: "See you soon."

I remained leaning against the wall with a strange sensation on my skin and the memory of his intense gaze that soon began to fade. A sudden cold shiver gave me goosebumps. Without Evan's heat to warm me, I realized I was still wet. Unsettled, I picked the towel up from the floor and quickly dried myself off.

It had been a weird encounter. Evan hadn't made me feel the sensations I always felt when he kissed me. I wasn't used to him being so insistent, and I wasn't sure I liked it.

30

SUBTLE DECEPTION

I pulled on my clothes, still confused, and knocked on the door to the workout room, from which came sounds so muffled they seemed far away. No one opened. I cautiously gripped the handle and opened the door just a crack to peek inside, but something struck it and slammed it shut. Before I could catch my breath Ginevra was beside me. "Gemma! What were you thinking? What are you doing here? It's dangerous for you!" she said, worried, almost reproaching me. I was about to reply but she cut me off, peering over my shoulder with an alarmed look on her face. "Someone's been here," she said, paying no attention to me.

"It was just Evan," I said, but she didn't look reassured.

"I thought he was gone."

"I thought so too but he surprised me." Ginevra continued to scan the room uneasily. "He had some spare time," I said. "Is Simon in there?"

A proud smile formed on her lips. I already knew what she was thinking. "Give him a little while to recover." She leaned toward me and lowered her voice. "I think I overdid it this time."

I shook my head and looked more closely at her body. There wasn't a scratch on it. It must be awesome to be a Witch. The door to the workout room opened behind Ginevra, who shot me a conspiratorial look.

"You're all in one piece, it seems," I said, smothering a laugh.

Simon looked at Ginevra, who shrugged. "Not a scratch," he shot back, throwing his girlfriend a challenging look.

"Good thing you heal fast," she taunted him. "We can go back in if you feel up to it."

"Okay, okay!" I said, smiling. "Don't you two ever get enough? I propose a truce. What do you say we go to the kitchen?"

Ginevra didn't take her eyes off Simon's for a second. "Sounds like a good idea." She smiled slyly. "Angels' bodies have their limits too. I wouldn't want you to exceed yours." Her sensual eyes sparkled at Simon, who tilted his head as he held her gaze. Suddenly he grabbed her wrist, yanked her toward him, and pinned her against the wall.

I'd seen Simon shirtless before but had never noticed how muscular he was. His tanned skin glistened with sweat. "See?" he whispered onto her lips, his strong arms tensed as they barred her way. "To catch you off guard, all I have to do is distract you."

I winced at the memory this scene brought to my mind. Blushing, I looked down, embarrassed. Ginevra sensually brought her lips close to Simon's without touching them, lingered a moment, and then nimbly inverted their positions, slamming him against the wall. "What makes you think I was off guard?" she whispered in response to his provocation.

Being able to read Simon's thoughts in order to know exactly when to strike was definitely an advantage for her. I shook my head as Simon smiled at her stubbornness; he clearly liked this aspect of her. "You never give up, do you?" He smiled against her lips, amused by their little game.

For Ginevra everything inevitably became an endless challenge, a competition in which she couldn't stand the idea of losing. Maybe it was part of her nature as a Witch. It was nice to see them together, but the more I watched them, the more I missed Evan. Though it had only been a few minutes since I'd last seen him, it felt like hours.

"I don't know about you, but I'm getting kind of hungry." I hoped one of them would take me up on the proposal. My eyes rested on Ginevra, who was quick to accept.

Simon shot me a glance and smiled. "You really have a Witch's appetite, Gemma," he teased.

Head down, I followed them upstairs. "It's the pool," I explained, feeling awkward. "Swimming makes me hungry."

The next two hours flew by so fast I almost didn't feel their weight on my heart. Simon and Ginevra were good company and our mutual affection was unconditional. Even so, Drake's absence was still keenly felt in every corner of the house. They all missed him, I was sure of it. Whenever one of us happened to mention his name a sad silence instantly filled the room.

Evan's lighthearted voice shook me from my thoughts. "Did you guys miss me?" I smiled. "Not much, it would seem," he said sarcastically, looking at the table that was covered with a cornucopia of leftovers. I threw my arms around his neck. "I guess somebody was celebrating without me," he teased, rubbing his nose against mine.

"What?" I exclaimed. "We would never celebrate without you." I shot a glance at Simon and Ginevra, urging them to back me up.

"Of course not!" Ginevra said as she popped another morsel into her mouth and chewed with delight. "How could you think such a thing?" Evan laughed and I kissed him as the others silently turned to go.

"Oookay, looks like we should leave you two alone," Ginevra said.

"No need," I was quick to reply.

Evan smiled and I noticed him wink at her.

"Someone doesn't agree with you, Gemma. Please, Evan. Spare me the details!" she groaned, pulling Simon by the hand. "At least wait until I've left the room!"

Evan laughed and turned to face me. Finally we were alone again. "It felt like an eternity," he said, gazing at me tenderly. I was in danger of melting whenever he looked at me that way. He almost seemed like another person compared to the last time I'd seen him. "Sorry I kept you waiting. It took longer than expected."

"You found it!" I cried with relief, noticing his dog tag was back in its place.

Evan didn't seem to understand. "Found what?" he asked, gently resting his lips on my neck.

"Your dog tag," I said.

"I never took it off," he whispered casually, his mouth making its way up toward my chin.

"Yes you did," I insisted. "You weren't wearing it by the pool." Evan froze and looked at me, frowning. "You said you'd left it up in your room," I reminded him, baffled as to why he looked so bewildered.

His eyes wavered in alarm as the truth began to dawn on me. "I don't remember saying that," he replied, standing stock-still and staring at me as if he were hoping to hear me say I was wrong. "Gemma, I've been gone for hours, you know that." He almost seemed to be trying to convince me it was true.

"No, you were—So, by the pool—" I put my hand to my mouth and felt my body turn ice cold with shock as I watched the rage grow in Evan's eyes. Hatred glinted in them.

"He came back," he snarled, tensing his muscles.

My hands trembled. "What—You mean it was Drake?" I whispered, horrified by the thought of our encounter. Evan fixed me with a wary gaze and I sensed his anger growing by the second. My body felt trapped in a block of ice.

It hadn't been Evan.

"What did he do to you?" he growled, his tone so harsh it made me flinch. "What did he do to you, Gemma?!" he repeated, raising his voice. A black fire burned in his eyes.

"I don't think you want to know," I barely murmured.

"Yes I do," he insisted through clenched teeth. "Did he touch you?"

I looked away and closed my eyes, unable to answer. Evan growled and slammed his fist into the cement wall. It cracked beneath his knuckles as I stood there, petrified. The look on his face told me there was no doubt about it: this time he wouldn't hold back.

"Evan—"

"He's crossed the line. It's not going to happen a second time," he said, his tone implacable.

"Evan!" Ginevra shouted, racing into the room. She stopped in front of us and looked him in the eye. "I need to talk to you."

"Not right now," he snapped.

"It's important. You need to listen to me. Drake is the least of our problems right now," she insisted. She'd read in our minds what had happened, but she didn't care; it seemed what she had to say was far more important. Finally Evan straightened up and paid attention. "The vial with the poison." Ginevra's tone was as grave as the look in her eyes. "It's missing. I can't find it anywhere, Evan!"

Her brother's face paled instantly.

"He was here!" Ginevra exclaimed. A cold shiver ran down my body. The Executioner sent to kill me had been in this house. "I don't know how he managed to get into my room without me noticing it," Ginevra said.

"Are you sure about all this?" Evan asked in alarm. "When was the last time you saw it?"

"I don't know, it's been too long. Since I gave you the poison to use on Faust, I guess. I haven't even thought about it since!" Ginevra cried in panic.

"But it was empty. You put the only drop of it onto the dagger—I saw you do it," Evan said, thinking.

"Evan, you're underestimating how potent it is. You have no idea how little it takes to kill a Subterranean."

"You should have destroyed it then!" he yelled. He fell silent for a long moment, lost in thought. "We don't know whether the Executioner came back after the last time or if he'd taken the poison even before that. We can't know if he intends to attack. We have to stay alert."

Simon nodded as he walked into the room. "Think you have a plan?" he asked.

Evan stood motionless for a moment before answering. "Something doesn't make sense. Too much time has passed since the last time he tried to kill Gemma." He continued to shake his head, processing the information.

"Maybe he wants to catch us off guard," Simon suggested.

Evan didn't seem convinced. "No. He's sly. He knows we'll never let down our defenses. He must have a plan." Evan's eyes narrowed to slits as if trying to see our enemy's intentions. "He has something in mind, but I won't let him get away with it. We need to stay alert and wait for him to make his move." A sudden spark ignited in his eyes. "When that happens we'll be here waiting for him."

"We don't even know who we're up against, Evan," Ginevra cautioned, "or even worse, what his power is."

Evan gave her a hard look. "I think I have an idea," he murmured to himself.

A frozen silence fell among us. I stared at Evan in shock, trying to decipher his expression. He came to me as if I'd called him, pulled me against his chest, and covered my head with his hand. "Don't worry," he whispered. "Everything's going to be fine."

A cold shiver raced over my skin because deep down I knew it wasn't true.

31

FIREFLIES IN THE NIGHT

I went to bed early and fell asleep without realizing it as the trees outside scratched at my window with their branches and the stormy wind howled like an angry wolf.

"Gemma . . ."

A voice echoed in my head, whispering in the silence of the night. I flinched. There was no way it could be morning already.

"Shh, don't worry. It's me," he whispered tenderly.

"Evan," I mumbled, my eyes still closed. I noticed him next to me and bolted upright in bed. "Evan, what is it?" I asked in alarm, wondering what could have happened to make him wake me up in the middle of the night. I blinked several times to allow my eyes to adjust and looked out the window where darkness reigned over the silent night. It had stopped snowing. "It's not morning yet," I said.

"Get dressed," he ordered, his voice kind.

Trying to understand, I looked into his eyes so he could see my concern, but he smiled reassuringly. "Are we going somewhere?" I asked, puzzled, continuing to look at the darkness outside the window.

Another smile spread across his face—this time a sweeter one. "Trust me," he whispered, never taking his eyes off me. "There's something you have to see."

I got out of bed and did as he'd told me to. "We're going out the window?" I asked in surprise when Evan opened it.

"As always." He smiled at me, but I still wasn't completely convinced of his proposal. It wasn't the first time we'd snuck out in the middle of the night, but when we'd done it before things had been different. Death hadn't been hunting me and we could count on Drake to replace me. Circumstances had changed.

"My folks might wake up! What if they notice I'm gone?"

He smiled disarmingly at my reluctance. "Why so worried all of a sudden? Come on, Gemma. We've done worse." I couldn't disagree. "I've already visited your parents. They won't wake up before dawn. I made sure of it."

I couldn't find any other objections to make, so I joined Evan at the windowsill. He cradled me in his flexed arms and a moment later we landed gracefully on the walk below. I didn't even feel us touch the ground. He must have defied gravity by controlling the air so it would waft us down. The only thing I felt was the cold wind stinging my cheeks.

The blizzard had subsided, leaving the yard blanketed with snow. The pure white mantle over everything was a beautiful sight. In the car I noticed two pairs of ice skates on the back seat—one pair small, the other almost twice as large—and instantly realized Evan's intentions. I stiffened in my seat as he glanced at me with a smile.

I thought of the Olympic Oval in front of the school. Every year when the temperature dropped it was filled with water that froze into a skating rink. What was he thinking? "It's three in the morning!" I said. "They'll think we've lost our minds!"

"There's nobody where we're going," he said, careful not to tell me more.

I was wrong; the car turned in the opposite direction from the school. I tried to pry more information out of him but gave up after a while and waited in silence to see where he was taking me. We continued toward the woods, away from Lake Placid and the city lights.

The darkness gradually swallowed us up as the car wound its way through the trees, the headlights casting a solid beam of light in front of us. A moment later I thought I glimpsed a soft glow deep in the woods, but it immediately faded. I leaned closer to the window, curious, trying to figure out where Evan was taking me and what had emitted that silvery light. He continued to steal glances at me, grinning the whole time because of my reaction.

The car stopped in the middle of nowhere and Evan opened my door. I looked around in bewilderment, daunted by the darkness. "Evan, what—" I stammered, unable to see anything.

His laughter rang through the night and his tone grew gentle. "Ready?" he whispered behind my ear. With a delicate touch, he lifted my chin.

As I stared at the dark leaves overhead, a silvery sparkle winked on. Slowly, the thick canopy came to life as hundreds of twinkling, luminous points appeared.

I was no longer sure if I was awake or dreaming. My eyes were dazzled by the incredible display. Like an infinitely large, delightful cave filled with fireflies, the forest had lit up all around us, thousands of brilliant specks shining through the treetops. From their pure white glow I could see they were tiny spheres of light. There were so many of them they banished the night, tiny little stars floating in the trees as though the heavens had descended and hidden there to watch us.

I pivoted slowly, my face to the treetops. They were a fascinating sight. I couldn't find the words to tell Evan how touched I was to know he'd already been there to prepare everything for me. I noticed he was staring at me, a smile still on his face as he waited for me to say something.

"Is all this real?" I murmured. "You know I don't like it when you confuse me like that—are we really here or are we in my mind?"

Evan laughed. "No, you aren't dreaming. If you were, I wouldn't have been able to take you wherever I wanted. Don't forget, in your dreams you're the one who calls the shots."

"You know how to take my breath away. It's beautiful," I exclaimed. "But why are we here?" I thought of the ice skates on the back seat of his car. There weren't any skating rinks in this area, and the school was far away.

Evan came up behind me and rested his hands on my hips. He glanced briefly at the lake through the trees, then looked at me, his expression uncertain but full of promises. "Have you ever skated on the lake under the stars?" he whispered, his lips brushing my ear. His hot breath tickled my skin.

"Of course," I said, thinking of the dozens of times Peter and I had stayed up late, skating on the lake and around the Oval outside the school.

I bit my lip, instantly regretting my impulsive reply, but Evan was quick to ask, "Have you ever watched it freeze over?" he whispered, pointing at Lake Placid in front of us.

Up until now I hadn't even thought about the lake. From the distance I'd seen the moonlight sparkle on its surface, but I hadn't been sure if it was frozen or if Evan was planning to make our skates glide across the water. With him, anything was possible.

"Are you kidding?" I said, turning my head to look at him. His chin was resting on my shoulder and my cheek brushed his. I already knew he wasn't, but his smile confirmed it. "You're not kidding," I murmured to myself.

"Come with me." Evan took my hand and led me toward the shore. I followed him. He let go only when we were at the water's edge, when he looked at me for a long moment, either to encourage me or more likely, to pique my curiosity even further. This was the part he always loved most. I watched him kneel down and reach out his hand until his palm was almost touching the water. I held my breath as the surface of the lake trembled below him, rippling slightly. Suddenly the water froze under his palm. I gaped as the ice spread out, stretching across the entire surface of the lake in crystal ripples, transforming it in seconds into a perfectly smooth mirror.

Evan turned toward me with a satisfied look on his face and I blinked, entranced. "You froze the lake," I whispered as if what he'd just done wasn't clear enough already.

"Nothing escapes you," he teased.

I opened my mouth, still amazed, and pointed at the shiny surface in front of us. *"You froze the lake!"* I repeated, dumbfounded.

"Yeeeaaaah." Evan frowned, looking puzzled. "I've done worse things in my life."

"I can't believe it."

"You don't like it?" he asked, sounding confused and concerned.

"No—Yes—It's just that it seems—" I struggled to find the words. "Unbelievable," I said, entranced. "It's really too much just for me, Evan."

"Nothing is too much for you," he was quick to reply, as if what I'd just said was silly. He stroked my cheek and disappeared. In a fraction of a second he was back and handed me my skates. He'd already put his on, though I was sure he didn't even need them. When I'd put mine on I took the hand he held out to me.

"Ready?" he asked, looking at me encouragingly.

I stared at the sheet of crystal that stretched out in front of me. "I'm not sure," I admitted, a bit worried.

"Trust me." He squeezed my hand. I rested one foot and then the other on the icy surface of the lake, moving hesitantly. It was harder than I'd imagined.

"Careful," Evan said softly, still clasping my hand. I'd always been good at skating, but he seemed like a pro in comparison. "This will be a bit different from the other times," he warned.

"I'd imagined that," I shot back sardonically, feeling like I was sliding across a soapy surface. No matter how hard I tried to keep my balance, it was impossible to maintain arm-leg coordination. The ice beneath us was perfectly smooth, as crystal clear as the icicles that hung like jewels from the tree branches.

"You'll get used to it in no time. Meanwhile, don't let go of my hand," he said, his voice deep.

"Okay." I struggled not to fall as I awkwardly made my way forward.

The air was so cold I couldn't feel my cheeks any more. My hand clasped in Evan's, instead, felt cozy and safe and its warmth spread all the way up my arm. I tried not to think of the cold, deep water beneath us; the layer of ice was thick and there was no reason for me to worry. With Evan I wasn't running any risks.

"Okay, I'm ready." When I felt fairly sure I could stay standing without his support I took a deep breath. "You can let go now," I told him. I didn't want him to leave my side, but I wanted to show him I could do it.

"You sure? It might be dangerous." My expression had probably given away my uncertainty. Evan relaxed his grip.

"I'll manage," I said in a low voice, mostly to reassure myself. He let go of my hand and I found myself teetering on my own.

It seemed easier when he was near to instill me with courage, yet I knew I could do it. I made my way forward determinedly, digging the blades in one after the other, faster and faster, pretending to have mastered the ice. The lake was immense, but it didn't matter how far out I went—Evan would be there to bring me back. In an instant he was at my side, skating in sync with me. Then, with a decisive movement, he swung out in front and skated backwards as if it were the most natural thing in the world. I'd always wondered how people could do that.

"This is fun!" I murmured, in spite of feeling a little dizzy from watching his face as we moved.

"You got used to it pretty quick," he said, pleased.

"Did you doubt me?" I grinned, finally finding my feet again.

"I'm still not so sure, actually."

Was he challenging me? With my next steps I pushed harder against the ice and moved faster. "Let's see if you can catch me," I said, taking up the challenge though I knew I'd already lost the race. Evan's laughter rang out behind me as I narrowed my eyes and focused on the ice in front of me. The air was so cold it took my breath away, but all I was worried about was not falling. I could hear his strokes behind mine as I gathered all my energy to stay out ahead of him. I knew perfectly well it was only a little game we were playing and that if he wanted to he could catch up with me in the blink of an eye.

Carelessly, I turned around to see how much of a lead I had. Wrong move. In a second I'd lost my balance and tripped over my own feet. Why did I always find a way to make a fool of myself? At this speed the impact with the ice was bound to be violent and painful. I instinctively put my hands out in front of me and tensed my muscles, bracing for the pain. From the corner of my eye I saw a blur shoot toward me at warp speed a second before I hit the icy surface and something cushioned the blow. I opened my eyes. It was Evan. He'd grabbed me and slid beneath me, his back on the ice, my body on top of his. For a moment I lay still, panting, my lips on his ear, my heart racing. Then I raised myself slightly and looked him in the eye, a cloud of breath escaping my lips.

Evan smiled, his expression tender. "Got you," he whispered, his eyes fixed on mine, his hands encircling my waist.

I bit my lower lip. Evan wasn't just talking about my fall. "I could have beaten you," I said defiantly, unable to handle defeat.

"No doubt about it," he said, an impish sparkle in his eye.

"Don't tease me. It's not my fault you're way faster. I'm just a mortal soul."

His smile softened and became more tender. With his hand he followed the curve of my face as he pushed back a lock of hair that had fallen over my forehead and swept it behind my ear. "You aren't just a mortal soul, Gemma. You're much more than that to me." My gaze locked onto his. "Otherwise I would never have fallen in love with you. You're—" He stared at me intently as if searching for the words inside me. "You're like a flower that blossomed from the snow." He stroked my cheek again.

I slowly lowered my head toward his face.

"A beautiful flower, so strong it defies the cold," he whispered, "but so delicate and fragile it needs protection."

I rested my lips on his. When I pulled back, he looked me in the eye, his expression proud. "And I *will* protect you from everything, at all costs," he said with determination.

I trembled at the memories his words conjured in my mind. There were moments when I could forget about everything else. At those moments Death stopped haunting me—there was no Executioner hunting me, threatening to kill me. There was nothing for me to be afraid of because Evan would always be with me. No one else. Just me and him, forever.

Then I would come back to reality. I couldn't escape my fate forever. Sooner or later I would have to pay the price. Deep in my heart, the only hope I nurtured was that I could avoid death as long as possible and spend what time I had left with Evan. That's all I wanted.

32

SCARLET DEATH

A snow flurry drifted through the air, caressing our faces as we lay on our backs, gazing at the sky. All around us, the spheres of fire glowed with their white light, hidden in the trees like fireflies peeking down at us from behind the leaves. Who knew how long we lay there on the ice, one next to the other, looking at the dark mantle overhead. I couldn't even feel the cold any more. Or maybe I simply didn't care. The warmth in my heart was enough to keep away the chill.

Evan had taken off his skates, disappearing and reappearing with his shoes on, but I'd decided to keep my own skates on a little while longer to prolong this magical experience. We hadn't spoken for a while now, maybe because the pure white moonglow had absorbed my thoughts, releasing them in a thousand reflections that touched the sky.

I wondered if there was some other place, apart from the earth, where Evan and I could live together without the constant threat of being separated. A world where my fate would be different from the one in store for me here. Then reason brought me back to the present. There was no other place I could seek refuge, and no matter how hard Evan tried to hide me, no matter how he struggled to protect me, Death would never stop hunting me down. It pursued me like a hungry feline, pulling down all the branches I managed to scramble up onto. I was its prey. How much longer would I have breath enough to run? It was impossible to say. But one thing was inevitable: the day would come when I wouldn't be able to endure it any more. I could only hope it didn't come too soon. I didn't want to lose Evan.

"What are you thinking about?" Evan rubbed his head against mine as he continued to stare at the sky.

I didn't want to drag him into the melancholy depths of my brooding mind. "Ice sculptures," I lied, but he must have realized it because he studied me silently for a long moment as if trying to probe my mind.

"You don't have to prove you're brave through all this. No one expects that of you, Gemma." I didn't reply. Nothing escaped him. "Besides, I already know you are. In fact, you're a lot braver than you imagine. It can't have been easy to face everything you've been through, but you've never given up."

"How could I? I had no choice, Evan," I said sadly.

"You know that's not true. Others would have broken down if they'd been in your shoes, but you've always taken everything with your head held high."

"Only because you're here to protect me."

He squeezed my hand and I understood what he was trying to say: he would always be there for me. We turned to look at each other and he smiled. For a fleeting moment, his smile seemed to be telling me everything would be fine—but now he was the one who was lying.

"So what were you saying about ice sculptures?"

I smiled at his attempt to change the subject. Playing along, I lost myself in my story. "I remember one in particular. I must have been seven or eight but I remember it like it was yesterday. It was this huge carriage made of ice—or maybe I was just really little so it seemed big to me. In any case, I remember going to touch it. It was so smooth and transparent it looked like crystal."

"I wish I could have seen you back then. And to think I was who knows where in the world, living an empty existence, while you were here," he reflected, the thought saddening him. "You must have been adorable."

"Actually, I was a little monster," I admitted.

Evan burst out laughing and propped himself up on his elbows. "I don't believe it."

"Ask my mom and dad. They'll be happy to tell you." I did as he had done, sitting up on the ice. My back was damp. "When they would come looking for me I was always out climbing trees with Peter. I was a total tomboy! It must have been his influence."

Mischief glimmered in Evan's dark eyes, so deep I risked losing myself in them. "A tomboy?" He raised an eyebrow. "That's hard for me to believe, especially after the other night."

Blushing, I changed the subject. "Anyway, there was this huge carriage and I assumed there were a prince and princess inside it. Peter made fun of me but I kept insisting. I can't believe I actually told you that, it's so stupid!"

My sudden embarrassment made him throw back his head back and laugh, but then his laughter became gentler. "I was right, though. Behind that tomboy façade, my sweet thing was already hiding," he said, grinning.

I tightened my lips, blushing at the confession I'd just made, revealing a tiny part of me I'd kept hidden among my memories.

"Hold on." Evan pulled himself up and rested one knee on the ice. I stared at him, puzzled, as he focused on the frozen surface, holding his palms over it.

"Evan, what—"

"Watch this," he whispered without looking at me, his sweet tone not allowing any objection.

"It's not another of your mind-blowing tricks, is it?" I joked nervously. He ignored me. "It's another of your mind-blowing tricks," I murmured. I stared at his hands, but nothing happened. Nothing except . . .

I squinted at the puff of white steam that rose from the cold surface beneath his palms, trying to remember if it had always been there. No, it was the ice that was steaming. The mist thickened beneath Evan's hands until I couldn't see through its silvery veil any more. It looked like something was moving inside it. I didn't understand. Evan's hands slowly moved up and the fog thinned out. The rest of his body followed his hand movements, straightening up as the ice changed shape at his command, leaving me breathless.

Only a moment had gone by. Before me stood a large statue that looked like it was made of crystal. I couldn't believe it—he'd sculpted it out of the ice as though it had been trapped inside it all along and he'd only freed it.

Despite all the astonishing things I'd already seen Evan never failed to surprise me. He'd left me wordless. "Your prince and princess," he announced with a flourish of his hand and a pleased smile on his lips. In silence, I looked from him to the sculpture, which was so perfect it was like I was seeing two actual people captured in the ice.

"Don't look at me like that—you know I can control the elements."

Without replying, I walked around it cautiously, complete astonishment on my face. I'd seen lots of ice sculptures in my life, but none of them came close to the graceful beauty before me now. It was perfect, right down to the smallest detail. There were no words to describe it. A prince was kneeling before his lady, holding a crystal flower out to her.

Reading my mind, Evan walked over to the prince and gently took the rose from his frozen hands. The flower came away as smoothly as if the prince himself had handed it to Evan. He offered it to me.

I hesitated before accepting it, not saying a word. Holding it in my hand like a precious gem, I examined it. "It's beautiful," I said, my voice barely audible. Each transparent petal was perfectly defined, the half-opened bud sparkling like a Swarovski crystal in the silvery moonlight.

How was it possible that all this was happening to me? It felt like I was living in a dream. I brought my other hand closer to trace its contours and stroke the petals with my fingertips.

"Careful," Evan warned me gently—but it was too late. I flinched at the sight of the blood. The petals were as sharp as they were beautiful. I hadn't even noticed I'd cut myself—there had been no pain. A scarlet droplet formed on my pointer finger, grew and slid down, leaving a crimson streak on my skin. As I watched the tiny red droplet, mesmerized, time seem to slow. I carefully observed every instant of its fall to the snow-covered ice. It struck the pure white surface and my heart skipped a beat as though I'd heard it make impact. Though the sound was imperceptible, it silenced my heart for a second.

A premonition. A horrible premonition writhed in my chest.

Evan watched me with concern but seemed unaware of the dark sentiment that throbbed in my veins, demanding my attention. Time froze as the strange sense of foreboding gripped my chest and stopped my heart.

"Everything okay?"

His voice pulled me back to his side as though someone had deactivated the mute button, snapping me out of my trance.

"Gemma, are you okay?" he insisted, alarmed, as I continued to stare blankly at the scarlet spot that had spread on the white carpet of snow.

"I'm fine. It's nothing," I stammered. What was going on with me? Why was I having these weird reactions? Why did time seem to suck me into a black hole where I couldn't breathe? Why did I feel these bone-chilling sensations on my skin? Was it a consequence of defying death and coming back to life?

"Let me take a look." Concerned about the cut, Evan examined my finger for a second.

"Beautiful and dangerous," I said, looking into his eyes. I wasn't talking about the flower.

Evan returned the look. "I can heal it in no time," he said solicitously.

"There's no need, really. It's just a scratch. It'll be fine," I reassured him.

Evan shot me a glance. "I told you you were brave." I wasn't sure whether or not there was mockery in his half smile. "But why wait?" Before I could reply he brushed his thumb over the cut. It closed at his touch. He flashed me a little smile and his expression abruptly changed.

I could tell from the expression on his face that something was wrong. He looked lost. Standing perfectly still, his muscles tensed, he moved his eyes as if to peer over his shoulder.

"Evan—"

"Don't move," he ordered.

My heart lurched. Inexplicably, my instinct had warned me. I'd foreseen it. The sensation I'd felt beneath my skin had been a premonition after all. All at once, I heard a strange, creaking sound. My heart pounded, making it difficult to breathe. Something moved on the slab of ice, too fast for me to make out what it was. I tried to get Evan's attention, but he looked through me, his face full of fury. I could see he was listening for something, but I couldn't tell what. Then I saw it on the ice: *a crack*. It was racing toward me.

"Evan . . ." I whispered, my heart in my throat. A whimper escaped me. He didn't move. The crack stopped at my feet and an eerie silence fell, hushing even the wind around us.

It was a threat.

I looked around, trying to control the panic filling my mind. My instinct already knew what to look for though my eyes hadn't yet managed to spot it anywhere on the ice. It had to be *him*. He must be here.

The Reaper Angel had come to kill me.

My alarmed eyes flew to Evan's. Up to now he'd worn a tough, focused expression but when I looked at him I saw a cunning smile spread across his face. He was ready to kill.

Bewildered, I stared at him, trying to understand, as he clenched his fists at his sides. Suddenly his voice rang out, breaking the icy, ominous stillness. "I should have expected this from a traitor like you." He spoke without turning around, as if someone were behind him.

"Nothing personal."

I jumped at the sound of the voice and whirled in the direction it had come from. My heart skipped a beat when my eyes met his.

Drake.

"Wha—How—" I stammered in shock. He was the Angel who wanted to kill me? No. It couldn't be true. I had to be wrong, yet I saw him clearly a dozen yards away, his cold, detached gaze fixed on us. In his shadowy face there was no hint of the fun-loving, carefree guy I had come to care about. My heart refused to accept it and yet there he was, his hostile gaze locked onto mine.

Drake was there to *kill me.* Something inside me shattered. For the first time I realized what was so different about the look in his eye: it was the look of a predator—and I was his prey. He'd just been waiting for the right moment to attack.

Drake took a step in my direction and Evan, his back to me, shielded me with his body, glaring at him threateningly. "I suppose it wasn't anything personal when you kissed her either," Evan accused him, bitter poison in his tone.

The corner of Drake's mouth rose in a crafty smile. "You mean the first time . . . or the second time?" He was clearly trying to provoke Evan. "Because I have to admit things were a lot more exciting by the pool. You should have seen the way she touched me."

"You pervert!" I accused him, stunned.

He tilted his head and locked eyes with me. "Come on, you mean to tell me you didn't like it?" There was a wicked glimmer in his dark gaze.

"I thought you were Evan!!!" I cried.

Drake shook his head as if to disagree. "Actually, I think part of you knew," he said.

I glared at him. This couldn't be happening. I couldn't believe those words had just come out of Drake's mouth. This had to be a trick—it was all too bizarre. He'd never spoken to me like this before. It couldn't be the same Drake who'd helped me so many times. I simply couldn't accept that he'd betrayed us all, that he, of all people, was my Executioner.

It hurt too much.

"Why?" Evan snarled, his muscles tensed.

"You know what?" Drake shot back in a mocking tone. Evan waited silently, his eyes narrowed to slits as he followed Drake's every movement. "I wanted to see what there was about her—what was so special about her, an insignificant mortal soul—that she deserved the protection of three Subterraneans and a Witch, against everyone and everything."

I winced at his harsh words. I didn't want to listen to him any more. It was too painful.

"And at what cost." He laughed to himself. "I thought maybe if I got close to her I could figure it out. But as I expected, she's not such a big deal—although I can't promise you I won't try her out again." His tone was even more provoking and a smirk spread across his face as he continued to challenge Evan with his eyes. "You know what I'm like—with me, bad habits die hard."

"Why?" Evan repeated in a snarl, his tone fiercer now. His resolute attitude made me guess he'd suspected this horrifying deception for some time now. There was no trace of surprise on his face—just rage.

Drake turned serious. "I'm a servant of Death," he said, as if Evan might have forgotten. "Just like you. Orders come first. There's nothing I can do about it. I can't deny my own nature."

Evan stifled a bitter smile. It was plain from the look in his eyes how difficult Drake's unfaithfulness was for him to accept, how much his brother's betrayal pained him. "You're right. I can't blame you for what they've ordered you to do," he said calmly, "but don't think I'm just going to stand by and watch you do it. You know I won't let you."

Drake cocked his head, his evil eyes locked onto his brother's, a look of amusement on his face. "You going to kill me like you killed Faustian?"

Evan clenched his fists. It had been difficult for him to kill Faust, and doing the same thing to his brother would be infinitely more so. Drake was aware of this and was using it to his advantage. Something flashed through my mind and I turned pale as my heart raced wildly. The poison. It had been Drake who'd taken it from Ginevra's room, and he would be prepared to use it against Evan if they battled. Panic left me breathless. I wished Evan could read my mind so I could warn him. I trembled at the thought of what might happen.

"I'll do what I have to do," Evan said, his tone steely. Vapor rose from the ice on which he stood, as if the fire burning inside him was melting it.

An evil smile spread across Drake's face, making me shudder. "Why don't you try it right now?" he said.

"No!" I cried. I had to prevent it. Drake clearly wanted to seize this chance to catch his brother off guard. I moved closer to Evan, alarmed. "Evan, don't do it," I whispered. "He's the one who took Ginevra's poison."

Evan didn't bat an eye. He attempted to reassure me in a low voice as he shielded me with his body, but there was nothing he could say to ease the panic consuming me. Terror descended on me, almost blocking out his words. His fierce gaze sought Drake's.

Without warning, the ice trembled and lurched beneath my feet. I jumped, a cry escaping me as I lost my grip on the flower I'd had in my hand the whole time. It shattered against the ice with a disquieting sound that penetrated my bones. Evan turned toward me.

"Evan!" I screamed in a desperate warning, but it was too late—I had distracted him.

A blast of ice-cold wind struck him in the chest, hurling him against the sculpture, which exploded in a thousand pieces beneath his weight. I tried to run to him but hesitated when he thrust his arm out in my direction without looking at me. He was already back on his feet. "Get out of here, Gemma. It's dangerous!"

I retreated, remembering the moment I'd distracted him.

The surface of the lake trembled beneath my feet again. All at once the ice exploded and a thousand fragments flew toward me. Evan hurled a fireball into the air, melting most of them, but a few remaining shards lodged in the ice. I turned toward Drake. His fiery gaze met mine, making me shudder with terror.

Evan charged him. They moved too fast for me to make them out clearly. All I could see in the dim light were two blurs battling it out on the ice. Drake hurled Evan in my direction as I watched, my heart shrinking in my chest. I felt small and powerless as he crashed backwards into a tree. It toppled over behind him, uprooted from the frozen ground. When he got up, there was something different in his look. He turned to me and winked, his face shrewd, evil.

I shuddered and recoiled. It was Drake in Evan's guise. The real Evan shot toward him like a bolt of lightning, stopping in front of him. I started. They were identical, like a reflection in a mirror.

Evan's fury was apparent. A vortex of wind blew around him and the ice steamed beneath his feet, creating spirals of fog that encircled him.

Drake changed his physical appearance again, his body smaller. "Why don't you attack me now?" Terror pierced my skin at the sound of my own voice: Drake had taken on my appearance. In his new body he challenged Evan. "Bet you can't." He laughed, an evil laugh that rang out icily through the chill night.

The air around Evan swirled restlessly as if expecting him to rush Drake from one second to the next. He was more enraged than ever.

"Nah," Drake said, "you don't have the guts. You're so predictable."

Evan ignored his provocation and his eyes seemed to ignite. All around him a vortex of air rose up like a barrier. The solid mass of air became fire, then earth, water, and again air. He hurled it at Drake, who still had my appearance, and it flung his brother far into the distance.

Evan turned to me. "Run! Gemma, you need to go!" His tone permitted no objections. "Hurry! Take the car!" he ordered, worried.

"No!" I protested. "I'm not leaving you here, Evan!"

"Gemma, do as I say!" he growled, glowering at me.

"I said no!" I insisted.

"Then at least get away from the lake. You've got to get off the ice!" he said agitatedly. "Go back to shore and wait for me there."

I flinched, realizing I needed to obey—staying there would only distract him. I rushed to him and kissed him desperately. "Be careful, I'm begging you." Evan rested his forehead on mine. "The poison. Watch out for the poison!"

"Wait for me," he said. His gaze hardened and I realized he wasn't speaking to me any more. "I have some dirty business to take care of," he added, raising his voice.

Out of the corner of my eye, I spotted Drake watching us, perfectly still, not far away. "What a romantic scene."

Evan gave me a gentle push, urging me to leave. "Jealousy can make life bitter. I have what you couldn't have. What's wrong, can't you accept that?" His tone had turned harsh and cruel. "You need to face facts—just because you lost Stella doesn't mean others don't have the right to love."

I glimpsed a glimmer of pain—fleeting yet intense—in Drake's eyes when he heard her name. I wasn't sure, but I thought I saw him flinch—or maybe it was just my imagination. This new Drake seemed incapable of feeling emotion. This Drake hadn't hesitated to wage war on his brother. He'd betrayed him. He'd betrayed us all.

I took a step back, slipping awkwardly on my skates, and skated as fast as I could toward shore, trying not to call attention to myself. I was stunned by how incredibly far away it seemed. All at once a low rumble put me on alert. A second later the ice cracked beneath my weight, bringing me up short. I fell with a crash and lay dazed, as a piercing pain gripped my belly and tore the breath from my lungs. I curled up to ease the pain. After a moment it began to lessen and I tried to get up, but the blade of one of my skates was stuck in the crack in the ice. I attempted to yank it out, shuddering at the metallic squeak it made each time it met with resistance from the ice.

I glanced nervously in Evan's direction, hoping he hadn't noticed. I didn't want to distract him; one false move and Drake could kill him with the poison. Cringing, I saw a tall, powerful figure towering in front of Evan, who staggered back at the sight, almost losing control. Drake had taken on yet another appearance. He was now shrouded in a red mantle that covered his entire body down to his feet. A broad hood concealed his face. Something inside me trembled unexpectedly as I watched the scarlet figure against the pure-white snow.

A deep, hoarse voice issued from the dark hood, uttering words that were incomprehensible to me, though Evan didn't seem to have a problem understanding them. I concentrated harder, a tingle spreading steadily over my skin. I could feel a dark, ancient energy flowing through those unnerving, primordial words that seemed to spring directly from the center of the earth as if they had existed since the beginning of time. Another shiver rushed up my spine. Some obscure instinct told me a much graver danger lurked behind this mysterious creature.

Drake resumed his appearance and Evan hurled a fireball at him. He crashed onto the ice a hundred yards away and the battle began again.

The crack in the ice advanced with an ominous groan, making my heart tremble again. In the blink of an eye, before I had time to realize what was happening, a gap opened and I slipped through it. I held my breath to avoid screaming, then gasped from the chill that sank into my skin. The water was so cold it took my breath away. "Ev—" I sputtered. Water filled my mouth, freezing my lungs. Something was dragging me down. I resurfaced for a few seconds, coughing up the water I'd swallowed, then gasped, filling my lungs with air. My legs felt heavy. I looked around, moving my arms in the water. I had just enough energy to hope I could do it alone, without drawing Evan's attention.

I grabbed hold of a slab of ice that had broken free from the surface and tried to catch my breath but slipped over and over. Something still seemed to be dragging me down. With difficulty I kept myself afloat, at times sinking into the icy lake, on the verge of blacking out.

The water was too cold. I felt like I was drowning. My legs had gone numb and my hands were starting to do the same. Just breathing took a tremendous effort. My chest expanded and contracted slowly and heavily, as if a strap were squeezing my ribcage. I clung to the slab of ice with all my strength but kept slipping.

"GEMMA!"

I heard my name being shouted in the distance. "Ev—" came from my mouth, barely audible. My throat filled with ice-cold water as the lake enveloped me in its freezing mantle. *Don't worry about me*, I wished I could reply as I surrendered to the darkness. But my wish was feeble, full of pain; Evan wouldn't be able to hear me any more.

Suddenly I felt light. My body was so cold now I could no longer feel the cruelty with which the water was freezing me. A wave of heat filled me like an electric charge and my body trembled in response.

I opened my eyes. I was once again on the surface and Evan was kneeling at my side. I felt the warmth of his touch but before it could sink in, something sent me flying. I crashed down onto the ice, where I lay sprawled for a moment, my energy drained. Moving was too painful and too difficult. Just opening my eyes took too much effort. My body wouldn't be able to resist the cold much longer, I could tell.

"Evv-vvv-vvv—" My teeth chattered so hard I couldn't even pronounce his name. Though I couldn't see him, I heard the sound of blows as he continued his battle with Drake and wondered if it would ever end. I struggled to keep my eyes open, knowing that if I fell asleep it would be the end of everything. For a moment the idea seemed comforting.

No. I couldn't lose consciousness, otherwise all Evan's efforts would have been in vain and Drake would win. I couldn't let that happen.

Slowly I forced my eyes open. Their lids were so heavy. Perhaps my eyes were deceiving me, but Evan and Drake seemed miles away, barely visible as they savagely battled each other. It was too difficult to bear. What would winning mean? Killing Drake? What a miserable price victory would exact.

No, there would be no victory in this battle.

I was devastated. I'd pitted two brothers against each other. My life wasn't worth this much. I was too tired to think. Every breath was exhausting and I couldn't tell whether darkness was all around me or if I was about to pass out again. Keeping my eyelids open was becoming more and more difficult; they felt as heavy as lead. All at once there was silence. I couldn't even hear the incessant spasmodic chattering of my teeth from the cold.

"Gemma!" As distant as an echo, Evan's voice tore me out of my isolation and I opened my eyes again. He and Drake were closer now, but it was still hard for me to make them out clearly. "You've got to keep awak—"

Darkness.

"Gemma! Stay with me, please!" he shouted again, desperation straining his voice.

I focused on Evan's face, twisted into a mask of hatred and suffering, bitterness and torment. His eyes mirrored his pain. I couldn't die now, of all times. This couldn't actually be the end of everything. And yet I was so tired . . .

My eyes went to Drake who was staring at Evan with a triumphant expression. If I died, Evan wouldn't be able to keep him from taking me with him. I couldn't let that happen. Gathering the little energy I had left, I fought as hard as I could to stay awake and lucid. I was determined not to surrender to my destiny.

Drake abruptly froze as if he'd seen something terrifying over Evan's shoulder, and vanished. His parting words, "We'll meet again soon," hung in the air. The warning note in his tone made me tremble.

Evan rushed to me, his face filled with concern. "Everything's going to be fine," he whispered tenderly. I opened my eyes and winced at the sight of the wounds on his face and body. Seeing the anxiety in my eyes, he shushed me before I could speak. "It's over." His tone softened, as did his expression, and my eyes closed again.

"You need to warm her," someone said in a kind, authoritative voice. Ginevra? I hadn't realized she was there too. I still didn't have the strength to open my eyes and make sure. Someone took off my skates.

"My God," Evan murmured.

"Her body won't hold out much longer. Look at her feet! She needs warmth."

Evan was already on top of me. "I'll take care of her," he said tenderly.

Heat spread slowly inside me, growing stronger and more comforting until it burst into a powerful energy that warmed every fiber of my being, filling my body from head to toe. A moment later, blurred images raced by in my mind as if my thoughts were whirling on an out-of-control carousel.

I opened my eyes. Evan's face was the first thing I saw. Simon and Ginevra were also leaning over me. "You're all here," I murmured, still dazed. "I sure keep you guys busy, don't I?" I joked, then became serious again. "Where is he now?"

It was Evan who answered. "He's gone." His eyes went to Ginevra's. "Seems he's afraid of you," he said intently, holding her gaze as if privately communicating with her.

"This is insane," Ginevra muttered as if to herself, a desperate look in her eyes. "Evan, tell me I'm wrong. Tell me your thoughts are lying, Evan!" It sounded like an order, though there was a pleading note in her voice.

Evan's expression hardened and Ginevra looked devastated.

"Would somebody mind telling me what's going on?" said Simon, intruding on their silence.

"It's Drake," I answered in a tiny voice, my heart crushed by guilt. I swallowed, trying to loosen the knot in my throat. "He's been the one behind it the whole time. He's the Executioner sent in to kill me."

A glint of ice flashed in Simon's eyes. He looked horrified by the revelation. "No," he whispered, gazing blankly over the lake, "you guys must be wrong." He continued to shake his head, seeming overwhelmed by shock and pain.

"I wish we were," I said slowly.

"It's impossible!" Simon insisted.

Evan looked directly into his brother's eyes. "No. It isn't." His hard tone banished every doubt. "The only way to get at Gemma was from the inside. The Elders knew nobody could get close to her with us around."

"Nobody except one of us," Simon broke in. He looked devastated by the reasoning behind the nefarious plan that had pitted us against each other.

"Exactly. Drake's the youngest member of the family and they knew it."

"No. I can't believe it. He would never do that," Ginevra said, looking as crushed as the others by the painful betrayal. "The fact that he's been with us for less time doesn't make him easier to influence. I can't accept that."

"You have to," Evan ordered in a growl, giving her a hard look. "Drake's made his decision. No matter how much he meant to me, I'll do whatever it takes to stop him."

"Evan!" Simon gasped reproachfully.

"Don't forget, Simon, *he* was the one who attacked *us*! He was about to kill Gemma tonight," Evan snarled. "And it wasn't the first time he'd tried."

"The poison," Ginevra said, suddenly gripped by the realization. "He's the one who took it from my room! I wonder why he hasn't used it yet."

"I don't know, but he won't hesitate to use it next time. That's why we need a plan," Evan stated, so determined, so confident it seemed impossible he was talking about killing his own brother.

"The last time you said that, things didn't turn out so well," Ginevra reminded him, sarcasm in her voice.

"This time we won't make any mistakes. What Drake is doing is reprehensible, but I can't blame him for not standing up to the Elders. I understand. I was on the verge of making that same decision to follow orders myself, though I already knew I loved Gemma. Why would he have disobeyed them?"

"For you," Ginevra was quick to say.

"His soul is on the line," Evan said, resolute.

"Still, it's insane. I would have bet no one would ever manage to separate us," Ginevra whispered, gazing sadly into space.

"Looks like you would have lost that bet." Evan's tone was matter-of-fact, as if he weren't bothered by the situation, but I knew that wasn't the case. "Drake was faced with a decision: with us or against us. He made up his mind, and we're going to act accordingly."

This time I couldn't justify Drake, not even to myself. What he'd done was inconceivable.

"Bullshit!" Simon burst out, overcome with rage. "Drake's never believed in Redemption! He would never have betrayed us for that."

"Seems he changed his mind," Ginevra said coldly.

"Evan," I ventured, goosebumps rising on my skin at the haunting memory, "who was that man with the hood? Why did Drake take on his appearance?" My words sliced through the air like the crack of a whip. They seemed to sting Simon and Ginevra more than the freezing air. Evan's face turned grim.

"It was an Elder," he said somberly.

Beside him, Simon tensed. "What are you talking about, Evan?" he said, shocked. "How can you be so sure? No one's ever seen an Elder!" I could hear in his tone that he wanted an explanation.

"You're wrong," Evan replied coldly. "I've seen an Elder before—when I summoned the Màsala to ask to be relieved of the mission to kill Gemma."

We could read the shock in Simon's eyes. His face turned to a mask of ice. "I thought you'd summoned them in your mind! My God, Evan, it was enough of a suicide mission as it was. But they—" Simon pressed his lips together as if trying to hold back a curse. "They *showed* themselves to you, for God's sake? Why didn't you tell us?"

"I didn't see any need to," Evan said.

Simon let out an exasperated sigh. "Where did it happen?" he asked.

"In the woods. What do you want me to say? I wasn't expecting it myself. They already knew what consequences there would be if I deserted, they already knew the feelings hidden in my heart. They'd already perceived them before I was aware of them myself, and they knew how many Subterraneans would pay the price. I guess that was why they thought it was best to personally intervene and try to change my mind, persuade me that it had to be done. They talked as if the fate of the whole world depended on Gemma's death, like it was a question of the utmost importance." Evan snorted, his lips twisted into a grimace, then faced Simon again, his eyes intense. "Not only did the Màsala refuse my request, they *demanded* I carry out their order—but I didn't."

"Wait a minute," said Ginevra, who looked as if she hadn't dared interrupt until then. "During the battle what you saw wasn't actually an Elder . . . but how could Drake have known what they look like?"

Our baffled faces shot to Evan's in search of an answer to the mystery but his expression had already darkened, shrouded by an impenetrable veil.

"He said something," I told Simon. "I couldn't tell what language it was, but it sounded ancient."

"Sanskrit," he deduced, looking grim.

"Evan, did you understand what—"

The darkness of Evan's expression made me cringe and the words died in my throat. He clenched his fists at his sides and his jaw tightened as he answered my unfinished question. "He's not going to stop until he kills you."

An eerie silence enveloped us all. A silence that extended to our hearts.

23

DARK OMEN

The sun hadn't yet risen over the silent town of Lake Placid. Snow blanketed everything in a fluffy white mantle. I stared at it through the picture window in Evan's living room, but all I saw was the dark halo encircling my heart.

Still in shock, the others continued their discussion, searching for a solution. Their conflicting emotions were keeping them from formulating a plan to kill the brother with whom they'd lived for such a long time—longer than my entire life.

I was miserable. Guilt gripped my heart like a tether pulled so tight it made it bleed. Even so, I tried hard to hide it, maybe because I was afraid the others would finally realize it was all my fault. Regret burned me like acid corroding my stomach. The feeling was unbearable.

From time to time, reflected in the window, I saw Evan steal a glance at me as Simon healed his wounds. Only after Evan had taken off his shirt had I seen the bloody gashes on his body.

"My God, look what he did to you," Ginevra had said, her voice broken with dismay over Drake's brutality. "I still can't believe it was him." Her comment had been met with silence.

Ginevra returned to the subject now, a new awareness in her eyes. "You already suspected him," she said, turning to Evan. It wasn't a question. "How could I not have picked up on your suspicions?" she wondered aloud, self-reproach in her tone. "When did you figure it out?"

I turned to look at Evan too, waiting for him to answer. He hesitated a few seconds, staring blankly ahead as if recalling the memory were painful. "He attacked us when we were in the café, but at that point I wasn't suspicious at all. I didn't sense the presence of any Subterraneans except him, but I thought he was there for the guy who'd been riding the motorcycle. That's what he wanted me to believe," Evan said as if just figuring it out now. "Then he caused the accident with my car. That's when I realized it wasn't over, that it was happening again." Evan paused, still shaken by the memory. "That afternoon he tried it again, in the woods."

"I still don't get it," said Simon. "What made you suspect Drake?"

"That afternoon, before the car accident, we went to a hangar not far from Lake Placid. I took Gemma up for a ride in the old fighter plane that used to be Drake's." I instantly noticed the surprise on Ginevra's face. She was wondering how Evan could have kept it a secret from her. "I was expecting to be attacked at any moment, although I tried not to let Gemma see how worried I was." He glanced at me. "What happened in the café had alarmed me. But then nothing happened."

We all gazed at him in silence.

"So I figured my suspicions were unfounded and that they hadn't come back to hunt Gemma down after all. It would have been the ideal opportunity for anyone who wanted to kill her. I'd offered them the perfect chance to attack. And if they had, I would have been prepared—but nothing happened." He stopped, gazing into space again. "Later the car went out of control and someone kept me from stopping it. That's when I thought of Drake and something he'd said just a few days before when I'd told him where I was going to take Gemma: he said he didn't want to see that plane ever again. He wanted me to get rid of it. I knew how much he suffered whenever he went near that place. Still, I couldn't accept the idea—it was so far-fetched. When he kissed Gemma my suspicions grew stronger, though I still wasn't completely sure. I went to Roomer's because I was furious about what he'd done and what I suspected he meant to do. I wanted to give him a warning, make him change his mind while there was still time. Or maybe deep down I still hoped I was wrong. Clearly I wasn't. In that case, I could at least have gotten him away from the house—that was already something."

"How did you manage to keep me in the dark about all this?" Ginevra was shocked. She still couldn't believe it was possible.

"I've honed my skills over the years," he said with dull sarcasm. "I can block my thoughts and keep anyone from getting into my mind. Besides, don't forget I have my powers too, including the power to influence *your* mind. I didn't want to worry you guys until I was sure. Until tonight," he repeated bitterly.

"What do we do now?" his sister asked.

I listened to them distractedly, staring blankly out the window as the first timid rays of sunlight began to illuminate the garden. Their voices reached me like a distant echo, almost as if I weren't part of the group right now. Maybe taking part in their pain was too much for me. Maybe I couldn't handle being the cause of it. I'd never seen them so upset before.

"First of all you two need to choose whose side you're on," Evan said steadily. I turned to look at him. The others' eyes were fixed on him. "You and Simon aren't obligated to stand by us. I won't ask you to do it. You're free to choose or declare your neutrality. I won't blame you if you decide not to get involved. Gemma and I can handle this on our own."

"No," Simon replied firmly. "What Drake has done is underhanded, atrocious. He had no right," he said, his voice stern. "He might have sided against us and chosen to follow orders, but he still should have treated her differently." He looked at me for a moment, righteous anger in his eyes. "Drake showed you no respect."

"I barely recognize him," Ginevra murmured distractedly. "Now I know why he was avoiding me all the time—he didn't want me to read his mind and find out his true intentions."

"The Elders thought of everything," Simon went on, still stunned. "I mean, he clearly isn't acting alone—I suspect he's working under someone's guidance. He's too young. They would never let him tackle all this on his own. It would be a suicide mission and *they* can't afford that. Besides, some of his behavior just isn't like him. He's always loved being surrounded by beautiful girls, but he would never have done anything so wrong to Evan, of all people."

For a moment a grim silence enveloped us. Simon and Ginevra still hadn't given a definitive answer, and the tension they felt about their decision was plain to see in their faces.

"We're with you," Ginevra stated, speaking for both of them.

Evan's face instantly relaxed and he let out a long sigh, as if he'd been holding his breath the whole time. Having Simon and Ginevra on our side was a far-from-negligible detail.

Simon rested his hand on his brother's shoulder. "We could never abandon you. You can count on us," he confirmed, though Ginevra had clearly spoken for both of them. "You're part of a team as long as you're playing on the right side of the field. Drake isn't on our side any more, though it pains me to accept it." His voice broke. "Personally, I don't feel like standing around doing nothing when someone needs me. Ginevra and I will be on the playing field with you," he concluded, sounding more confident.

"What do we do now?" Ginevra asked, turning to Evan. "We can't sit around waiting for him to attack. It's too dangerous. We need to be in full control of the situation." Her green eyes began to sparkle. "We need to act, and act fast." Evan looked absorbed in his sister's words. "But most importantly, we can't forget he stole my poison. That means that unless we stop him before it's too late, he'll use it against us. It's not just for Gemma any more."

"I wonder why he hasn't used it yet," Simon added, voicing the question we all shared.

"We're all wondering that," Ginevra said.

"The vial seemed empty," Evan said. "Maybe he thought it wouldn't be enough, that exposing himself that much was too risky. I mean, he was counting on our trusting him, and if we'd caught him with the poison it would have ruined that. No, it's crazy."

Ginevra shook her head. "Its odor was still strong. I could even smell it with the vial closed when I opened the drawer I'd hidden it in. I seriously doubt any Subterranean could survive if Drake decided to use it on them."

Evan and Simon exchanged puzzled glances, obviously not understanding. Then why had I understood instantly? I remembered perfectly well what Ginevra was talking about—the pungent smell was branded on my memory. Sometimes I even thought I could smell it when I woke up in the morning. It was probably because of the shock connected to the memory, the trauma I'd undergone that day. But I knew for a fact that Evan had told me the poison was odorless and tasteless. Was it possible it had a different effect on humans? Maybe it was a punishment for the Subterraneans—not being able to sense the only weapon capable of killing them.

Their conversation snapped me back to reality.

"He hasn't used it yet, which means he still has it, and that complicates everything." Ginevra was leading the discussion again. "We had an advantage over Faust, but this time we're fighting on equal terms." As she spoke, she shot Simon concerned glances, probably worried about him.

I stared at the floor, feeling guilty again. No one had anything else to say.

"Damn it!" Evan's furious voice sliced through the dismal silence we were lost in. "Not now!" he said through gritted teeth. After a moment, his expression became more resigned.

Ginevra gazed at him regretfully for a second. To my dismay, I understood. He had to leave. I looked him in the eye, forcing myself not to seem alarmed, though the idea that he was leaving me right now made me tremble. After everything that had happened today, I wasn't sure I could face anything else, especially without Evan's support. I was exhausted and couldn't even remember the last time I'd slept or eaten.

Evan looked at me, a mix of devastation and rage in his eyes. Without coming closer, he clenched his fists, his eyes on mine. The intense silence seemed to fill with his unspoken words.

"Evan," I murmured, almost to myself, in a frail voice.

"I'm not leaving now," he growled.

"We'll be here with her," Ginevra reassured him. "There's nothing for you to be afraid of."

Evan shook his head. "No. I said I'm not leaving," he insisted. "I can't. I can't leave her now, of all times."

"He won't attack right away," Simon pointed out. "He'll need to recover after tonight's fight too, and we still don't have a plan for how to face him. We need time."

Evan clenched his jaw, deep in thought. He looked torn. "To hell with it! I don't care!" He looked at me again and moved closer. "I'm staying here with you."

I wavered for a moment, confused by his expression. It had become tender but still had a touch of desperation in it. I didn't know what to say, though I was sure of what I wanted and sure of what would be best. Unfortunately, the two things weren't the same. "You should go," I said, my voice dull. It wasn't convincing enough. I tried to regain my self-control, even though I knew someone else in the room was aware of exactly what I was feeling. "Nothing's going to happen to me. I don't want you to compromise yourself for me even more than you already have." For a second, I thought my words had been almost believable.

"Screw the rules!" he exclaimed, still furious. Then his tone sweetened for me. "I have nothing more to lose if I stay, but I could lose everything if I go."

"It's not true you have nothing more to lose," I said. "You've already risked enough for me." Evan came closer still and my voice began to waver. "I won't—I won't let you throw away your only hope of redeeming yourself," I said in a desperate whisper as he rested his forehead against mine. "I want to know you'll be there when . . . one day—I don't want to lose you forever."

Ginevra spoke up. "Evan, she's right. We'll be here with her. You've been gone for far longer periods in the past, even days at a time."

"That was different," he snapped.

"We'll protect her. It's only a few hours," she insisted, trying to reassure him. Her concept of time was a little different from mine, though. What were a few hours to someone to whom time was of no importance? For me it would be an eternity. I could already feel the burden though Evan was still there with me.

He seemed to consider what Ginevra had said. After a moment he looked at me, his expression grim, and nodded slightly, though he didn't seem entirely convinced. He stroked my cheek and slipped his fingers into my hair, his face close to mine. "You sure?" he whispered, studying my face.

I nodded, hoping my eyes weren't giving me away. "How long will you be gone?" I asked timidly. I had to know.

"Until this evening. I'll be back at six." He glanced at the clock on the wall. "It's already seven in the morning," he said reassuringly.

"Seven? School!" I exclaimed.

Evan cut me off, his expression stern. "You're not going to school today. It's too risky. Besides, I'll be calmer if I know you're here with the others. Promise me you won't leave the house," he whispered, articulating each word.

"All right," I said. "Of course I promise. I promise." After all, skipping another day of school wouldn't be the end of the world. "Although my parents—"

"I'll use mind control on them," Evan said. "Don't worry. I'll stop by your place before leaving."

"Okay," I said, resigned. "See you back here at six, then." I forced a smile. There was something different in the way he looked at me: a profound sadness, a bitterness, shone through, as if he were afraid this would be the last time he saw me.

"I won't be a single minute late," he whispered, lifting my chin. He gave me a little smile, locking his gaze onto mine for a long moment. "I have to go," he said, louder, so the others could hear him too. Turning toward his brother and sister with the most serious expression I'd ever seen on his face, he said, "Protect her at all costs. I'm counting on you two. We've got to make the first move this time. Think of a plan while I'm gone. Meanwhile I'll do the same."

When Simon and Ginevra nodded, Evan turned back to me. I looked at him, a terrible feeling deep in my chest. My eyes locked onto his and a profound sense of desperation grew in my heart as tears welled up in my eyes. Suddenly I didn't want him to go any more—I wanted to keep him there with me. Part of me was screaming at myself to stop him. "Kiss me," I begged, forcing back the tears.

Evan moved his lips closer to mine, seeming to sense that I shared his desperation. Gripping my face in his hands, he kissed me ardently, as if no one else were in the room. For a moment the contact with his mouth made me dizzy. His lips, softer than ever, moved gently against mine. Small, tender kisses alternated with ones that were longer, more passionate—*desperate.*

When he pulled away and rested his forehead on mine, a shiver of terror ran down my spine and I felt a deep sense of loss. My gaze met his and again the terrible sensation that this would be our last kiss came over me. I shuddered from the power of the ghastly premonition.

Evan ran his hands down my arms and rubbed them gently because I had goosebumps. He took my hand and smiled at me, but it didn't dispel the awful feeling. Could it really be a premonition? Would I really die during the few short hours Evan would be gone? I looked into his eyes but couldn't see him; my mind was elsewhere, adrift.

He ran his thumb over my lower lip to bring me back to reality, shaking me out of my fog. I looked him in the eyes again, forcing a smile that he returned.

"I'll take the taste of your lips with me," he whispered, his face an inch from mine.

"And I'll be here waiting for you to renew it with another kiss," I said, hoping against hope it was a promise I would be able to keep.

His gaze didn't leave me for a second as he began to disappear before my eyes. The strange agitation stirred more fiercely inside me and my heart responded by accelerating its rhythm. I felt a sudden, desperate impulse to squeeze his hand and keep him there with me before he vanished entirely, but it was too late. Evan was gone. A blade of ice pierced my heart. Never before had I felt so alone.

34

EXTREME DECISIONS

"Don't worry," Ginevra told me. Though I could feel her close by, I barely registered my surroundings. Evan had been gone only a moment, during which I hadn't moved, staring blankly at the spot where he'd been, my mind wandering who knew where. It was as if a black hole had swallowed up all my thoughts. I felt alone without him, and the horrifying certainty that I'd lost him forever stubbornly persisted. Would I really never see him again? The very thought was enough to drain me of all my emotions.

"Gemma." A hand stroked my arm in the same place Evan had touched it a moment ago. I instinctively pulled back as if to protect the memory and looked at her, dazed. "Everything's going to be fine."

I looked into Ginevra's eyes and felt like I was seeing her for the first time. My eyelids fluttered nervously, as if I'd just awakened from a state of shock.

"We won't let anything happen to you. You'll see, the day will go by fast." Evan had said the same thing, but I wasn't convinced. "You should eat something."

"I'm not hungry," I said automatically. My stomach was in knots.

"Yes you are," she said sternly. "You can't afford to get weak now, of all times. You need every last drop of your energy." Her voice was raised in reproach and I didn't have the strength to put up a fight. "Besides, you look exhausted. You need to get some sleep. Let's go to the kitchen. I'll make you something to eat and then you'll go rest," she ordered me firmly.

Not wanting to waste my breath, I did as she said and followed her into the other room. After all, she wasn't all wrong. Maybe it was weakness that was clouding my mind, and that was the last thing I needed.

The silence in the kitchen made it seem even larger than it was. That it felt so empty, on the other hand, was for a completely different reason. I missed Evan. Unable to stop thinking I'd never see him again, tears stung my eyes. I could feel his absence in my stomach.

"The only absence you feel in your stomach is lack of food!" Ginevra said, replying to my thoughts and trying to boost my morale—but the look on my face told her it wouldn't work.

Only a few hours had passed, the minutes ticking slowly by. It seemed like an eternity since Evan had left. Simon and Ginevra moved around the kitchen nervously. I hadn't moved from my seat the whole time, listening to them. I wanted to help, but for some reason all I could think of was the look on Evan's face right before he'd disappeared and the terrible feeling of emptiness and loss he'd left behind.

"There must be something we can do to put an end to this whole thing," Simon was saying.

"Nothing that doesn't involve the one thing you're refusing to think about," Ginevra told him frankly. "You've got to accept it, Simon."

"You think I don't realize that? I'm not denying what has to happen."

"So why don't you say it out loud?" she rebuked him. "You can't, that's why! Simon, if you aren't convinced—"

“Of course I am,” he said firmly. “It’s just that—it’s hard.” His expression turned sad.

“I know, but we’ve already chosen sides. Now we just need to figure out how to play the game: offense or defense. As I see it, we can’t wait for Drake to make the first move. Don’t forget he has poison and he’ll use it against you guys. We’re all involved at this point. He might decide to use it on Evan.” Ginevra paused a moment, looking troubled. “Or on you.” Her eyes glimmered on his. “And I’ll never let him do that. I’m not putting your life in jeopardy. Drake is perfectly capable of making his own decisions and so are we. I’m not going to risk anything happening to you, Simon. We’re going to do what we need to do.” She looked straight at him, in her eyes a sharp light that shone with all the coldness of her true nature. “We’re going to kill him.”

At that moment she was a Witch and Drake was her ancient enemy, a Subterranean to kill. Her prey. The thought hit me so hard I shuddered.

Simon’s face turned grim, but the gleam of pain in his eye showed me he knew Ginevra was right. They would do what they had to do, no matter how painful it was.

Sitting in my corner, I felt smaller and more insignificant than ever. It wasn’t fair that my survival was causing so much grief to the people I loved most. Maybe there actually was some reason I was destined to die and they were making a terrible mistake by defying fate. How many more lives would be cut short because of me? How many more Angels would be killed so I could live? Who would be next? Because I was certain—it would never really be over. I wasn’t so sure any more that my life was worth that much. And yet I couldn’t stand the thought of losing Evan forever.

Hidden behind my feelings of guilt, my egotistical survival instinct reared its head from time to time, eclipsing everything else, urging me to fight, to cling to life tooth and nail, to do whatever it took to avoid losing Evan.

I couldn’t give him up. Not for anything in the world. Not for *anyone* in the world. I didn’t care how selfish or even evil what I wanted was; I wasn’t going to lose Evan, not even if prolonging my life meant sacrificing the lives of many others. Everything had its price. Someone else would pay the price of my destiny. I had to accept that because the alternative was inconceivable.

A shudder ran down my arms and for a moment I felt an odd sensation under my skin. Excitement mixed with something else I couldn’t decipher. Power, maybe? I quickly composed myself, shocked by my own thoughts, and looked around in alarm, hoping Ginevra hadn’t heard them. She was still talking to Simon, so wrapped up in their conversation she didn’t seem to be paying attention to me, though I couldn’t be completely sure.

I silently reflected on the strange, uncontrollable sensation I’d just had. It was like there was another Gemma inside me, one I’d never known, and my mind had temporarily shut down, letting her emerge, allowing some primitive instinct to take over—a dark instinct I could feel in my bones. It scared me because it felt like an integral part of me. The sensation wasn’t entirely new to me—it wasn’t the first time it had happened. I’d felt it before during the last few weeks, like a secret switch inside me had been flipped, instantly filling me with unfamiliar wrath. It was a rebellious, uncontrollable feeling that made me unexpectedly boil with rage. The last time it had made me scream at Ginevra.

What the hell was happening to me? Was it some kind of side effect of having come back from the dead? Maybe Evan was wrong—maybe I wasn’t as strong as he thought and I was falling to pieces.

No, I was just under stress. It was an understandable reaction. The emotional pressure I’d been subject to was clearly too much for me. After all, everybody has their limits. No matter how hard I tried to hide it, even from myself, I actually felt so fragile, beyond exhausted. My nerves were as taut as a strand of hair against a razor, trembling at the faintest puff of air. All it would take was one tiny movement for me to touch the razor's edge and snap. It felt like that moment was about to arrive.

"You're not getting involved." Simon's voice rang through the room, his fiery eyes locked onto Ginevra's.

"I know how to defend myself," she retorted. "Don't think I'm going to stand by doing nothing while Drake hurts you."

"I've already told you, nothing's going to happen to me."

"My poison is lethal to you too!" Ginevra shouted.

"Just like his fire is to you!"

"We've trained hard and we'll keep on training hard until the time comes. I'm ready. It won't be the first time for me—I've battled lots of Subterraneans before."

"That was ages ago!"

"You can't protect yourself against the poison, but I can protect myself from his attacks. Besides, you're forgetting that he's afraid of me."

"No," he repeated firmly. "It's out of the question."

"Simon, we'll train harder. Trust me, it's the best choice. Let me do this," Ginevra said, trying hard to persuade him.

Crushed by a feeling of powerlessness, I looked directly at Simon for the first time just as his crystalline eyes flickered and a sly smile spread over his face. It looked familiar for some reason, and I realized it was the same smile that appeared on Evan's lips whenever he had an idea. I tried hard not to let myself be overcome by nostalgia, since it threatened to drag me into the vortex that led to Evan. Maybe it was natural for every thought to lead me back to him.

I turned to look at Ginevra. Her eyes had narrowed to slits as she studied Simon's mind with keen interest. "What are you thinking?" I said, speaking for the first time.

They turned toward me as if they'd forgotten my presence. I looked at each of them in turn. Simon hesitated, giving Ginevra time to carefully assess his idea.

"Interesting," she whispered, deep in thought.

I glanced at Simon and then turned back to Ginevra, waiting for one of them to answer me.

"Drake is expecting a battle." Simon's expression gradually became more cunning and determined as he explained. The plan began to take shape outside his mind. "But he's in for a surprise."

"It's a desperate plan," Ginevra cautioned him, still probing his mind.

"Desperate times call for desperate measures."

They both turned their eyes on me. I looked back and forth between them, puzzled. The whole time they'd pretty much excluded me from their conversation, talking to each other as if I weren't there, but now they had a strange light in their eyes as they stared at me, as if I were the key to everything.

"What?" I asked in alarm, but their attention to me disappeared as quickly as it had come. I was invisible again.

"Would she go that far?" Simon asked Ginevra, almost in a whisper, without taking his eyes off me. I had the impression they were both studying me. "It might work but we need to assess all the risks," Simon warned her. "It would take incredible courage."

"I don't think that's a problem. She can do it. I know she can."

"How can you be so sure?"

"I just am, trust me. I can't explain why—it's like an instinct. Just believe me on this," Ginevra told him.

"But you saw how she reacted the first time!"

"This time it'll be different," she said, determined. "Things have changed."

I was lost. Simon wasn't so convinced of his own plan any more?

"Besides, I'm not even sure Evan would allow it."

"Would you guys mind telling me what you're talking about?" I blurted. "What wouldn't Evan agree to?" They both stared at me again. "What do you have to tell me?" I realized my voice was trembling. "You have a plan, don't you?"

"Not necessarily," Simon answered.

Ginevra rephrased his answer: "You'll be the one to decide that," she said gravely.

I looked at her, bewildered. What was going on? "I'm too tired to play guessing games," I said. Their mysterious discussion had left me exasperated. "What is your plan, exactly?"

They stared at me for a long moment, as surprised as I was by how calmly I'd asked. Ginevra was studying me, I was sure of it. There was nothing I could hide from her. "Simon has an idea." I waited for her to go on, my impatience mounting. "I think it's a good plan, but you would be directly involved." Her gaze, deep as a stormy sea, lingered on me.

"That's why the decision is up to you," Simon added. "No one will blame you if you decide to refuse."

They were both gazing at me attentively. What was going on? Could Simon read my thoughts now too? From the way he was looking at me, it certainly seemed like it. My heartbeat accelerated unexpectedly. What was with all the tension I saw on their faces? And why would Evan not accept their plan? My instinct gave me the answer: I was going to have to do something dangerous.

"Would you mind telling me what's going on?" I asked again, though I wasn't so sure I wanted to know any more.

"The idea might work. In fact, I *know* it'll work. It's an excellent plan," Ginevra exclaimed, "but it requires a courageous decision on your part." She moved a few steps closer. "And I know you're capable of handling it."

"Tell me something I don't already know," I shot back, out of patience.

"Gemma," Ginevra began cautiously, "you already know my poison is the only weapon that can kill Drake." I nodded without speaking. "But open battle might be too risky at this point for any of us. You know Evan won't hesitate to fight for you."

"We're almost positive somebody's got Drake's back," Simon added. "He isn't working alone, and that's definitely not to our advantage. We might lose." His tone hardened.

Was that really a possibility?

"And we can't forget he has my poison with him—enough for a lethal dose." Ginevra said. She paused to study my reaction and read the thoughts that whirled confusedly in my mind like a helium balloon at the mercy of the wind. Their plan must be far from pleasant if it was taking them this long to explain it. She continued. "That's why we need to avoid a direct battle . . . and set a trap for him. We need to catch him off guard," she concluded firmly.

"All right," I whispered, my voice barely audible, "but what's my part in all this?" I was starting to feel seriously worried.

"Actually, that all depends on you," Ginevra said gravely.

I turned to Simon who was staring at the floor as if avoiding my eyes. The idea had been his, and yet on his face was a look of . . . uncertainty? Guilt? I couldn't tell. And what were we talking about, exactly?

"I'll do whatever it takes." My voice trembled. I wasn't completely sure I would be able to keep that promise, but after all it was entirely my fault they were in this situation in the first place. "Tell me what you have in mind," I said, my tone more convinced this time.

"Good," Ginevra murmured, almost to herself, "because you're the only one who can slip Drake the poison without his noticing."

Her words hit me hard, like a punch to the gut. "Me? What are you talking about? H-how could I?" I asked, confused.

"With a kiss."

I jumped in my seat, my blood running cold. It was finally clear why they'd been so hesitant and mysterious. A mind-numbing panic filled me and I tried not to show how incredibly shaken I was. "You're saying I would have to *kiss* him?" I shot nervous looks at Ginevra and Simon, who was still avoiding my eyes.

"No one is forcing you, of course," he said, "but that's all we've got. For now, it's our only hope. We can't put the poison in a glass of water—Drake has no need to drink and would be suspicious if you asked him to. Not to mention how dangerous it would be if he discovered our plan."

It took me a moment to grasp what he meant. They had wondered out loud if I was brave enough and now I was wondering the same thing. Ginevra seemed convinced, but how could they be so sure, if not even I knew the answer to that question? I would have to let Drake come near me, and he could kill me with a wave of his hand. That in itself was enough to make me hesitate.

The thought of kissing anyone other than Evan of my own free will was hard enough already, but it was impossible to wrap my brain around the fact that this kiss would be fatal. No matter how many times Simon and Ginevra told me I wouldn't be forced to do it, I knew it wasn't true, at least in part. I had to do it whether or not I wanted to. It was my turn. I had to protect Evan.

It was up to me to kill Drake. I calmly repeated the thought in my mind as the two of them assessed my silence. Simon, who had stood aside, was also waiting for me to speak.

When I finally opened my mouth, I'd made my decision and it was final. "I'm the one who set you against each other. I'll do whatever you ask."

"Don't speak too soon," Simon warned. "First you need to hear the hardest part."

His harsh tone made me flinch. "What could be more terrible than kissing Drake . . . and *killing* him?" I asked, forcing out the last two words. How would I be able to kill Drake if I could barely stand the mere thought of doing it? I studied their faces and waited.

After a silence that felt endless, Ginevra explained all in one breath: "You wouldn't be immune to the poison."

A cold, bitter wave crashed over me even before I'd fully grasped what she'd just said. My body had understood and reacted instinctively. "You're saying—" I murmured in shock.

"The poison is going to kill you too," Simon said ruefully.

I was stunned. My thoughts echoed in my mind as they continued talking, freezing everything inside me. For a moment I felt cut off from them, like I wasn't in the room any more. I was alone—alone in my desperation.

So death would come after all, and not by chance. I felt myself wandering through the darkness of those absurd words. My mind seemed to be lost, or maybe it didn't want to return at all. I wished I could run away from this place, from these people, even from myself, and hide somewhere dark and safe.

I heard something in the background and barely managed to realize someone was talking to me, but I couldn't make out the words, still deafened as I was by the last ones. They whirled through my head, drowning out everything else. Everything was so distorted, so confusing . . .

Their voices echoed in my head, shouting the bone-chilling words I didn't want to hear: I had to die.

All at once the murmur stopped and the sudden silence tore me out the trance I'd fallen into, dragging me back to the room. "You're saying that—" I stopped, unable to go on.

Simon and Ginevra continued to watch me silently. "We told you it would be difficult," Ginevra said.

"And we'll understand if you decide to back down, though we don't have much time to come up with another plan. If Drake attacks again, we'll have to face him, and we're not sure how that will turn out," Simon explained.

I winced, thinking of Evan. He was all that mattered to me. Everything else—including my own life—was less important.

"Simon's plan is really good," Ginevra added, "and there's no way it can fail, unless you're discovered."

Did they really think I was capable of this? I would ruin everything like I always did one way or another, and put them in danger for the millionth time. Why didn't they realize that? Why did they trust me so much?

"The only person who doesn't trust you is you," Ginevra said, replying to my thoughts.

"What if I fail?" I murmured, the knot in my throat growing tighter.

"You won't. We trust you, Gemma," Simon assured me.

"What happens afterwards?" I said, my voice barely audible, forcing myself to hide my trembling.

Simon walked over to me and looked me in the eye for the first time. "You don't need to worry about that." There wasn't a trace of fear or doubt in his voice. "We'll be there with you, even though you won't be able to see us. When the right moment comes we'll get there in time. You just need to focus on what you have to do and it will all be over. We'll take care of the rest. We've already done it once before. We know now how to handle the situation and we'll be able to bring you back without any problems. You'll return, but he won't."

Simon's reassuring tone eased some of my tension. I felt drained. In a way, I had no words to say or questions to ask.

"You can always say no," Ginevra repeated.

I turned to look at her. *No, I can't,* I replied in my mind. I owed it to him—to them all. "I'll do it," I announced, forcing myself to sound determined. "Tell me what I have to do."

Simon shook his head. "This is insane," he burst out. My eyes shot to his. "Forget we even said it. We'll think of something else."

"Simon, there's no time," Ginevra rebuked him.

"Evan will never go along with it. We're wasting our breath."

"Why? Don't forget his last plan entailed risks, and they weren't any less drastic than yours. He was aware of the dangers but he accepted them." Simon looked torn and Ginevra studied his silence. "Fine. Do you have a better idea?"

Simon clearly didn't. "All I'm saying is that it's insane! We can't let him get so close to Gemma."

If they didn't even believe in the plan, how could I?

"It's dangerous, that's true, but we'll be there with her. It'll work and none of us will get hurt. Now cut it out, Simon—you're confusing her!"

"It's up to me to decide, right?" I said. They looked at me. "Simon, is there any possibility you won't be able to bring me back?" I asked, just in case.

Simon glanced at me, seeming unsure whether or not to relieve my doubts with his answer. "No. Your death will only be temporary. As far as that goes, you have nothing to worry about. It would be even briefer than last time."

"But last time," I said cautiously, "there were three of you there to heal me."

My point left him wordless for a second, but he composed himself. "We don't need Drake. This time we won't need to heal wounds all over your body, so it'll be easier. You'll only die from the effect of the poison. Other than that, your body will remain intact and unharmed."

"I don't see a problem then," I said firmly. I looked him in the eye, almost as if I were the one reassuring him. "I can do it," I said in a determined tone even I didn't recognize.

"You sure?" he asked, still wary.

I looked at him and then at Ginevra before answering: "I'm doing it." I stared at them hard to emphasize my decision.

"Fine. We have to act fast then. We can't risk his making the first move, so you need to be prepared to face him when the opportunity presents itself."

I flinched when I realized it was actually going to happen. I'd agreed. The *end* would be the solution. "When do you think he might show up?" I asked anxiously, turning to Ginevra.

"We can't know for sure. He'll need time to recover and I doubt he would decide to attack too soon, but meanwhile he might use his powers to get close to you again. I'll give you some of my poison. You'll need to take special care of it. You must keep it with you *everywhere* and *at all times*. Then, when the opportunity arises—and I don't think it'll take that long—you can't hesitate for even a second or Drake might guess our plan."

I trembled at the thought. Ginevra had been clear in the strict orders she'd given me. They were all counting on me. I couldn't let them down. "We need to tell Evan," I said, worried there wouldn't be time.

"We'll tell him when he gets back," Simon reassured me. "Don't worry."

I sighed with relief. I wasn't prepared for the possibility of carrying out the plan without his support.

"I wouldn't be able to bring you back without him," Simon continued. "I just hope Drake doesn't take advantage of his being gone to get near you," he said, looking concerned.

"What should I do if that happens?" I asked in alarm.

"Nothing risky," he warned. "You can't use the poison until Evan knows about the plan, otherwise you'll complicate things." Simon looked me in the eye to make sure I followed his instructions. "You risk actually dying, Gemma. I can't do it all alone. It's imperative that both Evan and I reach you in time to save you."

"We'll be there even if you can't see us," Ginevra explained. "We'll have to keep a certain distance. That way Drake can feel safe enough to get close without being able to sense our presence. Still, we'll be close enough to get to you in time."

"Fine. I'm ready." I swallowed and looked confidently at Ginevra. "Give me the poison."

She nodded slightly, her eyes fixed on mine. "Come with me."

I did as she said, but after a few steps I turned to look at Simon, puzzled. "Aren't you coming?"

A bitter half smile escaped him. "I don't think that would be a good idea."

"Right." I opened my mouth but closed it a moment later.

Simon was still smiling. "Don't get bitten before it's time or we'll have to scrap the whole plan!" he warned with a wink and a touch of sarcasm.

"If that happens I guess you won't need a plan any more," I reminded him in the same tone, returning the smile and leaving the room.

35

MYSTERIOUS INSTINCT

Ginevra opened her bedroom door casually, disregarding the furious beating of my heart that I was sure she could hear. My blood was pumping so hard I felt my veins throbbing in my temples. This was all so bizarre.

I'd been in this room a hundred times and knew it well—I'd memorized its every detail. Except one, obviously: the vault, which had always been strictly off limits. I'd never paid much attention to it, but now the door seemed larger and heavier, as if it continued to grow out of proportion before my eyes and wanted to crush me. Or maybe it was me who felt smaller and more helpless than ever. In a moment I would walk through that door toward an encounter with my fate.

I'd heard them mention Ginevra's serpent before, though rarely. Usually they preferred not to dwell on the subject. Ginevra came to a halt in front of the door. I was right behind her.

"You can wait outside if you want," she said.

"I'd rather go in," I replied quickly, yearning to give in to the strange instinct that continued to push me toward danger.

With a clack so loud it penetrated my bones, the lock opened and the vault door swung open. Shuddering as I followed Ginevra in, I looked around and realized we weren't in a room, but rather, an enormous, unearthly garden under a lead-gray sky. It was as though the door had opened into a parallel dimension.

When Ginevra moved I followed close on her heels, staying alert. I didn't want her serpent to lunge out and bite me. Of course if it did, it would spare them a few problems. In reply to my thoughts, Ginevra cast me an amused frown. "Just kidding," I said with a grin and a shrug.

All at once her expression turned serious—not worried, just serious. "Don't move," she warned, stopping in front of me calmly. At her words I froze in my tracks. Out of the corner of my eye I noticed a movement just over my shoulder. "Don't worry," she reassured me. "He won't hurt you."

Every fiber of my body trembled as the movement continued. I stood rigid and saw it: her serpent. It moved with Ginevra's grace, weaving in harmonious patterns through the branches above my head.

"He's under my control," she continued to reassure me. "He won't do anything to you. He obeys my thoughts."

I weighed her words and something dawned on me: it wasn't fear I was feeling. Something else was trembling inside me, some emotion I couldn't put my finger on.

The serpent moved toward Ginevra, slithering over a large branch so smoothly he almost seemed to float through the air. Ginevra held out her hand and the creature obeyed, sliding sinuously onto her arm. I would never have imagined it, but seeing them together was electrifying.

The serpent coiled gracefully around Ginevra's forearm. "Scared?" she asked me, her voice comforting as I stared at her, fascinated.

"No, I don't think so." It was the truth. "I think it's something else. He's so . . . *magnetic*," I replied as the animal formed a perfect spiral, gliding elegantly up to Ginevra's elbow. When he reached her upper arm, something unexpected happened. My eyes bulged as the serpent fused with her skin.

A glimmer spread over Ginevra's eyes, making them even greener. Their emerald-like light was hard to describe. For a fraction of a second her pupils narrowed and lengthened in imitation of her serpent's, leaving me breathless. She turned to me with the satisfied look an inventor might have when showing off their newest creation for the first time. Unable to believe what I'd just seen, I opened my mouth to speak, but not a sound came out. Ginevra continued to smile at me like someone who's just finished a long journey through the desert and finally quenched their thirst.

The serpent had disappeared beneath her skin, leaving a spiral-shaped silver mark around her arm. *Magnificent* was the only word my brain could come up with.

"You really think so?" she asked, looking honored.

I was even more convinced than before: there was something magnetic about her creature, so powerful and extraordinary. I nodded, unable to take my eyes off the spot on her arm where her serpent had disappeared.

"He's part of me," she whispered, her smile widening as she looked me in the eye in search of understanding.

I flashed her a reassuring smile. After all, I didn't need to read Ginevra's mind to guess how she felt. For centuries her only company had been three Subterraneans, and on top of that she'd always hidden the existence of her creature from them. She'd had to conceal an important part of herself and although Simon had always known her secret, Ginevra could never have shared with him the feelings that bonded her to her serpent. She'd even had to create an impenetrable barrier to separate them. It must have been nice for her to finally be able to share something so important, so personal.

The serpent rematerialized, gliding across Ginevra's skin before my captivated eyes, as if he'd also heard my thoughts and wanted to give me the chance to see him more closely. He spiraled down her arm toward me. Ginevra reached her arm out, a pleased look on her face.

I instinctively moved nearer. The serpent triggered a strong attraction in me, a powerful energy that even the most hidden part of my brain could detect.

We were so close. For a moment, the serpent swayed in front of my face as I gazed at him in fascination. His venom was deadly and he could bite me so quickly I would be dead before I knew it. Yet I wasn't frightened. There was no trace of fear in my body. Quite the opposite—it felt like the serpent was summoning me. The more I looked at him, the more I longed to touch him. It was a visceral need, a need I couldn't control . . .

"Don't get too close," Ginevra warned cautiously. This must have been a completely new experience for her too.

"So small yet so powerful," I murmured, my eyes riveted on the bewitching creature.

"True greatness doesn't depend on size. Sometimes the greatest power resides in the most hidden things, unseen to our eyes. This is the first time I've shown him to anyone in who knows how long."

"Yeah, that's what I would imagine."

"I even keep him away from Simon," Ginevra said as though she needed to explain. She had the serpent slide down into her hands and showed him a tiny glass container the size of a thimble. I admired her movements. I would have given anything for an ounce of her gracefulness.

"He's too dangerous for Simon," she went on, frowning in response to my thoughts. She thought it was crazy that I sometimes looked at her with such admiration. *I* thought it was crazy that she considered *me* to be on the same level as her.

"I thought you said you could control him," I said aloud after our silent disagreement.

"Yes, but I can't guarantee his reaction in such an extreme situation. Simon is still a Subterranean, after all, and it might be too much for a serpent to bear. If his survival instinct kicked in, I would have to—" Ginevra stopped abruptly. There was no need for her to finish her sentence—I already understood. "I do it to protect both of them."

As she said this, the serpent sank his fang into the vial, drawing my attention. The scent was so powerful and immediate it made me dizzy. I almost lost my balance, it was so intoxicating. It was just as I remembered it: intense, overpowering . . . *irresistible.* Who knew what it would be like to taste it. For a second, it almost felt like I was savoring its flavor. I would find out soon enough.

Ginevra raised an eyebrow and looked at me. "It's strange that you can smell it," she said with surprise.

"I thought Subterraneans were the only ones who couldn't," I said, confused.

"Actually, I've never tested it out on a . . . human." She said the last word cautiously.

"Go ahead and say it—I'm not offended. I know perfectly well I'm a human," I reminded her.

"It's just that Angels generally can't smell it."

"That must be an advantage for you Witches."

"I guess."

"Since they can't smell it, they can't anticipate the danger, or something like that," I said, still dazed by the scent. Who knew why humans were allowed to smell it? From the look on Ginevra's face, I deduced that she was wondering the same thing.

"Done," she told me, setting her serpent back on a large branch that hung directly over our heads. "We have the poison." She raised the vial to show me its contents and a sparkling droplet slid ominously to the bottom, almost dancing—elegant and lethal, just like Ginevra. It was hard to fathom how much power was contained in that tiny vial. I stared at it for a long moment, struggling against the seductive power that tried to pull me into its black coils.

Ginevra tore me from my thoughts. "Still think you can do it?" she asked. "You won't be able to change your mind. Once you've taken the poison you'll have to see it through to the end."

"Explain everything to me," I said without hesitating.

After a long, silent, intense gaze, Ginevra took my hand and cautiously placed the vial in my palm. A shudder ran through me at the contact with the cold glass—or more likely, the awareness of what it contained had triggered my reaction. I had just signed a contract with death and in my hand I held the weapon with which I would take my own life. The key to my own end—or might it be a new beginning? I wasn't sure.

"It's essential that Drake not realize your intentions," Ginevra warned as if I didn't already know that.

"Are you sure I'll have the chance to use it? Who says he won't attack me right away? He might not give me the opportunity to get close enough to kiss him."

"We create our own opportunities. Don't forget he can't come into our house in his real appearance and I don't think you have any intention of leaving for the time being. That means the only way he can get close to you is to take the guise of one of us. He could take on my appearance or Simon's, but that wouldn't make sense, given that he can get a lot closer to you by transforming into Evan. Unless, of course, Evan is already there with you—but I doubt he'll try that again, after what happened last time. My guess is he'll want to approach you when you're alone—that would make more sense. You'll have to seize the chance. Once Evan knows about our plan, we'll set the trap and pretend to leave you alone. I'm sure Drake won't let the opportunity pass him by. At that point you'll have to use all your powers of seduction to lure him close to you. It'll be an invitation I'm sure he won't be able to refuse. Then, making sure he doesn't notice, moisten your lips with the poison. You'll have a few seconds to kiss him."

As Ginevra gave me my instructions, I stared at the little vial and gulped. She rested her warm hand on my shoulder. "Don't worry. I'm sure you won't even have to make an effort. From what I've gathered from your memories, you won't even need to persuade him. It's Drake, remember. This is all part of the game for him. He'll kiss you first, but it will be too late for him by then."

I looked up in time to see a glint in Ginevra's eyes, preceded by a bitter smile. "We'd better not make Simon worry. He's still downstairs waiting for us. I can feel his impatience even through the walls." Ginevra locked the mighty vault and we left her room.

"Yeah, we'd better not." I shut the door behind me.

"You have it on you?" Simon asked, poorly concealing the nervousness in his voice.

I tightened my lips in confirmation and unconsciously gripped the little vial in my sweatshirt pocket. From the contact with my skin, the glass had grown warm and my fingers seemed to quiver with tension.

"Make sure you hold on to it," he warned me with a sardonic grin.

"Don't make me angry or I might kill you too," I teased, my tone serious.

"You want to kiss me too?" he shot back, grinning. "Because I don't think Ginevra would like that very much." He tipped his head at his girlfriend next to him, encircling her waist from behind.

"No offense, but one brother at a time is enough. I was just dying to say it, that's all."

Ginevra smiled and they exchanged a light kiss. "Aren't you tired?" she asked, worried about me as always. "You should get some sleep."

"I don't think I could manage that. Not now, at least." The blood was churning through my veins.

Simon and Ginevra glanced at each other. I noticed her nod slightly as if answering a question I hadn't heard. "Gemma," Simon began, his tone kind, "it would be wise if she and I used the next few hours constructively."

"We need to train," Ginevra said, turning to me, straightforward as always. "Until we tell Evan about the plan, there's nothing else we can do. We have to be ready in case something goes wrong. You can never be too prepared. You have the poison on you and you've got to be ready to use it at any moment. But now you need to get some rest," she insisted, giving me no choice.

"Can't—can't I go with you two?" I asked timidly even though I already knew the answer. I really didn't want to be alone, not in this state of alarm.

They exchanged another look.

"Okay, you can come with us, but you have to be extremely careful," Ginevra warned, her tone serious.

I could barely believe my ears. The workout room had always been off limits to me. It seemed impossible that Simon and Ginevra were being so accommodating. Or maybe I should consider it a bad sign—they were so afraid to leave me alone they were willing to bend the rules. Then again, her vault had always been off limits too and she'd just taken me there. It seemed as if all bets were off today, as though all the boundaries had been brought down.

Soon even the one between life and death would be obliterated. And it would take me with it.

The heavy door to the workout room closed with an ominous clang like the barred door of a prison cell. I kept looking around uneasily, unsure of what was going to happen. It wasn't the first time I'd been in this room—Evan had shown it to me over the summer, and a couple times we'd hung out there with the others, laughing amid the black punching bags filled with cement and the mats covering the dark marble floor. But I'd never been there when any of them were seriously training. When they did, for my own safety I wasn't allowed to enter for any reason. Now, for the first time, a sinister shadow descended on the room.

"Ready?" Simon stood in front of Ginevra. His tone was both challenging and determined.

For a moment their eyes frightened me: an Angel against a Witch, each prepared to receive the other's deadly blows.

"Always," she hissed, a smug look on her face.

My heartbeat suddenly accelerated. Had they forgotten I was here? I nervously shifted my weight from one leg to the other, not knowing what I was supposed to do in the meantime. Why had nobody explained it to me? All those times they hadn't let me in there were making me awfully uncomfortable right now.

"Gemma, stay behind me," Ginevra ordered, her tone far from comforting.

"Huh?" She couldn't be serious.

"Do as I say," she hissed, her eyes never leaving Simon's.

Ginevra actually wanted me to stand in the trajectory of Simon's blows? From the look on his face I could tell I didn't have much time to consider alternatives that might be just as risky. I followed Ginevra's order and darted behind her back. The tension between the two of them grew as taut as an electrical current across a silver wire.

Before I knew what they were planning to do, a violent explosion burst from Simon's body and a trail of fire came at us at breathtaking speed. I stifled a scream and held my breath, instinctively covering my face with my arms. The overwhelming force made Ginevra's hair fly back and the scorching heat of the fire hit me full in the face. My stomach felt as if it had been turned inside out. Ginevra's foot squeaked against the floor as she countered his attack.

I couldn't breathe. Suddenly the heat disappeared, leaving me trembling. I heard amused laughter and opened my eyes, allowing myself to inhale.

It was Simon. "Relax!" he told me, grinning. "I'm not planning on killing my girlfriend." I looked at Ginevra, disoriented. My breathing came in irregular gasps as if my body couldn't get enough oxygen.

"Did you think he was going to roast us?" she admonished me.

"I didn't have much time to think about it," I said, still in a state of shock. "The fear was enough to fry my neurons. But what—" I was dazed.

"The enemy never leaves you time to think—remember that. You always need to be prepared."

"Why weren't we hit?" I asked, still confused.

"Because I prevented it. I created a barrier and removed the air around us, which is why you couldn't breathe. Fire can't cross through it. That's what protected us," she explained, looking proud of her demonstration.

I stared at her, wordless with amazement. "It's incredible," I murmured to myself. "By the way, thanks for warning me," I scolded her, not hiding my sarcasm.

Ginevra snickered. "That was nothing. Managing to do it when I'm moving and under more difficult circumstances is even harder, but we've learned to defend ourselves. If you know the things that can destroy you, you can learn to protect yourself—some of the time."

Her discussion with Simon popped back into my mind. Ginevra was right—Subterraneans had no way to defend themselves against Witches' poison, whereas Witches could escape Subterraneans' attacks. *Witches were more powerful.*

I gaped at Ginevra, blown away by this new awareness, but she instantly rushed off, disappearing from sight. I tried to follow her with my eyes as she darted through the room, dodging the fireballs Simon hurled at her like lightning bolts, threatening to reduce her to ashes.

My heart in my throat, I flattened myself against the wall. The room must have been reinforced with a special material, because the missed shots hit the walls without leaving a mark. I couldn't remember ever having heard such a din.

Scaling the walls at warp speed as if gravity had no power over her, Ginevra deflected the fireballs even while spinning through the air. Occasional silver lights burst from her body and rushed at Simon like bolts of lightning, but neither of the two ever managed to hit the other. The floor trembled under their blows.

Ginevra chased Simon and when she reached him their bodies collided in a wild battle that led them from one end of the room to the other. They were spectacular, especially Ginevra. I couldn't stop staring at her in frank admiration. I'd never seen her like this before. One moment she was dodging Simon's blows with feline grace and the next she was on the offense, leveling swift, violent attacks against him. She was like a cougar ever ready to pounce. The power she emanated was perceptible, like an aura. It was everywhere, so evident I could almost see it.

I could barely follow them with my eyes. For a moment the whole room seemed to spin. All the noise had thrown me off balance, and both Simon and Ginevra noticed. They stopped and looked at me.

"Something the matter?" Ginevra asked, looking concerned.

I hadn't realized it was so obvious. "No, I'm a little tired, that's all," I said. "I feel kind of dizzy."

"You need to get some sleep," Simon said, almost reproachfully. "I know only one person who's more stubborn than you, and the two of you make a nice couple."

I smiled. "I guess you're right, but this whole thing is making me so nervous I don't know if I'll be able to—"

"I'm sure a hot bath will help," Ginevra suggested, her tone kind.

"Maybe that's what I need," I finally said.

"It's ready and waiting. Want me to come with you?"

"No, you guys go ahead and keep training. I'll be fine." They had already done enough for me.

"When you're finished, you can lie down in my room or in Evan's, if you prefer. Take all the time you need."

"Okay, thanks," I said.

I left the room, their concerned eyes still on me, climbed the stairs, and walked down the hall without relaxing my grip on the vial. Having it with me made me feel safe, to a certain extent. When I opened the door to the spa, a cloud of hot steam hit me. The room was filled with that particular spicy scent that made me think of Ginevra. The soft candlelight made the atmosphere so relaxing.

I carefully took the vial out of my pocket and rested it on the edge of the tub. With my hair tied up so it wouldn't get wet, I let my clothes slide to the floor and sank into the scalding-hot water. The relief was instant.

I rested my head on the edge of the tub, closed my eyes, and surrendered to the comforting sensation, letting myself be cradled by my thoughts. It was insane—I'd spent so much time and effort trying to escape death only to decide now to seek it out of my own free will. But it was what I had to do, a flaming hoop I had to jump through in order to bring the show to an end.

I'd made up my mind. No matter how much Simon's plan frightened me, I'd already made too many mistakes, rash decisions for which we would all have to pay the consequences. I couldn't continue to put the others in jeopardy and stand on the sidelines while they fought a battle that should have been mine.

The last time I'd acted on impulse and refused to accept Evan's plan, I'd almost lost him. It was a risk I was no longer willing to run, not if I could help it. If there was something I could do to prevent it, I wouldn't let Evan fight Drake again.

It was up to me now.

Evan was right. None of them were being forced to protect me and yet neither Simon nor Ginevra had ever shown a second's hesitation about it. From the very beginning they had always been prepared to support Evan and me. Even when Evan's decisions had seemed questionable to them, they'd been there. For that I would be eternally grateful to them.

But now I had the chance to do my part.

In spite of the circumstances, none of them were treating me like a fragile piece of glass. I could play a role in their lives just as they had in mine.

That's what I felt now—like one of them. We were fighting a war for my sake and only mine. It was only fair that I be the one to walk onto the battlefield. I would be the one to kill the Reaper Angel who was after me.

Of one thing I was finally sure: the constant fear of being hunted, of feeling him breathing down my neck, had made me tremble for months, but now that I was the one choosing death, I wasn't frightened any more.

When I came down the stairs I found the living room empty and silent. Simon and Ginevra must still be down in the workout room. I could have joined them, and would have if I hadn't suddenly felt sleepy and drained. The hot water had soothed every muscle in my body and I wasn't even sure I'd be able to find the energy to climb back up the stairs to Evan's room. I couldn't remember the last time I'd gotten any sleep and I'd never felt so tired in my whole life.

I took my phone out of my sweatshirt pocket and put it on the glass coffee table, sure that a few hours would be enough to get me back on my feet. Letting my body sink into the leather cushions on the couch, I forced my eyelids to remain open one more minute. All my body wanted was to lose consciousness.

I rested my head on a cushion, my fingers still gripping the vial I'd hidden protectively in my pocket. A second before my eyes closed, I glanced at the light-blue digits on the Blu-ray player. It was one o'clock. Only five hours left until six. When I woke up, Evan would be there.

EVAN

36

SPLINTERS IN THE HEART

Dark specks on the gray asphalt, sounds and silences dissolving in the air; my fists clenched so tight they hurt, my body as tense as my heart. From atop the building I absently watched the slow progression of thousands of bodies flowing like water in a river a thousand miles away. In my ethereal form I could even hear their heartbeats and footsteps. The sounds were so close and yet so far from where my mind was.

I knew I wasn't alone. None of them were there by chance. I could almost feel their ice-cold eyes on me, demanding I concentrate. It was almost time. The wind lashed at my skin, trying to snap me back to attention, but without success—because I wasn't really there. Or rather, my body was, but my heart was elsewhere, struggling with disappointment, grief, and fear.

Devastating disappointment over a brother I'd lost. *Brother*—maybe it was time for me to stop using that word.

Grief, bound up with her, with Gemma—the person whose life had become my sole purpose, the only one who could make me breathe again and take my breath away with a single glance. There are billions of people in the world, yet you can feel infinitely alone if you're deprived of the one who's important to you. I had lived for a long time, but only now did I realize it.

I felt so powerless when I was away from her, I felt I was going mad. I imagined her threatened by a thousand dangers and me unable to do anything to protect her. Without her, the frustration was tearing me to pieces, as unbearable as whiplashes against my naked, fragile heart.

And finally, fear. Fear of what might happen—of what was bound to happen. Because no matter how things turned out this time, no victory would be celebrated in my soul. With my heart bloodied from the pain I would sacrifice my brother, but part of me would die with him. Maybe it had already died from disappointment.

Deep inside I continued to struggle to accept the painful, ineradicable truth. Part of me still insisted on denying Drake's betrayal, considering it one of night's deceptions, nothing more than a nightmare. Like I might wake up any minute now and find it had never happened, that it had all been just a projection of a fear buried in my heart, a lie . . . and then Drake would be by my side again, as always, and we would fight this war together.

But that wasn't the truth. It was just an illusion to alleviate the unbearable pain that tormented me—as if that feeble hope might be enough to erase everything else. *Nothing could.* I couldn't go on lying to myself forever.

Up to the very end, I had repressed my doubts and reproached myself for my suspicions. I had hoped I was wrong—I'd hoped it with all my soul, which was why I hadn't said a word about it to anyone. Deep down I'd been afraid that giving voice to the unspoken thought would make it more real.

I'd known that sooner or later someone would come to claim Gemma's life. I'd lived with this torment every single moment, hoping she wouldn't notice as I'd forced myself to fill her days with memories of the two of us—special memories, unique experiences I didn't want her to forget.

My need for her was so insatiable I even stole her nights, like a greedy thief jealous of his treasure. I'd always wanted to keep her close because I was afraid someone would soon come to take her away from me.

But not him; anyone but him. Never had I imagined I would have to fight a member of my own family. Never, not even for a second. Not until that first, terrible suspicion—and even then the thought had been too painful. That night by the lake my heart had turned colder than ice when my suspicions had taken shape before my eyes like a nightmare come to life to torture me.

I didn't dare imagine where I would find the strength to kill Drake. I tried to stop thinking about it by visualizing Gemma's face in my mind, but there was no way to banish the terrible image.

I'd already put myself to the test in a battle against him and it had felt like every blow I dealt Drake had come back to strike me as well with just as much force, cutting through me like a double-edged blade.

What I couldn't understand was why the same true wasn't true for him. The merciless, detached coldness in his eyes was what hurt me most, as if someone had erased every memory of me from his heart along with the affection I'd thought he had for me. But maybe that was my mistake and I'd just been kidding myself, thinking I'd found in him the brother I'd never had. Now it was so difficult, so painful to accept the truth.

If I hadn't had Gemma to protect, Drake's betrayal would have destroyed me. She was the strength I clung to to avoid drowning in despair, in this cruel, grim twist of fate. No—fate was to blame for many things, but not for this. Fate guided us to certain events and led us to forks in the road, but we were the ones who ultimately chose which path to take. Our decisions led us to our destiny. I had learned that.

But no matter how terrible or painful it was, I couldn't be angry at Drake. When all this was over, would I also be able to forgive myself for my own sins?

I already knew the answer.

No. I would never be able to forgive myself for my brother's death. Nevertheless, I would keep on living. For her. Because nothing was more important.

Wars, epidemics, massacres . . . For long centuries, my heart, as hard as metal forged in the fire, had borne ever more difficult trials. It had carried too heavy a burden as souls slipped through my fingers—souls I tore away from their families, staining me with guilt I could never wash away. My eyes had witnessed tragedies I could never forget. And yet in the single blink of an eye my heart had stopped. I had surrendered to love at one look from a sweet, delicate, mortal soul. My life depended on this.

It depended on her.

Time crept by at a glacial pace. Never in my existence had it been so cruel. Ten endless hours of waiting. How would I be able to bear the last few minutes that separated me from her?

I had no reason to believe Gemma was in danger—I knew I could count on Simon and Ginevra—but that wasn't enough. For some reason, the painful thought that I wasn't there to protect her threatened to overcome me with every passing moment.

Nevertheless, I couldn't shirk my duty.

I had to make sure destiny was carried out, not because I was a Soldier of Death with no choice—not any longer—but because if I didn't keep Death from robbing me of Gemma, I wouldn't be able to join her after this life. It was the only thing keeping me away from her. I couldn't afford to give up the possibility. But neither the oceans nor the continents nor any execution order Fate could give would be enough to keep me from thinking of her every second—of the special way she looked at me, as if I were important—*me.*

Didn't she know that without her I was no one? I never had been. Yet at her side I felt so strong, so safe. All those lifetimes I'd wasted in the blind assumption that I had lived—God, how wrong I had been. You can't realize you've always been in the darkness until you find a spark that finally makes your heart beat. My blind eyes had been used to living in the dark. Then I'd discovered an unknown world full of light and hope, and only at that point had I realized I'd been wandering in the shadows.

It had taken only an instant to realize how devastating and irreversible the feeling was. I'd known in a heartbeat that it was impossible for me to return to the darkness. I knew I could never let anyone take from me the most precious thing I had in the world, the only spark that could light up my life: Gemma.

No. I would never let that happen. My eyes had been dazzled and I could never go back to the darkness I'd once known so well. Not any more.

Everything had changed since I'd met Gemma. I myself had altered, and the change inside me had been so deep, so radical, that I couldn't even remember who I'd been before I met her—as if I hadn't even existed. With all the emotions that had stirred inside me since she'd been in my life, this handful of months had been worth more than all the centuries I'd lived.

I didn't know how much longer we had to live together, but I would treasure each memory forever, her smallest gesture, the symphony of her voice, her radiant smile, her sparkling gaze, the warmth of her skin, the fragrance of her hair, the soft touch of her lips . . . Kissing them drove me wild and each and every time my desire, my need for her was stronger, deeper, impossible to deny.

And then that day at the lake house . . . I'd felt like I was losing my mind. I'd feared my heart wouldn't be able to contain such emotion, like it was on the verge of exploding.

I'd yearned for her for centuries without knowing it. It was as if all my life I'd wanted nothing other than that moment, nothing other than to be with her, holding her close, feeling her warmth against my skin. To merge with her. To disappear inside her. God, what a sensation . . . How could such a deep emotion be wrong?

I should have felt guilty for feeling this way—after all, I was still an Angel—but I couldn't. Not even the tiniest fragment of my spirit regretted a single instant I had spent with Gemma. There was nothing more *right* than being with her. It was as if I had been born for her and she for me—I could sense it in her every breath, because it was in her breath that I found my own. Simply embracing her in the silence of the night to hear her heartbeat was enough to make me breathe.

And then there was the incredible attraction that electrified me whenever her eyes met mine—so powerful it devastated me. Every time her deep, dark eyes gazed into mine I lost myself in longing. I surrendered to that desire because it was all I wanted, all I needed. I loved her so much even looking at her hurt. Was love so overwhelming, so absolute for everyone?

I was fighting a battle I couldn't afford to lose. What would become of me if I did? How could I continue to live without her? Like a tree stripped bare, its roots ripped from the earth, I would die along with her. I couldn't see any other solution. I would be consumed like wood on a fire until nothing was left of me but ash, what we had been burnt to cinders by pain.

No. I would never let that happen. There wasn't much time left now. I could sense it in this body that had never felt so mine before. Days, maybe hours, and it would all be over. We would belong to each other properly, without anyone hunting us down.

I would protect her forever, whatever the cost, and soon I would make her my wife. I would make my vows before God and with a trembling heart put my mother's ring on her finger. It couldn't belong to anyone but Gemma. I knew that now. With that simple act, her soul would be united with mine forever.

I already belonged to her just as she belonged to me. I could feel it in Gemma's every heartbeat. The thought that Drake or anyone else might go near her again made me crazy. The kiss that miserable traitor had stolen from her was enough to drive me insane. I would have killed him without batting an eye if it hadn't been Drake. Or maybe I might have anyway, if Simon hadn't come to stop me. At this point it was hard to say.

I'd been consumed with rage, overcome by a furious jealousy that had gripped my chest, a deeply rooted hatred impossible to eradicate. At that brutal moment I'd even lost control of my reason. I couldn't tolerate the idea that someone else might touch my Gemma—or even desire her. I was prepared to kill for her, even to die for her. No one would take her away from me. Fate wouldn't be enough to separate us.

Drake would be the last one.

No other Executioner would come looking for her because I would prevent it. In silence I had racked my brains for months, seeking a way to keep Death from taking her away from me, and had finally found a glimmer of hope for our future: the forbidden fruit. Ambrosia, the vital essence that nourished me. I was almost sure it would allow her to live forever too.

It would be dangerous. I had scrupulously evaluated every possibility and in the end I'd reached the right conclusion: if she ate of the tree, her soul would be forever barred from entering Eden. It would make her immortal. It would make her mine for always—if she wanted it.

It didn't matter whether or not the rest of the family approved. It didn't matter if I had to leave them all behind. My mind was made up.

I wished I could control time, bend it to my will so I could return to her. The thought that Drake might take advantage of my absence and visit Gemma made me frantic. Today might have been the longest day of my life, and my frustration rose every second as I bore the slow passing of the hours that separated me from her. But it wouldn't be long now. I just had to hold out and bear the torment a little while longer.

I could already feel the tension in the air—the kind I felt on my skin just before it was time to move into action. Looking up, I met the eyes of one of the others who was crouched on the roof a few yards away, staring at me with a puzzled look on his face as if he wanted to understand my secrets and frustrations.

He didn't understand, nor would he ever be able to—I realized that now. Our race had been created solely to kill, to liberate the soul from the shell that protected it during its brief stay on earth. Not to give up everything, like Simon had. Or me. We had a different objective: Redemption. Driven by such a motive, no Subterranean would give up everything to look for love among the extremely rare cases of women who bore the gene of the Subterraneans. And bonding with a mortal soul was inconceivable. No one could understand the devastating power of love until they had personally been swept away. None of these Angels could imagine the nature of my frustration.

There were lots of us today, maybe more than forty, scattered over a five-hundred-yard radius. I could sense them all around me. We were all there for the same reason, and for many of them it was their sole purpose in life—but not for me. Whereas they were eagerly awaiting the moment to carry out their orders and second the hand of Fate, I was longing for everything to be finished so I could return to Gemma. It was the only thing that mattered to me. But by now the worst was over.

We had spent most of the first hours making sure each of these people would end up in the right place at the right time. That was usually the hardest part. My ability to control people's unconscious minds gave me an advantage over the others; once I'd tracked down the mortal soul entrusted to me, making it go where I wanted it to had never been a problem. I could bend anyone's mind to my will with a simple glance. They all obeyed.

Sometimes a minor decision was enough to change someone's destiny. Missing a train, running a red light, going back for something left behind—trivial actions that determined their fates, mere seconds that decided everything, whether someone lived or died. All I had to do was look them in the eye to get them under my control. They couldn't see me, but their spirits would obey.

A high-rise. Today a high-rise would collapse, consumed by flames. We also had to take care of the people who weren't supposed to end up trapped in the fire, because there was no such thing as coincidence. Or better said, if it did exist, we were the ones who acted behind its mask, hidden in the fuse that started a fire, the breeze that fanned the flames, the first gust of wind that whipped up a storm capable of wiping out entire populations.

Our intervention was subtle and no one ever noticed us. The preparation in cases like this one took a long time. In these hours I'd discovered that the woman entrusted to me was a thirty-eight-year-old American named Jodelle with a successful career in Bolivia. She'd started at the bottom and had worked her way up, assuring her two children a good future.

That morning she'd dropped her kids off at school. Still in her car, she'd been about to leave for work when a strange instinct had made me suggest she call them back. They'd spent the whole morning together enjoying La Paz while I prepared the others. It was a gift I wanted to give her and her children. I couldn't do anything more. I was just Death's Soldier, a slave to its will. I didn't have the power to defy fate.

Death itself was a part of life, like the due date on a contract for eternal freedom. Because no matter how unfair it might seem, it actually wasn't. Humans had always feared death, mistakenly considering it a punishment, overlooking in their blindness the true key to happiness on earth: enjoying the journey. No one ever realized that death was only a new beginning. I was convinced that if we revealed this secret to mankind, the world would be a better place; once the awareness that life was transitory had rid them of their oblivious skepticism, every mortal soul would be more careful of their actions. You needed to know evil to be able to choose which side you were on.

We were ready, each of us in our place. Within seconds the fire would be kindled and no one would be able to determine the cause. Still I couldn't concentrate.

Gemma. She was the only thing on my mind. The more time that passed, the more agitated I became about not being there with her. I tried to focus on the building in front of me before the fire consumed it. Jodelle had just gotten back. The mirror she was looking into had to be the one in the bathroom. No one else was home; her husband had offered to take the children to their karate lesson that had been rescheduled for today. Once again, the delay had nothing to do with coincidence.

Everything was ready. Death was poised to engulf the building and we, its Soldiers, were ready to assist destiny. I didn't need to look at a clock to see what time it was. Jodelle would be waiting for me at ten to six, twenty minutes after the fire had trapped her in her home like a mouse in a deadly cage.

Suddenly, the air went silent. An instant later, I felt warmth dispersing from the bodies of my companions as a golden flicker in the building told me the device had been triggered.

It was the beginning of the end. The end of my wait to be with Gemma.

37

DEADLY TRAP

It took only minutes for the spark to become an inferno. The wind fanned the flames, driving them higher and hotter, and the building was soon engulfed in an impenetrable wall of fire.

I stood perfectly still, watching their eyes fill with the fear of death. But no one could escape, not if one of us was there waiting for them. Panic filled the streets. People ran from every direction and helplessly watched the building go up in flames. Some of the ones inside jumped out the windows and clung to the scaffolding outside the building. Though they didn't realize it, they would be the survivors that day. None of us were there for them.

Then I sensed her. Jodelle. She exhaled her last breath, drawing me to her like a magnet. Before I knew it I was in the thick of the blaze, surrounded by flames that whipped all around me, threatening to devour me. They couldn't, of course, because I was the one who controlled them.

Jodelle was facing me, looking down at her hands. I took a step toward her and her bewildered eyes locked onto mine for a long moment. Some instinct made her begin to turn around, but I reached out my hand just in time to stop her. I wanted to spare her the tragic sight of her body being consumed by the raging fire.

Though Jodelle was lost and disoriented, I could tell that somehow my presence was comforting to her. I could read her every thought, her every fear. Her lips moved slightly in the deafening crackle that surrounded us. "Who are you?" she whispered, terrified.

"I'm here to help you." I spoke reassuringly, my voice low and cautious, as I gave her a kind smile so she would trust me.

"Help me," she repeated to herself as if she didn't understand what I'd just said. Her expression changed abruptly and her eyes widened at the sight of something behind me. I didn't need to turn around to understand her sudden look of terror. She'd seen her body reflected in what was left of the broken mirror on the wall behind me. Her head began to waver, moving almost imperceptibly from left to right.

"Jodelle," I said.

"I—I can't," she whispered, in shock. "I can't leave them. I need to go back." She broke off, falling into a stupor, her unseeing eyes still locked on mine.

"There's no need. Your time is up, Jodelle. You did it. You can come with me now," I reassured her, my voice soft as I slowly held out my hand. "Everything's fine. You're going home." At my words, her eyes lit up and she finally seemed to see me for the first time. She stared at my hand, hesitating. "Give me your hand, Jodelle," I said, "and all this will be over."

Inside her I sensed a new emotion: hope. She looked at me again, but her face was calmer now, like she'd finally understood why I was there. Reluctantly, she began to extend her hand to me but then stopped. I waited without moving. I didn't want to pressure her. Each soul reacted differently and it was only fair for me to respect her personal need for time. It was the least I could do.

I sensed her intentions before she moved. Her hand drew closer and touched mine as I smiled at her warmly to let her know everything would be fine. The moment my fingers grasped hers, her silhouette changed shape like a cloud of smoke moved by the wind. She disappeared before my eyes, her gratified murmur echoing in my ears: *"Thank you."*

I smiled to myself before disappearing. My ethereal body was automatically pulled back to the last place it had been before Jodelle's soul had asked to be saved—the rooftop of the building across the street. The sweet awareness that my tormenting wait was about to end warmed me. I checked my phone. It was a few minutes to six in Lake Placid.

Bitterness unexpectedly filled my mouth, wiping away my joy like the swipe of a sponge. *"Goddamn it!"* I growled ferociously, my eyes stinging with disappointment. "No! No! No! Not now! Not now . . ." I raised my hands to my head, consumed with desperation, shaking with indecision. What was the right thing to do?

I wasn't sure any more. I'd been counting down the seconds waiting for this moment to arrive. They couldn't do this to me—not now, of all times.

"Another order." I sighed, my energy draining away. I felt powerless. Gemma was expecting me at six and I didn't want to break my promise. I had to explain my absence somehow, let her know I'd be late so she wouldn't worry.

Resigned, I picked up my phone and called her. Since I expected her to answer right away each new ring sent my mind racing to a thousand thoughts, a thousand dangers.

I tried again and again with no results and began to fall into a panic verging on madness. "Damn it, pick up!" I hissed. What had happened to her? What was keeping her from answering? When I tried to contact Simon and Ginevra all I heard from their minds was silence. There was no time, but I had to make sure she was all right before I went to carry out my next mission. Why the hell had they waited until the last minute to let me know I had another one?

A thought struck me and I went cold: it was a trap. They wanted to keep me away from her so Drake could work undisturbed. I cursed again, blaming myself for not realizing it sooner. They'd lured me into leaving her on her own and I'd fallen for their dirty trick hook, line, and sinker.

A shudder of desperation gripped me, making my skin crawl. I might already be too late and it would be all my fault because I hadn't been there to protect her. I was the only one who could prevent it. A sudden flash of certainty illuminated my mind: if anything had happened to her, I would turn heaven upside down, tear it apart. Because of their deception, no one would survive. *No one.*

Seething, I glared at the flames roaring up from the building across the street as a fire that was even more violent and consuming rose inside me. I concentrated on Gemma in order to reach her, wherever she was, and vanished.

The relief I felt was so overpowering it made my body ache: she was asleep. My legs shook from my misplaced rage. There had been no trick, no deception. I dropped my head into my hands, undone by my fear. Unfounded suspicion had blinded me completely and made my entire world collapse.

Gemma was right there, lying on the sofa in a deep, peaceful slumber. I couldn't stop staring at her. My whole life was enclosed in that single delicate being. I moved toward the sofa, noticing her phone on the coffee table. I'd imagined the worst, but she was just sleeping so deeply she hadn't heard it ring.

I reproached myself for how impulsive I'd been—I might have woken her. Who knew how long it had been since she'd last slept? I forced myself to take a deep breath, filling my lungs with air though I had no need of it. The fear of losing her had driven me to imagine some sort of conspiracy when the truth was that Drake and I were the only two in this battle. Soon, only one would be left. And there was no way I was going to lose to him, because I had something more important to go back to. Never again to see her adorable face that I couldn't take my eyes from now was out of the question.

I went to her. Stroking her cheek, I pushed a stray lock of hair out of her face. The touch of her warm skin sent a jolt through my entire body. It had always been like that with her. There was some sort of magnetism between us. Even back when I hadn't known her and sworn I would keep my distance, I could never fight my urge to touch her. Physical contact with her felt essential. It was an indispensable need for me. Even though I knew it was physically impossible, it felt like my heart started beating inside me again every time I gave in to my instinctive craving to touch her. Pressing my lips against hers, feeling the warmth of her body, sliding my mouth across her skin until I was kissing her belly . . . all it took for me to feel alive was simple contact with her. For me to feel my heart throbbing in my throat, beating so hard it almost hurt.

Fighting the urge to steal the kiss she'd promised me when I got back, I caressed her again. At my touch, Gemma moved her head, following my hand. I froze, not wanting to wake her for anything in the world.

I could have stayed there for hours, watching her sleep, but I had to go.

"Evan . . ." she murmured, still asleep.

Her eyes moved beneath her closed eyelids. She was dreaming of me. The peacefulness in her voice melted my heart. I could have joined her in that dream. Every last bit of me wished I could, but I didn't have time and I knew that if I didn't go soon I wouldn't be able to find it in my heart to leave her.

No. I wouldn't be able to. I would leave her a message. I had to let her know I would be late, but without disturbing her sleep. Gemma expected me at six, and if she woke before I got back she would be worried.

I picked up a sheet of paper and let the pen move under my fingers.

Fate is against us; it keeps trying to separate us, but don't worry—it can't. Nothing in the world could ever keep me away from you. You can't separate a body from its heart without killing it. One more hour, my love. Just one more hour and I'll return to you.

Yours forever,
Evan

I would definitely be back before she woke up. As I placed the note on the coffee table the light of the display on the Blu-ray player caught my eye. It read exactly six o'clock. I would be back by seven.

The air was filled with her scent. I inhaled it deeply. An hour—just one more hour. What could possibly happen in an hour? Calmer now that I knew she was safe, I looked at her one last time, feeling a pit in my stomach for having to leave her again. If it had been up to me, I would never have left her alone to begin with. I wanted to engrave in my mind the sight of her face as she slept so peacefully and have the memory to keep me company while I was away.

I would always be there for her, as long as there was breath in my body. I wouldn't let anyone near her. I would rewrite her destiny, binding her life to mine, defying fate. I didn't care how much longer I needed to fight or how many of them came looking for her—I would be there to protect her. I would kill them off until there wasn't a single one left on earth. But Gemma would survive.

I leaned down and touched my lips to her forehead. It was painful to pull them away again.

"This will all be over soon," I whispered. With bitterness in my heart I vanished.

GEMMA

A MASK UNSEEN

A violent sense of vertigo woke me up. I opened my eyes groggily and realized I wasn't alone in the room. It took me a few seconds to make out my surroundings clearly. Finally I saw him. Evan.

I smiled and studied him for a moment. His back was turned to me and he was holding something, a piece of paper, maybe.

"Hey," I whispered tenderly.

He started and turned toward me. "Hey," he replied, smiling.

"What's that?" I murmured, my voice still sleepy, nodding at the piece of paper in his hands.

My curiosity seemed to surprise him and he hesitated before answering, then smiled. "Just a note for Ginevra. Nothing important," he said casually, folding the sheet in four. He tossed it into a stone vase on the coffee table and held his hand over it. The paper began to burn.

I looked at him, puzzled. My thoughts were still bleary after my long nap and I didn't understand why he'd done that. Raising my head from the cushion, I turned toward the clock. It read twenty after six. "You're late," I said with a grin, not taking my eyes off his.

"I didn't want to wake you." Evan held out his hand. When I took it, he helped me up from the couch, gently pulled me against him and clasped my hips.

"Well? What are you waiting for?" I asked, a hint of naughtiness in my tone that he didn't seem to catch. He looked a little tense—maybe he was frustrated that we didn't have a plan. Simon and Ginevra probably hadn't spoken to him yet. They must still be downstairs, and Evan had likely come to see me first thing after getting back. "I owe you a kiss, remember?" I whispered, pressing my lips against his and sinking my fingers into his wavy hair.

"I think I deserve a little more than that, don't you?" he whispered back. He finally seemed more relaxed. His arms pulled me closer as he kissed me.

I smiled against his mouth and pulled back gently, resting a hand on his chest. "Hey, give me a minute. I just woke up."

"I've already waited too long," he said, his breath uneven, pulling me to him again.

"I mean it," I whispered with a smile, finally managing to pull away from his embrace. I took him by the hands and led him to the couch. "There's something I have to talk to you about." I sat down and pulled him down next to me. Now that he was there beside me, I felt calmer, stronger. Nothing could stop me. "I was afraid you wouldn't get here in time."

"In time for what?" he asked warily. "What are you talking about?"

"Drake."

I noticed that his pupils dilated slightly at my mention of the name. "We have a plan," I announced proudly, as if the plan didn't involve my death. But that was how I felt. For once, I wouldn't have to hide. I wouldn't have to fear my hunter any more. I would no longer have to dread death. And I couldn't wait for Evan to know every last detail.

He blinked several times, clearly not expecting this. "That's great news," he finally said with a nervous look on his face as if he already suspected the danger I would be facing. "I'm listening."

I swallowed, my throat suddenly dry. "Ginevra is convinced Drake will try to get near me again in your appearance."

"I agree," he replied, clenching his fists.

"Good. So you'll also agree we can use the situation to our advantage."

"How, exactly?" He tensed.

A knot in my stomach made me hesitate. Having agreed to the plan didn't necessarily mean banishing all my fear. "Since I'll be closest to him, I'll be the one with the best opportunity to kill him," I blurted out all in one breath.

Evan didn't laugh like I'd expected him to. "What? How do you plan to do that?" he asked, seeming shaken.

I hadn't imagined he would actually consider the plan so quickly though, judging from the look on his face, I wasn't sure he liked the idea.

"That's absolutely ridiculous," he said, frowning.

"No it isn't, and unless you've come up with something else it's all we've got." I touched the vial in my pocket, then took it out and showed it to him. Evan went rigid, his head snapping back instinctively. "It's not ridiculous if I have this." My eyes were sparkling from the power I held in my hand.

"Is that what I think it is?" he asked, still frowning, his eyes riveted on the little glass vial. He looked anxious.

I nodded and tucked the poison back into my pocket where it couldn't hurt him. "I can do this, Evan," I reassured him.

"It's risky," he said, his gaze abstracted.

"I know, but I have to do it."

"How do you plan on making it happen, though? Do you really think Drake would be that stupid?" There was a note of bitterness in Evan's voice.

"I'll pretend I don't realize it's him." I swallowed. Having seen Evan's reaction to the first time his brother had stolen a kiss from me, telling him I would have to kiss Drake again might end up being the hardest part of all. "I just need to wet my lips with the poison," I explained softly, letting him guess the rest of the plan.

Evan didn't react as I had expected him to. Continuing to stare into space, he slowly rolled his hands into fists.

"Evan, I can do this, trust me. Let me do it. I'm not afraid to face death." Finally he looked at me. "I'm not afraid, because I know you'll be there to bring me back."

He was lost in thought.

I waited. Suddenly, a glimmer appeared in his eyes and he looked at the clock. I did the same. Six forty.

"It's shrewd," he murmured finally.

"It'll work," I said, possibly more to reassure myself than to convince him.

"We'll make sure it works," he replied. "Now listen carefully: Drake is going to try to find out what we're planning, and we already know how he manages to get close to you. From now on you can't trust anybody—not even Simon. You have no way of knowing it's actually him. You need to be absolutely certain who's in front of you. With Ginevra it won't be hard—you can always ask her to tell you what you're thinking. Drake can take on her appearance, but he can't mimic her powers. He'll definitely try to trick you to find out what we're planning."

"Okay, but how do I know if he takes on your appearance?"

After a moment of thought, Evan took my hands and looked me straight in the eye, inches from my face. "How did you feel without me?" he asked, his voice hard.

"What?" I said, puzzled.

"How did you feel without me?" he repeated, articulating the words carefully.

"Terrible, like always when you're gone," I stammered nervously, still confused by his question. "Why are you asking me that right now?"

"Because that's what I'll tell you whenever you ask me that question. Remember the words carefully, Gemma—it's absolutely critical. You need to remember them to be sure it's really me. This is a decisive moment. My brother could be here any minute. We can't make mistakes. His eyes, his voice—everything will lead you to believe he's me. So before you use the poison, before you kiss him, you need to test him by asking him what I just asked you. 'Like always': that will be the right answer, your key to recognizing me. Otherwise it doesn't matter how much he looks like me or how much he acts like me,"—Evan looked me straight in the eye, deliberately articulating each word—"you'll know it's not really me. Do you understand?"

I nodded, surprised by the hard note in his voice. He tensed and searched the room with his eyes, then looked at the clock again. I wondered why he kept doing that.

"It's time," he warned me, his expression sharp. My heart began to race. "He's close. I can sense him," he whispered.

I blinked as panic gripped me. "What?! He's here?" I asked breathlessly, wrapping my arms over my chest.

"Not yet, but he will be soon. I'm sure he's waiting for just the right moment." He looked me in the eye. "Ready?" he asked point-blank.

"How soon?" I asked, my voice trembling.

"I can't say. Just don't forget anything I've told you." He got up from the couch.

"Where are you going?" I asked in alarm, too quickly for my anxiety to escape him.

"Don't worry." He took my hands. "I won't be far, but I need to get out of here or he won't come near you."

"Right," I murmured, shaken. "That's what Ginevra said too."

Evan nodded. "Because it's true. I'll go tell the others that I know all about the plan. We need to be ready when the time comes to bring you back."

I swallowed, my mind suddenly blank. He leaned over and kissed me on the forehead. His expression unexpectedly turned sly and I flinched at the dark glint that flashed in his eyes. "It's going to be the most unforgettable kiss he's ever been given." He smiled to himself. "Because it will be his last," he hissed, his eyes narrowed to slits.

A cold shiver gripped my stomach.

29

CRIMSON KISS

The room around me seemed to expand infinitely once Evan was gone. I sank my fingers into the leather couch cushions and clenched my fists. It was really about to happen. Everything was about to end. A shudder ran through my heart as the knowledge that the time had come sank in.

I was going to kill Drake, all alone. I didn't know why I hadn't been able to picture it in my mind before now. Maybe part of me had expected Evan to refuse to let me go through with it. What had I been thinking?

It was right that I should do it. The fact that Evan hadn't objected only showed how much he trusted the plan. Otherwise I was sure he would never let me run such a risk. So why was I trembling? I tried to get up but my head started spinning again, making me pause.

It was a few minutes before seven and I hadn't eaten for hours. I was sure it would do me good, but not so sure my body would be able to handle food. All this tension had left me nauseated. The room spun around me and I felt a pit in my stomach, showing that my body was protesting my decision. I leaned back, sank into the couch, and closed my eyes. The silence around me was bone chilling.

My hands shook. I couldn't remember ever being so nervous before. A million things whirled in my mind. I just wanted to get off the merry-go-round, just for a few minutes. That's all I was asking for.

I tried to think of Evan, the love I felt for him, the unforgettable moments we'd shared, and for a few seconds my tension eased. But that brief moment of peace made room for another thought that burst unexpectedly into my mind with devastating effect.

I bolted upright as the thought raced through my aching head, triggering a storm of conflicting emotions I wasn't sure I could handle, especially not right now.

A question throbbed in my temples.

When had I had my last period?

I desperately tried to do the math, to sort through the dates, but anxiety overwhelmed me and I kept getting confused. For a long moment I couldn't breathe.

The day Evan and I had made love for the first time had been the day I'd discovered they'd found me. Ever since then, my fears about their coming back to hunt me had absorbed all my energy and I hadn't had the time or the strength to think about anything else. Still, it was ridiculous—it couldn't be. Evan was an Angel, and I was just a mortal.

I instinctively rested my hand on my belly, my eyes unfocused as I considered the absurd notion. I hadn't had any symptoms, any pain or discomfort that might make me suspect. Or maybe I'd been too wrapped up in everything else to pay attention to the signals my body had been sending me. I wasn't sure.

The more I thought it over, the more I realized there was no mistake about it: my cycle had always been regular, and I was several weeks late.

How the hell could I not have realized it? My suspicions turned to certainty. I cautiously covered my belly with both hands and uttered the words in a whisper: "A baby."

I was expecting a baby.

Tears filled my eyes—tears born of a myriad of conflicting emotions. But foremost among them was a new fear: it wasn't only my life at stake any more. How could I also risk our baby's? Would Evan and Simon be able to save its tiny life too? My fingers gripped my belly more firmly as though that might protect it.

I blinked as three tears slid down my face. I had to tell Evan. All my certainties had slipped away and everything was more complicated now.

My legs trembling, I got up from the couch and headed into the kitchen. The clock on the wall was the first thing my eyes fell on as I dragged myself to the sink. It was seven sharp. The clock struck the hour just like the realization had struck my heart. Turning on the tap, I hung my head, leaning against the edge of the sink. I let the water run, listening to its comforting gurgle and hoping it would wash away my thoughts, my worries.

I couldn't focus.

Out of the corner of my eye I saw a glass near my hand. Almost unconsciously I picked it up and held it under the faucet, watching it as it filled. Turning off the tap, I drank a sip, then set the glass down and leaned over the edge of the sink again, resting all my weight on my arms while bowing my head and trying to think straight. But it was no use. It was like I'd fallen into a dark chasm. I looked for the light, but no matter how hard I tried I couldn't find the way out. The walls were closing in on me and I couldn't breathe. The chasm was so deep and dark it cut me off from my surroundings, and I didn't hear him arrive. I jumped at the touch of his fingers on my waist.

"Miss me?" he whispered sweetly in my ear.

I spun around and found myself pinned between his body and the sink. I paled violently. It was Evan . . . or was it? I was riddled with doubt.

His lips smiled at me, but my heart rate accelerated and my breath came fast. "Hey . . . calm down. It's only me." He stroked my cheek, drying the tears on my face.

"Evan," I whispered in a tiny voice filled with uncertainty. Suddenly I didn't know what to do any more. I felt uncomfortable, confused, and not at all ready for this.

"Hey," he whispered again, sweeping my hair over my shoulder. "Relax. You're on edge. You don't have to worry any more. Everything's going to be fine. I'm here with you now." He cupped my face in his hands.

His words aroused my suspicions. The real Evan shouldn't have been there. He'd gone to alert the others. He moved closer until our bodies lightly touched, blocking my way by resting his hands on the sink behind me as he gently kissed my neck. I stood there, petrified.

"We'll figure out a plan and everything will return to normal." He leaned back and looked into my eyes. "Do you know if Ginevra or Simon came up with any ideas while I was gone?"

Drake is going to try to find out what we're planning. Evan's voice rang in my head like an alarm bell. There he was, attempting to discover our plans as Evan had warned me he would. I looked into his eyes and tried to find Drake in them, but didn't see a trace of him. Anxiety stifled my breathing.

"N-not yet," I stammered.

Another kiss on my neck, this one more wary.

"Evan . . ." I whispered, almost without moving my lips.

"Yes?" he said softly.

My breath came even faster. I needed air. "How did you feel without me?" I whispered into his ear, my voice trembling.

He exhaled against my neck and his tone filled with pain. "Like I was in hell."

My heart constricted. *Wrong answer.*

He took my hand and squeezed it, rubbing his cheek against mine tenderly. "I felt like I was going mad," he said in a barely audible voice, his tone almost desperate, as I stood there unable to move.

Everything will lead you to believe he's me. The real Evan's words whirled through my head. *It doesn't matter how much he acts like me.*

I shook my head, in torment. It was obvious that after our last encounter Drake would be gentler, more cautious. I had to realize he would do or say anything to seem like Evan. Now I knew this wasn't the real Evan. He was lying—I knew it.

The vial felt like a ton of bricks inside my pocket. The others knew by now. Evan had gone to warn them. It was time.

"Your heart's beating so hard." He rested his hand on my chest.

He was so sweet, and yet I knew he wasn't really Evan. Why, then, was this still so difficult? Though I'd been trying hard not to do it, I inadvertently looked directly into his eyes, so close to mine, and my heart stopped. I wasn't sure I was brave enough. After all, it was still Drake. But then again they were all counting on me. I couldn't let this chance slip through my fingers. Drake was right there in front of me and the poison was burning a hole in my pocket. I couldn't back down. I had to do it. I owed it to Evan, to Ginevra, to Simon. I owed it to the baby growing inside me. I owed it to myself.

He rested his forehead against mine. The gesture broke my heart in two. Raising his hand with mine still clasped in it, he looked into my eyes. Palm to palm, forehead to forehead. "It'll all be over soon," he whispered, his gaze locked onto mine. "I promise."

I slid my free hand into my pocket and clenched the glass vial between my fingers. "I know," I murmured, resting my chin on his shoulder so he wouldn't see the teardrop streaking my face. "It'll all be over soon." I took the cap off inside my pocket. The smell of the poison rose into the air, so pungent it burned my throat. It took effort not to react. The aroma had suddenly captured my every thought. I felt an almost irresistible desire to move the vial closer and fill my nostrils with its scent.

Though I tried not to let myself get swept away by the strange sensation, there was no ignoring it. It was like a primitive instinct hidden in my gut.

This was wrong of me—I had to focus on Drake. But I could smell it, and it was going to my head.

I focused my attention on the body holding me close. I didn't want to give him a name any more.

Evan's voice whispered shyly in my ear: "You haven't answered my question: did you miss me?"

I cringed in silence at the tenderness in his voice. I thought of Drake, remembering his real face, all the moments I'd shared with him, the sincere affection that had connected us before he'd gone over to the wrong side.

I dipped a trembling finger into the poison. "I'll always miss you," I breathed into his ear as I brushed my finger over my lips, feeling an iron weight on my heart. It was over. We were both about to die. "Evan," I murmured, seeking his gaze. "Kiss me."

His mouth moved toward mine, stopping a fraction of an inch away. I closed my eyes as a hot tear slid down my cheek and I felt his lips part and then press against mine.

"Gem," he whispered in my mind with infinite sweetness, his lips still on mine.

A dagger cleaved my heart. I froze and tore my lips from his, my bulging eyes filled with shock and despair. A second later, his body jerked as if an electric charge had surged through it.

Simon and Ginevra appeared at the other end of the room. "NO!" Ginevra's shriek died in her throat. She covered her mouth with her hand, her eyes petrified.

My heart burst in my chest, forcing me to hear its message of desperation. Overwhelmed with panic, I grabbed his shirt collar and bared his neck. The dog tag jingled against Evan's skin. It was there. In its place.

No. It couldn't be true. What had I done?!

"Evan," I murmured in anguish, my tears overflowing while his eyes stared at me, full of terror. "Evan, no . . ."

His body began to shudder and he staggered backwards to the kitchen table. He tried to grab its edge but fell to the floor. I rushed to him, my hands shaking as I caressed his face and hair.

No! No! No! This was all wrong. Not Evan. No. Profound, violent torment consumed me. "You—You came back," I sobbed. "You told me to—"

Almost imperceptibly he shook his head as his body jerked again. "I left you a message," he murmured between spasms as I moved my hands over his body desperately. I had no idea what to do.

"Evan, no—Please!" I struggled between numbness and despair.

The spasms racking his body grew more violent. I grabbed his face with both hands. "Look at me. *Look at me!*" I pleaded. "Evan, I'm begging you—" Tears filled my eyes. *Maybe I can take back the poison*, I thought. "Kiss me." In torment, I pressed my lips to his, but his body continued to shudder. "Evan . . ." I sobbed.

"It doesn't matter," he whispered, kissing the palm with which I had been caressing his cheek. He pulled his dog tag off his neck and pressed it into my hand. "Maybe this is my punishment, but it"—his face was a mask of agony though he tried to hide it—"it was worth it."

"No!" I shook my head over and over, my eyes locked onto his in a hopeless attempt to keep him there. "I'm begging you, Evan, don't die! Stay with me!" My tears fell on his face as I clung to him in desperation. "Don't leave me, please. You can't leave me now!" I sobbed. "You can't, because . . . "

He rested his finger on my lips, his eyes probing mine. Like a miracle, a crystal tear slid from his eye. *"I love you,"* his voice whispered in my mind. *"Wherever I go, that will never change."*

I squeezed his hand tighter, but I couldn't keep him with me. "You can't . . . I'm having your baby!" The desperate whisper broke through my tears, but Evan vanished before he could hear it.

I fell forward, desolate, paralyzed by his sudden absence. I pressed my palms against the ground, my eyes staring unseeingly at the empty floor beneath me. My heart shattered. A maelstrom of memories hit me like a tornado, dragging me back in time. The first time he'd smiled at me, his gaze sweetening only for me, him shaking his wet hair as he came out of the lake, his body entwined with mine.

His voice filled my head like a distorted echo, putting me into a trance. *My name is Evan James . . . I love you—love you—love you . . . Damn me, then, with a kiss . . . Close your eyes . . . Those are Sephires . . . —phires—phires . . . God, you're beautiful . . .* To punish me, my mind was pulling me back through time. *Hold on tight—ight—ight . . . The Angel saw heaven for the first time . . . Everything's going to be fine . . . You're my star . . . Just to see you breathe—eathe—eathe . . . Don't forget us—us—us . . .*

I wanted it to stop; it was too painful. But Evan's words continued to whirl in my head and tighten around my heart. *Did you miss me? . . . You're all mine—ine—ine . . . I'll always be at your side . . . Gem . . . Marry me.*

The torrent of jumbled memories was killing me. They pierced my chest, as painful as thorns wound around my heart. The way he tenderly pressed his lips to mine, the scent of his skin, the gentle touch of his mouth when, behind the wheel, he would turn to look me in the eye while kissing the palm of my hand—he'd done that so often. It was a gesture that drove me wild—and one I would never experience again.

"It can't be . . ." I murmured to myself as Simon and Ginevra stood frozen a few steps away, their incredulous faces filled with horror. "This can't be true." I looked up at them. The pain was making it hard to breathe. *This can't really have happened!* I begged them with my eyes.

Something moved at the other end of the room.

Drake.

Simon's eyes, brimming with hatred and disgust, locked onto his. "How could you do this, Drake?" he screamed in outrage, fighting back tears. "He was your brother!"

Ginevra's icy voice cut him off. "That isn't Drake. It never has been."

I looked up, stunned, just in time to see Drake's evil smile vanish, along with the rest of his guise. In its place appeared a Subterranean I'd never seen before, his eyes filled with terror. An instant later, a flash of light shot across the room like a bullet.

Ginevra.

I held my breath. The Angel was gone. Where his feet had been was Ginevra's serpent. It slithered back to her and coiled around her ankle. They had disintegrated him with a single fatal blow. He hadn't even seen it coming. Her power was awe-inducing.

I could barely see through the veil of tears covering my eyes. My heart frozen, shattered into infinite shards that tore me apart with each breath, I stared at my hands, shocked and bewildered. "Why am I still alive?" I murmured, trembling.

It wasn't a question—it was a desperate protest.

I clutched Evan's chain in my fist as an infinite, agonizing pain settled into my chest.

My heart was bleeding. It would bleed forever.

BOOK THREE

BROKENHEARTED

THE POWER OF DARKNESS

A novel by

Elisa S. Amore

Translated by

Leah Janeczko

"But the Lord God called to the man [. . .]
And He said, [. . .] "Have you eaten from the tree
that I commanded you not to eat from?"
The man said, "The woman you put here with me—
she gave me some fruit from the tree and I ate it."
Then the Lord God said to the woman,
"What is this you have done?"
The woman said, "The serpent deceived me, and I ate."
Genesis 3:9-13

PROLOGUE

"Get a blanket-anket-anket . . . We need to warm her-er-er!"

Ginevra.

Her voice reached me from afar, like an echo distorted by the wind. I thought I saw figures scrambling around me. They left pale wakes behind them like objects moving through water—or maybe it was my body that was immersed in a murky, cold, corrosive liquid.

With effort, I recognized Simon's voice. It had the same tinge of desperation as Ginevra's. "She's still alive. Her heart is still beating-ing-ing . . . My God, she's burning up. We've got to help her-er-er!"

"She's in shock-ock-ock . . . Do something, Simon!"

"It must be the poison. I can't counteract it!"

"It's making her blood boil. Here! Quick, let's get her onto the table!"

A metallic noise drowned out their voices, the sound of thousands of nails crashing to the floor—I felt them being driven into my skull. Something cold pressed against my back. An even more piercing chill gripped my stomach. But the pain in my chest . . . it left me breathless. I was trapped in its coils of darkness yet I couldn't remember what had caused it.

"Gemma-emma-emma. You've got to respond-ond-ond! Gemma, please! Open your eyes-eyes-eyes . . . Simon, do something!"

"I'm trying! Damn it!" His frustrated growl filled my head.

Suddenly, all the noise stopped.

"Gemma . . ."

The whisper reached me like a caress. The voice was clear this time, crisp.

"Evan . . ." The impulse made its way from my heart to my lips.

I opened my eyes but found only Simon and Ginevra. I was in a bed. Dazed by the nightmare, I tried to remember how I had gotten there. My eyes finally met Ginevra's and glimpsed the anguish that flashed through them. Reality hit me like a jolt of electricity.

It wasn't a nightmare. A wail of desperation escaped me as a knot gripped my stomach and kept me from breathing. *Evan.* Panicking, I bolted upright and my gaze shot from one side of the room to the other.

"Gemma, stay down." Ginevra tried to calm me, but I couldn't hear her voice any more because a louder, more painful sound had filled my head. It took me a minute to realize it was coming from my heart. "You're not ready to get out of bed yet."

I tried to escape her firm grip but I was too weak and gave in. Still confused, my head throbbing, I looked up. "Evan . . . Where's Evan?" I asked, my voice hoarse with desperation and my eyes pleading for an answer I knew would never come.

Their silence struck me full in the chest, like a stab to the heart. My eyes darted back and forth between them, but neither Ginevra nor Simon could bear to look at me. I closed my tear-filled eyes and turned my head away as the pain washed over me and I abandoned myself to its icy coils, letting it drag me deeper and deeper into an abyss I'd never known before, wanting only for that black whirlpool to swallow me up.

Simon interrupted my tormented thoughts. "It's been six days. The poison you ingested left you with a high fever. It didn't kill you, though. You're still alive, Gemma."

"Your parents came to visit you every day," Ginevra said. She'd read in my mind that I didn't care whether death had spared me. "I told them you would be staying here until you recovered—or for as long as you wanted."

"She convinced them it was best for everyone," Simon added.

They continued to talk to me but I couldn't hear them. Their words made no sense. I was alive while *Evan was dead.* Why? Why was I still alive? Why had the poison taken everything from me, giving me no choice but to look on like an empty shell?

It wasn't fair. There had to be some kind of divine justice I could appeal to. I yanked off the covers and climbed out of bed, barefoot and dressed only in my underwear. Simon tried to bar my way but I was already out the door.

"Let her go." I barely overheard Ginevra's voice from the top of the stairs.

The air was bitter cold but I didn't care. Though I had on only thin white cotton underclothes, the night chill was nothing compared to the freezing pall that clung to my skin. Nothing could affect me compared to the pain that was tearing me apart inside. The wind lashed at me, freezing the tears on my cheeks and taking my breath away, but it didn't matter any more. All I wanted to do was run, afraid that if I stopped, the phantom of that nightmare would reach me. I couldn't let that happen; I knew the burden would be unbearable. I had to run—away from everything. I wasn't strong enough to face reality.

The snow-covered trees darted by as swiftly as ghosts. They tried to grab me but I didn't fear them. Part of me hoped they would snatch me up into their grim world, into the arms of Death, who would ease my suffering, where it wouldn't hurt so much.

Death. I had spent so much time trying to deceive her, and now, in a bizarre twist of fate, the queen of darkness I had so feared was eluding me. Why didn't she send out her loyal shadows to claim me? I wasn't afraid any more, because there could be no place darker than my heart.

I ran across the damp ground with its lingering patches of snow. My legs were numb but I continued to run as the pain inside me grew, swelled, consumed me with every cursed breath. Raindrops mingled with the tears that streamed down my face, washing away the salty streaks left behind by the wind.

I flung myself onto the cold, wet ground, barely registering it, my knees and palms pressed against the earth as my body spasmed in the fits of pain that gripped my chest. I stayed there, trembling, my head drooping like a now-dead part of my body.

I clenched my fists until they hurt and squeezed my eyes shut as a desperate scream rose from my chest. "Noooooo! *Whyyyyy?* I was supposed to die, not him!" I shrieked at the sky. "It was my fate, not his! Evaaaaan!" The pain was uncontainable. It hurt. It hurt unbearably and tore my heart in two.

I wished the earth would swallow me up, that I could just lie there in the hope that the snow would soon arrive to bury me. I let myself fall to the ground, allowing the rain—mocking consoler—to stream over my skin. Finally, I slipped into blackness, weary from the devastating torment I was certain would never end.

When I opened my eyes, snow framed the surface of the lake like a silvery halo while the sun beyond the horizon barely illuminated the dawn. Exhausted, I pushed myself up onto my side and dragged my body to the shore. I curled up and hugged my knees to my chest. I felt emptied. *Evan* . . . Tears returned to fill my weary eyes.

"I knew you would be here." Ginevra crouched down and sat beside me on the damp ground.

I lay there without moving, staring at the ripples on the water. "Why am I not dead?"

Silence lengthened the distance that separated me from her—that separated me from the world.

"We don't know. You ran a high fever for days and you were delirious the whole time. There were times when we thought you weren't going to make it." Ginevra fell into a strange silence, reliving the memory.

"Kill me," I hissed. Ginevra turned quickly toward me. "Look what I've done to your family—first Drake, and now . . . Evan." Uttering his name drove the knife that was lodged in my heart deeper into my flesh. "Kill me. Please." I turned to look at her, blinking as two teardrops escaped my eyes and slid down my cheeks. "I'm begging you, Gwen."

Ginevra reached out and stroked my belly. "Aren't you forgetting something?" She drew me toward her, cradling me in her arm, and I rested my head on her shoulder.

"It hurts too much. I can't—I can't breathe." Ginevra looked at me helplessly. "I didn't tell him. I didn't have time to tell Evan about the baby."

Unable to ease my pain, she said nothing. I lost myself in the somber silence. "He asked me to marry him," I confessed after a moment.

"I know. I always knew it, from the day he realized he loved you. He was just waiting to ask you until you were ready."

More silence.

"I destroyed everything. I don't deserve to live. It doesn't make sense any more. Kill me, I beg you."

"It wasn't your fault, Gemma. It was a trap. *They* kept him away! The Màsala knew he—"

Sobs shook my chest and I couldn't hear what she was saying. "How can I bear all of this? I . . . I can't do it."

"I don't know," she whispered into my hair, "but we'll face it together." She held me tighter as hot tears streamed down my cold face.

I stared at the rippled lake in front of me, my gaze lost between the blanket of fog and the horizon where the first rays of light reflected off its mirrored surface. It was daybreak, yet no light could ever free me from the darkness that imprisoned me. Outside, the sun was rising. Inside me, it had set forever.

Far away
where nothing speaks of you,
where everything tastes bitter,
where memory makes no sense,
it is as cold as ice
that knows not how to melt.
Where the silence of things deafens:
the darkness, the tick-tock of a sweet memory.
Far away, even farther than echo;
where those who think weep,
where every dream is the same color.

From the book of poetry written by my father,
Giuseppe Strazzanti

1

COMFORTING PROMISES

January

Mechanically putting one foot in front of the other, I walked down the steep path. In the dense, snow-covered woods, nature displayed her stark winter beauty as she always did. The forest was filled with a thousand sounds, but I could barely hear them. It was astonishing how the world went on, ignoring the suffering inside me, ignoring the rubble of my heart as it splintered into shards day after day and everything crashed down on me again and again. The sun went on rising and setting. Even my own body went on breathing—as if it too were mocking me.

I reached the water's edge, sat down cross-legged, and let the chilly morning air lash at my face. I closed my eyes, forcing myself to dam up the river of tears that constantly waited behind their lids to ambush me.

Each day at the same time my heart led me to that spot as it had the night I awoke from that horrifying dream. With a never-ending pain in my chest I watched the moon's melancholy attempt to reach the sun that eluded her every time. There on the lakeshore, in that spot where the memory of us twisted around my heart like barbed wire, the moon's desperate message touched me. I felt the burden of her sorrow as she watched her beloved sun from afar with her pale light before vanishing after her long journey. I imagined their forbidden desire to meet. Just one day. Just one time. A single moment together.

But no one could ever grant their wish, just as no one could ever again bring back my Evan. My life would remain an endless, bitter-cold night of darkness, devoid of light. My beloved sun had disappeared forever.

Months had passed since Evan's death—or had it been only weeks? I couldn't remember. Time didn't matter any more. I just wanted to disappear, to dissolve in the water like sunbeams at sunset. Instead I went on living. Walking. Breathing.

But every single breath burned my chest.

Unable to explain the actual how or why of Evan's death, Ginevra had told everyone he had driven off one night and never been seen or heard from again—that, worried something terrible had happened to him, we had searched for him high and low, but no one had found him. Other people murmured about a "missing person," but my parents realized the truth. They even offered to take care of the funeral arrangements, when they thought I couldn't hear them, but they'd been dissuaded since a body hadn't been found.

So there had been no ceremony, no funeral—it was as if it hadn't happened. Like it was all just a nightmare. The worst I could ever have imagined, but just a nightmare all the same, which the morning could have taken away. But every day the sun rose without him. I would wake up in his bed and feel like I was dying all over again. I would lie there clutching the covers without opening my eyes, as though I were dead too. Then the dark pit would rise up to fill my chest, brutally reminding me that it was all true, and I would curl up in the sheets and let it swallow me whole as I buried my sobs in his pillow. Evan was gone. Never again would I hear his voice breathe sweet nothings into my ear, never again would I feel his hands caress me, never again would I blush at his penetrating gaze after catching him staring at me with those little creases beneath his eyes. Never again would he tease me . . .

My devastating need for him made me long to die. Instead, I had no choice but to keep going, my heart shattering into a thousand pieces over and over, moment after moment, every single day.

I had lost everything.

The days dragged by, each more painful than the last. At school I would occasionally respond to my friends' worried looks by forcing a smile, but the second I looked into their compassionate faces my eyes would well up and my lips would quiver and I would have to press them tightly together to stop the tears. Feeling naked and fragile, I would run off before my heart fell to pieces right there in front of them. I couldn't let anyone get close to me—I was too vulnerable. Besides, no one could understand how desperate I was inside. It felt like a piece of me was missing, like someone had violently, unexpectedly ripped out a part of my body, an essential part without which it was too painful to go on living.

"Hey . . ."

I rested my head on my knees as Ginevra's calm, caring voice guided me back to reality. "Hey," I whispered.

"Time to go to school," she reminded me gently.

"I don't feel like going." I met her eyes and she understood. She sat down beside me and for a while we stared at the lake in silence. "You keep coming here," she said softly.

"I can't help it," I said, my voice weary. "It's like I need to experience the pain again, let it explode inside, to punish myself."

"Gemma . . ."

The torment I felt was inconsolable and somehow she sensed it as though it were her own, as though there was some sort of connection between my heart and hers. I stared at a colorful hot-air balloon drifting all alone across the sky and remembered when we had all taken part in the Adirondack Balloon Festival, a local event, rising into the air together with hundreds of other balloons before breaking away from the group.

"He wanted to stay," I said aloud, since Ginevra would have been able to hear my thoughts anyway.

After the battle on the frozen lake, Evan had received an execution order. He'd decided to stay by my side to protect me but I'd forced him to go. As we shared our last real kiss, I'd promised to give him another one when he returned, but it was with that kiss—when I'd thought it wasn't actually Evan but an impostor—that I killed him. If only he hadn't left in the first place . . .

"It was my fault. He didn't want to leave me, but I insisted."

"Because it was the right thing to do. You did it for him. You thought it was best for your future together."

"What future? Evan and I don't have a future together any more."

"You had no way of knowing he wouldn't be back before—before the kiss. Come on." Her voice was a barely audible whisper. "Let's go home, at least. It's freezing out here." I nodded, letting Ginevra wrap her arm around me and lead me to her black BMW X6.

Simon rushed up to us the moment we walked through the front door. "She did it again?" he asked Ginevra, as though I weren't standing right there. She nodded. "Gemma . . ." There was concern in his voice. "Gemma, I can help you. Why won't you listen to me?"

I shot him a fiery glare. "Don't come near me!" I threatened, shuddering internally at the idea. "If you can't undo the wrong I've done, I'll pay for my actions. You can't take away my pain too," I cried, partly in despair, partly as a warning. I didn't want Simon to erase my memories of Evan—that would have been unbearable.

"I would never do it against your will," he said, trying to reassure me, "but why won't you let me help you?"

"I never want to forget anything about him." Trying to sound determined, I fought back the tears, losing myself in a silence all my own. "Not a single second, not a single breath he took. Not ever. Not even if the pain kills me."

Ginevra rested her hand on my shoulder. "I know it's too soon, but sooner or later you'll forget Evan and your heart will open up to someone else. You can fall in love again. It happens all the time at your age. Life isn't over for you, Gemma." Encouraged by my silence, she went on. "Peter's a nice guy. Maybe with time you might give him a chance."

I looked at her with an expression that was as stunned as it was angry. How could she say something like that? Could she really think that?

"He's still in love with you. Don't let his love fade away while you're thinking about someone you can never have back."

"Could you ever forget Simon if something happened to him?"

"That's different," she said with a mix of obstinacy and compassion. "I'm not a human, I'm a Witch. We love differently from you mortals."

"Then I guess I'm not human either, because I know I'll never forget Evan. My heart will never have room for anyone but him."

Ginevra was about to say something but changed her mind when she saw the determination in my eyes. I didn't know about her, but as far as I was concerned the discussion was over.

"Gemma, right now it might not feel possible, but you'll get through this," Simon assured me.

"You're wrong, you're all wrong!" I took a breath, trying to keep my voice down. "I . . . I feel like I'm being crushed. I can't breathe."

"Simon's right. You've got to take your life back into your own hands, Gemma. You're still alive!" Ginevra insisted as though she could convince me. "Incredible as it might be, the poison didn't kill you. Faust didn't kill you. Neither did that other Subterranean who passed himself off as Drake! You should be happy; why don't you realize that?!"

I shot her a look, totally offended. How could she even think I might be *grateful* to fate for taking everything from me? It was inconceivable. How could she not understand? It no longer mattered if I was dead or alive. "How can I go on living when I already feel dead inside?" I stared at her intensely, tasting the poison in my words.

Ginevra leaned over and hugged me. "You're not dead, you just need to realize it. The fever is gone. I think it would be best if you went home."

"No!" I couldn't believe it. Was Ginevra actually kicking me out?

"Gemma, you can't go on hurting yourself like this. Living here is too hard on you. You'll never get over it if you keep refusing to let him go!"

A sob escaped me. What was she trying to tell me? I didn't want to let him go. I wanted to cling to him, to his memory, to his scent, which still lingered on his pillow. Losing that too would be too much for me to bear.

"Maybe we should leave town," Simon whispered, but I heard him.

"NO!" The desperate cry burst from my chest. "No, please! You can't! You can't leave me! It would be like dying all over again, I wouldn't be able to take it!" I felt like I was slipping into a chasm.

"Shh. Gemma, calm down. We're not leaving," Ginevra said softly, shooting Simon a reproachful glance. "I would never leave you. You're my sister and nothing can ever change that."

Simon nodded silently, seeing the truth in it. I forced myself to breathe to ward off a panic attack. "Swear it," I pleaded, looking at her, devastated. She let me go and looked at me for a moment. "Swear it!" I insisted.

"I swear it," she said firmly, stroking my hair. "I could never leave you. Besides, you're not safe yet. There's no guarantee they won't attack you again." She looked at Simon for a long moment. "It's up to us to protect her now. For the time being, I know what you need, Gemma. Follow me."

"Where are we going?" I asked hesitantly.

Simon gave her a nod of agreement. Ginevra turned to look at me, her hand on the door leading to the garage. "You could use a reminder that you're still alive."

2

THE VOICE OF CONSCIENCE

Ginevra's Lamborghini Reventón shot out of the garage with a feline bound as I tried to banish to a dark corner of my mind the memory that continued to surface whenever my eye fell for more than a few seconds on the leather-and-Alcantara-suede upholstery. The last time I'd been in that car was with Evan. After we'd spent the evening in the garage fixing it, he'd pulled me down onto the seat with him and things had quickly heated up. Time had slipped away unnoticed that night as we hid from reality . . . until my dad had called. It felt like years since then.

I slid my hand into the neck of my red sweatshirt and pulled out Evan's dog tag. I hadn't taken it off since he'd torn it from his neck and put it into my hand a moment before vanishing. I clenched it in my fist until it hurt.

"It'll get easier with time, you'll see." Ginevra was looking at me out of the corner of her eye. She could hear all my thoughts but I didn't care. It had been a while since I'd given up trying to censor them. It was pointless. Besides, it didn't matter any more. I didn't answer. She knew herself it was a lie. "I swore to you we wouldn't leave."

I turned to look at her, alarmed. I hoped she didn't want something in exchange. She couldn't force me not to suffer. She couldn't force me to forget.

"No, Gemma, I don't want you to forget Evan. I wouldn't want it for myself either. But you have to at least make an effort. Try to get a grip." I hung my head, acquiescing, though I didn't know how to go about it. "One step at a time, okay? Evan wouldn't want to see you like this. He fought so that you could live. Don't throw away the gift he wanted to give you." Staring out the window, I bit my lip and tried to swallow the knot in my throat. "Try to take your mind off things at least a little, just for today. Would you? For *me?*"

I gave a small nod, still staring at the trees as they raced past on the other side of the glass, their naked black branches seeming to reach skyward in supplication. "Where are we going?" I managed to ask, making an effort to indulge her. I couldn't repress the pain weighing on my chest, but I could at least force myself to camouflage it, to hide it from the others and keep up appearances. I didn't want Ginevra to have second thoughts and decide to leave me. I wouldn't be able to bear it. Ginevra could read my mind, but she would never be able to fully understand the pain and grief I was experiencing. Those emotions were all mine. I just had to force myself to ignore them for a little while, to push them deep down in my heart so Simon and Ginevra wouldn't leave me.

"I'm taking you to New York City," she said with a sincere smile. "A change of scenery for a few hours will do you good."

"Why isn't Simon coming with us?"

Ginevra laughed. "Guys aren't cut out for this kind of thing."

"*What* kind of thing, exactly? What's your plan?" I asked warily.

"Don't worry, it won't be anything horrible. We'll hang out for a while—you know, girl time. Just you and me. We can do whatever you want. Go shopping, walk through Central Park, admire the view from the top of the Empire State Building, check out the neon signs in Times Square—"

"No stores, please," I was quick to say.

"Whatever. In any case, Lake Placid is too sleepy, too quiet. You need to be somewhere that doesn't give you time to think, at least for a while."

I tightened my lips, not so sure it would be enough.

The cold, gray air of New York City welcomed us only four hours later. It usually took six to get there, but Ginevra had burned up the accelerator. When I got out of the car thousands of sounds hit me, almost throwing me off balance. Ringing phones, footsteps, honking horns, hundreds of voices fused together into a single, constant, incomprehensible buzz. I looked around and took a deep breath just as a hot trail of smells wafted by: hot dogs mixed with smog. My stomach twisted, unsure whether or not to listen to my hunger.

"Welcome to the Big Apple!" Ginevra's face was lit up with excitement, her eyes lost among the shop windows and the thousands of blinking lights. Suddenly a giant plasma screen filled with her image: a blond goddess with breathtaking curves and emerald-green eyes. "I've always loved this place!" she exclaimed, pulling me along by the hand as I rolled my eyes at her narcissism.

The passersby all seemed to be in a hurry, as though each had a specific destination, a direction. I, on the other hand, wanted only to fade into the crowd that packed the street, to lose myself among all the people . . . to forget who I was.

Every so often we stopped at one of the shop windows and each time it took a lot of effort to persuade Ginevra she didn't have to buy me everything I laid eyes on. I would inevitably end up resigning myself and waiting for her on the sidewalk until she came out again with yet another package.

At one point something caught her attention and she stopped so abruptly I almost walked right into her. "Oh. My. God!" she exclaimed, her eyes bulging.

"What is it?" I asked, alarmed. I was almost afraid to turn around and find out what she had seen.

"That dress is amazing! It's breathtaking!"

I followed her gaze to the shop window and saw what she was talking about. "Um, sure, if you live in the eighteen hundreds," I shot back on impulse, but then it dawned on me that Ginevra might actually *have* lived during the Victorian era. Frowning, I looked at her and realized I'd never asked her. "How old are you, anyway?"

A huge smile lit up her face. "You never ask a girl her age, hasn't anyone ever told you that?"

I blinked. "It doesn't count if it's another girl asking. Don't dodge the question."

Ginevra's smile widened into a grin. "Old enough," she replied as she dragged me into the store. Once inside, she squeezed my hand, excitement filling her voice. "Pinch me. I'm in heaven! There are so many of them!" A wave of memories made her eyes sparkle and she lost herself in a world all her own, stroking the fabrics and skipping from one dress to the next. All at once she stopped in her tracks. Her gaze darted around the room like lightning and finished on mine. I started shaking my head in alarm. I could guess from the light in her eyes what she had in mind.

"No way," I said. "Forget it."

"Come on, you promised you would make an effort. Besides, this dress is perfect for you!" She pulled me encouragingly toward a red gown.

"Gwen, I have no intention of buying this dress. I wouldn't know what to do with it."

"Nobody said you had to buy it." Ginevra motioned to the sales clerk who took the dress off the mannequin and handed it to her. She held it out to me, wielding her most persuasive smile. "Aw, try it on. I'm sure you'll look enchanting in it!" I rolled my eyes. "You promised you would humor me!"

"Actually, I never said that," I shot back huffily.

"Like you needed to." With a shrug, she turned to the clerk and pointed at the dress in the window that had caught her eye, then winked at me and disappeared into a changing room before I could respond. I took a deep breath and forced myself to go along with it.

The changing room was spacious—it had to be, otherwise no one would have been able to move around in there wearing one of those hot-air balloons. The curtains and furniture were also done in Victorian style. It was like going back in time.

With a resigned sigh, I took off my clothes, put on the fluffy gown, and smoothed the fabric with my hands. It really was gorgeous, I had to admit. I pulled on my ponytail and a soft wave of dark brown locks tumbled onto my back. For a second I let my guard down and allowed myself to get into the role.

"Miss, do you need any help?" The clerk had come to my dressing room. Her voice was muffled by the thick fabric of the curtain.

"I can't do up the corset." I opened the curtain just as Ginevra appeared opposite me. We stared at each other for a long moment, smiles appearing on our faces. Stunning in her white gown trimmed in gold, she took a step toward me, asking the clerk with a glance to leave us alone. As though she had received an order, the young woman obeyed without hesitation.

Ginevra stepped behind me and laced up the back of my dress so tightly I could barely breathe. I wondered if the clerk was curious as to how Ginevra had managed to lace up her own gown without any help. My eye fell distractedly on the microscopic price tag that dangled from the waist. The gown cost a fortune.

"You're a vision, *chérie*," Ginevra whispered behind my ear, continuing to tug and lace.

"You speak French now?" I said, grinning, as my cheeks turned red at the sight of my reflection in the mirror. I had never fantasized about what it must be like to live in an era totally different from my own, yet Evan must have been used to seeing girls walking around wearing luxurious gowns like this one. My heart skipped a beat at the thought of Evan just as Ginevra squeezed my shoulders.

"Aren't they amazing?" she asked in an attempt to distract me.

"I can't deny it. They're simply beautiful and you look like a princess."

Ginevra smiled happily, checking herself out in the mirror. Leaving her to admire her reflection, I wandered around the boutique, checking out the accessories and running my finger over the fabrics. My gown swished, dancing across the floor. On display on a small inlaid-wood table were elbow-length gloves grouped into different colors and materials. Another table showed off parasols in linen and lace.

I turned toward Ginevra. Her long blond hair flowed down her back in a golden cascade, curling at the ends. Smiling at her enthusiasm as she contemplated her reflection in the mirror, I turned back to study the store, then glanced out the window. The smile died on my lips and my heart turned to ice as my eyes met his.

Evan.

I rushed outside, desperately looking for the spot where I'd seen him, but the crowds seemed to be increasing. I hurried along, pushing my way through them until I found myself running. Everything around me began to spin, as though the hurrying multitude wanted to sweep me up into its vortex.

It was him. I had seen him. It wasn't a ghost. It was Evan *in flesh and blood.* His eyes of ice had found mine through the window. I'd glimpsed them for only a second but it was long enough for them to absorb all the other colors and turn everything else black and white.

I looked for him among the faces of the passersby, but he had disappeared. Why was he hiding? Had he *chosen* to leave me? Or had he been forced to go and couldn't come back? Utterly confused, I ran a hand over my forehead and grabbed my hair, clenching my fists. I felt like I was on a carousel spinning out of control.

A sinister sound stirred the air right behind my ear. I spun around in alarm. People steered clear, casting nervous glances at me. There came another breath of air on the opposite side that seemed to drift in on an ominous wind. I spun around again, trying to follow it. I felt like I was losing my mind. A cold shiver made my hair stand on end. The malevolent breath of wind seemed to be hovering nearby like a ghost. Then the infernal whisper crept into my mind:

Murderer.

Clutching my hair with both hands, I began to shake my head convulsively. I didn't want to hear it, but the voice continued to torture me: *Murderer. Murderer. Murderer.*

I sank down against the wall with my knees pressed to my chest, squeezed my eyes shut, and covered my ears as the tears battled to come out.

No. No. No!

"Hey, hey . . ." Someone touched my arm. A familiar voice, very close to my face. I raised my head and looked into her big green eyes. "Everything is fine." Ginevra was beside me, squatting on the sidewalk.

The sounds from the street suddenly returned, hitting me loud and clear, like someone had just unmuted the world. People hurried along the sidewalks and cars zoomed down the streets. I looked around, feeling like a frightened animal. I had no idea what had just happened or how I had gotten there—it felt like I had just lived through a nightmare. Was my desperation actually verging on insanity?

"Everything is fine." Ginevra continued to talk to me as I tried to convince myself I wasn't crazy. I nodded and rested my head on her shoulder. I must have been a strange sight, wearing a Victorian gown and sporting a pair of Nikes. People glanced at me, then ignored me and continued peacefully on their way. I, on the other hand, was in shock.

"Well? Want to tell me what happened?" Ginevra asked, her voice concerned and comforting. I shook my head, not sure I knew myself. "You ran out of the store. I looked everywhere for you but I couldn't block out the thoughts of all the other people to track down yours."

Suddenly I remembered everything. "Evan," I whispered, my voice breaking from the lump in my throat.

"Gemma." Ginevra sighed with exasperation and turned to look me straight in the eye. "Evan is dead. Do you understand what I'm saying?"

I frowned. I felt like I wasn't really there, but rather, suspended between the present and the insane moment I had just experienced. In my head I was still trapped in Evan's gaze. "I saw him," I whispered in a barely audible voice, not looking at her.

"That's impossible." Ginevra took me by the arms. "You *thought* you saw him. Your mind projected his image. You're still upset about what happened." But I wasn't listening, because another memory had made my blood run cold: the chilling accusation carried by the wind.

Murderer, it had said. I trembled as Ginevra held me tight. "I killed him. I killed Evan. I'm a murderer. I deserve to die."

"Gemma, you need to stop feeling guilty about what happened. It was an evil scheme *plotted out from beginning to end.*"

The tears returned to slide down my cheeks. "I should have known. I should have known it wasn't him." I looked at Ginevra desperately, my lips quivering. "I didn't recognize him!"

Ginevra lifted my chin as though I were a child. "Listen to me: there's no way you could have known! We fell into our own trap. It wasn't your fault. That Subterranean tricked us all right from the start."

I looked away, unable to let Ginevra's words in so they could touch my broken heart. Nothing could convince me it wasn't my fault. *I* had killed Evan. Death had come to him by my lips. I had taken his life with a kiss cursed by fate. The chilling whisper I had heard in my head was my own conscience screaming its reproach, reminding me of what I'd done.

We walked on for a few blocks. My fit of madness had driven me pretty far away. I felt incredibly awkward with my Nikes and the gown flowing imperiously over the rough asphalt. I lifted the skirt to avoid ruining it.

"What do you say we stop off somewhere to eat?" she asked in a considerate tone.

"I'd rather go home, if you don't mind."

Ginevra made a vague gesture and shrugged. I realized that if she went without food she risked turning grouchy, but I felt vulnerable and wanted to get home as soon as I could. "Besides, we need to take this dress back," I reminded her, though I could already see the gray of Ginevra's car in the distance.

"No need." A smile escaped her. "I bought it."

I blinked and shot her a disapproving glance. "You said you weren't going to!"

"No, I said *you* didn't have to buy it." The smile on her lips turned into a grin. "I never said I wouldn't buy it for you."

Resigned, I shook my head and carefully gathered up the skirt of the gown so I could sit down in the passenger seat. The Lamborghini took off, drawing only a few stares. In Manhattan it was easy to go unnoticed. We certainly weren't in Lake Placid, where all eyes were always trained on the five of us.

The three of us, I forced myself to remember.

"I can't wait to see how you manage to change now!" Ginevra smiled, trying to lift my spirits.

"Very funny! You know I have no intention of spending four whole hours in a car suffocating in this thing. Where are my clothes?"

She pointed at the hood of the car. "In the trunk, of course."

"What??"

She shrugged, her smile spreading into a grin, then gave in. "Don't worry, just kidding. They're right there under your seat."

"Would you help me?" I asked, pointing at my dress's laces. "I can't undo it on my own."

While Ginevra kept her hands on the steering wheel and her eyes on the road, the long laces began to float through the air and undo themselves, sending a tingle down my back. I slid off the gown and folded it up in the bag that had contained my clothes.

"Ah . . . at last!" Slipping on jeans and a sweatshirt felt like a dream. "Is your offer of food still good?"

"Forget it." Ginevra glanced at me. "Absolutely not."

"Come on!" I begged her. "You can't let me starve to death just to avoid getting a few crumbs on the floor mats! It'll take us hours to get home!"

She glanced at me and caved. "Oh, all right. What are you hungry for?"

"A burger and fries?" I asked, looking at her hopefully.

"You're disgusting," she shot back, jutting her chin toward the glove box in front of me.

When I opened it, two hamburgers and two sides of French fries almost tumbled out onto my lap. I looked at Ginevra. "For both of us? Didn't you just say I was disgusting?"

She shrugged it off. "Seemed rude not to keep you company."

"Yeah, right." I smiled to myself and picked up a bag of fries. She reached out, took one and popped it into her mouth.

Halfway home I fell asleep, switching off my mind for what felt like no more than an instant. I woke up with a start, feeling like I was drowning, just as Ginevra pulled through the gates at home. Groggy, I mumbled, "We're back."

The garage door closed behind us and the engine went silent. Simon rested his hands on the roof of the car and leaned down to greet Ginevra with a kiss. Lately they'd been careful not to overdo it with the PDAs when I was around, worried I would sink back into a pit of longing for Evan.

Simon headed to the front of the car. "How much stuff did you buy?!" he exclaimed in shock when he saw the number of boxes Ginevra had managed to fit into the Lamborghini's storage compartment.

"It's not for me. That's all hers," she said with a nod and a wink in my direction.

"I had nothing to do with it, I swear," I told him, raising my hands defensively.

"That's what I figured." Simon shot me an understanding look. "What is this?" he gasped, almost horrified by Ginevra's gown from the 1800s that was peeking out of its bag.

"Don't ask me." I pressed my lips firmly together, not wanting to get involved.

"My God! I was so happy when these things finally went out of fashion! Is she doing it to torture me?"

With a shrug, I followed them toward the living room door. Out of the corner of my eye I glimpsed the black motorcycle in the darkest area of the garage. The previous summer, in a race spawned by sibling rivalry, I'd gotten onto that bike with Ginevra and—who knew how—we'd won. The next day Ginevra had started to teach me how to drive a bike, but when Evan got back from the mission he'd been on he'd replaced her as my teacher. He'd said later he planned to buy me my own motorcycle so I could join in the races.

I stared at the spot beside Evan's bike—a spot that would forever remain empty.

"I'll pay you back sooner or later," I promised Ginevra, sitting on her bed as she put her purchases away in her walk-in closet. I had no idea how I would manage that, but I would find a way.

"You don't owe me a cent," she was quick to reply.

"That dress cost a fortune, not to mention all the other things! I told you not to buy me anything, but you never listen."

"You'll be thanking me soon enough when you don't fit into those any more," she said with a grin, pointing at my hip-hugger jeans.

"Hey!"

Ginevra laughed, but her eyes quickly filled with warmth. "You're still one of us. That hasn't changed," she said to convince me she didn't want me to pay her back. To judge from her words, she seemed to be avoiding letting Evan's name slip. "What's our is yours. You can take all the money you like whenever you need it."

"Don't be ridiculous. I could never take your money."

Ginevra's only reply was to turn and walk into her closet. From what she'd told me, her collection was nothing in comparison to the typical wardrobes of Witches, who liked to wear a different outfit for each occasion. "Third drawer down," she said abruptly.

I looked around, wondering if she was mad at me. "Huh?"

"Open it."

Puzzled, I went to the dark wooden dresser. "Do you need something in partic—" I froze when I pulled the drawer open. It was full of stacks of hundred-dollar bills. "What the hell?"

Ginevra appeared in the doorway. "Go ahead, take some and put them in your backpack. You never know when they might come in handy!"

"Ginevra, are you crazy? They're going to think I robbed a bank! I can't take your money!"

She strode over in a huff. "Empty it," she ordered me.

"Huh?! What for?"

"Go on, empty it!" she insisted.

"Why? I don't get what you're trying to pr—"

Before I could finish, Ginevra moved between me and the dresser. "Fine, I'll do it myself." In a flash, she dumped the contents of the drawer onto the floor, forming a pyramid of bills.

"What are you—"

She waved her hand over the money and before my shocked eyes the bills burst into flames, warming my face.

"Whoa-whoa-whoa! Wait!" I tried to stop her, but in the blink of an eye the fire carbonized all the money. I stared at the pile of ashes in shock.

Ginevra's laughter snapped me out of it. "It's only paper, Gemma!"

"Sure, go tell that to all the people who wage wars for centuries for some of that 'paper.'"

With a flick of her hand, the now-empty drawer slammed back into the dresser, making me jump. "Go ahead, open it again."

"You're kidding, right?" I turned to look at her, but my hands unconsciously opened the drawer. It was full of money again.

"That's how it works for us." I stared at her, floored, and blinked as a giant smile spread across her face. "It's a treasure chest," she explained, looking pleased.

"A *what*?" I still couldn't believe what I'd just witnessed.

"I've tried to convince Simon that times have changed, but he still insists on calling them that. There are several of them throughout the house. Once they were filled with gold coins, but now"—she leaned over, picked up a stack of bills, and waved it in front of my face— "it's only paper. Do you get it now? You can use the treasure chests whenever you want. I don't need to be present. They respond to anyone and will give you whatever world currency you want. Consider it a private—and bottomless—bank."

"It's like the leprechaun's pot of gold at the end of the rainbow," I murmured.

"What?"

"Never mind." I sat on the bed and Ginevra went back to focusing on what she'd been doing. I was still stunned, but also relieved there was no need to pay her back all that money after all. "I'm going to go draw a hot bath," I said, raising my voice so she could hear me from the closet.

"You just relax. I'll take care of the rest. Oh, and . . . I hung up your dress in my closet in case you feel like putting it on again."

I walked out the door with a smile, definitely doubting that would ever happen.

3

A CRY OF REMORSE

The spa in their house was like an oasis of peace. In the hot tub, the water burbled on the surface like little geysers emitting spirals of steam.

After my bath, I really needed to call my parents. I knew I had disappointed them over the last few weeks, so I'd decided to stay on at Evan's house and try to avoid them as long as I could, partly out of fear of facing them and partly because I didn't think I would be able to bear their pity. It wasn't fair—I knew that—but I couldn't help it. Ginevra had explained to them that something had happened to Evan, that he'd disappeared. Her powers of persuasion had come in handy in convincing them not to insist, to let me detach myself from Evan gradually. They had respected my decision and stepped aside. I couldn't imagine how much my mom must have suffered.

The truth was Ginevra wanted to keep an eye on me and study the effects the poison had had on my body—or rather, the effects it *hadn't* had; for some bizarre reason, it hadn't killed me. Maybe it was because of the baby. My mortal blood combined with Evan's Subterranean blood had probably generated something different, something stronger, that had protected me. No matter how many explanations came to our minds, nothing had solved the mystery.

Even so, Ginevra was right: I couldn't stay there forever. It was time for me to go home. I sank into the boiling-hot water, shivering at its contrast with the bitter cold in my heart. The memory of Evan's gaze as he stared at me through the shop window was like a needle stuck in my brain. How could it possibly have been only my imagination? Was I so tormented that my brain was responding to my heart's desperate need by generating hallucinations?

It was like living a nightmare. Part of me still cherished the hope that at any moment someone might wake me, but it never happened. I had fallen into a dark pit. Every day I sank deeper and deeper; the ground continued to cave in and I was farther and farther from the light—from my Evan. I felt like a fire deprived of oxygen that was gradually dying, condemned to be reduced to nothing but ash.

The heat of the water was so comforting it alleviated some of the chill I felt inside. All I had to do was let myself sink. Driven by that desire, I slowly slid down and the heat on my neck sent little tingles of pleasure through my body, caressing me in waves. I needed it so badly. If only that heat could reach the ice in my heart . . .

I slid farther down until my head was submerged. The surface of the water closed above me and I was swept up in a sensation of infinite peace, a sweet oblivion that enveloped me like a warm velvet blanket. It cradled me and gently rocked me in its warmth.

Evan.

His eyes smiled at me. There, in that dreamy, sleepy state I saw nothing but his face. He was waiting for me. The soft curve of his lips moved slightly, mouthing something in slow motion.

Gem. He was calling to me. *I love you.*

I felt tears sting my eyes but no longer felt any pain as I glided toward him, finally feeling him so close again. I wanted to cry out that I loved him too, that we would be together again, that soon I—

All at once something tore me away from him. Someone was clutching me. I opened my eyes and struggled to breathe as water streamed out of my nose, freeing my lungs.

"Gemma! What on earth were you doing?!" Horrified, Ginevra shook me. "My God. Are you out of your mind?! I was keeping an eye on you and all of a sudden I couldn't hear your thoughts any more!"

Only then did I become aware of where I was. "I—"

"Come here," she whispered, and squeezed me tight. Her embrace was the key that unlocked all my pain. Sobs suddenly wracked my body and a torrent of tears streamed from my eyes.

"I miss him," I whispered, my voice barely audible.

"I know." Ginevra stroked my hair.

"I don't . . . don't know how to live without him." She held me tighter. "I can't breathe. Without Evan, it's like I'm suffocating. I just want to die so I can be with him again. Help me, please."

"I'm here," she whispered comfortingly in my ear, trying to calm me. "I'll always be here for you."

"Sometimes I just want to disappear. "

"Look at me." She took my face in her hands. "You can't give up now. It's hard, I know, but you have to fight."

My chin quivered as more tears filled my eyes. "What sense is there in fighting? Don't you get it? Evan is dead! *Dead.* He's dead, and my will to fight died with him. Let them take me," I cried. I struggled to keep my voice steady, but the sobs returned to shake me and the pain to grip my chest, overwhelming me. "Why doesn't anyone come looking for me? Why don't they kill me so I can join him?"

"You wouldn't join him anyway."

"I pray for death to come free me from this living hell."

"You can't say things like that! You have to do it for Evan. Gemma, he sacrificed everything to keep you alive. You can't do this to him. If you gave up now, his death would have been in vain." Ginevra stroked the water with her hand.

Though I wanted to nod, nothing she had said eased my pain. Her eyes came to rest on my belly. She caressed it as though the gesture concealed a thousand words.

I sat up, trying to compose myself. "I'm not even sure it's there," I blurted. "It's been over three months but my body hasn't changed. I don't feel *anything*." It was a relief to finally admit it out loud. I had taken several pregnancy tests, but the total lack of symptoms had left me in doubt. Still, it wouldn't have been a good idea to see a doctor to confirm the pregnancy, let alone have sonograms done; none of us knew what a Subterranean's seed might generate, and Simon and Ginevra couldn't risk exposure that way. Day after day I would look at my belly, expecting it to grow, but it never did. There was nothing about my body that suggested I was pregnant except that I hadn't had any periods—but then again, major stress could make women skip periods.

Ginevra continued to stroke the surface of the water, gliding her fingers through the foam, swaying slightly as she traced wide lines. Her face wore an absorbed look. She raised her head and our eyes met. "It's there." She smiled at me. I stared at her in silence, bewildered by her confidence. I wanted to ask how she could be so sure, but words weren't necessary. She covered my belly with her hand and looked me in the eye. "I can hear its little heart beating," she whispered.

Her voice was like a caress. Something hit me right in the chest. An emotion. I sat there, dazed and silent as the echo of Ginevra's words made its way through my heart. Instinctively I raised my hands to my abdomen and the whole world seemed to stop. He was *really* inside me? I was stunned, as though just discovering it.

A part of Evan was growing inside me. I couldn't risk losing him.

As the unexpected certainty sank in, I looked up at Ginevra and we smiled at each other. I let out the breath I'd been holding and hot tears slid down my face uncontrollably.

"It might be a girl; I can't be sure," Ginevra said.

I slowly leaned back in the tub and considered Ginevra's comment. Suddenly her expression darkened, alarming me. She nervously pushed some foam aside with her fingers, as though searching for something beneath the surface.

"What's wrong, Gwen? Why are you looking at me that way?"

"How did you get that scar?" she asked, pointing at the wispy, silvery streaks on my abdomen.

"What, that? It's nothing, just a birthmark," I was quick to reassure her. "My grandmother used to tell me that in some parts of the world there's an old wives' tale that says that when you're pregnant, if you have a craving but don't satisfy it, the baby will end up with a birthmark in that shape on its skin. Ridiculous, isn't it? The funny thing is, it seems my mom was always asking for coconut or something like that when she was expecting me."

Ginevra blinked and looked at me again with a strange light in her eyes. It looked like . . . *concern*?

"What is it?" Did she not believe me? Suddenly I remembered when Evan had also noticed it the first time we made love. I struggled not to sink into the abyss. I hadn't even had the chance to tell him about the baby.

She composed herself and gave me a smile that looked forced. "Are you okay now, or do you want me to stay here with you?" Ginevra looked distracted, focused on something I couldn't grasp.

"No, no. Go back to Simon. I think I'll stay here a little longer."

"You sure?"

"Sure."

Watching her walk out the door, I tried to get a grip and banish the sadness. I cupped some water in my hands and rinsed away the dried tears that had left my skin tight.

I can hear its little heart beating. My heart trembled at the memory of Ginevra's words. I really *was* expecting a baby—Evan's child. Who knew why my body wasn't showing any visible signs yet. My belly was the same as it always had been. And none of us knew how things might turn out. Sooner or later I would have to start researching to find out if there had been other cases like mine. Would the baby be human? Or would it have powers like its father? A thought struck me like a lightning bolt: would he have to serve Death as an Executioner? I didn't want to think about it.

A strange sound outside the door put me on guard. I got out of the tub and wrapped a towel around me. Steam seemed to be seeping out through the gap under the door, drawn into the hall by some sinister power. I opened the door a crack and peeked out. There was an unearthly silence. An eerie one. I took a cautious step forward, groping for the light switch. I could barely see a thing.

In the utter silence, an ominous whisper drifted through the air and into my ear. A chilling whisper, like someone praying under their breath. A door slammed behind me. I spun around and jumped: a figure stood at the end of the hall. My heart racing, I squinted and tried to make out the face. His gaze came to rest on mine and when I recognized him my heart thumped and went still.

Evan.

My eyelids fluttered and a tear slid down my cheek. "Evan!" I cried, rushing toward him. In the spine-chilling silence of the dark hallway, my voice resounded off the walls, returning to me in a twisted echo. Before I could reach him, though, his face suddenly filled with terror and he pulled back, flattening himself against the wall.

"Evan!" I froze. I'd seen that fearful look before.

Gem . . .

I reached him and tried to take hold of him, but he staggered and collapsed to the ground. I leaned over him, wracked with sobs as his body jerked from the spasms caused by the poison.

No! Not again, no!

"Evan, I'm begging you, don't die. Don't leave me, please." Tears flooded my eyes as he shuddered, sprawled on the floor. It was happening again: the past had sucked me into its vortex of pain and I could do nothing to stop it. I couldn't keep Evan from dying.

"Evan!" I grabbed his head in both hands and continued to weep, drowning in desperation. I wanted time to stop. I wanted to keep him there with me, even at the cost of giving my life for his. His lips moved, his voice barely audible. Trying to understand what he was whispering to me, I stared at his lips forming the words and my heart turned to ice.

Murderer.

An explosion inside my chest left me shattered. I knelt there in shock as a breath of wind brushed my ear, sweeping past like a ghost. Following it with my eyes, I turned toward the dark hallway and started with fright. A little girl wearing a white petticoat stared at me, hidden in the shadows. Very slowly, she began to drift toward me. I stifled a shriek of terror and turned to look at Evan, but the spot where he had been lying was empty. I couldn't breathe.

The girl came to an abrupt halt. A single shaft of light barely illuminated the hallway and through the gloom I finally saw her face. I tried to scream but no sound came from my throat, my words frozen in terror at the sight. It was me at age five, but her face was pale as a ghost's. She had deep, dark rings under her black eyes and her hair hung loose to her waist. The sinister whisper filled my head once more as the little girl raised her arm and pointed at me. An accusation. She was *accusing me.*

I put my hands over my ears to block out the whispers, but it was no use: a thousand voices were murmuring a single spine-chilling word: *Murderer. Murderer. Murderer.*

I felt I might lose my mind. An icy wind lashed my face. My eyes shot up and found the girl right in front of me. Her eye sockets were empty and pitch black. I cringed and my heart leapt to my throat when her lips moved, joining the voices inside my head: "*Murderer.*"

A shudder rattled me down to my bones. Then, in the distance, another voice: "Gemma! Gemma! Wake up, damn it!"

I found myself sprawled on the floor, trembling, feeling like I had fallen from an incredible height. Simon and Ginevra were at my side, shaking me. I looked up at them in shock, my body still quivering.

"What happened?" I murmured, so softly I wasn't sure I had actually uttered the words.

Simon and Ginevra exchanged a glance. "Everything's fine now. We're here."

"Evan . . ."

Another fleeting glance. Was I going insane? "I think you had a hallucination. It was like you fell into a trance. I couldn't hear your thoughts again."

What Ginevra said shocked me. What was happening to me? Was one single moment of relief from my guilt enough for my conscience to wake up and fling accusations at me?

"No, Gemma." Exasperated, Ginevra forced me to look at her as though I had forgotten every word she'd told me, as though I had lost my senses. "Evan is gone," she said cautiously, without hiding her compassion.

"Maybe you should lie down for a while," Simon suggested, his gentle voice betraying his concern. "A little shuteye would do you good."

I couldn't disagree. Nodding, I let Ginevra help me dry myself off. As I got under the covers I felt like an automaton—a dry, empty, useless husk on the verge of cracking.

"Want me to stay here until you fall asleep?" I nodded again, or at least I thought I did. I was so tired. "Simon called your parents to let them know you're okay." She squeezed my hand. "You'll see, tomorrow you'll . . ."

Ginevra continued to talk, but I couldn't hear her any more.

4

THE EMPTY ROOMS OF THE HEART

Drake's cheerful face came into focus against the blurred backdrop of the lake at sunset. "You still here, sunshine?" When I turned toward him, I found him leaning over me and holding out his hand. "Why don't you come with us? We found an amazing place beyond the woods!" His smile was an invitation to follow him, so I took his hand.

"Finally," Evan's warm voice whispered in my ear as he slid his arm around my waist. "I couldn't wait any longer without you." His lips touched my hair and I trembled, shaken by a strange sensation. Something was wrong.

Drake's harmonious laughter rang through the trees as I followed Evan and him into the woods. Given their cheerful, perfectly calm expressions, it seemed there was no reason for me to be worried, but still, a vague presentiment nagged at me. From time to time Evan squeezed my hand. As though by magic, his touch banished my every fear. Even so, the treetops grew denser with each step we took, blocking the sunlight, and the air grew colder and colder. "Evan, what—"

"Shh. Don't be afraid." Suddenly the woods gave way before us, revealing blocks of worn stone that looked as old as the world itself.

"You can't change fate." Evan's voice touched my ear as gently as a breath of warm air. Still, something wasn't right. All at once I experienced a terrible feeling of loss, and when I spun around I was shocked to discover they were gone. I was alone, surrounded by the darkness. Even the woods had vanished. Fear filled me and it took all my strength to gulp down the lump in my throat that threatened to suffocate me. I moved through the rubble, trying to figure out where I was. All at once, there among the stones, I saw the entrance to a cave. I looked around, unsure of whether it was a hiding place or a trap. In the end I decided to risk it and ventured inside. The air was damp and a golden glimmer danced over the rock walls.

Trailing my hand over the craggy stone, I advanced slowly, my steps hesitant and my heart racing. In the distance I heard a faint lapping noise: there must have been water there. I raised my eyes. Thousands of glittering stalactites hung from the ceiling—a magnificent sight.

Suddenly I tripped and found myself sprawled on the cold rock. As I ran a hand over my forehead I noticed something on the ground—a strange groove. I traced it with my fingers and quickly brushed aside the dust, revealing a symbol carved into the rock. I stared at it. It looked familiar. Had I seen it somewhere before?

Something made me look up. Eyes. Jade ones, like Ginevra's. I flinched, but then realized they were kind. They belonged to a beautiful woman who was leaning over me, her hand held out. She had gorgeous, wavy, chestnut-brown hair that flowed over her breast and a braid around her head that framed her face, making it even more radiant. There was something in her eyes—something elusive yet familiar.

"Did I frighten you?" Her voice penetrated my bones with its harmonious sweetness. A strange power emanated from her. She laughed at my fear, the most beautiful sound I'd ever heard. "How silly. You shouldn't be afraid of me. Come, I'll help you up."

Concealing my uncertainty, I complied and took her hand. "Who are you?" I asked.

"My name is Anya."

"I'm—"

"Gemma."

"How did you—"

Her graceful laughter rang through the cave, which meanwhile had changed. It was as though the walls before us had pulled back to make room for a small, shimmering body of water. *The same color as her eyes . . .* Curiosity banished every thought: all I wanted was to go to the water's edge and admire the varied hues that dappled its surface. I had never seen anything like it. The little pond seemed enchanted.

Drake's words returned to my mind. Was this the amazing place he wanted to show me? "What place is this?" I asked Anya.

"You'll love it, you'll see!" she replied, her enthusiasm tinged with a trace of sensuality, like an enchantress. Did she want me to follow her?

In the blink of an eye Anya was on the opposite shore. I was left breathless by how swiftly she'd moved. She teased me, her harmonious laughter echoing through the cave again, then turned solemn. "You have to come with me," she announced. "You can't change your fate. Sooner or later you'll have to realize that."

Something in her firm tone sounded wrong to my ears. She materialized at my side again, making me jump, but then smiled at me. "Come. I want to show you something."

She took my hand and I let her guide me. I couldn't resist; my body was ignoring my instincts and obeying only her. But once we reached the water's edge I stopped, momentarily steeling myself against Anya's power over me. Just as I slipped out of her grasp, something glimmering beneath the surface caught my attention. When I recognized him I dropped to my knees and gripped the lake's rocky border, driven by renewed desperation.

"Evan . . ." The water was deep but I could make out his shape. He was chained to the bottom, his face turned up toward the surface as though he had heard my voice.

"EVAN!" I screamed, gripped by an uncontrollable impulse. I plunged my arm into the water to grab him but jerked it back when excruciating pain seared my flesh. The water felt corrosive. I desperately scanned the ripples in search of his face but could no longer see the bottom of the pool.

"What does it mean?" I asked Anya, trying to hold back my tears. "Where is Evan?" Was my mind playing tricks on me? Was it Anya, toying with me? "Who are you?" I shouted, trembling.

Anya slowly shook her head. "That's not the right question." She stared at me for a long moment. "Come with me, Gemma." She held out her hand and stepped barefoot into the water.

I looked into her eyes, my heart pounding. There was something buried deep within me that yearned to follow the woman, certain she could reveal mysterious secrets to me. Yet there seemed to be a threat in her invitation, making part of me rebel against that ancestral call. She emanated an aura of power like an alluring siren, and I was willing to follow her into the abyss like a sailor enchanted by her sweet voice.

I murmured Evan's name. For some insane reason, I thought following her would lead me to him. Driven by that desire, I reached out to take Anya's hand but my heart balked. Heeding its warning, I immediately pulled back.

"You have to come with me, Gemma," Anya insisted. "It's your destiny. It always has been, right from the start."

I blinked, entranced both by her gaze and the water, whose lure continued to magnetize the part of me unable to resist.

"You belong to us," she repeated more slowly, in a persuasive whisper.

I reached toward her. "I belong—"

"Gemma! Gemma, wake up!" The voice dragged me away from that enchanting place. I found myself staring into Ginevra's worried eyes in the semidarkness of Evan's room as the first light of dawn peeked in through the curtains.

"Ginevra." I stared at her, confused. "What happened? Why are you shouting?"

She heaved a sigh of relief as Simon appeared in the doorway, agitated. "It's been a hellish night." She cautiously rested her hand on my forehead. "You were delirious. You kept mumbling the weirdest things." Another concerned sigh. "You started screaming and we came running, but nothing could wake you. You had a really high fever again and we were afraid you were slipping back into that state of unconsciousness."

"Do you think it's because of the poison, still?" I asked.

Simon went over to Ginevra and took her hand to calm her. "Her body should have purged it from her system by now."

"We can't be sure," she said. "Something's wrong. I've never seen anyone survive such a high fever and wake up like nothing happened."

"I . . . I'm fine," I tried to reassure them. I touched the back of my hand to my forehead: it was beaded with sweat, but cool. When I met Ginevra's worried gaze, it felt like she was hiding something from me, but I immediately banished the thought. "Honestly. Everything's fine. Don't worry, guys."

"We'll stay here with you," Simon offered.

"Really," I was quick to reply, "there's no need."

"No, Simon is right. Besides, it's almost morning. We can go downstairs if you like," Ginevra suggested. "Unless you want to sleep a while longer."

For some reason, I had the impression that Ginevra wanted me to get up, that she actually thought my going back to sleep was a bad idea. *She was afraid it would happen again.*

"Fine with me," I said. "I wouldn't be able to fall back asleep anyway."

"Perfect," Ginevra murmured, not taking her eyes off me.

I distractedly tucked my hair behind my ear, embarrassed by her unusual look of concern. She seemed to be studying me. "Gwen, are you worried about something?"

My question seemed to startle her, but her expression remained calm. "No," she said casually. "Why should I be? You said you were okay, didn't you?" She got up from the bed, crossed the room, and leaned against the doorframe.

"Yeah," I said, finding her behavior a little perplexing.

"Perfect!" she exclaimed with a bit too much enthusiasm to be believable. She nodded to Simon. "Go prepare the TV. I'll take care of the food while Gemma is getting ready."

I bit my bottom lip, staring at Simon as he left the room. Ginevra followed. Before the door closed behind her, I called. "You're sure everything's okay?"

She wavered, showing her hesitation. "Everything is under control."

I couldn't see her face, but her calm, calculated tone betrayed how hard she was trying to hide her true emotions. As the door swished shut an uneasy tingle crept over my skin.

What was Ginevra hiding from me?

The second I walked into the kitchen their whispering abruptly ceased. "Hey!" Ginevra welcomed me aloud so Simon, whose back was turned to me, would know I was there.

The impression that they were hiding something from me was taking root in my mind. "Hey," I replied without much enthusiasm. I slipped my thumbs into the back pockets of my jeans and rocked back and forth to ease the unusual awkwardness.

Simon came over and pulled out a chair at the table for me. "Called your parents already?"

"Yeah. I promised to have lunch at home with them. We've been spending so little time together lately, I couldn't bring myself to say no. This whole situation must be really hard on them." Simon and Ginevra exchanged fleeting glances, confirming my suspicions. "Is there something I should know?" I asked. Their hesitation convinced me to insist. "Gwen, what were you two talking about before I walked in?"

Ginevra looked unperturbed but for a split second Simon's eyes wavered.

"Simon?" I pressed him.

"They found Evan's car." A blade pierced what was left of my heart. "It happened last night."

"This isn't good for her. She doesn't need to hear it," Ginevra said.

"Yes I do," I said. "I want to know."

Ginevra nodded, her eyes fixed on mine. "The police are dragging the lake for him. They think they'll find his body there. We saw helicopters and the chief of police stopped by when you were in the shower."

"He asked us some questions. Wanted to let us know he would keep us posted if they find him."

I gripped the back of the chair. Hearing someone refer to Evan as a corpse made my stomach churn. "He didn't want to talk to me?"

"Simon made him uninterested in you."

It took a few seconds for her meaning to sink in. I knew how easy it was for a Subterranean to influence humans' minds however they pleased. Simon could manipulate people's memories, so he must have made the police chief forget all about me.

"Maybe you shouldn't go to school today," Ginevra suggested.

"No, I could use the distraction."

"They might ask you all sorts of questions. I don't think being around people who feel sorry for you will be good for you."

"It won't be very different from what I'm already going through. I can handle it," I said, determined. For some reason, the thought of staying home scared me. I didn't want the nightmares to come back and haunt me. Besides, nothing could make me feel worse than the burden already weighing on my heart.

"I told Evan to get rid of that car! He must have forgotten, damn it!"

Simon's comment hit me straight in the heart. I stared at him, shocked by his irritable remark. How could he talk about Evan in that tone?

Ginevra sensed the indignation in my thoughts and rested her hand on Simon's wrist to make him understand. "It's better this way." It was incredible how she managed to keep her cool in every circumstance.

"She's right," I spoke up, drawing their glances. "They wanted an explanation. Now they've got one. At least they'll have something new to talk about." My voice sounded distant to my own ears. It felt like I was in a parallel dimension where nothing made sense, as if I were living someone else's life, one that didn't belong to me. A life that was bizarre, meaningless. Painful. Or maybe it was my refusal to accept having lost Evan that made it so unreal. I left my slice of buttered toast on my plate and grabbed my backpack. I felt drained of all emotion, and my appetite had disappeared as well.

"I'm going to school," I announced, walking quickly away from the table.

"Wait! I'll go with you!" Ginevra exclaimed. Simon held up his hand to say goodbye and I nodded at him.

Minutes later, Ginevra and I were walking through the school doors. I tried to keep my head down to avoid all the compassionate looks, but with every step I heard the other students' murmurs. Everyone's attention seemed directed solely at me.

"Gemma!" Jeneane and Faith caught up with me as I was pretending to put some books away in my locker.

"I heard what happened on the news," Faith began shyly. I hung my head, unable to look them in the eye.

"You have no idea how sorry we are. This must be awful for you." Jeneane put her arms around me and hugged me.

"I can't imagine what you're going through," Faith added. "If you need anything at all, day or night, we're totally here for you."

"What she needs is to avoid thinking about all this," Ginevra said, looking at them sourly, "and this attitude certainly doesn't help."

"Gwen!" I said with annoyance. "Take it easy. I'm not a child." I turned to my old friends. "Everything's fine. Actually, I already suspected something like that had happened, but I really appreciate your support. Maybe someday soon we could hang out."

"That's not a bad idea," Ginevra agreed.

"Count on it," Jeneane said while Faith nodded in silence, tears in her eyes. "Just let us know when."

"Thanks. See you in class." I shut my locker, thinking of how I had avoided everyone over the last few months and wondering how they could possibly still be willing to talk to me. Peter was silently waiting for me to be the one to start up our relationship again. Meanwhile, my parents always let me know when he stopped by to ask how I was. He also glanced in my direction whenever he thought I wouldn't notice. He always knew what I needed.

For some strange reason I found it comforting that everyone now thought Evan was dead, as though sharing an infinitesimal part of my pain gave me the strength to pretend I was all right when they looked at me. The news had formed a sort of shield—admittedly a fragile one full of cracks—around my heart that helped me hide my anguish from the world. But despite everything, beneath that shield the pain still burned and nothing could ever make it subside.

The hours dragged by as I watched the snowflakes perform a slow dance outside the window. The teacher's voice paused from time to time and I was almost sure his gaze had followed mine out the window, but I was too apathetic to find out.

"Hey." Ginevra tugged on my sweatshirt to grab my attention and tapped on some papers she was holding. "Check these out." She slid them onto my desk.

There was no need to look down for me to know what they were. Just to be nice, I thumbed through them but then gave a grunt of disinterest. "I don't want to go to some stupid college."

"At least give them a look!"

"What makes you think they would accept me in my condition?" I protested, trying not to raise my voice.

"No need to worry about that." Her tone softened, making me look her in the eye. "I'll be there to help you. We'll do it together, all four of us."

"Four?"

"The three of us and the baby. It'll already be born by then."

"Oh, right."

"We can babysit while you're out. Simon loves babies. He had a little brother. It was hard to leave him when he enlisted. If you don't want to go someplace far away, you could apply to Nazareth College in Rochester. Your grandparents live around there too."

"Gwen, I'm not even sure I'll be able to finish high school. Yale, Dartmouth, Boston? They would never accept me." My voice faded at the thought of how I'd used to dream of going to a prestigious university. It had been a sand castle that the wind had swept away, leaving behind only ruins. "In any case, I don't deserve to go to them any more. My grades would have done a nosedive if you hadn't insisted on doing my homework for me. Speaking of which, like I've already told you, you've got to stop doing it."

"Only when you feel ready to take your life back into your own hands. Until then, I'm not letting it fall apart."

"I'll never be ready," I mumbled, tears welling in my eyes.

"Yes you will." Her whisper was barely audible, but I heard it. "I promise."

I returned to my thoughts of Evan and the darkness in which my soul dwelled without his light to illuminate my path. If I closed my eyes I could almost believe for an instant that he was still there with me. I looked out the window as though he might reappear at any second. But the emptiness that had taken up residence inside me reminded me it would never happen.

I walked down the hall with Ginevra and realized for the first time how hard it was not to think of my pain when everyone around me did nothing but remind me of it. Despite her attempts to distract me, every look, every gesture, every whisper brought back the memory of what I had lost.

"Jeremy Lloyd is still head over heels for you," I whispered as we walked into the cafeteria.

Jeremy was a brawny sophomore who couldn't take his eyes off Ginevra. She was constantly teasing him. When he struggled to hide his shyness by acting cocky she would have fun turning the tables on him with little witcheries. Once in a while Jeremy dared to ask her out, to at least give him a chance, but she would just toy with him by making something fall to the ground between them so he would trip over it and look ridiculous.

"Looks like he's been working out, don't you think?"

"He's coming this way," I warned Ginevra under my breath, noticing she was hiding a sly smile. "Don't do it again, please?" I begged her, but her smile grew brighter and before I could stop her Jeremy tripped over a chair, probably wondering how it had gotten there.

"How you doing, Jer?" she asked with a smile he would never forget.

I rolled my eyes and held out my hand to help him to his feet, but he got up on his own, looking at Ginevra with adoration. "Always great, when you're around," he said, moving closer. "Still convinced you don't want to go out with me?" he asked point-blank, seeming unconcerned about coming on too strong. "Consider it an open invitation," he insisted, raising an eyebrow.

Ginevra moved dangerously close to him. "You know what, Jeremy? I would love it if you . . ." She whispered something in his ear. I could see he was having trouble staying on his feet with all the excitement that had to be running through him.

"Absolutely," he murmured, under her spell.

Ginevra smiled and turned her back on him. "Who knows? I might just give you a chance." She was only teasing him, but Jeremy's face instantly flushed. "Once you've learned how to walk without falling over yourself, that is." Her answer left him speechless as, amused, she wielded her most dazzling smile.

"And I bet you'll never let that happen," I muttered. "Give it up, Jer. She's already got a boyfriend." I pushed her away, exasperated by her sadistic game. "Ginevra, you really are unbelievable! This is insane! Your magnetism is surreal. All the guys hang on your every word. I'd love to know how you do it."

Ginevra raised a malicious eyebrow. "That's one of the advantages of being a Witch. You know, how you look isn't important, because everybody has their own personal taste when it comes to appearances. What counts is your allure, the energy you emanate. It's like a love potion that we give off with every glance. If you can feel the electricity, rest assured he feels it too. You just need to learn to use that power to your advantage. It's your attitude that makes the difference. Everything in life is seduction. If you know how to wield it, the world is in your hands. We Witches have complete control over our pheromones. It's lots of fun." She smiled.

"It's hard for me to agree, seeing how *you're* the only one who had any fun just now."

"That's not true. The whole cafeteria laughed when Jeremy fell." She grinned and patted my shoulder. "Don't get so bent out of shape about it. Besides, at the moment I have a mission to accomplish, so humor me."

"What would that be?" I cast her a glance as she sat down at a secluded table.

"Making you smile!" She winked at me and I stifled a laugh. "I managed, didn't I?"

As I shook my head, my eyes came to rest on a table in front of us and my smile vanished as quickly as it had appeared. Peter had just left his lacrosse team and was sitting there alone, frowning and looking glum.

Before I could open my mouth Ginevra had guessed my intentions. "Go talk to him," she said with an encouraging nod, probing my mind.

"I'm not sure that—"

"He's waiting for you," she assured me, knowing I was afraid he wouldn't want to speak to me any more. "He's been choosing to sit alone for a while now, hoping you'll feel ready to talk to him, hoping you know he's there for you—that he always has been. Don't be afraid, Gemma. Not with him. Fear is just an obstacle, and until you get past it you'll never know what's waiting for you on the other side."

Peter had probably heard the news too. It wasn't hard to imagine he felt bad for me. Though I'd known him my whole life, his sweetness continued to amaze me.

"It's time for you to go talk to him, don't you think?"

Giving a little nod, I stood up before I could change my mind. I walked over slowly, studying Peter's profile. He hadn't noticed me yet. "Talking to yourself?" I asked.

Peter raised his melancholy eyes for only a second and then stared blankly at the table again, as though convinced I was just a figment of his imagination. "There's no better company than yourself," he said. His tone was vaguely bitter but also defeated. I was sure he was referring to me, to my absence in his life.

"Sorry, I'm bothering you," I murmured, turning to go.

"No, wait." I stopped without turning around. There was a long pause. "How are things?" he asked.

The simplicity of his question defused my tension. I pulled out a chair and sat down facing him, grateful he hadn't mentioned Evan's car being found. We looked at each other without saying anything, tacitly trying to determine what remained between us. We hadn't seen each other for a long time, but shouldn't friendship be able to survive anything? Where would we pick things up? Would we act like nothing had happened? That was impossible—I had set off on a journey toward the universe and my world had crumbled too many times. The Gemma he'd once known was gone, even if part of her was still trapped in the ashes of a star that had exploded inside her.

"Seen the news?" I asked, my gaze wandering to his tray.

"I haven't been watching much TV lately," he said without asking what I was referring to.

"Never mind." When I looked up into his face I felt a strange, terrible sensation. We had become strangers. From the way his eyes wavered almost imperceptibly, it was clear that he'd realized it too. I could never have imagined it might happen to us.

"I heard you've been asking about me over the last few weeks."

"I shouldn't have, probably," he said after a moment of silence.

"No, I'm happy to know"—I struggled to find the words— "that you don't hate me."

His face lit up and his eyes shot to mine. "Why would I hate you?"

"Well, because . . . because of how things went."

"I could never hate you."

I rubbed my hands together, completely on edge, and glanced at Ginevra. She was looking out the window but I was sure she was listening to us. "I was afraid you would. Hate me, I mean." Peter frowned, surprised. This time, when our eyes met, they exchanged a bit of the affection that used to warm us. "You could call me sometime if you feel like it," I suggested.

"I've wanted to," he admitted, his tone still sad. "I dialed your number lots of times . . . stared at it, but in the end I didn't make the call."

"Why not?"

"You were holed up in that fortress. Sometimes I wondered if you were hiding from me." He smiled to himself but immediately grew serious again. "The truth is I was afraid you weren't ready. You certainly didn't need anybody else feeling sorry for you. Besides, I was sure you knew that when you were ready, I would be there."

A lump rose in my throat. My chin trembled and I tightened my lips to avoid crying, but a solitary tear escaped anyway. Peter reached his hand toward mine in a silent gesture of comfort—the only kind I could bear.

"You're right." I smiled through the tears. "You've always known what I need." I squeezed his hand. "Now I know how much I missed you."

Peter smiled at me tenderly as the bell rang for a long moment, our eyes locked the whole time.

"There she is. You see her talking with Turner again in the cafeteria?"

"They've always been *close*, Peter and her. He's the baby daddy, if you ask me. The other guy found out about them and ditched her."

As I listened to the two girls gossip in the hall, uncontrollable anger built up inside me. Ginevra squeezed my hand but I was about to erupt like a volcano.

"Great theory. Shame he crashed afterwards." The two girls laughed.

It was seriously too much. I rushed at one of them and slammed her against the lockers. She cried out and I looked her in the eye. "Don't even *think* of talking like that about him," I snarled right into her face. "Because next time I'm gonna rip your tongue out."

"Oh my God, did you see that?"

"What is she doing?"

"She's crazy, the poor thing."

Hearing the whispering behind me, I slowly came to my senses. "Gemma," Ginevra called. She hadn't tried to stop me. She'd probably wanted to shut them up too when she heard them insulting Evan. "That's enough. Let's go."

I released my grip on the girl, whose eyes filled with tears. Minutes later I heard my name over the PA system. I was being called to the principal's office. I let out an exasperated groan. Wasn't I going through enough already?

"Don't worry. I'll take care of it," Ginevra assured me.

I opened the door to the office and saw the girl I'd attacked, along with her friend. When I walked in she backed up like she was terrified of me. I rolled my eyes. I hadn't hurt her that badly—certainly not as badly as she'd hurt me with her poisonous words. Still, it came as no surprise; Mallory Gardner was in Jeneane's drama class. She was just putting on an act for the principal.

"Miss Bloom, is it true you assaulted Miss Gardner?"

"Yes, Mr. Reynolds, but she said—"

"What she said is irrelevant!" he bellowed, leaving me mortified.

"Mr. Reynolds!" Ginevra sat down facing his desk and crossed her legs. "Don't you think 'assault' is a bit too strong a word? All Gemma did was give her friend a great big hug."

"Whaaa?" Mallory sputtered. "She slammed me against the lockers! You saw it for—" Ginevra shot her a piercing glare and Mallory choked back the rest.

"Miss Gardner, have the courtesy to let her finish. What is it you were saying?" The principal was putty in Ginevra's hands.

"I was saying it might be better to consider the issue resolved. After all, Gemma is going through a terrible time. More stress wouldn't be good for her."

"But Gemma attacked her!" Mallory's friend said. "Mr. Reynolds, you saw the scratches for yourself!" She pulled the top of the girl's shirt down to bare her shoulder and I flinched at the sight of the red marks my nails had left. Had I actually been the one to make those?

My eyelids fluttered as they disappeared before my eyes.

"What the— They were right here!"

"She's making it up. She must have rubbed her skin to put on this little charade. She's the one who attacked Gemma with her gratuitous insults!" Ginevra snapped. "Mr. Reynolds should punish the two of you for your lack of moral support."

He considered Ginevra's words. Another glance from her, and he succumbed to her powers of suggestion. "She's right. You shouldn't have been so cruel to your classmate, especially in light of what she's had to endure recently. A one-day suspension will help you reflect," he said sternly, filling out two slips of paper.

"What? That's insane!" the two girls whined.

"Are you questioning our principal's judgment?" Ginevra asked, feigning innocence.

The two scowled at her. She smiled as they walked out the door carrying their suspension slips, then stood up and took me by the hand. "Mr. Reynolds, we're really grateful for your understanding. It would be better if Gemma's parents didn't learn about this little misunderstanding."

"Of course. No need to alarm the family over something that never happened."

Ginevra was unbelievable. Without my saying a single word, she'd turned the tables in our favor in a matter of minutes and had the girls *I* attacked be suspended. Actually, they deserved it. I smiled too, savoring our little victory.

As I stood up to follow Ginevra, who was already at the door, an old photo of a little girl on the principal's desk struck me. Noticing that it had drawn my attention, he seemed to shake himself free of Ginevra's spell, breaking the connection between them. "My little Caitlin," he said, his face growing sad.

The girl was on a bicycle and looked very sweet. "She's adorable."

"Gemma, we'd better go now," Ginevra said.

"Who's the boy next to her?"

"Gemma, I told you, let's go." She sounded nervous, but I didn't listen to her. I couldn't take my eyes off the photograph.

"It looks like he really cares about her." I reached out, uncontrollably drawn to the photo, but the principal snatched it away and stared at me like I was crazy. "What boy? Are you pulling my leg?"

Confused, I looked at him and turned back to the photo. "The boy squatting down next to her, in the green shirt. I was just saying that, from his smile, he looks really affe—"

"There is no boy in this photograph." A shiver ran down my spine. What was he saying? "This is the last memento we have of Caitlin. She died minutes after this picture was taken, hit by a car," the principal said, his eyes filling with tears.

I looked more closely at the picture. Was he kidding me? There was a boy right there! He had incredibly light eyes and long blond hair tied in a ponytail, and was crouching beside her as though . . . as though waiting for her.

As I stared at the photograph, stunned, it dawned on me: the principal couldn't see him because he was a Subterranean, there to claim little Caitlin's soul. "I don't—" I wanted to apologize but had no idea what to say.

How was it possible that I could see him? It was just a photograph!

Ginevra rested a hand on my shoulder. "Gemma, we should go now. Mr. Reynolds, as I mentioned, Gemma has been going through a very difficult time . . ."

"I'll write her a pass to go home," he agreed, still upset. I watched his hand as it moved across the slip of paper, but I wasn't actually there. I was lost—lost in doubt, in strange thoughts. Lost in my madness.

I dropped Ginevra off and parked the BMW in my parents' driveway. Before getting out, I took a deep breath. They must have already heard the news about Evan's car being found. Mom's suffocating hug confirmed my assumption. "Honey, we heard what happened. You have no idea how sorry we are." I looked at her, unable to speak. "I know you haven't wanted to talk about it, but Ginevra told me Evan unexpectedly disappeared and that no one knew where he was. She also told me the search led nowhere and that—that you suspected he was dead. But none of us could have imagined something like this."

Maybe out of egotism, I had never talked to my parents about Evan's death. How could I have confessed to them that I'd been the one to kill him, when not even I could accept it? "I know, Mom, but the news doesn't change anything. He was gone before and he's gone now, and there's nothing anyone can do about it."

"She just can't get over it," my dad murmured from the other room, disheartened by my mood.

"Honey, thank God . . . I'm so happy you weren't in the car with him," Mom added.

Her remark chilled my heart and my body reacted by freezing. I pulled away from her, furious. "Thank God for *what*?" I hissed. "You don't know what you're talking about. It was all my fault! I'm the one who should have died! Not Evan!" But Mom could never understand that. It was true: she simply didn't know. "I'm sorry." I fought back the tears, horrified with myself.

"Honey, it's not your fault. You're still shaken," she whispered, stroking my hair. But her words just twisted the knife stuck in my heart by reminding me of what I had done. She had no idea how wrong she was. It was *all* my fault. "You're still upset."

I pulled back and wiped away my tears. "No, I'm fine. It's just that I skipped a few meals, so all I want to do is eat, if that's okay with you," I lied, wanting the moment to end.

"Of course. Everything's ready."

"How's Iron Dog doing? I have to admit I kind of miss the little monster," Dad said, sensing my desperate need to change the subject.

"Couldn't be better. Ginevra loves him. Besides, their yard is a lot bigger than ours."

"I wish you would come home," Mom said softly, letting all her grief show. "But I realize that with work and everything else, you wouldn't get the attention you need right now."

"Simon and Ginevra are good people," I reassured her.

"I know, and I have no doubt they'll take good care of you. I've seen how much they care for you. Still, it's important for you to know that whatever you need, we'll always be here. You do know that, don't you? Please tell me you do," she begged.

"I know, Mom. Of course I do."

She had always felt guilty about the time she denied me because of work, and now her concern was off the charts. But there was nothing she could do. It was a good thing Simon and Ginevra had used their powers to convince her to let me stay at their place, otherwise she would have felt even worse. I was kind of sorry, but knew it was for the best.

"Besides, next year you would have left us anyway to go to college," Dad reminded me. Or maybe he'd said it for Mom's benefit. I took a sip of soda and looked down. "I mean, you still want to go to a good college, don't you?" Dad asked.

"Of course," I forced myself to say. I didn't want to disappoint them yet again, and the sigh of relief he and Mom drew made it clear that any other answer would have done just that. "Ginevra already got me some application forms." I just hoped the principal didn't change his mind and tell them what had happened at school. He probably thought I was crazy now too.

"Good. You know how much it means to us. You've worked so hard and it would be a shame to waste all the effort you've put in over the years."

"You're right," I lied again. "That's not going to happen."

I wondered how they would accept the truth when I didn't end up going to college after all. I decided that for the time being it didn't matter; I would cross that bridge when I came to it. For now, it was like I was watching my life through a fogged-up window. I couldn't see through the glass. I couldn't imagine a future without Evan.

Lunch lasted longer than usual, as though my parents didn't want to let me leave because they were afraid they would never see me again. They looked sad as they watched me go upstairs to my room, where I holed myself up for a little while.

I leaned back against the door and waited until I heard only the silence that told me they'd gone. Then, moving slowly around the room, I studied every detail carefully: the walls, desk, books, bed . . . Everything was just as I'd left it, but nothing was like it had been before. Every surface, every detail was filled with the memory of Evan, his scent, the sound of his laughter in my hair—

"Gemma?"

I jumped. "Mom! I thought you'd already left."

"Without saying goodbye?" She shut the door, stood behind me and rested her hands on my shoulders. "If I ask you how you are, will you tell me the truth this time? It's just me and you, like it used to be."

I looked at her. I always tried to avoid crying in front of others, to hide my pain, but that made it accumulate behind the door to my heart until it crushed my chest. So sometimes the door burst open, which was exactly what I felt was about to happen. "I'm not the same person I used to be, Mom."

"Of course you are. You might feel lost, but you'll find your path again, you'll see."

"Sorry, but there's no path for me any more," I confessed.

"Gemma, not all is lost. You have to have faith. Pessimism is an easier road than the tortuous one that leads to hope. Not everyone has the courage to walk that road, but you've always been a fighter. It might look like the end of the world to you right now, but that will pass. And when you fall in love again, Evan will be only a mem—"

I jerked away from her, feeling the rage build up inside me. "I realize it's not the end of the world. The world doesn't give a damn about me—it just keeps moving along like I don't exist, like none of this is important. But I know for sure it's the end of *my* world. I'll never have anyone else in my life."

"Honey . . ."

"Leave me alone, Mom! You can't understand."

"Don't hold back your tears. Not in front of me, please. Don't keep your emotions from me. I was just trying to encourage you. You can't give up hope—it's the only light we have left when life darkens our path. Without hope everything turns dark, and I don't want that for you."

"It's *already* dark, Mom! *Why can't you understand that?!*"

"*You're* the one who doesn't understand. You've got your whole life ahead of you. You can't destroy everything because of one boy! I know it's hard, but you'll come out of it, I promise."

"Don't promise me things that are out of your control." I moved away, desperately wanting to distance myself from her, from those words. "You once told me life is like a mountain: you only reach the top when you give up and stop climbing. When you think there's nothing left but to descend. Well, I'm there. I give up, Mom. I can't do it."

"Of course you can. You're going through a rough period, but one day everything will make sense again. You're only seventeen! You'll go to college, meet lots of other boys, and fall in love ag—"

"It's not going to happen, Mom!" I shouted in frustration. Why wouldn't she go? Why wouldn't she leave me alone?! I wished she would disappear. I wished they would all disappear forever.

Mom smoothed my hair behind my ear. "I'll try to explain it using an analogy you understand really well: love is like a book. When one story ends, you can't just lose hope. You close one book but you can open others—as many as you like. You're the one who chooses whether to reread the same book over and over or to move on."

I sighed. She was always ready to dole out advice, to preach from the pulpit of her perfect life. But mine wasn't perfect—just the opposite! Why couldn't she see that? "No, Mom. Let me tell you how things are. It's true, a love story is like a book you loved, but even when it ends you can always hide away in the pages of your memories whenever you want. That's enough because you know no other story could ever offer you the emotions it made you feel."

"No one can erase those emotions, but that doesn't mean you can't experience other, *different* emotions when you fall in love again. You can discover new stories, Gemma. If you close yourself off, you'll never know what new adventures await you."

"I'm not going to go out looking for another boyfriend or a father for my child. I'm raising the baby on my own," I stated, adamant. I had given Evan the keys to my heart and no one else would ever be able to unlock it.

"Gemma, the love we hold inside is precious. It's a little fire that keeps us alive. We need to watch over it, hide it sometimes, maybe, but never give anyone else the power to extinguish it."

"How *dare* you tell me something like that?! You, of all people, who raised me spewing your *stupid* theories about eternal love!" I could see my words had hurt Mom deeply. The tears built up inside me. "I'm sorry," I mumbled, feeling horrible. "Please, I need some time alone."

She clasped me to her and turned to go, stopping in the doorway. "Keep climbing, Gemma. Your peak is still far away."

I clenched my fists once she'd closed the door, feeling like everything inside me was on the verge of exploding. All at once I couldn't hold it in any more. Blind rage took over and with a shriek of frustration I let its fury rush through me. Gnashing my teeth, I hurled everything on my desk to the floor, picked up every object I could get my hands on and smashed it against the walls. I wanted to destroy everything. Taking a framed photograph from the shelf, I shattered it against the door.

The sound vibrated inside me, reminding me that I too was made of fragile glass. I fell to my knees and picked up the frame, not caring if I cut myself. Behind the shards, my image smiled, wrapped in Evan's arms. The moment was clear in my memory: we'd been on a boat, my feet dangling in the water. Evan had surprised me by sitting down behind me and pulling me close between his outstretched legs. I still remembered the thrill that contact made me feel. Evan had stroked my cheek with his nose and Ginevra had captured the moment. Running my finger over my smile, a smile I would never wear again, I wept. This time I didn't even try to stop the tears. I felt terribly alone. Empty. Robbed.

Torn apart.

"Evan," I murmured almost inaudibly. The room was blurry through my tear-filled eyes. "I miss you . . . You promised. You promised you would never leave me," I told him, sobs breaking my voice. "You said you would always be there. Please, give me a sign, be it a light or a shadow."

Silence. Deafening silence.

I tried to stifle my sobs, but all I could hear was the echo of my pain as it washed over me again. Suddenly a gentle breeze came through the window and caressed my skin, sending a shiver through me. My chin quivered as I remembered when it had been Evan who arrived in silence with his warm, penetrating gaze. I closed my eyes and let the tears stream down my face as, with trembling lips, I whispered to the wind, hoping it would carry my words to him: "I miss you to death. I don't know how to go on without you."

But when I opened my eyes, the room was empty. It had been all along. For the millionth time, I felt alone. My room had never seemed so big before—or maybe it was just me feeling the emptiness of being without Evan.

5

FRAGILE

From time to time I took one hand off the steering wheel of the BMW to wipe my eyes so I could see the road. The short drive from my parents' house to Simon and Ginevra's must have gotten longer somehow, because it felt like I would never get there. The snow had stopped falling, leaving the air damp and the streets slippery. Fluffy white patches had accumulated on the branches that raced by like ghosts outside the window, projecting me into a surreal landscape. Inside the car, Lana del Rey's melodious voice cradled me in my own dark paradise. The words seemed to have been written just for me. *There's no you, except in my dreams tonight . . .* It was getting harder and harder to ease the pain when it wrapped me in its thorny embrace. My guilt was killing me. I couldn't accept the fact that my lips had taken Evan's last breath.

I had always considered my own death the most terrible scenario of all—it was impossible to imagine a worse torment. Ever since I'd learned about the Subterraneans and the fate that had been written for me, it had occupied my mind. I'd learned to live with the awareness that each moment might be my last. It had never once occurred to me that I might be the one to go on living, without Evan. But now I was condemned to a fate worse than death; losing Evan so unexpectedly was a pain I would never learn to live with.

Fate had mocked us to the very end. I felt like I was living in an ironic fairy tale. In the silence of the car—Lana's song had ended—I answered my own thoughts out loud: "Yeah, but unlike with a book, you can't peek at the final pages of your life to see how things will end up. You can't rewrite the ending if something goes wrong." I sank into silence again, ruminating. The pages of your life turned all on their own, day after day, and all you could do was look on. I had ruined everything, and the pain, the guilt, the memories of Evan and everything we had lost—*the life I had torn away from him*—were driving me insane.

I wiped my eyes with the sleeve of my sweatshirt and the memory of his voice swept over me.

"You planning on eating the whole thing?" Evan gestured at my sleeve, which I had distractedly raised to my mouth. My sleeves were always too long for some reason, and when I was nervous I sometimes chewed on them without realizing it. "Won't be easy to digest." His mouth widened into a grin. "Don't be nervous. There's no need."

"You're not the one who's in danger of losing everything," I reminded him.

He stifled a cheerless laugh. "What would be left for me if you died? I'm not going to let him touch you ever again, Gemma. No one is going to hurt you. And I'm not doing it just for you—I'm doing it most of all for myself. I would be lost if I lost you."

I would be lost if I lost you.

I would be lost if I lost you . . .

A breath of air brushed my neck. My eyes flew to the windows, but they were all rolled up. I pulled my sleeves down over my hands to protect myself from the cold—or maybe from the chill the memory had left behind. Though I turned up the heat, another shiver swept over me. This time a strange noise accompanied it—an eerie, evil hiss—and the wind seemed to whisper directly in my ear. Alarmed, I glanced into the rearview mirror to check the back seat, but nothing was there. When I returned my eyes to the road my heart leapt to my throat: two eyes of ice stared at me from the center of the street.

Evan.

I slammed on the brake, scant feet from him, and the car came to a halt so abruptly I hit the steering wheel. Trembling and on the verge of tears, I raised my head. The road was deserted. I turned off the engine, got out, and looked around, my breathing ragged. A car zoomed past, but my heart was so swollen with disappointment I didn't even flinch. Even the wind mocked me, howling all around me.

"Evan . . ." I whispered, devastated. Hanging my head, I forced myself back into the car and allowed desperation to flood through me, clenching the steering wheel until my fingers were numb.

"Miss?" A rap on the window made me jump. I quickly dried my tears and struggled to compose myself before lowering the window. "I'm sorry, miss, I didn't mean to startle you. Are you all right?" asked the man standing beside the car.

I'd never seen him before, but judging from his accent I guessed he was a tourist. Lake Placid was full of them year round. In winter it was a perfect destination for people who loved skiing or snowboarding. Not only because of the Adirondacks, but also because we had hosted the Olympics not once but twice—in 1932 and 1980—and attractions like the Olympic Center and the Olympic Jumping Complex were open to anyone looking for a thrill.

"Thanks, I'm just a little tired," I managed to say, but the forlorn expression on my face must not have convinced him, because he insisted.

"You're really pale. Want me to take you home?" he offered in a kind tone.

"No, there's no need," I was quick to reply, forcing myself to hide the fear creeping up inside me. After all, the road was secluded and the man gave no sign of leaving. He could have been anyone.

"You sure you're okay to drive? And don't worry—my wife is with me, back there." My eyes followed his thumb to the side of the road, where a young woman waved to me from a car. I stifled a sigh of relief. At least he wasn't some maniac. "Thank you . . . really, but I'm fine. I'm already feeling better."

The man gave in. "All right, but take care, okay?"

Nodding, I started the engine. I watched his car pull away, then lowered the sun visor to look at myself in the mirror. A scream burst from me: Evan was in the back seat. I whirled around but there was no one there.

Sitting there, breathless, I buried my face in my hands. What the hell was happening to me? Was I descending inescapably into madness? With trembling hands I lowered the mirror again, gasping for air, my heart in my throat. This time it reflected only me. I slumped back into my seat. There had never been a reflection—unless my guilt, which had decided to torment me, had created it.

I quickly drove back to the house, trying to compose myself.

Irony trotted up to me, tail wagging. Ginevra was reclined in a regal position on the red couch while the vacuum cleaner danced back and forth to the rhythm of the music. In spite of how terrible my life was, the scene got a faint smile out of me.

"Why am I always the one who has to clean the house?" she called. I tossed my keys onto the entryway table, shaking my head at Ginevra's complaint.

"I'm not talking about *you*, of course," she said in a low voice as I passed her.

"You say it as if it took you effort."

"At least I managed to make you smile!" In my mind, Ginevra's words almost sounded like a reproach but she was quick to ease my sense of guilt. "Gemma, it's okay for you to smile every once in a while. Don't feel bad about it. Evan wouldn't want to see you this way."

Hearing his name threatened to drag me back down into the abyss, but Simon rescued me in the nick of time. "Hey! You'd better move or you might be involved in an accident," he warned me from the kitchen. Only then did I realize the vacuum cleaner was moving straight toward me as though possessed.

I went to join him. "Thanks, I'm not insured against that kind of thing."

"Well? How did it go with your parents?"

"Just like I expected." I sat down on a chair across from his.

He nodded, solemn. "I can imagine. And at school?"

"You should have seen her! She showed her true colors!" Ginevra said from the next room. "I liked how you acted this morning. We really can do it, if you want. Rip her tongue out, I mean."

"I think the suspension is enough. Besides, those *aren't* my true colors. Anger made me overreact, that's all."

"I'm almost afraid to ask, but . . . what happened?"

"Gemma taught a lesson to two girls who were dissing Evan."

"Seriously?"

"Yes. I'm so proud of her! C'mon, don't feel bad. They deserved it," she said to me.

"Yeah, maybe they did."

"I warned you that you were going to deprive her of her innocence," Simon teased his girlfriend.

"Malicious people only understand malice. Talk to them using other language and they won't understand a word you're saying."

"Nice theory," he said, rolling his eyes.

"You bet it is," Ginevra shot back.

"If you hadn't sweet-talked the principal, he definitely would have punished me," I pointed out, disproving her logic.

"But that didn't happen, and those two will think twice before saying anything like that again. Just remember: my offer is still good."

"We're not ripping out their tongues, Gwen."

"All right, all right, it was just a suggestion!" she said defensively, still sprawled on the couch.

"So how do you feel?" Simon asked me, turning serious again. I was about to answer him but when he saw the frustration on my face he quickly changed the subject, winking at me instead and nodding in Ginevra's direction. "I bet she broke some hearts, as usual?" Judging from his expression he wasn't the least bit worried.

"It's not my fault!" Ginevra called from the next room, loud enough to be heard over the music. "It's that Jeremy kid who just won't give it up!"

With an embarrassed shrug, I stared at my hands, unsure what to say. "I keep telling her to cut it out, but she thinks it's fun to fry his neurons." Simon burst out laughing. "You're not jealous?" I asked, lowering my voice in amazement.

"I don't have the slightest doubt about Ginevra's feelings for me." He smiled calmly. His words aroused a distant yet warm memory in me of the feeling of security I used to get when I looked into Evan's eyes. "Supernatural love—be it a Subterranean's or a Witch's—isn't like human love," he explained, his tone sweet.

"What do you mean?"

"How can I put this? Let's say that for humans, love is like the moon: fickle and inconstant. Its pale glow warms their lives that otherwise would remain in total darkness. Our love, on the other hand, is like the sun. Its light illuminates everything, turns everything into an explosion of colors. It's fiery. It's eternal—until it dies along with us."

I listened to him, wordless, fully aware that though I was human, my love was also like the sun.

"You were the only thing that mattered to Evan," Simon added, getting straight to the point. "He would have done anything to keep you alive."

"Even die?" I retorted bitterly.

"Even die. You know that. Just like I'm sure your love for him goes beyond normal human limits."

Grateful he understood me, I nodded and got up from the chair before the armor I had managed to build around me could fall to pieces in front of him. "I'm going to rest for a while, if you don't mind. I'm pretty tired." I left the room, secretly afraid of what I might be about to face.

I had no idea what was happening to my body or my mind, but something was definitely wrong. Sometimes it was like my brain hid away in a world all its own, a world where Evan still existed and the pain was only a memory, and when that happened nothing could snap me back to reality. But the illusion lasted only moments and then reality would hit me full force right in the chest, stoking the fire of my desperation, and my heart would end up bleeding even more. I hadn't spoken a word to anyone about my millionth hallucination, but I was sure Ginevra had already discovered everything while silently probing my thoughts.

I went upstairs to Evan's room, which had become my hideaway, and shut the door behind me. The room was filled with sunlight reflected off the snow outside, so I closed the curtains in order to feel more sheltered and lay down on the bed. My eyes closed, I took Evan's chain that I wore around my neck, turned it over in my fingers, and held it in my palm, like I did every night to fall asleep. All I wanted was not to think about it for an hour. Just one hour. To pretend it had never happened, that Evan was only away on a mission—because the way things actually were made me feel I was losing my mind. But then, letting myself forget his death would have been egotistical. I didn't deserve it. It was right for me to suffer because it was all my fault Evan was gone. How could I live with the burden? How could I forgive myself, when it had been my lips that had stolen his last breath? How could I wake up morning after morning feeling the pain of his absence? Every night I sought his touch yet found only cold fabric under my fingers. My life had been dyed a single color: in my future I saw only black.

I got up from the bed, went to the bookcase, and carefully took out the ancient volume of Tristan and Iseult. A tear silently slid down my cheek because I knew what I would find between its pages. I tried not to think of the afternoon when that book had kept us company, but my drawer of memories promptly ignored my command, breaking the seal I'd put on it. Evan's laughter filled my head, his voice caressing the words locked away in the book.

They were like the honeysuckle vine,

Which around a hazel tree will twine,

Holding the trunk as in a fist

And climbing until its tendrils twist

Around the top and hold it fast.

Together tree and vine will last.
But then, if anyone should pry
The vine away, they both will die.
My love, we're like that vine and tree;
I'll die without you, you without me.

I could practically feel Evan's forehead resting on mine like he was still there, his dark eyes full of promises. He had been right: just like the honeysuckle and its hazel tree, now that I was parted from him I too felt I was slowly dying. Still, despite everything, like the plants that grew from Tristan and Iseult's tombs, our souls would remain entwined forever. No one would ever be able to separate them.

In those moments, hidden away in that room, we had lived our little fairy tale, with no idea that that cursed day would be the beginning of the end. With no idea that, like Iseult, who died of grief over the loss of her love, I too would grieve for my Tristan forever, letting desperation slowly sap my life.

I opened the leather-bound book, revealing its little secret carefully tucked between the yellowed pages. With a trembling hand, I took the slip of burnt paper. I couldn't hold back any longer and a silent tear slid down my face and wet my hand as I crumpled to my knees. The book, now sprinkled with my tears, fell to the floor and I curled up with Evan's note clasped in my hand. *His last message.*

There was no need for me to reread it—I remembered it word for word. By now it was engraved on my brain. I had read it hundreds of times and yet my eyes insisted on going back over every line, trying to imagine what the message would have sounded like coming from his lips. But the flame had consumed the edges of the paper, so part of his words had disappeared along with him. I ran my thumb over the elegant handwriting, as though with this gesture I could touch his hand, and imagined him as he wrote it an hour before dying. If only I had read it in time . . .

As I clutched the slip of paper, his words whirled in my head as though he were whispering them in my ear.

You can't separate a body from its heart without killing it.
One more hour, my love.
Just one more hour and I'll return to you.
Yours forever,
Evan

I closed my eyes, my chest wracked with sobs, and imagined Evan there with me, his arms encircling my shoulders in a warm embrace. My heart was trapped in a cage that was growing ever tighter, so tight it couldn't pump oxygen through me any more. I couldn't breathe. I wished everything would fade away so I wouldn't feel the pain any longer. I wished I could shed my skin for a new one, but I knew it would be useless because he was in my bones. Whenever I closed my eyes the scene played over and over endlessly in my head. I wished it would stop. I wished *everything* would stop. And the worst thing of all was that I continued to live, even knowing that something inside me had died forever.

The only emotion as powerful as my anguish over losing Evan was my remorse for having killed him. My guilt ate at me like a woodworm and the pain was a fire that consumed me from within. It hurt. And nothing except death would ever make the hurting stop.

As the tears continued to flow, I ran my hand over my belly and realized there was only one thing keeping me from putting an end to the torture, only one buoy to cling to in the stormy sea that dragged me further and further from shore into deeper and deeper water. When you were adrift it didn't matter where you landed—all that mattered was the promise of a safe haven. And that's what the baby was to me: my safe haven. I raised my head with effort to look out the window and wondered whether one day I would be less fragile.

Once again I rested my hands on my belly. It was all I had left of Evan.

6

THE SCENT OF NOSTALGIA

Someone gently knocked on the door. I was still curled up on the floor with my head on my knees, my cheeks streaked from the dried tears that had left my skin tight. I looked up, waiting for the pain to ease, then stroked Evan's note one last time, tucked it back between the pages of the book, and stood up.

"Come on in, Gwen," I murmured. My voice was too low for anyone to hear it, but the door opened and a tuft of short hair peeked in. "Oh, Simon, it's you." I tried to compose myself but it was too late; he had already walked into the room and was staring at me, a desolate look of helplessness in his eyes. I was in pieces.

"I came to see how you were."

I rubbed my sides and shrugged. "A bit better," I lied.

His discouraged sigh told me I hadn't been very convincing. "Why don't you come downstairs and join us?" he asked, but I was too depressed to take him up on the offer. The fact that he and Ginevra were always together did nothing but remind me how alone I was. "Staying cooped up in here isn't doing you any good."

"Do you think there's something wrong with me?" I asked.

My question seemed to catch him off guard. His eyes wavered. Maybe he didn't have the answer to that either, or if he did, it couldn't have been anything reassuring. He swallowed and clenched his fists, clearly embarrassed, but then looked me in the eye, this time firmly. "Gemma, in a short amount of time, life gave you an amazing gift and then unexpectedly took it all away from you. You and Evan were so close that when he was torn away from you, a piece of you was torn away too. There's *nothing* wrong with you. You just need time to learn to live with the pain."

Simon had chosen his words carefully and I was grateful for that. He seemed to realize that my only option was to learn to accept the pain, to grin and bear it, because I was certain I would never get over losing Evan. "It'll get better with time. It'll heal, you'll see," he promised, stroking my shoulder.

"You guys keep saying that, but it never happens. It never will," I said softly, overcome by my pain. "It's like there's a knife still lodged in my heart and whenever I move, whenever I *breathe*, the blade tears away another piece of flesh."

Simon half closed his eyes and sighed, clenching his fists even tighter. He knew perfectly well how I was feeling. "I miss him too," he admitted, "but you really need to try to stay strong. Come downstairs . . . please?"

I looked up and the words came out before my brain could process my unexpected wish. "I'd like to go see Peter for a while, if you don't mind."

My request seemed to surprise him. He thought it over for a second and looked at the sky through the half-closed curtains, pensive. "In a few hours it'll be dark," he said, his frown betraying his concern. "It might be dangerous."

"I won't be gone long. I just really need a change of scenery," I insisted.

Simon's face darkened, but he nodded. My request clearly worried him, but at the same time he didn't want to refuse it. "Take your phone with you and if you need anything call me right away."

I didn't know where the impulse had come from, but as soon as the words were out, I realized I really did need to get out of that house and leave the past behind me, just for a couple of hours. Just long enough for me to breathe. I went into the bathroom and rinsed my face. Looking at myself in the mirror, I got ready to put on a new mask before going to Peter's.

I parked the car on the wet driveway that had recently been shoveled clean of snow. A string of unlit Christmas lights trimmed every inch of the front of the house—the echo of a holiday that, like a ghost, had slipped away without my even noticing. I wrapped my heavy sweatshirt around me and rang the bell.

"Gemma!" Mrs. Turner gave me a hug brimming with affection, almost as though she hadn't believed she would ever see me again. "Oh, sweetheart! I've been so worried about you." Tears that she tried to disguise filled her eyes. Maybe coming out of my shell hadn't been such a good idea. As long as the world continued to pity me it would be impossible to distance myself from the pain.

"It's good to see you again, Mrs. Turner. Is Peter home?" I asked, hoping she would give up her intention of consoling me. Actually, I'd known the answer to my question even before knocking on their door because I'd seen Peter's outline in his window. He was working out.

"Oh, of course. Come in, dear. He's up in his room." Exasperated, she pointed at the stairs, down which issued an infernal racket. "He's been in there for two hours with the music turned up full blast. I have no idea how he can stand it!"

"Have you tried telling him to turn it down?"

"The problem is he can't hear me—or maybe he's pretending not to. He hung his old *Keep out* sign on his door." I smiled at the memory of Peter and me making that sign. "But if I remember correctly, you're the one person authorized to ignore it." She winked at me as an invitation to go on up.

"Maybe I shouldn't. We're not little kids any more."

"Don't be silly. I'm sure your privilege is still valid"—she gave me an affectionate smile—"and that he'll be happy to see you. I'll be in the kitchen if you need anything. In case you want something to lure him downstairs, I made an apple pie. I always liked having the two of you in the kitchen."

"I'll try." I bit my bottom lip as Peter's mom walked into the other room and slowly climbed the stairs, gathering my courage. Before I knew it I found myself turning the knob on Peter's door.

My face was so used to tears that the smile that spread over it felt almost foreign as I leaned against the doorframe. The room was just as I remembered it, the walls covered with his drawings of Marvel heroes, the Blue Bombers banner above the lacrosse equipment hanging from a hook, waiting for spring, pencils and markers scattered over a sheet of paper on the desk, his comic book collection proudly lined up in the bookcase, and a pile of clothes on the chair. Peter had his back to me and was throwing punches at the worn punching bag hanging from the ceiling. He wore the blue pants from his lacrosse uniform and the muscles in his bare back flexed with every blow. From the sweat trickling down his still-tanned skin, I could tell he must have been at it for hours. The bag jerked wildly beneath his blows. He seemed to be taking out all his frustrations on it. I was used to seeing Peter work out for both hockey and lacrosse, his true passion. I knew every muscle in his back, having watched him many times, but recently he seemed to have kicked things up a notch.

I smiled and turned off the ear-shattering Iron Maiden music to get his attention. Peter spun toward the stereo and smiled the instant he saw me. I crossed my arms and leaned against the wall. "Trying to punch a hole in that thing?" I joked, gesturing at the still-swaying bag.

Peter pounded his fists together. I felt a void in my chest, remembering Evan and the afternoon in the workout room when I'd unwrapped the tape from his hands and he'd used it to pull me closer. Forcing back the thought, I looked at Peter and said with a grin, "I don't get why you're so pissed off at it. What did it ever do to you?"

Peter came closer, wiping his neck with a towel. His dark curls were dripping with sweat. Stopping in front of me, he looked at me with a sly smile. "Didn't you see the sign?"

"I thought it didn't apply to me," I teased. I ran a finger down his wet chest. "Ew! You're all sweaty!" Peter cocked his head and his broadening smile made me guess his foul intentions. "Don't you dare!" I warned.

He shot forward but I dodged him. Unfortunately, on his second attempt, he managed to grab me by the arms and lift me up. I burst out laughing. "Put me down!" I shrieked, and he obeyed. But his euphoria had filled my heart with memories and, overcome by nostalgia for a time gone by, I couldn't help but throw my arms around his neck and rest my head on his chest to feel the warmth of his presence. I just wanted to feel like I used to when we were children: free from sad thoughts. "Oh, Pet . . ."

He stood there for a second, surprised by my gesture, but then returned the hug and held me against him. He ran his nose through my hair and kissed me lightly on the head. It was so natural being with him. It felt like we were meeting again after having lived in two parallel worlds—and actually it was partly true. I was happy something was left of us, the old us, Gemma and her friend Peter. The boy next door who healed all my wounds without asking for anything in return.

"I've missed this. I've missed you, Gemma."

His embrace grew gentler and suddenly I sensed the heat his body was emanating. His heart thumped against my chest, its rhythm accelerating. I tried to pull back but Peter wouldn't let go and the silence grew deeper, as though we were both holding our breath. My eyes went to his Adam's apple that rose and slowly descended. I looked up slightly, inadvertently lining my mouth up with his. Taking a deep breath, I moved away, shyly trying to look him in the eye.

"Sorry." He swallowed and headed to the stereo. "I was thinking about you and when I saw you in the doorway, it almost didn't seem real. I let myself get carried away."

"No problem," I was quick to reply, sitting down on his bed.

Peter put on a Linkin Park album and lowered the volume so the music was only in the background. He took a sleeveless white undershirt from a dresser drawer, put it on, and leaned his elbow against the window frame.

"I knew you would come sooner or later," he said, undoing the tape around his knuckles.

"You always know everything, don't you?"

Still warm, his arm muscles swelled with his every movement. "Only when it comes to you."

I smiled at him and he winked back. "I needed a breath of fresh air."

"Then I guess my sweaty room wasn't the best choice."

"Actually yeah, I was thinking of something *fresher*," I joked, feigning disgust.

"Oh, sorry! Hold on, let me open the window."

"I was only kidding!" I protested, but he continued to yank on the window, which wouldn't budge. Something suddenly hit me. "Hey!"

Peter had turned around and thrown an old stuffed gorilla at me. It had bounced off my chest, without hurting me. "I was only kidding too, smartass! Didn't you notice it's freezing outside? I'm afraid you'll have to put up with my fragrance: *Eau de Macho*."

I raised an eyebrow and held back a smile. "Your self-esteem has definitely improved, I see."

He bit the inside of his cheek, like he always used to do. "So has your mood, *I see*."

"Yeah . . . In any case, it doesn't smell bad in here. I like your smell. It's—comforting."

"*Comforting*?" Peter grinned, and two deep dimples formed in his cheeks.

"It's familiar. It smells like you." I smiled as I picked up the little stuffed animal that had fallen to the floor. I stared at the toy for a moment, clasping it to me in a wave of affection. "You still have it." I'd given it to him ten years before, the day he fell out of a tree and broke his leg, and I'd been afraid he was going to die.

Peter took the stuffed animal from me and fell onto his bed. "Only because it reminds me of your face." He tossed it in the air and caught it like he often did with his lacrosse ball.

"Why you—" My jaw dropped and I tore the gorilla out of his hands to use it as a weapon. He grabbed my wrist and his eyes once again got lost in mine, still with that strange mix of desire and frustration. I pulled my wrist free and looked away. Maybe it hadn't been a good idea to visit him.

"We're playing hockey at the Olympic Center in a few days. You coming to the game?" he asked, filling the silence.

"Peter, there's something I need to tell you," I blurted. "It's one of the reasons I came."

He sat up beside me, ran a hand over his face and through his curls, and turned to look at me. "You're pregnant," he said with a smile.

"H-how did you know?" I gasped.

"Come on, Gemma. We're not in New York City. This is a small town, remember?" He shrugged.

"So everybody knows . . ."

For a long moment neither of us opened our mouths. Peter didn't seem upset; in fact, he looked calm. He must have already had enough time to digest the news. How long had he known?

After a long moment of silence, his hand slid across the bed and onto mine, interlacing our fingers on the blue blanket. "How do you feel?" he asked in a concerned tone.

I hesitated, but the warmth of Peter's hand reminded me that with him there was no need to lie. "In pieces." My voice was barely audible, but he squeezed my hand. "Sometimes all I want to do is scream," I admitted. My empty gaze found his, which suddenly sparkled with enthusiasm.

"Not a bad idea."

I cocked my head and stared at him, not understanding. "What do you have in mind?"

Peter winked at me and got up from the bed, his hand still in mine as his face lit up. "Come with me."

"It should be around here somewhere . . ." Peter continued to mumble to himself, studying a tourist map of the Adirondacks as I followed his directions, driving the BMW up a steep road through the woods.

"I still don't understand where you're taking me," I said, curious, as we ascended higher and higher.

"Pull over," he suddenly told me. "This should be the place."

"What place?" I asked, exasperated.

Without answering, Peter got out and double-checked the path that branched off from the road. "This way!" He grabbed my hand and pulled me through the trees.

"You sure this is the right direction?"

He stared at me, smiling with satisfaction. "Come on—you must remember this spot!"

"Remember it? You mean I've been here before?"

He nodded. I looked around, searching for some detail that might jog my memory, but I couldn't recall ever having been there before. Then the woods opened into a clearing and my eyes lit up as I was whisked back to the past. "I forgot all about this place!" I exclaimed, brimming with enthusiasm as I admired the view. Below us, the snowy treetops formed a mantle of white that enveloped Lake Placid. "I still don't get it, though. Why did you bring me here?"

"You said you remember being here before. Do you remember *when?*"

"Of course! We were thirteen," I said. That day we'd hiked to the top of Whiteface Mountain, one of the highest peaks in the Adirondacks, about fifteen minutes outside of Lake Placid.

"We were on a field trip," Peter added, "and while the others were checking out the view with binoculars, you wandered away from the group and I came looking for you."

"We got lost."

Peter nodded. "And ended up here."

"I remember. But why are we here now?"

Peter took a step and stood behind me, his lips on my ear. "Remember how our voices echoed off the mountains together?"

I turned toward him eagerly and he smiled back. His intentions were finally clear. That day many years ago, when he and I were still just kids, we'd screamed into the wind at the top of our lungs, hoping someone in the group would hear us. But fear soon gave way to excitement, and Peter and I had shouted over and over, feeling like we were flying. We'd left the world behind while our voices soared through the air and came back to us again and again, until someone found us and took us back to the group. I had completely forgotten about it.

"You said you wanted to scream. You can do it here. It's just you and me and our mountains," Peter encouraged me, studying my reaction.

I smiled, a little embarrassed by his suggestion. "Peter! We're not thirteen any more."

"Who cares? We're here. You and me, exactly like back then."

For a second I was convinced he was right. Time fell away: Peter and I were still together, just like back then. Only now there was a huge boulder separating us, and it was in my heart. And yet, just for a moment, I wanted to breathe the air of that distant past . . .

"It's going to work, you know," Peter said in response to my skepticism. "Trust me."

I looked down, unsure, and he walked up to the edge of the cliff. Shooting me a glance, he cupped his hands around his mouth and without taking his eyes off me shouted my name as loud as he could. Then he held his hand out to me as his voice echoed through the air. I approached him with hesitant steps. For some reason I was afraid to give in to the need to do it. I was afraid of what my heart might shout to the whole wide world.

"Go ahead, shout out a wish," he said. "It feels amazing!"

I smiled to myself, took a deep breath, and screamed with all the breath I had in my lungs, letting everything out, ridding myself of the pain. Shouting that I wanted to live, that I wanted to die, that I didn't want to suffer any more. Peter's voice joined mine. My eyes filled with tears, because all I could think about was Evan. I squeezed my eyes shut. Desperation continued to hound me, begging me to listen to it, but I flung it off the mountaintop.

Peter went silent, leaving only his echo ringing through the air. My eyes were still closed when I felt his hand grasp mine. I opened them, short of breath, but in my chest was a lightness I had forgotten.

"Well? How do you feel?" He smiled.

"God, what a sensation!" I said. "It was so *liberating*! I felt like I could have taken wing, and everything was so simple. How did you come up with the idea of bringing me here?"

Peter shrugged and sat down on a rock. "I don't know. I figured it would make you feel better. You needed to vent, to let it all out."

I went and sat down next to him, picking up a stone. I was still exhilarated. A strange breeze stirred my hair, almost like a caress. "What was that?" I exclaimed, suddenly uneasy.

"Relax, Gemma. It's just the wind." Peter smiled and I went back to focusing on the lightness that had filled me. I didn't want it to fade.

"You were right," I admitted, casting him a sidelong glance. Under his coat, Peter wore his white sweatshirt with the hood pulled up over his head, exactly like mine. Our warm breath condensed into little clouds. "Remember this?" He mimed smoking, blowing a stream of vapor through his lips. It made me laugh. You couldn't live in the past, but what harm was there, just that once, given that the present hurt so much and the future still frightened me?

I averted my gaze, focusing on my feet. "A lot of years have gone by since that day, you know," I thought aloud, "and a lot has changed, but there's one thing that's remained constant in my life." I turned toward him, searching for the two kids who had screamed into the wind. They were still there, I could feel it. "Knowing you'll always be there for me."

"It's true, I'll always be there for you. It doesn't matter what decisions you make—mine is never going to change."

"There's a secret I'd like you to share with me," I said. He stared at me, curious. "How is it you always know what I need? Please tell me."

"I don't know," he admitted, smiling. "I just do. Maybe it's because we grew up together." He shrugged again, suddenly becoming pensive. "Maybe we're more connected than you're willing to admit."

I shook my head. "If that were true, it should work the other way around too, but I've never been good at guessing what you need."

"Only because having you beside me is enough," he confessed in a faint voice. He took both my hands and his dark eyes bored into mine, so close and penetrating I couldn't escape them. "Gemma . . ." he said softly, and swallowed.

"Peter, I—" Though I wanted to stop him, the words died in my throat when I felt tears sting my eyes, anxious to show the world my pain.

Peter must have noticed, because he rested his forehead on mine and squeezed his eyes shut. A tear ran down my face and he wiped it away with his thumb, which lingered a second too long on my skin. I could tell he also felt we'd never been so close before. Not like that. Desperation gripped my heart, but I still felt it wasn't wrong to be there. I *needed* Peter. Another tear trembled on my lashes and slid down, coming to rest on my lips. He stared at it, holding his breath, and brushed it away, moving his finger slowly, doing nothing to hide his desire.

I took his hand and moved it from my face. "Please, Pet," I begged. I was afraid I wouldn't be strong enough to pull away from the warmth of his body, to resist the need to feel him holding me in his arms for a moment. It wouldn't have been fair, because in his embrace I would have closed my eyes and imagined it wasn't him. I would have told myself the warmth was coming from Evan, so I could feel him near me once more. I couldn't do that to Peter—make him believe my heart felt something it didn't. There was no one else for me but Evan. I knew Peter's heart beat for me, but mine pulsed to a different rhythm. And if one day the fire inside me went out, nothing would remain but ashes—it would be an arid, sterile place where nothing would ever grow again.

Peter squeezed my hand tighter and I looked him in the eye. "Pet," I forced myself to say. I didn't want a relationship built on lies. I needed a connection bound by the sturdy cords of truth, cords that might hurt at times, but kept a relationship together forever. "What I feel for him is so deep"—my voice trembled and I wasn't sure I would be able to get it out, but another teardrop fell and the knot in my throat loosened—"so deeply rooted inside me that not even death can dissolve it."

His eyes wavered as it sank in. No matter how much it might have hurt him, it had been the right thing to do. Death had taken Evan from me, but I wouldn't let it steal a single atom of our connection.

Peter gulped, his intense gaze darkened by conflicting, unfathomable emotions. "I know you chose someone else," he began, and I could see the words caused him pain, "but that doesn't mean I've stopped loving you." New tears flooded my face. "We have a lifetime of memories together that won't let me." He looked down at his hand stroking mine.

I closed my eyes and turned my head away, totally incapable of finding a reply as pain lacerated my heart like a steel blade. "Evan . . ." I thought I'd said his name only in my mind, but my lips had moved in a whisper that slipped away on the wind.

Peter clenched his fists at his sides and his expression hardened. He rested his hands on my shoulders, forcing me to look him in the eye. "Gemma, Evan is dead! You realize that, don't you? He's gone!" The cruelty of his words made me wince. "But I'm not. I'm here, and I love you. I've always loved you. Let me be the one to raise the baby."

I tightened my lips as my chin began to quiver and tears streamed down my face, quickly drying in the chilly mountain air. I felt the light touch of his forehead against mine and when I opened my tear-veiled eyes they found his. For a moment it felt like the world had come to a halt around us. Peter raised his chin slightly and his mouth brushed mine.

I turned my head away before it was too late, leaving his lips puckered in midair, and clenched my jaw. "I'm sorry," I whispered. "I can't."

Maybe my Peter was gone; maybe I'd lost him, because the person in front of me was someone else—more daring, more demanding. But I wanted my friend back, I didn't want another boyfriend. I would never replace Evan, would never even try to.

All at once my eyes went wide and a shudder ran down my spine. I panicked. "What was that?" I asked. An ominous, familiar, icy wind had just swept over my bones. Peter frowned, at a loss. "Did you feel it too?" I twisted around, searching for the source of the strange breeze, but knew it was useless. It was coming from my mind. It was happening again.

"Gemma, what is it?" he asked. A second later, he blanched violently and shoved me back, staring at the ground with terror in his eyes. "Watch out! There are snakes everywhere!" he screamed, darting away from me. His hood fell back and I saw that his forehead was dripping with sweat.

I nervously scanned the ground and looked back up at him, bewildered. Nothing was there. There were no snakes. Suddenly I heard him. Evan. My head shot in the direction his voice had come from, but no one was there—only the empty space beyond the edge of the cliff.

"Gemma, no!" Peter's shout pierced the air, but I barely heard it as my body moved toward the other voice.

"Evan," I murmured to myself. He called to me again. *I'm here*. Another step. I followed the comforting sound and looked down over the edge. Shock gripped my heart when I found myself looking into his terrified eyes. *Evan!* He was clinging to a tree trunk that stuck out from the side of the cliff, his body dangling in the void.

I inched toward him as Peter's anxious voice reached me: "Gemma, come back!"

"I have to help him!" I leaned over the cracked tree trunk, hoping it wouldn't give beneath our combined weight, and desperately tried to grab him. "Evan! Take my hand!" A shriek escaped my throat as his dark eyes, full of dismay and terror, met mine.

"Don't let me die . . ."

My eyes filled with tears. I gripped his hand with all my might but I knew I couldn't bear his weight much longer. "I'm not letting go. Hold on tight!" I screamed, pouring into my words all the anguish tormenting my heart. But Evan slipped away and plunged into the void.

"Nooooo!!" Desperation tore my heart in two. I lunged forward to grab him but lost my balance and tumbled over the edge.

7

MURMURS IN THE DARKNESS

"Hang . . . on!" Peter grunted through clenched teeth.

I looked up and felt my arm stinging. Peter had grabbed my wrist firmly as my body dangled over empty space. "Let go! Let me go! I have to go with him!"

"Gemma! What the fuck are you talking about?! I'm not letting you fall! Hold on tight. Gemma, look at me! Look at me!"

His voice was so harsh it brought me out of my trance. I stared at Peter for a long moment before slowly regaining my senses, like a sleepwalker who's just woken up. "Peter . . ." I murmured. All at once I became conscious of the void below me and thrashed my legs, panicking. "Peter! I'm going to fall! Help me, please! Pull me up!"

"I'm trying to!" He grimaced from the effort but couldn't do it. The veins in his arms looked ready to burst. "Shit! I can't! You're too . . . heavy! There's something—"

I felt myself slipping a fraction of an inch at a time. "Don't let go!" He gripped my wrist tighter. It hurt so much I thought it might snap in two. "Peter, don't let go of me, please!" I shrieked, overwhelmed with terror, slipping farther still. Tears streamed down my face as I thought of the baby growing inside me. Living didn't matter to me any more, but I couldn't let death take our baby too—that would be like killing Evan all over again.

"I'm not letting go," Peter snarled, his every muscle tense from the strain. "Take my other hand too!"

He held it out to me, but my attempt to grab it made my body lurch, loosening Peter's grip, which slid from my wrist to my hand. It felt like some dark force was pulling me down, undermining Peter's efforts.

"Hold on, please!"

"We'll get out of this, don't worry. We'll get out," he grunted, but when I looked him in the eye I saw it: a flicker of desperation. Peter was convinced he couldn't do it. I was going to fall. He strained his muscles once more, pulling back with his legs as the sweat continued to trickle down his temples, but my fingers slid even more from his grip.

"Gemma! Hold on tight!"

All at once a gust of wind, a mixture of hot and cold air, hit me, making me shiver. It swept me up into the air like a whirlwind. My brain felt foggy. Was I falling?

A split second later I crashed down onto the ground with a scream. I took a deep breath. No, it wasn't the ground. It was Peter. His hand was still in mine and I looked into his desperate eyes. Panting, he squeezed me against his chest so tightly I couldn't breathe.

He hadn't let me fall.

"Gemma . . ." He cupped my face in his hands. "I thought I wouldn't be able to do it. Are you okay?" I nodded, never taking my eyes from his. "It's over," he whispered, watching as the empty space beyond the cliff's edge darkened in the twilight. "I don't know who helped me pull you up, but it's all over now, thank God. Let's get out of here."

I tried to stand, but it took a minute for my legs to stop shaking. By the time we reached the car darkness had already hidden everything beneath its black shroud.

"Let me drive," Peter said, but I adamantly took my place behind the wheel. It was true my hands were still trembling and the tingle in my back had crept up to my head, but driving relaxed me. Having to focus on the road would take my mind off what had just happened.

"I said I'm fine. I just want to go home."

"Okay, but I don't want you to go alone. Let's go straight to Ginevra's."

"Your house isn't far."

Peter seemed determined not to listen to me. "I don't care. I'm coming with you. I'll walk home from there."

"Peter, are you kidding? That's ridiculous."

"It's not a suggestion, Gemma."

"Whatever," I said, giving in. "But at least let Simon give you a ride." Out of the corner of my eye, I saw Peter relax in his seat and look away from me. Regardless, I knew he was still shaken by what had happened; the tension between us was palpable.

He turned to face me again. "Now would you mind telling me what the hell you were doing back there?!"

"I—I don't know. I thought that—but you didn't see him, did you?" I whispered. I was almost afraid to say it out loud. Had I seen Evan . . . or hadn't I?

"All I saw was a whole bed of snakes that chose the perfect time to come out and attack me. I kept shouting but it was like you couldn't hear me, and I couldn't go after you because those monsters were slithering in from every which way. I was sure some of them even bit me, but I don't feel anything now." He looked down at his shoe, frowning.

"You're terrified of snakes. How on earth did you—"

"Why should I give a damn about snakes?! You're more important. I had to help you."

"Thanks," I said softly.

All at once, Peter jumped. "Whoa, whoa, *whoa*! What are you doing?!" he shouted, squirming in his seat.

I stared at him in bewilderment. "What's wrong? Calm down!"

But he looked terrified. He stared at me with wild eyes, clutching his hair. "What the fuck! Gemma, turn on the lights!" he bellowed. I stared at the road, not understanding. "The headlights! Turn them on, for fuck's sake! You're freaking me out!"

I did as he said and the road lit up as though it were daytime. "There, happy? I don't get why you're so upset."

"You *what*?!" He stared at me in shock.

"I didn't even notice they were off," I explained with a shrug, still confused.

"You didn't even—Oh! You're unbelievable, Gemma! It's pitch dark out. How the hell could you see where you were going?"

"I could see perfectly well," I insisted.

Peter drew a long, uncertain breath. "You sure you're okay?"

His question hung in the air between us. I wasn't sure I knew the answer.

I parked in the driveway. As I stepped out of the car onto the gravel, my knee gave way, but I managed not to let Peter notice. Strange tingles ran over my skin and crept up my back, tickling the nape of my neck. Peter walked me to the front steps of the sprawling house, but when I set my foot on the first step, the ground seemed to give way beneath me and I had to lean on him for support.

Suddenly everything became confused. "Gemma!" Peter's voice was distant, muffled. I sought his face but could barely open my eyes. There was only a blurred image. I realized Peter was lifting me from the ground. "Shit! You're burning up!"

"Quick, bring her inside!"

"What happened? Here, let me carry her."

Ginevra's voice was jumbled together with Simon's. Clearly concerned, he took me out of Peter's arms. My head spun faster and faster; it was like being on a carousel. Someone felt my forehead.

"She was fine a minute ago. What's happening to her?" Peter sounded bewildered and alarmed. "Why is she shaking like that?"

"She's having another attack."

"Attack? What the hell are you talking about? Why does she have such a high fever?"

"Quick, we need to cover her up. Peter, it would be better if you went home," Simon told him.

"Home? We need to take her to the hospital!"

"*No hospitals.* We'll take care of her." Simon rested me on something cool—the leather couch, I guessed. The words he had chosen for Peter were kind, but his tone had been stern. *Peter . . .* I tried to whisper, but my lips remained sealed, refusing to obey my command. "Now, would you like to explain to me what the hell happened?" Simon demanded.

I tried again to speak but realized it was impossible. Sleep wanted to tear me away and no matter how hard I struggled to resist it my mind faded in and out.

"I wish someone would explain it to *me*! Damn it, this is insane! So we drive up Whiteface Mountain and all of a sudden she goes out of her mind, talking nonsense. It was like she couldn't hear me, like she'd fallen into a trance. I didn't know what to do! There were all those snakes and she kept talking to herself, calling Evan's name. She seemed crazy. Then she leans over the cliff, loses her balance, and falls," Peter said, agitated.

Beside me, Simon was holding his breath. "She had another hallucination. Why the hell did you take her up there?!"

"How was I supposed to know she would try to throw herself off a cliff? We didn't even go all the way to the top. Somebody should have warned me about these attacks of hers, because it sounds like this isn't the first time it's happened, is it?" Neither of them answered. "I just don't get it. I'm strong enough. I'm in shape, and Gemma doesn't weigh that much. All the same, though I managed to grab her in time, it felt like it would've taken the strength of ten guys to hold her, like there was some invisible force dragging her down. Then suddenly she gets light, like someone is below her, pushing her up, and I manage to pull her back over the edge. It must've been all the adrenaline, I guess—I really was desperate." Peter was talking a mile a minute and his voice was fading in and out, as though he were pacing. "We headed back here, but she was fine. She even insisted on driving. Then, all of a sudden, outside the door, she faints and . . . Are you going to tell me what's going on with her or what?" he shouted. "Why am I thinking this has happened to her before? Am I right?"

For a moment, Peter's question received no reply. It was Simon who finally broke the silence, speaking in a low voice as though he knew I could hear every word. "Losing Evan has been rough on her. She still hasn't overcome the trauma."

"Okay," Peter said resolutely, "but the hallucinations and—" A hand touched my forehead. "Jesus, she's burning up!"

More silence. Peter was clearly asking for answers neither of them wanted to give him, but Simon tried to be reassuring. "It's a psychosomatic reaction. Her mind is trying to ease some of the trauma by expressing it through physical symptoms."

"How would you know? Are you a doctor or something?" Peter shot back contemptuously. "How can you be so sure?"

"Peter, calm down," Ginevra interjected. "It was sweet of you to take care of her. Simon and I will take it from here. Trust us, just this once. Gemma needs to rest. You were right: this isn't the first time it's happened, and we know what to do. Let Simon give you a ride home."

Peter was silent. Ginevra had put him in a tough spot. Or maybe she or Simon had influenced his mind to convince him.

"All right, I'll go. The only thing that matters to me is that she's okay. But tell her I'll keep my phone on tonight."

"We will if she wakes up before tomorrow." Something covered my body. "Let's let her rest." Simon's whisper was so soft I barely heard it. Or maybe it was because I was slipping away into the darkness. I heard the door close and let myself go, a fire burning inside my head.

8

SOUL TERRORS

Emerging from the deep state of unconsciousness into which I had sunk, I slowly began to perceive my body. At first it was just the frenzied beating of my heart. It surrounded me; I was its prisoner. It throbbed in my temples. Each beat shook me but I couldn't react, trapped as I was in the darkness. I squirmed. The surface beneath me was hard, and my warm, humid breath dampened my face as though the room had suddenly shrunk so small it was squashing me. Slowly but surely I regained awareness of the various parts of my body, of the sweat that left my back damp and my forehead beaded.

I tried to take a deep breath, but my throat closed up as if someone had used up all the air. With an effort, I forced my eyes open. To my terror, I found myself in absolute darkness. Where was I? Though I struggled to breathe, I was suffocating. There was no more oxygen. I attempted to move but my limbs felt hemmed in; I instinctively raised my arms and my hands struck a solid surface. Panic flooded me. Numb with shock, I groped around me, seeking a way out, but realized to my horror that my body was confined in a cramped space. I was trapped. The air grew heavier by the second. I gasped, in desperate need of oxygen, but it felt like steel straps were squeezing my chest. Raising my hands above me, I strained to push upward, leveraging with my whole body, knowing even as I fought to escape that it was hopeless. I was sealed in a cement casket.

I had been buried alive.

I pounded the rough surface repeatedly. My skin cracked open and blood oozed from my fists but it didn't matter—I had to get out before it was too late. "Get me out of here!!" I screamed, still pounding, my voice broken with sobs. "Gwen! Why did you bury me?! I'm still alive! Gwen!"

Suddenly I felt a noose tightening around my neck. My hands flew to my throat but there was nothing there. There was simply no more oxygen for me to breathe. Distant voices reached me, muffled by the thick layer of cement, as I struggled to avoid being crushed.

"Gemma! Come on, breathe!" Though Ginevra's voice was far away, I heard the desperation in her words.

"Gwen . . ." I tried to make myself heard through the stone slab, but my strength was abandoning me. "It's too cramped. I can't breathe. My . . . baby. Save my baby," I gasped, my ears plugged and my head on the verge of exploding.

"Come on! Come on! Try to react! Simon! She's stopped breathing!" Ginevra's voice was ever fainter, ever more distorted.

"Hang in there, Gemma! You've got to fight! Air! She needs more air! Quick, open the windows! We need to get her to breathe!"

The earth shook beneath my body, bringing me back to the surface. My eyes shot open and my lungs avidly gulped in the air. Only then did I realize it wasn't the earth moving—it was Ginevra, who wouldn't stop shaking me. I panted, inhaling the oxygen that every fiber of my body craved, then looked around, terrified by the horrific experience I had just undergone. I threw my arms around Ginevra's neck, sobbing. "Oh, Gwen! How did they do it? Why did they seal me up in there?"

"Shh . . ." She stroked my hair and held me close. "Calm down. You're safe now." I pulled back to look her in the eye, but her image was blurry from the tears. "It's all over."

"What happened?" I asked, but she avoided my gaze and exchanged glances with Simon.

"You were delirious," Simon told me, staring at the floor as though he felt powerless.

"I—" My weary voice cracked with anguish. "I . . . I was sealed in a cement casket. I couldn't breathe." Simon and Ginevra stared at me, slowly shaking their heads. "Someone sealed me in a casket," I insisted.

"There was no casket, Gemma."

I stared at Simon in shock, unable to believe him, then looked around. There was no trace of my prison. "But how—"

"You were hallucinating." Ginevra stroked my hair, speaking sweetly to sugarcoat the pill. I looked at my hands, certain I would find them covered with cuts from pounding against the cement, but there wasn't a scratch on them. "Here." Ginevra helped me sit up, but I was still stunned by her words. "You'd better get back to bed. It's the middle of the night and you need to rest." She tucked me in and handed me a notebook with a dark blue cover. On closer look, I saw it was a diary. "I made this for you. I thought it might help if you let out what you're feeling inside. In our language it's called an *epikor.* It means 'messenger' and it's connected to the deepest part of you. Sometimes we only realize what's inside us, *what we are,* when we talk about it with someone. Otherwise the truth remains buried within us, too deep for us to see or understand it. But it's not always easy to get everything out with other people. A diary, on the other hand, is like a part of ourselves where we're free to say it all. You have no idea how much this can help in handling life's challenges."

"I've never had a diary," I said softly, studying the embossing on the cover.

"You can pretend they're letters that—"

"Gwen, what's wrong with me?" She sighed, just as Simon came back into the room. "I can take it. I just want to know what's happening to me. I don't need you guys to protect me from this too."

Simon and Ginevra looked at each other. "We're not sure," she admitted hesitantly. "The poison is powerful. It didn't kill you on the spot, but that doesn't mean it can't still do it."

"Gin!" he reproached her.

"No, Simon, she has a right to know." I nodded, my heart trembling. "It must still be in your bloodstream and your body can't eliminate it. It's putting up a fight, though, which is why you're having hallucinations and running high fevers."

Simon looked at her out of the corner of his eye. Even in the state I was in, I could tell how little he agreed with her theory.

"Sorry, I haven't found any other explanation for all this," she said.

"Let's say you're right." I looked Ginevra in the eye to make sure she told me the truth. "What will happen if the poison gets the better of me?"

"You'll die," she confessed, her face ashen, as though it were more than a mere possibility.

"But that's not going to happen." Simon came a step closer. "Do you feel up to telling us what happened when you were with Peter?"

"Peter!" I'd completely forgotten how I'd gotten home.

"Calm down, don't stress. Peter is fine. He brought you here and then went home."

"I've got to call him!" I searched the nightstand for my phone.

"It's the middle of the night, Gemma. You can talk to him in the morning."

I nodded reluctantly and gathered my thoughts before returning to Simon's question. "I saw Evan. He was—" My voice broke and my sight fogged, his image reappearing before my eyes. "He was falling from the edge of the cliff. I tried to hold him up but couldn't." For a moment I feared my sobs would suffocate me.

"Evan wasn't really there." Ginevra pronounced each word cautiously, her eyes fixed on mine and her hands gripping my shoulders in the attempt to bring me back to my senses.

I shook my head because I didn't want to believe it, but inside I knew it was true. "I know—I mean, I get it. But I *saw* him!" I wanted to convince her I wasn't crazy, but I wasn't entirely sure of it myself. The memory of Evan dangling over the precipice was too vivid for me to think it was just a hallucination. It was real, not a mere projection. Or maybe Simon was right and my mind was too fragile to handle all the pain. "I'm losing my mind. I'm hallucinating, Gwen, it's not normal! Thank God Peter got to me in time." I rested my hands on my belly. "I honestly thought he wasn't going to be able to do it. It was like some dark force was pulling me down. But then I suddenly felt light, as if something was pushing me up." I clearly remembered what I'd felt. And then there had been that gust of wind, hot and cold at the same time. It had been like two conflicting forces whirling around me, waging a battle for my survival . . . as though something were trying to help me. Still, in a world where everyone was out to kill me, the thought that someone might want to save me seemed ridiculous. I could no longer count on anyone except Simon and Ginevra, and I hoped I wouldn't lose them too, seeing how everything around me died.

Ginevra smiled at me, breaking the tension. "He grabbed you despite his fear of snakes."

I smiled back, but then remembered another detail. "Looks like I'm not the only one having hallucinations, because there were no snakes!"

Simon and Ginevra's expressions suddenly darkened with alarm. "Gemma, what are you saying? Are you sure?" Before I could reply Ginevra scanned my every thought.

"Of course I'm sure. Even when I . . . hallucinate"—it was a struggle to say the word out loud, because it was admitting something was wrong with me—"afterwards I never forget anything that happened, not even the weirdest details. And there were no snakes, I'm positive."

"Hold on a second," Simon exclaimed. Ginevra and I instantly looked at him. He stayed silent, his eyes directed at Ginevra, who was listening carefully to his thoughts.

"Um, guys? I'm right here," I said a bit sarcastically, waving my hand. "Would you mind explaining what's going on?"

Simon came over and took me by the shoulders, his eyes boring into mine and his expression clearing. "Gemma!" He shook his head, trying to follow his own train of thought. "It's not the poison. It's happening again! How could we not have realized it? The crises you've had. Your hallucinations. Don't you get it? *A Subterranean is behind all this!*"

I gaped, unsure whether to consider this good news or a death sentence.

"I've already encountered a power like his," Simon continued. "It's powerful because it lets him act without coming out into the open. He gets into his victims' heads and persuades them to kill themselves. He's already doing it."

"Wha— Wait, hold on. I'm not following you."

Simon nervously ran his hand through his hair.

"I can barely believe it, but it makes sense," Ginevra murmured. "We should have realized it sooner. Just the thought of the risk you were running . . . He's feeding off your fears. Think carefully, Gemma: a moment ago you thought someone had buried you alive."

A shiver gripped my back as I recalled the experience. He was right. Simon was right. "That's why I keep reliving Evan's death."

Ginevra nodded. "He focuses on what torments you the most. It happened in New York, remember? That was the first time you saw Evan. It must have been his doing even then."

"And in the hallway . . ." I whispered, putting the pieces together.

"He's toying with your mind." Simon had a new light in his eyes, as if a burden had been lifted from him. Up until he'd realized this, I knew he'd felt he could do nothing about my suffering, and that had made him taciturn and short-tempered. But now the look on his face was determined because he knew how to battle my demons. "He wants to convince you to take your own life, and he almost succeeded. He used your suffering to convince you that you were going insane, but he made one false move: he outed himself to us by trying to stop Peter with the snakes."

"Peter . . ." I murmured.

"The Subterranean tried to use Peter's fear against him to keep him from saving you."

"But Pet managed anyway. He overcame his phobia for me," I said, amazed.

"He was brave." Simon still sounded proud about solving the riddle. "And it's a good thing he was, because the Subterranean definitely wasn't expecting that."

"You think he might actually have killed her that way?" Ginevra asked.

"Sure. What just happened is proof—you saw it for yourself. He made Gemma believe she was suffocating. Her mind was so convinced there was no oxygen that her body reacted accordingly. She definitely would have died if we hadn't shown up and driven off the Executioner."

I gasped. "You mean he was *here*?"

"Yes. Actually, the most dangerous aspect of a Reaper with a power like his, purely mental, is the ability to make himself invisible to anyone, even a Witch." Simon looked steadily at Ginevra. "It would take serious concentration for you just to detect his presence."

"So what do we do?" I asked, looking them in the eye warily.

"For now, you get some rest," Simon said, his voice firm. "You're still weak, and we need you to be strong enough to fight, now more than ever. It's not our fears that enslave us, but how we face them. He'll attack you again and you'll have to resist until we can catch him."

"Then what?"

Simon arched an eyebrow, a new fire ablaze in his eyes. "Then it'll be his turn to be afraid."

The time had come for him to protect me.

9

THE DARKNESS WITHIN ME

At last, the room is quiet. So quiet I can hear the pen move across this ivory-colored paper, forever staining it with my gloomy thoughts. Simon and Ginevra left so I could rest, both of them relieved they'd figured out why I've been so unwell. Maybe while I was desperate about losing Evan this whole time they were suffering for me.

So that explains it: another Subterranean. Another creature condemned to die just so I can stay alive. It all seems so unfair. How many more will suffer the fate meant for me before they realize my life isn't worth all this? How many others will have to die for me? Simon? Ginevra? Or maybe my baby? No. I'll never let them take him too.

Ginevra and Simon are relieved there's a logical explanation for my hallucinations, that they aren't caused by madness. But it doesn't matter to me. Knowing it does nothing to ease my pain. Quite the opposite, in fact. At least during my visions, I could fool myself into thinking Evan wasn't dead, and for a moment my desperation would subside, leaving room for hope—an emotion that's otherwise banished forever from my heart. But then he died again before my eyes, and each time it left me even more devastated.

The pain is changing me. Sometimes I'm almost afraid because I end up thinking horrible things. Like that time after my mom talked to me I caught myself wishing she would die. How did this happen to me? I told Simon about it and he says it's normal, that it happens to most people, and that the point is to decide not to listen to those thoughts.

I texted Peter to thank him for his help. I heard his voice when I was unconscious. He told Simon he would wait for news of me, but I don't feel like calling him this late at night. I still can't believe that after all these years he told me how he really feels, even though he knows I don't feel the same. There will never be anyone else in my life because my heart has been shattered and, like a broken vase, it's not capable of containing anything any more. I'll keep my Evan safe and warm, and when the baby is born, maybe I'll see Evan in him, a little piece of him to hold onto. I would give my life to see Evan just once more. One last time together so I could say goodbye. But there's nothing I can do to make amends, and that's the worst part. I feel like a piece of glass with cracks running through it that lengthen with every vibration of my heart, every breath, every tear. And no matter how hard I try not to break down, I'm on the verge of breaking into thousands of pieces. I'm a shattered piece of glass.

Sometimes at night I think I feel his touch and I seek his embrace in the darkness. Everyone asks me how I am, but nothing I can say would ever give them the faintest idea. Sealed inside an endless pain, cold and dark, with no way out. In pieces.

Trapped in a room full of memories, a room I can't escape from.

~~Evan. Evan. Evan.~~

He's all there is in my mind and the memory hurts so much that death would be a relief in comparison to what I'm experiencing now, to the thought of what I've lost. It hurts too much. And every beat of my weary heart, every breath, makes me wish everything would just end, because the pain is unbearable.

It's like it's raining inside me. A corrosive, incessant, suffocating rain. It pours down on me with a roar: deafening, deafening, deafening . . . like a shower of nails on my heart of ice.

The cord that connected me to Evan has been slashed and someone has torn up my roots. I move and breathe, but my heart pumps only poison that corrodes me down to my bones. It burns my blood, darkens my mind, devastates my soul and every part of me.

Soon the pain will annihilate me, and then the shadows will do with me as they wish—because at that point I'll be dead.

"How deep do you think it is down there?" Evan's dark irises stared at me, trying to decipher my expression.

My eyes lost themselves in his, so close my heart skipped a beat, two deep wells ready to swallow it up. "Evan," I murmured, barely moving my lips as he leaned over to examine the pool that stretched out endlessly below us. It was like a mother-of-pearl shell that had been carved into the rock and filled with water. He was squatting beside me on the rocky shore and the water's light reflected in his eyes that brimmed with enthusiasm.

"Come with me, Gemma. I want to find out what's down there."

"No! Evan, wait!" I exclaimed, my voice trembling, but he had already stood up and moved to the water's edge. I hesitated, staring at his back, which was crisscrossed with what seemed to be lash marks and burns. As he turned around to encourage me, I saw his hair was longer. It gave him a wild look.

"I'm tired of waiting, Gem." Evan's eyes filled with bitterness and he dove in. I lunged forward to grab him, but something held me back. I dragged myself to the edge of the pool and watched him sink further and further down until the darkness engulfed him and he disappeared.

"Evan!" I reached out my hand but instantly jerked it back: the water had burned me. When I squatted, a clang and a sharp pain in my ankles made me look down. "What the—" My ankles were shackled in thick iron chains that were making them bleed and squeezing them tighter with every attempt to pull free.

"How deep do you think it is down there?"

I looked up and jade-green eyes smiled at me, inches from my own. Though I couldn't remember ever seeing her before, the mahogany-haired young woman's face seemed familiar.

"Who are you?" I asked warily as she leaned over the surface of the water and peered into the depths. Her eyes were filled with awe, as though it contained some forbidden treasure.

"I'm Anya." She smiled at me. "Isn't it wonderful down there?" Her eyes sparkled so intensely they seemed to be illuminated by an inner light. "Come with me, Gemma! Let's find out where it leads!" she exclaimed, still leaning over the edge of the pool, her face full of promise.

I shook my head, dazed by the power of her voice. "I can't! I can't go with you." I looked down at my ankles, which were still trapped. The clank of the iron chains drew her attention.

She studied them for a long moment and looked at me again. "Why not?"

"I—I don't know."

"Don't fight it, Gemma. Come with us." I stared at her, unsettled. Her words seemed to be hiding a different meaning that eluded me. "It will be easier for you. Everything will end. The pain will stop. You just need to come with us." Her eyes continued to gaze hypnotically into mine as her voice crept inside me like powerful dark fog. "Make up your mind. *He's waiting for you.*"

"Evan . . ." Her words pierced my heart, but a sudden explosion in my head set my brain on fire and kept me from taking her hand. I gritted my teeth from the terrible pain and stepped away from her. My brain felt like it was about to melt from the intense heat. I tried to speak, but my chest was so tight I couldn't utter a sound.

"You have to choose, Gemma."

Maybe it was actually her voice that was burning my brain. It suddenly seemed like the whole world was being sucked into the pool of water as the pain in my head vanished, leaving me short of breath. I stared at the walls of Evan's room, the echo of Anya's voice fading in my mind.

I looked around, staggered by the strange dream, as my body forced itself to breathe steadily again. I touched my forehead. It was damp and my skin was still hot. I must have run a high fever again. Alarmed, I checked the room but knew that even if the Executioner was there I wouldn't be able to sense his presence, much less call Simon or Ginevra to come to my rescue. My only hope was to strengthen my mind's defenses, make an effort to ward off his attacks. It would be difficult, but I had to at least try, and deep in my heart I hoped that understanding what was causing my hallucinations would work to my advantage.

I pushed off the covers, catching the diary as it fell. I had left it on the bed when I nodded off. Before putting it back on the pillow, I stopped to look at its ivory-colored pages and decided Ginevra was right: laying out my pain like that, letting the paper absorb it like ink, would help distance it a bit from my heart, drain it away, even if only for a moment. Maybe seeing the words from a distance would make them less mine and help me breathe.

The touch of my bare foot against the wood floor sent a shiver down my spine. As I walked down the hall, Simon and Ginevra's comforting murmurs coming from behind a closed door momentarily ceased when she sensed my presence but then started up again as soon as she was reassured that my thoughts were calm.

A hot shower would help wash away the remnants of the night, which had left me with a deep feeling of discouragement and uneasiness. When the spa had filled with steam I stepped under the scalding stream of the shower and even my tiniest muscles began to ease. I wished I could stay there forever, enveloped in that sweet coziness that banished every thought and concern, drawing them down the drain with it. I felt so comfortable in the water, as though it were my element. I washed my hair, gently massaging my scalp, and rinsed it, letting the heat slide slowly down my face like a caress. It was soothing to stand under the water, holding my breath. Opening my eyes to take a breath through the spray, I suddenly jumped in terror.

Two jade-green eyes reflected in the glass of the shower stall stared back at me. I lurched back but then realized it was only my reflection—or maybe an image that had persisted from the strange dream I'd had. Gradually my heartbeat slowed and I almost smiled at my overreaction. My mind had dragged that night's bad dream into the real world. Would it never end?

It was then I noticed there was a dent in the stone wall of the shower. I stared at the cracks and the way they branched out, wondering what had caused them. I couldn't resist the impulse to touch them. An image flashed into my mind: Evan's arms resting tensely against the rock, his head bowed and water streaming down his bare back. He looked tormented. *It had been him.* Who knew how I could be so sure, but I was. I'd seen him brutally smash his fist against the wall. I touched it again, missing him desperately, and made myself get out of the shower.

As I turned off the water and opened the door a shooting pain gripped my belly, making me double over and grit my teeth. A scarlet trickle flowed down my leg, contrasting starkly with the white porcelain of the floor like a gruesome threat. Staring at my fingers with alarm, I saw they were stained red, and stifled a scream. My hands trembled and I could think of nothing except the baby.

I made myself take a deep breath. The Executioner. It had to be the Executioner. Terrified, I tried to wash away the blood and discovered it wasn't coming from between my legs. Just then, I heard Simon and Ginevra burst into the hallway. They began to bang insistently on the door.

"Everything's fine," I shouted to them before they could come in. "Everything's fine," I repeated to myself in an attempt to banish the tension. I used a washcloth to stanch the wound on my belly, then dropped it to the floor and buried my face in my hands, still trembling from fright.

Ginevra waited until I had put some clothes on before coming into the room. "Are you okay? What happened?" She studied the room, her eyes lingering on the washcloth on the floor.

"I don't know, it must have been the Subterranean. There was blood everywhere. I guess I managed to ward off his attack this time."

With extreme caution, Ginevra lifted the bottom of my shirt, her expression indecipherable. "No. I see it too. You're still bleeding." I looked down at the fabric. The bloodstain on it was expanding. Ginevra's eyes wavered and filled with terror. "It can't be . . ." The words escaped her in a barely audible gasp as I tried in vain to understand why she was so upset.

"Gwen, what's wrong? It's just a little blood." I grabbed another washcloth and realized as I patted the wound that the blood was coming right from my birthmark. "I must have cut myself with something. My skin has gotten really sensitive lately and— Gwen, are you listening?"

Ginevra forced herself to look me in the eye and helped me stanch the bleeding, all the while staring at me as though seeing me for the first time. I wasn't sure what was frightening her, but there was something in her eyes—a strange edginess that betrayed how upset she was.

"If the sight of blood has this big an effect on you, I'd better go change."

"Right." Ginevra nodded without picking up on my sarcasm. I walked around her, still baffled by her expression.

In the silence of Evan's room, I examined my belly. There was no wound on my skin and the burning sensation had lessened to a mild tingle, but the birthmark I'd had my whole life had turned translucent like a burn mark or a faint, pearly tattoo. Still, compared to all the bizarre events in my life, this was the least of my worries. I couldn't understand Ginevra's reaction. I decided it didn't matter—I was already too busy finding the energy to face my demons. To face the world. To breathe. I didn't have the strength to worry about other people too.

My thoughts shocked me. When had I become so egotistical?

Simon's voice came from behind the door. "Gemma, everything all right?"

"It's nothing, Simon." Ginevra must have let him know I hadn't felt well. "Nothing serious, don't worry."

He peeked around the door, waiting for permission to come in. I smiled at him, trying to ease the tension. "I saw blood on the floor in the spa," he said with a mix of embarrassment and concern.

"It was just a scratch. It's already stopped bleeding. The baby is fine. I think Ginevra's getting a little overanxious."

"She really cares about you. I mean, you know . . . about you and the baby. The three of us are all she has left, and she's already lost so much."

"Her Sisters, you mean."

Simon nodded. "Giving them up was the most difficult thing she'd ever done. It devastated her. You have no idea what she went through. She's very attached to you, so it's no surprise she's worried, especially given your condition."

"Yeah." I stroked my belly as though the gesture might protect the baby growing inside me. "I wonder if we'll manage to get through all this torture. Sometimes I think that even if the Executioner fails, my body will finish the job on its own by giving in to the agony." Utterly discouraged, I sighed and looked into Simon's eyes. "It's really too much. I can't—I can't find peace, day or night."

He pulled me against him and held me tight. I stiffened in surprise but the awkwardness quickly faded, giving way to a deep sense of calm. He ran his hand through my hair. "It'll get better, you'll see." His soft voice lulled me into some parallel world where the pain eased, muffled by a blanket of pure white roses. "Let yourself go, Gemma. You just need to let me help you."

All at once I noticed that the veins in his forearm were turning black, as though absorbing poison, and my heart began to bleed again, pierced by thousands of thorns. I shoved him away. Simon teetered, his arms in midair. "What the hell did you think you were doing?!" I screamed, violent anger surging through me.

"I just wanted to help you," he said, his voice tinged with guilt.

"I don't need your help! I don't need anyone!"

"Gemma, be reasonable. I just wanted to ease some of your pain. I didn't touch your memories. All this negative energy isn't good for the baby."

I glared at him, overcome by venomous rage. "That's not your problem."

"Gemma . . ." Simon reached toward my shoulder, but I knocked his hand away with a strength I hadn't known I had.

"Don't touch me!"

Simon's eyes wavered and he looked stunned by the contempt in my voice.

"*Never touch me again,*" I snapped.

"If that's what you want." Simon sighed, giving in, but something in his eyes—a shadow of sadness and defeat—brought a pang to my heart. Only then did I become fully aware of the tone I had used. I stood there as Simon turned his back on me and left in silence. Little by little, the cloud of poison that had been fogging my mind dissipated and was replaced by feelings of guilt. Why had I treated him so badly?

10

CHECKMATE

Simon appeared behind me so suddenly it made me jump. "Sorry, I didn't mean to startle you."

"Oh! You were—"

"Yeah," he was quick to reply, confirming my suspicions: he had just returned from a mission. Though I had lived in their world for months, the thought still made me shiver. "It was an elderly person, if that puts you more at ease." He sat down at the kitchen table and invited me to join him with a nod.

"Simon—" My eyes met his.

He clenched his jaw, his face full of resentment. "It's not a problem," he said.

"I don't—I honestly don't know what got into me. I'm so sorry. I'm horrified by how I treated you." I pulled a chair back from the table, gripping the wood tightly.

"Don't worry about it. It doesn't matter."

"You just wanted to help me, and I went and—I was a total bitch."

"It's water under the bridge."

I nodded and, hanging my head in embarrassment, sat down at the table. Ginevra came in, carrying something, but I didn't look at her. "It's just that all this is seriously fraying my nerves. As if that weren't enough, every time I close my eyes I find myself flung into a nightmare. I keep—I keep dreaming about a woman. It's like she's haunting me." I looked up and noticed Ginevra's expression freeze, though she was trying to look unperturbed. "I had them before too, but I've been having them more and more often lately."

"Is she always the same? Do you always dream of the same woman?" Simon asked.

"I can't remember. All I know is I have the feeling I know her."

"Ginevra, what's wrong?" Simon asked. He'd also noticed the worried look on her face.

"Nothing. It's nothing. Just thinking." Simon tightened his lips, perplexed.

"Do you guys think it's possible that I"—I hesitated because it was so hard to voice the suspicion that had weighed on my heart for some time—"that I could have had a premonition of Evan's death?"

"What are you talking about, Gemma?" Ginevra asked.

"I dreamed it before he died. I dreamed of him dying. More than once. That's why I'm so upset about the nightmares haunting me now—I'm afraid they might reflect reality. Maybe it's the price I have to pay for coming back from death."

Simon tried to reassure me. "Relax, Gemma. It was probably caused by your fears. It definitely wasn't a premonition. Hold on." A glimmer of illumination lit up his face. "Maybe that's also his doing. Maybe the Subterranean can enter your dreams, like Faust or like—" He left his sentence unfinished to avoid naming Evan, who had had the same power. "It would make sense. After all, he's already able to get past your mind's defenses when you're awake. Maybe he can do it while you're asleep too."

"You're right!" I exclaimed. Ginevra, on the other hand, didn't seem very convinced. "He probably takes on a woman's guise to hide his real appearance and confuse us," I said.

"It's possible," Simon agreed, deep in thought.

"I think he wanted to convince me to follow her," I added.

"He must have the ability to entrance people. It's a dangerous power that could lead you to surrender to him completely—an almost irresistible attraction."

"It sure is," I mumbled, remembering the sensation that had seemed to creep under my skin.

A metallic click made us turn toward Ginevra. She was polishing some weapons. "In any case, since he likes to play around, I've prepared some little toys just for him." She slid something across the table. It looked like a handgun but with a more complex structure.

"Guns?" I asked, surprised.

"Were you expecting bows and arrows?" Ginevra flashed a half-smile.

"No, seriously. What do you mean to do with *those*?"

"They're not ordinary guns," explained Simon. He seemed to understand what the weapons were, though I guessed he'd never seen them before, given how closely he was examining their details.

Ginevra pushed an iron case lined with black leather toward us. A grim smile hardened her features as we looked at the contents.

"They're perfect. You did an excellent job, *chérie*," Simon told her with a smile.

"Thanks." Ginevra winked at him while I frowned, still puzzled. Did they really mean to face such a dangerous Executioner with handguns?

Exercising extreme caution, Ginevra took out one of the projectiles and showed it to me. It was pointy, like a spearhead, and in the middle of its metal surface was a tiny glass section containing a drop or two of clear liquid.

"Your poison," I murmured.

"My serpent and I had our work cut out for us. I was busy all night making these."

"Think it'll work?" I asked skeptically.

"I don't *think*, I *know* it'll work. With these"—Ginevra loaded the gun with one of the tiny projectiles, the safety making an ominous click—"we're guaranteed a huge advantage. This way Simon can protect himself and I'll be less worried."

I stared at the gun on the table in front of me. Actually, I had to agree with them: it was perfect. Ginevra had created weapons with her poison to battle the Subterranean. "You're amazing!" I said, and sat back in my chair as she and Simon slid the guns into various holsters. She even had a little one strapped around her thigh. She winked at me, making me smile.

"What do we do about school?"

"No school today. Too dangerous."

"Okay, but what do we do? I mean, are we going to hang around here until we nail him? On top of that, if it's so hard to detect his presence, how are we going to catch him?"

"She's right. We need to lure him out into the open, set a trap for him." Simon's eyes lit up, relishing the new challenge.

"But how?"

Simon looked at me and smiled. It was a predatory smile.

"Let's saddle up." Ginevra loaded her gun and cast me a glance. "It's hunting time."

"I'm still not sure this is a good idea," I shouted, trying to be heard over the aggressive roar of the engines that filled the garage with foreboding echoes.

Simon rested his arms on the roof of the Lamborghini. Ginevra was revving the accelerator to warm up the engine. "You sure it'll work?" she asked him.

He nodded. "Trust me, the Subterranean is only waiting for the opportunity to attack Gemma. He's less likely to do it if we're at home."

"Why don't we all take the BMW?" I asked hesitantly.

"We need to split up. I'll go out first but I'll keep my eye on you. Gin, the second the Subterranean turns up, you and Gemma get out of there," Simon ordered. "I'll take care of him."

It warmed my heart to see how concerned they were about each other. Ginevra nodded and Simon slapped the roof of the car with his hand before climbing into his Bugatti Veyron. He pulled out next to us in his blue missile, his eyes locked on his girlfriend's.

The garage door closed behind us. It was too late to turn back now. We were going to hunt down my Executioner. It was dangerous, I realized that, but it was a match I couldn't miss out on.

The bright red traffic light kept our wheels glued to the street. It felt like the starting line of a race whose finish no one could imagine. Impatient, Simon and Ginevra revved their engines without taking their eyes off each other. Fearful, I stared at them in silence, wondering who would win and—most importantly—who would pay the price this time. I wouldn't be able to bear losing either of them.

Suddenly another sports car nudged its way between us and revved its engine challengingly. I leaned forward in my seat to look at the driver. Behind the wheel was a young woman who clearly didn't understand how dangerous it was for her to be doing that. She wore a sexy, skintight, dark-gray racing driver's suit. Her hair was blond and straight, and her big blue eyes stood out beneath thick black lashes. She looked to be around twenty-five but she might have been younger—one of those rich, spoiled, city girls whose daddy had bought her a fancy car. She was probably attracted to Simon's good looks and thought flaunting her car might be a good way to seduce him. We, on the other hand, were about to race toward death—a detail she certainly wouldn't have liked. The red light prolonged the tension as the woman continued to rev her engine.

I smiled to myself, finding the situation amusing. "What a weird-looking car."

"It's Italian," Ginevra replied, checking it out from the corner of her eye. "A Pagani Zonda R. Not too shabby! Central monocoque in carbon-titanium, 750 horsepower, and shifts gears in twenty milliseconds thanks to a magnesium-cased dog-ring gearbox. In a nutshell, a car designed for racing."

"Hey, check it out. Looks like she's got it in for you two," I told her, noticing that the young woman wasn't only trying to provoke Simon, on her left, but also Ginevra, on her right.

Ginevra tapped her fingers on the steering wheel and glanced at her impatiently. "Unless she's looking for trouble, I hope for her sake she stays out of our way. This is not the time."

The light turned green and the wheels of the three cars squealed as we all shot off like missiles amid the protests of nearby pedestrians. Just outside Lake Placid, Simon's car disappeared, pushed by its thousand horsepower, while the woman's dropped back behind us. Maybe she had realized that Simon and Ginevra weren't interested in racing her—or, more likely, she'd detected the threatening look in Ginevra's sharp eyes. I took a deep breath, holding back the panic that threatened to suck me up into its dark vortex. The more Ginevra accelerated, the faster my heart raced, beating in time to the roar of the engine as I wondered when the Reaper Angel would show himself.

In my heightened state of alert, I jumped when I saw the front of the Zonda pull up alongside the Lamborghini's back wheels. "I thought she gave up!" I complained. "Didn't you lose her?" The woman was putting her life in jeopardy by interfering in our plans. Her pearl-white car zoomed along, matching our speed. "What does she think she's doing?"

Ginevra ignored the woman, who instead looked at me with a fake smile that sent a shiver down my spine. The Zonda roared louder and edged toward the Lamborghini, forcing Ginevra to veer away so the cars wouldn't collide.

"What the—what the hell does she want with us?" Ginevra hissed between clenched teeth. She watched the car in her mirror, bitter irritation on her face. "Take a hike, blondie. You could get burned in this game." She accelerated more, but the woman insisted, pulling up alongside us again. "Damn it!" She tightened her lips.

My heart lurched. "Gwen!" I shrieked as a ball of fire burst from the woman's outstretched palm and shattered the window of the Zonda.

"Son of a—" The car swerved dangerously as Ginevra took us out of the trajectory of the fireball. It missed us by a hair.

"What the hell is going on?!" I screamed, panic surging through me.

Simon reappeared from far down the road, spun his car around and positioned himself opposite us.

"It worked." Ginevra's voice betrayed no emotion, her icy gaze locked on the road as a crafty smile spread over her face.

"A woman?!" I asked, trying to keep my voice down. "I thought Subterraneans were all males!"

"You did? Why would you think that?" Ginevra cast me an amused glance. "This will just make it more fun to get rid of her."

"Wha—" I put my hands on my head, more confused than ever. In the rearview mirror I saw Simon's Bugatti tailing the car behind us.

"They must *seriously* want you. I know from experience that the females are as lethal as they are rare." Ginevra continued to drive, keeping her eyes glued to the road. "Extremely lethal." She seemed pleased that the challenge was getting even more exciting and at the same time fully confident about how our deadly game would play out. I, on the other hand, had learned at my own expense not to take anything for granted. Suddenly Ginevra's eyes lit up.

"What is it?" I asked, nervous. I knew that look—I'd seen it on her face lots of times during their clandestine races.

"Simon has decided to make things a little more interesting."

"W-what do you mean 'interesting'? Isn't this interesting enough?"

"It'll be even better without powers." She winked at me, excited by the thought.

"You mean he's not going to attack her with his fireballs?"

"Yes, but the race on our end won't be run using our powers." She shrugged casually as though she were talking about the weather. "We like to let the engines do their own thing—the sound is so much cooler when the cars are under strain."

Despite Ginevra's apparent confidence, my heart thumped wildly and a knot gripped my stomach. I dug my fingers into the leather seat and jumped at every spark emitted by the two cars battling it out behind us. Simon did everything he could to block the Executioner's car so it couldn't reach our Lamborghini, but the woman must have been more skilled than he'd expected, because she was giving him a serious run for his money.

"Is she the woman you see in your dreams?"

Ginevra's question made me start. It hadn't occurred to me that the two might be connected. "I'm not sure. She might be."

"Maybe I was wrong," she muttered to herself.

"Wrong about what?"

Ginevra seemed surprised by my question, as though she hadn't realized she'd spoken out loud. "Nothing. Never mind." Her expression darkened momentarily and then cleared.

"How the hell could you not have sensed her?" Though I wished I could have asked more nicely, what came out of my mouth was an accusation.

"She has the power to shield her mind. I didn't perceive anything strange in her thoughts. I told you, she's going to be a challenge."

The Zonda eluded Simon's attacks and raced toward us at warp speed. "She's going to hit us! She's going to hit us!" I squirmed in my seat, cursing as the blond Angel shot toward us like a bullet toward its target, but before I could catch my breath the car zoomed past us. "Gwen, look out!"

A huge semi full of tree trunks suddenly swerved in front of us, cutting us off. It looked like an out-of-control giant about to crash down on top of us. Ginevra frowned, searching for possible escape routes, then smiled, barely touched the gearshift, and hit the gas. I held my breath and braced for impact as the semi skidded toward us, blocking all the lanes, but the Lamborghini roared louder and flew beneath the wheels of the semi. I stared at Ginevra's smiling face and struggled to control my breathing.

"Relax." Ginevra winked at me. "We've just started playing."

But another doubt gripped my stomach. "Simon!" I unbuckled my seatbelt in a second flat, spun around, and shot to my knees in my seat, terrified he hadn't made it through. Peering through the rear window I saw the semi lying on the road like a sleeping behemoth, enveloped in a cloud of dust. The tree trunks had scattered everywhere. "I don't see him, Gwen!" I shot her a glance and her lips arched in a captivating smile.

Just then, Simon came skidding out across the asphalt to the left of the semi. I collapsed into my seat and allowed myself a sigh of relief. Ginevra let out a laugh. "I told you to relax. It would require more than a truck to take Simon out."

Without losing speed, he pulled up alongside our car and traded glances with Ginevra. I looked around nervously, wondering where the Executioner was, and felt the earth disappear beneath me when a gray Ferrari identical to Evan's pulled up on our right. I bit down the pain seeing the car caused me and looked up. My heart lurched. Evan was behind the wheel. I threw myself against the window, shouting his name and pounding my fists on the door.

"Gemma, calm down! Gemma!"

"Let me out! Let me out, I have to go to him!" Completely hysterical, I jerked on the door handle again and again.

Gemma . . . His voice burst into my head. Desperate, I burst into tears. All at once my window exploded. Flying shards of glass were everywhere. Evan leaned over and reached toward me. "Take my hand, Gemma! Come with me!"

My seatbelt clicked closed around my waist as Ginevra continued to shout, "Gemma, snap out of it!" Fighting to maintain control of the car with one hand, she shook me hard with the other. "It's her! It's her, toying with you!"

I could barely hear her; her voice reached me in confused fragments. "Come on, Gemma! Take my hand!" Evan urged me, but I was lost halfway, unable to decide which of the two voices to cling to. The Ferrari continued to keep pace with us, despite Ginevra's maneuvers to avoid it. "Come with me, Gemma! Don't listen to her. She just wants to keep you away from me!" I impulsively grabbed the steering wheel.

"Gemma! Gemma, what are you doing? Snap out of it!"

"I have to go to him! Let me go to him! Please, pull over!"

The car swerved, threatening to go out of control. Suddenly, Simon's Bugatti appeared in front of us, aiming at the Ferrari. What was he doing? He risked hurting Evan! "Simon!"

"Your mind! Keep control of your mind, Gemma!" Ginevra screamed.

Little by little, her words penetrated the wall that the Subterranean had built around my mind. I turned to look for Evan but saw in his place only the blond Angel, who shot me a sly smile. The Zonda abruptly slowed and spun around, avoiding impact with Simon's car, which pursued it as Ginevra sped forward in an attempt to get me out of there.

"Gwen, I—" My guilt trapped my voice in my throat.

"It doesn't matter. Everything okay?"

I nodded, still shaken. "How does she do that? How the hell does she do that?!" I couldn't fathom the strength of her power. *I had seen Evan.* I had been completely convinced it was him, that he had come to save me. How could that woman instill such a sense of security in me that not even Ginevra's words had been enough to stop me?

"You have to focus and force yourself not to let her in."

"But I don't know how to shield my mind!" I wailed.

"Make an effort, Gemma! Now you know she can attack you at any moment, but you can be prepared when she does. Focus and keep her out!" Ginevra gritted her teeth and clutched the wheel. The asphalt burst open as we drove over it, as though we were racing over the mouth of an erupting volcano. "Brace yourself!"

I sank my fingers into the seat, lurching with the car's abrupt movements. Ginevra downshifted and veered off the road, pulling up alongside the Zonda. A bolt of lightning shot out at the Angel's car, but the blond swerved to avoid it, saving all but a lock of her hair from the lightning bolt. "Ugly Witch!" she hissed, her face dark with rage. She cranked the steering wheel, preparing to attack, and shot a fireball at the Lamborghini.

Ginevra nimbly sidestepped the attack, making the back tires skid. The incandescent ball shot between our wheels and crashed into the trees. "Wow! It passed underneath us!" I exclaimed with admiration. Ginevra sent her adversary a challenging smile.

"You've got to give me lessons someday. Where on earth did you learn to drive like this?"

Before she could reply the Zonda rammed our side so hard I lurched in my seat. Ginevra let out a string of curses. "You bitch! You are so dead." She pulled a lever next to the steering wheel, switching off the traction control and putting the car into sport-shift mode. The back of the Lamborghini tilted and the car negotiated a hairpin turn, its tires screeching against the asphalt as the Zonda shot toward us on our right. I gasped, panicking. In the midst of the confusion Ginevra took out her gun, raised her arm in front of my face and fired several shots through my window. The Angel dodged them. Ginevra jammed her foot down on the accelerator, her eyes ablaze, the threatening expression on her face making me shudder.

"Now let's make good use of every last horsepower." Ginevra focused on the road and the car shot forward like a fiery arrow. Through the back window I saw Simon blocking our adversary's way. A long hairpin turn put the two cars' tractions to the test. For a second I thought they had lost control, but then I realized Simon was trying to force the Zonda off the road. Mid-curve, his Bugatti swerved left and rammed the blond's door, making the windows explode in a shower of glass.

The Lamborghini entered a tunnel and the battle disappeared. The ominous echo of our engine was soon joined by the roar of the two other cars. Suddenly Ginevra screamed, losing focus for the first time. I turned toward her and my heart leapt to my throat. She was fluttering her hands over the steering wheel. "What's wrong?!" I cried, trying to grab the wheel as the car barreled out of the tunnel at breakneck speed. Behind me, Simon had overtaken the Zonda.

"The fire! It's burning hot! Don't touch it! Don't touch the wheel!!"

I looked at the steering wheel, bewildered. It was suddenly clear: Ginevra was under attack. "Gwen! Gwen! Listen to me!" I shook her shoulder while trying to keep the car on the road. But it was impossible; Ginevra was hysterically jamming her foot on the accelerator. The Lamborghini plunged off the road and into the trees. "Gwen! You've got to listen to me! It's not happening!" I shouted in an attempt to reassure her. "Everything's fine! There is no fire, you're not burning!" A tree ripped the driver's-side mirror off the car. *We were going to crash.* "Block your mind, damn it!"

My words finally penetrated the shield around her mind. Ginevra regained control of herself and grabbed the wheel. She swerved and skidded to a halt, dodging a tree a second before hitting it full on. I closed my eyes, relief flooding through me.

"I'm sorry," she whispered, letting her head fall back against the headrest. "I had no idea she was so . . ." She shut her eyes, clearly trying to banish the memory of the terrible sensation that had possessed her. Simon and the blond shot by us on the road flanking the woods at an insane speed.

"Breathe," I said, well aware of how the experience had shaken her.

But Ginevra started the engine, the light in her eyes fiercer than ever. "There's no time to breathe." The wheels spun threateningly, raising a cloud of dust, and the car took off through the forest.

At first the other two cars were blurry specks racing ahead in the distance, emitting sparks and swerving wildly, but the Lamborghini quickly caught up to them. We could see a single stream of energy flowing between the Zonda and the Bugatti. I held my breath but then noticed the beam was coming from Simon's palm. The blond Angel was resisting it with equal strength and the air between them trembled with energy. Simon attacked more ferociously, forcing the other car to swerve onto a side road.

Ginevra tried to pull up alongside Simon but braked when the Zonda reappeared on the overpass we'd just gone under. The blond swerved suddenly and the car flew off the bridge and over the low roof of the Bugatti in front of us. "My God! She drives even worse than you do!" I shouted, panic gripping me. The Zonda crashed back onto the road. Its door burst open and snapped off. "Look out!" I bit my lip.

Simon tried to dodge the door but it was too close. Shearing off his passenger side mirror, it continued to skid across the asphalt straight toward us, sparks flying. Ginevra steered around it, fire in her eyes.

As we sped by, the lake bordering the road churned and rose into a crystal wall. Nature itself seemed to be rebelling, a furious witness to the battle between two Angels in the service of Death. I shifted my attention back to the road. Fear pressed me back into my seat and I jammed my foot down on an imaginary brake pedal. Ahead of us, the gates of a railroad crossing were slowly descending.

"Oh my God, Gwen!"

Ignoring my protests, Ginevra shifted into sixth and stepped on the gas. I clapped my hands to my mouth as Simon, glued to the rear of the Zonda, slipped under the gates a split second before they lowered completely. Our way was now blocked but Ginevra continued to accelerate. I clenched my fists on my seat, my entire body stiff with panic and my lips moving quickly in a silent prayer. The Lamborghini was quite low-slung but I wasn't sure it could cross the tracks without smashing into the gates. Ginevra, on the other hand, didn't seem the least bit concerned. It was her against the train in a race we couldn't afford to lose.

We were scant yards from the tracks. "You can do it! You can do it! You can do it!" I urged her on, then held my breath and braced for the worst.

Ginevra's face twisted with rage. Her lips tightened and a curse unbecoming to her normally graceful demeanor escaped her. The car skidded to a dead stop parallel to the tracks. I flinched as the freight train sliced through the air.

"Damn it!" Ginevra pounded on the steering wheel with both hands.

I took a deep breath, my heart still trembling. "Did we lose them?" I asked, my voice unsteady.

"Don't count on it."

The Lamborghini zoomed off the highway and onto the flattened earth alongside the tracks, moving parallel to the train. From time to time, in the gap between one boxcar and the next, I could see the two automobiles chasing one other on the opposite side.

"Shit! The ground drops off up ahead!" My heart stopped beating when I heard Ginevra's snarl, but instead of slowing down she put the car in fourth and sped up.

"What are you doing? Stop!"

Ahead of us, the tracks continued onto a narrow bridge over a gaping ravine that looked like a giant had taken a bite out of the land. There was no way to get to the other side from where we were now.

"Gwen! Stop! Damn it! There's a ravine up ahead! You've got to stop!"

"Brace yourself as hard as you can! This time I can do it!"

"What the—" My body instinctively flattened itself against the seat as the Lamborghini leapt forward, challenging the train. "Oh my God! What are you doing, Gwen? We're going to crash! You can't—you can't mean to jump it?!" Ginevra said nothing, her eyes locked on the ravine ahead of us. The Lamborghini overtook the train. "You can't jump the ravine, Gwen! Tell me you don't mean to jump it!!"

The ground opened up in front of us like a demon opening its jaws, ready to swallow us. "Oh my God! Oh my God! Oh my God!"

Ginevra swerved brusquely and the car careened right, skidding up onto the tracks. The train whistle blasted behind us. I leaned out to look at the empty space below us as shivers ran through my body. Closing my eyes, I leaned back in my seat, gasping for air. "Has anybody ever told you you're utterly insane?"

Ginevra turned to look at me, a complicit smile spreading across her lips. "A few times." She saw something over my shoulder and her expression darkened. The blond Angel must be behind us. Her stubbornness far exceeded our expectations. Simon's continued attacks couldn't stop her, and she barely left him enough time to defend himself against her offensive.

A loud blast shook me out of my thoughts. Another train was rushing toward us along the opposite tracks, sounding its whistle in an ominous warning.

"Damn it!" The Lamborghini slowed just long enough for Ginevra to downshift as the locomotive behind us thundered toward us, then swerved sharply to the left, crashing down onto the ground on the other side of the ravine. The second train zoomed by like a ghost and disappeared behind the first.

All at once there was a huge explosion, followed by a loud screech. The ground shook beneath the Lamborghini's tires. I jumped in my seat in shock: a fireball had struck the train. It was threatening to derail and hit us.

"Christ, Simon. Be careful!" Ginevra's voice sounded worried, but she didn't allow it to affect her driving, simultaneously accelerating and pulling on the chromed handbrake to make the car sideslip. I held on as best I could as the car tilted onto its side, continuing alongside the train at top speed as Ginevra controlled our angle with the steering wheel. "And to think Evan always used to say the drifting brake was useless!" she cried excitedly. I bit my lip to push back the memory of Evan, afraid the Angel might use it to her advantage. "Damn it! The cops are here," Ginevra grumbled.

"Huh? Where?" I couldn't see any cop cars. She must have picked up on the officers' thoughts. We couldn't risk involving innocent people, not to mention what would happen if we drew attention to ourselves.

With incredible agility Ginevra downshifted into third. The tires squealed and the pistons screamed as if they would burst out of the engine. The Lamborghini took off like a missile in front of the police car and crossed the tracks in front of the train a nanosecond before it derailed. The police leapt forward in hot pursuit but the runaway train instantly cut them off. I leaned back in my seat in time to see the cruiser spinning around after being clipped by the iron giant.

"His doughnut's going to go down the wrong pipe." Ginevra smiled at me, easing the tension a little. We turned onto a highway and set off after Simon and the Subterranean.

The roar of our cars was like a war cry that instantly cleared the highway of other drivers. The Zonda tried to pull back and approach us, but Simon blocked it with his Bugatti. Right in front of us, the gate on the back of a long cargo truck broke open, dumping a massive amount of dirt on the road. As soon as the driver realized he was losing his load, he slammed on the brakes and slowed to a stop. He started to get out, but found the Zonda zooming toward him. The man paled and stepped back, leaving the door open. Meanwhile, Simon sped up on the opposite side.

A shriek escaped me. "Gwen!" Simon had spun his car around and was facing the Zonda. The two cars collided head-on. The Angel found Simon in front of her, his gun aimed straight at her face. Shots rang out as the Bugatti danced backwards across the asphalt, propelled by the Zonda. I squirmed in my seat as Simon pushed out the cracked windshield. Beside me Ginevra flinched. I knew she was seeing through Simon's eyes.

"What's wrong?!" I shouted, panicking.

"She's not in the car."

I leaned out the broken window to see for myself and the ice-cold wind lashed my skin. "Simon!" I screamed, to warn him of the danger.

The blond Angel materialized on the roof of the Bugatti, dressed entirely in gray. Grabbing Simon with one hand, she yanked him out of the car through its shattered windshield. It was easy to see she'd been trained to kill. The two Subterraneans began to fight on the roof as the two cars beneath them continued to move at top speed all on their own. Simon clutched his weapon firmly but she dodged his shots one after the other. Like a small semi-automatic, the transparent compartment in its center contained several poisoned bullets. I wondered if she also had a secret weapon. What if the Màsala had armed her against other Subterraneans? What if she too had a supply of poison capable of killing Simon? Horrified, I put my hands to my mouth. I couldn't let him die too. In a matter of months I had already killed off half the family.

Ginevra slammed on the brakes, making the tires squeal against the asphalt as a warning to Simon. Up ahead, the road curved sharply to one side and ran along the edge of a deep gully. Still gripping the gun, Simon rolled off the roof and leapt to the ground. The Angel also noticed the imminent danger and glanced at our car, flashing an ominous smile at Ginevra. "One down," she mouthed, provocation burning in her eyes as she dove through the windshield of Simon's Bugatti and agilely maneuvered the car away from the gully, allowing her Zonda to sail into the void.

Ginevra raced to pick Simon up. "She took my car. Now she's seriously pissed me off," he growled, his eyes burning with rage. Ready to kill, he leapt onto the roof of the Lamborghini and Ginevra peeled out after the blond Angel, reaching her in moments thanks to Simon's control of the elements. Ahead of us was a double-decker car-carrier trailer filled with identical cars. Simon slapped the top of the Lamborghini twice and Ginevra nodded. They had obviously formulated a plan.

"What's happening?" I asked anxiously. What was she about to do?

Ginevra gripped the steering wheel as the corners of her mouth curved into a sly smile. "We're wrapping up this hunt."

A violent crash drew my attention to the road and my heart leapt to my throat. A dozen vehicles were sliding off the trailer. As though we were a rock in the middle of a stream, the cars rolled past us one by one without hitting us. Meanwhile, the trailer continued as though nothing had happened. Simon must have been controlling the driver's mind so he wouldn't notice anything. Once the carrier was empty, a loading ramp slid down from the upper deck. Sparks flew. Only then, to my horror, did I realize what Simon had in mind. Before I could protest, Ginevra pressed her foot down on the accelerator, pinning me in my seat, raced up the ramp and soared through the air over the trailer. Simon leapt off the Lamborghini onto the roof of his Bugatti, piloted by the blond Subterranean.

I lurched forward violently when we hit the ground. Ginevra laughed as I gaped at her in disbelief. "Was that really necessary?" I asked. "Couldn't Simon simply have materialized on top of his car?"

She laughed again. "But why? We're having so much fun!" she replied, bursting with enthusiasm. Despite everything, I had to admit I was dizzy with excitement. I sank back into my seat, the Lamborghini roaring like a lion as it pulled up behind the Bugatti. Our enemy was zigzagging violently in an attempt to shake Simon off, but he clung tightly to the roof. Determined to put an end to the battle, he drew his gun but the Angel swerved and the weapon flew out of his hands, shattering under our tires.

"Shit! He lost it!" Ginevra fumed.

"But you gave him more than one, right?" I said anxiously, refusing to accept defeat.

"I read Simon's mind. He left the others in the car." The second the words were out of her mouth, Ginevra's eyes widened as she realized the danger Simon was in.

A shiver ran through me. Before we could try to stop him, Simon leaned down over the windshield to find the Angel aiming a gun straight at his forehead. Horror spread over Ginevra's face and she let out a whimper.

I covered my mouth with my hands, blinded by desperation. It couldn't happen again—not to Simon. Time seemed to stop as I stared at the scene, horrified: Simon on the roof, motionless and defenseless, facing the enemy who was about to kill him. Like a mirror, Ginevra's eyes reflected her boyfriend's terror. I could see him silently touching her mind, sending her a final farewell.

I held my breath, frozen in sheer terror, but the Angel vanished unexpectedly, leaving us all stunned. Only a second had gone by since she'd pressed the gun to Simon's forehead, but to me it had felt like an eternity of agony.

Ginevra let out a moan of pure suffering and pulled the car up, her hands shaking. I'd never seen her so upset. Simon grabbed the steering wheel of his own car to avoid going off the road and slipped in through the windshield. The Bugatti slid sideways and skidded to a halt a few yards ahead of us. Ginevra leapt out of the Lamborghini before it stopped, and the two met midway in an embrace that was so desperate, so intense and intimate I had to look away.

I rubbed my arms and realized they were trembling. When I looked back at Simon and Ginevra, they were standing in the middle of the road as though no one else existed. Simon held her close, one hand behind her neck, their foreheads touching. Neither spoke, lost in a silence all their own. Inside me a voice clamored, still terrified by the danger Simon had just faced. I gave them a few more moments and then walked over to them, discovering that my legs were trembling too.

"I would never have let her do it," Ginevra whispered. "Even if it meant making her head explode, I would never have let her. It all happened so fast, that's all. I was afraid that—"

"Simon!" I exclaimed. He extended an arm to welcome me into his embrace. I clung to him, trying to express all my concern and gratitude for how fiercely he'd fought for me and the risks he'd taken to save me. "What happened?" I asked, my voice breaking from the fear of losing another person I cared about.

Simon and Ginevra looked at each other. "She was pointing the gun at me," he explained. "She could have killed me right then and there, and for a second I thought she was going to.

Then, enunciating really clearly, she said, 'Checkmate.' She looked me right in the eye, then dropped the gun and disappeared. This whole thing obviously amuses her." Ginevra's face darkened and I could see her losing herself in the intensity of Simon's memory.

"She didn't say anything else?" I insisted, looking at them one after the other.

Simon nodded and stared at me, his face somber, as though resolutely shouldering the full burden of the message intended for me. "'Until the next match.'"

A shudder of foreboding turned my blood to ice. There would be no escape.

11

BLOOD RED

January 16

I've been staring at this ivory page for fifteen minutes, hoping to find some comfort in my diary. I'm waiting for my thoughts to come unstuck so I can unburden myself, but they seem to be frozen. This morning the risk of losing Simon was a brutal, unexpected blow that threatened to drag me down into the dark pit I've been trying to grope my way out of ever since I lost everything—since I lost Evan.

I'm so tired that sometimes sleep drags me away like a seashell rocked by the small waves at the water's edge. Strangely enough, I only realized after I wrote down today's date that tomorrow is my birthday. Like I care. There are far bigger things on my mind right now. Even though I knew Ginevra was monitoring my every thought when we were at the table, I couldn't keep myself from stealing glances at Simon as he lay stretched out on the living-room couch. This morning made me realize something: there's a very real danger of losing one of them. The image of Ginevra's terrified face in my mind still makes me shudder. They've both been endlessly loyal to me even though there's nothing connecting them to me any more, and—most importantly—in spite of the fact that I don't deserve their protection in the first place. Why are they doing it? They've brought me nothing but happiness while I, on the other hand, have brought them nothing but death and destruction, putting them in danger and jeopardizing their relationship. And yet the bond between us wasn't severed after Evan's death, like I expected—like I feared. Quite the opposite: in spite of everything, they've both kept protecting me, risking their lives day after day to save mine. And for what? How can they consider me worthy of their protection? I wonder when they're going to realize I've taken everything from them . . . and that I'm going to keep on doing it in spite of my best efforts not to.

Evan. Drake. Whose turn will it be when we play the next match? I do nothing but ask myself that, because I'm sure the game will go on until I die and put an end to this war with my own blood. For some unknown reason, someone wants my life. They've decided I need to die and they won't stop until they've taken me. So what sense is there in prolonging this agony, in risking the lives of the people I love most? There will never be peace, not ever. In the end it's bound to happen, even with all Simon and Ginevra's efforts to protect me. But meanwhile there will be more defeats, more victims . . . You can't always dodge a bullet and not expect someone else to get hurt. The anguish I saw in Ginevra's eyes when that Angel pointed the gun at Simon's head gripped my heart, which I thought had died, and threw it into a cold, dark cell. I realized at that moment I couldn't bear to cause Ginevra the same pain that fetters my soul. I wish I could find a way to keep them safe, a way to fight instead of standing passively by as they wage a war that's mine and mine alone. I wish I could turn back time and stop myself from making the mistake that drained the life from me. Instead I have no choice but to stay here and look on. Life gives. Life takes away. But it's partly our fault too. Our decisions, our mistakes, decide what we ultimately end up with. Sometimes I try to imagine what that cursed day would have been like if I'd been able to read Evan's note in time and keep all this torment from beginning in the first place. But no matter how many times I scream his name in my head I'm answered only by silence—a grim, gloomy silence that pierces my heart with its icy thorns, and I can't breathe because it hurts, it hurts too much. I clench my fists but all I grasp is emptiness. Bitter solitude plagues my heart. I keep seeing Evan's face in my mind, and all I want is to

The steady dripping of water woke me and I found myself on a hard stone floor. My side ached and my head throbbed. I tried to get up. It felt like the dampness in the thick-walled room had sunk into my bones. Only a dim light illuminated the cold, dark place.

I went over to its only window, which was protected by thick bars. Looking outside, I found I was incredibly high up. Below me, trees stretched out to infinity like a dark, threatening mantle. In spite of how far above them I was, though, I could tell something was wrong: the trunks were stunted and twisted as though the ground were poisoned. I backed away from the window, feeling a powerful sense of foreboding tingle beneath my skin.

A loud noise captured my attention.

I crossed the room with long strides but tripped over the irregular stone slabs and crashed into something hard. I felt its surface as my eyes struggled to penetrate the darkness. *Wood.* It wasn't a wall, it was a door. I could have cheered, but a voice made my heart stand still. I stared at the door, my eyes glazing over in shock.

Evan . . .

My lips had struggled to say his name aloud, but a furious whirlwind of emotions had struck me, paralyzed me, as my hands trembled against the door. I stood there listening and another voice came through the wood. A woman's. I froze. After a moment, I heard it again. Sensual. Velvety. Hypnotic.

No. It couldn't be true. I desperately searched for the latch and found a small bolt in the middle of the door. I fiddled with it until I managed to open a small view panel, also barred. My body turned to ice: Evan was pressed back against a stone wall and the woman was circling him like a hawk, stroking his bare chest.

"No!" I cried. The woman's eyes darted to mine, razor-sharp fragments of amber that illuminated a pale face framed by a cascade of hair of the same color. Evan didn't seem to have noticed me. He looked drugged or under the effect of some dark spell. The woman kept her eyes trained on me while she continued to stroke Evan's body as though to provoke me. Full of fury, I gripped the bars impotently.

There was something familiar about the woman's features, though I was certain I'd never seen her before. She touched her lips to his neck and made her way up to his chin, her eyes still watching me with feline stealth.

"No! Evan!" I screamed, clenching the bars in my fists as though I could crush them with the strength of my desperation. At the sound of my voice Evan raised his head, but before he could see me the woman shot to the door of my cell at warp speed. I could see annoyance at the interruption in her fierce gaze. Holding my breath, I tried to resist her commanding gaze and deep, hypnotic eyes. They were evil and had the power to subjugate. The woman seemed to probe inside me; suddenly her lips curved into a cunning smile. She moved aside slightly and it was then that I saw the shackles around Evan's wrists that chained him to the stone wall. I covered my mouth with my hands as he writhed, his terrified, helpless eyes staring into mine.

"You're the one who did this to him."

I jumped. The woman was behind me now, inside my cell. She gently pushed the hair from my face but I couldn't take my eyes off Evan. His skin was covered with bruises and cuts from the iron shackles gripping his wrists. His torn jeans were smeared with dirt and blood.

"Why don't you go to him? Can't you see he needs you?"

I whirled around, but the woman had disappeared. An eerie noise crept in through the silence of the cold walls. Fear kept me from turning back toward Evan. It was the low growl of an animal prepared to attack. I peered through the darkness and thought I saw a glint in the darkest corner of the cell. Something was lurking there, watching me. Something sinister and deadly, a creature ready to devour me. I flattened myself against the wall, a jolt of pure terror running through me and, as though it smelled my fear, a dark shape leapt from the shadows with an aggressive snarl, coming at me so fast it took my breath away. Its claws sank into my belly, tearing my flesh.

I shrieked with pain and opened my eyes, slowly recognizing the walls of Evan's room. My hands were still pressed against my belly, I was panting, and my body was covered with sweat.

The red patch on the panther's paw was still vivid in my mind. I forced myself to breathe and slowly lifted my top. My belly was still throbbing, burning as though the panther's claws had actually torn through me. I stared at my birthmark, where the pain seemed to be coming from. I touched it cautiously and it burned my hand. It was incandescent, like a fire was burning inside it. I stared at my trembling fingers. Could the Angel have done this to me?

In the silence of the night, murmured voices gradually became audible, making my blood run cold. I tilted my head, listening, hoping it was just another aftereffect of my nightmare. It came again: the most sinister sound I'd ever heard. Dozens of voices whispering, joining together in a dark, indecipherable prayer. A shudder of apprehension ran through my body, yet part of me felt helplessly drawn to it. I found myself automatically pushing the covers aside and looking out the doorway into the silent darkness. Slowly I crossed the hall, guided by the bloodcurdling sound—an ancestral call from which I couldn't break free. I longed only to reach it, merge with it.

"Treh. Immuaarimet. Lohe. Keh. Kuta Sih. - Treh. Immuaarimet. Lohe. Keh. Kuta Sih."

The sound led me to Ginevra's door. I hesitated, my hand resting on the knob, as though my mind were torn equally between two forces and didn't know which one to give in to. But then the dark chanting overpowered me and I stepped into the room. A dim glow instantly captured my attention—a summons that was irresistible, though it came from behind a door I knew was forbidden. The murmur grew louder, urging me to follow it, and my body moved toward Ginevra's vault. Driven by some arcane power of enchantment, I walked through the forbidden door and found myself in a garden at dusk. Something drew my attention to the center of a giant glass case and I yearned to reach it as the voices flowed through my mind, chanting faster and faster. In a mechanical gesture that felt inexplicably natural, I lifted the cover off the case and the voices melted into a single one that seemed to come from Ginevra's serpent. I stopped to stare at him, hypnotized by the magnetism he emanated, as if he were the most beautiful creature on earth. The animal slowly slithered onto a trunk, his gracefulness rivaled only by Ginevra's. He rose, swaying almost imperceptibly in front of my face in a hypnotic dance, his green eyes locked on mine. I sensed a mysterious energy flow into me through his gaze and I wanted to meld with him. I was at the mercy of a dark spell from which I didn't want to be released, some sort of powerful black magic that made my blood boil. His voice whispered a mysterious message that seemed to come from the depths of the earth.

One of us. There is no escape. It has begun. One of us. There is no escape. It has begun.

"GEMMA!!" A furious vortex sucked me back and hurled me against Ginevra's bedroom wall as the vault door slammed shut. I found myself on the floor, my palms on the ground and my breathing ragged.

"What the hell were you thinking?!" Ginevra shouted as she pulled me to my feet.

"I . . . I don't know," I admitted wretchedly. Suddenly I couldn't remember why I was there. Her presence seemed to have broken the enchantment I'd been under. "I *heard* him."

"What are you talking about?"

"The serpent. He was whispering something."

"You're raving." Ginevra touched my forehead, frightened. "Holy Christ! Your skin is on fire! You're burning up! Come on, let's get you to bed." Absorbed in her own thoughts, she put her arm around my shoulder and led me to my room. She helped me under the covers, looking at my trembling legs. After carefully checking the baby's heartbeat to make sure he was all right, she said, "Now, would you tell me why the fuck you went into the vault?! You have no idea of the danger you put yourself in!"

Simon rushed into the room. He was bare-chested, his perspiration bringing out the swell of his muscles. For a moment his presence left me dazed and I found myself staring at him: a fair-haired avenger Angel with disheveled locks hanging over his forehead. They reminded me so much of Evan's. "What's going on?" He came over, looking anxious as he wiped the sweat off with a gym towel.

"I found Gemma in the Copse, face to face with my serpent."

Simon paled instantly as his brow wrinkled and his eyes shot to mine. "How is that possible? How is she still alive?"

"I don't know," Ginevra replied, her voice grim.

"How the hell did she manage to get inside it in the first place? It has an armored door!" he added.

"That's what I'm wondering too." Ginevra peered at me, her eyes icy.

"I think the door was open," I managed to say before my voice went faint, "but I'm not completely sure. I don't remember very clearly what drove me there. I was awake, but it was like I was sleeping, in the grip of some sort of alien energy that forced me to move. I could sense its evil influence but couldn't resist it. Where were you two?" I asked, turning to Simon because it was hard for me to hold Ginevra's intense gaze.

She was the one who answered. "In the workout room. Where else would we be in the middle of the night? You were sleeping and we had to train. We need to be ready."

"Apparently, we need to watch over her at night too." Simon's tone was caring but left no room for objections.

"Do you guys think it was the Executioner?"

I noticed an unusual flicker of uneasiness in Ginevra's eye. Simon, on the other hand, seemed to have no doubt about it. "She waited until the two of us were distracted and then led you to the serpent so it could kill you. It was another of her tricks. It's a good thing Ginevra got there in time. Still, I wonder why the serpent didn't bite you."

Ginevra had been lost in thought but his last words snapped her out of it. "It really is strange. He's never behaved like that with anyone before," she admitted, frowning. Suddenly she composed herself. "Let's think about it tomorrow. Simon and I will take turns watching over you so you can rest. We can always work out individually with attack simulation scenarios."

Evan had shown them to me only once, but I well remembered how real the simulation scenarios were. The walls took on a new appearance, giving you the impression you were in another place, another dimension. You could be anywhere and with anyone. The guys often used them to work out because they weren't just passive images but solid figures that interacted with them, responding to their actions and decisions, recreating true-to-life situations like frontal attacks. The swimming pool was enchanted too. Ginevra had conceived it out of her innate love of nature. You could experience swimming in a river or a magnificent lake at the foot of a volcano. All you had to do was press a button to choose an illusion. They looked like holograms, but it was actually magic.

"Try to get some rest. It's four in the morning. You can still get in a few hours of sleep."

I sank my head into the pillow and pulled the covers up to my chin as Ginevra's voice faded away, dissolving into the darkness.

12

THE POWER OF THE MIND

After my sixteenth birthday and getting my license, I always imagined that eighteen would be an even more important milestone—a special day, after which I would feel different. Instead I felt nothing new. Just the opposite, actually. The painful fire that burned in my chest raged higher as soon as I opened my eyes. From the minute I woke up I did nothing but think of Evan, more ardently and more desperately than any day before. I had lost him forever. Nothing else mattered to me, and the fact that everyone kept telling me what a big deal my eighteenth birthday was only reminded me of it. *Because he wouldn't be there with me.*

Frozen in that torment, I jumped when I heard Jeneane's voice behind me: "Can we help the birthday girl celebrate?" she said cheerfully as she, Faith, Brandon, and Jake sat down at our table, their chairs squeaking.

"Sure, but maybe you're confusing me with someone else. I have nothing to celebrate." The words escaped me with a note of bitterness.

"Come on, Gemma!" Brandon exclaimed. "You only turn eighteen once!"

"Hey." Seated next to me, Faith rested her hand on my knee. "It's been months. You have to get over it. You're only eighteen! Why don't you try to move on?" she whispered, noting the sadness that had filled my eyes. Her concern was so sweet I forced myself to hide my anguish and smile at her.

"And what's this about not wanting to celebrate?" Jeneane pulled out a plastic container and put it on the table as Faith smiled beside me. She took off the lid and handed each of us a big chocolate muffin.

"They're huge!" I remarked.

Faith smiled, slightly embarrassed. "We knew you would never come to a party, so we decided to bring the party to you!" she said, sticking a candle into my muffin.

"Guys, you shouldn't have," I said, touched.

Ginevra, on my other side, smiled. "This way you can't refuse."

"And don't try to make a break for it. We've got a rope and we're prepared to tie you to your chair if necessary." Brandon winked at me, leaning over the table to light the candle with his lighter. His remark made me laugh. What on earth would they be doing with a rope at school?

"Faith made the muffins," Jake chimed in, looking at her fondly. Her cheeks turned pink.

"Yeah, well," she began, embarrassed, "it's not an actual birthday cake, but I'm better at making these."

"They're perfect." I smiled at her. "I'm really moved. It was so sweet of you guys to think of this. I figured you wouldn't even remember it was my birthday."

"We couldn't have forgotten even if we'd wanted to." Brandon tilted his chair back, his hands clasped behind his neck. "Peter wouldn't stop yapping about it all week lo—" He flinched. Jeneane must have kicked him under the table. Though I hadn't spent much time with my friends lately, some things hadn't changed.

Jake cleared his throat. "Here he comes now." I smiled and shifted my attention to Peter, who was heading toward our table, his hands tucked into the pockets of his Blue Bombers sweatshirt.

"Here!" Jeneane slid a muffin in his direction. "There's one for you too."

"Hey." Peter nodded in greeting, looking me in the eye.

"This sucks," Brandon grumbled. "I thought he wasn't coming. I wanted his too." He said it under his breath, but it was right during a lull in the conversation, so we all heard him. Jeneane kicked him again.

"Ow! Would you stop kicking me?!"

His expression was so comical none of us could help laughing, but Jeneane, as practical as always, shut them up. "Okay, okay. We don't have much time. She has to make her wish."

It's a wishing well. Make a wish.

"Gemma, come on!" Faith encouraged me, pulling me from my memories. "You need to blow out the candle. Close your eyes and make a wish."

I bit my lip and blew out the flame. I was all out of wishes, except for the one that would never come true—to see Evan one last time.

"Oh yeah!" Brandon held his muffin protectively as though someone might try to take it from him. "Finally we can dig in!" He scooted his chair back, probably afraid Jeneane might kick him again, and laughter rose from the table.

I looked up at Peter, noticing how tender his expression became when he smiled. His birthday text had been the first one I'd found on my phone that morning. It had been sent at 2:13. Since the accident on Whiteface Mountain, we hadn't spoken a word about what had happened, but he continued to shoot Ginevra strange looks. Sometimes I was afraid he might discover something about them and their world.

"You give her the present yet?" Peter asked.

"What present?" I exclaimed. "Really, guys, you didn't need to get me anything."

Jeneane pulled out a thin, elegant, black box. My eyes lit up.

"I told you to wrap it! She's already figured out what it is!" Faith said.

"That was just the reaction I was hoping for, if you want to know," Jeneane said defensively, already able to tell from my face that I loved it.

"You got me a Kindle!?"

"It was Peter's idea," Faith told me with a wink. She looked prettier than ever with her long red ponytail and fair complexion that brought out her green eyes.

When I looked at Peter he smiled and a dimple appeared in his cheek.

"Amazon is so awesome. I should use it more often," Jeneane went on. "It was delivered in two days and filled with books in two minutes flat!"

"There are books on it? Aw, guys . . ."

Though I felt guilty, I couldn't resist the urge to turn it on right away and find out what they had downloaded. I couldn't believe it. There were lots of my favorite titles and authors. Peter knew me all too well; he must have checked Amazon for my wish list. I would wait before reading some of the books, the ones that were bound to make me cry a river, since I already had enough reason to cry. In my friends' defense, they couldn't have known the plots like I did.

I held the eReader up to my nose and sniffed it, like I always did with paper books. Ever since I was little I'd been incredibly drawn to the smell of books. Back then I hadn't yet learned that it was because of the secret allure of ink. "There are so many titles!"

"We absolutely had to cheer you up."

"Thanks, you totally did." I smiled and Jeneane clapped her hands, bouncing in her chair. I glanced at Peter when I saw that *Jane Eyre* was on the list of titles. It hadn't been on my wish list because I'd already read it a million times, but he knew it was my all-time favorite book and had included it anyway so I could always have it with me. He smiled and winked at me.

"This is the one they made a movie out of, that one we saw last summer, right?" Faith asked, pointing at the second-to-last book of a saga I really loved about demon hunters. Actually, I had already read it but must have forgotten to take it off my list.

"Yeah, that's the one."

"Ah, Jace! I'm still in love with him!" Jeneane sighed. Jealous, Brandon pulled her close, making the whole group laugh.

I had also already read the story about Tatiana and Alexander, but I couldn't wait to reread it and continue with the trilogy because the first book was one of my favorites. I'd cried like a baby for hours.

The shrill sound of the bell made us all frown. "Oh, no! So soon?" Faith groaned.

"Why don't we all hang out at my house tonight?" Jake suggested. "My mom'll be visiting her sister and my dad's working down at the station. We could have a *Teen Wolf* marathon."

"One thing at a time, okay?" I replied, a bit overwhelmed by all the attention. And to think that when I'd first proposed watching the series, Jake had flat out refused. He'd ended up getting as hooked as me.

"Are you sure you don't want to celebrate tonight?" Ginevra got up from her chair. "We could do something nice, intimate, just a few friends and your parents."

"I really don't think it's a good idea," I said. "Besides, my parents already called me this morning. They invited us to lunch—me, you, and Simon, that is."

"Well, see you in class then, Gemma!" Faith waved goodbye as she walked off with the rest of the group.

"Sure, and thanks again, guys!" Jake flashed me a smile and Brandon winked at me before leaving the cafeteria.

"Hey, Gemma!" Peter came over to us and walked alongside me. "Think I could stop by your place this afternoon?"

I shot a fleeting glance at Ginevra to see what she thought, and Peter noticed. "It won't take long," he said.

"Okay, why not? You know where to find it."

"Perfect." Unexpectedly he stroked my palm, clasped my hand, and left a light kiss on the corner of my mouth. "Happy birthday," he whispered, never taking his eyes from mine.

Stunned by the gesture, it was only after Peter had walked away that I felt something hot in my palm. I instinctively hid my hand in my pocket, wondering what it was.

"What did he give you?" Ginevra asked, looking at my pocket with curiosity. Nothing escaped her. When I hesitated she instantly raised her hands in understanding. "Okay, okay! It's none of my business."

The classroom filled up quickly as Mr. Wilson, the Spanish teacher, stood with his back to us, writing the topic he was about to explain on the board. I struggled to focus on his voice and did pretty well for the first fifteen minutes or so, but then my eyes began to dart to the clock on the wall in front of me. A tingle spread over my palms, so strong I rubbed them together to make it go away, but it was no use. A moment later, an eerie murmur of voices sent a shiver rushing down my spine and left me with goosebumps.

"What was that noise?" Alarmed, I turned toward Ginevra who was sitting to my right.

"I didn't hear anything," she whispered back, looking around the room. "Relax, Gemma. She's not going to attack you in front of all these people. You're safe here."

I nodded, gripping my pen, and opened my notebook, forcing myself to concentrate on something other than the ghosts haunting me. I distractedly jotted down a few notes but the whispering started up again, whirling more and more frenetically in my mind. Taking a deep breath, I tried to drive it away but only felt more drawn to it. I wanted to listen to the sound. It seemed to promise to take me to a safe place far away, lulling me into a dreamy state where every painful thought faded.

The sound grew more intense, crisper, and I let myself go, losing myself in that chorus of low voices. I longed to be part of it. I sensed something hidden in the voices that offered me the possibility of unequalled powers. Behind the sound lurked darkness; I could feel it summoning me. I couldn't resist the mystical attraction. It suddenly occurred to me that I *already* felt part of it. It had put down roots inside me long ago and had been growing all the while.

Powerful. Ancestral. Dark.

One of us. There is no escape. It has begun. One of us. There is no escape. It has begun . . .

"Gemma . . . Miss Bloom, do you feel all right?"

My eyelids fluttered as I focused on the teacher's face. He was staring at me with concern. Dazed, I glanced around the room, trying to figure out what had happened and why everyone's attention was suddenly directed at me.

My classmates continued to stare at me, whispering to each other.

"Did you hear that?"

"What's up with her?"

"She was babbling like she's crazy or something. "

"Did you see her eyes? They looked really strange. She was staring into space while her hand kept moving all over the paper. Gave me the creeps."

"Yeah, she looked possessed. It's gonna give me nightmares tonight."

"It's gonna give me nightmares *forever*!"

"I wonder what she wrote."

"Poor thing. I feel so sorry for her."

"She hasn't gotten over it yet. And did you hear she's pregnant?"

"Miss Bloom, I asked if you felt all right," the teacher insisted. "Would you like me to call you a doctor?"

"Forget the doctor. Get an exorcist," someone said, covering their words with fake coughs. Everybody laughed. I looked down at my notebook and jumped at the symbol I saw scrawled on the page. There was something familiar about those lines and yet I was sure I'd never seen the drawing before. How had it gotten there? Could I possibly have drawn it *myself*? Even Ginevra was gaping at me. Though she was trying hard not to let it show, she seemed shaken. She was also probably wondering what was wrong with me. Meanwhile, the class continued to gossip.

"They say he ran off because of the baby."

"Yeah, but then they found his car."

"He staged it all just to get away from her, if you ask me."

I closed my eyes, devastated.

"Idiots." Ginevra murmured one curse after another as she reached for my hand under the desk. "I don't know what's keeping me from setting them all on fire." She shut the notebook. "Gemma." She squeezed my hand, encouraging me to look at her as I tried to emerge from my trance. "Mr. Wilson, maybe I should take Gemma home. She hasn't been feeling very well lately."

"That's a good idea." He felt my forehead and jumped. "*Madre de Dios,* she's burning up! Why would she come to school in this condition?! Take her to the nurse's office immediately!"

"She wasn't running a fever this morning. She just needs to go home. My boyfriend is a doctor," she lied. "He'll take care of her. If you'll just give us a permission slip . . ." Ginevra directed the power of her captivating gaze at the teacher who immediately gave in, entranced.

"Yes, of course. I'll fill it out right away."

Embarrassed, I tucked my fists into my sleeves as Ginevra helped me collect my things. I had never felt so awkward and out of place before. I forced myself to ignore the class's whispers as we walked out, followed by their stares.

"Where did you see that symbol?" Ginevra's voice sounded steady but I detected a trace of uneasiness she was trying hard to hide.

"I don't know. I must have dreamed it, I guess. Gwen, what's happening to me?" I pleaded, hoping she had an answer. "What is that symbol? And how did it end up in my notebook?"

Ginevra let out an exasperated sigh, as though she were hiding something from me and it was taking its toll on her. "It's like you get lost in some other dimension where I can't reach you. You sink into a trance state and I can't hear your thoughts because your mind is possessed. Right after that you get a fever. Come on." She squeezed my hand, but her words had accelerated my heart rate. "Let's go home."

Lunch had passed uneventfully, as though we were a normal family. Simon had turned out to be really funny, keeping up with all my dad's bad jokes. My fever had passed minutes after we left school, vanishing as quickly as it had come like it always did after my daytime trances. It was the same with the terrible nightmares of Evan that hunted me down like predators only to evaporate with the morning light.

I ran my fingers over the surface of the bathwater, watching the steam rise from the tub like a ghost. My parents had been less apprehensive than usual, welcoming me so calmly it caught me off guard. But then again, they didn't know my real mood. On days when I didn't stop by to visit they would call, asking Simon and Ginevra for news, and when I talked to them myself I was always careful not to let on too much about my problems. I felt kind of sorry for them because Ginevra had manipulated their minds so they would let me stay with her. But it was necessary. I couldn't destroy my parents' lives with my problems.

For my birthday they'd given me a gift card for a flight to any destination, with no expiration date. I had tried to refuse and managed to convince them I would never use it, especially in my condition, but they had insisted I keep it so that maybe soon I could at least visit my grandparents in Rochester. And so I'd put it away in a drawer along with my desire to celebrate.

The thought brought Peter to mind. I quickly dried my hands on a towel, leaned over the side of the tub, and searched the pocket of my jeans on the floor for his present. I clasped the small object between my fingers and pulled it out, curious. Under the soft spot lighting, the metal object sparkled in my damp hands like a tiny treasure.

A key.

It was very small—barely over an inch long. I turned it over, admiring the two letters interwoven in an intricate design that made it look like an antique. PG. Peter and Gemma. I clutched it tighter, wondering what he meant by it and imagining how much effort it must have taken him to find it. Peter never left anything to chance.

"Ow!" I gasped, suddenly in excruciating pain. My belly felt like it had been torn in two. The key fell from my hand and clattered onto the floor. I gripped the edge of the tub with one hand and clasped my abdomen with the other. It hurt so much I couldn't breathe.

I felt something hotter even than the bathwater on the inside of my thigh and froze, unable to look down, afraid of what I might see. Raising my hand from the tub, I slowly looked at it, petrified with fear. A crimson droplet dripped off my fingers and splashed back into the water with a sound that broke my heart.

Hot tears streamed down my cheeks and the pain that gripped my chest was so intense I thought my tears too must have been the color of blood. My baby. Something had happened to my baby. The water in the tub had slowly gone red, glimmering like a molten ruby. Sobbing, I thrashed my hands in the water, trying to push the blood away from me, but it was no use.

"Gwen! Help me! My baby! Please!! Help my baby! Gweeen!" I shrieked, stabbing pains piercing my belly. This time it was all over. I had killed Evan and now the baby too. The stress I had made him undergo had ended up killing him. "Gweeen!" I was on the verge of collapse, between the tears, my bloodied fingers, and the water that turned redder by the second, taking my baby from me. Taking all I had left of Evan. "Help me, please! Somebody help me!"

In a silent summons, light glinted off a pair of scissors that lay on the edge of the tub. I reached for them. I couldn't take it. I couldn't bear any more pain. It made no sense to deny myself the comfort of death if I had nothing more to live for. I opened the scissors, grabbed one of the blades and clenched my fist tight. The blood already on my fingers mingled with the blood that began to seep from my palm. It didn't matter, because soon I would no longer feel the pain. A murderer doesn't deserve to live . . .

"She's having another hallucination!"

The scissors flew from my hands and smashed against the wall.

"I lost him," my lips murmured, responding to the voice, though my glazed eyes couldn't see past the darkness into which I had fallen. "I lost my baby."

"Gemma, listen to me! She creates fears in your mind. Only with your mind can you destroy her. The fear is real only if you allow it to be. Fight back!"

"I lost my baby . . ."

"Look at me! *Look at me!*" Someone grabbed me by the shoulders and shook me hard. The instant my eyes met Ginevra's she held me tight. "You didn't lose him," she whispered tenderly, stroking my hair. "You didn't lose him."

Clinging to her words, I snapped out of it. I disentangled myself from her embrace and looked around. The water in the tub sparkled crystal-clear, tinged only by a few crimson droplets that had come from my palm.

Ginevra smiled at me and stroked my belly. "He's here. He's still inside you. I can hear him." I smiled, my eyes still full of tears. "His heart is beating like a tiny bird's, but he's strong."

"I thought . . . I thought he . . . I was about to . . . My God . . ." I covered my mouth with both hands and stared at Ginevra.

"It's not your fault." Ginevra pushed a strand of hair out of my face. Behind her, as still as a bronze statute, Simon was scrutinizing the room, his face stern and all his senses on guard. Relieved the baby was safe, I put both hands on my belly and looked around the room too, as though I could have perceived what had eluded both a Subterranean and a Witch.

All at once Simon lunged forward, moving so fast he was a blur, coming to a halt next to the wall and pressing his elbow against it.

Ginevra shot to her feet. The Angel suddenly materialized in Simon's iron grip, her lips curved into a ghoulish grin. I glowered at her. She'd been there all along, making me believe I had lost my baby so I would decide to take my own life. What kind of monster was capable of such evil?

"Fire . . ." Ginevra whispered, covering her arms with her hands. Judging from how pale her face had turned I guessed the Angel was attacking her again. In confirmation of my theory, the room burst into flames around Ginevra, showing me her fears. The fire rose up and blackened the walls as Simon, keeping a firm grip on the Angel, shouted at Ginevra to snap out of it. I covered myself with a bath towel and rushed over to shake her, desperate to tear her out of the darkness of insanity that had engulfed me until seconds ago. Who knew what Ginevra might do with her powers. What if the Angel made her believe Simon was an enemy? I shuddered at the thought. "Gwen! *Wake up!*"

I leapt back. The veins in her arms had swollen and something was coming out of her wrist. *Her serpent.* The animal dropped to the floor and moved toward the two Subterraneans. Simon tightened his grip on the enemy but his eyes wavered as Ginevra's serpent slithered up his ankle. Simon's worst nightmare.

Ginevra perceived the flash of terror that crossed the mind of her beloved and it snapped her out of her trance. Both the fire and the serpent instantly disappeared. "Simon!"

The Angel took advantage of Simon's distraction to escape from his iron grip. With lightning speed Ginevra whipped out two guns. Bullets peppered the stone wall from one end of the room to the other as she pursued our attacker. Simon caught up with the blond Angel at the far end of the room and pinned her against the wall. Ginevra threw him a gun. He caught it and jammed the barrel under the Angel's chin.

"Sorry." Simon raised an eyebrow, his eyes burning with satisfaction. "Your little mind games won't work on me." She froze, her proud gaze fixed on Simon's, clearly prepared to die.

"What are you waiting for, Simon?" Ginevra's insistent tone made it sound like a reproach, and yet he hesitated.

"I can't." Simon's jaw stiffened in frustration. He eased his grip on the gun but kept it trained on the Executioner. "I'm sorry—I can't do it."

"I don't see the problem." Ginevra flashed across the room and took Simon's place, pinning the Angel to the wall. "It won't be the first time for me." She cocked her gun and the metallic click echoed ominously through the silence.

"Wait!" I shouted.

Simon and Ginevra's eyes flew to mine, frowning slightly. I allowed the silence to build, drawing the gaze of our prisoner. "What if we don't kill her?" The Angel's eyes wavered in surprise.

I studied their faces. I could tell Ginevra was thirsting for revenge. Simon, on the other hand, seemed curious about my proposal. "Think about it: her death would just call down others." I looked from Simon to Ginevra. They were both torn, but for opposite reasons. "What if we kept her here?"

"It's a thought." Simon had guessed my plan. "It might work."

The blond Angel raised her chin a notch and Ginevra tightened her grip on the trigger. "Don't move, if you want to save your skin. I still don't know if I like the idea."

"Gwen, I've seen your serpent fuse with your flesh like he's a part of you. If his poison is capable of annihilating a Subterranean, your blood must be poisonous too." I let the sentence hang in the air, giving Ginevra a moment to let it sink in.

She seemed surprised by the implications of what I had said. "Poisonous, yes," she said, the shadow of a shrewd smile on her lips, "but not lethal."

"Think it would be enough to keep her under control for a while?"

A dark glint appeared in Ginevra's eyes and the mask that hid the Witch inside her momentarily slipped, letting her true nature emerge. "Let's find out, shall we?" Ginevra clenched her fist and drew her long fingernail across her palm. A scarlet trickle slid down her fingers. She pressed her hand against the mouth of the blond Angel who struggled in her grip, trying to resist.

"I told you to stay still," she ordered, raising her gun. "I can always change my mind."

The Angel gave in and stood still, staring at Ginevra defiantly until she moved her palm away from her bloodstained lips. The Angel spat, leaving a crimson splatter on the brown floor. "I am not a filthy vampire!"

When Ginevra let her go, the Angel doubled over and crumpled to her knees, weakened by the poison. I stared at the red splotch. The blood seemed to quiver with energy. It was a deep, hypnotic red with fine, golden, metallic-looking strands in it. That must have been the poison.

"What a shame." Ginevra leaned down to look her in the eye, unable to repress an evil grin. "I would have had loads of fun with crosses and wooden stakes." She pinned the Angel's wrists behind her back. "But I'm sure you and I will find other ways to amuse ourselves," she hissed.

I followed them downstairs to a passageway that led down from a trapdoor hidden in the floor of the workout room. "I had no idea this was here. Where'd it come from?" The walls and worn floor brought to my mind the terrible dream I'd had the night before. Torches in sconces that lit up as we neared them cast our shadows on the walls, transforming them into ghoulish silhouettes that looked like they might escape us and move with a will of their own.

"Torches? Seriously?" I whispered to Ginevra as Simon pushed the Angel down the foreboding passageway. "I mean, modern lighting wasn't good enough?"

Simon's lighthearted laugh echoed off the walls. "Don't bother, Gemma. I've already tried. With her it's a lost cause."

Ginevra shrugged, amused. "What can I say? Once in a while I get nostalgic for the old days." A loud noise made me jump. Simon had unbolted a heavy wooden door that looked like it opened into a medieval prison cell. I shot Ginevra another look of silent reproach and she held up her hands. "I wanted to recreate the atmosphere!"

I shook my head as Simon bound the Angel's hands with a chain that he attached to a ring set into the wall over her head, forcing her to keep her arms raised. "You mean to leave me down here?!" asked the Angel. She seemed disoriented from the effect of the poison.

"No. We're just trying it on for size. Then we'll let you go," Ginevra replied with bitter sarcasm. The Angel glared at her, her eyes full of contempt. At this, Ginevra walked up to her and bit her bottom lip. "Want a little more?" A drop of blood swelled on her sensual mouth. The Angel's attitude changed as she grasped the threat, but Ginevra insisted, placing both hands on the sides of her head and looking her in the eye. "Drink," she commanded in her most entrancing voice. Staring at Ginevra as though she worshipped her, the Angel obeyed and sucked the blood from her lip. Simon smiled to himself and Ginevra winked at him as she left her adversary in a state of torpor.

"Come, Gemma," Simon told me, leaving the room as I stood stock-still beside the Angel, feeling a vague uneasiness. "We have to go." I walked past her, feeling her eyes on me like those of a vulture waiting to devour its prey. I couldn't hold back a shudder.

"Try not to do anything foolish while we're gone." Ginevra glared at her and slammed the door. In the lugubrious silence, the sound reverberated off all the walls like a clap of thunder shaking the sky before a storm. "Good night," Ginevra whispered maliciously, staring at her through the small barred window.

The torches died out behind us and darkness engulfed the cell and what it concealed.

A scream pierced the silence, but we sealed it inside.

13

SECRETS UNDER LOCK AND KEY

Back in the living room, we heard a knock on the front door and exchanged fleeting glances. "Someone's here," I murmured, like it wasn't obvious already.

"What a genius!" Simon tousled my hair playfully, visibly relaxed from having locked up the danger.

"It's for you." Ginevra looked at me and pulled Simon away by the hand, leaving me alone in the living room.

"Anybody home?" When I opened the door, Peter's fist was poised in midair. His eyes found mine. "Hey!" he lowered his hand and let it hang at his side.

"Pet, this really isn't a good time," I admitted regretfully. I knew him well enough to pick up on the disappointment that flashed across his face.

"All right. I can come back some other day," he said, careful not to look me in the eye.

I sighed. "No, come on in. Simon and Ginevra just went upstairs."

"You sure?" I nodded and a solitary dimple appeared near his smile. "I'd rather stay here in the yard, if you don't mind. Feel like coming outside?"

Tightening my lips, I nodded again and closed the door behind me. As we walked along the path, the only sound was the damp gravel crunching beneath our feet. A breath of wind made me jump. "What was that? Did you feel it too?"

"It was just the wind. You sure you're okay?"

I had to stop seeing ghosts everywhere. The Angel was locked up, so I had nothing to fear. For once, I could relax. "Of course, I'm great." I forced a laugh to banish the tension.

Peter sat on the low stone wall in the garden to the west of the house and I did the same, crossing my legs. "Did you find it?" he asked. I realized he was referring to the present he'd tucked into my palm as though it were to be kept a secret.

I pulled the key out of my pocket and held it up. It was so small it looked fragile. "What does it mean?"

When he saw I had it with me, his face lit up. "What, you didn't figure it out?" He moved his face close to mine and gazed at me. "It's the key to my heart, Gemma. Okay, maybe it's a little silly . . . but I gave it to you so you'd know it'll always belong to you. No matter what." His voice trailed off, but in his eyes I glimpsed a flicker of hope that told me he still harbored the illusion I might change my mind.

I stared at it on my palm. It was so tiny and yet so meaningful to Peter. With that gesture, he had wanted to offer me his whole self, to give me his heart. "I wanted to make it out of silver," he added, interrupting my thoughts, "but I didn't want it to tarnish over time. It's pure titanium, which wasn't easy to find. My dad showed me how to shape the mold. Then I melted the metal and waited for it to cool. It left me with this." He showed me his hand, still marked by a burn.

I brushed my fingers over the scar, speechless. "You *made* it?" I gasped, seeing the key in a new light, as touched as I was amazed.

"You know I've been helping my dad out more often lately. In a few years he's going to hand the smithy over to me." He looked at me to underline the responsibility that would be entrusted to him. Noticing how I was staring at the key, he went on. "I wanted to make it look really old, like our friendship, and to forge it with a material that was strong—like the bond between us." He looked up and into my eyes. "*Indestructible.* Then I decided to interlock your initial and mine to let you know what I was offering you." Peter hung his head and stared at my hands, as though now that he'd explained everything he felt embarrassed. Stroking the scar, he said, "I know it's small and it's not worth much, but I spent a week making it."

I was quick to disagree. "It's priceless." I had loved the key the moment I saw it, and discovering all those things about it filled my heart with emotion. "'What is aught but as 'tis valued?'"

"A line from one of your books, I imagine?"

That got another smile out of me. "Shakespeare. *Troilus and Cressida.* I don't know how to thank you, Peter, really. I'll take good care of it."

"Happy birthday, then." Peter stared at me for a second, his head tilted. Then he smiled, and the dimples in his cheeks made an appearance. "I have to admit I didn't come here only because of your present. There's something I want to ask you, but first you have to swear you won't give me an answer right away."

"Go ahead, Peter. Don't keep me on pins and needles!" I punched his arm affectionately like I always did. It was so nice talking to him. Sometimes it made me feel like I was a little girl again.

"Marry me, Gemma. I can take care of the baby."

A little grin spread over my face. I couldn't hold it back. It was funny, seeing Peter so serious. In my eyes he was still the little boy who used to chase me through the trees, yelling at me for climbing too high.

"Peter, are you actually *proposing*?" I couldn't believe my ears. So that was why he had told me his dad's shop would soon be his—he wanted to prove his commitment. Looking him in the eye, I realized I'd been wrong: Peter wasn't a little boy any more. He had become a man. And he was offering me a future together with him.

"It'll be great, I promise. I won't let anyone make you suffer ever again."

"What about your plans for college?"

"I can always decide to stay here."

"I would never ask you to give up your future for me."

"You wouldn't be asking me to."

"Pet . . . we've already talked about this."

"That's not true. We started talking about it but got interrupted when—actually, I'm not really sure what happened. You fainted and your friends wouldn't let me stay with you. Since then we haven't had a chance to finish the discussion."

"My life is too complicated. You think you know me, but a lot has changed over the last year. *I've* changed. You have no idea how I feel, what I'm going through. It's like I'm falling: I just keep sinking lower and lower—every single day."

"I'll always be there to catch you. I'll help raise you up again, if you'll let me."

"I don't want to drag you down with me." I looked him in the eye.

"Gemma, when are you going to understand I already hit rock bottom when I lost you?!" he asked, suddenly angry. "I don't want to get back up unless you're by my side."

"Don't ask me that, Peter. I can't."

"It's not fair. You can't raise the baby all alone. You can't *reject* me. I don't deserve it!"

For a second the light in his eyes alarmed me. Rarely had I seen him so angry. But then I understood the bitter sorrow he was hiding. I couldn't give him what he was asking for. There was nothing I could do and he had finally realized it.

He ran his hand over his face, looking resigned. "Sorry. I don't know what came over me," he said wearily. "At least promise you'll never leave me. I still want to be part of your life anyway, like it's always been."

"Like it's always been." Hiding a tear, I smiled and leaned over to nudge him with my shoulder. "Otherwise who would be here to lift my spirits?"

Peter wrapped his arm around me and I put my head on his shoulder. When I talked to him, I almost forgot the supernatural pall that hung over my life. For a second, I let go of my apprehension and forgot about Executioners, Witches, serpents . . . It was restful to immerse my mind in clearer, calmer waters and think about college, summer vacation, and plans for the future, though I couldn't see any for myself. Listening to Peter, I even managed a few smiles. But then the sun set, warning us of the lateness of the hour, and the darkness lowered a curtain between us, returning me to Angels under lock and key—and my own ghosts that I couldn't imprison.

"Now? But we have to celebrate our big catch," Ginevra whined, sitting on Simon's lap. She kissed him as though it might convince him to disobey Death's orders.

"We can always celebrate when I get back," he whispered, breathing the words against her lips. She continued to tease him with tiny kisses on his earlobe. He smiled sheepishly because I was right there, but he couldn't help it—he was unavoidably turned on by her.

"Want me to leave the two of you alone?" I paused, my fork halfway to my mouth, and raised an eyebrow.

"Hear that? She'll leave the two of us alone," Ginevra said provocatively.

My jaw dropped at her audacity. "For your information, that was a rhetorical question," I teased.

Simon laughed as Ginevra stuck her tongue out at me. "For all I care you can stay and watch." She winked at me, enjoying my shocked reaction.

"Much as I would love that, ladies, I'll have to take a raincheck."

"Simon!" I gasped.

He spread his arms, grinning. "Just kidding, Gemma. We're in a great mood because we captured the Executioner. I'd rather have a few hours free, but there's going to be a tornado in Nebraska. When I get back we can all celebrate together. And don't get me wrong—I'm not talking about sex, obviously," he was quick to point out, embarrassed.

"Just out of curiosity, I've often read about fallen angels. Is that another way to define Subterraneans?"

Simon stifled a smile and tried to cover his laughter with a coughing fit. "What you read are just stories, the fruit of able writers' imaginations. Actually, Fallen Angels do exist. They're an all-female circle."

Ginevra's lips curved into a seductive smile. "He means us. Witches are the Fallen Angels. I imagined you'd figured that out. Or at least, the first of us was 'the Angel who fell by the hand of God,' though many continue to refer to us all that way. But believe me, it's not the most ridiculous name we've been given. In the past, some called us 'Witches from beyond the water.' Over the centuries they've used more names for us than I can remember. Valkyries, Sirens, Amazons, in stories, legends, myths—that's us. It's always been us. Most of the tales arose from the experiences of those who survived a Reaping, a gaze from an enchantress, a promise from a huntswoman . . . My Sisters use fear, superstition, ***temptation***, to get what they want."

"And what do they want?"

"Souls."

"It's a never-ending battle between Witches and Subterraneans," Simon added. "Speaking of which, I'd better go before I leave too many of them at their mercy."

Ginevra pouted and got off his lap. "Aw . . ."

"Address your complaints to your Sisters, not to me," he shot back.

Another question came to my mind. "You said there was going to be a tornado. Does that mean that earthquakes, tsunamis, and things like that are the work of Subterraneans?"

"Not always. Our nature isn't destructive. Subterraneans aren't interested in spreading chaos or destroying the Earth. Just the opposite—it's our duty to preserve it. Though sometimes we use our powers to wipe out entire populations if we're ordered to."

"But most of the time it's our fault," Ginevra added.

"Witches are the ones to cause catastrophes and natural disasters?"

"We control the atmospheric agents and Witches often have fun toying with nature—toying with *you*. Their aim is to destroy not the Earth, but humans, especially when they don't respect it. Sophìa, in particular, has a deep connection with nature, which bends to her will," Ginevra explained.

"And *we* intervene to mitigate the disasters and repair the damage," Simon put in. "We make sure the missing whose time hasn't yet come are found before the Witches can claim their souls; we look for new Subterraneans before they become their prisoners; and we liberate the Souls who need us. That's why our role is so important. We're the cord that binds Eden to the earth. This would never happen, of course, but if there weren't a single Subterranean left to ferry Souls there, all hope would be lost. The Witches would end up ruling the world and all mankind, including future generations, would be their slaves."

"But would all those people die even if it wasn't their fate?"

"Good and evil are two sides of the same coin. Witches can also act on fate's behalf by shuffling the deck however they like. Actions on both sides need to be calibrated to maintain balance in the world. They know what destiny holds in store, who has to die, and whose time hasn't yet come. Humans don't necessarily have to die for Witches to get what they're after. All they need to do is put them in a position where they'll be willing to barter their souls. Fear is the most precious currency."

"What happens to someone who's not ready to cross over?"

"If we don't manage to save them and they're unable to resist the Temptation, they fall into the Witches' hands and compromise their souls. When they die, there will be no Subterranean there waiting for them," Simon explained.

"Did you do those things, Gwen?"

"I couldn't help it. Actually, if you want to know the truth, I enjoyed it," she admitted with a shrewd smile.

"Do you think evil might ever take you over again?"

"Sometimes I think it might, but then I look at Simon and realize that love is the only invincible power there is. If you let love fill you, there's no room left for evil."

After dinner I went upstairs, seeking the comfort of Evan's room. I felt calmer, probably because I knew the source of my episodes was locked up and I could afford to abandon myself to my memories. Though I wasn't sure why, I couldn't stop picturing the house on the lake, with Evan sitting on the shore, smiling and ready to tease me like always. And yet it only took a moment for the image of the two of us to grow distorted, like a reflection in the lake's perfectly still surface when it was rippled by the rain. The memories began to burn in my heart—memories held together by a cord so worn it threatened to snap at any moment; memories that faded, sputtering like a fire that's devoured everything in the dark of night and is eventually reduced to ashes, darkness, and death . . . all that was left to me now.

"Gemma?" Ginevra peeked in as she knocked gently on the door.

I waved her in and she stared at me for a long while as though about to reveal something important. Something *difficult*. "I have something for you," she said, confirming my suspicion. "It's still your birthday." She approached me, reached into her pocket, and pulled out a little silver case that looked like an antique jewelry box.

With a sigh, I quickly looked away. "I don't want anything," I whispered, my voice breaking.

"Gemma." Ginevra came closer and forced me to look her in the eye. "You have to stop suffering." I tried to hold her gaze but quickly lowered my eyes, attempting to swallow the knot in my throat before it suffocated me. "Try to get a grip on yourself."

I looked up into her eyes. "You can't tell a fire to stop burning," I said matter-of-factly, fighting back the tears. What she was asking me to do was impossible.

Ginevra held my gaze. She opened her hand and a tiny golden flame rose from her palm. On an impulse, I brushed my fingers over the fire, but Ginevra moved it closer and made the flames tremble on my palm without burning it. "There's nothing we can't do in our minds. Find the strength inside you, Gemma."

I pulled my hand back without taking my eyes off her and the fire went out. "There are places the mind can't go when the heart has darkened them," I said firmly. "I . . . I feel like a dead tree."

"Not dead. Just bare. When the time comes, the leaves will grow back—you'll see." Ginevra respected my silence and put the case on the desk next to the portrait of Evan and his family in 1720. Then she turned to the door and rested her hand on the knob. "It's not from me. He would have wanted to give it to you. I read it in his mind."

I teetered a little as a tremble warmed my heart and my eyes filled with tears. Ginevra slowly closed the door behind her. I stayed where I was, staring at the case, frightened at the thought of what it might contain. I stroked it as my heart begged me to stop, screaming no, screaming that if I opened it I wouldn't be able to stand the pain. In the end, however, I gave in to the temptation. The silver box opened with a little click. I hesitated, shuddering, and slowly raised the lid.

I blinked and three crystal droplets slid down my face. My lashes wet with tears, I clutched the case in my fingers, unable to take my eyes off the ring inside it. It was small, dainty, with a pearl glowing in the center like a tiny version of the moon. I clasped it against my chest and let the pain wash over me. Overcome, I fell to my knees and clenched my fists against the floor, as though its solid surface could keep me from sinking. The ring pressed into my palm as I squeezed it tight—the ring Evan had vowed to give me when he'd proposed. The one on his mother's finger in the centuries-old family portrait. I closed my eyes and could almost feel Evan's arms around me, the heat of his body fusing with mine as we made love in the secluded place where we'd hidden from the world: on a military tarp in an old hangar, his voice caressing me like a sweet melody, promising never to leave me.

"I'm the one who was supposed to die," I sobbed in a tiny voice. "You promised." I curled up on the floor as though that would be enough to make me disappear. "You promised me, Evan. You promised you would never leave me." I silently waited for his reply but, like all the other times, I heard nothing but the silence of my heart.

The emptiness left by his absence was acid corroding me from the inside, slowly devouring me. Nothing would ever be able to give me back my Evan. The past had swallowed him up forever and iron chains imprisoned me in a limbo from which I could no longer escape, a cold place without light.

Heartbroken, I looked up and saw through the veil of my tears the blue cover of my diary that had fallen under the bed. I stared at it for a second before reaching for it, the ring still clasped to my chest like a little treasure I would never part with. That ring was the most precious gift I could ever have received. Despite the excruciating pain, I still belonged to him.

I went to the window, pushed the curtain aside, and let the air sweetly fill the room as I sought comfort in the night, silent and solitary. Just like me. I leaned back against the wall and slid down to the floor, my knees drawn up to my chest. As I closed my eyes, a breath of air snuck into the room and caressed my hair. I opened the diary and teardrops dripped from my chin, marking the page with my pain. The ink glided across the ivory paper, staining it with the poison distilled from my blood, imprisoning my agony forever on those pages.

~~January 17~~

Ginevra is right. It's still my birthday. Everybody keeps telling me I should move on, loosen my desperate grip on the past, and open myself up to what the future has in store for me, but all I keep doing is thinking about what I've lost, what no one can ever give back to me. It's as if my lifeblood has been drained away, leaving me lifeless: an empty shell deprived of its true essence.

Sometimes—but only sometimes—a breath of air brings me his scent and I breathe it in. Then I close my eyes and he's behind me, his hands on my waist, his lips on my neck, the warmth of his body so vivid that the disappointment kills me when I open my eyes and discover he's not there . . . that he never was.

What no one understands is that the comfort of that short-lived moment when the memory of him warms my heart is so intense, so necessary, that I would rather continue this slow death day after day for that brief illusion than awaken to the constant awareness that he's not with me any more, he'll never touch my face again, his lips will never smile against mine again. Evan. His very name threatens to disappear, smeared by a teardrop that's dripped onto the ink. I don't want to forget his laugh. I don't want to forget the feeling of his hand clasped in mine. But his features are beginning to fade and I'm scared—scared of losing the memories too, because they're all that's left to me. Without them, my heart will wither completely. I won't be able to bear it.

I wish I had never wanted Evan to save me, not at this price. It was his love for me that ultimately destroyed him. Evan's death was a mistake for which I and I alone am responsible, and I paid for it with my heart. If only I knew why fate is so set against me, the reason behind my death sentence . . . But no one can ever lift this burden from me.

No, actually. Maybe there's someone who can.

I shot to my feet, my diary falling to the ground. Drying my tears, I crossed the room and peeked into the hall to make sure no one was around. Simon and Ginevra couldn't discover my intentions or they would try to stop me. I tiptoed out, groped my way down the stairs in the dark, and crept across the living room. My hand trembling, I reached for the knob to the door leading downstairs and slowly turned it.

Someone owed me some answers.

An Angel under lock and key.

14

DANGEROUS TRESPASSES

I shut the door behind me and quickened my pace in the direction of the workout room. My chances of reaching the dungeon without obstacles were slim, but my fears vanished when I heard the sound of lapping water mingled with soft laughter from Simon and Ginevra. They were in the swimming pool enjoying some privacy, temporarily freed from the constant burden of my presence. Now that the Angel could no longer cause me problems, their voices sounded more carefree, as though a load had been lifted from their shoulders. I hurried past before one of them could notice me.

Staring at the trapdoor, I felt unsure about whether to continue, but before my common sense could reassert itself and change my mind, I followed my instinct and crept into the depths of the house. Once the pitch dark had swallowed me up, the reasons that had driven me to break the rules didn't seem so important any more and I considered the thought of going back upstairs. The air smelled so strongly of earth it was almost unbreathable, its dank odor filling my nostrils. Still, my curiosity was overpowering. Though Subterraneans didn't always know the reasons behind an execution order, Simon was almost certain that this one had been in contact with the Màsala, so I had to at least try. Putting one foot in front of the other, I ventured into the darkness, accompanied by the ominous echo of my footfalls in the lugubrious silence. I groped forward, tripping over the rough floor, trying to get my bearings from the memory of the only other time I'd been down there. Had it really been only a few hours earlier? It felt like months.

My fingers recognized a curve. I turned the corner and a faint glow guided me to the heavy door that confined the Subterranean. My heart trembled. I didn't know if it was from fear or the hope of finally learning my destiny. Gripping the door tightly to keep my hands from shaking, I undid the latch. It clicked open with a sinister sound that penetrated my bones. I grabbed a small torch from its sconce on the wall of the passageway. The door opened with a blood-curdling squeal.

"You were reckless to come here alone."

Her voice made me cringe even though I had prepared myself to face her. "I brought you a little light." I hung the torch on the cell wall, trying to appear calm.

The Angel's mocking laughter rang icily off the walls, making me shudder. "I am not afraid of the dark." She tilted her head and flashed me a spine-chilling look. The torch flickered. "But you are."

For a second, the shadows cast by the torch tricked me into thinking her eye sockets were empty. I knew how beautiful and alluring she was, but just then she looked like a monster spawned by the darkness. No—not a monster. An Angel of Death.

I took a deep breath and spoke in a steady voice. "I didn't come here to taunt you, and I don't think you're stupid enough to gamble away your only chance of staying alive—at least for a while. Don't forget, I'm the one who kept Ginevra from killing you." My hands wouldn't stop shaking so I slid them into my sweatshirt pockets, hoping she wouldn't notice. My fingers clutched the silver case as if it could instill courage in me.

"Why did you come, then?" She struggled not to seem weak, but her face betrayed her. "Unless you mean to free me, I suggest you leave. I do not socialize with humans." She looked away, her expression cold yet entrancing.

"You've never been human?"

A glimmer of surprise appeared in her eye. "Long ago, but it is a memory I care not to recall," she replied disdainfully.

I moved closer and she stared at me, her eyes veiled with wickedness. "What's your name?" I asked impulsively. Something about the Angel drew me to her just as strongly as it frightened me. Actually, *she* didn't frighten me—it was the emotion that stirred within me the moment I got close to her, some strange energy I could tell was wrong. Evil. Had I gone there driven by the same longing for revenge I'd seen in Ginevra's eyes? Was it possible that part of me was ready to vent all my rage on this chained creature that now looked so vulnerable?

"Is that what you wish to know from me?" The Angel interrupted my train of thought, bringing me back to the darkness of the cell.

"No, but I felt it was right to know your name before talking to you." It was insane how determined my voice sounded, so free from uncertainty, when actually every fiber of my body was trembling, begging me to get out of that accursed place.

The Angel chuckled. "You were brave to come here, I will grant you that."

"And you were a bitch to make me think I'd lost my baby." The instant the words escaped me I felt satisfied, freed from a burden. It wasn't so difficult to face her with my head held high under these circumstances. I wondered if I would have had the same courage if she hadn't been under the influence of the poison.

To my astonishment, the Angel laughed and her voice echoed off the walls. "Desna."

"What?" I asked, puzzled.

"My name. It is Desdemona, but you may call me Desna."

"Fine. I imagine you already know mine."

"Now that we have introduced ourselves, is there a reason you came here or do you simply have suicidal tendencies?"

I took a deep breath. I wasn't sure I could ask the question—not to someone who could actually give me the answer. I summoned up my courage, though, and asked, "Why?" I had murmured the word, but when I looked up into her eyes my voice began to rise, filling with bitterness. "Why are they so determined to see me die? Is my life so important? How many of you have died already trying to kill me? How many more will die? Are the Màsala willing to pay any price to kill me?" To my horror I noticed I had moved too close to her face, but Desna smiled, not the least bit intimidated by my reaction.

"The point is not why you must die"—she looked me straight in the eye as though giving me a warning—"but why you must not *live*."

I took a step back, stunned by how promptly she'd replied when I'd been so sure she wouldn't answer my question. Still, it wasn't enough. "It doesn't make sense. What did I ever do to deserve such a terrible sentence?"

Desna chuckled. "I cannot give you that information. Not without receiving something in exchange." Her eyebrow raised, lighting up her face. "What you ask of me has a price."

I held my breath. Could it actually be this easy? Would she really give me what I wanted? I was prepared to promise her anything, but what could she possibly want from me? "What can I give you that you don't already have?"

"Free me."

"I might be reckless, but I'm not stupid. The first thing you would do is kill me."

The piercing, crafty look in her eye sent a shiver through me. "I cannot deny it."

A despondent sigh escaped me and I turned my back on her to hide the bitter sorrow on my face. The Angel was of no use to me. I had been wrong to take the risk.

"Perhaps you do not want to free me, but . . ." Unwilling to listen to her any more, I headed for the door, resigned. " . . . would you leave your beloved Evan chained up down here?"

"Gemma!" I flinched at the sound of Evan's voice but squeezed my eyes shut and forced myself not to turn around. I knew the Angel was trying to penetrate my mind again. Weakened from the poison, Desna had less influence over me. I covered my ears with my hands to block out her voice and ran toward the half-closed door.

"Gemma! Free me, please! It's me, Evan!" I turned toward him and a shock ran through my body, freezing me in my tracks. "Free me, quick! Before she gets here!" he pleaded, his eyes locked on mine.

"Evan," I murmured, stunned. It was so wonderful to look into his eyes again. At last I had found him! He wasn't dead! The urgency in his voice made me leap into action. I grabbed the key from where Simon had hidden it and unlocked the shackles, trying to keep my hands steady. I took the cuffs off Evan's wrists and he toppled forward onto me as I braced myself to take his weight, anxious to help him. But the moment he raised his head Desna's evil grin petrified me, releasing me from her spell.

A shiver ran through me. I had set her free. I gasped, but the Angel had already disappeared through the door, swift as a ghost. I fell to my knees, my hands on the floor and my head hung low. Beaten. How could I have been so stupid?

The door creaked open, tearing me from my torment. My head snapped up. Desna was cautiously backing into the room. My eyes bulged: Ginevra's serpent slithered across the floor in pursuit, ready to lunge at her. The door slammed shut, sealing us inside. I pressed myself against the floor, unable to take my eyes off the serpent. He was so hypnotic, so fascinating. My desire to touch him was so powerful it left my throat dry. Was this the seduction used by evil to bend a mortal's will? How could mere humans hope to resist such power?

The Angel's terrified expression shook me out of my thoughts and I saw Ginevra. I shrieked and flattened myself against the wall, a jolt of pure terror running through me: her face radiated evil and her body was levitating inches above the floor. The pure energy she emitted made her hair whirl around her head, and darkness filled her eyes. Like a bolt of lightning she rushed at Desna and slammed her against the wall, doubling her over.

I had never seen Ginevra unleash the Witch inside her. The raw power she gave off inspired both admiration and dread in me. "Where did you think you were going?" Ginevra's eyes filled with brilliant streaks that extended into the whites like rays from a dark sun. The green of her irises came to life, vibrating with golden reflections, and her pupils elongated, like a cat's . . . or a snake's.

She put Desna back in chains, jerking them tighter this time. Her serpent slithered back up to her arm as the Angel cringed in terror against the wall. "I thought my blood would keep you under control, but I can see it wasn't enough." Sensing his adversary's fear, the serpent hissed.

"Gwen!" I shouted before her serpent could bite the Subterranean. She looked so different. I'd never seen that darkness in her eyes before. "You're scaring me! Stop it!"

The animal froze, coiled around Ginevra's upper arm twice, and disappeared beneath her skin as she stared at me sternly, her eyes still filled with liquid emeralds.

"Ugly Witch!" Desna screamed, but before she could say anything else, her captor struck her violently, knocking her against the wall. Ginevra broke open the skin on her palm with her teeth and pressed it to the Angel's mouth. "Maybe you didn't have enough. Did you lure Gemma down here?" Ginevra gritted her teeth and glared at her, seething.

"I did nothing." Desna broke free of Ginevra's grip and spat out the blood. A drop landed on my skin. "But you already knew that, did you not?" She threw her captor a challenging look.

Ginevra turned to look at me. "What the hell were you doing down here?"

"I wanted to see if everything was okay," I replied warily.

"Jesus Christ! What's wrong with you? She's not our *guest*, Gemma, she's our *prisoner*! Get it through your skull! What made you think she would give you the answers you wanted?" she accused me, searching my mind. "She tried to kill you and she won't hesitate to do it again the second she finds the smallest opportunity! Carrying out orders is the only thing that matters to Subterraneans. You should know that by now!"

"But I didn't think—"

"*What* didn't you think? You entered the wolf's den. What were you expecting?"

Suddenly I thought back to when Ginevra had asked me if Desna was the woman I'd dreamed of. Maybe it was true. In my dream I'd also seen Evan and she had taken on his appearance. She wanted me to follow her. *He's waiting for you*, she'd said. But Evan was dead. I couldn't have followed him unless I accepted death by her hand, the hand of the blond Angel who had come to kill me.

"I'm sorry. You're perfectly right, it was thoughtless of me."

"Thoughtless?!" Ginevra closed the distance between us, glaring at me. "I'm trying to protect you, but you're not helping."

I nodded, suddenly aware of the seriousness of my actions. Simon and Ginevra were risking their lives to protect me, and I was putting myself in danger. She was right on all counts. What had I been thinking?

"Come on." She helped me to my feet, her gaze softening. "Let's get out of here."

"Wait! You cannot keep me imprisoned here forever!"

"You're right." The door slammed shut behind us and Ginevra tilted her head, staring through the bars at the chained Angel, a cunning smile on her lips. "It won't be forever, just until I decide to kill you." A gust of wind blew out the torch. Desna's shrieks grew fainter, swallowed up by the passageway, until the trapdoor silenced them.

15

FRESH AIR

The school bell announced the end of classes and the empty halls were soon flooded with students who couldn't wait to leave the building and start the weekend. Though I didn't share in the general enthusiasm, the collective chatter emanated a contagious energy that in the end managed to make a dent in my shell. I had a strange feeling of freedom. Probably some of my uneasiness had been wiped away along with my fear of another attack by the Angel. Or maybe I just felt relieved that after what seemed like forever, I'd slept through a whole night without bad dreams. On top of that, I had expected to be greeted by a multitude of strange looks and whispers after the disturbing episode of the day before, but it hadn't happened. The students at Lake Placid High had turned out to be unusually supportive and hadn't brought it up. Was it out of pure compassion? Or had Simon had a hand in it by manipulating their memories? It didn't matter to me as long as they left me in peace. It was also the first day Ginevra had decided not to come with me, loosening the strings of her strict surveillance. She'd even given me the afternoon free. After all, with the Angel locked up I had nothing to fear apart from the ghosts haunting my soul.

Earbuds in, I pulled out my SLR camera and took a few shots for the assignment Mr. Madison had given us for photography class. We had to pick a theme—like faces, locations, or animals—and take a series of pictures using different lighting and lenses. I had chosen nature as my subject, so I zoomed in on some hoarfrost that had crystallized on a tree branch and noticed a little white flower growing through the ice right at the foot of the tree. I knelt down to take a few more shots, cranked the volume and lost myself to Sia singing *She Wolf* by David Guetta. I added a blue filter and the effect was amazing: the picture came out exactly the way I wanted. The little flower looked sad and solitary . . . just like me.

I looked up and noticed Peter waving to get my attention. I pulled out an earbud. "Gemma!" He beckoned me over, waiting for me beneath the twisted branches of a bare maple with the rest of the group.

"Hey, you're all here." I walked over to them, dropped my backpack on the ground that had been cleared of snow, and used it as a stool, sitting down next to Faith.

"Get any interesting shots?" asked Peter, who must have been watching me. I handed him the camera and he carefully studied my photos.

"Oh, shit! The assignment for Mr. Madison!" Jake groaned. "I forgot about it."

"Why do you take that class if you don't like it?" I asked. To me, taking photographs was more of a passion than an obligation, so it was hard to imagine anyone finding it a drag.

"Great question!" Brandon threw something at him and I understood: he must have signed up for it because of Faith. Jake, Peter, and Brandon were the stars of the Blue Bombers. They played hockey in winter and lacrosse in summer. Between practice and games they spent a lot of time together and they definitely confided in each other.

"Hey, this one's great! It looks like a flower from heaven," he said. I looked at the picture and a flashback filled my mind:

"No, Evan. Stop it!"

We'd been crossing the river inside a giant water lily that was blue streaked with silver, and when it closed over our heads, Evan had immediately moved closer to tempt me. I'd been afraid that any show of affection was forbidden in that sacred place, though.

"Come on, no one can see us."

"We can't make out like this, not here."

Ignoring me, he'd pressed his body against mine and kissed my neck, making my head spin. *"I would make love to you right here."*

"Evan!" I had avoided his kisses, pushing him away and laughing. *"You dope!"* I'd bitten my lip, burning with passion.

"Did I say that out loud?" Despite his attempt to cover for what he'd said, his sly smile had betrayed him.

"Gemma. Gemma!" Peter's insistent voice roused me.

"Yeah?"

He handed me my camera. "Here you go."

Evan and I had been in Heaven, but now it all seemed like just a dream. "Oh. Thanks."

"What should we do, guys? I'm bored!" Jeneane complained.

"Update your Facebook status," Brandon teased her. She threw a snowball at him.

Peter rested his arm on the tree, studying the necklace I wore, his expression pained as he searched for his pendant. I raised my arm, pushed back my thick sweatshirt and shook my wrist to show him his present, which dangled from a thin silver chain. He smiled at me, grasping my tacit message, and stared into my eyes as the group's voices became an indistinct murmur in the background.

"Gemma, why don't you come with us?"

"Huh?"

"Yeah, that would be great!" Peter exclaimed, looking hopeful, his gaze locked on mine.

"I don't know what you're talking about."

"What do you mean?! It's all over town!" Jeneane squealed. "There's a Lana del Rey concert at Bandshell Park tomorrow night. Everyone's going."

So that's why no one paid any attention to me at school today. "An outdoor concert? With all the snow?"

"That's why it's called the White Concert," Brandon said. He was sitting with his back against a tree, hands clasped behind his head, chewing gum.

"I don't know . . ." For a second, the invitation was tempting.

"Come on, you *love* Lana del Rey!" Faith insisted. It was true—though we'd already gone to lots of her concerts, since she'd grown up in Lake Placid.

"Well, at least it's not a no," Jeneane said, glancing at Peter. Taking his cue from her, he came over and crouched down in front of me.

"You're. Coming. With. Us," he said, taking advantage of the indecision I'd shown.

"Hey, Pete!" Brandon threw a snowball at him, startling him. "What are you trying to do, hypnotize her? I doubt it'll make her fall in love with you."

"Shut up, dumbass." Jeneane said, giving him a reproachful shove. Something flickered in Brandon's eyes and she ran off with a shriek, but he pinned her to the ground over her protests.

Peter let out a laugh. "Your approach is way more effective, I see. At least Gemma didn't try to escape!"

He threw a snowball at Brandon, starting a snowball fight that spared no one, not even me. When a well-aimed projectile threatened to hit me full on, Peter darted in front of me protectively, but lost his balance. A second later his body was on top of mine, my back against the damp ground. The smile on his lips slowly faded, yet in his eyes the warmth of the bond that had always connected us persisted.

"Sorry I knocked you over," he said, his gaze as tender as his tone.

"That's okay. You did it to pro—Look out!" A snowball flew toward us and Peter leaned closer to me to dodge it. He swallowed slowly, his gaze locked on mine. Silence enveloped us like a dome, shutting us off from the amused cries of the others.

"Will you come to the concert?" he asked, turning serious. "With me?" His eyes lingered on mine for a long moment as I thought it over. After all, what could happen to me now that the Executioner was no longer a problem? Maybe some company would do me good, especially if the whole group was going.

"Maybe." I hid a little smile and Peter raised an eyebrow, dimples appearing in his cheeks. "But now you have to let me go."

"Maybe?" He grabbed my wrists, threatening to keep me there until I'd given him a better answer.

"Okay! All right, I'll go! Happy?" He hadn't given me much choice.

"Hey, you two!" Brandon interrupted us, his wet hair sticking to his face as the others grinned. "Keep that up and you'll melt all the snow, and then we won't be able to play any more. Does that seem fair?"

I shifted on the ground, embarrassed by what the others must think at the sight of Peter and me off on our own, and in that position.

"Shut up, Bran," Peter shot back. "If you behave, one day I might teach you my hypnosis techniques, seeing as how they work better than yours."

"So you're coming with us?" Faith hugged me tight, bursting with enthusiasm. "I'm so happy! We'll all bring blankets and lie down on the lakeshore. I know you won't regret it. We'll have loads of fun!"

"Okay, okay! Don't suffocate her." Peter reclaimed my attention, holding out his hand to help me up.

"Hey, what do you say we get some shooting in?" Jake suggested. He was the police chief's son and had always loved going to the firing range. There were several of them scattered around the village, but his favorite was in a clearing where people practiced for deer hunting. I hated hunting almost as much as Faith did, but shooting at inanimate targets was fun so we did it often, mostly during spring and summer.

"Feel like it?" murmured Peter, who had come much closer as though to protect me. I tightened my lips to confirm his suspicion and he understood at once. "Doesn't seem like a good idea. Besides, we've got the hockey game later on."

"So what? You know we're going to destroy them!" Brandon said confidently.

"You bet we will. But right now Gemma needs a hot shower. Her clothes are damp and this cold weather isn't doing her any good in her condition."

"Oh, of course," the others agreed, instantly solicitous.

Not knowing how to respond to all the attention, I looked at my hand clasped in Peter's. He knew me so well. Ours was a bond that challenged every physical law, because even if all the parameters changed, he was a constant.

"It would be nice if you came to the game too." Peter lowered his voice as he spoke just to me again and stroked the back of my hand with his thumb. His question hung in the air as we looked each other in the eyes. His face was so close I could feel the warmth of his breath. Suddenly, he touched the edge of my mouth with his thumb. "A snowflake," he explained, his face serious. When I raised a skeptical eyebrow, he gave himself away, a dimple appearing in his cheek. "Want me to take you home?" he asked sweetly.

I never used to miss Peter's games and I knew how much they meant to him, but I wasn't sure I wanted to be around so many people. He must have realized that even though I hadn't given him an answer.

"Thanks, but Ginevra left me her car. Besides, I'm having lunch with my parents today."

"Great!" he exclaimed, baffling me. He tried to compose himself. "I mean, it's great that you're spending more time with them. It means you're feeling better, and since they've been so worried—"

"Right."

Of course Peter didn't know the real reason I'd been forced to undergo such strict surveillance. My being away from home wasn't because of my mood but because the Angel of Death had put me in grave danger. Now that she was locked up I could grant myself a little more liberty. Peter probably thought I was distancing myself from Ginevra—and the memory of Evan. The truth was, not a minute went by that I didn't think of him. Still, I felt the need to go out with my old friends, to breathe some normal air. *Human* air. Otherwise I risked going insane.

"Honey, have you thought of where you'd like to fly with the voucher we gave you?"

I raised my fork and filled my mouth with mashed potatoes, trying to avoid answering Mom's question, but she ignored my silence and insisted. "Your father made sure we got one without a destination or an expiration date so you could do whatever you wanted with it. We're good friends with the owner of the travel agency, you know, so you can go to him whenever you like."

"Actually, Mom, I—"

"You could use it to visit your grandparents in Rochester. They're not so young any more, and a change of scenery would do you a lot of good."

"Thanks, Mom, but honestly I—maybe it would be better if you guys used it. It's been years since you and Dad took some time off work."

Dad took my hand. "You don't have to use it now if you don't want to. Josephine, you're pushing her too hard."

"No, it's okay. Please don't fight because of me."

"Your mother is just concerned about you—like I am, for that matter. We know you're going through a hard time. It's been hard for us too, facing so many changes all at once. Your being away from home . . . your pregnancy." Dad ran a hand over his face. "I still don't know how I ended up agreeing to letting you leave. Oh God, you're still my little girl," he said, his tone grief-stricken. I'd never seen him so upset before.

"Dad, of course I'm still your little girl. I always will be."

He squeezed my hand and I returned the gesture. "You'll always be my Squirrelicue. When Ginevra told us you would be staying at their place for a while, my first reaction was to be mad at you, but then when she explained how badly you were doing, we felt like the whole world was crashing down around us and everything else was put on the back burner—including our shock at hearing you were expecting a baby. You must've gone through such awful moments, you poor thing, but now we're happy to see you're starting to get better."

"Thanks, Dad."

"No need to thank me. I'll admit I've always been pretty strict and maybe a bit apprehensive when it comes to you, but believe me, that's just because I love you so much." He looked like he was about to cry. I wondered how long he'd been waiting for me to become strong enough to tell me how he felt. "You'll be a parent soon too and maybe it'll help you understand what I'm trying to tell you."

"It's just— Well, like you said, I went through some awful times. You can't imagine how terrible. And I'm happy I can count on you two. Other parents in your shoes would have been furious. After all, I'm only eighteen and I'm already pregnant and the father is—I only wish you'd found out about it differently. I wish everything had gone differently. Evan—" I swallowed. My mom, behind me, squeezed my shoulders comfortingly. "He disappeared before I could tell him and—and there are so many things I'll never be able to forgive myself for."

"You'll manage, sweetie. Time heals all wounds, I promise."

"Okay, but for now let's change the subject before I start crying again."

"No tears!" My dad flashed one of his encouraging smiles, but not before I caught him turning to quickly wipe his eye. "How about a game of chess, like the good old days?"

"But it's late. Shouldn't you two already be at work?"

"My daughter is more important than any job in the world, especially if she's about to give me a fine grandson."

"Dad!"

My mom slapped his shoulder with her oven mitt. "Leave her alone, Josh! Can't you see you're embarrassing her?"

"Woman, go to the living room and get me the chess set so I can play a game with my daughter," he teased her.

Another slap, this time on the head. "You, *man*, drag your behind out of that chair and get it yourself."

I laughed as Dad massaged the back of his neck, flashing her his most charming smile. "Come here, little dictator!" He tried to grab Mom by the wrist but she slipped out of his grasp.

"No way!" She turned her back on him to hide her smile.

"I love it when she plays hard to get." He waggled his eyebrows and leaned over the table so she wouldn't hear him. "The problem is she figured that out a long time ago."

I smiled, but then made myself turn serious. "Dad, would you mind if I took a rain check on the chess? I'm exhausted."

"That's normal, sweetheart." Mom came over to me. "I was the same way when I was expecting you."

"Really?"

"Of course! Sometimes I would even fall asleep smack dab in the middle of a conversation. It's the baby that's sapping your strength. That's why you need lots of nourishment."

"I hadn't imagined that might be causing it."

"It is, especially toward the end, and my pregnancy lasted almost ten months! Everyone in Lake Placid was talking about it."

"The doctors wanted to induce labor," Dad interjected, "saying you might be in danger, but your mother flat out refused. She said you would be born when you were good and ready. That's where you got your stubbornness from."

Another slap to the head.

"I didn't want to force my baby if she didn't feel ready to come out of her shell yet. And now look—she turned out just fine. In fact, she's always had something special, different from all the rest."

Was my mom right? Could my ability to see Subterraneans possibly be due to that? Maybe during the extra gestation time my body had developed extra senses.

"Don't listen to her," Dad said, grinning. "She just came up with that theory to justify being so obstinate. Your baby's going to come out healthy and intelligent even if he only takes the normal nine months. As for the game, you're right, maybe we should do it another time. I forgot that little Davey is having his birthday party this afternoon."

"Mr. Burns's son? Isn't that Peter's youngest cousin?"

"Oh, right—Peter! How is he?"

"Great. Tomorrow I'm going with him and the others to the White Concert."

"Why, that's wonderful! You have no idea how much that boy cares about you. Lately he's stopped by every day to ask how you are. Only when we told him about the baby did he seem upset. He didn't turn up again for a week, but then everything went back to normal."

"He just needed a little time to let the news sink in. He's a fine young man. It'll do you good to spend time with him again."

"The whole group is going, Mom—Faith, Jeneane, Brandon, and Jake will be there too. Don't start getting any ideas, because for me there will never be anyone but Evan." My reply was so unexpectedly sour it left them wordless and I instantly regretted it. "In any case, tomorrow's Saturday and I don't have anything to do this afternoon. If it's okay with you I'll stop by the diner to give you a hand."

"Are you kidding?" My dad's smile broadened, lighting up his face. "It would be great if you came to spend time with us. Besides, it'll be packed, so an extra set of eyes will come in handy—if you feel up to it."

"Why shouldn't I? I'm pregnant, not sick. I like to feel useful. It'll do me good."

"Then it's agreed," Mom said, "but first Gemma needs to get some rest, otherwise she might fall asleep on one of the tables."

"Like mother, like daughter," Dad said in a singsong voice.

"I don't believe it! Did that *really* happen to you, Mom?"

"Um . . . only a few times," she said, caught off guard and looking embarrassed.

Dad covered his mouth with his hand and yawned. "A few times *a day,* that is."

"It wasn't my fault! Gemma was already a tomboy inside my belly. She drained all my energy. In the beginning I even lost weight!"

"Oh, thanks, Mom." I shot her a look brimming with sarcasm.

"Come on, don't tell me you've forgotten how your father and I always had to go searching the treetops for you when it was lunchtime."

Her words made my heart lurch. The memory of Evan lying on the snow came into my mind, so clear that for a second I felt the earth move under my feet. I had spent one of the most wonderful nights of my entire life skating on the lake that he himself had frozen over before my amazed eyes. We'd stayed there for hours talking, watched over by the starry night. I told him about how my parents had resigned themselves to my rebellious tomboy nature and Evan had seized the chance to tease me yet again, but then he'd surprised me by crafting a magnificent ice sculpture. But after that, the memories became tinged with blood. Back then I'd had no idea it would also be the most terrible night of my life—the last one I would spend with Evan.

"Sweetie, are you okay?" My mom must have noticed the change in my expression because she suddenly looked worried.

"It's nothing, Mom. Like you said, I'm just a little tired."

"Let's go to work, Josh," she said, pulling his arm, "and let Gemma rest. She can join us later."

"See you in a few, Squirrelicue." My dad touched his lips to my forehead and a moment later silence filled the room.

I set my feet on the dark ground with extreme caution. The air was thick and cool, the sky veiled with an ominous gloom. With no idea where I was, I had the terrible feeling I was lost, both physically and emotionally. At times I couldn't even remember who I was or what world I belonged to. The foliage rustled at my feet and all around me the forest became denser. The trees seemed to stretch out infinitely.

Something moved behind me, making me jump.

I spun around and peered at the dark silhouettes of the tree trunks, as still as soldiers in the night. My eyes wandered through the semidarkness but the forest seemed deserted. Still, I couldn't shake the feeling there were a thousand eyes spying on me. Threatening, hostile eyes. Creatures ready to pounce.

I turned back and my heart leapt to my throat. Someone was there in the distance—a figure blocking my path. I instinctively took a step back, but a fierce snarl behind me made me freeze. I fought the instinct to scream. The figure moved further away and something inside me urged me to follow it. However, as in a dream, the closer I got the more unreachable the hooded figure became. It seemed to be moving without touching the ground.

"Wait!" I cried.

The figure stopped. I slowed my pace, stepping forward warily.

"I'm lost. Can you show me the way home?"

Without turning around, the figure turned its head enough that I could see it was a woman. Her jade-green eyes shone like beacons in the night.

"Who . . . who are you?" I took a step forward, unexpectedly drawn to her.

A pleased smile appeared on her lips. "That's not the right question." A shiver ran through me at the sound of her hypnotic voice. I wanted to reply, to ask what she meant, but my brain was imprisoned by the sound. It had trapped me like a dark spell. I stood there, unable to stop her as she turned and moved away as silently as a ghost, disappearing into the night. Shaking myself out of my daze, I tried to follow her but my mind got lost again. I clung to the memory of her voice, following the sound like a path that would lead me back to my own world.

Suddenly the forest thinned and I came out into a clearing full of ruins. Pausing, I looked for the woman among the rubble but there was no sign of her. I wandered among the crumbling stones strewn everywhere until I saw her again. She stood at the mouth of a cave, her face turned toward me as though waiting for me. When she saw me she entered the cave, allowing the darkness to swallow her up.

"Wait!" I hurried to catch up with her. I had to exert myself to scramble over the huge rocks and kept falling. When I finally reached it, the mouth of the cave opened up before me like the gaping jaws of an animal preparing to gobble me up. Two conflicting forces struggled within me: should I go forward or turn back?

Part of my psyche continued to send out warning signals, making me shudder at every breath of air, but there was another, more compelling part that insisted I go on, as though the cave could lead me to fascinating, inaccessible places. Under the control of that arcane instinct, my foot took a step toward the darkness. Where had the woman gone? Where would she take me? The questions yearned to be answered.

I advanced through the darkness, my hands touching the walls, accompanied by the eerie sound of my echoing footsteps. A sudden flickering light showed me the way and I continued, taking care not to trip. From time to time I felt strange carvings in the rock. Fascinated, I ran my fingers along the grooves but couldn't decipher them, as if the markings were in some unknown language.

The path took a sharp turn, revealing the place the light was coming from. I flinched and stepped back when I saw a bare-chested figure crumpled on the ground. A whimper escaped me, and with a growl of exasperation the man stirred, the chains shackled to his wrists and ankles clanging.

"Who's there?!" he shouted, his proud voice devoid of fear.

My heart thudded violently against my ribs. "Evan!" A river of tears spilled from my eyes as I impetuously rushed toward him. "Evan . . ." I buried my face in his bare chest that was covered with slashes and burns.

"Gemma . . ." His arms held me tight, filling me with warmth.

"Evan, I've missed you so m—"

The earth trembled ominously beneath our feet, drowning out my voice. As I clung to Evan, another quake thwarted our embrace and the rock gave way beneath him. A huge dark chasm opened up. I screamed as Evan grabbed the edge of the pit that threatened to swallow him up.

"Hold on, Evan! Please don't fall!"

"Don't let me die, Gemma! Help me!"

Gritting my teeth, I tried to pull him up but the heavy chains around his wrists and ankles dragged him down into the void.

"Gemma!!"

"Evaaaan!!!"

As he fell he stared at me, his eyes filled with terror, until the darkness sucked him in and vanished. I fell backwards, my heart drained of all emotion. A gurgle rose from the crater, steadily increasing in volume. I leaned over the edge, my eyes darting everywhere as they tried to spot whatever was swirling in its depths. The sound grew closer and closer, louder and louder, until I could finally tell what it was: a powerful jet of water surging up from the crater, headed straight toward me. I screamed and pulled back as it hit me with the fury of a hurricane. Though I tried to resist, the current swept me into its very center. It felt like it was corroding my skin. I thrashed around in search of oxygen as the water threatened to drown me.

"Evan!!" I cried, desperately attempting to reach him across the barrier of death. Then the water filled my throat.

"Gemma!"

"Evan—" I coughed as someone shook me gently by the shoulders. I tried to focus, my lungs still screaming for oxygen. The ceiling of the living room brought me to my senses. I was at my parents' house.

"Simon." With a sigh of resignation, I looked him in the eye and leaned back into the couch. "Everything's okay."

The look on his face told me he wasn't convinced. "Another nightmare?" When I nodded he looked at me sympathetically.

I still felt a pit in my stomach from having let Evan fall. I had killed him. Again. "I keep dreaming of losing Evan," I said. "He loves me, he's in danger, but I can't save him and he—he dies right before my eyes and there's nothing I can do. It's like an obsession."

"I'm sorry. It's your feelings of guilt that are giving you the same nightmare over and over. It'll stop when you finally understand it wasn't your fault. He didn't die because of you," he repeated, his tone firm, though he knew I would never believe it. *I* had killed Evan. Nothing and no one could ever free me from my guilt.

I shook my head. "But I was having these nightmares even before Evan died, whenever he left me alone." My face darkened as my lips gave voice to a suspicion that had been buried in my heart for far too long. "Maybe coming back from death has consequences. A price. We played against too powerful an opponent. Maybe no one can really escape death."

Simon smiled at me affectionately. "We're going to keep trying."

"Ow!" I doubled up, grabbing my belly.

"Is it the baby?" Simon quickly asked, concerned.

"No, it's just my"—I looked down at my abdomen—"my skin. It *burns*."

Simon seemed alarmed but I reassured him. "Don't worry, it's already gone. Anyway, what are you doing here, Simon?" I asked, banishing the lingering memories of the horrible nightmare that had come back to haunt me.

"I came to make sure everything was all right." Simon touched my forehead, worried. "When I got here you were just waking up. You had a massive fever again, but your temperature is already going down."

"Sometimes I think it would have been better if I'd never met Evan. Maybe it's better to be born blind than to go blind once you know what light is."

"Why are you saying that? He wouldn't want—"

"He died because of me. Drake died because of me. You might be next. I'm not worth all this."

"Maybe you don't think so, but the two of them did. And so do I. Otherwise we would never have *chosen* to protect you in the first place. Evan was aware of the risks, and he fought for you right from the start. He didn't care about dying—he just wanted you to live. He chose *you*."

"What about Drake?"

"He cared a lot about you too."

"I know that, but if the Angel who took on Evan's appearance wasn't the real Drake, then what happened to him?"

"He died. Who knows where, who knows when. We'll never find out what happened." Simon's face suddenly darkened. I could see that not knowing the details about Drake's death pained him. "The only way to get to you was from the inside, and they knew none of us would betray you, so they killed him. Another Subterranean stepped in, passed himself off as Drake, and tricked us all. The very idea is insane. The Màsala must have helped him. They sent Evan away so the impostor could take his place too. None of us could have prevented it. In one fell swoop he would have been able to kill Evan and guarantee you couldn't come back from death, because I could never have managed to bring you back to life all on my own. They would have won on all fronts."

"But something went wrong with his plan too because despite the poison I didn't die."

"No one could have expected that. How do you feel?"

"Like someone who keeps reliving their worst nightmares. I can't take it any more, Simon. I honestly feel like I'm in danger of going insane. I—I'm afraid." It felt like I was on the edge, on the verge of slipping into a pit of madness. "He's there in everything I do, everything I see, everything I hear."

Simon opened his mouth but closed it a second later. He knew I would never agree to the only remedy he had to offer me. I preferred to suffer rather than forget everything. "Shall we go home now?" he asked.

"No thanks. I think I'll take a shower. You go back to Ginevra. I promised my parents I would help them out at the diner later on."

Simon shot me a telling glance. "You sure you're okay?"

"Of course," I said firmly, though the listlessness of my gaze betrayed my true feelings of resignation. "I'm starting to get used to it. It'll all stop soon, you'll see. I might not be able to ward off the attacks of a Subterranean who makes me confront my worst fears, but I can cope with the nightmares—though I don't know how much longer I can battle my guilt. Sometimes it feels like it's slowly killing me." Simon was right: the nightmares were a manifestation of my guilt over Evan's death. That was why I never found peace, not even at night.

"Okay, but call if you need us."

"I will."

His eyes locked on mine, Simon vanished. I took a moment to compose myself. Then I gathered my strength, got up from the couch, went into the bathroom, and locked the door behind me.

16

SCRATCHES ON THE HEART

I gripped the steering wheel and a solitary tear slid silently down my cheek. It was hard to compose myself with James Blunt's lyrics touching the pain I bore inside. I wiped away the tear with the back of my hand and parked the BMW behind the diner.

Inside it was packed with adults and kids. I noticed Alex, the young woman who waitressed for my parents on the weekends to pay for college expenses. She waved to me, then gave a tiny shrug and shot me a regretful glance to let me know she was too busy serving all those customers to come say hello.

"Here I am!" I leaned over the counter where my mom was staring down at the reservation list. She hadn't noticed me walk in.

"Honey! I thought you'd changed your mind."

"No, I overslept, that's all. Pass me that apron. I'll give you a hand."

"Oh, don't bother. You shouldn't exert yourself. Have a seat somewhere. We've got everything under control."

Just then a little boy raced past me and banged into a table, knocking over a stack of napkins. Alex raised her hands and ran over to pick them up, grumbling.

"It's not a bother. Besides, I'd be bored sitting there while you're all buzzing around like bees. I could wipe down the tables or load the trays—anything."

"All right, then. Here." Mom pulled an apron out of a drawer and tossed it to me. I put my hair up in a high ponytail with the hair tie I always wore around my arm and slipped on the visored dark-red cap that matched the uniforms.

"Alex!" my dad shouted from the kitchen. "Orders up for tables twelve, fifteen, eighteen. C'mon, let's get those hungry kids fed!"

"I'll do it, dear!" Mom called back, seeing that Alex had her hands full: she was holding two little boys at arm's length to keep them from getting into a tussle. "Gemma, watch the register, would you?"

"Sure, go ahead. I'll take care of their wallets." I smiled at her before she disappeared behind the counter. I straightened out the pastries in the case—something I did often, almost automatically. It relaxed me as my mind wandered through its winding, endless corridors. Right at the moment, though, they were too dark to explore and I had decided that for one afternoon I would do everything in my power not to let my parents see the burden that weighed on my heart. And so I focused on details, carefully examining the pralines on the brownies, counting the berries on the pies—anything that might help me forget my sadness.

"Aargh!" Alex leaned against the counter, exasperated. "Those brats are terrible!" I smiled at the funny face she was making. "It's impossible to keep them under control. There are too many of them!"

"Want me to give you a hand?" I said, still smiling.

"Are you kidding? Your dad would kill me. All he's done today is tell me to keep an eye on you and stop you from doing any kind of work you might get it into your head to do."

I gaped, surprised by how openly she'd admitted it, but then closed my mouth and smiled affectionately at Dad's thoughtfulness. And to think he had always been so stern.

"Don't tell him I told you, or he would—"

"He would kill you," I teased, imitating her voice. "Don't worry, your secret is safe with me."

"Hey, little boy! Climb down from there this second! I gotta go." Alex rolled her eyes at me and hurried off, leaving me with a smile on my lips.

A customer motioned me over and ordered three slices of pie and two large orange juices. I glanced at Alex and then at my mom, but they both had their hands full, so after preparing the order and putting it on a tray I decided to serve it myself before someone decided to run and help me. I couldn't stand the idea that they were acting differently because of the baby. I knew it was because they cared, but I wasn't used to being treated like a piece of fragile crystal. I lived with an Executioner and a Witch, and in my new world danger was an everyday thing. But they couldn't have known that.

I slowly picked up the tray, my eyes glued to the glasses, careful not to let the orange juice spill. I felt a little awkward, as though it were my first time, probably because of everyone's apprehension. As I came out from behind the counter, I checked the aisle both ways to make sure there weren't any little kids underfoot. Relieved, I looked up so I could see past my visor, but a hazy figure blocked my path. The sight of its green eyes gave me such a fright that I dropped the tray. The noise of the dishes crashing to the floor stupefied me. I knelt down to pick them up and realized no one was in front of me any longer.

"Gemma! Are you all right?" my mom cried in alarm as she rushed over to help. My hands moved quickly to clean up the mess I'd made, but my mind was still absent, bewitched by the jade-green gaze that had just electrified me.

"What happened? Don't you feel well?"

The voices around me were muffled. Only when it was too late did I realize my mom was feeling my forehead. "My God, you're burning up!" She took my arm, helped me up, and led me away. "Leave it, leave it there. Alex, would you take care of this? I'm calling you a doctor right this second."

"No!" Her offer was like a threat, snapping me out of it. I couldn't let a doctor examine me and put Simon and Ginevra at risk. "Freaking hallucinations," I muttered to myself. "Please, no doctor. I'm already a lot better. It was just a dizzy spell. I probably didn't sleep enough today."

"Then let me take you home."

"You can't leave Dad and Alex all on their own. Don't worry, Mom," I pleaded, hoping she would give in. "It's . . . it's been happening a lot lately. I'll be fine in no time, you'll see."

"Gemma, you're running a *high fever.* You need to go home."

I touched my forehead and showed her the heat was already fading, leaving my skin damp, as usual. "Trust me, I'm already better. I'll call Ginevra and ask her to come get me. Simon has a medical degree, you know that," I said, repeating the lie we often told. Actually, Simon could heal people better than any doctor on earth. It was just that my affliction remained a mystery; not even he could do anything against the effects of Witch poison.

"You're right, you aren't burning up any more. Go ahead and call Ginevra, but remember to get in touch later to let me know how you are or I might go crazy with worry."

I walked away from Mom and slid into a booth, realizing only then that my legs were shaking. Damn hallucinations. I forced back the tears. I felt so frustrated. Weren't the nightmares enough? Were they going to torture me when I was awake now as well?

Many people in my situation would have broken down. Maybe my time had come too. Without Evan to shore up the walls of my sanity, my protective shell was crumbling, leaving me fragile and defenseless on the edge of a dark, fathomless sea that led to madness. Like an anchor, the words carved on the table before me kept me from drifting away from shore on that sea of desperation: *Rise up and gather the brightest stars.* Evan had carved them there, maybe to bring me back to reality when I got lost. Back then, the hardest thing I could imagine was giving in to my longing to talk to him. I stroked the tabletop, remembering that moment, and shook myself out of it to focus on the vision I'd just had.

Those eyes . . . I had the funny feeling I'd seen them somewhere before. Could the hooded woman I'd glimpsed in front of me be from the dream that was haunting me? I couldn't remember. And why did the nightmares make my skin burn the way they did? Was it because of the poison too? Was my body really unable to fight it? Or maybe it was the Executioner—had she escaped and tracked me down? I shuddered at the thought and sent Simon a message, asking him to come get me.

He walked through the door minutes later, cordially saying hello to my parents. After reassuring them, we took the BMW back to the house—the only place I could feel the least bit safe.

My phone vibrated and I took it out of my sweatshirt pocket. There were four missed calls from Faith and Jeneane, plus a message Peter had sent an hour before.

Coming to the game?

"Simon?" I began hesitantly. He looked at me. "Turn back." He frowned, confused. "Do you mind if we stop somewhere first? I don't feel like going home. Not yet, at least."

"Where else do you want to go?"

"Peter's team is playing hockey at the Olympic Arena. It'd be nice to go see some of the game."

Simon ran his hand over the back of his neck, unsure. "It's not up to me to tell you what to do, but I'll come along if you don't mind. That way I won't need to worry."

"Of course, no problem. I'd love to spend some time with you."

"Great."

He parked outside the Olympic Arena. It was early evening and the big display on the side of the building said the game had already begun. A strong wind was blowing and along the façade flags from all over the world fluttered as though cheering on the teams. I ran up the steps, counting them in my mind. *Ten*, as always. I smiled. Once in a while it was nice to relive my old everyday routines. I paused to look at the five Olympic rings above the majestic entrance, savoring the sweet nostalgia.

The roar of the crowds hit us as we entered. The stands were packed. The Saranac Lake High team was our biggest rival and the fans were going crazy. According to the scoreboard, the Blue Bombers were winning 3-1 over the Red Storm and there were only seven minutes left in the game. I looked around and texted Faith.

Where are you?

She replied right away.

Look to your right.

I spotted Faith and Jeneane in the front row, waving to get my attention. As I led Simon through the crowd he held onto the hem of my sweatshirt to avoid losing track of me.

"Gemma! You made it after all!" Faith excitedly threw her arms around my neck just as the crowd cheered. The Red Storm had scored but we were still up by one point.

"What are they doing?! We've only got two minutes left! Come on, Bran! Move your ass and score another point!" Jeneane hollered. I smiled. She had always loved making a lot of noise. "Hey Gemma! You got here just in time. The game's in the bag! Peter scored two of our three points," she said.

When she noticed Simon beside me, her expression changed and she shifted into Barbie-doll mode. "Ooh . . . If I'd known you'd be bringing company I would've called you even more times."

Simon caught her innuendo and chuckled, touching his thumb to his nose sheepishly.

"Why didn't you tell us? We would have saved him a seat," Faith said apologetically.

"I wasn't planning on coming. I decided at the last minute and he tagged along."

"Oh, no problem. We can always squeeze together!" Jeneane was quick to say. "There's room for him in my seat." She batted her big blue eyes at Simon and scooched over to make space for him. The red seats were comfortable, but not big enough for two—not unless she sat in Simon's lap, and I suspected that was exactly her plan. I shot Jeneane a sidelong glance and pulled Simon away, giving him my spot. I couldn't stay standing very long or the people behind us would complain, so I sat down in the space between their seats.

Jeneane tugged on my arm and whispered in my ear, all excited. "Wow! How can you live under the same roof with a guy like *that?!*"

"Jeneane, you might as well stop drooling. He's with Ginevra."

"So what? She's been turning on all the guys at school since day one. Besides, she's not here." She winked at me, hiding who knew what intentions. It seemed that Jeneane felt threatened because Ginevra had stolen her place as queen bee. Was this her way to take revenge? I wasn't sure whether to be more afraid for Jeneane or Simon.

"Lucky for you! I wouldn't want to be in your shoes if Ginevra were here."

Just then the crowd burst into cheers and shot to their feet. The Blue Bombers had won. Jeneane grabbed my hand, pulled me down the stairs, and pressed herself up against the partition separating the stands from the rink, gesticulating to catch the attention of the boys gathered in the center of it. Peter, Brandon, and Jake were ecstatic, banging their hockey sticks together and letting out a battle cry. It was their victory ritual. When we were younger, we girls would make fun of them because it was so crude, but we'd since learned to love it. They skated across the ice to us and Peter triumphantly banged his head against the partition several times. Jake grabbed him and put him in a headlock, cheering for him, and Brandon did the same, because Pet had won the game almost singlehandedly. They pulled off their helmets and raised their sticks in our direction as Faith and Jeneane clapped their hands excitedly.

"It seems they won," Simon remarked next to me.

"Yeah, they rarely lose, though the Red Storm always gives them a real run for their money," I said.

"Gemma, hurry up! They want us to go meet them!" Faith took my arm and pulled me away. I noticed the boys were heading toward the locker room.

"Coming?" I asked Simon.

Jeneane seized her chance and linked arms with him. "Of course he's coming! Where else would he go?"

He nimbly shifted his weight, casually detaching himself from her without being rude, and rested a hand on my shoulder. "Actually, I'd rather wait in the car, if you don't mind." He shot me a telling look and I bit my lip. Simon was a gentleman and would never do anything to offend Jeneane, but he wanted to get her off his back.

"Oh, what a shame!" she whined.

Simon leaned over and put his mouth close to my ear. "Sorry, don't get me wrong, it's just that your girlfriend's got the wrong impression of me."

I smiled. Simon was always such a proud, self-confident guy—a perfect soldier—but he seemed so abashed around Hurricane Jeneane! "Don't worry, she gets that impression of practically every guy she meets. But come anyway. I don't want to make you wait in the car. It'll be quick."

"Okay," he said, giving in.

I took him by the hand and led him along as the crowd was still dispersing. "Jen, we can't go into the guys' locker room! Let's wait for them here," I said, but she probably wasn't listening. She pushed her way into the corridor. Just then Peter came out, pulling on a shirt. He instantly noticed my hand in Simon's and it seemed to bother him.

"Hey, hold the door! I didn't come all the way here for nothing!" Jeneane complained, peeking into the locker room.

"Go on in if you want. Brandon's still in there," Peter said.

"Who said anything about him?"

Jeneane threw the door open wide and I turned away, blushing. The entire team was bare-chested and some of them were only in their shorts. I shook my head as she actually walked into the locker room.

"Jeneane!" I shouted after her, but she ignored me. She was so self-confident. Her attitude never failed to amaze me. She'd dragged Faith with her, her red ponytail swishing through the door just before it closed and they disappeared inside. Faith was probably blushing—she was far shyer than Jeneane, though she would go along with things when encouraged.

Simon let go of my hand. "I'm going to take a walk around. I'll be back soon."

"Okay, but don't go too far. We won't stay very long."

Peter smiled at me. Simon must have redeemed himself in his eyes by giving us some time alone. "You came."

"I wish I could say 'Great game!' but I only showed up at the end. Sorry, it was already late when I read your message."

"The important thing is that you're here now."

"I heard you scored two points. You're still going strong!"

"Yeah, it was tough this time. The Red Storm is really good." Peter rubbed the back of his neck, as though trying to say something difficult. "So tell me, you and that guy have grown pretty close, I guess. He was holding your hand a minute ago."

"He's not 'that guy,' he's Simon! He cares a lot about me and I care about him. Come on, you can't be jealous." I nudged him affectionately and added defensively, "You always used to hold my hand." From the look on his face I could tell that was precisely the point. Peter had always felt something for me and his gestures had always meant something deeper than I'd realized—until recently. "In any case, it's not what you think. I've been through some bad times and Simon and Ginevra were there for me."

"You sure you know what it meant *to him?*"

"Yes: that he couldn't put up with Jeneane one more second!"

He raised an eyebrow and I smiled. I hadn't imagined the conversation could take such a ridiculous turn. Peter had finally confessed he loved me and now he felt threatened, but he knew nothing about Witches and Subterraneans. He couldn't imagine how Simon and Ginevra's love could withstand anything and how the bond between the three of us had strengthened over the recent months.

Brandon came out of the locker room followed by Jeneane, Faith, and Jake. They all looked worried. Brandon said, "Guys, we need to go watch a movie at the Palace. Bob's having problems and the theater might go out of business."

"What do you mean, it might go out of business? The Palace is legendary. It can't go out of business!" I said, alarmed.

"It will unless we find the money," he said. They've already launched a campaign to support the theater and tomorrow there's going to be a parade on Main Street. I found out this is the real reason for the Lana Del Rey concert."

"It's true. They were talking about it in the locker room," Faith said. "Unless the Palace comes up with enough money to switch to digital, it'll be shut down for good."

"The whole team's going there to celebrate and help Bob out," Jake added.

"We have so many memories there!" Jeneane put in. "Guys, we've absolutely got to go! It might be our last chance!"

"What, right now?" I asked hesitantly.

"The next showing's in fifteen minutes."

"I don't know . . ."

"Gemma, you can't say no. It's for a good cause."

"Yeah," Peter said. "Besides, I'm sure you'll love the movie. It's *The Hunger Games: Catching Fire*. They held it over."

"Simon?" I hoped he would back me up, but he shrugged.

"Fine with me, if you feel like it."

He probably wanted me to hang out with my friends a little while longer. After all, if he was there to protect me, he didn't see a problem with it. But going to the movies without Evan? And last time we'd taken Drake too.

"Come on, Gemma! Don't be a buzzkill," Jeneane groused.

"Oh, all right, we'll come too," I said. "I would've gone to see it anyway."

"Awesome!" she exclaimed. I could already see her figuring out a way to sit next to Simon.

"Going to see a movie won't kill me—unless you plan to offer me as a tribute, that is."

"Huh?"

"Maybe I should have waited until after the movie to crack that joke. Never mind."

Jeneane shrugged. I doubted she'd seen the first episode in the series—I'd seen it with Peter. She only went to the movies to drool over the hot guys on the screen. By the end of the second one she would no doubt be in love with Finnick.

"Should we ask Ginevra to meet up with us there?" I whispered to Simon as we headed to our car.

"No. It's best that she stay to watch over the Subterranean. We can't leave her unguarded—it's too dangerous."

"Shouldn't you at least let her know?"

"I already did." I looked at him, puzzled. "We don't use phones. That is, with her I don't need to. If I call her in my mind, she can hear all my thoughts."

"Oh."

Simon laughed and tousled my hair before getting behind the wheel. Faith and Jeneane came with us and Jeneane talked nonstop the whole way there. The guys, on the other hand, took Brandon's jeep.

We parked across from the Palace, a large red-brick building. People were lined up at the door, and on the sides of the marquee a message of support welcomed moviegoers:

Please help save the theater.
Go digital or go dark.

We paid for our tickets and went in. As I suspected, Jeneane swooped toward Simon like a falcon, but Brandon grabbed her by the hips and pulled her close. She laughed and in the end went with the flow and kissed him. I sat next to Simon and Peter took the seat on my other side.

The lights dimmed and music filled the theater.

"Want me to get you more?"

I turned to look at Simon. He was staring at me, seemingly amused by my expression. I froze with a fistful of popcorn halfway to my mouth. In no time at all I had polished off a giant tub. "Yeah, thanks, if you don't mind," I whispered gratefully. Simon got up to buy more, a smile on his lips.

"Psst! Hey, Gemma!" Jeneane leaned over Peter. "Let's switch seats."

"No, Jeneane. Stay there and watch the movie," I admonished her, hiding a smile. She stuck her tongue out at me and Brandon put his arm around her shoulders. That girl was incorrigible!

I looked over at Faith and Jake, further down in our row. Their eyes were trained on the screen, but there was a strong vibe between them and I wasn't so sure they were paying attention to the story. From time to time Jake moved his fingers to stroke Faith's on the armrest.

"Like the movie?" Peter asked, leaning toward me. We were so close our heads were touching.

"The adaptation is pretty faithful to the book, so yeah, I like it. *Hunger Games* is one of my favorite trilogies and I don't like it when they distort a book that's important to me."

"I know." He smiled and tried to take my hand, but Simon came back just then and I took advantage of his arrival by reaching for the popcorn. I couldn't let Peter hold my hand. Not there. He loved me and I understood his attempts to bring me closer to him, but the last time I'd been to the movies my hand had been clasped in Evan's, and my heart still ached too much. I was only there to help Bob. I didn't even care about seeing the movie.

Simon suddenly grabbed my wrist and gripped it tightly. I spun around and my heart leapt to my throat. It wasn't Simon, but a man I'd never seen before. "What do you want? Let go of me!" I hissed. I tried to pull my hand away, but he held it tight, his pleading face close to mine. He looked like a desperate vagrant.

"Help! They're going to get me!"

"Stop it! Cut it out!" I managed to break free and the man suddenly seemed to be suffocating, choking.

"They'll get you too," he gurgled, turning my blood ice-cold. Inside his mouth something moved. A butterfly. Its legs popped out through his lips and it crawled out. It was black. Completely black. The man seemed to be in agony. I reached out, but when I touched him he exploded into hundreds of black butterflies, making me jump in my seat.

"Gemma, everything okay?" The voice brought me back to reality. Simon. I looked around and everything was normal. Only Simon and Peter seemed to have noticed anything. Everyone in the room had just jumped in their seats when the monkey mutts burst into the frame.

"Want me to get you some water?" Peter asked with concern.

"No thanks. Everything's fine. This scene is just creepy, that's all."

While Peter seemed convinced, Simon suspected something had actually happened. "Another hallucination?" he asked.

I nodded and he reached for my hand, sensing my desperate need for comfort, but the second he touched me he jerked his hand back as though he'd been burned. We looked each other in the eye and he clasped my hand in his, ignoring the powerful heat I was emanating.

"What's wrong with me? Why am I seeing these things?"

Simon slid his arm around me and I rested my head on his shoulder, feeling safe. "It'll stop. Sooner or later it'll stop."

We were all heading for our cars, talking about the movie. "Why should Katniss have to choose? I mean, they're both in love with her. She should make the most of it. That's what I would do," Jeneane said.

"Oh yeah?!" In protest, Brandon grabbed her hand and pulled her against him.

"What's wrong with it? Until she makes up her mind she can be with both of them. That happens a lot in the movies!"

I rolled my eyes. "I can't stand love-triangle stories. Who knows why they're so popular these days. The main characters discover 'true love,' they promise each other the moon and swear they'll never part. As soon as there's the slightest problem they grow apart, break up, or—in most cases—someone else shows up and comes between them. It shouldn't be that way."

"Love is an immense emotion. You shouldn't squander it on only one person," Jeneane shot back, convinced.

"True love isn't like that. When you really love someone, it doesn't matter how many people knock on your door. You don't let them in, because there's only one key that opens that lock, and it belongs to the person you love. There's no room for anyone else." Peter's face clouded at my words.

"Well, Jeneane, looks like the door to your heart comes with a skeleton key," Jake joked. Brandon shoved him in her defense, hiding a smile.

"Have I ever told you you're a dumbass?" she said, though she didn't seem offended.

"It depends on the circumstances, though," Faith said, her shy gaze studying Peter, to encourage him, perhaps, or maybe to persuade me.

"The heart knows no circumstances," I said firmly. Evan was dead and yet my heart had never stopped beating for him and him alone.

"I propose an Xbox challenge!" Peter said. "Let's get a pizza at Bazzi's and go to my house. I got the latest Halo!"

"Last time I creamed you, if you'll remember," I teased him.

"Oh-ho! That sounds like a dare!" Jake exclaimed, winking at me.

"Nooo, not another multiplayer game, please? There's no dragging you guys away from them!" Faith groaned, a hint of a smile on her lips. She'd always liked spending evenings at the boys' houses.

"Gemma, why don't you come in the Jeep with us? That way Simon can go pick up his girlfriend."

"Um . . . I wasn't thinking of going. Sorry, Pet." We had almost reached our cars and I really couldn't wait to get home.

"Come on! We still need to celebrate our big win!" Peter said. "Simon, why don't you go get your girlfriend and meet up with us there?"

This time Simon realized I didn't want to go and came to my rescue. "It's late. Maybe another time, but thanks for the invite."

We waved goodbye, got into the BMW, and headed home.

A dizzy spell had made me lie down, but since I didn't feel like holing up in Evan's room I opted for the couch. Meanwhile, worried about the visions I'd told them about, Simon and Ginevra had gone down to the dungeon to check on our captured Subterranean and, I imagined, to give her another dose of poison to make sure she stayed put.

I distractedly stroked Irony as I watched an episode from the fifth season of *The Vampire Diaries*. He seemed to sense I wasn't feeling well. I loved the show and never missed an episode but I was tired of watching TV, so I heeded the grumble in my stomach and went to search the kitchen cabinets for something to curb my hunger. I was devouring a chocolate hazelnut bar when a sinister murmur made me jump.

"Simon?" I stepped cautiously into the living room. "Gwen? That you?"

Another sinister whisper. Finding the living room empty and silent gave me goosebumps. I continued to listen and a moment later the sound returned, this time stronger: it was the ghastly hiss of a chorus, a symphony of barely audible voices whispering together in prayer.

"Who's there? What do you want from me?! Leave me alone!"

A sudden breeze coming from behind me caught me off guard. I spun around and the shadowy figure of a woman cut my breath short. She was right in front of me, yet it was like she wasn't there. I gasped, panic seizing me as the sound grew stronger and more threatening. It exploded in my head as her eyes stared at me from the shadows of the golden hood she wore—two jade-green gems so intense they sent a jolt through my entire body. The mysterious, magnetic energy they emanated paralyzed me. Only then did I recognize her: it was the woman who tormented me in every dream—but now she was right there in front of me, so powerful I was afraid I might be electrocuted if I moved too close. Her lips were motionless and yet the strange murmur continued to gain strength in my head. Her body flowed toward me, her long golden cloak barely touching the floor. Frightened, I backed up but tripped and fell.

All at once Simon was there. He ran to me, crossing through the woman as though she didn't exist. She dissolved in the air like a cloud of smoke.

"Gemma, everything okay?" His voice sounded wary, as though he could tell I felt lost in a place from which I couldn't return. "Christ, you're running another fever. Ginevra!"

"She said I have to go to her." A tremor gripped my body when I realized the distant sound had come from my own lips.

"Who did?" Simon looked confused. He rested his hand on my knees, still pressed to my chest. I finally managed to raise my head.

"The woman with the hood." A tingle arose in the back of my neck and crept through my head. Then the image clouded over and everything went black.

"She's waking up."

I barely heard Ginevra's low whisper. Her voice was flat and strangely distant. I propped myself up on my elbows, slowly realizing I was on the couch in the living room. Had it only been another bad dream?

"What happened?" My voice was almost unrecognizable and my head wouldn't stop burning.

Simon and Ginevra came over. "You fainted." Simon stared at me with an indecipherable expression, like he couldn't understand who—or what—I was. Ginevra, on the other hand, had a waxy pallor, her gaze lost in some distant world.

"What? Why?!"

"No clue. You were raving and then you went unconscious."

"For how long?" I asked, wringing my hands nervously.

"Ten minutes, tops."

"Was there a problem with the Subterranean? Did she find a way to escape?" I asked, looking back and forth between them.

"No. Nothing like that." Simon's voice was devoid of emotion, while Ginevra seemed to have lost the power of speech.

"Then the poison you gave her must be wearing off and she—"

Simon shook his head, discarding the possibility. "She's out of commission. Her mind is lost who knows where. She could never regain enough lucidity to attack you—not right now. Ginevra's blood is a powerful drug."

I gulped, desperately searching for another explanation. All the while Ginevra remained silent, as though afraid to speak to me. "Gwen, what is it? What's that look on your face? I know you. There's something you've figured out and you don't want to tell me." Simon quickly looked toward his girlfriend, but she just pressed her lips together. "It's still the poison, isn't it? Is that why I keep having hallucinations? It's not normal for my temperature to shoot up so high and then drop back to normal a minute later." I waited for an answer, but none came. "If the Angel has nothing to do with it, what's wrong with me? Gwen, answer me, I'm begging you!"

"I honestly don't know what to tell you," she whispered. Her gaze was still distant, unable to meet mine.

"Just tell me the truth. If the poison I ingested is slowly killing me, I want to know. Do—do you think I'm going to die? I need to know."

"No, Gemma. I won't let you die," she announced firmly, as though it were out of the question. For the first time, she looked me in the eye. "That's a promise."

What was happening to me then? I hugged her desperately and she returned the hug just as intensely.

"I won't let you go. You're the only sister left to me. We'll get through this, you'll see." She stroked my hair affectionately as I nodded like a little girl. "One way or another, we'll get through this. No one is going to take you from me."

"What was that sound?" I freed myself from Ginevra's embrace and instinctively rested both hands on my belly.

"I didn't hear anything." Simon looked around, circumspect, before turning back to stare at me strangely.

"It's a boy," I whispered, clasping my fingers over my belly. Ginevra's eyes lit up and met mine.

Simon shrugged. "Sure, it might—"

"No, I know for certain. I *heard* him." My eyes filled with hot tears. "How is it possible for me to hear him?" I asked in disbelief.

"It must be some power the baby possesses. Maybe it lets him communicate with you through his mind. After all, he's inside you." Ginevra's face had regained its color. The revelation had wiped away her apprehension and filled her with enthusiasm.

"I can't believe it. I can hear his mind. He sent me a short, confused sound—a meaningless message. But I heard his voice! I'm not even showing yet but his mind has already developed. How is that possible?"

Simon tried to recover from his astonishment. "It's not a human embryo, we know that for sure now, but there's no way we can know how he's developing inside your body. Maybe he's what's causing the fever and the hallucinations," he added, thinking aloud, though he didn't seem entirely convinced.

Maybe we should take her to a doctor after all, someone we can trust. With our powers, it wouldn't be difficult to make—

"No doctors, please," I exclaimed. They turned to stare at me, shock on their faces. "What's wrong?" I asked.

For a moment, Simon looked at me in silence. "I didn't say anything."

My blood ran cold and my body turned to ice.

"He only *thought* it," Ginevra explained, her expression as shocked as it was bewildered. She had heard the remark in both Simon's mind and mine.

"*You* can hear my thoughts?" Simon was staring at me as though seeing me for the first time.

"I don't know . . . No! Come on, that's insane." I looked from one to the other, feeling more and more like a circus freak. "It's probably because of the baby. Maybe his powers are starting to develop and they're affecting me too." What the hell was happening to me? "Gwen?" Unable to handle their stares any longer, I tried to cling to Ginevra's help, but her face had grown grim and her mind seemed unreachable.

Simon leaned over as though to put his arm around my shoulders, but I pushed him away. "Leave me alone!" Suddenly overcome with anger, I jumped up from the couch and stormed off. I wished I could hide away in some distant place or even disappear if it meant I wouldn't have to feel the weight of their eyes on me. I grabbed the car keys in the foyer before either of them could stop me.

"Where do you think you're going? Gemma, wait!" Ginevra tried to reason with me, but the blood was boiling in my veins, shooting up to my head and clouding my brain.

"Don't try to follow me," I warned them in a low growl. "I need some time alone. Please." The way my voice broke when I uttered the last word forestalled any attempt on their part to change my mind as I shut the door behind me. My hand still on the knob, I squeezed my eyes shut as a wave of anger and frustration shook my body, making it tremble.

From behind the door I heard Simon's voice, tinged with compassion. "Let her go. With the Subterranean locked up she's not in danger."

There was no reply from Ginevra. Or maybe I'd taken myself out of earshot so I wouldn't have to hear her. I started the engine, unsure which way to head. After all, where could I possibly go? Peter's house? The diner? No matter where I went there was no escape from everything that was overwhelming me. There was something wrong with me. It didn't matter what it was or why none of us could figure out the reason behind it. What mattered was that instead of getting better, I was getting worse by the day, sinking further and further into it. I wondered when I would reach the point of no return. It wouldn't be long, I could feel it.

Looking up, I realized my hand had turned off the engine in an automatic gesture. I got out of the car, not surprised by the place my body, on autopilot, had brought me. As I made my way to the edge of the lake I shot a bitter glance at the house that stood in solitude among the leafless, snow-covered trees. Our hideaway. Mine and Evan's. My heart constricted, thinking it would never be that again, that it was all part of the past—a memory that time would eventually consume. It would disappear, like ashes in the wind.

Long icicles dripped from the frost-encrusted branches as the gray winter afternoon gradually waned, making way for the queen of the night: a fiery-red full moon that slowly made its solitary ascent to claim dominion over the heavens. Even the stars seemed to be missing; only two lonely specks shone in the darkening sky.

What would become of my life? I couldn't imagine the sun ever warming me again. It felt like nothing would ever be the same, as if the real Gemma had died along with Evan, leaving behind a useless shell emptied of all feeling.

Moved by a deep desperation, I went back to the car and sank into the seat. I felt defeated. There was nowhere for me to go. I didn't want to go back to Simon and Ginevra's and let them feel sorry for me. My eye fell on a flashlight wedged between the seats. I grabbed it and quickly climbed out of the car before my common sense could force me to reason. Twilight thickened the air and darkened the path leading to the old wooden house. The gate let out an unsettling creak but nothing scared me any more except my own demons. Once inside, the door shut out even the faint evening light. The darkness engulfed me. For a minute I stood there, steadying my breathing, trying to ignore the shapes created by the shadows. I switched on the flashlight and the beam illuminated the fireplace. Moving the flashlight back and forth, I scanned the room and slowly crept across the hardwood floor that creaked beneath my shoes. I wished I had a lighter so I could start a fire but I would just have to make do. I knelt on the red rug in front of the fireplace and a knot formed in my throat as I ran my hand over its soft surface. The most precious memory of my entire life burst into my head.

If my heart could beat, right now it would be out of control. I closed my eyes, abandoning myself to the sweet whisper. I could almost feel the warmth of Evan's breath on my skin.

This has been the most romantic afternoon I've ever spent. I wish it would never end.

It doesn't have to.

I lay down on the rug, curled up, and clasped my knees to my chest. Evan's voice was so loud and clear in my head I almost believed he was really there.

God, you're beautiful. I love you to death, Gem.

I squeezed my eyes shut and a hot tear slid down my face. I rested my hand on my shoulder as though I had actually just felt the gentle touch of his lips on me. In my heart, Evan was still there at my side, whispering his love into my ear. It was a lie I would never stop telling myself. How could it actually be over? I refused to believe he was gone. I couldn't accept having to live only with his memory.

"Evan . . ." My lips moved, whispering in the darkness as the tears silently slid down my cheeks. "You promised. You promised you would never leave me . . . I can't go on without you. I miss you too much." I bit the sleeve of my sweatshirt and a sob shook me. "*Antar mayy as,*" I murmured in a tiny voice. As I lay there, exhausted from the pain, suffocated by the sobs, sleep slowly pulled me away with it as I imagined Evan's body nestled behind mine, enveloping me in its warmth. Wakefulness slowly gave way to sleep and I felt his body heat, fooling me into believing it was real. I tightened my embrace around myself, pretending it was his, and surrendered to slumber, cradled by the soft whisper of his voice.

The crack of a whip pierced the air, making me cringe. I tried to discover where it had come from, but an eerie whisper filled my head, confusing me. A shout of rage made my heart constrict.

Evan. I had no doubt it was him.

I tried to stand up but something held me back. A heavy chain bound my ankles. Another piercing scream sent a pang through my heart. It was Evan, I was certain of it. He must be around there somewhere, and someone was torturing him. Driven by desperation, I dragged myself across the cold stone floor to the edge of the rock wall that imprisoned me. A whimper rose straight from my heart when my eyes confirmed my terrible suspicion. Evan was at the bottom of what appeared to be a crater, wrists and ankles chained to the wall, his muscles jerking uselessly at every blow inflicted upon him. His head was hanging, and his hair—longer and wilder than I remembered it—covered his face. Standing before him was a woman with a thick mane of copper-colored hair, clad in a brown Amazon-style dress that looked like it was sewn onto her skin. She brandished a heavy, lethal-looking whip, her face lit up in a sadistic sneer.

"Evan . . ." I wanted to scream his name, but all that issued from my mouth was a whisper. The redhead's hand rose into the air and my heart beat faster, as though rebelling against the sight. The whip sliced through the air and cruelly slashed Evan's defenseless body. He gritted his teeth in a howl of rage and glared at the woman. Hot tears streaming down my face, I squeezed my eyes shut so I wouldn't see, tugging fruitlessly on the chains around my ankles. Another cry of pain from Evan pierced my heart like a dagger as an explosion of energy burst from my chest and a primitive howl of frustration gripped me. Like a flash of lightning on the darkest of nights, a figure darted toward me, halting at my side. My furious eyes shot to the woman like the lash of a whip. She studied me with a slight smile of satisfaction. Her full-length golden cloak flowed over a green bodice gown.

"What do you want from Evan?!" The snarl that escaped me was unexpectedly fierce, but the woman said nothing. She just stared at me with that enigmatic look on her face, her jade-green eyes piercing. The longer I looked at her, the more I was convinced I'd seen her somewhere before. "I know you," I whispered, studying her intently. "Who are you?"

She leaned over and gazed at me with an expression that didn't seem quite as hostile. Then she smiled and her voice filled my head. "*I told you, that isn't the right question.*"

Trying to rebel against the power of her gaze, I twisted under the chains binding me. "Why are you holding us prisoner?! Free me and let me go to him!"

The woman's eyes lingered on my shackled ankles. "We aren't the ones keeping you imprisoned. You are. All you need to do is make the right choice and you'll finally be free of all your suffering. Only you can unlock those chains."

Confused, I frowned. Evan screamed again and rage blinded me. "What do you want from him?!" I hissed. "Leave him alone! Let him go! Torture me instead! Take me!"

The anguish of another lash made Evan roar like a caged lion. All at once something inside me exploded. My face transformed into a mask of pure evil as a dark energy crashed down on me like a tidal wave. From my chest emerged an unfamiliar sound like the snarl of a ravenous feline. An electric current streaked through my body and my hair rose over my shoulders as though swept up by some mysterious windstorm. The chains around my ankles burst and crumbled at my feet. The deafening noise snapped me out of my stupor and I instantly regained control of my body.

Disconcerted, I stared at the remains of the chains. My hand moved cautiously to pick up some of the iron scraps. They were still hot. What had happened to me? An unknown force, powerful and dark, had suddenly possessed me. How had I managed to free myself? Slowly, I raised my eyes to the woman. She was watching me, a smile as captivating as it was approving on her face.

The whispering returned with even greater intensity as I looked down at my hands, stunned at what I had just done. "Who am I?" I whispered in dismay amid the chorus of voices chanting inside my head.

The woman's smile broadened with satisfaction. "*That* is the right question."

Bolting upright, I found myself sitting in the pitch dark, my heart threatening to burst through my chest. My lungs gulped in oxygen as my hand trailed over a soft surface. Where was I? The blackest darkness shrouded everything. Slowly, my memories resurfaced and the phantom of my nightmare vanished. I was still at the lake house. I must have fallen asleep. As I groped for the flashlight, a shiver ran through my body.

There was a slow creak. In that grim darkness, a spectral sound arose in the silence like the hissing of a thousand snakes. Another shiver swept over my back as my hand searched desperately for the flashlight. The hiss grew louder and I shuddered, my terrified eyes trying uselessly to penetrate the darkness while the voices murmured their ominous message like a whispered litany, as though I were still caught in the nightmare.

I froze. It was as if the sound had penetrated my head and was controlling my movements. Possessing me. Suddenly I couldn't remember who I was. All I wanted was to listen to those voices, let them fill me, let them complete me. They were everything for me.

Come with us. You cannot stop it. It has begun . . .

My body slowly rose, moved by some dark, irresistible power. A strange burning sensation in my hands gradually rippled up my arms. I couldn't tell what was causing it. The pain intensified, and I clenched my teeth. It was as if something was flaying my fingers, grinding them down to the bone. I didn't care; a new desire had taken over not only my body but also my mind. Every trace of fear had left me, making way for an overwhelming feeling of power. If I wanted to, I could bend the whole world to my will . . .

"What are you doing?"

Ginevra's voice burst into my head, releasing me from the evil that had possessed me. I shook myself free of it as a lacerating pain gripped my hands and shot to my elbows. In the glow of Ginevra's flashlight, I read shock and consternation on her face. I looked down slowly to discover the cause of the pain and was stunned to see blood covering my hands and trickling down my arms.

I saw a flash of resignation cross Ginevra's face, and something died in her eyes. Warily, I turned for the first time to look at the wall illuminated by her flashlight. The world crumbled beneath my feet. "Oh my God."

"What's going on?" Simon appeared in the silence and stopped dead in his tracks in front of the wall where my fingernails had gouged a deep, blood-smeared furrow with intersecting lines to form an arcane symbol. *The same one I had sketched at school.*

"Fuck," he swore, but I wasn't listening to him.

"They're coming," I said in a faint voice, my gaze fixed on the macabre scarlet symbol that grew distorted as the blood dripped down the wall. It looked like a V with scratches traversing it, enclosed by a misshapen crescent moon. *A panther's claw marks*, I thought instinctively.

Clenching her fists, Ginevra turned to face Simon. "We have a problem."

17

THE POWER OF DARKNESS

The noise of a thunderstorm howled through the room and the doors and windows banged open and shut with a deafening clatter. All at once silence fell. From the semidarkness rose a vaguely familiar voice. "Is that what you call your Sisters now? A *problem*?"

A shiver made my blood run cold. *The Witches.*

"Anya." Ginevra dropped her flashlight. It fell to the parquet floor, casting a single cone of golden light across it. Conflicting emotions battled for control inside me as I watched her face. Caught between bitterness and dismay, Ginevra's gaze was fixed on the darkness.

Three women emerged from the shadows and walked toward us in black leather jumpsuits. The image of three panthers crossed my mind. The woman in the middle had long ebony hair with silver tips and eyes that glittered like two sapphires in the night. Another gazed at me arrogantly, her honey-colored eyes ablaze and her long hair an indefinable shade somewhere between blond and auburn. The one Ginevra had called Anya had riveting eyes the color of jade-green diamonds. She wore her long, chestnut-brown hair in braids that hung over her breasts, with a crown of finer braids crisscrossing her forehead. Of the three, her gaze seemed the least hostile.

Simon stepped protectively in front of Ginevra, his face twisted into a threatening expression as he glowered at them.

"No!" Ginevra cried, terrified by the thought of a conflict between Simon and the three Witches. They emanated such power I could feel it under my skin; they could have disintegrated Simon in a split second.

Instead, a contemptuous smile escaped the middle Witch, who I imagined was their leader. It was the smile of a black wolf gripping its prey in its jaws. "Brave of you, minion of Death, but never fear—we aren't here for Ginevra." The Witch kept her piercing, crystal-blue eyes riveted on me, making my heart shudder. "We're here to claim what belongs to us."

I frowned in bewilderment and a friendly smile spread across Anya's lips. She winked at me.

"No!" More than a protest, Ginevra's shout was a cry of desperation.

The woman with the black hair let out a bitter, scornful laugh, her eyes glittering like a million fragments of lapis lazuli. "No? Haven't you noticed the signs? Five hundred years have passed, but the memory should still be vivid in your mind. We are united by an ancient calling. Our lives are bound together in time."

The Witch's voice reverberated inside me, clouding my mind. What was she trying to say?

"It's not going to happen. I won't let it!" Ginevra said defiantly.

The Witch smiled again, but this time an evil light glinted in her eyes as she stared at Ginevra with a challenging air, as though irritated by her words. "You would not dare oppose us again. We will show no leniency this time. I would tell you how many centuries we have waited for her, but I suspect you already know. We have already lost one Sister. It will not happen again."

The Witch shot me a fiery look and instantly a stabbing pain in my belly doubled me over.

"Gemma!" Ginevra and Simon both rushed to help me. I raised my head to look at the Witch, wondering what her intentions were. She smiled at me, a bewitching smile.

"It burns, does it not?" The pain eased at the sound of her voice and I struggled to my feet, trying not to look weak. The Witch pointed a finger at my belly and I instinctively covered it to protect the baby. What did she want with my son?

"Why do you not raise your shirt?" Her question, spoken with a seductive smile, took me by surprise. I turned to Ginevra, who looked aghast. The Witch spoke again. "It is the serpent inside her. He is already forming."

A tremor in my heart gave me all the answers as she continued to fix her eyes on me as though I belonged to her. Her voice began to whirl in my head and my mind traveled to another place as I lost myself in her words. What was she insinuating? Could it be that—

You are correct, Naiad. You and your Dakor will be one. You cannot prevent it. The strange voice filled my head. I was certain it wasn't my own. Suddenly everything, no matter how dark and frightening, made sense.

I was one of them.

I was a Witch.

"Now I see . . . The nightmares. The premonitions. The terrible sensations—"

"No, Gemma! Snap out of it!" Ginevra shook me by the shoulders. "Listen to me. You've got to resist them!" She glared at the Witch. "She'll never choose to join you!"

The Witch laughed at Ginevra's brazenness. "She will when the time comes. She cannot elude the call of power. It has begun. You cannot stop it."

"It can't be her—it's impossible! You're making a mistake. Only four hundred and ninety-seven years have passed. There are still three left to go!" Ginevra sounded on the verge of desperation.

"Evil is inside her and the poison awakened it. That is how we detected her presence. It happened months ago. Its scent awakened her senses and we perceived her, though it was not yet time. When she later ingested it, her inner nature began to rebel. Direct contact with the right dose of poison will complete the process, and it will be irreversible. She belongs to us." The Witch shot me a piercing look. "The task of all the Subterraneans sent to kill you was not to make you *meet* your fate—it was to *prevent* it. You must choose. Do not deny what you truly are. One serpent bite will bind you to us forever."

"I'll never allow it!" Ginevra screamed.

The Witch replied calmly, "Never is such a long time, dost thou not agree? And we are so good at waiting." She threw me a look full of promise. "Remember that dreams hide many secrets . . ."

"Go to hell, all of you!" Ginevra growled contemptuously, but the Witches simply smiled at her.

"Count on it." The power of three evil gazes penetrated my bones before vanishing into the darkness, leaving my mind adrift in unknown realms. A flashback filled my head. I had dreamed of them—that was why their faces were so familiar. I had also seen Evan in those same dreams.

And if *they* really existed . . .

No one knows what happens to a Subterranean's soul. Everyone assumes it winds up in Hell . . . in Hell . . . in Hell. Evan's words surged among my thoughts, engulfing me like a river in flood.

Hell. Evan had spoken to me about it one summer day. Why hadn't it occurred to me before? If Eden existed—and I had seen it with my own eyes—its opposite also had to exist.

What if he was there?

Something stirred inside me. Buried by months of suffering beneath a thick crust of pain, a new emotion emerged from the dark abyss of my heart. Hope. If there was even a remote possibility Evan was in that place, I had to go there and find him.

EVAN

18

THE WOLF AND ITS PREY

For centuries I had served Death as its dutiful soldier, yet I'd never known its bitter taste. Not even when it came to me under false pretenses, offering me refuge in the comforting thought that it might free me from the torment of life if the inauspicious star that guided our love ever took my Gemma from me. Back then I'd fooled myself, thinking death might quench the fire that consumed me every time I thought of her. To my dismay, I discovered that nothing would ever relieve my suffering. It was just a lie, an illusion my mind had created to keep desperation from driving me insane. Now I knew that Death—faithful ally of the blackest shadows—had locked my heart up in its darkest dungeon and taken everything from me.

I didn't care how hard or how long my body was tortured. I couldn't feel the pain any more. I couldn't feel the burning sensation eating at my wrists, trapped in poisoned shackles. I couldn't feel the lashes of the whip. I couldn't feel the hunger. I couldn't feel the consuming fire when their accursed serpents sank their fangs into me. Their accursed Dakor. I couldn't feel anything any more. Or maybe it was that the pain didn't matter to me because a far more intense, more unbearable agony devoured me from the inside every time I thought of her, my Gem, my sun. Without her, I discovered the darkness of the shadows. I lost the heart I had rediscovered after centuries. It had been torn from me in a vile deception of fate. Not a second went by that I didn't think of her, wavering between reason and madness in the desperate awareness that I had left her alone in a world where Death had already drawn its bowstring and trained its black arrow on her. The thought of not being able to protect her any more drove me mad. Just as much as the knowledge that I would never see her again. Like a poisoned woodworm, the thought bored into my mind relentlessly, even during the moments following the serpent bites when my mind was lost to me.

How would Gemma survive without my protection? How would I be able to live without her, consumed by such torment for all eternity? Would Simon and Ginevra continue to protect her or had they already left her to her fate? After Drake's betrayal, I could be sure of nothing.

Flashes of a tortured existence alternated with moments of total bewilderment when I couldn't even remember who I was. I would try to fight, to get up, but my strength was gone and I would collapse, at the mercy of the dark spell that kept me trapped in that place, forcing me to lose myself in the darkest corners of the bitter-cold rooms of my heart. And yet, like a star in the blackest sky, a glimmer of light continued to bring me back, whispering a single name, and for one instant my heart would delude itself into believing it had begun to beat again.

Subdued laughter reached me in the darkness.

I could barely make out the murmur of voices, but after so many serpent bites I couldn't even count them, my mind was probably refusing to return to that godforsaken place.

"He's really good-looking even with all those scars, don't you think?"

More stifled laughs, followed by the menacing crack of a whip that pierced the air. A tingle crept up my legs; my body automatically cringed at the blood-chilling sound.

"Silence!" shouted a hostile, poisonous voice I'd learned to recognize: Devina, the cruelest, most capricious of the harpies keeping me prisoner.

"What's the big deal? Calm down. If you ask me, all you want is— Oh! The empress is coming." The voices fell silent.

"What is happening here?"

"I was just teaching these two vixens a lesson."

"Oh, listen to her! All hail the queen of the vipers! Why don't you drink some chamomile, Dev?"

"Enough! Suri, Nausyka, why are you not on patrol? And you, Devina, should not use that tone with your Sisters."

"We just got back. The hunt went well. It's just that when we saw this prisoner, we wondered why he hasn't given in yet. Maybe Devina isn't the right one to deal with him."

"That does not concern you. There are other matters that require my presence. Devina will take my place while I attend to the Reaping. Obey her every command."

"It will be done, my lady," the two Witches chorused.

"And you, Devina, make sure the prisoner is always under your control. You may torture him if you wish, but keep your distance from him."

"Why?!" Devina's voice reached me loud and clear. I wasn't sure if she'd raised her voice out of irritation or if my mind was beginning to emerge from the abyss. "None of the Sisters has claimed him! He's just a slave, like all the others!"

"He doesn't belong to you!"

It was another voice that had replied scornfully to Devina's protest. I recognized it at once. *Anya.* Courageous and kind—the only one in that madhouse.

"Who does he belong to, then?" Devina sounded beside herself with anger. "That half-Witch who doesn't even know we're keeping him here?"

"*Do not try to seduce him,* Devina. You had your chance with him centuries ago. It is too late now. That is an order, and it is to be obeyed," Sophìa thundered, adding something I couldn't understand in the ancient language of the Witches. It was the only tongue Subterraneans didn't know.

Devina whined with frustration as soon as their empress was gone.

"What do we do with these?" Nausyka asked, more cautiously this time, probably intimidated by Devina's expression that I imagined was brimming with hatred.

"Are you two still here? What else do you want?"

"Sophìa said we had to report to you. This week's hunt for Subterraneans went better than we had hoped. We captured seventeen more of them. They're already in their places, but these three aren't entirely convinced yet." There was a loud metallic clang, followed by grunts. "They refuse to bend to our will."

"Lock them in the dungeon," Devina said, her tone still bitter from the insult. She couldn't stand having to take orders from someone else—she preferred to issue them herself. "Make sure your Dakor keep them company. I'm sure it won't take them long to decide which side they're on. Now go. I'm getting a headache."

The room fell silent and I thought they'd finally left me alone. Then a murmur, distant, more confused, filled my head.

What was that? Did you feel it too?

It was just the wind. You sure you're okay?

I couldn't tell where it was coming from, but a new emotion suddenly stirred violently within me, as if my heart had started beating again.

Of course, I'm great!

A shudder electrified me. Gemma! Her voice, so full of life, pulled me out of the dark abyss I was often forced to wander in, lost, thanks to the effects of the poison. Unlike all the other times, though, this time I hadn't imagined it. I had actually heard her voice, so clear it made its way into my heart. As if she were right there next to me.

The lash of a whip brought me back to Hell. I gritted my teeth, steeling myself against the pain as my body reawakened.

"Welcome back, my little Angel."

A mocking grin welcomed me as I awoke. I jerked on the chains that gripped my wrists and ankles, ignoring the burning sensation caused by the poison that coated them.

"It took you a while. I didn't think you were going to recover this time. But maybe it's my fault. I'm afraid I overdid it with the doses of poison—but you make me so *angry*."

"You damned Witch!" I snarled, but mine was just the frustrated roar of a defenseless caged lion. If I had been able to free myself I would have torn her to shreds.

"Don't get so excited, Spartan, it'll only turn me on. I've always liked renegades. I didn't know how to get your attention any more, but I see my strategy woke you up this time."

You made *it?*

It's not worth much, but I spent a week making it.

It's priceless.

"Gemma . . ." I murmured, devastated. Her voice rang through the grotto and echoed off the rough walls like a boomerang that mercilessly returned to split my chest open.

"Don't you think it's cruel of her? Here you are being tortured because of her while she's living it up with her little childhood friend. *Peter*," she spat. "Unless I'm mistaken, that's his name."

The air shimmered before my eyes, blinded by frustration, thickening until it took on the appearance of two hazy figures.

I rebelled against my chains with a growl of dismay as Peter and Gemma's faces appeared, floating like ghosts. They were sitting next to each other and their closeness made me burn inside. Gemma was distractedly stroking Peter's hand, clutching something like it was a treasure. *Go ahead, Peter. Don't keep me on pins and needles!* She punched his shoulder and let out a carefree laugh.

"Turns out she's not doing so bad without you, don't you think?" Devina's lips twisted into an evil grin as I shot her a fiery glare.

"I don't believe you! Your tricks won't work on me!"

"No tricks. What you see has really happened. She really is with Peter. After you died she let herself be consoled by running into his arms."

"Gemma . . ." A jolt of pain traversed my heart. "That's impossible. She would never do that," I said, though I was actually trying to convince myself, not her. Gemma couldn't have forgotten me so quickly.

"Of course she could. She's already replaced you"—she came closer and stared at the shadowy figure—"with *him*. Humans are so weak, so vulnerable, they don't know what true love is. They've started a life together."

Marry me, Gemma. I'll take care of the baby. Gemma smiled slightly and my heart shattered.

"A baby? Gemma's expecting a baby?" I whispered, my mind lost in those words. It suddenly seemed I'd never known any Hell worse than the torture tearing me apart at that moment.

"It's yours." Devina smiled. "But someone else will raise it."

Blind fury pervaded me. Screaming until my voice was hoarse, I tried to wrench myself free from my chains. I'd never felt a more excruciating pain in my entire existence.

"Don't you think it's the right thing to do? Don't you want the best for her and the baby? You have nothing to offer her any more. It's selfish of you to hope she won't rebuild a life for herself without you. After all, why shouldn't she?" The Witch let out a treacherous laugh and moved closer until her lips touched my ear. "Believe me, what you see is the reality. No tricks. I let their spirits reach us so you could see with your own two eyes what's going on with your beloved Gemma. You need to give up and let her go. Forget her and move on—with me." Her hand slid down my bare chest. "Why serve Death when you can serve *me?*"

I whipped my head up and shot her a defiant glare. "Didn't your mistress tell you to keep your hands to yourself?"

The determination in my voice punctured Devina's fantasies. She'd clearly believed she had subjugated me. At the crack of her whip, the image of Gemma and Peter faded and died.

"She is not my *mistress*. The Empress is a *Sister*, just like the rest of us. I don't necessarily have to do what she tells me." She sneered at me. "We're not in Heaven, little Angel, and obedience isn't one of our strengths." She stroked my chest again, moving her hand all the way down to my belt. "There are other highly appreciated qualities around here that might please you, if you let yourself go." She moved her lips closer, breathing on mine.

When I jerked my face away, she bit her lip and offered it to me to drink her blood. Her hand slid slowly between my legs and came up my inner thigh. A crimson droplet made its way down her lip. I stared at it, attracted against my will by its power. It swelled and fell, landing on my bare foot. I followed it with my eyes but the Witch promptly drew my attention back to her lip. She was so close I could smell her blood.

"Go on, taste me. You'll regain a bit of strength. Just imagine it's ambrosia."

I swallowed, attracted to the magic of what she was offering me, but forced myself to spit my refusal in her face. "Your blood is only poison. It's nothing compared to the nectar of the Gods. Deal with it."

"Do you realize how many Subterraneans would kill for a single drop of this?" she whispered on my mouth. "In large doses, the pure blood of a Witch can dull your senses. Given in tiny doses, though, it can take an Angel to a paradise he's never known before. No substance is more intoxicating and gratifying. It's the most potent of drugs, the sweetest of spells. Not even man, despite all his efforts, has ever concocted anything with a similar effect. It can take you to distant, mysterious places where your body can soar, experience the thrill of the purest pleasure . . . and I'm offering it to you. All you need to do is swallow the slightest bit to surrender to your instinct for passion. To know *love*." She pressed her lips to mine.

For a second her blood left me dazed, but I yanked on the chains to break free from her grip and spat out the scarlet liquid. "You don't know what love is. What you're offering is worthless to me. You'll never bend me to your will. And for your information, the pleasure promised by a Witch like you is nothing compared to that of a Subterranean who lives only to love you. But you'll never know what that's like, because you're impervious to love. You'll never have what you want from me. You'll have to kill me—if you can."

Devina smiled and a sharp pain filled my head, making me shriek. My skull felt like it was about to explode. "Don't tempt me, Son of Eve. This tough attitude of yours won't help you. In fact, you should have realized by now I like it. Hard, determined, dangerous, and sexy. I might decide to keep you here forever. I could make you my personal manservant."

I spat a drop of blood-tinged saliva at her feet as I held her gaze. "I'll never be anything of yours."

"Don't be so sure. You struggle so hard to reject me and in the meantime you're already becoming my champion. In the last fight you were so brutal. It was so exciting to watch!"

"Every head I rip off, I imagine it's yours," I growled.

She laughed. My insolence amused her. "You have extraordinary strength. Taking on the Circle and beating them all like that without a single drop of our lymph? Imagine what you could do with my blood in your body."

"I'm not so sure you'd want to find out." I shot her another defiant look.

Each Witch had her champion for the battles in the Opalion. They called it "the Circle" because some of the Witches would gather in a deadly circle to seal off the field, from which only one of the combatants would emerge alive. They tore to shreds the souls of those who lost or any challengers who got too close to them. Though the floor inside the Circle was continually changing shape and size, their sinister symbol was always at its center, interwoven with that of the Subterraneans, like an ancient threat testifying to their power and the submission of our race. The Opalion consisted of different contests in which we faced off using weapons or even our bare hands, depending on the difficulty, and the Witches would hold a celebration for the games. Since I'd been there, I'd battled every kind of Soul found in Hell, and one after the other I had defeated them all. Still, that didn't make me Devina's personal champion—I would only become that if I battled with her blood in my body. But I would never give in to her.

The Witch slid her finger down my neck but I continued to stare straight ahead, the anger seething in me making me squeeze my eyes shut. "There was a time when you couldn't resist me." Her voice was once again a murmur. "I still remember our first encounters, and I would wager you haven't forgotten them either. You were so frightened and confused. Maybe I should have been more insistent back then when you couldn't take your eyes off me."

"You're wrong. I never wanted you."

"Are you so sure? Maybe I should start all over again to see what happens." Devina slowly drew closer and touched her lips to my temple. At the contact, her serpent stirred beneath her skin and slithered around her neck excitedly.

When I opened my eyes, the grotto had disappeared. We were in an orchard and she was facing me, clad in a full-length lace gown, leaning against a tree with a seductive expression.

"Why do you run from me?" My heart leapt in my chest: I could feel it, alive and pulsing as though I were still a mortal Soul. I had been the one to say those words. Confused, I tried to move toward her, but I'd lost control over my body. I wasn't myself any more—I was the me from my past. Devina had taken me back to 1720, to one of the dreams in which she'd visited me ever since I was a boy, the ones where she had power over me.

No! I had to oppose her! If I gave in to her in the past, the present as I knew it would be in jeopardy.

"It's you who keep running away," Devina said, pulling me toward her.

I tried to resist but my body moved on its own, without my consent. I watched my hands place themselves on the tree trunk on either side of Devina's head, imprisoning her, and I felt the desire to possess her growing in me. I stroked her neck with my fingers and my youthful will wavered. Thoughts from the past began to cloud my thinking and suddenly I was no longer sure who I was. Was Devina actually capable of crushing my will like that? Of imprisoning me in the past so she could have me in the future?

No. I couldn't let it happen.

I summoned the most precious image stored in my heart and showed it to him, to the Evan William James of that distant past. I couldn't let him succumb to Devina. He had to resist, just as he'd done then, so that one day he would meet Gemma.

Your heat burns my skin when you're near me.

Gemma's voice filled our minds and the young Evan hesitated. He pulled away from Devina, confused, his heart racing from the vision that had come from he knew not where, the vision I had transferred from my heart to his. Gemma's eyes had dazzled him for a single moment. He didn't know how, but he'd recognized them because his memories were connected to mine.

But Devina came back with a vengeance. "Don't run away, my lord. Stay here with me. You will be mine and I will be forever yours. I can show you worlds you do not yet know."

She pulled the young me against her and I felt desire rise within him. I struggled to emerge, to bring him back to his senses, but Devina's power was strong. She wanted me to accept the new reality she was trying to create, determined to seduce the young Evan and, in so doing, defeat Gemma so she could claim me for her own.

I would never have met Gemma. I would lose all memory of her, all I had left. With a surge of desperate defiance, energy filled me and my mind cleared. My sight sharpened and I found myself in the young man's body. I grabbed Devina's wrists and pinned them against the tree, a look of determination in my eye. I wasn't going to allow her to take my memories from me too.

I was myself now, in control.

I want to be with you and no one else.

The memory of Gemma filled the mind of the two Evans, coexisting in that ancient dream. I could feel his heart beating faster from the emotion. He didn't know Gemma but somehow he knew he belonged to her. I pulled back and let him experience the memory so it would be branded on his mind forever: Gemma and me in the old aircraft hangar, making love, her beneath me, stretched out on a military tarp, her bare skin touching mine, flooding me with emotions, and her big dark eyes fixed on me, making me her prisoner. Yes, I was hers and hers alone. It didn't matter how Devina schemed, how long she tortured me or tried to keep me away from Gemma. *She was mine, all mine. Forever mine.*

"Gem . . ." The young me uttered her name, amazed by the love that had exploded in his chest for a girl who was still unknown to him.

Devina cracked her whip, bringing me back to the present. I looked her straight in the eye and smiled. Once again, I had won. "Well? Did you find what you were looking for, rummaging around in my head?" I asked her contemptuously. She grunted and clenched the whip in her fist. "Sorry, *milady*. You can't control me. Not in the past, not now . . . not ever. No one can dominate me."

She placed her hand beside my head, her amber irises expanding over the whites like tentacles and her pupils gradually lengthening as rage overwhelmed her. I had never seen her so furious before. "I can control everything!" she thundered, smashing her palm against the rock in frustration. The whole grotto trembled.

I stared at her steadily, flaunting my calm. "That's not true. You can't control *me*."

Her golden pupils quivered with anger and I laughed, satisfied. "That remains to be seen!" she hissed.

"Did you really believe manipulating dreams in my past would be enough to subjugate me? Don't forget—I'm good at that game."

Devina had used my power to enter others' dreams to delve inside me and bring me back to that memory. To ward her off I'd done something she could never have imagined: I had planted the seed of the memory of Gemma in the young Evan, effectively changing my past. I smiled in wonder: I actually had a memory now of waking up and telling my mother about Gemma and how I had dreamed of her. It pierced my heart to know that as of that moment Gemma had become a part of my past—but never again would she be part of my future.

"You've managed to resist me, but you won't always be able to. Your mind is strong and resistant to persuasion but sooner or later you'll give in. We have all the time in the world. I will be your *Amìsha.*" The whip sliced through the air and violently slashed my bare chest. The sound was bone-chilling. The pain made me clench my teeth, but my eyes didn't leave Devina's for a second.

"Screw you, you ugly bitch."

The blaze of irritation that darkened her face twisted my lips into a grin as I ignored the pain burning every last inch of my body. All at once her gaze lit up with evil, as though she'd found the key to dominating me. I flinched when her serpent materialized from her belly. It sinuously wound its way down her leg and slithered gracefully over to me. I moved as far away as the chains would allow.

"It seems that while the wolf was out hunting it fell in love with its prey. Rather amusing, don't you think? Dangerous, mostly. It's a shame you'll be the one to pay the consequences, because there's something you still don't know about your betrothed." I grunted to drown out her venomous voice. "You should have killed her when you had the chance, because soon your roles will be reversed and you'll no longer be playing the wolf." I looked up at her, furious, and my sudden interest made her smile again. "She belongs to us. She already bears our mark."

A shudder wracked my body. It felt like she'd plunged an icy hand into my chest and squeezed my heart until it bled.

"Every time she came near you, some obscure power gripped your heart, didn't it? You couldn't resist her, and your desire for her clouded your mind. Her *eyes* made you her prisoner . . . That power comes from us."

The serpent shot toward me, threatening to drag me back into the darkness. My body recoiled. "Relax, Spartan. The poison can't kill you here—you've hit rock bottom. Where else would you want to go?"

The rage inside me burst free in a ferocious howl, my fiery glare challenging the Witch's. "You'd better hope I never break free, because you have no idea what I would do to you."

"I can't kill you." Her face twisted into a mask of pure evil, the gold of her eyes glowing until it turned to fire. "But I can always try."

I pulled back further, but the serpent attacked with lightning speed, sinking its fangs into my flesh. A groan escaped me and flames consumed me. The Witch's face blurred before my eyes.

"Sweet dreams, little Angel."

GEMMA

19

BETWEEN DREAMS AND REALITY

There was complete silence on the ride home. None of us had dared speak once the Witches had disappeared, not even Ginevra, though she had read every thought of mine—I could see that from her shocked expression.

The last piece of the puzzle had finally fallen into place. While my daytime torment was thanks to the Subterranean we were holding captive, at night it had been the Witches torturing me. I'd finally discovered the reason behind everything: I was destined to become a Witch. The thought should have terrified me, but instead the only thing I could think about was Evan and the possibility he was still alive. I would think about everything else later. It was only when we got home that the tension sought escape through my lips, as though the kitchen light had forever banished the darkness and awakened us all from a strange nightmare.

"Gwen?" I shot her a piercing look that demanded her full attention.

"I know what you're about to ask. Forget it." Her answer was as sharp as her crystal-green eyes. It was unexpectedly hurtful. I took in the pain and just as unexpectedly felt it burst inside me, ruled by a savage force. A *dark* force.

"What's happening, ladies? We're all in shock. I don't think it's the time for us to be fighting among ourselves." Simon's face was wan, showing he hadn't yet recovered from the experience we'd just had. He didn't realize what conclusion I had come to either.

"It's an insane idea!" Ginevra railed at me, ignoring him. Her growing anger was intertwined with frustration, like a vine creeping around a tree, hard to eradicate.

Dreams hide many secrets. The Witch's voice continued to whirl through my head, confirming the terrible truth that part of me must have always known.

"I . . . I still can't believe it. *My nightmares*. They kept haunting me and they were *real*, weren't they? I dreamed of them. I've always dreamed of them! They were torturing him," I murmured, trying to follow the stream of thoughts flowing through my head. It was a reverse journey in which everything took shape, finally acquiring meaning.

"The nightmares were nothing but their attempts to turn you toward evil."

I looked at Ginevra, my eyes fiery, and the determination on my face made her cringe. "But that's not all, is it? *You knew*." I wanted to shout into her face all the pain inside me, but all that came from my lips was a feeble sound. My doubts and fears had given way to certainty. Like a star exploding in the night, the future I'd been unable to see, blinded as I was by a dark cloud of pain, suddenly sparkled with a thousand colors. The sun had begun to shine again.

The thought that Evan was out there somewhere, still alive, banished the fear of what I was becoming. I would bring him back, even if it meant sacrificing everything, if I could just see him again one last time. In the blink of an eye, the warmth that flooded my heart melted away all the tension I'd accumulated. A river of tears filled my eyes, blurring their faces.

"He's still alive." I blinked and the tears streaked my cheeks. "You saw how much I was suffering. You kept telling me to move on, and all the while you knew he was still alive."

"Gemma, I—"

"Don't—don't try to play the part of the protector with me. You already know what I want." I'd tried to keep my voice from trembling, but in the end anger had gotten the better of me.

"Forget it. I won't let you do it."

A stream of energy flowed from my eyes to hers and everything else fell away. A wave of power that felt superhuman began to mount inside me. It lifted me from the ground as my hair lifted and fluttered in the air at the mercy of a wind that blew only inside me. Suddenly I was aware of every cell in my body, the whirlwind of emotions rushing through me, but I couldn't contain or control them. All I could do was let them explode.

"Gemma . . ." Concern edged Simon's voice as I noticed that several objects around the kitchen had risen into the air, moved by the dark energy possessing me.

"You don't have the right to decide about my life!" I enunciated each word as a snarl rattled in my chest and burst forth like a demon from hell. My body trembled at the realization that the sound had come from my own lips. The objects suspended in the air burst into a thousand fragments of glass, wood, and porcelain. Simon ducked as every window in the kitchen exploded in a hostile warning. My fiery glare was still locked on Ginevra. She stared back at me in shock, defeat mixed with resignation in her eyes.

"She's out of control," Simon whispered nervously.

Gemma, don't let it possess you. Ginevra's voice rang out clear and persuasive, but her lips hadn't moved. I could read her mind.

You should have told me! I growled mentally. My vehemence caused a short circuit and made all the lights go off.

"Damn it, would you two calm down?!" Simon shouted, but not even the deepest darkness could break the visual contact between Ginevra and me. I could see so clearly it might as well have been daytime. "Get a grip, Gemma."

I looked at Simon and my feet settled to the floor as the dark energy drained from me. Looking at their helpless faces, a tremendous urge to run away made me turn to go, but Simon moved like lightning and pinned me against the wall. He observed me, relief on his face, as I realized to my horror what had just happened and how I had demolished the room.

"Why don't you both try to relax? We can talk about this later when we're all calm," Simon suggested, but our thoughts were still engaged in a fierce battle.

"Evil is already inside me! I can feel it growing day by day and there's nothing I can do to stop it," I said.

"You can fight it!" Ginevra answered severely.

"Why should I, when it can give me back what I love most in the world?!" My voice softened, weakened by tears. "Why should I renounce what I am when what I am is what can give me back my *life*? You don't understand, Gwen. I *have to* go, with or without you. *I can't back down.*"

Ginevra grabbed her hair in frustration as she nervously paced the room. "You're the one who doesn't understand. What you're asking me to do is *impossible*. I can't! I can't go back there. It's forbidden to me. I swore an *oath*. If I went back they would kill Simon without thinking twice and I can't let that happen."

"I would never ask you to risk all that. I'll go alone."

"Out of the question," she promptly replied.

"*I'm going alone*. If I have to search all of Hell to find him, I'm bringing Evan back."

"He can't come back. *No one* can come back from death."

"I did." My determined eyes met hers. "Evan brought me back and I'm going to do the same for him."

"You don't know what you're talking about. That place is cursed! It's full of dark magic and terrifying creatures!"

"I don't care."

"I can't let you go."

"What would you do if it were Simon?"

Ginevra was torn. Her eyes wavered.

"I only have two choices, Gwen: go and save him, or stay and die with him." I wasn't afraid of death any more. This new hope had clarified everything, illuminated a passageway inside me. I had to cling to it with all my strength until my very last breath. It didn't matter what I had to do—I was going to bring him back. The thought of never returning didn't frighten me, not if I could see Evan again one last time. That was all that mattered.

"Gemma."

I noticed Simon's hand resting on my shoulder only after he said my name. Having realized the nature of the connection between Ginevra and me, he hadn't dared come between us. "We can't know for sure he's even there."

I looked at him and shook my head. It was obvious Ginevra had kept him in the dark too. I shot her a challenging look. "We can't know that? Is that so, *Gwen?*"

She hesitated, overcome by guilt. Simon looked at her as though seeing her for the first time. "You knew?" he whispered, bewilderment and a touch of contempt in his voice. "You knew all along? Ginevra, how could you keep quiet about something so important?!"

"I couldn't break my oath! The price is your *life*."

"You knew Evan was still alive and you did *nothing*?!" Simon clapped his hands to his head in disbelief. "Sweet Jesus, Evan is still alive and you knew it?! How could you?!"

"You think I didn't suffer from keeping you in the dark? I had to choose! It was a burden I've been carrying for months all alone, Simon." Ginevra took him by the shoulders and forced him to look at her. "I couldn't risk putting you in danger. What did you expect me to do, go get him? *You don't know them.* You have no idea what they're capable of! They let us go once—they won't do it a second time."

Simon pulled out of her grip. "You should have talked to me!" he growled, his voice hoarse with frustration.

"Come on, Simon. Don't tell me it never crossed your mind."

Despite Ginevra's attempt to calm him, his anger grew. "I'm a Subterranean, like all the other servants of Death, but none of us knows what death looks like. We can't hope for forgiveness like mortals can, and none of us know where the road your poison takes us on ends up. But it seems you do."

Ginevra had no answer. She hung her head and he intensified his attack. For a second I saw them for what they were: a Subterranean and a Witch, mortal enemies since the dawn of time. "I've always respected your wish not to talk about your Sisters or your world, but damn it—you should have told me about this! We could have come up with a solution together, for Christ's sake!"

"There is no solution, Simon! Not one that doesn't lead to your death."

"We're talking about Evan!" Simon exploded, looking her straight in the eye, almost as if he wasn't sure she was understanding him. "You should have told me!"

"I couldn't! Subterraneans can't learn that our venom is a door leading straight to Hell. If Gemma hadn't had those dreams, no one would ever have suspected it. I had to consider Gemma's wellbeing, and the baby's. I was sure that if she knew she would go there to get him, despite her condition. I had to protect them. I had to protect *you*, and I knew you would never let me."

Simon ran his hand over his face in frustration and turned to me, at a loss. "I'm sorry, Gemma, I didn't know anything about it. And she's right: I would never have let her."

Ginevra didn't seem willing to discuss it any longer, but I was prepared to do anything to convince her. She picked up on my thoughts. "If you went down there I wouldn't be able to help you, and I can't—*can't*—let you go there alone. Try to realize once and for all we're talking about Hell! You have no idea what dangers you would be up against!"

"Oh, you *bet* you're going to help her!" Simon's stern voice cracked in the air like a whip. "Whatever Gemma has in mind, we'll talk it over and deal with it together like a real team, because that's what we are, Ginevra: a team. A family. Get it through your head: this isn't all about you!"

"Have you both lost your minds? Am I the only one left with any common sense? This is insane, Simon! Gemma wouldn't survive a single hour down there."

"She's one of them. Your Sisters would never hurt her. If Evan really is their prisoner, I'm going to help Gemma find him, with or without you."

"But how? No one except a Witch can take her there."

"I'm sure Gemma can summon them. Their connection is strong and the process has already begun. Either you help her or Gemma can take things into her own hands: the choice is yours."

Faced with this concrete threat, Ginevra went deathly pale. "Well, let's hear it. What do you have in mind?"

"You know perfectly well what I have in mind," I said, giving her a hard stare, "and I'm going to do it with or without your help. They're already there—I can feel it. They've awakened the evil inside me."

"They can try to persuade you but they can't take you by force. It's up to you to decide."

"Then I don't see the problem."

Simon studied my face, trying to understand my intentions. Grateful to him for supporting me even without knowing what I wanted to do, I sighed and answered all in one breath: "The Witches want something from me and I want something from them. I'm willing to grant their wish if it means getting Evan back. We'll make a deal. I'll agree to become one of them. My life in exchange for Evan's."

Simon gasped, shocked by my plan. He was probably wondering whether Ginevra hadn't been right after all in trying to stop me.

"There! You hear that?! It's insane!" Ginevra burst out. "Why can't you two realize that?"

"They're going to take me anyway! It's what I am."

"That's not true—otherwise they would have taken you already. As I said, whether you become one of them or not is your decision."

"Has there ever been a chosen one who didn't become a Witch?"

Her silence gave me the answer. Witches waited five hundred years for the arrival of a new Sister. I was sure nothing would stop them until they had convinced me to accept evil.

"Gemma, everyone has an evil side hidden inside them. Some ignore it, others repress it, but no one is completely without it. It's a part of human nature and has been since original sin. And life on earth was begun so you could choose which side to listen to. According to an ancient Indian legend, there's a battle going on inside us between two wolves. One is evil, self-centered, full of envy and guilt; the other is good, full of joy, love, hope, truth . . . faith. Only one will emerge victorious in the end." Ginevra looked me in the eye. "The one you decide to feed."

An icy silence descended on the room. I didn't want to give in to evil, but I had no choice.

"There's always a choice," Ginevra replied, having read my mind.

I was quick to disagree. "I can't choose to live without Evan. I just can't."

"Gemma," Ginevra lowered her voice to a protective whisper, "the seed of evil is inside you. Don't let it grow."

I sighed and looked into her eyes. "It's already sprouting."

"You must conquer your emotions if you don't want to be suffocated by them. Think it over carefully, Gemma. Saving Evan won't bring you two together again. The Witches will separate you."

"I don't care. It's my fault Evan died. It's up to me to bring him back, even if that means sacrificing everything." I tried to keep my voice steady but failed.

"Don't think I don't realize what you're hoping, Gemma. Once the transformation takes place, you won't be able to turn back."

"You did."

Simon and Ginevra exchanged glances. "It's different. I had centuries to fight the evil inside me. Only my love for Simon managed to overcome it."

"Exactly. Love is the only invincible power—you said so yourself! My connection with Evan is powerful," I told her. I tried to convince her, but not even I was sure of what I was saying. I'd seen how powerfully they could possess me and I suspected I would never be able to defeat the Witches, but it didn't matter to me. I was willing to do anything in order to see Evan again, in order to bring him back.

"That won't be enough, Gemma."

"Are you sure?" Simon, who had been staying out of the conversation, tried to persuade Ginevra. "Maybe Gemma is right. She can't just repress evil." My eyes shot to his expectantly. "She has to let it emerge and then fight it. That's the only way she can eradicate it from her heart. Otherwise it will fester inside her forever."

"Whose side are you on?!" Ginevra asked, incredulous. "She can't give them the opportunity to possess her!"

"But she has to face them! You didn't repress your nature—you faced it and defeated it. There's no other way for Gemma to beat the Witches except by letting evil take root in her too, to then rid herself of it. They'll never stop hounding her—you saw for yourself how zealously they're anticipating her surrender. She can't defeat evil if she keeps repressing it. The Witches will torment her for all eternity. She needs to let it explode if she wants to gain control of it." Simon looked at me, full of hope. "Each of us has Heaven and Hell inside us."

"Quoting Oscar Wilde won't help convince her," I warned him, "but I agree. He also said: 'The only way to get rid of temptation is to yield to it.' Gwen, it was my fate to find you guys. Some strange power summoned me to you the first time I came to this house. It was you—I know that now. My connection to you is what drew me here. It also explains the burst of light I saw in the sky. I sensed your energy, the energy that united us. It was inevitable."

"Well, you can't summon them to offer yourself up. It would be a pointless sacrifice. They would seal the deal with deception—that's their specialty. And once transformed, not even you would let Evan go free. The only way to bring him back is to go down there and get him. They would never just hand him over to you. A promise given by Sophìa within her realm, on the other hand, is an indissoluble oath." Ginevra sighed, devastated. "If only you could bring him back before making a pact . . ."

"Then help me! You know Hell, you know the Witches. If you're on my side I can save him without being transformed!"

"I'll always be on your side. That's why I can't let you go. Once you're inside the Castle, they'll never let you leave until they've gotten what they want. No one who's ever been there has returned to tell the tale—no one who isn't a Witch, that is."

"But I *am* a Witch," I reminded her.

"Not yet, you aren't. And going down there would be a fool's errand. It's *forbidden*."

"I don't care. They won't hurt me."

"Yes they will, if you refuse to surrender yourself to them."

"If there's even a remote chance of finding Evan, I won't give up until I feel my heart stop beating."

Then Ginevra said something that touched my heart: "I don't want to lose the only Sister left to me." She hung her head, her voice breaking with emotion and her eyes brimming with tears.

"That's not going to happen. I have too much to come back for. I'll find a way."

"But—" She looked up and for the first time I saw a hint of surrender in her green eyes. "Think of the baby. The last few months have been very hard on you. One more trauma and you might lose him."

I smiled reassuringly at her so she would see how confident I was in my decision. "I'm sure he would die sooner if I stayed because he can feel my pain. I was on the verge of collapse, Gwen. Now I know Evan is alive, that there's hope! Believe me, nothing frightens me more than living another day without him. I'll be careful. Besides, the baby is so strong—half his blood is Evan's. That will protect him."

Nodding, Ginevra exchanged glances with Simon and my heart leapt as she finally gave in. "All right, Simon, I'll do as you ask. Gemma, I can't go with you, but I can explain everything you need to know. Just remember: you'll be alone and you'll have to endure a long, difficult journey before you reach Evan."

I nodded, not the least bit swayed by her attempts to talk me out of it. "I'm not afraid. I'm ready." I pulled out a chair and sat down, ready to receive her instructions.

20

REVELATIONS

"Man is so self-centered he's only ever wondered about his own nature. No one has ever really been interested in knowing what might have inspired God to create the human race in the first place." Ginevra rested her hands on the table, gathering her thoughts. Before beginning, she'd made little braids in my hair, telling me how Witches loved them because they were like snakes coiled around themselves, just like the Dakor encircling their arms.

"You're right, people always talk about mankind, about the reasons for life on Earth, but never about God, about *His* reasons or His wishes. What I do know is that He created us out of love, right?"

Ginevra smiled and began to pace the room. "God deemed it necessary to create woman for man. Do you think He didn't feel the same need as well? Before even creating man, He made a being that was immortal, like Himself—a being to love and be loved by. But something went wrong. He created the perfect woman for Himself and gave her great abilities, a power almost equal to His own. He called her Sophìa, which means 'wisdom.' Sophìa's grace and beauty exceeded His expectations, but so did her thirst for knowledge. Since power derives from knowledge, little by little Sophìa became insatiable. She wanted absolute power. She wanted to know all of God's secrets and couldn't stand being inferior to Him. One day she tried to usurp His powers and His kingdom. Grief-stricken by her betrayal, God imprisoned her in a cage made of Diamantea, the celestial essence, hoping her spirit would be purified and she would repent of her sins. She was fascinated by the cage's splendor, but when she touched it the diamond turned black and God suspected her soul was already too dark for redemption.

"And so He passed His sentence and banished her to a distant place that He named Hell. To console Himself, God created man, and when man asked for a woman, He was unable to refuse. Nevertheless, God's heart feared the worst, so He took a precaution: having discovered that knowledge might lead man and woman to thirst for power, He left them in the dark about everything. That way they would be free to live solely on their reciprocal love, which they did . . . until Sophìa decided she wanted those creatures for herself.

"When she learned of their existence, partly from boredom, partly from her longing for omnipotence, Sophìa decided she wanted to rule over mankind, so she sent a serpent to tempt Eve and make her crave knowledge. The serpent said to Eve,

'The river water blinds your soul
Let power be your children's goal
For rulers they are bound to be
By eating of the sacred Tree

"Sophìa hoped Adam and Eve and the children they had had would be damned to Hell like she was. That way she could rule over them. They would be her creatures. *Her slaves.* Sophìa began to see her world no longer as a punishment but as a wonderful opportunity. Those people would be her first subjects, and after them there would be many more.

"But Sophìa had sinned of her own volition, while man had been driven to evil by her treachery. And so, heartbroken about this new betrayal, God took all His rage out on Sophìa and the serpent that had done her bidding: from that moment on, they were to be a single being, and their souls, poisoned by evil, would be connected for life.

"But man wasn't free of guilt either, nor did he deserve the purity of Eden. However, since God loved His creatures and didn't want to deliver them to Sophìa, He gave them another chance, leaving them in a world halfway between Heaven, where evil didn't exist, and Hell, the kingdom of darkness. It was a world where man would neither be forced to serve Sophìa nor to love God, a world where he would be free to *choose* which side to be on—God's or Sophìa's. Eden would be the reward for those who loved God of their own free will. He granted men a mortal existence, giving them a set amount of time to redeem themselves."

"Incredible." I had listened to Ginevra, breathless with fascination. Great hatred could only have originated from great love. "He gave us free will to let us make a choice, but He also gave us a limited time to do it. So Earth is a sort of Purgatory."

"Exactly."

"Then theoretically Sophìa would be Satan."

"That's one of the names she's been given over the centuries, like Lilith and Hades. You know her better as Lucifer, which actually means 'light bearer,' or Satan, meaning 'she who opposes.' Only we call her by her real name: Sophìa. But it doesn't matter what you call her. She's evil incarnate. She's the devil. Her power is almost limitless and her heart is cold and ruthless. No one knows her better than I do. She even betrayed God, her Creator and only love, so He set his hopes on mankind, hoping they might experience the dream He hadn't been able to."

"Pure love," Simon explained, taking the words out of my mouth.

"But if she was God's wife, doesn't that mean she's a goddess?"

Ginevra shook her head, a poorly concealed smile on her lips. "*Empress.* She prefers to be called that, since she rules over her empire. There's only one God. A God can't be created."

"So what about the other Witches?"

"When she saw her plan had failed, she managed to wrest a promise from God by begging Him not to leave her all alone. And so, every five hundred years, a new Witch awakens on Earth to serve her. Sophìa wanted God's creatures, but He granted her only one every five hundred years—a female, who would also have the power to choose. Every mortal Soul the Witches seduce increases their power. They're getting stronger and stronger. Their abilities have improved over the centuries. Or maybe it's because mankind is forgetting where it came from."

"So those who believe in God have a better chance of not being corrupted by evil? Is that what you're telling me?"

Ginevra couldn't hold back a smile. "Believing in God isn't enough to save someone. Even Witches believe in him. As I said, it doesn't matter what you call the two parts: God, Witches, darkness, light, damnation, salvation. What counts is not losing sight of what they represent: good and evil. Every action, even the smallest, entails a decision that leans to one side or the other, though at times we don't realize it or we simply pretend not to notice. But inside, you know when something is right or wrong. You can tell from how the action makes you feel. It's a never-ending battle. Those who renounce evil and prove they're worthy of God's love can return to His kingdom. But don't think it's just a question of not committing this or that crime. Every mortal Soul has a moment in life when they find themselves facing a decision that will mark their fate. Everyone is eventually tempted by evil, some more often than others. The Witches often win Souls over gradually, luring them one step at a time along the path that leads to Hell. Other times it's a single major decision. What makes the difference is how a person behaves when they're tempted, the *choice* they make when the path of evil lies before them. A mortal might never have committed a sin, but they might sell their soul to the devil in exchange for what they desire most."

"If the Witches have so much power, what's keeping them from taking over the world?"

"What makes you think they aren't already doing it? Man will bring his own world to an end. He's already destroying it by choosing to comply with evil, driven by his lust for knowledge and power. By thinking only of himself and ignoring the consequences his decisions will have on those to come."

"Okay, but why haven't they taken it over already?"

"Because of the few humans who choose to renounce evil. There are always some who decide to follow the path of God, Yahweh, Jehovah, Elohim . . . whatever name they give Him. What difference does His name actually make? All that matters is that they follow the laws, choosing good over evil, love over hatred, hope over resignation. Believing means hoping—hoping there's something after death and it doesn't all end. Behaving accordingly in order to deserve Redemption. Resisting temptation. Their faith is what's keeping the world from falling to pieces. If someone doesn't hope a better place exists, they'll be unlikely to try to deserve it. Witches can't force Souls to follow them, just as God can't force them to love Him. That's why men have a conscience, the spokesman of the soul, though they often choose to ignore it."

"What would happen if everyone stopped believing in a reward?"

"Then there would be no hope for the world and even Earth would follow Hell's rules. It's already happening."

"But why do the Witches want men so badly? For what purpose, after all these centuries?"

"To make them their slaves."

A powerful shudder crept through me. I tried to control it but couldn't keep a tremble out of my voice. "Slaves?"

"The Witches don't want to rule the Earth because it's a place where there is and always will be free will. It's neutral territory, halfway between Heaven and Hell. No, they want to lead Souls into their empire, Hell. Only then can they become Sophìa's slaves, like she always wanted. That's why when the Witches discovered that Eve's banished children had been ordered to take redeemed Souls to Heaven, the Witches began to hunt them down. But I think you already know that part of the story."

"Right. Tell me more about the Witches instead."

"Their powers are almost limitless. They can read minds and nature bends to their will, but the most powerful weapon at their disposal is seduction. Subterraneans are capable of resisting it because they're warriors by nature, but for mortals it's very difficult."

I thought of the day Ginevra had shown up at school and how no one could take their eyes off her, how they'd all hung on her every word. She cast me a reproachful glance and continued. "Once a mortal's soul has been corrupted, Sophìa comes into possession of it when he dies. In Hell, the souls of the Damned are no longer free, the way they would be in Heaven. Witches promise eternal life, but it's a lie—only God can offer such a gift. Actually, all Sophìa wants is to prove that God's creation isn't worthy of His love—that it's easy to buy him off. Some humans even follow her spontaneously."

"How is that possible?"

"There are more humans than you would believe who will sell their souls just to see their dreams come true. They don't realize that in most cases they could do it all on their own if they only made the effort. But many choose the easy way: they invoke the Witches, surrender to them in exchange for their worthless promises, and end up in Hell, where they're nothing more than playthings. Mere puppets the Witches use for their amusement. Slaves—or, if you prefer, *zombies*—as soon as they completely lose their humanity."

"But they go on living."

"If you consider that a life. At first they still have a trace of humanity in them, but it fades with time. However, they maintain a glimmer of awareness that keeps them from forgetting what they were and what they gave up. It's the worst kind of torture, believe me, a condition that leads to madness. It would be easier if they were empty shells, but instead they're forced to exist while retaining the memory of what they once were. They're conscious of what they've become but can't fight it. And that's what they miss more than anything else: free will. Those beings no longer belong to themselves—they're slaves to fear, to hunger, to Hell. They're slaves to Sophìa."

"And they live like that forever?" I asked, almost afraid to hear the answer.

"No. Their souls are corrupt and therefore perishable. Theirs is an empty, ephemeral existence that the Witches can put an end to whenever they like."

"What happens then?"

"They disintegrate. They turn to dust and rejoin the earth."

"Maybe it's a form of liberation, then."

"Maybe, but not even that is their choice. Their instinct forces them to fight for their survival. But listen, this is important: the Damned aren't all the same. As I said, occasionally during a moment of temptation, a mortal who otherwise lives a good life isn't strong enough to battle evil and sacrifices Redemption to see his dreams come true. These are individuals whose will isn't strong enough to resist the Witches' coercion. Some people call them corrupt. But Hell is full of far more dangerous creatures: murderers, maniacs, thieves, lechers—beings you could never imagine meeting. From all epochs, from all eras."

A shiver penetrated my bones.

"Some of them band together in small communities. Others—the ones who have completely lost their humanity—wander aimlessly in search of other Souls to ease their unquenchable thirst for blood. Hell is full of hidden dangers, treacherous Souls, ferocious beasts. There are no rules there, except one: survival. It's chaos."

I gulped. I had suddenly felt a shiver beneath my skin and discovered my hands were trembling under the table. I clutched my knees and forced myself not to give in to fear. Whatever obstacle arose, I would overcome it, led by the new light I carried inside. Nothing and no one would keep me from reaching Evan. Now that Ginevra had begun to tell me about Hell, though, I needed to ask a question that had been weighing on my heart. I couldn't bear the burden any more. "What do Witches do to Subterraneans?" I asked, my voice trembling.

Ginevra broke off the silent conversation she'd begun with Simon, to which I wasn't invited, and looked at me, her face wary. Her expression suggested she'd been dreading the moment I would find the courage to ask her that. Simon ran his hand over his face and through his hair. Maybe he was thinking the same thing.

"They keep many of them in the Castle," Ginevra said, trying unsuccessfully to keep her voice from wavering.

"But . . . for what purpose?" I didn't take my eyes from hers for a second. I had the strong impression she was doing everything she could to hide something. I didn't know if she was doing it for my sake or Simon's.

"For their amusement. The Witches gain strength from the Subterraneans' power and they often have fun using it against them. They keep some as slaves and choose others to do battle for them or take part in their games. They have an army of Subterraneans ready to satisfy their every whim. Unlike other Souls, Subterraneans are immortal, so they're stronger. But most often they're chosen to pleasure them," she said cautiously. A shudder ran through me. "It doesn't matter if their heart belongs to someone else. If the Witches want to be with a

Subterranean—or even two or three at the same time—they're forced to obey, since they're the Witches' property. Everything in Hell is their property."

"Some Subterraneans might not think that was so bad," Simon joked, trying to coax the frozen expression off my face. He only succeeded in earning a glare from Ginevra.

"None of it is pleasant when you're being forced. And bear in mind that becoming a Witch's sex slave isn't the worst thing that can happen to a Subterranean. In fact, that only happens to the weakest, the ones who let themselves be ruled. Since Subterraneans are immortal, they can 'decide' whether to give in to a Witch's seduction. They keep the rebellious ones locked up in the dungeons and torture them until they bend to their will."

"My God. Evan . . ." I groaned. The thought of Evan being the Witches' slave had seemed unbearable at first, but now it felt like it might drive me insane.

"Don't worry. I don't think he's given in to evil," Simon added, trying to reassure me.

What actually scared me most was the thought of his being tortured. "No, you're right. I saw him," I said, lost in the memory that had suddenly returned to my mind. "I dreamed they were torturing him, but now I know it was actually happening. I have visions, you know."

"Those are your powers starting to manifest," Ginevra said in an attempt to calm me.

"Did it happen to you too?"

"At times, but my transformation happened differently."

"What do you mean?"

"I mean I had already chosen. Maybe this is all partly my fault. I should have prepared you sooner, but I ignored the signs. I was the last Sister to reawaken, but it hasn't been five hundred years yet, so I kept hoping I was wrong, that you weren't really one of us. That first time you met Evan in the woods marked your fate. The closeness with a Subterranean and then with a Witch kindled the nature buried in your soul. Later, the poison you came into contact with when we killed Faustian triggered something inside you. They sensed you. They heard the call of the Sister destined to awaken and the process began sooner than expected—which is exactly what the Màsala wanted to prevent."

"I was having prophetic dreams. They were warnings. I kept seeing Evan's death. It happened that night by the campfire too, remember? The Witches were already inside my head. When Evan entered my dreams they couldn't approach, but whenever he was gone they would find a way in." I suddenly remembered the nightmares I'd had whenever he was away on a mission. "If only I'd suspected he was in danger . . . my God." I buried my face in my hands, mortified.

Ginevra hugged me. "Hey, it's all right. There's no way you could have known. You had already perceived the essence of evil. Smelling the poison awakened your powers, but ingesting it when you kissed Evan sped up the process. That must be why the nightmares became more frequent. The serpent is forming inside you and that's what's causing your high fevers. Whenever the Witches make contact, that part of you reawakens. It's the Bond. When we discovered there was a Subterranean behind your hallucinations, we imagined that was also the cause of your nightmares—at least that's what I hoped. I hoped it with everything I had. Instead you were under two attacks: the Executioner's by day and the Witches' by night."

It was true. At times I'd even been able to feel the difference on my skin, like hot and cold—two obscure forces battling for my soul. The fever would always come after a nightmare or a premonition, but never after one of Desdemona's attacks. "But then I started having the visions even during the day."

"Right. The more you lost hope, the more power the Witches had over you."

I nodded in confirmation. Dropping my head into my hands, I tried to stifle the pain tearing me apart. I couldn't banish the mental image of Evan chained to the wall, bare-chested, his torn jeans streaked with blood as a Witch tried to seduce him only to whip him when he rejected her.

"Don't worry, Gemma. No matter how much they torture him, Subterraneans can't die in Hell, unlike mortal Souls. The only way a Subterranean can truly die is if he fails to eat of the Tree while he's on earth. In that case his soul is lost forever to oblivion."

"You mean they're going to torture him for all eternity?" I cried. Ginevra's attempt to comfort me had had the opposite effect.

Simon came to my rescue, a determined look on his face. "No. We're going to get him out of there, Gemma."

"First of all, I'll teach you how to block your mind," Ginevra said. "It's essential that they not discover your plan to renounce them once you've saved Evan. They have to believe in your sacrifice: your soul in exchange for Evan's. They can't suspect any kind of trick or you won't make it out alive." I nodded. My heart was beating like crazy. I didn't know if it was because of Ginevra's solemn tone or my impatience to see Evan again. "Renouncing evil will be very difficult once it's possessed you. Everything you've been—everything you've believed in—will disappear. The Gemma you've always known will cease to exist. Only your love for Evan will keep you from giving in."

Terror seized my heart. "Do you really think I'll come out of it?"

"I said it would be difficult—not impossible."

Simon rested his hand on my shoulder. "Ginevra and I hadn't known each other very long, but our love was still strong enough to break her bond with the Witches. The feeling you and Evan share was already powerful, and it's had time to grow and strengthen. I'm sure it'll be enough to prevent evil from subjugating you. You can do it. I've always suspected your love for Evan exceeded human boundaries. You have a supernatural soul—that's why you couldn't forget him. Losing him almost drove you insane because your relationship isn't a human one." I nodded, comforted by Simon's words. He smiled at me confidently. "And don't forget you're carrying his child. That's not a negligible detail. Your love for him will bring you back."

I covered my belly with both hands. I would never let anyone take my baby from me. He and Evan were my whole life. I nodded again. My heart trembled from the fierce battle being waged inside it between yearning and fear. The fear that I wasn't as strong as Ginevra, that I wouldn't be able to cast off the evil taking root inside me. That it would grow until it made me its prisoner. Would I be able to eradicate it once I had allowed it to smother me? Once I'd allowed it to *annihilate* me? Would I actually manage to emerge from the darkness?

There was one thing I was certain of: I wasn't going to let fear keep me from trying. I would bury it, crawl over it, choke it, but nothing was going to keep me from seeing Evan again. I would brave Hell and risk my life to bring him back. Even if it meant not coming back with him.

21

TIME PRESERVES ALL SECRETS

I moved slowly, trailing my hand over every object in Ginevra's room as though part of me knew for certain I would never see them again. I wasn't sure how much time had gone by since she'd asked me to wait for her there, but I was bursting with impatience. Until yesterday, the sun's rays had offered no warmth. Everything had lost its appeal. But now my heart had begun to beat again. The world was filled with colors once more because Evan, my Evan, was still alive, and I would soon be with him. For the first time we would all be together: he, I, and our baby.

After discussing it all night long, Simon and Ginevra had convinced me to lie down for a few hours. I was so anxious to see Evan, though, that I hadn't shut my eyes for a minute.

My hand stroked the covers of the books stacked on Ginevra's desk as if that touch were enough to reveal their secrets. The scarlet spine of a particular volume sparked my curiosity. I picked it up and a shiver ran down my spine, almost as if the book had given me an electric shock. I slid my fingers down the blood-red cover, slowly following the impressions of the strange symbols embossed on the leather, as I struggled between the almost irresistible urge to leaf through it and the awareness that I should put it back. As though it had a will of its own, my hand ignored the voice of reason and opened the book, revealing the secrets hidden in its ivory pages.

7 December, 1516

Tonight I dreamed of her again. It is the same woman, I am certain of it, as her image still consumes me now that I am awake.

A shudder ran through me and I flinched. I checked the cover, suddenly unsure whether I'd been the one to write those words, but it was Ginevra's diary. Both fascinated and frightened by the discovery, I let my eyes return impatiently to the page.

I hear voices in my head yet fear to tell a soul, as I know it would be the end of me. I would be burned, like the others. Their screams awakened me at dawn. They burned seven more and I knew one of them well. She was not a witch.

I couldn't stop the tremor that invaded my body. I knew I should stop reading but I couldn't. My eyes flew over the lines, grasping snippets here and there, while my mind, hungry for information, tried to memorize as many details as possible. All at once my hand paused on a page that was a slightly different color, dotted with dark splotches. I knew well what had caused those marks: they were tears.

12 January, 1517

This morning they took her away. Father sought to stop them and was arrested. God protect her, poor little soul. They will kill her. I know they will kill her, just as they killed all the others. Why have they not taken me? My heart is certainly more impure than Jana's. How I wish I were a real witch so I could annihilate them all. My sister is innocent. Her only fault is her love-stricken soul. It was not the Devil that led her out into the night, a captive of her tormented slumber. May my brother be damned for seeing her. I would kill him with my own hands for shouting out and waking the whole village, letting them all see the poor thing fainted away in the underbrush. The Devil had not possessed her—it was her love for Cédric that troubled her in her dreams. If only I had noticed her in time, I would never have let her go outside and her life would be spared. Instead they will torture her, and all that will remain of her body is ash . . .

"My God . . ." I swallowed, deeply shaken by Ginevra's thoughts, preserved on those pages for centuries. Appalled by the cruelty of men, I read on. As I turned the pages, I gradually sensed a new strength resonating between the lines. The words conveyed an energy that hadn't been there before, as if something in Ginevra had profoundly changed.

3 November, 1517

I feel invincible, as though the energy of a star had flowed into me, giving me new life. At first I was no longer sure who I was. Everything around me was unfamiliar, which frightened me somewhat, yet it no longer matters. I feel like a queen on a throne. I can do whatever I wish. I can punish whomever I wish. My dear Anya brought me this diary again that it might help me rediscover myself, yet rereading it has been like reading the accounts of a stranger, full of thoughts that belong to another. I know not the Ginevra Nesea Seraina Moser hidden in those pages, yet I *feel alive as never before.*

Last night I killed him. I killed the man who was once my brother and I claimed his soul, then left him at the mercy of the Insane to fend for himself. It was not difficult to win him over. Besides, no one deserved his fate more than he. I have no memory of his affection, as if we'd never met. Reading of the abominations he forced upon me and my poor sister convinced me it was his rightful place.

The diary slid from my hands and I stared into space, my mind trapped in those memories as if they were my own. My hands shook. I couldn't believe Ginevra was capable of committing such an atrocity. Had she really killed her own brother?

Fear crept into my heart like a woodworm, devouring every certainty. Would I become like that too? Would I really no longer be able to feel affection for my family? My friends? Evan? How could I forget the love that filled my heart for our baby? I couldn't believe evil might annihilate me completely. I would never allow it. I would fight with all my strength to emerge from the darkness and find the light. Ginevra had done it. There were too many things I wasn't willing to give up. I would never let anyone take those things from me, much less myself. Maybe there was a secret hidden somewhere in the pages of that diary that had allowed Ginevra to free herself from evil.

I picked it up from the floor and thumbed through it until my eyes found what they were looking for.

17 May, 1632

Today, for the first time, I hesitated.

I spared a Subterranean. That has never happened before. I must return to him and remedy the error before anyone learns of it. My head is so full of thoughts! Something new is growing inside me. My human side is struggling to re-emerge.

I am beginning to recall fragments of my past. I carefully checked this diary, yet the images I continue to recall are not contained in any of its pages. They are only in my head. Memories I had buried are unexpectedly surfacing, disorienting me. My mother's smile, steam rising from the bowls as we supped together . . . Jana's cheerful laughter.

I can sense it: not long hence I will find myself again.

3 June, 1632

I could not bring myself to do it. He was ready to succumb to me and yet I did not take him. I set his soul free, though he would have offered it to me willingly. It was unlike the other times. There is something in him, something I cannot elude. I seduced him yet wished for him to be free, wished for him to desire me of his own accord. And now I feel it is he who is holding me prisoner. I made love to him. I made love with him. It was as though our bodies became one.

When he asked to see me again I felt something deep in my heart. A quiver. Never before have I desired one of them. Not like this. What the devil is happening to me? I cannot have such feelings for a Son of Eve. I should have killed that soldier, seduced him and torn out his soul to prevent him from becoming a Subterranean. Only then could I have made him mine. Sophìa will punish me even for hesitating. I cannot risk losing her trust in me. Devina would enjoy that. She lies in wait for one false move so she can take my place.

I must come to my senses.

27 June, 1632

I no longer know who I am. I no longer know what is happening to me. Maintaining control over my thoughts is becoming more and more difficult, as I do nothing but think of him: General Adrian Simeone Dahlberg. I have been unable to get him out of my mind and my body burns anew at the thought of his hands on me. Thanks to us Witches, his Swedish troops have occupied Munich. The war is spreading and the Reaping has been more productive than we hoped. Souls spontaneously offer themselves to us on the battlefield, either so their lives will be spared or to ensure victory. The other night Simeone was slain in battle and instead of carrying his soul to Sophìa, I took it to safety. I hid him in a cave in the mountains. Though I know not yet how to have him eat of the Tree, he will be safe there, at least until my thoughts betray me. If anyone discovers him, I will die.

What is happening to me? Something is changing within me, something important, and I know not whether to repress this feeling or nurture it, for I fear the direction in which it is guiding me.

I feel I have betrayed my Sisters. Why did I not claim his soul when the opportunity presented itself? What is different about him? I continue to return to him as though compelled. Why have I allowed him to make love to me again and yet again? Perhaps there is another question I should ask myself instead: why did I make love to him? And most importantly, why was it so passionate, so overwhelming?

Adrian Simeone Dahlberg. There is no way to forget him.

20 January, 1721

The time when I must make a decision draws near, I can feel it. Many years have passed, yet the question still consumes me: how will I be able to eradicate such an important part of me to make room for another—indispensable to me now, a thousand times sweeter? I can no longer keep our secret now that Simeone and I have hidden another Subterranean, Evan. How am I to decide between myself and

"Gemma, what are—"

I snapped the diary shut and looked up to see Ginevra staring at me from the doorway, visibly shocked. "Did you really kill your brother?" I asked before I could stop myself, almost accusingly. I fixed my eyes on her, hoping she would say it wasn't true.

Ginevra hesitated, glancing at the diary, and then seemed to study me. "How did you know that?" she asked cautiously.

I blinked nervously and looked at the diary I'd read without permission, still in my hand. "I'm sorry, Gwen. I knew I shouldn't, but I couldn't resist."

Ginevra strode across the room and snatched the book from my hands. To my surprise, she opened it and held it out in front of my nose. I peered at it, puzzled, and instantly realized the reason for her astonishment. My eyes were immediately drawn to the page, but I couldn't read a single thing on it. It was a jumble of strange symbols.

"How were you able to read what's written there?" she repeated, carefully enunciating every word.

I paled. Not even I knew the answer. "I—I don't know. I have no idea. All I know is—"

"—is that you can," Ginevra finished for me. I couldn't utter a word; my mind seemed suddenly drained. "It's the Witches' ancient secret code," she continued. "To anyone else's eyes it's nothing but an incomprehensible jumble of symbols. For centuries mankind tried to decipher the rare fragments they came across, but without success. Some tried to transcribe a few imprecise snippets, but not even those could be deciphered. Not a trace of this written code survives today—the few examples they had in the past were destroyed. Your powers are getting stronger, Gemma. Your mind is beginning to accept the transformation, granting them access to your body."

Deep in my heart I'd always harbored the suspicion I was a little odd compared to the few girls I was friends with. No, not odd. *Different*. Only now did I understand the reason: the strange power that had started to awaken in me . . . a power that gripped me. *The power of darkness.*

Repressing my fear, I looked up at Ginevra. "Then it's true? You really did kill your brother?" I swallowed, my eyes on hers as I waited for her answer.

She gave it to me without hesitating. "I wasn't myself—I wasn't aware of what I was doing—but yes. I killed him without pity after I'd shown him what a *real* Witch was and what we were capable of. Because that's what Witches do. They have no scruples or human emotions except for the ones that bond them to each other. They're driven solely by the evil that lives within them. That's why I'm begging you to reconsider. Agreeing to become one of them means eradicating every trace of love from your heart."

"Only until you find something that can make it germinate again," I said, resolute.

"It's not easy to free yourself. I should know—I've been there myself. Witches are the essence of evil. They led Eve astray so she would betray her Adam. And who do you think convinced Judas to betray Christ? *I killed my own brother*. Only when my former self began to resurface did I understand the devastation I'd wreaked, but by then it was too late. That's why I started to consider leaving my Sisters and giving up that life when I discovered I loved

Simon. It took almost a century for that to happen. But in doing so I betrayed Sophìa and was sentenced to death."

"How did you m—"

"It's a long story. I'll tell you another time. Right now we need to focus on you."

I saw the pain in her eyes and nodded. "I read about your sister. Your real sister, I mean. I'm so sorry. What they did to her was terrible."

"You have no idea what my little Jana had to endure. In the early 1500s there was mass hysteria over Witches. Many innocent women were accused of serving the devil and killed." Ginevra looked down, devastated by the memory. "My sister did nothing wrong," she said, her voice trembling. "My brother betrayed her innocence by accusing her of witchcraft. The same brother who abused her for years sent her to her death. He might as well have personally lit the fire beneath her stake. Back then all it took was a single accuser for someone to be found guilty."

"They burned her at the stake?" I was horrified.

"Not before they'd subjected her to unbearable torture and humiliation. When they took her away, she was stripped naked. They even shaved her head to look for the devil's mark on her."

My hand automatically covered my belly where the devil's mark had been left on me. From time to time the scar burned; it was my serpent, trying to come out.

Ginevra smiled, amused by my thoughts. "Humans couldn't even recognize the sign of a real Witch. Often a common birthmark or some other mark on the skin, together with another person's testimony, was enough to have someone sentenced to death. My sister, for example, had a mole on her inner thigh. They imprisoned and tortured her to force her into confessing. She suffered the 'witches' chair,' a diabolical chair of red-hot iron on which she was forced to sit completely naked. Her fingernails were torn out along with the little hair left on her head, and in the end they burned her at the stake to grant her 'the salvation of purifying fire.' Such bullshit!"

"Did it ever happen that a real Witch was accused?"

"Only one time. That time gave rise to the first witch-hunt. It happened in 1017, an infamous year in the history of our Sisters. It was a Subterranean, driven by his thirst for revenge, who began the hysteria that killed thousands of people over the course of the following centuries. His name was Gareth. Legend has it the Màsala sent him to kill a girl before she transformed—just like what happened to you—but the Angel took advantage of people's inherent wickedness and amused himself by killing her in front of everyone. He had her burned in the public square after accusing her of serving the devil and showing them her distinguishing mark. From that time on, humans became hell-bent on exterminating women with suspicious marks."

"How horrible!" I couldn't believe a Subterranean could outdo a Witch in terms of cruelty.

"As I said, he was looking for revenge. It seems that when they were both still human they were married and she was unfaithful to him. Maybe that was why he stripped her naked and humiliated her like that before burning her. But the real hysteria broke out centuries later. In spite of the Subterranean's actions, the Màsala didn't punish him, since he'd done his duty, but he was relieved of all assignments and forced to hide in Eden to escape Sophìa's wrath.

"Five hundred years later Gareth began to thirst for revenge again. He was afraid his wife's spirit might return in the body of another woman, so he returned to Earth on his own and incited men to resume the hunt. Eventually it reached the village in Switzerland where I lived. After all those centuries of isolation with no purpose, with only his tormenting thoughts for company, Gareth had lost his mind. He wanted to find the next chosen one before she transformed so he could kill her like he'd killed his wife, with purifying fire. Word traveled quickly and panic spread. But this time Sophìa found him in time and killed him. She couldn't let it happen again.

"Meanwhile the hunt had taken on a life of its own, costing thousands of people their lives and—to Sophìa's delight—turning Soul after Soul to evil. As you see, I lived in times that were far more difficult and brutal than yours. Unlike you, I hadn't had any contact with the poison before my transformation, but the evil around me was enough to awaken what lurked inside me. You have no idea of the atrocities that were committed in my village. Evil spawns evil. When you've undergone more than your heart can bear, there's not much room left for love and you end up allowing yourself to be subjugated. That's why I was happy to transform. Back then all I wanted was revenge—revenge for my sister, revenge against the world. Jana wasn't a Witch and yet she was slain for being one. The day they killed her everything that was human in my heart vanished along with her, destroyed by my hatred for those heartless men. No one deserved to live more than Jana. She was so sweet and helpful to everyone. I had the opportunity to exact justice. All I had to do was make a decision: to hate mankind. It was a decision I'd already made in my heart. At that time, though, I couldn't have imagined to what lengths I would go. Hatred fed off me and I off it, day after day. I wasn't myself any more. I lost control over my mind. I didn't realize it until I met Simon. Back then he had such a funny, pompous name!" Ginevra smiled. "He reawakened the part of me that had been trapped deep in my heart for centuries, buried under evil—my humanity. It took some time, but fortunately in the end I realized life wasn't worth living without love and I made a different choice—the right one." She gazed at me as I silently absorbed every detail of the new world that awaited me. "And don't worry, you will too."

I nodded to convince myself and took a last look at the pages of her diary, noticing a symbol that appeared more frequently than the others. It piqued my curiosity. Ginevra read the question in my mind. "That's the symbol of the Subterraneans," she explained.

I ran my fingers over the strange, twisted X, fascinated by its lines, elegant yet foreboding. As I put the diary down, I wondered why the pages showed no signs of aging. "How have you kept it so well preserved over the centuries?" I asked, still trying to regain my self-possession. It seemed like the words had always been there.

"I put a spell on it so it would withstand the effects of time. It was my sweet Sister Anya who brought it back to me to remind me of who I was. That's why I gave you one when I guessed what was happening to you—though I was still hoping I was wrong about it." She disappeared into her walk-in closet, re-entering the room a moment later with an old trunk, her eyes locked on mine.

"What's in there?"

A new and tender smile lit up her eyes.

22

SURVIVAL LESSONS

"Gwen, what's inside it?" I repeated. Ginevra seemed lost in another world, gazing at the old trunk as though it contained a rare treasure. She set it on the bed and waved her hand over its ancient lock, which opened by magic.

She gently raised its lid and I leaned over, wondering what secrets it contained, then looked at her in surprise. She smiled. "In here you'll find everything you need."

I looked at her, mystified, then studied the objects carefully tucked away inside the trunk. "A dress? Why would I need a dress?"

Ginevra lifted the threadbare gown out and held it in her hands like the most precious of objects. "This isn't just any dress. It's mine. It's the dress I wore when I escaped from Hell. Witches are very particular about their outfits. They often dye their hair too: pink with black streaks; violet with purple streaks; black and red; navy blue and powder blue—sometimes even three or four colors together. Mortal women spend time painting their nails; Witches pay the same attention to their hair color. They have a different outfit for each particular event or time of day: hunts, ceremonies, games, the Opalion. Most of them are made of some kind of leather, even the weirdest kinds, but they're all very sexy. This, on the other hand, was my first normal dress—a sort of first step toward my new life together with Simon. It's also what I'd been wearing when I transformed. When I was still with my Sisters but had begun to remember my past, I liked to put it on from time to time. My mother made it for me for my twenty-fourth birthday. I was engaged at the time, but then Jana was killed, I transformed, and everything changed. Sorry, it's a bit threadbare; it was prettier before. When I was expelled from Hell and deprived of my powers, it got a little worn."

"Do I really have to wear it? Can't I go dressed like this?" I asked, horrified by the thought of walking around in a dress from the sixteenth century.

"Sure you can, but they'll kill you right away. You need to go as unnoticed as possible. Modern clothing will give you away—it will let the Damned know you've just arrived, a lost Soul whose last remaining shreds of life are there to be sucked clean. You need to blend in, Gemma, and not attract attention. In this old dress, at first glance you'll look like you've been there for centuries. As long as you keep your distance from the other Souls, that is. The longer a Soul has been in Hell, the more the others fear it because it's managed to survive. On top of that, the Damned don't like old flesh."

"But if this dress means so much to you, can't you use magic to make me a new one?"

"This one already has the odor of Hell on it. It'll help cover up your own scent a little, in case they get near you. New Souls are already a delicacy, but you're still *alive*, Gemma. You have no idea what that means. You're fresh meat, and the blood flowing through your veins will be irresistible to them. Oh God—" Ginevra ran a hand over her face, looking horrified. "This is crazy. It's a suicide mission! Why did I agree to help you?!"

"Gwen, listen to me: I don't care how dangerous it is! You'll never talk me out of it, not now that I'm so close to finding Evan."

"But it's insane! They'll smell you and hunt you down!"

"I don't care."

"Hell is a madhouse full of deadly traps and ferocious animals. Even if you manage to go unnoticed among the Damned, you'll never be able to hide from the Molock if you encounter any."

"Molock? Who—"

"They're creatures spawned from Hell. Half man, half beast. Extremely dangerous, bloodthirsty creatures. They'll smell your blood from miles away. And they aren't the only terrifying creatures down there, believe me! Think about this very carefully, Gemma. Once you're in Hell, there will be no turning back. Are you absolutely sure you want to do this? Even if you save Evan, once you transform, that will be your world."

"I'm not going to let Evan pay the price. Everything that happened was my fault."

Ginevra was silenced as much by the determination in my thoughts as in my eyes. "All right, then." She sighed, placed her hand on my belly, and closed her eyes.

"What are you doing?"

"Casting a spell on the baby. Until it's broken, he'll remain in a deep sleep. This way he won't be able to sense your emotions. If you're afraid, he won't know it. If you're anxious, he'll sleep peacefully. This way your pregnancy won't be an extra concern for you when you enter the Copse. Whatever happens, my magic will protect him. But listen carefully, Gemma: not even my spell will be able to save him if you get yourself killed." I nodded, grateful for the unexpected gift. It would be unbearable if he were hurt. I would never let that happen.

"Prepare yourself, because you're going to feel like you're inside your worst nightmare ever. Forget all those fairy tales you've heard about monsters. Everything you're going to encounter will be far worse."

"Well, after all, it *is* Hell. It's not like I can expect songbirds and rainbows."

"No, Gemma. You mustn't have *any* expectations; they will inevitably fall far short of the truth. Remember: never be fooled by appearances and never let your guard down. Here, take this."

I looked at the small, dark instrument in her hands. It appeared to be a sort of whistle, made of a strange alloy—black stone or metal, I couldn't tell—with a deep groove all around it. "What is it?" I asked.

"It's called a Phœbus. If you need help, use it and help will come. But be careful because it's risky. It's better to forget you even have it. Only use it if your life is in imminent danger. Do you understand, Gemma? Only use it if you really need to escape, and fast. Otherwise you risk drawing too much attention to yourself."

I took it and studied it for a few seconds. Ginevra handed me a small leather shoulder bag. "Put it in this satchel. We'll fill it with everything you need: food, water, and—most importantly—this."

My eyes were drawn to the strange amulet Ginevra was holding up, a stone coiled around itself like a serpent. I had the feeling I'd seen it somewhere before. "What's it for?"

"It's a key. You'll need it in order to come back. If you've already transformed you won't need it for yourself, but you'll still need it to let Evan through. There's no other way he can leave Hell. The portal only opens for Witches or those who have a key. Otherwise all the Subterraneans would try to escape." Ginevra gripped the amulet, concerned. "Come to think of it, you'd better wear it around your neck. It'll be safer there. You can't risk losing it. Listen to me carefully, Gemma: this is your ticket home. Lose it and both of you are done for." She had me put the amulet on, then looked down, her gaze unfocused. "I keep hoping you'll find a way to get out of there without sacrificing yourself to evil."

"Don't worry, Gwen. I won't let the Witches get the better of me. Even if I agree to transform, my love for Evan will prevent evil from possessing me. I won't leave him once I find him again—not if it depends on me. The only thing in life we can control is ourselves."

"I wish I were as confident as you."

I smiled. To me her words were comical. "Since the moment I met you, that's all I've thought about *you*."

"Don't be ridiculous, Gemma. You have a strength few people have. You've grown so much since we first met and your courage and determination have grown with you." Hearing this from Ginevra of all people sent a shiver of emotion through me. "Speaking of courage, you'll need this too."

Another shiver—more hostile and foreboding this time—replaced the first one. "A dagger? What will I do with that?"

"Defend yourself, if necessary."

I took it from her and examined its leather sheath. It looked so small . . . yet I'd learned that power and strength didn't depend on size. I slid it out for just a second. Its blade was black, of the same material as the whistle, while its grip was spiraled like a snake.

"Tie it to your arm or your calf, if you prefer, so it stays hidden under your dress."

"My arm. I'd rather it be around my arm," I was quick to say, praying I wouldn't need to use it.

"Aim for this spot here." Ginevra rested two fingers just below my ear where the blood pulsed through my carotid artery. "It's a small blade, but if you slip it in right there, your enemy will dissolve in a matter of seconds. Speaking of which, I advise you not to breathe in the ashes—they're toxic. Naturally that doesn't go for Molock or other Hell-born creatures. There's only one way to kill them, and that's with a direct blow to the maseolum, in the center of the chest. It's like an elongated root or a beating heart. I doubt you would even be able to get that close to one of them without it devouring you."

"What will happen if I don't stab one of the Damned in just the right spot?"

"You can wound him wherever you like—chop off a leg, an arm—but he'll recompose unless you lop his head off. Or decide to make a fire and eat him."

"Huh?"

"Don't worry—just kidding. Only the Lucid cook the Damned before eating them, and you definitely aren't one of them," she joked.

"What do you mean?"

"That you're already out of your mind, naturally. With the exception of Lucid Souls, everyone else prefers raw meat."

I pressed the back of my hand to my mouth, fighting a wave of nausea. "What are Lucid Souls? And what do you mean 'everyone else'? Is there a difference?"

"I told you, there are many dangerous creatures in Hell. There are lots of sins, and even more kinds of sinners. I couldn't name them all even if I wanted to. The enormous variety of transgressions leads to the formation of new species of Damned Souls. As if that weren't enough, many of them mutate and evolve over time. Quickly, if they have to. Usually, Souls tend to band together according to their natures. It's a sort of selection process based on 'species' or, if you prefer, on how serious the wrongs they committed during their lifetimes were. But each species has various subspecies. It's been that way since time immemorial. It's a nightmarish jungle teeming with danger. A damned place."

"Yeah—okay, okay, I get it. Keep going," I said, recognizing her millionth attempt to talk me out of it.

"All I'm saying is you shouldn't expect to find the souls of the Damned safely behind bars enduring whatever form of torture corresponds to their sins—you can run into them at any moment. In fact, it's bound to happen. They aren't immortal spirits or even dead bodies. They need to eat, but even more important, they need to avoid ending up as someone else's meal. That's their punishment: the constant struggle for survival. Some sinners have additional punishments as well. Egotists, for example, are forced to offer themselves to others as food, suffering the terrible torture of seeing parts of their bodies removed and devoured. The Damned often hunt them down, but the slyest Souls keep one hidden for times when food is scarce. Then there are the Lechers, who in life succumbed to the pleasures of the flesh. They're forced to offer their own flesh in exchange for pleasure."

"That's disgusting," I gasped, horrified by her words.

"That's Hell." The look on Ginevra's face was one of utter revulsion.

"Hold on a second. Egotists? They go to Hell too? Who hasn't been egotistical at least once in their life?"

"You're right, but that isn't the point. It's how far they were willing to go and what they were prepared to sacrifice in their own interests. What counts isn't so much the crime itself as the motivation that drove the Soul to commit it. Take Murderers, for instance. Murderers of the highest order don't need to be persuaded to take someone's life—they have death in their blood already and kill of their own free will. When they die, all the Witches have to do is collect their souls. They're the most dangerous ones, and the most ruthless among them are often chosen for the Circle. However, many other Souls are in Hell because they took a life not of their own free will but by allowing themselves to be seduced by the Witches. They're Murderers too, but that's not all they are. Souls are classified according to the intention that drove them to act. Someone who takes another person's life to save his own will be punished as an Egotist. The same thing goes for many other species. A person who runs away, for example, causing someone else's death as a result, is classified as a Coward. According to this system of classification, a group of Souls condemned to the same punishment may have committed completely different crimes. What counts is how they chose to behave when they were tempted. If someone is egotistical, sooner or later that will lead them to make a decision that hurts others. The Witches wait for this moment. They know which strings to pluck to bring evil out in people."

"So a sin isn't defined by the act itself, but by the emotion that motivates you to commit it, like tarnish on the soul."

"Exactly. It's emotions that rule over all else. Witches leverage them to turn a Soul to evil. They feed off people's weaknesses—wrath, pride, envy, avarice; also guilt, shame, and so on. The human soul can nurture an endless range of dark emotions, and the Witches understand their every nuance. They're enchantresses and weavers of illusion."

"Practically an infinite classification."

"More or less. It's Sophìa who sorts through the Souls from the Reaping. No pastime could be more gratifying to her. I've been there many times while she was doing it. I learned that there are three overarching Echelons. Those who have evil in their blood to begin with belong to the first one, the 'Great Echelon.' She considers them purebreds, Souls who don't need the influence of evil to do wrong. All the groups include purebreds. They're the most ferocious, most feared of all. Souls who give in to evil under the Witches' influence fall into the second Echelon. You can find every species in the first and second Echelons. In the third you'll find only the souls of the Corrupt—the ones who sold themselves to the Witches in exchange for personal gain. Even though most of them didn't commit other evil acts during their mortal lives, in Hell they have to fight for survival just like everyone else.

"As I said before, some species tend to seek each other out. There's a secret shared by the Damned: 'Better to know the color of the soul than the shape of the body.' It doesn't matter what action someone might take—what counts is the intention driving that action. By focusing directly on that, Souls know exactly what to expect from those around them. They often gather in villages, while others prefer to remain hidden, far from their enemies. Then there are the

Insane—those who've lost every trace of their humanity. They wander aimlessly in search of food, guided entirely by their instincts."

"Wait, back up. There are villages?"

"Lots of them. Usually they're made up of the Sane, shrewd Souls who still possess a glimmer of reason and attempt to preserve some semblance of civilization. Every Soul—regardless of species or Echelon—is in imminent danger of being overtaken by madness and losing what's left of his humanity. Basically, Souls can either maintain their sanity . . . or go insane. Some of them are in between. Generally, the Souls who during their lifetimes weren't completely consecrated to evil, those who committed lesser crimes, tend to have a better chance of keeping their sanity. Consequently, the Sane, for the most part, fall into the Corrupt category. But listen carefully to what I'm about to tell you: whether they're murderers or people who succumbed to evil as a means of achieving their goals, they all need to eat in order to survive—and there are no candy bars in Hell, if you get what I mean. You can't trust anyone."

I nodded, disconcerted.

"If they're unable to kill others, Souls are forced to do things to survive like feed off themselves. Eating parts of their own bodies causes them atrocious suffering, and when those parts grow back it's unimaginably painful. When they first arrive in Hell, all Souls are still partly human, though deprived of free will, but the more they feed on others, the more they lose their humanity. They gradually turn into the Insane. Zombies, Gemma, slaves to themselves and the evil that led them to that Godforsaken realm in the first place.

"In spite of all this, there *is* another species of Sane Souls that's purer: the Lucid. They're Souls that haven't let themselves be taken over by demonic influences. They aren't immune to evil, of course, but they struggle every day not only with the other Damned but also with themselves, because they refuse to succumb to evil. Their will is stronger. They grow vegetables, hunt game, but most of them don't last long. That's why there are so few of them."

A ray of hope touched my heart. "They're like humans, then."

"In a certain sense. There may also be Souls from the second Echelon among the Lucid, but for the most part they fall into the Corrupt category. As I told you, few of them last long."

"How can I find them?"

"Don't get your hopes up. Hell isn't a place to go looking for solidarity. No one trusts anyone—the Lucid even less than the others. Generally, they're solitary Souls who live in hiding. Even if you ran into one you certainly couldn't consider yourself lucky. In the end they're just like all the other Damned: ready and willing to kill."

What Ginevra said next caught my attention: "Subterraneans are the least dangerous because they don't need to eat. On Earth they served Death because of the curse on them, but in Hell they have no connection to evil. They preserve their identities, though many of them choose to suppress them in order to serve the Witches. They aren't wicked, but Witches' blood is such a powerful drug it reduces them to puppets at the mercy of their desires. The more Witch blood they consume, the harder it is for them to go without it and the deeper they sink into slavery. Some Subterraneans take refuge in the villages."

My heart leapt. "You mean Evan might be in one of them?"

"No, Gemma. With rare exceptions, they're ones the Witches have already tired of. They claim so many of them that a single escaped slave doesn't raise much interest. Don't delude yourself, Gemma. I doubt they would let Evan go that easily. I'm almost positive he's being kept inside the Castle under strict surveillance—maybe by Devina herself. They weren't born yesterday: they want you, and Evan is their bargaining chip. He's not just another Subterranean, he's the key to getting you. The other Executioners are used as slaves at the Castle, tortured and drugged so they'll satisfy the Witches' every whim, including sexually, and most Subterraneans are willing to do anything in order to have their blood. The poison stupefies them, but a few drops of Witches' blood sends them into ecstasies when ingested in proximity to the power the Sisters emanate. It's a rare commodity and many Subterraneans feel fortunate to serve them if it means they can suck a little of it like filthy vampires."

"Evan would never give in to them," I said, trying hard to convince myself. "You're right, chances are he's at the Castle. I saw it in one of my nightmares. You just need to explain how to get there."

"If all goes well, you should reach the Castle after a couple hours of walking. You probably won't even need food. All you have to do is follow the river downstream. It leads to the moat around the Castle. But be careful—it may not be that simple. Hell changes constantly. It's a crazy place, and if I know the Witches, any one of them might try to stand in your way."

"But why? I don't understand."

"That's because you don't know Devina. You need to watch out for her. She's eccentric and unpredictable. When I was one of them she harbored a deep hatred for me."

"How is that possible? Aren't all the Sisters connected by a powerful bond?"

"Evil corrodes all bonds, even the strongest ones. Also, envy is a difficult beast to tame. Devina is especially evil. She was the first Witch. That made her extra close to Sophìa and less so to the others. She's blinded by jealousy. Evil is inside us, Gemma, but not all Witches know how to handle it. She wanted to be the Empress's favorite and claim special rights, but Sophìa had a weakness for me that drove Devina crazy. Sophìa waited a thousand years for me to arrive, since the Witch who was supposed to awaken before me was killed before she transformed. It was the first time in the history of the Sisterhood that something like that had happened. I filled a void, which made me special in Sophìa's eyes. I was her Specter, which is like a second-in-command. That was why Devina enjoyed screwing things up for me. She was the one who exposed my betrayal. I'm sure she took my place once I left, and I have no doubt that if you transform she'll hate you too, no matter what you do, because you'll fill the void I left behind. The Bond is a gift God granted Sophìa after her exile, and it's the most powerful thing in the universe, second only to true love. Yet Devina is different from all the other Witches in history. The Bond doesn't seem to have the same effect on her. She can't control her deceitfulness even when it comes to Sophìa. She's completely blinded by her own hunger for omnipotence, kind of like Sophìa was towards God. Even though the Bond among Sisters is strong, the most powerful connections of all—which can't be eradicated from the heart of any Witch—are the ones with Sophìa and our own Dakor, since they're born of our essence. At the other end of the spectrum, there are Witches like Anya. She was the best of my Sisters."

"Anya. The name sounds familiar."

"I'm not surprised. I'm sure she's the Witch who visited you in your dreams."

"She must have been the one who called you Gwen," I said, remembering her words the first time I'd called her by that name.

Ginevra nodded. "There are days when I still miss her. She was a trusted friend and a loyal Sister. In any case, you don't have to worry. No matter how many obstacles you encounter, the Castle will show itself to you. Whatever happens, just keep following the river. As I said, Hell is an unstable place. It's crazy; it defies all logic. You might think you've reached the Castle only to see it vanish before your eyes. The landscape changes so suddenly it'll make you feel like you've lost your mind. As you make your way through the forest, the paths may become shorter or longer, but they'll inevitably lead you to her, to Sophìa, the High Empress."

"The devil," I corrected her.

Ginevra smiled. "Exactly. The important thing is never to lose sight of the river. I'm sure Sophìa is waiting for you."

I nodded and she bit her lip. "Once you and Evan are out of the Castle, you'll need to retrace your steps along the river until you reach the summit of Mount Nhubii. It stands above the tallest waterfall. Many call it Hell's Crown because its jagged peaks rise into the sky in a ring, like a barrier protecting what's hidden within it. You'll only have your own strength to rely on. Evan's powers will already be sapped since he hasn't eaten of the Tree for so long."

"Can't I take food with me for him?"

"No, Gemma, you can't. Ambrosia can't leave Eden. Simon will take care of that once you've both returned."

"You didn't say 'if.' That's comforting."

"Now you need to focus. There's a level area on the summit. There you'll find a circle of standing rocks with another circle inside it. We call it the Dánava. It's a passageway between dimensions. Long ago men on Earth, enchanted by the Witches who were toying with them, built a crude imitation of it, but obviously it never worked. What remains today is what humans call Stonehenge. Mankind has never learned what its true purpose was. In any case, you and Evan need to reach the center of the Dánava. Then it will be time for you to use the key, the Dreide. Don't worry, it will show you the way."

I nodded, overwhelmed by all the information. "Okay. River. Mountain. Key. I can do it."

"Whenever we make a decision it's a sort of bet between ourselves and the world. Winning and losing are two sides of the same coin. When it's tossed into the air, it's not only chance that decides whether it turns up heads or tails—the result also depends on the hand that flips it and on how hard it's flipped."

"I'm all in."

"I realize that. That's why I know you'll come back to me. You *have to*, Gemma. I'm counting on you. *Come back to me*. I don't want to lose you and the baby."

I hugged her. Ginevra snapped the hair tie that had fallen from my upper arm to my forearm. "*This* should have made me realize it."

"What does that have to do with anything? I've always worn it, even when I was a little girl."

"Exactly. I bet it makes you feel secure and you miss it when it's not on you. Every Witch wears her Dakor around her arm. That's the point of contact where the serpents prefer to merge with us. They say that when God cast the serpent into Hell for corrupting Eve, it bit Sophìa's wrist, crept inside her and took her soul. From that point on she was bound to her serpent for life. If you kill a Dakor, his Witch dies too. You've always worn a hair tie where your deepest essence says your Dakor should be. Though you didn't know it, your soul instinctively felt its absence. Like nostalgia."

"How can you be nostalgic for something you've never known?"

"Because your Dakor is inside you."

I wasn't sure whether the idea fascinated or frightened me. I'd seen Ginevra's serpent merge with her after coiling around her forearm. The thought that it would happen to me too was mind-boggling.

"I wish I could help you more."

"You've already done so much, Gwen. Now you just have to tell me where the entrance to Hell is."

Ginevra sighed as though she'd deliberately saved that detail for last, still hoping to change my mind, then gave in to the inevitable. "There's only one way in: the gateway that remained open when God banished his wife: Hell's Mouth, in the Yucatán."

"In the Yucatán? We have to go to Mexico?"

"Men have always searched for a passageway to the underworld. The Maya came close. There was a time long ago when some Witches had fun toying with men by showing themselves to certain tribes and revealing secrets unknown to the world, for the sheer joy of being worshipped as goddesses. They would grant men's wishes in exchange for their souls. The people didn't realize they were making a pact with the devil, just like people today who are drawn in by their empty promises. Sex, money, power—in exchange for what? A gratifying yet fleeting existence on Earth only to become slaves to their own hunger and that of others. Many sacrificed other Souls in addition to their own, so women and children were thrown alive into cenotes as offerings to the 'goddesses.'"

"How horrible!"

"Beliefs make the world go round. They're mankind's most dangerous weapon. Many of those peoples' prophecies and dogmas derived from the Witches, or at least from their interpretation of the Witches' promises. They took advantage of the people's ignorance, threatening to destroy the world. So the Maya built an important ceremonial complex named—and not by chance—Chichen Itzá. It literally means 'at the mouth of the well of the water enchantresses.' It was called that because they were on the other side of the well. Even today, there are winding tunnels and hidden passageways leading to underground temples beneath the complex. There, in the throne room, the Witches would show themselves to the Mayans to amuse themselves. Later, the Temple of Kukulkan was built in the center of the ruins, atop an earlier temple. It's a pyramid with stairs going up all four sides. During the spring and fall equinoxes, at sunrise and sunset—when the Witches would show themselves—the edges of the steps cast a snake-shaped shadow that appears to slither along the northern stairway. The pyramid was designed this way as a sign of respect for the Witches and to honor their Dakor. For the Maya, the universe was divided into three parts: the underworld, the earth and the heavens. For centuries they tried to find a way into the other worlds, searching for passageways in the cenotes and building temples over them. But no one ever discovered the location of the only way into Hell: a cenote hidden in the earth that no one has ever seen."

"Ready, ladies?" Totally fascinated by Ginevra's explanation, I hadn't noticed Simon standing in the doorway.

"Impatient, actually. 'Ready' is a big word. I don't think I ever will be."

Simon smiled, but only to ease the tension. "I'll wait for you downstairs."

"You don't need to come with us," Ginevra was quick to say.

"Why shouldn't I? This is as important to me as it is to you two," he said.

"It would be a lot wiser for you to stay here and keep watch on the Subterranean."

"I can go with you and come back to check on her whenever I want."

"We can't risk it, Simon!" Ginevra seemed anxious to do everything she could to keep Simon away from the Witches. To protect him, just like I would have done with Evan. She opened a drawer and took something out. "Here. You might need this."

Simon stared at the syringe she had handed him and smiled teasingly.

"Hey, watch it, I'm reading your mind. Don't try to have fun all alone. It wouldn't work anyway."

"I'm sure it wouldn't, *chérie*. It wouldn't be the same without you." Simon looked seductively into his girlfriend's eyes and stifled a smile as I wondered what was going on between them. Actually, I wasn't sure I really wanted to know. It was a good thing my mindreading powers weren't fully developed yet, since the erotic charge their bodies emitted was already enough to unsettle me. They looked like they were constantly on the verge of pouncing on each other.

"Um, guys? I'm right here!" I warned before the fire in their eyes could set the room ablaze.

"Agreed, then." Simon's eyes were locked on Ginevra's. "I'll wait for you here." It probably eased his mind to know that Ginevra would be far from Desdemona, since she was just as great a danger to her as the Witches were to him. He hugged me and I could feel his tensed muscles and his disheveled blond hair tickling my skin. "Come back soon."

I nodded as my heart began to race, though I didn't know if it was from excitement or fear. Probably both—that's what Evan would often say.

"Now what? How does it work?" I asked Ginevra, not knowing how she might use her powers to take us to Yucatán. The two of them exchanged an amused glance as I waited for an answer. "Well? Do we teleport ourselves there?"

23

FLASHBACK

"The airport?! We're at the airport?"

Ginevra hid a grin. "Were you expecting something more biblical? Your body hasn't transformed yet. You can't use teleportation."

"Great! Right when my transformation could come in handy. But nooo—my powers have to manifest only as premonitions, terrifying nightmares, and sinister apparitions."

"Calm down and enjoy your humanity while you still can."

I sighed and got out of the car as Ginevra handed me a backpack containing the satchel with my supplies and her dress that I would put on once we reached Yucatán. If I'd known we'd be flying somewhere on a plane, I would have brought along the flight voucher my parents had given me, though I strongly doubted Ginevra would have let me use it.

The wind howled outside as Ginevra and I waited patiently in the check-in line. On the other side of the large windows was a row of planes lined up on the tarmac like soldiers at the mercy of the storm. I couldn't believe I would soon see Evan again. Tears threatened to suffocate me at the thought, though they were sweeter than the bitter pain that had been slowly sucking the life out of me until just days before. "If this keeps up, I'm afraid they'll cancel all the flights," I said, worried, staring out at the storm that raged with growing intensity.

"Don't worry, it won't stop us. Look, there's our plane." Ginevra pointed at a large Boeing outside with mobile stairs being pushed up to it. They had just sprayed something on its wings, and Ginevra explained that it was a de-icing procedure.

All at once I noticed something unusual. Outside, right on the runway, men I hadn't seen a second ago had suddenly appeared, seemingly out of nowhere. They were scattered everywhere. One of them near the window turned toward me, almost as though I'd called to him, and his piercing gray eyes probed my soul.

He was a Subterranean.

"What do you th—Gwen!" I shouted suddenly.

In an instant the waiting area filled with screams. A plane in the process of landing had lost control and was racing toward us at top speed. Someone screamed that it was a terrorist attack and panic exploded in the terminal. Ginevra grabbed my hand and pulled me out of the way of the horde of hysterical people as the plane crashed through the parked aircrafts, mowing them down like soldiers felled by the enemy.

"Gwen!" I shouted again as the mob crushed me. A paralyzing pain burst in my temples as the crowd shoved me every which way, leaving me breathless. The shrill noise of a thousand voices poured into my head and I felt as helpless as a mollusk being dragged away by the current in a river full of fish.

"Don't let go of my hand, Gemma!" Ginevra called. But the pain made me double over and clap my hands over my ears in an attempt to block out the noise piercing my temples. Even the deafening crash of shattered glass when all the windows throughout the airport exploded couldn't block it out. I thought I was going insane.

"It's your powers, Gemma! You're hearing their minds," Ginevra explained, fighting her way into my thoughts. "Look at me. Isolate my voice. Cling to the sound of my voice and shut everything else out." Her instructions slowly helped me breathe again and I managed to look up at her. She gave me a sideways hug.

"What happened?" In shock, I watched the crowd scatter in all directions.

"I'm sorry, their panic triggered it. Fear is the strongest summons for a Witch because mortals are willing to do anything when they fear for their lives—even sell their souls. I'll teach you to block your mind, but right now we have to get out of here. The planes are all damaged. It was the Màsala, I'm sure of it. Come with me." She grabbed my hand and pulled me through the mass of people heading in the opposite direction. A policeman came toward us and barred our way. It seemed no one was allowed to leave the airport, but Ginevra didn't look the least bit intimidated.

"We need a plane. *Now*," she said to him.

"Follow me." With just one glance from her, the policemen blocking the exits stepped out of our way and escorted us onto the tarmac.

Like a bird huddled in the cold, a private jet hid in a corner, its wings covered with snow. A man came toward us, bracing himself against the wind. I thought he meant to stop us, since the storm had gotten worse, but Ginevra squeezed my hand reassuringly and walked up to him. Obeying the power of her eyes, he gestured for us to climb aboard and took his place in the cockpit.

I buried my face in my hands. "What the hell is going on?" I was terrified. It had all happened so fast I was still reeling.

"I thought at least this part of the journey would be easy, but I guess not. They tried to stop us and I'm sure they'll try again."

I leaned back in my seat, staring out at the lines racing by on the runway. The jet nosed up and took off. "Are they dead? All those people on that plane, are they dead?" I asked, begging for her to say no. Amid the general chaos I hadn't had the courage to look at what had happened after impact. Not to mention that I'd been the one who'd made all the windows in the airport explode. And then the Subterraneans! There were dozens of them. I'd seen them on the runway a moment before the plane crashed.

"I don't want to lie to you. Help arrived in time for some of them, but many didn't make it. Hey—" Ginevra moved my hands away from my face and looked me in the eye. "It wasn't your fault."

"How can you say that? It was! Come on, Gwen, everything keeps happening because of me. Sometimes I think it would be better if I were dead." My words trailed off. "It's just—I don't want to die before seeing Evan again," I admitted wearily.

"Don't talk like that, Gemma. Don't give up now that you're so close to finding him. The Màsala might try to get in our way, but they can't stop us. Those people's fates were already written."

I nodded, but before I could reply a sudden drop in altitude made me swallow my words. Clinging to my seat, I looked at Ginevra, but the pilot quickly reassured us by saying that the bad weather would be causing a little turbulence, that was all.

"Try to get some rest now," Ginevra suggested with concern. "It'll take us at least eight hours to get to Yucatán. The bad weather will soon be behind us and the flight will be smoother. Take advantage of it to sleep for a while. You'll need all your strength for what you'll be facing."

I nodded as my eyelids closed obediently.

From time to time my active mind unsettled my body and I woke with a start, wondering where I was, but Ginevra smiled at me from her seat and I returned to oblivion, wandering between wakefulness and slumber.

"Simon!" Ginevra's alarmed voice abruptly woke me. I had no idea how much time had passed since I'd dozed off.

"What's wrong!?" I bolted upright, trying to overcome my grogginess.

Ginevra looked at me gravely. "Desdemona. She managed to break free before he entered her cell. The effect of my blood must have partially worn off, allowing her to regain some strength, but not enough to disappear. She waited for Simon to arrive, surprised him from behind, and escaped."

"What happened to the syringe with your blood? Simon didn't manage to administer it to her in time?"

"No, she caught him off guard. She was faster and injected it into Simon."

A moan escaped me. "Don't worry, he'll be fine." Ginevra smiled mischievously. "It's no big deal. Simon is accustomed to the power of my blood. Intimate relations between a Subterranean and a Witch can be rather . . . unorthodox."

"Okay, spare me the details."

"If you insist. Anyway, if I'm not around he'll just have a nice long sleep."

"So you can hear him even from this far away?"

"Our bond is very strong."

"And how do you plan to—Gwen!" I grabbed hold of my seat just in time as the plane shuddered violently. An entire flock of large birds had just crashed into us.

Ginevra disappeared suddenly and was back in a fraction of a second. "Damn it!" she exclaimed, then grumbled something in a language I didn't understand. I was sure she was swearing. "They're giving us a run for our money. The pilot's gone."

"Gone?!" I jumped to my feet. "What do you mean *gone*?"

"I mean dead, Gemma. And unless you know how to fly an airplane, I'll have to take over the controls."

"Unless someone stops you."

I cringed, my blood running cold at the sound of the familiar voice. My eyes bulged as the blond Angel materialized behind Ginevra. "Gwen, look out!"

Desdemona hurled a fireball and I ducked, but Ginevra dodged it and cast a lightning bolt that smashed through one of the windows. The wind howled through the gaping hole it left in the side of the jet and we quickly lost altitude. Panic threatened to overwhelm me as Desna and Ginevra battled furiously between the seats. The Subterranean shot another fireball at Ginevra but she generated a shield around her body. Though the fire didn't burn her, the impetus pushed her farther and farther back toward the hole.

I let out a wail of terror when I saw treetops through the windows. On the verge of hysteria, I had a sudden thought. Clinging to whatever I could, I grappled my way to Ginevra's backpack and rummaged through it with trembling hands while behind me raged a ferocious battle in which I would be the victor's prize. Finally my hand closed around cold metal and my index finger quickly found the trigger. Before the Angel could stop me, I raised the gun, took aim and fired. Desdemona's back jerked. Ginevra gaped at me over her shoulder as the gun with the poisoned ammunition slid from my hands. A spasm gripped the Angel. Ginevra pivoted and with one finger pushed her through the hole in the side of the plane. "Bye-bye, blondie. It's a real shame I'm not in Hell any more. It would have been fun to play with you."

Desna dematerialized and vanished before hitting the ground. Ginevra rushed to me and swept me up in a hug. I was still shaking. "You saved me! You were fantastic, Gemma."

"Okay, but now would be a great time to repay the favor—in case you forgot, we're about to crash!"

Ginevra smiled. "Don't worry. We're not going to crash." She leaned out through the hole and the massive air current hit her, whipping her hair back.

"Hey! You planning on jumping without me?"

Slowly, the howling of the wind calmed and the plane seemed to go silent, as though we were a UFO in descent. Ginevra was using the power of the earth below us to cushion our landing. A few minutes later, almost delicately, what remained of the jet floated to the ground before my amazed eyes.

"We're there." Ginevra smiled at me affably, helping me climb out through the hole in the fuselage.

Still stunned, I looked around. My surroundings triggered a flashback, shocking me.

"I've been here before."

24

A LEAP INTO THE VOID

"How—how can I possibly be *positive* I've been here before?" It was unbelievable that the place could seem so familiar. "It's not just a funny feeling or déjà vu—I have a perfectly vivid memory of it."

We were in a clearing surrounded by dense jungle. The trees looked like they had withdrawn in reverential fear of the huge, ancient, stone blocks strewn around the open space, survivors of what once must have been a majestic temple. It now lay on the ground in ruins, the trees watching over it like guardians of a bygone empire. In the distance, peeking over the treetops, I caught a hazy glimpse of the main temple of Chichen Itzá.

"The Witches were the ones who led you here. They tried to win you over in your sleep, the only time I couldn't protect you from them," Ginevra explained.

"You mean I could have delivered myself to them even during my nightmares? How is that possible?"

"Come with me." She led me past the timeworn blocks that looked like sleeping giants. It felt like I could hear them breathing. "It doesn't matter if it's real life or only images created in your mind—what counts is your will. If you had *chosen* to go with them, you would have already delivered yourself to them. You would have already transformed. In dreams they can reach your unconscious, your deepest self, the part of you that makes decisions. Every one of their apparitions was nothing more than their attempt to turn you to evil, to convince you to join them, to conquer your soul."

"That's why they showed me Evan," I murmured. "They were hoping I would follow them. There was a pool of water, I remember now. Hell's Mouth." My eyes shot to Ginevra's as I connected all the dots.

"The Witches are trying to seduce your mind, but your mind is also a weapon you can use to fight back. They showed you what you most desired, but your will was so strong it resisted their attempts to persuade you."

"I was in chains," I suddenly remembered, "but why didn't I follow Evan to the other side of the well? I don't understand . . . I would do anything to be with him again—I'm sure I would."

"Because part of you knew the consequences of that decision and they can't force you, they can't deprive you of your free will. It was your unconscious that put you in chains. They couldn't just take you by force—it had to be your decision to follow them. But don't forget that loyalty and virtue aren't part of their ethical code. Once you're in Hell, you won't be in one of your nightmares any more. No one will be able to wake you up. You've decided to venture into the wolf's den at your own risk and peril. The Witches will play dirty and try everything they can to make you give in so they can keep you with them."

"They can't take from me anything I haven't already lost."

"As they see it, you belong to them, Gemma. Don't forget that. And they're not going to give up until evil has possessed you."

"But I might find a way out, escape together with Evan. What will happen if I don't give in to them? If I refuse?"

Ginevra looked at the ground and then fixed me with a piercing look. "You'll die."

"How is that a choice, then? Isn't it supposed to be my decision?"

"They'll never accept a flat-out refusal. Then again, a Sister has never denied the call. They have the power to get into your head, to make you promises no human can resist. If you oppose them they can decide to drive you insane. So no, they can't force you, but they would rather see you die than accept defeat. In any case, if you decided not to succumb to them, Simon and I would be there to protect you and the baby until death."

I gave Ginevra a sidelong glance and raised an eyebrow. "Mine or yours?"

"This isn't the time for wisecracks. I'm not sure you honestly realize what you're going up against, Gemma."

I smiled, ignoring Ginevra's tension. "Though you can read my mind I think you're the one who doesn't realize something: for the first time in a long time, I feel alive again. I'm not afraid, Gwen. Not any more. For months I lived in terror of everything, every day, every breath, but now I'm finally hopeful again, and nothing and no one can keep me from finding Evan. I've listened to everything you've told me, memorized every scrap of information. I know what I'm doing—and I can't wait to begin."

"Good, because we're almost there." Ginevra stopped before a high wall built of blocks of stone, which puzzled me, since the temple stood quite a distance from where we were. The dense jungle lined the clearing like a theater curtain concealing ancient secrets. "We need to go up there."

I raised my head to follow Ginevra's eyes and could barely make out an opening high up in the rock. I opened my mouth to speak, but a violent gust of air tore the words from my mouth and swept me up off the ground. I only realized what had happened when I was on my feet again: Ginevra had hurled me all the way up to the opening.

My head spinning, I looked down. Ginevra was just a distant speck. "Would you mind warning me next time?" I shouted to her from the edge of the opening in the wall.

Ginevra made an incredible leap and landed beside me with feline grace. "I thought I did," she replied with a dazzling smile. I turned around to peer into the darkness of the cave. It seemed to summon me in a whisper that was hostile yet seductive. "Didn't you say there was only one way into Hell's Mouth? This doesn't look like the temple in Chichen Itzá. That seemed pretty far away."

"Weren't you supposed to not be afraid of anything? All I said was that the temple was built *over* Hell's Mouth—not that we would reach it from there. Too many tourists. No one knows about this path. We'll reach the entrance through an underground passage. Now follow me. We've got a long way to go."

"Not to nag, but doesn't 'underground' mean we should be going down? Why are we so high up?" I stiffened at a sound as ominous as the groan of a mountain on the verge of collapsing. "What was that?" In the darkness of the cave, my alarmed voice rang out behind Ginevra, who was strangely silent. The ground shook beneath our feet. "Gwen, something's moving down there."

"Everything's under control. Try to relax." She came to a halt. I quickly caught up to her and focused on her face, which was shrouded in darkness. Her lips were moving quickly, her hands suspended in the air, palms down.

"This would be easier if you explained what's happening," I whispered as an unknown instinct warned me not to move. The ground shook harder. "Gwen?" I wasn't sure whether the tremor in my voice was caused by the quaking ground or my fear of what was moving beneath it.

"Would you shut up for a minute? I'm asking the terrestrial powers that guard the entrance for permission to go in."

"Right! Great! Now everything is clear! Let me know when they ans—"

All at once the earth cracked open beneath my feet as though angered by my sarcasm, swallowing up the rest of my sentence. I let out a shriek and clung to the edge before the darkness could devour me. Ginevra grabbed my arm and pulled me up. "Seriously? What is it with you today? All you had to do was take one step back."

"An occasional heads-up would be nice."

"Oh, sorry, I figured you would notice the earth gaping open beneath our feet."

"Forgive me for not having eagle eyes. I can't see a thing in here!"

Ginevra laughed at my sudden awkwardness. "You're right, my bad. Sometimes I'm so convinced you're my Sister that I forget you haven't transformed yet. It sure would come in handy if you could learn to control your powers."

"But how? My body hasn't transformed yet. It only happened to me once—I could see so well that Peter freaked out, thinking I was driving in the pitch dark. But no, sorry, I can't control them yet."

"No problem. I'll make a little light for you."

That wouldn't be bad. Before I could say the thought out loud, a shimmering sphere of light flickered to life and floated around us.

"My God . . . What place is this?"

"A place where it's not very wise to say that name."

I couldn't believe my eyes: an intricate, crumbling, stone stairway wound around the walls in a downward spiral that grew narrower as it descended. The bottom was hidden in darkness.

"Why didn't you think of that sooner? And would you mind telling the glowy thingy to stop circling around me? It's making me dizzy."

Ginevra laughed and took me by the hand. "Come on. We'd better start down."

"Is that a will-o'-the-wisp?" I asked, fascinated by the waves that flowed across its spherical surface. "I've seen Evan make spheres of light, but this looks different."

"Don't touch it unless you want to end up roasted," Ginevra warned, cutting short my attempt to take a closer look at it. "It's a sphere of pure energy. It can carbonize you in a split second." Her laugh rang crisply against the close walls, which smelled of mildew.

"What's so funny?"

"You should see your hair," she teased as I tried hard to match her pace.

"What's wrong with my hair?" The instant I raised my hands to my head, my fingers were zapped by static electricity.

Ginevra continued to make fun of me. "Told you not to get too close."

"Maybe you didn't tell me soon enough."

"Maybe . . ."

A shudder crept down my back and I couldn't smile along with her. The walls grew more humid with every step downward and—contrary to what I had feared—the air grew colder. A blood-chilling rumble warned us the earth was moving. I looked up in time to see the rock sealing shut above us.

"Gwen, what's happening? It's closing! The ground is closing up above us!"

"I know. Stay calm. Everything is under control. Breathe."

"But we're trapped underground! How will—"

"Gemma, *relax*! You're about to walk into the mouth of Hell and you're worried about a cramped space? Take a deep breath and don't look up. Focus on the descent."

I did as she said, but my heart was still pounding and I had the nagging doubt I wouldn't be strong enough.

"Of course you are. Don't let panic overwhelm you or you'll lose control over it. Fear is like a lion in an arena: unless you tame it, it'll kill you in two seconds flat. Keep that in mind."

"You know I'm claustrophobic. Besides, couldn't we just go down the same way we went up the wall? I mean, why don't you make me do another one of those super jumps?"

"I can't. Your body needs to adjust itself to the changing oxygen levels gradually, otherwise you risk suffocating down here."

"Well, that's really annoying. We'll never get there. This hole is endless! Where does it end up, at the center of the earth? Professor Lidenbrock would be ecstatic!"

"Jules Verne had an incredible imagination, but this isn't *Journey to the Center of the Earth.* Try to relax, Gemma. I can understand your impatience, but I can use the time to explain a few more things about Hell."

"What else is there to know?" I asked, still exasperated but resigned.

"I don't think I've told you about Devil's Stramonium yet."

"I'm almost positive you haven't. A name like that is hard to forget."

"It's a plant that grows only in the infernal realms, though you might have already seen some in my vault."

"What am I supposed to do with it?" I asked, puzzled.

"You can use it to protect yourself. It grows in thick tangles like thorn bushes. Its flowers are black, graceful, and dangerous. Its pretty appearance masks its true nature. Just like with Witches."

"Lethally beautiful, basically."

"Irresistible and deadly. Devil's Stramonium once existed on Earth too—Witches planted it there—and they say the flower was so beautiful it destroyed humans' free will. It could even capture their souls. But the Earth had to remain neutral territory for God and Sophìa, so legend has it that because it was so attractive and so dangerous to humans, the flower was separated from the plant.

"To render its magic less powerful, its essence was divided into two different species: the one humans know as the black bat flower took on the appearance of its blossom—elegant, majestic, and black. Many still call it 'the devil's flower.' Datura Stramonium, on the other hand, retained some of its poisonous properties, as well as the shape of the plant from which the blossom grows. It causes hallucinations and even death in large enough doses, but it's no longer a gateway to Hell, although many continue to call it Witches' Weed.

"In compensation, Sophìa was allowed to grow Devil's Stramonium in Hell, where no flower had ever grown before. Witches worship nature in all its forms, but the poison of their souls had made the land barren, preventing plants from sprouting. It was one of their curses: to hopelessly yearn for Eden, where nature flourishes. There are still vast, arid areas in Hell, like the Stone Forest, where not even the Damned dare hide.

"Even so, trees began to grow in Hell after that, though their trunks were deformed by the poison they absorbed from the soil. Various other plants of different shapes and properties grew too, all of them irresistible and dangerous, but none of them as powerful as Devil's Stramonium. Our Dakor crave its seeds, but in order to eat them they need to inject the flower with their venom, which spreads through the stalks down to the roots, making the plant extremely poisonous. Sophìa is particularly fond of them. She has many of them growing in one wing of the Castle. It's a vast garden planted in the interior courtyard where you'll find the Well of Souls, Sophìa's greatest joy. Anyway, the plant can help cover your scent. On top of that, the Damned are afraid of it because even brief contact with it sears their skin and cooks their flesh."

"How revolting."

"Wait until you see it. Some of the Damned lure less clever prey into a patch of the plants so they won't have to eat them completely raw."

"When I get back from Hell I could write a screenplay. I bet Joss Whedon could make an awesome movie out of it."

"Who?"

"The director of *Buffy the Vam*—Never mind. What else do I need to know?"

"Not much. I've explained everything I can. The rest, I'm afraid, you'll have to find out for yourself. Oh, one more thing—watch out for the raptors."

"Raptors? Like, birds?"

"Giant, ferocious ones. The trees should offer you shelter if you come across one, but don't be fooled if it doesn't seem to notice you. Once it sets its sights on you, it'll stalk you and attack when you least expect it."

"Nasty birds. Seek shelter under trees. Check. Next tip?"

"Try not to die."

Meanwhile, we'd reached the end of the staircase, a narrow, funnel-shaped vortex that led into an enclosed circular space that forked in two different directions.

"This place gives me the creeps." In the distance, I could hear the faint dripping of water. "Abandon all hope, ye who enter here . . ." I said under my breath, staring at the gloomy walls that seemed to want to imprison us.

"We're still on Earth, Gemma. Wait till you're actually in Hell."

"Should I expect the ground to crack open under my feet, fire and brimstone and all?"

"Not at all. Hell is a place you'll feel irremediably drawn to—but don't trust its appearance and remember everything I've told you. This way."

I followed Ginevra into the cavern on the left, which was darker and more cramped than its twin. The sphere of light quickly lit up what was hidden there.

"Whoa!" I exclaimed, looking around. Stalactites and stalagmites reached out toward one another, creating a magical display of colors the instant the light touched them. Fascinated, I went up to a wall. Arcane symbols covered the rock like an ancient parchment. "I've seen these markings before, but I can't—What does it say?"

Ginevra smiled at my curiosity without slowing her pace. I hated it when she did that. "I heard you, you know." Her voice reached me from around a curve, echoing through the tunnel.

"It's about time you taught me to block off my thoughts."

"But every now and then you come up with a good idea."

"Very funny. Come on, teach me so I can finally keep you out of my mind when I feel like it. No offense."

Ginevra looked back at me, pouting. "Am I really that bad?"

"Only once in a while." This time it was my turn to grin.

"Shut up!" She slapped my arm, smiling again. "Otherwise I'll leave you here in the dark."

"You would never do that. I know how much you care about me deep down," I teased.

"Don't put me to the test. If you started counting instead of babbling, we would make much better use of our time."

"I'm not babbling! Or am I? It's just that, I mean—I have so many things inside my head I could scream."

"Don't you dare. Instead, do what I told you."

"You mean count? Why should I count?"

"So you'll shut up, for starters, since you need to use your mind to do it." Ginevra chuckled.

"But you would hear me anyway."

"Okay, it's time to really focus. I'm not kidding. You're inside your mind now. Imagine erasing all your thoughts. Count slowly. Numbers will take the place of words. Imagine your brain is a blackboard. It's dark and shiny and the numbers are written down in white one by one as they appear in your mind. It's hard at first, I know, but it'll be easy once you've learned how to do it."

I tried to pay attention to Ginevra's voice as I followed her instructions, but I wasn't sure I could.

"Now picture the blackboard inside an empty room that's completely white. Imagine the walls—solid, all around you. Impenetrable walls. There's a door, see it? Focus on it, shut it, and lock it. Good. Now you can fill the room with whatever you want. Everything else will stay outside. No one can go in until you unlock the door and allow them access to your thoughts."

"How am I doing?" I asked shyly. I hadn't closed my eyes but was concentrating so hard I couldn't even see where I was walking.

"Either the Witches have possessed you again or you're successfully keeping me out, Sister." I smiled at her, hiding my enthusiasm. I hadn't thought it would be so easy. "Okay, but now let me in. I taught you so you could keep the other Witches out, not me."

Forget it, I told her in my mind. *You have no idea how long I've been waiting for this moment.*

"Hey, I heard that!" *Damn it, she still hasn't learned to block off her thoughts.*

"What makes you think I didn't let you hear that on purpose?" Suddenly I realized there was something different about her voice. "Wait a second, Gwen. I heard that too. I just read your mind."

Ginevra's lips tightened, then relaxed into a warm smile. "That's not surprising. We're near the source. Don't forget that we're Sisters and our mental connection is going to get stronger and stronger. When you reach Hell, your spirit will struggle to emerge. Your body may be affected."

"Like when I run a high fever?"

"I imagine so. Your mental powers will get sharper—the Witches may even sense them—but your body still isn't ready because it hasn't transformed." Ginevra heard the note of discouragement in my mind and squeezed my hand. I realized I would be facing a daunting challenge, pitting myself against God only knew how many and what kinds of dangers. I hoped my body wouldn't fail me; that would make everything even more difficult. I raised my hand to my neck and clasped my chain to build my courage. Before setting out, I'd put Evan's ring back in its little silver case. Now, carefully concealed beneath the thick fabric of my sweatshirt, I wore my butterfly pendant with the diamond from Heaven, interlaced with Evan's dog tag and the serpent-shaped amulet, the symbol of what I would soon become—three realms that were inseparable now.

"We're there."

Ginevra's voice made me look up and my frown vanished as my eyes were dazzled by our enchanting surroundings.

25

THE MOUTH OF HELL

"Oh. My. God."

"Haven't I already said it would be best to use a different exclamation?"

I wanted to reply but couldn't find the words. I had imagined Hell's Mouth as an ominous black hole that would try to gobble me up. Instead, the cavern had led us to a grotto hidden in the heart of the rock, dominated by a pool of water that reflected the myriad hues of a diamond. No longer necessary, the shining sphere had disappeared, allowing the cenote to sparkle with its own light. Golden shafts danced beneath its surface, creating a network of iridescent reflections as though the water was run through with strands of light. I couldn't believe such an amazingly ethereal place could contain the only entrance to the Underworld.

"This is it." I suddenly remembered seeing it before. It was unquestionably the focal point of my dreams. "This is where they always tried to bring me." A shudder ran down my spine. I had been dreaming of that place for a long time, even when Evan was still alive. "So all I had to do was cross through this and they would have made me their prisoner?"

"Not their prisoner—their loyal ally."

"What difference would it have made, if they'd taken Evan away from me?"

"You're here now," she reminded me, "and unless you save him you'll be forced to sacrifice yourself to them in vain."

"It's a price I'm willing to pay to see him again. We've already talked about this, Gwen. Tell me what I have to do."

"Be patient." Ginevra slid the backpack off her shoulders and pulled out my things. "Meanwhile, get ready. We can't overlook a single detail."

For practice, I tried to block my mind as I took off my jeans and put on Ginevra's old dress. She didn't even seem to notice that my thoughts had gone silent. My Sister suddenly looked lost, sitting on a rock across the grotto from me, her sad face reflected in the surface of the cenote. I put on the long green cloak, its hood falling heavily against my back, then slung over my shoulder the satchel containing food, water, and the strange whistle Ginevra had given me. I approached her, giving myself a few seconds to watch her from afar. It was clear from her expression how difficult it was for her to go along with my plan. She must have cared about me a great deal, judging from how upset she seemed to be.

"Gwen?" She slowly turned to look at me. "Would you mind?" I held out the sheathed dagger so she could help me put it on.

Ginevra took it and fastened both its buckles around my forearm. "I hope with all my heart you won't need it."

"Don't worry, Gwen. Everything is going to go fine. Soon we'll be a family again and no one will be able to separate us. I'm not going to give up everything over something I can learn to control."

Ginevra forced a nod and clasped me in a warm embrace. "I only wish I could help you more." A solitary tear slid down her cheek. I'd never seen her cry before.

"I know." I stroked her face, sensing in that tiny crystalline droplet the intrinsic energy that united us. I had never seen Ginevra so vulnerable and her pain tugged on my heartstrings. "Just wish me luck."

"The goddess of luck is blindfolded. If you don't guide her she won't find you."

"I'll do my best."

"Make sure you come back in one piece. You're the only Sister I have left. I don't want to lose you."

"That won't happen. I promise."

Ginevra smiled as another tear spilled over. "While you're at it, bring back that hardheaded boyfriend of yours. I miss making fun of him."

My heart skipped a beat, telling me the time had come to go get him. I knelt at the edge of the cenote, gazing at it with reverential respect as though it could return my look. Then I stood up and clenched my fists at my sides. "I'm ready."

I took a deep breath and Ginevra's powerful energy slowly lifted my body inches above the ground. Closing my eyes, I felt the energy surge through me from my toes to the tips of my hair that blew around my face as I levitated over the surface of the water. Sensing an arcane force stirring beneath me, I opened my eyes and saw the cenote churning, moved by a dark power.

From the water's edge, Ginevra watched, powerless, as the whirlpool forming beneath me roared, grasping at me with invisible hands that pulled me down toward the abyss.

I raised my eyes just in time to glimpse a man standing at the mouth of the cave, his face covered by the hood of a sweatshirt. "Look out!" I shouted. A fireball raced toward Ginevra while a second one headed in my direction. "GWEN!!" My eyes bulged as I felt its heat searing my skin, but a wall of water shot up in front of me, protecting me. I struggled to catch sight of Ginevra on the shore battling the dark Angel who had appeared out of nowhere in the Màsala's final attempt to keep me from reaching the Witches.

A second wall of water crashed down onto the Executioner. He staggered, fell to the ground, and dissolved instantly.

"Go!"

For the last time I looked into Ginevra's eyes in a silent farewell, then the abyss consumed me, pulling me into its depths. The sharp pain of a thousand needles pierced my skin, making me shriek. It felt like the water was burning me.

"It's the poison!" Ginevra's distant voice reached me as my senses grew weaker.

"It burns," I whispered, unsure whether she could hear me.

"The water's tainted! It's filled with poison! Hang in there, Gemma! It'll be over soon."

I jerked my head out of the ferocious whirlpool that was swallowing me up and tried to breathe, but my lungs filled with water as I caught one last glimpse of Ginevra huddled on the shore.

What came to me first was a feeling of lightness, as though my body were suddenly weightless. I opened my eyes a crack, and a stinging sensation burned them like salt, reminding me where I was: in Hell.

My lungs screamed for air. I thrashed my legs, but it only made me rotate in the water. I had no clue which way the surface was; I seemed to be going down rather than up. The whirlpool in the cenote had sucked me down and dumped me into the depths of a river. The heart of the Earth had ejected me directly into Hell. My foot touched something and my arms automatically reacted, striving for a way out in the opposite direction. My face emerged from the water. I coughed and sputtered, then filled my lungs with air, but the current was strong and soon pulled me back under. Losing hope, I searched for something to cling to as my skin burned from the poison. I had to find a way out of there or my head might explode. Suddenly the sound of the water grew louder, deafening me. A horrible suspicion gripped me but before I could even look around my head struck something solid, leaving me dazed. A moment later, as the water swiftly pulled me away, my vision blurred, I glimpsed the rock I had hit. I struggled against the current but felt consciousness abandoning me. I surrendered and plunged down an unfathomable void.

I shook my head dizzily. It felt like a swarm of bees was buzzing in my brain. The low rumble of a waterfall came from the distance but it was hard to figure out where, exactly. When I finally managed to open my eyes it felt as though the bees I'd heard in my head had attacked me all at once with their poisonous stingers. Doubling over from a pain that was so strong I could barely breathe, I curled up, expecting to pass out.

Instead, the burning feeling eased gradually until it throbbed only at my temples. I rested my palms on the dark sand and attempted to stand. My whole body ached as though a train had run me over. Only when I got to my knees did I see the waterfall in the distance and remember that the current must have swept me over its edge.

I checked to make sure nothing was broken and put my hands on my belly where my baby was sleeping under Ginevra's protective spell. There was no cut on my head and my clothes were dry again. I had no idea how long it had been since Ginevra and I had said goodbye. The sky was dark and a sinister twilight threatened to fade into the gloomiest of nights.

"Well," I mumbled to myself, "no flames or lakes of fire. Seems like a pretty good start." I was happy that that part of the stories about Hell wasn't true. I looked around. Despite Ginevra's warnings, it didn't seem like such a hostile place. Quite the opposite. There was a strange tingle under my skin as though Hell's dark magnetic power were reaching its tentacles out toward me. What scared me the most, actually, was that, deep down, I felt I belonged there.

A giant prehistoric-looking creature flew across the sky and my heart leapt to my throat. I wasn't sure whether to be frightened or fascinated. Suddenly the ground trembled beneath my palms, tearing me from my thoughts. At first it was only my fingers, but soon my whole body began to vibrate and a deafening noise filled the air—the sound of a stampede of wild horses.

I shot to my feet, my heart thumping to the rhythm of the approaching hooves. I had to find shelter fast. Instinct led me toward the forest that skirted the river and, panicking, I hid in a patch of prickly bushes that scratched my skin. The noise grew louder and louder, shaking the air as I held my breath and hoped they wouldn't see me. I squeezed my eyes shut as they crossed in front of me, their hooves pounding against the ground. They looked like men riding horses.

Slowly I began to breathe again, relieved they hadn't discovered me. Not far away, though, one of them stopped in his tracks and my heart went still with terror.

"My God." I instinctively backed up, my eyes wide. They weren't men on horseback. They were man and beast fused into a single monstrous creature. Beings like centaurs, but half buffalo instead of horse, their faces distorted by sharp teeth and murderous expressions.

Blood. The spine-chilling whisper crept into my head. It didn't sound like a word uttered in a human language but I understood it all the same. My senses must have sharpened. Uncontrollable terror made my stomach clench but my eyes were so paralyzed at the sight of the infernal creature I couldn't move a muscle.

"Blood!" This time the shout pierced the air, snapping me out of my trance, as the one who seemed to be their leader gestured for the others to follow him. I backed up and fled. I felt that I'd never run so fast in my life, but their hoof beats came closer and closer. I could feel them shaking the ground as their ghoulish roars rang out. Ginevra was right, they had smelled my blood. The creatures had to be Molock. I'd hoped never to come across them and instead they'd tracked me down before I even had a chance to take in my surroundings. What hope could I ever have against these Hell-born monsters?

Evan . . . Had my attempt to save him failed already? I doubled over as a stabbing pain lacerated my abdomen, then hid behind a tree to catch my breath, squeezing my eyes shut in desperation. There was no way for me to defend myself. I was about to die in that cursed forest. The thunder of the approaching hooves spurred me on, and I began to run again, holding my belly.

Suddenly the ground swallowed me up. For a few moments all I heard was crackling and rustling. When everything stopped, I realized the earth had given way beneath my feet and I'd fallen into a ravine choked with strange-looking spiny bushes. I could hear the Molock drawing near. Curling myself up in the brambles, I waited for the end.

When they were directly over my head, the thundering hooves abruptly went silent. Trying to control my breathing to avoid giving myself away, I raised my eyes. The Molock had stopped at the edge of the ravine and were uttering hoarse noises in a language that this time was incomprehensible to me. Something warm dribbled onto my cheek, maybe blood or drool, and a moan of disgust escaped me. I stiffened when I saw that my reaction had drawn the attention of the leader, who turned to look in my direction.

For some reason he couldn't see me, but I had a clear view of him. His enormous mouth took up most of his face. Large upper and lower fangs protruded from his lips like a saber-toothed tiger. His nose was completely flat, almost absent, and his nostrils were two slits that ran along his cheekbones. His demonic eyes were dark and bloodshot. He didn't have actual hair, but the fur that covered his body spread from his back up to his head and chin. His powerful limbs were totally covered with long fur in colors ranging from black to brown to reddish. His skin was black as a buffalo's. On his skull, small horns formed a spiky crown. His chest was a frightening mass of muscles that looked powerful enough to kill someone with a simple squeeze. The only hairless section of his body, it was covered with scar-like furrows that met in the center. He had no navel and instead of nipples I saw a single tiny hole in the center of his chest that opened and closed. That must have been the maseolum, the weak spot Ginevra had told me about. But there was no way I could ever have gotten close enough to try to attack him without being devoured in the process. I had never imagined—not even in my wildest dreams—that such horrifying creatures could exist.

To my amazement, the beasts began slowly to turn away and leave, snorting with dissatisfaction and grunting something incomprehensible. A familiar smell filled the air, though I couldn't put my finger on what it was. It was so powerful it almost made me dizzy. I held my breath without moving until their hoof beats faded into the distance. Only then, all my strength drained, did I pass out, blotting out my surroundings.

When I opened my eyes, I was relieved to discover I hadn't been dragged off in the jaws of some wild animal. I found myself inside the thorn bush, exactly where I'd lost consciousness. Even the sky was unchanged. I had no idea how much time had passed, but night still hadn't replaced the ghastly twilight. Instinctively I raised my hand to the bodice of my old dress, afraid I might have lost Ginevra's amulet, but it was still there. Suddenly thirsty, I pulled the canteen out of my satchel and took a gulp of water. Only when I looked up through the branches of the bush I was hidden in did I see it.

A village.

26

THE JAWS OF SILENCE

Before going out into the open, I pricked my ears, listening for even the slightest movement, but everything was shrouded in spectral silence. I brushed off my dress, hoping I hadn't ruined it, and set off down the path that led to the village, repeatedly looking over my shoulder.

I didn't know what kinds of creatures inhabited it. Maybe the souls of the Damned there had kept their humanity. At first glance it looked abandoned, but I still advanced cautiously and slowly, moving between the tiny stone houses, their roofs, doors, and window frames made of finely woven branches. The silence was deafening. I swallowed, scrutinizing every corner. A well sat at the point where the roads intersected at the center of the village while just beyond that a wooden swing hung perfectly still, abandoned, just like every other thing in that bone-chilling ghost town watched over by eternal twilight.

I passed the houses one by one, looking for a sign of life, but the doors and windows were all boarded up and there was no trace of anyone. I convinced myself it was a good thing, though deep down I harbored the hope I would find Souls that weren't completely evil.

Behind me an ominous hiss sliced the air, making me jump. I spun around but saw nothing. With horror, I discovered that the swing had begun to slowly move back and forth with a foreboding squeak, though there wasn't even a breath of wind. Goosebumps rose on my arms and my eyes darted around, searching for whoever had pushed it, but there was no one in sight.

Further along the street a house caught my attention. Unlike the others, its windows weren't boarded up. I walked up to it, peered inside to make sure it was actually abandoned, and gripped the door handle, then warily opened the door and closed it behind me. I rested my back against the wood and slid down to the cold floor. Only then, in the total silence, did I realize how hard my heart was pounding. Taking a deep breath, I rested my head on my knees. Maybe I could hide there until it was daytime. The twilight in Hell was more foreboding than any dusk I'd ever seen and shrouded everything in a ghoulish gloom.

A squeal made me start. My head shot up and I held my breath. Cautiously I rose to my feet, trying hard not to make a sound, but the dry wood of the door betrayed my presence by emitting a sinister creak.

Another squeal, this one louder. I checked the house's only other room, which must once have been a bedroom, but it was deserted. It contained only a crude mattress and a crib. I went back to the front door. All the furniture was made of finely interwoven twigs and branches. It looked solid, though worn by centuries of use. Four chairs and a table stood in the center of the room while a bookcase covered an entire wall. In it were a few stone objects, others of wood that looked hand-carved, and some books. I touched one. It was bound in some sort of animal skin and something was scrawled on the pages in black ink as though with a quill pen. I sniffed it and gagged. *Demon blood,* I thought, but instantly banished the idea. I turned around and noticed the giant fireplace that took up almost the entire wall opposite the bookcase.

It looked like a comfortable hideaway. Who knew why whoever had lived there had abandoned it. And yet . . . I rested my hand on the table and something dampened my fingers—a viscous liquid. My body went ice-cold, gripped by the terrible presentiment that it was blood. A strange sound from the bedroom made me return to the doorway. I peeked into the room and saw the cradle rocking gently. Repressing a shudder of fright, I took a step forward as my mind screamed at me to run. A strange prickle warned me to stay away from the cradle but I couldn't stop myself. A baby girl turned her round face to look at me, moving her little hands. I covered my mouth, shocked. Could someone actually have abandoned her there? She couldn't have been more than a year old.

Without thinking twice, I picked her up and cradled her tenderly. My eyes closed, I snuggled my head against hers. How could a babe in arms have ended up in that accursed place? What sin could possibly have stained such a tiny creature? Still holding the baby, I turned around and my heart leapt to my throat. Another child, this one around four years old, was standing there, perfectly still, staring at me through the gloom. I tried to steady my breathing but my instinct returned to warn me not to get near him. He must have been her brother and, given that there were four chairs in the other room, the children probably weren't alone.

"Don't worry, I don't want to hurt you. Wh-what's your name?" I forced myself to ask in a comforting tone, but the little boy continued to stare at me without speaking. "Do you understand what I'm saying?" He nodded but remained silent. "Where are your parents?"

His answer came only after a long pause. "They're dead," the little boy told me, his voice emotionless, his eyes glued to mine.

Dead.

It was so horrible that two little creatures had ended up all alone in that infernal place. "Did you see who did it? Who killed them?" I asked.

I soon regretted my question. He raised his arm and pointed his finger at the baby just as I noticed the terrifying noise she was making. She was *sniffing me*. Shocked, I held her out at arm's length and my heart lurched when I saw that her eyes had turned completely black. I let out a scream and tossed the baby toward her brother, but the creature landed on the floor on all fours and scuttled toward me, her eyes locked on mine.

She did it. She was the one who had killed her parents.

The two children watched me intently as, horrified, I tried to back up into the other room, but tripped and wound up on the floor. When I looked up they were gone. I peered around, searching for them in the gloom, still petrified by the memory of those eyes.

Getting hurriedly to my feet, I took refuge behind the table, but the little boy surprised me from behind. I spun around. His eyes were completely black now too. He smiled faintly, baring teeth that were narrow and came to a point, like a shark's.

"Do you want to play?" His voice came out in a dark, hair-raising snarl. It wasn't a sound made by a little boy, but by a demon.

I threw a chair at him and made a break for the door, but he was there waiting for me. Frantically looking for another way out, I noticed a door I hadn't seen before and threw it open. Inside a cramped closet, a tall man in his thirties wearing medieval-looking clothing gaped at me with bloodshot eyes. "Eat thy fill, but prithee, kill me not!" I stared at him in horror as he offered me his arm, which already had chunks of flesh bitten out of it.

I slammed the door shut and the baby scuttled over to me at a frightening speed. I let out a shriek and scrambled up the bookcase to escape her, but she crawled up after me, grabbed my leg and bit me. *She wanted to eat me alive!* The burning sensation was as immediate as it was intense. With a howl, I grabbed a heavy book and struck the baby with all my might, trying to make her release her grip, but her teeth were sunk deep into my flesh. When she finally let go, she twisted her head all the way around, leaving me in shock. I suddenly remembered the dagger. My hand shot to my forearm and I whipped it out. The blade plunged into the baby's neck with a sickening gurgle. She let out an inhuman screech. Black liquid filled her eye sockets and oozed from her nose and mouth, suffocating her. Seconds later, her body exploded in a cloud of grayish dust. I began to spasm and cough uncontrollably, my trembling hand still brandishing the dagger. I remembered Ginevra's warning about the toxicity of the ashes of the Damned, so I instantly held my breath and scrambled down from the bookcase.

The second I turned my back to the wall I saw him. Everything had happened so fast, I had forgotten about the boy. We stared at each other across the kitchen table, my eyes locked on his. He backed up and I took a step in the opposite direction. I'd seen how fast he could move but now he was slow, looking almost frightened. Without breaking eye contact, I stepped past the table and we moved in a circle. When his back was against the wall, he turned around, rested his hands and feet against it and began to crawl up it like a spider.

I was next to the front door. Opening it, I rushed outside and continued to advance cautiously through the village. It still looked deserted, but sinister hissing noises that sounded like the whistle of arrows suggested the opposite. They were all lurking in the semidarkness, moving so quickly they were only a blur. As I walked forward I held the dagger well in sight. Blood still dripped from its blade and I hoped it would frighten them off. Once I'd passed the last of the houses, I sprinted as fast as I could, leaving the horrifying village behind me.

Now I knew it: I was in Hell.

27

HIDING PLACE

Once I was a good distance away, I stopped to catch my breath and leaned against a tree, exhausted. Among a nearby cluster of rocks I saw the mouth of a small cave that might offer shelter. I gathered what was left of my energy and crawled inside it. Only then, far from everyone, did the tears stream from my eyes.

What had I done? A baby! I had killed a baby. I looked at my hands. They were shaking. I covered my face with them, sobs wracking my chest. The long skirt of Ginevra's dress was splattered with my blood, its odor so pungent I could smell it. I grabbed the canteen and rinsed some of it off my wounded calf, hoping no creatures would smell it. Not even the stinging pain in my leg bothered me as much as the guilt I felt over what I had just done. When Ginevra had given me the dagger I'd hoped I would never need to use it—but I had used it, and to kill an infant. What kind of horrible mother would I be? I felt like a monster. I was alone, devastated, and incredibly frightened. What would become of me? I felt farther and farther away from Evan, and the terrible fear that I might never see him again assaulted me.

Wiping my eyes, I tried to be brave, making myself remember that my current fear was nothing in comparison to how much I'd suffered at the thought of having lost Evan forever. Now that I knew he was alive—wherever he was—I was determined to cling with all my strength to the hope of finding him and never let it go. I was going to fight, and nothing would keep me from seeing him again.

I left my hiding place just as something darkened the sky, like a black cloud crossing in front of the sun. The leaves on the trees around me began to tremble.

"What the hell . . ."

The words died in my throat as the sky filled with extraordinary creatures that had human bodies but long feathered wings that were blacker than night. An entire swarm of Angels of darkness. No—not Angels. Demons. Terrified, I sought shelter under the trees and watched them soar across the sky. The instant the last of them was out of sight, I hurried off in the opposite direction, ignoring my exhaustion.

I walked for what felt like an eternity, trying to find my way back to the river that I'd distanced myself from in my flight from the Molock. By then it was clear that night was never going to arrive to dispel the twilight, nor could I hope for day to break. The sky seemed to be stuck at dusk. Even the moon and stars refused to cast their light on those accursed lands.

Though I'd walked a long way, I still hadn't reached the river. Without its precious guidance I was lost, with no idea of which way to go. The Castle could have been anywhere. Besides, with each step I was growing more convinced someone was following me. I had the terrible feeling I was being watched, as though the forest had a thousand eyes trained on me. I couldn't see anyone in the vicinity but I couldn't be sure, and I had the impression something was lurking in the bushes.

Ginevra was right—it was a mad, dangerous place. All my certainties began to fade. What if it really was a suicide mission? What if I never managed to reach Evan? I would be responsible for my baby's death.

I couldn't give up and accept that possibility. It didn't matter what became of me, I had no intention of losing either of them.

Something warm trickled down my calf. I raised my skirt to check and was horrified to see that my wound had reopened and blood was dripping to the ground, leaving a trail that led straight to me. *Forgive me, Gwen.* I tore off a strip of the hem of her beloved dress and bound the wound to stop the bleeding. I couldn't afford to leave any trace of myself or it would be the end of me. Little water remained in the canteen, and soon my food supply would run out too. What would I do then? I absolutely had to find the river as quickly as possible unless I wanted to end up as someone's next meal.

The forest looked endless. The trees grew denser, then opened up into clearings only to become dense again, but there was no sign of the river. If only I could utilize the power growing inside me—but I couldn't, though I felt its dark, constant presence hidden in a corner of my mind.

I tripped and fell to my hands and knees. Though my mind warned me to get up immediately, all my strength was gone and my body refused to continue the desperate search. I tried over and over but couldn't get to my feet. Desperation took hold of me: I had no idea where the river was hidden, Evan was the Witches' prisoner, and I was still convinced I would never reach him. Exhausted, I crumpled to the ground. Clenching my fists, I tried one last time, but my brain shut down, carrying me off to an unknown place. To safety.

In the dream, a chorus of voices was mixed with inhuman grunts. Slowly, my eyes made out a grim landscape with trees grayed by the approaching darkness. I didn't know where I was, but a hair-raising snort suddenly brought everything back. I wasn't in a dream. I shot to my feet, wondering how long I'd been lying on the ground. Frightened, I looked around. Then I heard it again.

It was distant, I was sure of it, but for some reason I heard it clearly. My senses had sharpened. I crept to a large rock not far away and the grunts grew louder. My instincts begged me to run away, but the instant my eyes fell on the macabre source of those sounds I was paralyzed: a herd of Molock were fighting over pieces of what once had been a man, snapping the bones apart and devouring the flesh. And he wasn't their only prey. There were others inside the circle of beasts. Some were still alive, kicking and trying to free themselves. Though I knew they weren't actually men—just other Damned Souls who in all likelihood would try to kill me if given half a chance—the sight still made me shudder.

A shooting pain throbbed in my temples and made me double over. I leaned against the rock as a groan escaped me. Raising my head with an effort, I cursed myself as the Molock scanned the area. Taking a few steps back, I kept my eyes locked on the monsters as they sniffed the air with their cheekbone nostrils, trying to pinpoint me, but the pain in my forehead made me stagger and collapse against a tree. Just then someone rushed past. I shook my head and the pain lessened and slipped away like a ghost. Another figure darted by, but this time I recognized one of the Molock's captives. My presence must have distracted the beasts, allowing a few of the Souls to escape. A shuffling of hooves forced me to take off at a run, my heart pounding almost hard enough to burst through my chest.

Suddenly a Soul grabbed my arm. Desperate, I pulled back with a strength I hadn't known I had, broke free, and ran away. Rather than wanting to help me escape, he no doubt wanted to insure himself a food supply in case he managed to escape the Molock. Just as the forest grew denser, the last handful of Souls overtook me and then—

All at once they were gone.

In front of me the trees opened into a round clearing. I came to a halt. The others had all vanished into thin air. I had nowhere to hide and the Molock were about to catch up with me. I still had no idea how I'd managed to elude them the first time but I wouldn't be so lucky a second time, not with the bleeding wound on my leg that even I could still smell.

The ground trembled beneath the Molock's hooves, announcing their imminent arrival. I shook myself out of my daze and started running again. Suddenly something grabbed my ankle and I crashed to the ground. I looked behind me to see what it was and froze. A woman had appeared from a trapdoor in the ground and was gripping my leg with inhuman strength, staring at me with a haunting expression. I tried to kick her away but she grabbed me with her other hand and began to drag me underground.

"Let go!" I screamed desperately. "Let me go!"

"Shh! They're coming. You have to hide!"

At the sound of her voice I stopped struggling and turned back toward her. Her face was gaunt and her deep-set eyes had dark bags under them. It looked like she hadn't eaten in weeks. Her complexion was waxy and her copper-colored hair was cropped close to her head. Was she honestly offering to help me?

"Hide in here, quick!" I searched the woman's face, trying to decide which was worse—the creatures hunting me down or her. "Quickly, there's no time! Do you want those monsters to eat you alive?"

The Molock's ever-closer hoof beats convinced me. I let the woman pull me down beside her and the trapdoor closed over our heads.

"What is this place?" I asked, looking around at what seemed to be a room carved into the rock.

The woman held a finger to her lips for me to be silent but when I heard hoof beats immediately overhead I couldn't hold back a whimper. I scrambled back from the trapdoor and the woman smiled. "Don't worry, they won't find you here. They're too stupid. They've never discovered our hiding places."

"You mean this is—"

"My home."

I ran my fingers over the strange mineral that illuminated the room. Its glow was dim but bright enough for me to make out my surroundings. At first glance it looked like a normal dwelling: a table with one chair, an unlit fireplace with a pot hanging over it and, in the back, a niche in the rock made up as a bed. "In this hellhole, if you're clever you stay in hiding as much as you can. You must be new around here. There's something unusual about your smell," the woman continued.

She had quite a human appearance, but I wasn't sure I could trust her. Was it possible she was a Subterranean? Ginevra had said they were the only ones who weren't wicked, and I still hoped to find someone to ease my overwhelming discouragement and solitude. Suddenly I remembered: the woman had mentioned there were other hiding places. So that was why the Damned who had escaped the Molock had vanished before my eyes—they must have hidden in other underground caves.

"Thank you. You probably saved my life, at least for the time being. My name is Gemma. Yours?"

Her reply came after a moment of silence that sent a shiver down my spine: "Xandra." I wasn't sure, but in the dim light a strange glint seemed to appear in her eye as she tried to hide a smile. She pushed back a curtain attached to the wall. I thought I glimpsed someone hidden behind it, but she merely took something from inside the cubbyhole.

A sudden sound made us both jump. "By all Hell's devils!" Xandra rushed to the trapdoor and barred it with wooden planks, cursing in some unknown language. I heard a low growl that made me shudder with terror in the dark room.

"What's happening?!" I cried, panicking.

Another clatter of hoof beats rattled the trapdoor. "They tracked you down!" she shouted, trying to be heard over the war cries of the Molock gathered overhead. "They must have followed your scent. Quick, open that jar next to the basin!"

"What for?"

"Just open it!"

I grabbed the large clay jar and pulled off the lid, my hands trembling. A familiar smell filled my nostrils, leaving me dazed. Hearing the urgency in Xandra's voice, I slid my hand into the jar as the Molock stomped on the trapdoor more violently. Finally my fingertips touched a tangled clump inside it.

"Quickly, rub it on yourself! It'll cover your scent!" I pulled my hand out and in the dim light saw some familiar-looking black petals and leaves. "What are you waiting for?! We don't have time! Hurry, or they won't go away!"

A massive blow from a hoof smashed open a hole over Xandra's head, compelling me to do as she said. I scrubbed the plant against my skin and my temples began to throb again. The pain doubled me over. I raised my eyes to the woman and saw her face fill with an emotion I wasn't expecting: astonishment.

Her thoughts filled my mind. *What in Hell is happening? Why isn't the Devil's Stramonium burning her?!*

"What? This is Stramonium?!"

Her eyes bulged and from her lips came a gasp. *"Witch!"* The Molock pawed the ground over our heads, trying to widen the hole they had smashed in, but she continued to stare at me, petrified.

"You wanted to kill me," I whispered in shock. My hopes that the woman might be a Subterranean vanished. "You thought this stuff would burn me! I heard you!"

Finally it dawned on me how I'd managed to escape the Molock the first time: the plants around me in the ravine were Devil's Stramonium. Ginevra had told me it might protect me since the Damned were afraid of it. Xandra, however, couldn't have known I was a Witch. Thinking I was a Soul like her, she'd told me to rub it on my skin not to save me but so it would cook my flesh. I shoved the plant into the satchel slung over my shoulder and smashed the jar to the ground at her feet, glaring at her in disgust as the Molock raged above us. Xandra stared at the remains of the jar and then looked up at me. On her gaunt face, an unnerving smile appeared beneath her hunger-darkened eyes.

"I too must eat," she whispered, sending an eerie shiver down my spine. More pounding on the trap door made me back up. The Molock were on the verge of knocking it in.

"You said *they* would eat me!" The catch in my voice betrayed my disappointment. I shouldn't have trusted her. After all, what could I have expected?

"I said they would eat you *alive*. Xandra doesn't like her meat raw. You should thank me!" She smiled again, but disappeared a second later as a giant beast dropped down onto her, crushing her. The Molock had gotten in.

I screamed and flung myself through a partially hidden door in the wall, trying not to look at Xandra's body being torn apart. As I ran, I plugged my ears to avoid hearing their grunts and the crunch of bones. At the end of a short tunnel I came out into a circular chamber illuminated by the same glowing rocks I'd seen in Xandra's hideaway. Tunnels and doorways led out of the chamber. It looked like an entire village dug into the rock, an intricate system of caves in which the Damned hid while remaining in contact with each other.

The doors along the tunnels must be entrances to other dwellings, which meant that sooner or later someone was bound to notice me. I had to find a place to hide, and fast, though by that time I'd realized there was nowhere I could feel safe down there. Ginevra was right: mine was a mad endeavor, a suicide mission. Hell was too dangerous. That was why I'd seen her cry for the first time: she was saying goodbye.

My legs trembling, I forced back the tears and ventured into the darkest tunnel, away from the dwellings.

28

HEAVEN AND HELL

I walked for hours, resting only to take tiny sips of water. Even my supply of dried meat was almost gone. I couldn't tell if I'd been there for hours or days. My hope of seeing Evan again was steadily fading. Would this tunnel become my tomb? I didn't want to give up but was beginning to think there was no choice.

Every so often the tunnel branched out, forcing me to choose a new path. At first it felt like I was going in circles but then I realized I hadn't seen any doors lately and concluded that the underground village was behind me at last.

Small animals occasionally scurried past my ankles, making me squirm, though I soon learned to recognize their noises and keep them at bay. As I turned into one of the galleries, a swarm of what I thought were bats attacked me, making me shriek, but on closer inspection I realized they were just butterflies—huge black butterflies. Soon I ended up in a cave full of chrysalises at least as big as me. I stood there staring at them, petrified, then ran off.

After a long time spent groping through the pitch dark, my sight suddenly sharpened inexplicably, allowing me to see just enough to gain my bearings. From time to time my skin felt feverishly hot—it was my nature rebelling as it recognized where I was—but my temperature soon returned to normal.

In the distance a barely perceptible glimmer illuminated the darkness in which I was lost. At first it was so dim that for a second I thought it was just my imagination, like a mirage in the desert. I hurried toward it but when I got close I also heard a crescendo of grunts.

The light was coming from above. It had to be an exit—the first one I'd seen in hours. I couldn't pass up the opportunity. Even though the noises made me think I might be throwing myself into the jaws of some horrible creature, I went toward it.

Just as I was nearing the exit, a bitter laugh escaped me at the sight of some Souls coming out of one of the tunnels behind me. I still had a chance—with a little luck I might reach the opening before they could turn me into their next meal.

I quickened my pace. When I reached the opening, I grabbed hold of a crack in the wall and climbed up with a strength I didn't know I had. I could already smell fresher air that cleansed my nostrils of the earthy stench that impregnated the walls underground. Making a final effort, I hoisted myself up, but one of the Damned beneath me grabbed hold of my calf. I let out a shriek that was like an explosion in the cramped space.

The Soul let go. Looking down, I saw his face crack and shatter like porcelain. I stared at him in astonishment as his head exploded in a cloud of dust. *He had covered his ears.* Could my shriek have been what had carbonized him? I touched my forehead. It was burning. Maybe Ginevra was right and my powers really were starting to emerge.

When I wedged my foot into the uppermost crack, the rock gave way beneath my weight and I fell back. I could hear footsteps approaching. Someone was coming. I struggled to shake the cloud from my mind as a ghoulish smile loomed over me, but I didn't have the strength and darkness washed over me.

Through the blackness I was submerged in came the murmur of soft, vaguely cheerful voices and for a second I deluded myself that the nightmare was finally over. I clung to those sounds as I slowly came to, a sharp pain lacerating my head. I rubbed the nape of my neck, the spot where the pain radiated from, and found that my hair was dry and matted. Then I remembered. I must have hit my head when I fell from the rock wall. Ignoring the pain, I tried to get up from the old wooden bench on which I lay. The room was packed with all sorts of people. Whoever had found me must have carried me to some kind of tavern where everyone seemed to be having a good time.

It took me no more than a moment to figure out where I'd ended up. Where I was could only be one specific, terrifying place, and the creatures that surrounded me could only be one species of Damned.

Lechers. The air was heavy with the smell of sex.

At first sight the place might have been mistaken for a "normal" house of ill repute except that no one was acting normally. Everywhere I turned, people were indulging in every aspect of carnal pleasure: between the tables, on the benches, against the walls. A woman straddling a man stared at me steadily as she whispered something in her lover's ear, giving me the creeps. I noticed that the glasses were filled with a reddish liquid that definitely wasn't wine. Terrified, I looked around for a way out and noticed to my horror that the skirt of my dress was raised. I quickly covered myself, painfully aware that whoever had taken me there had done so for a specific reason. I had to escape. I hoped it wasn't too late, that they hadn't abused me while I was unconscious.

"Awake at last." I jumped at the clear sound of a male voice and focused on a young face. His eyes, black and hypnotic, instantly sent a shiver through me as they gazed at me. His lips curved into a smile.

I instinctively pulled my knees to my chest and scurried away over the long bench. Touching my neck, I felt the medallion. It gave me an instant sense of security. "Don't come near me," I warned the young man, looking him in the eye.

His long, raven-black hair was tied into a low ponytail with a leather thong. "Come now, don't get worked up. I don't mean to harm you or"—he looked around and grinned—"whatever it is you think I have in mind."

Though his expression wasn't hostile, I couldn't trust anyone any more. "Who are you? What is this place? Was it you who brought me here?"

Another grin. The guy's cocky expression made me think he was laughing at me. I was frightened and couldn't hide it.

"You ask a lot of questions for a girl who just banged her head." He put his feet up on the table, tilted his chair back, and clasped his hands behind his head, a cunning smile on his lips. His eyes were glued to mine. "Ahrec. Jigol's. No."

"What's that, a riddle?" I said acidly.

His laughter rang out. "Just answering your questions, Peachskin." His eyes unabashedly studied my neckline. "My name is Ahrec, this is Jigol's tavern, and no, I'm not the one who brought you here."

"Don't call me that again." I looked at him warily. "My name is Gemma. Who's Jigen? And if it wasn't you, who brought me to this place?"

"*Jigol* is that fellow over there." He jerked his head toward a massive, broad-shouldered man who was bald and dressed entirely in buffalo pelts. "And that's the answer to both questions."

I gulped when I saw the burly man slide his hand between the thighs of a woman sitting on the bar with her legs spread wide. She really seemed to be enjoying his attentions. Ahrec followed my eyes. "Ugly fellow, isn't he? Don't worry, I kept my eye on you the whole time. No one laid a hand on you." I swallowed again and my eyes darted to Ahrec's, grateful he had answered my thoughts and relieved my most horrifying fear.

"I think he wanted you all to himself. Luckily I showed up in time." He winked at me, broadening his sly smile.

"What do you mean?" I cocked my head and shot him a piercing look, suddenly frightened by his expression.

"I claimed you for myself." My eyes widened in shock as my hand moved toward my arm. "I have to admit it wasn't easy. I had to fight to get you. I'm sure you'll thank me later." I clutched the hilt of my dagger. "Whoa, whoa, whoa! You're dangerous, it would seem," he joked, but my eyes didn't leave his for a second. "Don't worry. I was only kidding!"

I continued to stare at him warily.

"Truth is, Jigol was just waiting for you to come to. He's not too fond of passive lovers, you see."

"What?!" My uneasiness was beginning to verge on despair. Was that nasty-looking guy actually just waiting for me to be awake before raping me?

"Drink a bit of this." Ahrec offered me a tankard of the strange red liquid they were all drinking. Still distraught, I refused, so he tilted his head back and took a long drink. "That's a pity." He wiped his mouth with the back of his hand as a scarlet trickle ran down one corner of his lips. "It would help you relax." He stared at me as though wanting to worm his way inside me, probe me for answers to questions I couldn't even imagine.

"What is that stuff?" I asked, nodding at the cup with a hint of disgust. I had the feeling I wasn't going to like the answer one bit. The liquid was thick and scarlet with golden streaks, and my instincts told me it wasn't cherry juice.

"It may not be the nectar of the gods, but this 'stuff' can definitely take you to paradise." Ahrec shrugged and finished it in a single gulp. "It's forbidden around here—rare goods—but it would seem Jigol has connections. That's one reason his tavern is always full."

The more Ahrec talked, the clearer it became to me what the red liquid was. Ginevra had talked to me about her "little games" with Simon, and I'd already seen those golden streaks when we captured the Executioner.

It was Witch's blood. My heart skipped a beat at the thought that they might use it on Evan. What effect would it have on him? Would he really succumb to them? Was it powerful enough to break down his defenses like some dark spell? Or did the Witches use it to dull his senses, like we'd done with Desdemona?

"Welcome back, princess." A huge hand gripped my shoulder. I whipped around and a shiver of terror raced down my back when I looked into Jigol's hard, hungry eyes. "It was about time. I was getting tired of waiting."

I tried to break free but he held me tighter and slid his other hand down my bodice. Frozen in terror, I sought Ahrec's gaze. He sat there without moving, seemingly caught off guard, but there was a determined look in his eyes that darted furiously between me and Jigol. I shot him a pleading look, though there was no reason to hope for his help. Even if he tried, Ahrec wouldn't have a chance against him in a fight; he was toned but lean, whereas Jigol was built like an ogre.

"Hey, don't be like that." Jigol tried to pin me down as he began to rub his body against mine. His tongue slid down my neck as I squirmed with disgust. "Relax, we're in my kingdom now. There are no Flesh Fiends allowed in here. We can have some fun. I bet nobody offered you a bit of my elixir yet. I'll have to chop off some heads for their lack of hospitality."

Out of the corner of my eye I saw his hand grab a tankard full of it. I sealed my lips tight, but Jigol pressed the tankard against my mouth, forcing it open. "It's magic," he insisted. "You wanna stay in this living hell or let me take you to paradise?" He grabbed my bodice, ready to yank my dress off, and the medallion popped out.

Suddenly an inhuman howl silenced the room. I immediately spat out the blood and turned around. The shriek had come from Jigol. He was clutching his arm that was now missing a hand. I let out a scream when I realized his fingers were still clawing at my shoulder. With horror, I shrugged off the hand.

I looked up and Ahrec grinned at me cockily. "Don't worry. He'll grow a new one." With a single, flowing movement, Ahrec had snatched the dagger from me and chopped off Jigol's hand. He'd done it so quickly I hadn't even noticed he'd moved toward us.

Jigol continued to moan, clutching his arm. "Get them!" he bellowed, his voice even hoarser from the pain.

Ahrec grabbed my arm and yanked me toward the door. "We'd best be leaving, and fast." He clasped my hand firmly in his, without giving me the chance to object, and led me across the room. Some of the Damned rushed to stop us and he fought them off by hurling tables at them, lifting them with one hand and making them seem as light as papier-mâché.

Once we neared the door, however, a group of men blocked our way, putting an end to our escape. Before I knew it, Ahrec had grabbed me by the waist, hoisted me onto a counter, nimbly leapt up beside me and with a firm kick smashed in the wooden planks of a boarded-up window. He took me by the hand and a moment later the twilight air cooled my face.

I ran after him as he headed toward the forest. He was going so fast I could barely keep up with him. Suddenly something moved in the darkness. I tensed, but Ahrec started to laugh.

I squinted and a gasp escaped me. "My God!"

A man with long black hair and the body of a Greek God was taking a woman against a tree while two other women contended for his mouth in anxious anticipation.

"He's a Flesh Fiend," Ahrec explained. I wanted to look away but couldn't. "The ladies, on the other hand, are Nymphs. During their lifetimes they were slaves to sex."

"You're kidding, right?" Ahrec laughed again. "Nymphs? I thought Nymphs were some sort of—I don't know—*fairies!*"

"They are. Fairies who lure unwitting victims to do their sexual bidding, like it or not. Even the Witches are called Nymphs sometimes, because of their powers of seduction and their unbridled lust. Where do you think the word 'nymphomaniac' comes from? Those Nymphs want nothing more than to copulate with him, at all costs. I recommend you not watch. It won't be a pretty sight."

"Watch? What do you take me for—some kind of creepy voyeur?"

"Do as you please. I only said it to spare you the shock of seeing him feed on them."

I teetered and slowed my pace, bewildered. "What do you mean, he's going to feed on them?"

"Exactly what you think."

"But they're together, they're all over him, and—"

"And he's going to rip their heads off and eat them. Eat them alive. Devour them. I'll draw you a picture if you like. I have all the time in the world."

"But that's insane! You mean one minute she has his tongue in her mouth and the next he'll be gobbling hers up like it's no big deal?"

"I would have described the scene differently, but I'll admit you do have a lively imagination," Ahrec joked.

A shudder crept down my spine. "It's horrifying. Can't we warn them?"

"No need. They already know."

"Why are they still there, then?! Why don't they run away?" I stared at the three women. Another of them was pressed against the tree now. The man was taking her vigorously, making her shriek with pleasure.

"They can't help it. I told you, they're slaves to their own lust."

I blinked and turned toward Ahrec, forcing myself to take my eyes off the spectacle that would soon be tinged red.

"Don't look at me. It's the price Lechers have to pay—male and female alike. They're slaves to sex and here they're forced to pay for it with their lives. They can't help it. For the most part they only dally yet often they can't stop, and once they've sated their appetites they meet with a gruesome end. Just like these ladies. Lucky for them they didn't encounter a female Flesh Fiend."

"Why? What's the difference?"

"The females are also called Praying Mantises. People say they can give you the most phenomenal sex you'll ever experience, yet during coitus they bite your head off in chunks. They don't have the brute force of male Flesh Fiends, so their victims experience a slow, agonizing death—along with rapturous pleasure. So it's not such a terrible end after all."

"God, how revolting!"

Ahrec shrugged. "There are Flesh Fiends lurking everywhere around these parts, yet Jigol's tavern is a safe haven. Those three women were probably headed there and didn't make it."

"Wait." Instinct made me stop before we made our way into the trees. "Why did you do it?"

His face didn't look hostile, but his black eyes flashed like a wolf's that's tracked down the hiding place of its prey.

"Did you rescue me so *you* could be the one to devour me or . . . who knows what else?" I asked defiantly.

His laughter rang out crisply through the cool air, like the first time I'd heard it. "You think I rescued you from Jigol so I could devour you or . . . *who knows what else?*"

"Shouldn't I think that? It wouldn't be the first time it's happened to me down here. Besides, why should I trust you?"

Ahrec came closer. Having him so near made me stiffen. "For at least two reasons." I arched an eyebrow, waiting for his explanation. "The first is that I just saved you from Jigol. You can always go back to his tavern if you'd rather discover the paradise he promised you." This time he was the one to arch an eyebrow. The shadow of a smile appeared on his lips.

"And what would the second reason be?" I asked suspiciously.

Ahrec cupped my chin in his hand and turned my head in a surprisingly gentle gesture. "The second would be those fellows over there." I jumped at the sight of a horde of men in the distance advancing inexorably in our direction. Ahrec took my hand again and I was forced to look him in the eye. "I don't believe you have much choice."

I sighed in frustration. He was right. I didn't want to trust him, but what alternative was there? I let him lead me into the forest and away from the men following us. I would just have to be careful never to let my guard down.

"Why were you there?" We had walked for a long time in silence, seeking the shelter of the forest to shake our pursuers.

"Beg pardon?" Ahrec must have grown so used to my silence that my question took him by surprise. Or maybe he just wanted to stall or avoid answering.

"What were you doing there, in the tavern? Are you one of them?"

Another mocking laugh. Ahrec was starting to get on my nerves. "Are you asking me if I'm a Lecher? Deep down, who isn't a bit lustful?"

I instinctively backed away from him. Ahrec looked around to make sure we were alone. "Don't worry, I'll give you all the time you need." He came closer, his eyes slightly wild. "However, sooner or later you'll have to show me your gratitude for saving you. Don't tell me you wouldn't enjoy it too."

My panic was so overwhelming I couldn't move a muscle. Ahrec was inches from me, his eyes not leaving mine for a second. Then his lips spread into a smile and he burst out laughing as I stood there blinking. "Come on! You didn't really believe me about my 'reward,' did you?"

"It's not funny." As I stomped past him I punched his shoulder, but hidden under his sweater were rock-hard muscles. My wrist hurt, but I didn't let it show. I didn't know whether I should be afraid of Ahrec or feel safe. Every ounce of me hoped it was the latter.

"Come on now, don't pout," he shouted after me as I stormed away. "Hasn't anyone ever told you what fun it is to tease you?"

Something contracted inside me but I was careful to hide how upset I was. "Yes, actually. Someone used to tell me that all the time."

Evan.

A quiver in my heart reminded me what was at stake. "Who are you and why did you save me?" I insisted. "The truth this time."

Ahrec caught up with me and clasped his hands behind his neck without slowing his pace. "I saw you slung over Jigol's shoulder and followed him. At first I had no intention of saving you—I was simply curious. Don't know what came over me. Challenging Jigol wasn't wise of me, yet I couldn't help it."

"You seemed at home back there. How did you know about Jigol and his tavern if you're not one of them?"

"When you're in a place like this for a long time you learn to know your enemies. It's not easy to survive unless you watch your back."

I jumped over a strange stone that protruded from the ground in my path. Only then did I notice that all around us were hundreds of small skulls dangling from spiny tree trunks. I froze in terror.

"*Antirrhinum Skull.*"

"Huh?"

"That's their scientific name. They're just flowers." Ahrec laughed, enjoying my expression.

"So you're a botany expert, are you?" I asked with sarcasm, given that it was the only language he seemed to understand.

"I'm an expert on skulls—at least enough to know that those aren't skulls."

"But how do you know their name?"

"It's better if you don't ask." Ahrec winked at me and I sighed, deciding to drop it. All his answers did was prompt more questions in me, while I should have been focusing only on what really interested me.

"Who are you?" I tried again, but Ahrec continued to tease me.

"You do like to repeat yourself! I'm the fellow who saved your life, isn't that enough?"

"Are you a Subterranean?" I asked point-blank.

Ahrec let out a long whistle. "My, you are direct."

"I didn't ask you what color underwear you have on."

"Who says I have any on?" He grinned at me mockingly as I rolled my eyes at his insolence.

"Are you or aren't you?" I insisted. I couldn't trust him unless I knew what kind of Soul he was.

"You're asking if I'm a Subterranean?" Ahrec looked at me out of the corner of his eye. Once again, I suspected he was considering how to answer. He must have survived thanks to his shrewdness in addition to his incredible strength. "You know a lot for someone who's still a mortal."

"How do you know I'm a mortal?" I shot back warily.

He smiled, not taking me seriously. "Anyone could tell that. I'd wager they could even smell your scent underground. You're rare goods around here. And by rare I mean *unique*."

"Is that why you want me with you?"

Ahrec chuckled. "Again?! Look, I've already told you I'm not after your blood or your body—though I'm not saying I wouldn't like it if you were to have second thoughts."

"Hey! You dodged my question again. Are you or are you not an Angel?"

"We're all *Demons* here, Peachskin." He paused before going on. "Perhaps there was a time when I used to be one; however, in this accursed place it doesn't matter which race you're from. All that matters is which races you have to steer clear of to avoid being—Look out!"

There was a sputter and a hiss. Ahrec grabbed me and shoved me against something before I realized what was going on. I tried to breathe but he was squeezing my chest. When he eased his grip I looked around, frightened. I was backed against a tree and he was in front of me, his arms still wrapped around me. "This would be a fine time for you to have those second thoughts." He arched an eyebrow as an amused grin appeared on his lips. I glared at him and shoved him away.

He moved aside and seemed uncomfortable, but only for a second. "You should be more careful. One false step and—*poof*." He gestured with one hand and I noticed his palm was burned.

"You're hurt!" I pulled away from the tree trunk, which prickled like a million needles. I noticed it was covered with tiny thorns. They must have been poisoned and he'd leaned his palms against them to protect me—from what, I still didn't understand.

Without replying, Ahrec started walking again and I followed him. Soon another sputter caught my attention, but this time I saw where it was coming from and stopped to watch it. A column of steam burst from the ground, pulverizing a big black butterfly flying over it. They were geysers. Poisonous geysers hidden in the black earth. Dazed and suddenly breathless, I looked at Ahrec, who simply shrugged.

He had saved me. Again. "Who are you?" I insisted.

Ahrec looked me in the eye, this time serious. "I'm just someone who's trying to survive, like everyone else." He pulled out my dagger and I stiffened. Holding it by the blade, he handed it to me, still looking into my eyes. "You can trust me." I glanced at the hilt and then at him. "Otherwise why would I give this back to you? You might even kill me with it. I know you've used it before—I smell cursed blood on it. Take it if it makes you feel more at ease."

It was then that I spotted something beneath his left sleeve and my heart filled with hope. Slowly, without taking my eyes off Ahrec's, I took the weapon and slid it back into its sheath, then swiftly snatched his wrist and bared his arm. The mark of the Children of Eve appeared before my eyes like a promise. I was right: Ahrec was a Subterranean.

"My! Don't you think you're moving a bit too fast? Want to see me naked already, do you?" Ahrec pulled his arm back, away from my scrutiny. "If you want me to strip, you could have simply said so."

"Sorry. I have to admit you seemed *human*, or at least different from the others I've run into so far. I had to do it."

Ahrec whistled. "Two points in my favor, then. I'll take that as a compliment."

"Why is your tattoo so distorted?" I asked, hoping he wouldn't be offended.

Ahrec's face darkened and he paused in stubborn silence. Just when I thought he wasn't going to answer, he admitted: "They captured me and disfigured it."

I had other questions, but I was clearly making him uncomfortable. Besides, all things considered, it wasn't important. Ahrec was a Subterranean—that was all that mattered to me. He might really be able to help me after all.

"Think you could help me find the river?"

Ahrec shrugged obligingly. "I have no other commitments."

My heart leapt with hope. "Really?! I mean—thank you! It's very important for me to get there."

"Come on, calm down. There's no saying I won't change my mind about that reward." He winked and smiled at me mockingly while inwardly I chastised myself for revealing all my enthusiasm.

"I'm not going to give you that kind of reward," I assured him, serious again.

"Really? I have a little of Jigol's elixir, if it'll help you unwind a bit." I glared at him and he shrugged. "A pity. You don't know what you're missing."

"Are you going to help me or aren't you?" I insisted.

"Very well, I'll help you find the river. However, first we'd better stop for a while. I haven't eaten in days."

"I hope that's not a threat," I warned.

Ahrec's laughter rang through the trees. "You're beautiful *and* witty." I shot him a glance and he moved his face close to mine, lowering his voice. "In case it wasn't clear, that was a compliment."

I blinked, his nearness making me uncomfortable. He took a couple steps back with an ill-concealed smile on his lips.

"Want to eat?"

With one hand I rummaged through the satchel slung over my shoulder and found myself considering his offer. As though he'd read my mind, Ahrec smiled at me and disappeared into the shrubbery.

Suddenly I felt alone in the darkness, lost without him, as if Ahrec had been with me from the first second. I'd almost convinced myself that I'd grown used to the agonizing screams that broke the silence from time to time, but without him at my side they frightened me again. I rubbed my arms, looking around warily, and thought I saw a shadow moving among the trees.

"Ahrec," I called, a terrible presentiment taking hold of me. "Ahrec . . . someone's here."

In front of me a shrub stirred, sending an eerie shiver up my spine, but before I could give in to panic, Ahrec reappeared, still in the shadows, carrying an animal he'd caught. There was something strange about him, something sinister. I backed up and a stifled cry escaped me. His eyes were ravenous and in the darkness his pupils had dilated, turning blacker than night, as though he were there to kill me. "I th-think there's something in the trees," I warned him as he approached.

He whipped his head to the side in an unnatural movement. A second later, he emerged from the shadows of the trees and the dim light illuminated his face.

"For a moment I thought—" Realizing his face was normal, I let out the breath I'd been holding. Fear had clouded my thinking to the point of making Ahrec look like a monster to my eyes.

He peered around, clearly alarmed someone might be out there. Then he came and showed me what he had caught. It looked a bit like a fox but was the size of a rabbit.

"How did you—"

Ahrec wiped his mouth with the back of his hand and tossed the animal at my feet. "It's better if you don't know."

"I don't eat raw meat," I warned him, trying not to retch.

"You're always jumping to conclusions. Actually that wasn't what I had in mind." He sat down cross-legged and in seconds a flame flickered up between his palms.

"How did—" I stammered, puzzled.

"How do you think the cavemen did it?" He showed me the sticks he was holding. "It's something so rudimentary, I didn't expect it would amaze you."

"Another point in your favor." I crouched down to take in some of its warmth as Ahrec fed the flames with kindling until it had grown into a small fire.

I watched the flames dance in the twilight. Their heat seemed to ignite all the emotions I held within, and they exploded inside me as I sat, my face immobile, my gaze trapped in the dazzling lights that danced in the air. Finding Evan, the hope that held my heart prisoner, seemed farther and farther away.

I closed my eyes and imagined Evan beside me. Every fear disappeared when I was with him. Right now I felt in danger of losing him forever. Searching Hell for him was a desperate endeavor. I was risking everything just to chase after that glimmer of hope. Despite all the hardships, fears, and uncertainties, though, I would never give up. I stroked my belly, thinking of my baby—a part of Evan growing inside me, protected by Ginevra's magic, in case his half-Angelic blood wasn't enough to keep him safe.

Thinking of my baby brought to mind the baby girl I'd killed, and I struggled not to sink into depression. Suddenly I couldn't remember why I'd done it. Had I honestly not had any way to escape? Had I really been forced to do it, or had it been my evil nature taking control of me? Would evil really annihilate who I was without leaving me any alternative? Would I lose the capacity to choose? Or, even worse, would it happen without my realizing it?

"Was it hard?" Ahrec's voice was muffled and distant to my ears, but it was a lifeline I could cling to and pull myself out of the pyre of guilt in which I was burning. I raised my eyes and found his waiting for me. I'd been so absorbed in my thoughts I hadn't realized he was studying me. "It must have been hard for you," he continued, his direct gaze telling me he didn't need confirmation.

"You were right," I found myself whispering. The words had slipped out without my permission.

"About what?" Ahrec's tone was cautious but comforting.

"About the dagger. When you said I'd used it. I've been forced to do horrible things since I got here." Ahrec nodded understandingly. "I even—" I struggled to admit it out loud. "I killed a baby." I paused for so long I thought I wouldn't go on, but then I said, "It was terrible and I can't forgive myself."

Ahrec chucked a stone into the fire, stared at it a moment, and turned to look at me. "You shouldn't feel guilty about it. This place isn't your world."

For some reason, hearing the truth from someone else startled me. Maybe deep down I *had* been forced to do it.

"Your rules don't apply here," he added, the tension on his face slowly easing. "You must have ended up in the Forge of the Antichrist, the village of the Unholy. There are no other babies down here. You were right to defend yourself—they would have killed you otherwise. Many are fooled by their appearance, yet those Souls aren't really little children. They're the Damned who didn't receive purification, the Divine Blessing, on Earth. It doesn't matter what rite it's done through—every religion has its own way to consecrate one's life to God. Also the souls of those who lost faith in God and never found it again, like atheists. No belief in Heaven, no interest in going there."

"You mean even innocent children who don't know anything about life yet end up in Hell just because someone else didn't purify them? That's ridiculous."

"It would be ridiculous, if it happened that way. Not receiving purification isn't enough for a Soul to end up in Hell. Don't forget, a personal decision is always involved. Mortals have free will, and only a freely made choice can damn them forever. Many unbelievers or unpurified people are pure in spirit and at the moment of temptation make the right choice, so their souls are saved. The Unholy, on the other hand, are the souls of the unpurified or atheists who during their lifetimes chose to live in evil. While they're here, they slowly experience what we call the Dwindling: they grow younger and younger until they ultimately look like infants. Though no one knows why, a few keep their adult appearance—perhaps because they've retained a bit of their humanity. However, most of them get littler and littler until they cease to exist. They aren't babies. The younger and smaller they are, the more skillful and dangerous they are. Despite their appearance, they're strong, fast, and deadly. You're lucky you're still alive. They're a ferocious race because they've never known the divine touch. With a few exceptions, of course. I still don't know how you managed to escape from them alive." Ahrec looked at my amulet and I instinctively raised my hand to my chest to cover it.

I nodded, silently thanking him for convincing me I wasn't a monster.

The flames crackled and lit up our faces. From time to time I would take a piece of meat I had cooked over the fire and put it in my mouth. The flavor wasn't the best, but I needed nourishment.

"There's something I have to confess," I blurted. He remained silent, waiting for me to go on. Up until then, I hadn't wanted to take the funny feeling I'd been having too seriously, but I felt safe with Ahrec, so it was easier to face my fears. I peered around at the darkness. "Ever since I got here I've had the feeling someone was following me."

To my surprise, Ahrec stiffened. His eyes scanned the shadows under the trees.

"Once in a while it's like I can see eyes hiding in the darkness—an animal's eyes, like it's stalking me. Who knows, maybe it's just my imagination. Sometimes it feels like this place is making me lose my mind," I admitted. Ahrec tried to hide his uneasiness behind a forced smile, but his face was rigid. "But basically, if there really was something out there, it would've already had lots of chances to attack me, wouldn't it?" I smiled, but the eerie silence that suddenly surrounded us made a shiver crawl beneath my skin.

"No doubt." Ahrec continued to smile, though he still seemed to be forcing it. "It must be your imagination. Why don't you get some rest now?"

Instinct made me peer into the darkness again. No one was there—the forest was silent—but the presentiment was strong and I felt vulnerable. My predator was hiding out there, waiting for the right moment to attack. Something was hunting me down, I was sure of it.

"I'll stand guard while you sleep. It's a long walk to the river and you'll need your strength to make it there."

I lay down on the ground, using my satchel as a pillow. There was something hypnotic in Ahrec's dark gaze. "Don't worry, I'll watch over you." Suddenly I felt incredibly tired and all the strength drained from my body.

"Now sleep, Peachskin."

His words lulled me like a dark spell, persuasive and comforting, until the coils of darkness enveloped me completely.

29

POISON AND BLOOD

When I gradually began to awaken, I had no idea how long I'd been asleep. Time didn't seem to count in that place. I felt something tickling my skin and slowly returned to my surroundings as the fire crackled and the flames danced in the half-light, casting sinister shadows on the ground. Squinting, I made out a figure doubled over on itself. No—crouched over something it held in its hands. The figure seemed to be contemplating whatever it was with a mix of desperation and satisfaction, as if it were his own still-beating heart. The palpable intensity of his gaze made me tremble . . . or maybe it was something else causing that feeling in me.

Suddenly I felt naked and vulnerable. Something was missing. My hand flew to my neck and a shudder turned the blood in my veins to ice. The medallion was gone. "Ahrec—"

He spun around in surprise, but his face was . . . *different*. I scrambled backwards with a shriek of fear, but he didn't move. His eyes followed me ravenously, as black as those of an animal poised to kill. My medallion was clutched in his hands.

I stared at him in terror. It was as though Ahrec was gone, as though every trace of humanity had vanished from his eyes. I stealthily reached for the dagger, but Ahrec must have guessed my intentions because he vanished in the blink of an eye. I scanned the darkness, afraid he might attack me from behind.

"Looking for this?"

I raised my eyes. Overhead, perched on an incredibly high branch, Ahrec stared down at me, his shoulders leaning against the trunk. He slid the blade of my dagger over his tongue, licking off some blood that still looked fresh. Ahrec had tricked me. He was a monster like all the others. And this time I had no way out.

"You told me you were a Subterranean," I cried, my voice cracking with horror.

Ahrec shoved the blade of the dagger into the tree. "I lied," he said in a low growl that didn't sound like his voice. "You shouldn't give your trust so easily. After all, we *are* in Hell." He leapt down and moved closer. "Besides, you wanted so badly for it to be true. Why not let you believe it? I certainly couldn't have told you I was an Unholy Soul."

"You're a—" His words wrenched a groan from my chest.

"Of a sort, actually. I received a holy blessing yet later I stopped believing and lived only by my own rules." The reddish glow of the fire made his face even more threatening as he inched closer. "They didn't know what to do with me, so they damned me as one of them. It's just that I'm stuck at this age. Though I've no idea why, I've never undergone the Dwindling."

"It can't be. I saw your tattoo."

"What, this?" Ahrec bared his arm, smiling. "It's not hard to brand your own skin."

"You did that to yourself? Why?"

"Survival. Subterranean Souls are the only ones who can't die here. No one is daft enough to challenge them—no one except me, naturally. I had to capture more than one of them to finally get the tattoo right. Took me years to perfect it." His eyes were those of a monster, like they'd been when he'd returned with the food. I should have realized it then: Subterraneans don't eat. What a fool I'd been.

"Y-you tricked me. But if all you wanted was the medallion, why didn't you kill me right away?"

Ahrec continued to creep forward. "I wasn't quite sure what you were. First I had to understand what risks I was running. You're human, yet you wear a Witch's trinket around your neck. I was a bit confused by that. Then I thought that perhaps if you trusted me enough to lower your guard—"

"Give it back! That medallion doesn't belong you!"

"Yes it does. You have no idea what it means to have been damned to this place for centuries. Every. Day. Every. Minute. *This*"—he held up the amulet, which he was clenching so tightly his hand had begun to bleed—"is my ticket to freedom. No one is taking it from me. Taking it from you proved easier than I thought. Can you believe I was actually going to keep my word? Before stealing it from you I truly was going to take you to the river, yet when you said you were being followed I realized I had to act quickly." He took another step forward and I scooted myself backwards across the ground. He was so close I could see his teeth. They were incredibly sharp and deadly.

"Do you mean to kill me?" I asked, my voice trembling. Shivers spread over my entire body when Ahrec didn't answer. He just stared at me.

"They're pro—" Sudden terror flashed across his face as something lunged from the darkness and landed heavily on him, knocking him brutally to the ground. I saw it was a large feline. I tried to move away, shrieking with horror as the beast sank its fangs into him. When Ahrec's body stopped twitching, the creature turned its head and looked me in the eye. I cringed, terrified it would tear me to pieces, but instead it continued to stare at me, perfectly still, as though trying to tell me something. I blinked, unable to focus on anything else.

Suddenly all my fear left me. A single thought filled my head: the animal was magnificent. I felt a strange desire to move closer and merge with it. It had fur darker than night and green eyes that emanated a glow that was somehow familiar. Could this be the animal that had been following me? Where else could I have ever looked into a black panther's eyes before?

Acting on an irresistible impulse, I leaned toward it, holding its gaze, but the panther leapt gracefully over the fire and disappeared into the darkness. I crumpled to the ground, speechless, still unable to believe it hadn't slain me too.

A gurgle distracted me from the thought. *Ahrec*. I went to him, trying to avoid looking at the gaping wound in his chest, the deep slash in his neck, and the blood that gushed from it. He wasn't dead yet. He reached out his arm, slid his hand over the ground and touched mine. When I opened my palm he rested my amulet on it.

"Ahrec . . ." I murmured, my voice trembling. His eyes were once again the eyes of the trustworthy young man I'd known, and seeing him like that tugged at my heartstrings.

"I . . . just . . . wanted . . . to be free," he said with effort. A tear streaked my face. I took his hand in mine and he squeezed it tightly. "Take care of yourself . . . Peachskin." He smiled at me affectionately and vanished.

I stared at the cloud of dust into which he had dissolved and new tears slid silently down my cheeks. I had held them back for too long and suddenly I couldn't contain them any longer. I wept because deep down Ahrec hadn't really wanted to kill me. I wept because I had lost even the tiniest hope of finding the river.

Once again, I was alone and vulnerable, trapped in a world without Evan. A world without light. He was out there somewhere, but I hadn't managed to find him.

I had failed—I had no choice but to accept it.

When the ground had absorbed every last tear, I opened my eyes, utterly exhausted. It felt like there was nothing worth fighting for any more. I might as well wait right there until someone came and put an end to my suffering. Even the fire had died out, depriving me of its warmth.

My unfocused gaze lingered on a shape that stood out against the twilit sky, a darker patch against the dreariness, but I was too depressed to pay attention to my flights of fancy. There was nothing out there beyond the hills, nothing I could cling to to help me recover my courage and determination. Just images projected by my mind that, like me, had been beaten down by disappointment.

Blurred by my tears, the shape split in two, then fused into one again. I blinked. The dim light had to be playing a cruel joke on me. And yet . . . I pushed myself up on my palms, electrified. It was still there. *The Castle.*

It wasn't a mirage. It was really there, beyond the hills. Like a giant, it rose into the sky and towered over everything, staring at me as though to guide me to it. The blood began to pulse strongly through my veins again and my heart pounded so hard I felt it would burst from my chest. The joy that flooded me almost knocked me over. Evan was there and I still had a chance to save him. The Castle was far away, but *it was there.* I had found it. And after everything I'd faced already, those last miles wouldn't be enough to stop me. I would conquer the two hills that protected it like soldiers guarding a fortress. I would brave the forest and the dangers lurking there. I would walk for days on end, climb the Castle walls if need be, but in the end I would reach it. Nothing else mattered any more.

Without realizing it, I had already started walking. My feet were moving on their own, my eyes riveted on my destination, fearing it might fade away. I felt as if I were flying. Suddenly every dismal thought vanished. Soon I would see Evan and nothing would ever separate us again. I still had the feeling that hidden eyes were following my every movement from the forest, but I didn't even care about that. I was prepared to face and kill anything that dared attack me.

I felt invincible.

The forest was swarming with creatures—I could hear every little sound—but they all shied away from me, as though they too sensed the energy I was emanating.

Something glinted on the ground. I looked down. At the foot of the tree Ahrec had climbed lay my dagger. How strange—I remembered his leaving it lodged in the trunk high up on the tree. Had he made it fall just for me? I looked around warily before picking up the weapon and sheathing it. My eyes instantly returned to the Castle in the distance. It was so imposing it even challenged the sky. Not even the thick treetops could cover its majesty. A flock of ravens soared overhead, but instead of being afraid I watched them, fascinated, until they disappeared beyond the trees.

I couldn't believe I would soon see Evan again. For a long time my heart had faltered, like an old clock on the verge of dying. But now, with my renewed hope, it threatened to burst through my chest.

From the corner of my eye I saw something move in the semidarkness. A shiver ran down my spine but I did my best to ignore it and continued walking. Another movement—quicker this time. I tried to follow it with my eyes but saw only the gloom of dusk. A low, hair-raising growl filled the air but I couldn't tell where it was coming from. I instinctively rested my hand on the hilt of my dagger, my eyes scanning the gloom, but the sound seemed to surround me, coming from several directions at once. All at once, dark shadows crept out into the open, their hackles raised and their throaty growls growing louder.

Wolves. An entire pack of wolves prepared to lunge at me. The blade sang as I drew it from its sheath. I wasn't afraid. I stood there waiting, challenging them with my eyes. Nothing would come between me and Evan.

I gulped as the pack surrounded me. The largest wolf snarled louder than the rest and drew ever closer. I prepared myself to face it, but it leapt onto my chest and knocked me to the ground as the rest of the pack looked on. I struggled, but the wolf was too strong. It aimed its massive, powerful fangs directly at my throat as a scream escaped me.

Suddenly the animal pricked its ears and backed away, whining faintly. I narrowed my eyes, trying to understand what had just happened and what could have caused the wolf to retreat. What creature could be terrifying enough to frighten that wolf?

It was still right there in front of me, only now it regarded me with a completely different attitude. Its eyes studied me with curiosity. I propped myself up on my palms and the wolf bowed its head in what seemed to be a show of respect. I cocked my head, baffled, trying to understand its behavior as I slowly rose to my feet.

The wolf withdrew to rejoin the pack and a howl pierced the night. Their frightened, uncertain eyes didn't leave mine. I realized their instincts were telling them something that their sense of smell couldn't fathom: my body smelled of human blood, but there was a Witch buried inside me. I cautiously stepped forward and the wolves moved back as if in some dark dance until they disappeared into the forest. It seemed impossible they could be afraid of me. Could it have been something else that frightened them? I looked around. I didn't see anyone, and yet I had the impression there was someone else out there, hiding.

I sheathed the dagger and continued walking, marveling at how brave I'd been when facing the wolves. I hadn't been afraid at all, as though inside me lay the certainty I would be able to subdue them. The feeling of power was perceptible beneath my skin. Had that been enough to drive them away? Had they actually sensed it too?

I noticed suddenly that all the trees in the forest were bare, and stopped in my tracks. Hundreds of thick branches all around me were twisted like bodies paralyzed by terror. Abruptly, the rooftops of a village that had been hidden behind two tall hills appeared in the near distance. An irrepressible shudder ran through me. I knew it was better to steer clear of villages—the very thought of going through another one terrified me—but I had no choice.

I looked beyond the hills and the village. The Castle was getting closer. It seemed to stare at me, as though to encourage me—or frighten me away. I swallowed and my heart sent a message to my brain, ordering it to banish my fear. A moment later, my legs moved toward the village.

30

TRAPPED

People scurried in every direction, staring at their feet, their faces covered by long hoods. For a long time I'd remained hidden behind a cart, observing them, waiting for the right moment to go out, but it seemed the coming and going would never lessen, so I raised the hood of my green cloak and blended into the crowd. Being so close to so many Damned Souls made my heart race. Maybe it was just my nerves, but they seemed to be casting me grave looks as though they sensed something different about me. Something wrong. I continued along the street, anxious to leave the village behind and reach the Castle and Evan. But no matter how hard I tried to keep a low profile, I gradually realized an empty space had opened up around me as though the people, afraid of me, were keeping their distance. I walked on, as frightened as a rabbit in a wolf's den, their murmurs haunting me.

"What is she?"

"Can't you smell that she's human? It can't be!"

The sudden, ominous blast of a horn pierced the air, making me shiver. The next thing I knew chaos broke out all around me. What the hell was going on?

Then I saw them. A shudder ran all the way from my legs to my neck: a swarm of dark Angels was flying toward the village. I froze in terror and looked around for a place to hide but a woman in the crowd suddenly stopped and fixed her gaze on me. The whole world seemed to grind to a halt around us as the fire in her eyes burned into mine.

"Stop!" she thundered without taking her eyes off me. "The Indavas have never attacked us before." She raised her hand in my direction and everyone stopped to listen to her. Panic gripped me. "'Tis *she* who brought them here! Let us deliver her to them!"

The silent crowd seemed confused, unsure of what the best course of action would be.

"Ofelia is right!" a man's deep, powerful voice shouted. "They'll kill us one by one until they've taken her! Let's feed her to them!"

The crowd cheered in unison and charged in my direction. I backed up, terrified, but the men were on top of me before I had time to react. I struggled to break free, but their grip was too tight.

"Quickly! They're coming!" someone said anxiously. Despite my attempts to escape they shoved me against a post, knocking the breath out of me.

"Let me go!" I screamed in dismay, but none of them paid any attention. Someone pulled my hands behind my back and a rope was wound around my wrists and then my ankles. I felt like Andromeda, chained up with no Perseus to save me.

"Set me free! Please! I just wanted to cross through the village!" I looked overhead: the Indavas, as the villagers had called them, were getting closer and closer. "Let me go and I'll lead them away from here!" I tried to convince them in a steady voice, but there wasn't a shadow of hesitation in their eyes. Instead, they stared at me as though I were some strange monster.

A man came over, reached out toward my medallion, and exchanged glances with his friend. "'Tis true, 'tis the Dreide she wears. But why did she not fight back?" I tried to squirm away from his hand as someone let out a sudden scream of terror.

The man jumped and pulled back his hand. "They're coming!" Screams filled the square again as the crowd scattered in every direction.

"Let me go!" I shouted, trying to pull free of the ropes. "Don't leave me here, you cowards!" But no one listened to me and in seconds the only sound was the echo of my desperation. The streets had gone silent. They had all run off to hide, leaving me bound to a post as their sacrifice.

A living, pulsing dark cloud appeared overhead. Seconds later, the swarm of dark Angels had obscured the sky, covering the twilight with their mighty, bat-like wings. A shudder ran through my body as the creatures plunged down to attack the village.

No—not the village. To attack *me*. I tugged against the ropes over and over in an attempt to free myself but soon realized it was no use. I began to sob, not with tears of terror—there wasn't a trace of fear in me—but of desperation. I would never see Evan again or hold my baby in my arms.

One of the Angels swooped toward me. It wasn't until it was very close that I could make out its features. A single word filled my mind: vampire. It was a vampire with a reptile's face, a long serpentine tail, razor-sharp claws, and a beak lined with teeth. A strange horn stuck out of its head, occasionally emitting an unearthly bioluminescent glow. I wanted to close my eyes to avoid the sight, but instead I tilted my head and held my breath as the Angel of darkness wrapped itself around me. I felt its strong body squeezing me, forcing the air out of my lungs. I moaned from the pain and tried to break free but the creature's long tail was coiled around my body, crushing me as it prepared to sink its vampire fangs into my flesh. I screamed with all the breath I had left, and the monster slashed my cheek with its beak.

Unexpectedly, something hurled the demon away from me. I stared at it in shock, its body crumpled on a rooftop, its tail still twitching. A spark shot out of its body. The fire quickly spread and in the blink of an eye the whole house was engulfed in flames. I looked up with a mix of terror, relief, and confusion as two jade-green eyes bored into mine.

Anya.

My heart leapt as a group of Witches on winged steeds chased off the Indavas, shooting thunderbolts and lightning that briefly lit up the sky. Meanwhile, the fire slowly destroyed the village, consuming the houses one after the other. The Souls ran into the street, screaming in terror and fleeing in every direction.

My head was throbbing frantically, trapped in a tangle of emotions. It was over. The Witches had saved me from the Indavas and they would finally take me to Evan. In exchange, they would demand my surrender, but it didn't matter. I didn't care about sacrificing myself to them as long as I could finally reach the Castle. It was my last hope for Evan to be set free.

Once the village was rid of the horrible Indavas, Anya flew her steed toward me, but a bolt of lightning sliced the air between us and the animal reared in the air.

Anya's gaze turned furious. I followed it and found myself looking into Devina's fierce, icy eyes. I would have recognized them from among a thousand others. The amber of her irises seemed to have caught fire.

"No one is to go near her."

Her voice rang out like an order—hard and implacable—while she studied my face with interest. I did my best to block her from my mind, but I could feel her tentacles unfurling in my brain, trying to bring down my defenses. I held on, though; I couldn't let her discover my plan, not now that I was so close to Evan, and after a long moment of silent struggle, she cracked her whip in frustration and gave up.

Devina pulled on the reins of her strange armored steed and turned to leave, followed by the other Witches. Only Anya didn't move, her face filled with resentment. I looked over their shoulders and was almost overcome with desperation: the Castle had vanished, as though it had been only a mirage.

"Wait!" At the sound of my voice, Devina stopped without turning her steed around, granting me only a sidelong glance. "Take me with you!" I cried, my back still pressed against the post. I tried to sound confident, but my voice betrayed my desperation. "I have a message for your Empress."

Devina's only response was mocking laughter. "What do you take me for, your carrier pigeon?" She looked at me, tilting her head, and her smile twisted into a mask of pure evil. "I'm afraid you'll have to find her on your own"—she raised an eyebrow, her expression challenging—"at your own risk and peril."

"Devina! You can't leave her here!" Anya said reproachfully, shooting her a defiant look, but Devina wasn't the least perturbed.

"Anya is right," said a third Sister with big eyes and straight raven-black hair. "Sophìa won't be happy when she learns about this."

"Then don't tell her," Devina said to silence her, a hint of derision in her voice.

Anya spurred her steed and rode over in front of Devina, lowering her voice. "Have you gone mad? What are you thinking?"

The two Sisters silently challenged each other for a long moment. I wished I could read their minds but was afraid that if I tried to Devina might be able to penetrate mine.

"Sophìa left *me* in charge." Devina's voice was as sharp as her gaze. "You've already helped her enough. We do as *I* say now." She cocked her head and cast me an icy look that sent an involuntary shiver through me. "Leave her there and wish her good luck." She spurred her steed and took flight.

Anya gave me a look full of regret. It was clear she wanted to help me but couldn't go against Devina's orders, since Sophìa had left her in charge. Suddenly the pressure on my wrists eased. I looked at Anya, both confused and surprised. She smiled back.

The well, Gemma. I jumped when her voice filled my head. Once Devina was gone, I'd lowered my defenses and Anya had managed to reach my mind. *There's a tunnel beneath the well. It connects to the river. Follow the river and it will lead you to the Castle. Don't give up, Gemma. You're almost there.*

As I shook the ropes off my wrists I smiled and looked into her eyes with my own tear-filled ones, trying to express my gratitude. Anya returned my look, then spurred her steed and rose into the air, joining her Sisters.

I watched her figure grow smaller until every trace of it was swallowed up by the twilight. Then I untied the ropes from my ankles and went over to the well, which wasn't far away. I peered down into it, struggling with fear and uncertainty, but there was no time to hesitate. I felt I could trust Anya. I grabbed hold of the wooden bucket and lowered myself into its depths until darkness engulfed me.

At the bottom I rested one foot on the ground, shuddering. I was standing in an icy pool of water. A stinging sensation crept up my legs but the water was so cold that the discomfort soon vanished. After one last glance up, I took a deep breath and made my way into the tunnel. It was narrow and less dark than I'd expected, though it was possible I was seeing clearly only because my encounter with the Witches had reawakened some of my powers. A strange smell that reminded me vaguely of something I couldn't identify pervaded the air.

After a while, overcome with thirst, I leaned over to examine the water that reached my ankles. I wasn't sure I wanted to drink it, but I was so parched my tongue felt like it had crushed glass on it. I scooped some water into my hands and squinted as I raised it to my lips. It took only a second to finally recognize the familiar smell.

Poison.

The water must have contained only a small amount because my skin wasn't burning like it had when I'd fallen into the river. An idea occurred to me: I leaned over again, took the canteen out of the satchel, and filled it as full as I could. If nothing else, it could at least serve as a makeshift weapon, though I hoped I wouldn't have to use it.

I lifted the bottom of my skirt to wash away the dried blood between my calf and ankle. When the water touched the wound I gritted my teeth and bit my lip to keep from screaming, but the pain disappeared as quickly as it had come. I checked my leg to make sure it was clean and my eyes bulged with surprise: the wound inflicted by the Unholy Soul was gone. Had the poison actually had a healing effect on me? I couldn't believe it.

I stroked my cheek where the gash was still throbbing and poured some poisoned water over it, squeezing my eyes shut against the pain. It only lasted a second and the wound vanished beneath my fingertips. I straightened up, shook my head in surprise, and started walking again.

A short while later, something brushed against my ankle. I jumped, but saw it was only a small animal, which scurried off. It probably thought I was too big to tackle. As the hours wore on I came across a few other animals, but none of them were any larger or braver than the first. They inevitably ignored me and crawled away, so I stopped jumping at every strange grunt and squeak and continued to make my way down the narrow tunnel, trying to focus solely on the sound of the water dripping steadily from the walls.

Another sound, however, gave me chills. I wasn't sure if it was real or just my imagination, but I had the impression someone was whispering in my ear. The sound paralyzed me and I looked around in alarm. The water continued to drip with an eerie sound, but there was no one else in the passageway, I was sure of it. All at once something touched my arm. A shiver spread from the spot I'd been touched through my whole body like an electric current, making me shriek.

"Who's there?" I shouted, but the only reply was my own echo coming back to haunt me. I swallowed, listening as silence returned to the tunnel, and another whisper touched my ear. I spun around and saw it: a partially visible face peering at me, inches away. My heart banged against my ribs and I flattened myself against the wall. I should have fled, but I couldn't take my eyes off the strange being. The face moved closer to mine and I let it study me. There was no telling what it was—an ethereal creature that looked like it was made of water, or air that had changed consistency and crafted itself into a human semblance. It didn't look at all hostile. The way it flowed through the air with soft, graceful movements fascinated me. Before I realized it I'd raised my hand, drawn by my desire to feel the curious creature's consistency beneath my fingertips.

"Don't touch it!" I whirled around and caught my breath at the sight of the hooded figure before me. I knew that voice. "Shh . . ." Slowly, she pulled back her hood and raised a finger to her lips.

"Gwen!" My heart did a somersault when my eyes met hers. Though I longed to rush to her and hug her, the ethereal creature swirled around me, recapturing my attention. I was entranced by its enchanting movements. The almost irresistible urge to touch it came over me again, blocking everything else out.

"Stop, Gemma!" Ginevra insisted.

"Why? I just want a closer look. " My voice sounded muffled and distant even to me—it was like being under a spell.

"Don't touch it. It's a Pariah. Look at me, Gemma. Focus only on me."

Ginevra's presence was enough for me to listen to her and ignore the overpowering attraction the creature was exercising on me. I flattened myself against the wall, eluding the strange, wraithlike creature. "What's a Pariah?" I asked, tearing my eyes away from the creature with an effort.

"They're the souls of those whose sin in life was being so vain they sacrificed everything else. *Don't let it touch you,*" she warned as the creature circled me again. It seemed to be performing a graceful, hypnotic dance. "The proud, the egocentric, narcissists, those in love only with themselves, those who see nothing but themselves are ostracized here, condemned to virtual invisibility."

"What would happen if I touched it?"

"Your essence would flow into it and your body would dissolve. That's how Pariahs feed. They need others to survive, although the effect wears off fast and they need to feed again. They can't take you by force, no matter how much they would like to or how hungry they are—they can only try to draw your attention. They're masters at the art of enchantment. It's a gift granted them in memory of their previous lives. If you stare at one for too long you won't be able to look away. Because of its hypnotic powers you'll ultimately fuse with it. They're capable of bonding any Soul to them."

"But it's so pretty . . ."

"Gemma!"

"What do I do?!" I cried, frightened of the translucent creature for the first time.

"I can only warn you and guide you. I'm a projection of your mind. I've been trying to establish a connection with you ever since you got here, but this is the first time I've achieved it. Your powers are getting stronger."

The Pariah came closer, blocking my way.

Ginevra stared at a spot deep inside the tunnel and her eyes widened in fear. "There are others. Run, Gemma! Quick! They're coming. I can't help you! You have to get out of here. They can't leave the tunnels."

I automatically darted forward, dodging the Pariah, and rushed down the tunnel. Ginevra had disappeared, but her voice still filled my head: *Run, Gemma! Get out of there!* The Pariah moved swiftly, as though one with the water. I knew it was behind me because I could hear its eerie whisper in my ear.

To the right! Turn right! Ginevra ordered, guiding me into a broader tunnel that suddenly forked into two smaller ones. From the end of one of them came a pale glow, but my enthusiasm disappeared when I approached it and found it was a dead end. An opening at the end of the other tunnel led outside toward the river, but boulders blocked it. I tried to crawl around them, but it was useless. I was trapped with my back to the wall, and the Pariahs were quickly approaching. I felt like a rabbit in a wolf's den.

Then I remembered the Devil's Stramonium. I searched the satchel for the plant I'd saved, but my hands were shaking too hard. When I finally had it in my fingers, a ghastly whisper echoed through the tunnel, making me start, and the plant slipped from my fingers and disappeared into the water lapping at my feet. I felt for it frantically, but was too panicked to find it.

"Gwen!" I pleaded. "Come back! Damn it!"

I looked over my shoulder to see where the Pariahs were and rushed off in the opposite direction. All at once, a light caught my attention. There was another tunnel! I took it and raced breathlessly toward the twilight as a strange roaring noise grew ever louder, echoing off the dripping tunnel walls around me. I was almost there—I could see the exit. Sprinting the last few yards, I readied myself to jump—and came to a screeching halt before I could plunge into the void. The sound of the waterfall below hit me full on.

I'd almost ended up being washed over it, and it was higher than any waterfall I'd ever seen. Feeling like I'd been punched in the face, I wheeled around, frantic. I was too high up to jump. Taking a deep breath, I realized I had no choice but to go back the way I'd come. A whisper filled the tunnel and brushed my ear. I repressed a shiver and forced myself to continue the desperate search for a way out, but the farther I went the smaller the passageway became until I was ultimately forced to get down on all fours. I felt as if I was living a nightmare. The air grew thicker and danker and my lungs cried out for oxygen.

One of the Pariahs touched my ankle. I pulled it away instantly with a scream that echoed through the cramped space, desperate and grim. The whispers returned in unison, warning me of their arrival en masse. Suddenly it felt like all the air was gone. I coughed. My legs were heavier and it took tremendous effort to drag them across the damp ground.

There's an exit! I jumped when I heard Ginevra's sharp voice in my head, realizing only then that I was on the verge of passing out. *Come on, Gemma! Hang in there. You're almost there!*

I gritted my teeth in a final effort and a dim light reached me from the end of the passageway. I crawled forward, staring at it, afraid it would vanish. I'd learned by that time that nothing could be taken for granted in that accursed place. When I finally made it to the opening, I dragged myself out on my knees, exhausted, and avidly gulped down the air of twilight.

Get up, Gemma! Get out of there! The urgency in Ginevra's voice made me look behind me. The Pariahs had slipped out of the tunnel and flowed over to me. I looked at them in fear as they surrounded me.

"You said they couldn't come outside!" I shouted at Ginevra.

It used to be that way! They must have evolved! she said, panic in her voice. *Run, Gemma! Run away! Now!* Her voice faded, carried away by the wind until it vanished.

I got up and began running through the forest, but the Pariahs followed me like ghosts, whispering in my ears in an unknown language. I could sense their longing to possess me. They must not have eaten for months, because they clearly had no intention of letting me go.

"Gwen!" I cried out for Ginevra's help, afraid I couldn't hold out much longer, but she was nowhere to be found. Our connection had been broken. I squeezed my eyes shut in an effort to contact her.

Suddenly the threatening growl of a big cat sliced through the air and filled the forest. I opened my eyes and froze. The black panther stood in front of me. We stared at each other for a long moment. I lifted my eyes and my heart shot to my throat. Behind the panther, beyond a thick patch of trees, surrounded by a forest of black stone, stood the Castle, challenging the sky. How absurd it was that I would die there, only a few steps from it.

The panther moved toward me and I stepped back, but a spine-chilling whisper touched my ears. The Pariahs were closing in. I found myself between a rock and a hard place, unsure which fate would be worse—dying by their hand or being devoured by the feline.

All at once, to my amazement, the panther bowed its head without taking its eyes off mine, just like the wolves had done. I stared at it, mystified, and saw something familiar in its green eyes. I felt I'd seen them before, but the idea was too ludicrous to be true. Was it possible that—

I pushed the thought out of my mind and moved toward it warily. The panther didn't move. Instead, its eyes lingered on mine as though to convey a message—an urgent one. I stepped around it and proceeded toward the Castle with long strides, urged on by the murmurs coming from behind me. I couldn't believe it was actually there. A vast, black castle. Foreboding. Magnificent. And dangerous.

A threatening growl made me spin around. My heart skipped a beat when I saw the panther had disappeared. In its place was a hooded figure, its back turned to me. I stared in shock as a wave of energy burst from the figure's palms, disintegrating the Pariahs.

We were the only ones left in the grim surroundings. The figure turned to look at me, its face concealed by the hood.

Do not resist me. The voice was sensual and hypnotic in my head as I struggled to block it. *Let me in.*

A shiver ran through me as the figure quickly covered the distance separating us. Unable to move a muscle, I braced for impact but instead it stopped in front of me and lowered its hood. Two jade-green eyes smiled at me. A strange warmth filled my head and suddenly I could no longer feel my legs.

"Gemma!"

I felt her arms around my body as consciousness left me. Yet there, comforted by Anya's voice, for the first time I felt safe. I closed my eyes and let the shadows carry me away.

"Was it you who brought her here?"

A voice forced its way into the darkness I drifted in. It sounded muffled and distant, from another dimension. I was confused, with no idea where I was.

"She got here on her own," another voice said defiantly.

"Certainly not without your help."

The hostility that oozed from those words penetrated the dark cloud fogging my mind and I recognized the voice. Devina.

"Sophìa told me to protect her!"

Anya.

I tried to force my body to react, but my mind seemed unable to find a way to communicate with my muscles.

"The Empress won't be pleased when I tell her how you tried to get in her way; how you left her in danger, at the mercy of the Damned. Do you have any idea what she had to endure?! You may be Sophìa's Specter, but that doesn't give you the right to disobey her orders."

The crack of a whip pierced the air: Devina's threatening response to Anya's scornful accusations. I felt my body grow heavier, as though I was slowly regaining my senses.

After a pause, Devina's voice came again, her tone dramatically different. "Oh, good." She gave a light laugh as I struggled to emerge. "The Spartan is coming to."

Something in those words sent a shock through me. I struggled with all my might until the veil separating me from them began to dissolve. My eyelids fluttered. When I finally managed to keep them open I found myself in a giant chamber full of cushions, draperies, and tapestries that adorned the walls with mystical elegance. I blinked, trying to focus. The ceiling was so high that looking up at it made me dizzy. With an effort, I pushed myself up onto my elbows and discovered I was lying on a pile of black cushions that felt like silk to the touch.

A soft creak made me turn and notice a door. It was ajar. I got up and took a step toward it but froze when I spotted two panthers guarding it on the other side. One of them had faint leopard spots on its black fur.

"Keep your hands off him, Dev."

I started, surprised to hear the voices again. So it hadn't been just a dream, I really had heard them. I tried to follow the sound and found myself facing another massive wooden door, closed this time. I leaned against it so I could hear better.

"Don't you think you're taking this protective role a bit too seriously? You're a Witch, not her nanny."

"She's one of us, whether you like the idea or not."

I gripped the handle, hoping the room would stop spinning, and found that the door wasn't locked.

"Do you honestly think I care?" Devina's voice was suddenly more sensual, dropping an octave. "After all, he and I have spent a lot of time together lately. Enough for me to claim him."

I opened the door a crack as the silence was broken by another, more familiar sound. I couldn't be sure I hadn't just imagined it, though, because at that moment a shooting pain gripped my temples. I squeezed the door handle, waiting for the pain to ease, then looked around for Devina and recognized her copper-colored locks.

She was standing beside a bare-chested man, clearly trying to seduce him. There must have been someone else with them but the image continued to blur before my eyes. I felt dazed like never before and couldn't make any of them out clearly. On top of that, my head was pounding excruciatingly from the effort of blocking off my mind. I couldn't risk letting Devina discover me.

The man growled at her. That growl, the sound of a ferocious animal trapped in a cage, echoed through the dark rooms of my mind and shook the part of me that was still at the mercy of the shadows. I summoned my courage and opened the door a little more.

The blurred image split into two and then grew clear . . . and I saw him. "Don't touch me, bitch." A tremor rocked my heart when I heard his voice.

Evan.

I wanted to shout but could only do so in my mind. My low groan, however, drew their attention. My eyes instantly locked onto his as a single tear made its way down my cheek.

"Gemma?" His lips whispered my name, his eyes filling with astonishment. I stood frozen, overwhelmed with emotion, afraid it was only a dream. "GEMMA!" Evan's desperate shout thundered off the walls and trembled in my heart as he struggled to break free from the chains that bound him to the rock.

"EVAN!!" The barrier holding back my emotions burst and I flew to him, tears flooding my eyes. The two panthers instantly leapt out in front of me, blocking me, but an uncontrollable wave of dark energy washed over me, hurling the beasts out of my path. My body collided with Evan's. He threw his arms around me and held me tight.

"Evan!" I rested my forehead on his, my tearful eyes prisoners of his loving gaze. Everything else faded into obscurity.

"Gem . . ." He sank his hand into my hair, clasped the nape of my neck, and pressed his lips against mine in a desperate kiss. A kiss that tasted of salt and blood. A kiss that tasted of pain and infinite love. Of us.

"You're here." Hot tears continued to slide down my cheeks as every part of me trembled, once again wrapped in his embrace. "You're here. It's really you . . ." My voice broke with emotion. I thought I had lost him, but there he was with me.

"You have to get out of here." His eyes bored into mine, desperate. "It's dangerous," he whispered onto my lips, cupping my face in his hands as I shook my head between them.

"No. I'm not going anywhere without you."

Evan stroked my bottom lip with his thumb and closed his eyes. "Gemma, you've got—"

"Enough." Our eyes darted to the side in unison at the sound of Devina's icy voice. "I have had quite enough."

"Wait, NO!"

Devina ignored Anya's shout and hurled a thunderbolt at me. My eyes widened and I couldn't move. With a savage howl Evan ripped the chains out of the wall and shielded me with his body, taking the blow on his bare back. His scream shook the room.

"Evan!"

He clung to me, his muscles jerking from the pain. "You recovered quickly this time," Devina told him mockingly. Evan turned and fixed his eyes on hers, maintaining an icy calm.

"Devina, stop it!" Anya shouted. Her Sister ignored her, her face transformed into a mask of evil. Evan gritted his teeth and crumpled to his knees as a new attack from Devina tore a shriek from him.

"Evan!" I threw myself onto him, but I could see his suffering was excruciating. He seemed to be burning up from the inside.

"I said stop it. Now!" Anya shouted.

"I don't take orders," Devina replied icily. "Much less from you."

"Stop it, please!" I begged her, my eyes filled with tears as Evan tensed his muscles, though he defiantly held Devina's gaze. "That's enough! What are you doing to him?!" I was on the brink of despair.

"If you really must know, I created a force field inside him," she replied with a sly smile. "I can make it expand until he explodes." Evan howled again, wracked with pain.

"You're killing him! Stop it!" I pleaded, distraught.

Devina laughed. "He can't die any more than he has, not if he's already here. But I can inflict a great deal of pain on him." Vindictiveness flickered in her eyes. "Of course, if I did it to you . . ."

"Don't. Touch. Her," Evan growled, his silvery eyes aflame with rage.

Unexpectedly, Anya stepped protectively in front of us and Evan crumpled forward, exhausted.

"Evan!" I tried to hold him up, clasping him in my arms, and he squeezed my hand.

"You've had enough fun," Anya told Devina firmly.

Devina shot her an icy glare. "Get out of the way. This is none of your affair," she warned.

"I don't take orders from you either—not when they go against Sophia's. The *Empress* ordered me to protect her, and that's what I'm doing."

They stared at each other, nose to nose, in a tacit challenge.

"She may have given you instructions but while she's gone I'm the one giving orders. *I'm* her Specter. Where the hell are the Drusas?!" she called without taking her eyes off Anya.

Two panthers padded over and stopped at Devina's feet, their heads bowed. From what I had gathered, Drusas were guards. Each of the Sisters had her own role to play. There was no internal hierarchy—except when Devina was around.

"Safria! Nerea! Throw them into the dungeons," Devina ordered. Her face twisted into a grin. "Separate them, naturally. If one of them speaks on the way there, punish the other one."

The panthers bowed their heads submissively. A second later their bodies lengthened, taking on a human appearance. The two Witches looked like Amazons. They wore dark-brown leather shorts and vests of reddish-brown fur and were barefoot, with only a strip of brown leather running from their big toes to their ankles. From there it wound its way up their legs like a serpent. One of them had yellowish eyes like the Dakor coiled around her wrist and long blond hair spotted at the tips like leopard's fur. The other had dark skin, blue eyes, and thick, curly, artfully braided hair. Her Dakor was wrapped around her thigh. Each wore a small braid across her forehead like a diadem or a symbol.

A hostile energy crept up my legs and suddenly I found myself standing, Evan beside me, as an invisible force pushed us to move against our will. I looked back at Anya and she stared at me, an expression of regret on her face, until we went through the door and she disappeared from view.

The two Witches escorted us through the Castle in single file, our hands behind our backs. Evan's wrists still bore what was left of the chains that had imprisoned him. Their occasional clank comforted me, reminding me he was still behind me though I couldn't see him. The thought that he was there with me was all that counted. Suddenly everything had regained meaning. It didn't matter if I stayed there forever as long as he was alive.

We made our way down a hallway that seemed endless, its walls made of some kind of polished black stone I'd never seen before. The entire fortress seemed to have been carved out of a massive black diamond. Black silk drapes covered its broad windows and crystal sconces illuminated the rooms. The black floor had a strange glow to it that almost made it look like it was lined with silk. Even the butterflies I saw fluttering near the ceiling at times were black. They seemed frightened, as though they also wanted to escape.

Outside, we found ourselves in an inner courtyard enclosed by various wings of the Castle, joined together by tall, ominous-looking towers. The courtyard looked like a battlefield: lots of Witches wearing Amazon outfits were facing each other in open combat; it must have been where they trained. One of them turned toward me, her expression still fiery from battle. She moved like a panther in her black outfit, but her incredible blue eyes stood out like bright stars and her long white hair was tipped with a dazzling cascade of black diamonds.

Nausyka. The name filled my head. I didn't know where it had come from, but I was sure it was what the Witch was called. A black panther leapt at her with a roar and the two Witches resumed their fight.

Some of them used magic, transforming in midair and turning the forces of nature to their advantage, while others engaged in hand-to-hand combat, moving in a dark dance like graceful felines battling over their next meal. I found it spellbinding. At first I was appalled by how ferociously they were fighting, but then I stared at them, fascinated, until we were taken into another wing of the Castle.

We entered a vast hall full of silk cushions and draperies. It must have been some sort of temple of pleasure: hordes of Witches were entertaining themselves with their lovers. The males must once have been Subterraneans, but now they were mere playthings in the Witches' hands, helplessly addicted to their mistresses' blood. I thought I glimpsed a familiar face among them, but what they were doing forced me to look away in embarrassment.

Leaving the pit of perdition behind, we walked down another long hallway. Just as I was wondering if they would lock us up in one of the black crystal towers I'd seen from the courtyard, we started down a flight of stairs that seemed to descend infinitely into an even darker and more ominous Hell.

The passageway was so narrow I could feel Evan's warmth right behind me. Neither of us dared speak out of fear for the other's safety, but I could hear his breathing and that was enough for me. The farther down we went, the less light there was. Finally we reached a long hallway full of cells. I jumped when a prisoner slammed against the bars and reached out to grab me, his face gaunt and his eyes darkened with hunger. Evan rushed at him in my defense, pushing past one of the Witches. His body touched mine for a second, filling me with warmth, but the Drusas shoved us forward toward an isolated wing of the dungeon at the end of which were two thick wooden cell doors similar to the one Ginevra had imprisoned Desdemona behind.

"We're there," one of the two Witches said, her tone flat.

"Evan!" I broke free from the Witch's grip and ran toward him. His arms held me tight. As though he'd never left me, our bodies enmeshed like two perfectly fitting halves of some mechanism. I couldn't bear for them to separate us again, but the Drusa yanked me away by the shoulders.

"Let her go!" Evan tried to fight, but could do nothing against the Witches' dark powers.

"Why don't you take a nap, little Angel?"

"No!" I screamed as the Dakor coiled around the Witch's arm sank his fangs into Evan's flesh. "Evan!"

The Witch shoved him into one of the cells and slammed the door shut. I screamed his name in desperation, squirming in the Witch's clutches, but she pushed me into the cell next to his, freed my wrists, and closed the door. I slammed my body against the wooden door, pounding it with my fists, cursing at the two Witches.

Before walking away, one of the Sisters bowed her head slightly. "I'm sorry." She looked at me, her eyes full of remorse. "Devina's orders." From her expression I could tell there wasn't anything she could do about it.

I leaned against the door, my forehead pressed to the hard wood, and felt the tears sting my eyes. "Evan . . ." The cell was dark and cold and not a sound came from the adjacent one. I rested my shoulders against the door and slid down to the floor, burying my head on my knees. The cell seemed so familiar to me—it felt like I'd already been locked up there. Then I remembered: it had happened in a premonitory dream the Witches had induced. Overcome, I sobbed harder, my tears choking me. They had foreseen everything—how could I fight against their power? My ridiculous plan had no chance of working. Evan and I would never find a way to escape from the fortress together. There was only one thing I could do: sacrifice myself so they would set him free and hope I could resist the evil that would attempt to annihilate me. For a long time my one wish had been to see Evan again, even if it was only one last time, and now I had to keep my word. A tear wet my lips, bitter as poison. I'd found Evan, but fate would part us again, because I would have to swear my loyalty to the Witches. I had no choice. Suddenly the thought of escaping with Evan seemed absurd. We were children of two different worlds: good and evil. I belonged to the Witches and no one could change that. But I would find a way to bear it. Anything, to save Evan. Anything, to know he was alive, somewhere in the world, even if he was far from me.

Wracked with sobs, I huddled on the stone floor. Slowly but surely my exhaustion won out and I slid into sleep.

When I opened my eyes, I realized I was shivering from the cold.

"Gemma!"

A tremor shook my heart at the sound of his voice. "Evan!" I bolted awake and searched for him in the darkness.

"Over here!"

I turned toward his voice. In the wall separating us was a narrow floor-to-ceiling gap with thick iron bars through which I could see Evan's eyes. I rushed to him. "Evan!" I clasped my hands over his fists that were gripping the iron bars and stroked his wrists, still prisoners of the chains. It broke my heart to see him like that, his knuckles bloodied and blood encrusted on his face.

Evan unclenched his fists and touched his palms to mine as our eyes—silent messengers—bridged the painful distance between us. "I waited for you to wake up." He reached out and stroked my cheek, his eyes on mine, as though afraid I might disappear. "You're so beautiful." I was filthy, my hands worn and my dress ripped, but he didn't care. There was pain in his whisper. The pain of nostalgia.

I rested my forehead against the bars and he did the same. I couldn't believe he was actually there, that it wasn't just another dream. So close and yet so infinitely far away. I stared at his lips. Feeling the warmth of his breath so near made me quiver, though I knew I couldn't bridge the distance between us. As though shaken by the same desire, he stroked my bottom lip with his thumb. I closed my eyes, emotion trembling through me.

"You need to drink something."

I slowly opened my eyes. His voice still seemed like a figment of my imagination, but the instant my eyes met his caring gaze, the tears threatened to overwhelm me again. After everything I'd been through, I couldn't believe Evan was finally there.

He slid his hands through the bars, cupped them, and concentrated. I waited silently, wondering what he was doing, looking back and forth between his face and his hands. A small bubble of water slowly surfaced on his palms. "It's not much, but drink it."

I moved my lips to his hands, pressed them together on his palm in a light kiss, and tilted my head so he could caress my cheek. "I felt like I was dying without you," I confessed, my eyes closed as I remembered the desperation that still lived in my heart.

"I serve Death, but I had never truly known what death was until the day I lost you. I never stopped hoping I would see you again, even for a second," he said softly. "But you shouldn't have come here. Sooner or later I would have found my way back to you. This place is too dangerous for you."

"I don't care. How could I leave you here after what I did to you?"

"It wasn't your fault," he said, trying to convince me, but my remorse over his death was inconsolable.

"You took the poison from *my lips*. I should have realized it was you. And instead I—I killed you. The day you died I died too."

"You didn't kill me," he whispered, moving his hand to stroke my cheek. "I'm here with you now. No one can separate us ever again."

My eyes shot to his, stricken. How could I bear to tell him that we would soon have to part? Fate had been against us from the beginning and now it had won. Like the sun and the moon that pursued each other eternally without success, Evan and I weren't destined to be together, and I had to accept that.

"Evan, I—"

A sudden clang drew our attention. In the semidarkness, the door to my cell creaked and opened, admitting a hooded figure. I cringed, but Evan squeezed my hand tighter. As she approached me, the woman raised a finger to her lips and uncovered her face.

"Anya! What are you doing here?" I exclaimed in surprise.

"Shh," she said, keeping her voice low. "We don't have much time. Move away from the bars."

Still kneeling opposite each other, Evan and I exchanged wary looks. Then I nodded. "We can trust her," I reassured him, but every trace of doubt had already vanished from his face.

"I know." Evan looked at Anya for a few seconds. "She's been a good friend to me. At least she didn't torture me when she was on guard duty."

Anya gave him a little nod of recognition as he and I moved away from each other. The bars bent before our eyes, creating an opening wide enough for Evan to squeeze through. His shackles broke apart and clattered onto the stone floor. Evan rubbed his wrists in surprise and looked into my eyes. His lips instantly found mine as he held me tight, his hands wandering desperately through my hair.

"You have two hours."

We stopped, suddenly remembering Anya was still there. She raised her hood but paused by the door, her back to us. "Then I'll have to put things back the way they were. I'm sorry. I wish there were more I could do."

"Wait!" I said. Anya looked over her shoulder at me. "It was you," I said, voicing the certainty that had taken root in my mind. "In the forest. It was you all along. You followed me. I could sense you."

The Panther has dwelled forever in each of our spirits. The thought filled my mind. It was spoken in my own voice, confusing me momentarily as to its origin. Anya gave a little nod, confirming my suspicion.

"Then it was you who killed Ahrec. But why? He wasn't going to hurt me." I let the sentence hang in the silence and waited for her reply. That was what Ahrec had been trying to tell me: *They're protecting you.*

Her emotionless voice broke the silence of the cell. "The Dreide wouldn't have given him his freedom. He could never have left this place. No one goes back. If he had crossed through the gates his body would have disintegrated, but he didn't realize that. I read his mind: he was struggling with himself," she explained. "His human part was fighting not to harm you, but the other part was ready to attack. He was on the verge of losing control and I couldn't let him do that. I watched over you from the start, though Devina constantly tried to prevent me from doing it. Watch out for her," she warned. She turned to go, but Evan stopped her again.

"Thank you," he said. Anya paused, waiting. "For taking care of her," Evan finished.

She nodded and reached for the door, but something seemed to be holding her there. "How is Gwen?" she asked after a long silence.

Gwen. Anya was the only one of her Sisters that called Ginevra by that name. "She told me about you," I said. Anya smiled beneath her hood. "I could tell she cared a lot about you. That's what made me trust you."

"I've never stopped thinking about her," she said, a hint of bitterness in her voice. "But I'm happy about the choice she made. I wasn't as brave."

"You mean—"

"His name was Alexey, but our lives were destined to part."

"I'm sorry," I whispered, dismayed.

"Don't be." Poised on the threshold, Anya turned to look me in the eye. "I'm the one who should have fought for him. But that was long ago." I gulped, wondering if her words were meant as a warning for me.

"I'll return in two hours. Meanwhile, I'll make sure no one disturbs you." She cast me a last glance and closed the cell door, leaving us on the floor clinging to each other.

My eyes lingered on the door as I tried to understand what she'd been attempting to tell me. Was there possibly a way out of my predestined fate? How could I save Evan if I refused to succumb to them?

"What are you thinking about?" Evan's low voice made me start. He tenderly brushed my hair from my shoulder. "Judging from the look on your face, it can't be pleasant."

I took his hand and clasped it in mine, not wanting him to think I wasn't happy he was there with me. "Evan—" I looked into his eyes and he frowned, puzzled.

"Why are you staring at me as if this is the last time you're going to be with me?" I turned away and his hand gently slid into my hair, reclaiming my attention. "We're together now." He rested his forehead against my temple and a light kiss caressed my skin. I closed my eyes, unable to explain to Evan what I was going to do. "Gemma?"

"I'm one of them," I blurted. His hand froze on my neck. "I . . . I'm a Witch. I belong to them."

A tear slid silently down my cheek and Evan slowly brushed it away. "You're mine," he said, contradicting me. "You belong only to me."

I shook my head in his hand. "I'm going to have to swear an oath of loyalty to them. My blood is already infected. All that's left for the transformation to be complete is for me to agree."

"Why on earth would you?" he asked sharply.

I raised my eyes to his. "I won't leave you here to be tortured by Devina."

Evan clenched his jaw, instantly understanding my intentions. "You're not going to agree to join them to save me," he said sternly. It almost sounded like an order. He grabbed my face in both hands and his eyes hardened, inches from mine. "I'll never let you do it, Gemma."

In spite of his words, I knew I had no choice.

"If we ever leave this place—whether it's in a day or a lifetime—we're leaving it together. I'm not going without you." My eyes brimmed with tears. I blinked and another teardrop silently descended. "We'll stay here together until we find some way out," he reassured me.

I was quick to protest. "They'll torture you to convince me to join them!" My voice broke from the pain I bore inside.

"Who cares?!" He gripped my shoulders, demanding the eye contact I was trying to deny him. "My only hell has been being away from you. If I can't have you I'll find my way back here."

"I can't, Evan. I can't allow them to torture you. They're already inside me. My nature has already awakened."

His eyes wavered as the truth dawned on him. "So that's why you were able to see me and sense my presence."

I nodded, despondent. "I can't stop it."

He stroked my palm with his thumb like he'd always done, then interlaced his fingers with mine, lowering his voice to a whisper. "Yes you can. We'll stop it together." He looked steadily into my eyes, sealing his vow.

I smiled and held back the tears. Would I be able to fight the part of me that would try to annihilate me? At Evan's side, I felt I could challenge the world.

"They told me, but I thought it was just another one of their tricks," he said. "It must be terrible for you. I can't imagine what you've gone through."

"Can you believe that when I found out, seeing you again was the only thing I could think about? I considered it a fair price to pay."

Evan tenderly stroked my cheek and his face filled with pain. "The very thing that allowed us to meet is the same thing that's threatening to divide us now," he whispered, devastated. He touched my lip with his thumb and gazed into my eyes.

"No one will ever separate us." I squeezed my eyes shut, trying to convince myself. "Now that I've found you again I'll never let you go. Even if they take me, they'll never be able to remove you from my heart. I'll stay by your side. I can fight it."

"If you become a Witch you'll only want to kill me, Gemma. Evil will take you over and you won't even realize it."

"No."

"You won't be able to resist!"

"I'll find a way. Everyone has a dark side, but most people manage to overcome it."

"The people you're talking about don't have the devil's venom in their bodies, Gemma. You can't let them transform you. At that point the evil will be unstoppable."

"Ginevra did it!"

"But after how long? I'm not leaving you in those harpies' clutches for centuries."

"Meeting Simon changed her. I already have you. The love that unites the two of us will save me from them—save me from myself. We each have our own demons to fight. I just need to find the way to face mine so you can be safe. They'll never separate us."

"I won't let you do it," he whispered against my lips, resting his forehead on mine.

"There's nothing you can do to stop me." Another tear slid from my eye and Evan wiped it from my lip. I raised a hand and touched his chest, which was black and blue. "What did they do to you?" My finger followed the deep scars on his shoulders and torso. His jeans were torn and his skin caked with dried blood. It was unbearable. "I'm so sorry," I murmured, but Evan rubbed his forehead against mine and sought my gaze.

"Physical torture I can bear. The real torment was in my heart," he said softly, closing his eyes, a prisoner of the memories. "I suffered the tortures of Hell knowing you were far away without my protection. I'm never going to leave you again."

"Simon and Ginevra risked a lot to protect me."

"And they have my eternal gratitude for that, but I'm going to take care of you from now on." His hand slid down my side, slowly, and his thumb brushed my belly. He looked into my eyes. "Take care of you both."

I stared at him for a long moment, astonished. *He knew*. Evan knew about the baby. "How did—" I began.

He put a hand behind my neck, sank his face into my hair, and drew a deep breath. "Then it's true." His voice told me what was in his heart.

"Does it scare you?" I asked.

Evan stroked my belly with extreme tenderness. "A tiny creature is growing inside you, testimony to the love that binds us. How could that scare me? It's extraordinary. This baby has a part of you and a part of me, and in order to be happy it needs both of us." His voice grew serious. "I'm not going to let you make such a huge sacrifice."

I wanted to nod, but I knew his words wouldn't be enough to release me from my fate. Evan had protected me long enough. The time had come for me to save him. My eyes traced the scars that the poison had burned into his skin. Some were recent. I almost burst into tears at the thought of what he'd endured. It was never going to happen again, I would make sure of that.

Without speaking, I took off his dog tag and put it around his neck, looking him in the eye. "This is where it belongs," I whispered, touching the metal. My fingers lingered on his skin, stroked his chest, and slowly rose to his shoulders. I had longed to have him beside me so many times that my heart ached merely from touching him and reminding myself he was actually there.

I ran my fingers down a scar on his shoulder, then touched my lips to it and sealed them in a tiny kiss. Evan's muscles tightened—whether from pain or emotion, I didn't know. My mouth moved over his skin, alighting on his chest, his abdomen . . . on each and every mark, as though my kisses could erase them. Brimming with desire, our eyes exchanged silent promises. Evan's hands slid down my back, making me tremble. I could happily have died right then, cuddled in his embrace.

As though Evan had heard my thought, he swept the hair from my shoulder and gently touched his lips to my neck, as though asking for my consent. I felt their warmth on my skin, their every movement, as he kissed me tenderly. I closed my eyes and felt his hand slide the dress off my shoulder, baring my skin so his lips could explore it. "My God, have I missed you . . ."

The soft whisper against my skin made me moan. I caressed his abdomen and let him kiss me. Moving of their own free will, my hands slid down and undid the button of his jeans. In the silent cell, Evan breathed deeply, trembling with emotion. Resting a hand on the floor, he gently pushed me back, his mouth lingering on my breast. I closed my eyes and felt his warm hands on me, sliding under my skirt.

A wave of emotion washed over me when he pressed his body against mine. Yearning to erase the distance between us, I could have ripped off the scant fabric of the underwear separating us, the heat of his hard body setting me aflame where our bodies touched. I felt feverish, on the verge of catching fire beneath him.

"I never want to be away from you again. Promise you won't leave me," he whispered against my lips, at once determined and desperate as he laced his fingers with mine. "*Samvicaranam. Samyodhanam.* Stay together. Fight together." He rested his forehead on mine. My heart raced, anxious for me to seal the vow, convinced the evil within me would never be able to penetrate me deeply enough to eradicate my love for him.

"My heart belongs to you forever," I murmured, and suddenly I was certain of it: not even the transformation could end my love for him. That was all I could promise.

Evan closed his eyes, brushed his cheek against mine, and was inside me. I quivered, tingles of pleasure flooding my body. I sank my fingers into his shoulder as he moved inside me, setting me aflame until I lost my mind. His warm chest brushed against my breasts, making me shudder with ecstasy. I clung to him, fusing my body to his, skin on skin. His heat was so familiar . . . I yearned to merge with him, disappear inside him so we would be joined forever. The heat of passion flooded my head, bringing me to the verge of delirium. I gazed at his chest, his arms, trying to memorize every contour, every flexed muscle. The Subterranean tattoo stood out on his forearm, creating a sweet nostalgia in me, imprinting on my mind the ardor of his body, the strength of his arms as he held me, the quiver his hands left behind when they touched me. I'd missed him so much . . .

"I love you, Gem."

I stared at the soft curve of Evan's lips as they uttered my name, then felt their warmth on my mouth. He took my hand, rested it next to my head and clasped it as though wanting to fuse it forever with his own as he plunged deeper and deeper into me, generating a surge of pleasure with each thrust.

A new heat inundated my body as Evan climaxed inside me, waves of passion surging through every fiber of my being. I quivered as my contracted muscles relaxed. Evan rested his forehead on mine, smiling at me as I lost myself in his gray eyes, longing for a world where no one was after us, a world where we would never have to part.

But no such world existed.

The twilight filtered in through the small barred window that opened to the outside, barely illuminating Evan's features. He was still lying on top of me, his head propped on his palm, his eyes gazing into mine. I couldn't remember ever being so happy and so frightened at the same time. Frightened of what I would be confronting. My heart had already known the pain of separation and couldn't bear it again. Part of me feared I wouldn't be able to banish the evil that would try to separate me from him. Yet I had no choice. I only hoped I would be strong enough to face my demons.

Evan brushed his fingertip over my skin, drawing imaginary lines on my tummy. His face was relaxed, his lips hinting at a smile. I wished I could read his mind, reach wherever it was that he was wandering. Given the look on his face, I presumed it was someplace nice.

"I can't believe it's happening," he said softly before I could ask him. "A baby, Gemma. Before meeting you, I wasn't even sure life made any sense. Then you arrived, and now . . . a baby! It's amazing." I smiled. "How do you think it's possible? I mean, I never thought, never had the faintest idea my life could be so full with—with so many things. But—a baby?" His rambling made me laugh. He was so happy and surprised he couldn't even express his emotions. He ran a hand over his head. "God . . . I never even dared hope something so big might happen to *me*."

"Why shouldn't it have?" I asked, smiling.

"I didn't know I was physically capable. After all, I'm not human."

"You're capable of taking a life with a single touch of your hand. It's not so far-fetched that you could create a life too."

Evan smiled and cast me a strange glance. "Speaking of taking lives, who the hell is *Ahrec*?"

At the sight of the new expression on his face, I couldn't help but smile. "Some guy who helped me escape from a seedy bar full of Lechers, that's all. Your age, more or less."

Evan blinked, looking confused. "What was he doing there? What did he want from you? Down here, nobody gives anyone something for nothing."

I raised an eyebrow, deciding to keep him on pins and needles a little longer. "I'm not sure, but all things considered, he wasn't as bad as the other Souls I ran into." He narrowed his eyes. "You're jealous," I teased, playing with a stray lock of his hair. It was so long and wild it fell down over his silvery eyes, giving him a dangerous look.

He grabbed my wrist and pinned me to the floor, fire in his gaze. "If I hadn't heard he was already dead, I would have tracked him down and killed him."

I looked into his eyes and fell captive to them. He was so handsome, I could have stared at him forever. He was propped up over me, holding my wrists against the floor. From that position his hair fell forward and in the twilight his eyes seemed sharper, inaccessible. No—not inaccessible. *He was mine.* The dog tag dangled between us. I had the urge to grab it and pull him against me; I couldn't stand even that small distance between us. I wanted to fuse with him and not let anyone separate us.

His eyes rested on my lips and my heart leapt to my throat at the unexpressed desire I read there. As though he sensed my heart rate accelerating, Evan leaned down and his mouth found mine with new passion, as though he could never get enough.

He released his grip on my wrists and his hands slid into mine, over my head. I opened my fingers and let him clasp them, interlacing them with his own. He didn't need to be afraid I wasn't his, because I would be forever. His and his alone.

"I can come back later if this is a bad time."

Startled, we looked toward the window from where the male voice had come. I scrambled to pull my dress over me and then propped myself up on my elbows because I couldn't see his face clearly—or more likely because I couldn't believe it was actually who I thought it was. Evan burst out laughing and walked over to the bars to grip his forearm.

"Hey, sunshine, you just going to lie there or are you coming over to say hi?"

My heart raced when it heard the voice again. "Drake?" I gasped, approaching the window cautiously as though he were a ghost.

"At your service, baby doll." He winked at me, a smile lighting up his face. "Need a hand?"

"Drake!" I exclaimed, so excited I risked dropping my dress. Luckily, he noticed in time and turned back to look at Evan.

"It's good to see you again, bro, though I would have chosen a different place—and a better time."

"What are you doing here?" I blushed at the question. Like it wasn't obvious.

Drake cocked his head and checked out the cell. "I could ask you two the same question. This is a pretty weird place to hook up—unless you have *freaky* tastes."

I flushed, trying not to think of the possibility that he'd seen me half-naked. I would definitely have remembered it as one of the most embarrassing moments in my life.

Evan clapped his hand over their locked fists, still smiling. "Good to see you again, bro."

"Okay, we'd better save the thanks for later. We haven't got all day."

"Thanks for what?" I asked, still stunned by his unexpected appearance.

"I'm breaking you out of here—unless you've got any objections, that is."

Evan pulled me in close, his arms around my waist, in a gesture that silently expressed his thoughts. Drake was our only hope. Suddenly the weight of the world was lifted from my shoulders, letting me breathe again. I wouldn't have to sacrifice myself to the Witches in order to save Evan!

"Told you we would find another solution," he whispered in my ear. Then he said to Drake, "All right then, get us out of here. I don't want to stay in this place one more minute."

All at once the door opened with a groan. I jumped as someone slipped into the cell and quickly closed it behind them. The delicious scent of freedom quickly faded. Evan stepped in front of me protectively. My heart did a somersault when I found myself looking into the newcomer's eyes.

"We meet again. Imagine that."

Hearing the sound of his voice rise from the gloom made me shudder. *Faustian*. Encircled by a black mustache and goatee, his lips curved into a smile that in the dim light made my skin crawl. Though the memory of Faust was buried deep inside me, it had never vanished. I could never forget the gleam he'd had in his eyes while he was torturing me. "So you ended up here as well," he said.

Evan kept me behind him. He was ready to spring into action, his muscles tensed and his sharp eyes trained on Faustian.

"Not for long," I replied icily. "I'm only passing through."

"I know. That's why I'm here."

Evan and I looked at each other, confused.

"He's with me," Drake explained.

Evan shot his brother a glance, looking hesitant. "You sure he—"

"He's on our side. It's okay, you can trust him," he repeated, not a shadow of doubt in his voice. "He's the one who brought me here. He saw them taking you to the dungeon, recognized you, and came to find me. Evan, I can't get you out of this place alone. My powers are gone and I'm too weak. He, on the other hand . . ."

"I indulged in a little treat before coming here." Faust raised his eyebrows and headed for the window.

Evan and I stepped aside to let him pass. The treat Faust referred to must have been the Witches' little games, meaning he'd fed on their blood. When we passed through the Witches' temple of pleasure I'd had the vague impression I recognized someone. It must have been him.

Before our wary eyes, Faustian bent the iron bars and turned to look at us as I slipped the sleeves of my dress on and covered my shoulders. "Well? What are you waiting for, a letter of recommendation? Hurry, we don't have much time. If they discover me they'll fry my brain."

"Why are you doing it, then? Why run such a risk, and for us, of all people?" I asked disdainfully, still not sure I could trust him. After all, Evan was the one who had killed him and sent him to Hell.

Faustian looked me in the eye, his expression suddenly serious and tinged with sadness. "There's nothing they can take from me that I haven't already lost." He ran his hand down his neck and seemed to relax. "I understand your misgivings but believe me, I don't resent the two of you for anything that happened. In fact, I was asking for it."

"You couldn't get out of it. It wasn't your choice," Drake said, his voice charged with urgency, "and they realize that." He stared first at me and then at Evan.

Faustian stepped toward us, the dim light from outside illuminating his face. "I was following orders, that's true, but what I did to you *was* my choice." He offered me his hand. I stared at it for a long moment, then looked him in the eye again.

"This is my chance to make amends, if you'll allow me."

I nodded slightly without taking my eyes from his, but couldn't bring myself to shake his hand. I was afraid that if I touched it the past might come back to haunt me. He let his arm go slack at his side.

Evan took me by the waist and lifted me up to the window through which Drake was looking in. I grabbed hold of the bars and Drake pulled me up toward him and out. Even the toxic air of Hell smelled fresh and wonderful after the cell, but I was instantly anxious to see Evan again, to have him at my side and never let him go. I still couldn't be sure it wasn't a trap.

"Get him out, Drake! Get him out!" I begged, but quickly realized there was no need to ask: seconds later I saw Evan at the window. He jumped down beside me and hugged me as though he too had been afraid of never seeing me again.

"You're not coming?" Drake asked Faust.

We looked up at Faustian, but he shrugged. "I wouldn't know where else to go. Besides, there's nothing lacking here."

"There's a cave just past the thicket where we met if you change your mind."

"I'll keep that in mind in case something goes wrong," Faustian replied, not taking his eyes off Drake. "Now go or they'll discover you."

"But what if they discover *you*?" I couldn't help but ask, suddenly worried he might betray us.

"They won't learn anything about you, if that's what's worrying you. I know how to block off my mind—mine and others'. You know that for yourself." I remembered with a shudder how Faustian had kept the others from finding me after he'd kidnapped me. There was no need for him to remind me. "I don't have all my powers any more, but I'll be able to keep them at bay," he added.

"What will happen to you?" Evan asked.

"I'll manage somehow. There was only one Witch standing guard at the back of the hall. I covered my hand with a piece of cloth, pretending to bring you food. I don't think she even noticed me. In fact, this might sound strange, but she seemed to be *pretending* not to notice me."

Anya. It must have been her. My heart warmed at her millionth attempt to help me.

"My friend, that stuff they're giving you must have some pretty nasty side effects if you actually think a Witch pretended not to notice you," Drake joked. "Now get going and be careful. It's not bad having somebody on the inside."

Evan gave Faustian a silent nod of gratitude. "Thank you," I whispered through the semidarkness, "and good luck."

Above us, Faustian winked at me before twisting the bars back into place. "You'll need that more than I will."

I turned and hugged Drake tight, pouring into the gesture all the pain of those months spent without him. The nightmare had begun when we thought he'd been the one ordered to kill me. Though we'd discovered at the very end that he'd actually never betrayed us, we still didn't know the full explanation.

The instant I let go of Drake, Evan took my hand and squeezed it. "Let's get out of here." He smiled at me and joy and hope filled my heart.

"Come on," Drake said in a low voice. "The place I live isn't far away." He turned to look at us, his face unexpectedly bright. "Stella's waiting for us."

31

DRAKE

"Stella?" Evan asked, voicing what we were both thinking. "Am I understanding you right? You mean *your* Stella?"

"That's the one," Drake replied, a new light in his eyes.

"There are a lot of things you need to explain to us, Drake."

"We've got all the time in the world. Right now we'd better not make her worry."

Amazed by the news, we followed Drake into the mouth of a cave and crossed a dark, foreboding passageway. Evan kept his arm wrapped around my waist reassuringly. I heaved a sigh of relief when we saw a faint light at the end of the tunnel.

The light came from the same luminous rock I'd seen in Xandra's hideaway and later in the underground caves. Drake noticed me staring at it and explained that it was very hard to come by. It was foelstone, a luminous substance that hardened in contact with the air secreted by a ferocious animal. I thought of the glowing cocoons I'd seen in the spider's lair and shuddered.

Drake said Stella had also discovered that Dakor venom—which polluted everything in the area—was highly flammable, and she'd come up with a way to extract it from the spring inside their cave. For a long time she'd used it for heating, to make weapons to defend herself, and also to purify the water. That was how she'd survived.

The room we were in was small but looked comfortable. It seemed to have everything necessary: a table carved out of the rock, two small chairs that stood next to each other, a rudimentary hearth and, in the back, just beyond the spring, a large bed covered with thick furs. Of Stella, however, there was no trace. Evan and I exchanged a look, suspecting that Stella was actually a figment of Drake's imagination, a companion his mind had created to cope with his solitude.

Drake, though, looked around, pensive. "She must have gone out on reconnaissance," he said, a hint of concern in his voice. "I'm sure she'll be back any minute."

Evan and I looked at each other again. He rested a hand on Drake's shoulder. "Hey, bro, you sure you're okay?"

At first, Drake looked at Evan as though he was insulted, but then he smiled. "Yeah, why shouldn't I be?"

Evan shrugged and looked away, embarrassed. Was Drake delusional? "You've been here alone for such a long time . . . I mean, you know . . . It must have been rough on you."

"Absolutely. You can't even imagine. This place can drive you nuts." Drake sat down on a rock outcropping and shook his head. "Fortunately I found my Stella, otherwise I don't know what I would've done. And now I've reunited part of my family! You have no idea how much I missed you guys."

Evan rubbed his neck, embarrassed. "You still have to tell us what happened," he said, probably to avoid talking about Drake's mental state. After all, it was easy to imagine how hard it must have been to suddenly be hurled into that infernal place. I had experienced it for myself and understood his need to seek refuge in a beloved—albeit imaginary—figure. Once he was home, his mental state would stabilize and we would all remember the experience as nothing more than a bad nightmare.

"Just to be clear," Evan continued, subtle sarcasm in his voice, "that wasn't you who kissed Gemma, right?"

"What?!" Drake turned to stare at him, shocked by the question, and Evan's laughter filled the cave.

"Nothing, never mind." Evan looked suddenly relieved, as though a weight had been lifted from him.

"Sounds like I'm not the only one with lots to tell," Drake joked as he started a fire.

"The thing is, I'm not exactly sure when the other guy took your place."

"Hold on." I looked at Evan, a new doubt gripping me. "How did *you* know it wasn't the real Drake? We all thought it was him. We only found out the truth when it was too late—by then you were already gone."

"It's true, I believed it too. I believed it for a long time," he admitted. "During one of her guard-duty shifts, Anya told me what had happened."

"Sorry about that," Drake said as a tiny flame ran along a groove carved into the floor, warming the cave. "It was partly my fault. He caught me off guard and I couldn't stop him. I wanted to warn you but they don't have phones down here—can you believe it?"

I smiled at his carefree tone. I'd missed Drake so much.

"I'm the one who needs to apologize," Evan said. "I should never have doubted you. When I found out the truth, I couldn't believe I ever had."

"There was no way you could've known, and you were right to protect Gemma. I would've done the same thing in your shoes. I'm the one who should have been more alert. I just wasn't expecting an attack. It had been months since anyone had come looking for her and I figured they'd given up. I made the mistake of letting my guard down."

"We all did, so don't feel bad," Evan said.

"Hey, look where we all ended up. You have no idea what I've been through. The guilt and all the worry about what could happen—I knew what that bastard intended to do, but I couldn't help you or warn you. It all happened so fast. Simon and I were down in the workout room training and, like always, I was kidding him about his twisted relationship with Ginevra. She wanted his company during a race that day, so in the end I had to give in. You know what G is like—she always has to have her way. So Simon went to be with her and I started working out alone. I'd just activated an awesome exotic scenario—complete with hot girls cheering me on—when Simon came back. Or at least I thought it was Simon."

Bitterness suddenly filled Drake's face. He couldn't have known it wasn't really his brother. He ran his hands over his shaved head, his gaze lost in the memory. As he spoke, the images of that fateful day filled my mind so vividly I felt as if I were personally witnessing the scene:

"What, back so soon? Your girlfriend give you permission to play with me a little longer?" My laugh echoed off the walls of the workout room, but Simon was strangely serious.

"Something like that," he said.

"Don't worry. This'll be quicker than you think."

"We'll see."

"I'm all yours, bro." I smiled.

We were circling each other, ready to attack, but it was like something about him had changed during the minutes he was gone. I couldn't put my finger on what because he was pretty much ignoring my banter—he just kept staring at me like he was studying me or something.

"Go ahead, gimme all you got . . . or are you waiting for her permission to do that too?" I said to provoke him.

That was when Simon struck his first blow. It was so brutal it knocked the air out of my lungs. I realized something definitely wasn't right.

"Whoa, a little cranky, are we?" I said. He ignored me and continued to attack, barely giving me a chance to defend myself. He was way overdoing it. "Wow, you mean business today. Guess blondie didn't wear you out enough last night?" No response. "C'mon Simon. Is it something I said? Awww, I didn't mean to hurt your little feelings!" I zigzagged to dodge his attacks that were destroying the virtual forest around us. One of his blows grazed my ribs and I stared at him, shocked. I suddenly got serious and asked him, "Can't we talk about it?"

I didn't even see it coming: Simon lunged at me and I ended up sprawled on the floor. My eyes bulged from the excruciating pain fogging my brain, and when I looked down to check out what was causing it, I saw a knife sticking out of my ribs.

Simon had stabbed me. No—not Simon. I realized it couldn't be him. "Who the hell are you?" I stared at him in horror as my body started to lurch and spasm: the knife must have been poisoned. Whoever that bastard was, he'd thought of everything.

Simon's face vanished and the Subterranean showed me his real appearance. "Nothing personal—I just needed a way to become part of the family and get close to the mortal girl. She's so safe here in your fortress, watched over 24/7. I had to come up with something."

"They'll—" A shudder kept me from continuing and rage boiled up inside me as I realized I was dead meat. "They'll never let you near her!" I hissed, my teeth clenched and my body wracked with tremors.

"The poison must have already fried your brain if you haven't figured it out yet: that's why I needed you. *As I see it, Gemma is as good as dead, though I'm curious to get to know her a little better. Maybe I'll take my time before killing her."*

"They'll hunt you down."

"I'm not afraid of anyone."

"If you kill her, there's nowhere you'll be able to hide from Evan. He'll find you and show you no mercy." I coughed, my sight growing blurry.

"What a shame for him that he'll never find me." I looked up at the Subterranean and flinched at the sight of my own image. "Because it won't be me *he'll be hunting down."*

"Next thing I knew, here I was," Drake concluded. I rubbed my arms, unable to stop trembling after hearing his side of the story. "Using my appearance, he'd come into the house and stolen the poison from Ginevra's room. There was no way I could've known the blade was poisoned. He'd planned everything to take my place—that way he could get near Gemma and you guys wouldn't be able to track him down because you wouldn't know what he looked like. When I woke up, I was at the Castle."

"How did you manage to get out of there?" asked Evan, who had listened to the entire story with his elbows on his knees and his head in his hands.

"When I first got here, they gave me an ultimatum: surrender to them or resist and be tortured. The first option had its perks, so I decided not to put up a fight, hoping they'd give me a little breathing room. I'd seen other Subterraneans walking around the Castle wherever they wanted, and I figured it would be a good way to plan an escape. Usually they don't keep any of them under surveillance. After all, if there's no reason for them to rebel against the Witches there's no reason for them to try to escape either. On top of that, their minds are constantly monitored by those harpies. The really hard part was pretending to be subjugated by Kreeshna, the Witch who was supposed to have claimed me back in the day. As you know, when a mortal with the blood of the Children of Eve dies, a Witch comes to tempt him. If he gives in, she becomes his *Amìsha*—she owns his soul and has more privileges with him than her Sisters. In a sense, he becomes her property. Witches are spoiled brats. When they fail to claim a Subterranean's soul they'll stop at nothing until he's theirs."

"Is that why Devina considers you her property?" I asked Evan in a low voice.

It was Devina who centuries ago had had Evan killed and tried to steal his soul, but failed. *The redheaded woman.* Suddenly I realized she'd been sneaking into my dreams for a long time—even before Evan died. When the Witches had come to me in my dreams, their aim had been to awaken the Witch nature hidden inside me. *Her* goal, on the other hand, had been to make me understand she was going to take him from me.

"Exactly. To Devina, Evan is hers, just like I was Kreeshna's. For some of them the pursuit verges on obsession, at least until the Subterranean finally succumbs. Then in most cases they forget about him. Anyway, the first chance I got, I escaped from the Castle. There are so many Subterraneans who've surrendered that often the Witches don't even bother to go looking for the few who disappear. Still, I'll bet Kreeshna is still out hunting for me. She always looked at me like she wasn't convinced I'd really given in to her. I knew I was taking a serious risk by going back, but when I heard about you guys being there I didn't think twice. So now, tell me about you." Drake looked at Evan. "How'd you wind up here? I imagine the Subterranean used the same trick on both of us?"

"Something like that," Evan said vaguely, but Drake insisted on hearing the details. Evan slid his hand behind his neck, thinking out loud. "I took Gemma to see Eden, and when we got back Ginevra and Simon came into my room, talking about racing. That must have been right when the other Subterranean was attacking you. And it was my transgression that must have triggered the hunt for Gemma."

"Of course!" I exclaimed. "While you guys were out I went to the kitchen to get something to eat. Drake surprised me there but I could sense something strange about him." Drake shook his head, confirming my suspicion: it hadn't been him.

"After he got rid of you, he took your place and tried to seduce Gemma before attacking her," Evan mused.

"Which would explain your weird question about me kissing her."

"Yeah. I couldn't get over it—I was devastated. I thought you'd betrayed us, so I threw the fake Drake out, but he attacked us. We should have figured out right away it wasn't you because of how he was avoiding Ginevra. He was afraid of being discovered by her. She could have read his mind or at the very least known from the sound of his voice in his thoughts that he wasn't really you."

"So he killed you in battle? That's hard to believe. He must have—"

"No," I cut in. "Actually, I was the one who killed Evan."

Drake closed his mouth and looked back and forth between us, stunned.

"He outsmarted us," Evan explained, taking my hand. "He tricked us all, and by the time we figured it out it was too late."

I hung my head, overwhelmed with remorse.

"Who's hungry?" The unfamiliar voice filled the little room. Evan stepped in front of me protectively.

Drake shot to his feet and swept the girl up in a hug. "Guys, meet Stella."

Evan and I exchanged a fleeting glance as Drake squeezed Stella again as though he hadn't seen her in days.

"Easy does it!" she said, breathless. "I was just out hunting."

Drake rested his forehead against her, his reproach sweet: "You know you're never supposed to go outside without me."

"I survived for decades without you and I have no intention of dying now. Besides, I imagined Gemma would be hungry!" Stella held up the game she'd caught and Drake smiled at her tenderly.

"Actually, she's not all wrong," I said, hunger twisting my stomach into knots.

Drake took Stella by the hand and led her over to us, beaming.

"So you're Stella—and you actually exist," Evan blurted.

Drake frowned, looking confused. "Huh? What do you mean?" Evan tightened his lips and shrugged nonchalantly.

"We thought some wild animal had eaten your marbles," I joked, and we all burst out laughing. I could barely remember the last time I'd heard the sound of my own laughter. Out of the corner of my eye I looked at Evan, his face illuminated by the firelight, the tattoo standing out on his arm, the golden skin of his bare chest . . . With him there, everything was so simple. The meat even tasted better. The food Ahrec had caught had merely filled the void I'd had in my stomach, but this time I savored each bite because every worry had vanished and in my heart the sun was shining again.

"What about you, Stella? How did you end up here?" I asked as we were eating, unable to imagine why her soul had been damned to Hell. She seemed like a warrior. She had dark skin and exotic charm, and her cheerful nature instantly made me think of a female version of Drake.

"I ran away from my Subterranean," she replied breezily.

Evan couldn't help but laugh. "What do you mean you ran away from your Subterranean? Now there's a first!"

"She sure is something, isn't she?" Drake wrapped his arm around her shoulders and she leaned her head on him. "She refused to leave me. I was still in the war back then and had no idea she'd been killed."

"A woman offered me protection. She asked me what was dearest to my heart—but there was no need to tell her. She *knew*. It was you. She promised I would see you again if I went with her, and I believed her."

"A Witch," I was quick to say.

"Yes, but I didn't know that. She used deception to corrupt me. At least that's what I thought for a long time."

"I'm sorry," I murmured. For some reason I felt I owed her an apology.

"You shouldn't be. I'm grateful to her now. If she hadn't done it, my Drake and I wouldn't be together again."

"Actually, now that you put it that way . . ." I looked around the bare cave walls. "How do you pass the time here? I mean, when you're not busy getting gnawed on by ferocious animals."

Drake and Stella exchanged a complicit glance and I blushed. "We have everything we need here." I was sure Drake was going to crack a joke, but instead he caressed her cheek. It was a side of him I'd never seen before.

"I saw you in the Cowards' village," Stella suddenly confessed. I frowned. "I'm sorry for what they did to you. There was nothing I could do to help you."

I'd been right. The village had seemed to be populated by humans, and that was probably how they preserved some of their humanity. They were too cowardly to kill, but they hadn't thought twice about serving me up to the Indavas in order to save themselves.

"That's okay," I reassured her. "I understand."

"She ran back to tell me what had happened," Drake added. "She didn't know you. Word had spread that you were wearing a Dreide around your neck, but we couldn't have known it was you, of all people."

My eyes shot to Evan's. He was also staring at me, probably wondering what Drake was talking about. Hiding a smile, I shrugged and showed it to him. "This is what Ahrec wanted from me. I was only teasing you before," I explained in a low voice, grinning.

He raised a surprised eyebrow.

"You must be tired," Stella said with concern. She picked up a strange brush that looked like it was made with blunted porcupine quills and began to run it through my hair. "You can take a bath, if you like. Our well is safe, and it's always clean."

"It's true. Every day we use Stella's invention to draw water from the spring and purify it—which leaves us with fresh poison that we turn into fuel, weapons, and food. The rock already filters out most of the poison, but we still need to completely purify the water to get as much as we need."

"It was so brave of you to decide to come here and save Evan. I can imagine what you must have gone through. You must be exhausted. Why don't you lie down on our bed for a while? It's not very comfortable but—"

"Actually I've never been so awake in my whole life. What do you say we start walking? The medallion will help get us out, but first we need to reach the crest above the river, at the source of the waterfall."

Evan moved closer to me and whispered sweetly in my ear: "Do you feel up to it? If you want, we can wait a while longer until you've rested."

"What I want is to get of this place," I said readily. I took his hand and looked him in the eye. "With you."

"What about the baby? Wouldn't it be better for him if you conserved your strength?"

I shook my head. I couldn't wait to get out of there and forget that nightmare forever. "Don't worry about him. Ginevra put a protective spell on him before I left." I stroked my belly and Evan looked into my eyes. "He's safe." I smiled, reading the sweetness in his gaze.

"A baby?!" Drake boomed. "No way, guys! Seriously?" He strode over and suffocated us in a warm embrace. "I'm gonna be an uncle and you don't even tell me?!"

I smiled at him and Stella clapped her hands, full of enthusiasm. "That's wonderful! Congratulations!"

Evan and Drake high-fived, clasped forearms, and gave each other friendly slaps on the back. "Who would of thought?!" Drake exclaimed, still astonished.

"Yeah," Evan said. "I still can't believe it myself."

"Guys?" I was forced to interrupt them. "You'll have all the time you want for congratulations later on, but right now we'd better start walking. It won't be easy to reach the portal," I warned. I was eager to get home as quickly as possible.

"I agree," Evan said. "Simon and Ginevra will be so happy to see us all together again!"

Something in his words made Drake's face darken. "I'm afraid you're going to have to say hi to them for me."

Evan and I looked at each other in alarm. "What do you mean? Aren't you and Stella coming with us?" Stella went to Drake, took his hand, and rested her head on his shoulder.

"Drake, what's going on?" I gasped.

"Sorry, sunshine." He shrugged sadly. "Stella can't leave this place. We've seen other Souls try it. They get disintegrated on the spot. She doesn't have a human body to go back to, which means she has to stay here. And I have to protect her. My place is with her."

Evan and I continued to stare at them, helpless and unsure what to say.

He smiled. "All things considered, it's not so bad down here." He slid his arm around Stella's waist and gazed at her tenderly. "I've got everything I need."

"Drake—"

"I left her once—I'm not going to leave her again." His voice was so determined I couldn't reply.

Evan approached his brother and clasped his fist in his, chest to chest. "You sure you're going to be okay?"

Drake nodded. "When I found her she was on the verge of losing her humanity, and I would have met with the same fate. Finding each other again saved us both. We're safe here. We hunt for game so we don't hurt anybody. We live a private life—socializing around these parts isn't a good idea. Besides, I'm hoping to run into my Subterranean impersonator one day so I can give him the warm welcome he deserves."

"We'll never forget you. Your absence is going to leave a void in our lives, but I would do the same if I were in your shoes."

"Sooner or later we're bound to meet again, bro, don't you think?"

"Yeah, just don't count on it being sooner!"

I walked over to hug Drake and a teardrop escaped my control.

"I'm going to miss you too, sunshine. Hey, don't be sad for me—I've never been so happy before."

"I understand," I murmured, nodding.

"Good luck, bro." Evan hugged him, clapping his shoulder.

"Good luck. Be careful and keep a low profile. And every so often tell the little guy who's on the way about old Uncle Drake!" He winked at me, making me smile through my tears. "But now, get going. I'm sure Simon and Ginevra are worried about you guys."

I hugged Stella too. Evan took my hand and led me out of the cave. I turned around to give them one last look. I couldn't believe I would never see Drake again.

Evan squeezed my hand, drawing my gaze, and I smiled at him. I knew exactly what he was thinking, what he was trying to tell me. It didn't matter where we were—Heaven or Hell—as long as we were together. Deep down, I knew Drake had also found his happiness in Stella.

32

TOWARD FREEDOM

"Do you think Anya's noticed we're gone? She said she would be back in two hours. How long do you think it's been?"

Evan kissed my temple and squeezed my hand. "I don't know. When I'm with you time doesn't matter any more—it disappears along with the rest of the world."

I smiled. I'd forgotten how Evan could free my heart of all its agony. "I still can't believe I found you." It was like a dream. I held Evan's hand tight, afraid he might disappear, but his warmth was so real my heart continued to skip beats. For months I'd believed I'd lost him and my world had turned black. The pain was still vivid, and part of me would preserve the memory forever. But now he was with me again, his hand in mine. Every time his silvery eyes sought mine I felt like I was flying. Even if it were a dream, I thought, I would want to live in it forever and never wake up, because the real life I'd endured without Evan was too painful. It seemed impossible that the nightmare was over and that we would soon be home together.

"I always told you you were brave." Evan touched his thumb to the tip of my nose. "But I had no idea *how* brave. Until now, I was always the crazy one—but you fought your way through *Hell* to come get me."

"You're wrong," I said. "I came here to escape the hell I was living in day after day without you."

I'd faced dangers Evan couldn't even have imagined, but my biggest fear had vanished the second I'd discovered he was still alive. And I had done it. My heart leapt at the thought. Despite everything, I had found Evan. Nothing would ever come between us again.

"I can't help thinking about how insane and dangerous your plan was," he said reproachfully, his jaw clenched.

"Aren't you the one who always said we needed to experience emotions to the fullest, no matter how crazy they were?"

"Yes, but not without me. If something had happened to you I wouldn't be able to bear it. I'm the one who's supposed to protect you, not the other way around."

"I would never have left you here alone, not even if it meant having to stay here myself. When I lost you something broke inside me. I thought I would never heal. But then I found out you were still alive and the wound healed, because nothing and no one could have kept me from coming to find you."

Evan stopped in his tracks, pulled me against him, and held me tight. My body clung to his, feeling every muscle. He breathed into my hair, pouring out all the tension he'd accumulated. "I've lived for over three centuries, but the last months without you were the longest, hardest ones of my existence," he whispered, touching his lips to my ear. "I'll never let anyone separate us again."

"As long as I live—whether it's a day or eighty more years—the only thing I want is you by my side," I told him. Nothing else mattered to me.

Evan moved his head slightly, stirring my hair. "Not even death will be a threat to us any longer." Puzzled by his reply, I leaned back to look him in the face, and his silver-gray eyes narrowed on mine. "I've thought it over and I think there's a solution that will end all our problems. I could go on protecting you forever, but I don't want your life to be constantly in jeopardy—I can't bear it. No one's going to hunt you down again."

"What are you talking about, Evan? What's your plan?" I stared at him eagerly.

"I spent a long time thinking about how to solve the problem. I came up with the answer before I died, but I didn't have the chance to tell you. Ambrosia. It will give you eternal life."

"The forbidden fruit?! Evan, are you crazy?! Do you have any idea what that action might trigger? Haven't you thought about the consequences?"

"I don't care. To hell with rules and consequences!" he growled in exasperation. "I can't lose you again—not a day from now or even a hundred years from now." His gaze grew tender on mine as he stroked my cheek. "I want you with me, Gem." He leaned in until we were forehead to forehead, his gray eyes on mine. "This time forever."

"Evan . . ." I couldn't let him take such a foolish risk for me—not without knowing what might happen as a result. "They might punish you." I was almost pleading. He didn't seem to be leaving me much choice.

"I don't care." He shook his head, his forehead still resting on mine. "I don't care," he repeated in a whisper. "I never want to lose you."

"I have the seed of evil inside me," I reminded him. "I can't go back to Eden. That's how they found me the first time."

"You're not one of them and you never will be. Ambrosia is the divine fruit—it'll sever all your ties with them, cancel every trace."

"Are you sure about that? How do you know they won't separate us to punish us?" A cascade of doubts filled my head, but Evan tenderly brushed his thumb across my lip.

"Everything's going to be fine," he whispered against my mouth. "I promise. Everything's going to be fine, Gem. Trust me."

I nodded and then his lips were on mine, banishing every other thought. Heaven, Hell, Witches, Subterraneans—all the barriers shattered and everything blended together as I lost myself in Evan's embrace. The forest whirled around us and I forgot who I was.

"Let's find a place to rest," he said in a low voice, separating his lips from mine.

"I don't need to. I'm not tired," I lied, but my face gave me away.

"There are some caves down there." He took my hand and guided me toward them. "You might not be tired, but my powers are gone and I wouldn't mind a few hours of rest." He smiled, but this time I suspected he was the one lying.

I followed him because actually I wasn't sure myself I could keep going much longer. Sleeping for a little while wouldn't change anything. We'd already walked for hours, staying beneath the thick treetops to avoid being seen, but this time we never lost sight of the river. I realized how difficult our lives might become if we did.

"Here, this looks perfect," Evan said as we entered a small cave. I peered around through the darkness and suddenly realized all my fear had vanished because with Evan I finally felt safe.

He sat down on the ground, his back against the wall and his arms resting on his knees, looking authentically tired. I sat down between his legs, curling up against him, my back against his chest. His arm encircled me, making me feel protected. Suddenly my eyelids grew heavy and I had to fight to keep them open.

"Sleep." He interlaced his fingers with mine, filling me with warmth. "I'll be right here when you wake up." Evan rested his head against the wall behind mine and, as if by magic, every part of me surrendered to sleep.

"What was that?" I bolted awake, gasping for air, my heart racing at the spine-chilling murmur that had woken me.

"Shh . . . it was just a nightmare." Evan ran his hand over my head and I calmed down. He was still there. "It's nothing. Just a bad dream." He kissed my forehead as a shiver carried off the remnants of the dream.

I raised my head to look at him and he smiled at me. Then I heard the murmur. "There it is again!" I said in a low voice, the blood draining from my face. Evan pricked his ears and scanned the darkness of the cave.

It hadn't been a nightmare. I'd heard the sinister murmur of mingled voices. His muscles tensed, telling me the noise had reached him too. "How could you have heard it in your sleep?"

"It seems my senses are sharper here in Hell."

He cautiously got up and gestured for me not to move. "Evan," I whispered, but he held a finger to his lips, peering through the darkness.

"You're right. Someone's here. I heard it too."

"Let's get out of here," I begged him, but he continued to advance cautiously toward the sound. "Evan," I urged, frightened. We had no idea what kind of creature might be lurking in that cave and I had no intention of finding out. But he seemed undaunted and determined.

"Let's just go, please?" I joined him and the murmur grew stronger.

"Stay back," he warned in a low voice, turning a dark corner.

"This is no time to go snooping." I took his hand. He turned to look at me and seemed to understand.

"All right, let's get out of here," he agreed. I nodded and gave a sigh of relief.

Just as we headed toward the mouth of the cave, something grabbed Evan by the shoulder. We spun around and a scream escaped me at the sight of the hideous faceless creature before us. Reacting instinctively, Evan knocked its head off its shoulders with one swift blow. The creature fell to its knees, let out a deafening shriek that echoed through the cave, and vanished. Alerted by the first one's cry, an entire group of the creatures that were huddled up as though in prayer in a corner of the cave, whipped their heads around toward us.

"Run!" Evan ordered. A shudder ran down my spine, but he'd already grabbed my hand and pulled me outside.

"I told you we should have ignored it!" I said, my breath coming in gasps. Maintaining my speed, I turned around and saw the group of creatures spilling out of the cave in pursuit. They moved in fits and starts as though following us based only on our scent. "They're following us! Run! Don't stop!"

"What the hell are they?!" Evan exclaimed without slowing his pace. He cursed under his breath.

"Zombies!" I screamed into the wind as a shiver ran over my skin.

"How do you know that?!" he asked, surprised.

"It's not like I took a bus tour to the Castle," I shot back, rolling my eyes. "Did you think braving the terrors of Hell to save you was a joyride?" Evan shook his head, both concerned and impressed. "The river, Evan! We've got to follow the river! Don't lose sight of it or it'll be the end of us!" I shouted, panicking.

"Damn it!" Evan yelled, looking back at the zombies. "Faster! They're gaining on us!"

I took another quick look behind me and trembled. Tattered clothing dangled from their lacerated, blood-spattered bodies, and their unnatural gait alone gave me the creeps. Their faces—deformed by their total lack of humanity—consisted of two small, closely set cavities that served as nostrils, and wide, threatening mouths. I held back a shudder at the thought that they used them to devour their prey whole, like snakes.

"Evan!" I shouted, terrified by how close they were. Something occurred to me and I let go of his hand. Still running, I searched my satchel, trying not to trip in the process, and pulled out the canteen full of poison-tainted water.

"What are you doing?!" Evan shouted. "Keep running, Gemma!"

My hands trembling, I turned to the closest zombie and splashed some of the water in its face. The creature jumped and pounced on me, knocking me to the ground. I wailed in horror, but in seconds it exploded in a cloud of dust. I coughed and covered my mouth to avoid breathing in the toxic ashes. Evan raced back and helped me to my feet.

"There are too many of them! We'll never make it! We've got to shake them, Gemma, run! Run!" Evan shouted. "We need to get out of here, and fast!" I looked around frantically for a way out. We could have jumped into the river, but the current would have swept us away.

And fast . . . Evan's words triggered something inside me and suddenly I heard Ginevra's voice in my head: ***It's called a Phœbus. Only use it if you really need to escape, and fast.***

I searched the satchel again, but my hands couldn't distinguish between the objects. At last my fingers closed around a small crystal cylinder. My heart leapt.

"Don't slow down! Run!" Evan called to me. I pulled out the Phœbus and raised it to my mouth. A high-pitched whistle cleaved the trees. "What are you doing, Gemma, trying to hypnotize them?!"

Looking over my shoulder, I saw that the zombies were bothered by the noise and slowed down, but after a moment of confusion, once the echo had faded away among the leaves, they resumed their hunt. "I don't understand. Nothing happened," I said wearily. All at once the sound of galloping hooves shook the earth beneath our feet. I looked up and saw something in the distance.

"What the—" Evan's surprised words hung in the air as I let out a hopeful cheer without slowing down.

"It's Ginevra's horse! It's coming to help us!" I exclaimed, panting. A huge stallion was galloping toward us at breakneck speed.

A low curse escaped Evan. "It's not going to get very far unless it can navigate that current!" My eyes went wide. He was right. I'd been so happy the horse was coming to our rescue that I hadn't noticed it was on the other side of the river.

"What do we do?" I asked, panicking.

"We jump into the water," he said. "I don't think those zombies can swim."

"They wouldn't try—the river's full of poison. Infernal creatures are afraid of it."

"It's perfect, then."

"No! We can't get in, either. It would kill the zombies, but it would burn you," I said, still running. "Besides, the current is too strong. It'll drag us away."

"Then you'd better find a way to stop him too," Evan said, pointing at the horse that looked like it was about to jump into the river. "I don't think Ginevra would be happy if we killed her steed."

"No!" I shouted, but the stallion leapt into the void.

Evan and I froze at the river's edge, our eyes locked on the animal. At the last possible moment, it unfurled a pair of wings, leaving us open-mouthed.

"Oh my God." I couldn't find any words.

"That is not a horse," Evan stated, looking stunned.

"Definitely not," I whispered without taking my eyes off the mighty beast that had soared into the air before our amazed stares.

With a clatter of hooves, the stallion landed on the shore a few steps from us. From its mouth issued a sound that made me think of a prehistoric animal. I blinked with fascination at the magnificent black angel with outspread wings. Now that he was close to us, I realized he wasn't exactly a horse. His face wasn't long and his features were more like a lion's. On his head were three small horns made of some sort of black crystal that looked like a magical diadem. His neck was long and mighty, his body muscular and strong. He had large hooves with talons on them, and his tail also ended in a claw. His skin was so black and shiny it looked like a suit of armor, and his wings were as broad and powerful as a dragon's. Thinking about it now, I realized I'd seen the Witches riding the same beasts through the air over the Cowards' village, but the dim twilight, along with my panic, had kept me from taking in their features.

The animal shook his head and let out a long call: an invitation to snap us out of our frozen state. I turned around and saw that the rest of the zombies had almost reached us. Crouching with their noses low to the ground, they scurried along as swiftly as spiders.

Evan took my hand and led me to the stallion. He tried to leap onto its mighty back, but the animal threw him off with a neigh of disapproval. "He doesn't seem to like me," he muttered.

"Hurry, Evan! They're almost here!"

He tried again, but the creature refused to be mounted. "He won't let me. I think he wants *you* to guide him."

"What?! I don't know how to fly that thing," I said, confused.

"Come on, Gemma!" he urged anxiously. "There's no time for a crash course. Get on!"

Snapping myself out of my daze, I climbed up onto the creature, who this time stood still. The instant I stroked his coat, which was soft—unlike what I had imagined—I felt a subtle chemistry between us.

"Think I can get on now too?" Evan asked ironically.

I gave him my hand and helped him climb up behind me. Just then, a zombie lunged at us but our steed opened its jaws and let out a cry so shrill it was barely audible. The zombie dissolved in a cloud of dust.

"Thank you!" I cried in surprise.

The creature shook its mane. Evan shouted for me to hurry. Unsure of what to do, I tried nudging the animal's side with my heel and he set off at a gallop. Evan whooped with joy as the zombies disappeared behind us. "This thing is awesome!" he exclaimed, as excited as a little boy. "Why didn't you think of this before?"

"Ginevra told me to use the whistle only in an extreme emergency," I shouted over the hoof beats.

Evan rolled his eyes. "Like those zombies weren't a big enough emergency?"

"Okay, so maybe I kind of . . . forgot I had it?" I was forced to admit.

"Shit. Go! Go! Go!" Evan shouted, suddenly panicking.

"What is it?" I looked over my shoulder. Evan didn't need to explain. The zombies were on all fours now, bounding after us with incredible speed. It was as though they'd evolved in a matter of seconds, adapting to the conditions demanded by the hunt. In all likelihood, those beings hadn't seen food in months. They looked like ghoulish gorillas thirsty for blood. *My* blood. "How the hell did they do that?!" I screamed.

"Where did they come from, a Steven Spielberg movie?" Evan shot back, disgusted by the sight of them.

"Evan! Look out!"

One of the zombies had leapt up behind us and was about to land on Evan but disintegrated in the air not a second too soon.

"What just happened?" I said, astonished. Evan had carbonized him with a wave of his hand.

"I'd like to know that myself. I'm probably not as out of shape as I thought!" He gave a dismissive laugh.

"So why didn't you think of trying that before?" I mimicked him teasingly.

Evan looked over his shoulder and cursed. "Damn it! They won't give up. Don't they ever get tired?!"

The bizarre creatures were gaining on us, leaping from one tree to the next with frightful agility. "We'll never lose them," he warned. "You've got to make him fly, Gemma!"

"I don't know how!" I cried. The stallion continued to race along the river.

"Talk to him! Maybe he can understand you," he said. Seeing the derisive look on my face, he insisted, "We'll never find out unless you try!"

"Okay," I said, unconvinced. I looked down at the big black lion running like a mighty war machine under us. "Fly!" I shouted, spurring him on with my legs.

Nothing happened. "It didn't work!" I turned and saw Evan laughing. Nudging him with my shoulder, I protested, "Hey! I only did what you told me to!"

"I know," he said, still grinning, "and it was hilarious."

"At least one of us is having a good—" I shrieked at the sight of another zombie lunging at us.

Our mount noticed in time and dodged it at the last second. The zombie splashed into the river. I watched with disgust as it emerged, its huge mouth frozen in a howl and its burnt skin dissolving in the water.

"This is no time to kid around," I murmured, becoming serious. It was wonderful to hear the sound of Evan's laughter again and that particular tone he used to tease me, but we had to focus and find a way to get out of there or we would end up as those zombies' next meal. I stroked our steed's back and a strange tingle rose up my arm as though his energy had flowed into me. I closed my eyes, the comforting sensation flooding through me. *Come on, Argas, take us away. We need you—*

"Wa-hoooo!" Evan's victory whoop brought me back and I opened my eyes.

"What is it?" I exclaimed with a start, clinging to Argas's back when I saw the ground rapidly becoming more distant beneath us.

"You did it!" Evan said excitedly. "Let's see if you guys can fly now too!" he shouted at the zombies who had halted, watching us as we rose into the sky. One of them took a giant leap toward us, but Argas's barbed tail suddenly burst into flame and blasted the thing into oblivion with a single blow.

"Did you see that?!" Evan exclaimed.

Dazed, I blinked as the air lashed my face. *Argas*. I didn't know why I'd called him that. The name must have been buried in my soul and crept through my thoughts like an ancient instinct.

Evan rested his chin on my shoulder and a shiver spread through my body. The tension slid away. The zombies were growing smaller, receding into the distance. I heaved a sigh of relief. We'd done it—though I had no idea what had just happened.

"You did it! But how?" he asked, smiling.

"I don't know. I simply . . . thought it." I stared at Argas, soaring majestically across the sky. With every wingbeat I felt a quiver inside. It was crazy, but I had the impression I was part of him, as though there was some invisible connection between us.

"It's amazing!" Evan murmured, fascinated.

I stroked Argas's back and he let out a soft nicker of pleasure. "Yes," I whispered, "it's amazing." I smiled and closed my eyes. *Take us away from here,* I whispered, lightly touching

Argas's mind. He responded with an almost imperceptible whinny. I opened my eyes and a sly smile curved my lips. "You'd better hang on tight!" I warned Evan.

"What?" he shouted over the wingbeats.

Without warning, Argas swerved sharply, forcing Evan to grab hold of me. I burst out laughing. "Think it's funny, do you?" he asked, hiding a smile.

"It's time for me to start making fun of you!" I teased. His laughter rang out in the sky, joining mine. Suddenly everything was wonderful. I had found Evan and we were flying toward home together. Soon the nightmare would be over. Even the landscape that scrolled away behind us was free of that ominous shroud of darkness that had terrified me for days. Magically, it wasn't scary any more. Beneath us, the forest extended infinitely, dotted here and there by villages. Who knew what other terrible creatures were lurking there or how many bloodthirsty Souls and infernal beasts prowled the forest, but seen from above it all seemed so distant. I felt free, safely out of reach. Towering mountains challenged the sky that loomed over everything in its eternal twilight. As far as the eye could see, the river snaked across the land like a venomous Dakor, occasionally thundering over cliffs in broad waterfalls. I held my breath as Argas flew over an erupting volcano. A liquid that looked like molten crystal burst into the sky, filling the air with shimmering golden reflections. *Poison*, I thought instinctively.

Then I saw it: Mount Nhubii. Tall and majestic, it watched from afar, awaiting our arrival. "Evan, look!" I cried, full of enthusiasm. The enormous waterfall plunging from the summit seemed to descend infinitely.

I couldn't believe it was all about to be over. It felt like centuries had passed since its waters had dragged me there. But I'd challenged everyone and everything and ultimately accomplished what I'd come for. I'd risked it all for Evan, and soon he and I would be home. A tear of joy escaped my eye and flew into the air as, behind me, Evan held me tighter.

"I told you, Gem." His whisper caressed my neck. "Nothing can ever separate us."

A shiver running beneath my skin, I closed my eyes and snuggled my neck against his head, smiling. We flew over the waterfall and my heart filled with hope. At last I could see it, the highest point: freedom.

"That must be it, over there!" I shouted to Evan, pointing at a majestic stone circle protected by the mountains' ragged peaks.

"Why do I have the impression I've seen that somewhere before? It looks like Stonehenge. What is it?"

I tilted my face toward him and smiled. "Our road to freedom." It was exactly like Ginevra had described it: a more complete version of the stone circle in England. "And this"—I pulled the medallion out of my dress and showed it to Evan—"is our return ticket. It'll take us home."

Evan unleashed a mighty laugh that filled the air around us. Argas joined in with a whinny of satisfaction.

"Well, what are we waiting for?! Let's get out of this place!" I closed my eyes, a smile on my lips, and concentrated on Argas.

Following my thoughts, the animal flew in circles and made a running landing. I spurred him on to keep him moving, my eyes never leaving the Dánava, and as though we were one being he obeyed, galloping straight toward freedom.

All at once a wild squeal from Argas sliced through the twilight like thunder in a cloudless sky, piercing my bones. I lost sight of the Dánava and suddenly found myself on the ground. It all happened so fast I didn't have the chance to wonder why Argas had suddenly thrown us. Dazed, I held my head, trying to regain my bearings, when a voice stopped my heart, clutching it in its icy talons.

"Going somewhere?" Devina leaned over me and grinned, her expression excited, ravenous.

"Gemma!" Evan cried, and my heart ached as he ran toward me.

"No!" I screamed. With a wave of her hand Devina sent him crashing into a tree. The branches writhed and twisted around Evan's body, pinning him in place like steel straps. I raised my eyes and glared furiously at Devina. "Let him go!" I snarled, but all she did was throw him a scornful glance as she picked something up from the ground.

"This looks familiar." I shot her a defiant look at the veiled accusation against Ginevra. "Did you honestly think you would get very far using *this*?" She dangled the Phœbus over her palm and then clenched her fist. The whistle shattered. "I've always said you weren't very bright. You were free again and you might even have made it if you hadn't called for his help." Argas uttered a disconsolate grunt, almost as though he felt guilty. "Your calling Ginevra's Saurus led me straight to you." *Saurus*. So that was what the Witches' steeds were called.

She was right—I'd been a fool. Ginevra had warned me that the whistle would draw attention. Once again, I had ruined everything. Devastated, I watched Evan struggling to free himself, his fiery gaze locked on Devina's.

Coiled around her arm, Devina's Dakor hissed. I stared at the serpent, hopelessly drawn to him, but then my eye fell on the whip Devina was holding. I pictured her lashing Evan and a blinding rage built up inside me, but she just laughed and stroked my cheek with her lethal weapon. "Isn't she *magnificent*?"

I cried out from the pain. *Poison*. All she had had to do was touch her whip to my face and it made my skin burn.

"That is what you must call her from now on."

"You named your whip?" I said with a mocking sneer.

"It's made from Molock hide. I killed the beast myself without using magic." In a veiled threat she slowly traced a circle around my neck with the whip, then showed me the handle, which glimmered in the twilight. It was carved from the same black crystal as Ginevra's Phœbus. "You continue to hide your thoughts from me, but I *know* you're attracted to it. It's the most precious substance in Hell. We once brought it to your world to study the effects of its purification. You can still find rare fragments of it on Earth, but this is of a purer, more resistant quality. The Castle itself is built of this material. Only our magic is capable of destroying it. But I see you also have a piece of it." Using her whip, Devina raised my butterfly necklace, but I jerked away. "Witches yearn for Heaven and the material it's made of: diamonds. They're our most irresistible temptation, but here they lose their light. They absorb the black magic and turn into carbonado, the substance of darkness. Such a terrible punishment."

I looked at my necklace and my eyes widened. She was right. The little diamond Evan had given me had turned black. When I looked up again, I found myself staring straight into the eyes of Devina's serpent. They were the same color as his Witch's: liquid amber.

"I must admit it's been amusing, but I'm tired of playing with the two of you. Sophìa will be back soon, we can all feel it." Devina narrowed her eyes and came closer, forcing me to step back. "Can't you feel it too?" she whispered, her eyes locked on mine and her voice suddenly hypnotic. She twisted her hand and a stabbing pain shot through my belly.

"Gemma!"

The pain prevented me from reacting to Evan's voice. The wound throbbed under my fingers: the mark of Sophìa. I forced my eyes open, defying the pain, but the only thing I could hear was her voice. "Can't you feel it inside you?" Devina whispered.

"Gemma!" Evan's voice was muffled and distant, as though a wall had risen around her and me, isolating us from everything else.

"It's the Power. Don't fight it, Gemma. Everything will make sense." I felt at the mercy of her words, as though nothing else mattered.

"Don't listen to her!" Evan's shout slammed into the wall separating us, shattering it.

Devina's expression turned bitter and the wound in my belly burned again. "Why do you insist on renouncing it?" She turned to glare at Evan. "Tsk. In order to be with *him*?"

Evan howled in pain and my heart constricted in my chest. I shot her a fiery glare. "I was about to say it was to avoid being like you, but that would have been my second answer."

Devina bent down and tore the medallion from my neck. "You won't be needing this any more." I continued to glare at her. "We'll see how witty you are when I take you to see Sophìa. Now move." She yanked me forward and I collapsed on the ground, on the verge of tears. Devina forced me to my feet, but I broke free and ran toward Evan, crying his name as he writhed in his prison.

"Gemma!" The tears blurred my vision but I continued to run. "Gemmaaa!"

My attempt proved as useless as it was desperate. A sharp pain shot through my temples and I crumpled to my knees.

"Gemma!"

I raised my hands to my head. It felt like it was on fire. I struggled to look at Evan. He fought so desperately against the branches that bound him like chains, it seemed he would uproot the tree. Then the pain clouded my vision.

I'd reached my limit. I'd found Evan, but Devina had torn him away from me, once again denying us our freedom. It couldn't be true, it couldn't really be happening to us. I was imprisoned in a nightmare from which I couldn't awake, a nightmare with no end.

"Evan . . ." I murmured, my cheek pressed against the ground. And together with my whisper, it seemed my life was being torn away from me.

I had no idea where my mind had wandered; I couldn't even feel my body any more, beyond the vague impression that I was lying on a slab of ice. My only certainty was the emptiness in my heart, the undeniable feeling that something had been torn out of me, leaving behind a dark hole.

A loud noise jolted me awake and I found myself lying on a floor, my palms and cheek pressed against the cold stone.

"About time." I blinked wearily as Devina strode into the cell. "At last you're awake. Don't get your hopes up—you're not going anywhere this time, not unless you learn to fly."

I glanced up at the tiny slit of window and realized what she meant. We must have been very high up, in the tallest tower.

"It won't be long now. Sophìa is almost here." It sounded like a threat, and I pictured the evil grin on her lips. "You would have been better off being a good girl. The Empress doesn't care for betrayal."

I struggled to my feet so I could look her in the eye and for the first time realized there was someone else with her. A prisoner. "Evan—" I could barely speak. My heart trembled, surrendering to the hope that it might be him, but the prisoner didn't move or speak, shattering my dreams.

"Where is Evan? What have you done to him?" I screamed, overcome with desperation. "Did you leave him there to die?" I rushed at Devina, tears in my eyes, but she grabbed my wrists and overpowered me. "You can't have left him there to die!" I screamed, on the brink of madness, but Devina shoved me to the ground, unperturbed by my agony.

Beside her, the prisoner let out a strange grunt, drawing my attention. Unlike the Witch, he seemed upset by my tears. I stopped to look at him. The torch outside the door cast a shaft of light onto his face, revealing gruesome scars. I flinched and stepped back, frightened, as my last hope that it was my Evan shattered into a thousand pieces. He withdrew, hiding his face under the hood of his long cloak, as though ashamed. It couldn't be him. It was just another wretched creature spawned from Hell. My longing for Evan began to feel like a physical pain: the agonizing need to have him beside me.

"I'll be back soon." Devina's icy voice echoed off the cell walls. She shoved the prisoner by the shoulder, knocking him to the ground. He crawled as quickly as he could into the darkest corner, dragging the chains shackled to his ankles behind him as Devina turned back to me with a sneer on her lips. "Meanwhile, enjoy Gromghus's company. I picked out his name. It means 'monster' in our language. It suits him, dost thou not agree?"

The door slammed shut. I burst into tears and huddled in another corner. It was over. This time it was all over.

EVAN

33

POISONED THORNS

"Sorry, did I keep you waiting?"

I heard the Witch's voice and looked up at her, furious. My attempts to break free from the branches trapping me had drained every ounce of my strength, but if looks could have killed, Devina would have been burnt to cinders in a split second.

She came over, rested one hand on my chest, and stroked my face with the other. "Did you miss me?" she whispered near my lips.

I turned my face to avoid looking at her, filled with loathing for that creature who could have single-handedly ruled over all of Hell as its unrivaled queen of cruelty. "Where did you take her?" I hissed. Devina scrutinized me as though trying to grasp my essence, then pulled back and smiled, a dangerous gleam in her eyes. "Where did you take her?!" I screamed with all the rage in my body.

"Calm down." Devina circled me, her eyes fixed on me, as I seethed with hatred. "In a way, we're on the same side, you know. Why do you think no one came close to Gemma for five whole months? We were the ones protecting her. At least, some of us were." She leaned her face close to mine, her accursed Dakor hissing as it anticipated my taste. "Actually, let's say all of us except *me*. You were protecting Gemma, but without our help you wouldn't have stood a chance—let alone your family, after you died. To protect her we eliminated more Subterraneans than you can imagine.

"I bet you're still wondering why your disobedience went unpunished. They could have denied you access to Eden because of what you did. You wouldn't have had any way to eat of the Tree and you would have died a slow death that ultimately would have condemned you to eternal oblivion. But that didn't happen, and here you are now." She touched her nose to my ear. "Do you want to know why?" I glared at her in contempt and she laughed. "What, you haven't figured it out? There was no legitimate order for Gemma's death. It wasn't her fate. *She wasn't supposed to die.* They could never have denied you access to Eden because the cause of your desertion would have given away their deception. The Màsala wanted only to prevent her transformation. They knew she was going to become one of us."

"That will never happen!" I shouted, jerking against the branches trapping my arms.

She laughed louder. "Your willpower is captivating, I must admit, but it will get you nowhere, don't you realize that?"

"Do what you want to me. But *leave Gemma alone!*" I snapped, still glaring at her. I knew what Devina wanted from me. I'd never been willing to give it to her, but if Gemma was in her hands, I would do anything to save her.

She flashed me a mocking smile. "I'll do what I want to you all right, but the Empress will see to the girl—it's none of my affair now. This, on the other hand, I'll keep as a memento." She yanked the dog tag from my neck and stared at me with a strange light in her eyes, like she had special plans for me. "You're still splendidly intact." She let her ravenous gaze slide down my body, still imprisoned by her magic restraints. "A pity. I'd hoped that with you tied up here someone would have taught you the lesson a fugitive deserves." She smiled, amused. "Maybe easy prey isn't enjoyed around here. The hunt is always enticing for a predator, dost thou not agree?"

I shot her a defiant look, wondering what she meant to do with me, but she went on, a mocking smile still on her lips. "But then again"—she glanced at Ginevra's Saurus, which, to my surprise, had protected me the whole time, keeping the Damned that wanted to attack me at bay—"traitors are lurking everywhere. You never know who you can trust these days. A Witch's Saurus protecting a Subterranean? Tsk!" She raised an eyebrow, her expression stern. "That means I'll have to take matters into my own hands once again."

An agonizing burning sensation engulfed me from head to toe, plunging me into the center of my very own bonfire. I gritted my teeth, struggling to withstand it. I'd never felt such intense pain before, not even when Devina had tortured me. It felt like the skin was being flayed from my body, like the scars that marked me everywhere were lengthening, wrapping around me like tentacles, tearing me apart. The venom from all the bites and lashes she'd inflicted on me was moving, coursing through my veins. I clenched my fists until the pain subsided, leaving me drained. All at once the branches of the tree released me from their grip and withdrew. I fell to my knees, devastated.

"You could have been at my side for all eternity." The pain had been so overwhelming I'd forgotten Devina was even there. It felt like I was in the center of a tornado of fire. "I had great plans for us. But now I wouldn't know what to do with you."

With effort, I raised my head and she peered down at me, grinning a demon's grin. "Gemma's going to choose to join us rather than stay with you."

Her words made me shudder because some part of me grasped the threat. My muscles were still twitching beneath my filthy, torn, threadbare clothes. I could tell something about me had changed—and not in a good way.

"Not even she will want you near her now." I looked at the backs of my hands and cringed with horror, instantly covering my face. "Because you're a monster. Gromghus—that's the perfect name for you." Devina laughed, her evil voice echoing through the twilight. She cracked her whip and the air around her thickened into a mirror and then shattered into reflective shards. She kicked a piece of the glass toward me and I scrambled for it like a hungry man for a piece of bread.

I looked at my own reflection and my world ceased to exist. I was a monster. Devina had turned me into a hideous monster, one that Gemma would rightfully be afraid of. My body was covered with deeply gouged scars that snaked from my chest in all directions, running over my arms, my neck, my face . . . I touched my head and to my horror discovered no trace of the thick hair that had covered it. My skull was completely bald and deformed by furrows. I clenched my fists and charged at Devina but froze, terrified by the sound of my own voice. Clasping my hands around my throat in horror, I found that I could only grunt like a wild beast. I stepped back, shocked and defeated by the terrible truth: Devina had made me a monster.

"Not so tough now, are you?" she said with smug satisfaction. I gripped the shard of glass so hard blood oozed from my palm. "What a shame I won't see you in action again in the Opalion! How I adored it when you ripped your adversaries' heads off with your bare hands . . . I can't wait to see the face Gemma makes when she sees your new look."

I cringed and took a step toward her to beg her not to do it. Looking her in the eye, I took her by the shoulders. For just a second I thought I saw a glimmer of compassion in her amber eyes, but then she said, "You're right—I'd better not let her know what I've done to you. After all, she'll be my Sister soon." She smiled, pleased with her plan. At her words, I stepped back, defeated.

"Don't make that face. Gemma will be better off if you can't explain it to her, dost thou not agree? If she found out who you really were she would stay with you, but only out of pity. Is that what you want for her?"

Her voice pierced my heart like poisoned thorns. "No one would want to be with you of their own accord. Let her keep the memory she already has of you. Once she joins us, I'll grant you the gift of allowing you to stay near her—though there's no guarantee you'll always enjoy seeing her, especially when her lips are on those of her Claimed. She'll be transformed and you'll remain at her side, serving her, watching her with other Subterraneans she's enslaved. And she'll never know you exist. But you'll have to make do with that—after all, one can't have everything. Here." She threw me a long cloak to cover myself with. It unfurled in the air, blocking out her image momentarily before falling on the ground in front of me. "You're a monster now, don't forget." Devina laughed at my utter defeat.

The idea that Gemma might be afraid of me was unbearable. The very thought was devastating. Devina was right—my appearance would repulse her. What future could I ever offer her by choosing to stay with her? By *forcing her* to stay with me? No, I couldn't allow it. I would continue to love her, to watch her in silence, but I had to stand aside. Gemma would never find out what had happened to me.

We had lost. I *felt* lost. Even if I found a way to explain to Gemma what Devina had done to me, I couldn't ask her to make such a huge sacrifice. My only choice was to give her up.

Give us up.

34

A FINAL FAREWELL

I cringed when I saw her lying on the ground and my heart withered because I couldn't run to her. I had to hide. I couldn't let Gemma see the monster I'd become.

"At last you're awake." Devina's icy voice broke the silence of the cell. "Don't get your hopes up—you're not going anywhere this time. Not unless you learn to fly," she warned, discouraging any possible thought of escaping Gemma might have had.

I'd tried to fight back on the way there, but Devina had forced me to follow her to the Castle's tallest tower. She could have thrown me into any other cell and left me there to die—it didn't matter to me—but her cruel imagination had inspired her to lock me up in that particular one, together with Gemma, inflicting on me the torture of having to look at her without being able to reveal my true identity.

"It won't be long now. Sophia is almost here," Devina said. "You would have been better off being a good girl. The Empress doesn't care for betrayal." She glanced at me, but I was distracted by Gemma's movements as she struggled to get up. It took all the willpower I had not to run to her. Instead, I clenched my fists at my sides until they bled and focused on the pain.

"Evan . . ."

Hearing her whisper made my heart ache. I squeezed my eyes shut and forced myself not to move a muscle. Discovering what I had become would devastate her. I didn't want to deprive her of the hope—the *illusion*—that I had managed to escape. I didn't want to steal from her the memory she had of me. Of what I'd once been.

"Where is Evan? What have you done to him?" Her voice broke with frustration as she lashed out at Devina. *She didn't recognize me.* The knowledge triggered both relief and disappointment inside me. "Did you leave him there to die?" Gemma screamed, rushing at the Witch in desperation. I closed my eyes so I wouldn't see it. "You can't have left him there to die!"

That wasn't supposed to happen. Gemma wasn't supposed to believe I was dead. I would have to find a way to reassure her and make her believe I was safe. I would stay at her side so she wouldn't suffer, but without letting her know who I was.

Devina grabbed her by the wrists and threw her to the floor. A groan escaped me, drawing her attention, and I was ashamed. It was the grunt of an animal, the sound of a monster. As if mocking me, the torchlight touched my face just as Gemma turned in my direction. Her look of curiosity and hope transformed into one of horror. I hated Devina for how those dirty games amused her. Though I had already imagined Gemma's reaction to my face, her shocked, frightened expression was still a stab to the heart.

Gemma pulled back, cringing, and the world fell to pieces at my feet. I quickly covered my face with my hood so she wouldn't see me any more and huddled under the cloak. In the hundreds of years I'd lived, I'd never felt such pain or such a sense of loss. Gemma was right there in front of me but I couldn't have her any more.

"I'll be back soon." Devina shoved me like a rag doll and I tripped over the chains on my ankles. "Meanwhile, enjoy Gromghus's company," she told Gemma with a sneer before turning and closing the door behind her, leaving us alone in the dark.

Together, but hopelessly alone.

I didn't even try to react. I had lost everything, irrevocably and forever. My only concern was that Gemma might look at me again. I was afraid she would recognize me and want to stay with me anyway. Devina was right: I couldn't ruin her life; I had to let her go. Defeated, I scurried back into the darkest corner of the cell, hiding from her eyes—those big, wonderful eyes I would never have the chance to look into again. Eyes that would never again light up for me, never again probe my heart—because I wouldn't let them. I would have to cherish in my heart the memory of her gaze on me as I'd once been. I would fight so that at least wouldn't be taken from her. I would continue to love her forever though she would never know it.

The sound of her weeping in the silence of the cell broke my heart. I'd deluded myself into thinking the worst was over, but hearing her cry renewed the pain, making it unbearable. Seeing her so fragile, defenseless, and hopeless devastated me. Each gentle sob, each tear, felt like losing her all over again, infinitely. The heartache was more agonizing than the physical pain I'd undergone during the transformation or any other torture they'd ever inflicted on me. I tried to ignore her, covering my ears with my hands, curling up against the wall, but I couldn't. I could bear the burden of my own pain for eternity, but I couldn't stand the sound of hers. I couldn't bear to hear her cry. After everything she'd endured, it was clear she couldn't take it any longer. She was on the verge of collapse.

Overcome by the power of my love for her, I moved closer. She had her head on her knees and didn't notice me, even when I reached out to touch her. But then I realized my nearness would bring her no comfort, so I moved back, hoping she hadn't noticed anything. My chains rattled, though, betraying my presence.

Gemma raised her head, alert. "Wait." I instinctively covered my face, hiding it under my hood, but she insisted. I could feel her gaze on me in search of answers. "You don't mean to hurt me, I can tell. At least let me see who you are." She reached out and pushed my hood back onto my shoulders. Her expression remained frozen. I desperately covered my face again and a hostile snarl rose from my chest, echoing in the cell, mocking me. It felt like I was hearing it for the first time: the sound of a beast. When the echo faded, Gemma's weeping returned to torment me, filling the air. What had I done? I'd frightened her. Out of fear of her seeing me, I'd reacted like a monster, aggressively. Maybe that was what I'd actually become. Was it possible that Devina had transformed more than just my appearance? I couldn't stay near Gemma if there was a possibility of my hurting her, if I couldn't control those terrible new instincts.

I flinched when I felt her hand rest on my knee. I'd been so overwhelmed by grief, I hadn't realized Gemma's weeping had stopped and she'd moved closer to me, drawn by my desperation. I grabbed my hood and pulled it well down over my face.

"You don't want me to see you?" she whispered, as though afraid of frightening me. My breathing accelerated at the gentle sound of her voice so close to me. I hadn't dared hope she would speak to me again. I shook my head slowly, keeping my emotions in check, and she understood. "Who are you?" she asked kindly.

I almost lost myself to despair when I tried to reply, because I had no words. How I wished I could shout *It's me! I'm here!* and embrace her and promise her nothing would ever separate us again, but it would be a selfish gesture, because Gemma didn't deserve to be with a monster. I shook my head again helplessly and hid behind my new mask.

"You can't speak?" she asked. A groan of dismay escaped my throat as I huddled there. "Gromghus. Is that your name?"

I was forced to nod.

"I'll just call you Gus. After all, who we are isn't important in here," Gemma said wearily. "We've all been defeated. Everything is lost . . ." She looked down. Hearing the sadness in her voice, I involuntarily reached out and took her hand to comfort her. When Gemma saw it, ruined by scars, she flinched imperceptibly. I began to pull it back, but she stopped me and held it in her own. I'd never known anyone so brave. For all she knew, I could have been a beast ready to devour her, yet she hadn't let herself be frightened by my appearance. She thought of me as a poor creature spurned even by Hell. A creature that, like her, was at the mercy of Devina's cruelty. Much as I longed to, I couldn't look her in the eye. I could never have stood to read on her face the only reaction I feared more than fear: pity. Gemma pitied me.

She stroked my hand again and I fought the desire to pull her to me and never let her go. Being able to touch her skin again filled me with a painful warmth full of nostalgia for everything we could never be again. I closed my eyes and pretended for just a second that nothing had changed. I stroked her palm tenderly like I always did, suddenly realizing it might be the last time I would ever touch her skin, clasp her hand in mine, feel her so close to me. The two of us alone in a dark cell, prisoners of an impossible love, bound to a cruel fate that, despite all our efforts, had vanquished us.

I'll love you forever, Gem. That emotion filled my head, my heart, my soul, until they overflowed. Everything inside me was screaming out my desperation because I couldn't tell her who I was or feel her lips on mine one last time, tell her I would love her forever. I couldn't wish her farewell.

Gemma slowly raised her head as though she'd sensed my pain and her eyes met mine. Emotion hit me like a hurricane and I couldn't look away. Her gaze lost itself in mine and for an instant I forgot everything else. Slowly, I raised my hand and tucked her hair behind her ear, an instinctive gesture I couldn't stop myself from making, driven by my desperate longing for her. My hand lingered on her skin, barely touching it, and she started, as though a shiver had run through her. For a single egotistical second, I hoped she'd understood, but the delusion vanished when I saw her eyes resting on my wrinkled, scarred hands.

She looked up, her eyes going wide. She hadn't recognized me. She was only afraid of me. The pain ran me through like a sword.

A loud noise made both of us jump. Devina threw open the door and burst into the room like a demon come to execute us. "Sophìa awaits you," she announced sternly to Gemma. Their Empress had arrived. Her expression lit up with a cunning smile when she saw that Gemma and I were so close together. "You come along too," she ordered me. She waved a hand and I fell at her feet. "It will be amusing."

To my surprise, Gemma rushed at her in my defense but Devina shoved her away and yanked on my chains, laughing. "You made friends with the monster, I see," she said with a sneer.

Devina crushed my hand against the hard rock and from my chest came a snarl that made Gemma pull back in fear. I felt dead inside. I had just proved Devina right: Gemma would always be afraid of me. Furious, I lunged at the Witch but before I could attack her she tore off my hood to humiliate me. I wanted to throw myself on Devina and tear her to shreds, but the fear that she might reveal what I had become forced me not to defy her. Instead, out of love for Gemma, I would let her tyrannize me. I backed up and quickly put on my hood in a desperate attempt to cover myself. It was a feeling I'd never experienced before: I couldn't fight back, I could only hide. Revealing myself to Gemma would condemn her to being with a monster, and I couldn't allow her pity for me to ruin her life. I'd always been a soldier and, like a soldier, the time had come for me to withstand torture rather than give the enemy what they wished.

"We've already wasted enough time. The Empress doesn't like to be kept waiting." Devina pushed me out of the cell and Gemma stepped around her to follow me, her face proud and fearless. Two Witches appeared, though, and inserted themselves between us to escort her while Devina, behind me, forced me to keep my distance. She took every chance she got to mock me in front of Gemma, who from time to time would peek over her shoulder, making me hide my face under my hood. No torture during my imprisonment had ever been so unbearable and Devina was perfectly aware of it. As if we were in a terrible dream, Gemma walked in front of me, ignoring my presence, and I continued to follow her, desperately aware that I could never reach her again. I'd lost her.

We crossed through dozens of rooms, each more bizarre than the last. Some were furnished with cages and other threatening-looking instruments for the Witches' games. Many looked like gardens full of branches from which Dakor peered out everywhere. By then I'd been in the Castle long enough to understand that it was a sort of academy where the Witches trained, entertained themselves with their slaves, and tortured those like me who rebelled against their dominion.

After walking down a long hallway we finally reached a massive door that opened on its own as the two Witches escorting Gemma approached it.

"Don't try anything funny. Stay here and don't move. I'm not done with you yet," Devina said, shoving me inside and leaving me in a corner of the room with two of her Sisters. "You two, keep an eye on him."

Gemma glanced at us but continued to the center of the hall. It wasn't particularly large compared to the other rooms in the Castle, but there was something eerily fascinating about it. I could see a dark opening in the ceiling and directly beneath it on the floor, a shining semicircle containing the Witches' symbol. Large, dark branches snaked up the walls, twisting around themselves all the way up to the ceiling. A majestic throne stood proudly at the far end, glittering like a black diamond. Its back was tall and had sharp points like cathedral spires.

The Witch seated on the throne watched Gemma approach. I'd seen her a few times before. Her icy gaze was magnetic and her hair was long and raven-black except for the locks that grew at her temples, which were as pearly as moonbeams and gave her a venerable, regal air. She wore a majestic black gown that flowed into a wide train made entirely of black butterflies and flower petals of the same color. Lilith, worshipped by her Sisters and disciples, better known as Sophìa, the bride of God and Empress of the Underworld. Coiled around her arm, her Dakor hissed. It alone sent shivers down my spine with its lapis lazuli eyes identical to its mistress's. A thin crown of black butterflies that barely touched her forehead was woven into her hair like a diadem. She stood and turned slightly, and I noticed that her dress opened behind her shoulders, leaving her back completely bare. The butterflies were fluttering all over her, creating an incredible effect.

I looked around and noticed for the first time that there were butterflies everywhere: on the broad windows, the walls, the ceiling. From time to time, one of them rose from Sophìa's gown and fluttered around her as she silently contemplated it.

Unexpectedly, Sophìa's gaze came to rest on me, then darted to Devina, vaguely amused. It must have taken only a second for her to realize what had happened. Only Gemma was unaware of my presence now. And those who wished to claim her as their Sister did nothing but ridicule her.

"Naiad, it is a pleasure to have you here with me," Sophìa said to Gemma, her hypnotic, imperious voice filling the hall, a glint of satisfaction in her eyes at having obtained what she wanted.

Gemma, who had crossed the room with her head held high, never taking her eyes off Sophìa, stared at her defiantly.

"It is unkind to take one's leave before being received, is it not?" Sophìa asked maliciously, referring to our escape. The other Witches bowed their heads in reverential respect for the

Empress. "Perhaps you do not care for my Empire of Darkness?" She raised an eyebrow and awaited Gemma's reply.

It was promptly given. "I certainly can't say I was given a friendly welcome."

Sophìa smiled at her boldness; Gemma was in the presence of the devil incarnate yet didn't seem the least bit intimidated. "There is something you were perhaps not told. *No one* leaves my realm without my permission."

"Then I ask for your permission."

Sophìa laughed out loud. "You are daring. That is why I am so fond of you. If you wish to receive my permission, however, you must give me something in return." The Empress stroked the feline at her side—a large, fierce-looking panther. "Bring him in," she ordered, her gaze fixed on Gemma as though studying her in detail. She seemed amused.

I stared at them in silent surprise as I wondered who else Sophìa meant to receive. Drake? Stella? No. Neither of them. When I realized what Devina had in mind, my heart trembled and turned to ice, then stone, and finally ash.

An identical copy of me—of who I'd once been—was escorted into the room by a Witch. He stopped in front of Sophìa, not far from Gemma. His chest was bare and the dog tag Devina had torn from me after my transformation hung around his neck. I was shocked to notice that Gemma was staring at it, suddenly looking disoriented. They looked at each other for a long moment, making me wish I was dead, but neither dared speak before the Empress. Devina would finally have her revenge for my rejection of her.

"You came here to take him back. You are brave, but that comes as no surprise. What fascinates me is how you succeeded in hiding your true intentions from me." Gemma continued to stare at her without replying. "My dear Ginevra betrayed us once when she decided to leave us, and now she's betrayed us again by allowing you to come here and defy us."

"Ginevra has nothing to do with it!" Gemma said angrily. "It's me you want. Leave everyone else out of this."

Sophìa smiled. She'd hit the bullseye. "You are correct. And I wish it to be clear that unless I receive what you intended to offer me in return, I shall not grant you permission. Not with him."

No! I tried to break free from the Witches guarding me, but they held me back. I knew what she was asking: she wanted Gemma to agree to join them in exchange for freeing the man she believed to be me. They were tricking her!

"You are free to go," Sophìa challenged her. "He, however, remains with us." The impostor who had taken my place played his part, struggling in the Witches' grasp. Devina smiled and cast me a look of smug satisfaction.

"Remain here, and he may go," the Empress continued. "You are much more precious to us than you are to him. It's simple. The choice is yours."

I had to find a way to stop her. It was a trap. Sophìa was actually leaving her no choice; Gemma would never leave on her own. She would sacrifice herself, believing she was saving me, but instead it would all be in vain.

I was desperate. I couldn't let Gemma give in to the Witches but I had no way to stop her. Selfishly, I'd thought I could continue to have her near me, keeping my true identity a secret, but I'd never stopped to think of what it would mean if she decided to stay with them—or me, in my present guise. I didn't want Gemma to transform. I wanted her to escape from this terrible place and never return, even if it meant giving her up forever.

"I can't."

I jumped, emerging from my torment, when I heard Gemma's firm refusal. She'd remained silent, reflecting on the proposal, and must have reached the conclusion that, despite everything, joining them would be madness. I would lose her, but Ginevra and Simon would take care of her and the baby, and just knowing they were safe would have to be enough for me.

"I won't agree to become one of you." Sophìa stared at her, a smile on her lips as though Gemma had said just the opposite. "Not while I have Evan's child in my womb."

It hit me like a bucket of ice-cold water. I realized why Sophìa was so calm: Gemma hadn't entirely refused her offer, and the Empress must have read that in her mind. "I'll do it. I'll become one of you," Gemma continued.

A snarl escaped me, drawing their attention. I struggled in the Witches' grip in spite of their accursed serpents that were coiled around their arms, hissing angrily. I didn't care any more if Gemma discovered me so long as I could manage to stop her. The Witches held me back and I realized Gemma was staring at us, her eyes brimming with regret. She seemed to be struggling to hold back tears. Almost as if forcing herself not to look, she bowed her head. At the end of the day, no matter how much she might pity me, I wasn't her problem.

She raised her head and I could hear renewed determination in her voice. "I will agree to let you transform me, but on certain conditions." Meanwhile, the other Evan was silent, a puppet in Devina's hands.

"Ah!" Looking vexed, Devina stepped forward to stand between Gemma and Sophìa. "She's not yet one of us and she already wants to dictate the rules!" The Empress shot her a glance that silenced her on the spot, then looked back at Gemma, prompting her to continue.

"I propose a deal: the transformation will take place only after the baby is born. I ask for three days after the birth," Gemma proclaimed. Sophìa narrowed her eyes. "What are three more days to you?" Gemma insisted.

The Empress nodded. "Granted. We have waited for centuries. Three more days will make little difference."

But Gemma wasn't finished yet. "My son must not be involved."

"That I cannot guarantee. Your son was conceived from the seed of a Subterranean, yet a part of us also dwells within him. How great that part may be we do not know. It is a situation we have never encountered before."

"I'm not willing to negotiate."

"I shall promise you one thing," Sophìa said. "He will be the one to choose. You have my word."

"Your word means nothing if you use deception to make him choose like you've done with me."

"No tricks. We shall leave him free from all constraints."

"No dreams or apparitions?"

"We shall not influence him in any way. You must realize, however, that if he offers to join us of his own free will, naturally we will not refuse that alliance. Besides, one day you might also wish for him to be here with you."

Gemma stared at her for a long while, studying her as if she too were able to read minds. "Time will tell. But I have one last condition. I came all the way here alone, journeying through Hell battling your creatures. I'm not willing to leave here all alone."

Devina snorted and I glimpsed the hint of an evil smile on her face. "Of course! Take your slave with you, by all means. I have no need of him." She contemptuously shoved the impostor, who tripped and fell into Gemma's arms.

I stared at them, petrified. Their eyes met and my heart shattered into a thousand pieces. Even the possibility of loving her from afar was being torn away from me. Gemma would transform and I would have to live with the knowledge that *he* had taken my place in her heart.

"Not him."

I started and looked up at Gemma. She extricated herself from the impostor and her eyes swept the room until they rested on mine. "I'm taking Gromghus with me."

I blinked, paralyzed, as she ran to me. I closed my eyes and held her tight. It seemed unreal and I didn't want her to slip away. Leaning back, I looked into Gemma's eyes, ashamed of my hideousness. She lifted her hand and caressed my cheek, but I pulled away. Her eyes filled with tears.

"Evan," she whispered. Hearing my name on her lips again caused a pang in my heart. "What have they done to you? My love."

A tear slid down her face and I wiped it from her cheek. I attempted to speak but had no voice, so I tried to tell her with my eyes what I was feeling: a love that had no end.

"I'm sorry. I'm so, so sorry. It's all over now," she whispered comfortingly. "I'm taking you away from this place."

Sophìa's laughter rang through the hall, breaking the invisible cord connecting our eyes. "It would seem your little trick failed, Devina," she said contemptuously.

Though she struggled to hide it, Devina looked livid. "Could you really still love him with such a repulsive appearance?" she asked scornfully, voicing the torment I felt in my heart.

Gemma smiled at her. "I don't expect you to understand what love is. You could have turned him into an insect and I would have continued to love him. Love isn't in the eyes, but in the hearts of those who are capable of experiencing it."

She looked at me and I stood taller. "When I thought you were dead, all my hope vanished along with you. I just wanted you back, whatever it cost. I'd already lost you once—I wouldn't be able to bear it again," she said, gazing into my eyes. Turning toward Devina again, Gemma said, "I don't care what he looks like, but I don't expect you to understand the depth of such an emotion, so I won't waste any time explaining it to you."

Devina snarled with frustration and vented her anger by attacking the Subterranean with my appearance who no longer served her purpose. He doubled over in pain and crumpled to the floor, unconscious.

Sophìa laughed. "I played along with your little game, Devina, though naiveté is not usually one of your weak points. Did you really believe it would be so easy to deceive her? She *is* one of us, after all." The Empress's face showed her derision.

"Not yet—she's only half Witch! Why are you listening to her?!" Devina growled, furious that her plan had failed. "Kill the baby and get rid of that worthless servant! That way she'll have nothing left to live for and will choose evil! I can do it for you." In the blink of an eye, she shot across the room and grasped Gemma's belly.

Don't touch her!!!

The howl filled my head, trapped by my inability to voice it, as I lunged at Devina to stop her. She noticed my movement and a sudden thunderbolt hit me in the chest, knocking me all the way to the other side of the room.

"Evan!" I heard Gemma's stifled scream in the distance, but the pain left me reeling, forcing me to the floor. I knew my face was exposed, but didn't have the strength to cover it or even get to my feet.

Meanwhile, Devina held Gemma captive, preventing her from coming to me. "Sophìa, listen to me! You have no reason to give in to her whims when you can take what you want and give her nothing in return."

"No!" Another voice rang out, fierce and authoritative. It took me only a second to identify it. I turned to look at the Empress and saw Anya at her side where the panther had been a moment earlier. "Sophìa, don't listen to Devina. If you do what she asks, Gemma will never forgive you."

"After the transformation she won't even remember it!" Devina shot back, trying to convince the Empress, who was listening closely to them both.

Anya ignored her and focused all her attention on Sophìa. "I've seen their love. It's strong. The venom won't be enough to rid her heart of the longing for revenge. Listen to me, I beg you. Devina is afraid someone will steal her place." She turned to her Sister and shot her a piercing look. "The truth is she wants to prevent Gemma from becoming one of us. She's trying to hide it, but I know it's true. Sophìa," she continued, her voice low and respectful, "you have what you wished for. Let him return to how he was and give them time to say goodbye."

"Why should I undo the spell? He means nothing to me."

"But *she* means something to you. Devina only transformed him out of spite because he rejected her advances while you were gone." Sophìa looked at Devina. I remembered when Sophìa had ordered Devina not to try to seduce me, but Devina had deliberately ignored the command. Witches were protective about their claims to Subterraneans, and Devina had never gotten over the fact that she hadn't been able to make me hers.

"There's no point in leaving him this way. It only gives Gemma another reason to hate you," Anya continued. "Give them a little time. What difference can a few months make? They'll soon pass and then Gemma will belong to us for eternity. Why continue to make her suffer when she's already decided to follow you? It's only a matter of time before she joins us. Consider it your gift to her."

Sophìa looked at Gemma as she reflected on Anya's suggestion. Finally she nodded, forcing Devina to release Gemma, who immediately ran to help me up. I raised myself up on my elbows as Sophìa spoke again: "Your advice is always wise, Anemone. I shall ignore the fact that you helped them to be together. However, I shall not follow your suggestion in its entirety; I will grant them both their freedom, but the slave will receive no additional favors from me. That is all I am willing to concede."

"I don't care," Gemma said, to everyone's surprise.

I stared at her in shock, hope rising in me. Her eyes told me she *truly* didn't care what I looked like. It would be difficult, but maybe she might find some way to still love me.

Sophìa smiled at her, fascinated by her reaction. "Naiad, never have I doubted your strength or your courage, yet today you remind me of a lesson long faded by time: the eyes of love see beyond appearances, just as those of the heart see beyond betrayal. I accept your terms and grant you both permission to return to your world, but do not forget that you belong to us. It is only a matter of time. You will have three days after your child is born and then we will come for you. You will comply with these conditions under pain of death—your own and that of all those you love: your child, your precious beloved, your family. No one will be spared, and their souls will be ours."

"That won't be necessary." Gemma stood up and looked at Sophìa with a determined air. "I will keep my promise."

"Then I shall see you soon." Sophìa locked eyes with Gemma, the words sounding like a threat. "Anya, Devina, escort them to the portal." When Devina opened her mouth to protest, Sophìa glared at her. "That is an order," she said sternly. "You have already caused enough problems. Do not make me regret my magnanimity."

Devina stared back at her defiantly but dared not speak. All at once the air crystallized in front of her, creating a mirrored passageway.

Anya smiled at Gemma and me as she guided us to it. Suddenly the contours of Devina's body faded before our eyes, a black panther appearing in her place. She lashed out with a menacing paw, challenging us to move closer, but in a flash Anya assumed the same shape and barred her way with a fierce growl that echoed off the walls. The two panthers faced each other, displaying their lethal claws that I knew from experience were tipped with Dakor venom, just like their fangs. A red patch on one paw distinguished the amber-eyed panther from Anya, a graceful black feline with a sharp emerald gaze. This sort of transformation in the past must have been what gave rise to legends, prophecies, and superstitions about black cats.

Sophìa put an end to their quarrel, urging us through the mirrored passageway. Gemma and I took a last look back and I saw the satisfied smile on her cunning face. Gemma had sworn an oath—made a pact with the devil—sacrificing herself to save me. But I would find some way to break that pact.

A second before the large hall disappeared behind us, I saw Sophìa rise from her throne. Keeping her eyes on me like a threat, she spread her arms wide. The sleeves of her gown fanned out into butterfly wings. She brought them back to her sides and rose rapidly into the air, disappearing through the hole in the ceiling.

"Here." Once again in human form, Anya smiled at me and opened her hand. On her palm was the dog tag she must have taken from the impostor. "I think this belongs to you." Looking at her, still stunned, I took it and put it around my neck with a nod of gratitude.

"That's all I'm able to give back to you. I'm sorry," she said softly, clearly upset she hadn't convinced Sophìa to change me back to normal. "You have to be careful," she warned us, casting me a glance. "Now that Gemma has agreed to join us, the Màsala will stop at nothing to prevent her transformation. Sophìa would rather have seen you transform right away, to avoid possible risks—we already lost one Sister in the past—but she decided to give you a little more time. It must have been a difficult decision for her."

"It's thanks to you that she agreed to my conditions," Gemma said.

But Anya shook her head, looking concerned. "That's not the point. What I'm trying to tell you is to remain alert. We'll try to help you, but it won't be easy. Be prepared for confrontations with far more Subterraneans than you've faced up to now," she said gravely. I nodded in silence, hoping my intense gaze would communicate to her my commitment to protect Gemma even at the cost of my own life.

While Devina paced irritably across from us, Gemma ran to embrace Anya. "Ginevra was right about you," she said.

"Tell her I haven't forgotten our promise. But now hurry, before Sophìa changes her mind."

The glass portal had taken us directly to the Dánava, and Anya led us to the center of the two rings of stone. She moved away, tossing Gemma the strange serpent-shaped medallion that Devina had torn from her neck.

Gemma stared at it, unsure of what to do. All at once the relic let out a hiss and stirred. Gemma and I watched as the tiny serpent came to life and slithered across her palm. It coiled around her finger in a gentle caress, then dropped to the stone beneath our feet and aligned itself in the symbol carved in the rock.

Lightning split the sky and the twilight thickened as the air began to churn. Gemma's dark hair lifted and rose into the air, whipped by the harsh wind howling around us. She looked at me warily and my hand slid into hers. I wished I could speak to her, but I would have to content myself with simply drawing her to me. The wind had grown so violent, though, that I couldn't even embrace her. I looked up and saw blurred figures like black ghosts whirling above us, creating a dark vortex, a barrier inside the stone circle. I finally managed to wrap my arms around Gemma, but the vortex swept us up and wrenched her away from me.

"Evan!" Gemma shouted, trying to be heard over the howling wind. I roared, holding on to her hands with all my strength as the cyclone flung our bodies through the air, the wind trying in vain to separate us. The spirits spun around us with increasing fury. No—they weren't spirits. I could see them clearly now. They were huge butterflies. They filled the air, surrounding us, then merged into one another, condensing into a pool of black water into which we plunged. I screamed in pain, my body on fire.

"Evan!!!" Gemma cried. My sight clouded and the current tore me away. Gemma continued to call my name and I fought to emerge from the furious whirlpool and find her, but it was useless. *Gemma . . .* The whisper filled my head as my strength abandoned me. It was as if the water was draining all my energy.

"Simon, quick! Pull him up!" I felt someone grab me by the arms and drag me out of the boiling cauldron. I forced my eyes open and Ginevra's face filled my field of vision. "Gemma . . ." I gasped, begging Ginevra to help her. Then I collapsed at the water's edge and everything went black.

A caress brought me to my senses like a soothing balm that instantly healed every wound. I opened my eyes to see Gemma leaning over me, her big dark eyes on mine.

Ashamed, I felt the impulse to cover my face because the current had torn away my cloak. I still couldn't bear the thought of Gemma staying with me out of pity, but I would have to learn to live with that overwhelming burden.

"We're home," she said softly, caressing my face.

"Gem . . ." The whisper traveled from my heart to my lips and I jumped at the sound of my own voice. Gemma smiled at me and I bolted upright, touching my face in astonishment, my heart racing with the hope that the rest of me had also returned to normal. I held up my hands and saw smooth skin. Looking into Gemma's eyes, I saw she was still smiling. I couldn't believe the Witch had changed her mind. "But Sophìa said—"

"Anya must have convinced her after all," she said. I pulled her against me and crushed her in my arms.

"Hey!" Ginevra slapped Gemma on the shoulder, a huge smile on her face. "What took you so long?" Gemma looked at her, her face filling with the memory of her odyssey. "That was the longest five minutes of my entire life!" Ginevra said teasingly.

Gemma relaxed, relieved. "Was I really gone only five minutes?"

"That's how much time elapsed between one portal and the other," she explained. "In Hell there's no time."

"Then it was the most intense five minutes of my entire life too." Gemma looked at me and a smile lit up her face, smoothing away all signs of her torment. I couldn't even imagine everything she'd gone through in Hell during her quest to find me.

I raised my hand to her cheek and stroked it. "It's over," I whispered, but her image doubled before my eyes.

Someone propped me up. "Quick, he needs to eat of the Tree." *Simon.* I hadn't noticed he was there. I hadn't even noticed I was on the verge of passing out. He slung my arm over his shoulder and picked me up as Gemma fixed worried eyes on me.

"Don't worry, I'll be back soon," I mumbled, my eyes locked on hers as I vanished. Gemma's answering smile made me feel I was in Heaven again.

Our Hell was over. No one would ever separate us again.

EVAN

35

THE SUN WITHIN

Framed by a snowy backdrop, everybody in town was gathered around the lake, forming a multicolored patchwork that moved to the hypnotic rhythm of Lana del Rey's *Young and Beautiful*. The music filled the night.

On the drive back from the airport, I watched them through the car's tinted windows and thought of the emptiness I'd felt in my heart when my friends had invited me to that concert. All I'd been able to think about was Evan and the fact that I would never see him again. Only one day before, the most I could have hoped for was to momentarily assuage the immense pain by spending a night out with friends, pretending that the snow that had frozen my heart would one day melt. Today, my heart had begun to beat again. No sun could ever warm me more than the realization that Evan was with me.

It felt like an eternity had gone by rather than just a handful of hours. The world seemed to have stopped during my odyssey through Hell and held its breath as it waited for me to bring him back. I hadn't slept a wink during the flight home, despite slumber's attempts to envelop me. Evan had slipped his hand into mine and hadn't let go. Part of me still feared it was all an illusion, that his presence there was one last island on which my mind had sought refuge before sinking into the depths of madness. I didn't want to fall asleep, afraid my Evan wouldn't be there when I woke up.

When I paused to reflect on everything I'd faced, it seemed impossible that I had actually done it. And yet Evan was beside me. I could feel the warmth of his breath. Against all odds, I'd brought him back. It had been a mad, arduous endeavor, but I'd done it. And despite all my fears, deep in my heart I'd always known that no Witch and no creature from Hell could ever keep me away from him.

I didn't want to waste a single minute of our time together.

"It's yours. I brought it in case you wanted to call your parents." Simon, behind the wheel, handed me my phone, though I hadn't even noticed it beeping. I'd sealed myself in a bubble where the only things that existed were Evan and me and my hand clasped in his on the back seat of the BMW, waiting for our months-long journey to come to an end.

Simon had already told my parents that Evan had been found—that the car accident had left him with amnesia, unable to contact us—and that we hadn't been able to track him down until he'd finally regained his memory. When I entered my PIN, eighteen missed calls lit up the display and an envelope icon blinked above. I opened the most recent of the twelve texts Peter had sent me over the last few hours.

Where are you?

I stared out the window, watching the crowd. Beside me Evan squeezed my hand. I was supposed to have gone to that concert but I'd been busy with something far bigger. I rested my head on Evan's shoulder and my heart smiled as I read the reply I'd instinctively written.

I went through hell but I'm finally back in heaven.

EPILOGUE

"What happened to all the snow?" I asked Evan, raising my voice to be heard at the end of the path, where he'd gone ahead on his bicycle. The vague suspicion that winter had stopped just for us occurred to me, making me laugh.

Evan jammed on the brake and skidded over the damp forest floor. "It must have melted when it saw you." This time he was the one to laugh at my awkward attempt to dodge the flying dirt as I pedaled behind him. "Besides, it's not safe to ride your bike if the ground is slippery, don't you agree? We can't risk your falling!" he said, looking amused as he teased me. That must have been one of the things he'd missed most during our separation—teasing me. He was wearing black cyclist's gloves that left his fingers bare and had tied his long, overgrown hair into a samurai ponytail. *He looked so sexy . . .*

"You thought of everything," I shot back, trying not to let him see me blush.

A week had gone by since our return from Yucatán and Evan had had all the time he needed to recover and regain his powers. That meant that even if I had fallen, my chances of ending up on the ground were zero, so Evan must have had something else in mind. When he'd woken me that Saturday morning, his eyes full of childlike enthusiasm, his suggestion that we ride our bikes to the lake house hadn't seemed so strange. But the closer we got to the shore, the more convinced I was that Evan was up to something.

It hadn't snowed for two days. The sun shone high in the sky, casting its light on the lake's icy surface. The leaves stirred in the breeze while the snow melted on the damp ground right before our wheels, clearing a path like a theater curtain rising on a play performed only for us. Only small patches of snow scattered here and there in the forest watched us, silent spectators of our newfound love. The scent of the woods was intoxicating. At last I could smell it again.

"Wait for me!" Struggling to keep up with Evan, I tried to curb his enthusiastic race through the trees as he popped wheelies and spun around like it was an obstacle course. "You still haven't told me what we're doing here," I reminded him when we'd reached our hideaway.

His carefree laughter echoed through the trees as he rode back and came to a skidding halt in front of me, a smile in his eyes. Dropping his bike close to the edge of the lake, he tossed his gloves to the ground and, after helping me off my bike, took me by the waist and lifted me into the air, holding me close. I slid down his body and the forest spun around us as his lips fused with mine.

"I love you. Will that do for an answer?" he whispered against my lips.

"It would if I didn't know you well enough to recognize that strange smile."

"What smile?" he replied teasingly.

"The one you're trying to hide right now!" I retorted, and he kissed me again.

"Nothing gets past you," he whispered.

"Glad you finally noticed," I said sardonically.

"If I really have no choice but to give in to your insistence"—he took my hand and led me to the shore, looking at me out of the corner of his eye—"I hear the Snowball Hop is coming up soon." He raised an eyebrow, a half grin on his lips, sat down at the water's edge, and pulled me down onto his lap. "I'm officially claiming every dance on your dance card. Think you can scare up a Victorian dress by next Saturday?"

"No more dances, please. The last prom I went to didn't end up among my fondest memories," I reminded him.

Evan smiled—he'd probably been expecting me to say that. "This time it's going to be different." He drew me closer, his words sounding like a promise. "Want to take the risk?"

"The only risk I'll be running is not being able to fit into the dress any more. Ginevra has a couple of them in her wardrobe, and my guess is that the theme of this year's hop isn't a coincidence."

"I wouldn't snub vintage dresses if I were you. You were so sexy in Hell with that outfit on." He raised an eyebrow and I thought back to when we'd made love in the prison cell. God . . .

Evan laughed, guessing what was on my mind. Blushing, I replied quickly, "At this point I'm afraid I'll have to make a few alterations." I looked at my belly, which over the last week had begun to swell.

He smiled. "I'm sure you'll be gorgeous," he assured me, and I almost lost myself in his dark eyes.

"I'd better be, otherwise I'll look horrible next to you!" I said, grinning. His expression became serious, and I knew he was trapped in past torment.

"Did I say something wrong?" I asked cautiously. Something in my words seemed to have upset him.

"Would you really have still loved me if I'd stayed a monster?" Sadness darkened his face as he waited for me to answer, but I had no doubts.

"My eyes could never see you as a monster"—my hand slid to his chest and rested on his heart—"because it's your heart that joins me to you. We're bonded together and no spell could ever change how I feel."

What I said seemed to reassure him only partly, as though something in him was still afraid he might lose me. "Will that always be true? No matter what happens?"

The question hung between us and Evan looked into my eyes as though searching them for my answer. I realized he was referring to my transformation, but once again I had no doubts. "*Antar mayy as.* I'll always love you, Evan. It couldn't be any other way." I rested my chin on his shoulder and felt his chest against mine as he held me close. No transformation could destroy my love for him. "Of course, I can't deny I would have missed the sound of your voice—but then again, you wouldn't have been able to tease me any more." I gave him a sly smile.

Evan smiled tenderly and put his mouth to my ear, making me tremble with emotion. "Well, I'm afraid you'll have to put up with me for a long time, because I'm going to make sure you never have a reason to miss *any* part of me. *Yatha tvam mayy asi,*" he whispered, sending a tingle over my skin.

I closed my mouth and swallowed, gazing into his eyes. They were so close to mine I risked being trapped in them. "It will be sweet suffering," I murmured against his mouth.

"When did you realize the other Evan wasn't me?" he asked softly. I watched his lips move, hypnotized. When my brain had processed the question, I looked up at him and smiled. I'd been waiting for him to ask me that for a while. "I recognized you when we were in the cell."

Evan looked at me in surprise. I could see him trying to figure out whether or not I was serious.

"Your gestures made me suspect it, when you . . . you stroked my palm with your thumb," I said with difficulty. The memory was still so vivid in my heart. I'd spent such a long time thinking about his caresses, yearning for his touch, that it would have been impossible for me not to recognize it. When he had touched me, a tingle had spread from his fingers and touched my soul. "At first I wasn't sure." Through his shirt I slowly stroked the scar that ran down his right forearm, losing myself in the memory. The marks left on his body by the poison would never fade, a constant reminder of Devina's cruelty. There was nothing in the world that could make me want to become like her. "It seemed impossible, but then I looked into your eyes and every doubt vanished. I realized it was you, but I thought it would be better not to let Devina know. I had to make her think her plan was working, at least until I was with Sophia."

Evan continued to stare at me, surprised by my revelation. He didn't realize the most incredible part was yet to come. "And, I heard your thoughts," I confessed all in one breath, and waited for his reaction.

"You . . . what?" he asked, stunned.

I shrugged, smiling. "I heard your voice in my head. You called me Gem. No one else calls me that, so there was no doubt it was you."

"You can really read minds?"

My confession had astonished Evan more than I'd expected, but I couldn't tell if he was pleasantly surprised—or scared. Evan had always conveyed his thoughts to me, but in Hell he'd been without his powers, whereas mine had begun to develop.

"I can't control it yet," I said regretfully. "I don't know when it's about to happen." Actually, the only two times I'd read someone's mind were both right after being in the presence of Witches. My body must have sensed the bond and activated the powers hidden within me. "I suppose that'll happen once I've transformed."

Evan stiffened. "You're not going to transform," he said, his voice firm, his gaze commanding.

I stared at him, unable to reply. I didn't want to shatter his illusions because deep in my heart I nurtured the same hope. Instinctively, I pushed up the sleeve of my sweatshirt and began to fiddle with the black hair tie around my arm. Now that I knew what it meant, I should have taken it off, but it was something that had always been part of me.

"We'll keep it from happening." Evan's gaze softened on mine. He kissed my forehead and I closed my eyes, surrendering to our very own utopia. "We're part of each other, Gemma. We need to fight to make that true forever. *Samvicaranam. Samyodhanam.* Remember?"

"Stay together. Fight together," I translated. No one was going to separate me from him. I would fight against everyone—even myself—but we would stay together.

Sitting on Evan's lap, I stared at the lake, my gaze sweeping to the distant horizon where the snow and ice gave way to the colors of a clear sky full of hope. My fingers instinctively clasped the pendant I wore around my neck. The diamond sparkled once again; the evil that had darkened it in Hell had been purged. Would I, in the same way, also manage to emerge from the darkness? I didn't know what would become of me, but one thing was certain: all I wanted was to stay with Evan and our baby.

Seeming to sense my thoughts, he pulled me more snugly against his hips and held me tighter. Then he slid his hand under my sweatshirt and stroked my back, following the shiver he'd caused. He was so close his lips brushed mine with every movement.

I stroked his ear with my nose and took a deep breath, inhaling his scent. "Evan, would you do something for me?"

"Anything. Whether it's permitted in this world or forbidden."

He rested his forehead against mine and my fingers played with his hand, stroking it and drawing imaginary symbols, then moving onto his forearm, tracing the marks tattooed there. Evan let me study them.

"I'd like you to give me a tattoo. I want to have those words on me so I can remember this moment—remember the two of us—whenever I read them." *After my memory has been obliterated*, I thought, but didn't dare say it out loud. I needed it. I was more afraid than ever before of losing him again. Afraid of myself, afraid of the transformation.

His forehead still touching mine, Evan took a deep breath and slid a hand behind my neck, holding me tight. Then, slowly, he held the other one near my face, offering me his palm as I continued to stroke his arm. My fingers slid up over his wrist until they mirrored his. Palm to palm. A burning sensation stung my thumb and spread down the side of my hand, but I didn't take my eyes off Evan. Our gazes remained locked until the pain subsided and he smiled against my lips, brushing his nose over mine.

Clasped in Evan's lap, I turned my head and smiled in amazement. Our palms were still suspended between us, and along the inner side of my right hand was engraved in elegant writing:

संविचरणम्

The mark rose to my thumb, encircling it twice. But it wasn't the entire phrase I'd asked for; on Evan's left hand was another tattoo that lined up with mine, completing it.

संयोधनम्

He'd given himself one as well, uniting us even in that small gesture. The phrase could be read in its entirety only when we joined hands. "*Samvicaranam,*" Evan whispered, running his thumb over the writing on my hand. *Stay together.*

I looked him straight in the eye and brushed my finger over his new tattoo to seal the vow. "*Samyodhanam.*" *Fight together.*

"For eternity." Without taking his eyes off my face, Evan interlaced his fingers with mine.

I looked at the tattoo and my breath caught in my throat as I understood for the first time the meaning of the symbol Evan had created for us. If we held our thumbs apart, each of us had a simple oval that came to a slight point on the outer side, but when we interlaced our fingers my oval joined with Evan's to form the infinity symbol.

"Did it hurt?" He looked at my face warily. Inside me a thousand different emotions struggled to prevail, and the winner would probably be tears.

"Yes—it made my heart ache. It's wonderful."

Evan had given me the tattoo I'd asked for, but only half of it; he would keep the other half. Now, along with the mark of the Children of Eve on his forearm, he carried on his left hand *our* symbol, the symbol of our bond and our battle. We had grown to know each other through our shared battle, and we would continue the struggle together. Fate had given us no peace and we knew we might never achieve it, but we would continue to fight for all eternity—whatever it took—to stay together.

My eyes shining, I stroked his tattoo and moved my hand to the mark of the Subterraneans. Then I slid it up his arm to his shoulder where, beneath his black cotton shirt, I knew there was another one of the lash marks left by Devina, the Witch who might one day be my Sister. I ran my fingers over it, promising myself I would never become like her. Now I too had left my mark on Evan—a mark that spoke of love, not of death and destruction, like hers. Never would I want to be like Devina. That possibility might be what frightened me most about the thought of transforming.

"You know . . ." Evan had watched me as I reflected, but for some reason he was smiling. He swept a lock of hair from my face and reclaimed my hand. "Devina left me with a lot of scars, but one of them hurt her more than it did me. Inadvertently she gave us a gift, because now you're also in my past."

"What? What do you mean I'm in your past?" I laced my fingers with his, sealing them in our own special infinity, and snuggled against his chest, playing with the dog tag around his neck.

"I remember having a memory of you the night before I died in 1720."

I stared at him in astonishment, my hands on his chest. "Did she implant that memory?"

"No, I did—to remind myself that you're my fate."

I found my smile again. How had I been able to be without Evan for so long? My heart ached at the mere thought. "And it had an effect on the present?"

"Exactly. I have new memories now. In one of them, I'm telling my mother about you. In a way, it's almost like I introduced the two of you." I thought I might burst with emotion and he smiled, seeming happier than ever. "And it couldn't be any more perfect, because actually"—he lowered his voice to a murmur—"I didn't bring you all the way here to invite you to the dance."

I pulled back to look Evan in the eye and he offered me his hand to help me to my feet. "Before coming to wake you up this morning I went to see your parents at the diner," he said.

"To see my parents?" I stared at him, puzzled. "What for?"

"This time I wanted to do things properly." Evan stepped closer and my heart raced. "This place is full of us, don't you think?" he said softly, resting his forehead on mine. He opened his hand and showed me the little silver case he'd been hiding in his palm.

I swallowed, staring at the little box as it slowly opened upon his command. "Evan," I murmured, but he took my wrist, making me tremble, as his ring slowly slid onto my finger.

"Marry me, Gem," he whispered with incredible tenderness. "It's all I want." His dark eyes probed mine and I wished the moment would never end.

"It's all I want too." The words flowed directly from my heart. I closed my eyes as a feverish heat swept over me, filling my mind.

Evan's lips tenderly touched mine again and again, playing hide and seek, sealing his vow and testifying to our love. "Should I take that as a yes?" he murmured, smiling against my lips. He squeezed my hands at my sides as I bit my lip, pretending to be thinking over his proposal.

"Couldn't you tell already?" I smiled, unable to help it.

He lifted me into the air and spun me around as his laughter filled the forest. "Come on, quick!" He took my hand, led me to my bike, and climbed onto his own. "I want the whole world to know!"

Smiling at his enthusiasm as I followed him, I stopped to look at the little ring on my finger. My heart was still pounding with emotion. I looked up at Evan who was zigzagging through the trees, freestyle.

"Hey! Where are you going?" I called after him as he charged up the rugged terrain.

Evan whipped his bike around and skidded to a halt in front of me. "Wherever I go, I'll always come back to you."

BOOK FOUR

EXPIATION

THE WHISPER OF DEATH

A novel by

Elisa S. Amore

Translated by

Leah Janeczko

"The universe will never be extinguished
because just when the darkness
seems to have smothered all,
to be truly transcendent,
the new seeds of light
are reborn in the very depths."
Philip K. Dick

PROLOGUE

"Simon, behind you!" I shouted from atop one of the boulders, but my voice was drowned out by the explosion of the fireball hurled at my brother. I held my breath in alarm, but moments later Simon emerged from the cloud of dust, a thousand shards of rock still raining down.

"Where'd he go?!" he shouted, agitated, shielding his eyes with his arm to avoid the shower of shattered stone.

I hadn't seen where the Subterranean had gone, but a fleeting movement caught my eye. "Over there! By the wall!"

Simon narrowed his eyes and disappeared into a crevice in the rocks.

"You take care of him, little brother," I murmured. "I'll keep climbing."

I had no idea what that hellish place was. It looked like a world in ruins from one of Drake's video games. The wreck of an old galleon stood among the rocks like a sentry and small pools of water dotted the sandy earth. Around me, the rocks rose in a circle all the way up to the ceiling of the cavern, where light streamed in through a hole. It was as though a giant hand had descended from above and punched through the rocks, opening a passageway to Hell while groping with its fingers to dig channels all around it. The result was a bizarre labyrinth of tunnels that made their way up toward the surface.

A movement to my left. I gripped my dagger and stood motionless, all my senses alert. The Subterranean materialized behind me but I spun around in time, blocked his fist, and slammed him against the wall. He shot to his feet and rushed me at warp speed. My blows were brutal and direct, but the young redheaded Subterranean put up a good defense. He broke off a jagged piece of rock and wounded my bare chest with it. I gritted my teeth, absorbing the pain.

I jumped up, grabbed hold of a vine dangling among the rocks, and pinned the Subterranean's head between my legs. I whipped him around, releasing my grip and dropping him several levels. Keeping my eyes trained on him, I opened my hand and summoned the poison-tipped dagger that had slipped to the ground.

The Subterranean shot me a glare brimming with contempt and raced off through one of the infinite number of clefts in the rock. I slid my weapon into my belt and set off after him, swinging from vine to vine. Barehanded, I climbed up one of the vertical passageways that looked like a tunnel burrowed through the ground by worms. The place hadn't actually been designed for escaping; it was a prison, and sooner or later the Subterranean I was chasing would realize it. I'd seen the flicker of fear in his eyes when he discovered he couldn't dematerialize any more, that he couldn't escape me. The perimeter had been sealed off. It wasn't time to run—it was time to fight. And we were going to exterminate every last one of them.

I followed the sound of his footsteps racing through the unpredictable twists and turns. A mortal wouldn't have been able to handle the dizzying pace of the obstacle course, but with me chasing him, that Subterranean was doomed.

"You can't keep her away from us forever," he shouted.

I pounced in front of him and shoved him against the wall. "But I'll never stop trying." As I drew my dagger its blade hissed and I pressed it against his throat.

"Others will come," he warned, his eyes full of fear.

"I have a plan for that too," I shot back, my expression threatening.

We'd spent a whole week, day and night, formulating a plan, studying every detail. Now that Gemma had sworn loyalty to the Witches she'd never been more in danger. The Màsala wanted to take her before she transformed, but I wasn't about to let anybody touch her.

The Subterranean cringed, bracing for the blow. Instead I grabbed his hands and pinned them to the rock. An arrow whistled past my ear. I spun around and her eyes pierced me, as golden as those of the hissing Dakor coiled around her wrist.

A Witch.

The Subterranean let out a wail of terror but she continued to stare at me, a mix of excitement and bitterness in her eyes. She had a proud face, dark skin, and a long ponytail as black as ebony.

Bathsheeva.

She set another poisoned arrow against her bow and took aim at me, but a second before she released it her arm tipped up and she hit her real target. The Subterranean who'd just materialized in midair crumpled to the ground, the arrow protruding from his leg.

Like a bolt of lightning, another arrow flew straight toward us and lodged inches from the head of the Subterranean I'd immobilized. With a fierce snap, a black leather cord whipped around his wrists, binding him to the wall. The Angel of Death howled with pain from the poison the cord had been soaked in and passed out, scarlet trickles of blood streaking the mark of the Children of Eve on his arm.

The Witch narrowed her threatening eyes at me once again, then took a mighty leap and set off to track down her next prey. The Subterranean she'd hit in the leg was writhing on the ground just steps from me, his flesh sizzling from the arrow's poison. Framed by long black hair, his face was covered with welts, painful testimony to his personal battle with the Witch.

I clenched my fists. He was about to die, but in his gray eyes there wasn't a shadow of fear or remorse—only the proud awareness that with his death others would come to complete the mission. I raised my foot and kicked him hard in the face to erase that satisfied smirk.

The sounds of the battle echoed off the walls. There was no time for long farewells because we weren't done fighting yet. I ran in the direction of the shouts and leapt off the rocks into the void. Aiming for one of the two Subterraneans Simon was battling, I landed on him with all my weight, like a hungry lion pouncing on its prey. I was well aware of my peers' blind dedication during battle, but my strength had another source, another energy, another name. My need to protect Gemma was unstoppable. I could feel the fire grow stronger inside me every time I struck. And struck. Again and again. I would slaughter them all, each and every one of them. No one was going to take her away from me again.

I dragged the Subterranean back and slammed him against the ground. My hair fell over my face, my breathing ragged and my muscles quivering as I held him in place.

He stared at me in terror as the earth cracked beneath him. What scared him most, I could tell, were my eyes. They were the same ice-color as his, but mine held a fire he'd never seen before.

Someone clapped, deliberately, and I slowly raised my eyes.

"What an exciting show. I'd almost forgotten how ardently you used to battle in the Opalion." Devina emerged from the shadows, moving with feline grace as four black panthers stalked from different crevasses in the rock and positioned themselves in a circle.

Terrified, the Subterranean beneath me tried to break free, but I tightened my grip. "Too bad the show didn't feature you," I shot back at the Witch, my sarcastic voice overflowing with hatred.

She leaned over and stroked my cheek with her black-painted fingernail. Her fiery eyes told me she still desired me. She slid her finger down my neck and across the long, deep scar on my shoulder. A dark shadow veiled her gaze at the memory of when she'd left her marks on me, almost as though she'd branded me as her property. Her Dakor slowly slithered out of her thick red hair and hissed close to my face.

I grabbed the hand she was touching me with and glared at her with contempt.

"Such bitterness," she lamented, her voice honeyed. "After all the time we spent having fun together . . ." One of the panthers roared and she sneered.

In a silent challenge, I held her ardent gaze as her serpent circled down her arm. The blond Subterranean struggled beneath me, terrified, as the Dakor slithered closer and closer to him and the air filled with tension.

Another panther roared, and this time the sound filled the entire cave.

"Oh, all right! You're all so tiresome!" Devina stood up and cracked her whip, winding it around the Angel's throat. She jerked it back and smashed him against the galleon's fragile wooden hull, shattering it and revealing what was hidden inside: a cluster of Subterraneans bound to tall posts.

I went to stand beside Simon, my muscles tensed. He too had captured a Subterranean. The two panthers facing them transformed into Witches, seized his prisoner, and bound him to a post beside the others as more Sisters leapt down from the rocks with their prey.

Devina smiled at me, in her eyes a glimmer of nostalgia and a hint of promise. I turned to follow Simon, but something stopped me. The burning pain registered before the crack of the whip; Devina's poisoned lash had coiled around my wrist. "Leaving so soon? The fun is barely starting."

Simon and I exchanged glances. He seemed worried about my intentions, but I grabbed the whip, ignoring the pain, and jerked it out of Devina's grip. Before she realized what I was doing, I threw myself on her, forcing her backwards with my body and pressing the whip tightly against her throat. "We're not in your world now, *Witch.* Just because we've formed an alliance doesn't mean I'm willing to put up with you. Try that again and I'll incinerate you."

Three panthers crept toward us threateningly. "Evan," Simon called.

I looked at the Witch again. Would I ever manage to wipe that smug smirk off her face? I turned my back to her and followed Simon to the waterfall above. There, behind the curtain of water, was the way out. I opened the door and behind me Simon pressed the black carbonado button. Our surroundings changed: the ruins slowly turned into the familiar walls of the workout room. The rock beneath our feet flattened out to form the floor, like a lake gradually freezing over, sealing the Subterraneans in our dungeon below, guarded by a group of ferocious panthers who were prepared to devour them.

"Luring them here was a great idea, bro. Well done!" I told Simon, throwing myself down onto the sofa in the living room. He straddled a chair and started munching popcorn. After various days of nonstop battling the Subterraneans sent in to kill Gemma, we'd come up with a strategy. Originally, we'd only had to deal with one Executioner at a time, but this time they'd sent in nine of them at once. The Witches had helped us secure the training room area, and one by one the Executioners had fallen into our trap. Once they'd been lured in, they had no way out. Now they were under round-the-clock surveillance by a group of Drusas—guardian Witches—who were keeping them in a weakened state with their powerful venomous blood.

Even if they broke free, the perimeter of the workout room was sealed off so they couldn't dematerialize. We had them in the palm of our hands.

"At least we're playing on our home field now," Simon replied. "The enchanted workout room is a perfect battlefield."

"Yeah. There's no better way to train, and the simulation scenarios made everything more fun. Let's hope the plan works and more don't turn up."

"I'm sure this'll keep them at bay for a while. Besides, we had no choice. There were too many of them this time. I counted seven prisoners."

I too had counted the posts to which we'd bound the Subterraneans. Two were missing. "One died right before my eyes. He was about to attack me when a Witch ran him through."

"Eight Executioners in one night? Not bad. What sons of bitches. The Màsala have decided not to cut us any slack."

"Nine, actually," Devina called out nonchalantly, suddenly appearing out of nowhere.

"You mean you killed another one?!" I shot to my feet and confronted the Witch. I'd assumed one of them had escaped, but instead Devina had killed him, risking ruining our plan.

"Calm down, Spartan," she said in a lilting voice. "I understand the rules: only prisoners."

"Couldn't you have understood it before?" Simon reproached her.

"Don't you realize what this might mean for us?!" I growled, inches from her face. "We have a plan. Follow it."

"Evan is right, Dev," Anya spoke up, walking through the door with two other Sisters. She was the one who, in panther form, had growled at Devina when she provoked me. I'd recognized her by her emerald eyes. "We can't kill them any more. For every Subterranean we get rid of, another one will show up. Or maybe more. Who knows?"

"Imprisoning Desdemona worked," Simon reassured her. "It'll work again this time."

"I think so too, but we need to be careful and not let our instincts get the better of us." Anya cast a reproachful glance at her Sister who hadn't been able to hold back in battle.

"What a bore! You're taking all the fun out of it!" Devina complained. Anya rolled her eyes. "I killed a Subterranean, but I wasn't the only one. Why are you taking it out on me?!" She looked accusingly at Bathsheeva.

"Hey, it's not my fault!" Bathsheeva protested. "I saw you, you killed him on purpose. I *had* to do it. There were three of them and that bastard was making things rough for me. He was armed to the teeth and he wounded my Dakor. He had these strange razor-sharp brass knuckles—I'd never seen anything like them. They got smeared with my Dakor's poison. While I was capturing the other two he got away. He was about to attack Evan with that weird weapon of his and would have killed him if I hadn't shown up in time." The Witch sent me a fleeting glance and I nodded to her in acknowledgement.

"So what? Sophìa's orders are to protect Gemma, not her boy toy," Devina said with a sneer.

I glowered at her. I couldn't stand how she jeered at me like she owned me. I knew what she was thinking: if the Subterranean had hit me with his poisoned weapon, I would have ended up back in Hell where she could do with me as she pleased.

"Forgive her," Anya said. "She's a real Witch when—No, she's like that practically all the time."

"It's nice to know you speak so affectionately about me behind my back, little Sister."

"I wasn't speaking behind your back. You know for yourself you act like a bitch. It's what you do best."

"Touché." Devina gave a shrug of satisfaction.

"Do I really have to stay here?" Simon asked.

The grimace that twisted Devina's face got a smile out of me. Maybe once in a while it had to get to even her to know her company wasn't enjoyed.

"Is Gemma with Gwen?" Anya asked, suddenly worried again. I nodded to reassure her and looked outside. Beyond the hexagonal picture window, darkness shrouded everything.

"Nerea, Safria, join Gwen upstairs. We should reinforce our surveillance."

The two Witches nodded and left us, morphing into panthers before climbing the stairs. I nodded to Anya, grateful for her consideration. Though Gemma hadn't transformed yet, most of her Sisters were already treating her as one of their own. In recent days I'd been surprised by how loyally the Witches had helped us protect her.

"We have to keep up our guard," Anya said. "Bathsheeva killed an Executioner to protect Evan, and Devina slew one because . . ." She looked at her Sister reproachfully. "Well, because otherwise she wouldn't be Devina."

"Blah blah blah," Devina said, responding to the accusation in a singsong voice.

"We've imprisoned seven, but we know for certain two more will soon be after Gemma. Over the last few nights we've had time to study each of them, but we have no idea who they'll send in now. We don't know when they'll attack next. Still, there's no doubt that—" A sudden hiss sliced through the air, cutting Anya short.

We spun around in alarm and Devina smiled at us, pleased. "Problem solved." The Witch filed her nails with the shaft of her whip as we all stared at her, wordless. On the ground, an Executioner who'd appeared from nowhere writhed beneath the iron grip of her heel, while another hung from the wall, unconscious, behind the Witch. "You might consider thanking me at this point."

Simon's relieved laugh filled the room and I shook my head, my tension draining away. He loathed Devina, maybe even more than I did—she was the one who had betrayed Ginevra and made the Sisterhood drive her out of her world, putting both their lives in jeopardy. However, crossing the latest two Subterraneans off our list would make life easier, and for once it was thanks to her.

"Great job, Dev," Anya said sincerely. "Now let's take them down to join the others."

"I'm not guarding the Children of Eve if I can't even kill them," the redheaded Witch complained, heading toward the workout room.

"Yes you are, if you want at least to have a little fun with them. I bet you can't wait." Anya winked at me. They dragged the two unconscious Subterraneans through the door leading downstairs and closed it behind them. I was infinitely grateful for her gesture: it finally left me free to go to Gemma.

"The best way to start the day, don't you think?" Simon slapped me on the shoulder and I grimaced from the pain of the cuts and bruises on my chest. "Nice work with that Carpathian," he said, grinning.

"Carpathian?"

"That's what Drake would have called him. You see how big that guy was?"

"Yeah, I'm sure Drake would have had a blast this time." I missed my brother Drake terribly—we all did—and the awareness that I would never see him again was devastating. Still, I couldn't blame him for deciding to stay in Hell with the woman he loved. If I were in his shoes I would have done the same thing. "Things aren't so bad for him down there. He has his Stella. I wish you could've met her. She's a tough one."

"Just what Drake needed to get his act together!"

We both burst out laughing.

"Anyway, you weren't bad yourself, though that gash in your side is pretty gruesome," I said, teasing him. We were both bare-chested, our skin dirty and scratched from the battle.

"Yeah, those fireballs sure are annoying when they hit you."

I laughed. Annoying? I well remembered how blindingly painful it was when a Subterranean struck you with his angel fire. The battle with Drake's impersonator had really put me to the test. "Want me to give you a hand with that?"

"Stay away," he warned me with a little smile. "We both know you can't wait to run up those stairs. Besides," he said, waggling his eyebrows, "battle wounds are the world's most powerful aphrodisiac, didn't you know? Now get out of here. And while you're at it send the blond down to me. Go on, leave me alone before this gash heals." He added in a whisper, "Ginevra goes crazy for little games like this."

"You two are completely insane."

"What can I do?" Simon shrugged.

I shook my head, leaving him in the living room. I'd battled Subterraneans all night long, so I should have been exhausted. Instead, the thought of going to Gemma filled me with pure energy. I took the stairs three at a time, electrified at the idea of being with her. I still hadn't forgotten the feeling of that terrible void deep in my heart when they'd torn her away from me. At times, when the memories of Hell filled my head, that same terrible sensation of loss returned and it felt like I was losing my mind. Now that we were together again, I wanted her beside me every second.

I stopped outside the door to my room where she was sleeping. Two Drusas—Nerea and Safria—were standing guard in their feline form. They had shiny black fur and sharp yellow and blue eyes that glinted in the half-light. Beneath Nerea's coat I glimpsed a faint spotted pattern, while Safria's was as clear as night. They both bowed their heads and moved aside for me. Inside the room, a large black panther with jade-green eyes rose majestically to its feet and a shiver ran through me. I still wasn't used to seeing Ginevra in her feline manifestation. In animal form, the Witches could better perceive their Subterranean enemies, which was why they often transformed when given the task of acting as Drusas. I studied her, fascinated. Within the walls of the house they looked larger, yet they moved so gracefully. If you stared at them for too long, you were in danger of being bewitched. Ginevra was beautiful and intimidating at the same time. Her threatening green eyes struck fear into the heart. On her forehead, a white droplet-shaped patch stood out against her black fur. She moved forward elegantly and assumed her human appearance.

Simon had insisted she be the one to watch over Gemma so she would stay out of the battle. I'd immediately backed him up, because with Ginevra guarding her I would feel more secure, more able to focus on the fight. It was surprising to see the bond that had formed between her and Gemma while I was away. Ginevra had been at her side and had protected her like a Sister even before she'd known Gemma was destined to become one. Even Simon had proven to be protective toward her, and for that I would be eternally grateful to them.

When I'd lost everything, including myself, they'd taken me in and given me a new life. I realized part of Ginevra's affection toward Gemma was due to the dark nature buried inside her—a nature they shared. Yet I'd known Ginevra for centuries, and seeing her so attached to the person I loved most in the world filled me with pride. It was unique, sensational.

Ginevra smiled at me, reading in my mind how anxious I was to be alone with Gemma. "Shouldn't you take a shower first?" she joked, gesturing at my bruised, soot-covered chest.

"Somebody told me war wounds are really sexy." I ran a hand up my neck, grinning. "Speaking of which, that somebody is waiting for you downstairs." I winked at her.

"Better not keep him waiting, then." Smiling, she stole out of the room.

"Hey, Gin," I said before she shut the door behind her. "Thanks."

"I'll have the Drusas stand guard downstairs. That way you can have a little time to yourselves. Just be sure you don't make too much noise—you and your *war wounds*," she teased with a sly grin. I chuckled and she closed the door softly to avoid waking Gemma.

A blue book lay on the floor. I picked it up. It was her diary. She must have dozed off while writing in it. I stroked the embossing on the cover and set it on the nightstand, then stared at her in the dim light. Her skin glowed like silver and her ebony-black hair was spread out on the pillow. I clenched my fists to contain the wave of emotion that flooded me.

Gemma was lying on her side, fast asleep. I moved closer to the bed. The sheet was pulled back, leaving her legs bare. I stroked her knee and thought of covering it so she wouldn't be cold, but instead my hand slowly rose up her thigh, moving the fabric away. I breathed deeply, forcing myself to get a grip, but just then Gemma parted her lips and desire threatened to overwhelm me.

I lay down behind her, our bodies nestling together like two perfect halves, and stared at the soft curve of her bosom as it rose and fell to the tranquil rhythm of her heart. Brushing the hair from her face, I touched my nose to her ear and breathed in her scent. I closed my eyes, overcome with love for her. My hand ran down her side and slowly slid to her belly, where a tiny creature was growing inside her—a creature I already loved with all my soul. I sought her hand beneath the covers and squeezed it, impatient to join her in her dream.

Do not destroy this tacit silence
but leave me, I beg you,
to these melancholy shadows.
Let me perish with the sun.
Giuseppe Strazzanti, my father.

1

THE COLORS OF THE SOUL

"Hey." Gemma opened her eyes and squeezed my hand, turning to face me.

"Hey," I whispered back, stroking her palm with my thumb. I raised her hand to my mouth and kissed it, gazing at her the whole time.

She closed her eyes, turned all the way over and slid her knee between my legs. The gesture set my blood on fire. I drew her to me and was on top of her in a flash, my lips on her neck and my hips pressed against hers. "Gem . . ." I sought her mouth and she arched her back, yearning for my body. I cupped her bottom with my hand and pulled her against me roughly, responding to her need as our breathing mingled, trembling with desire.

Gemma clutched my dog tag in her fingers and kept me pulled against her, burning with the same passion that consumed me. She kissed me sweetly on the mouth, quenching my instincts. I prolonged the kiss, moving slowly. Resting my forehead against hers, I tried to regain control of my breathing. "Good morning." I looked her in the eye and she smiled at me.

"This is a great way to wake up. Just be careful—I'm going to expect this every morning."

"Well, I don't know about that. I'm a pretty busy guy." I shot her a teasing grin and she punched me on the shoulder.

"Hey!"

I laughed, swept her up in my arms, and pulled her on top of me. "I'm yours. Every morning of every day to come." I fixed my eyes on hers to make sure she knew I meant every word.

Gemma pretended to think it over and then decided to smile at me. She ran her finger down my chest, looking me in the eye. "Now will you explain why you're half-naked in my bed? What are your intentions?"

"To unleash your most deeply buried instincts. Wasn't it clear?" I raised an eyebrow, still teasing her. Her jaw dropped in pretended shock. "I must say I'm surprised by how easily I managed to do it. Clearly some of your instincts aren't buried so deeply after all." I laughed, enjoying the range of reactions Gemma was trying to hide from me, even though I could sense her every emotion. "Besides, have you always slept in only your underwear?"

She let out a playful gasp, covering herself with the sheet.

"It's not my fault you got uncovered in your sleep."

"And you didn't even bother to cover me, I bet!"

"Uh . . . Yeah, sure. I mean, I was just about to."

"You . . . !" She pulled the pillow out from under my head and started to hit me with it.

Unable to block the blows, I grabbed her wrists and both of us laughed like little kids. When we finally ran out of laughter, she turned on her side, facing me.

"She was haunting his soul and he vowed to haunt her dreams," I murmured. I tucked a lock of hair behind her ear as she watched my every movement, mesmerized. How could love cause such restlessness deep in one's heart? Immense joy, tumultuous passion . . . the agonizing fear of losing her. Love was a generous thief. It had stolen my heart, taking me prisoner, but never had a prison been so sweet and so necessary. It didn't matter how long I'd fought it or how hard I'd tried to control it. In the end, it had conquered me, my instincts, my desires. All I had to do was look at Gemma to understand that my world had changed. She was both my Heaven and my Hell.

There could be no Evan without Gemma.

"You didn't answer my question. Did you think I wouldn't notice?" Gemma raised an eyebrow slyly. "Well? Why are you shirtless? And more importantly, why do you have blood and dirt all over you?"

My wounds had healed, but maybe I should have taken Ginevra's advice and washed off all traces of the battle. "Let's just say last night was a bit *lively*."

"What happened? Did they hurt you? Why didn't you wake me?" she asked, agitated.

"We carried out our plan," I said, point-blank.

"Last night?!"

"They tried to attack us all at once again. It was the perfect opportunity. One of them even came in here."

"What? How?!"

"Don't worry. He didn't even touch you. Ginevra took care of him. We had to act fast. The Witches relaxed their defense of the house, convincing the Executioners they'd found a way in. At that point we lured them into the workout room."

"Did the simulation scenarios work? And the defenses?"

I nodded. "It was a perfect battlefield. None of them managed to dematerialize and we got them all."

"All of them? You mean nine Subterraneans captured *in just one night*?!"

"Actually, there was a slight delay with two of them, but Devina handled the problem."

"Devina? You mean redheaded Devina the Witch slash Cruella de Vil?"

"That's the one."

Gemma closed her mouth and I smiled. She was so sweet when she got jealous. I pulled her by the wrist and rubbed my nose against hers to ease the agitation that the memory of Devina and me in Hell caused her. "Hey, weren't you the one who had the idea of imprisoning the Subterraneans instead of killing them?" She nodded, pride sparkling in her eyes.

"What was the name of the one who tried to off you when I was gone?"

"Desdemona. Have I told you I was the one who killed her?" she replied, secretly pleased.

I feigned surprise and shock. "And how did you do that, pray tell?"

"I shot her." She shrugged, as if she'd just told me she'd made scrambled eggs.

I laughed and pulled her closer. "Well, you did fight your way through Hell to save me—I always knew you were brave," I whispered, my mouth close to her ear.

"What choice did I have? I had to go get you and she was in my way!"

"A terrible decision, really." I shook my head, pretending disapproval.

"Moron!" She laughed too when she realized I was joking. She covered my face with her hand but I pinned her wrists against the pillow and stole a kiss from her.

"When are you going to stop teasing me?"

"When the moon meets the sun. Now get up—I have a plan."

Gemma rolled her eyes. "Every time you say that I have good reason to be scared."

In spite of her words, I could sense her enthusiasm growing from the beating of her heart. "Don't lie to me."

She climbed out of bed, instantly noticing the many cans of paint I'd stacked up in the back of the room. The floor was covered with a white drop cloth.

"What does all of this mean?" She looked at me, surprised.

I smiled and led her toward the paints. "It means we're going to paint your room."

The walls of Gemma's room were covered with photographs. In many of them she was with Peter. I would never have asked her to take them down because, all things considered, I was grateful to the guy for being there at her side as she grew up. Peter had been as important to Gemma as Ginevra was to me, though the feelings Peter had for Gemma had led her to loosen the bond between them. Every so often we would all meet up—our group and Gemma's friends—and at school sometimes the two of them would even spend time alone. Inevitably he would take the opportunity to make a move on her, and when that happened I would have to fight the urge to break his neck. Knowing that he wanted her made a fire burn inside me. If it hadn't been for Ginevra I probably would have slaughtered him long ago. But then I would look at the pictures of Gemma and me sharing our everyday lives together, and the fire would die down. She was mine and no one else's.

"Well? What color should we start with?"

I turned to look at Gemma and my breath caught in my throat. Her golden skin glowed in the light coming in through the window. She still wore the clothes she'd slept in: a soft blue satin camisole and shorts. She walked toward me, barefoot, and showed me her index finger tinged with red paint. While I'd been trying to control my homicidal instincts toward Peter, she'd already cleared all the walls, taking down the photos and removing the books from the shelves. She was so electrified by the thought of painting her old room! She'd wanted to do it for a long time, but the thought unsettled her. Gemma was very attached to the memories objects held for her. She was afraid that if she changed the color of the walls, hiding the scattered pencil marks or flaking paint, she would erase part of her life. There were even lines on the wall marking her height and Peter's as they'd grown up over the years.

"What do you say to this?" She slid her finger across the wall, leaving behind a wavy line of red paint.

"Actually, what do you say we use them all?" I suggested, heading toward her laptop. Typing in the password—*Gevan*—I started up her playlist. I adjusted the volume and the sound of Passenger's *Let Her Go* filled the room.

"All of them? What do you mean?"

"That you don't have to choose the color you want right away."

Gemma moved closer, suspicious. "Okay . . . So what do we use to paint?"

With a flick of my foot, I swept two long paintbrushes off the ground and caught them in mid-air. I twirled them in my fingers and offered them to Gemma. They were thin but as long as her arm.

She looked at them, puzzled, before taking them. "Where do we start?"

"Let's play a game." I took her hand, pulled her in front of the cans of paint and stood behind her. "Close your eyes," I whispered in her ear.

"Huh?" She turned to look at me, confused.

"Shh . . ." I squeezed her hands at her sides. "Close your eyes."

"How can I paint if my eyes are closed?"

"Trust me. It'll be fun."

Gemma took a deep breath and did as I said. I rested my palms on the backs of her hands and laced my fingers with hers, holding the brushes along with her. Guiding her hands, I had her dip the tips in two different colors—yellow and red—then raised the brushes, marking two spots on the wall.

"Ready?" I whispered again. Gemma nodded. "Now free your mind and follow your instinct. Let yourself go, move as though it was just you and the paints. There's only one rule: never take the brushes off the walls and don't open your eyes for anything in the world."

"Those are *two* rules."

"Just focus on yourself."

"Okay," she murmured trustingly. After a few seconds, she moved one of the two brushes over the wall and the other one followed close behind.

I also closed my eyes and breathed through her hair, surrendering to her movements. Gemma followed the rhythm of the music and the paintbrushes danced through the air as though she were an orchestra conductor.

She took a step and then another, and I followed, my fingers still intertwined with hers as though we were one being. Under my control, the yellow turned to orange, the red transformed into green, then blue and purple. The colors blended together from wall to wall, morphing into still other hues as Gemma advanced slowly, following her need to fill the entire room. My eyes still closed, I let myself be guided by her movements, melding with her, her heart beating against my chest almost as though it were my own. From time to time Gemma trembled, and her shiver spread to me.

Antar may as. Yata tvam may asi.

She was inside me, in my heart, in my soul.

Finally she stopped, satisfied. Slowly, I raised her hands over her head and ran mine down them. I stroked her neck, her shoulders, then moved down to clasp her hips. When I kissed her softly behind the ear, she turned slightly, rubbing her head against mine, then lowered her hands as the notes of Lana Del Rey faded. I opened my eyes and smiled, my lips on her ear. "Now you can look."

Gemma raised her eyelids and trembled. I could sense her amazement even before reading it in her eyes. She didn't say a word, just turned around, her mouth slightly open and her gaze captivated by the walls full of colors. The lines were as soft as the harmony she felt deep in her heart, marked here and there by sharper segments that expressed her uneasiness. Some areas stood out more than others. I'd perceived feelings of fear and distress arise in her when she painted them. The lines ran parallel, followed each other, parted, and then rose up together to touch the sky. To the rhythm of *Glory and Gore* by Lorde, Gemma had painted the boldest segments. With Adele's *Set Fire to the Rain*, she'd let herself go with long, interwoven lines. Lana Del Rey had reawakened grimmer thoughts, bringing out her fears. At those moments, even the sunbeams had grown dimmer and the darkness behind her closed eyelids had turned to gloom.

"Evan, it's . . . Did we do this?" Gemma continued to stare at the stunning weavings of colors on the walls, fascinated.

"I didn't do anything. It was you."

"Incredible," she murmured to herself.

Smiling with satisfaction, I took Gemma's hand and whirled her around. She locked her big dark eyes on mine and for a second I was left breathless. I pulled her to me gently and moved her away again, guiding her movements to the sound of Ed Sheeran's voice in an unplanned dance. Colorful droplets of paint rose from the cans into the air, drifted through the room and encircled us. Amazement and wonder filled her eyes as she watched them.

Taking me by surprise, Gemma did a spin, never letting go of my hand, and leaned back against my chest, swaying to the rhythm of *Thinking Out Loud.* I closed my eyes and rubbed my head against hers, overcome by the sensations.

The song ended, interrupting that brief moment, and the faster rhythm of Pink boomed against the walls. Gemma turned to go, but I pulled her back, spinning her around quickly and back into my arms, laughing. "You can tell the drops of paint to stop now too. One of them was about to land on my face."

I caught a drifting sphere of paint on my finger and smeared it on her nose. "What, like ***this***?"

"Why you . . . !!" Gemma's eyes opened wide and her jaw dropped with surprise. She caught a droplet of her own and drew a line down my face with it. I let her do it and then raised an eyebrow: a clear warning that she should run, and fast. Gemma understood and let out a shriek before rushing over to the paint cans and dunking both brushes in them, challenging me.

"You sure that's a good move?" I said, letting a this-means-war grin escape me. I shot toward her. She let out another shriek and ran, dropping both paintbrushes. I chased her around the room and in a flash grabbed her from behind and spun her around as she squealed with laughter. I pinned her to the ground beneath me, her sweet laughter filling my soul. She tried to defend herself and counterattack but I showed no mercy, painting her arms, legs, neck. Each touch triggered something inside me. I caressed her inner thigh and moved my fingers upward, leaving a blue streak on her skin. Gemma's laughter grew softer when I rose to her belly. In a single movement I ripped her camisole in two, her beauty leaving me breathless. Her chest moved quickly, her breathing ragged from what had just happened—or maybe from what was about to happen. Like a tidal wave, her emotions crashed down on me: anticipation, impatience . . . desire.

I gently stroked her belly, then kissed it over and over. Gemma smiled at me. My immense love for the baby filled her with joy. But instantly my eyes found hers, like those of a wolf. My hand rose over her middle and found the clasp to her bra. I propped Gemma up and slipped it off her as she slid her hands down my chest, then sat on the floor and drew her to me, holding her tightly by the waist. Gemma watched the little drops of paint floating around us. She lifted her hand and moved her fingers through them.

A sweet melody filled the room. I brushed the hair from her face and sought her eyes, whispering the lyrics: *"'Cause all of me loves all of you. Love your curves and all your edges, all your perfect imperfections."*

Gemma closed her eyes and rested her forehead against my cheek, then lowered her hand, dipped her finger in the little pool of paint that had formed there, and drew symbols on the white drop cloth that covered the floor.

"Give your all to me. I'll give my all to you. You're my end and my beginning. Even when I lose I'm winning." I stroked her fingers, following her lines, weaving together our movements, seeking her hand. Our thumbs playfully touched and clasped together to complete the tattoo that united us. *Stay together, fight together:* the writing connected to the two rings in the infinity symbol. I rested my palm on her hand and led it to the drop cloth, our laced fingers dancing together, creating new colors. I felt like we were making love. It was the most sensual moment of my entire life. Every movement was so erotically charged that the paint almost felt hot against our skin. Or maybe it was me, boiling with desire for her. I raised our clasped hands, spread open her palms and gently took her wrists, pulling myself against her skin as our fingers continued to seek each other out, touch each other, slide at times tenderly, at times with need. I felt I was losing my mind: it was a sweet hell from which I wished no redemption. Overcome by those sensations, I squeezed her bottom and pulled her on top of me.

In my ethereal form my emotions were more intense—they flooded me with a force that was uncontrollable, devastating, vital. A multitude of tiny explosions that changed my universe. I sought her lips and our tongues touched, teasing each other playfully. She moaned and I let out a long breath, yearning to rip off the fabric still dividing us. As if sensing my need, Gemma undid the button on my pants and unzipped them, leaving me breathless. Anticipation was killing me like never before. My hand slid into her shorts, stroking her underwear. Gemma trembled with pleasure, gripping the mark of the Children of Eve on my forearm. She arched her back, yearning for contact, and rubbed her hips against mine, her hot panties pressing against my erection. I moaned, her reaction leaving me stunned, and kissed her intensely on the mouth as our bodies burned, melting together. I grasped her nape with one hand while with the other I pushed her underwear aside and penetrated her, groaning with pleasure.

Gemma panted, driving me wild. I gripped her nape tighter and she raised her chin, letting my lips slide down her neck in slow, sweet agony. With my other hand I pulled her against me more firmly, her hot breasts on my chest sending quivers through me as I moved inside her. I could feel Gemma's emotions growing with mine, so powerful they clouded my senses. I perceived the exact moment when her pleasure reached its peak and at that very moment I climaxed inside her, overwhelmed by the intensity of the emotions.

Cradling her neck, I rested my forehead against hers and a smile escaped us both. I swept her hair out of her face, tucked it behind her ear and kissed her—a long kiss, sweet and necessary—as shivers of pleasure shook my body once more. A star had just exploded inside of me. Its name was Gemma.

2

POTENTIAL

Gemma laughed. "You have my handprint on your back."

"Where? Oh, that's okay. It'll be my spoils of war."

"Hey!" She hit my shoulder. "What do you mean?"

"Well, you know, I did fight for you all night long." I raised an eyebrow to provoke her. "This way I can show Simon it was worth it." I laughed, teasing her.

Gemma's jaw dropped and her face turned bright red. "You're not showing Simon," she warned me. "Now go straight to the spa and take a shower!"

I moved my lips to her ear. "Only if you'll join me," I whispered, gently sucking her earlobe.

Gemma trembled and closed her eyes, at the mercy of her emotions. Then she pushed me away and laughed. "I bet Simon would get himself injured on purpose just to have Ginevra heal him."

"You would win that bet."

"So tell me, did the two of you plan all this last night? Otherwise why would you want to show him my handprint on you?"

I raised my hands. "I didn't tell him anything. I came here with honorable intentions, I swear." I tried to hide a grin but failed.

"Yeah, right. You expect me to believe you weren't planning on *this*?" she said, gesturing at our entwined bodies on the floor.

I leaned over her and nibbled her neck. "I *always* plan on this."

Gemma laughed and let out a shriek when I pinned her beneath me and tickled her. I stroked her belly, growing serious again. It was unbelievable that a tiny creature was growing right there inside her. Gemma toyed with my dog tag but I continued to stare at her belly, enchanted. I leaned down and rested my ear against it as I continued to stroke it.

"Hear anything?" she asked, curious.

I listened to Gemma's breathing, then heard a rapid flutter and smiled. "I can hear his heart beating. Tell me again about how you heard him. Are you really sure it's a boy?"

"Not a hundred percent, but my instinct says so. I heard something while I was talking to Simon and Ginevra. I thought it was because the baby had powers, but instead they were mine. *I* was the one reading his mind. But it hasn't happened again since then."

"It must be amazing." I kissed her belly, but as I caressed the silvery streaks on it I grew sad.

She instantly realized why I looked concerned. "Evan, do you think the baby will be human?"

"I ask myself that question every day." I raised my head to look her in the eye. "Whatever his nature is, he's ours and we'll protect him together." Gemma's eyes moved to the matching tattoos on our hands, her expression a mix of fear and concern.

Stay together. Fight together.

She'd made a pact with the Witches to save me, but I still couldn't accept it. Gemma was convinced the transformation wouldn't obliterate her, that she would manage to cling to our love to drive the evil out of her, but I was consumed by doubt. I couldn't allow her to transform. I couldn't run the risk. I had to come up with a way to prevent it.

"A penny for your thoughts," she said, stroking my head.

"I'm thinking about how happy we'll be together with him."

Gemma smiled. "Do you think the Màsala will ever give up and let me be?"

Only two things could make the Màsala stop hounding Gemma: her transformation or her death. In either case, I would end up defeated because I would lose her. I propped myself up on my elbows and moved closer to her, looking into her eyes. "No," I admitted, "but we're not about to give up either."

Gemma nodded in silence. I stroked her cheek. I would have turned Heaven and Hell upside down to be with her—no one was going to take her away from me. I pressed my lips to hers and our kiss burned with passion, kindled by our caresses. I slid my hand up her thigh, ready to start all over again. Gemma clung to my biceps, letting me kiss her neck and breasts. I sensed the desire growing in her, but suddenly it was replaced by something else: astonishment and wonder. She darted around me and rose onto her palms.

"Oh my God." Gemma's jaw dropped, her eyes widening as she peered up. On the ceiling had appeared the image of the two of us entwined in a starry sky. She got to her feet, still staring at the painting, entranced.

"Wow." I also looked up, stupefied.

"You mean it's real? It's not my imagination?"

"Well . . . Define *imagination*."

"Don't kid around, Evan. It's—"

"It's us," I whispered, holding her from behind, "and it's magnificent."

"But how? *When*?"

I laughed and moved my lips to her ear. "Want me to tell you a secret?" She nodded eagerly. "I didn't do anything."

Gemma turned to look at me, amazed. "What? You mean . . . ?" I nodded for a long moment as she reflected. "It was *me*?" she asked, still confused.

It was the truth. As we made love, the paints had danced across the ceiling, creating the incredible image of the two of us locked in an embrace in our universe. Gemma's soul was what had given life to that magical dance.

"Looks like you gave it a finishing touch." I smiled at Gemma.

She ran her hands through her hair. "But I don't get it. Usually I realize when my powers are awakening. Oh my God! How am I going to explain this to my mom?"

"I bet she won't even notice." I winked at her, still teasing her. I'd given Gemma clues, but it still hadn't dawned on her.

"What do you mean she won't notice? How could she not notice? It looks like a paint bomb exploded in here! Maybe I should've left my room the way it—Wait a second . . . I always sleep at your place. What are we doing in my old bedroom?" She turned to look at me and her eyes slowly went wide, the smile gradually spreading across her face as she figured it out. "I'm . . . dreaming," she murmured to herself. "This is a dream, isn't it? We're inside my head."

I nodded and smiled back at Gemma. She was electrified. Few times before had I made her aware she was dreaming because I didn't want to deprive her of the emotions she would have missed out on. In dreams, my soul was closer to hers. I could read her subconscious and perceive her slightest sensation as though it were my own. To me, it was a parallel universe in which everything was amplified. Gemma knew that on those occasions I could read inside her, so if she realized she was in a dream she held back, reluctant to stay so open to me. Instead, I wanted her to experience every emotion to the fullest.

"If you meant to tell me, you could've done it sooner!" she reproved me with a little smile.

"Well, looks like you played your part anyway," I teased, gesturing at the ceiling. In her dreams, Gemma had always had the ability to recreate incredible scenarios and this time her spirit had painted a picture of the two of us.

"So when I wake up everything will be like it was before? What a shame."

"Will you remember it?" I whispered in her ear, squeezing her from behind. She nodded. I could sense her heart brimming with joy. "We can always redo it, if you want . . . but for real."

Gemma turned around and folded her arms around my neck. "No, I don't want to risk spoiling this memory."

"You never could." I kissed her on the lips but she pulled away.

"Besides, from now on when I look at my old room, I'll see it with different eyes."

"Why's that?"

"Well . . ." She slowly moved away, holding my hand. "Because now I know its potential. I know what it could become."

Potential. The word had a double meaning: Gemma was trying to distract me, but I realized she was actually referring to ***her own*** potential. She had something in mind and I could already sense her attempts to keep me from picking up on it. She'd always been good at that.

"Hey, where are you going?" I asked suspiciously.

She smiled and opened her bedroom door. Sunlight burst in. Before us was a white beach gently lapped by waves. "It's my turn to play."

I smiled, shaking my head. Gemma shut the door behind her and disappeared. I gave her a few seconds' head start and then ran after her.

3

HIDE-AND-SEEK

Telling Gemma we were in a dream gave her enormous power and she knew it. She could do anything she wanted, go anywhere. She had full control over her desires and this time she'd decided to take advantage of them.

"Gemma . . . Come on! You can't hide from me," I called out. I heard her laughter in the distance. "You're going to regret that joke you played on me with your father!"

When I'd opened the door after Gemma closed it behind her, I'd found myself in the hallway of her house. Her father had just come out of his bedroom and went ballistic when he saw me barefoot, shirtless, and covered with paint. I'd bidden him a rather sheepish goodbye and opened various doors before ending up in the dream where Gemma had hidden. We were in her mind and she was having fun playing hide-and-seek with me.

The sand was so white it blinded me, the sea an endless expanse of blue and green.

"Gemma . . . Do you really mean to leave me here all alone?"

You're not alone, her voice whispered on the wind. *I'm right here.*

I spun around, but the beach was deserted. "Okay, keep on toying with me." Gemma laughed, amused. "You know what I'm going to do to you the second I catch you?" I concentrated on her soul like never before as I waited for her reply.

First you have to find me . . .

Guided by the sound of her voice, I lunged to one side and grabbed her. Gemma laughed, pinned beneath me. "Well? What were you saying?" I raised an eyebrow, satisfied.

"You found me." She smiled, her gaze provocative.

"I will always find you." I rubbed my nose against hers and she touched my lips. "You can't escape me," I warned.

She looked me in the eye and kissed me more passionately. Resting a hand on my chest, she deftly inverted our positions, rising up and straddling me. "Are you so sure?" she whispered against my mouth. I tried to kiss her but she pulled back, forcing me to lean up to follow her lips.

"You bet," I said, grinning.

Gemma bit my lip, leaving me in a momentary daze during which she pushed me down, leapt to her feet, and raced off. "Start running, then!" she challenged me, dashing away across the beach.

"You know I'm going to catch you!" I shot off after her.

It didn't take me long to catch up with her. She tried to escape me, laughing and shrieking at every attempt to grab her. She ran along the water's edge, hoping to gain ground, but there was no way she could elude me for long, and soon I grabbed her by the waist and picked her up, cradling her in my arms. I waded into the water until it was up to my hips, ignoring Gemma's protests as she clung to my neck, afraid to get wet.

"So, did I win the bet?" I asked.

"It's too soon to say!" she replied stubbornly.

"Oh yeah?!" I raised an eyebrow, a threatening look on my face.

"No, wait! No!" she cried, guessing my intentions.

Ignoring her, I bent down and stood up again with Gemma dripping wet in my arms. She shrieked from the contact with the water and then laughed, kicking her legs as she tried to get free, but I dunked her another time and then another.

"Hey! I'm not a teabag, you know!"

"And yet I would willingly drink you."

Gemma managed to pull me down and throw me off balance. We toppled into the water and a splash fight ensued, both of us laughing like crazy. All at once I grabbed her wrist, just because I felt like it, and pulled her against me. Even with only that small distance between us I already missed her. I missed touching her, missed the contact of our joined bodies. She responded by holding me tight.

"I knew I should never let you know when we're in a dream," I whispered into her hair.

She looked at me, resting her hands on my chest. "Because I can do whatever I want?"

"Because you always trick me."

Gemma smiled. "I always trick you when we're awake too."

"It's true, you're right." I touched my forehead to hers.

Gemma stroked my chest, washing away the paint. I did the same, pouring water over her shoulders and seizing the opportunity to touch her, because there was no denying it: I never tired of her.

"You wanted to take a shower together, right? Well, we're getting clean," she said provocatively.

I looked at her, a sparkle in my eye. "My idea of a shower was a little different, if I'm going to be honest."

"Because you never get enough."

I leaned closer and kissed her neck. "Because I never get enough of *you*," I whispered, brushing my lips against hers. I grabbed her thighs and lifted her up. Gemma wrapped her legs around my waist, our bodies wet and our tongues touching. All her emotions exploded inside me and she let me explore them: the infinite joy she felt, the hope she nurtured, her fear of losing me—the same fear that lurked inside me. Yet there, in the dream, it was just the two of us holding each other tight, hidden from the whole world. Just for that moment, I wouldn't let fear overpower us. We deserved to be happy. We'd been through a million trials and tribulations so we could be together and that moment was all our own.

With Gemma still clinging to me, I walked toward the shore, set her down at the water's edge, and lay down beside her as the waves caressed us only to draw back fearfully.

"Evan, are there hierarchies among Angels?" she asked out of the blue.

"Not exactly. There's us and there's them, the Màsala. The orders come to us like a whisper and the information appears directly in our heads."

"So no guardian Angels?"

"Those are legends dreamed up by humans to satisfy their need to feel at peace. True peace, if you earn it, isn't in this world, but humans feel comforted by the belief that someone's watching over them. Life on Earth wasn't made for peace—it was made for decisions. Every decision or reaction—even the smallest one—is a step toward good or evil. Only decisions made toward good will lead man to the peace he seeks by nature. Still, not everyone is strong enough to resist the power of darkness. So no, there are no guardian Angels. There's good and evil. Life and death. You, however, can consider me your own personal guardian Angel." I winked at Gemma and she smiled at me.

"You already were. How much longer do we have before the alarm goes off?" she asked. "It's so nice here."

"Not long, I'm afraid."

"If we could stay here I would sleep forever."

I smiled and took her hands on the sand, staring at the sky. "If you did, you'd miss the Winter Carnival," I teased her. Gemma had fought long and hard with the school faculty. Because of her pregnancy, they'd told her she couldn't participate in the school games, but the tomboy in her had rebelled. If it had been up to her, she would even have signed up for broomball and the alligator walk, but in the end they'd reached a compromise.

"They don't want me to take part this year anyway. I'll read about my classmates' heroic deeds in the *Blue Bomber Times*."

"They're only keeping you from competing in a few events," I reminded her.

"I'm not good at singing, and you're better than I am at ice sculpture."

"I can always make one for you. Besides, you're forgetting the pie-eating contest. If you sign up for that, my bet is your team will score tons of points!"

"Hey!" I laughed and barely dodged her blow. "Why does everyone keep saying that? Do I really eat so much?"

"Only slightly above average." I grinned. Staring at the sky, I squeezed her hand. Recently Gemma's appetite had grown to amazing proportions. It wasn't only because of the pregnancy but also because of the Witch nature buried inside her. Gemma's body was burning lots of energy and producing just as much. Luckily for her, the food burned off quickly and had no effect on her figure. Quite the opposite, in fact; she was five months pregnant but it was barely noticeable. Still, pregnancy had left her glowing. Gemma's curves had softened and she was sexier than ever. Looking at her made my heart race but scared me just as much, because it meant that with every passing day she was closer to her Sisters.

To protect Gemma we'd formed an alliance, but their presence stimulated her senses, like a summons her body couldn't resist. The Witch in her was waking up and I could do nothing to stop it. Gemma was certain the transformation wouldn't drag her away, that she wouldn't leave me to follow them to Hell. If I'd been as certain of it as she was I would have wanted her to transform so we could stay together forever, like Simon and Ginevra. That was what she was planning on: transforming and then renouncing evil. But I saw the doubt in Ginevra's eyes and that was enough to convince me: I wasn't going to let Gemma transform. No matter what it took, I would prevent it.

A little bird flew overhead, tweeting a relentless melody. It turned back and flapped around us. Gemma propped herself up on her elbows. "Do you hear that strange chirping? I've never seen that kind of bird before," she murmured.

I laughed. "I know that sound . . . and so do you. Open your eyes, sleepyhead. It's time to wake up."

I opened my eyes and Gemma grumbled in my arms. We were back in my room. "No, no . . . let's stay here. Go away, nasty old bird!"

I laughed into her hair and switched off the alarm that Gemma still believed was a strange bird. She relaxed, pleased because it had flown away and stopped bothering her. I hugged her from behind and she slowly opened her eyes.

"Good morning," I whispered.

"Mmm . . . Why are we here? Let's go back to sleep . . ."

"You can't go back to sleep. It's late. Ginevra's already waiting for you."

Gemma bolted upright and looked at me. "Aren't you coming too?"

I shook my head. "Maybe later." I only had a couple of missions but I wasn't sure I'd manage to get to school in time.

Gemma grumbled and got out of bed. As she dropped her shorts to the floor and took off her camisole I couldn't take my eyes off her. She was so sexy in her gray cotton underwear . . . I clenched my fists on the bed, fighting off the impulse to reach for her and keep her from going to school. She sensed my intentions and laughed. Her camisole hit me in the face, surprising me. "Peeping Tom."

"It's not my fault I can't resist you."

"Oh, really?" She raised an eyebrow and came closer, her gaze seductive. "Are you saying it's my fault?" She moved my knee aside and slipped in between my legs.

"I'm saying you should buy longer pajamas if you want to keep me away from you."

"I never said I wanted to keep you away from me."

My hands slowly slid up the backs of her thighs, unable to stay still. I rested my head on her belly, breathing in her scent. Gemma rested her knees on the bed and sat down, straddling me. Provoking me was becoming her favorite game. "He tried to resist her, but she wouldn't let him," she murmured, her arms around my neck.

I raised an eyebrow. She didn't realize what she was getting herself into. I grabbed her by the bottom and swept her onto the bed, my erection pressing against her. My hands slowly moved over her body. "*Correction*," I replied, playing along. "He would never try to resist her. He wanted her and didn't hide it. He knew he would never be able to control himself, as his fire was fueled by the very air she breathed." I stroked her lip with my thumb. "An undeniable need."

"So you're saying you can't resist me, *despite yourself*?"

"I'm saying I don't want to and never will, unless you decide to stop me."

"Then I'll have to follow your suggestion and buy longer pajamas," she teased. "You sure that will be enough to calm your instincts?"

"I'm afraid it won't help at all." I lowered my mouth to hers and surrendered to a kiss, my hands clasping her bottom tightly. "Gem . . ." I kissed her neck and groaned, on the verge of losing my mind.

"Hey . . . you two!" Ginevra knocked insistently on the door and Gemma laughed.

"Not a good time. Go away," I grunted.

"It's morning and Gemma's going to be late for school."

"There's no school today," I called back, continuing to kiss Gemma.

"Get out here or I'll be forced to come in!"

I ignored her and Gemma rolled on top of me. She started to kiss my chest tenderly, looking me in the eye as Ginevra continued to knock, undeterred. "Don't say I didn't warn you!" She opened the door and stood there, arms crossed. I plopped my head onto the pillow and Gemma smiled at her Sister.

"Good morning to you too."

"Man, what a pain in the ass!" I grumbled loud enough for her to hear it.

"Gwen, why the big rush to get to school?" Gemma asked.

Ginevra smiled and clapped her hands, bouncing. "The games start today. Put some clothes on or I'll take you to school as you are!" she goaded her, literally dragging her away from me.

"Trying to cause a mass extermination, are you?" I retorted. The thought of Gemma naked in public made my blood boil. No one could see her without clothes on and live. She was all mine. Gemma turned to look at me and shrugged, powerless.

The Winter Carnival games were a perfect occasion for Ginevra to prove to everyone that she was the best. "Try not to attract too much attention," I warned her. "These aren't the little games you play with your Sisters in the kingdom of darkness."

"It's broomball, Evan. Why are you so worked up?" she scoffed.

"There are mortal Souls there and somebody could get hurt." That day they would be taking Nausyka and Anya to school too, to protect Gemma. I just hoped Ginevra wouldn't get carried away by her enthusiasm. "Don't let Gemma out of your sight."

"Relax, Evan. The Subterraneans are under close surveillance. Gemma will be safe with us and we'll have loads of fun!"

Gemma, who meanwhile had gotten dressed, came over and planted a kiss on my mouth. "Don't worry, I'll be there to keep an eye on them," she whispered. "You go do your duty, Soldier." She winked at me and hurried out of the room. Ginevra stuck her tongue out at me and followed her.

I interlaced my fingers behind my head and lay back down on the bed, listening to the noises in the house. For days, the Executioners who'd come to kill Gemma hadn't let up for a second. They'd even attacked her at school once, but Simon had protected her, knocking the Subterranean out with a single blow. Gemma, who was the only person able to see him, had let out a scream during class, drawing everyone's attention. She'd flicked an imaginary spider off her desk and the teacher had resumed the lesson. They hadn't attacked at school since then but, as a precaution, at least one of us was with Gemma at all times.

I heard panthers growl in the hallway and, a second later, voices. Things would go better now that all the Subterraneans were under our control. Once the simulation scenario was deactivated, the galleon had gone back to being a normal cell and the prisoners found themselves chained to the walls with a group of black panthers guarding them. The Drusas had to be careful not to injure them because their teeth and claws secreted their serpents' venom. A single scratch was enough to kill a Subterranean, and if that happened, others would show up. In any case, they wouldn't escape, as dazed as they were by the Witches' blood. I'd learned the hard way the effect it could have on our minds. The Witches had the power to modify it based on what they wanted from us. In some cases, it could even enhance our strength, like it did during the Games—or it could annihilate us. The prisoners would never be able to rebel.

Hearing the engine of the BMW starting up, I jumped out of bed and went to the window. From the looks of the girls' clothes, they'd had a snowball fight. Gemma was laughing with her Sisters and was so calm as she got into the car. I should have been happy, but instead I was jealous—jealous and worried they would take her away from me. Gemma's bond with them would make the transformation easier for her, but it would also make it harder for her to renounce evil.

Ginevra, on the other hand, didn't seem the least bit worried. Being reunited with her Sisters had given back to her something she thought she'd lost. She was beaming. On top of that, though at times she harbored doubts that she didn't dare voice, she had endless trust in Gemma. She was convinced that once Gemma transformed she wouldn't lose herself, that our love and her love for our baby would eradicate the evil inside her. Gemma wouldn't be human any more—she would be a Witch—but she would keep all her memories and human emotions. Still, not even Ginevra could be sure.

Gemma noticed me staring at her and waved to me from the front seat. I returned her smile and waited until they drove off. Then I balled my fists against the windowpane, frustrated. I couldn't risk it. No, I would never allow Gemma to transform.

4

FOUL PLAY

I got into the shower and washed away the dirt from the battle. Maybe it wasn't appropriate to feel this way, but I'd had an awesome time fighting the Subterraneans. Simon and I had worked as a team, defeating over half of them, though many of them were strong and battle hardened. Still, they hadn't been as determined as I was. Once we'd subdued them, the Witches had taken over. It wasn't that long ago I would never have believed it if somebody had told me I would form an alliance with the Witches—with *Devina*. I hadn't forgotten the 'special treatment' she'd given me in her world to try to dominate me, and I couldn't wait to repay her the favor.

I put my head under the jet of water and tilted it back, hoping to rinse away my anger at Devina. We were allies. I had to force myself to remember that. And although we'd imprisoned the nine Subterraneans who'd attacked us over the last week, I had to stay focused and never let my guard down.

The Màsala were willing to do anything to kill Gemma. What they might not realize was that *I* wasn't going to let a Subterranean take her away from me. If they managed to make her soul cross over, I would lose her forever, and with her, our child. The stakes were too high. An unexpected smile spread across my lips. A hundred Subterraneans wouldn't have been enough to stop me. I was willing to kill them all.

The blood and dirt washed away, tinting the water, and my chest trembled at the memory of the paints blending together in our hands, the warmth of our intertwined bodies, the intense emotions that flooded me when I was in my ethereal form. It had been an otherworldly experience. I smiled, remembering the picture of us that Gemma's soul had created. While the entire world tried to separate us, Gemma and I became more and more closely bonded. Our love was growing as intensely as the passion that burned whenever we were alone. I rested my palms on the stone wall and closed my eyes, the sensations sweeping me away. Gemma satiated me, yet I was always hungry for her. Her attempts to seduce me made me lose my mind . . . and all control. She'd realized that and had fun toying with me. Most times desire consumed me and I let it take me over, burning together with her.

I shook my head and ran my hands over my face. Making love in her dream had been all-consuming and I still felt a bit dazed. I should have been focusing on the orders I was about to carry out but I couldn't think of anything except her, the scent of her skin, her lips on me, my hands on her body. Gemma was my obsession. It had always been that way and I had no intention of resisting it. I was hers. Mind, soul, body . . . and my stilled heart, which beat only for her.

I turned off the water and got out of the shower, wrapping a towel around my waist. I looked at myself in the mirror as I dried my hair with a towel and noticed writing on the fogged-over glass:

I'll be waiting for you ∞

I smiled when I recognized Gemma's handwriting and walked out of the room barefoot. I was a Soldier of Death who was about to kill two people, but Gemma made me feel like a little kid who couldn't wait to finish his homework so he could see her. The towel still around my waist, I went into my room to get dressed, tossing my dirty boxers onto a chair.

The door closed behind me and I straightened up. I didn't need to turn around to know who had followed me. "If you're looking for cat kibble, the kitchen is downstairs," I snapped.

Devina walked up and touched my shoulder, stepping around me. "I'm hungry for something else right now." She slid her finger down the scar she herself had inflicted on me.

I stood stock still, my jaw clenched and my eyes burning into hers. "I'm afraid you'll have to make do," I said curtly. "I'm not on the menu."

She sat on the bed, hoping to seduce me, but I turned my back on her and went over to the dresser where I let the towel fall to the floor. She whistled. I pulled on boxers and jeans without blinking an eye.

"I'm confused, Evan. Undressing isn't the best way to get me out of here—you should know that."

I approached the bed and grabbed her by the throat, catching her off guard. "And you should know that I'd like nothing more than to tear you limb from limb. Now get out of here before I decide to follow my instinct. I haven't been very good at holding back lately." I jerked my hand away.

She rubbed her throat, vexed. "Mind your manners. I just stopped by to say hello."

"Stay away from me, Witch. I'm trying hard not to incinerate you, but you're not making it easy."

Instead of leaving, she spread her legs and snapped her whip between them, her eyes glittering like molten gold. "You've already lit a fire inside me, right here. Only you can put it out."

"You can burn for all I care."

"Why don't we let bygones be bygones? We're allies now, aren't we?" She stroked the bed with her hand suggestively, looking me in the eye. "We could seal our deal right here . . ." Her whip cracked again. "I like the thought of doing it in your bed."

I snorted. "Aren't you Witches bound by claiming rights?"

"We'll talk about that when she's a Witch and she's claimed you. Until then, she isn't your Amìsha." She raised her eyebrows and a subtle scent wafted in my direction.

"Keep your pheromones to yourself—they have no effect on me."

Devina stood up and came close. "Are you so sure? I heard your thoughts while you were in the shower and figured you might need someone to have a little fun with," she whispered in my ear, touching my bare chest. "We're alone. Gemma will never find out."

"Have fun with you? What, are you offering me your head on a platter?"

"I'm offering you much more than revenge, don't you see?" Her hand slid up the inside of my thigh until it reached my crotch. "I'm offering you *expiation.* I can give you much more than myself. I can give you my heart." Devina stroked my lip with her thumb and tried to kiss me. On her mouth sparkled the trickle of blood with which she hoped to subjugate me.

I grabbed her wrist and looked her in the eye. "The only place I could want your heart is in my fist," I growled. "You're insane if you think you have the slightest chance with me."

The amber in her eyes seemed to melt, extending over their whites, and her pupils lengthened like a serpent's. "Be careful how you speak to me, Child of Eve. Your princess is still sweet and vulnerable."

The second she mentioned Gemma, a burst of rage blinded me. "Threaten her again and I'll personally scatter your ashes in Hell," I hissed, snatching my shirt off the chair and heading for the door. "Oh, and have fun on your own. The bed's still warm. Use your imagination."

Devina cracked her whip and I smiled without turning around. I went down the stairs just as Simon appeared in the kitchen.

"Morning. Long night?" he said, grinning.

"Not long enough," I shot back, pulling on my shirt. "What happened to your battle wounds?"

"A sweet young maiden cured them for me last night."

"Just like you'd hoped."

Simon filled two shot glasses with bourbon and held one out to me. A panther nonchalantly glided through the room and I cast my brother a glance.

"I'm afraid we'll have to get used to that," he said.

"I'd rather die."

Simon laughed and raised his glass in a toast. "To the battle."

"And to those to come." I downed the liquor in a single gulp to celebrate our victory. Another panther jumped onto the railing at the top of the stairs and leapt down. Simon and I stared at her and she snarled. I didn't need to check for the red patch on her paw to know who it was: Devina. Her eyes challenged me, glittering like drops of amber.

"You're right. I'll never get used to this." Simon refilled our glasses. The panthers exchanged growls, crossed the living room, and headed toward the dungeon. The door closed behind them.

"You, on the other hand, should clean yourself up," I suggested. Simon didn't seem to have washed away the blood or dirt from the battle.

"I know. I just need to recharge my batteries first."

"Nine Subterraneans too much for you?" I joked.

"No, Ginevra on her own is enough to zap my energy. Being with her is like taking on a hundred Executioners all at once. Speaking of which, I checked on Gemma at school before coming back here. She's fine, having fun with the girls." I nodded to thank him, but my face clouded. It didn't escape Simon's notice. "You worried?"

"Wouldn't you be?"

"Take it easy, Evan. Ginevra's there with her. Besides, if Gemma is finally able to have fun it's only because you're back here with her."

I looked at Simon, thankful for his words. He lowered his voice, though there was no risk the Witches would hear him, since the workout room was soundproof. "Do you have any idea what she went through when she thought she'd lost you? She didn't want me to take the pain away because she didn't want to lose a single memory of you. Do you think she would accept the thought of losing you forever to join them? That's insane. Gemma would never give you up, Evan. She would never give up the *two of you*. She would accept the transformation but she would stay herself. I believe it, and you should too. Her plan is going to work."

"What if it doesn't? What happens to me?"

"It *has to* work—it's all we've got."

"Wrong. What if there was an alternative?"

My brother looked at me. I had his attention. I clenched my fists, preparing to lay it on him. "What if Gemma ate of the Tree?"

"Have you lost your mind?! You've always had insane ideas, but this one tops them all."

"Why? It might work! What if the Divine Fruit eradicated the evil inside her? What if it purified her soul? She would be one of us: immortal."

"Okay. You must have ingested too much poison in Hell," he said, raising both hands. I sighed. Why didn't Simon understand me? "Evan, did you hear how many *what ifs* there are in your plan? Here's a couple more for you: what if you were both punished for it? What if it had catastrophic consequences?"

"What punishment could ever be worse than the one I'm already suffering? Anything would be better than this. I'm not going to let the Witches obliterate her."

"Evan, no one who isn't a Subterranean has ever eaten of the Tree."

"Then she'll be the first," I shot back, determined.

"Evan . . ."

"I hoped at least you would understand me!"

"And I do." Simon rested his hands on the table and looked me in the eye. "But you have to think of the consequences this might have for her and everyone else."

"You think I haven't?" I stared at him steadily. "I think about that *every minute*. And for now it's all I have to cling to. I need this hope." I knew my brother was right, that I should assess everything down to the smallest detail, but no one could give me any certainties. "Simon, I've thought it over long and hard, honestly, and I'll keep thinking it over, but it's a possibility we need to consider."

"All right. We'll talk about it later. Give me some time to reflect."

I nodded, grateful that he was at least making an effort. "It's late. I've got orders to carry out."

"And I'd better take a shower," he said. We fist-bumped and I disappeared behind him.

The conversation with my brother left me with a bitter taste in my mouth. It was true, my plan still needed to be ironed out, but at least it was something. I refused to give in to the idea of losing Gemma. Only a few months were left before she would transform into a Witch and begin to hate me. The thought was devastating. I ran a hand over my face. I had to concentrate. I focused on the flickering lights illuminating the night and went to the scene of the accident. My assignment had taken me to Japan.

The headlight of the downed motorcycle cast a sinister shaft of light across the asphalt. The families of the two kids hit by the car had just arrived. The boy driving the bike was loaded onto one of the three ambulances while his mother wept at his side, calling his name. I walked past him. The life was gone from his legs, but no Subterranean was there for him. The girl was loaded onto another ambulance and I got in with her. The rear doors closed and the inside filled with the sobs of her mother, who was gripping the girl's hand. The sirens screamed their urgency as the vehicle began its desperate race against time. *Against me*. It was a race they wouldn't win.

"Mmm . . . mmmom," the girl moaned.

The mother wiped away her tears, forcing a smile. "I'm right here. I'm here, sweetheart."

"I'm . . ." The girl's chest rose and fell with effort.

"Don't strain yourself. We'll be at the hospital in no time and you'll get better."

A tear slid down the girl's cheek. "I love you."

The woman burst into tears. "I love you too. Now don't talk. You'll be better soon. You'll be better soon."

"I'm . . ."

I held my hand over her chest and paused, waiting for her last words.

"I'm sorry, Mom."

I lowered my hand and the life left her body. Her eyes stared blankly into space and her mother began to shriek, tears of despair running down her cheeks. The paramedics intervened to resuscitate her daughter as the mother huddled in the corner, but there was nothing they could do. The girl, Sachiko, was already staring at me from the far side of the ambulance, ignoring the chaos around us. She came over and tried to touch me. "Who are you?"

"I'm here for you. I'll take you to safety."

Sachiko thought over what I'd said and seemed to understand. She looked at her mother, who was clutching her daughter's jacket to her mouth to stifle her sobs. "Is she going to be okay?" she asked.

I stared at her, searching for an answer. I couldn't guarantee that in this life she would forget her pain, but if she made the right decisions on Earth then yes, she would be all right and the two of them would be together again. "One day," I reassured her.

Sachiko hung her head. "It's all my fault. We got into a fight. I ran out of the house with Takeshi, my boyfriend. Mom didn't trust him. She wanted me to dump him . . . Is he okay?"

"They only entrusted me with you."

She huffed. "He only had one helmet and said it would be too big on me."

I balled my hands into fists, wishing I could change ambulances. "Parents often understand things their children aren't willing to listen to."

"I get that now, but it's too late," she said softly.

I held out my hand and she took it, vanishing like a puff of smoke. After I'd guided her through the worlds, the sounds in the ambulance hit me again, like someone had turned up the volume with a remote control.

The paramedics had stopped trying to revive Sachiko and were now holding the mother still as one of them sedated her. I sat down beside her and held her hand, hoping to give her a bit of comfort. Would she feel better if she knew her daughter would be all right in the place I'd led her to? If she knew that one day they would be together again, in a world without corruption, without pain, without darkness . . . a world that was denied to me.

All I wanted—all I had ever wanted—was to know that even if Gemma died I wouldn't lose her. Instead I was condemned to an existence of solitude. Not a Soul in Eden could see me. To me, a descendant of the Children of Eve, it was a deserted place. Gemma and I could be together only on Earth. If she crossed over, I would never see her again.

My power flowed into the woman and she fell asleep. The thoughts that had been running through my head triggered within me the compelling urge to see Gemma. I would have to make it fast, since I still had another execution order, but I couldn't resist my need for her. I concentrated and the ambulance disappeared.

Gemma was sitting in front of me, so engrossed in the story she was reading she didn't notice me. The seats in the auditorium were dimly lit, so when I was sure no one would spot me I materialized. The only lights were pointed at the stage, where Jeneane was singing a number from the musical she would be performing in. The boy at the piano played the notes wrong, angering her and leading to a heated argument. Gemma didn't move, as though she couldn't even hear them. She seemed to be in another world—a world where there were no Executioners who wanted to kill her. It was nice that she had a means of escape and could hide away in a place where negative thoughts wouldn't hound her. For a second, sorry to pull her out of that world, I considered leaving, but then she smiled. I leaned toward her, wondering what she was reading.

"You going to stand there spying on me all day long?" Gemma turned. She'd smiled because she'd noticed I was there.

I smiled back at her and folded my arms behind my head. "I was just wondering whether I should leave you to your book boyfriend or demand your attention."

"What did you decide?" she asked, raising an eyebrow.

I shot forward and snatched the book out of her hands. "That I'm better." I planted a quick kiss on her mouth and darted away, the loot in my hand.

"Hey! Give that back!"

"Let's see, who do we have here?" I opened the book to scan a few words as she leaned over the back of her seat. "Damon and Kitty. Interesting names . . ."

"That's not all. If you must know, he's quite the hunk," she teased.

"Oh, is that so?"

"Yep," she said, her expression sly.

"Are you saying I should be jealous?" I dematerialized to change places and seconds later she was sitting on my lap. She looked around, confused. I'd moved so fast she couldn't even tell how she'd ended up there.

"Well, actually . . ." She touched my nose with hers. "Damon's a really hot alien. On the other hand, you're here in flesh and blood."

"Oh, is that the only reason?!"

She shook her head and moved her mouth to my ear. "It's also because . . ." She stroked my arm provocatively and nimbly whisked the book out of my hands. "Gotcha!"

I laughed. "So it's true? I'm competing with that guy? I'll have to work hard to capture your complete attention."

"C'mon, cut it out!" Gemma laughed and hit me on the chest. A tremor ran through my body the instant she touched me.

I went serious again and brushed my thumb against the paint on her cheeks. "These look good on you. They remind me of last night." With her so close, sitting on my lap, I was in danger of losing control.

Gemma touched the yellow streaks on her face. "Yeah. I look like a warrior."

"You *are* a warrior," I replied in a heartbeat, and she kissed me. I slid my hands under her loose yellow jersey and she stopped, laughing against my mouth.

"Hey . . . People can see us, you know!"

"So what? I don't care." I pulled her closer and continued to kiss her.

"Evan!" She looked around to draw my attention to the kids on stage who were stealing glances at us.

I relaxed in my seat and raised my hands. "Okay, you win this time, but only because I can't stay for long anyway." She nodded without asking questions. "Aren't you going to the game?" I asked, pulling at her jersey.

"My class is outside playing snow volleyball in the Olympic Oval and I'm not allowed, so I'd rather stay here."

"Why's your friend still up on stage?"

Gemma looked at Jeneane, who had started reciting her lines. "It's the guys' team on the field. They're holding auditions for the spring musical in a few days and she wants the lead role."

"Doesn't she always get the lead role?"

"Yeah, but this time she has competition. There's a freshman girl who's really good and might steal the part from under her nose."

"Jeneane's giving it all she's got, I see."

"Yeah. She won't stop rehearsing. By now I know all her lines by heart."

"How'd the pie-eating contest go?" I asked, hiding a smile.

"I didn't stand a chance. Ginevra, Nausyka, and Anya creamed everybody. To compensate, Jeneane outdid everyone at the opening ceremony and clinched our team's victory during the sing-thing."

"Which would be . . . ?"

"A competition among all the classes to see who sings the LPHS Alma Mater best. It's what kicks off the Winter Carnival, and the winners get a ton of points."

"What else is planned?"

"Let's see . . . they've already done the relay race, the tug-of-war, and the alligator walk."

"Sounds like a dangerous game," I joked, making Gemma laugh.

"I didn't take part in it, anyway. The broomball match starts in half an hour. Today it's the girls' team's turn and I'll just be cheering them on. What a drag."

I glanced at the stage. Her friend also wore the senior team's yellow uniform for the Winter Carnival games. I could read in Gemma's subconscious how much she wanted to play. She'd always been a tomboy and she liked a challenge. It must have been hard for her to accept the faculty's decision, but after all they had no way of knowing the baby could withstand far more than a game of broomball. Gemma's fear of having to leave her life behind was right there around the corner and she clung to the need to live every day to the fullest.

"I bet they'll win, with you cheering them on," I said, trying to boost her spirits.

She crinkled her nose. "There's no way they can lose, with Ginevra, Anya, and Nausyka on the team."

I looked over my shoulder. From the back row, Nausyka shot me a scornful greeting. She was pretending to read something as she watched over Gemma. "But they aren't even on the team," I said in disbelief.

"Ha, that's nothing! You should see what they did to their uniforms."

"I can imagine." I grinned. There was nothing surprising about that. With three Witches in the rink, I was sorry to miss the game. It would have been fun to watch. I pushed the hair from her face and smiled. I adored the feisty side of her. I'd probed the souls of thousands of mortals, but Gemma's was like no other. "I'd better go. I wouldn't want someone to miss their big date," I joked.

"Well, whoever it is, I bet they'd be more than happy to miss their date with death."

I laughed, assuming my angelic guise. It was quite rare for Gemma to manage to joke about my duties as a Subterranean. That aspect of me still upset her—which was understandable, given that she herself had been one of my targets.

"See you later," I murmured, just as Jeneane called from the stage: "Hey, you two!"

We turned to look at her. She shook her head and squinted, confused. "What happened to Evan? He was there a second ago."

Gemma cast me a fleeting glance, smiling. My eyes must have been shining like liquid silver in the half-light, but Jeneane couldn't see me. "Yeah, and angels have wings. Evan left a while ago. You were just too wrapped up in yourself to notice."

"Hey, is the pregnancy turning you into a bitch?"

"If that's what causes it, then you must be pregnant too," Gemma called back.

"Very funny!"

I wasn't sure whether I should laugh at how they were needling each other or worry that Gemma was becoming more like Ginevra.

"So tell me, did you even listen to me singing? That's why you came here, wasn't it?"

"For that and to have some peace and quiet so I could read."

"You mean you prefer make-believe stories to my beautiful voice?"

Gemma smiled. "A story is a big lie that everyone loves listening to."

"Not me. Close that book and experience the real world—that is, *me*."

"No, you get down here or we'll be late for the game."

"Is it so late already?" Jeneane jumped down from the stage and walked up the aisle to her. She was glowing. "Well? How was I?" she asked casually.

Was Gemma becoming more like Ginevra? Maybe I was just imagining things. I was getting more nervous with every passing day. Jeneane bounced up and down, clapping her hands. "C'mon, I'm psyched for the game! We're going to bring home lots of points, I know we are!"

"I bet you're right," Gemma said softly, glancing my way. She also knew they were bound to win, thanks to her Sisters. I took her hand in mine and she squeezed it to say goodbye before I vanished. It was time for me to focus on my other assignment. My work wasn't done.

I found myself in the corridor of a hospital, in front of the heavy door that separated me from my target. Something caught my eye. I turned and saw a man staring at me through the window of one of the ORs. He was an Executioner, like me. Hospitals were always full of us. Still, it had become hard for me to look at other Subterraneans without suspicion, without thinking they were my enemies. Once I used to ignore them. The only thing that had mattered to me—the only thing I knew—were orders. But Gemma had changed all that. She'd changed me. My dedication to my obligations as a Subterranean hadn't changed; ferrying Souls to prevent the Witches from claiming them was still an essential principle of my nature as a Soldier, but now my priority was to protect Gemma. That was why I could never let my guard down. In every Subterranean I encountered, an enemy might be hiding.

A gurney was rolled out of the OR and the Angel of Death followed it. I went back to focusing on my mission and entered my operating room. I walked slowly among the doctors, who moved cautiously. A twelve-year-old girl, Yoko, was lying face down as the doctors stitched up her skin after having operated on her kidneys.

I moved farther into the OR, to another bed where a young woman was lying in the same position. Her name was Corinne. She was twenty-two years old and American, the one who'd been driving the car that had crashed into Sachiko's motorcycle.

A single heartbeat ran across the monitors, letting out a steady *beep*. It was the little girl's. Corinne, on the other hand, had been dead on arrival. She must have been an organ donor because the doctors had just removed one of her kidneys to give it to the girl so at least she might live.

I waited for the doctors to finish with Yoko and then freed the Soul trapped in Corinne's body.

"Hands off, perv." I spun around. Corinne was behind me, glaring at me. "Well? You one of those types who's into corpses?"

A smile escaped me and I stood up straight. "You're pretty lively for somebody who just died."

"Oh, no!" She touched her face, pretending to be shocked. "I'm dead? Gasp! Why?!" A second later she was serious and condescending again. "I figured out I was dead when I was screaming my head off and nobody even noticed, Einstein. I mean, c'mon! They could at least have covered me up, don't you think?! I'm dead for ten minutes and the first thing they do is take my clothes off. Practically the story of my life," she grumbled, waving her arms in the air. "Speaking of which, shouldn't I be transparent?" She turned her hands over and back again, examining them.

"Would you stop pacing?" I asked with a smile. "It's making me dizzy."

She stopped and took a closer look at me. Her hair was black, cut short, and she had big blue eyes. "So who the hell are you, anyways?! Was it you who freed me? If it was, then thanks. I couldn't keep on screaming like that. I was out of breath."

"I can believe that," I muttered, given how much air she was using even now with her nonstop talking. "Just so you know, you don't need to breathe any more."

Her eyes bulged. "You don't say!" She closed her mouth and pretended to hold her breath, then exhaled hard and shook her head, rolling her eyes at me. "You think I hadn't noticed that?! It's the first thing you notice when you die. So where'd you get your Undead License anyway? I've never seen the handbook, but I'm pretty sure the first rule is: always answer questions. Well? You want to tell me what you're doing here? Are you a voyeur or what?"

"What," I replied, grinning.

"Right, so this is a guessing game? Okay, let's see . . . Are you my spirit guide? Are you here to teach me all the tricks of being an evil poltergeist?"

"In a way."

"I bet you're like that guy in the movie *Ghost*. What was his name? You know, that guy, the ghost in the subway."

"I don't know what you're talking about, but no, you're not an evil poltergeist. If you were, I wouldn't be here."

"Buddy, if you don't know the movie *Ghost* you definitely are weir—He didn't have a name! That's why I couldn't remember it! *No name*, can you be more pathetic than that? So what about the tricks?"

"I'm not here to teach you tricks." I tried to dam the raging river, but the woman was a hurricane of energy.

"Then what do you want from me?! Who are you?" she asked, finally serious.

"I'm your ride." I smiled.

Incredibly, Corinne finally closed her mouth. My revelation seemed to have stopped her in her tracks, but it only lasted a second. "Whoa! So I have to come with you in order to go . . ." She moved her hands up and down, simulating scales. I took one of them and raised it to show her we were going up and not down. She twisted her mouth and nodded, pleasantly surprised. "Can't say I expected it. Nice that they sent me a hottie!"

Her brazenness made me laugh. I held my hand out to her. She looked at it hesitantly. "So now what happens? I take your hand and we start flying around the room?"

"Something like that."

Corinne glanced one last time at little Yoko and her face fell. "She'll have to find another nanny. I won't be much good to her dead," she joked, but the sarcasm couldn't hide her sadness. She loved the little girl.

"She won't forget you," I promised. I took her hand and she smiled, but then, just as she was fading, something crossed her mind.

"Hang on! I've got more ques—"

I shook my head and ran a hand over my neck. Rarely did you encounter spirits like Corinne. I materialized in the corridor and glanced at the other rooms again. There was no trace of the Subterranean I'd seen before, but in a quiet, dimly lit room, a woman was kneeling at the foot of a bed, praying under her breath. I paused to study her, listening to her words. She wasn't praying for her elderly father to get better—she knew he was suffering and there was nothing more they could do to help him. She was praying for his soul, asking her God to give him peace and put an end to his pain. The woman had no way of knowing it, but a Subterranean was already there for him, waiting beside the window.

A group of doctors ran toward me and I dodged out of their way, then walked to the waiting room, where a doctor was talking to the little girl's mother. She'd left her husband to pursue her career, but it hadn't left her with much time to dedicate to her family. I didn't need to enter her dreams to know she was reflecting on her decisions—I'd learned to read the human soul. Later that night she would phone her husband. If the nanny's kidney wasn't compatible, their daughter might not survive either. But that wasn't what was written; her time hadn't come yet. The little girl had been very lucky because my work was done for the day. I smiled and turned away, anxious to return to Gemma.

It was pitch dark in the little room I materialized in but I could already sense Gemma's heartbeat as she neared. I opened the door a crack and saw her. She was walking with Nausyka and Jeneane, who was talking nonstop. The Witch seemed interested in her chatter and was giving her advice better left unfollowed. Gemma, on the other hand, was engrossed in her book. The hallway was deserted. The students were all at the game. When she was close enough, I grabbed her hand and pulled her inside.

Gemma let out a shriek but I covered her mouth, gesturing for her to be quiet. When she realized it was me she nodded, so I let her go. I pricked my ears toward the hallway, where Jeneane had just noticed she was gone. "Gemma? Where are you?! Where'd she go? Did you see her?" she asked Nausyka.

The Witch didn't reply but I knew she'd spotted me. In fact, she'd sensed my presence even before hearing my thoughts. It was almost impossible for a Subterranean to hide from a Witch. I could, though. Gemma laughed and I pulled her against me. "Shh . . . or they'll find us," I warned her in a whisper.

"Evan, what are you doing?!" she reproached me, still laughing.

"I thought that since you can't play games with the others, you could still have a little fun with me." I kissed her neck.

"Are you going crazy?"

I kissed her again. "I've always been crazy."

"Evan, they might see us!" she protested, laughing. She tried to break free but I held her tighter.

"Nobody's going to see us in here." I drew her close, my breath coming quickly against her neck.

"What do you think you're doing? We're at school!" She put her hands on my shoulders to push me away but then sank her nails into my skin, her breathing growing ragged from my kisses.

"I have every intention of making you forget that guy Damon."

Gemma's breath came fast when my lips closed on her earlobe. Her fingers gripped the tattoo on my arm. "I forgot him the moment you grabbed my hand to drag me in here."

I smiled and pulled back. "Good: mission accomplished."

"What are you doing? Why did you stop?" she protested. She stumbled and I pulled her against me to keep her from falling. She reached one hand over her head and with a click a dim light barely illuminated the cramped closet we were in.

"Didn't you tell me to stop?" I loved teasing her, especially when she looked at me with those mischievous eyes.

She rested a hand on my chest, but something happened when she touched me—an image burst into my mind: *the two of us, our skin sweaty and our breathing mingled as we made love in that broom closet. My lips moved over her, my hands touched her all over . . .* Gemma pulled away from me and the vision vanished. We stared at each other for a long moment, stunned, trying to understand what had just happened. My ravenous eyes were drawn to her lips and desire overwhelmed me. In a flash, my mouth found hers and I pushed Gemma against the wall almost brutally. She returned my kiss passionately and yanked my shirt up. I pulled it off, trying to maintain the contact between our bodies, and she did the same. My dog tag clinked against her necklace, both of them cold against our burning-hot skin. I grabbed her by the thighs and lifted her up, wanting to meld with her. Overcome by the same need, Gemma wrapped her legs around my waist and sank her fingers into my hair.

"Oh, Gem . . ." I panted against her lips.

All at once, the door flew open and Gemma let out a shriek, crossing her arms over her bare chest.

"What the hell's going on here?!" the janitor bellowed, looking back and forth between us.

I clenched my fists and pushed Gemma behind me to hide her. Locking my fiery gaze on the man's, I saw the fear in his eyes, almost as if he realized who was hiding inside me. "Get. Out. Now," I snarled.

He stood there stock-still, taking in every word. *Take what you need and don't come back,* I ordered him in my mind. Nodding, the man grabbed a bucket and some sponges. "Now go and forget what you saw."

The janitor closed the door and I relaxed, running a hand down the back of my neck. I turned toward Gemma, who was putting her shirt on. "Hey . . . What are you doing?" I pinned her hands to the wall. "We're not done yet." I kissed her neck and she smiled, lacing her fingers with mine.

"You're going to drive me crazy, Evan James," she said softly, sliding her hands out of my grasp. "But now we'd better go to the game." She slipped away, leaving me with my hands on the wall.

"I should have killed him for interrupting us," I growled with annoyance.

"You wouldn't," Gemma said matter-of-factly.

I pulled on my shirt and drew her against me, this time tenderly. "For you, I'd kill anyone," I assured her, my eyes lingering on hers.

"Even if he didn't do anything?"

"He got between you and me. That's reason enough." I winked at her and grabbed her hand, pulling her out of the broom closet. "You okay? Your hand is scorching hot."

"It's nothing. It'll go back to normal in no time." My face darkened. *It was the power.*

Two girls in red uniforms stared at us, whispering to each other with smiles on their lips. Simon and Ginevra had told me how everyone at school had talked behind Gemma's back when they thought I'd abandoned her. If I could have followed my instinct I would have killed them all. But they'd already been taught their lesson. I smiled, listening to their whispers; now they were jealous of her. When one of them turned to look at us, I put my arm around Gemma's shoulder and pulled her to me. Gemma was special. But most importantly, she was mine. And I was all hers. Everyone needed to know that.

When we opened the doors to the Olympic Arena, a deafening roar hit us. The game was in full swing and the spectators were shouting and cheering on their teams. The stands were full of color because each class was wearing their team jersey. It was my first Winter Carnival at Lake Placid High but Gemma had explained everything to me with the enthusiasm of a child. It lasted two days, with all the high-school classes competing for points. On the third day they held the Snowball Hop, at which they announced the winning team and crowned the king and queen.

The senior players wore jerseys and shorts in yellow, matching the two streaks on their cheeks and their headbands. The same thing went for the juniors, though they wore red, the sophomores blue, and the freshmen green. The seniors scored a point and Gemma cheered, hurrying to reach the stands.

"Looks like it's almost over," I said. A moment later the referee called the end of the game. The stands exploded into cheers, including the rival teams. The Witches must have put on quite a show out there in the rink, dazzling everyone.

"So tell me, has that uniform always been so short?" I asked Gemma, jealous when I noticed how short her skirt was.

She blushed. "Nausyka did it. She altered the sweatshirt too, but I wore my spare." The oversized sweatshirt she wore was definitely cozier than the tight ones Anya, Nausyka, and Ginevra had on.

"Hey, what—what's going on?" Gemma asked, suddenly worried.

The spectators sat down again and a low murmur replaced the cheering. The senior women's team had gathered together opposite the senior men's team. I pricked my ears, canceling out every other sound around me. "The guys just challenged them," I told Gemma.

"What?!" She stood up, both frightened and excited. "That wasn't in the program!"

"It was Peter's idea. Brandon and Jake backed him up. What did you expect? Ginevra's team creamed their opponents."

The two senior teams, now opponents, went out onto the rink. The crowd stood up and cheered.

"If they think they can beat the girls playing like that, they've already lost." Gemma pointed to one of the male players. I laughed. He'd practically passed the orange ball straight to Anya.

"Hey, what the fuck are you doing?!" Brandon shoved the boy and his reproach could be heard all the way from our seats.

"Oh, nice. They're even fighting with each other," Gemma murmured.

"It's the Witches. That's the effect they have."

"You mean they're turning the boys against each other?"

"They're guys. With three girls that look like that in the rink they would have been at odds anyway, but yes, the presence of Witches triggers negative emotions in mortals."

The crowd cheered and Gemma stood up. "I don't believe it! Peter scored!" she cried, jumping up and down.

"Really?" I asked, scanning the rink for him.

The Witches' eyes glinted with defiance, but he stared back at them with more fighting spirit than I'd ever seen in him before. In the rink he knew his stuff. I'd always known he had it in him, but scoring against three Witch opponents was commendable. The entire men's team was fixated on their every movement, but he was focused on the game and wasn't letting himself be bedazzled. His love for Gemma must be so strong it left no room for little games of seduction.

Faith and Brandon were contending for the orange ball, gliding across the ice with their long sticks. He'd just about reached his opponents' goal when Jeneane blocked him, catching him off guard. The boy fell to the ice amid the crowd's shouts. Nausyka skidded to a halt beside him and held out her hand, but he got up on his own, scowling. The women's team was massacring them.

"It's not fair. The guys will never beat them," Gemma said.

The Witches moved gracefully, like seductive panthers. "Even when they aren't using magic, Witches are a thousand times stronger than mortals—not to mention the power they wield over their souls simply by being near them. This isn't a game; they're just having fun toying with the guys." Nausyka passed a boy and whispered something in his ear. They were playing dirty, and I wasn't happy about it. "But Peter's giving them a run for their money."

Just then, with Brandon backing him up, Peter managed to score another goal and the crowd went wild. "Way to go, Peter!" Gemma cheered. "You're right. I bet they weren't expecting this. The Witches can read the guys' minds and foresee their every move, but he's managed to score anyway."

"Funny, Peter's never been the unpredictable type. It must be the girls' strategy to avoid boring the crowd."

"I don't think so. Nausyka looks pretty pissed off," Gemma pointed out, suddenly worried. All at once she froze, her gaze unfocused. "There's something in the air. Can't you feel it too?"

I touched her hand to reassure her and a spark flew between us. Just then, in chorus, the spectators let out an *oooh* of concern. We looked around, but everyone had rushed down to the rink. I did the same, pulling Gemma by the hand, and leaned down to look. I had a bad feeling. A boy was stretched out in the middle of the ice, unmoving. My eyes scanned the rink. When Nausyka's eyes met mine, I slammed my fists against the railing and a growl of frustration escaped me. I knew what was going on but I wasn't going to let it happen. Grabbing hold of the railing, I leapt down and pushed through the crowd that had gathered around the boy. The coach held me back, but let me by after one fiery glance from me. I went up to the boy. His heartbeat was weak; the Witch was drawing him to her. Soon he would be dead. As I pretended to check his eyes, I rested a hand on his chest, counteracting Nausyka's efforts to take his soul. The boy shot bolt upright, avidly gulping in air, and an audible sigh of relief spread through the crowd.

I looked up at the Witch. *Don't try to mess with me again,* I threatened her mentally. I knew she could hear me. The coach knelt beside the boy and I stood up, leaving him to the others to take care of.

I followed the Witches into the dark hallway. "Sorry, Evan. I tried to stop her," Ginevra said softly. She'd also heard my thoughts and knew what I was capable of doing in order to keep Gemma safe.

I walked past her and stopped, my face inches from Nausyka's. "What did you think you were doing?!" I hissed.

She smiled contemptuously. "Was it against the rules? I'm new and not very familiar with your games . . ."

I punched the locker by her head, crumpling the metal. "You guys are here to protect Gemma," I reminded her sternly.

"No one told us we had to stop being what we are."

"*I'm* telling you."

"He was mine. I'd already claimed—"

"No souls," I said. She raised her chin, irritated. "Not in this school. Not when Gemma's around," I emphasized. We couldn't risk drawing in more Subterraneans.

"Evan." Gemma touched my arm and I pulled my fist away without taking my eyes off Nausyka.

"He's right," Anya insisted. "You seduced that boy's soul despite my objections. Why didn't you stop when we told you to?"

"Because I don't take orders from you," her Sister shot back.

"It wasn't an order," Ginevra intervened. "You can take his soul some other time. He's yours to claim."

"If he's stupid enough to listen to you again," I added, drawing looks from them.

"Right now," Ginevra went on, "our priority is protecting Gemma. I was wrong too, to let myself get wrapped up in the mortals' stupid game, but you crossed the line."

"Oh, come on, what did I do, anyway!? The kid's fine now, isn't he?"

"No thanks to you," I grumbled. "Anyway, let's get out of here before we attract too much attention." I put my arm around Gemma's neck and we all headed toward the door.

"You sure he'll be okay?" Gemma asked, watching the boy being loaded into an ambulance despite his protests.

"He'll be great," Nausyka interjected, passing me to get into the BMW. Ginevra and Anya got into the back. Ginevra had had a new light in her eyes ever since she'd started spending time with her Sisters, as though she'd rediscovered a part of herself.

"Gemma!" someone called as she was about to climb into the car. "Hey, guys! Wait up!"

We turned toward the voice. Faith was walking toward us, followed by Jeneane. "You disappeared. We were looking all over for you!" she exclaimed when she reached us.

"Great game! You guys were amazing!" Gemma cheered.

"I know!" Faith said excitedly. "It was unbelievable! I've never felt so charged up before, or so *strong*." Out of the corner of my eye I glanced at Nausyka, who was smiling to herself.

"The guys must have taken the defeat pretty hard," Gemma said with a grin.

"We'll be making fun of them literally forever!" Jeneane enthused, and all three of them laughed. From the car, Ginevra called to Gemma to hurry up.

"We're going to Saranac Lake tonight to see the Ice Castle. Coming with us?" Faith asked.

"I don't know . . ." Gemma said, looking at us questioningly.

"Why not?" I replied.

Jeneane cheered. "I heard they built a maze in it this year, too. It'll be so much fun!"

"Okay." Gemma smiled. "See you later, then."

"We'll go find the guys and let them know!" Faith said.

"And make fun of them!" her friend added as they hurried off.

I shook my head, grinning, but when I looked at Gemma I noticed she was smiling. It was nice that once in a while she could live the carefree life of an eighteen-year-old with her mortal friends, temporarily forgetting the fact that a horde of supernatural creatures was battling for her survival while the other half wanted her dead.

We got into our seats and I started the engine. Gemma turned on the stereo and *Thinking Out Loud* by Ed Sheeran filled the car. We exchanged glances, hiding a smile, both of us thinking of how we'd danced in her dream to the notes of that song.

"Hey, you two, hold off on the thoughts. We can hear them, you know," Nausyka groaned.

I smiled and took Gemma's hand. "So what? I'm not holding off on anything for you," I replied with a sneer. I raised Gemma's hand to my mouth and kissed her fingers, gazing into her eyes.

The Witch snorted in disgust. Though they'd already witnessed what had happened between Ginevra and Simon, they still couldn't stand the sight of a Witch and a Subterranean together. *Gemma isn't a Witch yet*, I reminded myself.

When we reached the driveway of our estate, I turned off the car as the gate was closing. "Gemma, going to school with you was fun. When can we do it again?" Anya asked, her voice eager.

"Never," I said sternly. "Not if you guys intend to cause trouble."

Gemma and Ginevra had arranged with the school principal for Ginevra's "cousins" to be able to attend class with us during their visit. Ginevra, whose powers of persuasion seemed unlimited when it came to the principal, had even gotten his permission for them to join in school sporting events like the Winter Carnival games.

"Come on, Evan!" Anya took my arm and walked beside me toward the front door. "Nausyka won't cause any more problems, you have my word. We want to go to the Ice Castle too!" she said enthusiastically.

How could these creatures be the same ones I'd met in Hell? They seemed like a group of silly adolescents with raging hormones. Yet I hadn't forgotten the time I'd spent with them in Hell: the torture, their filthy blood games. I hadn't forgotten they wanted to take Gemma away from me. No, there was nothing silly about them. I couldn't trust them. They were Witches. And I was a Subterranean.

"I've got a better idea," Nausyka said. "Why don't you stay here like a good little Soldier? We'll take care of protecting our Sister."

I rushed at her, but Anya stepped between us. "Calm down, she was only kidding," she said, casting a reproachful look at Nausyka, who was smirking, her long white hair blending in with the snowy background.

"All right, you can go, but I have no intention of babysitting you. You're not here for a guided tour—you're here to watch over Gemma."

"That's what we're going to do," Anya assured me happily.

I opened the front door and two panthers stopped to stare at us. I still had to get used to them. *No*, I thought. I never would.

Gemma leaned over to pet Irony, who'd waddled up to her, tail wagging. For some reason the big felines' presence didn't scare him. Maybe it was because Witches were in tune with nature and all its creatures bent to their will.

"Welcome back." Devina slunk down the stairs toward us.

Gemma was laughing with Anya and Ginevra, but her mood changed the second she saw her. "Well, well, if it isn't the Wicked Witch of the West," she said, dumping her backpack on the ground. "What were you doing upstairs? You don't have permission to go wandering around our rooms," she reproached her threateningly.

Without blinking an eye, Devina drew closer to me. "Oh, I only stayed in his bed for a little while . . . after he left." She looked at Gemma to provoke her and I clenched my fists. "Speaking of which, you left these in your room when you got dressed again." She rested her hand on my chest, her nails digging into me, but I didn't take what she held in it. I wasn't about to play along.

Gemma strode over to her and tore my boxers out of her hand. All at once something made her freeze, as though she'd gotten a shock. Her eyes became unfocused and for a second her pupils seemed to lengthen like a feline's. Devina smiled and moved her lips to Gemma's ear. "He's so sexy without them," she whispered.

A sconce on the wall exploded. Gemma tried to control her breathing. I'd never seen her like this before. She seemed to be trying to tame a demon raging inside her, like she was on the verge of making Devina's head explode through the power of her mind.

"Gemma . . ." I said, but her eyes remained locked on the Witch's, as if in communication with her. I noticed red drops dripping from her palms and went to her, breaking the dark spell between them. "You're hurt." I took her hands and ran my thumb over the cuts in her palms. She'd clenched her fists so hard her nails had pierced her flesh. I scowled at Devina. "You know, some bastards put collars on their dogs to make them stop barking. I'll get you one. I'm sure it would work on cats too."

"I'd be happy to wear it if you put it on me yourself. Electric shocks make everything more interesting," she replied mischievously.

"Devina, that's enough!" Ginevra broke in. "None of us likes staying under the same roof, but we've got to deal with it for as long as necessary, and you need to understand your place once and for all."

Devina cast her a haughty glance. "Who ever said I didn't like staying here?" She winked at me and walked away, leaving the door that led down to the dungeon open. She wanted us to watch her as she made her exit.

Ginevra closed it with a mental command, grumbling over her Sister's behavior. "It's hopeless. She'll never change."

"Was it just my imagination or did the little Witch make a lamp explode?" Nausyka asked. Gemma still looked shaken but her eyes had gone back to normal.

"Gemma . . ." I said.

She turned to look at me. "You undressed in front of Devina. I saw it," she hissed. I swallowed, shocked by her words. The dismay in her voice paralyzed me.

She hung her head and left me there, staring at nothing.

5

UNCONTROLLABLE INSTINCT

I had hurt her. I'd gotten undressed with Devina in the room, but only to make her suffer a little. Instead, I'd made Gemma suffer. Upstairs, my bedroom door slammed shut, snapping me out of my trance. With the eyes of all three Witches trained on me, I took the stairs three at a time to get to Gemma.

Outside my room, I froze. I could sense she was there, leaning against the door. I rested my palms on the wood, right where I knew hers were on the other side. I could hear her breathing. "Gem . . ." I whispered. I was so connected to her soul that I could perceive her anywhere. This time, though, there was more than just a door between us—there was a painful silence I wished I could fill. A distance that was killing me. I made a fist and materialized behind her.

"Why did you do it?" she hissed, sensing my presence. She didn't turn around.

"It doesn't—"

"You undressed with her in the room!" She turned to face me and her hard glare turned me to ice.

"Nothing happened!" I assured her, angry at myself. Overwhelmed, I hit the desk with my fist.

"Getting undressed is already something. You shouldn't have done it, Evan! You know she wants you, and you go and provoke her?"

The shutters burst open. I went up to her and rested my fists on either side of her head. She was losing control and I had to bring her back. "Gemma, this is what Devina wants: to divide us. Don't let her do it." I grabbed her hands and looked her straight in the eye.

Her irises went back to normal, driving off the darkness. I kissed her fingers, never taking my eyes off hers, and she hugged me tight. Closing my eyes, I rubbed my head against hers.

For a few seconds I'd thought I'd lost her, and it had been terrible. The darkness was already extending its tentacles to take her from me, but I was going to hold her close.

"Forgive me, Evan," she murmured.

I stroked her hair. "It's my fault. I shouldn't have provoked that Witch. But believe me, the only thing I wanted to do to her was disintegrate her."

"I know. I've never doubted you or forgotten what she did to you. I never will forget it. Maybe that's why I lose control so easily when she's around. Sometimes, inside me, I know what I'm doing is wrong, but I can't control myself. I'm scared, Evan," she confessed.

I sighed and held her against me so she wouldn't see the fear on my face. How could I reassure her when I was terrified myself? The proximity to her Sisters was stimulating Gemma's powers. The Witch buried within her was awakening and we could do nothing to stop it.

But then again, it was often Devina who provoked it, and we could at least stand up to her. I cupped Gemma's face in my hands and looked her in the eye. "You can't let that Witch get the better of you."

She nodded as I brushed a tear from her cheek with my thumb. "Do you think it was her who showed me the vision?"

"No, it was you, but she triggered something in you that caused it—a spark that ignited your powers."

"Anger."

"Yeah. That's what they do, isn't it? Incite people to hatred and violence. Anger leads to more anger."

"I feel like Dr. Jekyll and Mr. Hyde. There's so much chaos inside me . . ."

"You must have chaos in you to give birth to a dancing star," I whispered.

"Friedrich Nietzsche."

"I was sure you would know that."

Gemma smiled.

"So what happened at school, then? In the broom closet, I also had a vision, at the same moment you did," I said.

"You mean it wasn't you?" I shook my head and she seemed to lose herself in a distant memory. "It's happened before," she murmured.

"When?"

"On the veranda." She pointed at the door. "The first time you brought me here. When you finally told me who you were. I touched your back and we saw the same thing in our minds. I projected the image into your head. I guess the same thing happened today at school."

"That must be what happens when a Subterranean desires a Witch—she can project into his mind what will happen if he follows his instinct."

"I *bewitched* you."

I smiled and stroked her ear with my nose. "You don't need any powers to do that," I murmured. "You do just fine all on your own."

Gemma laughed and held me away from her, both hands on my chest. "Be good. We need to dig deeper into what causes these visions. It was my nature that tried to seduce you, you see?"

Kissing her neck, I held her tight. "So there are positive aspects to your nature," I murmured, my lips on her skin.

"I need to learn how to control this desire effect," she said, deep in thought. "Let's try it again! Maybe I can project another image into your mind," she exclaimed, sounding determined.

But I was even more determined than she was. Following my urge, I lifted her up and sat her down on the desk. "I'd rather do it my way." I kissed her, pressing my hips against hers.

She bit my lip and squeezed her legs around my body to hold me tighter. "I'm afraid I'm not going to stop you," she moaned, giving in.

I pulled off her sweatshirt and undershirt at the same time, blinded by desire. Gemma pulled off my shirt, unbuttoned my jeans, and lowered them slightly. My hands made their way under her skirt, unable to resist as my desire pressed impetuously against her.

Just then her phone rang, vibrating inside the sweatshirt on the floor. "I should get that," Gemma said softly.

I clasped my hand around her bottom and pulled her tightly against me while caressing her back with the other. "It'll stop." I grabbed the back of her head and pressed my lips to her neck, making her moan. With a few tugs I got her out of her skirt. I couldn't stand to be separated from her by the stupid fabric any more. I wanted to touch her skin. I wanted to feel her against me.

The phone insisted, distracting her again. "It might be important," she mumbled.

I didn't stop. "I don't care."

"It might be my parents!" she exclaimed, jumping down and wriggling free from my grasp. I rested my hands on the desk, frustrated. "It's Faith," she told me.

I turned around and the sight of her left me breathless. *God, she was beautiful.* Why did she have that effect on me every time? I'd never experienced anything like it. My body, my senses, all of me felt overpowered by her. Her pearl-colored lingerie stood out against her golden skin: a lace bra and underwear that shouldn't have been legal. Gemma certainly knew how to drive me wild.

She'd taken the phone from her uniform on the floor and stood there in the middle of the room, focused on the message she was reading while I died with longing for her.

"She says they'll be here in half an hour." Gemma looked up. "I'm afraid we'll have to take a raincheck on our little chat. Hey, why are you looking at me like that?"

"Like *what*?" I moved closer, one eyebrow raised.

She stepped back, smiling. "Like someone who wants to eat me."

I trapped her against the wall and sniffed her neck. "Maybe because it's true. You're driving me wild—what can I do?" I whispered against her skin. I nibbled her shoulder and she trembled.

"Hey, you're not playing fair." Gemma rested her hands on my shoulders to calm me and smiled, her eyes still closed. "If we go to the Ice Castle in this state we'll be in danger of melting it all down."

"Then let's not go." I continued to kiss her. I loved to tease Gemma, to slowly drive her as wild as she drove me, kissing her everywhere, following the shivers I sent through her body. "Still want me to stop?"

"No," she whispered. "I don't want you to . . . But there's no time." She slipped away, pulling on her skirt and looking at me, a grin on her face. "Are you getting dressed or are you going like that?" She pointed at my bare chest. Gemma liked teasing me too. She couldn't even imagine what it triggered in me, the feelings I would have to overcome to manage to stay away from her. Quickly tying her hair up, she planted a kiss on my lips. "We've only got half an hour. I'm going to run and take a shower!" She left the room, carrying her clothes in a bundle.

I sighed, staring at the door that had just closed behind her. A sudden smile curved my lips. Did she really think she could slip away from me like that? I pricked my ears and heard the shower being turned on in the other room, the sound of the glass door closing, the melody she was humming to herself.

I took off my shoes, then my jeans, with the concentration of a wolf watching its prey from afar. The instant my boxers fell to the floor I disappeared and materialized behind her. Her eyes were closed and steam was billowing through the room, carrying with it the sound of that delicious melody. I would have liked to stand there watching her a little longer, but my hand moved on its own and rested on her back, slowly ascending.

She tensed slightly but immediately realized it was me and only turned her head. I moved closer behind her and took her hand. She half closed her eyes when I stroked her cheek with my nose.

"Did you really think I'd let you leave?" I whispered into her ear. I reached out and rested my hands on the wall in front of her, trapping her.

"I was hoping you wouldn't," she confessed. I kissed her earlobe, pressing my desire against her. Gemma turned and joined her lips to mine in a slow, hot kiss full of promises as her hand slid down my chest, lower and lower, and our tongues touched in a sensual, hypnotic dance.

A groan escaped me when Gemma stroked my erection. I felt like I was losing my mind. Gemma triggered unfamiliar instincts inside me. I was a Soldier of Death, but when she was around all that remained was a man.

I stepped across the shower and pressed her against the wall, my hands on the verge of pulverizing the rock from the emotions racing through me. I rested my forehead against hers, breaking off our kiss to try to regain control. Her big dark eyes probed mine and I swallowed, completely at the mercy of her power. I scooped up some lather and began to caress her, very slowly, running my hand up her back, over her shoulder, and then up her neck as she moved her head slowly, surrendering to my caresses. I followed the curve of her jaw and my thumb lingered on her lower lip. My hand descended to her collarbone, her breast, her waist . . . before slipping between her legs. Gemma reacted with a moan, sinking her nails into my biceps and pulling me closer. I felt undone by the sensations; the knot in my stomach her gaze provoked, the dizziness the touch of her hands on me triggered, the burning deep in my chest that begged me to meld with her.

I caressed her bottom and slid my hand down her thigh, which I lifted to make room for me between her legs. Gemma cried out my name but I almost didn't hear her, my mind clouded with passion as I entered her. I gripped her bottom, holding her tightly as I moved inside her. With my mouth I explored her neck, thirsty for her, her skin, her scent. I slowly sucked her earlobe as she moaned and twisted to mold her body to mine, to fuse with me, feeding off my own need. A fiery storm raged inside me. I grunted and clung to her, losing myself in her as I thrust harder and harder. Gemma's breathing grew more ragged. She again cried out my name and the storm exploded inside me. I sank my hand into her hair and kissed her chin as I climaxed inside her, slowing my movements.

I sucked Gemma's neck and she sank her nails into my back, groaning with pleasure, clinging to me, keeping me inside her. My hand slid between us, clasped her breast, and then went down to her belly, between her legs . . . I stroked Gemma's desire with my thumb and she cried out with pleasure, her muscles contracting and shivers running across her skin.

Gemma raised her eyes to mine, her breathing still uneven as the fog in her head lifted. I took her hand and raised it, holding it against the wall. I smiled at her and she squeezed it tightly. We'd just been to heaven and hell together, emerging from our own ashes. The fire that had enveloped us was so all-consuming it still burned in my chest.

"I don't want to lose you, Evan," she whispered unexpectedly.

"It's gratifying to hear that at moments like this," I said, grinning. I stroked her thumb and she turned to look at our joined hands. Resting my forehead against her temple, I kissed her cheekbone. "I won't let it happen," I whispered.

Gemma took a deep breath, her heart still racing. Her gaze was lost on the rings of our tattoos that together formed the infinity symbol, renewing our vow each time we joined hands.

Stay together. Fight together.

GEMMA

6

BLOCKS OF ICE

I got out of the shower and wrapped a towel around me, my cheeks aching from the huge smile that refused to leave my face. I let my hair down and opened the window a crack. The steam soon cleared and the mirror reflected my image. I ran a hand over my face, still grinning like a moron. It was bright red! Why did Evan inevitably have that effect on me?

Sweeping my hair to one side, I suddenly froze and leaned closer to my reflection, my hand on my neck. My eyes widened at the hickey Evan had left on me. Part of me was turned on by the sight of it—it reminded me of the electrifying moment when I'd felt his lips on me—yet I suspected a little part of him had done it because we were about to go out with Peter. By that point Evan should have realized he didn't need to leave his mark on me to know I was his. I still had butterflies in my stomach, thinking back to a few minutes earlier, to what had happened in the shower and how passionately he had desired me. I closed my eyes. I could still feel his hands on me, caressing my wet skin as the water slid down our bodies and the steam enveloped us. It was as though he possessed the code to activate all the sensors in my body. I saw myself stroking the tattoo on his arm. At my touch, a shiver had spread across his forearm, tracing the intricate design, his muscles flexing every time he thrust himself into me. I'd always been drawn by his mark. It aroused me and frightened me at the same time. Part of me wondered if it was because of what I was going to become—a Witch on the hunt for her Subterranean—but whenever that happened I reassured myself with a reminder that I'd never felt a similar attraction to the marks of other Subterraneans. My connection to Evan went beyond our roles, and love would overcome the dark power inside me. I would defeat the powers of evil—I wouldn't let them obliterate me. Though Evan was determined to find a solution that would prevent me from becoming a Witch, I was well aware that the darkness was inside me and only I could defeat it.

I'd already experienced what it meant to lose Evan and I wasn't willing to accept it again. I would respect the pact but would remain on Earth. I was more and more convinced I wouldn't change. It wasn't possible to erase the memories I'd built together with Evan. He couldn't be eradicated from my heart.

I ran my fingers over the hickey, remembering his mouth's fiery touch. Raising my eyes to the mirror, I found I was still smiling. Deep down, it warmed my heart that Evan felt the need to leave his mark on me, the need to make me his. He'd never stopped romancing me. We'd been through so much together, our relationship had evolved and our bond had strengthened, yet he was still the enamored and slightly crazy guy I'd always known. Even if I'd realized in time that he was giving me a hickey, I knew I would have let him do it, just like when he'd snuck into the shower even though the others were about to arrive. He was impulsive and stubborn—maybe even more than I was. After making love, we'd started fooling around again, and it had taken every ounce of my self-control to resist him and kick him out of the shower.

Downstairs, the front door closed and murmurs filled the living room. "Oh, *shit*," I murmured. They'd arrived. I dressed in a hurry, knowing I had to get downstairs, and fast, before Evan and Peter got into a fistfight in the living room. I hopped into the hallway, tugging my snow boots on, but something stopped me.

A sensation.

Slowly, I turned around as a shiver ran down my spine. The hallway was dark, illuminated only by a faint glow from one of the bedrooms. I felt a sudden gust of wind. Evan must have left his window open. I walked toward his room to close it, but my heart leapt in my chest from fright. Someone was staring at me through the crack in the door.

Blinking, I advanced cautiously, but the eyes were still there. It looked like a little boy. The door swung shut, closed by a puff of air, but I threw it open. Evan's sweatshirt swung back and forth on the doorknob. I heaved a sigh of relief. The room was empty and the window was, in fact, open, letting in the cold. I shivered, partly because of the draft and partly because of that nasty sensation.

"Hey, Gemma."

I jumped, my heart beating like crazy. "Simon," I said, still stunned.

"What are you doing here? Your friends are already downstairs. If I were you, I wouldn't leave Evan alone with Peter."

"Actually, you're right." I smiled at him. "Aren't you coming with us to the Ice Castle?"

"I'll catch up with you in a bit. First I'm going downstairs to make sure everything's under control."

"You mean the prisoners?"

"I mean the prisoners' *guards*. Better not to trust them too much."

I nodded. "Be careful," I warned him, serious.

He smiled and tousled my hair. "No need to worry. Everything's under control. Go have fun with your friends." I returned his smile and headed for the stairs. Casting a last glance at Evan's sweatshirt, I shook my head. I was getting paranoid.

"Here she is, finally!" Faith exclaimed as Jake pulled her against him, making her protest.

"Hey!" I said as I hurried down the stairs.

Peter was sprawled on the couch with Brandon, while Evan was drying his still-damp hair with a towel. I sighed with relief: no blood on the carpet. Peter had a strange look on his face. He seemed worried, or maybe confused—I couldn't tell. Irony had hopped into his lap, but Peter was focused on something else. When he saw me, though, his agitation vanished and he looked calm again.

"A little longer and nobody would have been able to drag these two off the couch," Jeneane exclaimed, climbing over Peter's legs to be closer to Brandon, who suddenly grabbed her hand and pulled.

"Hey!" she cried, toppling onto his lap. He laughed and held her tight.

"Sorry to keep you waiting. There was a slight holdup." Instinctively, my eyes sought Evan's. He smiled at me, making me blush. Faith and Jeneane must have noticed because they whispered something to each other. Peter glanced at me and then at Evan before looking away, irritated.

"I told you there wasn't time," I murmured, moving closer to Evan. I wished I could have avoided making a big entrance, with everyone's attention focused on me. They could read on my face what we'd just done.

He smiled, sensing my embarrassment, and moved his mouth to my ear. "Then you should choose your words more carefully. 'I'm going to take a shower' isn't the best way to get rid of me."

"I have the impression you wouldn't have given up no matter what I said," I teased, raising an eyebrow.

"You're right," he admitted. "And I'm sorry about *this*," he whispered, running his finger over the hickey.

I raised the neck of my sweatshirt and looked around. No one was paying attention to us, but Evan still had that saucy grin on his face. "You're completely insane," I said, grinning back at him.

"I know, that's what makes me irresistible." He winked at me, took me by the hand and pulled me away.

"Get your lazy asses off the sofa, it's time to go," Ginevra announced, coming down the stairs. I hadn't heard her upstairs. She must have been in the Copse, a little corner of Hell she'd recreated for her serpent in her bedroom—an area that was off limits for all of us. She opened the front door and motioned to us impatiently.

"For crying out loud," Brandon grumbled, still sunk into the couch, "why can't we stay here and watch the ga—" All at once he jumped in his seat, shocked, and pointed at the picture window in the kitchen, his eyes bulging. "Did you guys see that?! A black panther just walked by!" The others stared at him in silent disbelief as he clung to the couch, still scared. "It was there! You've got to believe me!"

Ginevra and I exchanged tense glances but then burst out laughing, followed immediately by the others. "I told you not to smoke that stuff, dude. It's too strong," Jake said, jeering.

Brandon composed himself, looking annoyed. "I saw it, okay?!" he insisted. Ginevra walked over to the window. He tried to stop her, more frightened than ever. "Are you crazy?! Get away from there!" he warned her, not bothering to hide the fear in his voice.

Ginevra ignored him and opened the window wide. Everyone held their breath. Peter had a grim look on his face again, like he felt he was in enemy territory, almost as if he suspected something. Evan and I exchanged looks. Maybe it hadn't been a good idea to invite a group of mortals to a house full of Witches, panthers, and imprisoned Executioners.

"There it is! It's right there! I can see its tail!" Brandon cried. "Close it, or—"

"She'll devour us all?" Ginevra turned to us, cradling a big black cat that flicked its tail in irritation. Everybody laughed and Brandon ran a hand up his neck, embarrassed but relieved.

"Maybe you really did overdo it with that stuff," Faith chided, one eyebrow raised.

"It was just a big, stupid cat," he muttered.

Ginevra held the cat up to his face and it hissed, making him pull back. "She must not have appreciated the word 'stupid.'"

"Come with me, champ." Jeneane grabbed Brandon by the shirt and pulled him away.

"Dude! Seriously? There are no panthers in the Adirondacks. At most it might've been a black bear!" Jake joked.

"I hate bears," Faith said. "They can rip your head off with a single blow."

"You've never seen what a panther can do to you," Ginevra said mischievously.

"There are no panthers around here," I repeated.

"You have to admit it's really big for a cat," Brandon insisted.

"Yeah, we will when you admit we destroyed you during the game!" Faith teased.

"You didn't *win*. The game wasn't over yet!" he said, annoyed.

The entire group started a heated discussion about how the game had gone and Evan took my hand, distracting me from the chatter. We exchanged a complicit glance. With our "slight holdup," we'd risked really messing things up, and Brandon had almost had a heart attack.

"Wait for me!" Nausyka ran out the door after us. She must have been the panther guarding the grounds. "You can't go to the Castle without me. I'm the main attraction!" she whined arrogantly, striding ahead of us. Actually, Nausyka did seem like an ice queen.

Evan rolled his eyes and both of us smiled. With all the Witches, supernatural creatures, and bloodthirsty Reaper Angels, one thing was certain: in that house, nobody ever got bored.

We arrived at the Ice Castle at dusk. The parade had already begun and the floats were making their way down the streets filled with music and groups of people wearing masks. After leaving the house, we'd gone to the North Elba toboggan run, where some middle-school students were still hanging out. They didn't take part in the Winter Carnival, so during the two days of competitions they would go sledding and have fun in the snow. Before leaving for the Ice Castle, we had some hot tea at my parents' diner.

In Saranac Lake they celebrated the Winter Carnival with two weeks full of events like the Ladies' Fry Pan Toss, musicals, great plays, and a parade complete with fireworks. But the most spectacular attraction was the Ice Castle on the shore of Lake Flower's Pontiac Bay. It was built out of two tons of ice blocks and had tunnels, mazes, and ever-changing surprises. I loved it. It was massive and majestic, one of the most magical parts of the Winter Carnival, and it made me feel like I was in a medieval fairy tale.

I took snapshots of the parade and my friends. Some of them complained because I was constantly taking pictures, but then they struck a pose, making funny faces for the camera.

Jeneane let out a sudden shriek and we all turned around, worried. "I can't wait to go inside!" she exclaimed, jumping up and down. She left us behind and slipped into the Castle with a huge smile.

"Wait for me!" Brandon broke away from the group to follow her.

"Relax," Evan whispered to me. He squeezed my hand and I took a deep breath. We were too tense. Ginevra and Simon also had serious looks on their faces. Anya, on the other hand, was looking around with her eyes full of enthusiasm while Nausyka was beaming and self-confident. On the way there, Evan had been very strict in reminding her that the only reason we were taking her with us was for my safety. She couldn't let the mortals' souls distract her. She was there to protect *me*. Evan had repeated it over and over again. Still, none of us were sure she would manage to restrain her instincts.

"What do we do, go track Jeneane down?" Faith asked, gesturing at the Ice Castle.

"I'm sure Brandon's checking the Castle for a cozy little room where he can be alone with her," Jake said.

"Not a bad idea," Nausyka said, her voice suddenly velvety. She rested her hand on Jake's shoulder and caressed his muscles. I looked at Faith. Her cheeks were practically purple, contrasting with her pale skin. Jake, on the other hand, paid no attention to Nausyka. The Witch suddenly turned to Peter and took his hand. "What do you say, want to go with me?"

"Nausyka, enough!" Ginevra said, stopping her and continuing the rest of the conversation mentally.

"*Can't I have even a little bit of fun? I'm not doing anything wrong*," she huffed. "*Besides, he's adorable!*" She pulled Peter closer, still holding him by the hand.

"Evan . . ." I murmured, worried. I turned to look at him but he was concentrating on something else.

"Don't worry. She won't tempt Peter's soul," he told me. Like Ginevra, he must have communicated telepathically with the Witch to remind her of the rules of the game.

"Okay," I said, though I still wasn't completely convinced she would abide by them. I'd noticed the constant glances she'd thrown at Peter during the game at school, and I wouldn't have had any objections if she'd been a mere mortal.

Peter readily accepted her attentions, though I saw caution in his eyes. He continued to hold her hand and from time to time even squeezed her waist, peeking in my direction. Chances were he was hoping to make me jealous, though that was impossible. My heart belonged to Evan and no one else. My only reaction to Nausyka's being so close to Peter was concern. Evil lurked inside her, and he didn't know it. The last thing I wanted was for Peter to lose his soul because of me.

"We're going to look for Brandon and Jeneane," Faith insisted, taking Jake by the arm. She was clearly doing everything she could to keep Nausyka away from him.

"We'll come with you." Peter glanced at Nausyka for confirmation. "Feel like it?"

"*Go ahead*," Evan told her in his mind, letting me listen in, "*but no tricks with the kid*."

"*I don't take orders from you*," she hissed as she passed him. They exchanged an icy glare and she grabbed hold of Peter's arm. The two of them headed toward the Castle.

I knew Nausyka's presence bothered Evan and he was probably happy to be rid of her. I went up to Anya, but there was no need for me to voice my concern out loud. "*Would you . . . ?*"

"*Don't worry. I'll keep an eye on her.*" Anya smiled at me and followed her Sister into the Castle.

"Anyone else want to join their group?" Simon joked, irritated that the Witches hadn't stayed there to protect me.

"I'm just fine here with you guys," I said. He winked at me. Evan, Simon, and Ginevra were a more-than-capable surveillance team. Nausyka could go ahead and have some fun in the world of the mortals . . . just as long as it made her forget her Witch instincts.

I moved closer to Ginevra. "Gwen," I said in a low voice, "can we trust her?"

She'd already read the concern in my thoughts. "She won't claim Peter's soul—don't worry about that. Anya's there with them. Besides, I'll continue to keep an eye on their minds, if it makes you feel better."

I nodded, thankful for her help. I didn't want anyone else to pay the price for my destiny again. Drake's sacrifice was still a dagger piercing my stomach. We missed him every second of the day, and it was my fault. Protecting me had landed him in Hell.

"And thanks to that, he found his beloved Stella," Ginevra reproached me, listening to my thoughts. "Relax, Gemma. Nothing's going to happen to anyone today. We should all be like Nausyka. After all, we came here to have fun. The Executioners are all under lock and key, so we have nothing to worry about."

I took a deep breath, the cold air chilling my lungs. "You're right. I have no reason to be this nervous."

"Hear that, Evan?" Simon said. "Your girlfriend's really nervous. Why don't you warm her up a little?"

"Ooooh . . . " Ginevra said, provoking me.

We'd been left on our own and all things considered, it was a good thing, because I felt more comfortable. In the past I would have found Simon's allusion embarrassing, but now we were all so close it was natural for us to tease each other in every situation. Evan, Simon, Ginevra, and I were a family—close-knit and inseparable.

"Hey, that was a private conversation." I punched Simon on the shoulder and clung to Evan's arm. "But he's not all wrong—it really is cold. I wouldn't mind a bit of your warmth."

Evan laughed. "Careful, I might take you at your word." He winked at me and we headed toward the Ice Castle. I fell behind to snap a few shots, and the others told me to hurry up. At the entrance, a big sign carved into the ice, lit up in blue lights, welcomed the visitors:

SARANAC LAKE
WINTER CARNIVAL

The air was even colder between the mighty walls of ice. I caught up with the group, snapping pictures of the amazing ice sculptures. There was a magnificent moose, a giant spider web, and even a motorcycle meticulously carved in the smallest detail. I turned the corner and found myself before a crystal carriage like the one I'd seen as a little girl. I couldn't help but remember the moment when I'd shared that memory with Evan and he'd created a prince and princess just for me on the frozen lake under the stars. The halls were full of incredible creations: a magnificent angel with unfurled wings, an archer with his bow pulled taut, and even a unicorn reared up on its hind legs. I turned another corner and found the sculpture of a ferocious beast in front of me. It was a wolf with its jaws open wide. A shiver ran down my back. I took a picture of it and realized I was all alone. Where had the others gone? I must have gotten too distracted. It was so easy to get lost while daydreaming in that enchanted kingdom. I turned around, still peering through the viewfinder, and a little boy's face filled the lens. I jumped in surprise. He seemed to have appeared out of nowhere. I smiled at him, but he continued to stare at me in silence. He must have been around four, and he was adorable, with eyes so blue they looked like ice. Instinctively I raised the lens to frame him. I had just snapped the picture when someone behind me grabbed me by the waist. "Boo!"

I whirled around, frightened. "So this is where you've been hiding." Evan's smile shone reassuringly but my heart was still pounding.

"Evan, you scared me to death."

"Relax, I was just teasing you. You shouldn't go wandering around all by yourself. Ginevra's keeping track of your thoughts, but even you know that sometimes your mind manages to block her."

"It's not my fault they designed a maze worthy of James Dashner this year."

"Who?"

"Nothing, never mind. I must have gotten lost," I said, gesticulating with the camera in my hand.

Evan grabbed it and took it from around my neck. "Maybe if you looked with your eyes and not through your viewfinder it would be easier for you to see where we're going." He pointed the lens at me as I held back a smile, pretending to pout. "You're beautiful," he said softly, snapping a couple of pictures.

"What are you doing?!" I protested.

"There's only one thing in this whole Castle worth immortalizing, and that's you."

"Cut it out!" I laughed and covered the lens with my hand. It was embarrassing to be on the other side of it. "Come on, give it back!"

"No, for today I'm holding it hostage." He pulled me into a secluded corner. "What do you say we melt a few blocks of ice?" he whispered into my hair.

I shivered. "What, is sneaking me into cramped spaces becoming your favorite pastime?"

"You're my favorite pastime." I closed my eyes in ecstasy as Evan's lips traced sweet kisses on my neck. "Kissing you," he went on, "touching you"—his hand slid up my thigh and came to rest on my bottom—"making love to you." He pulled me roughly against him and a moan escaped me.

"Evan, everybody will see us!"

"I can't do without it," he murmured against my skin, holding me tight.

"That's pretty obvious," I joked. He brushed his tongue over the hickey he'd left on me and I closed my eyes, tingles running through me. I clung to him and dug my fingers into his back. When he nibbled at my neck I broke free. "Evan, that tickles!"

He took my hand and his resonant laugh echoed through the tunnel as he backed away with a little smile on his lips. "Stay close to me or the next time you get lost I'll be forced to melt down the whole Castle to find you." I stuck my tongue out at him. "Try me if you don't believe it."

"I'd better not—I wouldn't want to spoil the fun for the whole town." I didn't dare challenge him. As stubborn as he was, there was a serious risk he would really do it.

Suddenly I remembered the little boy. "Wait a sec!" What if he'd gotten lost too? In that maze it wasn't hard to do. I turned around, but he was gone.

"What's wrong?" Evan asked, stopping to stare at me.

I walked back a few steps. He couldn't have gone far. I turned the corner and froze. It was a dead end. Where had the boy gone? Had he walked by us while we were fooling around?

"Gemma, what's worrying you?"

"I don't know where he went."

"Who?" Evan asked, puzzled.

"The little boy who was here with me."

"There was no boy when I got here."

"Yes there was—he was right there. I should've helped him. Maybe he was lost."

Evan drew me against him. "Relax. If he was, I'm sure he's already tracked down his parents."

I'd become hypersensitive when it came to children. Making it seem like a casual gesture, Evan touched his hand to my forehead. On the occasions when my power emerged, my body reacted with a high fever, more intense than any human being could bear. Sometimes just being near a Witch was enough to set it off. At first the fits had been so strong I'd passed out. With time I'd learned to control the power, especially once I'd accepted my true nature. Even my hair had grown darker recently.

"I saw him, Evan. I'm not seeing things!" I snapped, rage rising inside me. Why did everyone blame me whenever things weren't like they said they were?

"All right, all right! I didn't say anything. Calm down," Evan whispered, stroking my hair. He cupped my face in his hands and made me look at him.

Only when I'd begun to think clearly again did I realize I was trembling. I read the concern in his eyes and my anger vanished. "I'm sorry," I whispered, burying my face in his chest.

"Shh, everything's okay. It'll all be fine."

I wasn't so sure of that any more. If I already slipped toward evil so quickly without realizing it, how would I ever manage to resist the darkness once the serpent had sunk its fangs into me? With its venom in my bloodstream, rage and hatred would banish all the rest, just like everyone kept telling me. But I was stubborn. I'd convinced everyone it would be all right. Now doubts were starting to creep into my mind.

Evan took my hand. "Come on, let's catch up with the others."

I nodded, remaining silent. What if he'd been right all along? He didn't want to risk losing me in the transformation and was determined to find a solution that would release me from my promise to the Witches. Why did I never listen to him? I'd asked him to trust me when I didn't even trust myself. I had to rethink everything. I had to consider his idea. I had to trust Evan.

Simon and Ginevra were laughing, walking along cheerfully hand in hand. How I wished I could stop time, eliminate all the evil from our lives, bring back Drake and Stella, and let everyone live happily ever after. Unfortunately, we weren't living in a fairy tale and my destiny was more and more uncertain. All our destinies were. Yet they were still there, smiling as though our lives weren't about to change in a few months, as though we weren't in constant danger . . . because I wasn't the only one who had to escape death. Every day I was more aware of how much all of them were risking their lives to save me. When would they realize I wasn't worth it?

"Stop torturing yourself and take a picture of me and Simon." Ginevra tugged on my hair in an affectionate reproach and gave me my camera back.

"Sorry, I can't help it."

"Yes, you can! Enjoy the night, the hunk next to you, and your inseparable ball-breaking Sister who loves you." Ginevra hugged me from behind, resting her cheek against mine. *I loved her so much!*

"Hey, don't forget about me," Simon whined.

"You stay where you are—for today you're all mine." She winked at him and ran to hug him as I centered them in the frame. Ginevra was radiant with her long golden hair, dazzling smile, and sparkling green eyes. She definitely looked like an ice queen.

"Wait! I'll take one more. Hold it . . . Perfect."

"Let's go," Evan told us. "We should find the others before the fireworks start."

"Just a sec," I said, checking the pictures I'd taken of Simon and Ginevra. I smiled when I saw I'd managed to capture the light sparkling in Ginevra's eyes. I couldn't have been more satisfied. Clicking through the photos, I also found the ones Evan had taken of me. My colors were different from hers, but my big dark eyes stood out just as nicely against the white background, as did my cheeks, kissed by the blush only Evan could bring out in them.

The next shot was blank. I must have taken it by accident. I was about to delete it when I remembered and the smile died on my lips. It wasn't blank. It was the picture I'd taken of the little boy. What did it mean?

"Gemma, what is up with you today?" Simon groaned. "Do we have to drag you behind us on a sled?"

Meanwhile, Ginevra had already walked off. Evan squeezed me from behind and I forced myself to banish my concern. "It's nothing. I'm a little tired, that's all. It must be normal enough in my condition."

"Want me to carry you on my shoulders?" Evan joked.

I punched his arm. "I'm not a four-year-old."

"So what? I can still bear your weight . . . for the time being," he said, grinning.

"I'll dare you to do it when I'm a total blimp."

Evan laughed and held my hand. "I'll still carry you then."

I smiled at him but couldn't force down my nervousness for long. I kept thinking about the little boy.

I let go of Evan's hand and went back to looking at the pictures. He was right—there was no boy. Had I imagined him? Had he been another of my visions? What part of my subconscious had conjured him up? And why? Maybe it was because of my pregnancy . . . Could he be a projection of my future? Could he be my child? Who could say how far my powers might go?

A strange instinct tingled under my skin, the same one that had gripped me earlier. While before I hadn't wanted to give it any importance, now I was certain: it hadn't been the sweatshirt hanging from Evan's doorknob—I really had seen a little boy staring at me through the crack in the door.

I heard a whimper in the distance and slowed down, pricking my ears. It was coming from behind me. I turned and my heart contracted when I glimpsed the little boy disappear around the corner. I rushed through the maze after him, afraid he would disappear again. Instead, there he was, huddled on a slab of ice, crying. Just in case he was only in my imagination, I looked around to make sure no one could see me before asking, "Hey, everything okay? Are you lost?" He continued to cry. I moved closer and leaned over him. "What's your name? I'll take you to your mommy. Do you know where she is?"

"She died," a grim voice behind me said. "Two thousand years ago."

I spun around and found myself facing a little boy identical to the first. There were two of them. When I turned back, his brother slowly raised his head and his eyes of ice pierced me, shattering every doubt. "Soon you'll be dead too," he murmured with a crafty smile.

My heart twisted painfully in my chest. They were Subterraneans. And they were there to kill me.

7

FIREWORKS

"Evan!" I shouted. All at once a slab of ice fell from the ceiling behind the boy. I was trapped. Panicking, I tried to catch my breath, but it seemed an impossible task. Raising my hands to my throat, I crumpled to my knees.

"Gemma!" Evan's muffled shout reached me from outside my ice prison.

Evan!! I tried to scream but to my horror realized I couldn't. A drop of blood splashed onto the snow. *What . . . What are you doing to me?* My eyes shot to the two children as a sharp burning sensation spread through my body, making any movement impossible.

One of them smiled with an evil look in his eye. "Resisting is pointless." His voice didn't sound like a child's. It was deep, like a demon's.

Gwen! I shouted in my mind, *I'm here! Help me! I can't hold out much longer!*

The other boy walked slowly around me as I huddled on the ground, terrified, unable to move a muscle. "Don't bother trying to fight."

I gritted my teeth, trying to resist their power, but it was no use. My heartbeat began to slow inexorably as fire set the veins throughout my body ablaze.

Was everything truly about to end?

"Gemma!!" The desperate shout made its way through the walls as something hot trickled from my ears. I kept my eyes locked on the little boy as the world around me grew blurry, slowly fading. He smiled as craftily as a hungry wolf. Blood leaked from my nose and a crimson droplet splashed onto the snow, staining it red. I began to lose consciousness, barely noticing when my cheek struck the white ground. The pain had made me its own, gripping me in a vise of ice. *I was so tired . . .*

My eyelids blinked slowly and opened with effort. All I could think of were Evan and my baby, but their image grew ever fainter and more distant. Once they disappeared I knew I would lose them forever.

All at once the ground beneath me trembled, sending a shock through me. I opened my eyes but couldn't focus on anything. The cold stung my cheek. There was a burst of light and a loud noise that sounded like an explosion. The voices were close now, as though they were all around me, but there was something else: a chorus of shouts that filled the night, like a crazed crowd. A blond angel approached, hand outstretched. The children fell to their knees, powerless. Arms gently picked me up.

"Gemma, Gemma! Hang in there, stay with me." A hand brushed the hair from my face as a sweet warmth slowly spread through me. *Evan.* I struggled to focus on his face but lacked the strength. He cradled me in his arms. "We've got to get out of here. We've got to take her away!" he shouted, making my ears throb. I closed my eyes, amazed I could do it. Evan rested his forehead against mine. "You'll be fine. I'm here with you now," he whispered. I could sense the mix of emotions battling within him—anger, relief, and concern—while I felt as though I were enclosed in a bubble, separated from everyone else.

Evan kissed my forehead and an explosion of colors filled the sky. Then another . . . and another, coloring my world of confusion.

"You're in danger. Get out of here!"

Evan's gaze went to the Witch who'd just arrived—Zhora.

"You're late," Ginevra said.

"I'm sorry. I came as soon as I could."

"How the fuck could this have happened?" Evan burst out, furious. If more Subterraneans had shown up, it meant the Witches had killed at least one of their prisoners.

"Evan, calm down. We don't know what happened," said Simon.

"This is not good," grumbled Ginevra, who'd already read her Sister's mind. "We have to separate the prisoners. They're stronger together."

"Did they escape?" Simon asked.

"They committed suicide," Ginevra replied icily.

"Oh, great!" Evan fumed. "Just what we needed: kamikaze Subterraneans."

"But how could that happen?!"

"One of them sacrificed himself for the cause," Zhora explained. "He provoked our Dakor and got bitten on purpose. Another tried to do the same. We attempted to stop him, but were unable to . . . and he died. What happened here?" she asked, looking around.

"We showed up just in time. A few more minutes and they would have had her."

"How is she?" The Witch walked up to me. She stroked my cheek and kissed me on the mouth, leaving me dazed. A strange tingle filled me.

"She'll be okay," Evan replied, barely able to hide the bitterness in his voice. He gestured at the two unconscious children on the ice, guarded by Ginevra and Zhora's Dakor.

"For now we've stopped them. I'll take care of them later," Ginevra snarled. "Right now, let's get out of here." Evan nodded. I could see him more clearly now, as the fireworks lit up the night.

"Gemma! Gemma! Jesus! What happened to her?!" It was Peter.

I turned my head a little and smiled at him. "Pet . . ." I said, amazed I could speak again, though my voice was hoarse. "I'm fine. Don't worry."

"What happened?"

"We saw an explosion. The police blocked our way, but you guys were trapped in here!" Jeneane explained, shaken.

Faith covered her mouth with both hands as Jake gripped her shoulders. "My God! Who are those two little boys? We've got to get them to the hospital!" She moved closer but let out a shriek when she saw the serpents.

"Brandon, get the police!" Jeneane cried.

"Stop," Evan ordered, and Brandon stopped. "Everyone calm down," he continued, his voice grave as he crept into their minds. He was controlling them. *"You guys split up from us and we didn't meet again. We left early because Gemma had a dizzy spell. It was a great night, but the Castle collapsed and you were all scared. Go home and get some sleep."*

"C'mon, guys," Jake said. "You heard what the cops said, we can't hang around here."

The others nodded and walked toward their car. Brandon pulled Peter by the arm, but Peter yanked himself free. "Let go of me!" he barked, looking very concerned. "I have to call Gemma. Something happened, I can sense it," he muttered. He couldn't see me any more, yet Evan's words hadn't completely reassured him.

Evan and Simon exchanged a long look. Simon went over to Peter and rested a hand on his shoulder, looking at him intently.

He was about to use his power. I held my breath. Only a few times had I seen Simon erase someone's memory. It wasn't the same as the Subterraneans' ability to control people's minds.

Evan had planted false memories in their minds, making them believe they'd had those experiences. Simon's power, on the other hand, went well beyond that. He acted on people's actual memory.

Don't worry. Evan's voice filled my head. *Simon will only erase his memory of us.*

"Why didn't he have to do that to the others, too?"

"Because Peter is so attached to you. My order only partially convinced him. He must have been too worried. It happens, sometimes."

I looked at Peter. The veins on his neck were turning black and flowing toward Simon's hand, as if Simon were sucking away the memories from that very spot.

"Will he be okay?" I said softly. I still felt very weak.

Evan nodded. "Tomorrow morning he'll have a bad headache, that's all." I smiled at him. Still filled with concern, his eyes never left mine.

"Guys!" Ginevra called, drawing our attention. "We have a problem." A gasp escaped me. The little boys were gone.

8

GIFTS FROM HELL

"They're very strong," Ginevra noted as we entered the kitchen. "They almost killed Gemma—and kept us out at the same time."

During the trip home, I'd regained my strength and they'd explained what had happened. The two Subterraneans had frozen me in a sort of prison they'd created and had been draining me of my energy until Ginevra and Anya broke down their barriers and Evan shattered the Castle to pieces. Simon had managed to evacuate almost all the people inside, but many were injured.

They looked like little kids but it had taken two Subterraneans and two Witches to defeat them. Ginevra was right: they were very strong.

"But who are they?" Simon asked, frustrated.

"Could they be shapeshifters, like Drake?" I guessed. They must have taken advantage of my sensitivity toward children to lure me away from the others.

"No," stated a voice behind me. A black butterfly alighted on my hand. I shivered and turned around. *Sophìa.*

"Shit," Simon muttered.

The queen of darkness advanced. All the panthers bowed and the Witches around the table lowered their eyes as a sign of submission.

The devil incarnate was in our house. And she wanted me with her.

Ginevra froze, but didn't bow. She held her gaze until Sophìa approached me and took my chin in her fingers. Evan stepped forward, but Simon stopped him. I kept my gaze steadily on hers as her incredible lapis lazuli eyes probed mine, penetrating my soul. She was so close I could smell her scent. She smelled like flowers—an obscure, forbidden fragrance. She leaned in slowly and kissed me on the lips, leaving me dazed. A current of electricity branched through me, tingling under my skin. When Sophìa's lips left mine she smiled at me, inches from my face, but I couldn't move a muscle. In the room, silence had fallen.

"What did you do to her?!" Evan snarled, stepping in front of me.

"At ease, Spartan. I come in peace," Sophìa replied, her voice so charismatic and warm it made me quiver. "It was merely a greeting for my Naiad."

"She isn't yours," Evan growled.

Sophìa laughed. "Yes she is. It is only a matter of time."

"Why have you come?" Ginevra asked.

"Is this how you welcome me to your home?"

"You aren't welcome here," Simon reminded her.

"I was certain I understood there was a truce between us, Soldier. Is that no longer the case?" Sophìa stared at Simon.

He glared at her threateningly in turn. Ginevra intervened before things got out of hand. "Of course it is. We weren't expecting to see you here, that's all. What can we do for you, my lady?"

Sophìa smiled. Ginevra had subjugated herself to her, though her eyes burned with pride. Yet she didn't hate her—I could sense that. She was doing it out of fear for Simon. Still, there was another emotion. It was hidden deep down but I could sense it: nostalgia. Despite everything, she missed Sophìa.

"I am here to warn you. The two you saw are no ordinary Subterraneans."

"You mean they aren't Executioners who took on the appearance of children?" I asked.

"As I have already said, no. That is their true appearance. They are Asvins. They are not like you," she warned, speaking to the two Subterraneans in the room. "They are divinities. Celestial creatures. And they are very powerful. They never work together, but for you, Naiad, they seem to have made an exception."

"I've never heard anything of the kind," Simon murmured.

"They are Soldiers. Ferrymen of Souls, like you, but from a . . . *purer* species." A veiled insult glimmered in Sophìa's eyes.

"What does that mean?" Evan grunted. "And how do we kill them?" After what they'd done to me, he didn't even care about the fact that if we did so others would arrive.

"You can't," another voice said. We all turned to look at Devina, who'd just appeared in the living room. "My lady." Devina bowed to Sophìa, who gave her a long, sensual kiss on the lips.

Evan snorted, clearly disgusted. "Can we focus on the topic at hand or do you have to do that whenever you guys meet? If you want, we can leave the two of you alone."

Sophìa simply smiled, fixing her blue eyes on Evan. Her long, black, silver-tipped hair was tied up in a ponytail that reached her bottom, and the curves of her toned body were brought out by an extravagant gown in lace as black as her lipstick and pointy fingernails. She looked no older than twenty-five. No one would have guessed she was the devil.

"You can't kill them," Devina said again. "They're Deva twins, as old as time. They were among the first Subterraneans ever to exist and their name is legendary. They almost killed off two of us at the same time. They're very strong and have fun toying with Souls, terrorizing them before taking them away. For them *everything* is a game, but it's no laughing matter. They're immortal. Some legends say they obtained divine favor, while according to others their souls have been redeemed. Killing them is impossible. We've tried to subdue them several times," she admitted, "but since they're children, our seductive powers have no effect on them."

"However, I know a way to stop them," Sophìa concluded. "That is why I am here."

"We're listening," Evan said.

"There is only one thing that will keep them at bay. Your paltry underground prison will not be enough to trap them. You require something special: a cage forged of a substance as ancient as they are."

"Diamantea," Simon said under his breath.

I held back a smile. Sophìa herself had been imprisoned in a cage made of the divine stone.

"No," Sophìa said. "I have something better. Something more powerful." She opened her palm, showing us a tiny black crystal. I recognized it instantly. It was carbonado, the substance from Hell. She clasped it in her fist and the prism lengthened into a sharp stick that unfolded and changed shape, transforming in seconds into a cage of black diamond, impregnable and lethal. "Be careful, Subterraneans, not to cut yourselves on it unless you wish to pay us a visit in Hell. In that case, you are always welcome." She turned and winked at Simon. "The cage will deprive the Twins of all their powers. Including immortality." She smiled, her eyes flashing blue.

"We can't kill them," Simon spoke up, to calm Evan's anger. "Others would come. We can't risk it."

"In that case I will accept them as a gift when Naiad is safe . . . at my side." She fixed a sly smile on me before vanishing into the darkness.

"At least she was useful," Evan said sardonically.

"It was forged from Sophia's venom, Simon. Don't touch it!" Ginevra warned, seeing that he'd moved closer to it than he should have. In the middle of the living room, the bars of the big black cage twisted like serpents, forming an intricate lattice that blocked much of the view of the inside.

"How do we move it?" I asked shyly, but no one answered. "You don't mean to leave it here, do you?"

"Why not?" Evan joked. "It's not bad. It goes with the rest of the furniture."

"Except that, unlike the rest of the furniture, it can kill you," Ginevra shot back.

"That would be such a loss . . ." Devina goaded him.

I glared at her, knowing she couldn't help but hope Evan cut himself on its poisoned edges, because if he did he would return to her in Hell. "Go lick your tail, you ugly bitch," I snarled at her.

Standing behind me, Evan rested his hands on my shoulders to calm me. Devina moved her face close to mine. "Or I could lick *him*," she whispered, touching my ear with her tongue. "He liked it so much last time . . ." Black rage boiled up within me and the light in the living room exploded.

Evan leaned over me and held me tight. "Shh . . ." he murmured in my hair. "Don't listen to her. Breathe." His soothing voice managed to keep the darkness from suffocating me.

Devina's eyes were locked on mine, the trace of a smile on her lips. "I wish I could transform right now just so I could tear you to shreds," I hissed at her.

"We'll see who you want to tear to shreds once you're one of us. My bet is I'll be your best friend." Devina cast a sly glance at Evan. "What role will *you* play, Evan?"

"That's enough, Devina!" Ginevra warned her. "This isn't a game. Get it through your head!"

"No matter what happens, I'll never play on your side, that's for sure," Evan told her contemptuously. Devina shrugged, pretending to let his remark slide. But it had been a fierce clash, and Evan hadn't come out of it unscathed. I took his hand and he forced a smile. I knew that what he most feared about the transformation was the chance that I might hate him. But that could never happen . . . or could it?

I wasn't so sure any more.

9

DANGEROUS NOSTALGIA

After Sophìa had left us, Simon and Evan received execution orders and went off on their missions. Meanwhile, Ginevra went downstairs with the other Witches to check on the remaining prisoners and make sure none of them had attempted suicide. Lying on the couch with one arm over my eyes, I distractedly petted Irony. The big cage was still there in the middle of the living room. It was so strange, being there all alone in its presence. It emanated a strange energy, as though it weren't just an object but a living being.

I felt someone staring at me and opened my eyes. A large panther rested its muzzle on my cushion and let out a low, vibrant growl. I smiled. It was Anya. Her jade-green eyes stared at me, inches from my own. I moved my head closer and she rubbed hers against me, purring. Just a year earlier if someone had tried to tell me something like that could happen I would have called them crazy. Instead, I was face to face with a large panther . . . *and I loved her so.* Recently my bond with Anya had grown stronger, partly because we'd been living together. It felt like I'd always known her. She nudged Irony over with her muzzle and curled up at the foot of the couch to guard me, though it wasn't necessary. The Deva twins had escaped, but they wouldn't attack me at our house. For a long time I stared at the cage, attracted by its power. How could a simple object be powerful enough to stop two immortal beings? Without realizing it, I had moved closer, driven by the urge to feel it beneath my fingers. I could sense Sophìa's power flowing though the carbonado and was drawn to it—helplessly.

I raised a hand to touch it and my fingers cautiously traced the curves of the bars. I could feel the blood racing beneath my skin. I took a deep breath, overwhelmed by the intensity of the energy, loving the sensation of strength it created in me. All at once the black stone came to life, slithering at my touch like serpents in a dark dance. The cage door opened and I held my breath, eager to enter it.

"What are you doing?" Ginevra burst into the room and I took a step back.

"Nothing," I said defensively. "Just admiring the cage."

Ginevra's face darkened and she glanced at the panther, secretly communicating with her. "We'd better take it down," she finally murmured to herself. "You know, it might be dangerous . . . for Evan and Simon." *I don't know what kind of power it might have over her.*

"Don't lie, Gwen. I heard you," I said.

"Your powers are growing stronger."

"It's inevitable, with all these Witches around."

Ginevra wrapped her hand around one of the carbonado bars and the cage folded up, collapsing into a prism of black diamond.

"How will it happen?" I asked her point-blank. I didn't need to say anything else for her to understand that I was referring to my transformation. "Will I have to . . . die?"

Anya leapt off the couch and left us alone. Ginevra smiled. "No, Gemma. That's not going to happen." I followed her up the stairs and into her room. "Our bodies don't die like a Subterranean's. They transform. It'll be a rebirth. The venom will flow through your veins, making your body stronger. Invincible. You'll have full power over yourself and your senses. And the energy that now controls you will become part of you. You'll be in control of it."

I sat down on her bed. "Will the others notice anything different? My parents, Peter . . . ?" I didn't want the change to take away my old life and the people I cared about.

"They'll all see you in a new light. No one will be able to say no to you any more. Your charm will dazzle them. There are four different kinds of pheromones and the Witches control them all. You'll have sway over mortals . . . and all the Subterraneans."

That was what unsettled me the most. "Gwen, do you think the love between Evan and me is tainted by my power?" It was clear there was a very specific explanation for the wild attraction I'd felt for Evan the first time I saw him—I just hadn't realized it yet.

"The feelings Evan has for you are pure, Gemma. You two didn't fall in love because of your nature. I've never had any doubt about it, and neither should you." When Evan had been in Hell, Devina had tried to convince him it was true. "Devina just wanted to separate him from you. That was her goal all along, but she never succeeded. The connection between you two doesn't depend on what's inside you—otherwise you would have felt the same thing for Simon, or for Drake. The same thing goes for Evan. He fell in love with your soul. I saw it. He was lost the moment he realized you were capable of seeing him. The only thing your power did was make it possible for you to meet."

I nodded, thankful for what she'd said. "Have you ever missed sleeping?"

"Are you kidding? There are so many things to do and learn that I can't even imagine wasting half my life doing nothing."

"Sleeping *isn't* doing nothing," I protested, getting a wink from her in response. "What else is going to change with my transformation?"

"I'll show you something you'll like." Ginevra raised her hand and a book flew into her palm. When she looked at it, it snapped open and the pages flipped over rapidly before her eyes, which now sparkled green. The book closed and she smiled at me. "Ask me what it's about."

My jaw dropped. "Don't tell me you—" She nodded. She'd read the entire book in seconds. "I've always wished I could do that—there are so many books out there!"

She looked at me affectionately and then grew serious, finally answering my question. "Lots of things will change with the transformation. Your skin will become impenetrable. Nothing will be able to scratch you—nothing human, at least. Your senses will sharpen, you'll smell more smells, hear more sounds, taste more tastes. You'll have a powerful relationship with food."

"More powerful than it already is?"

"Actually, I wouldn't count on it." She laughed. "Anyway, whatever substance you put into your body after the transformation will be burned off by the venom in your blood." Ginevra gazed at me. "And then, the powers, obviously. And your eyes . . ."

"What's going to happen to my eyes?"

"They'll still be the same, but they'll have a sparkle no one can resist. And whenever the power flows inside you, your pupils will lengthen, showing the animal souls that rule within you: the panther and your Dakor."

When the power possessed the Witches, their eyes glinted with energy like molten metal and their pupils took on the threatening shape of panthers' pupils or the lethal ones of venomous snakes. My eyes would transform like that too. The thought made me tremble, yet part of me was secretly excited.

"Tell me about the powers." *What will it be like to be able to read anyone's mind at any time?* I wondered.

"It's not always fun to know what people are thinking. It can be frustrating sometimes."

"You can't really believe that."

"Sure I can. You have no idea what it's like, hearing *every thought*, knowing *every emotion* of the people around you, even people who mean a lot to you."

"I thought it was the coolest part of all."

"No, it isn't. Everyone has something they'd rather keep to themselves, even out of politeness." A bitter smile escaped Ginevra. "But with me around, no one can do it. When you have an argument with someone you can decide to keep the nasty remarks to yourself, but you can't control your thoughts. And sometimes you don't want to hear them because they hurt more than words—they go straight to your heart." She sighed and sat down beside me. "I won't lie to you, Gemma. I don't want to tell you I don't like what I am, that you should stay away from my world and renounce your nature, because that's not how I feel. My connection to you is strong, and if the possibility you'll be able to transform without leaving us turns out to be true, then I couldn't be happier. But I don't want to lose you, Gemma, and the risk of that is high. The powers and everything else are extraordinary, but there's also a dark side you'll have to reckon with. Witches are spellbinding creatures who awaken the evil in every human on Earth. Sooner or later everyone faces their Temptation, and Witches are lying in wait, ready to creep into their consciences. They instill doubts, feed insecurities, pull out the dark side lurking in each mortal. They're corruptors of Souls. Some mortals, the weaker ones, can't resist, and the Witches work on them slowly. Others, the ones who are already too corrupt, are taken at once."

"I thought it was the Màsala who determined the time allotted to each mortal. Do Witches work on Death's behalf too?"

"Of course. If a Soul is corrupt, a Subterranean isn't assigned to it. The Witches decide how and when to deal with it, and it dies by the Witches' hand. Death has two faces: Subterraneans bring Radiant Death with them; Witches are Dark Death. The difference is that for the Children of Eve, killing and ferrying Souls is a duty while for the Witches it's a pleasure. Gemma, you can't let yourself be dazzled by the desire for powers, even if it's difficult to resist. I have to admit I would never want to be a normal person, but only because I've already won my battle against the darkness. For me the worst is over, but you still have a world of challenges to face. I would give up my powers if it was enough to guarantee your redemption."

"Oh, Gwen . . ." I hugged her tight and a tear streaked my face.

Ginevra wiped it from my cheek and kissed me affectionately on the lips. A comforting warmth trembled in my heart. It wasn't a kiss like Sophìa's, which had been one of possession, brimming with erotic undertones—it was a kiss of love. "I'll never let them hurt you."

"Thank you. Though I haven't transformed yet, you're a real Sister to me. You, Evan, and Simon are my whole world."

"Hey, don't forget about the baby." Ginevra stroked my belly and I smiled through my tears.

"I never could. He's a part of me." The thought of the baby brought to mind a more disturbing one. "How are we going to capture the Deva twins?" I asked. "What powers do they have?"

"We had our suspicions after they attacked you, but Devina confirmed it. As you know, all Subterraneans have powers that help them ferry mortal Souls and cause the natural death of their bodies. The twins have the power to paralyze. One of them can influence the muscles of the body and the other controls circulation. Generally one of them is enough to accomplish a mission, but—"

"But for me they sent both," I finished her sentence, and she nodded grimly.

I understood now. One of them had paralyzed my muscles while the other worked on my circulatory system. I'd bled from my nose and ears. When Evan healed me once we were back home, he'd been particularly careful to check whether they had damaged my internal organs.

"We'll get them," Ginevra reassured me. "We'll come up with a plan tomorrow. But now you need to rest. You're safe here—the house is protected. Take this." She held out her hand and put something into my palm. "You can keep it if it'll make you feel more at ease."

I opened my fist and stared in surprise at the black diamond. "Thanks. Though I already feel safe with all of you."

"Stay here in my room, if you want. I'm going down to have a snack. All this agitation has made me hungry. Want me to bring you something?"

I smiled. To Ginevra any excuse was a good excuse to eat, and I was becoming more and more like her. "I'm fine, thanks."

"If you change your mind . . ." Ginevra winked at me and walked out the door.

I got up from the bed. I would rather rest in Evan's room, where I could smell his scent. In the hallway I almost screamed with fright when a panther leapt down in front of me. A red splotch stood out on her right paw. *Devina.* "Hey, carrot top. Next time use the stairs." She bared her fangs and growled, the harsh noise echoing off the walls. I turned my back on her and walked toward Evan's room. It was horrifying to think that if I transformed, my mind would be connected to Devina's. I didn't want to read her thoughts. If there was one person I hated most in the world, it was her. Not even Sophia made me feel such deep hatred.

Turning the knob on his bedroom door, a strange nostalgia suddenly gripped me. I hadn't read *Jane Eyre* in months, and in the state of tension I was in, the thought that I could hide away in its yellowed pages was comforting. In the margins were notes I'd written when my life had been normal, when Witches, Heaven, and Hell existed only in novels.

I kept walking. I missed my Rochester, especially now that Evan was gone. I climbed the narrow ladder that led to the attic, where Evan had stored all the things I'd brought from my parents' house. I had no idea when he would be back from his mission. No matter how many crushes I'd had during my lifelong career as an avid reader, no book boyfriend could hold a candle to Evan, as far as I was concerned.

With effort, I pushed open the wooden door in the ceiling, climbed through it and immediately turned on the yellow lightbulb hanging in the middle of the room. A gust of wind crept in through the round window. I shivered and hurried to close it. Outside it was dark and had started to snow. I rubbed my arms from the cold and examined the large storage boxes. I had so much stuff in there! I closed my eyes and let myself be enveloped by the smell of the books, the paper, the ink . . . the smell of stories. The most wonderful fragrance in the world. I knelt down and looked through a few of the boxes, reliving with a smile the memories the old books' covers conjured up in me.

Something behind me moved.

I spun around, my heart leaping in my chest, but the attic was deserted and surprisingly eerie. I filled my lungs with courage. There was nothing for me to worry about. Kneeling down again, I went back to rummaging around and finally found the old Charlotte Brontë book when a sudden noise made me start. I jumped to my feet. Something was moving in the corner. A box. I fought the urge to flee and reached out to see what it was hiding.

A gray squirrel chattered with fright and I let out the breath I'd been holding. "What are you doing up here, huh?" The squirrel hid in the corner, clawing the wall as though wanting to dig a hole in it. I reached out to pick it up and the window banged open, letting in a gust of snow.

"Ow!" The squirrel bit me and I yanked my hand back. "Hey, what did I ever do to you?" I grumbled. The wind made the lightbulb sway on its cord, illuminating the squirrel's face intermittently.

I tried again, lowering my voice. "C'mere. I'm not going to hurt you." I picked it up and found it was trembling. "Don't worry, little fella. You know, when I was a little girl they used to call me Squirrelicue? Actually, they still do, though I can't stand it." I stroked its head and something dampened my fingers. When I stared at my trembling hand, my eyes went wide. It was blood. It wasn't the finger it had bitten—there was too much of it. It was the squirrel, bleeding from the ears. Its gray fur was matted with red. I gagged as the squirrel squeaked in pain, and a terrible suspicion took root in me.

The light flickered and went out. I whirled around and the little boy of death stared at me, his eyes of ice glinting in the darkness. With a shriek I threw the squirrel at him and bolted, but his twin materialized in front of me, blocking my way.

"Want to see who can run faster?" he asked in his demon's voice. I grabbed the black diamond from my pocket and jammed it into the shoulder of the Deva behind me, taking him by surprise. Howling with pain, an inhuman sound that gave me goosebumps, he fell to the floor. With a shocked look on his face, he watched the blood gush from the wound, then raised his hate-filled eyes to me as he yanked the sharp prism out of his flesh. His brother raised his hand at me and I fell to my knees, paralyzed. Though I struggled to move my muscles, it was no use. The wounded Deva hurled the black stone away and laughed in the darkness as a drop of blood slid from my nose.

Just then a roar made the attic walls tremble and a panther landed on the Deva who was paralyzing my body. "Gemma!" Ginevra rushed into the room with two other panthers. In seconds their snarls filled the air. I wasn't strong enough to move, though the twins had released their grip. One of them was on the floor, grappling with a panther. The wounded Deva tried to escape, but Ginevra stopped him.

She summoned the black crystal to her and hurled it at his feet. He stared at the stone, at a loss, fear in his eyes for perhaps the first time in his entire existence. The carbonado came to life, unfolding around the Devas . . . and me. The panther bounded out before the cage door could close. One of the twins tried to rush out but the panthers snarled and he retreated.

"Gemma! Get out of there! *Now!*" Ginevra screamed.

I didn't move. The cage sealed itself up . . . with me inside.

10

THE DARKNESS SUMMONS

Though I knew I was no longer the victim of the Devas' power, since they—like me—were trapped in the cage, I felt a strange force inside me. Lying on the floor of the cage, my disheveled hair covering my face, I was trying to understand what it was when I heard a low growl. The twins backed up. I hid a smile because the sound had come from me.

And I liked it.

"What the fuck?" Simon gasped, but I barely heard him. I wanted to focus only on myself.

"It's the carbonado's power. It's awakened the evil inside her."

I could hear them, hear them all. It was like I was everywhere. They were holding their breath. Slowly, I raised my eyes to look at the Devas and terror spread across their childlike faces. They were powerless inside the cage. I, however, felt invincible. I crept toward them. One of the twins tried to attack me but my power hurled him away before he could even come close. *I had done it.* I felt the power flow through me like black lava. It burned but it made me stronger.

"Gemma, what are you doing? Get out of there!" Ginevra shouted. She opened the cage and tried to draw me to her with magic, but I blocked it and the barred door slammed shut.

"Go away! Go away, all of you!" I screamed. I didn't want to leave. I didn't want to give up that sensation, give up the *power.* The power was irresistible. The power satiated me. Someone shrieked and I spun around. It was Anya, who had just covered her mouth with both hands. I tilted my head because all at once I realized I was seeing her upside down. Somehow I had ended up on all fours on the ceiling of the cage. I leapt down to the floor as the cage door flew open and someone rushed inside and grabbed me by the waist.

"No! NO!" I shrieked, and my voice seemed to come straight from Hell. Strong arms dragged me away against my will. I clung to the cage with all my might, making my abductor scream in pain, but I continued to kick and struggle.

"Evan, get her out of there!"

I heard a grunt of effort and fell on top of someone. My body quivered. Hands clasped my face. My eyes met Evan's, and then . . . nothing.

"She's coming to."

I blinked and slowly opened my eyes. A small crowd was leaning over me. There were Subterraneans and Witches, but Ginevra told them all to move back so I could breathe.

"Evan . . ." I murmured. I tried to get up from the couch but felt drained.

"Good," Simon snorted irritably. "Now she can explain what the fuck happened!"

Evan stood up straight and faced his brother. "Hey, what's your problem?"

"We'd better call in an exorcist. We can't handle this kind of stuff," Simon hissed, his voice hard. My eyes widened. His comment had cut me to the quick.

"Simon!" Ginevra said reproachfully. "That's enough. Calm down, both of you."

Simon ran a hand over his face. "You're right. I don't even know why I said it. I'm sorry, Gemma. I've never even thought anything like that."

I happened to catch sight of my reflection in the mirror and my heart skipped a beat. My eyes . . . They were completely black, without whites. "It's my fault," I said in a tiny voice.

Evan immediately leaned over me. "What are you saying? None of this is your fault."

"Yes it is. Simon reacted that way because of me. Didn't he, Gwen?"

"Probably," she admitted regretfully.

But I ***knew*** it was because of me. I had felt the evil spread from me to Simon. I'd tried to stop it but couldn't. He'd said those nasty things because I'd generated a negative energy in him. Was that what was in store for me? Wasn't it enough for evil to darken my life? Did it also have to affect the lives of the people I loved? I didn't want to drag everyone else into my own darkness.

"Sophia's kiss must have awakened your power and the cage brought it out."

"That bitch!" Evan snarled. The panthers growled, advancing threateningly.

"Enough!" Ginevra stopped them. "You're not here to fight."

"He cannot insult the Empress in front of us."

"Then leave. If you stay here only to fight you're not helping."

I swallowed, dejected. I'd heard Ginevra speaking with Devina in her panther form. It was already happening. Every day I was closer to my transformation.

The panthers departed angrily, closing the door leading to the dungeon behind them. I let my head drop and breathed deeply. "I'm sorry, Simon. I didn't mean to influence you."

"It's not your fault," he reassured me. He'd come back from his mission just in time to see Evan pull me out of the cage.

"Tell me what happened," I said.

"The twins paralyzed you. We managed to stop them and hit them with the fragment of carbonado, which turned back into a cage, trapping you inside it too," Ginevra told me. "When they lost their powers you wouldn't come out. We tried to pull you out with magic, but you fought us off. You even injured Devina."

My eyes bulged. "I remember. Now I remember everything. I was the one who did those things."

"You weren't yourself. You were possessed, Gemma. Possessed by evil. Even I had never seen anything like it. Your voice was . . . different. You put the twins out of action. You hung them upside down inside the cage and came close to killing them. Fortunately Evan arrived in time."

Evan. I remembered him grunting with pain as he tried to drag me away. "You're hurt!" I exclaimed, taking his hand in mine.

He squeezed it tight. "It's nothing. All that matters is that you're safe now."

"That's not true. You risked your life for me! You could have died!"

"I could have lost you, which is worse."

"If you'd cut yourself on the black diamond, I—"

"But I didn't," he said, his eyes probing mine.

"How did you manage to get me out?"

"Not even we Witches were able to do that with our magic," Ginevra admitted. "Evan came back from his mission and when he saw you in the cage, he rushed in without thinking twice. He didn't have his powers in there and had to sling you over his shoulder against your will, but the poisonous bars left burns on him when you struggled to break free."

"Gin, why are you telling her this?"

"She needs to know. There can't be secrets among us."

I covered my face with my hands. "Forgive me, Evan."
"Everything's okay. It's going to be fine, I promise."
"Is this what's going to happen to me, Gwen?"
"No," said Anya, the only other Sister who'd stayed in the room. "It's the darkness trapped inside you that's possessing you. Once you accept the transformation, you'll set it free. You'll control it."
"I saw my eyes in the mirror." I shuddered at the memory of those big black pools staring back at me. "I looked possessed by the devil."
"You were—it's just that the devil is a part of you."
"My eyes aren't like yours. Why not?"
"For the same reason, I suppose." This time it was Ginevra who spoke. "You haven't undergone the transformation yet. What's happening to you is new for us too. Your closeness to our world jumpstarted the process. Your Dakor's venom will complete it, when Sophìa baptizes it. At that point your eyes will be his eyes and you'll have a single heartbeat."
That was why I'd seen fear on Anya's face. A tear slid down my cheek. "Evan, how can you—" I couldn't find the words. I'd even frightened myself when I saw my reflection.
"It wasn't the first time I'd seen you like that."
"What are you talking about?" I asked, shocked.
"I've seen that darkness in your eyes before," he admitted.
"It happens whenever the power summons you," Ginevra said.
"Why didn't you tell me about it?"
"There was no point in scaring you," Simon explained.
"So you let me be around other people and risk being seen?!" I shouted. "Are you trying to ruin my life?! How could you do that to me?!"
Evan took my face in his hands and his eyes focused on mine. When I looked into them, so deep and intense, a knot formed in my throat. *I was about to lose control again.* How could it be happening so soon? A river of tears filled my eyes and I let them flow. "I'm sorry," I sobbed. "How can you still bear to be near me? You should lock me up in a cage too. I'm a monster!"
All of them filed out of the room, leaving me alone with Evan. "Don't say that," he whispered. He laced his fingers with mine and our tattoos joined, forming the infinity symbol. "Remember? Stay together. Fight together. I'll never give you up."
I clung to him, unable to hold back the sobs, and he held me tight until I fell asleep.

The lake shore shimmered amber. The sun was setting, kissing its surface in a warm farewell. Evan emerged from the lake, as handsome as a god. Beaded water sparkled on his golden skin. The mark of the Children of Eve stood out on his left forearm. With my finger I beckoned to him, on my lips a seductive smile.
Evan rested his palms on the sand and locked eyes with me. He pressed his wet lips against mine, coaxing them open. I did as he wished and our tongues touched. Still kissing me, he made his way between my legs, pressing his erection against me, and I came alive with desire. I took him by the shoulders, swiftly pushed him to the ground, and straddled him, staring at him with a provocative look on my face. He grabbed my bottom to pull me closer, but I pinned his hands against the sand. I moved my mouth close to his, without touching it, savoring his yearning for me. Provoking him gave me intense pleasure. My hand slid down his arm. I felt the veins in his flexed muscles, my nails sharp on the tattoo of the Subterraneans. Moving very slowly, I ran my tongue over his lips. He couldn't hold back any longer. Moaning with

pleasure, he took my lower lip lightly between his teeth. I was *so* aroused, I wanted him. I wanted him inside me, to feel he was mine.

"Can I join your little party?" My head shot up. Evan came out of the lake house and walked up to me with a saucy little smile on his face.

If he was there, who was I . . . I looked at the Evan lying beneath me: he was still smiling at me but began to fade like a puff of smoke. The real Evan sat down beside me and I smoothed my hair, unable to meet his sly gaze. "So this is what you dream about when I'm not around." He grinned.

My cheeks burned. *It was a dream.* And he'd seen everything. "You looked a lot better shirtless."

"I can always take it off," he teased.

"You know, you shouldn't spy on my dreams like that," I reproached him, embarrassed. "Besides, why did it take you so long to show up? I mean, while I was making out with the other you."

"You fell asleep—I picked you up and carried you to bed. But you didn't waste any time." He raised an eyebrow. "And for the record, I wasn't spying. I came to visit you and you were with that guy. If you want I can leave you two alone. I saw how you came onto him. Maybe I should be jealous."

"*That guy* was you. Or better," I stammered, "it was you as my imagination sees you."

A sexy smile appeared on Evan's face. "I'm really here now. What do you say we pick up from where you two left off?" he suggested, his voice provocative.

I laughed and punched him on the shoulder. "Stop teasing me!"

"I'm serious!" Evan protested, but I was still too embarrassed to consider his proposal. When Evan burst into my dreams, the line between reality and make-believe disappeared and everything became possible. It was just that he could read every emotion, every mood, so not only had he seen my attempt to seduce him on the beach, he must have also perceived my desperate need for him, to have him inside me. I blushed again.

"So I'm dreaming," I said, to break the tension. "At least I realize it now."

"Well, don't go running away," he warned, smiling. The last time I'd realized we were in a dream, I'd seized my chance to play around with him by hiding behind the doors of my mind. He'd found me. He always did.

"I would never run away from you," I whispered.

Evan's face suddenly darkened. "I wish I could believe that."

Strangely, though he was the custodian of dreams, I'd always been able to read Evan's soul almost as well as he could read mine. Who knew, maybe it was another one of the lethal secrets in my Witch nature. What I did know for sure was that Evan was afraid, and right then I could sense it. "You know, there's something I really miss, something I'm sure I'll never stop missing."

"What?" he asked.

He turned to look at me but I continued to stare straight ahead at the water. "Heaven." I took a deep breath, letting my heart warm at my only memory of Eden. It had been an incredible journey full of comforting sensations. Never again had I felt like I had there: complete and at peace. It was an amazing gift Evan had wanted to give me so I would be part of his world. Back then I hadn't known that evil lurked inside me. My presence there had given us away, though, and Evan had paid the price. I was a Witch, and my world would soon be Hell. There was no place for me in Heaven. Yet the longing for it was part of our punishment—mine and my Sisters'.

Evan squeezed my hand and stroked my palm with his thumb. "We can still go there."

I whipped my head around. What was he talking about? "Sure, if we want to enrage the celestial forces." I smiled. "More than we already have, that is."

Evan remained serious. "Come with me."

"What are you doing? Stop, this is crazy!"

He took my hands and rested his forehead against mine, giving me a smile. "We're not going to unleash any celestial forces. Trust me." I smiled back and nodded. The world all around us disappeared.

11

POETRY IN THE SKY

"Evan, where are we?" I looked around, breathless. The familiar sights of our little lake had disappeared and now, spread out before us, was a seemingly endless landscape. We were high up on a snow-covered mountain. The night concealed the ocean but its song reached us nonetheless.

"What place is this?" I insisted as he savored the infinite sensations filling me.

"We're in Norway," he finally answered, casting me an enquiring glance.

"In Norway? You brought me to *Norway*?!" I exclaimed in disbelief.

"Well, technically *you* brought me *here*, given that we're in your dream," Evan joked, but then became serious. "It's the closest place to Heaven there is on Earth. Look."

I looked away from him and my eyes filled with the magic that lit up the sky. "Oh my God . . ." I murmured. Above us, the colors of the aurora borealis danced in the dark night like rays of hope. The darkness was a theater curtain that lifted to reveal the display of lights performed just for us, like a poem recited by the sky.

"They call it the dance of the northern lights. I've always wanted to bring you here," Evan confessed. "Isn't it amazing?"

"Divine," I said, because there was no other word to describe it.

Pleased, Evan smiled. "Subterraneans love to come here. All the legends about us began in Norway. People can't see us, obviously, but some of them with slightly sharper senses can feel our presence. Coming here is a way to ease the burden of our punishment. It's not Heaven, but we can pretend it is. Though the Souls we've ferried aren't here, we can at least meet up with other Subterraneans." Evan laughed. "It's a lie I like to tell myself."

I took his hand and squeezed it, looking up at the sky again. "You're right. It's not Heaven. It's much more, because we're here together. Thank you for showing it to me."

Evan leaned over and brushed my ear with his lips. "It can be our Heaven," he whispered, and a shiver tickled my neck.

"I love you, Evan. I love you like I've never loved anyone." I rested my forehead against his and he closed his eyes.

"Say it again."

"I love you," I whispered against his mouth. I kissed him and a tear dampened our lips.

"*Samam*." As do I. Evan slowly pushed my hair from my face, his fingers lingering to caress it. "Being away from you is like having a noose around my heart: it hurts, but I know you'll always show up to loosen it. If I lost you now, the noose would turn to barbed wire and my heart would bleed for eternity."

"No, Evan." I shook my head, tears filling my eyes.

"For me, there can be no worse punishment than losing you."

"You're not going to lose me," I assured him.

"You can't be certain, Gemma. You saw what happens to you when the power controls you."

"Only because I haven't transformed yet. At that point *I'll* be controlling *it*. I'm not going to leave you, Evan. I'll never leave you."

"I wish I could believe you, but I can't. Even if you don't forget all about me, how will you renounce Sophìa? Who says she'll let you go?"

"Our agreement is that I transform. I never said I would live in Hell with them."

"Once the Bond is established, nothing will be more important to you."

I shook my head. What he was saying was unacceptable. "You and the baby are everything to me, do you understand that?"

"It's true now, but the venom will erase us from your heart."

"That's impossible. No power could ever erase you from my heart."

"Yes it can, if you don't remember us." Evan clenched his fists and growled with frustration. "Gemma, I've lived with Simon for a long time and I know what I'm talking about. Lots of times I've seen what happens when a memory is erased. The heart and mind are connected. If a memory is removed from the mind, no trace is left of the emotion it was connected to. You're deluding yourself."

"Ginevra believes in me. Why can't you? She's been through it herself!" If Ginevra thought I could do it, transform without the old me disappearing, there was hope. It wasn't just a delusion. I would become a Witch, and Evan and I would live on Earth together with our child. With Simon and Ginevra. Maybe one day we could even find a way to bring back Drake and Stella and then we would be a family again. A tear emerged, streaking my face, and at the same time, a doubt: what if Ginevra's confidence was influenced by her desire to have me as a Sister? No, that couldn't be. She would lose me too, in that case. I couldn't give in to doubt or I wouldn't be able to do it. I would respect the pact, but would do so by my own rules.

Evan cupped my face in his hands. "Things don't necessarily have to go that way. I'm begging you, at least consider my proposal."

"Drink Ambrosia?" I asked. He nodded. "Don't you realize how risky that would be for you? I won't let you fight my battles for me any more. Last time you paid far too high a price." I rubbed his shoulders. Beneath the fabric he still bore the marks of Hell, where he'd been captured and tortured over and over. I couldn't let that happen again. The very thought was unbearable.

"I don't care about the risks if I know you're safe. Ambrosia will eradicate the evil inside you. It'll purify you."

"But you can't be sure, can you? Your plan doesn't give us any guarantee that I'll be able to escape the transformation either. It might unleash even worse forces against us."

"How could it get any worse than it already is?!" Evan raged. Frustrated, he ran his hand over his face. "I don't want to lose you."

"You won't. I'll always love you, Evan. It's inconceivable that that would ever change. No spell will ever take me away from you." I looked him steadily in the eye and he swallowed. "I made a promise and I'm going to keep it—that way I'll be immortal and we can stay together forever."

Evan hid from me in grim silence, his mind filled with the demons that tortured him. Ever since he'd discovered my true nature, something in him had changed. There was no longer fear in his eyes when he battled the other Soldiers of Death. He was fierce and self-confident. The only thing that frightened him now was my transformation.

I raised my head, drawn by a sudden new gleam in the sky. The green of the aurora slowly faded to red, like a dark omen. Evan stared at it for a long while and his voice dropped to a melancholy whisper: *"In nocturnal skies a blood-red light glows / with dark, livid rays that stream through the air / whilst languish, uncertain, 'neath veils of rose / all seven suns of the frigid Great Bear."*

"That's beautiful," I said softly, my eyes captivated by the tongues of fire that pierced the darkness. The sight was magnificent yet also frightening, like the second life that had been granted to me—a destiny that sooner or later would be tinged the color of my blood, just like the red in the sky that night.

"A poet wrote it in 1870," Evan explained, to banish the dismal thoughts from my heart. "Red northern lights are the rarest kind. They appear every ten years, sometimes even less frequently. The color is caused by the gases present in the atmosphere, their electrical state, and the energy of the particles that strike them."

"What causes the color red?"

"Molecular oxygen. Atomic oxygen, on the other hand, causes the color green."

"Blue is my favorite," I admitted. *Because it reminds me of your eyes.*

"Blue isn't as rare as red, but not as common as green, either. It's caused by nitrogen."

I covered my belly with my hand and Evan rested his hand on mine. He sat down behind me and continued to hold me while in the sky coronas and brilliant rays of light moved like a huge veil that painted the night. *What color would our baby's eyes be?*

"Evan . . ." I laced my fingers with his. How I wished I knew what would become of us and the baby I carried. "Do you ever wonder what he'll be like?"

"Every day."

"And?"

"It's not important if he's a Subterranean or a simple mortal. He's the living proof of our great love—that's all that matters." I squeezed his hand tighter, listening to the sounds of the northern lights. "Hear that?" he said softly, behind me. Distant whispers drifted through the air. When Evan's lips brushed my ear I closed my eyes. "That's the auroral chorus. You can't imagine how many incredible legends it's inspired."

"Tell me one," I encouraged him, knowing how much mythology fascinated him. I thought back to the night we'd spent beneath the stars, long ago, when I was still oblivious to the terrible fate in store for me and he was preparing to say goodbye forever. It felt like centuries had passed since then.

"I don't know any," he said.

I smiled. "Liar," I accused him, but he remained serious.

"There are lots of different beliefs. Some indigenous tribes, for example, thought the lights were reflections of a 'dance of fire' performed by sprites. To the Inuit in Greenland they were the spirits of children who had died violent deaths or on their birthdays. The Vikings, on the other hand, thought it was the work of the Valkyries who rode through the sky in shining armor on their steeds."

That was why he didn't want to talk to me about it. "So it's my fault, is it? Well, my Sisters', I mean, of course," I said with a grin, but the comment seemed to hit Evan hard. "I'm sorry. That was a lame joke."

"Don't worry," he reassured me, holding me tighter. "You know there are people who go aurora hunting? They wait up for nights on end to see them and then race over the snow following them."

"I guess it must be worth it. Seeing them has been such an exciting experience."

"For me too." Evan stood up and held out his hand. "Come on, I want to introduce you to someone."

I frowned but took his hand without questioning him. We walked down a hill and I smiled in amazement when I saw what awaited us. "What's this?!" I asked, electrified.

"Your carriage, my lady." Evan smiled and let go of my hand.

I went toward the five exquisite white wolves in front of the little sled. Fascinated, I approached them cautiously. Their eyes were as clear as ice, as if they too were Subterraneans, their fur snow-white streaked with gray. As I neared them, the wolves bowed to me. I knelt down and they came closer. At first they sniffed me, but then began to lick my face. I laughed as they rubbed against me.

"What should we call them? We have to give them names!" When Evan saw my enthusiasm his laughter filled the night. In my dreams, my emotions became his, because he could perceive them. "Hey, champ," I whispered to the lead wolf. "I bet you're the bravest. I'll call you Balto."

"Like one of the dogs that brought diphtheria serum to Nome, Alaska during the epidemic of winter 1925." I nodded, even though Evan hadn't really posed it as a question. He'd probably been there when those people died, but I didn't dare ask.

"'Endurance, fidelity, intelligence,'" I said, quoting from the inscription dedicated to the dog in New York's Central Park. They'd even made a cartoon about him, and it had made me cry rivers of tears. "Yes, it's decided: I'm calling you Balto," I repeated, stroking his thick fur. Another wolf licked me. It tickled. He had eyes so clear they looked like crystal. "And you'll be White Fang."

Evan stared at me inquisitively. "Another hero of the ice?"

I smiled to myself. Evan wasn't as well-versed in fictional characters as he was in historical ones. "In a way, yeah. He's the title character of a Jack London book. When I was four, my mother would read it to me every night." Maybe that was why I had become so passionate about reading.

"We have to go," Evan said. "Come on. Want to take a spin?"

I smiled and took the hand he was holding out to me. He raised mine to his lips, turned it over and kissed my palm, his gray eyes locked on mine, then walked me to the sled and bowed gallantly.

I laughed. "Do I sit here?" I pointed at a tiny seat big enough for only one person.

"No, stay close to me." He raised an eyebrow, inviting me to join him on the footboards. "The view is better from here. Careful." He showed me where to put my feet and I took hold of the handlebar in front of me. Evan took his place behind me and wrapped his arms around me, resting his hands on top of mine. "Ready?" I nodded, my eyes sparkling with joy. "Hold on tight. We're going to chase the aurora."

Evan perceived my thoughts and held me tighter, breathing against my neck. "Cold?"

I shook my head. "I grew up in the Adirondacks. I'm used to the cold."

"The cold in Scandinavia is different, though."

"We're in my dream," I reminded him. "You're all I need to keep warm." Evan laughed, tickling my skin. He nibbled at my neck, sending a wave of tingles through my body. "Evan, stop it!"

"Stop what?" His teeth tickled me again. He was smiling.

"You're teasing me."

"I would never!" he cried.

"Just warn me if you plan to make this thing fly at some point."

Evan burst out laughing. "Who do you think I am, Santa Claus?"

The wolves stopped beside a wooden cabin half-buried in the snow. Evan looked at the cabin and then at me, confused. I smiled and took him by the hand, leading him inside.

"I wasn't expecting this, but it's an excellent change of plans," he said, pleased.

"After all, it's *my* dream, isn't it?"

"I agree. Let's let it end the way it began." He took me in his arms and the door closed behind us. I laughed as he opened it a second later only to hang out a do-not-disturb sign.

"There's a little stardust in each of us, but you must have more of it than other people," Evan whispered against my neck.

I closed my eyes as the shiver lingered against my skin. "Do you think we'll ever find this kind of peace in our waking life?" I asked as we listened to the fire crackle. I would gladly remain asleep if it meant I could stay there, embracing Evan in our dreams. Only there could we find peace. As soon as I woke up, harsh reality always returned to overwhelm us.

"That's what we're fighting for. As long as we're together, there's hope."

I stroked his Subterranean tattoo, running my fingers along the lines that marked his muscles, and Evan kissed my forehead. We were naked, on the floor, the fire burning in a stone brazier in the middle of the room. We had made love as though it were our last night together and then started all over again. I didn't know how much of the night we had left, but I wanted it to be endless.

"Will you always love me, Evan?"

"Yes, my love."

"Until when?"

"Beyond death."

I breathed in against his chest and closed my eyes, my hands clasped around his dog tag.

12

STAY WITH ME

"A sleigh drawn by white wolves!" I laughed, thinking back to the magical night I'd spent with Evan just hours earlier. "How'd you come up with the idea, anyway?"

Evan walked beside me down the school hallway, where the walls, lockers, and even the floors were decked out for the Winter Carnival. On the floor, wide strips of tape in yellow, red, green, and blue indicated the various teams while decorations and streamers in the same colors hung from the ceiling—though a sign on the wall read:

Yellow, red, green, or blue,
whatever color you choose,
we all represent our high school!

"You sure seemed to enjoy it . . . judging from the reward you gave me," Evan said with a sly smile.

"Shh! Do you want someone to hear?" I reproached him, looking around. I blushed and chewed on the sleeve of my yellow sweatshirt. But it was true—it had been so romantic that in the end I'd practically pounced on him.

"I bet I know what you're thinking about," he teased me, one eyebrow raised.

"Why, you . . . !" I shot back, punching his shoulder. "I was just saying that knowing *you,* I would have expected a snowmobile instead."

"But I know *you* and knew you wouldn't be able to resist a pack of pure-white wolves." He smiled.

He was right, though I wished I could wipe that mischievous little smile off his face. Evan was the real wolf—and I was his prey.

"Anyway, there's something I was going to ask you last night. Who knows why I forg— Would you stop smirking?!" Evan laughed out loud. "Okay, okay. I know why I forgot. Happy?"

"Very," he replied, pleased.

The memory of his hands on me, his mouth on every inch of my skin, our naked bodies entwined in front of the fire made me lose my train of thought for a second. The mental image left my blood boiling.

"Well? What is it you wanted to ask?"

"Huh?" I blinked. Evan had stopped, leaning his shoulder against my locker. "Oh, yeah, right. Your birthday. You've never told me what day it is."

He smiled and shook his head. "I'm not telling you."

"Aw, come on! You know I won't stop asking until you do!"

"I have all the time in the world."

"Then I won't let you touch me until you've told me," I threatened.

Evan grabbed me by the shirt and pulled me against him. "You sure you'll be able to resist me?" he murmured, inches from my face. He touched his nose to mine and I felt butterflies in my stomach. I was lost to him. The problem was that he knew it. The wonderful thing was that he felt the same about me. I was about to kiss him when he smiled against my lips. "I would have bet." He was being so cheeky I could have hit him, but he pressed me back against the lockers and kissed me passionately. "Sorry. I can't resist you either," he admitted.

"So will you tell me when your birthday is?"

"No."

"Damn it!"

"It might even have been last night. What difference does it make?"

My eyes opened wide. "Was it last night? If it was you *have to* tell me."

"If it was, it means you've already given me a gift. More than one, actually." He laughed. "In any case, no. It wasn't last night."

"Promise me you'll tell me some time, at least. I know you're just doing this to spite me."

Evan laughed again. How he loved teasing me. After all the time we'd spent together, that had never changed. I groaned in exasperation. I was stubborn, but he was unbeatable. "Any chance I could sweet-talk it out of you?" I raised an eyebrow and stroked his chest to provoke him.

He took my hand and kissed my thumb. Gazing into my eyes, he brushed it with his tongue. "Alas, I fear you would only forget the question yet again, m'lady," he replied, his voice sensual but his eyes glinting with mockery.

Pouting, I pulled back my hand. "What if an Executioner suddenly popped out of nowhere and offed me? You'd let me die without knowing when your birthday is?"

"First, I would kill him before he could even get close to you. Second, we're not going to see any more Subterraneans around here for quite some time."

"Right." That was what I hoped, and the others seemed convinced of it too. While Evan and I had been fooling around in the mountain cabin the night before, Ginevra and the other Witches had reinforced the security measures. After the suicides of the two Angels of Death and the attack of the twin Devas, no precaution was too much.

"Hey." Evan took both my hands and rested his forehead on mine. "You're safe now," he whispered. I nodded. "This is an important time, your last year of school, and our baby is growing inside you." He rested his hand on my belly. "I mean to spend every minute with you. No Subterranean is going to cheat me of any more time with you or he'll be dead before he's even given his orders."

I smiled and Evan stroked my lip with his thumb while keeping his other hand protectively over my belly. Just then, we felt a movement. Our jaws dropped. *The baby had kicked.* "Did you feel that?" Evan asked, a look of wonderment on his face.

I nodded, my eyes glistening. A silent tear slid down my face and Evan wiped it away with his thumb and hugged me, both of us smiling.

"Hey guys!"

"Jeneane at three o'clock," Evan warned me.

I quickly tried to dry my tears before she could see them, but it was too late. "Hey, what's up?" She hurried over and took me by the shoulders, then shot a reproachful glance at Evan. "If I find out you hurt her, you're going to have to answer to me, Mr. Hunk," she told him. Evan raised his hands defensively, hiding a smile.

I laughed and the tears returned to fill my eyes. "Don't worry, Jeneane, they're tears of joy. The baby just kicked for the first time."

"Oh my God!" she squealed, holding me tight. "No way! Let me feel . . ." She rested a hand on my belly but nothing happened.

"Sorry, I can't control it."

"No problem." She hugged me again. "And here I figured the pregnancy was just an excuse for you to get out of class once in a while!"

"What?" I gasped, confused.

"Come on, I'm not the only one! There are even bets being made around school. Tons of people don't believe you're really pregnant. You're in better shape than my mom."

"Oh, thanks. You mean that as a compliment?"

"Hello! My mother's a knockout. I work up a sweat trying to keep up with her. You eat like an elephant and you've only gained, what, five pounds? I gain weight just by looking at food. So yeah, it was totally a compliment."

Everything considered, Jeneane was right. In my ample sweatshirt for the games, no one would have imagined I was expecting a baby. "I've got a fast metabolism. It's true, my belly hasn't grown much, but he's right here." I touched my middle. "And today he let us feel his presence for the first time."

Just then, Faith, Brandon, and Jake came walking up behind her. "The baby kicked!" Jeneane told them before they could even say hi.

"Perfect," I grumbled to Evan. "Pretty soon the whole school's going to know."

"Don't worry, it's wonderful."

"Okay, but the two of us aren't through talking about your birthday." Evan laughed.

"Dude, cool!" Jake exclaimed, moving closer.

"Out of my way, I want to feel it too!" Brandon exclaimed. "Can we?" A moment later the two huge jocks were leaning over my belly, listening.

"Move it, champs. You look like a couple of little girls!" Jeneane teased, pushing them aside.

"Hey, you two." Evan stared at them. "I think that's enough. Keep your hands to yourself."

"Okay, okay," I said, moving away from the little group gathered around me. "That's enough for now."

"But I haven't felt it yet!" Jeneane protested. She sighed. "I want to have a baby in my belly too."

"I can put one there for you if you want," Brandon said, seizing the moment as he raised an eyebrow.

"Pervert!" she snapped, hitting him on the head.

"Ow! You said you wanted one! I was just offering to help. You should be thanking me!" Jeneane hit him again. "Ow! What did I say?!" The whole group laughed as he rubbed his head.

Jeneane took his hand. "Come on, the dodgeball game starts in half an hour. If we beat our opponents, maybe afterwards I'll show you my boobs." A broad smile spread over Brandon's face and he waggled his eyebrows at us as she dragged him away. "Gemma, bathroom in five minutes," Jeneane ordered me before disappearing into the crowd.

"What an asshat!" Jake sneered. "We'd better go keep an eye on them. He would get himself embalmed for that girl."

"Coming with us?" Faith asked, her long red ponytail contrasting with her Winter Carnival outfit. Yellow was definitely her color.

"You guys go on ahead," I said. "We'll meet up in the bathroom in five."

"Okay—I wouldn't miss it for anything in the world," Jake said.

"You're not invited."

"Here you are." Ginevra turned the corner just then. She was with Camelia, the most eccentric and sensual of the Sisters. In her altered uniform she was stunning. Someone had snitched on them to the principal, who had come charging out of his office to explain to them that it was against the rules. Needless to say, he'd forgotten all about it the second he'd seen them approach.

"Just in time for the war paint."

"Sounds interesting," Camelia exclaimed. "What are we waiting for?" Anya and Nausyka had stayed to guard the Subterraneans and the Twins, but Camelia had wanted to come with me. She and Nausyka together would have been too much.

"War paint?" Evan asked, looking amused.

"That's what Jeneane calls it. Why do you think she's waiting for us in the bathroom? Stay here. She's liable to paint you too," I warned him, giving him a peck on the lips.

"I'll take your advice, then. See you later!"

"And don't forget your promise!"

Evan smiled. "What promise?"

I headed to the bathroom with Ginevra and Camelia. Everyone turned as we walked by, astounded by the magnetism the two Witches emanated. Of course, their close-fitting outfits and tall boots helped. Even I had a hard time taking my eyes off them. Part of me was secretly electrified about becoming like them, about mastering my sensuality like they did and finally feeling more confident.

"Look out," Camelia said to a boy a moment before he ran smack dab into an open locker. She shrugged, a sexy smile on her lips. "I warned him." I laughed with my Sisters as he touched his forehead, still unable to take his eyes off us.

My Sisters. It was strange how easily I managed to think of them that way. Though I hadn't transformed yet, I could already feel the power connecting us. Ginevra said it was because of the Bond—the mystical connection that would be cemented by a bite from my Dakor—and I already sensed its power. Being with them made me feel good, and I could tell the same thing went for Ginevra. She'd been beaming lately, ever since they'd started fighting together to protect me. And I was happy it was because of me. I'd given her back part of her old world.

"I heard people are getting ready for a war here." Camelia walked into the girls' room, drawing the attention of Faith and Jeneane, who was painting yellow lines on her face.

"Not the kind you're thinking of," Ginevra communicated telepathically to rein her in. I stared at her, shocked. I'd heard her!

"Relax, little Sister. I just want to have some fun."

"As long as you remember your place. This isn't the Hunt, after all."

"What do you mean, the hunt?" I thought, and they both turned to look at me.

"A more exciting kind of competition." Camelia winked at me, tacitly promising I would soon find out once I was in Hell. "Well? Is it my turn yet?" she asked, this time aloud.

"Get in line, Miss America. I'm going first," Jeneane replied, intent on doing up her face in the mirror. The big yellow pencil slipped in her hand, leaving a broad smear across her cheek all the way up to her ear.

"*Now* is it my turn?" Camelia asked, a little smile on her lips. Faith laughed but tried to hide it from her friend. Jeneane couldn't have known it was the Witch who'd made her mess it up, but she shot her a deadly glare all the same.

"C'mon, hand it over," I said, stepping forward and taking the pencil out of her hand. I had to be careful around Camelia. Though they all did their best to control themselves, they weren't accustomed to interacting with mortals, and Jeneane might end up paying a serious price. Wiping off the smear, I made a new mark and colored her lips yellow while Faith drew little flowers on her temples. That morning the two of them, like almost all the girls in school, had dyed one or more locks of their hair yellow to imitate Camelia. With her orange hair streaked with yellow, her head looked like a sunset. I was sure she was proud of how she'd influenced my friends . . . and the rest of the school.

"I'm used to it."

"Huh?" Jeneane asked.

"Nothing," I quickly answered for Camelia, casting a reproachful glance at my Sister for responding to my thoughts out loud. She laughed, not caring in the least.

"Do you have only one pencil?" I asked as I finished touching up Faith's face.

"We gave the other one to the guys."

I did Ginevra's face and then started on Camelia. She stared me straight in the eye the whole time and I felt a strange energy filling me. That always happened with them. They looked at me like someone would look at a lover.

"Your turn," she murmured, her voice hypnotic. I gave the pencil to Ginevra so she could do me but Camelia snatched it out of her hand. "Leave it to me."

I blinked. She was so close I almost felt embarrassed. She drew on my face and then leaned over me.

"*Don't.*" Ginevra's voice burst into our minds. I shook myself free of Camelia's spell. She ran her thumb over my lip, staring at me with a slight smile, her eyes gray and sensual.

"Hey, is your friend a lesbian?" I held my breath at Jeneane's remark, afraid of how Camelia might react, but she just laughed and moved closer to her.

"Never say never." Sliding her hand from Jeneane's neck to her chest, she whispered against her lips, "Want to try something new, little mortal?" Captivated by Camelia's lips, Jeneane didn't reply.

"Gwen!"

"That's enough, Camelia! You can't bewitch the girls. You can't do it to anyone. *We've already talked about this,"* Ginevra ordered her in her mind.

Faith walked out of one of the stalls and stared at them, confused. "Um, what's going on?"

Reluctantly, Camelia moved away from Jeneane. "Nothing fun, it seems," the Witch complained.

"Where's Peter?" I asked, to change the subject.

"Oh, I think I heard he was with a girl," Faith said.

"Wow! Peter, with a girl? Anyone I know?" I asked excitedly.

"She's a friend of yours. The one who was with you yesterday," Jeneane said.

"We aren't friends. We're Sisters," Camelia replied contemptuously. I barely heard her. My happiness had been shattered by Jeneane's words. I looked at Ginevra, who shrugged.

"Sorry, I don't know anything about it. I thought she was guarding the prisoners."

"Gwen, you've got to tell Nausyka to stay away from him. What does she want from him, anyway?"

"Calm down. I'll talk to her."

I was able to communicate mentally with Ginevra more regularly now. My powers were growing stronger. Or could it have been my anger that intensified them?

"Hey, Gemma, what's wrong?" Faith asked, bringing me back to them. She rested her hand on my shoulder and I realized I was shaking.

"Nothing. Nothing's wrong," I replied, trying to calm myself.

"You're jealous!" Jeneane exclaimed. "What have I always told you, little Joey? Why choose between Dawson and Pacey when you can have them both?"

"That's what I always say! I underestimated you," Camelia chimed in, "even if I don't know who those people are."

"You're crazy, Jeneane. Evan, Peter, and I have never been a triangle and we never will be. Get that through your head once and for all. I'm expecting Evan's baby!"

"So what? What are you going to do? Get married? Live happily ever after? Sooner or later you might want a little diversion."

"What the—"

"Chill, okay? I was only kidding! There's never been a more lopsided triangle than yours. Nobody could come between you two. Romeo and Juliet! You're disgustingly inseparable. Still . . . you're really not jealous about Peter? Not even a little?"

"Not even a little. I'm just a bit worried about him. We grew up together and I care about him. You don't know Nausyka. She can be a real witch."

"Speaking of witches, who was the redhead at your place last night? She seemed like a total bitch."

Camelia stepped in front of her, her expression threatening. "Don't you dare say that again. Devina is my Sister."

"I could've guessed that," Jeneane shot back sardonically. "What'd they feed you when you were babies?" *All as pretty as they are bitchy,* she thought.

"Okay, time to go!" I exclaimed before things got ugly.

"Hey, Gemma, how are you?" Faith asked as we walked out the door. "After your dizzy spell at the Ice Castle, I mean."

"Fine. Evan just took me home. Why, did you stop by to see me?" I asked, suddenly remembering that Evan had ordered them to go home.

"We were on our way home, but Peter was really worried about you. He wanted to make sure you were okay."

"He didn't mention it. He texted me this morning but didn't say anything about you guys stopping by."

"Because that girl wouldn't let us in. She practically kicked us out." Faith laughed, but I was thinking of Peter. His brain had obeyed Simon's order, but his love for me was so deep that he'd stopped by to see me first. He couldn't get near Nausyka. I had to protect him because there was only one thing that Witch wanted from him: his soul.

"I can't believe the baby kicked and I wasn't there to feel it!" Ginevra whined as we headed toward the gym. We'd stopped off at our lockers so Jeneane could put away the makeup, while I'd picked up my camera and—just in case—the novel about aliens I hadn't finished yet. "I'm not leaving your side until I've felt it too."

"Don't worry. It'll happen again, Gwen."

"Have you chosen a name yet?"

"Yes, but don't go rummaging through my brain because I have no intention of letting you find out what it is."

"Oh, come on! I didn't teach you to block your mind so you could use it against *me*. We're Sisters. There shouldn't be secrets between us."

I smiled. I'd inadvertently given Ginevra a challenge and I knew she wouldn't give in until she'd won. "We're not Sisters with a capital S yet."

"Yes we are. You and I always have been."

"You'll find out the name when the time is right."

"But—"

I slipped into the gym before she could try to persuade me. A murmur filled the large room, peppered with the squeal of the players' sneakers as they warmed up on the court. The dodgeball game was about to begin and the stands were filling up fast, taking on the colors of the various teams. We were about to battle the sophomores.

"Root for us, Gemma!" Faith exclaimed, to sugarcoat the pill. She knew how much I loved dodgeball and the Winter Carnival in general. I'd always been athletic. Competition exhilarated me and when I went out onto the field, the rest of the world disappeared.

"I bet you won't need it." With Camelia and Ginevra playing, their opponents didn't have a chance. "Hit them all!"

"Come on, I can't wait to try out this new game!" Camelia exclaimed excitedly as she strode onto the court.

"Don't worry, Gemma. I'll keep an eye on her. She's just here to have fun."

"Nausyka was too, but you saw what happened at the game yesterday, didn't you?"

"Relax. It won't happen this time. I'll keep her under control."

"Okay, I trust you." All my friends were there in the building, people I'd grown up with and cared a lot about. I didn't want any of their souls to be compromised purely on a whim.

"I said relax!" Ginevra insisted, following my train of thought. I looked around, searching for Camelia, and spotted Peter. He was already on the court with Brandon and Jake. No sign of Nausyka. *Thank Heaven.*

The referee gave them instructions as they got ready. I'd already explained the rules of the game to Ginevra and Camelia, and they'd found them pretty funny. I was sorry I couldn't play too, but when I thought of the little kick I'd felt earlier, my disappointment disappeared. I stroked my belly and smiled.

The referee blew his whistle to alert the players and I rushed to the sideline to snap a few shots for the yearbook. Along the central line—the dead zone—a number of balls were lined up. The rival teams were positioned on opposite sides behind the end lines, ready to race to the center and grab as many balls as possible for their own team.

When the referee blew his whistle again, officially starting the first game, the players charged toward the balls and hurried back to their respective fields. Seconds later, a full-fledged war broke out on the court.

I took some snapshots: players on the ground, doubled over laughing, others flying through the air with funny looks on their faces as they dodged a ball just about to hit them. I even managed to capture the moment a player was taken out by enemy fire, the ball frozen on his chest and his eyes bulging. The players could defend themselves only by warding off an attack with a ball. Those hit directly by a ball were "killed" and had to leave the court until one of their teammates brought them back in by catching one of their adversaries' balls. By the end of the games, there would be a few bruises and lots of laughs.

Ginevra and Camelia were having loads of fun. It was easier for them to catch the balls and at times they even helped out members of our team. Peter hit the last of our remaining adversaries and the referee blew the whistle, announcing the end of the first game.

The players traded sides and the balls were once again placed mid-court. We had to win seven three-minute games to win the entire match. I zoomed in on Faith in her starting position and focused on her lily-white face, green eyes, and freckled nose. She could have been a Witch, she was so pretty.

I got ready to steal a few more shots when someone grabbed me by the waist. "Hiding from me?" Evan whispered in my ear, pressing up against me so tightly I couldn't turn around. A quiver ran down my back.

"There's no place on Earth I could hide from you. And I would never want to anyway," I assured him, smiling.

"Hey, you two, that's not a sporting event we practice on my court. Back to the stands," the gym teacher told us.

"Come with me." Evan took my hand and I blushed, seeing that the teacher was watching us.

"Where? The stands are over there."

"We'll hide together." The sexy smile I couldn't say no to appeared on his lips and he winked at me before pulling me toward the boys' locker rooms.

"Evan, no! I can't come in here!" I protested, embarrassed.

He took the camera from around my neck and put it on a bench together with my book. "Yes you can, if you're with me." Pushing me against the wall, he began to kiss me with burning desire, drawing me into his whirlwind of passion.

"Oh, Evan, stop," I panted as his lips touched my neck to then nibble my shoulder and his warm hands explored my body. *Oh, Evan, please don't stop,* I thought, consumed by the fire he'd ignited. "Someone might come in. The match is almost over."

His hands slid under my skirt and I moaned. Unable to hold back, I took off his shirt and stroked his bare shoulders as he devoured me with kisses. In a flash he'd freed me of my sweatshirt. I arched my back, dying to feel him closer, to feel him inside me, and he pushed me against the wall, pressing his erection against me.

"Oh, Gem," he whispered as I melted.

"What's going on here?!" The gym teacher's voice boomed through the locker room and Evan pulled away from me to face him, his expression suddenly violent.

"Get. Out. Now," he warned, his face an inch away from the man's. "Gemma went home. You gave her a permission slip. Stop looking for her."

The teacher glanced at me and blinked, deep in thought. I sheepishly covered my chest with my arms. Nature hadn't been generous with me as far as that went, but recently I'd been spilling out of my bra. He left the room. A crowd of boys walked in on his heels and my eyes widened.

"Put your shirt on," Evan ordered me. I quickly slipped it on, but one of the boys spotted me in the process and whistled. Evan rushed him and slammed him against the wall before the boy knew what had hit him. "Don't even look at her," he threatened.

"Calm down, bro. I didn't do anything." The boy raised his hands, scared. No one in the room dared get close to Evan.

The locker room door opened and Peter walked in. His smile of victory died the moment he saw me there. "Gemma, what are you doing in here? What's up with your—" He moved closer, studying my eyes. I blinked, afraid the darkness had returned, and he pulled back, confused.

"Pet, I'm fine. Don't worry. We were just leaving."

Evan let go of the boy and picked his shirt up from the floor. "Yeah," Peter replied, staring at Evan's bare chest, "I can see that."

"Let's go, Gemma." Evan took my hand and I squeezed his with both of mine.

"Talk to you later," I told Peter as we left the locker room. Looking deflated, he nodded and disappeared behind the door as it closed after me.

"But it isn't over yet! I have to take pictures for the yearbook. What was all that about a permission slip?" I asked Evan, following him down the hall.

"I'm taking you away. They'll survive."

"Away? But where?"

"Where no one can disturb us." Evan stopped and pulled me against him. "I want to be alone with you," he whispered in my ear. "I can't stay away from you any longer."

My knees trembled from the desire his warm, sensual voice aroused in me. "Okay," I murmured, at the mercy of his spell.

He let me get my things from my locker before dragging me out of the school, where he took my hand again and led me to his car. I got into the big BMW, my heart pounding. I had made love with Evan a thousand times, but the desire I could see in his eyes sent an electric current through me, melting me. Two fires were poised to merge and spread, and the anticipation was as scorching hot as the air separating them. *When I Was Your Man* by Bruno Mars was playing on the radio. As we drove off, Evan lifted my hand and kissed my palm, taking his eyes off the road to look at me. It was one of the gestures I'd missed most when he was in Hell, and a smile spontaneously blossomed on my lips.

"Now would you mind telling me what got into you back there in the locker room?" I'd felt the wall shudder when Evan slammed the boy against it. I hoped someone had taken him to the nurse's office.

Evan looked at me and kissed my palm again. "You're mine," he said, looking me in the eye.

"I think everyone already knows that," I joked. After all, the guy hadn't done anything wrong. Evan's reaction had been a bit harsh, and yet part of me was smiling at how he'd defended my honor. He'd been jealous because I was stripped down to my bra in front of a bunch of other boys. I recalled how his back muscles had tautened when he was holding the kid against the wall, and for a second I got lost in the memory.

"Hey." I shook myself out of my thoughts and realized Evan was staring at me. "You with me?"

"What is it?" I asked, worried, quickly lowering the visor to check my face in the mirror. "Are my eyes okay? Is something wrong with me again?"

Evan laughed. "No, Gemma. There's nothing wrong, believe me." His eyes slid down my body, stopping on my miniskirt. I was wearing over-the-knee socks, but my thighs were bare. "I was just admiring how sexy you are in that outfit. I'm jealous of my own eyes, because they can explore you while my poor hands are forced to stay on the wheel."

His impatience made me smile. "We're almost there, Evan. In a matter of minutes they'll be able to touch me all they want."

He rested his hand between my thighs and when I slowly opened them he slipped it beneath my skirt and stroked my underwear with his thumb. I held my breath, my heart skipping a beat, and a wave of heat flowed like lava to the spot where he was touching me.

"I'm going to do a lot more than that," he said, his gaze brimming with promises.

My body trembled. When he stared at me, Evan never hid his desire for me. *He wanted me.* He wanted me to be his. At every moment. He never got enough. Neither did I. We were hungry for each other's vital essence.

The car stopped outside our hideaway, the house on the lake. I reached over to open the door, but Evan put out a hand and stopped me. "Aren't we going in?" I asked, confused.

"No, it's snowing. Let's stay here. Have some alone time." Evan raised an eyebrow and leaned in to kiss me. His lips still on mine, he climbed over the gearshift and sat down beside me on my seat. He was so close it made me tremble. I slipped my knee between his legs to entwine mine with his. Evan gazed at me tenderly, the creases under his eyes driving me wild, and swept the hair off my face. My lips were so close to his I could smell the scent of his breath.

"People seem to interrupt us nonstop," I murmured, impulsively raising my chin to kiss his lips.

"No one will do it here," he assured me. He kissed me back, gently brushing his tongue against mine.

Just months ago, I'd been afraid an Angel could never succumb to his carnal desires, that it was forbidden to him. Even if that had been true, it wouldn't have mattered to Evan. Together we had explored the universe, losing ourselves and rediscovering the light. Every time.

"Evan, will you ever get tired of risking everything for me?"

"I've already broken all the rules I know of to be with you, and if I discover more I'll break those too."

"Will it always be true? Even if I—" He rested his finger on my lips, keeping me from going on, but I took his hand and lowered it. "Even if I get lost during the transformation?"

He swallowed and looked me straight in the eye. "Then I'll find you and bring you back." He slid his hand down my nape and rested his forehead against mine. I knew his outer confidence was only a mask and that just beneath the surface hid the fear it might actually happen.

"I'm afraid I was what set you off in the locker room," I confessed bitterly.

Evan chuckled and stroked my hair. "The only fault you have is being so beautiful it made me lose my mind. Your power didn't drive me to go at the kid, Gemma. If it had, I would know it. I've *always* felt the urge to kill anyone who gets close to you. You don't know how many times I've been on the verge of doing it. Especially with your friend Peter. I'm an Angel of Death, Gemma. It's an innate impulse. When those guys walked in and saw you half-naked, I . . . I lost it. Forgive me."

"Don't feel bad." I smiled and kissed him, holding him tight. "I like it when you fight for me," I admitted as the radio whispered the notes of *Young and Beautiful* by Lana Del Rey. I thought back to when I'd heard it in that same car on the way home from the long journey that had given me back my great love. After all the hardships and challenges, he was still there, supporting me, protecting me. *Loving me.* My future was uncertain, but there was one thing I had no doubt about: he would always be there.

"Think it's wise to skip school to be here?" he asked me suddenly.

"In my future there are Witches, a horde of celestial creatures dead set on killing me, and it's highly likely I'm going to become a plague to humanity. I don't care if it isn't wise to be here."

Evan leaned over and buried his nose in my hair, speaking in my ear. "I meant being here with me."

"I'm not afraid of you. I never have been."

"I'm the one who's afraid of me and what I might do to you, if you only . . ." he whispered, staring steadily at my lips.

"You don't need my permission," I replied, at the mercy of my emotions, and Evan kissed me passionately.

"It's cramped in here. Are you comfortable?"

"I'm fine," I murmured. He shifted and straddled me to leave me more room. "Do you ever think about your Ferrari?" I asked out of the blue. It had ended up in the water below the bridge after our accident. Ginevra could have gotten it back or given him a new one, but he didn't want her to. "You know, I have to admit I do miss it myself sometimes."

"Me too. But then I remember we couldn't do this in it." He reached out and the seat swung back. I laughed from fright and rested a hand on Evan's chest as he laughed too. A silence fell between us and my eyes found his. How was it possible to love someone so much? To the point that my heart ached every time I looked at him? Like this, with him on top of me, his arms extended to avoid crushing me and the dog tag dangling from his neck, he was more handsome than ever. Suddenly the distance felt unbearable. I wanted to have him closer, to meld with him. I pulled him to me as the notes of *All of Me* filled the car.

Recognizing the song, he looked at me and smiled, whispering the words against my skin like he'd done in my dream when we'd made love immersed in the magic of the colorful paints. *What would I do without your smart mouth? Drawing me in, and you kicking me out. You've got my head spinning, no kidding, I can't pin you down. What's going on in that beautiful mind? I'm your magical mystery ride. And I'm so dizzy, don't know what hit me, but I'll be all right. My head's underwater but I'm breathing fine. You're crazy and I'm out of my mind.* His hands slid down me, slowly exploring my body, his voice caressing my neck. I closed my eyes, swept away by emotion, and his lips touched my ear, sending a thousand shivers through me.

Give your all to me. I'll give my all to you. You're my end and my beginning, even when I lose I'm winning. I wrapped my arms around his neck and pulled him against me, erasing the distance between us. My hands made their way under his shirt and pushed it up to caress every muscle in his firm abdomen. He straightened up, grabbed it behind his head and pulled it off, refocusing his attention on me. Taking off my sweatshirt, he swiftly unhooked my bra. My heart pounded at the touch of his hot body against mine, skin against skin, as the snowflakes brushed against the car windows, peeking in at us.

"Want to make love with me?" he whispered against my skin.

"Every second," I said softly.

His hand slipped beneath my skirt. Suddenly it was very hot, and not because the heater was on. I unbuttoned his jeans and lowered them, grabbing his behind to move him closer. He held me tight and rubbed his erection against me, making me melt.

"Oh, Evan . . ." I whispered, intoxicated.

He pulled off my underwear. "Say it again," he whispered in ecstasy. "Say my name. Tell me you want me."

"I want you, Evan. I want you inside me." I slid my hands into his boxers, pushed them down and clasped his firm buttocks. He parted my legs with his knee and I arched my back, offering myself to him. Sensing my need, he entered me, drawing a moan from me and then another as he kissed my neck, my shoulder, my breast. I surrendered to him completely, to his lips that sent hot tingles all through my body, to his ragged breathing that mingled with mine, to the heat, all our own, as the forest all around us turned white.

His hand gripped my arm, his fingers grasping my hair tie and pulling it tight as though wanting to tear it off me. I sank my nails into his skin and he accelerated his pace, thrusting harder to fuse with me, filling my entire being with quivers.

"Stay with me, Gem," he begged, rubbing his forehead, damp with perspiration, against my chin.

"Forever," I promised. No transformation would stifle our love. Evan gripped me tighter and his heat flooded my body as he climaxed inside me. He kissed me passionately and trapped my lip between his teeth. I moaned against his mouth, reaching ecstasy, and our breathing became one.

Evan rested his cheek against mine and cradled me in his arms as I wrapped my legs around his waist to stay connected to him. "Stay inside me, Evan," I begged, demanding from him a promise I desperately hoped I would be able to keep myself. Whatever his answer was, though, it would be a lie, because the choice wasn't up to him. Still, it was a lie we both needed.

He looked at me, his dark eyes probing mine, and swept the hair from my face. "Forever."

13

A SOLDIER OF DEATH

"April thirteenth," Evan whispered in my ear as I drew a heart on the fogged-up glass.

"Huh?" I turned to look at him, confused.

"My birthday. It's April thirteenth."

"Oh, so that explains it." I pretended not to be interested in the fact that, after my countless requests, he'd finally told me.

"Explains what, pray tell?"

I shrugged, keeping him in suspense. "You're an Aries."

"If we consider Western astrology, yes, I am an Aries. So what? Does that tell you anything?"

"It tells me everything!" I burst out, amused.

"I didn't know you believed in astrology."

I laughed. "Actually, I don't. I was just kidding."

"Ah, all right. And, just out of curiosity, what are Aries normally like?"

I ran my hand down his arm to his tattoo. "Brave . . . romantic, and also very protective," I stated, still drawing the heart on the glass with my other hand.

Evan reached out and finished my drawing, writing our combined name in it.

Gevan.

"I don't need a horoscope to know you're all those things and much more," he whispered when he was done.

"Yours is a fire sign," I continued. I, on the other hand, was an earth sign, which was why I was so pensive.

"All good qualities, basically." He raised an eyebrow, looking cocky.

"Don't get your hopes up. Aries are also very hotheaded and incredibly stubborn."

"Me? Hotheaded?"

"Says the guy who just beat up another guy for merely looking at his girlfriend."

"He would always be possessive of her because she was his."

"She was," I said softly, looking into his eyes, "and forever would be."

Evan's hungry gaze slid down my bare body as he touched me with his fingertips. "She couldn't blame him. She was naked in that locker room and no one else had permission to look at her."

"She didn't want anyone except him to look at her."

Evan rested his forehead against mine and sighed. "And yet he was desperate," he confessed, his voice trembling.

"Why?" I asked. I slid my hand into his hair and made him look at me.

"Because he was desperately in love with her. I have a desperate need of you, Gem."

I closed my eyes and kissed his lips, losing myself in him. I knew what was hidden in his sweet declaration: fear. It continued to surface, haunting us like a ghost. Deep in my heart I hoped our love—born and raised amid trials and tribulations—could also survive this, the hardest of all ordeals. "No one can tell us what the future holds. Day after day, we need to live in the present, always hoping we'll have another tomorrow together," I murmured, quoting something Evan had said to me some time before.

He recognized it and chuckled. "Wait." He pulled his phone out of his jeans pocket. "I want to take a picture of this moment." Sliding his arm under my neck, he put his face next to mine and gazed at me for a moment, then snapped the shot. Eternal moments of fleeting bliss.

Evan and I stayed there in each other's arms for hours, listening to music as snow drifted through the branches like little sprites who'd come down from the sky to spy on us. We talked about our baby, about the Witches who'd invaded our everyday lives, about Devina who'd never stopped longing to claim Evan's soul. We talked about Peter and my parents, who continued to worry about me.

At first my father had been against my living with Evan, but no human will could resist the power of a Witch like Ginevra, and she'd convinced him that letting me live with him was the best solution, especially for the baby. My mother was overjoyed to see me smiling again thanks to Evan. She was fine with my going to live with him on the condition that I stopped by to see them or called them every day. And that I finished high school, naturally. I lived up to my word and studied hard, though when I did my homework Evan often came to distract me from my obligations and I could never resist him for long.

"What are you thinking about?" Evan asked, noticing my smile.

"How stubborn you are."

"Again with the horoscope? And for the record, I didn't beat up that kid. I just threatened him a little."

"Lucky him. If you'd punched him, I doubt we'd be here talking about it. He'd be in the morgue and you'd be locked up."

"Only you can put me in chains." He winked at me and I punched him on the shoulder.

Evan climbed back into the driver's seat and got dressed, a smile on his lips. I'd promised my folks I would stop by the diner to see them, and judging from the noises my stomach was making, it had gotten late. Evan had yellow streaks on his forehead and along his cheekbones, and I couldn't help but giggle.

"What is it?" he asked, realizing I was laughing at him.

"You'd better clean up your face or my dad might get pissed off at you."

"More than usual?" Evan joked, not even glancing in the mirror as he put the car into reverse. He knew what I was talking about but didn't care.

"What were you just saying about not being stubborn?" I reached out and wiped his cheeks with my fingers. "Besides, my dad likes you. I know he doesn't show it, but that's only because he's always been really protective of me. Despite that, he gave you his blessing."

"I'm afraid he's going to change his mind about me if you show up looking like this." He flipped down the mirror in front of me so I could see myself.

"Oh my God." My eyes bulged and I covered my cheeks with both hands. My cheeks were red, my hair was one big tangle, and the yellow makeup was smeared ear to ear. What had happened between us was practically written all over my face. As Evan set off, I quickly cleaned myself up, combed my hair, and put it up in a ponytail with the hair tie I kept around my arm.

"You still wear it," he murmured, a fiery sadness in his eyes. Ever since we'd discovered why I never parted from my hair tie, Evan had looked at it angrily. I'd noticed how he'd clung to it while we were making love, though.

"I can't help it," I admitted. Putting it on was an unconscious response to my connection to my Dakor. Now that I knew that, I should have stopped wearing it, but it was hard. Looking at Evan, I rested my hand on his and changed the subject. "Can we stop by Adirondack Popcorn? I've got an incredible craving for Moose Crunch."

He relaxed and smiled. "Weren't you drooling over the thought of your mom's potato puff a second ago? Didn't you ask her to make it for you?"

"Sure. I'll eat that too. Why wouldn't I?"

Evan smiled. "Right. Why did I bother asking?"

"Hey, what are you insinuating?" I said, frowning. "It's not my fault I have a healthy appetite!"

"Anyone would already have gained sixty pounds with all you eat," he exclaimed with a grin.

"Shut up. I'm so hungry I could eat you too," I warned, giving him a dirty look.

He pulled up outside the popcorn shop at 2520 Main Street. Next to it was the Cabin Grill, and at the thought of French fries my stomach growled again. I lowered the window and the smell of caramel corn wafted over to me in the car. "Mmm . . . What sweet torture," I said, breathing it in deeply. "Hurry up or I'll make good on my threat."

Evan laughed and got out of the car. I watched him walk into the shop with its wooden façade and display window filled with treats. He came back minutes later with various bags of my favorite flavors of popcorn: peanut, caramel, and chocolate; maple, bourbon, and bacon; and toasted hazelnut.

"You're my angel." I almost ripped them out of his hands and stuffed my mouth like a glutton. "Oh my God," I whispered, closing my eyes. "I'm in heaven." Evan shook his head and chuckled. "Laugh at me all you want—it doesn't matter. I've got these." I clasped the bags to my chest and wolfed down more popcorn as the car headed toward my parents' diner.

"Wait. You've got some crumbs here." He leaned toward me and touched my lip with his thumb. Then he moved closer to kiss me, lingering as though tasting me. "Your mouth is like the nectar of the gods. It goes straight to my head."

"It's the popcorn. I told you it was good." Evan laughed again but then his expression slowly turned grim. "What is it?" I asked, worried I'd upset him somehow. "Sorry, I really am being a glutton."

"You're adorable," he reassured me.

"Then why do you look so serious? Is something the matter?"

"No, it's nothing. I was just concentrating, that's all." He looked at me with a little smile. "Mind if we take a quick detour?" He turned right, heading away from the diner.

"Why?" I asked with alarm. "Has something happened?"

"Nothing you need to worry about." The car came to a sudden halt. Evan turned to look at me and his eyes turned a silvery gray. A shiver ran down my back. He'd transformed.

"I'll be back in a sec."

I nodded and watched him get out of the car. He walked around to the other side, his eyes on me the whole time. No one on the street could see him in his angelic form, but I could. He stopped on the front walk of a house, took one last look at me, and disappeared.

I raised more caramel corn to my mouth, one piece after another, completely on edge. I didn't want to know where he'd gone. With me he was always so sweet, which made it hard to accept that inside him was a Soldier of Death.

Suddenly, Evan materialized in the driver's seat, making me jump. "That was fast," I said. He pressed his lips together, still serious. As he started the engine, someone inside the house screamed and I whipped my head in that direction. Evan switched on the radio so I wouldn't hear. A shiver turned my blood to ice as I realized what had happened. "You just killed someone," I murmured, petrified.

"Sorry," he said sadly. "For some orders we have very little advance notice. I didn't have time to drop you off and come back, and I didn't want to leave you alone. If it's any consolation, he was elderly and passed on quickly."

I nodded and blinked, shaken. For him it was so normal, but I still hadn't gotten used to his dark side. How could Evan accept mine? Maybe he wouldn't be able to either. I leaned back in my seat and an icy silence fell over us.

14

HEAVEN AND HELL

"Here you are at last!" My mom came up to me and gave me a big hug. "I hope my Squirrelicue is hungry, because I made her favorite dishes!"

"I could eat a horse," I assured her. The funny part was that it was true.

"Hello, Evan. Please have a seat." My mom took him by the arm and led him to his chair, casting me a look of approval. She'd always liked Evan in spite of everything. "Give me a second. I'll be right back."

"I'll come with you," I said. "That way I can say hi to Dad."

"I'll wait for you here," Evan said.

I followed my mom into the back and gave my dad a hug. "Careful, you'll get custard all over you," he warned, but I didn't care. "You here alone?" he asked warily.

"I'm with Evan, and our friends will be here any minute."

Dad grumbled something as Mom burst with enthusiasm. "Great! I'll go get the tables ready." She adored not only Ginevra but also her Sisters.

Our Sisters, suggested a voice inside me, but I instantly banished the thought. I helped Mom take out the food she'd made for Evan and me. She didn't know he didn't eat our food, but I would polish off all of it before she even noticed.

"Oh, the redheaded girl is already here," Mom told me.

Strange, I hadn't told Faith we'd be there. I looked up, but instead of Faith I saw Devina. "*Get away from him now,*" I ordered her telepathically. She turned toward me and smiled, resting her arm on Evan's shoulder.

"Why is it that Ginevra's cousin is so attached to Evan? Are they related?"

"No, she's a bitch, that's all," I grunted. The dish in my hands trembled. My mother shot me a concerned look; I didn't usually talk like that in front of her. A couple near me suddenly raised their voices and the girl slapped her boyfriend across the face. *It was my fault.* My anger had extended to them. I had to be more careful. I risked losing control.

"Don't worry, Squirrelicue. Evan only has eyes for you," Mom reassured me. "I have to go help your father, but I'll be back soon."

I took a deep breath to calm my nerves and went to sit next to Evan, but he grabbed me and made me sit on his lap. "You'll be more comfy here," he whispered, completely ignoring Devina. I rubbed my head against him and inside me clear skies returned. Evan was my beacon. He always managed to guide me through the darkness.

"You two are disgusting," Devina complained, leaning back in her chair.

"Either that, or you're dying of jealousy," I said insolently.

She snorted. "Don't delude yourself. I'm only here for the food. Your mother's cooking is divine."

"You have powers. Use them to cook for yourself."

"I like being served."

"Then here. Feed your face with this." I rudely shoved a dish at her and focused on Evan, kissing him sensually. Without objecting, he kissed me back as Devina watched. In her presence, Evan was always very affectionate with me—partly to reassure me, partly to make her understand that he was all mine.

"A-hem . . ." *My father.* "Let's not overdo it, okay?"

Devina smiled. She must have lured him out front. I shot her a lethal look and pulled away from Evan. "Sorry, Dad," I murmured, sitting in my seat.

"I brought you fries with black pepper, just how you like them."

"Thanks! You're the best." I got up to kiss his cheek and he calmed down.

"You're still my little girl. Don't forget it."

"I won't." I squeezed his arm affectionately and he disappeared into the back.

Just then, Ginevra and Simon appeared in the door along with four Witches: Safria, who had amazing violet-blue eyes that stood out against her black skin; Nausyka, with her silver hair and eyes of ice; Zhora—whom many of the Sisters called Suri—with her short mahogany-colored hair and incredible emerald-green eyes; and finally Camelia, who on that occasion was showing off both light- and dark-blue hair.

It must have been strange for them to be there, keeping their instincts under control. Maybe they considered it a game, a challenge to themselves that they didn't want to lose. And yet I saw the way their eyes caressed the other customers as though they were all potential prey. Everyone around us was fascinated by our group. If they'd been normal people dressed in the Witches' sexy, extravagant outfits, there would have been an outbreak of gossip in our town, but they charmed everyone. They were breathtakingly beautiful.

The Witches praised my mom's cooking, polishing it off as though they hadn't eaten for months, and she was so enthusiastic she kept filling up their plates, proud of their constant compliments. Once again, Ginevra assured me her Sisters wouldn't put the mortals' lives at risk. They were only there to spend some time with us and protect me if need be. Some of the Drusas, in the form of panthers, had stayed to watch over the prisoners in the dungeons, while other Witches had stayed with Sophìa because, like it or not, the evil in the world couldn't take a vacation. Their work had to go on.

"Gemma, you absolutely have to try this," Camelia told me. "It's *divine*!"

Her excitement made me smile. "It's all yours. I grew up with my mom's potato puff. I know what it tastes like."

"Don't you want even a little bit?" she asked sadly, almost as though I'd told her I didn't want to be her friend.

"Okay, I'll take some." A radiant smile lit up her face and I couldn't help but return it.

Ginevra squeezed my hand under the table and for a moment it felt like it was just her and me in the room. I knew exactly what she was feeling. She was happy to be there with her Sisters. *With me.* It must have been so hard for her to choose to leave them. I felt the bond and I hadn't even transformed yet. They already treated me like a Sister. People were spellbound by them. They looked at them, their eyes brimming with admiration, as though they were princesses. And maybe they actually were—they were princesses of darkness. And soon I would be one of them. A part of me that I tried to keep hidden wanted to be part of it, but then I remembered that the price was being separated from Evan. I would never be willing to pay that price.

The line between good and evil had grown so tenuous it was hard to tell them apart. The Witches were evil . . . yet they wanted to protect me. The Màsala, on the other hand, had done nothing but try to kill me. Where was my place? Who was I supposed to defend myself from? Sometimes I no longer knew.

And then there was Evan, there were Simon, Ginevra . . . and Drake. They were sacrificing everything for me. They'd protected me from the Subterraneans and the Witches, from both warring factions. It had always been a battle for souls between them, and now they both wanted mine—the Màsala, to send it to Heaven, where Evan and I would never be able to see each other again, and the Witches, to send it to Hell, where *maybe* there was still a chance for us.

Noticing I was in a daze, Evan squeezed my hand. I looked into his eyes and every doubt vanished. We were caught at the midpoint of the battle between good and evil. That was where our love was. Nothing else mattered.

The candles cast quivering lights and shadows that danced across the walls. The water in the tub was hot and the little cascade flowed from the rock with a sound that soothed my spirit.

Evan had gone on a mission to the other side of the world. I'd gone home with Simon and Ginevra, but then he too had been called to duty. Even with everything happening around us, they were Soldiers and their orders came before everything else . . . except me.

I smiled, thinking of how affectionately Evan and Simon protected me. Two Soldiers of Death battling for a mortal soul. A soul everyone was vying for. When it was all over, who would it belong to?

To me, I promised myself. That was the only way I could stay together with Evan. I moved closer to the little waterfall and let the water run over my head, filling me with its warmth, relaxing my every muscle. I moved my head to the right, then to the left. Suddenly I sensed a presence in the room and my eyes shot open.

"You going to stand there watching me?" I asked provocatively without turning around, my eyes on the rock wall.

Evan came over and rested his hands on the tub. "That was one of my options." I turned and looked into his eyes, which were as gray as the storm of desire that I knew raged inside him. God . . . Why did he stare at me like that? It drove me wild.

I moved closer and raised myself slightly, dangerously close to his face. "Or," I whispered against his mouth, "we could explore the other options."

Evan swallowed and his hand stroked my wet side. "I agree," he whispered, mesmerized by my lips. I grazed them just barely against his, igniting his desire, but instantly pulled back, toying with him. "Option one: I stand here and watch you take a bath for me," he murmured.

"The idea sounds enticing," I said playfully, still provoking him. I'd realized that I loved arousing him.

"Option two: I get undressed and take a bath with you. It *has* been a long day, you know . . ." He raised an eyebrow, his expression telling.

"I think I'll choose option three."

"Which is . . . ?"

I smiled and grabbed him by the shirt. "The one where I pull you in still dressed!"

"Wait, stop!" But it was too late. He emerged from the water, a saucy smile on his lips, and slicked back his hair. "You're getting mischievous! You want war?"

I shrieked when Evan lunged at me, splattering the floor. I tried to escape, but he grabbed me by the waist and pinned me down beneath him. "Now you're my prisoner."

I challenged his eyes of ice. "And what will you do with me?" I teased him again, moving my lips closer and then pulling them back.

Evan cupped my head in his hand and kissed my chin passionately. "I'll take you to heaven."

I moaned when he nibbled my shoulder, sending an electric charge surging through my entire body. Clinging to him, I hurriedly pulled off his wet shirt and unbuttoned his jeans, flinging them to the floor. We were naked, immersed in the hot water, one against the other. His hands moved over me, leaving shivers on my skin. All the while devouring me with kisses, he grabbed me by the bottom and pulled me astride him. My core throbbed with desire; I squeezed my legs around Evan's hips to feel his erection against me. Lifting me up slightly, he penetrated me, staying motionless, holding me tight. "Oh, Gem. Why do you do this to me?" he whispered, clasping one of my breasts in his strong, warm hand. He stroked my nipple with his thumb and I felt it stiffen at his touch. He kissed it and rested his head on my chest. "You break down all my defenses," he murmured in desperation.

I cupped his face in my hands and kissed it, taking my fill of him. He was inside me, satiating me, completing me, like he always did. Grabbing the hair at the nape of his neck, I moved against him, pursuing the pleasure only he could give me.

"You'll take me to hell," he grunted, letting desire overwhelm him. He grabbed my buttocks and squeezed me tighter, thrusting with tender force. Our cheeks brushed together, our foreheads touched, our lips sought each other. We were in another world, a bubble all our own, intoxicated by the love that united us. It inundated us, touching our souls.

He bit my lip, panting in my ear, and a quiver made my heart tremble. I clung to Evan and a cry escaped me as I peaked. Evan gripped my bottom tighter and climaxed inside me with a groan roughened by desire. He held me tight, rubbing his cheek against mine. "You are my goddess," he whispered, his lips brushing my ear.

I smiled and kissed his shoulder. "Didn't you just say I would take you to hell?" I left more kisses on his neck, moving down to his chest, following the scars.

Evan nodded. "But I promised you heaven, remember?"

"You kept your promise, then, because I was just there."

15

DUSTY MEMORIES

"Why didn't you tell me right away when your birthday was?" I asked Evan. We were still in the tub, the soft light barely illuminating the room. He was behind me, stroking my back with a sponge, immersed in a cloud of white foam.

"It wasn't important," he replied, his voice suddenly sad. "So much time has gone by since I celebrated it that I barely remembered it."

"Tell the truth, Evan."

He remained silent, running the sponge over my neck before answering. "That was also the day my mother died." He dropped the sponge and caressed my arms, soothing the shiver that his confession had triggered. "There was a chance for me to see her," he continued in a whisper, "to say goodbye to her the way I hadn't been able to before I died. But I was out on a mission. Her soul left her body and I could have spoken to her, but I wasn't there. And so she passed to the other side. I missed my only chance."

"I'm sorry," I murmured in a tiny voice. A tear slid down my face. I should have realized there had to be a reason he hadn't wanted to tell me. My stubbornness had hurt him.

"You couldn't have known. Besides, like I said, it's been a long time. It's not important any more." I turned to look at him and nodded. He wiped a tear from my face and smiled. "I don't want to see you cry," he warned me. "Let's think of the present. It's much more . . . comforting." He raised an eyebrow and pulled me back against him, kissing me tenderly, then took some shampoo and applied it to my hair, his strong fingers gently massaging my scalp.

I closed my eyes, surrendering to the pleasurable sensation. "I like taking baths with you."

"I'm better than a spa," he boasted. "Full service." He winked at me and smiled.

"Will you visit me tonight?" I looked at him hopefully. Every time his gray eyes probed mine, I lost myself.

"I don't think I can. I'm going on a mission and won't be back in time. Sorry."

"Oh . . . " A bitter sigh escaped me. "So you'll be gone all night long?"

"And all day too, I think."

"I'll have nightmares." That always happened when he was gone. When he was in my dreams, he drove off all my demons.

Evan tucked my hair behind my ear. "I'll ask Ginevra to stay with you."

"No, there's no need. I'm safe now. I can handle a bad dream. Let's let her enjoy a little free time."

He nodded, though I wasn't sure he would listen to me, and asked, "Is there something I can do for you?"

I already had the answer to that. "Actually, there is."

"I'm all ears."

"Would you go up to the attic with me?"

Evan looked puzzled. The twins were in the attic, still imprisoned in the carbonado cage.

"I don't want to do anything rash," I reassured him.

"Of course not. Otherwise you wouldn't need to ask—you would have just gone and done it."

"Very funny."

"What's so important up there?"

"Something I wanted to get yesterday, but then they attacked me and—"

"When you say 'something' you mean a book, I presume."

I shrugged, holding back a smile. "You know me well."

"Don't you have two of them on the nightstand?" Evan was probably a little scared to take me there—not because of what the twins might do to me but because of what the carbonado might awaken in me.

"I've already finished those," I said, thinking about the series on aliens that I'd left in Evan's room. I bit my lip and batted my eyelashes.

"All right, I'll take you up there. Otherwise, knowing you, you'll probably go on your own."

I clapped my hands happily. I couldn't wait to have my *Jane Eyre* back. If I had to be alone that night, Rochester would keep me company.

We climbed out of the tub and got dressed. A big black panther was guarding the door and I smiled when I saw the red patch on its paw. It was Devina and she must have heard everything. Picking up on that thought, she flicked her tail at me and walked off with a low growl. *He was mine.* Sooner or later she would get it through her head.

Oblivious to our little battle to mark our territory, Evan took my hand and led me to the trapdoor that went to the attic. He opened it, went up the ladder first, and peered into the darkness. Pulling himself up, he offered me his hand to help me up. The lightbulb was gone—I'd made it explode—and outside a cold darkness had already fallen. Evan opened his palm and a sphere of light came to life, dimly illuminating the room. *Angel fire.* I stood there staring at it, almost hypnotized by its silvery glow. How could I be so fascinated by something that was such a serious danger to me? Once I transformed, that fire—so pure and radiant—would be the only weapon capable of killing me.

My heart beat faster. No. The energy making me quiver was coming from elsewhere. I followed my instinct and turned toward the cage at the far end of the attic. The two children were sitting on the floor, leaning back against the bars with their heads lolling forward as though sleeping . . . or dead. I truly hoped that wasn't the case. That cage was our only hope of living a peaceful life during our last remaining months. As though he'd sensed my thoughts, Evan squeezed my hand. "Well? Where do we start looking?"

"I-it should be over here," I stammered. "I don't understand. It was right here." Evan stepped forward and helped me look through the storage boxes as the energy that filled the room continued to prickle me. Maybe going up there hadn't been such a good idea. Fighting the instinct to turn toward the cage, I continued to rummage around.

"Looking for this?" asked two hoarse voices.

"Don't turn around," Evan warned me between clenched teeth.

"It must be important if you came all the way up here to get it," one of the Devas continued. Pages rustled and I turned around. The little boy stared at me. *He had my book.*

"Give it back." I slowly stood up and looked him in the eye.

"Why don't you come get it?" he challenged me, his voice eerie. I moved a step closer.

"Gemma, no!" Evan blocked my way, facing me. I remained calm. "I'll take care of this." He raised his hand, bending the air to his will . . . but nothing happened. He frowned with frustration and the Deva grinned, clutching my book in his hands. Evan's power couldn't go past the barrier.

"I'm bored in here. Maybe I'll tear out some pages. It might be fun."

I clenched my fists.

"Gemma, forget about it. Let's get out of here!"

The little boy ripped the corner of one of the pages and Evan shot across the room. "I wouldn't provoke her if I were you," he warned, but the boy boldly ripped out the rest of the page.

"No!" I screamed. My dark power hit him full force, slamming him back against the bars. The sound of the paper being ripped had torn my heart.

"Gemma, that's enough," Evan shouted, rushing back to me. "I have it. I've got the book." He showed me the volume and the torn page, and I blinked, finally breathing again. The Deva fell to the floor of the cage with a thud and didn't get up.

"Let's get out of here." Evan put his arm around my shoulder and kissed my forehead. I nodded and looked around. It looked like a hurricane had torn through the room. Had I done that? A shudder of terror ran through me at the thought that such a destructive power lurked inside me.

We reached the trapdoor, where the panther with a red splotch on its paw awaited us. If she'd been in her human form just then she would have had a smug smile on her face. But I didn't want to be like that. Like her. *Like them.* I didn't want to destroy things . . . or people, by stealing their souls. I held Evan's hand tight, less and less sure I would remain myself.

"Why does this book mean so much to you?" Evan asked me as I tried to carefully tape the page back in. He stopped me and without saying a word used his powers to repair it. I stared at him, amazed, and he winked at me. "Well? Why is it so important? Was it a present from an admirer?" he joked, but I remained serious, clutching the book to my chest.

"My grandmother gave it to me. See?" I opened it and showed him the first page, which had her name on it. *Gemma.*

"Oh, I thought that was you," Evan said.

"It is, but not only. We wrote it together when I was eight. She said that that way the book would be ours. The margins are full of notes, reflections, questions, thoughts . . ."

"Now I understand."

"There are two kinds of books: ones you can't wait to finish and ones you wish would never end."

Seeing how much I loved the story, Evan had once given me his copy of *Jane Eyre*, a first edition from 1847, which I took special care of. Nevertheless, not even that priceless volume was as precious to me as my own copy, which was irreplaceable.

"Thank you for fixing it."

"Well, you were the one who got it back," Evan joked, but a second later his expression darkened. "You're getting stronger and stronger."

"Does it scare you?"

"The only thing that scares me is the thought of losing you."

"That's not going to happen," I promised, taking his hand to reunite our tattoo. "*Samvicaranam,*" I whispered, and he rested his forehead against mine.

"*Samyodhanam,*" he murmured against my lips.

Stay together. Fight together.

"I'll find myself and you'll be there too. I swear it."

Evan looked at me. He wanted to believe me, wanted to with all his heart, yet part of him couldn't. So how could I be so sure?

"I have to go now," he said softly, and I nodded, still shaken by all those emotions. "Promise me you won't go back up there."

"I wouldn't even think of it," I reassured him.

"A whole day without you. How will I live?"

"How will I not die?"

Evan hugged me to him again, his dark eyes transforming, turning to ice. Giving me a kiss on the lips that sent a tingle through me, he vanished, leaving me alone in the silence.

"I wouldn't even think of it," I repeated to myself. But the demon I feared wasn't in the attic.

It was trapped inside me.

16

PARALLEL WORLDS

I wandered through the trees of the snowy forest, wrapped in my long red cloak that stood out against the pure white snow like a drop of blood. Its broad hood covered my head. It was chilly and the night was preparing to slice the air with its sickle of darkness, bringing with it cold and death, because not far away one of its Executioners would claim a soul. Evan was on a mission and wouldn't be there to protect me. I wrapped the cloak around me more tightly, though the devastating cold was not around me but inside me.

The tree trunks stood like silent soldiers, and yet there was something eerie in the air, a sinister shiver that followed me everywhere, as though death were passing by me time and time again.

Someone grabbed my wrist all of a sudden. "You lost, Little Red Riding Hood?" I spun around and Evan was in front of me, his silvery gray eyes shining in the darkness like a wolf's.

"Evan!" I sighed with relief. "What are you doing here? Didn't you have to go on a mission?"

He smiled. "I couldn't stay away from you." He kissed my neck and moved toward me, forcing me to take a step back.

"Orders come first—isn't that your motto?"

"*You* come first—that's my motto." I laughed and returned his insistent kisses.

He pulled back and took me by the hand. "Let's go."

"Where?"

"Someplace warmer, so I can take off your clothes." I laughed and ran with him through the trees. As we passed, the forest shed its white mantle and the lake showed us its shimmering waters. I turned around. Winter had disappeared, leaving in its place a crisp spring night. "Come here, Gemma. It's fun," Evan called out.

My gaze found him on Peninsula Trail, a path that crossed the lake. It was so nice to stroll along it, surrounded by the calm waters. It was like being at the ends of the earth.

"Come back!" I shouted to him. "The water's freezing."

"Come get me!" he dared me.

Sometimes Evan was worse than a little boy. I laughed and took off my shoes, pulled up the hem of my cloak and dress, and walked down the path barefoot. It was the long dress Ginevra had lent me for my journey through Hell, though I couldn't remember putting it on . . .

The water rose to my ankles, the current tickling my skin. "Here I am! I made it! Happy?"

Evan grabbed my waist and smiled. "I'm always happy to see you, Peachskin."

"What?" Why had he called me that? I looked up and found myself staring into Ahrec's ink-black eyes. The Unholy Soul smiled at me, his tiny teeth jagged like a shark's. *Was I in Hell?* I backed up, frightened, but my foot slipped on the mossy rocks and I fell into the shallow water.

"Come. I'll help you cross the river." *The river.* I had to follow the river to find Evan. Ahrec held out his hand but I let out a scream and backed away. I struggled to my feet and the current pulled off my cloak, sweeping it away from the shore.

I turned back, running barefoot along the path. Ahrec suddenly appeared right in front of me. Unable to come to a halt, I tumbled onto him. He tried to restrain me, but I broke free and scratched him hard. Blood splattered my face but instead of stopping I continued to tear at his flesh. My nails were as sharp as a panther's. I slashed open his chest and with a suffocated gurgle Ahrec fell to his knees.

His eyes had gone back to normal. "Well done, Peachskin." He fell face-down into the water. A dark red pool spread out around his body and the current dragged him away. I thought of my cloak and stared at my hands, trembling. They were covered with his blood but it wasn't black, like the blood of the Damned. It was red. I washed them obsessively in the river, getting my long dress wet. What had I done? I ran away without turning back, wanting to return to the car, but I couldn't remember where I'd parked it.

I spotted the hideaway in the distance and my heart leapt with joy. As I looked over my shoulder, frightened by a dark presence I continued to sense, I crashed into someone. I looked up, dazed by the impact. It was Evan. "It's you!" I threw my arms around him.

"Hey, calm down. Why are you so on edge?"

"Where have you been?"

"On a mission. I told you I had an execution order. But I'm here now." He stroked my head and I let myself breathe. I looked at our hideaway on the shore. Through the window I glimpsed the glow of the fireplace, defying the darkness. Smoke rose from the chimney. I'd thought he was alone there, but from the house came the roar of a group of panthers that pierced the night.

"Aren't we going inside?" I asked Evan, puzzled.

He kissed me on the lips. "No. Let's spend some alone time," he murmured, stroking my cheek. "Just you, me, and Devina." I leapt back, my heart pounding in my chest, but bumped into someone behind me. I spun around, panting.

Devina smiled and leaned in to kiss me. "He'll be all mine," she whispered against my lips. Her honey-colored eyes challenged me, as narrow as a panther's.

"No!" I shouted, taking another step back and continuing to stare at them. Evan took her hand and led her to our hideaway. A tear slid down my face when the door closed, leaving me all alone.

I turned and started running, hoping the darkness would ease my pain, but I felt a strange presence at my heels. Soon the air was full of hostile, deafening hisses. I stopped, exhausted, as the air all around me shimmered and took shape. It was then that I recognized it.

A Pariah.

I knew I couldn't pay attention to it or it would absorb my soul, but I couldn't help it. Its evanescent figure hypnotized me, circling me slowly, as though in a dance. Whispers filled my head. It wasn't alone. I looked around and a group of them emerged from the thick of the forest. Though I tried to resist their call, I was mesmerized, at the mercy of some dark power. The first Pariah quivered, excited by my interest. My yearning overpowered me and I reached out my hand.

"DON'T TOUCH IT!"

I woke with a start, Ginevra's voice still echoing through my mind. Raising my hands to my head, I took a deep breath, still shaken. *Just another bad dream.* Another horribly bad dream.

The house was quiet. I looked around. Through the half-opened door came a shaft of light that barely illuminated the darkness. In the hall, a panther stood guard outside the door.

Everything was normal. *Except for the fact that my life was a horror movie,* I thought. I pushed off the heavy covers and headed to the bathroom. Evan hadn't come back yet. I went to the sink and rinsed my face. Suddenly I had a strange sensation: I felt drawn to the mirror and slowly raised my face. In the reflection, my eyes captivated me. They were dark and powerful . . . as though they weren't mine. My heart skipped a beat. There was no trace of their whites—they were two deep pools summoning me, the eyes of the demon within me. Suddenly I wanted to free it. I wanted to touch it. I wanted to *be it* and absorb its power. I reached out, rested my fingers on the mirror . . . and they sank into it. Looking at them, confused, I noticed that the black eyes in the mirror continued to stare at me as dark bulgy streaks slithered across my face like snakes. It was the demon absorbing *me*, absorbing my energy. Frightened, I tried to pull my hand back but couldn't. Something was blocking me. The darkness wanted me for its own. The streaks on my reflection grew darker and darker. It was going to annihilate me!

Panicking, I tried once more to pull back my hand and the mirror cracked. I tugged on my wrist with my other hand and finally jerked my hand free, shattering the mirror into a thousand pieces. As I stared at my bloody fingers, a voice hissed through the silence: *"You cannot escape me."*

My body went cold. *It was my voice.* I spun around. In front of me was another me, in flesh and blood. Terror trapped the air in my lungs. "I'm you," she hissed, her black eyes pools of evil.

"No!" I screamed.

A slow smile spread over her lips. "It's too late. He's inside you. *He's growing!*" A hiss broke the silence and a serpent slithered out of her mouth. I jumped back, but the animal darted forward and lunged at me.

My eyes shot open. It had only been a nightmare. It was already daytime. Outside, the sunlight reflecting off the pure white snow was blinding. My heart still beating fast, I suddenly realized my arm was raised, suspended in the air and swaying like a snake hypnotized by a snake charmer. I pulled it down, bewildered, and sat up in bed.

A large panther put its head around the door. It was Anya, with her marvelous eyes of jade. I smiled at her. "Good morning." She gave a little bow, came over, and rubbed her head against my legs. I stroked her and she rose onto her hind legs, trapping me on the bed. She licked my face, which tickled, and I giggled like a little girl when she didn't stop.

"I get it! I get it! It's a good morning for you too." The panther purred and I petted her some more. The sun was already high in the sky. How long had I slept? It didn't really matter. It was Saturday and I wouldn't have to worry about school. Anya walked back to the door and flicked her tail. She wanted me to follow her, but first I had to get ready.

I let her out, closed the door, and headed to the bathroom, avoiding the mirror. All of a sudden I was afraid to look at myself, afraid of the darkness . . . *I was afraid of myself.* It had been a spine-chilling sensation, staring into my own evil-filled eyes. Fear was starting to become a reality and my unconscious was sending me signals. What if I really didn't manage to stay myself? More and more often I'd seen evil possess me and had done nothing to stop it. The power that flowed through me was exhilarating. Evan had always been the one to pull me out of the clutches of darkness. But I could no longer ignore the doubt that had begun to hound me: what if evil really did manage to obliterate me?

I dried my face and looked at myself in the mirror, my heart pounding. My eyes were normal. I sighed with relief. What had I expected to see? In an automatic gesture I let down my hair and put the hair tie around my upper arm. A shudder raised goosebumps on my arms as I remembered the serpent that had crawled out of my mouth. It had been shiny and as black as night.

He's inside you. He's growing, my voice had said.

I touched the scar on my belly and it throbbed. My fingers felt wet and I looked at them. *They were bloody.* Like in my dream. Nervous, I checked the wound. A stream of scarlet trickled from it. I hurriedly cleaned it with some washcloths, opened the medicine cabinet, and took out some cotton, pressing it against my skin until the bleeding stopped. I leaned against the sink, still shaken. Where would all this take me?

I closed the cabinet and jumped at the sight of my reflection. And yet it was just me—not the demon inside me. Was I actually afraid of *myself* now? I brushed my hair, never taking my eyes off my reflection. I needed to overcome my insecurity, otherwise I would never manage to face my future—it would be too frightening. But the more I stared at my eyes, the more I sank into their depths, as if they no longer belonged to me. Suddenly I thought I saw my lips curve in a little smirk of power. My heart skipped a beat.

"Gemma, everything okay?" Ginevra's voice shook me out of those thoughts. "Breakfast is ready. You'd better hurry if you want to find anything left. They're polishing everything off down here!"

"Coming!" I put down my brush, casting a last glance in the mirror. I'd battled Subterraneans and Witches. I'd even battled death. I was strong. But that meant that so was *she*, the other me. Which of the two of us would prevail? The answer wasn't so easy to see any more.

The aromas reached the stairs. Festive chatter filled the living room. Simon wasn't there. He must have been away on a mission too. There were only women in the house. *Witches*, I corrected myself. "What is this, a pajama party?" I asked, joining them in the kitchen. Irony trotted over to me, wagging his tail, and I leaned down to pet him.

"Gemma!" Anya called to me. "Have a seat. We were waiting for you."

I looked at the girls, whose mouths were all full. "That's clear to see," I joked, making them freeze and stare at me with guilty expressions. "Don't worry, I was just kidding. Don't let me stop you."

Anya laughed. "We're definitely not short on food," she assured me. "There's all you could want."

"Oh, fries!" Only Witches would think of having them for breakfast. I immediately ate one, chewing with delight. "Say what you want, but to me this is heaven. It's still a mystery how you guys don't gain an ounce, given everything you eat."

"Look who's talking." Nausyka winked at me. "You should be a blimp by now, given everything *you* eat, but you're still in good shape for someone who's expecting a baby."

I blushed. It was a huge compliment, coming from one of them. "You're one of us, Sister," Camelia said in response to my thoughts. I smiled at her. It was really nice to have them around. They were so closely knit that, in spite of myself, I felt flattered by the thought of being part of their group.

Ginevra picked up on my thought and smiled at me. If I transformed, would I love them all as much as I loved Ginevra? The answer was obvious. *It was already happening.* But I wasn't going to follow them into Hell. So would separating from them be painful?

The answer to that was also clear: never as much as separating from Evan and Ginevra would be.

"Did I miss anything?" Just then, Simon appeared behind me, reminding me that he was also on my list. I would miss him at least as much as I did Drake. I smiled at him and banished my thoughts before the Witches discovered them.

"Take a seat, if you can get near them, but I'm warning you: be careful. They're pretty dangerous when someone eyes their food."

"More dangerous than normal?" Simon joked, pulling his beloved Ginevra to him. "I missed you," he whispered to her, resting his forehead on hers.

I looked away to give them some privacy. A pang in my heart reminded me Evan wouldn't be back until that evening. Who knew where he was or what he was doing? Was he in some distant corner of the world or only miles away? What kind of Souls did he need to help that it was taking him so long? Whoever they were, I was jealous of the time Evan was spending with them instead of me. He was mine and I wanted him all to myself.

"He will be, once you claim him," someone whispered in my ear. I looked at Zhora, surprised she'd heard my thought. Something trembled in my chest. *Desire.* Deep down, I found the idea enticing.

The Witch smiled at me and winked, but Devina, at the back of the room, glared icily at both of us. "Evan will always be *free* to love me," I told Zhora adamantly. "I would never want him to be subjugated to me."

The Witch laughed. Did she not believe it, perhaps? For Simon and Ginevra it had worked.

"Hey, Gemma," Simon put in just then, "I ran into Evan last night. He wanted me to give you this." He held out a piece of paper folded in two. I took it, trembling with emotion as I opened it.

I miss you.
E.

I sighed, butterflies fluttering in my stomach over those three little words that meant the world to me. I missed him to death. My soul was so entwined with his that being apart was always painful.

"Couldn't he have texted you?" Devina said, rolling her eyes. "Did he forget this is the twenty-first century?"

"I think it's so romantic!" Camelia sighed, earning a glare from Devina. "What did I say?!" she protested.

Ignoring them both, I went into the living room, clutching the note to my chest, and stared out the window, where everything was covered with white. It was only one day. What was one day? Still, I missed him terribly. I kept telling myself it would all work out, but actually I was quivering inside. Our future was more uncertain than ever. We had only a few months left. What would become of us?

"Simon, are you going to see him again?" I asked, hoping I could reply to his note.

"Sorry, I don't think so, but he'll be back tonight. Don't tell him I told you, but he was pretty excited about your big date," he admitted, winking at me.

I smiled. Some time before, at the lakeshore, Evan had asked me to the Snowball Hop and I had accepted, despite having less-than-fond memories of the last school dance I'd gone to.

The Winter Carnival games were over, and that night we would crown a king and queen who would officially kick off the dance.

Simon rested his hands on my shoulders. "Everything will go fine. And I don't just mean tonight," he reassured me, reading on my face the fears that tormented me.

"Thanks for being a snitch, then. I'll keep your secret."

He gave me a peck on the forehead and stroked my belly. As he did, the baby kicked. Simon pulled away, his eyes going wide and his face lighting up with joy. "Did you feel that?"

I laughed. "Yes, I felt it. He doesn't do that for everyone, you know—you're one of the privileged few. If you ask me, he already loves you a lot."

"I hope so!" he exclaimed happily. "I intend to teach him all sorts of little tricks."

"Um, what exactly do you have in mind?"

"Being an anxious mother already? Parents can't always know everything," he said, teasing me.

I thought about the little Subterranean boys locked up in the attic and couldn't help but wonder what would become of my son. Would he have to serve Death, like them? Or would he be human? Would good claim him, or evil? Would he even be able to choose between the two? Only time would tell.

Simon's voice interrupted my musings. "Can I ask you something? Why did you ask the Witches for three days after the baby's birth? Why not five—or seven, for that matter?"

"I figured that by then we would have come up with a plan to prevent the transformation. I couldn't ask for months—that would have been too long. Once the baby was born and taken to safety, three days seemed like more than enough time to put our plan into action. Besides, Ariel managed!"

"Who?"

"The Little Mermaid. In three days she got her voice back, defeated the evil witch, and won the prince's love."

"You're forgetting that your evil witch is the devil and you aren't in a Disney movie."

"Right." I sighed with resignation. "I'm more like an episode of *Final Destination*," I joked, a bitter smile on my face.

"Gemma. I want you to know I've never thought what I said the other night. I was being controlled by some power that *forced* me to say it."

"It was me." I looked down. "That power came from me. I'm sorry. I didn't want to hurt you, Simon. I should run away, but I'm not brave enough."

"You could never hide from us."

"Sure I could." A tear slid down my face. If I were dead, they would never be able to find me and they would all be safe.

"Don't even think that." Simon hugged me, stroking my head.

"No one else should suffer because of me. I'm not worth it."

"Do you really not see how special you are? The forces of Heaven and Hell have mobilized to claim you. It's not all your fault I said those things. It's partly mine too."

"What do you mean?"

"I admit that your bond with Ginevra scares me a little. She's very protective of you."

"You all are."

"I know. That's not what I meant. Something in her has changed since she found out about your nature. She feels *the Bond.*" A shudder ran through my body. "And I'm a little jealous."

"What are you talking about, Simon? For her, you come before everything else."

"What if that wasn't true any more?"

"That's crazy." The love between Simon and Ginevra was my benchmark, the rock to which I clung to convince myself the transformation wouldn't drag me away.

"I know. I'm sorry. I'm just afraid of losing her."

I stroked his arm. I'd never seen him so vulnerable before. "That'll never happen," I reassured him.

"That's probably true. What I'm saying is that your power wouldn't have had any influence on me if I didn't feel the way I feel."

"You're in love, and everything around us is changing. We can't know what's going to happen, but the one thing I'm sure of is that you two are going to stay together. Nothing can break the bond between you," I stated without a shadow of doubt. "It's normal for you to have thoughts like that, but *I* made them come out. It's all my fault. Don't be mad at me for what I am."

Simon hugged me. "You shouldn't be mad at yourself either. We'll get through this." I nodded and sank into his hug.

"Sorry if I'm interrupting." Nausyka came over and Simon left us alone. "Gemma, I just wanted to let you know your friend Peter asked me to go to the dance with him."

"What did you tell him?" I asked, upset.

"I accepted, of course."

"You *what*?! You can't go to the dance with him! Call him and tell him you changed your mind."

Nausyka turned her back on me, her expression pleased. "I wasn't asking for your permission. It was just an FYI."

I felt steam coming out of my ears. "What do you want from him?" I growled at her.

"I just told you: I want to go to the dance with him."

I clenched my fists, overcome with anger. "No. You won't. He's like a brother to me. Leave him alone." The window exploded and an icy wind blew into the room. I could feel myself rising off the floor, my fiery eyes locked on the Witch's.

In the blink of an eye she was right there in front of me. "Think these little tricks scare me?" she hissed, her ice-colored eyes transforming into those of her Dakor. "You have no idea who you're dealing with." The serpent materialized from her flesh and hissed in my face.

"That's enough!" Anya shouted. The wind stopped blowing and my feet touched the floor. I looked at Anya and she shot me a complicit look. "Nausyka, I challenge you. Choose your competition. The prize will be the boy." I opened my mouth to protest but she interrupted me. "Only for tonight, that is. If you win, you can take him to the dance. Otherwise he'll go with me."

"Don't worry," Ginevra whispered in my ear. "Nausyka's a wimp compared to Anya. Whatever challenge she proposes, she has zero chance of beating her."

I looked at Anya and my heart warmed at how she'd come to my rescue. I smiled at her and she smiled back. I would never have managed to convince Nausyka to change her mind, whereas Anya had been shrewd. I was certain that if Nausyka had gone out with Peter that night, she would have somehow jeopardized his soul, and sooner or later she would have returned to claim it. Anya, on the other hand, I trusted. I knew Peter's soul would be safe with her.

"Coming upstairs with me?" Ginevra asked me.

"Aren't we going to watch the competition?"

Ginevra laughed. "I strongly advise against it."

"Oh." I followed her up the stairs, watching Nausyka and Anya turn and walk away, both in panther form. "Where are they going?"

"The workout room," Ginevra told me after reading her Sisters' minds. "Nausyka chose a pretty cool simulation scenario. I bet Peter wouldn't mind being there with them."

"And I bet that's all I should know about it."

Ginevra laughed and opened the door to her room. "You win that bet."

"But wait, in the workout room? Aren't the prisoners there?"

"No. They're on another level. That's how the simulation scenarios work, like parallel realities."

"Like a multiverse."

"In a way." Ginevra stopped to look at me. "Have you thought about what to do with your Dakor? Even if the transformation doesn't obliterate you, he'll be part of you."

"I'm willing to destroy him," I said confidently.

"That won't be so simple. Besides, it's not like you need to. In any case, you can take your time and decide. Meanwhile, there's a safe place where you can set him free." Ginevra deactivated the vault door's locking mechanism and I gaped.

"What are you doing, Gwen?"

She turned to me and smiled. "Taking you into my own personal Hell."

Hesitantly, I took the hand she held out to me and followed her. "That's not very reassuring, as far as invitations go."

"Were you expecting a welcome mat?" she shot back as we made our way into the Copse. The door thudded closed behind us and I spun around. "It's safer this way," she explained.

Of course. We couldn't leave a door to Hell open—not with Simon around. The atmosphere was grim and eerie, like a haunted forest at twilight. Roots twisted on the ground and, farther in, a strange trunk was bent over on itself, its boughs so thick they formed an impenetrable cocoon. Only when I drew close to it did I realize it was a nest: her Dakor's lair. The last time I'd gone into Ginevra's secret hiding place the Dakor had been in a glass case, but she must have transformed it. Now the animal was trapped in the tree, but its forked tongue flickered through the branches, making me shiver. Ginevra stood in front of him. When he saw her he froze, as though hypnotized. They stared into each other's eyes for a long moment and suddenly the branches retreated.

I took a step back, shuddering at the thought of the dream I'd had the night before. The serpent sensed my nervousness and hissed at me, but Ginevra reached her right hand out to him and he penetrated her palm. She let her head fall back, on her face an expression of pain mixed with intense pleasure. When she looked at me again, her eyes were different. They were like her Dakor's. The pupils had lengthened and the green of her irises seemed to come to life. It moved, as brilliant as liquid jade, spreading over the whites like claws about to seize it.

I stared at her, as fascinated as though seeing it for the first time. But now there was also another feeling: fear. I raised my hand to my belly, where my scar was. Soon my body would also spawn a Dakor and he and I would be one.

Just then, Ginevra extended her left hand toward me and the serpent emerged, ripping her flesh. I stared at it in shock. "Don't be afraid," she said softly.

In spite of everything, I found her Dakor irresistibly attractive. I wanted to touch him. I wanted to feel him on me, absorb his power. As if he'd heard my thought, the serpent moved toward me and coiled around my arm. I closed my eyes, exhilarated, and let him slither over me, going up my arm, wrapping around my neck and creeping into my shirt, moving down between my breasts . . . to my belly, right where my scar was. A hiss of excitement shook the serpent, who knew what was lurking there: my Dakor. And yet my baby was there too. The thought snapped me out of it.

"Gwen." My eyes flew to hers and, sensing my concern, she summoned her serpent with her mind. What if he didn't manage to control his instincts? What if he'd detected Evan's genes in my baby?

Cautiously, Ginevra slipped her hand under my shirt as I stood still. The serpent coiled around her arm and slithered up to her neck, staring at me intently. "Don't worry. The baby isn't running any risk," she assured me, but I'd already forgotten every concern as my eyes fused with the animal's. They were so hypnotic and powerful, as though they hid some dark, fascinating, mysterious energy, the door to a magical place full of promises.

I was burning up. "That's enough for today," Ginevra said softly.

I looked at her, still dazed but free from the Dakor's spell. "Why did you bring me here?" I asked.

She put her Dakor back into his nest and the branches sealed up around him. "There's too much power in you, Gemma. You might be able to learn to control it, though, a little at a time. I'll help you."

"Do you think it'll make it easier to resist the transformation? That it won't obliterate me?"

"It's possible. We can at least try. Your body is slowly getting accustomed to it. You used to end up unconscious for days when the Witches established contact, and now your fever doesn't run nearly as high as it used to. Maybe your mind can get used to it too."

She was right. I nodded, grateful for her precious help. "What was your transformation like?" I asked.

"I wasn't so attached to my life. I wanted to slaughter everyone. Back then, my power awoke on Earth and the Sisters sensed it. They began to invade my dreams, tempting me with their promises, and I was happy to listen to them. When the time for my transformation came, I had no doubt about the choice I would make. I wanted to be like them, to be with them. And that was what happened, just like it had with all the others, one every five hundred years. With you, though, everything was different right from the start. The process began long before it was expected to. Your proximity to me and to the Subterraneans awakened your power. When you ingested the poison to kill the guy we thought was Drake, the transformation began and things got worse and worse. We all changed from mortals into Witches in a single night, whereas you're transforming slowly. And with every passing day you grow more powerful."

"You think that might help me avoid losing myself, don't you?"

"A gradual process might be less invasive than a more drastic one, but that's just my hope."

"What effect will the Bond have on me?"

"The Bond is an unbreakable force that will connect you to the Sisters. It compels you to protect and defend them. It's all of you against the world, and nothing can break it." Ginevra still suffered from being away from her Sisters.

"Where are we going?" I asked, following her up a hill.

"Let's stay here for a while, if you don't have other plans." She helped me climb onto a rock and a huge valley opened up before us, taking my breath away.

"No plans," I whispered, hypnotized by the incredible landscape. Ginevra laughed and motioned for me to join her, sitting on the summit of the peak and leaning back against a large tree. It seemed like the whole world was spread out below us.

"What do you think?" she asked excitedly.

"It's breathtaking."

Something moved in the distance, approaching us. A big black bird. No, it wasn't a bird. I jumped to my feet with a mix of surprise and excitement. "Argas!" I exclaimed, a lump in my throat.

Ginevra smiled. "I knew you'd be happy to see him again."

Ginevra's Saurus landed on the peak, folding his big black wings, and came toward me. I ran over and threw my arms around him. He whinnied and rubbed his head against mine. "I can't believe he's here." I'd missed him so much! I could never have survived Hell without him. Though he was Ginevra's steed, a connection had formed instantly between us. He'd also defended Evan from the Damned.

I sat down again and he curled up at Ginevra's feet, his giant head on her lap. I looked at Ginevra and saw a tear slide down her face. "Gwen . . ." I whispered, surprised. She stroked her animal, her eyes veiled with sorrow.

Only then did I understand. "This isn't the real Hell." Ginevra shook her head, still stroking Argas. "And he isn't real," I murmured. "So that's why you lock yourself up in here so often. Not only to train, but—"

"To remember. It's not easy to eradicate such an important part of you."

Ginevra had recreated a corner of Hell and hidden it behind the bars of her "forbidden door." She'd done so not only to give her Dakor a safe place to stay, but also to have a memory in which to seek refuge. I'd always believed it was a door that led to a little portion of her world. Only now did I realize it wasn't true. It was a lie she told herself to hide the pain. She missed her world terribly. "So this is just another artificial scenario?"

"Yes."

"And he's not really here," I said, this time louder. "He's just an illusion?"

"Yes." Her voice was sad.

I sighed. "You'd like to see him again, wouldn't you?"

"More than anything in the world."

I sighed again and stared at the valley that stretched beyond the mountains with their waterfalls and lush vegetation. "I really admire you for the decision you made," I said. "I can tell how much it makes you suffer, but despite that you chose Simon."

"He counts more than anything else," she stated without hesitation. And yet, though hundreds of years had passed, her connection to her world was still deeply rooted in her and the distance made her suffer. I too remembered the feeling of belonging I'd had once I was there.

"I wish I had half your courage," I admitted. If I were as strong as she was, maybe I would be able to avoid letting the transformation obliterate me.

Ginevra laughed and looked at me with affection. "If courage were enough, you'd have nothing to fear from the transformation. You're the bravest person I know."

"That's not true. I'm always filled with doubt, I never know what the right thing to do is, and most importantly . . . I'm afraid, Gwen. I'm even afraid of myself."

"*Fear* makes us strong. Every time you face it, you win a battle with yourself. And you're the strongest warrior I've ever seen."

A tear slid down my cheek.

"You faced Death with your head held high when it came to take you. You took the poison, knowing it would kill you. You even went all the way to Hell for your love. Without help. Without powers. Just you and the immense strength you have in your heart. You mean to tell me that isn't courage?"

I smiled through my tears. "Thanks, Gwen." I rested my head on her shoulder and she hugged me.

"I'm happy you're here with me," she suddenly said. "I can never go back to Hell, and this is the only way we can be there together."

"I'm not going there either," I assured her.

She squeezed my hand. "I hope not. I don't want to lose you, Gemma."

"That's not going to happen. I'm not giving up." I wasn't going to let evil obliterate me. I risked losing so much, *too* much. I wasn't willing to give in.

Argas whinnied and I trembled. Of all the challenges I'd faced, the hardest one was yet to come: the battle against myself.

17

THE SNOWBALL HOP

"Were we gone so long?!" I exclaimed as we came out through the vault door. I couldn't believe it was dark out already.

"Time flies when you're with a Sister."

I smiled at her affectionately. The bond between us wasn't because of my nature—it had grown strong long before. "What happened to Nausyka and Anya?" I asked, curious, hoping Ginevra would track down their minds wherever they were in the house.

"We can find out later. First let's eat something. I'm famished," she protested, walking down the stairs.

"You're always famished."

"Look who's talking!"

I stuck my tongue out at her and she shoved something in my mouth. My eyes bulged and I took a bite out of a chocolate muffin. It was delicious. Ginevra had used an effective argument to come out of the conversation a winner. The table in the living room was piled high with food, but we were so hungry that in minutes there was almost nothing left.

"Aren't you two ready yet?"

Sprawled on the couch, our bellies about to burst—at least mine—Ginevra and I turned toward Anya, who'd just appeared in the living room. I usually jumped whenever one of them popped up out of the blue, but I was too full to do even that. The Witches didn't gradually appear and disappear, like Subterraneans—they went *poof*.

I struggled to my feet, surprised to see how stunning Anya looked in her luxurious gown. A big smile spread across her face. "You like it?" She twirled around. With her long, green, Venetian dress and her curly hair, she looked like a princess. She was all set for the Snowball Hop, while I still had to get ready—and there was no sign of Evan.

"Mmm . . . Pizza!" Nausyka took a slice and savored it voluptuously, as though making love to it. I cast a questioning glance at Anya: Nausyka was also dressed for the dance. She wore an elegant black gown with a plunging neckline and a mermaid train. Her white hair was plaited in a long braid that hung over one shoulder. Its tip looked like it had been dipped in black ink. She looked like an evil, sexy twin of Elsa from *Frozen*. I didn't dare imagine the reaction she would get in a room full of mortals ready to fall at her feet. One of them, however, worried me more than the others.

"Are you going to tell your friend about the change of plans or do you want to give me his number?" Anya winked at me and smiled. She'd won! *Thank you*, I mouthed to her. Nausyka glared at me icily. "But now, what are we waiting for? I don't want to miss the coronation!" Anya took me by the hand and pulled me up the stairs.

"Wait for me!" shouted Ginevra, hurrying after us.

"Don't take too long," Nausyka grumbled. "I'm tired of being cooped up in this house."

Anya pushed me into a chair and started to put makeup on me while Ginevra styled my hair. Strangely, I didn't feel like a rag doll in their hands—I felt like a princess with her ladies-in-waiting. I felt loved.

"Was it easy to snatch Nausyka's date away from her?" I asked Anya.

"I have to admit she gave it her best shot."

"What does she want from Peter? Why is she obsessed with him?"

"She's not going to compromise his soul," Ginevra said. "Trust me."

"It's her I don't trust. I want her to stay away from him. I'm a lot happier that he's going to the dance with Anya."

She smiled, continuing to put eye shadow on me. "To tell you the truth, you shouldn't be wondering what she wants from him, but what *he* wants from *her*."

"What do you mean?"

"Your friend's a really bright kid—above all, he's very curious."

"We've known that for a while now," Ginevra said, grinning. Peter had always pried into their business, but I was sure he did it to protect me. "He only wanted to go out with Nausyka because he thinks he may uncover something strange. He's not the least bit interested in her, aside from the physical attraction . . . which she has every intention of satisfying."

"Yeah, I can imagine," I said.

"But you don't have to worry about it any more. With me around, she'll stay away from him and I can assure you I won't seduce him."

"Anya, I know he's just a mortal Soul to you, but I don't want him *not* to have a good time. With you he can. You have my blessing."

Anya stopped, a black eyeliner pencil poised near my eyes. "That's really kind of you. I know how close you two are."

"That's true, but I don't think about him like *that*, so it's okay if he goes to the dance with you and has fun. Who knows? Maybe you and he could deepen your new *friendship*." I looked at Anya with a mischievous air.

"You mean you wouldn't be even a little jealous?"

"Not even a little," I said confidently. "I would be happy if Peter found someone who deserved him."

"That someone can't be me," Anya reminded me. She was only there temporarily. Once her mission was finished, she would return to Hell with her Sisters.

"I know," I admitted a little sadly, "but it certainly can't be Nausyka. If Peter has to have a good time, I'd rather he have it with you."

"It's natural for you to want to protect him," Ginevra said, busy braiding my hair.

"*Et voilà!* Mission accomplished," Anya exclaimed excitedly. Ginevra looked at me and for a second seemed shocked.

"Gwen, everything okay?" I asked with concern.

She smiled at me, banishing my fears. "Yes. You're spellbinding." She helped me put on the voluminous Victorian gown and laced up the back. "Remember when we bought these dresses?" she asked affectionately.

"When *you* bought them," I reminded her. "I didn't even want to try mine on!"

"Turns out they came in handy, didn't they?"

"Yeah, and I'm sure you had nothing to do with it."

"I don't know what you mean." Ginevra shot me a sidelong glance, hiding a smile. My dress was red, the color of blood. We'd bought it in New York during a day trip. Back then we hadn't known what the theme for the Winter Carnival dance would be, but I suspected Ginevra had had a hand in the decision.

"All done. Now you can look," she said as Anya gazed at me with delight.

I raised the hem of my skirt just above my ankles and walked over to the mirror, where I slowly raised my eyes, almost fearfully. I instantly realized why Ginevra seemed so shaken. *I looked like one of them.*

"You look divine," Anya whispered behind me, squeezing my shoulders. I blinked, astonished. Mascara enhanced my long lashes and eyeliner as black as my eye shadow brought out the curve of my eyes. The line continued to my temples, creating a design. It almost looked like an elegant mask—no, not a mask. *Butterfly wings.* My gaze had become deep and incredibly magnetic, and my hair was gathered into a soft wave of curls that flowed over one shoulder. Peeking out here and there were little braids that held the hairstyle in place. I couldn't believe it was me.

"That dress is perfect. I would never be able to tell you're expecting a baby," Anya said.

I touched my abdomen. She was right. With that dress, my belly wasn't noticeable at all. There were girls at school who looked more pregnant than I did—even though they weren't. Though I didn't know why, it really was hard to tell on me. Now I just hoped Evan got back in time. When he'd asked me to the dance I wasn't sure whether it was a good idea, but then, like a little girl, I'd let excitement wash over me. It was our first dance together. The first dance to which someone other than Peter had invited me. And I was crazy in love with my date. I had a bad feeling, though. Something inside me told me he wasn't coming.

"He'll come," Anya reassured me, though there was no way she could be sure.

"Knowing him, he'll be there in time to kill every guy who checks out your cleavage," Ginevra added. I burst out laughing. "I wouldn't laugh if I were you. Believe me, it'll be a slaughter." She smiled, pointing at the plunging neckline that brought out the curve of my breasts.

"I say he'll be the one to die—the minute he lays eyes on you. You're going to be the prettiest girl at the dance. After me, naturally." Anya winked at me and I smiled. Evan had captured my heart and held it tight, but I knew it was safe in his hands.

The doorbell rang but before I could wonder who it was they already knew. "It's Peter," said Anya. "We'd better go down before Nausyka seizes her chance."

"You two finish getting ready. I'll take care of it," I offered. I hurried down the stairs but the bell rang again and Nausyka opened it.

"Hi," I heard Peter say to her.

"Thanks, Nausyka. I've got it," I exclaimed before she could try anything on him. *"You lost your bet, remember?"* I told her in my mind.

"It won't be the last one," she replied, glancing at me before walking off. Peter watched her leave, confused, and then his eyes rested on me.

"Hi," I said, but he seemed to have lost his power of speech. "Change of plans. Nausyka isn't going with you any more." For a second his eyes lit up.

"Anya's going with you," I hurried to add before he got any ideas.

"It doesn't matter," he replied, his eyes fixed on mine. "She wasn't my first choice anyway."

I looked away, embarrassed. "Come on in. Anya will be down in a minute."

Peter walked into the living room. He looked handsome in his elegant nineteenth-century suit: a black waistcoat over a blue silk shirt and, for the first time, a tie. It wasn't just the clothes—there was also something different in his bearing. He was becoming a man.

"You're not wearing your hair tie on your arm," he noticed.

I'd forgotten how attentive he was when it came to me. "I can go without it tonight," I said. The truth was that the dream I'd had the night before had upset me so much that I'd started to be afraid of myself, of what I would become. The hair tie had always been part of me, but as a response to the summons of evil. Just for one night I wanted to escape the darkness. I hoped it wouldn't pursue me.

"Funny," Peter exclaimed. "I think I've only seen you without it a few times."

"Lots of things about me have changed lately, Pet."

His eyes fell to the tattoo on my hand. It hadn't escaped him that Evan had one just like it. "Right, everything's different. Strange, don't you think? This is our first dance *not* together." *Finally, he'd said it.* Naturally it had occurred to him too. Peter gave me an affectionate smile. It made me realize one thing hadn't changed: despite everything, he would always be my best friend.

"Yeah." I smiled back. "It really is strange." He and I had always gone to school dances together, from the Halloween dance to the Snowball Hop to Prom. Every year, every event.

"Where's your date?"

"Oh, Evan's meeting me later on . . . I hope. He had an important commitment."

"More important than you?" he asked, suddenly annoyed. He'd never stopped being protective.

"He'll turn up in no time, really."

"Tell the truth, Gemma," Devina said, magically appearing behind him. "You're not even sure he's coming. Why don't you go to the dance with your friend here?"

"Is what she says true?" Peter blurted.

"No, she's only saying it to make me angry." I shot her an icy glare. There were times I wished I could transform just so I could take her on in a battle to the death.

"Seriously, Gemma." Peter took my hand. "If Evan's not here you can go with me. As friends. Like we've always done."

I freed myself from his grip, trying not to hurt his feelings. "I'm sure he's coming. Besides, you can't bail on Anya, can you?"

"He certainly can't. He's my knight in shining armor!" Anya said, making her entrance. She curtsied and Peter, acting the gentleman, kissed the back of her hand, but secretly continued to stare at me. Was he becoming bolder?

"It's not his fault. You're breathtaking tonight," Ginevra whispered in my thoughts. I turned and she winked at me with a broad smile as she walked down the stairs. She was radiant in her white-and-gold gown, like a sun goddess. Her blond hair was gathered back, a small braid crossing her forehead like a diadem. She had once explained that Witches had the habit of braiding their hair, and that a braid across the forehead was like a symbol of the Sisterhood.

"Look who's talking," I whispered to her when she approached me.

"I'm not kidding," she insisted. "You have an aura of power around you. I can feel it. Your body is producing loads of pheromones." My mouth dropped open in concern. That was why Peter couldn't take his eyes off me. Ginevra nodded, picking up on my thought. "It must have been your visit to the Copse. It made you stronger."

"We're going in Peter's car," Anya broke in. "See you there!"

"We'd better get going too," Ginevra said, changing the subject. "Don't worry. Relax and enjoy the dance. Everything will go fine, you'll see." I nodded, hoping with all my heart that Evan would show up soon to make sure of it. I always felt safer when he was with me.

"Well?" Camelia appeared in the room in a dreamy powder-blue gown. "Are we going to the dance or aren't we?" She'd dyed her hair the same color, leaving the roots darker. Her outfit was complete with a delightful little pink hat. Her enthusiasm made me smile, but the mischief in her eyes worried me. "I missed these dresses so much!" she exclaimed, twirling around.

"I didn't, not one bit." Simon appeared behind Ginevra and kissed her bare neck, pulling her against him. She turned and kissed him passionately. "I think I'm going to get rid of it, and fast," he whispered, his hands on her hips.

She bit his lip. "I'm not sure I can wait that long."

"Hey, we're still here, you know," I warned them. They smiled at each other, taming the fire that consumed them.

"Okay, if you're so scandalized . . ." Ginevra told me, a sly grin on her face.

Actually, I was missing Evan terribly. "Gwen, I have a bad feeling about this. Maybe we shouldn't go without Evan."

"He's just on a mission, Gemma."

"Do you really think he'll get there in time?" I asked as we opened the garage door.

"I don't know," she admitted, taking my hand, "but whatever happens, we're going to have fun." I returned her smile and got into the back between Camelia and Nausyka. Simon sat down behind the wheel, with Ginevra in the passenger seat.

I put on my iPod earbuds to shut myself off from the group for a moment. My mind continued to return to Evan. I picked out an Avril Lavigne song, *When You're Gone*. I'd always liked listening to songs that matched my mood. Music was like a good friend: it understood me, no matter what. And I missed Evan so much . . . The fear of losing him through the transformation seemed more real when he was gone, because I knew no one else was capable of pulling me out of the darkness.

We reached the Crowne Plaza Resort in no time. The atmosphere inside was magical. All the students from the high school looked so elegant, and the Victorian theme had been implemented to perfection, with draperies and fabrics from that era, big candelabras, and even an area for the orchestra with a piano and various instruments. Some of the boys wore hats and carried canes while others even had fake mustaches or beards. It was really like being in the nineteenth century.

Peter was at the back of the room with Anya. He took her hand when the coronation was announced.

"Just in time!" Nausyka exclaimed.

"Don't get your hopes up. The queen can only be chosen from among the seniors, and you're a little bit older," I teased her. "Besides, you're not even enrolled in this school."

"Oh yeah?" she replied, annoyed. "If I want to, I can get myself crowned this very—"

"Faith Nichols!" the principal announced.

"Aw, too late," I said, one eyebrow raised.

"You did that on purpose. You distracted me!" she said, stunned. Surprisingly, there was no trace of anger in her voice. In fact, she seemed to find it funny. "You're learning," she admitted, realizing I'd done it intentionally. Knowing that Nausyka wanted to make the principal say her name, I'd stolen that little victory from her.

I searched the crowd for my friend Faith. She was climbing the steps to the dais that had been set up for the occasion. I forgot about Nausyka and smiled. I was so happy Faith had won the title of Winter Carnival Queen. I'd voted for her myself a few days before. Though she tried to hide it by wearing her magnificent red hair in a tight bun or always staying in Jeneane's shadow, her beauty hadn't gone unnoticed. The truth was that Faith didn't like to have everyone's eyes on her—too much attention made her uncomfortable. She preferred to be with the horses on her family's ranch. I'd seen her with her mare, Hope. Together they seemed invincible. That night, like it or not, everyone had noticed her. She'd worn her copper-red hair down and it flowed over her peach-colored dress. She was gorgeous. I'd always known she was. She went to sit on the throne that had been prepared, waiting for them to announce the king.

" . . . and the Winter Carnival King is . . ." the principal continued. Brandon stepped toward the stairs. "Peter Turner!" the man announced in a booming voice.

I gaped, ecstatic, as Peter rubbed his neck, embarrassed. He hadn't been expecting it. He looked at me from across the room and I clapped for him. *It was the tie*, I mimed. He laughed and walked toward the dais. As he passed Brandon he slapped him on the shoulder. "Next time, dude," he joked, regaining his confidence. Brandon reached out to give him a playful punch on the shoulder, but Peter dodged it.

He thanked everyone, as Faith had done, and went to sit on the throne beside her, but the principal asked them to open the dance. Peter held his hand out to her and she let him guide her to the middle of the room, where they began to dance.

"My knight has become a king!" Anya exclaimed, joining us.

"That doesn't make you a queen," said Nausyka, who hadn't yet gotten over her defeat.

"At least I *have* a knight."

"*Had*," the Witch pointed out, gesturing at Peter and Faith, who were dancing close together.

"You could be his secret lover," Camelia suggested, looking amused.

I shook my head and went off in search of the punch, hoping no one had spiked it. "Want something to drink?" I asked the three of them, but they paid no attention to me.

Ginevra and Simon danced by to the rhythm of a Venetian rondo. Simon wore a white-and-gold suit, probably an original. Everyone's eyes were on them. They really did look like a knight with his princess. He stood out with his dark allure, a blond Angel of Death dressed in white. He looked like an officer—and, come to think of it, he was. I'd read in Ginevra's diary that before they met Simon had been a soldier in the Swedish forces. *General Adrian Simeone Dahlberg.* The girls from school weren't used to seeing him and he left them dazzled.

Faith and Peter also danced by as I was sipping my punch. I raised my glass to toast them and Faith smiled at me cheerfully. They danced off, but a moment later Jake asked to cut in and Peter relinquished Faith, taking off the crown and giving it to his friend. It wasn't a secret to anyone that Jake was in love with her and that Faith loved him back. The mystery was why they weren't together. Peter came over to me and I smiled at him.

"Congratulations," I told him. "Winter Carnival King! Who would have guessed?"

"Was it that unlikely?" he asked, pretending to be offended, but two dimples soon appeared in his cheeks.

"No, not at all. You look great tonight."

"So you do."

The silence grew awkward.

"Those two are perfect together," I said, nodding toward Faith and Jake.

Peter laughed. "He's nervous. He's about to ask her to be his girlfriend."

"Finally! Let's hope it happens."

"Your date's not here yet?"

"Ahem . . . Here you are!" Anya emerged from the crowd and linked her arm in his. "Gemma, do you mind if I steal him for a moment?"

"Of course not," I said as she led him away.

She looked back and winked at me. "So tell me all about the coronation . . . Speaking of which, where's your crown? Have they dethroned you already?"

I laughed as they walked off. I wasn't sure Peter would be able to handle her Witch's exuberance. Still, they were cute together. Watching them as they moved across the dance floor, I knew for certain that I wouldn't mind if something romantic started between them. Maybe my friendship with Peter would go back to what it had once been. I smiled. Yes, I liked the idea.

All at once, a sharp pain in my abdomen made me double over. Unable to breathe, I gripped the tablecloth in one hand. Glasses of punch crashed to the floor, spilling their contents. I looked at the crowd dancing and the room started to spin.

I'd do anything to go out with him.

I'm going to get back at that bitch.
Please, kiss me. Go on, kiss me.
What I would give to get her into bed.
If I find out they hooked up it's over between us.

I gasped for air. Where were all those voices coming from? People's faces passed me like ghosts and their laughs jumbled together, filling my head. I closed my eyes and everything stopped. In the darkness I could hear only my breathing; all the other sounds had faded away. Even the pain was gone. When I opened my eyes I found myself in the center of the room. A couple in front of me was arguing.

"You've been staring at him all night. I saw you!"

"That's not true! I don't even know who you're talking about!"

I walked around the boy. Though I didn't know him well, I suddenly felt attracted to him. I wanted to see him from closer up. As I moved nearer, his breathing accelerated and he shouted at the girl, his eyes bulging, "Don't lie!" He was on the verge of losing control.

"I'm not lying! I swear, I only care about you." A tear streaked the girl's face and he wavered. I couldn't tolerate it.

"She wants to go to bed with him," I whispered in his ear.

"You want to go to bed with him!" the boy repeated. A sensation of immense power surged through me. "It's the truth, isn't it?"

"Maybe she's already cheated on you."

"Or you already cheated on me," he continued. He pulled his hand back and slapped his girlfriend across the face. She fell to the floor and everyone turned to stare at them. I smiled, but something distracted me: a distant voice.

"Gemma? Hey, Gemma, you okay?" I felt myself being dragged away as though at the mercy of a raging river, the frenzied beating of my heart returning to drown out all the other sounds. My eyes shot open and the voice became clear. It was Jeneane. I looked at my hands clutching the paper tablecloth, now torn, and felt my heartbeat slowing down. "Hey, do you feel okay?" she asked again, worried.

I struggled to my feet and saw the couple fighting, but . . . they were on the other side of the room. What had just happened? My head spun faster and I felt like I was falling.

"Gemma!"

"Step aside, people. I'm a doctor." It was Simon. His warm hands raised my head and in the background I heard Ginevra and Anya coaxing the crowd to stay back.

"Gemma!" Peter said, resisting their efforts. "What's wrong with her? Is she okay? Let me through!"

"She just had a dizzy spell. It's natural when you're expecting a baby. Give her a moment," they told him.

Someone loosened my bodice and I started breathing again. I slowly opened my eyes to see Simon gazing at me. "Welcome back." He smiled. I stared back at him, unsmiling, as a silent tear slid down my cheek. What had just happened? I knew the answer. It had been me. I'd incited that boy to slap his girlfriend, even though she hadn't done anything. How could it be?

"Calm down now," Simon whispered, using his healing power on me. The only problem was that what was wrong with me couldn't be healed. "Think you can stand up?" I nodded, letting him help me. He walked me to the hallway and the Witches followed us.

"What happened?" I asked, exasperated and frightened. No one answered. *"What just happened?"* I insisted.

"Gemma." Anya rested her hands on my shoulders. She'd read the guilt in my mind. "It's nothing. Calm down. This isn't good for the baby."

"How can you say it's nothing? It was me! *I* made that guy hit her. It might not be a big deal to you, but to me it's a *very* big deal."

"You'd better get used to it," Nausyka replied curtly.

"What?" I turned to face her.

"That's enough. You guys can't mean to argue here, I hope," Ginevra intervened.

"I refuse to console her," her Sister insisted.

"She's upset."

"She has no reason to be. What's going to happen later?"

"She's still a mortal. Her soul isn't ready yet," Ginevra hissed.

"It's her nature and she's going to have to deal with it."

I covered my ears and Nausyka went back into the ballroom, Camelia at her side.

"I'm going too," Anya whispered. "I'd better keep an eye on them."

Ginevra put her arm around my shoulders and tried to look me in the eye. I stared into space, though, lost in the darkness lurking inside me. "There were two of me," I murmured in shock. Ginevra let out a long sigh.

I'd had an out-of-body experience. "Tell me I imagined it, Gwen. Tell me it wasn't me who caused their fight."

"It wasn't you." I looked at her, in my eyes a hope that faded the second they met hers. "You didn't cause their fight, but you heard it and . . . you fanned the flames." Ginevra put a hand to her forehead, remorseful. "It's my fault. It's all my fault. I was wrong. Taking you to see my Dakor wasn't a good idea—it just made things worse." My eyes widened. She was right: taking me into her world had exposed me to evil, and my soul had absorbed it, accelerating the process.

"But I split in two. How could that be?"

"Your soul felt drawn to their argument and went to it. Your body isn't yet ready for power like that, so you passed out. It's my fault. I'm sorry."

I touched the mark on my belly that was still throbbing. I'd felt a knife plunge into my flesh there. That mark belonged to the devil, as did I. I'd already sworn, but suddenly I wanted to take it all back. I didn't want to transform any more. I didn't want to risk turning into a monster. Evan was right—I couldn't control the darkness. It would force me to remain there, watching, feeding off me as I lost everything. As I lost Evan.

I remembered everything about the fight between the couple. Every crude, appealing sensation. The scary thing was that during it I hadn't remembered anything about myself. All I'd wanted was to continue to feel that power.

I'd been deluding myself. I would never manage to battle the evil inside me, because I wouldn't want to battle it any more. My doubts dissolved, leaving way for a terrible certainty: the transformation would obliterate me. I'd been all wrong and everyone else had been right—most of all Evan, who had never accepted the thought of my transforming and was desperately looking for another solution. I'd always thought he didn't trust in us, in our love, but he was just afraid of losing me. He didn't want to risk it. He understood that no matter how strong our love was, it didn't depend on us—only on me. I never listened to him and always complicated everything. But this time I couldn't be wrong again, because everything was at stake. Not even I wanted to risk it any more. I wasn't going to transform.

"Guys . . . " Ginevra's whisper shook me from my thoughts as a shiver ran down my spine.

Simon and I leaned toward her, worried. Ginevra looked like she'd seen a ghost. "Gwen, what's wrong?"

Distraught, her eyes met mine. "It's your Dakor," she said, her voice low and frozen from shock. "His heart has started beating."

A shudder of fear chilled me to the bone.

18

THE FIRST DANCE

"Want to go home?" Ginevra asked me, worried. I hadn't said a word since she'd revealed the terrible truth: my Dakor had awakened. With every passing day, I was closer and closer to the transformation. How would I manage to prevent it? Whenever I wondered that, I felt a knot in my throat. I was afraid. I didn't want to lose everything.

"We can leave, if you want," she insisted.

"No. I want to stay."

"It doesn't look like Evan is going to make it after all," Simon told us. It was strange he hadn't shown up yet, and by now it was clear he wasn't coming.

"I'm sure his mission delayed him," Ginevra said. "Let's go home, Gemma. You're still upset."

"I said no." I wiped my tears with my hand. "You guys got all dressed up for me. I don't want to ruin the party. Nausyka would never forgive me."

"We didn't get dressed up like this just for you," Ginevra said, looking at me out of the corner of her eye. I smiled. She loved that dress.

"We'll stay if she wants to," Simon spoke up, "but on one condition."

"Which is . . . ?" I looked at Simon, curious.

"That you'll do me the honor of granting me the next dance."

"What?" Simon had gotten a smile out of me. "You don't have to do that for me, really."

"I don't have to, but you do. You have to do it for me."

"Why would our dancing be a favor to you?"

Simon took my hand in his white-gloved one and kissed the back of it with a bow. "Because I come from a distant time in which a lady wasn't permitted to leave a ball without having first danced with at least one gentleman."

Smiling at his sweetness, I looked at Ginevra and she nodded her approval. I squeezed Simon's hand and walked at his side to the center of the ballroom. "But we're not in your time," I finally said.

"Let's pretend we are, shall we?" He bowed slightly, without taking his eyes off mine, and I curtsied to him.

Everyone was lined up, ready to begin the magical dance. I was sorry Evan wasn't with me, but at least having Simon there was a consolation. I cared about him so much. He'd protected me, risking his life so many times. I'd never forgotten how afraid I'd been at the sight of Desdemona pointing that gun at his head. He could have decided from that point on to abandon me, but he never had. He'd been at my side physically and morally, and I loved him for it. Not like I loved Evan or my baby, but with a deep, fraternal love, as though we shared the same blood.

The music began and Simon smiled at me. "Ready?"

"I promise not to step on your toes."

We moved to the rhythm of the violins, executing the dance steps. Stepping toward each other, we pressed our palms together before taking a step back. Simon twirled me around and knelt down like all the other boys, while the other girls and I circled them. Another step forward and another back. Then we both raised our right hands, palms facing without touching, and made a full circle, looking each other in the eye. We smiled the whole time, but when the circle was finished the line of boys moved down and I found myself facing another dance partner. He bowed, I nodded, and the dance began again. I danced with a boy I didn't know and then with Jake, who was surprisingly gallant. Next came Brandon, who ogled my neckline the whole time. I had to give him a slap on the back of the head when he knelt down. I tried not to let the others notice, but he yelped and clutched his head, making the whole line of dancers grin.

Then it was Peter's turn. "Hi," I said.

He bowed before replying. "Hi." We came together and he looked me in the eye. "You okay?" We joined palms and took a step back.

"It was just a dizzy spell," I assured him. He smiled, kneeling in front of me. "You going to ask for your crown back?"

"That kind of stuff isn't for me. I'm more the trophy type."

"Right." I laughed. Peter was a jock and in his room he had a collection of cups and medals.

He stood up and we looked each other in the eye, following the choreography. "I'm happy I got to dance with you."

"Even if just a little," I reminded him.

"Even if just a little," he said, laughing before growing serious again and bowing to his new dance partner. I curtsied to the boy in front of me and jumped when I saw it was the boy from the fight. A tumult of emotions rose within me and I felt like running away. I tried to control my breathing and overcome my fear. The boy took my hand and turned me around, but then let go. Had he recognized me too? Impossible. In fact, a second later I felt him take my hand again while my back was still to him. I completed the circle and my heart skipped a beat.

"My lady," Evan said, smiling. He was right there in front of me, my hand in his. He bowed and I circled him, my heart pounding. He'd sent the boy away and taken his place. Evan looked so dashing in his Victorian clothes that it felt like I was lost in an ancient dream. He wore a white silk shirt beneath a black jacket from that era. A filmy neckerchief in black silk completed the look. We joined palms and when we neared each other he interlaced his fingers with mine. "I missed you," he whispered, touching my forehead with his.

Tears filled my eyes, releasing all my tension. "I missed you too," I said. I raised my right hand and he stroked it as we turned around, gazing intently into each other's eyes. He wasn't supposed to touch my hand but the energy between us wouldn't allow that distance, so our fingers touched and then parted, like two secret lovers who feared being exposed.

The circle finished and we changed dance partners again, but the whole time his eyes never left mine, nor mine his. Before the time came for us to move down to another partner, Evan grabbed my hand and pulled me away.

"Hey!" my new partner protested, but Evan paid no attention to him. Putting his arms around my waist, he led me in a dance all our own. Far from the others. Far from the world.

The music stopped and the hall burst into applause. We took refuge in a secluded corner at the back of the room. A slow song came on, met by a chorus of approval. Evan took both my hands and placed them around his neck. Holding me by the waist, he stared at me intensely. We hadn't seen each other for a whole day and I'd missed him as if he were oxygen; I needed him to breathe. "Oh, Evan. I thought you weren't coming."

He rested his forehead against mine. "I wouldn't have missed this for anything in the world. I was hoping to get here in time for the first dance, but the mission took longer than expected."

"You made it. That was my first dance."

"But I wasn't your first partner."

"You were the last one—that's all that matters. Just for your information, Simon was the first."

He smiled. "Remind me to thank him. Did you get my note?"

"Yes, it made me so happy, thanks. Now I know you're thinking of me too when you're on a mission."

Evan brushed a lock of hair off my forehead. "I can go to the ends of the earth, but my heart stays here with you." He gently took my hand and placed it on his chest. "Hear that? There's only silence here. Now listen." He took my hand again and this time placed it on my chest. My heart was beating powerfully. "Your heart beats for us both."

I shook my head. "No, Evan. You shouldn't say that." I knew the message hidden in those words. If I died, he wouldn't go on living without me. I couldn't accept that. I needed to know he would be safe. "Take back your heart. If it means you would die without me, I don't want it." A tear streaked my face. Now more than ever I felt the end was near—the end of everything.

Evan wiped the tear from my cheek. "Hey, why are you crying? What's going on?"

How could I tell him that everything I'd believed was wrong? That he was right and the transformation would be the end of everything? That it would be the end of us . . . "I'm scared, Evan."

He clasped my face in his hands and looked into my eyes. "I'm here now. I'm not leaving you."

I shook my head. "I can't control it. You were right. The power is going to annihilate me."

Evan's eyes widened. I could see he was shocked by my confession, torn. For such a long time I'd been saying just the opposite, and now, for the first time, I was casting doubt on everything. My life was in his hands. It depended on his decisions.

"Help me, Evan. I don't want to transform. I don't want to forget you forever."

Evan held me tight. "I won't let it happen. I would never have let it happen," he told me. "I'm taking you with me to Heaven and you're eating of the Tree. No matter what."

I rested my forehead against his. "Are you with me?" he whispered in my ear.

"No matter what," I repeated. For once, I would listen to Evan and go along with his plan. It was our only chance. The divine nectar would rid me of the evil inside me. I had to cling to that certainty.

"I wouldn't have given up anyway, but I'm thankful you finally changed your mind," Evan admitted.

"I should have listened to you before."

"One way or the other I would have convinced you. I wouldn't have let you go, Gemma. I was *desperate*." I looked him straight in the eye. On his face I could read his fear of losing me. "Because I'm desperately in love with you," he continued in a whisper.

I pressed my lips to his and he kissed me tenderly, brushing my tongue with his softly one moment and passionately the next. His hand slid into my hair to hold me closer as our mouths sought each other, hot from our forbidden love. The world around us disappeared. It was just me and Evan, locked in an embrace.

"Marry me, Gem." He gazed at me intently, our breath mingling.

"I've already said yes. I will marry you, Evan."

He shook his head, still resting on mine. "I mean here. Now. Marry me, Gemma," he whispered against my lips.

My heart skipped a beat. "But how—"

"We'll do it in secret. Just us. Simon will perform the ceremony, if you'll agree to do it here. I don't want to wait a second longer." I closed my eyes, my heart ready to burst with emotion. "Say yes, Gemma. Be mine."

"I'm already yours," I whispered, and kissed him.

"It's you and me. We don't need anything else."

I looked at him. "My mother's going to kill me."

"She won't know. No one will know," Evan whispered, smiling. "We'll have a big ceremony once all this is over. Until then"—he took my hands and stroked the ring I wore on my finger—"only we will know. It'll be our secret. So is that a yes?"

I smiled and he didn't take his eyes off mine as his voice filled my head: *"Simon, you need to come here."* My heart began to pound. Were we really about to do it? Yes, yes, and again yes. I wanted to marry Evan. I wanted to join my soul with his; that was where it belonged.

Simon soon reached us. "What's going on?" he asked, worried. Anya and Ginevra turned up a second later and let out a cry of surprise when they mentally read our intentions.

I smiled at Simon, the only one who still didn't know what was happening. "Would you marry us?" I asked him point-blank.

Unsurprised, he smiled back at me. "It would be an honor."

"We don't have rings, though," I pointed out.

"There's no need for anything new. Do you have something here with you that can serve as a testament to your love?"

Without thinking twice, Evan grabbed his dog tag and pulled it over his head, laying it in Simon's open palm. I took off my butterfly necklace and handed it to him. We couldn't have found anything more symbolic. Both chains had been with us from the start: I never took mine off, even at night, and he never went without his either. They'd been there for our first kiss, when Evan had come into my dream to say goodbye forever; they'd been there when he'd declared his love and engraved our names on them; when we'd made love for the first time . . . and all the other times after that. They'd been there when he asked me to marry him and when I'd followed him all the way to Hell to give his dog tag back to him and we'd made love in the dungeon cell. Those chains were the emblems of our great love. I didn't need anything else.

Simon held them and began to recite an ancient litany I imagined was in Sanskrit. I gazed at Evan. He held my hands, his dark eyes lost in mine, as mine were in his.

Simon held out our keepsakes, now consecrated. "Repeat after me: *Tavātmānam upadhehi. ahaµ taµ saµdadhe."*

Evan took my chain from Simon's palm and, without taking his eyes from mine, whispered: "Entrust to me your soul and I will watch over it."

"I entrust my soul to you," I said softly. Evan put the necklace around my neck and smiled. I took the dog tag from Simon's palm and noticed there was another engraving on the back of it now, beside our names.

अत्यन्तम्

"Tavātmānam upadhehi. ahaµ taµ saµdadhe," I went on, this time in Sanskrit. *Entrust to me your soul and I will watch over it.*

"Tubhyaµ mamātmānam upadadhe. I entrust my soul to you," Evan replied. He leaned down slightly to let me slip the chain over his head and took my hands. My heart was beating so hard I was sure he could hear it. *"Mamātmā mari, yati tvayā saha.* My spirit will die with you and rise again with you." He stroked my palm and a sigh of love filled my chest.

"Mamātmā mari, yati tvayā saha," I repeated, enchanted. The whole time his eyes had never once left mine.

"*Atyantam*," Simon decreed. "Your souls are united. Now and forever."

"Now and forever," Evan whispered before kissing me. I rested my forehead against his and he held me tightly around the waist.

"Now and forever," I repeated, smiling against his lips.

In the background, the lake watched us through the picture window, a silent witness. No one in the ballroom had noticed anything. They'd all been dancing while we joined our souls right before their eyes.

I had become his wife.

"Hey, make way for the maid of honor," Ginevra exclaimed. "I need to congratulate the bride!" She came up to me and gave me a big, strong hug.

"Congratulations, brother." Simon shook Evan's hand and gave him a friendly slap on the shoulder before hugging him.

"You didn't know anything about this?" I asked Ginevra, thinking she might have read Evan's mind.

"I knew he wanted to marry you, but I didn't think he'd be crazy enough to do it here."

"What does it matter where they did it?" Anya spoke up. "It was so romantic!" She hugged me and I returned the gesture. "Congratulations. I'm rooting for you," she said, wiping a tear from her eye.

"I love you, Anya."

"Oh, if you knew how much I love you!" She squeezed me so long I started to laugh.

"Okay, she gets how much you care about her," Evan remarked, reclaiming my attention, "but now the bride's coming with me." He took me by the hand and led me away as violins played the notes of *Odissea Veneziana.*

"Hey!" the girls grumbled, while Simon laughed.

"Wait, where are we going?" I exclaimed, raising the hem of my long gown with one hand.

Evan opened the front door and nodded at his motorcycle parked outside. "On our honeymoon," he said with a sly smile. I smiled and followed him. He took off his jacket and offered it to me. I slipped it on and closed it snugly, though I knew he would warm the air around us so I wouldn't be cold, the way he always did. He offered me a hand to help me onto the bike while holding the handlebar with the other.

Ginevra and Anya watched from the door, smiling, and I waved goodbye. "Wait!" I took off the red lace garter that matched my dress and climbed on, holding him tight. The engine started up with a roar that filled the night. Evan gunned the accelerator and set off as I tossed the garter behind me. I saw Anya catch it.

I hugged Evan, my heart warming at the thought of what had just happened. We had just secretly wed. He was my husband and I was his bride. Nothing could deprive us of that certainty. For the first time, I felt like everything would be okay. The Ambrosia would purify me and the nightmare would be over, replaced by our dreams. As though he'd heard my thoughts, Evan accelerated, racing toward that new hope, toward a new world where he and I would be together . . . this time forever.

Atyantam.

EVAN

19

WAITING

July 9th

I gazed at Gemma, who lay on the bed in my room as I played the violin. Five months had gone by since the night of our wedding, and it had been the most wonderful time of my entire life.

"Don't stop. Keep playing for me, Evan."

"As you wish," I whispered. I tucked the violin back under my chin, my damp hair falling over my forehead. My eyes were prisoners to hers as my melody filled the room, pursuing our eternal love. I couldn't stop staring at Gemma as she lay there, relaxed, her cheeks flushed after we'd made love. The sun had just risen but the summer light was already streaming into the room. The song came to an end and I walked over to her.

"There's nothing sexier than a handsome, bare-chested man playing the violin while gazing into your eyes."

". . . Said the woman who had bewitched him." I touched the bow to her neck ever so slightly. "Will that suffice or would you have more, my lady?" She smiled at me, raising her arms over her head as the bow moved across her skin, sliding down to her breasts. It rose again and pushed the bra strap off her shoulder.

"I could watch you play for hours," she said. It had become her favorite thing, asking me for a song after we made love. She would lie there gazing at me while I poured my love for her into the strings, playing brand-new notes.

"That last song reminded me of an old movie I used to adore. *Canone Inverso: Making Love.*"

"I've never seen it, but we could watch it together."

"It's really touching. I'm afraid I would cry more than usual. We'd better wait until after the baby's born. You can listen to the soundtrack, if you like. It's by Ennio Morricone."

"Speaking of the baby, do you still feel nothing different? I mean, he should've been born by now." Over the last few weeks my tension had grown with each passing day as the time drew near for the big moment . . . and for Sophìa to claim Gemma's soul. No other Subterraneans had attacked us, and Gemma was safe, but the baby was overdue and it worried me not to know why.

Gemma smiled. Unlike me, she was calm. "I told you, Evan. It's normal in my family. My mother had a really long pregnancy too."

"And you're special," I said without thinking.

"Does that mean you think he will be too?" she asked. That seemed to be the only thing that still upset her. We didn't know if the baby would be human or if he would have powers. Ginevra had tried using magic to find out more, but the baby was protected by an impenetrable shell.

"We'll find out soon enough," I reassured her, and she nodded. I was happy Gemma had agreed to follow my plan and not transform. It had been hard to keep the secret all those months. The Witches continued to stay at the house, but Gemma had gotten good at keeping them from reading her mind. I'd helped her perfect the technique and together we'd hidden our true intentions, letting them believe Gemma intended to keep up her side of the pact with Sophìa. Not even Simon and Ginevra knew. We did it to protect them—both from the Witches, who were always prowling around, and from the consequences of our decision.

Once the baby was born, I would take Gemma to Heaven and she would eat of the Tree, casting evil out of her heart forever. In recent months, our plan had helped her stay strong whenever the darkness spread its tentacles around her. The closer the time to transform drew, the more strongly the power of evil writhed within her, threatening to tear her away. But soon it would all be over.

"There's something you haven't told me."

"What?" she asked.

"Why did you ask the Witches for three days after the birth?"

"Funny, Simon asked me the same thing."

"Really? What did you tell him?"

"That's how they do it in Disney movies."

I laughed. "Is that the real reason?"

"Well, not only that."

"Tell me the rest," I encouraged her, pushing the hair from her forehead. I sought her eyes until she raised them and looked at me. "I wanted to spend time with the baby. No matter what happened, I wanted us to be a family, at least for a little while."

Her answer left me wordless. I held her close and kissed her head. "We will be. And not for three days, but forever."

She pressed her lips to mine to seal the vow. "A while ago you said you'd gotten orders?"

I bit her lip. "I only take orders from you," I whispered.

Gemma laughed. "At ease, Soldier. We can't spend the whole day in this room making love."

"You're right." My hand slid down to her hip. "There's the spa and the living room . . . and the kitchen. What about the garage?"

She punched my shoulder and broke free from my embrace. "We've already done it in the garage, remember? And in the workout room and the swimming pool and the music room." She leaned in again to tease me, which she loved doing so much. "But the part I love most is when you steal into my dreams," she admitted.

"Why?" I asked, curious.

"Because that way we can be together all the time, day and night. I don't want to waste even one minute."

She kissed me sweetly and I took a deep breath, preparing to leave her. "Speaking of which . . ."

"You have to go," she finished for me. "You have a mission and you can't stay, I know. Orders come first. What's wrong, Evan? Why that look? With Anya and Ginevra here I'll be fine."

"No, not this time." She stared at me, puzzled. It was hard to give her the bad news. "I never thought I'd say this, but you need to spend some time with your friend Peter. I'm going over to take his father."

"No . . ." she gasped in shock. "Mr. Turner . . ."

"I'm sorry. I have to follow orders. His time has come."

Gemma blinked and a tear slid down her face. "Can I at least say goodbye to him?" I nodded. "How much time does he have left?"

"I'll be at his house in an hour."

She leapt out of bed and pulled on her clothes. "Take the car. I won't be needing it," I told her.

"Thank you," she said softly. I knew she was talking not about the car but the fact that I was giving her the chance to say goodbye. She kissed me on the lips and left the room. I heard her run down the stairs, open and shut the front door, and start the car. It couldn't have been easy for her. She'd grown up with Peter and had known Mr. Turner since she was a little girl; it was right that she be there for her friend, though the thought of the two of them together put me on edge. To avoid upsetting her too much, I'd waited until the last minute to break the bad news to her, but the time had come. I went downstairs to the living room.

"Everything okay?" Simon asked. "I saw Gemma run out the door. She all right?"

"Yeah, she's fine. She went to Peter's. In a little while I've got an appointment at his house."

"I see. The mother?"

"Father. I gave Gemma the chance to say goodbye. Besides, the kid's going to need her."

"That was a nice thing to do. I know how hard it is for you."

"Yeah."

"The baby? Any news?"

"Nothing yet. I wonder if his being overdue has anything to do with his nature," I told him, worried.

"We've already talked about that. There's no way we can know until he's born. In any case, Gemma ingested the poison and the baby survived anyway. That should give us hope. It means he's immune to the poison and he's not a Subterranean. Besides, Gemma conceived him as a mortal. Maybe he'll be a baby like all the others."

"We can't say that for sure." Ginevra appeared in the room. "Evil was already rooted inside her. Maybe your genes combined to generate something unique. His powers might prove to be immense. He has the blood of a Subterranean and the blood of a Witch."

"You know what that means?" Simon asked her, without actually expecting an answer. "It might put an end to the feud that has shed blood on both sides for centuries."

"Or it might trigger a war," Ginevra said. "The bloodiest, most ferocious one ever seen."

I clenched my fists. If there was one thing that was sure, it was that no one was going to take my son from me.

"The day is coming, Evan," Simon reminded me. "Gemma could give birth at any moment. Have you thought of how you're going to face the Witches if she really does manage to go through the transformation without being obliterated? Do you really think they'll agree to let her go without a fight?"

Ginevra gave me a hard look. "She's not going to transform, is she?" I frowned in frustration. Distracted, I'd let a bit of my concern show and Ginevra had picked up on it.

"What's she talking about?" Simon asked, surprised.

"We'll talk it over when I get back. Right now I have to go."

"Evan!" Ginevra called after me as I disappeared. But it was too late.

20

A SAD FAREWELL

I materialized at the Turner home. They were all in the living room—Peter, his parents, and Gemma. When I arrived she flinched, but instantly realized from my gray eyes that she was the only one who could see me, so she tried to hide her emotions as best she could. We stared at each other for a few seconds and then I nodded my head. Her lips tightened and her eyes filled with sadness because the time had come. I was there for Mr. Turner and soon I would take his soul.

"*Get him out of here,*" I told her with my mind.

She took Peter by the arm and pulled him up from the sofa. "Why don't you show me your latest drawing?"

Peter was instantly enthusiastic. Gemma knew how to handle the guy. "You're going to like it. It's in my room. Come upstairs with me."

They turned to go but before leaving the living room, Gemma stopped. "Mr. Turner?"

"Yes, sweetheart?" he replied. He was a tall, broad-shouldered man with gray hair and a slight paunch. His son didn't much resemble him; he'd inherited his mother's traits.

"I'm happy you decided not to move to Europe."

The man's face lit up. "Fortunately, that good-for-nothing brother-in-law of mine came to his senses."

"My uncle took over Grandpa's business so we didn't need to relocate any more," Peter said.

"Last year we were on the verge of packing our bags who knows how many times," his mother said. "My brother wouldn't hear of working in the fields and we couldn't let everything fall apart. Still, my father isn't as strong as he used to be and needed help."

"I understand, Mrs. Turner. You're Italian, right?"

"Yes, I'm from a small town in Tuscany."

"Peter told me about it. It must be a wonderful place."

"Oh, you can't imagine!"

"Let them go, dear. You can tell them all about it some other time," her husband said, as though he had a more pressing need.

"In any case, thank you," Gemma concluded. "It's great that you stayed here."

"You're such a sweet girl," he replied.

Gemma shot me one last glance before leaving the room with Peter. I went over to the man, who had started chatting with his wife, believing they were alone. He had no idea I was there for him. No one knew it, except Gemma. I found the thought a bit disorienting. It was strange to carry out orders knowing she was there in the house with me.

"It's such a shame Gemma got pregnant by another boy."

"What are you saying, Matthew?"

"I know my son. He'll never give up on that girl, and with a baby on the way it'll be harder for him to win her over." I clenched my fists, tempted to put an immediate end to the conversation.

"Gemma's a fine girl, but she's with another boy now and they're about to have a baby together. I'm sure Peter has already gotten over it and that one day he'll find someone more fitting for him."

"What, are you blind? Can't you see how he looks at her? He's not going to give up until he gets her, Angela. Either that or he'll suffer in silence for the rest of his life. Between the two alternatives, I prefer the first."

"What do you want him to do?"

"I don't want him to suffer. I hope Gemma has a change of heart and finally recognizes what there is between them."

"Do you really want Peter to raise someone else's child?"

"Why not? I did it." My eyes bulged with surprise. So he wasn't Peter's real father?

"Shh . . . Do you want him to hear you?"

"You're the one who never wanted to tell him. I never had a problem with it. He's my son, as far as I'm concerned."

"He's not ready yet," the mother said softly, tears in her eyes. "He'll find out when the time is right. The truth might upset him now."

"Or it might give him the strength to—Ah!" Mr. Turner raised a hand to his head. His coffee cup fell to the ground.

"Matthew! Matthew, what's wrong?!" His wife knelt in front of him.

"My head!" he groaned between gritted teeth. "It feels like it's been split in two with an ax. It . . . hurts."

His wife jumped to her feet, grabbed her phone, and called 911. "Help! My husband needs help! Hurry!" She gave them the address and went back to comforting him, trembling. He was on his knees now, his elbow propped on the sofa. I clenched my fists tighter to finish what I'd begun. The man gave a cry of pain and crumpled to the floor.

"Matthew!" Angela screamed, bursting into tears. "Peter! Peter, come here! Hurry!"

"What's wrong?" he shouted, rushing into the room. Seeing his father lying there, Peter stood paralyzed in the doorway for a moment. "Dad . . ." he murmured.

In tears, his mother looked at her husband. "They're on their way," she said, stroking his face. "Everything will be just fine. You're going to be just fine." She'd rested her husband's head on her lap, tears streaming down her cheeks.

Peter ran across the room and knelt before his father. "Dad!" he said anxiously. I looked up and met Gemma's eyes. She'd never seen me during a mission and she hadn't taken her eyes off me for a second. Was she afraid of me? What was she thinking? Was all she saw a Soldier of Death who'd come to tear away the soul of her friend's father? Or did she realize it was still me?

"You don't have to watch this, you know," my voice touched her mind. I didn't want her to see the darkness that lurked in me. She shook her head slowly. She was going to stay put.

"Dad!" Peter's voice broke the connection between us. We both looked at the boy, who was leaning over his dying father. "Don't worry, they're coming." He didn't cry, but his voice was distraught.

His father, who'd realized his time had come, shook his head and motioned him closer. "Take care of your mother. You're the man of the house now. Understood?"

A tear slid down Peter's face. "Don't say that, Dad! You're going to get better."

"There's something you should know."

"Matthew . . ." His wife tried to stop him but her sobs prevented it.

"Your mother was already pregnant when I met her. I . . ." Suddenly he let out another cry of pain.

"Don't talk, Dad. Don't talk . . . They're on their way."

"No. You need to know. I'm not . . . I'm not your father," he confessed, his eyes filling with tears.

"Yes. Yes, you are. I've always known, but I've never cared. You *are* my father." The man's eyes wavered with surprise and his heart beat faster for a moment before going forever silent. "Dad!" Peter cried, but the man's gaze was already lost and his hand dropped out of the boy's.

The mother bit her fist, unable to hold back a grief-stricken sob. She hugged her husband, shaking him through her tears. I looked at Gemma, who was standing in the doorway, a hand clasped over her mouth and her eyes full of tears.

"I'm sorry," I whispered to her mind. Why had I thought bringing her there was a good idea? I knew the answer: she would never have forgiven me if I hadn't told her.

Something behind me drew her attention. The sorrow vanished from her eyes, replaced by astonishment. I turned to find Peter's father's soul standing beside me, his gaze locked on his family. I looked back at Gemma, stunned. *She could see him.* A shiver crept through me as I lost myself in her eyes. They were turning black.

"Gemma, stay with me," I whispered in her mind. What the hell had I been thinking, bringing her there?! *"Gem, Peter is suffering. Your friend needs you."* My words managed to break through to her heart, driving the darkness away. Gemma knelt beside Peter and held his hand without saying a word.

"Have you come for me?" Mr. Turner stared at me, waiting. "Thank you," he said quietly. "I never would have been able to tell him any other way."

I nodded. He'd suffered so much about not being Peter's biological father that he'd only been able to tell him with his last breath. If he'd found the courage to do so sooner, he would have realized it didn't matter much to Peter. Mr. Turner's soul was now free of remorse and fear. The confession had liberated him and his soul was at peace.

"Can she see us?" His question snapped me out of my meditative trance. I stared at Gemma, still shaken, and she immediately looked away.

"No. None of them can," I lied.

He took a closer look at me. "I know you. You're—"

"You're mistaken. You've never seen me before."

"I've never seen you before. Who are you?" he asked, influenced by what I'd said.

"It doesn't matter. Your time here is over. Take my hand and you'll finally be free."

The man looked one last time at his family. "Will I see them again?"

"One day, perhaps." I didn't want to lie to him again. I didn't know if there would be Subterraneans waiting for them when their time came. If they gave in to Temptation, they would find a Witch waiting for them instead.

The man reached out and took my hand, slowly vanishing. My eyes went to Gemma's. She'd seen the whole thing. I had no idea what she was thinking or how she saw me just then. I was Death. Had she truly understood that before? The ambulance's siren announced its pointless arrival. Gemma hugged Peter, staring at me over his shoulder. *"Stay with him for a while,"* I suggested in her mind, *"but then come back to me."* She nodded slightly, her big dark eyes fixed on mine as I disappeared.

21

DISAGREEMENTS

"Well?" Ginevra snapped the second I reappeared in the living room. "What's going on? And why have you kept us out of the loop?"

I walked past her and went to pour myself a bourbon, which I tossed back in a single gulp before pouring another one. "I did it to protect you. It's not safe with them here," I growled, nodding at the door leading down to the dungeon. The Witches were still underfoot. It would be easier for them to discover the truth if all of us knew about it.

"What are you planning, Evan?" Simon admonished me, grabbing me by the arm.

"I'm going to have Gemma eat of the Tree. She's already agreed."

Simon stepped back, gripping his hair in his hands. "You're out of your mind. We already discarded that idea, remember?"

"We said we'd talk about it one day, but we never did."

"I thought you'd gotten a hold on yourself! Damn it, you never think of the consequences."

"Well, you think about them too much."

"Because everything is at stake!" he yelled.

"I'm not going to sit around while she transforms and erases me from her heart completely. You and Ginevra were enemies once—you should know what it means."

"This is different. Everything is different! Gemma isn't going to erase you from her heart."

"We can't know that for sure, and I don't want to lose her. I'm willing to lose myself. I'm even willing to lose you two if you're not with me on this. I'm sorry, but not her—I can't lose her."

"Evan," Ginevra said. Reading the desperation in my thoughts had calmed her. "There's a good chance it won't happen. I wouldn't tell you that if I didn't believe it. Gemma is strong and can withstand evil."

"But she doesn't want to go through with it," I snarled. "She's afraid. She's afraid of herself; I can feel it. Every night in her dreams I feel the terror consuming her. She doesn't want to undergo the transformation any longer because she's afraid she can't do it. I've seen how powerfully evil possesses her—you two have seen it for yourselves."

"That's because she hasn't transformed yet. Once she has, she'll be capable of controlling all that power, but she can't do it as long as she's still human. Evil is like a beast trapped inside her."

"And I'm not willing to set it free. Not if it means Gemma could become my enemy. I'm sorry."

"She made a deal with the devil herself, Evan. There's no turning back."

"Ambrosia will free her."

"That's insane!" my brother roared.

"Why don't you ever agree with me?!" I groaned in frustration.

"Because you're reckless," Simon retorted, "and because your love for Gemma is making you desperate."

"I'm not crazy and I'll prove it to you."

"Evan, think about this." Simon struggled to stay calm, hoping I would listen to him. "If making Gemma drink Ambrosia was enough to prevent her from becoming a Witch, don't you think the Màsala would have done that already—not only with her, but with all the other Sisters?!"

"The Màsala can't go against what God Himself has decreed. The Witches are His gift to Sophìa. One every five hundred years. He made a promise," Ginevra put in.

"But they also decided to intervene by trying to kill her before she could transform, and who has to pay the consequences for their dirty tricks? We do!" I shouted, beside myself. "A random accident that happens to a soon-to-be Witch goes unnoticed, whereas purifying her with the Divine Fruit would expose them, revealing their treachery, which would mean another Witch might get called in to replace Gemma and they'd be back at square one. For the Màsala, nothing would change. For me, everything would."

"Purification didn't work on Sophìa," Ginevra reminded me. "Not even the Diamantea cage eradicated evil from her heart."

"Gemma isn't the devil. It might work on her."

"But then what happens?" Simon asked. "You don't know."

"You're still in time to reconsider," Ginevra added. "Maybe Gemma can undergo the transformation without losing herself. There's still hope."

"Hope isn't enough for me, Gin. I need to do something."

Simon shook his head. "I can't let you. It's too big a risk for you."

"She's already agreed. If you want to prevent it, you'll have to go through me." I stared at Simon, my eyes brimming with defiance.

"Fine, if it'll knock some sense into you." Simon took off his shirt and I did the same, assuming a defensive stance. He materialized behind me and grabbed me by the shoulders, but I warded off his attack and tried to shove him off balance.

"My mind's made up," I said resolutely.

He threw a punch but I blocked his arm and knocked him to the floor. He deftly dragged me down with him and the battle ensued amid broken glass and shattered stones. I grabbed Simon and slammed him against a wall, which cracked under the blow.

"That's enough!" Ginevra yelled.

But with a snarl Simon struck me full in the chest, sending me flying backwards, gritting my teeth from the pain. I fell to my knees, panting. He'd burned me with white fire. "You bastard," I murmured.

"I can't believe this. You're like two little kids. We've got to stick together! You even agreed to join forces with the Witches and now you're fighting each other?"

Simon held out his hand to help me up and I took it, groaning from the pain. "Sorry, bro," he said, nodding at the scorch marks the fire had left on my chest.

"You play dirty," I said reproachfully.

"I did it for you. I can't let you do something so crazy." He rested his hand on my shoulder and the burns slowly healed.

"Sorry, but there's no talking me out of it. Not this time." When I'd fallen in love with Gemma, my only fear had been that she would be afraid of me, but now I had a bigger fear: that she would see me as an enemy.

"It's not up to us to decide, unfortunately," Ginevra said. There was a hint of sorrow in her eyes. I knew that deep down, a small part of her wanted Gemma to transform. "Is that really what she wants?"

"Yes."

"She did a good job hiding it. She had a good teacher." Ginevra looked at me sharply.

"No one's better than me at keeping you out, remember? I've thought a lot about the possible consequences, believe me. I know there may be a high price to pay, but my mind's made up: once the baby is born, Gemma is going to drink Ambrosia."

"Making a decision is always an act of courage," Ginevra said softly.

"Sometimes courage lies in backing down," Simon countered, still far from convinced. He turned to me. "What makes you think she won't transform all the same?"

"I *need* this hope. Don't take it away from me. It's all I've got. Some risks are worth fighting for."

"Such vehemence in your eyes." I jumped at Devina's voice and glanced at Ginevra. How much of our conversation had she overheard? I could see Ginevra looking at Devina, searching her mind. She looked at me and shook her head.

Devina circled me, stroking my bare chest. "Aw, did my Champion get wounded in battle?" She gazed at me with tender eyes while I glowered back at her. I grabbed her wrists roughly, taking her hands off me.

She smiled. "You always did know how to turn me on."

"I'm not your Champion."

"Not yet. Hope springs eternal." With a wink, she turned her back on me and cracked her whip.

I need this hope. The words I'd just said a minute ago whirled through my head. What if Devina was capable of hiding the truth from Ginevra too? No. She couldn't have overheard our conversation. My sister would have realized it.

"Don't you knock before *appearing*?" Simon asked her curtly.

Devina looked him over from head to toe. "You're not so bad yourself," she said provocatively. "We could have a nice party here, just the four of us. What do you say?" She winked at Simon.

Ginevra stepped in front of her. "Why don't we have one, just you and me?" she challenged, her eyes burning into Devina's.

"Okay, blondie, don't get all worked up."

Anya walked through the door leading downstairs. "What's going on? Haven't you told them yet?"

"I was just about to," Devina said.

"Told us what?"

"We're going to have a problem pretty soon. The Subterraneans are fading because they haven't eaten of the Tree for such a long time."

"So soon?" I asked, worried. "It's only been a few months."

"It's our poison. The blood we give them and the magic we use to keep them under control saps their energy. That's why we think they're going to fade away soon. I don't know how much longer they have. The baby should have been born by now. We didn't expect things to go on this long. Soon they'll begin to disappear into Oblivion."

"What a waste!" Devina groaned. "Let's at least claim their souls before they disappear—that way they'll end up in Hell instead of vanishing. Some of them have even begged me: 'Please, I don't want to end up in Oblivion!' Cowards! Still, it's been torture, not being able to give in to their wishes."

"Cut it out, Dev," Anya told her. "That's not the problem. If the prisoners die . . ."

"Others will come," Simon thought aloud.

"So we fight them," I continued, resolute. I was prepared to do anything. No one was going to stop me.

22

THE FOREST AWAKENS

"Is Gemma still with Peter?" Simon asked me as he walked into the workout room.

The punching bag was still swinging from my blows. I stopped it with my forearm. "Yeah. It's a rough moment for him. He needs her."

"How's Gemma handling it?"

"She's strong. She'll manage to help him through it."

"Not that." Simon sent me a knowing look.

Gemma had watched me carry out an order. The sight of her eyes filling with darkness had shaken me, but I didn't tell Simon about that. I grabbed a long steel staff and began practicing with it, twirling it in front of me. "It wasn't the first time it had happened, actually. She'd already seen Drake take somebody right before the accident in my Ferrari," I said, mostly trying to reassure myself. I spun the stick and shifted it from hand to hand.

"That's not the same thing," Simon insisted.

"What do you want me to say, that I'm scared? Yeah, I am. Happy now?" I exclaimed in exasperation. "I took that man's life right in front of her eyes and I have no idea how she's going to see me from now on."

Simon removed his shirt and started punching the bag that hung from the ceiling, glancing at me from over his rear fist. "Why don't you ask her?"

I stopped, the staff slamming to a halt in my palm. "You're right. It's been hours. I'd better get Gemma some lunch."

"Otherwise she might eat some of her friends," Simon joked. I shot him a dirty look, holding back a grin, then focused on Gemma. A second later, I frowned.

"What's up?" he asked, seeing my expression suddenly go grave.

"I can't find her," I said, worried.

"What do you mean you can't find her?" He too tried to search for Gemma's soul, but a second later his eyes met mine. "You're right. I can't sense her aura."

I searched for Peter's soul and quickly found it: he was with his mother, but Gemma wasn't there. "What the fuck is going on? Where did she go?" I materialized upstairs in the living room and Simon followed me. "Gwen, try to find Gemma. I can't."

"What do you mean, you can't?"

"I mean you have to track down her thoughts, damn it!" I snapped, out of my mind with worry.

Ginevra stood there listening, combing the whole town in search of Gemma's mind. She stared into space for a moment before finally turning to me, disheartened. She couldn't find her either. I grabbed my hair in desperation.

"Calm down, Evan. It doesn't mean anything," Simon reassured me.

A surge of rage filled my chest. I struck the glass coffee table with my fist, shattering it into a thousand pieces, furious at myself for having been so careless. "I shouldn't have let her go! We can't find Gemma. How can you think I could possibly calm down?! Do you know what this means? She might even be dead!" I shouted in despair.

"Evan, you know that's not the only possible explanation," Ginevra said. "Evil has probably taken her over. That's been happening more and more often lately."

I tried to calm myself. She was right. Gemma couldn't be dead—the Subterraneans were all under lock and key. She wasn't running any risks. But then where was she? Her experience with Peter's father must have brought back the darkness. When her mind was possessed, not even the Witches could sense her. She disappeared as though she no longer existed. At Peter's house I'd seen her eyes transform. I shouldn't have left her alone. What a fool I'd been!

"She's in the forest," Devina said, materializing next to us.

I rushed at her and squeezed my hand around her neck, shoving her against the wall. "How do you know that? Did you take her there?" Her serpent burst through her skin, poised to attack me, its fiery eyes defiant.

"Enough! You're losing control," Ginevra shouted, stepping between us. "Evan, you need to calm down. Devina knows where Gemma is. That's a good thing." Devina smiled at me, her catlike eyes locked on mine.

"And you, try to be clearer and tell us exactly where Gemma is," her Sister said.

"Only when the Spartan gets over his urge to kill me."

"Then we'll never know," I snarled through clenched teeth. "Put your serpent away," I warned her.

She smiled, her gaze provocative. "Why don't you take yours out? Please?"

"Tell me where Gemma is!" I slammed my palms against the wall on either side of her head, cracking it.

"She's in the forest," Ginevra said, reading the Witch's mind, "near the Peninsula Trail by the old Howard Johnson."

"I know where that is." We'd been there a thousand times before, alone or with her friends. But why had Gemma gone there?

"We'll come with you," Simon was quick to offer.

"No," I said. "I'm going alone. I'll contact you if I need you." He nodded, realizing that after what had happened at Peter's house I needed to talk to Gemma alone.

I vanished and rematerialized in the forest, unsure exactly where Gemma was—I still couldn't sense her soul. I wandered through the trees, calling her name, but there was no sign of her. A boat was making its way across the river. There seemed to be injured people on board but I didn't have time to look into it. Gemma wasn't with them.

Then I saw her.

"Gemma . . ." I murmured, my heart in turmoil. She was curled up on the ground, head down. "Gemma!" I cried as I rushed to her. She heard me and raised her head. A second later I was holding her in my arms. She clung to me as though afraid she would sink into the earth.

"Evan," she sobbed.

"My love, what happened? I was going out of my mind."

She clung to me harder and wept, shattering my heart into a million pieces. "It was terrible," she whispered. "I don't want to be like this. Save me, Evan, I'm begging you."

I stroked her hair and closed my eyes. How could I even think of letting her transform? "It's over. I'm here now," I said softly. Feeling the desperate need to keep her with me, I held her close. There was dirt under her fingernails. She must have sunk her hands into the ground as she abandoned herself to the tears. "Tell me what happened."

"I don't even know where to start."

"What were you doing here?"

She shook her head, drying her tears. "I don't know. I found myself here. The other night I dreamed of the Peninsula Trail—maybe that's why. I felt this shooting pain in my temples and suddenly my mind was filled with the thoughts of people I didn't know. Prayers, desires. My head was about to explode. And then I heard your voice. It was you, guiding me through the darkness."

"It wasn't me."

"I know, but at the moment I believed it was. I must have imagined it."

"Or maybe not." Gemma looked at me and frowned, seeing the fire in my eyes. "Did you happen to see Devina while you were coming here?"

"No, but . . . You're right. Now I remember clearly. I thought it was you, but it wasn't really your voice. It was hers. She was telling me to follow my instinct."

"I'm going to kill that bitch!" I snarled, gritting my teeth.

Gemma took my hands and I tried to remain calm. "You can't hold it against her. They want me with them—they've never made a secret of that. It's my fault. It's what I am," she murmured, distraught.

"No it isn't, and it never will be," I said with conviction. I wouldn't let evil drag her away. I couldn't bear to see her like this, defenseless. I would offer myself in her place if it meant saving her from the darkness.

Gemma stared at her hands, still trembling. "Evil is inside me. I can feel it growing every day." I clenched my jaw. At that moment—more than ever before—I longed to have her drink the nectar of the Divine Fruit. I didn't care what Simon thought. I didn't care what the consequences would be. "Maybe there's no hope for me any more. The darkness is consuming me," she whispered, tears in her eyes.

"Don't say that. Please don't."

Gemma looked at me. The sorrow in her eyes was a knife driven into my heart. "You don't understand," she murmured in a barely audible voice. "I killed him."

My eyes widened. "What are you talking about, Gemma? Who did you kill?"

Gemma wasn't listening to me. She seemed lost in the memory. "I wanted his soul." An icy shiver crept over me, trapping my breath in my lungs. She continued: "It was so easy. I saw a boat. On it, a dog was whimpering. Someone had hit it. Blind rage flooded me and I felt I couldn't allow it. A second later there I was, on board with them. Not my body, just my soul. My dark, dangerous soul. The owner of the dog had rushed the guy and I told him not to stop. *'Hit him! He's a filthy bastard!'* And so he hit him.

"Their wives were screaming, trying to get them to stop, but the two kept fighting and the boat rocked on the current. Then the guy fell and the dog's owner grabbed him, glaring at him with bloodshot eyes. He held the guy's head over the side of the boat, blinded by the rage that I was fueling. 'Stop it!' the women screamed. But he didn't stop, because I didn't want him to. I wanted him to keep going. I wanted him to kill the guy.

"'Not so tough when you're the one getting beat up, are you, asshole?' he shouted, repeating the words I put into his head. He slammed the man's head against the boat. The dog was barking. The women were crying. I was electrified by his energy.

"'Okay, you win,' the other man said, pleading. 'I shouldn't have hit your dog. I'm sorry.' His teeth were covered with blood and he could barely breathe. The dog's owner loosened his grip, so I went up to him. *'Kill him. Otherwise he might do it again. He deserves to be punished,'* I whispered in his ear.

"He shouted, 'Fuck you, you ugly bastard.' 'Richard, no!' his friend's wife begged. But it was too late. He slammed his head harder against the boat and the women shrieked at the sight of the blood. Then a force pulled me back and I was here again." Gemma stared at her hands, as though they were drenched in blood.

I hugged her and she burst into tears. "I killed him! He hadn't done anything and I killed him. Evan, I don't want to be this way. Save me, please!"

I cupped her face in my hands, wiped away her tears, and rested my forehead against hers. "Look at me, Gemma. You didn't kill him. You got that?" She frowned. I had her full attention. "I saw the boat just before I found you. Someone was injured but no one was dead," I reassured her.

She gaped at me. "It was you. You brought me back." She hugged me tight. "Only you can drag me out of the darkness. Be my light, Evan. Don't leave me in the shadows."

"I won't." I kissed her forehead. "I never will. Forgive me—it was all my fault."

"What do you mean?"

"You came into contact with a Soul. I showed you his passing. It reawakened the Witch buried in you," I admitted. "It was all my fault."

Gemma shook her head, seeing how guilty I felt. "Don't say that. You did something wonderful, letting me be there for my friend. I'm the one who always ruins everything."

"You mean you don't see me differently now?"

"What? Why should I?"

"Because you saw the Executioner. You saw me when I killed a mortal and took his soul. That's why I told you to leave. I didn't want you to see the darkness in me," I admitted wearily.

Gemma looked at me, her expression calm again. "You've seen mine and you haven't run away. Why would I do it to you?"

"I'm Death, Gemma."

"You're still you, Evan. And to me you're everything," she said, looking me steadily in the eye.

"I realize that part of me has always scared you, and today I showed it to you. We're going to stop the evil inside you, but no one can ever change what I am: I'm a Soldier and I bring death with me. I took your friend's father, whom you also cared for. How can you not hate me?"

"Hate you? Seeing you in action was *magnificent*," she confessed.

"Magnificent? I killed that man right in front of your eyes, Gemma. Weren't you even a little afraid for him? You knew I was there, that he was about to die."

"How is it you don't understand? You saved him."

"I understand that. I'm just amazed you do too." We Subterraneans were clear about our mission: to liberate Souls from their bodies and guide them to eternal peace. It was mortals who usually didn't understand death. "What else did you feel?" I asked, eager to know her emotions.

"I saw how you convinced Mr. Turner I couldn't see the two of you. I almost believed it myself. It was weird . . . and exciting."

"Exciting," I repeated, laughing.

"Don't make fun of me!" Gemma punched me on the shoulder.

"You're right. This is no time to kid around. How's Peter?"

"Shaken, but he's trying to be strong for his mom. I was with him all morning. Jeneane, Brandon, Jake, and Faith came over too."

I nodded. Jake and Faith had finally become a couple and were inseparable. It had happened at the dance: he'd kissed her, and seeing how eagerly she'd kissed him back, he wouldn't take no for an answer. "Where's Peter now?"

"Running errands. He had to help his mom make all the arrangements, so we left. She's devastated and needs him right now, poor thing. The funeral is tomorrow."

"I'm sorry."

"Me too."

I stood up and held out my hand. "What do you say I get you something to eat?"

Gemma smiled. "What were you planning to get for me here in the forest, hmm?"

"Fish, birds . . . how about a little squirrel meat?"

She took my hand, stood up, and punched me on the shoulder again. "I don't eat squirrels!"

I laughed. "I know. I was only kidding—though I bet right now you could eat a horse. I heard your stomach growl a couple times."

"Moron!" Gemma walked past me, pouting.

"Only joking! But you really should eat something. Our hideaway isn't far from here. I could ask Ginevra to bring you something."

"All right, but I'm not a bottomless pit. I don't know why you guys always say that."

"If you say so." I shrugged, hiding a smile.

"Oh, all right, I admit it. Happy? I like food. I could eat a—Ahhh!"

I flinched, petrified by her scream. She doubled over, her hands on her belly. "Gemma, what's wrong?" I asked anxiously.

She cried out again, this time louder. "It's the baby," she managed to say, gritting her teeth against the pain. "He's coming."

"What? Here? *Now*?"

"Ahhh!"

I looked around. What was I supposed to do? I didn't have the faintest idea! I'd seen many lives come into the world, but I'd never felt so nervous before. Our baby was about to be born. It was both exciting and frightening.

"Evan!" Gemma's shout brought me back to reality.

"Hold on to me," I told her. "I'll take you to the hideaway. It's not far." I took her in my arms and she cried out even louder.

"No. No! Put me down!" she cried, panting. "Here. We need to do it here."

"All right." I gently rested her on the ground and she clung tightly to my arm.

"Don't leave me, Evan. I'm afraid."

"I'm here." I took her hand and kissed it, looking into her eyes. Gemma needed me; there was no room for doubt. I had to give her strength now. "Stay calm and breathe normally. I'll help you. You're safe with me," I whispered.

She nodded, clenching her teeth against another contraction. I took off my shirt and used it to cushion her head. "You trying to turn me on? Because this is not the time," she joked.

"What a shame—I was hoping it would work as a distraction." I winked at her and she laughed. "Now you need to focus, Gemma. Don't worry. Everything's going to be fine." She nodded several times and let me spread her legs apart.

"Gin! Simon! I need you, now!" I shouted in my mind. Removing Gemma's underwear, I saw it was drenched with amniotic fluid. The impenetrable shell that had protected our son for all those months had broken. I knelt there, perfectly still, a shiver running down my spine. For the first time, I could sense my son's soul. The emotion threatened to overwhelm me.

"Is everything all right? What is it?" she asked, concerned by my expression.

"It's our baby. The time has come to meet him. It's time, my love. Now you have to help him come out, okay? Here, let me help you. When you feel the pain, just—"

She squeezed my hand in a death grip. "Ahhh . . ." The earth shook beneath us. I looked up. All at once, clouds gathered in the sky and the forest came to life. Leaves whirled through the air, driven by a dark force. It was as though Gemma and I were in the eye of a hurricane that raged all around us. The lake churned, the water rising into giant waves. Nature was witnessing an extraordinary event; never before had a Witch given birth.

"What's happening, Evan?"

"It's nothing. Just focus on the baby. Here he comes! I see his head!" I exclaimed, my hands trembling. "You're doing great. One more push. We're almost there! That's it!"

The forest howled around us as though Gemma's energy had transferred itself to the trees. I let go of her hand, preparing to catch the baby. She screeched between clenched teeth and bore down in one final, exhausting push.

I caught the baby and cradled him in my arms. The forest filled with his cries. The leaves trembled and the wind howled even more fiercely, like a wolf acknowledging its leader. All the elements seemed to awaken at the force of his life's shriek. A flock of birds rose in flight and filled the air. I raised the baby to my chest. He looked at me and the wind stopped howling. The clouds dispersed and sunlight streamed down on us as my soul touched my son's. Tears flooded my eyes and I had to squeeze them shut and open them several times to make out his face.

"Evan . . ." Gemma murmured, breathless. She was exhausted. "Quickly, I want to see him," she begged me, in tears. I cut the umbilical cord, healed the end of it, and rested him, still covered with blood, in Gemma's arms. "It's a boy," I whispered. "Just like you always said."

She clasped him to her chest and wept. I couldn't stop staring at him. He had big, blue, slightly almond-shaped eyes and thick, curly, dark hair. And those tiny hands . . . I felt a primordial need to protect him. I healed Gemma's wounds, sat down behind her, and held her close as together we admired our little miracle, with only the forest as witness.

"Thank you," she said softly. "I couldn't have done it without you."

"I wouldn't have missed it for anything in the world." I kissed her.

The baby wailed. "See that, Evan? He's looking at us."

"He recognizes you," I said as mother and child gazed at one another.

She smiled. "Hello, sweetheart. Welcome to the world," she whispered.

"Do you already have a name for him?"

Gemma nodded. "He's always had one. His name is Daniel Liam James."

My eyes went wide. "Daniel. Like Danielle, my mother."

"And Liam from William, like his father. For us he'll just be Liam."

"What do you say we also add Drake, after his uncle?"

"I bet he would call him Double D." Gemma laughed through her tears and then gazed at the baby again. "Drake Daniel Liam James. It's a bit long, but I like it."

I kissed the baby on the forehead. "Liam," I repeated.

Gemma caressed his face. "Hold me tight, Evan."

"I'm right here," I whispered behind her.

A tear trickled down her cheek. "I . . . I don't want to leave him. I don't want the Witches to take me away from you."

"I'll never allow it. We'll follow our plan and everything will go fine, I promise. No one's going to separate us."

Gemma went back to stroking the baby. "Don't worry," she whispered to him. "We'll protect you."

"Guys, where the hell are you?!" I called out in my mind. A second later, Simon and Ginevra appeared behind Gemma. "You guys missed one hell of a show," I exclaimed.

"Oh my God!" Ginevra saw Gemma on the ground and rushed to her side.

"There's someone who wants to meet you," she said.

"Shit." Simon quickly took off his shirt and wrapped it around the baby, who was still in Gemma's arms.

"Hey, would you wait a few days before teaching him swear words?" she joked.

"How did it happen? Why didn't you call us earlier?" Ginevra asked me reproachfully. "I can't believe I missed it!"

"Don't worry, you'll be spending a lot of time together," Gemma assured her.

"I did. I tried calling you. I figured you were in the workout room."

"No, we didn't want be out of reach."

"So why didn't we hear you?" Simon asked me.

Ginevra's eyes shot to mine. We were both thinking the same thing. *It must have been Gemma.* During the birth, it was as though Gemma's energy had exploded all around us. Her power must have interfered with my thoughts, preventing them from reaching the others.

"Can I hold him?" Ginevra asked. Gemma smiled and let her take him out of her arms. "Of all the forms of magic, this is the most extraordinary one," she whispered, cradling the baby.

Simon leaned over and kissed the child on the forehead. "He's adorable. Have you chosen a name?"

"More than one, actually: Drake Daniel Liam James, but to us he'll just be Liam."

"Liam," Ginevra repeated. "You're one of us now."

"He's perfect," Simon told us.

"Simon, bring the baby here," I said. Gin, take care of Gemma."

"Evan, don't leave me," Gemma begged.

"I'm not going anywhere. I just need to get a little water, okay? I'll be back in a second." She nodded and let Ginevra clean her up.

I went to the edge of the lake with Simon, who knelt beside me holding the baby. I raised my palm over the water and it rose up in a gurgling arc. With the heat of my fire I sterilized it, then cooled it enough so Simon could bathe Liam and wrap him in his shirt again.

"Congratulations," he told me, slapping my shoulder. "You're a father now."

"Yeah." I smiled. It was strange to actually hear it said.

"How do you feel?"

"Never been happier," I said.

"As we all are."

"Come on, let's take them someplace more comfortable. Gemma needs to rest." Simon nodded, cradling the baby. I picked Gemma up in my arms and we walked toward our lake house, which wasn't far away.

"We have to tell my parents," Gemma exclaimed when we arrived.

"Simon, would you?" I laid Gemma on the sofa. The sun was still high and sunshine was coming in through the windows, lighting up the room.

"Liam must be hungry," Ginevra said. "I'll get him some milk."

"No," Gemma said. "I want to feed him myself."

Simon handed her the baby and turned to give them some privacy as he phoned Gemma's parents. She bared her breast and snuggled Liam against her. The baby opened his eyes and gazed at his mother for a long moment. He nuzzled her skin, finally found her breast, and began to suckle. Gemma held her breath with emotion and a tear slid down her face. I couldn't imagine her feelings as she fed him.

Our lives were hanging by a thread, held together by an unacceptable oath. The baby was born. We had three days before the Witches returned to claim Gemma. But I wasn't going to let it happen. I was going to take her hand and together, we would let that thread snap and fall into the void—wherever we ended up.

23

LIGHT AND DARKNESS

Gemma's parents were overjoyed by the news of the birth. They closed the diner and hurried over to the lake house. It took a bit longer than expected to convince them there was no need to take Gemma and the baby to the hospital. To reassure them, we made them believe Simon—who everyone believed was a doctor—had delivered Gemma's baby there because there hadn't been time. The two of them couldn't stop thanking him. They had no idea that the baby had been born in the middle of the forest and that I was the one who had delivered him.

Peter's father's funeral was the next morning. We promised we would stop by to see Gemma's parents the next afternoon before leaving town. We'd used a little persuasive mind control to make Gemma's parents believe—and accept—the idea that we were going on a vacation once the baby was born. It was a necessary lie, given that we didn't know what the future had in store for us. They accepted our decision, though reluctantly, and insisted that upon our "return" we get married. They didn't know we already had.

Anya was also with us all afternoon, along with two panthers that prowled the room nervously. Fortunately, the panthers had waited for Gemma's parents to leave before making their appearance. The time was drawing near and the thought was making me nervous. Having them around was risky. At any moment they might discover our plans and ruin everything.

When the sun finally set the visitors left, leaving us alone to admire our son. I was a father. It made me so proud, I could think of nothing else. To Liam I would be the father I'd never had. I would love him, protect him. And maybe one day he would look up to me.

I gazed at Gemma. She'd slept peacefully on the sofa for most of the night, the baby nestled in her arm. She couldn't bear the thought of being separated from him.

Simon and Ginevra had finally come around. It was important for us to have them as allies in our war against the Witches.

"Look, Evan. He woke up," Ginevra whispered. I slowly went up to Liam and took him in my arms, rocking him beside the fireplace. "He looks so sweet, and so human," Ginevra said, caressing him.

"Sure does," Simon added at her side.

"What's he thinking?" I asked Ginevra.

"He's too young. He doesn't have actual thoughts yet, but he's processing everything around him, the images, the sounds . . . I can interpret his sensations."

"How does he feel right now?"

"He feels safe."

"You're my son," I whispered as he studied my face.

"A son born from the union between good and evil, light and darkness," Simon added solemnly. "Whatever his nature is, he's the emblem of that balance."

Ginevra leaned in for a closer look. "And the whole world will kneel to him."

"Liam . . ." Gemma mumbled, waking up.

"He's here," I said reassuringly, going over to her.

"Do you think he's eaten enough?"

"I think so, but maybe you should eat something now. You need to regain your strength."

"I already have," she assured me, "though I'd gladly have some pizza anyway." She cast a hopeful glance at Ginevra.

"You've got an appetite—that's a good sign." She winked at Gemma and pointed at the kitchen table where the pizza was waiting for her. Gemma made a beeline for the food. She was wearing a white nightgown and her long black hair flowed over her shoulders. Her figure was fantastic. No one would have imagined she'd just given birth to a seven-pound bundle of joy. Everyone had been worried that she'd barely gained weight and the pregnancy had lasted so long, but we knew it was because of her nature. Now that the baby was born, there was no longer any sign of the pregnancy, and after the delivery I'd healed all her wounds.

"Simon, would you mind holding Liam?"

"Of course not. We're already best friends," he said.

"Mmm . . . This pizza's delicious. Evan, you brought your violin!" Gemma exclaimed, beaming.

I smiled. "I thought the baby might like a little music." I rested the instrument on my shoulder and played a new melody, sweet and slow, like a soothing lullaby. Liam stared at me attentively, filling my heart with emotions I'd never experienced before. Pride, mostly. His eyelids soon drooped and he surrendered to sleep. I smiled and walked toward his mother, moving the bow over the strings as I looked into Gemma's eyes. Notes from the mahogany piano joined mine. I didn't need to look to know it was Simon accompanying me.

"It's beautiful," Gemma said softly when the music stopped.

"It's for you." I took her hand and kissed her palm, gazing into her eyes. "The love I feel is captured in its notes."

"If Drake were here right now, I bet he'd be grousing about all this lovey-dovey stuff," Ginevra said, grinning.

"She's right, bro. You've completely lost it," Simon added with a smile. He stroked Liam, who was in Ginevra's arms. "But with a miracle like this, I would too."

"We'll all raise him together," Gemma said. "After all, he's also a little bit yours. If it hadn't been for the two of you he wouldn't be here today."

I smiled at Gemma and squeezed her hand. "Come on. Feel like taking a walk?"

"Outside?" She looked at the baby, her expression apprehensive.

"Don't worry, he's in good hands."

"I know." She relaxed, went over to Liam, and stroked his head. After tenderly kissing his forehead, she joined me by the door. "It's strange not to have him inside me any more," she admitted.

It was still dark out, but the sun was preparing to rise, slightly illuminating the sky.

"I feel an emptiness inside. It's like I miss him. I can't stop looking at him."

"Yeah, I know what you mean. But you kept him all to yourself for long enough. It's my turn to get to know him." I winked at her and she laughed as we neared the lake shore, barefoot.

"You're right. I can't imagine being separated from him, that's all."

"No one is going to separate you from him . . . or from me. We're a family now, and soon we'll make sure no supernatural force will ever threaten to divide us again." I rested my forehead against hers and took a deep breath, the water lapping at my ankles. "Sometimes I think it's all my fault," I admitted.

"What are you talking about, Evan?"

"If you hadn't gone to get me in Hell, you wouldn't have been forced to swear loyalty to the Witches, and you and the baby would be able to live normal lives."

"There's nothing normal about my life, Evan. This is my fate. Without you, I'd be lost in the darkness. I made the pact with the Witches because I knew your love would keep me here. There's hope only if you're here at my side."

"No, hope isn't enough for me. We'll do it my way."

"I know, we've already agreed."

I hugged Gemma around the waist. "What are we waiting for, then? Let's do it now. I don't want to waste another second."

"We still have two days before the Witches come to force me to make good on my promise. Let's at least wait a few hours."

"Why? You and the baby are fine. There's no reason to wait any longer."

"I . . . I'm afraid, Evan. We don't know what the consequences of our decision will be, and I'm not ready to part from Liam yet. Just a few more hours, okay? For just a little while let's pretend everything's normal."

I held her tight and stroked her head, breathing in the scent of her hair. "Everything's going to be fine, Gem."

"I know. As long as you're with me, I won't be afraid."

"Want to go inside?"

"No, let's stay here a little longer." Gemma took my hands and waded into the lake, her eyes never leaving mine. She immersed herself and the morning light made the beaded water on her face sparkle like diamonds. I stroked her cheek and my thumb lingered on her lip.

She gazed at me provocatively and guided my hand to her breast, her stiffened nipples peeking through her transparent nightgown. She looked like a water nymph who'd come to bewitch me. I drew her to me and breathed against her neck. "Why are you doing this to me?" I whispered, pressing my arousal against her.

Gemma bit her lip, smiling. "I want to make sure you still desire me."

"I desire you more than ever now that you've given me a son," I whispered against her mouth before kissing her passionately.

"You'll have to keep your distance for a while, I'm afraid."

"It'll be sheer hell." I kissed her again and she laughed, resting her hands on my chest. The dog tag had grown cold beneath my wet shirt. Or maybe it was the contrast with the fire racing through my veins.

"We'd better get back," Gemma whispered. How she loved to tease me.

I blocked her path and lifted her up by the thighs, drawing her against me. "Where do you think you're going?" I raised an eyebrow and my mouth traced the curve of her chin.

"It's almost day, Evan."

"No it isn't. It's night. The stars are out."

Gemma looked up at the sky and laughed. "Where do you see any? There are no stars."

I sought her hand beneath the water and squeezed it, gazing into her beautiful eyes. "You're wrong, because I'm looking at two of them right now." I kissed her tenderly on the mouth and she responded, biting my lip.

"I wish I could make love with you," she whispered, lighting the fire that dominated me. I pulled her hips against mine and felt the heat of her desire. I kissed her more ardently, mingling our breath.

"Hey, little mermaid!" Ginevra called out. "The baby woke up and is demanding breakfast. And you, Adonis, behave yourself! Can't you even wait one day? By Lilith! The woman just gave birth!" She went back inside, muttering, and Gemma and I burst out laughing.

"Looks like the little guy is going to have what I can't," I joked, fondling one of her breasts. "He's already one step ahead of me."

Gemma laughed. "I'm sure you'll teach him all sorts of things, *Adonis*. As for the two of us, later on we'll pick up this conversation where we left off. But now, Soldier, at ease."

I raised her hand to my mouth and kissed her palm, looking her in the eye. "As you wish." I waded toward the shore, Gemma behind me.

"I'd better put something dry on before nursing the baby," she thought aloud.

"No problem. Ginevra can get you a change of clothes." I emerged from the lake and shook the water from my hair, wetting her even more.

"Evan!" I smiled. I couldn't help it. I had no idea why, but I loved teasing her. Sometimes it made her mad, but she never held a grudge for long. "Wait!" Gemma called out. I turned around and saw her leaning over, searching for something on the lakebed. "How on earth . . . ? My necklace fell off. Ah, there it is!" she exclaimed, relieved.

Just then Liam's wails reached us. "As impatient as his mother when it comes to food. I'll go on ahead," I told her as she groped through the sand for her chain. I strode to the door of the hideaway where Ginevra smiled at me, my son in her arms.

"Got it!" Gemma exclaimed, still in the water. I turned to look at her as she stood up, the necklace clasped in her hand and a smile on her lips.

A sudden hiss pierced the air.

Too fast.

Too unexpected.

"Gemmaaa!!!" Her eyes locked onto mine. Then they moved down to the large arrow lodged in her chest. I raced toward her but a cold wind pushed me back, turning my heart to ice. "Gemmaaa!!!" I screamed, my chest splintering into shards of pain.

"Fuck, no!" Simon shouted. "Gin, don't leave Liam!" He joined me and together we tried to break through the barrier. Gemma raised her eyes and stared at me, devastated. I knew that look—I'd seen it a million times on the faces of mortals about to die. *No. Not Gemma, no!*

A tear slid down her cheek. "Liam," her lips murmured as a patch of red spread out around the arrow. She fell to her knees, her eyes trained on mine. Everything around me vanished as I drowned in the chaos inside my mind. All I could hear was the sound of her heartbeat that grew slower and slower.

"Gemmaaa!" I screamed.

A man appeared behind her, a bow in his hand. "Die, Witch." He grasped her head and snapped her neck. Gemma's eyes wavered and went blank.

"Noooo!" I screamed at the top of my lungs.

Anya appeared beside me and froze. Shaking herself out of it, she rushed at the man, but the barrier repelled her. The man raised his eyes, looked at me with a sneer, and disappeared. I raced into the water to Gemma, who was floating face down with the arrow sticking out of her back. Her heart had stopped beating.

I turned her over and dragged her to shore as Simon and Anya rushed to us. "Simon, help me! We've got to heal her!" I snapped the arrow in two and pulled it out of her body. It had pierced her heart. "No, Gemma, no! Don't leave me now, of all times." I tried to close up the wound but she didn't respond. "Come on, Gemma! Fight!" I screamed.

"No! This wasn't supposed to happen!" Anya said, leaning over Gemma.

Simon rested his hand on my shoulder. "Evan, stop."

"Don't tell me to stop!" I shouted. "Keep healing her, Simon! Don't give up!"

"She's dead, Evan."

"We'll bring her back. We've done it before. Where's her soul? Why isn't her soul here?!" Simon stared at me, devastated, and I covered my face with my bloody hands.

"Gemma!" Ginevra ran to her and threw herself to her knees. "Gemma, no! How could this happen?" she screamed at her Sister who'd had the task of watching over the Subterranean prisoners.

"I don't know. The Subterraneans are all still there. They're fading, but none of them has died. I don't understand."

"Then why did another Executioner show up?"

"That wasn't just any Executioner. I recognized him," Anya said. "That was Gareth Kreihn. We call him Absolon, which in our language means . . . "

"Witch hunter," Ginevra murmured, turning pale.

"How is that even possible? He died centuries ago," I exclaimed.

"It seems not." Ginevra grabbed the arrow and sniffed it. "This is poisoned."

I clenched my fists. "Why didn't he take her? Why didn't he help her cross over?"

"It's too late for her soul. Evil has claimed her. By dying, Gemma will now be a Soul damned to wander Hell."

"It can't end this way!" I snarled. I had denied Gemma Heaven, denied her immortality with her Sisters, and now she would be nothing but another of the Damned in Hell? Was this the future I'd promised her? I'd been such an egotist! My love for her had destroyed her.

I couldn't accept it. "Transform her." I looked at Anya, determined.

"What did you say?"

"Transform her," I repeated firmly. There was still a chance. I had to act fast.

"Evan, think this through," Simon warned me.

"Shut up! She can't die like this! Not now!"

Anya and Ginevra exchanged glances. "Simon, take the baby," Ginevra told him. "Take him away. Go back home."

"I'm not leaving you here."

"Yes, you are! Take him away, now! You have to keep him safe." She shot him a pointed look and he nodded. She leaned over and tore open Gemma's nightgown. A knot formed in my throat at the sight of Gemma so defenseless, with a hole in her chest. I bit my fist to fight back the pain.

"Evan, move back," Ginevra ordered. "Move back, I told you!"

I took a step backward as they tried to summon Gemma's Dakor so it could bite her. Her heart wasn't beating any more and her soul was lost somewhere in the darkness. There was no choice. I would rather she transform than be dead. Maybe the transformation wouldn't obliterate her after all. Maybe there was still a chance she would choose me.

"It's not working!" Ginevra growled.

"What do you mean, it's not working? Try again, damn it!"

"She has to be alive to transform," Anya said sadly.

"This shouldn't have happened," Ginevra murmured, leaning over Gemma's body.

I crumpled to my knees as my soul slowly died. No. It couldn't actually have happened. I dug my fingers into the earth and a scream tore my chest in two: "LILITH! You can't let her die! I'm begging you!"

A burst of lightning streaked through the sky and Devina materialized in front of us. "Sophìa is preparing to wage war. The Màsala will regret what they've done to Gemma."

"No," Ginevra gasped.

I clenched my fists. "Take me with you. I want to fight."

"Evan, what are you talking about?" Ginevra exclaimed. "A war against the Màsala won't accomplish anything. It won't bring Gemma back!"

"She's right," Anya said. "It'll be a massacre. The battlefield will be Earth. Many will die."

"I don't care," I shot back icily. Gemma had died and my humanity had died with her, leaving behind only the Executioner. I wanted revenge. For months we'd fought to protect my love. Now it was time for me to hunt.

"Evan, listen to me!" Ginevra shouted. Her voice was distant, as though she were speaking from some faraway place, but she was right there. It was me who was lost. "You're blinded by rage! Think of the baby. Who's going to protect Liam? He's your son. He needs you." I eased my grip, my fists loosening. Ginevra had managed to penetrate the black shroud around my heart. "Wait. Devina isn't here just to tell us that—are you?" Ginevra added, picking up on her Sister's thoughts.

"There's still a way to prevent war."

"She's right," Anya said in a low voice, her expression focused as she read her Sister's thoughts. "Maybe we still have a chance to save Gemma." She stared at Devina, who laughed to herself.

"The Empress gave me *this* for her. She tore it off her finger before my very eyes. You'd better hope it works." Devina showed us a small object, black and sharp.

"What is it?" I asked.

"The Devil's Claw."

"Will it work?" Ginevra asked anxiously.

"We have to try," Anya said.

"Try what? What's going on?" I asked, apprehensive.

Anya looked at me. "Ginevra and I can't awaken Gemma's Dakor . . ."

"Only the devil can bring the dead back from Hell," Devina added.

"Well? What are you waiting for? Do something!" I yelled. Anya slowly looked up at me. What did that look mean?

"Evan, Sophìa's poison will cancel every last trace of Gemma," Ginevra warned me, voicing her Sister's thoughts. "There's no chance she'll still be herself. Are you sure you want this?"

I looked at her. "Do it." Ginevra nodded and Devina smirked at me.

"I'm sorry," Anya said softly, looking at me regretfully.

Devina went up to Gemma, holding Sophìa's claw. She took her wrist and carved the mark of the Witches into her skin while murmuring an ancient litany whose meaning I couldn't understand. *"Treh. Immuaarimet. Lohe. Keh. Kuta Sih."*

"Treh. Immuaarimet. Lohe. Keh. Kuta Sih," Ginevra and Anya echoed. *"Treh. Immuaarimet. Lohe. Keh. Kuta Sih."*

The mark sizzled like seared flesh and Gemma's outstretched body levitated into the air. The water in the lake churned; the wind blew fiercely. Something rested on my shoulder: a black butterfly. No, not one. They were everywhere, filling the sky, a vortex created by a dark force. All the windows in the lake house exploded. I took a step back as a burst of lightning lit up the sky. Gemma's head jerked back as though her neck had snapped again. Her eyes were pure black, wide open, and trained on me as they changed form. The darkness retreated from their whites and her pupils lengthened like a serpent's before returning to normal. A myriad of water droplets rose from the lake and hovered until another stroke of lightning pierced the sky and they crashed down like an explosion. A shriek of pain burst from Gemma's mouth. I rushed toward her but someone held me back. It was Devina. For once she was right: I couldn't interfere.

The wind was so strong it threatened to drag me away as Gemma continued to shriek. Something stirred in her belly, creeping beneath her skin, finally rupturing it to emerge. *Her Dakor.*

"It's black," Ginevra whispered to her Sisters, as though that were something unusual for them. The serpent slithered across Gemma's belly and she stopped screaming. Aroused by the power, the animal moved swiftly, longing to feed, longing to be part of Gemma. It opened its fangs and sank them into her wrist. She seemed struck by a jolt of exhilaration mixed with anguish as the serpent penetrated her arm and disappeared inside her once again.

The wound disappeared. Gemma straightened and stood, keeping her head down for a moment as she avidly gulped in the air. We all held our breath. She slowly raised her head and fixed her gaze on me, her eyes lengthening like her serpent's and glittering like carbonado.

"Gemma," I whispered, and part of me died forever when I realized it was no longer her. Her black eyes, streaked with purple, remained fixed on mine as a challenging sneer spread across her face. She was still disoriented, but one thing was clear: she saw me as her enemy. The new beginning for Gemma was the end for us.

Anya rested her hands on Gemma's shoulders, looking sadly at my lost expression. "We have to go," she said, turning to Devina. "We have a war to prevent." I looked at Gemma one last time as she disappeared before my eyes, leaving me petrified with pain.

They had used Sophìa's own poison to awaken Gemma's Dakor. While before we'd had some hope Gemma might transform yet remain herself, that hope was now gone.

Ginevra looked at me, in her eyes her sorrow over the undeniable verdict. "We've lost her."

GEMMA

24

THE AWAKENING

I felt my heart beat wildly as a powerful energy flooded me. My first instinct was to fight it, but instead I surrendered to its power and let it fill me. A hot shiver ran through my body. I opened my eyes. Light was all around me, while shadows gathered inside me.

My head bowed, I tried to control my breathing and with it, the energy surging within me. I smiled, enraptured by the power I felt flowing through my veins like lava, regenerating me. It was dark and magnificent. I slowly raised my eyes and was instantly drawn to the Soul before me. It was unlike the other three; instinct urged me to annihilate it. I had no idea where I was or even who I was. My gaze remained locked on the young man's gray eyes while inside me violent impulses raged.

A young woman with green eyes rested her hands on my shoulders, preventing me from unleashing my fury on him. "We have to go. We have a war to prevent."

Before I could stop her, the man vanished. The journey lasted only a moment. When I looked around, we were in a different place. "Who are you?" I asked warily. "Where are we? Why have you brought me here?"

The green-eyed woman looked closely at me and took my hand. "I'm Anya. Don't you remember?" Should I have? She looked at me as though I should, or at least as though she hoped I would, but I had no idea what was going on.

The redhead beside her laughed. "Of course she doesn't remember. It erased everything. Absolutely *everything*." She seemed pleased by it. Should I be too?

"It was Sophìa's poison that awakened her. How could she remember?"

"I know. I was just hoping."

"Hoping for what?"

I stared at them, bewildered. I'd heard their voices, but neither of them had opened their mouths. Had I only imagined it? The redhead took me by the hand and led me away from the other woman. "Come, dear. Someone is expecting you."

I looked back, where Anya still stood. She had a look of irritation on her face, as though she were angry at the redhead. Someone clapped their hands and the sound filled the large circular hall. There were windows everywhere that reached to the ceiling, letting in the twilight.

Then I saw her. A woman sat on a majestic black throne. She wore a long gown with a V-shaped neckline that plunged to her navel. The powerful energy she emanated drew me to her. My heart began to beat harder. I wanted to go to her, to touch her.

As though she'd heard my thoughts, the woman with the gaze of ice smiled at me and stood. Her waist-long hair was black at the roots, gradually fading to gray, until it became white at the tips, like a splendid partial eclipse of the moon. At her feet, two big black panthers watched my every movement.

I had no idea who the women were or where I was, but for some reason I didn't care. I felt at home. The two women at my side bowed to her and I did the same, but she raised my chin. Her eyes were such an intense shade of blue it took my breath away. Her long lashes stood out against her fair skin and her lips, painted black, bewitched me. They were so perfectly contoured they seemed magical. I felt as though I were a bee and she was my queen. That was all I knew. Moving her lips close to mine, she kissed me, sending an electric charge through my body. "Welcome," she said, her voice captivating. "Do you know who I am?"

I looked into her eyes. "No." I neither knew nor cared. Whoever she was, I was hers.

She smiled. "Do not worry. Soon you will know all." She seemed so pleased to see me. "You will blossom, my little chrysalis. You will spread your wings and become a magnificent black butterfly. Your arrival changes many things. It was good of your Sisters to bring you home."

My Sisters. So that was why I felt that energy between us.

The woman turned and the panthers watched her as she walked back to them and seated herself again on her throne. "Prepare her. Later there is to be a great celebration."

"Yes, my Empress," both women replied.

She smiled at me and suddenly burst into an explosion of black butterflies that rose into the air. I watched them, fascinated, as they disappeared through a hole in the ceiling, then dropped my eyes again to the now-empty throne. She had transformed. I should have been afraid, but instead I was exhilarated.

"Where are they going?" I asked, but a pain gripped my head, doubling me over.

"She asks so many questions . . ."

"I have to find a way to . . ."

"Did you see? She's here . . ."

I clapped my hands over my ears and looked around, confused. Where were all those voices coming from? They were in my head. That was why it ached so badly.

". . . on me . . ." Anya was trying to speak to me. ". . . other voices." I didn't understand. What was she saying? "Gemma, listen to me!" Her voice rose above the chorus of others in my mind. "Focus on me . . . Good, that's it. Breathe and watch my lips moving."

I did as she said and managed to isolate the sound, banishing the other voices. "What's happening to me?" I asked in alarm.

Anya smiled. "It's perfectly normal. You'll get used to it soon. Come. I'll take you to your chambers."

"I'll stay here," the other Sister said, "in case any new prisoners to play with show up."

"As you like," Anya replied. "See you at the celebration."

"Gemma, I'm happy you're finally home." The redhead smiled at me and I nodded.

"Thank you," I said before Anya led me away.

We went through several rooms and I understood almost immediately that we were in a castle. There were lots of people, mainly women in combat outfits. I wore a white nightgown that was torn and bloodied. What could possibly have happened to me?

"Don't worry about that," Anya said, as though she'd read my mind. "We'll bring you some suitable clothes in time for the festivities."

"What festivities?" I asked hesitantly.

She beamed. "The ones in your honor, the Welcome Ceremony. All of us have one."

"All of you? How many of you are there?"

"Oh, you'll find out soon enough. You're very confused, I know, but you'll like it here with us, Gemma. I guarantee it." I stared at Anya. *Gemma.* She kept saying that. It seemed to be my name. Why couldn't I remember it? "Come on, let me show you something fun." She pulled me into a small hallway where voices filled my head:

"What gorgeous hair!"

"And look at that complexion!"

"Hands down, she's the most beautiful of all the Sisters."

"What is this place?" I asked, confused.

"The Hall of Flattery. Each of us hears what we'd like to hear. It boosts your self-esteem. Not that any of us need it, but compliments can't hurt, and most of us can't go without them. If you like this, wait till you see the Chamber of Mirrors."

We reached a large wooden door at the end of the hall. Anya opened it and showed me the room. It had a high, high ceiling where black butterflies fluttered. The walls were almost entirely covered with mirrors. A large fireplace set into one wall lit up the room while another wall had a window framing a clear sky at twilight. In the center of the room stood a big black bed with blood-red silk sheets. All the walls were black—as were the ceiling and floor—and made of a material that sparkled like a dark diamond.

Two young women bowed to me and smiled. "We've been expecting you, my lady," another one said, ushering me inside.

"Who are you?"

"They're Mizhyas."

"Are they my Sisters too?" I asked, though I didn't feel the same connection to them that I did to Anya.

"No, but you can consider them your handmaids. They're very loyal and are always at your service."

The three women bowed. I realized I could perceive their emotions: veneration mixed with fear. One of them kissed my hand. "I am Emayn and I will be honored to serve you." I stepped back, studying her carefully. She had olive skin and a sensual gaze. An artistic tattoo on her right hand made its way up her arm.

Another, her skin snow-white, stepped forward and lowered her eyes fearfully. "My name is Meryall. Ask of me what you will and I will do it." I raised her chin and looked into her big blue eyes.

The last of them had remained in reverential silence. I approached her. She had a small face and a sharp expression. Her eyes showed no fear—only caution. "And what is your name?"

"Freia, my lady. At your service."

I studied them from head to toe. All three wore leather ankle boots and sexy, close-fitting, brown uniforms, and their hair was braided, like the other women I'd seen in the Castle. Each had a band tattooed on her arm in a different shape, like a distinctive marking. Their bodies were toned and muscular and they looked like battle-trained Amazons.

"Actually, they are," Anya replied.

I turned to her, surprised. Now there was no doubt about it. "You can read my mind?"

She smiled. "Cool, isn't it? Pretty soon you'll be doing it too. And that's nothing!"

"I have powers?" The idea thrilled me.

"Of course you do. You have a great power buried inside you. We're going to teach you to control it."

"Who am I?" I asked, sensing that the answer was the key to everything.

"You're one of us." Anya hugged me. "And you're finally home."

25

BLOOD BOND

The Castle was abuzz. Everyone seemed excited about the party. From time to time Mizhyas came to peek into the room. Anya had directed me to put on a special gown, the same one they'd all worn the day of their ceremony. It consisted of black leather shorts with a fluffy, full-length train that looked like it was made of interwoven butterfly wings, black knee-high boots, and leather laces that crisscrossed up my thighs.

My maidservants had given me a long, hot bath and a massage before carefully doing up my eyes with black shadow, enhancing them greatly. Now Anya was giving my hair a final touch-up, gathering a few locks and braiding the style into place.

"Why don't I remember anything about my past?"

"Because you were generated by Earth to join us."

"You mean I didn't have a life before this one?"

Anya hesitated, as if choosing her words carefully. "You did, but you swore loyalty to us."

"Did I know it would make me lose my memory?"

"Yes."

My life must have been horrible if I'd wanted to run away from it. This place, on the other hand, made me feel strong.

"Your life begins now." Anya looked me in the eye. "With us. You're special, Gemma. Only one mortal every five hundred years receives this gift."

"What gift?"

"The power. Immortality. Sisterhood. We're Witches, Gemma."

Witches. A quiver of pleasure ran beneath my skin. "Who was that man with the gray eyes in the forest?"

"Your greatest enemy: a Subterranean," said the redhead, who'd just appeared. So that was why I'd felt such hostility toward him.

"Devina, are you already tired of waiting for new prisoners? Why don't you go out and find some yourself?"

"No, stay here," I told her. "Please." I felt a strong affinity toward her. I had the impression she had much to teach me. She emanated power and I wanted to absorb every drop.

Devina smiled at me. "Of course, with great pleasure."

The two Sisters looked at each other challengingly. I was sure they were having a mental conversation without including me. A constant murmur filled my mind but I couldn't distinguish the voices. "Will I always have these voices in my head?"

"You'll get used to it. Focus on your own thoughts and everything else will fade into the background."

"When will I start understanding your thoughts too?" I asked, frustrated by their silent conversation.

"After your Dakor's baptism, once you've sealed the Bond with us. Sophìa will officially unite you to us and the transformation will be complete."

"Sophìa is the woman who was on the throne, isn't she?"

"She's our Great Sister," Devina replied. "A Witch, just like you and me."

"But she's also our Empress, although Devina sometimes forgets it."

"Can we do what she did when she disintegrated?" For some reason, I'd been bewitched by her butterflies.

"No. Only when we die—but that's a remote possibility."

"Each time it's like a tiny death for her," Devina added. "It's just that she can't die."

"She's the queen of darkness. Death belongs to her."

"But it's the only thing she can't have herself. That's why she likes it so much."

"You're ready," Anya said.

I looked into a large mirror and smiled at my reflection. I didn't know who I'd been before, but what I saw now pleased me. I was pretty. And soon I would become very dangerous.

Anya turned to her Sister. "What do you think?"

"I think she's missing something." Devina smiled and turned around. "Follow me."

I obeyed, letting her guide me down a long hallway that took us to a huge courtyard where a grim twilight ruled. The place was in commotion, with Amazons running in and out of it.

"Are there only women here?" I asked.

A half-smile appeared on Devina's face. "No, but we keep the men out of our way. We don't need them. If anything, they're the ones who need us. Depending on a man is a sign of weakness, but making him depend on you is an indicator of power. Every man you see in the Castle subjugated himself to us of his own free will . . . either that or he's our prisoner." I smiled. It was an interesting topic.

I followed her down broad staircases leading to an underground door. When Devina opened it, a flame ran along the stone walls, lighting them up. "Here. This is it."

"What is this place?"

"This is where we keep a few of our toys." I looked around and my jaw dropped. "This is the weapons room. You can't go to the ceremony without having chosen a weapon."

"Have I ever battled before?"

"You have it in your blood. For you, it'll be like breathing."

All the walls were entirely covered with weapons. There were so many of them! "How do I choose?"

"You can use all the weapons you want, whenever you want, naturally, but each of us has a special one we always keep with us."

"What's yours?"

Devina brought her hand to her thigh and a second later a whip cracked through the air. The sound was so sharp its echo filled the room. "Once you have your toy, you can personalize it with symbols of your battles. I perfected my *Magnificent* with Molock skin."

"What's a Molock?"

"It's a creature from Hell—one of the fiercest. It was fun to see the terror in its eyes while I was flaying it. You'll have fun too, I'm sure of it."

"You chose the perfect name. It really is magnificent," I admitted, staring at the whip in her hand. "How will I find mine?"

"It'll find you. When you touch it, its energy will come to life and you'll be able to feel the power that unites you."

"What are we waiting for, then? Let's start right away!" I smiled at her and began to look around. There were weapons of all kinds, eras, and sizes. I picked up a sword and weighed it in my hand. It was incredible how confidently I handled it. I spun it around in one hand as Devina watched me with a proud look on her face. Putting it back, I grabbed a long iron staff.

I followed my instinct and the staff moved in my hands as though we were one. I made a feint at Devina, who nimbly dodged it and pinned me to the wall.

She smiled, pleased. "You're a natural, but you still have a lot to learn."

"When?" I asked impatiently. I felt strong. I wanted to become invincible.

"Soon. Very soon," she promised. "Have you found what you were looking for?"

I was about to say no when my eyes fell on a pedestal at the back of the room. A crossbow sat atop it, a beautiful black crossbow that begged me to come closer. "There it is," I murmured to myself, heeding its call.

"Excellent choice," Devina said, a touch of admiration in her eyes.

After a moment's hesitation, I reached out and picked up the crossbow, almost with deference. It adapted perfectly to my grip and I felt its lethal power flow into me. It looked like it had been carved from a black diamond, the same stone the Castle was made from. Looking at the crossbow, I noticed there was a tattoo on my hand. It was composed of strange symbols, but somehow I knew what it meant: *stay together*. It must have had something to do with my Sisters.

"It's a rare object," Devina said, pulling me out of my thoughts. "Sophìa forged it centuries and centuries ago. No one has touched it since, but I was there when she made it. I saw the power it possesses." She picked up a small, all-black arrow and showed it to me. "Its arrows are unstoppable and deadly. You'll have to be careful how you use it, because it's a weapon that takes no prisoners."

I smiled, my eyes locked on my new weapon. "*Khalida*," I whispered. *Unstoppable*. The language that had suddenly filled my mind was unfamiliar to me, but suddenly I could speak it.

Devina nodded with satisfaction. "I think it's perfect."

"I want to try it," I said excitedly.

"We'll do that soon. Right now we need to go to the ceremony. You're the guest of honor, so you can't be late." She winked at me and motioned for me to follow her.

I strapped on a sling and hung the crossbow on my back. I was about to follow Devina, but something stopped me. "Wait!" I picked up two daggers with crescent-shaped blades, spun them around, and tucked them into the strips of leather laced around my thighs. "I'm taking these too."

Devina smiled. I liked that room. I would have to go back soon. Outside, I looked around the empty courtyard. "Where did everybody go?"

"They're in the Pantheon. The ceremony is about to begin." Devina led me inside the Castle to a massive door of carved black stone. "Ready?"

I nodded and the door slowly opened at her command. We were once again in the throne room, only this time everyone was there, clad in long golden cloaks with broad hoods, their eyes trained on me. I raised my chin and made my way into the room with my head held high, gazing steadily at the Empress. It was as though I was bound to her by some mystical connection. As I passed, everyone around me bowed: women, men, and majestic black panthers. I stopped only when I reached the throne.

Silence reigned supreme. A tongue of fire ran along the walls, casting lights and shadows on my Sisters' beautiful faces. A flock of black butterflies circled through the air and alit on the throne, drawn by its power, but my eyes didn't waver.

Sophìa smiled, her expression radiant. As she stood, everyone held their breath. A black serpent slithered around her neck. *Dakor*, my instinct said. His incredible lapis lazuli eyes peered at me from close up, hypnotic. They were identical to Sophìa's. She glanced at my crossbow and nodded, as though satisfied with my choice. All at once, her voice filled my head.

"Naiad. I have waited so long for you, my little warrior."

"I am yours, my Empress," I said resolutely, bowing my head.

She slowly spread her arms and proclaimed, "May the ceremony begin!" A chorus of drums and shouts filled the room. "Come," she said, holding my hand. "Take your place. It is time for you to unite with your Sisters." She walked me to a throne next to hers. It was smaller but just as majestic. At its sides, two panthers bowed to me. There was something familiar about one of them . . . It must have been the color of its eyes—jade green. A moment later it changed form and I realized why I had had that sensation: it was Anya. I stared at her, amazed. The other panther also took on a human form, but I'd never seen her before.

I sat on the throne and Sophìa took her place at my side. "Today is a great day," she proclaimed as the crowd listened, ecstatic. Once again she wore a gown that appeared to be made of black butterflies, but the design was different, as if it were molding itself to her body. "After five hundred long years, one of our Sisters has awakened from Earth to join us. She has been given to us and we welcome her as blood of our blood, now and for eternity." The crowd cheered and stamped their feet. "And now introduce yourselves, Sisters! Let us present Naiad's new family to her."

Anya knelt before me. "She is Anya," Sophìa said, "but I know you have already met her. She is loyal and wise. She will be a good Sister to you."

My new Sister stood. Her hair flowed over her shoulders in soft chestnut-brown curls with a contrasting blond streak that crossed through them like a shaft of light. She gazed at me for a moment, the serpent coiled around her arm peering at me with the same incredible green eyes, then kissed me on the lips. "Welcome," she whispered before winking at me and stepping back. She stopped before the throne at the edge of a red symbol on the floor, the symbol that represented us. No one had explained that to me but somehow I knew it.

"Devina. The first Sister . . . and my Specter," Sophìa announced. "She has the spirit of a warrior and will guide you in your ascent."

Devina made a little bow without taking her eyes off mine and kissed me. Her kiss wasn't tender like Anya's, but electrifying and sensual. Her lips were painted red, the same color as her hair. Even her eyes seemed to be made of fire.

Then came Bathsheeva, whom the Sisters simply called Sheeva. She had a long ponytail that reached her ankles, caramel-colored skin, and eyes of molten gold. She too knelt before me and kissed me on the lips to welcome me. Next was Zafirah—Safria to the Sisters. Her blue eyes with their hints of purple stood out against her black skin and crown of braided black hair. Kreeshna, also dark-skinned, had a long braid that hung over her shoulder. Zhora followed, with very short, bright, mahogany hair and emerald-green eyes that glowed like those of the Dakor wrapped around her wrist. Nerea was next. She had long blond hair with speckled tips and incredible yellow eyes; then Camelia, as sensual as a siren with her big gray eyes, fair skin, and pastel-pink hair that turned lilac at the tips. Last of all came Nausyka. Her hair was platinum blond and her blue eyes sparkled like pole stars. They each wore a lock of braided hair across their foreheads like a diadem. I counted nine of them, plus Sophìa and me. Though I'd never seen most of them before, I felt the strong connection uniting us. They were my Sisters and I was one of them. A Witch. Each had her own serpent, some coiled around arms, others around necks, still others around thighs.

They stood there waiting until the Empress spoke again. "The time has come," she announced solemnly. The entire audience knelt as Sophìa stood and offered me her hand. She led me to the center of the circle of Witches where the symbol was carved into the black stone. A maidservant appeared carrying a black chalice covered with a red silk cloth, which Sophìa removed. The Mizhya took it, bowed, and retreated, joining a long line of maidservants. The Witches' serpents hissed. Only they stirred inside the hall. Everyone else held their breath.

Sophìa approached Devina and offered her the chalice. As Devina looked at me, her eyes as ardent as fire, her serpent opened his jaws and bit her wrist, disappearing inside her. Her irises expanded like tentacles, filling the whites of her eyes, and her pupils lengthened. Devina held out her wrist and let a drop of her blood fall into Sophìa's cup. Anya did the same, and all the other Sisters followed suit. When the last drop of blood had been offered, Sophìa came to me and handed me the cup. I took it and her serpent hissed, fixing his eyes on mine before opening his jaws, striking, and then slithering into his mistress. The Empress's blue eyes glittered for a moment, becoming just like her Dakor's, as her blood dripped into the cup, sizzling. "This is the blood of your Sisters," she recited in an ancient tongue that I was able to understand. "Drink it and receive them inside you."

I raised the cup to my lips, looking at the Witches one by one. They looked back at me with respect and anticipation. I allowed their blood to flow onto my tongue and its aroma enraptured me down to my soul. The Mizhya returned and carried the cup away. My head was spinning.

Sophìa took my wrist and slid her long black nails over my skin, cutting my palm. "Though everywhere he is forced to crawl, in this his realm he rules over all." My heart was thumping and I felt like I'd taken a powerful drug. "Come to me," Sophìa whispered.

Then it happened. A serpent, like those of my Sisters, slowly emerged from my palm. He was black—completely black. I stood there staring at him as he slithered up my wrist. He hissed, gazing at me intently. His black eyes were streaked with violet and I instantly felt he was part of me.

A murmur swept through the crowd.

"Do you see that? It's black."

"It can't be . . ."

"It's just like the Empress's . . ."

They were right. My serpent wasn't green, like my other Sisters'.

Sophìa looked at me and smiled. "You are not only one of us," she said, her voice solemn. "You are the thirteenth Witch and I have been awaiting you a long, long time." She took my hand and raised it to her lips, kissing my bloody palm. "Offer your blood to the Sisterhood to seal the Bond." I went around the circle of Witches and one by one they leaned in to drink from my palm. "It is time," Sophìa announced.

All the Witches, including the Empress, held hands, closing the circle around me. *"Kaameh. Tika nun kàa. Saeth rith,"* they chanted as one. The serpents crept out of their bodies as the prayer grew more rhythmic and intense. It was Kahatmunì, the Witches' secret, ancient code. And I understood it.

The Bond has now been consecrated and cannot be eradicated.

"Kaameh. Tika nun kàa. Saeth rith."

"Kaameh. Tika nun kàa. Saeth rith."

All their Dakor came to me, slithering across the floor and encircling me. My serpent was excited, responding to their call. The crowd began to stamp their feet in a hypnotic rhythm, faster and faster.

"Blossom, my little chrysalis."

Silence filled the room once more as my Dakor opened his jaws and sank his fangs into my wrist, penetrating me. The train of my dress exploded into a myriad of black butterflies and I threw back my head, overwhelmed by a mix of pain and pure pleasure. My eyes burned as he fused with me and the butterflies whirled around me. I felt his heart beat and synchronize with mine. I heard his hiss whisper inside my head and sensed his soul bond to mine. We were one.

"You will have the strength of a panther. The shrewdness of a serpent. The grace of a butterfly," Sophìa proclaimed.

"She's magnificent," one of the Sisters was thinking.

"A worthy warrior."

"I'll teach her everything," Devina added.

"I must protect her," Anya thought.

They were inside my mind, all of them. I was a Witch. The transformation was complete.

When the tingling stopped, I turned to look at Sophìa, who awaited me, beaming. She moved closer and pressed her lips to mine in a long, sensual kiss. "You are officially one of us now. Nothing can break our bond."

"Yes, my Empress."

The Witches cheered and lifted me onto their shoulders, letting out a battle cry. I smiled, letting their enthusiasm infect me. I remembered nothing about my past, but I was certain I'd never been so happy before.

26

A NEW WORLD

"Where are we going?" I asked them telepathically. The ceremony was over and the Witches were carrying me out of the Castle, tossing me into the air from time to time and letting out war whoops.

"This is when the real party starts!" Devina told me.

I could hear their every smallest thought. The voices of the other people present also filled my mind, and if I concentrated, I could make out one or another, but with the Witches it was different. Their voices were loud and clear, as if we were all a single, inseparable being.

They led me to what looked like an amphitheater. There were already lots of people looking out from the balconies of the surrounding buildings, in the stands, in the center of the arena. Bare-chested men beat drums while others performed an acrobatic tribal dance that was crude and incredibly sexy. The Witches put me down and Devina rested her hand on my shoulder. "Here, try this." She offered me a chalice containing a clear liquid and I gulped it down.

My eyes went wide and my throat burned. "What is it?!" I exclaimed, but a second later the liquid warmed my stomach and spread through my entire body, causing a quiver of pleasure. I savored the sensation and longed for more.

Devina smiled. "It's poison. Something exquisite."

I looked around and saw that everyone was having fun. "It's really strong!" I exclaimed, tipsy.

"Cider is lethal, but not for us."

Beside me, a bare-chested man belted back the contents of a glass. "Not for them either, I see."

"What they're drinking is different from ours. Small amounts of our blood filtered of its poison is a delight, if properly distilled."

"They're drinking our blood?"

"Only a few drops. There are certain Souls—Apothecaries—who are in great demand because they're skilled at preparing a special blend. Here they call it Elixir. Our blood is the most powerful drug that has ever existed."

I watched the bare-chested men as they danced, feeling incredibly drawn to their good looks and virility. My Sister looked at me with a twinkle in her eye. "Wait till you see them in the Arena. *There's nothing sexier than two warriors battling to the death for you."*

"Who are they?" I asked, curious.

Devina laughed and took the cup from my hands. "Don't overdo it your first time or you'll get a headache. Those are Subterraneans," she explained, bringing to my mind the distant memory of the young man with gray eyes.

"I thought they were our enemies."

"Not here in the Castle. On Earth, the Children of Eve hinder our mission and must be stopped. Every Subterranean you see here, on the other hand, has chosen to subjugate himself to us." Devina stopped beside one of the men and kissed him. He took her by the hips and squeezed her bottom, but she slid her finger down his neck and sank her nail in, leaving a line of blood. The Subterranean fell to his knees.

"You can have as many as you want at your command. I'll bring you the finest Soldiers from which to choose. It's your party—tonight you should have company," Devina promised.

I looked at the Subterranean and smiled, arousal growing inside me. But something else she'd said had caught my attention. "What's our mission?"

"Souls," she replied, a light in her eye. "There are many of them on Earth and the number continues to grow. Over the last century there's been a dangerous decline in the perception of evil. Dangerous for them, naturally, not for us. Our task is to bring them here."

"How?"

"With our power. It's still early for you. First you'll have to train. But when the time comes, you'll feed off that power. You won't be able to do without it. You'll wonder how you ever managed to live without it." I listened to her, fascinated. I wanted that day to come as soon as possible. "It will come," she promised, reading my mind. "Meanwhile, let's enjoy the party." Devina picked up two cups of poison and offered me one. I smiled at her, drank the liquid in a single gulp, and let out a whoop.

"There you are," Sophìa exclaimed, coming over to us. Everyone bowed as she passed and so did I, but she stopped me, raising my chin. "Please, Naiad. This is your party. It is I who should bow to you. Your presence here brings me immense joy. It has been centuries since I was as excited over something as I am over your arrival."

"I am honored, my Empress."

Suddenly I couldn't hear Devina's thoughts any more. I looked in her direction, but she was still there, staring at Sophìa. With a cross expression, she turned and walked away.

"Where is she going?" I asked, but no one replied.

"Come. I wish to give you a gift," Sophìa said.

I followed her across the courtyard, through the crowd. I recognized two of my Sisters, Zhora and Sheeva, who were battling some Mizhyas. A small circle had gathered around them. I felt a strong urge to join them, and Sophìa smiled.

"You will have much time to fight. Soon your training will begin. I am certain you will prove to be an excellent warrior. The strength of your soul is extraordinary. Never before had I seen a fire like yours in a mortal."

"Are the maidservants mortal?" I asked. My eyes could see their strength, but my spirit detected their weakness. Not even the Subterraneans were as strong as us—at least the ones there at the Castle—yet I had perceived in them the flame of immortality.

"Mizhyas are nothing but Damned Souls brought in to serve us."

Just then, Sheeva slit one of their throats and the crowd cheered. Black liquid gushed from the wound until she fell to the ground and disappeared in a cloud of dust. "We train them to fight for our entertainment, but none of them last long. Nevertheless, they are happy to serve us. Being with us is a fine way to go. Outside our walls it is true 'Hell' for them compared to this." Sophìa smiled, her blue eyes glittering in the twilight.

Her words piqued my interest. "When may I leave the Castle?"

"Whenever you like. That is why we are here."

"May I ask a question?"

"There is no need. I already know what you wish to ask."

I frowned. I felt the need to ask her out loud. "During the ceremony you said I was the thirteenth Witch, but there were only eleven Sisters, counting you and me. Where are the other two?"

Sophìa looked at me, deep sorrow clouding her eyes. All at once her voice filled my mind: *"In the past we lost two Sisters and the pain over their loss still flows strong in the blood of each of us."*

"What were their names?"

"Tamaya and . . . Ginevra." The names echoed in my mind. I didn't know them, but somehow I felt the pain in my heart as well.

"We have arrived. After you," Sophìa said, this time aloud. We'd reached the top of a tall tower that rose up, challenging the sky. I stepped out onto its broad terrace and the crisp air hit me. I closed my eyes and breathed in deeply. I felt so free . . . and happy.

A whinny drew my attention. I looked around and for the first time noticed there were covered stalls on the roof of the circular tower. Yes, now I could hear it: their breathing. There were creatures inside the stalls and they had to be enormous.

"Where are we?" I asked, surprised.

"The stables. This is where you are to receive your gift, a Saurus."

A chorus of whinnies filled the twilight as, all around us, magnificent steeds spread their wings and bowed to the Empress. Excitement filled my chest. "These Sauruses belong to your Sisters, but tonight a new creature will rise from the darkness to serve you . . . and protect you."

One of them whinnied and pawed the ground, awakening in me the desire to move closer. I stroked his nose and he relaxed. He was majestic, strong, and graceful—a perfect warrior of the shadows.

Argas. The name burst into my thoughts. I didn't know where it had come from, but suddenly I was sure it was his. "Argas," I whispered, following my instinct. He whinnied and nuzzled me. "I want him," I said, resolute. It was a selfish thought. The creature belonged to one of my Sisters, but I didn't care. I felt a deep connection to him the second I touched him.

"So be it," Sophìa granted.

"I'm willing to fight for him." A fire burned in me: the yearning to excel, even at my Sisters' expense.

Sophìa smiled. "That will not be necessary . . . this time. He lost his Witch centuries ago." I stroked his coat. It was soft, though it looked as hard as armor. Argas rubbed his head against me, tickling me. "It would seem that it is he who has chosen you. Here." She tossed something to me and I caught it. It was a small whistle made of carbonado. It was old, and one end of it was chipped, but I loved it. I stroked it, wondering what its story was.

"Thank you," I murmured. "It's the most beautiful gift you could have given me. Along with the rest, naturally."

"What are you waiting for, then?" she asked with a big smile. "Your new world awaits you." I smiled excitedly and mounted Argas, who whinnied and reared before galloping to the end of the terrace, where he plunged off the edge and swooped through the air.

Sophìa's voice filled my head. *"Spread your wings, my butterfly, and* soar.*"*

27

QUEEN OF THE SKIES

"Yahooo!" The wind swallowed up my shout as we rose into the sky, exploring my new world. I felt strong and full of life. This place was my home; I could feel it in every fiber of my being. Argas kicked out his hind legs and whinnied to catch my attention. He was also happy to be there with me. I laughed, filling the air with the wonderful sound, and leaned down to stroke him as he carried me higher. Spreading my arms, I closed my eyes, the air whipping at my face. I held the world in my hands and power flowed through me like an electric charge as I inhaled the scent of the twilight—the scent of home.

Suddenly my eyes stung. They were transforming. I opened them, an evil grin on my lips. My Dakor was inside me—I could feel him. His poison was powerful, intoxicating. "Yah!" I spurred Argas and he responded at once by plunging downward. The sight below us was breathtaking. The river twisted and turned between the valleys; the volcano erupted, celebrating my presence; Mount Nhubii, with its waterfalls, watched me in silent reverence. And then, the Castle: a majestic, menacing needle pointed at the sky. Sensing my need to return there, Argas beat his mighty black wings and headed toward the tall tower so swiftly I feared we would crash into it, but at the last moment he pulled up, his claws brushing the black wall. I could hear and see everything, even the smallest creature running to hide from me. I spotted the torches at the celebration and circled the courtyard. The crowd saw me and cheered, raising their cups in my honor. I swooped down to be closer to my Sisters, who let out war cries. Flying past them, I joined my voice with theirs. Suddenly, whistles filled the air and huge shadows clouded the sky. I looked up in time to see a magnificent flock of Sauruses beating their wings and racing toward us.

"The Kryadon!" Anya shouted, jumping onto her own. All our Sisters echoed her, their shouts filling my head. Even Sophìa joined them. Hers was the only Saurus with shades of gray. All the others were black.

"*What's the Kryadon?*" I asked of no one in particular. Their Sauruses all rose into the sky to join Argas.

"Get ready for the Games, princess," Devina replied.

I spurred my Saurus on and flew alongside her. "What games? I don't know the rules."

A grin spread across her face before she angled her Saurus downward. *"There's only one rule that counts: kill."* I smiled and plunged after her.

A group of Souls raced across the ground as fast as their legs could carry them, seeking shelter. Devina's Saurus rushed at them and captured one. The Soul tried to kick free, but her whip was wrapped around his neck. She charged back into the sky, tearing his head off.

"What a cruel game," I murmured to myself, feeling a smile emerge. "I like it."

"Gemma, this one's all yours," Zhora shouted. She rushed at an escaping Soul and grabbed him, hurling him head-first into a tree. I instinctively whipped out my crossbow and nocked an arrow, shooting him in the throat. The Soul disintegrated on the spot and my Sisters cheered. I smiled as a powerful energy grew inside me. The arrow dislodged itself from the tree and returned to me on its own. I caught it and let out a whoop, brandishing it like a trophy.

"So this is the Kryadon?" I asked.

"No, we're just warming up." Nausyka smiled. "Hone your weapons! It's time to have fun!"

I leaned low over Argas's back as he flew into a narrow tunnel. Seconds later he burst out the other side, a swarm of black butterflies following us and a magnificent cascade tumbling down beneath us. Argas followed it straight down, continuing along the river.

"Gemma, come here. We've found a village." The voice was Anya's.

I spurred my Saurus and joined the other Sisters circling a village carved into the rock. From the looks of the square it seemed deserted, but Sheeva shot a flaming arrow into one of the grottos and a Soul rushed out, screaming and consumed by flames. He was soon followed by many others. Panic ensued as they began to turn to ash. I did as my Sisters did, spreading chaos and death. In Sophìa's thoughts I could sense her pride that I'd learned so quickly. She was proud of me. And I would have done anything to please her.

I plunged down toward a little house hidden among the rocks and summoned the power of darkness. I felt it grow inside me, pervading me with its incredible energy. Focusing on my target, I sent a burst of light crashing into it, destroying everything. The other Witches cheered, struck by my boldness. I felt as though I'd been reborn. Anya's Saurus flew up alongside mine. "Is this how you have fun here?" I asked.

She smiled at me. "Do you like it?"

"I don't think I can do without it any more!" I exclaimed, the poison setting my veins on fire.

"I told you you'd be happy here with us," she said with a smile before challenging the wind.

"Catch me!" shouted another Sister. I turned to the right. It was Camelia. She'd stood up on her Saurus's back and spread her arms. Before I could even wonder what she was doing, she let herself fall backwards into the void. I spurred Argas and swooped down beneath her. Everyone's laughter filled my mind. Grinning, Camelia did a backflip and landed on my Saurus.

"You guys are all insane!" I exclaimed in my mind.

"Then welcome to the madhouse." Camelia winked at me and jumped into the void again. A moment later she was back on her Saurus, which passed me as it ascended. "Thanks for the ride!" she shouted to me, smiling. I shook my head.

"There aren't any here," Devina told the group.

"What are we looking for?" I asked.

"Recruits," Anya said.

"Recruits for what?"

"For the Opalion, naturally. This is the Kryadon. We call it the Hunt. It's the preparation for the Games."

"Look, over there!" Nerea shouted. Suddenly something gripped my shoulders and head while my skin felt like it had been stroked with a paintbrush dipped in ink. I touched my body, surprised. Armor had appeared on me, but I wasn't the only one. All the Sisters were now clad in strange armored helmets with antennas like a butterfly's, and tattoos had appeared on their faces. While earlier my Sisters had looked like Amazons, now they were fierce knights.

"Hold on tight!" Anya told me.

A second later my Saurus did a nosedive, following his companions. He hit the ground at a gallop and entered a cave. I could hear the cries of Souls running away, as well as their thoughts, a confused jumble of fear. It was too dark for the Damned to see, whereas our eyesight was perfect. I could even make out the color of their eyes as we rushed alongside them. "Gotcha!" Nausyka exclaimed, and emitted a strange cry. We emerged from the tunnel and I saw a Soul hanging from her Saurus, his feet bound.

"There are two more!" Sophìa alerted us, scanning the crowd, but I didn't understand which Souls in particular she was talking about. Sheeva charged one of the Damned but Devina unsaddled her with her Saurus. With a snap of Devina's whip, the Soul fell to the ground, screaming in pain. She flew up, dragging him into the air until he disintegrated.

I heard another strange shout, and another still. I flew over to Anya, who'd just caught another Soul. "Who are they?"

"First-Echelon Sane Souls," she explained. "They're prized fighters for the Opalion because they're particularly aggressive. They've survived years of trials and tribulations without joining the ranks of the Insane, that is, without losing their minds. It's a perfect combination in a combatant: strong but also controllable. They hide among the Lucid—the ones we killed in the cave. The Lucid have no hope of serving evil, though we occasionally toss a few of them into the Arena to amuse the crowds. But Kreeshna's outdone us. She caught a Subterranean. He'll be useful, and he's worth twice as much."

I looked at Kreeshna's prisoner. When she'd captured him, her victory cry had been different from the others. It must have been a signal. The prisoner was a young black man with a strange tattoo that branched out on his right arm. His silvery gray eyes shone through the darkness like those of all the other men I'd seen at the celebration. Like those of the young man in the forest.

"Subterraneans are better at hiding from us because they're not afraid," Anya went on.

"How do you find the Sane?"

"By attacking villages and killing everyone we come across," Nausyka replied, flying alongside us with a satisfied smile on her lips.

"I mean, how do you distinguish them from the rest of the Damned?"

"You probe their minds. It takes practice, though. You need to learn to understand Souls in order to discover their fears. It'll get easier for you after your first Reaping."

"Look, there's one down there," Anya said, pointing. "Each Soul is worth one point. Whoever returns to the Castle with three wins." She plunged downward.

"I didn't know it was a contest!"

"Everything's a contest!" she called back.

Two Sisters were already contending for the prey, but Anya swooped down between them, clearing the way for me. I turned to look at her and she winked. *"Go ahead! Don't aim at the throat!"* she called out in my mind.

Beside me, Nerea and Safria also rushed at the Sane Soul, so I clung to Argas and spurred him on. When I was close to the Soul, I grabbed the two curved daggers strapped to my thighs and threw them, pinning him to a tree by the shoulders.

Argas landed at a gallop and reared in front of our prey. I leapt off his back and summoned the knives with magic. I liked their threatening shape. The sharp blades flew back to me as obediently as boomerangs. The Soul fell to his knees. I licked one of the blades, cleaning the black blood off it, and spat it in his face. He glared at me defiantly, the affront sending a powerful anger surging through me. I raised my foot and smashed it into his face, sending him sprawling. The Soul gurgled . . . and burst into a cloud of ashes. I looked around, confused, as my Sisters galloped over to me.

"What a shame," Nerea said. "He could at least have been mine."

"I only kicked him. I didn't think it would reduce him to ashes," I protested, defending my actions.

Sophìa smiled, her eyes glinting with satisfaction. "The Hunt is in your blood. I am not surprised. Yet you must use the proper amount of force."

"I couldn't control myself," I said in my defense. It hadn't been my fault.

"You will learn."

"Where's Devina?" I asked, noticing she wasn't with us.

"She went hunting for ferocious beasts. Those are worth three points." Sophia grinned, seeing me burn with curiosity.

"So one of them is enough . . . What's the reward for the winner of the Hunt?"

"She becomes the prize of the Opalion and initiates the Games." Sophia mounted her majestic Saurus and took flight. Fascinated, I watched her ascend into the sky. My Sisters followed her like bees behind their queen.

"Sheathe your weapons because the Opalion has its queen," Devina said in our minds. She'd caught one. A moment later she emerged from behind a mountain with a big, odd-looking creature dangling from her Saurus. A single catch and she'd won the competition.

"When can I take part in the Reaping?" I asked, anxious to win. I had to learn to recognize Souls' fears as quickly as possible.

"You must first prepare for it, but do not fear. Your training will begin today," Sophia promised. Her laughter tickled my mind. She knew my most intimate thoughts, and there was only one thing I could think about: at the next Opalion, *I* would be the queen.

EVAN

28

PROMISES

"That way, Simon!" The motorcycle slid beneath me as the flaming arrow intended for my brother lodged in the asphalt. I drove around it and set off again, rising onto my back wheel while Simon and Ginevra dodged the attacks of the bastard who'd been chasing us for weeks. I'd had enough of him. I prepared a fireball as the roar of our engines filled the night. *"Simon, get ready!"* I shouted to him in my mind.

He positioned himself behind me, waiting for our target to reappear, while Ginevra, who knew what I was about to do, conjured a vacuum sphere around her. When our adversary materialized on the road in front of us, I threw my fireball and Simon manipulated the air so its flames branched out, surrounding us in a protective bubble that moved at the same speed as the bikes.

I stared into the Hunter's dark eyes as we approached. He didn't move—only his dark-brown ponytail stirred in the wind. In his brown leather clothes, he looked like a warrior who'd escaped from another era.

The Executioner ran toward us, breaching the barrier. "What the fuck?" Simon muttered. In a flash Absolon was in front of me. He grabbed my handlebars, swung himself up from the ground and landed behind me on the seat, putting me in a stranglehold with his bow.

I lost control of the bike, which leaned to the side and slid across the asphalt, sparks flying, dragging me with it. I struggled against the Subterranean, but he was strong—stronger than anyone I'd ever encountered. Simon reared up and zoomed toward us, but Absolon was prepared: setting an arrow against his mighty bow, he released it. It lodged in the bike's gas tank, which exploded. The arrows were dipped in poison, like the one that had killed Gemma, and the fire spread instantly. I searched for Simon among the flames while fighting off the Hunter. Fortunately, he'd already materialized on Ginevra's motorcycle.

"He's mine!" she shouted. Her wheels squealed against the asphalt and the bike skidded to a halt scant yards from us. Ginevra moved swiftly, her green Witch eyes slicing through the night.

"No!" Simon shouted, but it was too late. Ginevra's serpent emerged from her flesh and lunged at the Subterranean. In a split second Absolon turned and, to our astonishment, grabbed the serpent by the head.

"Shit, no!" I exclaimed in shock.

Ginevra's eyes bulged as the creature wriggled in his grip. All the Hunter had to do was crush its skull . . . and Ginevra would die. Terrified, Simon didn't hesitate. With a barbaric shriek he reared up on his bike and shot toward the Hunter, but before he could reach him Absolon vanished, letting the serpent fall to the ground. Simon hit the brakes, confused.

I stared at the Dakor. It was battling the same enemy as I was, but did that mean there was a truce between us? The serpent hissed and approached me threateningly. "Guess not," I muttered. Ginevra summoned her Dakor. It went back to her and disappeared under her skin.

"What the hell just happened?" Simon snapped before letting out a string of curses. He kicked the bike, making it slide across the ground, and turned to face Ginevra. "Damn it, he was *this close* to killing you! Do you realize that?" he screamed in her face.

"Did you expect me to stand around and watch him kill Evan? His arrows are poisoned!"

"I told you to stay out of it!"

"Gin, he wouldn't have killed me and you know it. It's you he wants. He's a Witch Hunter. You have to let me protect you," I reminded her, backing Simon up.

"You were really risking it," he added.

"How could I know he'd catch my Dakor in midair?"

"That's true," I agreed. "I've never met anyone who could do that. He's really strong and he could have killed you in the blink of an eye. So why didn't he?" I picked up my bike. It was falling apart. A surge of rage overtook me and I slammed it to the ground again.

"The bikes are totaled," Simon remarked.

"I'll take care of them," Ginevra said. "They'll be as good as new."

"I don't give a shit about the bikes!" I growled. My tension was mounting. The Subterranean who'd killed Gemma had been hunting us down relentlessly for weeks, stalking us like mice. I grabbed my hair in my fists and howled at the night, overwhelmed with exasperation.

It had been three months since the Witches had taken Gemma and there hadn't been a sign of her since. I was losing my mind. Beyond all logic, I'd even started dreaming. I dreamed of touching her, of brushing my lips across hers . . . but every night those images turned into terrifying nightmares.

Ginevra took my hands in hers. "Evan, calm down. You can't lose it now, of all times. Liam needs you." I forced myself to look at her and filled my lungs with air. The thought of my son was the only thing that could make me think clearly again. "Let's go home," she murmured, "before that bastard Hunter comes back."

I nodded. Ginevra was right. Her life was in danger. I couldn't let anger cloud my judgment. She needed me and I had to protect her. I owed it to Simon—he'd protected Gemma while I was gone, and now they both needed my help . . . and my focus. I had to stay lucid and fight, though what consumed me more than the fire of a thousand Hunters was the terrible awareness that I had lost Gemma.

"And so the princess saved her prince from the castle in which he was imprisoned and—" Anya stopped when she sensed our thoughts. She raised her eyes and gave me a sad smile.

"Thanks, Anya," Ginevra told her. "I knew I could count on you."

She gently rested Liam in his crib. "He just fell asleep. Don't make any noise."

I went over to look at him and every shadow disappeared from my mind. His big, almond-shaped eyes were closed, his cheeks flushed from sleep, and his hair curled on his forehead. Whenever I got lost, he had the power to bring me back.

"Why has that Subterranean got it in for us?" Simon hissed. "Wasn't Gemma enough for him?"

"He's not a Subterranean like the others—he's a Witch Hunter, and Ginevra's the only Witch dwelling on Earth now. It's her he wants," said Anya, who knew him well.

"I know how dangerous it is for you to come here," I told her, "and I'm grateful for your help." The Witch nodded. A painful silence developed between us. "How is she?" I asked. I knew she wasn't allowed to talk to me about Gemma, but if I didn't find out I might lose my mind.

"She's fine," was the only answer I got.

"Is there any trace of us left in her?" Even a little would be enough for me: a memory, an image that had resisted the transformation.

"None, sorry." I clenched my fists, letting my defenses down in front of her. "The Devil's Claw wiped away every last feeling in her. There's only room for the Bond."

"I don't believe it," I said, my voice tight with frustration. "I—I can't accept it. It's been three months! Why hasn't she set foot on Earth again?"

"She's finishing her training. That's how it works."

"No, that's not true. You're trying to keep her away from me."

"Evan . . ." Ginevra tried to calm me down, but it was a lost cause.

"How can I hope to win her back if I don't even get to see her?"

"Actually, you can't. She made her choice, Evan."

"No she didn't," I snapped.

Anya gaped as she read the truth in my mind: Gemma had decided to drink Ambrosia. She locked eyes with me. "Sophìa would never have let you two go. In any case, things turned out differently. You yourself asked me to transform her. You yourself invoked Sophìa. It was the only way to save her life."

"Give her this." Anya stared at the diary in Ginevra's hands. In it were hidden Gemma's deepest thoughts. "It might help her remember," Ginevra said quietly.

"I doubt it," she replied, looking sorry, "but I can try."

"Wait." I went to Anya and pulled out a letter. I'd written it for Gemma months earlier, just in case she ended up transforming. She looked at it for a moment and slipped it into the diary.

"Take care of her, please," Ginevra begged her.

"I'll try, though Devina has taken her under her wing." Ginevra's eyes widened. "Gemma trusts her and there's not much I can do about it."

"That bitch!" I snarled.

"Don't worry. I'll keep looking out for her."

I nodded my thanks and she disappeared. Simon and Ginevra also left, closing the door behind them softly. I wasn't sure Gemma's diary or my letter would help much, but at least it was something, though not what I hoped for: I wanted to see her. I needed her and knew that deep in her heart Gemma also needed me and our baby. Maybe I'd done everything wrong. Maybe I should have let Gemma pass on rather than allowing her transformation. I'd battled Subterraneans who wanted to take her away from me, I'd battled the Màsala who had condemned her to death, but I'd been self-centered. I'd spent all that time keeping her from dying so I wouldn't lose her, but by doing so I'd denied her the peace of Eden. Now all that awaited her was eternity in Hell. And there was no guarantee she would come back to me.

Her eyes looked out at me from a snapshot of us together. I'd taken it on a snowy day after we'd made love in my car. Beside the framed picture on the dresser were Gemma's ring and necklace. I'd picked them up from the lakeside when she'd disappeared. I turned the pendant over and read the inscription on the back of it.

Gevan. Forever.

The little diamond sparkled as I turned it in my fingers. When she'd transformed, the diamond had absorbed her dark essence and become carbonado. I'd stared at it for a moment as the sun rose over the lake, mocking me. Like Gemma, the diamond had lost its light, surrendering to the darkness. Moments later, though, it had begun to sparkle again. I gripped the pendant in my fist until my palm ached. No, it wasn't the end. I couldn't accept it. I would never give up. Like the diamond, Gemma would also find her light again.

Liam wailed and I went over to the crib. He looked at me with his deep, curious, blue eyes. I was sure he missed his mother too. "I'll bring her back to us," I promised, stroking his cheek. He smiled at me. I picked up the violin and played the song I'd composed for him and Gemma the day of his birth. A lullaby. Liam loved it. The sound of the violin calmed him, so every night I would play it for him.

We were alone, the two of us. A father with his wonderful child. If only I'd purified Gemma immediately after the birth . . . Waiting had been a mistake. But how could I have imagined I would lose her? My whole world had changed in a single night . . . in a single instant.

Ginevra was leaning against the door, listening. She often did that. I continued to play. She was suffering too. I let the final note linger, sighing as the room fell back into silence. Ginevra waited a moment and then walked away. I looked at Liam, who'd fallen asleep. Physiologically, he was completely normal. Despite our expectations, he was human. He was the sweetest baby in the world and looking at him made my heart ache because everything about him reminded me of Gemma. I had promised to protect him. That was my mission now, the most important one I would ever carry out.

There was only one way to keep my promise to the very end: find Gemma and bring her back. At all costs.

GEMMA

29

DANGEROUS TEMPTATIONS

I dodged Nausyka's staff as Sheeva attacked me from behind in the form of a panther. I saw her just in time, did a backflip, landed behind her, and looked up at my Sisters. "I'm afraid you're too old for me," I provoked them smugly.

"Don't count on it, newbie. You've still got a lot to learn."

"You've taught me everything there is to know. When can I come with you to the Reaping?" I groaned.

"Sophìa will be the one to decide. You can't contend with Subterraneans unless you're adequately trained—otherwise you'll get yourself killed by their fire."

"I didn't ask to go on Recon. It's mortal Souls I'm interested in," I insisted.

"That would be even more dangerous, because you'd be running not into fledgling Subterraneans but Soldiers of Death prepared to battle for the soul of whomever you want to take possession of."

"I'm ready. I can face them if I need to."

"We'll see," Nausyka said.

I raised the staff using the power of my mind and spun it through the air challengingly. My Sister looked me straight in the eye and snatched it. I turned and leapt high into the air, climbing barehanded up the black stone of the Castle until I reached the floor where my rooms were. I wanted to take a hot bath. I was dirty and the training had been more grueling than usual. Still, I couldn't complain—I'd been the one to push myself beyond the limit. I felt like a caged lion. I wanted to fight. I wanted to face our enemies. But more than anything else, I wanted to take part in the Reaping. I *thirsted* for Souls. It was a desire that had grown in me day after day to the point of being unbearable.

The moment I arrived at the entrance to my chambers, I froze: the door was ajar. Someone was inside. I blocked off my thoughts and peeked through the gap. Anya and Devina were there. The former was holding a book with embossing on its blue cover. She held it tight, as though it were something important.

"She's forgotten him! Get over it!" Using magic, Devina whisked the book out of her hands and set fire to it. It burst into flames and fell to the floor in a pile of ash.

"No!" Anya gasped, leaning over it. "What have you done?!" She was furious. Her green panther eyes flashed and her Dakor hissed.

"Do you want to challenge me, by chance?" Devina asked, facing up to her. "Or do you want me to tell Sophìa that instead of working on the Reaping you were playing nanny to a Subterranean's son?"

What was going on between them? What were they talking about? Why were they behaving like that?

"He's her son too."

"That's not important any more."

"She might want him here."

I burst into the room, flinging the door open wide. "What's going on?"

They turned to look at me, stunned, probably mystified as to why they hadn't sensed my arrival. I was able to block off my thoughts almost all the time, something that continued to surprise them. They certainly hadn't taught me how; closing off your mind to the other Sisters was forbidden. Not officially, of course. It was more of an unwritten law. Nevertheless, I couldn't help it. It was an innate gift, one that not all of them possessed. It was as if I'd learned how to do it in my past life.

Devina smiled at me as though nothing had happened. "You're back. We were waiting for you." She came over and put her arm around my waist. "How did training go today?"

"As usual. I beat Zhora, Nausyka, and even Bathsheeva. I think I'm ready for the Reaping."

"I agree with you. Come, let's go to the spas. You can take a nice hot bath and then we'll convince Sophìa you're ready." She turned to look at Anya. "If I promise to go along and keep an eye on you, she'll listen to me."

"That's the greatest thing you could do for me!" I exclaimed excitedly.

"I'm your Sister. You know that we help each other out."

"Anya, are you coming with us?" I turned toward her and noticed she was staring at us with a fiery gaze.

"I'll catch up with you."

Why was she acting that way? Was she jealous of my relationship with Devina? Like me, she too often blocked her thoughts, so I had no way of knowing what was going through her mind. Devina, on the other hand, was more transparent. Her thoughts weren't always commendable, but at least she didn't hide them. She'd been my role model ever since I arrived at the Castle. I wanted to be like Devina.

The heat could already be felt in the hallways. When Devina and I made our entrance in the Spa Parlor every head turned. Devina was respected in the Castle—almost as much as Sophìa. I admired her for that, though I had to admit I was jealous of her power. I wanted it to be mine . . . and one day it would be. The Subterraneans bowed to us and let us through. I watched them, attracted to their well-trained bodies. They weren't simple Children of Eve like all the others; visiting the Spa Parlor was a privilege granted exclusively to Champions. Almost all the Witches had one, and maybe soon I would have my own.

Emayn, my Mizhya, knelt at my feet and undid the laces wrapped around my high-heeled boots. Then she stood up to undress me, but Devina grabbed her hand. *"Get lost,"* she hissed, then turned to smile at me. "I'll take care of you."

The maidservant bowed and retreated rapidly, cringing, afraid Devina would kill her. That happened often, even for far less. I was growing fond of my maids but Devina considered them chattel, and when she tired of hers she would slay them brutally. I knew that for her the only bond that counted was the one with her Sisters. Maybe she was right, like she was about everything else. I smiled back at her and let her unlace my brown bodice. It fell to the floor, freeing my breasts. Devina also got undressed, revealing her generous bosom.

We sank into the tub. Devina slowly moved toward me and our breasts touched. She picked up a pitcher and poured scalding hot water over my neck as I melted in its heat. I looked into her amber eyes, hiding a smile. I knew what she was doing. The others' Champions were watching and she wanted to arouse them. I enjoyed feeling desired; it turned me on. Playing along, I slowly ran a sponge over her shoulders and down to her breasts as she closed her eyes, letting me touch her.

"Come on. Let's give them a little show," she whispered in my mind. I leaned over and kissed her sensually on the lips. "Choose one."

"What?" I asked.

"Choose a Champion. Which one do you want to be with?"

"But they belong to my Sisters. It's against the rules."

"I'll take care of them, don't worry. It's my gift to you for completing your training." Devina moved her lips to my ear and her voice became a murmur: "Come on, don't tell me you're not tempted. Choose one. Which one excites you the most?" I studied the Subterraneans. Their thoughts were a tangle of arousal. "I could give you mine . . . or would you prefer Anya's?"

My eyes lingered on a dark-skinned Subterranean. He had a penetrating gaze and sexy creases below his eyes. "Careful, princess—that's Sophìa's Champion. None of us can touch him. But if you want him, I can arrange for a secret encounter."

"What's going on here?" Anya hissed with irritation. I pulled away from Devina. How much had Anya overheard? I wasn't sure how far I could trust her. Loyalty to Sophìa counted a lot for all the Sisters . . . a little less for Devina.

"We were just relaxing a bit," Devina replied. She slid into the water, immersing her shoulders. "You should too. You could really use it," she said to provoke her.

"Do you want to take a bath with us?" I asked.

"There's no time. I came to tell you I spoke with Sophìa about your training. I proposed taking you with me to the Reaping."

"Really?" I jumped to my feet, excited by the news. "When can we start?"

Her lips curved in a smile. Anya's smile was always sweet and affectionate, unlike Devina's, which was sharp and most times full of contempt. "You're ready," Anya said. "Even today, if you like. But first the Empress wishes to see you."

I got out of the tub and my Mizhyas ran over to dry me. "Well? What are we waiting for?"

"Hang on," Devina said. "I said I was going to speak to her on Gemma's behalf. That was my prerogative."

"Gemma isn't your property. She's as much my Sister as yours."

"What difference does it make who takes me to the Reaping? All that matters to me is going. There's no need to fight over this. In fact, why don't you both come?"

"That sounds like an excellent idea," Devina exclaimed, her amber eyes locked on Anya's.

"Let's go," she said, annoyed. "The Empress awaits us."

"Let's not keep her waiting," Devina replied, winking at me.

I sheathed my daggers and crossbow and followed them, casting one last glance at Sophìa's Champion. I'd just discovered something important about myself: I was drawn to things that were forbidden.

30

THE WHISPER OF EVIL

"No." Sophìa stopped us at the entrance to the Pantheon. "Only Naiad." Anya and Devina looked at each other. I couldn't take my eyes off the Empress. Her beauty was spellbinding. None of us could hold a candle to her. "Come now. Come forward," she said.

I walked toward her and my Sisters stayed behind. Sophìa rose from her throne and I bowed. It was then that a panther attacked me from behind. I leapt back just in time as another two crept toward me, on their guard. *She was challenging me.*

I smiled: challenge accepted.

All three panthers lunged at once, but I managed to avoid their claws and counterattack. In a few quick moves I sent two of them—Nerea and Kreeshna—to the ground. That left only Bathsheeva, who watched me with her golden eyes. I channeled my power and unleashed it on her, generating a shock wave that struck all three panthers, hurling them away. The force of my attack even made Sophìa's hair fly back.

It was clear what was happening: Sophìa wanted to see with her own eyes how far along I was with my training. It was a test, and I had every intention of passing it. I materialized behind Sophìa and attacked her. She blocked the blow in time and smiled at me, her gaze captivating. If she wanted war, she would have it. The Sisters were shocked.

"What's she doing?"

"She's challenging the Empress?"

"Is she out of her mind?"

"Go on, Gemma. Show her all you've got." It was Devina, backing me up.

Smiling, I drew my daggers and tried to strike Sophìa. She was very agile, and stronger than anyone I'd ever fought before, but I wasn't about to give up. The entire hall became our battleground, our rapid attacks a dark dance. Sophìa smiled, cast me an amused glance, and with a single blow sent me crashing into the wall. The impact was so powerful it felt like it had come from a sledgehammer. I sank to my knees, feeling like every bone in my body was broken. She hadn't even used her powers—only her physical strength. I saw Sophìa's feet approach and stop in front of me. "You are ready."

I raised my head, surprised, and she smiled at me and held out her hand. I took it, looking into her blue eyes. "You mean I can take part in the Reaping?"

"We train for two purposes: attacking Subterraneans when we are on Reconnaissance and defending ourselves from Subterraneans during the Reaping. This is the most difficult, most dangerous part. The Children of Eve do not always hinder our work, but when they do we must know how to defend ourselves, and you have proven you are capable of at least trying to do so. It was brave of you to challenge me. I admit I expected it from you—you have war in your blood. I would be a fool to force you to suppress it any longer."

"I've been waiting for this for a long time."

"Anya and Devina will go along to protect you."

I looked at my Sisters, who had joined us. "I don't need to be protected." I fixed my eyes on hers to emphasize my confidence.

"You are very skilled. Not even Devina learned so quickly," Sophìa said.

"Thank you, my Empress." I bowed to her. Though I sensed Devina's thoughts were in turmoil because of the provocation, I couldn't decipher them. The competition among us Sisters was always fierce. Sophìa said challenges brought us to life, which was why she constantly stirred up rivalries among us. Despite it all, the Bond among us was solid. Nothing was stronger.

My Sisters had taught me everything. Every day they trained me in the field and helped me practice using magic. Sophìa had revealed the secrets of the world to me and finally I was ready to discover it with my own eyes.

Anya rested her hand on my chest and my brown clothing changed, wrapping around me like the skin of a serpent—a black serpent, just like my Dakor. I'd already seen the outfit on my Sisters. It was what they wore to the Reaping. It was exciting to finally be able to wear it. My eyes were aflame, burning with poison. In my mouth I could almost taste the flavor of the Souls I would make mine.

"Have a good Reaping, my wicked little butterflies," Sophìa told us. "Show mercy only to yourselves and to the thirst of your Dakor." We bowed to the Empress. She leapt up and disintegrated into a hundred black butterflies that disappeared through the hole in the ceiling.

Someone took my hand and I turned around to find Anya giving me an encouraging smile. I nodded to let her know I was ready, then took Devina's hand as darkness engulfed us. *"Follow your instinct,"* Devina told me in her mind.

The chaos lasted only seconds. When the light returned, we were no longer in the Castle. I looked around. I was in a cluttered apartment. Anya and Devina weren't at my side any more, but even though I couldn't see them I knew they were there with me. I felt the power of the Bond. However, something just as powerful was summoning me, clouding everything else. An intoxicating sensation. No—perhaps it was a scent. It was nothing and everything, together. The pure essence of evil. I felt it flowing inside me and my blood boiled at its call. I focused on that sweet song and swiftly reached them: a young married couple fighting in the kitchen.

It was my first Temptation, yet I knew perfectly what to do. My instinct cried out for me to do as it wished. I moved closer and studied them. Within seconds I knew everything. I knew their dirtiest secrets. She looked desperate, her eyes red from crying and her face covered with bruises. She'd waited up all night for him and when he'd gotten home he'd beaten her.

"I told you I had a meeting!"

"He's lying," I whispered to the woman. *"You smell perfume on him. He was with another woman."*

"A meeting with your whore! Liar!"

"You're crazy. Tomorrow I'm sending you back to your mother's!" he shouted.

I fed the woman's suspicions: *"So he'll be free to go to her."*

"So you'll be free to go to her, right? Answer me!"

I looked into the man's eyes. I was enjoying the game more and more. *"Is that how you let a woman treat you? Put her in her place!"*

"Shut up, bitch!" He smacked her face so hard it sent her flying to the ground. She crawled across the floor in tears and I returned to fan the flames inside her.

"I bet this is how you fuck her, huh?! You used to love doing it with me on the floor. Or do you two do it on your desk?"

"Don't hide," I whispered to the man. *"You're in charge here and she has to accept it. Tell her how it was. Tell her how hard she made you come."*

"You wanna know how we did it? We did it on the floor and on the couch and in the bathroom and in every corner of my office. While you were here at home I was making her ride me. I fucked her every single day. Happy?"

I felt her heart break and reach the point of no return. *"He fucked her every single day. He's just a filthy son of a bitch. Make him pay!"* The woman shot to her feet, grabbed a knife, and rushed at him with a shriek of rage, but the man stopped her in time and disarmed her, wounding her in the belly in the process. They stared at each other for a long moment. Her eyes were full of fear now. The man's were bloodshot. He'd lost all control.

I smiled and whispered my Temptation: *"Kill her. Kill her or for you it'll be the end."*

"No! Wait!" the woman begged, in tears.

"Stab her. It's too late to back out now. She's just an obstacle. She'll leave you and press charges. You'll lose everything. Your life will be over."

"I can't lose everything," he hissed to himself. Raising the knife, he plunged it into her body again and again, venting all his anger on her. The woman's eyes opened wide with terror and then went blank. I slipped out of the man's mind.

As though emptied, he stood there, perfectly still. He looked at the bloody knife in his hand and flung it to the floor. "What have I done?" he gasped in horror. "Nadine! Nadine!" He tried to revive the woman, but it was useless. The man straightened up, wiping a tear from his eyes, his cheek smeared with the woman's blood. "Why wouldn't she believe me? I didn't do anything with that woman! Nadine . . . I shouldn't have provoked her like that! I wanted to reassure her and instead I killed her! I'm a monster!"

Now that I wasn't clouding his conscience, guilt was consuming him. He stared at the knife for a long moment, then leaned over, picked it up, and plunged it into his heart. His soul came out of his body and looked me straight in the eye. "Who are you?"

"I'm the evil inside you," I whispered.

The man's eyes bulged and his soul was sucked back into his body, which fell to its knees in a puddle of blood. Something stirred in his mouth. I smiled smugly as a black butterfly forced his lips open and crawled out—his now-damned Soul. I leaned over and picked it up, watching it wriggle between my fingers.

A powerful energy surged through me like lava, setting my veins aflame. The exhilaration went to my head more strongly than pure poison. How had I ever managed to exist without that sensation before? My Dakor slithered beneath my skin, broke through it near my collarbone, and hissed at the Soul. I could feel my serpent's heart beat faster. I could sense his thirst. Guided by instinct, he opened his fangs wide and devoured the butterfly.

The Reaping had begun.

31

INSATIABLE THIRST

I closed my eyes as my Dakor devoured the man's damned soul and dark energy flooded through me, leaving me in bliss. Everything I'd done up to that point, all the incredible sensations I'd experienced since I'd been in Hell, were suddenly *nothing* compared to the power surging through me. Not the Hunt, not the Opalion, not all the fun I'd had with my Sisters . . . nothing had quenched my thirst. It was as though I'd been awaiting that moment forever. I realized it was my calling: Souls—leading them to perdition was pure pleasure. I wanted to seduce them. I wanted to make them mine and quench my thirst.

All at once, something tore me away from those thoughts. Someone was there with me. I turned and found the woman's soul staring at me, perfectly still. She was frightened—I could feel it. No Witch had corrupted her over the course of her life, though she'd faced Temptation many times.

Just then, a Subterranean appeared for her. "Hello there," I said, my voice provocative. My Dakor hissed uneasily.

"Who are you two? What do you want from me?" the woman asked, trying unsuccessfully to conceal her terror.

"Come with me. Can't you see what he did to you?" I showed her her body on the floor, lying in a pool of blood. "I'll take you to him so you can get your revenge."

"Where is he? Where have you taken him?"

"Come with me and I'll show you."

"Don't listen to her!" the Subterranean boomed, glaring at me with fiery eyes. The woman, however, was tempted. "If you follow me, I can save you from the darkness. I'll show you the light and you'll find peace," the Subterranean went on.

"There is no peace without revenge," I whispered to her. "Deep down, what do you want?"

"I . . . I want to make him pay," she murmured to herself. She looked up, determined. "Take me to him." With those words, her soul was sucked back into her body and regurgitated as a splendid black butterfly.

Well done, little mortal. There's a bit of Witch in each of you. I smiled at the Subterranean. "Step aside, ferryman. Her soul is mine."

"Her soul isn't yours to take! I was sent here for her!"

"Oops, did I ruin your mission?" I goaded him.

He shot me a piercing look and my eyes burned with poison. I wasn't afraid of him. Devina and Anya appeared just then and he backed up in fright before disappearing, still furious. My Dakor opened its fangs and devoured the woman's soul.

Looking around, my Sisters stepped over the two bodies. "Not bad for her first time," Devina said. "She even managed to corrupt the woman after she'd been entrusted to a Subterranean. See that, Anya? She's a fast learner."

"Faster than you, it would seem," Anya returned, repeating the Empress's words. "Why didn't you leave after you took the man's Soul?" she asked me reproachfully.

"I took the woman's too. Aren't you pleased?"

"Of course, but there was a Subterranean. A battle over Souls is too dangerous for you."

"She worked it out just fine," Devina said in my defense.

"What's the problem? I won and I took her Soul."

"It could have ended badly."

"But it didn't. The situation was under control."

"Only because we showed up."

"Then next time stay out of it. That way I can prove you wrong. You're not my babysitter."

"Oh, you're going to break her heart," Devina said, smirking. "Babysitting is becoming her favorite pastime. Isn't it, Anya?" She sent her a look I couldn't decipher. What were they saying in their minds? And why weren't they including me in it?

"I don't understand why you can't be proud of me like Devina," I grumbled.

Anya came closer. "You're wrong—I'm very proud of you, really. I care about you more than you can imagine. That's why I worry about you." I nodded. I could tell her affection for me was sincere. It wasn't only because of the Bond. "How do you feel?" she asked.

"Intoxicated," I replied.

"Do you want to go home now? I know how draining the first time can be."

The power that had surged through me was fierce, but it hadn't slaked my thirst—it had intensified it. "Not at all. We've only just begun."

"Why not just one little glass? Go on, drink it!"

"Marcos, cut it out. Justin has to drive!" A redheaded girl took the glass out of his hands. She was drunk. "This stuff's too strong for him. It's better off in my stomach than his. Otherwise who's going to take me home?"

The statement hurt the boy, who had a crush on her. He hated that she was treating him like a chauffeur, a little boy she could put in a corner and take advantage of whenever she liked. He felt left out but didn't have the courage to do anything about it. I was going to give him that courage.

I stepped forward, stoking the anger secretly smoldering inside the boy. *"She doesn't think you have the guts to do it. Pick up that glass. Show her you're brave too. Show her you're no coward."*

"Screw it, Sara! Hand me that glass!" Justin knocked the drink back in one gulp. The girl cheered excitedly and dragged him through the crowd.

"Time to go home, people. Party's over." An adult had come into the room. The kids all moaned. "Come on, out you go. Which of you is the designated driver?"

"That would be me," Justin replied, slurring his words. That single drink had been enough to dull his senses.

The kid's drunk. Maybe I should drive them home myself, the man thought.

"But the game's starting soon," I whispered in his mind.

He checked the clock and shrugged. *Aw, who cares? They'll work it out.* I smiled. The man had potential. Soon I would return to tempt him as well.

"Justin, I thought you didn't drink," said another girl named Melanie.

"Shhh. I'm fine. Never better."

"Maybe we should call a taxi."

"I'll take you. I know the way. Let's go. See? I can stand on one leg." They got into the car and I got in with them.

"Dude, you drive like a little kid," Marcos teased him.

I'm not a little kid, he thought.

"Prove it to him. Go faster. It'll impress her." Justin obeyed, blinded by his desire for her. Sara whooped enthusiastically and raised her hands in the air. He turned up the music on the stereo and stepped harder on the accelerator, satisfied.

"Whoa, dude, now you're overdoing it," Marcos complained.

"C'mon, Justin. Slow down," Melanie added.

"What's wrong with you two? Scared of a little adrenaline?" Sara said.

"You're going too fast, for fuck's sake!" Marcos exclaimed.

All at once a moose stepped out onto the dark street and Justin slammed on the brakes. The tires squealed across the asphalt as the car jerked to a halt. For a second there was silence, then someone started laughing and the others joined in.

"I thought we were done for."

"Gotta tell you, dude, you're insane."

"Guys," Melanie murmured in a tiny voice. "The train!"

"Huh?"

"The train's coming!" she cried. "We're on the tracks! We have to get off them!" The train whistled, its lights coming closer and closer.

"Drive, Justin!" Marcos shouted. "Get this fucking car moving!"

"I can't! It won't start!" he cried.

"Let's get out of here, quick!" I smiled and jammed the locks.

"They won't open!"

"I don't want to die!" Sara whimpered. Justin grabbed the fire extinguisher from under his seat and smashed his window. He scrambled out of the car and stood staring at the other kids as they tried to get out, then raised his eyes to the train. It was coming closer and closer.

"Justin, help me!" Melanie screamed. He looked at the train again, gauging the distance.

"You can't make it. You'll die too. Leave her there."

Justin stood there for a moment, paralyzed by my Temptation. Then he shook his head and rushed back to get her. Anger grew inside me. I'd lost him. He helped Melanie out and they both fell to the ground as Marcos smashed the other window and pulled himself out as well.

"Marcos help me! I'm stuck!" Sara pleaded.

"I'm sorry," he whispered, in tears, his conscience deadened by evil.

"Marcos!" she shrieked.

The train plowed into the car, sweeping it away with Sara inside it.

"Why didn't you help her?" Justin screamed at him. "She was right next to you! You could have gotten her out!"

"There wasn't time!" the frightened boy said.

"My God . . . She's dead . . ." Melanie covered her mouth with her hands.

"Sure there was time. You didn't help her!"

"I . . . I'm sorry," Marcos whispered. "I was afraid of dying."

"Don't apologize," I whispered. *"He was the one driving."*

"You were the one driving. It's your fault! We all could have died! I'm telling the cops. I'm telling them everything."

"No you're not," Justin hissed.

"Guys, cut it out! What's wrong with you?! Sara is dead!"

Down the track, the train was slowly grinding to a halt and we could hear sirens in the distance. Marcos pointed his finger at Justin. "We're all in deep shit. We're going to stick together, got it? We need to come up with an explanation." The other two nodded.

Anya and Devina materialized beside me. "Having a good Reaping?"

"I lost him." I gestured at Justin. "He resisted my Temptation."

"It happens," Anya said.

Devina went up to Marcos. "In compensation, I see you tarnished him."

"Better than nothing," I said. The purer they were the more fun it was. That taste of the forbidden . . . I'd thought Justin was weak because they'd talked him into drinking so easily. Nevertheless, instead of succumbing to my evil temptation, he'd saved the girl.

Marcos's soul, on the other hand, was now tarnished. He could still redeem himself, but we would make sure he was tempted again and, when his time came, one of us would claim him.

A Subterranean came for the girl. I gazed at him for a long time, fighting the urge to attack him, but I had more urgent matters to think about.

"Let's go. We're done here," I told my Sisters. I was anxious to begin again.

I should stay and turn myself in, thought the man in front of me. He'd just killed his girlfriend over nothing.

"Get out of here," I whispered in his mind. I smiled, watching him run away. If he'd stayed, maybe he would have had some hope of redemption, but he'd fled. One day he would be mine.

We'd collected the souls of dozens of mortals, tarnished those of hundreds more, but I could never get enough. My thirst grew with each new conquest, my Dakor was getting stronger, and I felt more alive than I'd ever felt. Entering the minds of mortals was child's play. They were so easy to manipulate! Only a few—those with the strongest spirits—managed to resist our Temptation. All the others gave in to our lethal whispers. We listened to their thoughts and quickly discovered what tormented them most. Secrets, lies, hidden desires. Evil had a thousand disguises and we assumed them all in our efforts to corrupt the mortals. We leveraged their emotions, their fears, their weaknesses. Some wanted money and some wanted power, no matter the cost. At that point we came into play. Each granted wish was a deal with the devil. We'd amassed First-Echelon Souls, Cowards like Marcos, Egotists, Corrupt Souls, and Lechers. They were the most fun of all.

"That's enough for now," Devina said.

"No," I insisted. "I'm not done yet."

"It's time to go back to the Castle. Sophia will be anxiously awaiting our Reaping."

"One more Soul, then we can go back," I said resolutely. I wasn't ready yet.

"Agreed." Devina gave in.

We materialized in a luxurious apartment where a party was going on. The noise was deafening and colorful lights chased each other all around the room to the rhythm of the music.

"Why don't we have a little fun?" Anya suggested. Appearing in the middle of the crowd so even the mortals could see her, she winked at me, inviting us to follow suit.

I smiled and turned to Devina. "Finally an idea I like."

She, on the other hand, looked vexed. *"What are you doing, Anya? We're exposing ourselves too much."*

"Relax, Dev. You could really use it," she shot back wickedly, dancing between two young men.

But Devina was adamant. *"He'll come."*

"We can't hide her forever."

I looked at my Sisters. What were they talking about? Hide who? And from whom? Did they think the music could drown out their thoughts? Or did they think they'd blocked them off from me, like they were doing more and more often?

"Come on, Gemma!" Anya encouraged me. "Come dance! It's fun!"

I made my way through the crowd to her, dragging Devina behind me. She grumbled but then saw a man she liked and started coming on to him. We went wild in the crowd, flirting, our pheromones drawing all the males to us like bees to nectar. No one could resist our dark allure.

"Hey, Gemma, check out that guy over there." Devina pointed to a man who was dancing with his girlfriend but couldn't take his eyes off me. I probed his mind. She wasn't his girlfriend. She was a professional dancer, and this was his bachelor party. The next day he was getting married, but just then it was me he wanted. *A lecher.* As my final prey I couldn't ask for anything better than a cheater.

"The honor is yours," Devina said.

I wafted my pheromones over to him, inducing him to come closer, then danced with him, using my provocative movements to turn him wild with desire. Completely bewitched by me, he was ready and willing to cheat on his fiancée. He moved his lips toward mine but I dodged them and pushed him to his knees in front of me. He looked up at me ecstatically as I danced around him. Taking off his shirt, he reached out and put his hand on my behind, but Devina cracked her whip and trapped his wrist in it. Though he shouted from the pain, he was instantly excited when Devina joined me in my sexy dance. "Nice costumes," he told us both, trying to pull me against him.

Suddenly someone rushed him and dragged him away from me. The crowd around us pulled back as the man was brutally smashed against the wall. I sensed at once it was a Child of Eve. "By Lilith! What the—" I stopped mid-sentence when the Subterranean turned and his silvery gray eyes locked onto mine, burning into them.

"At last I've found you." His voice filled my head.

"You again," I murmured to myself. It was the young man from the forest.

"Let's get out of here!" Devina ordered, but he strode over to her and grabbed her by the neck.

"You're not going anywhere," he threatened.

"Care to bet?" Devina slipped free from his grasp and materialized beside me and Anya.

"Anya, no!" an unknown female voice shouted in our minds. I spun around and met her incredibly green eyes. By Lilith, it was a Witch!

A second later we disappeared.

"What's going on?" I demanded when we materialized at the Castle.

"I don't know what you're talking about," Devina retorted icily as Anya went to tell Sophìa we'd returned.

"Maybe if you stopped blocking off your mind you'd be able to read mine. That woman was a Witch! One of us! I felt the Bond." Finally I remembered—I'd seen her in the forest too, but my hostility toward the Subterranean had distracted me and I hadn't given her another thought.

"There is no Bond. In any case, I'm not allowed to talk about it."

"Fine. That means I'll ask Sophìa. At least tell me why we ran away. I don't understand—we've faced lots of Subterraneans before."

"He's different. He's not just any ordinary Subterranean. He's dangerous."

"Even better, then. Next time I want to fight him."

"No! You need to stay away from him."

"Why? Didn't you say Anya was too protective?"

"He's mine," she admitted. "I've been after him for centuries but he's never bent to my will. It's only a matter of time, though."

"He wants to kill you. I read it in his mind."

"I know. He's the most ferocious Subterranean I've ever encountered. Sexy and ruthless—that's why I want him. He's been hunting me down to kill me, and he'll try to kill you too. He has the power to creep into your mind, but you mustn't let him in. He'll try to convince you he's ready and willing to be claimed, that he worships you, and a whole bunch of other lies, but you mustn't listen to him. It's a trick. The minute you lower your defenses he'll attack and kill you. If we ever run into him again don't let him into your mind. It's his greatest power." Devina took my hands and looked me in the eye. "Do you trust me?"

I smiled. "Of course. More than anyone else in the world."

32

FIRST REAPING

"Welcome back," Sophìa said when we arrived. "Did you have a good Reaping?"

"See for yourself," I replied, a smug smile on my lips. I summoned my Dakor, who crawled out of my wrist and dropped to the floor, slithering over to the symbol of the Witches carved in red in the black floor. Anya and Devina's Dakor followed him.

"Come to me!" the Empress exclaimed, raising her arms in her elegant black gown. The serpents opened their jaws wide and three swarms of black butterflies flew out, merging into a single vortex like a dark tornado. Sophìa's laughter filled the hall as the myriad of Souls whirled about. "Fly, my little butterflies! This is your new realm."

The butterflies danced before the Empress. She clapped her hands and the Souls encircled her before flying up and disappearing through the opening in the ceiling. Finally she looked at me. "Excellent work. I could not be prouder. Especially of you, Naiad." I bowed to her, grateful, and looked her in the eye again. "Now tell me: did the Reaping meet your expectations?"

"It far exceeded them," I told her. My Dakor had quenched his thirst. The Souls had given him strength and I felt invincible.

"Good. Very good. Then tell me, what is it that troubles you?"

Though I'd closed off my mind, the Empress had detected my emotions. "Not what, but who. Tell me about Ginevra." Her name had come to my mind when her green eyes met mine; my soul had recognized the Bond. Sophìa cast a questioning glance at Anya and Devina. Or maybe it was one of reproach, because the two stepped back and went away, leaving me alone with her. "You told me my Sisters were dead! I'm confused, because I just ran into one of them."

Sophìa didn't reply, but instead fixed me with a guilty look. "Come," she finally said. "Let us find a quieter place to speak." She descended the steps and stood right in front of me, on the symbol. The floor trembled slightly and rose like an elevator. I looked up with surprise as the opening in the ceiling grew closer. We emerged into a well made of carbonado and the platform came to a halt. I looked around in wonder. It was the most luminous place I'd ever seen in the Castle—maybe in my entire life.

"Where are we?" I asked in astonishment.

Sophìa smiled. "Welcome to my garden." Part of the low wall surrounding us crumbled away to let us out. I took a few steps and turned back to look at it.

"It is the Well of Souls," Sophìa said as the carbonado sealed up again. "It is here that the Souls of all the Damned in the Castle converge. All my beloved butterflies." She raised her arms and let them flutter around her. Butterflies were everywhere—on the walls, on the huge glass ceiling, and most of all . . . "Come. I shall show them to you," she said, noticing my interest. Spread out in front of us was an incredible field of Devil's Stramonium. I'd never seen so much of it before. Its presence was almost frightening, as though it was alive. "You are fortunate. Few have seen my beloved crop of Devil's Stramonium." Sophìa plucked one of the blossoms and held it out to me. It was black and regal, just like her.

"The Witches' flower," I murmured. I inhaled its scent and instantly felt intoxicated. My Dakor heard the call and materialized from my skin. He too sniffed it and then gulped it down.

Laughing, Sophìa plucked a black butterfly from a flower and held it up near her eyes. "And you, were you a bad boy, my little Lecher?" It flapped its wings and fluttered away as the Empress watched it.

"This is where the Sorting of Souls is done," I said. It wasn't a question. My Sisters had told me about Sophìa's garden. I knew she often spent time there, entrusting command of the Castle to Devina, her Specter. She spoke to her Souls, cultivated Devil's Stramonium, and sorted the Damned before casting them out into Hell, where they would return to their human forms.

"Precisely," Sophìa said, confirming my thoughts. "But at times I also come here to relax. It is heavenly, is it not?" She laughed and I agreed.

Sophìa knew how to be eccentric, especially when it came to her butterflies, but I was there for another reason. I wanted an explanation. "You told me they were dead," I repeated, point-blank.

She stopped and turned her back to me. "To me they are," she replied, her voice once again serious.

"Tell me more."

"Ginevra left us."

I frowned. I would never have expected an answer like that. "How is that possible? It's madness."

"And yet it happened. She betrayed our trust and I banished her." It seemed impossible to me that a Sister could forswear the Bond like that. Sophìa was everything to us. "Not to her. When she left, my heart broke."

I snorted. "What heart? Your heart is made of ice."

"But to me, all of you are fire—the only thing that can melt my heart. You Sisters are everything to me."

"As you are to us." She was right. I knew how much she cared about us all. I shouldn't have been so unkind.

Sophìa nodded. "No other interesting encounters apart from Ginevra during your Reaping?" she suddenly asked, studying me closely.

What did she mean? "No . . ." I thought it over. "I don't think so."

"No other powerful emotion apart from your Bond with her?"

"Of course, as always, the seduction and Temptation and then the Reaping all went straight to my head."

"Excellent."

"What about the other Sister?" I said, switching to a subject that interested me more. "You said we lost two of them. Did the other one abandon us too?" The idea still seemed absurd.

"No. Tamaya was slain before she transformed. It was her husband who sacrificed her after he became a Subterranean. One cannot trust the Children of Eve. They are uncontrollable."

"What happened to him?"

"I dealt with him myself. Now that you have had the answers you sought, I wish to give you a gift."

"Being able to live in your kingdom is already a tremendous gift," I replied on impulse. Sophìa had been saddened by our conversation and I couldn't bear it.

"Do you mean you would refuse the gift I wish to give you?"

"I didn't mean that. I would never turn down a gift from you."

She smiled. "Very well. Come."

I followed her down a narrow hallway. The light had returned to normal—it was dimmer and gloomier than it had been in the field of Devil's Stramonium. The butterflies followed us, fluttering everywhere. Lining the walls were huge glass display cases, full of mounted butterflies. Only then did I notice that beneath each of them was a small, engraved carbonado plaque. I stopped to study them and Sophìa came back to join me, a smile on her lips. "It is my private collection . . . A little whim of mine. Do you like it?" There were butterflies big and small. All of them were black. I read a few of the names: *Caligula. Maximilien Robespierre. Joseph Stalin. Nero. Heinrich Himmler.* "These are—"

"My pride and joy. They are the foulest of the Damned that humanity has ever encountered, the most ferocious, most heartless mortals who ever existed on Earth. My masterpieces, if you prefer. They are those with whom I established a fruitful alliance. Some were even excellent lovers. They spread panic, terror, and death. They made people lose their faith. Under their rule, my kingdom flourished. Until, that is, their time came and they returned to me. Adding a new piece to my collection is always a momentous occasion. When it happens, I preside over an Opalion as queen in honor of my victory."

"Wow," I murmured. I'd participated in various Games in the Circle, but none of them had ever been held in Sophìa's honor. Maybe that was why I'd never seen her Champion in action. The thought of him stirred something inside me—the desire to watch him do battle.

"You have met Zakharìa," Sophìa said, sensing my interest.

I'd lost control of my thoughts. "I'm sorry, my lady."

"Do not be sorry. You know the rules of the Sisterhood: upon request, a Subterranean claimed by a Sister may be loaned to another who desires him."

"But . . . I thought it didn't count for Champions, much less yours. Devina said—"

"Indeed, that is true, but I could make an exception for you if you wish."

I stared at her, surprised. Was the Empress granting me her Champion? I couldn't imagine a greater honor. "Thank you, my lady, but for the moment I'd like to focus on Souls. Reaping is my vocation. I can't stop thinking about it. When can I go again?"

Sophìa burst into a laugh that brimmed with pride. "Soon, my black butterfly." She stopped beside a small altar and picked something up. "It is tradition for each Witch to receive the sacred token after her first Reaping. And you have proven yourself worthy to wear it." She opened her palm.

My eyes widened. In her hand was the ancient medallion I'd seen my Sisters wear: the Dreide.

EVAN

33

THE ILLUSION OF HAVING YOU NEAR

"All this time waiting for a sign from Gemma and when I finally find her I let her slip through my fingers!"

"Calm down, Evan," said Simon. "You'll have another chance."

"I shouldn't have blown this one!" I snapped.

"Don't shout or you'll wake Liam. He was crying all night long."

"You're right. Sorry."

Simon had stayed with him while Ginevra and I went looking for Gemma. Tracking her down had been hard even for her, and she could rely on the Bond. Gemma's power was strong—darkness shrouded her like a mantle. We had to be patient, wait for an opening. Without Ginevra I never would have managed. My connection to Gemma had been broken because her soul had been corrupted.

"They're ready." Ginevra appeared with an arsenal of weapons. She dropped them on the table and looked at me. "We'll see if he can catch a bullet in mid-air too."

I picked up the projectile and studied it. Inside it was venom from her Dakor. "Nice work. It's ingenious."

"It was easy, once I worked out the mechanism."

When we were still together, Gemma had told me about how they'd used weapons Ginevra designed to defend themselves from Desdemona, the Angel of Death sent in by the Màsala to kill her. They were dangerous for us and therefore effective against our enemies.

Ginevra strapped a holster to her thigh. Simon and I had already put on our shoulder holsters. "There are two guns each, plus this." Ginevra pulled out a Kalashnikov. "I'll keep this, if you don't mind. I have a score to settle with that Hunter."

"Be our guest."

"Careful with that thing," she warned, alluding to the bullet in my fingers.

"What, it might explode in my hand?" I joked.

"You never know. Your nerves haven't been reliable lately, and we need you alive." Ginevra was talking about my incident with the guy Gemma had been seducing at the party. I hadn't been able to help myself. When I'd seen his hands on her I'd lost my head and had come close to killing him. I was fierce, frustrated, and willing to kill to get her back.

I slid the cartridge into one of the guns and loaded it. "With these, the bastard doesn't stand a chance."

"Guess who's back," Ginevra suddenly said.

"He's here? Where?" Simon and I turned to look at her, gripping our weapons.

She was concentrating, listening. "Not him. It's Gemma. She's on Earth."

Emotions filled my heart: joy, fear . . . *urgency*. I holstered my weapons, staring at Ginevra. "What are we waiting for, then? Take me to her," I said resolutely.

"Good luck," Simon murmured.

Ginevra took my hand and together we dematerialized. Gemma's eyes were the first thing I saw, like two magnets that drew me to them the second I appeared. She, in contrast, glared at me with hatred, annoyed by my presence. It was like being shot in the chest with a poisoned bullet. In front of her was a newly born Soul, his dead body lying next to them.

The sight of Gemma seducing another man threatened to send me out of control again. I couldn't stand it. Fighting the instinct to shoot him, I grabbed the guy by the arm and helped him cross over, showing him the way.

"How dare you?" Gemma hissed. "He was already mine."

"Don't make me regret not killing him," I shot back threateningly.

She raised her arm to strike me but I blocked her wrist. We stared at each other for a long moment. I didn't know what was worse: the fact that she didn't remember me or the hostility I saw in her eyes.

Devina attacked me from behind and I was forced to defend myself.

"Gin, don't let Gemma get away!" I shouted, struggling with the redhead. I shoved her against the wall and pinned her there. She sneered at me as her Dakor emerged to challenge me. I tightened my grip, not even afraid of the thing. "I'll take care of this Witch."

"I know some fun games you could entertain me with," she whispered, touching her lips to my neck.

"You just don't give up, do you? What's wrong with you?"

"Sooner or later I'm going to claim you."

"Or maybe somebody else will," I said to provoke her. Her eyes burned with hatred. I'd never given in to Devina, but Gemma had a power over me Devina would never have.

"It wouldn't be a good idea for you to come back to us in Hell," she hissed, regaining her confidence.

"You're right. I'd better bring her back here to me."

Devina smiled and broke loose, attacking me again. "You'll never achieve that goal!"

"Then I'll die trying," I snarled, counterattacking.

"Evan, leave her to me!" Ginevra shouted, rushing at Devina. Until then, she'd kept Gemma, who refused to strike her, at bay. I jumped in front of Gemma. I had to keep her there. I wanted a chance to talk to her—just one. She launched an attack and then another, but I blocked them all without striking her. I barely recognized her. She'd always been a fighter, but now she was a fearless warrior. The Witches had trained her well; she was giving me a run for my money with her poisoned, curved-bladed daggers. Time was running out. I had to seize my chance. I disarmed her and trapped her against the wall, pinning her wrists to it. For a long moment we looked at each other as she caught her breath.

"You know your stuff when it comes to fighting Subterraneans."

"Especially the ones who want to kill me," she hissed.

I gripped her wrists harder. "I don't want to kill you."

"You're lying—I know you are. What else could you want of me?"

"To have you by my side," I said, determined, staring into her eyes. She held my gaze and a sneer formed on her face. She moved her lips close to mine, driving me wild. How I longed to kiss her again . . . just one kiss. Her hand rested on my thigh and slowly rose, disintegrating my every last shred of willpower.

"You're aroused by me," she whispered, thrusting her hips against me as I lost my mind. The brief contact disarmed me, but then I looked into her eyes. A glimmer of violet flashed across them, returning me to my senses. In a flash, I spun Gemma around and held her face against the wall, pressing my erection against her.

"I'm always aroused by you," I whispered behind her ear. For a moment I'd let myself be bewitched, but now I was in control again.

"You'll never have me," she said, her tone confident.

"Evan, look out!" Ginevra shouted. An arrow whistled past my ear. I grabbed Gemma in my arms and held her tight, rolling across the wall with her. Absolon was back.

Gemma stared at me, confused by my gesture, and the Hunter attacked again. "Go! Run!" I shouted to her.

"We need to get out of here!" Devina materialized beside her and they vanished.

I brandished my guns and prepared to face the Hunter. He was going to pay dearly for interrupting my encounter with Gemma. I shot at him and he dodged the bullet, surprised.

Ginevra pulled out her Kalashnikov, but the Hunter appeared behind me so she couldn't open fire. Not only was he strong, he was also agile and extremely sly. I tackled him and a furious struggle ensued. Suddenly, he tore a gun away from me, but I managed to kick it out of his hand before he could shoot.

I was trying to keep him away from Ginevra. There was no way I could go back to Simon without her. I'd experienced for myself what it was like to lose the person you love. I launched another attack and Absolon defended himself by throwing me to the floor. I slid across the ground and pulled out another gun, firing a shot that hit him straight in the gut and passed through to the other side. His eyes went wide with shock. Ginevra and I held our breath, waiting for him to disintegrate. Instead he slowly raised his head and stared at me, his lips twisted into a sneer. We stood there, stunned. The bullet hadn't killed him?

The Hunter prepared to attack again and Ginevra reacted by showering him with all the ammo in her Kalashnikov. Yet he continued to rush me, disappearing and reappearing as swiftly as a ghost. He tackled me and grabbed my shirt, but Ginevra cast a spell that hurled him away. An instant later she materialized at my side and got me out of there.

"What happened?" Simon asked, looking frightened when we appeared in front of him in the kitchen.

"The Hunter," I burst out, my nerves on edge. "He attacked us."

"The bullets, Evan!" cried Ginevra, who still couldn't believe it. "Did you see what he did? I've never seen a Subterranean like this one. How can we face him now? We have nothing that can stop him!"

"Would you two explain what's going on?" Simon insisted with exasperation. "We've faced lots of Subterraneans. One more shouldn't scare us."

"He's not like the others. My venom doesn't kill him," she explained.

Simon's eyes bulged. "How is that possible?"

"I have no idea. I hit him with an entire arsenal but it didn't leave a scratch on him. No Subterranean has ever had such power."

"But he isn't any ordinary Subterranean," I reminded them. "He's a Hunter. His priority isn't helping Souls pass on—what matters to him is killing Witches. He must have developed some sort of immunity to their venom."

"I've never seen anything like it," Ginevra murmured, incredulous.

"Yeah. He's become a serious problem."

Simon locked eyes with Ginevra. "This game is getting too dangerous for you."

"You can't ask me to stay holed up at home just because it's protected," replied Ginevra, who must have read his mind. "I'd rather risk my life than be imprisoned."

"Well, I'm not willing to run that risk," he said sternly.

"Evan needs me. Gemma might—"

"*I* need you," Simon shouted. "The topic is closed. Until we kill the Hunter, you're not leaving here." The fire in his eyes kept Ginevra from protesting, though I knew it wouldn't be so easy to keep her still—not when Gemma was involved. Bringing her home was almost as important to Ginevra as it was to me.

"Gemma? Did you find her?"

I nodded wearily. "It was no use. She doesn't remember *anything*." I sighed, at a loss.

"What now?"

"I'll keep trying. I have no intention of giving up." Somewhere beneath that Witch's exterior was my Gemma, and I would find her again.

"I spoke to her while we were fighting," Ginevra said. "In her mind."

"I'm listening," I said. What had she told her? Maybe she'd unearthed some glimmer of a memory . . .

"No, I'm sorry. She sees you only as a Subterranean, an enemy."

"No need to be so direct," Simon told her reproachfully.

"That's all right," I reassured him, sitting down on the sofa. "I already know how Gemma feels when I'm near her." Great bitterness, followed by the deep desire to claim me as her slave. My mind lost itself in the memory of her fiery gaze. "What did she tell you?" I asked Ginevra, driving the image from my thoughts.

"She was confused. She doesn't understand why I'm with you two." Ginevra chuckled. "She wanted me to come to my senses."

"What did you tell her?"

"That she was the one on the wrong side. Then I realized that only you had any chance of bringing something out in her, so I handed her over to you."

"It didn't work," I said softly, resting my head on my knees. "I can't believe this is actually happening. Me, fighting against Gemma. It's a nightmare."

"What will you do if she never comes back? Have you ever thought about that?"

"That's not even a possibility." I gave Ginevra a hard stare, almost as if her question were an insult.

"You should think about it, though."

"Never." I shot to my feet, furious. Had she lost her mind?

"You don't understand. The Sisters' Bond has taken possession of her. I felt it. Gemma was reborn through Sophìa's venom. I'm not sure there's any chance she'll be able to renounce evil."

"Shut up," I ordered.

"What, you don't want to hear it? Well, you have to. We've all got a lot on the line."

"You can back down whenever you want," I growled.

"That's not the problem! I care about Gemma as much as you do. I want to bring her back too, but you need to open your eyes and face facts."

"I'd rather be blind than lose hope."

"I don't want you to give up, Evan. I just want you to stay focused. You were on the verge of letting yourself be claimed today. They were on Recon and you're a Subterranean." My eyes widened at the memory of the power Gemma had had over me. "If you let her tricks work on you, it'll end up being *you* who gives in to *her* and not vice versa. Are you understanding me? *You* need to be strong. That's the only way you'll manage to bring her back. You need to see Gemma for what she is now: a Witch. What got into you back there, anyway?"

"I . . . I lost my head," I confessed. Having her so close after such a long time had disarmed me. I'd touched her—had been on the verge of kissing her. I'd longed to hold her again so badly I'd let myself be overpowered. Her lips had been so close to mine I'd believed I'd found her again.

"Instead, she had you in the palm of her hand. She was *this* close to making you hers."

"I'm already hers."

"You know what I mean. The more you gave in to her, the more your energy flowed into her. Her lips would have made you her prisoner."

"Maybe I should let her do it," I murmured, feeling defeated.

"Don't even say that," Simon reproached me. "What would become of Liam?"

I ran my hands over my head. What I'd said was ridiculous—I would never abandon my son. "You guys are right. I'll be more careful next time."

Unless I was willing to succumb, I would have to see things for what they were. I couldn't keep on deluding myself that I'd found her again just because she seemed to give in to me. It was a trick. Gemma was a Witch and I was a Subterranean. Once again we were pitted against each other, like when it had all begun—only now our roles had been reversed: I was the prey and she was the hunter. Gemma had tried to claim me. I'd felt my soul yearning to run to her, to give in to those lips, so inviting, so desirable. Overcome with frustration, I punched the sofa. Gemma's power was so strong it overwhelmed me even when she wasn't there. Ginevra was right. I couldn't let her get into my head or I would lose sight of my objective. *I had to stay focused* to avoid surrendering. I had to see Gemma for what she'd become: a Witch. There was one thing, though, that I was wrong about: in our battle, I wasn't the only prey. We were both predators. One of us would subdue the other. Either I would bring Gemma back or she would take me.

The hunt had begun.

GEMMA

34

A NEW DESIRE

The doors to the kitchens flew open and all the Damned bowed, frightened, as I made my entrance. I was hungry. Very hungry. Soon we would all gather together to eat, but I couldn't wait. I pointed to one of the Gluttons. "You. Bring me what you prepared. At once."

"As you command, my lady," he said ceremoniously, fear in his voice.

I sat down on a table and tasted the meat he placed before me. It felt like I hadn't eaten in centuries, but that was nothing new. There was never enough food for me. Still, that day I was particularly on edge, which made things worse. The Damned watched me enviously as I raised the food to my mouth. They were all as thin as sticks and their sunken, bloodshot eyes disgusted me.

"Don't stare at me like that, dog," I snarled at the one who'd served me. I threw a dagger at him and it lodged in his skeletal neck. He gurgled and exploded in a cloud of smoke as all the others groaned with terror. I picked up the platter of meat and smashed it against the floor. "It's too tough." The dagger returned to me like a boomerang. I caught it and jabbed it into the table. Then I pointed to another of the Damned. "You. What do you have for me?"

"Everything I have is yours, mistress." He bowed, offering me his platter.

"Nothing you say will earn you any pity from me, bootlicker." I dug my heel into his shoulder and he fell to his knees in pain. Picking up a candy apple from the platter he'd held out to me, I examined it. "But maybe this will." Its sweetness exploded in my mouth. "*Divine*," I moaned, closing my eyes. "Gluttony is without doubt the most delicious of all sins." I hopped off the table and tossed the rest of the apple to the floor at his feet. "Here. You've earned it."

He lunged at the food and grabbed it, holding it tight. "Thank you, my lady, thank you."

He knelt down to kiss my feet but I shoved him away. "Make more for me and my Sisters!"

"As you command, mistress. Right away."

"Now get lost before I change my mind." He crawled away, not daring to stand up. "What are you all doing, idling around?! Back to the kitchens!" At my command the other Gluttons hurried back to their posts. Actually, we Witches could have made all the food we wanted magically appear, but that wouldn't have been as much fun. Because of this, Sophìa had built huge kitchens and filled them with the finest Gluttons found during the Hunt. It was more satisfying to have others wait on us. During their lives, Gluttons had committed incredible atrocities to satisfy their insatiable appetites—not only for food, but also for money, power, and so forth. In Hell, their souls were ravenous, in a state of endless hunger that couldn't be satiated. Their lives there were very short. They lacked strength, they lacked the power they'd always yearned for, and for the other Damned they were easy prey, the littlest fish. However, some of them were granted the privilege of waiting on us, and in exchange we allowed them to live longer—at least, as long as their dishes were worthy of our palates.

Hung on a wall in the kitchens was Drugo, the first chef who'd set foot in the Castle. Legend was that, hoping to amaze Sophìa, he'd prepared an elaborate dish made of butterflies. Obsessed with her butterflies, she'd been outraged and had hung him there without killing him as a warning to all the others. Over his head she'd placed a plaque, as she did with all her beloved lost Souls, bearing the inscription "The Profaner." Since then, everyone had called him that. His suffering would be eternal.

I looked out the window and saw twilight ruling in the forest. Opening my palm to summon my Dakor, I felt the venom burn in my eyes as they transformed. The serpent hissed and slithered up my arm. It was comforting to feel him against my skin. Maybe he could banish the uncertainty that had left me so on edge: why had the Subterranean saved me from that arrow? I'd smelled the aroma of our venom on its tip. It wouldn't have had any effect on me unless the archer had used pure fire . . . and yet the young man had shielded me with his body, even though for him the arrow would have been fatal. Why? It made no sense. It must have been a trick to make me lower my defenses. Devina had warned me about him. Everything she'd told me had been right: he was dangerous—more dangerous than the other Subterraneans—because his mind worked differently. What Devina had hidden from me, though, was that his soul had such a delicious, satisfying scent. Now I understood why she wanted to make him hers. She'd tried for centuries without succeeding. It had taken very little for me to get close to achieving that goal, on the other hand. He wanted me. I'd sensed it. I'd sensed the emotions struggling inside him, utterly different from those of the other Subterraneans we'd claimed. They all reacted either with total hostility or a complete willingness to surrender, but in him there was more. He was full of desire, but his willpower was incredibly strong. He wanted to have me, yet maintain control. His was an absurd thought . . . but it excited me.

I smiled. Growing inside me was the sweetest whim, the most exciting challenge. I would bring down his defenses. I would claim him.

35

MILLICENT AND PRISCA

Voices touched my mind. It was Anya and Devina, and they were arguing. Again. Was it starting to become a habit? And why did I have the impression they were hiding something from me? After Devina had burned Anya's book in my chambers, I'd found a tiny fragment of paper. The words in Sanskrit were cut off and I couldn't decipher them, but the graceful handwriting belonged to neither of them.

I drew my daggers and spun them around in my hands. The gesture relaxed me. Closing my mind so my Sisters wouldn't notice my presence, I listened to their thoughts more carefully. I'd gotten good at it.

"Don't you dare, or I'll tell Sophìa," Devina threatened. She sounded confident. *"I thought you knew me better. Do you really think Sophìa would accept it? It's against her rules. Since when have you been willing to break them?"* she asked mockingly.

"Right—that's usually more your department," Anya mocked back.

"That doesn't matter any more. In that life she's dead. She came here to us and here she'll stay."

"You think I don't realize that? I just want her to find herself."

"She already has. She's a Witch."

"She could be both."

"Nonsense."

"Do I seem like nonsense to you? It wouldn't change anything for us if she knew!"

"It would change for me."

"*Or maybe you mean* for him? *You're deluding yourself."*

"Not any more than you are. No little fairy tale could undo the Empress's venom. Do you think Sophìa is a fool? She took precautions."

"What does that mean? What do you know?"

"Good!" said another voice, interrupting Anya. It was Camelia. "You're here. I'm dying of hunger. When are the others coming?"

"Gemma's already here," Devina said.

I jumped. How had she sensed my presence? I sheathed the daggers behind my back and stood up straight, entering the Hall of Sisterhood. "These Gluttons are a bunch of crybabies. They're starting to get on my nerves," I said in a steady voice. "They'd better bring me something good to eat or I'll make heads fly." I glanced at Devina and then at Anya.

Devina was pleased with me—it was clear from the way she looked at me. Anya, on the other hand, always seemed disturbed. Why? Because she was jealous of how close I was with Devina, that was why. However, neither of their opinions interested me. I was who I wanted to be, and soon I would become even more.

"Welcome, my black butterflies." Sophìa appeared in the room in an elegant black gown that left her thighs bare. The long sleeves covered her hands, showing only her sharp black fingernails. The Empress always wore magnificent gowns. At times they were sumptuous and strange, at others sober and refined. They were all made by her black butterflies, who modeled their creations directly on her body. They often changed their arrangement from one moment to the next, based on her mood, and they all gave her an irresistibly sexy look. Sophìa was the devil, but to anyone who saw her she was a goddess—the most enchanting, most dangerous creature in the entire universe. When she sat down, the strange hat on her head changed shape. As always, it was composed of butterflies. "Take your places and tell me of your victories and your failures."

"A failure is merely a victory not yet enjoyed," we replied as one.

"Excellent." Sophìa smiled, looking at us with satisfaction.

The Hall of Sisterhood was one of the most luminous rooms in the Castle. It wasn't particularly large, but in compensation it was high-ceilinged, and black butterflies fluttered far overhead, their wings producing a sound that delighted our Empress. A large chandelier hung over the table around which we sat, a perfect ring of black carbonado at which we all had the same importance, including Sophìa. Whoever sat at the Ring of Sisterhood was equal to all the others. "Tell me, Sisters, tell me everything," the Empress insisted.

Having dinner together gave us the chance to share our experiences, to tell Sophìa everything we'd done. That night Nerea and Safria began with anecdotes about the Reaping—some amusing, others gruesome. Our maidservants served the dishes the Gluttons had prepared and went to stand behind us, one for each Witch. The ring began to turn, allowing us all to taste each of the dishes the Mizhyas continued to serve. Their tasks also included keeping our cups constantly full of Cider, but this time one of them—Millicent—spilled some on Devina's shoe. My Sister cursed, furious, and Millicent dropped to her knees to clean it as the others held their breath.

"I'm sorry! I'm sorry! Forgive me, my lady," Millicent pleaded in fright.

Devina studied her shoe and smiled at her Mizhya. "Don't worry. It happens," she said. The maidservant looked at her, stunned, and relaxed slightly. Devina did away with servants for far less. Millicent would be wise not to get her hopes up. "Now fill my cup," Devina told her, holding out her black goblet.

"As you command, my lady. At once." The maidservant obeyed, Devina's amber eyes on her all the while.

"Go on, take it," the Witch ordered her with an affable smile. Millicent stared at her, confused, but obeyed. "Now *drink it*," she snapped, her smile curling into a sneer.

Millicent stiffened. "But . . . it's poison. If I do, I'll die."

"I said *drink it!*"

Millicent looked at us Sisters one after the other, hoping someone would offer her a pardon, but no one spoke in her favor. She cast a desperate glance at Prisca, one of Anya's maids, and raised the goblet to her lips, hands trembling.

"No!" cried Prisca. She ran across the room and tore the cup out of Millicent's hands. "I'll pay for her mistake." Before Millicent could stop her, the other Mizhya gulped down the poison.

"No! What have you done?" Millicent cried, bursting into tears. Prisca gurgled, burning up from the inside out, and fell to her knees as Millicent embraced her. Seconds later she exploded in a cloud of dust.

"What a touching scene," Devina scoffed, making some of us laugh. Millicent and Prisca were lovers—we all knew that. "Still, I've never understood martyrs. Dying for someone else?" She snorted. "That's nonsense, dost thou not agree?"

"No!" Millicent dared to contradict her. "She was my great love," she whimpered, still on the floor.

"No one deserves love more than we do," Devina said. Her whip cracked through the air and wrapped around the Mizhya's neck. "It's a pity her sacrifice was pointless. I'm not one to make compromises—she should have known that." She yanked on the whip and Millicent fell at her feet. Devina shoved her heel against her neck, preparing to finish her off, but Anya rose to her feet.

"Stop!" she ordered. We all turned to look at her. "Millicent has my pardon."

"Stop getting in the way all the time. You're spoiling my fun," Devina groaned. She pressed harder, all the maidservants in the room watching breathlessly.

"You killed Prisca. She was my Mizhya, and a good one. You owe me another."

"But I didn't kill her. She did it on her own."

Everyone laughed at Devina's joke. Everyone except the Empress. "Obey your Sister," she said sternly. "If she wishes to take the servant as her own, it is her right."

Devina fumed, but lifted her foot, freeing her. Head bowed, Millicent struggled to her feet, went to Anya, and kissed her hands. A tear slid silently down her cheek and Anya wiped it away. "In your place now," she told her tenderly.

Millicent nodded and went to stand behind her. Another Mizhya came into the room and took her place behind Devina, looking frightened because she knew what she was up against; Devina was the most capricious of the Sisters, and her Mizhyas either never did enough for her or didn't battle-train hard enough.

"Very well, my fearless butterflies," the Empress said, bringing our attention back to her. "Who has another interesting story for me?" Meanwhile, the swarm of Souls descended from the ceiling and began to flutter over the table, creating amazing formations. Art in movement. Sophìa adored it.

"I have an interesting story," I began. The Empress smiled at me. "Devina and I went on Recon today."

"How did it go?"

"Excellently, I would say." I looked at Devina, who smiled at me, her amber eyes aimed straight at mine.

"The chrysalis has blossomed," Devina said, nodding. "She's getting better and better."

"We claimed various Subterraneans and brought home eleven prisoners."

"A praiseworthy achievement. I am very proud."

"Still, I'm not satisfied." I opened my mind to let Sophìa read my thoughts, but also told her aloud, "There's a Subterranean I would like to claim more than any other." I glanced at Devina, who now looked furious. But I didn't care. I had decided: he had to be mine. "He's stubborn and disrespectful. There's not the slightest trace of fear in him—only strength, determination, and desire. I want him to be mine."

"Very well, then. You have found your Champion."

"No!" Devina protested, quickly rising to her feet. "I'm going to be the one to claim him."

"You are free to try," Sophìa said to calm her, "but so is Naiad." I shot Devina a challenging look. Only one of us would manage to win him—and it was going to be me.

"I told you how long I've been after him. How can you do this *to me?*" Devina said bitterly.

"Following your own instincts above all else is the first thing you taught me," I answered, resolute. ***Your instinct is the most powerful weapon, the most reliable shield. Always follow it and you'll find your way.*** Giving in to my whims was more important than heeding hers. And now, ***he*** was my whim.

Devina pretended to calm down and addressed the Empress with greater deference. "My lady, this is madness. May I remind you how dangerous he is?"

"Don't pretend you care about her," Anya spoke up. "You just want Evan for yourself." *Evan.* So that was what the Subterranean was called. I had to remember the name.

"Devina, your concerns are unfounded. There is no chance that this Subterranean could endanger our Naiad or the Sisterhood more than any of the others. She is special. She is a powerful Witch and within her flows my own venom. She will be with me forever. No one can change that," the Empress stated matter-of-factly.

Devina and Sophìa looked at each other for a long moment. Why was Devina so worried about that Subterranean? It wasn't only jealousy—there was something else, I knew it. Was he really as dangerous as she'd always claimed? She herself had trained me so well that I could face him. Why, then, was she so concerned? Sophìa didn't seem to have any doubts—quite the opposite. Anya, who had defended me, now looked sad again—disappointed, maybe.

"Then it is decided," the Empress proclaimed. "The Subterranean will be less dangerous under our control. If Gemma succeeds in claiming him, he may become her Champion."

Devina cracked her whip. Frightened, the swarm of butterflies dissipated and flocked to Sophìa. We all watched as Devina stormed out of the room.

Our challenge had begun.

EVAN

36

ABSOLON

I watched Simon make his way through the wreckage of the plane crash. Neither of us could wait to finish the mission and get back to Ginevra and Liam. Since our discovery that the Hunter was immune to her venom Simon had been out of his mind, knowing how reckless Ginevra became when it came to Gemma. This time, though, he hadn't given her any choice: until we found a solution she would stay at home, where she would be safe. We had no idea how to rid ourselves of Absolon. Maybe we could lure him into the magic simulation scenarios, like we'd done with the other Subterraneans who'd been after Gemma.

Simon disappeared, accompanying a Soul into the other world. I walked among the mutilated bodies in search of other Souls to ferry over. In the wreckage I noticed a young man with his back turned toward me, crouching beside his body. I approached him and noticed he was weeping. Another frightened Soul. "Can you save me?" he suddenly asked me, his head bowed.

I rested a hand on his shoulder, but nothing happened. He looked up and I saw his black eyes.

A bitter sigh escaped me. "I can't. I'm sorry." His Soul was irremediably tarnished. It was too late to help him. I felt a dark energy surround me a second before the Witch materialized in front of him.

"Who are you?" the man asked, terrified by her ominous presence. Or maybe it was her golden serpent eyes that scared him.

"You offend me. Don't you remember me any more? We've spent so much time together."

The young man didn't recognize her face, but he must have given in to her dark whispers, offering his soul to her. He tried to run, but the Witch paralyzed him with her magic and dragged him across the ground as he screamed. She swept him over to his corpse, which sucked him back up. Moments later, out of its mouth crawled a big black butterfly—one of the largest I'd ever seen. Her Dakor lunged out and gobbled it up.

"What a delight," the Witch murmured. I narrowed my eyes and she smiled at me seductively. "Bathsheeva." She materialized in front of me, her expression menacing.

"Go back to the Castle, princess of darkness. There's nothing more for you here," I told her.

"You never know what I might find in the wreckage," she replied, turning her eyes to the soul of a woman. If she wasn't completely compromised, one of us still had a chance to save her. I wasn't about to let the Witch take her. When Bathsheeva sensed my intentions, her expression hardened. "Step aside, Child of Eve. This time there's no truce to rein in my instincts." Her serpent hissed close to my face, but Simon materialized beside me, ready to hurl the fireball in his hand. The Witch glanced at it and turned to look at me. "Your reinforcements have arrived."

"You have your allies and I have mine," I told her. She withdrew her serpent and, with one last challenging look, vanished.

"Evan, look out!" Simon cried.

An arrow whizzed right by my head and lodged in the plane's fuselage where the Witch had been a moment before. I slowly turned and looked the archer straight in the eye. "Absolon."

Simon kept his fireball burning and remained at my side expectantly. "What a shame," he said. "You barely missed her."

The Hunter narrowed his eyes at us in a tacit challenge, nocked another arrow, and pointed his bow at us.

"Why are you still here? You miss the good old days of being a Soldier?" I asked mockingly. He pulled back on the bowstring but I materialized in front of him and grabbed the arrow before it could leave the bow. "Or did you want to train with us for a while?"

Throwing me a malevolent look, he tried to punch me. Simon jumped over the debris of the plane and hurled him away. My brother and I exchanged a complicit glance and split up to catch him off guard. While Simon diverted his attention, I climbed onto the roof of the plane to lie in wait for him. Immune or not, sooner or later I would find a way to make Absolon pay for what he'd done to Gemma. The second he went after my brother I caught him off guard and slammed him to the ground, but my victory was fleeting. He was too strong and would soon manage to overpower me. We struggled amid the wreckage and Simon rushed in to help me. He opened his fiery palm and clamped it onto Absolon's shoulder, burning through his leather tunic. The Hunter gnashed his teeth from the pain and with a single blow hurled Simon away, returning his focus to me. "Ye have thick skins, ye two."

"We're fighting for a good cause."

He smiled. "As am I." A dark, sharp blade slid out from his ring. He moved to stab me with it but Anya appeared behind him and dragged him away. The Hunter looked at us and tried to break free from Anya's grip, but she shoved him against the plane. Her Dakor opened its fangs.

"Anya, no!" Simon shouted with alarm. "He's immune! Your venom can't kill him!"

She whipped out a long dagger and pinned his hand to the plane with it. Absolon shrieked in anguish. Anya pulled off his ring and pointed it at his throat. "Well, maybe this can." Absolon stared at her, his eyes aflame, and tried to dematerialize, but it was no use. His skin began to shrivel, as if the Witch were desiccating him from the inside.

"Going somewhere?" Anya challenged him.

I approached them, stopping abruptly at the sight of the ring. "What the fuck?!" I muttered. Simon and I stared at each other in shock. It was the Devil's Claw.

The Hunter hadn't come for the Witch. He was there to kill us.

37

HIDDEN TRUTHS

"Where did you get this?" Simon shouted, pointing the ring at the Hunter's throat. The Claw glittered, dark and sharp as a razor—a messenger of death for those of my race. Its poison could banish a Child of Eve to Oblivion.

Absolon sneered in reply. He was sitting on the ground, leaning against the wreckage, his body immobilized by Anya's power. "Answer me! How did you get your hands on this?!" Simon shoved him to the ground with his foot. I'd never seen him so furious before.

"The same way he got the poison for his arrows," Anya replied, thinking out loud. "Sophìa recruited him."

"His arrow was for me, not Gemma," I murmured, remembering the last time we'd met, when I'd protected her from the Hunter's attack. "We were his targets, Simon."

"That's crazy. Not only is he a Subterranean like us, he's also a Witch Hunter."

"Only the devil in person could have given him the Claw. That's the only explanation," Anya insisted.

"Why would he want to kill us?" Simon replied, still incredulous.

"To keep me away from Gemma. How did I not see that?" I said. "Anya's right. Sophìa is behind all this. She always has been. ***She*** ordered Gemma's death." We'd been wrong—it hadn't been a last-ditch attempt by the Màsala.

Anya's jaw dropped in horror. "Tell us everything you know," I snarled, turning to Absolon.

"Why do ye not ask the Witch? I can feel her trying to enter my mind." I looked at Anya, but she shook her head.

Absolon laughed. He was obscuring his thoughts. "When ye spend centuries locked up like a cur ye learn to master true solitude."

Enraged, I hoisted him up and slammed him against the side of the plane. *"Tell us what you know!"*

Paralyzed by Anya's spell, he had no choice. "Why should I help ye? What have I to gain?"

Without taking my eyes off his, I summoned the ring to my hand and pointed it at him. "Is your life enough?" The Hunter tilted his head back, distancing himself from the lethal blade.

"Was it Sophìa who ordered Gemma's death?"

Absolon stared at me for a long moment before giving in. "Aye."

A sob escaped Anya. "I'm sorry, Evan. I had no idea."

"It's not your fault, it's mine. I should have been more careful. Devina must have overheard me while I was telling my brother about the plan to purify Gemma, and she ratted me out. Is that right?" I asked the Hunter, pushing him to confess.

"'Tis," he confirmed, "yet 'twas not that made her do it. Lilith had already recruited me. She personally trained me for months. Said the risk of losing the new Witch was too high. Your plan but added more urgency to hers."

My eyes went wide. "Sophìa saw how strong our bond was—that was why she didn't want to run any risks. If she hadn't intervened, Gemma might actually have been able to resist evil."

Absolon nodded. "She feared the transformation alone might fail to steal her away from ye. I saw it when she tore off her fingernail and gave it to the red . . . A demon, that one, she is."

"Wait a minute. You were with them? You mean Devina knew everything? She knew you were going to kill Gemma? *She knew* you were still alive? How is it possible Sophìa spared you after what you did to Tamaya?" Anya hissed, tears in her eyes.

"The red interceded. Once I had reduced Tamaya to ashes, 'twas *she* who saved me from the devil's wrath. She would call on me in my cell, though I cursed her every visit. I would rather have rotted alone than lie with her. At times it made me regret not being dead."

Anya looked shocked. "She's never cared about anyone, not even the Sisterhood."

"Or maybe she thought he might come in handy one day," Simon remarked.

"Aye," the Hunter confirmed, looking proud about having killed Gemma before our eyes.

I lunged at him, but Anya stopped me. We needed him alive. "What was her plan? What did you hear?" she asked, still shaken.

"She sent me out to slay the half-Witch so ye would resuscitate her with Lilith's venom. That way the lass would be hers forever."

"There was no war," I murmured.

Absolon smiled. "All an act. Lilith knew ye would never let her die. She tore a nail off her finger. Howling with pain, she was. She's mad. All of ye are mad."

"Then you know what you're risking if you don't cooperate," Simon replied.

"Tell me what she said," I growled as the anger inside me grew.

"'He himself will beg me to transform her.'" I punched the fuselage, overcome with rage, and left a dent in it.

"Evan, calm down. We were playing with the devil. What did you expect?" Simon asked. "It was obvious she didn't want to let her get away."

"What happened after that?"

"Use your imagination." The Hunter stared at me, sneering.

It was Simon who deduced the answer: "After using the Claw to bring Gemma back to life, Sophìa must have given him a new mission. So she gave him the Claw to get rid of us. She knew we would never give up. Did I guess correctly?"

Absolon looked at me. "Why are ye chasing after her so relentlessly? She's one of them now."

"She's my wife," I roared, furious.

He snorted. "Ye fight so fervently for her when your 'wife' does naught but betray ye with other men."

"Are we still talking about me or are we talking about you now?" I said to provoke him. Once he became a Subterranean, Absolon had slain his wife Tamaya before she could transform into a Witch, publicly humiliating her for betraying him.

He looked at me and smiled. "I wager she's already doing it." I grabbed him by the throat and squeezed.

"Evan, we're wasting time," my brother reminded me.

I stared at Absolon for a long moment, trying to calm my nerves. "I'm going to bring her back."

I let go of him and he slid down and crumpled to the ground, his body as dry as stone. "Did ye not hear what I said? Evil has darkened her soul. 'Tis an irreversible curse. There's no hope for her. A Daughter of Lilith, she is," he concluded with a triumphant laugh.

My good humor had run out. I planted my foot on his shoulder and kicked, smashing his head against the plane. "She's coming back to me." Fists clenched, I turned to Anya. "We have to let her know it was Sophìa who plotted her death."

"She'll never believe you," she replied bleakly. "Besides, she wouldn't care. Sophìa's power over her is very strong. Gemma was forged by her venom. She was reborn from her. The Hunter is right: Gemma's soul is an extension of the Empress's. There's no way to bring her back. I'm sorry."

"Gemma's soul belongs only to me," I hissed.

Anya hung her head, unable to reply. She wanted to believe me but couldn't. "What should we do with him?" she asked after a moment.

"Let's lock him up in the dungeon," Simon replied. "He'll be safe there."

"Now that we've captured him, nothing will keep me from seeing Gemma again."

"You're forgetting Devina," Anya said. "Gemma trusts her too much. The situation is spiraling out of control."

"What about you? Will you help me talk to her again?" Sometimes not even Ginevra could hear Gemma. We needed all the help we could get.

"I already am. *I* was the one who made sure she materialized at the party. From now on I'll let you know whenever she returns to Earth. I'm sorry, that's the best I can do."

"It's already a lot." I took the ring and studied it. The Claw was as sharp as a panther's and as black as carbonado. I cast one last look at the Hunter. "We'll keep this." I pressed the little button in the metal and the blade retracted. I tossed it to Simon. "Later on we'll figure out what to do with you." I raised my foot and kicked him in the face again. He fell to the ground, his eyes wide open, as Anya used her powers on him until she'd petrified even his face.

The Hunter had fallen into his own trap.

GEMMA

38

MIND AND SOUL

I was reclining on red cushions in the Hall of Perversions while my Mizhyas massaged my body with hot stones. My mind, however, was elsewhere, trapped in the eyes of ice of that Subterranean. *Evan*. Their color was the same as the other Children of Eve, yet a different sparkle animated them.

You have found your Champion. Sophìa's words continued to whirl in my head. I had witnessed dozens of Opalions and some had even been held in my honor after I'd won the Hunt, though I still hadn't found a worthy Champion. But now I wouldn't give up until I'd claimed Evan, w;hether he liked it or not. I would make him my prisoner and lock him up in the dungeons, if need be. Sooner or later I would bend him to my will. The fact that I was challenging Devina for him would make everything more exciting.

My maidservants stopped and I opened my eyes to find out why. Devina had shooed them away and was standing next to me, together with two bare-chested Subterraneans wearing only the standard leather pants of claimed Executioners. All at once her black outfit changed, transforming into a long skirt in white and gold. A delicate necklace dangled to her bare abdomen and her breasts were covered only by a thin strip of fabric the same color as her skirt.

"Did you come to make me change my mind or to remind me how dangerous Evan is?"

"Nothing of the sort. I thought our challenge should be celebrated with a little party just for us." She gestured to the two Subterraneans, who began to massage my body. I closed my eyes, moaning with pleasure. Their hands were warm and strong—nothing like the maidservants' small, cold ones.

"What do you say we have a little fun? You did well today on Recon. You deserve it." Devina lay beside me and the two men admired her. One of them had blond hair tied up in a ponytail, the other short dark hair and a scar along his cheekbone. Devina spread her legs, inviting the blond Executioner to come forward, and he began to massage her hips. I took a closer look and for the first time noticed that the two were part of our most recent catch. I had claimed one of them myself, and he would obey my every order. He would do anything to give me pleasure . . . and ask for nothing in return. They'd become our love slaves, like all the other claimed Executioners. Once they succumbed we entered their minds and their souls, and all they wanted to do was please us. Only Champions had special privileges.

I pushed my hair to one side and allowed him to caress my back. His movements were slow, his hands rough and exciting. Devina ran her sharp fingernail down her chest, making a rivulet of blood seep out. He sank his head between her breasts to lick it and she closed her eyes, aroused.

"Thanks for the peace offering," I told Devina, though he wouldn't have been my first choice. We had also taken eleven prisoners, and I definitely would have preferred one of them to a claimed Subterranean. It would have been more exciting to bend him to my will.

No, said a little voice inside me. Only one of them could quench my thirst. Up until then, I'd never paid much attention to the Subterraneans. Though Devina had offered me the most intrepid of her warriors as a gift, I always ended up tiring of them and killing them before they got too close. None of them could excite me. The truth was that the Children of Eve left me bored. I preferred action, going into battle, fighting . . . stealing mortals' souls. That was what I found exciting. To Devina, sex was an obsession. She always said lust was the sweetest of sins. I, instead, was always focused on the Bond, on the Reaping, on the Hunt. *On Sophìa.* One of my greatest wishes was to please her. The biggest challenge of all was to become her Specter. Nothing mattered more to me, and one day I would reach my goal. However, now that I had chosen my Champion I was beginning to understand Devina's lustful desires. I wanted to see him kneeling in front of me, feel his mouth between my legs as his eyes gazed at me, full of desire.

The Executioner with the scar kissed my shoulder and I closed my eyes, aroused by the pictures in my mind. When I spread my legs, his hands slid up to massage my thighs. He took my foot and I watched him unlace my boot, but when he raised his eyes to mine, the spell broke. I rested my heel on his chest and shoved him away, anger growing inside me. That Subterranean was attractive, but he wasn't ***him***.

"What a waste of time," I grumbled, standing up.

"Where are you going?" Devina exclaimed, sounding annoyed.

"You take him. I'm going to look for something that really amuses me."

Just then, Anya appeared. "Sophìa wishes to speak to you in private," she told Devina.

"I'll go later. Can't you see I'm busy?" she answered, intoxicated by the attentions of the Subterraneans, who were now both focused on her. "In fact, why don't you join me? These two are new. Let's teach them a little about our customs. They're fast learners."

"The Empress doesn't like to be kept waiting, and she said she wanted to see you at once," Anya insisted sternly. The looks she was giving Devina were more irritated than usual.

"A little R and R would do you good, Sister," Devina goaded her. "Are you jealous because I didn't offer them to you first?"

"You just want her to be like you," Anya said accusingly.

Devina shot her a piercing look. "She already is like me." Her lips spread into a sneer.

"Stop talking about me like I'm not here," I put in. "I'm no one's trophy. I'm not like anyone. I'm just myself. Accept it, both of you."

"She's the one who needs to accept it, given that she keeps bringing you her Soldiers," Anya said.

"They're a gift. She should appreciate it," Devina retorted.

"You just want her to lose her purity and betray him. Don't think I don't realize that."

Devina laughed. "Are you listening to yourself? She's a Witch, Anya."

"That doesn't mean she can't be herself too."

"What you're talking about no longer exists. It's a dead body in a forest. It's the past. We're her future. All this is in her nature."

"And he's in her soul," Anya said.

My eyes went to them. What were they talking about?

"Her soul belongs only to Sophìa now. She was reborn from her venom," Devina replied, sneering. "Nothing can change how things are."

"Why is it so important that it was Sophìa who transformed me?" I asked them. "All that matters to me is my life here with you. My past existence, before I was bitten, is of no importance to me now."

Devina smiled. "Forgive her, Gemma. Anya likes to brood over insignificant problems. She should learn to relax," she said, returning to the attentions of the two Subterraneans.

"Do as you like." Anya turned her back on her.

I followed her out of the room. "Anya, can I talk to you?"

She looked at me for a long moment and nodded. "First let's find someplace quieter." She took me by the hand and the entrance to the Hall of Perversions disappeared. We materialized in an abandoned wing of the Castle. I had been there only once before, during my first days there.

The large double doors opened with a creak and closed behind us, sealing us inside. We all called it the Chamber of Enchantments, not because it had powers but because it was where we stored all the magical objects created over the centuries to satisfy mortals' whims. For Witches, making deals with them was an irresistible pastime. They would grant mortals wishes . . . in exchange for their souls. Over the centuries, they had created all sorts of magical contraptions to amuse themselves, many of which were collected in that room. It was a giant circular grotto with a large oval table in black stone in its center, illuminated by a skylight in the ceiling. Energy vibrated on all its walls, which were full of niches carved to order to accommodate the various devices. There were objects that slowed time or sped it up and others that commanded the forces of the sky and earth: staffs that brought rain, stones that invoked the benefits of the sun and moon or controlled the wind, amulets that tricked the light, making whoever wore them invisible, not to mention enchanted weapons capable of annihilating armies of soldiers: swords, war hammers, spears and shields . . .

"Look, this is one of Devina's favorites: a Mirror of Shame." I looked at it, curious. "It not only shows one's reflection but delves into the heart of the person looking into it and lays bare their sins. Some mortals have used it to accuse their adversaries, others to save their own lives . . . or to get out of trouble."

"Extortion is a delicious form of wickedness," I replied, instantly grasping her allusion.

"This, on the other hand, is its twin: my favorite."

"What does it do?"

"It's the Mirror of Courage. It shows people the part of themselves they're keeping hidden. The one they'd really like to be. Some Souls lose themselves to the desire to be what they see reflected in it. Certain mortals might stray because of their longing for what they've seen. The weakest ones even go insane."

"I prefer the first mirror. It's more fun," I said as we made our way through the room. "What's that one up there?" I asked Anya, drawn to an object that sparkled high above. I jumped onto the wall and climbed almost all the way to the top, where I grabbed it and leapt down, landing in front of my Sister.

"That's a Soul Sphere."

I studied the sphere. It was sparkly, created with a myriad of carbonado prisms. "What does it do, predict the future?"

Anya laughed. "No one can predict the future—it's the result of millions of decisions. Choices are the future."

"Not even Sophia can?" I asked. I couldn't believe there was a limit to the Empress's powers.

"I can't answer that, but I wouldn't be surprised if she could. She's the queen of the underworld, after all."

"So what is the sphere's power?" I asked.

"It's the key to Nirvana, a transcendent world suspended between our worlds."

"Does it really exist?"

"Only in the mind of he who finds it. But that's not all." Anya took the sphere from my hands and held it in front of her face, turning it slowly. "This sphere can connect the mind of whoever possesses it to that of anyone she desires, creating a path where the two Souls unite. It transcends their bodies, leaving their spirits free to follow their desires. To find peace. Soul and mind in a world all their own."

"Isn't Nirvana a state without passion or desires?"

"Not *without*, but above. It's the achievement of desires. It's an otherwise unreachable state of inner peace. It's pure ecstasy."

"If one of us infused that kind of power in this sphere to satisfy the desires of a few mortals, does that mean we have it inside ourselves too?"

"No. Sophìa made this sphere. It's one of the few objects she personally forged for men. We Sisters are strong, but she has powers beyond whatever you could possibly imagine. None of us has ever been able to connect to someone's soul like that."

"Do you think I could keep it?"

"No, I'm sorry. Sophìa's very jealous of her toys. You can ask her permission to use it, if you like. She'd probably let you."

"It doesn't matter. I was just curious."

"Did you want to talk to me about Ginevra?" she asked point-blank.

"Huh?" I replied, my eyes still captivated by the energy the sphere was emanating.

"You said you wanted to talk to me."

There was so much I had to ask her. Anya was a trusted Sister. She might have been the wisest among us, but she also had a very strong spirit: she was one of the few who could stand up to Devina. Plus, Sophìa completely trusted her and her decisions. I couldn't choose a better confidant.

"I saw her," I explained, a knot in my stomach. "I ran into Ginevra and felt both happiness and sadness."

"I know," Anya said, her face full of sorrow.

"So basically, she's our Sister. How can she refuse to stay here with us? What happened to her? Why did Sophìa banish her?"

"For the Empress it was the hardest decision, but it was either that or death. At first she'd sentenced her to die."

"You were the one who changed her mind, I'll bet." Anya smiled, returning to that memory. "I don't understand. I read the suffering in her mind. She felt the Bond uniting us too, so why is she acting this way? *This* is her realm! Her place is here, with us. Maybe if I talked to Sophìa I could convince her to let her come back."

"Even if you convinced Sophìa, Ginevra would never want to. She chose to leave us . . . so she could live with a Subterranean."

"What?! You mean she betrayed us to be with an enemy? Did she lose her mind?"

"Sophìa was deeply disappointed by her behavior. For her, the Bond is the most important thing there is."

"I understand. It is for me too."

"However, there's a bond that's even stronger, if you have the good fortune to experience it."

"What are you talking about? That's absurd."

"Love. God gave Sophìa the Bond with her Sisters, but because she hadn't returned His feelings for her, He couldn't allow her to feel toward others an emotion that surpassed the power of true love."

"You've experienced it," I murmured, reading the story Anya had hidden away in her mind.

"That's not important any more." Though she turned away to escape my eyes, I caught her wiping a tear from her cheek.

"You're right," I said, trying to reassure her. "The past doesn't matter."

"That's not always true," she told me. "Sometimes the past can help us understand who we really are."

"It's true for me. I know who I am. I know what I want and how to get it. I don't care about the past. Only together with all of you does my life have meaning. I'll never understand how Ginevra could have made that decision." Anya looked down sadly. "You and Devina have been arguing a lot lately. Sometimes I have the impression it's because of me. Tell me why."

"Nothing I could tell you would change anything. You were created by Sophìa. Her venom runs through your veins. You belong to her. Besides, I'm forbidden to even think about certain things. Only you can probe inside yourself."

"Why would you want to change anything?"

"Because you're becoming more like Devina by the day."

"What's wrong with that?" I hissed with frustration. Why was Anya always so jealous of Devina? I cared for them both, but it was very clear to me who I wanted to be. "You're a good Sister, but when Devina's around you behave differently. What's the problem between you two?"

"We often want different things."

"Different things for me too?"

"Especially for you," she admitted, making me furious.

"Well, don't worry yourselves about it. I can manage all on my own!"

"I know," Anya replied with conviction. "You're very strong. You always have been. I just want to make sure you're always in charge of your own decisions."

Our eyes met and I suddenly felt like a willful child. Anya, instead, was mature, and her affection for me was sincere.

"Forgive me," I told her. "Sometimes I get carried away."

"That's all right. You still have a lot to learn."

"How do you manage to resist the power? Evil never takes control of you—you're the one to control it."

"I'm the second Witch that awakened for Sophìa. I've had a long time to learn to control myself."

"But Devina transformed before you did. She's the first Witch, but there's so much darkness in her. She doesn't have your wisdom. Why not?"

"Because I listen to my heart."

"The first thing Devina taught me was to listen only to my instinct."

"You're a Witch, Gemma. Your instinct will always lead you toward evil, toward what you are."

"What's wrong with that?"

"Nothing," she assured me, "but sometimes you need to listen to both to be sure you're making the right decision. Don't let the darkness blind you, Gemma."

"I'll try," I promised. She hugged me. I closed my eyes, overwhelmed by my love for her.

"I see you've received your Dreide," she said with a smile.

I stroked the medallion I wore around my neck, a small black serpent in the center of it. "Yours is nice, with those shades of green."

"It's the medallion that creates its colors for us."

"I know." When I had held mine in my hand for the first time, the serpent had stirred, coloring itself black. "I haven't discovered all its powers yet."

"Oh, they're limitless. You'll use some more than others."

"Tell me about some of them," I asked, curious.

"As you saw today on Reconnaissance, the Dreide stores the purest essence of the Subterraneans we claim. The moment they succumb to us, their souls are trapped within it and as of then they belong to us. But the Dreide is also their only key to get out of Hell. A real paradox, don't you think?"

"What do you mean?"

"The Dreide controls the door to the underworld—the only way in, the only way out—on Mount Nhubii, the Devil's Plane. The Damned can't cross through the passageway between the two worlds. The Souls who try remain trapped there forever. However, Subterraneans can, once the medallion has opened the portal for them."

"Why should they do that? I don't understand."

"Not alone, obviously, but with one of us. Some Sisters have fun taking their Champions to Earth from time to time."

"But why?"

Anya smiled. "For us they're trophies. Or maybe it's simply to spite the Màsala. Don't bother thinking about it."

"Speaking of our Champions . . ."

"I heard what you said at the Ring of Sisterhood." Anya turned, hiding her face. "Are you sure *he's* the one you want to claim?"

"Do you think I'm not strong enough, like Devina does?"

"No, just the opposite. And she knows it."

"All she does is tell me I should stay away from him, that's he's dangerous."

"Because she's afraid. The challenge you proposed is more dangerous for her than it is for you."

"What do you mean?"

"She knows she might lose."

"So why do you think I shouldn't claim him?" I asked, having read her mind.

"Are you still convinced your past doesn't matter to you at all?"

"What does my past have to do with it?"

"He was part of it."

I gaped at her in shock. "What does that mean?"

"Dig deep within you, Gemma. Maybe there's still hope."

I locked eyes with Anya's, offended. "This is how I am now, whether you like it or not. I have no connection to the past. All that matters is the future, and there's one thing I can see clearly: he's going to be my slave."

EVAN

39

THE LIGHT OF THE SOUL

Gemma leapt up to the window of the cathedral and turned to look at me, her eyes snapping with malice. *Until next time,* she mouthed. She blew me a kiss and hurled herself against the glass, which shattered in a shower of colorful prisms. The crowd screamed in panic and swarmed outside as I continued to stare at the spot where she'd disappeared.

We were in Rome . . . and she'd escaped me yet again. I growled in frustration. I'd followed her to Thailand, Singapore, through Africa, to the farthest reaches of Earth. Each time I came closer and closer. She and her Sisters destroyed sacred sites to diminish faith among believers, spread terror, and stained mortal Souls with their poisonous whispers. Then I would show up and our game would burst into flames. She battled to kill. I tried not to harm her.

Gemma had changed since I'd protected her from the Hunter's arrow. At first I'd deluded myself that she remembered me, but then I'd realized her true intentions. Ours had become a sensual hunt in which neither of us had any intention of giving up. I wanted Gemma back by my side on Earth. She wanted me with her in Hell. She'd decided she liked my tenacity and wanted to claim me. She was both bolder and more elusive, and this made everything more difficult. It seemed like each time we met she was sexier and more dangerous, and I was more in danger of losing my mind. Every time we encountered each other I managed to pin her down, but she was the one leading the game. She would brush her lips against mine to absorb my energy, and for a moment I would lose myself in her, because that closeness was everything I wanted. Many times I was on the verge of giving in to her beguiling power, overcome by desire for her, by the overwhelming attraction she exerted on me, but then I would think of Liam, think of my Gem, and everything I would lose if I gave up. That was when I would rebel. At times I was brutal, but I had no choice.

Our encounters were increasingly fleeting—a matter of seconds or, at most, minutes, during which each battled to gain control over the other. I wanted to make her remember. She made me forget myself.

Anya told me there was no hope. Their Empress had even given Gemma her blessing to claim me. She no longer feared I might steal her away because she was certain the old Gemma had been obliterated. I, however, refused to give up. As long as I lived, I would fight for us. All it took was for her to set foot on Earth and I rushed to her. I would follow her to the ends of the Earth.

I materialized in the garden where Simon, Anya, and Ginevra were sitting on the lawn, playing with Irony and little Liam. It was already April and spring had sprung all around us. Liam loved all the colors.

"News?" Simon asked. I shook my head, frustrated.

"Evan, maybe you should—"

"No!" I growled at Anya. "Don't even say it."

"You've been trying for nine months," Simon agreed.

"And I'm going to keep on trying. I'm never giving up."

"This whole time, nothing has changed. Maybe Anya's right," Simon urged. "Maybe Sophìa's venom irremediably obliterated her. She would never let Gemma return to Earth if she risked losing her to you."

"She doesn't care about the past. She doesn't want to remember," Anya admitted to me with sorrow. "Nothing can bring her back unless she's the one who wants it to happen."

"What if we let her see Liam?" Simon proposed.

"Out of the question. It's too dangerous," I answered.

"You're right. She might decide on a whim she wants him for herself."

I clenched my fists, making up my mind. "Simon's right. It's been too long. We need to do something, try another approach."

"No!" Ginevra protested, reading the plan in my mind.

I ignored her, staring hard at my brother. "Simon, you need to use your power on Gemma."

Ginevra stood up. "We've already tried that. You don't know what happened the first time. It's too dangerous!"

"I would risk my life to do it, but my power only works on mortal Souls," Simon replied. "It doesn't work with Witches because their souls are corrupt. We've already talked about this."

"That's true," Anya said. "Centuries ago they tried to use it on Devina to make her forget she'd seen Simon and Ginevra together, but it was useless . . . and dangerous."

"We need to at least try!" I shouted in exasperation.

Liam babbled something and we all turned to look at him. He smiled and took a few steps toward me. I sighed and tears stung my eyes. Only he could calm me. "Come here," I said softly. He laughed in contentment. I knelt down and opened my arms to him, smiling at his awkward attempt to reach me. He toddled over to me and then clapped for himself, making us all smile.

"He's modest! Just like his Aunt Ginevra," Simon remarked, earning himself a glare from her.

"We'll bring your mommy home," I whispered to Liam. I rubbed my nose against his and he tried to bite it. "I hope you didn't get her appetite too." I lay down and held Liam above me to make him fly like an airplane. He loved that game. Time had flown by in the blink of an eye and Liam was already nine months old. He was a good-natured little boy and incredibly curious. But most importantly, he was human. There was no trace of supernatural power or energy in him.

"Here." Ginevra handed me a baby bottle full of milk. "It's feeding time." I leaned back against a tree and cradled him in my arms. He looked at me as he gulped down the warm liquid and his eyelids slowly grew heavy. I spent all my free time with him. I played with him, took him with me while I worked out. Watching me do handstand pushups gave him fits of giggles, especially when I pretended to fall and hurt myself. Often I would read him the old copy of *White Fang* I'd found in Gemma's storage boxes in the attic. It was the first book she'd ever read, and I hoped that by reading it to Liam, he could in some way feel more connected to his mother.

Some time ago he'd started to babble "dada," filling my heart with emotions I hadn't thought I would ever experience. I played the violin for him, fed him, and a few times even took him for a ride on my bike in the driveway. Then there were Ginevra and Simon, on whom I knew I could count. When I was carrying out orders or chasing after Gemma, one of them stayed there to protect him. The house was well defended, but you could never be too sure, which was why we never took him outside the walls of our fortress.

As far as Gemma's parents knew, we'd moved to London be with my relatives. I sent them photos of Liam and once in a while Ginevra would talk on the phone with them, simulating Gemma's voice. It would have been different if Drake had still been around to go visit them. But then I thought it might be harder for me to be face to face with her ghost, knowing I'd lost her.

I looked at Liam and Gemma's voice filled my head: *I wanted us to be a family.* "We will be," I murmured, stroking Liam's sweet face as he slept. "It doesn't matter how long it takes." I was going to keep my promise. I got up and went into the house, opening the sliding windows in the kitchen before putting Liam into the playpen we'd set up in the living room and going back out to my brother and sister.

"I was serious before," I told Simon, looking at him resolutely. "I want you to use your power on Gemma. Only you can probe deep inside her and reach her memories."

"Not if they've been wiped out."

"You've got to try!" I shouted, pleading. "She's still there. Somewhere in her heart she'll hear you. She can't have vanished forever. No magic can take her away from me. Part of her still loves me, I know it. I just have to help her remember."

Now that Gemma had transformed, I could no longer take her to Heaven to have her drink Ambrosia, but if she managed to remember, nothing would separate us ever again. Now that she was immortal we could live together for all eternity, like Simon and Ginevra.

"All right." Simon gave in. "We'll give it a shot as soon as Gemma returns to Earth."

"She's already here," Anya told us.

Simon and Ginevra looked at each other for a long moment. She still didn't agree with letting him do it, but she wasn't going to stand in his way. Simon looked at me and nodded. I held my hand out to Anya and she guided me to Gemma. A moment later she was in front of me, at her feet a young mother who was smothering her baby.

My eyes went wide in shock. "Don't do it," I begged her.

Gemma peered at me and smiled. "I'm not doing anything," she replied, dark sensuality in her voice. The baby boy cried, squirming beneath the pillow his mother was pressing over his face. He was younger than Liam. Simon had also frozen at the sight, but we could do nothing—it was the woman who had to decide not to follow evil. Now she began to weep and shout: "Enough! Stop crying! Stop it! Stop it!"

But Gemma was there to strengthen the woman's resolve, instilling her venom in her: *"He'll never stop,"* she whispered, staring at me. *"He'll ruin everything. George can't stand him. He knows. He knows it isn't his baby. He'll leave you."*

A man materialized at the back of the room. It was a Subterranean. He'd come for the baby. "Simon, do something!" I ordered.

Despite his horror, Simon reacted instantly. Though the woman couldn't see him, he cupped her face in his hands. Beneath her skin, her veins moved like little snakes as Simon evoked memories of her and her baby in her mind. She stopped, her eyes going wide, and for a second I almost had the impression she looked Simon right in the eye. Finally realizing what she was doing, she let out a scream, flinging the pillow away. She took the little boy in her arms, trying to revive him, and called 911. "I'm sorry. I don't know what got into me . . ." she said. "I heard a voice . . ." She wept, but now they were tears of desperation.

The Subterranean in the back of the room disappeared and I heaved a sigh of relief. The child was no longer in danger, nor was the young woman's soul. Gemma looked at me with hatred in her eyes. She seemed to be deciding whether to attack or leave. Before she could escape us I rushed up behind her and pinned her hands behind her back. "Simon!" I shouted.

Gemma tilted her head toward me and smiled. "If you wanted to have a threesome, you could've told me so right from the start." Simon materialized in front of her and grabbed her face, pressing his thumbs against her temples.

"Do it! Now!" I ordered. Gemma fell to her knees and I let her go as Simon held her tight. Her face became a black spider web as Simon's power flowed through her veins. Suddenly her Dakor hissed somewhere inside her and Gemma's eyes transformed.

"What's going on? You're hurting her!" I shouted.

"She's fighting me!" Simon growled. "I can't, I'm sorry."

"Keep going! Dig deeper!" Blood trickled from my brother's ear, but he didn't stop. "Simon!" I shouted, a second before a dark force hurled him away from Gemma. I ran to him and helped him to his feet.

"I'm sorry," he murmured. "I dug deep but found nothing."

Gemma stood up and shot me an icy glare. She pulled out her curved daggers and spun them around in her hands, ready to fling them, but I was faster; I materialized in front of her and held her wrists against the wall. I couldn't accept that even the last trace of hope had vanished.

Weakened by Simon's spell, Gemma dropped the knives and looked at me, still short of breath. Maybe it was my only chance to talk to her before she could escape. "Gemma, they're tricking you."

She wormed her hands free, her gaze hard. "How dare you? They're my Sisters. They're all I have."

"That's not true. You have me," I said. "You have Liam. Do you remember him?" I asked desperately, hoping Simon's power had had some effect on her.

Gemma seemed to think about it, her brow knit, but then her ice-cold eyes returned to mine. "I don't know any Liam. And I don't know you either."

"Your Sisters did this to you."

"They made me strong and invincible."

"They tore you away from us," I contradicted her.

"I *chose* to join them. There's no other way to enter the Bond."

"That's not true. They had to kill you to have you with them."

"Sophia saved me!"

"I begged her to!" I shouted in desperation, squeezing her wrists against the wall.

Gemma stared at me, confusion in her eyes. "What do you want from me?" she asked, studying me carefully.

I loosened my grip on her wrists and opened my hand in hers. Palm to palm. "I want you," I whispered, stroking her thumb with mine. "Just you." My gesture drew her gaze to our joined hands, to the tattoos that completed each other, the symbol for infinity that formed only when we were together. She studied it for a moment, surprised, and her big black eyes fixed on mine, digging inside me, leaving a deep furrow. I clasped her hands tighter, not wanting to let her go, but she vanished, her gaze still on mine, leaving me on the verge of tears, brimming with rage, vain hopes, and frustration. I hung my head and rested it against the wall, balling my fists against the stone as the emotions mushroomed inside me to the point of devastation, then struck the wall, which shattered from the impact. The anger was too great for me to contain. Each time Gemma ran away from me it was like losing her all over again.

"Hey." Simon rested his hands on my shoulders. "I'm sorry." Once again, Simon had risked his life to help me, but despite his best efforts he'd failed.

I rested a hand on his. "Thanks for trying." What was left to me now, if even this hope had been taken from me? Was it possible my Gemma truly didn't exist any more? No. No. No! I would never accept it. I would never allow it.

For such a long time, Gemma had been my light. Now she was lost in the darkness, unable to return. But somewhere inside her, her soul still shone. I didn't care what Simon thought. It was a lie, another attempt by evil to take her from me. She still existed. I would find her and bring her home. By my side. It was the only place for her.

GEMMA

40

THE EYE OF DESTINY

I went up to one of the tallest windows in the Castle and crouched down, breathing in the cool air. It almost seemed like I could see the entire kingdom from up there. The thick expanse of trees, the twisted trunks in the Marsh of Stillness, the waterfalls with their comforting rumble . . . the huge volcano that watched over us like a surly giant.

I felt like queen of the world . . . yet something disturbed me, though I couldn't put my finger on what. I stood up and spread my arms, contemplating the void beneath me, then closed my eyes and leaned forward, entrusting myself to the darkness. "*Argas*," I whispered in his mind.

I felt his heartbeat. When I opened my eyes, he was beneath me. He spread his mighty wings and I landed on his rock-hard back. I smiled and he whinnied, carrying me up to where the scent of freedom could banish the doubt that tormented me.

Argas and I were deeply connected. I spent all the time I could with him and together we explored Hell, following the rivers upstream or flying over mountains and waterfalls. It felt like he'd always been a part of me, not only since I'd bonded with my Sisters. With him I felt invincible and complete.

We quickly left the Castle behind us, soaring over hidden dwellings and underground villages. I could sense the fear of the Damned who sought shelter there. It was useless: no one could hide from me. But that day they didn't interest me.

A group of Souls fled at the sight of Argas descending. While he was still galloping, I leapt off his back and walked to the river's edge, observing my reflection in the swiftly flowing water. All I could see was a blurred outline. Maybe that really was what I was. Maybe it was all an illusion.

They had to kill you to have you with them. The Subterranean's voice filled my head like a ghost determined to haunt me. What did he want from me? Why did he hunt me down so insistently? Devina had wanted him for centuries, but he had chosen me. *Just me*. Why?

Sophia saved me!

I begged her to!

His frustrated shout exploded in my head. Nothing seemed to matter to him except convincing me of his sincerity, but it was absurd. A trick. I shook my head, banishing my doubts. Devina had warned me. She knew him well. She'd told me he would try to get into my head. I had to be careful.

Lost in the image of his gaze, both proud and desperate, I bent down and picked up a clod of earth. A flower blossomed at my command. It was black, like my tormented soul. I shouldn't listen to his lies. I knew where my place was—nothing else mattered. I stroked the stem and the Stramonium lengthened, obeying my order. At my touch, the flower spread into a lush fan. I stroked its velvety petals, but my eyes were drawn to the tattoo on my hand.

Another image filled my head: my palm against the Subterranean's, the lines on our juxtaposed thumbs forming a single design.

Stay together. Fight together.

A shiver crept up my back. I had always imagined it was a promise connected to my Sisters. Why did he have the same tattoo? And why had he been so intent on making me notice? Was it another of his tricks?

They tore you away from us. What did he mean by that? For months he'd been trying to subdue me, and now I was letting him penetrate my barriers? Why was I allowing him to plant doubts in my mind? I couldn't let him fool me. Witches had only one enemy—Subterraneans—and he was one of them. My Dakor stirred inside me, plucking the cords of my reason. Drawn by the scent of the flower, he crept out onto my palm and did a slow dance around it, then opened his fangs and gulped it down, staring at me intently. Our eyes were identical at that moment. I felt them burn, reminding me where my place was. He and I were two entities but a single being. I belonged to this place. What importance could the past possibly have?

An arrow hissed through the air and a small creature squealed. I was instantly on my feet, waiting for the hunter who'd shot it to emerge from the forest in search of her prey. Her thoughts were near. Maybe I would take home some fine plunder, a fierce new maidservant who could take my mind off my dark doubts. When she appeared in the bushes, my eyes locked onto hers.

"Gemma," she murmured, caught between surprise and happiness. I frowned, confused. How did this Soul know my name? Something moved in the trees, distracting me from her.

"Don't get mad if you didn't catch one bigger than mine. You can try again next time!" a man said cheerfully, approaching her.

"Drake, look," the woman said softly.

He saw me and froze. It was a Subterranean. His grey eyes pierced me as I studied them carefully. I probed his mind, losing myself in his memories—a confused tunnel of images in which I too was there, smiling with the other Subterranean, Evan. The power of his emotions was so astonishing I couldn't move a muscle.

"Let's get out of here, quick," the man urged her, and they disappeared into the forest together, leaving me with a new doubt to paralyze me: who were those two? And most importantly, how did they know me? What possible reason could a Soul and a Subterranean banished to Hell have for knowing me, a Witch? On Earth, Subterraneans might be untruthful, showing me lies in order to confuse me and prevail over Souls. But what reason would that Drake have to do so here? Besides, our encounter had been accidental, unexpected for both of us. It made no sense.

I looked once again at the tattoo on my hand. *Stay together.* Who was I, really? Would learning about my past help me find out?

There was something I was missing. I couldn't go on lying to myself and ignoring the need stirring inside me. I craved answers. Things needed to be clarified and there was only one person I trusted, more than anyone else in the world.

I leapt onto my Saurus's back, suddenly burning with the desire to unlock the doors of my mind. And Sophìa had the key.

It was easy to find her. The Bond united us like parts of the same body. She was the heart and her heartbeat gave us energy. When I appeared in the large arched entrance, she welcomed me with a big smile. She had known I would come.

"My respects, Empress," I said, bowing to her.

Sophìa raised my chin. "Please, do not bow to me, my pet." She took my hand and kissed it, looking me in the eye intensely as I lost myself in her dark allure.

"You know why I'm here."

"For some time I have known this moment would arrive," she said. "Tell me, do you have any doubts about where your rightful place is?" she asked, though she already knew the answer.

"No. Nothing could make me doubt that my place is here at your side."

She smiled, pleased, and led me into the room that she called the Eye of Destiny. The ceiling sparkled, dotted with thousands of stars that reproduced the galaxies. In the center of the room ruled a giant black globe where millions of tiny lights twinkled, some blinking on, others blinking off. They were the pride and the torment of Sophìa, who spent hours studying them, the souls of the Subterraneans we claimed and those who rebelled against us, unleashing her fury.

"Knowing one's past is a whim that every Sister longs to satisfy sooner or later, though all that matters to us is our life here at the Castle."

"It is, my lady. I can't stand it that the others know things I don't, but the past won't change what I am."

"That is certain." Sophìa smiled, confident. "The transformation cancels all memories. For some the effect lasts longer than for others. No one can make them return, yet with time they often resurface on their own. Nevertheless, that does not change what we are."

"Do all my Sisters remember who they were before the Bond?" I asked.

"All of them except Devina, because I transformed her myself and my venom is the most powerful weapon. Devina was the first of the Sisters."

"You mean after all these centuries she's never remembered anything?"

"Nothing has ever mattered to her except her place beside me."

"I understand. Nothing means more to me either," I confessed. "I was just curious."

Sophìa studied me carefully. "Devina has her moments, but she is a loyal and trusted Sister. It is for this reason that for centuries she has been my Specter."

I nodded, agreeing with her description of Devina. The Empress turned the globe slowly, reflecting on what she'd told me. Her mind was closed to me, a dark, unfathomable well. The globe stopped and her eyes locked onto mine with a mischievous smile. "I know you would like to take her place. The time has come for you to be honored with that privilege."

My eyes went wide and my heart pounded. "I've never wanted anything else," I declared, deeply proud at her words. The Bond among all the Sisters was strong, but I knew I loved Sophìa more than anyone else, and she too had always shown a special affection to me. All I had ever wanted was to please her and become her Specter—her second-in-command—and at last I had succeeded. I would be in charge of the Castle when Sophìa willed it, and everyone would take orders from me. The idea of all that power was already going to my head and I couldn't wait to put myself to the test. "How will Devina take the news?"

"Devina must accept it. Moreover, she has always suspected you would replace her," she conceded. She approached me and kissed me on the lips. "I have never hidden my preference for you, and now that you are finally ready, it is your right to be by my side."

"I swear I won't disappoint you."

"I am certain of it. Now, come. I have a special task to entrust to you. It will satisfy your curiosity."

I smiled at her. "I am yours, my lady."

"Not even I can give back to you what has been lost forever, such as your memories. However, I can give to you a gift you will deem precious. Nothing can satisfy your thirst to know your past more than the person who lived it with you. Someone who shared everything with the old Gemma. Today you may claim his soul and he will not resist you because he already loves you." Sophia turned the black globe and with her elegant black fingernail touched a tiny village on Earth nestled among the Adirondack mountains. "His time has come. He is already yours. You need only to go and take him."

Send me to him. A white speck lit up on the globe, revealing the young man to me. I smiled. Peter was his name. And his soul would be mine.

EVAN

41

POINT OF NO RETURN

"Are you *sure* you didn't find anything?" I asked Simon. We'd just returned from our encounter with Gemma.

"I'm sorry, not a trace. Gemma is—"

"Don't say it!" I shouted in exasperation. "Don't *think* it."

He tried to bring me to my senses. "Evan! You need to calm down, please."

Tears started to my eyes. I grabbed my hair and pressed my lips together to prevent the words from escaping. I'd been so convinced Simon's power could change things! I couldn't accept that it wasn't so. I couldn't accept that he'd searched inside her and hadn't found a single trace, a single memory that might bring her back. I couldn't accept that all hope was lost. "I thought I saw something in her eyes."

"That's what you say every time, Evan. With every desperate attempt you make, you think you've found her again, but it's only a lie you tell yourself and it's putting you more and more at risk. She's going to end up capturing you unless you can control yourself."

"I . . . can't," I said. A tear slid down my face. "I want her back, Simon. Every time I think I've lost her, I can't breathe."

Simon was right: I was gradually losing control. I could feel I would soon go mad with rage, frustration—and nostalgia. Most of all nostalgia. I missed Gemma terribly. Every day was worse than the one before, because she was farther away, more elusive. "I have to see her again. Now."

"It won't help anything!" Simon shouted.

"What are you saying, that I should give up? That one day I should look Liam in the eye and tell him his mother's gone because I gave up on her?" How could I? "I'm sorry, I can't do that."

"What can you possibly do that we haven't already tried? Seeing her again won't have any effect on her, but you'll keep getting worse."

"The worst thing of all is being away from her." Despite the fact that Gemma had changed, seeing her lit up my heart. I couldn't stay away—my desire for her was too painful. How could Simon ask me to give up all hope? "I need her. I'm going to go look for her. I'll even summon her if I need to."

"You don't," Ginevra said, entering the room with Liam in her arms. "She's back. And she's very close." I looked at her questioningly. "She's at Peter's. You'll have to hurry, because she wants his soul."

"You mean she remembers him?" I asked, full of hope.

"No. Sophia sent her to him on a whim. I can hear Gemma's thoughts. She's seducing him and he isn't stopping her. It won't take her long to claim him. He loves her—he's not going to put up a fight."

I clenched my fists, shaking off the thought of Gemma and Peter together. "Just what I needed: an excuse to get rid of the kid once and for all."

"Don't talk nonsense, Evan," Simon admonished me. Given how things were turning out, he knew there was a risk I might actually do it.

"Now go," Ginevra urged us. I went over to her and kissed Liam on the forehead. "Good luck, Evan." My eyes met hers and I nodded before vanishing.

When Simon and I materialized in Peter's smithy Gemma instantly sensed our presence, though she didn't move. All she did was raise her malicious gaze to us over his shoulder. I had to summon all my self-control to keep from rushing over and killing him when I saw his hands on her. Gemma smiled, grasping my thoughts as I tried to calm down. "Good. The game is more exciting."

"Don't," I ordered her. Waking from her spell, Peter turned to look at us.

"What are you doing here? Go away."

"Stay out of this, kid," Simon warned, knowing my nerves were on the brink of snapping.

"You're the ones who should stay out of it. She wants *me* now."

"She's not who you think she is any more," I told him. "She's dangerous."

Gemma smiled and slid her hand down Peter's chest. "What do you imagine I might do to him? Kill him? I can give him everything he desires." Peter looked at her, captivated by her bewitching power yet confused by her behavior.

"Your offer has a steep price tag," I shot back coldly.

"What price isn't worth paying to satisfy our desires?"

"The soul," I replied, intransigent. "Gemma, listen to me. You can't take his. You don't realize it now, but you would regret it forever."

"What the fuck is going on? Is this some kind of joke? Gemma, would you tell me what's happening? And why are you dressed like that?" Peter exclaimed, now completely free of her spell.

She caressed his face, wafting her pheromones over him. The guy was tough for a mortal. Gemma's power dazed him but couldn't pull him in completely. "Peter," she whispered, "you and I are connected, you know we are. Who do you trust more: me or them?" He gazed at her, at the mercy of the passion she'd aroused in him. "Show me," Gemma whispered against his lips. "Kiss me."

Black rage rose inside me, compelling me to act. I couldn't stand around watching. I rushed at Gemma and she pushed Peter away in order to defend herself from my attack. Simon joined the fray, but she was fast, agile, and managed to hold her ground against us both. I tried to grab her, but she eluded my every attempt. She whipped out her daggers as I grabbed a long iron pole from a table and bent it to my will. "Step aside, Simon. This is between her and me." The pole glinted, turning into a sharp sword.

Gemma was more and more excited by the game. She honestly had no idea what I'd just prevented her from doing. If she'd taken Peter's soul, she would never have forgiven herself. Just like I would never forgive myself if I let her go.

"You're the one who never gives up," she said, lunging at me with her dagger.

I blocked her blow with the sword. "Never, when it comes to you." We moved swiftly around the smithy among the equipment and sharp metal objects.

"It's a shame there's still something you haven't realized about me." She did a backflip and I followed her, launching another attack.

"I know everything about you," I said.

"Then you know I don't like to lose." She stretched a hand out toward Peter and it took me a moment to understand.

"Peter, no!" I shouted. A pointed pole flew from behind him and ran him through.

Peter looked at us, his expression desperate, his hands gripping the bloody pole that protruded from his abdomen. "Gemma . . ." he murmured, dropping to his knees. Simon rushed to heal him, but Peter's mouth filled with blood and he crumpled to the ground, his eyes still wide.

"He's dead," Simon announced, unable to help him.

"What a great loss," Gemma said, a grin on her lips. With a scream of rage I attacked her again. The Gemma in front of me had nothing to do with my Gem. She was ruthless, and the only voice she heard was the voice of evil. Maybe it was time for me to listen to it too. I'd tried in every way possible to bring her back, to rekindle her memories of us, but nothing had worked. Maybe it was time to try more extreme measures.

Gemma eyed me with a little grin as she dodged my blows, which for the first time were brutal. "Reaper Angel versus Reaper Witch. Round one."

"Evan, what are you doing?!" Simon shouted. He'd never seen me really attack Gemma, but maybe there wasn't any other option.

We were on a perfect battlefield. I didn't want to seriously injure her but I had to at least try to shake her up. The more I attacked, the more amused she seemed. She began to use magic. Every tool in the room became a weapon. Around us rose a cloud of dust, trapping us inside a little hurricane. Gemma hurled me to the far end of the room, but I sprang back to attack her. A wall of nails flew toward me. The metal melted before it could hit me, so the coast was clear to rush her and knock her to the ground once more.

"I knew I had chosen my Champion wisely," she told me in my mind, satisfied. She'd used my power.

"That isn't surprising—you've always chosen me. It's with the family that you made the wrong choice." The remark enraged her, but she immediately looked away, distracted by something.

"Evan!" Simon cried. Peter's soul had left his body. He was looking at his hands, confused by the new sensations running through him. Slowly he raised his head and his eyes pierced us, as gray as molten silver.

"What's happening to me?" Peter fell to his knees and howled in pain as black ink seared his arm like a brand. Simon and I stared at each other, astonished. *He was a Subterranean.*

Gemma freed herself from my grip and reappeared beside Peter. "I'll be back for you," she whispered in his ear, her eyes locked on mine. Then she disappeared, a victorious smile on her lips.

42

HEART OF ICE

"All this is insane! Tell me I'm dreaming," Peter burst out, in shock. "What the hell is this thing on my arm? Am I a ghost? And why does Gemma look like she came straight out of an episode of *Xena: Warrior Princess?*"

"Calm down. We'll explain everything," Simon replied.

"Wait a minute. If I'm dead, how is it you two can see me?" Peter took another look at his old body that lay on the floor in a pool of blood.

"Look." Simon showed him the mark on his own arm. "We've got one too. You've been chosen. You aren't a mortal Soul. You're one of us, a Subterranean."

"So you guys are dead too," he said. "I always knew there was something strange about you."

"That's not the point."

"Is the blond a 'Subterranean' too, whatever that is?" he asked cockily.

"She's a Witch."

"Oh, well, that explains everything."

"Gemma wasn't here for his mortal soul—she wanted to claim him as a slave," I reasoned aloud.

"Souls? *Slaves*? What the hell is a Subterranean? Either this is a nightmare or I've ended up in one of my comic books."

"Get him out of here before I kill him a second time," I said.

"Hey, you can't talk to me like that."

"You'll understand everything once you've eaten," Simon explained. "Let's go. I'll show you the way."

"Hold on! What's going to happen to me and my life?"

I crossed the room with long strides and shoved my face into his. "That's your life, right there," I growled, pointing at his corpse. "Forget about it, because it's already gone."

Showing unexpected courage, he didn't back down. In fact, he glared at me bitterly. "My mother can't bury another body. I'm all she's got left."

"What does that mean?"

"I don't want to *die*."

"It's too late. In case you haven't noticed, you're already dead."

"Okay, I get it—I'm dead, but why does anyone have to know that? Nobody knows you guys are. If I'm not a common Soul, if I am what you say I am, why should I disappear?"

"You're a Soldier now. You'll be given orders and they'll be the only thing that matters to you."

"I'm a *what*?" he asked in shock. Not even the sight of his bloody body had upset him so much. "I want to be normal. I didn't ask for this."

"None of us did. And you're not normal. You were chosen to serve Fate. Orders come first," Simon insisted.

I sighed in exasperation. "We're just wasting time."

"Peter, trust us. When you eat of the Tree you'll understand everything. You'll know what your place is and you'll be a lot stronger than you've ever been."

"What would happen if I didn't eat?"

"You'd get weaker and weaker until you disappeared. Evil would seize its chance to claim you and you wouldn't be able to fight it."

Peter was stressed out, but not as much as I was. I'd had enough of the guy. I didn't have Simon's patience, much less in this situation. "Do you have any idea how lucky you are? By this time you would have already been in Hell if we hadn't been here to save you. Like it or not, death exists, and we're its Soldiers."

Peter reflected a moment and nodded. "Okay, but we'll do things my way. I'm not going to leave my mom all on her own." His words impacted me, clearing a path back to the memory of my own mother. "I can be both things. You even go to school. I just need to learn your rules."

"All right. Do what you want."

Just then, the door opened and a woman entered the room. "Mom," he murmured, aghast. She couldn't see us but she immediately spotted Peter's bloody corpse. Her scream echoed through the room and she fainted. Simon rushed to her, catching her before she fell.

"It looks like I don't have a choice any more," Peter said, tears in his eyes. He leaned over his mother and stroked her cheek, looking at her as though for the last time.

"Yes you do," I told him. "Simon can erase this memory from her mind."

"Can you really do that?" Peter asked, his voice full of hope.

Simon nodded. His power hadn't been able to bring Gemma back, but it could save the connection between Peter and his mother.

Peter turned to look at me, gratitude filling his face. "I guess I owe you my thanks."

"It's not the first favor I've done for you today," I retorted. It was true. If Simon hadn't been around, I'm pretty sure I would have killed him when I saw him with Gemma.

Simon leaned over Peter's mother and rested his fingers on her temples. The woman's face filled with thin back veins that quivered beneath her skin as he extracted her memory.

"What . . . what's he doing to her?" Peter asked in alarm.

"Don't worry, she'll recover. When she wakes up she won't remember any of this."

Peter nodded gratefully. "We need to get rid of my body. Nobody can find out I'm dead."

"We could bury it somewhere in the woods, make it unrecognizable," I reassured him.

"I've got a better idea." Peter shoved open a heavy iron door. "We'll burn it in the incinerator."

I went back to the house alone. I'd left Simon with the task of showing Peter the way between the two worlds. He wouldn't be able to accompany him all the way to the Tree of Knowledge so he could eat of its fruit, but he would explain how it was done and Peter's instinct would take care of the rest. Simon would wait for him to return and then bring him here to us, at least for the time being. More than anyone else, I understood his need not to abandon his mother, especially after I'd personally taken his father from him. But it wouldn't be easy for Peter to pretend to still be human and take on his new duties as a Soldier at the same time. No matter how hard he tried to cling to his old life, it no longer belonged to him, and sooner or later he would realize it.

The house was unusually quiet. Liam must have been sleeping. I checked his playpen in the living room but he wasn't there. Disappearing and materializing in the boy's room, I found it empty as well. *"Ginevra, where are you?"* I called in my mind. The only reply was silence. Normally she would have materialized beside me instantly. It was strange to think she'd gone out and taken the baby with her. I concentrated on Liam's soul to reach him, wherever he was. I couldn't find him. The world came crashing down around me and the room began to spin. No. It couldn't actually have happened.

"Evan . . ." My ears detected a faint murmur. It was Ginevra, in the pool area downstairs. I materialized beside her in the blink of an eye. She was on the floor, wounded and semiconscious. All around us was an imaginary forest full of life, but in my heart there was only silence.

"Ginevra! Ginevra, wake up! What happened?" I tried to bring her to, but my power didn't work on her.

"Liam . . ." she murmured in anguish.

I jerked away from her, my eyes full of tears. "No . . ." I whispered, "It can't be true. Tell me it's not true. I beg you . . ."

I turned around and saw him. Everything inside me turned to ice. "NO!" I screamed. A flock of birds took wing, frightened.

Liam's little body was floating face down in the simulated lake, his arms limp at his sides, swaying in the current that tried to push him to shore. I leapt into the water and carried him out, resting him on the rock and turning him over to look him in the face. He was so tiny, so defenseless! His heart had stopped beating. "Liam!" I cried, attempting to use my healing powers on him. It didn't work. His soul was gone; someone had already helped him cross over. How could it have happened? "No!" I screamed in desperation. I clasped him to my chest, weeping in pain. "Liam, no . . ." I repeated, holding him tight. I kissed him on the forehead and pushed the hair from his face. It was thick, like his mother's.

I had lost them both. I couldn't believe he was gone, that I would never watch him grow up . . . that I hadn't been there to protect him.

The hiss of an arrow touched my ear. I spun around and caught it, my eyes burning into those of the Hunter. Absolon. He'd broken free. I clenched my fist so hard it crushed his arrow. The shaft was metal, but within a split second I'd pulverized it in my fury. "You have no idea what you've got coming to you," I threatened.

He glanced at the baby as I rested his body gently on the ground, never taking my eyes off Absolon. Standing up to face him, I balled my hands into fists. A strong wind blew through the trees, making the forest shudder. Wild rage blinded me and pain crushed my chest with its bands of steel.

In a flash, Absolon nocked another arrow and pointed his bow straight at me. I disappeared only to reappear right in front of him, my chest touching his arrowhead. "You're going to sorely miss the Hell you came from," I promised.

He lowered his weapon and attacked me, but I was faster. No man, Subterranean, or celestial creature could have escaped my wrath. Absolon tried to defend himself but I struck him mercilessly again and again, slamming him against the rock wall, shattering stones and uprooting the trees. I wanted to tear him limb from limb before sending him back to Hell. How dare he take my child from me?

Absolon tried to escape by leaping to the top of the waterfall, but I beat him to it. As soon as he landed, I hurled him to the cold stone at the edge of the cliff and wrapped one hand around his throat. With the other I took one of his arrows and pointed it at his jugular as he tried to distance himself from me by craning his neck into the empty space below him. I knew the poison wouldn't kill him, and in any case I didn't want him dead. Not yet. First he would have to experience for himself the suffering he'd inflicted on me, that he'd inflicted on my little Liam. I wanted him to taste at least some of the Hell that had emerged inside me.

Tears returned to fill my eyes. "How could you take it out on him?" I snarled, desperate. "How dare you take him from me?!" I screamed. Blood trickled from the spot where I was pressing the arrowhead.

"'Tis only ye I'm after," he replied, undaunted.

"Then you shouldn't have taken it out on him, because all you've gained is your own death," I shouted in fury, my demoniacal eyes brimming with pain, rage, and loathing for the bastard who had stolen everything from me—first Gemma and now Liam. A shriek rose from my chest and echoed through the forest as I slit his throat with his own arrow.

He gurgled, but a burst of lightning streaked the sky above us, which suddenly darkened. "Stop!" a voice shouted.

I was so lost in my fury I didn't recognize it. I had to turn toward her to realize it was Ginevra. "He has to die," I hissed, "but first he has to endure Gemma's suffering . . . and Liam's. And mine."

"He wasn't the one who killed Liam," she revealed gravely.

I released my grip on the Hunter and dried my tears. He gurgled, pulling the arrow from his neck. I stood up and leaned over the waterfall. Ginevra had my full attention. "Who was it, then?" I snarled, seething. Whoever it was, I would find them and tear them to shreds.

"It was one of the Màsala."

43

A PAINFUL GOODBYE

I sank to my knees and embraced Liam for the last time, the excruciating fact of his absence bringing fresh tears to my eyes. "Why did they do this to me?" I sobbed, kissing his tiny cheeks. I had failed. I should have brought Gemma back so we could be a family but I had failed miserably, and now she would never see our child again. I couldn't bear it, it was too painful. Too devastating. "Liam . . ." I murmured. "He had nothing to do with this, any of this." My tears dampened his face.

Ginevra rested her hand on my shoulder. "He's in Heaven now. He'll be fine. At least he won't grow up in the middle of this war."

"I'll never see him again. I've lost him forever," I said, my voice dull.

"I'm sorry," Ginevra said. "I tried to stop him but I couldn't." She stroked Liam's forehead and her armor crumbled. She burst into tears. "I fought back, used all my magic, but it was useless. He took him away. Liam called out for you before vanishing. Then I passed out."

I squeezed my eyes shut, overcome by pain. "It's not your fault," I reassured her. "Thank you for protecting him and loving him," I murmured. Together we shed bitter tears, little Liam's body lying motionless on our laps.

"No!" Simon shouted when he appeared beside us. Ginevra and I looked at him. Peter was at his side but Ginevra didn't even notice. Nothing mattered more than our loss.

"It was the Màsala. They took him," Ginevra told him. But it wasn't the time for explanations. Simon knelt over the child and kissed his forehead, hugging Ginevra. He ran his hand over her cheek and healed her wound.

"I'm sorry I wasn't here for him," Peter said, but Ginevra shook her head to silence him.

I stood up and gathered pieces of wood. Ginevra watched me bind them together as she cradled Liam. Absolon was tied to a tree, unconscious. Ginevra had paralyzed him again with her magic. I built a little boat, making sure the structure was sturdy. Liam loved boats. Simon had carved him a wooden toy boat, and Liam loved to watch it float in the pond at the back of the gardens. I gently rested him inside it and a tear slid down my cheek as I prepared to say goodbye.

"Wait." Ginevra touched the wood and a bed of flowers appeared around his little body. She leaned down and something sprang from the ground. A white orchid. She knew how much they meant to me. It was my mother's favorite flower, and she'd always kept one on her piano. I would sit beside it and stare at it as she composed new melodies just for me. Ginevra plucked the orchid and offered it to me. I kissed the flower and rested it on Liam's body. My mother would protect him. A new shudder of grief left me sobbing as a white flame emanated from my palm.

Seeing that I couldn't bring myself to move, Simon set the boat adrift. When it had moved onto the lake, I cast my fireball onto it and the wood burst into flames, shrouding Liam in the heat of the fire. My fire . . . my last embrace.

Goodbye, my little warrior.

44

SEDUCTION AND TEMPTATION

I was sunk into the sofa, cradling Liam's toy boat in my hands. I would cherish it forever as the most precious of treasures. "How are you?" Ginevra asked, sitting down beside me. We'd watched the funeral pyre all night long, until Liam's little body had turned to ash. Only then did the others manage to pull me away. Ginevra had deactivated the forest simulation scenario and my dream of fatherhood had vanished along with that illusion. I'd spent hours in the darkness on that sofa, contemplating my suffering. Irony stayed beside me the whole time, as though he understood what had happened. We'd lost Gemma and now Liam as well.

"Tell me again," I begged her, my voice empty. The fire of my pain was beginning to give way to ice. "Tell me everything you know."

"His name is Adhémar. He's one of the twelve."

"Sounds like you know them well."

"Only because I was Sophìa's Specter and, like her, I had privileges. It's never a pleasant experience meeting members of the Brotherhood. The mere presence of the Màsala leaves you petrified. Few have seen them, since they're superior beings and never show themselves to anyone—they always wear a red hood to hide their appearance—but I have. It's like they have no face. Their eyes look like glass. They're blind, because they see through Souls. Their voice is as dark as the depths of the abyss, their power immense."

I understood what Ginevra must have felt. I'd met with one of the Màsala when I wanted to back out of my orders to execute Gemma. I'd summoned them, imagining they would pay no attention, but one of them had actually shown himself to me. The entire forest had reacted to his presence and time had frozen. His eyes were hollow, empty. Meeting his gaze was like staring into a hole that looked out onto the universe. It made me dizzy. Back then I hadn't known how important she was to them—important enough to show themselves to me to make sure I killed her. What they couldn't have foreseen was that she would fall in love with me.

"We don't know why they took Liam's life. I doubt his time had come, but at this point even they are breaking the rules. Maybe they were afraid Gemma would take him with her and use him in the name of evil."

"To do what? Liam didn't have any powers. He was human," I said. "He was only a baby."

"Maybe they weren't sure of that."

"So just to be on the safe side they took his soul?!" I shouted, furious.

"They saved it," Simon reminded me, a firm believer in his Subterranean values.

Right. Why was it so painful, then? Once again, the desire to keep someone with me had taken precedence over my principles as a Soldier. It was just like when I'd spared Gemma. Saving her back then would have prevented her from transforming and serving evil. By killing her I would have spared her Hell. Still, I would have done it a thousand times if it meant being able to be with her. It was self-centered, but there was nothing I could do about it. Liam wouldn't have had to die so soon either. I balled my hands into fists. I'd lost my son forever, but Gemma was still out there and I had no intention of letting her go.

“I know what I have to do,” I declared. Ginevra looked at me, shaken. She already understood. “There’s nothing keeping me here any longer. I’m going to Hell and I’m going to bring her back.”

“Are you out of your mind?” she said. “It’s madness and you know it.”

“Evan, you’re devastated over losing Liam. Please, think carefully,” Simon cautioned me.

“I already have.”

“You can keep trying from right here, you know.”

“For how long? What has it gotten me so far? Weeks, *months* of frustrating expectation, to spend how long with her? Five minutes? No. That’s not enough. I need her. I have to see her, *touch her*, convince her to unearth her past with me. I can’t do it unless I have enough time.”

“Not even Simon’s power worked. You may never succeed.”

“Then I’ll stay with her in Hell.”

“You’ve already been there. They locked you up and tortured you. You can’t have forgotten. You still have the scars.”

“The scar I have in my heart right now is more painful,” I growled in frustration.

“Are you even willing to accept that it might be Gemma who inflicts all that pain on you this time? Will you be able to bear such suffering?” Simon warned.

“I won’t go as a prisoner.” I looked him straight in the eye. “I’ll let her claim me.”

“That won’t help anything. It’ll only be surrendering,” Ginevra murmured.

“My mind’s made up, so save your breath.”

“I don’t want to stop you, but you need a better plan than that.”

“Sorry, I don’t have one. I’ve tried fighting to bring her back, but that didn’t work. I have to go. I owe it to Liam. It’s not going to end like this—I’m not giving up on us.” I ran my hands through my hair. A silence fell among us. Simon and Ginevra realized that nothing could change my mind. “It doesn’t matter where. My place is with her.” *Stay together. Fight together,* I thought, gripping my thumb in my fist. The promise wasn’t just tattooed on our hands—the words were also branded deep in her heart. I knew they were. They still burned, and I would reawaken their power, no matter what it cost.

Simon rested his hand on my shoulder. “You’re right. You have to go.”

I raised my eyes to him and even Ginevra nodded in resignation. “Just don’t ask me to say goodbye to you.”

I smiled at her. “I won’t.” I got up from the sofa, hugged her, and fist-bumped Simon.

My thoughts returned to the cenote where the mouth to Hell was located—a timeless place whose dangers lurked beneath its dark waters. Back then I’d been escaping from a nightmare. Now I was about to enter it willingly.

“That’s not a plan. It’s a suicide mission,” Peter said, his tone critical.

“Why are you still here?” I said, annoyed. I’d forgotten he was even there. Peter had eaten of the Tree, thereby gaining the knowledge of our worlds. Still, everything was new to him and what had just happened had floored him, leaving him wordless this whole time.

“Hey, why are you always so pissed off at me?” he shot back, frowning at me as he approached. I stepped up to look him square in the eye, ready to take him on.

“Calm down, you two,” said Simon. “Fighting won’t help anyone.”

“You guys are crazy,” Peter scoffed.

I snorted. “What, you would abandon Gemma to evil? Didn’t you used to claim you were her best friend?”

“That’s exactly why I think it’s crazy for you to go there alone. I want to help you. There must be a better solution.”

“What would you know? You haven’t spent the last few months looking for a way to bring her back while your family was being torn apart.”

"Evan, you can't blame him for thinking it's risky. He's right," Simon put in.

"I don't need him, and I don't need to stand here explaining it to him either."

"Actually, you do," Ginevra contradicted me. "You need him." I looked at her, dubious.

"How are you going to get yourself captured, Evan?" Simon asked. "We can't wait for Gemma to return to Earth—that could take weeks."

"Maybe not," Ginevra said. "She killed Peter to claim him, and she won't give up so easily. She'll come back looking for him soon enough."

I thought it over. All things considered, Ginevra was right.

"I have to act as bait?" Peter protested.

"Whoa, you're a genius—I never would have guessed it!" I said sarcastically.

"Guys, don't fight," Ginevra yelled. "We have far more important things to discuss."

"You said you wanted to help," Simon reminded Peter, who nodded.

"Do you feel up to facing Gemma?" Ginevra asked him. "Think carefully—Witches will entrance you with their beauty and subjugate your mind unless you defend your thoughts. Seduction and temptation are their most powerful weapons. Think you're strong enough to resist Gemma's power?"

"I can do it," he said, determined. "I'm not afraid and I'm not backing down."

"I still can't believe you're a Subterranean," I muttered. It was strange seeing him there in our living room, talking to him about things like Hell, Witches, and being claimed.

"It explains why he's always been drawn to us . . . especially to Gemma," Simon replied. "He grew up at her side because the Màsala *knew*, and they put him near her."

"It also explains why he had something against me right from the start," Ginevra said, throwing him a provocative look.

"Plus his fear of snakes," I added, taking full advantage of this opportunity to point out his weaknesses. I couldn't bring myself to see him as an ally or dispel my urge to kill him, especially now that he had so much power over Gemma.

"He's always been fairly resistant to our power," Simon pointed out, "but we never imagined he had the Subterranean gene in him."

"Only Sophìa can track down the descendants of the Children of Eve. She poured some of her power into a large globe so all her Sisters would be able to identify their enemies. It's also the tool she uses to bend the forces of nature to her will. Sophìa is obsessed with Earth and likes toying with mortals. All she has to do is choose a spot on the globe and toss a little water into the air to cause a storm, flood, or tsunami, spreading panic, death, and destruction. It's been the most complicated of her magic spells. Right after creating it, she burst into thousands of fragments—butterflies as black as her soul. She managed to reconstitute herself, but only partially," Ginevra told us, evidently reliving the memory. "I was with her at the time. Her beautiful face was like a puzzle with pieces missing. She lost consciousness for a long time, though I was the only one who knew it. I was her Specter and took her place until she returned."

"What does a Specter do?" Peter asked.

"She takes over command of Hell and all its creatures," she replied, her tone solemn. "The Sisters are connected by a bond of equality, but even they must bow to the Specter's orders. Whoever has been appointed Specter holds vast power, and not everyone is capable of handling it. That's why Sophìa's Specter is ruthless and unscrupulous."

"Who took your place?"

"Devina. No one deserves the scepter of evil more than she does. I think she's still the Empress's second-in-command."

"Do you think she'll try to subjugate Evan again once he's back at the Castle?" Simon asked.

"If Gemma claims him, she would have to leave him alone—though knowing Devina, that can't be ruled out. What's certain is that she will try to stop you, Evan, since she knows your true intentions. Gemma trusts her—it won't be easy to compete with that."

"Devina has no power over me and never has. I'll fight her like I've always done."

Ginevra nodded.

"What do we do now?" Peter asked.

"We wait. She'll come looking for you when the time's come," Ginevra said. She gave Simon a telling look. He went over to Peter, placed his hand on his neck and looked him straight in the eye. The veins on Peter's face squirmed as a dark memory ran through them, flowing toward Simon.

"Go home," Simon ordered. Peter nodded and disappeared.

"Why did you do that?" I asked hesitantly.

"I only canceled his memory of this conversation. It's better that he not know our plan, or Gemma will discover right away that he's only acting as bait. He hasn't learned to block off his mind yet."

"It's more dangerous for him. Will he be able to resist Gemma's power?"

"He's a Subterranean," Simon replied. "He knows where his place is."

"But he loves her, and that hasn't changed. He won't hurt her even though he knows she's a Witch—but she might hurt him."

"That's why we need to act fast."

"I agree with you," Ginevra said, nodding. "I doubt he'll be able to resist Gemma's seduction. We need to get to them before it's too late or we'll have another problem. We need to be prepared."

"How long do you think it'll be before she comes back for him?" Simon asked her.

Ginevra smiled. "There's one thing all Witches have in common."

"What's that?"

"We hate to wait."

"She's already here," I murmured, frowning. Inside our house, Peter had been hidden by our protective barriers, but once he'd left she'd tracked him down.

"This is it." Ginevra came up to me, in her eyes a trace of bitterness. This might be goodbye. None of us knew if I would return. I would let Gemma claim me, and there was only one way she could do it: with a bite from her serpent. The first time Witch venom had killed me, death had torn me away from her. Now it was my only hope of winning her back. The burn was still vivid in my mind, like fire in my veins. But I wasn't afraid any more.

Ginevra locked eyes with me. "Are you ready to die for Gemma?"

"I have been since I first met her," I replied confidently.

Simon gave me a bear hug. "Good luck, brother."

I pulled back to look at him, my eyes turning gray as I transformed. "I'm afraid I'm going to need it this time." He and Ginevra silently watched me as I disappeared, guiding my steps toward death. Toward Gemma.

GEMMA

45

KISS OF DARKNESS

Around me danced a swarm of black butterflies, fawning over me. They felt the power I emanated and fed off it. Sophìa had left, leaving me in her garden right in the middle of the Reaping. Only she could sort through the Souls, but I was her Specter now so I had certain privileges. No one else had permission to witness the Sorting. For some, Sophìa's garden was a forbidden utopia. I closed my eyes and spread my arms, allowing the Souls to alight on me, venerating me and clinging to my body like they did with the Empress.

One of them came to rest on my hand and I eyed it carefully. It had bold, powerful wings. My Dakor sensed its power and materialized. The other butterflies all rose into the air at once, like an explosion, but the one on my hand didn't move. It must be an interesting Soul. My serpent hissed, creeping toward it, but I called him back, calming his impulses. I wanted it for myself. I knew it was forbidden, but I felt an overwhelming curiosity to know who it was, so I released my pheromones, immediately drawing the swarm back. The butterfly sensed my energy and bit me, wanting to feed off it. A second later a man took form before my eyes. He had well-developed muscles, a shaven head, dirty skin, and a scar along his cheekbone. He looked like a barbarian warrior and had such a virile air it seemed impossible he was the Soul of a mere mortal and not a Subterranean. The man bowed to me, resting one knee on the ground. "At your command, my queen," he said, subjugating himself to my power.

He was a First-Echelon murderer—I had felt it the minute he bit me. That was how Sophìa sorted Souls: with the Butterfly's Kiss. Sophìa plumbed their depths, knew their souls' darkest hue, and sorted them, based on the crimes they had committed, assigning them to an Echelon—the punishment they would have to undergo. First Echelon, Second, Third—she classified them into hundreds of subcategories. The butterflies would dance through the air, obeying her orders as they avidly awaited their turn. The large windows in the ceiling would open like a blossoming flower from whose heart they would be spit out into Hell, their new realm.

A Soul like the warrior before me would be in great demand during the Hunt for the Opalion, but before they were recruited, Souls had to endure the great trial of Hell: surviving so as to prove themselves worthy. If they remained sane, they proved their strength. Only the toughest endured. Rarely during the Games did the Damned survive the Subterraneans, let alone our Champions. This one, however, had a fearless air and a powerful body. Maybe I should keep him for myself . . . The temptation was strong, but I knew Sophìa wouldn't approve. I would definitely go out looking for him later, though. *If you're strong enough to resist, one day I'll find you and you'll return to me.*

"What are you doing here?" Devina's voice sounded behind me. My Dakor lunged and bit the warrior, who vaporized in a cloud of dust.

"What a shame," I sighed, shrugging.

"You're not allowed to awaken the Empress's Souls. It's not your task."

"I was only contemplating them. Is that forbidden too?"

Devina's mind was in turmoil. She knew Sophìa had passed the scepter of command to me, and it had to have incensed her. However, her thoughts were distant and unfathomable. Why did she continue to keep me out? I already knew she was furious with me—what else did she have to hide?

"I heard Sophìa has given you a great gift."

"Yes, soon there will be an Opalion in my honor and everyone will learn that I am the new Specter."

"My congratulations. But I wasn't talking about that." Devina studied me, her expression sly. "I mean the boy, Peter. You didn't manage to claim him, it seems."

"Not yet," I corrected her. "He's already mine. It's only a matter of time."

"I hope so, or it would be a real disappointment for the Empress." I glared at her. "What about the other one, Evan? You haven't claimed him yet either? Didn't you want him to be your Champion?"

I thought of the Subterranean and his impertinence. There was something about him that irritated and attracted me in equal measure. Devina had tried to subjugate him for centuries and failed. Perhaps I should leave the tedious task to her, since he'd done nothing but make doubt creep into my mind. I was Specter now; I'd obtained what I most desired. "You can keep him," I said. She smiled at me enthusiastically, forgetting our conflict. She was my Sister, and after all, I had to make it up to her for taking command away from her.

On the other hand, Peter seemed like a fine prize to claim. I hadn't sensed him again after he'd disappeared. Those two killjoys must have shown him the way to eat of the Tree. Now he had Knowledge, and he must also have acquired his Subterranean powers, but that wouldn't keep me from subjugating him.

As if he'd sensed my need for him, I detected his soul again. "Well, I suppose you have unfinished business to take care of," Devina remarked, having read my mind.

"Would you see to Sophìa's Reaping?" I asked.

"Of course." Devina smiled at me. "After all, I always have."

I went up to her and kissed her on the lips. "Thank you. You're the best of the Sisters. Well, I'm off. A gift was given to me. The time has come to claim it."

I followed the young man's call and materialized next to him. He was turned away from me, but when he sensed my presence he spun around. "Turn around again—I was admiring you," I told him mischievously. He had firm buttocks and a well-trained body.

"Gemma . . ." he murmured, shaken. His breathing suddenly went ragged. Though he no longer needed air, he was still attached to his human habits. Novices were so sweet. He leaned back against the workbench, gripping the edge of it in a useless attempt to maintain control.

"Were you expecting me?" I asked, my voice charismatic.

Seeing me approach, he didn't budge and allowed me to move in between his legs. "You have to go. I don't want to fight you."

I pushed the curly locks from his forehead as he stared at my lips, at the mercy of his emotions. "I don't want to fight either. There's a bond between us. Can't you feel it too?" I whispered. "I won't hurt you. All I want is a kiss." I moved my lips closer and he stood there, paralyzed. I hadn't yet unleashed my powers of seduction, but he already seemed utterly at my mercy. I smiled. Taking him would be child's play. But maybe I could amuse myself with him a little more first. "You can touch me, if you want," I whispered to him, guiding his hands onto my sides.

He ran his nose down my neck, his hands trembling. I could read his desire for me in his thoughts. He wanted me—he always had. And now he could have me. Still, part of him resisted me; the Subterranean in him was rebelling against the Witch.

"Maybe Devina is right," I said softly. He listened to me carefully. "What Sophìa gave me is a great gift."

If I took him it would satisfy that part of me that wanted to reconnect to the past. Claiming him would be enough to quench my thirst. Peter was a fascinating Subterranean. He had always loved the old Gemma and he would learn to love the new one too. Soon there would be an Opalion in my honor and I needed a Champion. I stroked his bulging biceps. He was strong and would be trustworthy and loyal. I moved my mouth to his ear and emanated my seductive power. My Dakor emerged, hissing with impatience, but Peter didn't even notice.

I bit my lip, causing a drop of blood to seep out. "At last I've found my Champion," I whispered. I moved my lips close to his and he was on the verge of touching them.

"Stop!" A voice thundered in the room, interrupting our tête-à-tête. I whirled around and my eyes locked onto Evan's, which were as sharp as ice. "I'll be your Champion," he told me in a determined voice.

In a split second I was in front of him. "You're lying." I studied his face and he made no objection, allowing me to explore his mind and comb through his thoughts.

"I have nothing left to lose," he said, his voice low and resolute.

Behind us, Peter stepped forward in protest, but I stilled him with my powers. My Dakor drew near Evan's face and he didn't move, his dauntless gaze locked on mine. There wasn't a trace of fear in his eyes. "A tempting offer," I admitted. Devina had chased that Subterranean for centuries and now he was offering himself to me—not as a prisoner but as my Champion.

"Don't miss your chance, then," he provoked me, his gaze proud and sharp.

"Normally we're the ones who hunt Subterraneans, but you're different from all the rest. You're stubborn. Why are you willing to die of your own volition?"

He looked down and took my hand. "Sometimes you have to die to be reborn."

I studied our joined palms and shook my head, banishing my doubts. "Fine. Then you'll die for me." I touched my finger to my lip, dabbed it in the blood, and raised it to his mouth. He accepted it, caressing it with his tongue, and an image exploded in my mind.

I never want to be separated from you again. Promise you won't leave me. Samvicaranam. Samyodhanam. *Stay together. Fight together.*

My heart belongs to you forever.

I jerked my hand back in shock as a shudder gripped me. I had been the one to say those last words. I looked him in the eye. What had happened? What had I seen? It was the two of us locked in a desperate embrace, as though it were my own memory.

No. It couldn't be—he was deceiving me, and I wasn't about to fall into his trap. I grabbed his chin and touched his lips with mine, absorbing his essence with my kiss of darkness.

"Evan, no!" Ginevra screamed, appearing in the room, but it was too late. My Dakor attacked, sinking his fangs into the neck of the Subterranean who stared at me, wracked with the first tremors. Through his mind I sensed the pain he was experiencing—but there was no fear.

He vanished, destination Hell. I clasped the Dreide I wore around my neck and studied it as it filled with a soft light.

I smiled. His soul was mine.

46

SWEET POISON

I materialized in one of the rooms we reserved for rebels—or, as we called them, Torture Caverns. Usually only Subterraneans who refused to bend to our will ended up in them. Those we claimed were set free in exchange for having surrendered their souls to us. Different accommodations, though, had been prepared for Evan. He would pay for that last little trick he'd attempted to play on me. Ginevra had read my mind just before I took him and had tried to stop him.

Evan appeared, his back to me. He looked around and instantly understood where he was. Spinning around, he stared at me boldly. "What's going on? Why am I here?" he asked, furious.

Smiling, I grabbed his shirt and tore it off him. "You won't be needing this." As I studied his body he didn't take his eyes off me. Two Drusas approached to discourage any attempt at rebellion.

"Seize him," I ordered, turning my back on him.

He struggled and broke free from my Sisters, grabbing me roughly by the wrist. "Gemma, wait!"

Two panthers landed beside him, growling threateningly. "Halt!" I ordered them. I tilted my head toward the Subterranean without turning around. "Let go," I hissed, my voice so icy he released his grip. "Lock him up. But first give him a shower."

"As you command," my Sisters replied, bowing to me.

"As you command?" Evan asked with surprise. "What does that mean?"

I smiled and turned toward him. "That I'm in charge here." The Subterranean's eyes went wide, his mind grappling with what I'd just said. My Sisters forced him to his knees and bound his hands behind his back with poisoned chains.

I turned my back on him and leapt up to one of the high windows. Giving him one last look, I found his gray eyes trained on me. I grunted with annoyance. Who did he think he was? He was a Subterranean like all the others. And now I had claimed him. If he thought he could make demands, I would put him in his place. Slipping out the window, I drew my knives and jammed them into the wall above me. Pulling myself up, I began to climb the Castle wall.

The air was cool in the gloom of the kingdom. I liked being high up—higher and higher. What I needed, after all those strange emotions, was my Saurus. When I reached the roof, I went into the stable to wake him and he welcomed me with an enthusiastic whinny while all the others bowed before me. I stroked Argas and he unfurled his mighty wings. Pulling myself onto his back, I spurred him to a gallop, his hooves echoing through the silent twilight.

"Away, Argas," I whispered in his mind. *"Carry me far away."* He took wing, sensing my need. I wanted to feel free, but I hadn't been able to for a while now. My mind was imprisoned by the past, by my doubts, by those eyes of ice. I lowered my eyelids and tilted my head back, letting the wind lash my face. I hoped it would wash away the thoughts tormenting me, but it was no use. The image I'd seen returned to fill my mind.

Promise you won't leave me.
My heart belongs to you forever.

What was that flashback? Could it actually be a memory?

Argas flew over the volcano and I ordered him to descend into it. I quieted the rage of the eruption, which diminished to a sputter on the surface. Nature bent to my every wish because I was its queen. My Saurus landed on a rocky outcrop and let me dismount. The scorching heat reddened my cheeks. The air was incandescent, but not even those temperatures could scathe my invincible body. Quite the opposite—a strong dose of boiling poison was what I needed. Maybe it would clear my mind. I unfastened my corset and took off my weapons, along with all my clothes, then sank down into the liquid, feeling its energy envelop me. The poison was just like me: lethally dangerous. Below the surface I felt the heartbeat of my Dakor, intoxicated by all that power. I slowly emerged, my eyes burning and glinting with purple tones, the eyes of my Dakor, who exulted inside me. I *was* a creature of Hell. I was Hell.

I swam inside the volcano, thinking of Evan. The flashback had occurred the moment his tongue had touched my thumb. The contact had triggered some sort of energy between us—or maybe it was something else.

What was it that had changed in me lately? My encounter with those two Souls by the river must have destabilized me. Through their minds I'd also seen images of Evan and me together. What could it mean? It had been a mistake to let them go. I had to find them and kill them. She would be easy prey since she was just another one of the Damned, but as for the other—Drake—he was a Subterranean and couldn't die. Still, I would find a way to silence him. Our dungeons always had room for rebels. That was where I would have Evan locked up. It had been a great victory. I couldn't wait to show Sophìa my trophy. I smiled. Devina wouldn't believe her eyes.

I should have ordered that Evan be brought to the spa, where the Champions entertained their Amìshas. Instead I had decided to grant him access only to the showers where the rebels were sent, despite the fact that he'd given himself to me and my Dreide now contained his deepest essence. Why couldn't I treat him like the others? Why did I still feel the need to fight him? I closed my eyes. He had clouded my mind, forcing me to remain vigilant. Yet now that I'd claimed him I could no longer hide my desire for him, my desire to carefully watch him subjugate himself to me.

I opened my eyes. The landscape around me had changed. I was no longer in the volcano. I looked around, confused. Hearing water crashing down furiously against rocks, I advanced and peeked around the wall. Evan was turned away from me, completely naked, his hands resting against the wall, muscles tensed, head bowed as the water ran down his golden skin in a sensual caress. My heart was pounding. How had I ended up there? And why was I experiencing those strange sensations? I felt vulnerable.

I approached him, obeying my desperate need to touch him, the burning desire to feel his hands on me . . . like sweet poison. He turned, the hair hanging over his forehead dripping wet, his gray eyes locked onto mine. He swallowed, at the mercy of his emotions, and gazed at my naked body. His thoughts lost themselves, drifting. I wafted my seductive power to him as I advanced beneath the stream of water. He seemed dazzled by me, but in a different way from the others. There was a glimmer of awareness in his eyes.

He ran his thumb over my wet lips and contemplated them for a moment, letting me read the desire in his mind. Then he kissed me—a sweet, sensual kiss that soon turned into a desperate need. Evan rounded on me and trapped me against the wall, our naked bodies touching as I surrendered to his kiss.

A whinny from Argas filled my mind, bringing me back. I looked around, disoriented. *I was still in the volcano.* What the hell had happened? Had I imagined it all? It hadn't been another flashback. It had been a vision of the present. It seemed so real I couldn't believe it had happened only in my mind. Still dripping wet, I went to Argas. Had all that poison made me hallucinate?

Dressed again, I leapt onto my Saurus's back, still shaken by the vision. Maybe I'd been wrong to claim the Subterranean who'd hunted me down so stubbornly. Maybe I really should have left him to Devina. But I couldn't resist. Challenges excited me, and he was different. He triggered sensations in me that made me fight yet also attracted me. Was that why my mind had so avidly sought him out?

I flew to the Castle and hurried to his cell, slamming the door behind me. He was sitting on the floor, his back against the wall and his chained hands resting on his knee. He raised his head and his gray eyes shone through the half-light, instantly finding mine. "Welcome back," he said sardonically.

I probed his thoughts. He was still unsettled by my role as commander and the reception he'd been given. Still, he wasn't giving up. I'd never met a more stubborn Subterranean. Nevertheless, sooner or later I would bend him to my will.

"Is this how you treat your Champion?" he asked with arrogant defiance.

I approached him and planted the heel of my boot between his legs. "You'll have to earn that title first." He slowly rose to his feet, brushing his body against mine, and looked into my eyes. The sparkle illuminating his own was maddening. Neither rebellious nor subdued, I could see he didn't want to bend. He wanted to bend me, but I would never let him. "Your mind is different from the others. It's not trustworthy enough. What most distinguishes a Champion is his loyalty to his Amìsha."

"You can trust me," he replied, "but I bet that's not your real problem. Maybe you're afraid you won't be able to trust yourself."

"Nonsense!" I replied irritably, looking away. "Don't think you're the only one to aspire to the position." I walked over to the Subterranean standing guard, staring at us through the bars of the cell. Upon my command, one of the bars disintegrated and he made his way toward me through the thousands of metal shards, utterly at the mercy of my power. "I've claimed many of you since I've been here. Any of them could become my Champion." I touched the Subterranean's muscular chest, staring steadily at Evan in a tacit challenge.

He looked furious, his thoughts a black cloud that threatened to unleash its power. His gray eyes were tempestuous. Smiling, I pulled the guard to me and brushed his ear with my lips. He reacted and grabbed me by the hips, yearning for my kiss, but a howl of rage filled the cell as Evan lunged at him and hurled him to the floor. He pinned me against the wall, his hands still bound and his gray eyes locked on mine. The Subterranean got up to face him, prepared to protect me, but I raised my hand and stopped him. He bowed before me as my gaze remained steadily on Evan's. I was more curious than ever about him. Perhaps the key to discovering the secret behind him was to go along with it. "At ease, Soldier. What makes you think you're so special?"

"Your body," he replied impertinently. "You're attracted to me."

"I'm attracted to all Subterraneans."

"No one attracts you more than I do—admit it," he dared me.

I locked my eyes on his, standing up to his insolence. "You have no effect on me," I lied, enunciating each word.

"You didn't seem so indifferent back there in the showers." I jumped in shock. What was he saying? It hadn't only been a vision in my mind? "You look surprised."

"Did you do that?"

"No, not at all. It was you who came to see me. I was in the shower. I was thinking of you and all of a sudden you were there. You let me kiss you," he added, pleased. "Then you disappeared and I found myself with my hands against the wall again, as though it had never happened. But I know it's not true."

"How do you know that?"

"Because you've done it before."

I turned my back on him, nervous. "You're lying."

"No I'm not, and you know it. Read my mind if you don't believe me."

"I don't trust your mind."

"Don't you trust your own? You experienced that moment in the shower with me too. It was our desire that broke through the confines separating us."

Nirvana. It liberates spirits from their bodies, leaving them free to follow their desires. Soul and mind in a world all their own.

"That's impossible," I murmured. "Only Sophìa has such great power." It was the same power she had imprisoned in the sphere. That Subterranean was capable of awakening it in me.

Evan walked up behind me and his mouth brushed my ear. "Our minds are bonded together."

I rubbed my cheek against his, overcome by the energy that quivered between us, but then shook my head. "There is no bond!" I snarled, furious.

He took my hand and held it up before our faces. "So how do you explain this?"

I stared at our two tattoos. He didn't take his eyes off me. There was no doubt they had the same calligraphy. But why? It made no sense. How could my life before Sophìa be connected to a Subterranean's?

"Give me a chance," he whispered.

"Why should I believe you?"

"Because I'm your husband."

"That's absurd."

"No it isn't. I bet your Sisters didn't bother to tell you that."

"Even if they had, I would never have believed such blasphemy. You're a Child of Eve."

The Subterranean ran his chained hands over my head and drew me to him tenderly, trapping me in his arms. "You haven't always been here. Before, you were with me," he whispered against my lips. *"Mamåtmå mari, yati tvayå saha."*

I frowned. *My spirit will die with you and rise again with you.* The words meant nothing to me but they seemed important to him. There was something I was missing. His lips teased mine hungrily. Maybe he was trying to cloud my mind. Devina had told me he was dangerous. And yet . . .

I rested my hands on his chest and pushed him against the wall, taking control. I instantly felt his erection against me and touched it through his pants as he bit my lip. As swiftly as a ghost, he grabbed my bottom and drew me to him, inverting our positions. His mouth moved avidly down my neck, his body pressed against mine, his hands inflaming me as they gripped me firmly by the buttocks.

My Dakor awoke, inebriated by Evan's presence, and his hiss snapped me out of my daze. I grabbed my dagger and shoved its blade against his throat, stopping him instantly. His eyes bored into mine, full of challenge. Part of me was irresistibly attracted to him. He'd given himself to me, surrendered his soul to me so I could claim it, yet I couldn't subjugate him.

That rebellious spark still lingered in his eyes of ice. "We're the ones who hunt you down," I hissed furiously. "We're the ones who toy with you. Not vice versa."

"This isn't a game," he insisted.

"It is for me." I broke through his chains and strode past him, still clutching my dagger, but before I could walk out the door a shadow in the corner caught my attention. Nothing was there, but the second I looked at it an image burst into my head.

Gromghus. Is that your name?

Who we are isn't important in here.

"Gemma, what's happening?"

I emerged from the vision and turned to look at Evan, who seemed worried. "Gromghus," I murmured to myself, to remember it. I felt the name was important, though I didn't know why. What had just happened? I'd seen a strange creature hiding its face under a long hood, and I'd been speaking to it.

"What did you say?" Evan asked, now looking shocked. Might he know the answer?

"Who is Gromghus? Stop putting images in my head!" I snapped.

"They aren't images. They're memories," he exclaimed in surprise, his eyes lighting up. "Simon's power is working!"

"What power? What have you done to me?!" I felt a fire building inside me, ready to explode. A wave of energy burst from me and struck Evan full in the chest, sending him crashing against the wall.

I stared at him as he hit the ground on his hands and knees. This Subterranean was poisoning me. Why did I keep seeking him out? I gripped my dagger. The whole thing had to end. It wasn't important any more whether they were lies or whether this Child of Eve really had been part of my past. Hell was my world now, and I was its queen. I went to him and leaned over him. He raised his head slightly, his dark hair falling over his forehead. "I'll send my maidservants to prepare you," I told him icily. "You'll soon have an excellent opportunity to demonstrate your loyalty. If you wish to become my Champion, you'll have to prove you're worthy."

My Dakor lunged and sank his fangs into Evan's flesh. He raised his eyes to look at me one last time, then collapsed onto his side. I stood up and walked to the door as he struggled to resist the poison and stay conscious. "Now rest, Soldier," I told him before closing the door. "The Games are about to begin."

EVAN

47

UNFORGIVABLE INSULT

A murmur brought me back to the light. "He's so cute!" What had happened? Had Gemma really recalled an old memory? Or had it just been a dream?

"Shh! Do you want to get yourself killed?"

"Freia's right. The mistress claimed him. You're not allowed to say such things."

"Well, if she claimed him, why is she treating him like a prisoner?"

"Be quiet! He's coming to!"

I struggled to emerge from the darkness. When I finally managed, the three young women smiled at me. "Welcome back," one of them said. The others laughed, putting away some herbs which they must have used to wake me—they were still smoldering and my nostrils were full of the sweet, spicy odor.

"Who are you? What do you want from me?"

"I'm Emayn," the liveliest of them said. "Her name's Meryall, and she's—"

"We're Mizhyas," the last one said, cutting her off. "We need to prepare you for the Opalion."

I'd heard her name as I was waking up: Freia. "Why? This isn't the first time I've taken part in the Games," I told them. When I'd been a prisoner before I'd participated in them many times, in what they called the Circle, but I'd never needed any preparation. They'd simply thrown me into the arena and I'd battled to defend myself for as long as my strength held out.

"This time it's different. You were chosen by our mistress, so you'll be battling as her Champion. She's Sophìa's Specter now, and today everyone will bow before her when they hear the news."

A pang of bitterness ran through me. It meant the devil in person had recognized the evil inside her. I sighed, thinking of the serpent's bite. I'd suffered the torture it inflicted on me and its poison had hurt even more than Devina's. "Where is she now?"

"That's none of your concern. She'll come to you when it's time."

I shook my head, trying to remember what was true and what I'd dreamed after losing consciousness. If Gemma was beginning to remember, maybe there really was hope. "Where are we?"

"In the gymnasia around the Circle. All the other Champions are preparing as we speak." I looked around. It was a well-lit room full of weapons and equipment. "Don't even think about it," Meryall warned me, thinking I wanted to make a break for it. "The panthers are already outside."

"I have no intention of escaping," I reassured her.

"Good, you're better off that way," Emayn continued. "I don't know why my mistress is keeping you prisoner after choosing you, but this is a big opportunity for you and you'd be wise to seize it. You're lucky. Our mistresses' Champions are the only ones who enjoy certain *privileges*, if you know what I mean." The maidservant winked as she spread salve on my arms. "On the other hand, if you rebel, you're done for."

"Thanks for the warning," I said, giving her a smile.

"Don't mention it. Here, eat these." Emayn offered me a bowl full of seeds. I looked at them dubiously. "They might not taste like Ambrosia, but you can't be fussy here. They'll give you strength."

I swallowed them as the other woman, Meryall, smiled sheepishly. "Our mistress's vital essence—that'll definitely boost your strength."

"Gemma's blood," I murmured, remembering all the times I had refused Devina's.

"You have to drink it if you want to fight as her Champion. She'll transmit her energy to you. If you win, she'll personally train with you. It's a great honor."

"How long has the Opalion existed?"

"As long as Hell itself," Emayn answered. "For fun, Sophìa also took it to Earth, though in a primitive version, without levels or enchanted scenarios—just battles and death. The mortals called the Games *Munera*, lethal battles among armed gladiators or even against animals, in which case they called them *Venationes*. The most famous of them were held at the Coliseum in Rome. I was there back then. I was a Mizhya to the Empress, along with Freia. You can't imagine the atrocities mortals are capable of under the influence of a Witch."

"That's enough talking," Freia said. "Leave him be." The whole time she'd been silent, busy with a mortar and pestle, engrossed in crushing black flowers to extract their poison, which she spread onto various weapons. Just touching them would have burned her flesh, and if she cut herself it would be the end of her.

"Don't worry," I reassured her. "It's not a problem."

"For you, maybe, but we know our place and we mustn't forget." Freia cast a glance at the other two maidservants who looked down before backing away.

"They'll come for you when it's time. Meanwhile, I advise you to warm up your muscles." She nodded at all the equipment. "In case we don't see each other again, good luck." The Mizhyas bowed and left the room, closing the massive wooden door behind them.

I sat on the cot and looked around. The room was huge, with weapons and equipment of all kinds. There was still a trace of venom in my body. My muscles were burning and I knew what to expect in the Opalion. It was best I took the Mizhya's advice and warmed up before the battles. I would have to fight bloodthirsty Souls captured during the Hunt, then a ferocious beast, and finally I would come up against one of their Champions. Whoever won would bring glory to his Amìsha and obtain her as a reward. The Witches claimed Subterraneans for their amusement, often sharing them with each other. The Champions, on the other hand, were the only ones to whom they gave themselves completely. And the only way to achieve that was to win the Opalion. But the Witches were lusty creatures, so the Opalion just happened to be held frequently. They were also capricious and competitive, which was why they held a Hunt before being able to satisfy their needs. One of them had to win it to become the Witch of Honor at the Opalion, which meant she became the "prize" and could lie with her Champion. Watching Subterraneans engage in mortal combat aroused them.

If the competitor made it through the first two trials, a Sister challenged the Witch of Honor with her own Champion. Sophìa was the one to choose the challenger. If the rival Champion won, the Witch of Honor lost her title, passing it to her Sister, who could then lie with her own Champion and obtain glory and the envy of the others. At the end of the match, true victory didn't belong to the Champion but to the Witch who'd outdone her Sisters.

The Witch of Honor could send in whomever she wished, and Devina had always chosen me—a prisoner—though I refused to drink her blood to fight as her Champion. I fought for myself. I'd beaten all my adversaries except the challenging Champion—not because I hadn't been capable, but because I preferred to be defeated rather than give Devina the satisfaction of seeing me win for her.

This time it was different. The Opalion was being held in Gemma's honor. She would be the prize and this time it meant only one thing to me: I had to win.

I jumped off the cot and tested my hand muscles, opening and closing them. There were metal bars suspended from the ceiling, positioned at different heights. I went over to one of them and jumped up to grab it before slowly pulling myself up. I could feel my back muscles tighten with every pull, but the more I warmed them up the more my strength returned as my blood rid itself of the last remainders of the poison. I hoisted myself up and stood on top of the bar. In front of me wound a path all through the room, rising and falling at different heights. With a leap, I grabbed the next bar and used my abdominals to swing myself over to the next. I continued upwards, climbing and spinning through the air. Grabbing hold of a bar with my legs, I dangled my upper body to work my abdominals in a long series of pull-ups.

"By Lilith, what a show."

I vaulted to the ground and grabbed a gladius from the wall, pointing it at Devina's throat. She didn't move, staring at me steadily with interest. "At ease, Spartan. The Games haven't begun yet. You'll have time to vent all your ardor."

"What do you want? Why are you here?" I snarled, still aiming the blade at her throat.

"What silly questions. I'm here to enjoy the show, like everyone else." She moved away from the weapon and circled me, moving her lips to my ear. "However, I was hoping to watch it from closer up." She stroked my chest as I stood still, muscles tensed.

"Gemma claimed me. You should know that," I reminded her, clenching my jaw.

"That doesn't mean she can't share you with me. We Sisters are very generous among ourselves. It's part of our blood bond. I myself have shared my Soldiers with her many times," she whispered in an attempt to provoke me.

I spun around and pushed her against the wall, pressing my forearm against her throat. Her serpent emerged to threaten me but I didn't move a muscle, continuing to look her in the eye. "Don't you dare say that again."

Devina smiled. "You're so sexy when you get rebellious."

"What's going on?" I turned toward Gemma, who'd just entered the room. The sight of her left me transfixed. She wore a tremendously sexy black gown worthy of a queen of darkness.

"I just stopped by to wish the new competitor good luck, but he turned out to be rather *hostile*," Devina told her with a malicious air. I pressed my arm harder against her throat.

"Let go of my Sister at once," Gemma commanded me. I glared at Devina and she flashed me a smile. "Step away, I told you. Immediately." I gave the Witch one last shove before loosening my grip and lowering my weapon. Gemma nodded at the gladius and it flew to her hand. "You don't need this yet. Devina, leave us, please."

"Wait," her Sister said. "I thought maybe you'd allow me to share the prisoner with you this time."

"He isn't a prisoner. He's my Champion."

"Not yet," her Sister reminded her. "He hasn't yet drunk your blood. He hasn't battled and won for you. He's not your Champion yet. You're his *Amìsha*, that's true—you claimed him—but he may be asked for by your Sisters as long as he's a Soldier like all the others. And this is my last chance, is it not?"

"I have no intention of going along with it," I warned Gemma. "She's a witch."

"We all are," Gemma replied icily, "and you may not disobey me."

"After all, you owe me," Devina insisted.

Gemma reflected. "You're right, dear Sister. It would be selfish of me not to share with you the Subterranean you hunted for centuries and I ultimately claimed."

"Gemma, what are you saying?" I protested in shock.

She raised her chin and looked me straight in the eye. "So be it," she declared.

Smiling, Devina grabbed me roughly and flung me to the other side of the room. Seconds later I found myself on a large round bed hidden behind broad curtains. The red silk sheets contrasted with the black carbonado background. It was adorned with plush cushions and draperies that hung from the ceiling. I stared at the two Witches as they approached.

"Do not disobey my command or I will not think your loyalty worthy," Gemma warned.

Devina dropped her long black cloak to the floor. She pulled out her faithful whip and rested her knee on the bed. I was petrified. I'd always rejected Devina and now Gemma was surrendering me to her. I looked her in the eye, hoping to find a trace of regret. "Is this really what you want?"

Gemma climbed onto the bed and moved toward Devina. "It's what we all want." She touched her Sister's lips with her own. "It is my gift to you, Sister," she whispered.

Devina smiled at her and came toward me, crawling sensually over my body. I never would have thought that one day she would make me her own, but she'd been very good at manipulating Gemma's trust, and now I was forced to give in to her dirty tricks.

The Witch brought her lips to mine and I indulged her, staring at Gemma, who didn't take her eyes off us. I rested my hands on Devina's hips and she brushed her whip across my chest. "I knew sooner or later this moment would come," she murmured against my mouth. Pointing her fingernail at my bicep, she traced the scar she'd left on me the last time I'd been in Hell. "I'm a very nasty Witch. Punish me."

I grabbed her wrists brusquely and inverted our positions, trapping her on the bed. If they wanted to play, I would do it my way. Devina squeezed my buttocks and pulled me against her, moaning with pleasure. She undid my pants and sank her nails into my sides, scratching my skin.

"Enough!" Gemma snapped, stopping her.

"What's the matter? Why don't you come and have fun with us?" Devina said, irritated.

My gaze locked onto Gemma's. "I've changed my mind," she said, still staring at me.

"You can't!" her Sister said, cracking her whip in the air. "You owe me."

"Evan, move aside," she insisted, enunciating each word. Hearing my name on her lips again hit me straight in the heart. I rolled over, freeing Devina from my grip. The Witch looked furious. "Now get out," Gemma ordered.

"You can't give me a gift and then take it back like this," her Sister retorted, her pride wounded.

"Yes I can. I'm the Specter now and you will obey me."

Devina got up from the bed and approached her Sister, defiance in her eyes. *"Nïak suh hamet."* I didn't speak the Witches' tongue, but her tone was definitely full of resentment.

"I'm telling you for the last time: get out of this room."

Devina bowed to her contemptuously. "*Kaahmì.*" That one word I knew well. I'd heard it often during my imprisonment. *As you command.* Without moving, Gemma held her gaze until she walked away. Before leaving the room, Devina turned to cast me one last glance and her lips mouthed the words *Goodbye, Soldier.* Then she leapt forward and turned into a panther, ready for the Opalion.

"Why did you do that?" I asked Gemma. She turned her back on me but I grabbed her wrist and made her look at me. "Why did you stop Devina?" I insisted.

Gemma looked away. "It was bad timing. The Games are about to start."

"You had another flashback," I murmured. "You remembered something else, didn't you?" I let go of her wrist.

"I've already told you I care nothing about the past." She moved away but I followed her and took her by the arm, forcing her to face me.

"But I care."

Gemma broke free from my grip and slammed me against the wall, furious. But I knew what was hiding behind her anger: fear. She was starting to remember snippets of us and couldn't explain what was happening to her.

I wasn't about to give up. I grabbed her and trapped her against the wall. "What did you see?" I insisted, holding her tight.

"It's your fault. What have you done to me?!" she snarled. "You've polluted my mind. Rid me of your poison!"

"*I'm* your poison, and you're mine. There's no antidote for us. There's nothing we can do," I whispered against her lips and kissed her passionately. She struggled but I could feel her resistance waver and held her hands against the wall. She was aroused and I risked losing my head right there. Outside, an entire arena was waiting to watch me do battle. In there, I could have died of love just for her.

"You're a Subterranean. It's normal for you to be in love with me," she said, reading my mind.

I cupped her cheek in my hand and stroked her lip with my thumb. She couldn't hold back and brushed her tongue against it. "And you're a Witch, so why do I set fire to your venom?"

"I feel nothing for you."

I kissed her neck and her breath came faster. "Liar."

She grabbed my arms and a second later I was on the bed, Gemma straddling me. "All I want," she purred, her voice sensual, "is for you to be my Champion."

"I'm ready to become your Champion."

"Receive my blood inside you," she whispered, looking me in the eye. She bit her lip and leaned over me. I could hear her heart beating quickly, our breathing becoming one. "*Taste me,*" she whispered. I licked the blood from her lips, losing my mind, then closed my eyes, pervaded by a powerful feeling of ecstasy. She smiled and sank her nails into my shoulders as I kissed her again, hungry for her vital essence, a venom so powerful it broke through all my defenses.

"Easy, Champion, or you'll pass out."

"You have no idea how long I've waited for this moment. How long I've waited to touch you again, to feel your lips on mine . . ."

"Fight for me. If you win the Games, you'll have what you want for an entire night."

"I'm not willing to wait," I said, determined. I slipped her daggers off from behind her back and tossed them onto the floor. She allowed me to take off her crossbow while looking me in the eye, probing inside me to discover my intentions. I pulled her against me and rolled over, pinning her to the bed. I nibbled her neck, her shoulder, descending toward her breast.

"Stop," she whispered, at the mercy of her emotions.

"No."

"I command you."

"Your voice lies. It's your body I'm listening to. Your lips." I kissed her and she let herself be drawn in. "Your eyes." I stroked her lashes with my thumb, gazing at her intently. I leaned over her ear and touched it with my mouth. "*Your breath.*" My hand slid over her breast and she looked at me, helpless. "Your pulse. Listen to how your heart is racing."

"You have no effect on me," she replied defiantly, rebelling against the sensations she was experiencing, but I knew her well—I knew everything about her.

"You keep lying." I lowered myself onto her and brushed my nose against her cheek, sliding my hand up her thigh. "Make love with me," I whispered against her lips.

"No. It's forbidden."

"If you remembered, you would know I've never cared about the rules. Your blood flows within me. I am your Champion."

"You have to win for me before you can have me."

"I'm going to win for you. I'll kill them all just so I can touch you again." I kissed her on the neck and she closed her eyes, excited by my promise. Clasping her buttocks, I held her tight against me so she could feel how much I desired her. "But first tell me why." She looked me in the eye, weighing the answer to the question she'd already read in my mind. "Why did you stop Devina? It was a serious insult, but you did it anyway. *Say it.*"

"Because you're mine," she hissed, staring at me intensely, leaving me on the edge of insanity.

"You're wrong." I spread her legs roughly and pulled her even closer. My fingers clutched her undergarment and tore it off. "It's you who are mine." I entered her and kept her tightly pressed against me as she cried out. I rested my cheek on her chest, on the brink of exploding from the emotions rushing through me. Gemma clung to the cushions, her muscles clenched to hold me close. Her nails scratched my back as I moved inside her. All my frustration faded, swept away by the passion only she could nourish. I held her hands over her head and kissed her with desperation.

Unwilling to be tamed, she was on top of me in a flash. For a moment I was afraid she was going to make me stop, but then she gazed into my eyes and removed her bodice, freeing her supple breasts. My hands slowly moved up her sides to stroke her nipples and she moaned, moving slowly on top of me. I was breathless. I'd spent months chasing her, longing for her. And now she wanted me. I was inside her and didn't want to let her go ever again. I propped myself up to be closer to her and caressed her back through her long hair.

"You're a madman," she murmured, her arousal growing. "I should kill you for this affront."

"You won't," I assured her. "You'll come to visit me every night, against all the rules." I ran my thumb over her lip and she took it into her mouth. "Because you're like me: we aren't made for rules."

"Why are you doing this to me?" she gasped, crying out with pleasure. "You've taken my body. Let my mind be free."

"I am in you as you are in me," I told her in Sanskrit. "In my heart. In your soul. I'm not giving up until you remember." I began kissing her again passionately and she scratched my chest, her poisoned nails leaving marks. I groaned, caught between pain and pleasure. "Were you with others before me?" I asked, the blood boiling in my veins at the thought.

"No one," she replied, a helpless victim of the power that ruled us both.

"Devina's Soldiers?" I insisted. "Tell me and I'll kill every last one of them."

"You're my Champion. No one else."

"Gem," I moaned.

She squeezed her legs around my waist and arched her back, reaching the climax of her pleasure. I rested a hand on her nape and ran my lips down her neck. "I missed you so much," I whispered, brushing my cheek against her skin as our intertwined bodies trembled from having found each other again. "It's amazing to hear your voice again. Keep talking to me. I've waited an eternity. I thought I would die without you."

She was silent, letting my words wander inside her. For a moment I deluded myself that I'd finally found her. Her fingers stroked the tattoo on my thumb, so similar to hers, then rose up my arm and traced the deep scar that ran from my bicep to my shoulder. When she lowered her eyes to the one on my chest, her brow furrowed. "You've already been our prisoner," she said softly, guessing it for the first time.

"I'm not your prisoner," I stated, drawing her against me to kiss her. But she moved away and stood up, her back to me. I admired her naked body, her long hair flowing down her back, her toned muscles and golden skin. She was a goddess. "I'm here only for you, to remind you of what we had . . . to take you back."

A maidservant burst into the room. "Everything is ready, my lady." It was Meryall. She went to Gemma and helped her dress, stealing glances at my naked body.

"Inform the Empress that she may announce me." Her command called the young woman to attention and she immediately looked down, embarrassed. "Today a new Champion battles in the Opalion."

"Yes, my lady." The maidservant bowed and left the room.

"Forget the past, Soldier," Gemma said, sheathing her weapons behind her back.

"No!" I got up from the bed and approached her from behind, taking her by the arms.

"We're here in the present and you will battle as my Champion. My blood flows inside you. What more could you possibly want?" she said without turning around.

"Your body isn't enough. I want your mind. Your heart belongs to me and sooner or later you'll realize that for yourself," I promised. I wasn't willing to give up now that I was so close.

Gemma moved away, stopping at the door. "My heart belongs to Sophìa. You will never have it. And you'd better fight well or you won't have anything else either. Go and kill them all, my Gladiator. Be my Champion or die for me. Good luck. *Gahl sum keht.*" She looked me in the eye one last time and left the room, leaving me alone.

I knew those words in Kahatmunì, the Witches' tongue. They meant "Forge your glory." I couldn't believe that after making such passionate love to me her coldness had returned so quickly. If her expression had been a blade, it would have pierced my heart.

I laced up my brown leather pants and sat on the bed, disheartened. In those moments when I'd been inside her, I'd deluded myself that everything had returned to what it was before, that she was mine again. I rested my elbows on my knees and covered my face with my hands, frustrated. I couldn't give up. Not now, of all times. I would win the Opalion for her—with her blood in my body nothing could stop me. During battle she would ignite it, making it burn in my veins, giving me supernatural strength. I would slaughter them all just to be with Gemma again, because the thought of not being able to have her again was killing me.

"Evan."

My head shot up as a hooded figure stepped before me. I recognized the voice instantly, there was no doubt about it. "Ginevra. What are you doing here?" I gasped, approaching her.

She pushed her hood back, revealing her face. "You're in danger, Evan."

I looked around, on my guard, and tried to touch her but found myself grabbing only air. She was an illusion. "What's going on? Why are you here?"

"There's no time for questions. Listen carefully. Simon's power is working. It took root inside Gemma and continues to unearth her memories. Sophìa knows it and you've become a threat to her. She's afraid of losing Gemma because of you. That's why she called for an Opalion in Gemma's honor and is letting you fight for her—she wants to get rid of you. Anya warned us just in time."

"I'm going to fight," I growled fiercely. Nothing was going to keep me away from Gemma.

"No. We won't let you. Sophìa gave the order to kill you, Evan. You're going to die in the arena today."

"Does Gemma know?" That possibility alone was enough to kill me.

"No, of course not. She chose you as her Champion—she would never accept it. But if you die in battle she won't be able to object."

I clenched my fists. If Sophìa felt I was such a threat, that meant I had an actual shot at getting Gemma back. "I can't give up now, of all times. She's starting to remember!" I insisted.

"That's not enough for her to cast off evil. She needs to remember everything before she can find herself. I've been through it."

"I need more time."

"You don't have any! And neither do I. We need to act fast, before they discover I'm here."

"Here where?" I asked, voicing a terrible suspicion.

"In Hell, Evan. I'm already here, with Simon, Drake, and Stella."

I knit my brows in shock. "Are you out of your mind? What does Simon have to say about this? I can't believe he approved something so insane."

"It was his idea and I backed him up."

"You were both banished. Sophìa put a death sentence on you."

"We're prepared to fight—for you and for our lives."

"It's too risky. You have to get out of here!"

"It's too late. We're not going to let them kill you. We're going to attack the Castle."

"No! I can do this. Don't risk your lives for me. I can't allow it!"

"It's already been decided. We've gathered an army under my command, and there's an entire militia of rebels inside the Castle who will help us. We're getting you out of here."

"I'm not going anywhere without Gemma."

"You won't be any good to her if you're dead!"

"I don't want to put you in danger. It was my decision to come here. I'm going to see it through. I'm fighting."

"You can't. They'll kill you!"

"I'll die if I have to. I'm not leaving here without Gemma."

"We'll take Gemma with us," Ginevra said.

"How?"

"We'll take her, I promise you. Trust me, Evan. Trust all of us. There's only one way to save your life: by forcing Sophìa to let you go."

"How can anyone force the devil to do something?"

"By declaring war." Ginevra stared at me, in her eyes pure determination.

"You know what a war would mean, don't you? Your Sisters would be in danger. Are you willing to run that risk despite the Bond?"

"My bond is with you now. My Sisters gave me destruction and death—the death of those I loved, of those I didn't know, the death of my soul. You gave me back myself. You're my family now. Besides, don't think it's so easy to face them in battle. They know how to defend themselves from your angel fire, though for them it's as lethal as the death of their serpents."

I nodded. It must have pained her greatly to say it. "Kill a Witch's Dakor and the Witch dies with it."

"I hope it won't come to that," she murmured, distraught. I could see that the idea of joining forces against her Sisters caused one part of her tremendous pain—but the other part had chosen Gemma and me. She looked at me. "What about you? Are you ready to battle the Witches?"

"I've been training with one of them for centuries," I replied with a laugh, feeling not a shadow of fear. "What's the plan?"

"We're attack—"

The doors swung open all at once and I spun around. Ginevra vanished an instant before four Soldiers burst into the room to escort me out. The horn blew, announcing the beginning of the Games. The Subterraneans gathered my weapons and walked me to the threshold. For a moment there was silence, then the doors were opened. I strode out and everyone in the stands cheered when they saw me.

The courtyard had been transformed into an amphitheater. I made my way to the center of it and looked around. All of Hell seemed to have flocked to the event. The stands were packed with the Damned—brave Souls who were risking death just to experience the thrill of witnessing the Games. The Opalion was the only occasion for which Sophìa opened the Castle gates, and for this one she must have spread the word far and wide throughout the kingdom. I scanned the crowds, searching for my friends among the hooded faces. Ginevra hadn't had time to explain their plan, but her promise was enough for me: *We'll take Gemma with us.* Until then, there was only one thing for me to do.

Fight.

The Witches were already in position—nine black panthers in a circle, staring at me. Devina's amber eyes flashed at me. I would have recognized them in whatever form she took. Even now they had a defiant gleam and suddenly I remembered what she had said as she took her leave: *Goodbye, Soldier.* So she'd known about Sophìa's plan—she must have.

"Silence!" thundered a commanding voice. The entire arena fell silent. I turned and saw her. Sophìa was standing on a dais reserved for the Witches. Beside her was Gemma. They both wore bizarre steampunk outfits with dark yet sexy tones and, on their faces, black markings that looked like tattoos.

Sophìa and the Witch of Honor were the only ones who would preside over the Games in their human form until they were joined by the Sister who would offer up her Champion for the duel. The others had the task of guarding the edge of the Circle in their animal form, prepared to tear to shreds any of the Damned or Subterraneans who dared set foot outside of it.

"My dear lost Souls," the Empress began. "I am pleased you have come in such great numbers, as today is an important day—not only for the Sisterhood but for all of you. What better occasion than an Opalion to give you such happy news? It is with immense pride that I announce to you that the kingdom has a new commander: our Sister Naiad." Gemma rose to her feet and the crowd cheered for her. "Honor her as you have done with those who came before her over the centuries. Obey her commands and be willing to die for her."

The snarl of a panther filled the arena—Devina opposing the affront—but the other panthers instantly drowned her out, rejoicing for Gemma and her new appointment.

"This Opalion is for Naiad and it will determine the valor of her new Champion. He will undergo grueling trials and challenges. If he is valiant enough a worthy opponent will be chosen to face him in a duel. Only one will be declared the victor, rendering honor and glory unto his Amìsha. May the show begin! Good luck, Champion. Forge your glory."

Sophìa sat down and I prepared to fight.

48

THE OPALION

I stood at attention, muscles rippling, as I awaited the first challenge. A swarm of black butterflies flew in my direction. I watched them as they circled me and immediately flew away. Each transformed into a threatening-looking Soul. In a flash I was surrounded. The spectators held their breath until the first one came forward. He was a tall, dangerous-looking man wearing seventeenth-century clothing. He'd been the first to make a move, but that didn't make him any braver than the rest—it just made him my first victim. I smiled, my eyes trained on him in an ominous invitation. The man leapt toward me and attacked with a dagger he whipped out at the last second. I dodged it though he dealt me a glancing blow. I grabbed the Soul by the arm and head-butted him. Black liquid gushed from his forehead and he fell to the ground, dazed. He tried to get to his feet, reaching for the dagger he'd dropped, but I crushed his hand beneath my foot. Tearing away from him a piece of sharpened wood he'd kept hidden behind his back, I swiftly slashed his throat.

The crowd remained silent for a moment, stunned by how quickly I'd killed him, and then burst into enthusiastic cheers and shouts. The decapitated body fell to the ground and exploded in a cloud of smoke. I raised my eyes to the other Damned, daring them to make their move. One of them let out a cry of fear and fled toward the edge of the Circle, but a panther chased him and tore him to pieces. Seconds later all that was left of him was ash.

Two of the Damned advanced together. They must have been brothers, because they resembled each other greatly. They too were armed. With my foot I flicked my first opponent's dagger into the air and caught it. I flipped the weapon in my hand, waiting for the brothers' move. They looked bloodthirsty, and with good reason: their survival was at stake. But I had an even stronger motivation: I was fighting for Gemma.

One of them gave a war cry and launched his attack, but I wasn't about to be intimidated. I waited until he was close and grabbed him, using his own momentum to flip him and send him crashing into his brother. They got up and attacked together. I blocked a punch from the smaller one and used his arm for leverage as I jumped up and delivered a double kick to the larger one, who ended sprawled on the ground. But my grip was too brutal; the smaller one's arm snapped and he fell to his knees, screaming in pain. I seized my chance and drove the dagger into his throat.

"Sorry," I told his brother. "Didn't want to make him suffer."

He glared at me with hatred and launched another attack. Just then the smaller one turned to dust and I snatched up the dagger as the second Soul rushed at me, sinking the sharp blade into his neck. He gurgled, black blood gushed from his mouth, and he too was reduced to ashes.

Overjoyed, the spectators went wild, but I was just warming up. I raised my eyes to the Panthior, the platform of honor, and Gemma gave me a pleased look. *"I'm going to win for you,"* I told her in my mind, and she smiled at me, her Witch eyes glittering craftily.

At her side, Sophìa stared at me with fire in her eyes. At the tournaments she acted as Stage Director, transforming the playing field and increasing the difficulty of the trials. When she made her move, I wouldn't be unprepared. She flung out her hand in a challenging gesture and heavy bars sprang from the ground and bent around me, sealing me inside a small cage together with my new adversaries: the most ferocious Souls selected during the Hunt. Against some other Subterranean they might have had a chance, but not against me. I was the most ruthless of them all. In that arena, I was the lion.

Some of them climbed onto the ceiling of the cage and crawled over my head while others crept up behind me. I studied their movements. All my opponents were armed and I was surrounded. My only defense was to attack. I charged at one of them, dropped to my knees, and slid across the ground. Wresting the sword away from him, I struck a brutal blow, chopping two adversaries in half. Black blood spurted from their bodies. As I was getting up I threw a right hook at another one and took his sword. I spun around and two heads tumbled to the ground. With Gemma's blood in my body I felt invincible. A Soul swooped down onto me from the ceiling of the cage but I shot backwards and slammed him against the bars. The blow left him dazed and he let go, but two more dropped down and held my arms as a third came and bludgeoned me in the face. Blood filled my mouth. I slowly turned my head until my eyes met his. The ferociousness on my face was enough to leave him unsteady on his feet. I spat out the blood and freed myself with a backflip as the third Soul fled—but he wasn't going to escape me. I chased him down and slit his throat.

Only two were left. I looked from one to the other. It was clear from their faces that they were wondering which of them would be next, but I was tired of playing. Spinning both swords in my hands, I threw them at the same time, pinning both Souls to the bars. Like two filthy, impaled vampires they disintegrated, returning to ashes.

The crowd cheered for my victory. I'd exterminated them all. I looked around, still trapped behind the bars of the cage, and a black butterfly fluttered up to me. I watched it as it landed on the ground nearby. Before it could transform I picked up a dagger and stabbed it. The creature wriggled and flapped its wings. I raised my eyes to Sophìa and twisted the blade in my prey. The last of the Damned.

49

MORTAL CHALLENGE

The bars withdrew, signaling the end of the first challenge. The spectators were delirious and couldn't wait to see me face my next trial: a battle against a beast. After a momentary pause, flames rose up all around me and the ground began to shake. I picked up a javelin, squeezing my fingers around its grip.

A blood-chilling grunt announced its arrival behind me. I spun around and saw it. Instinctively, I tried to back up but the flames blocked me. The crowd had fallen silent, holding their breath. The beast was huge. It looked like a giant buffalo with leathery skin and massive horns on its head. Even worse, it was staring at me as though it hadn't eaten in months and I was its next meal. "Sit, boy, sit . . ." I said in a low voice. Enraged, the beast grunted and charged. I hurled the javelin, but it parried the blow with a head butt and continued its advance.

I dodged it in the nick of time and ended up sprawled on the ground. "Oh, sorry, are you a she? Didn't mean to offend you!" Maybe it wasn't the best time to crack a joke, but a fire was burning inside me that was hotter than the flames surrounding us. Gemma's poison was instilling confidence and strength in me.

When the creature charged again I ran toward the fire and at the last second did a backflip out of its path while the beast continued through the wall of flames. Seconds later it returned, moving slowly toward me through the incandescent tongues of fire that hadn't harmed it in the least.

As though offended by the affront, the circle of fire broke up and dozens of flames began to dance across the battlefield like whips that lashed to and fro, making my every movement perilous. However, the fire was a problem only for me. The animal didn't fear it and was ready to attack once more. I looked at Sophia and she smirked. Was this how she planned to kill me? I would never give her the satisfaction of dying right before Gemma's eyes. I focused on the beast and prepared myself for its next charge, which came soon. When it was close enough I grabbed hold of its horns and tried to leap onto its back, but the animal shook its head fiercely, making the endeavor impossible. In the end it won out and flung me away.

I rolled away from the flames and crumpled to the ground, surprised by a shooting pain. Touching my side, I stared at my fingers. They were bloody. The beast had gored me. I gritted my teeth, the dirt making the gash burn.

The ferocious creature snorted, stamped its hooves, and launched another attack, forcing me to spring to my feet before it could crush me. I staggered to where the dagger lay on the ground and picked it up. At the first opportunity I drove it into the beast's chest. "Now we're even."

The animal reared up, letting out a strange wail of pain. I seized my chance and climbed onto its back. It tried to throw me to the ground again but this time my grip was firm. I drew my dagger and plunged it into its skull. The beast's eyes went wide and it froze, then crashed to the ground like a huge boulder, sending up a massive cloud of dust that covered everything. I pulled myself to my feet and waited for it to settle, my hand firm on the bloody dagger and my eyes locked on Sophìa's. I was ready for the next challenge.

Gemma rose, gazing into my eyes with pride. The panthers roared in their circle. In the stands, the spectators were ecstatic—not because I had bravely triumphed in the first two trials, but because the most difficult one awaited me: the duel against another Champion.

All around the arena, the massive doors to the gymnasia opened and a band of Subterraneans emerged. They were all barefoot and bare-chested, clad in brown leather pants like mine, muscles tensed and prepared to do battle. Each panther came onto the field and positioned herself beside her Champion, all anxious for the Empress to choose my challenger. She rose and stood beside Gemma, offering me a contemptuous smile. For a second everything fell silent in expectation of her verdict.

"You have battled valiantly," she admitted, her gaze as sharp as a blade. "I must choose your opponent carefully. Naiad is my Specter now, and our new commander's Champion must prove that his valor goes beyond that of all others. Only a Soldier worthy of her may be by her side. That is why you are to fight Zakharìa, *my* Champion." A gasp escaped the crowd and Sophìa smiled.

Another door opened—the largest one—admitting the last of the Subterraneans to the arena. The panthers roared angrily while all the spectators' eyes turned to him. He was a tall, powerful man with dark skin and gray eyes as sharp as ice that challenged me. He strode to the center of the arena and knelt before his queen. I glanced at Gemma: her expression was concerned but she didn't protest the choice.

This was what Ginevra had been trying to warn me about: Sophìa's Champion wasn't just dangerous—his blood was lethal. Since time immemorial he'd been nurtured on his Amìsha's vital essence and, like her, he could send a Subterranean to his eternal death in Oblivion. That was why the Empress had decided to send him out: to kill me.

"What is it? You look concerned. Do you wish to ask me to withdraw you, perhaps?" the devil provoked me, her tone mocking.

I trained my eyes on her fearlessly. "I'm ready to fight." Gemma nodded, her eyes gleaming with pride.

"Your courage is admirable, I must admit. It will be a true pity for Naiad to have to give you up."

My eyes locked with Gemma's for a long moment, and then a group of guards marched onto the field and escorted me out of the arena.

50

TO THE DEATH

Ginevra's last words filled my mind. That was what she'd been about to tell me: I would be up against Sophìa's Champion. The Empress had planned this from the start. I'd gone through the first two trials wondering how she intended to get rid of me, and now I knew—by pitting me against Zakharìa in the most difficult challenge of all: the duel.

Soldiers escorted me back to the gymnasium, where Gemma's Mizhyas awaited me to dress my wounds. I scanned the crowd in search of my friends, but there was no sign of them. I tried to concentrate on the battle ahead. I couldn't lose focus. A million reasons could have prevented Ginevra from reaching the Castle with her army. It was almost insane to think they might come to our rescue. I could count only on myself. The doors closed behind me and the three maidservants greeted me and had me sit down. They examined the gash in my side and prepared an ointment, then stanched the bleeding on my cheeks and shoulders and oiled my muscles. I let them do it, my mind fixed on Zakharìa's gaze and its promise of death. I clenched my fists. I couldn't let him kill me with Gemma watching. I had to fight and defend myself. It was my only chance of being with her again. I had to become her Champion. I tried to free my mind, but her blood was a powerful poison that obscured every other thought except those connected to her.

I raised my head when the doors opened and Gemma entered the room. "Leave us," she ordered without taking her eyes off me. The Mizhyas made a little bow and left. I strode to her and pressed my lips against hers. She kissed me back, taken by surprise. I closed my eyes and rested my forehead against hers, forgetting everything around me—the bloodthirsty arena, the duel I was about to face. I could do it all if I had her.

"You fought bravely," Gemma said in a low, sensual voice. "I knew you would be a fine Champion." She turned her back to me and walked away, her skirt's long train leaving her sides bare. "However, you're quite presumptuous in your ideas about your prize. You must first win the tournament for me if you wish to be rewarded."

I went up behind her and was about to grasp her shoulders to turn her around, but stopped with my hands suspended in midair, limiting myself to touching her arms. She didn't move. "You can't ask me to stay away from you," I whispered into her hair, closing my eyes.

She turned and stroked the cut on my face. "Win for me," she said, probing my soul.

Everything was about to be decided out there in that arena. Our fate would change forever if I lost. All we'd fought for was at stake. Gemma didn't know my opponent was planning to kill me. I might die, but I was prepared to do so for her.

"*Kaahmì*," I replied. *As you wish.*

An irresistible smile appeared on her lips. I stroked them with my thumb and she moved them close to mine, igniting my desire. Drawing her against me tenderly, I demanded another kiss. My tongue touched hers and I no longer knew who I was. Gemma bit her lip and I sucked it, hungry for more of her vital essence. All I needed was one drop . . . She gave it to me, making my head spin and my body turn to flames, burning with desire.

Gemma rested her hands on my chest and her fingers traced the scars for a moment. Then she pulled her lips from mine, leaving me breathless. She looked at me and her voice enveloped me: "I wanted to give you another taste. Do not disappoint me."

She turned her back on me and walked out, leaving me in a daze. I tried to control my breathing as the blood burned inside me, igniting all my senses, but there wasn't time. The doors opened again and guards burst into the room. To my surprise I recognized one of them. It was Faustian. What was he doing there?

As he passed he bumped my shoulder and slipped something into my hand. I closed my fist, looked away and straightened up. The doors reopened and the spectators cheered in anticipation. Keeping my arm at my side, I opened my palm a crack to see what Faustian had given me. My eyes bulged. It was Absolon's ring—the Devil's Claw. I stared at Zakharìa at the opposite end of the arena and smiled. Now it was a fair fight.

The Empress rose to announce the beginning of the challenge but I didn't take my eyes off him. "Fight, my Gladiators, and may the more valiant of you win. Forge your glory!"

The guards escorted us to the center of the Circle and I found myself face to face with my adversary. I'd never seen the Empress's Champion take part in the Games; it was certainly a rare occurrence. The panthers were already in their positions, tensely prowling back and forth, patrolling their assigned areas. I glanced at Anya and touched the ring I'd hidden in my pocket. She nodded slightly. The duel was the final challenge, and only one of us would come out of it victorious.

I looked Zakharìa straight in the eye as the crowd held its breath. "It honors me to know that Sophìa had to inconvenience her Champion in order to defeat me." He stared at me in silence. We were both on guard, a gladius gripped in our fists, as the first round required. "What a shame," I continued. "I was hoping we could get acquainted before I hacked you to bits."

My opponent gritted his teeth and charged, knocking me on the shoulder so hard I fell right next to the edge of the Circle. The stands exulted while, with a ferocious roar, a panther bared its poisoned fangs and raised its paw toward me. If it wounded me I would lose consciousness and Sophìa would win the tournament. I would, however, remain alive. Only the Empress's venom could send a Subterranean to oblivion, and Zakharìa's body was full of it.

I stood up and faced him again. "I get it, you don't care for introductions," I said with a challenging smile. "Shyness is a terrible thing, you know? Your mistress should let you get out more often."

The mention of Sophìa made him react. He charged again, but this time I was more prepared and dodged his attack. I leapt onto him from behind, toppling him backwards, and dragged him toward the Witches. The crowd gave a start of surprise.

I turned to stare at Sophìa on her platform. She had a victorious expression on her face, but I was going to wipe it off. All the spectators and even the Witches thought the Opalion's final battle was being waged. She and I knew the truth: there was much more at stake. The real prize was Gemma, and Sophìa and I were the ones fighting for it.

Zakharìa got to his feet and I shifted my attention back to him. Every shred of humor in me had vanished. I had to defeat him before he defeated me. This time I was the first to attack. He took the blow and counterattacked. He was the most skilled opponent I'd ever fought, but I knew how to defend myself. The second I shoved him to the ground the horn signaled the end of the first round.

I continued to hold him down until the Soldiers pulled me off him. They handed us two long metal-tipped staffs as the ground shook beneath our feet. The pavement crumbled and a gaping chasm opened up all around us. We found ourselves on a pillar of earth with smaller ones nearby. Around those, empty space. The horn blew once more, marking the start of the second round of the duel.

All my senses alert, I searched my opponent for a weak spot and launched my attack. I was good with a staff—I'd trained long and hard using them with my brothers—but my opponent was the Empress's worthy Champion and skilled at expert maneuvers. I leapt onto a nearby column and he followed suit, jumping onto the one beside it. Our staffs collided, their pointed tips threatening first me, then him. My muscles strained from the effort, but Gemma's blood was an inexhaustible source of energy. A mere glance at her set it on fire, making me fight with new vigor.

He dodged my lunge and began to run, jumping from one pillar to the next. I chased him until he reached the edge, one step away from the panthers. Turning just in time to see me leap onto his column with my weapon pointed at him, he parried my blow but lost his balance and fell. I pounced on him and we rolled across the ground until he managed to overpower me, pinning me down and pressing the shaft of his staff against my throat. I tried to shove him away but he was too strong. Zakharìa pushed me forward and I found myself with my head dangling over the void. The crowd cheered for the Empress's Champion. I looked him in the eyes, which for the first time sparkled with the anticipation of victory. I couldn't accept it. Driven by desperation, I struck him with all my might and swiftly broke loose. He spun around but then froze, disconcerted—another sharp point was now pressed against his throat: the Devil's Claw. Just then the horn blew, decreeing the end of the round. I hadn't defeated him, but at least now he too knew it was a fair fight.

I turned to Sophìa with a defiant glare as the abyss sealed up. She'd risen in alarm. Still, there was nothing she could do to stop me. I picked up the sword that had appeared on the ground, my eyes locked onto Zakharìa's. "You are shrewd," he said, speaking for the first time. "Now I see why the Empress feels you are a threat."

"You'd better focus on your own problems, because I intend to give you lots of them," I shot back, attempting a lunge. He parried, giving rise to the most ferocious of duels.

A layer of water formed beneath our feet, soon turning to muck. There was no rule limiting the number of rounds—they could be infinite, as could the scenarios Sophìa conjured up for the duels. They would continue until one of the two contenders was defeated. However, now that I'd revealed my secret weapon to Zakharìa, he and I knew this round would be the last one. It was either him or me.

Our swords sang with each increasingly brutal blow. "You're good with a sword, I'll give you that," I told him as he warded off my attack by thrusting his sword against mine. The force was so great it sent me staggering back into the mud, dangerously close to the edge. A panther snarled, prepared to pounce. Seizing his chance, Zakharìa disarmed me and kicked me hard, sending me to my knees.

The spectators burst out in a deafening roar. They too realized the end was near. I raised my eyes and through my mud-splattered hair watched the Damned going into raptures. "What, no one's rooting for me?" I joked before turning back to look at my opponent.

He ran his sharp blade across his chest, making a long incision, and then pointed it—now edged with his poisoned blood—at my throat. A hush fell over the crowd as I stared him straight in the eye. I looked at Gemma, who had risen from her seat to witness my execution.

In the silence, a single voice rose. "*I'm* rooting for you."

Drake. I whipped my head up as a panther pounced on Zakharìa, tearing him off of me. In seconds, Ginevra's army swarmed into the arena, attacking everyone and everything. I raised my eyes to Sophìa, whose expression was one of utter shock, and this time I was the one to smile at her.

The Games were over. The war had begun.

51

THE WHISPER OF DEATH

The panthers rushed to attack, ripping a group of the rebel Damned to shreds. In seconds the arena had turned into a battlefield on which chaos had exploded. Drake ran toward me but darted to the side at the last second to knock down one of the Witches' Soldiers. He reached me as a new group surrounded us.

"You took your sweet time," I joked, leaning my back against his.

"You know Ginevra. It takes her ages to get ready," he said. Together we attacked. "I have to admit"—he did a backflip, landed behind an enemy, and slashed his throat—"you put on a good show."

"I was practically phoning it in." I parried a lunge and rammed the Claw into my adversary's throat, then spun around and did the same with a Subterranean who was closing in on Drake. Both the Soul and the Subterranean exploded in a cloud of ash. Drake and I gave each other a bear hug. "I missed you, bro," I said.

"Sorry you had to come all the way back here to hang out with me again." He grinned. "Anyway, I missed your ugly mug too."

"We'd better save the sweet nothings for when we're out of here." I ducked to avoid the arm of a Soul someone had lobbed at me.

"For once, I agree with you."

Around us, the war raged. Ginevra had gathered an incredible army: the Damned, zombies, and various types of ferocious beasts defended our cause, battling the Witches' army, which was composed of subjugated Subterraneans and a multitude of battle-trained Amazons. In the fray I recognized many prisoners I'd seen before in the Castle, including Faustian, who had joined our side. The rebels confronting the Witches were in the thousands, but our adversaries seemed infinite. The Witches summoned Hell-spawned creatures that swarmed in from all corners of the underworld. They conjured up statues of animals, which they then brought to life.

Ginevra battled like a lioness, Simon and Peter at her side, while Drake had joined Stella. She was so skilled and so fierce in battling the Mizhyas that she seemed like one of them. I scanned the battle for Gemma and spotted her not far away, keeping the Souls of the Damned at bay. As I struggled through the crowd to reach her, my sword turned even against my allies to defend her. I would allow no one to harm her. "Gemma, we need to get out of here. My friends will help us escape."

"You will all die for this affront to the Empress!"

"We're taking you away from here whether you like it or not!" I shouted over the din. She pulled out her crossbow and aimed it at my face. "Please, come with me," I pleaded. "Your place is with me."

"My place is here. With Sophìa."

"Sophìa betrayed you, can't you see that? She didn't hesitate a second to order the death of the Champion *you* chose."

A mighty boom drowned out the frenzy of the battle. We stopped, alert, and a large blue-eyed gorilla barreled toward us, raging. Gemma leapt out of the way and I dodged it a second before it could crush me. I watched her rush to her Saurus that had swooped down to her rescue. She grabbed hold of it with a single hand and leapt onto its back. Argas took wing. I struck down every creature in my path in my attempt to follow Gemma. She came to a halt above her Sisters, who were battling in the form of panthers, slid off Argas, and joined forces with them. One by one, the Witches morphed back into their human forms. All at once, the sky darkened and a barrier surrounded them, advancing with them and destroying everyone it touched. All the Damned retreated, but Ginevra stood her ground and faced them.

"Step aside," Gemma ordered her.

"Come away with us and no one will get hurt," Ginevra promised.

"You've lost your mind!"

"You're the one who's not thinking straight! You're blinded by love for Sophìa. She ordered the death of your Champion. We're here to save him *and* you."

"I don't need to be saved."

"I'm your Sister."

"No you aren't. Not any more. They're my Sisters. Did you really think you could defeat us with a bunch of rebels? Consider them dead meat."

"Don't count on it—they all have my blood in their bodies."

"Then this means war."

A lightning bolt streaked the sky and Ginevra's entire army returned to the fray. I found Simon and Drake and joined them in battle. The Witches weren't ordinary adversaries; their powers were immense. The air itself was imbued with black magic and it took all our strength to withstand it. Each Subterranean summoned the elements to help: air, earth, water, and fire—the fire that the Witches so feared and that now threatened them in their own territory, within their Castle walls. Their serpents hissed, sinking their fangs into Damned Souls and rebel Subterraneans alike. They fell like leaves in the wind. Peter was on his knees, Devina's whip coiled around his neck. I hadn't yet learned what his special power was but it must have been strong, because he freed himself from the whip and pinned the Witch against the wall.

Absolon was also there, longbow in hand. He quickly killed off the Empress's guards and headed straight for the Witches. Somewhere in the distance the massive volcano erupted, making the ground quake. I used my power over the earth to summon the poison that impregnated the soil. It rose up, forming a giant arch. Simon set it on fire and hurled it against the Witches, who defended themselves by creating a vacuum around them so the fire would have no oxygen to feed on. But the spell weakened their protective shield, opening a gap that we took advantage of to launch a new attack. Against their Soldiers we used the poisoned weapons Ginevra had prepared. Our lances and arrows burned with angel fire.

A Witch hurled a lightning bolt straight at me, but at the last second Argas pushed me out of its path. Gemma looked in our direction, surprised by her Saurus's action. Anya also came running. She'd stayed close to Gemma since the revolt had begun. Though she hadn't openly joined our side, she had to have been the one who gave Faustian the Devil's Claw. Anya was there not to stand in our way but to protect Gemma, and I hoped she would help persuade her to come with us.

A Subterranean nocked two flaming arrows. I realized too late whom he was aiming at. "Gemmaaa!!!" Horror filled my eyes. I tried to stop them, but one of them flew toward her, the fire piercing the twilight. Anya looked at me in shock and pushed Gemma out of the way, taking the arrow in the chest. A tear slid down her cheek before a wave of flames engulfed her. Her body instantly exploded into thousands of black butterflies.

"Anyaaa!!!" Gemma screamed, kneeling where her Sister had been a second before. In despair, Ginevra slew the Subterranean who'd killed Anya. Sophìa's shriek echoed throughout the realm. For an instant the battle halted as the sky transformed, filling suddenly with a tempest of lightning bolts that hurled their fury down on us. Gemma's eyes transformed, becoming inhuman, as she flung herself at her adversaries.

All at once something stopped her and she crumpled to her knees. For a second I feared someone had hit her, but then she raised her head and her eyes met mine. It was like finding each other again after centuries. She clenched her fists against the ground, her eyes fixed intensely on me, as a burst of emotion struck me full in the chest. "Evan," she murmured.

She remembered. Tears filled my eyes. *"Gem."*

My Gem—I had found her! I ran toward her, killing anyone who got in my way, but a swarm of black butterflies descended upon us like the darkest of prophecies, lifted some of the Damned from the ground, and tore them apart in midair before lashing out at me and hurling me away.

"Sophìa, no!" Gemma screamed, her voice cracking with desperation.

The Empress materialized in front of me, in her eyes all the world's evil. "*You* are the cause of this!" she thundered. "Now *die*, Soldier!" She hurled her serpent straight at me and I realized that this was the end. Now that I had finally found my Gem, I was about to die.

Gemma's agonized shriek shook the sky. "Noooo!!!" As Sophìa's Dakor opened its fangs, there was a deafening boom, like a wave of energy holding back time. Gemma's voice filled my mind. *"He must live."*

"It will be forever and there will be no return."

I cringed, my blood running cold. It was the Màsala.

"It doesn't matter. As long as he's alive, my soul will be at peace."

The strange power subsided. I glimpsed another blurred form darting past me and realized to my horror it was Gemma's serpent. I turned toward her, desperate, but it was too late. A tear slid from Gemma's eye an instant before Sophìa's Dakor sank its fangs into her serpent, ripping off its head.

Gemma's eyes, still fixed on mine, grew wide as the pain her Dakor had felt flooded through her. Ever so slightly, her lips moved: "*Atyantam.*" Her body exploded into a swarm of black butterflies.

My mind reeled from the shock and tears flooded my eyes. I clenched my teeth and let out a shriek of pain that pierced the sky. Dazed, I watched the battle raging all around me. Ginevra was on the ground, sobbing and clutching the earth where a moment earlier Gemma had been. Sophìa sank to her knees, paralyzed.

No! No! No! It couldn't end like this. I couldn't finally find her only to lose her again. Why had she done it? She'd sacrificed herself for me, dying in my place. I sobbed. The pain was unbearable; it wracked my chest. I turned toward the battle and realized I'd undertaken a journey with no return. Without Gemma, nothing had meaning any more. I began to run, tearing a sword out of the hands of one of the Damned, lopping off heads and venting my rage on anyone who stepped into my path. Argas's cry of anguish rose up in the night as he circled in the air above us. I ran to him and he swooped down so I could leap onto his back and continue my massacre, hurling fireballs at the accursed Witches as the Saurus charged ahead in a futile attempt—like my own—to escape the pain. Subterraneans, Witches, the Damned—I didn't care who I struck down. I didn't care about anything any more. I had lost everything. No one deserved to live more than Gemma. They all had to die.

Brandishing my sword, I was rushing at a group of Soldiers when a voice filled my head. *"Evan, stop."* A shiver crept through me and I froze. It was Gemma. I turned around and her big dark eyes locked onto mine. "Enough," she said softly.

I slid off Argas's back and rushed to her, wiping away the tears that blurred my view of her. I crumpled to my knees at her feet and wept. She cradled my head and I held her tight. She too knelt and I stroked her hair with the desperation of a man condemned to death. I rested my forehead against hers, our eyes exchanging forbidden promises.

"How . . ." It was Gemma's soul I was embracing. She wasn't there to stay.

"You're free. Your soul no longer belongs to me." Gemma touched her neck. The Dreide with which she'd claimed me was gone.

"I don't want to be free of you. My soul will belong to you forever."

"Evan . . ." she murmured, taking my hand. I squeezed my eyes shut as more tears flooded them, shaking my head because I knew what she was about to tell me—what was about to happen.

"No. Don't say it. Please don't say it," I begged her.

"I'm here to say goodbye to you."

I held her tight against me, clenching my fists. I couldn't accept it. I couldn't let her go. "Stay with me," I whispered, on the verge of madness. "Stay with me, I'm begging you. I can't lose you now that I've found you again."

"I can't stay. I prayed for forgiveness and it was granted to me." She stared at me, her eyes mirroring my desperation. "I couldn't leave without thanking you for fighting for me up to the very end."

I shook my head. "Without you, nothing I did means anything any more."

"It means something to me, Evan. You freed me."

"It wasn't supposed to end this way. We were supposed to be together forever."

"This was how it had to end all along, but meanwhile you gave me the world. Death has whispered its last song to me."

"I didn't save you."

"Yes you did. My soul will be at peace now."

A hooded figure appeared behind Gemma. It was one of the Màsala. Her great sacrifice had delivered her from the darkness, but crossing over into the light would take her away from me forever. I held her tight, refusing to let her leave me. "No. I won't let you go." A tear slid down my cheek. Never had I been so desperate. "This shouldn't have happened." I shook my head. "It shouldn't have happened."

"We fought to prevent it but fate was against us, Evan. I'll never regret having tried. I've lived moments with you I'll never forget."

"There won't be any more. There won't be any more moments for us together!" I whispered. "You know the curse I'm under. If you pass over, I'll lose you forever. Why did you do it? Why did you stop fighting?"

"I only stopped fighting for myself. Now it's time for me to protect you. If you had died today, I never would have forgiven myself. There won't be any more wars to fight, Evan."

"This is the end—the end of everything."

Gemma took my hand in hers and raised it, gazing at our joined palms, our vows interlacing for the last time. "There will never be a true end for us."

Our palms pressed closer, caressed each other, explored each other for the last time. I looked at her fingers, stroking them, trying to memorize her touch. I would never experience it again. The Màsala behind her approached. Gemma's gaze plumbed mine in a final farewell as a tear slid silently from my eyes. Then she disappeared.

I sank to my knees. I had lost her forever.

"Enough!" A commanding voice resounded through the night, and the battle all around me ceased. I was still on the ground, dazed and heartbroken. Slowly I raised my head, but only because it had been Ginevra's voice.

I started when I saw she was at Sophìa's side. "The war will come to an end. Now!" she ordered. Everyone looked around, suddenly freed from her dark spell. I stared at her, bewildered, and she detected my thoughts. "It's over, Evan," she whispered, looking devastated. "We lost, but at least you can save yourselves."

"There's nothing left in me to save."

"Yes there is. I led this revolt. I'll be the one to pay the price . . . in exchange for your lives."

"No!" Simon stepped forward, emerging from the crowd.

Ginevra turned to look at him and a tear slid down her cheek. "Earth isn't a good place for those like us. I'm sorry. I have no choice."

"But I do," Simon replied, and she nodded. If Ginevra had decided to remain in Hell to put an end to the war, Simon would stay there with her. A band of panthers surrounded me and a Witch bound my wrists behind my back. I stood and let them lead me away, casting a final glance at Simon and Ginevra.

The air shimmered in front of me as the portal opened. I saw Drake staring at me from his position at the head of our army. He was covered with blood and ash, and his powerful body was shielding Stella's protectively. We looked at each other one last time. Driven forward by the Witch and the panthers, I crossed through the portal and all the chaos disappeared. The Witch didn't speak; the panthers made not a sound. They too were mourning. I allowed them to lead me to the center of the Dànava, my eyes lost in the void as the mechanism was activated and a whirlwind of butterflies came to life around me, dragging me out of Hell.

But a worse Hell dwelled in my soul that had been darkened forever. I had lost Gemma. I had lost everything.

Thunder. Inside me and out.
Bolts of lightning. They crash down onto the confines of my reason.
Light. Darkness. Shadows.
Vain hope.

52

A FINAL PROMISE

I stared at Gemma's casket as they covered it with dirt. It was empty, like my heart and everything else that remained of me. Even the sky wept, bathing the black umbrellas of the community that had come together to say a final farewell to my wife and our child. I let its tears fall on me. I didn't deserve its consolation.

Breaking the news to Gemma's parents had been the hardest thing I'd ever done. Their grief was like salt in my bleeding wound. Her father had collapsed to the floor in tears. Her mother had hit me over and over, refusing to believe it. At the end she had clung to me as we wept bitter tears together, tears that burned like the deadliest of poisons.

I gripped the violin tighter, squeezing my eyes shut as I moved the bow across the strings, playing a final lullaby for Gemma and Liam. I would never see them again. The notes cut into me, exposing my pain as Gemma's eyes returned to fill my mind. Every time those eyes looked at me, my heart broke in two to let her in. She was inside me and no condemnation could ever move her from there. But death had breathed its last whisper into her ear. There would be no happy ending for us—for any of us.

Ginevra had sacrificed her freedom in exchange for my life and Simon's. He too had made up his mind, refusing to leave her. And so he'd stayed with her in Hell.

Someone rested a hand on my shoulder. It was Peter. When I looked up, I saw that the crowd had dispersed and we were alone. "I'm sorry," he said.

"They let you go," I remarked.

"Simon intervened for me. He stayed in the Castle with Ginevra."

"He'll get by. He's strong."

"I know. Ginevra imposed some conditions."

"You fought well. Thank you for protecting Gemma."

"I didn't do it for you." He looked down. "You know, when I got back from Hell I went to eat of the Tree," he admitted. He was talking about Eden, but not even he dared say the name aloud, almost as though it had become a forbidden place. "It's strange, knowing she's there and I can't see her." I closed my eyes. I hadn't found the courage to do the same. "I stayed a while, listening. I tried to imagine her there next to me. Maybe she really was there and I didn't know it. It's frustrating. But you—you haven't eaten of the Tree since you got back from the war, have you?"

I didn't reply. Peter was right, but I couldn't go back there. I'd once told Gemma there was no world where we could be together. Inside me I'd always hoped it wasn't true, but it was. We were separated, in two different worlds, lost Souls who would never meet again.

It had happened. What I'd feared from the very start had happened: Gemma had crossed over. I'd lost her. Like a dream that fades with the morning light, it was the end. The end of everything. The end of *me*.

"I know I can't replace your friends, just like no one could ever replace the one I lost," Peter continued, "but I want you to know you can count on me, for anything." I nodded my thanks. "I have to go now." Peter turned and walked away, leaving me alone with Gemma.

I stared at the engraving on her headstone. Leaning over, I stroked the stone. The words transformed beneath my fingertips and my final promise to her appeared.

Atyantam

A year later

I turned down the car stereo as I stopped at the light. Pink Floyd was playing *Wish You Were Here.* I looked out the window. Outside, standing on the sidewalk, Gemma gazed at me. She smiled . . . and then vanished. I gripped the steering wheel. Her soul lived on inside me.

53

ETERNAL PEACE

I went to the lakeshore to watch the water ripple as the wind caressed it like a lover. Filling my lungs with air, I closed my eyes and smiled. Gemma's image was still vivid in my mind, a salve for my soul tormented by her absence. I sought her inside me whenever the pain filled my chest as I waited for it all to be over. I'd been waiting for such a long time, but now the end was near—I could feel it. Soon I too would find peace.

I looked at the lake house and imagined Gemma standing in the doorway, waiting for me with Liam in her arms. It was a lie, I knew it—a lie to lessen my pain. I couldn't be honest with myself.

After Gemma's funeral I'd gathered her things from the family manor, set fire to the house, and watched it burn until nothing was left. Drake, Simon, Ginevra, Liam . . . Gemma. One by one they'd vanished like ghosts, leaving the huge house empty. When all that remained was ash, I'd returned to the house on the lake, seeking refuge in the memory of us, and waited for Death to finally claim me as well. Without having eaten of the Tree, I'd lost first my powers, then my strength. I struggled against gripping hunger and my blood burned with the desperate need for Ambrosia.

A few days before, Devina had returned to me, proposing I stay with her, speaking to me for the first time in a serious tone. I even noted a glimmer of sadness in her eye. She'd promised me peace, but for me, peace had one name only, and that name had been eliminated from that world. I no longer wanted to be there.

I'd been left all alone because of the decisions I'd made. That April morning when Gemma had missed her appointment with Death, I'd destroyed the lives of everyone I cared about: Drake, Simon, and Ginevra had ended up in Hell; Gemma and the baby were in Heaven, far from me. I was trapped, exiled from everything I loved. I should have gone to Hell to receive the punishment I deserved, but I wasn't brave enough. Not because of the torture—I could have withstood the Witches' torture for all eternity if there had been hope—but I couldn't live another day knowing I'd lost Gemma and Liam forever. My heart had disintegrated and the crumbs were too small to piece back together. And so I had decided I would dissolve. A few more hours and everything would end in Oblivion. I would have peace—a peace I didn't deserve, but without which I could no longer continue.

Ginevra had snuck back for a visit and begged me to eat of the Tree, but my mind was made up. I wasn't even carrying out my orders any more. What was the point? Even worse, the idea of helping a Soul cross over was unbearable, knowing that everyone could see her except me.

Since the dawn of time, the sun had risen and set every day and time had moved inexorably forward as millions of Souls passed through life, one after the other. Gemma was one of them. Her time was up. And though I'd tried everything to keep her with me, nature—the nature she'd loved so dearly—had taken her, to restore balance. In the order of the universe, she was but one of countless Souls. To me, she was the whole universe.

I raised my hand to my neck and took off my dog tag, to which I had linked Gemma's necklace, and looked at them one last time, reading the engravings.

Gevan
Atyantam

I tied the two chains into a knot that would never be undone, eternal witness to our love, and cast them over the water. At the peak of their arc they sparkled, kissed by the light of the sun as it gave them its blessing. They hit the surface of the lake and sank, settling on the lakebed where no one would separate them ever again. Together. Like Gemma and I could no longer be. A solitary tear slid down my face.

I lowered my hand and examined it in the morning light. It was almost transparent. I smiled. I was beginning to fade, and there was no better place for it to happen than the lake house, our special hideaway. It was there that we'd made love the first time, there that our child had been born. It was there that I wanted it all to end. I would finish in Oblivion, but a shadow of me would wander the woods for eternity, reliving the magic of our times together. The first time she'd promised herself to me as I held her against that tree. I stroked its bark, where she once had stood, as though I could touch her again . . . just one last time before vanishing forever.

Her laughter still filled the air. Her gaze burned inside me each time I closed my eyes.

Are you here to protect me? Is that your mission?

A reckless Angel.

My heart belongs to you forever.

Inside, I was happy because no one could deprive us of our memories. They were a priceless gift. They were my expiation.

Keep playing for me, Evan.

Wherever I went, I would take them with me. And even if the two of us were apart, those memories would be eternal.

Out of the blue, someone grabbed my leg. I spun around and my eyes went wide with surprise. It was a Subterranean, on the verge of vanishing. "H . . . eeelll . . . help . . . me . . ."

Thoughts crowded my mind. He needed to eat of the Tree. I could help him cross over—but I couldn't go back there because in my condition the lure of the fruit would be too powerful to resist. I had to decide fast. The young man fixed his eyes on me, pleading for my help. Suddenly I thought of Liam, of the man he might have become, and of whoever one day might have had the power to decide whether to spare him or end his life.

I reached out and rested a hand on his shoulder. The world around us transformed and disappeared. *"Go. Follow your need,"* I told him in my mind.

"Thank you." I could hear his voice, but he'd already vanished.

I was back in Eden. Alone. I looked at the row of pillars surrounding me where I'd once been with Gemma. They called it the Celestial City, but inside me everything was dark. Knowing she was there and I couldn't see her drove me mad. Maybe she was talking to me and I couldn't hear her voice. I closed my eyes, praying for her to speak louder so I could hear. The scent of the fruit filled my nostrils and I clenched my fists. I had to be strong, one last time. I had to leave before the temptation became too difficult to ignore. Soon I would disappear—it wouldn't be long.

I prepared myself to return to Earth, but a sudden stinging sensation spread over my left arm, a pain I'd never felt before. Had Death come to take me? Would I disappear right there, with Gemma so close to me, hidden from my eyes by my curse? It was a good place to die.

The stinging grew stronger. I turned my hand over and my eyes widened in bewilderment. I wasn't vanishing. It was the mark of the Children of Eve that was burning. Its claws withdrew like a snare unraveling, freeing me from its punishment. In shock, I examined it, trying to understand what was happening to me.

A voice broke my eternal silence: "Finally." I stood stock-still. Was madness claiming me just before I vanished? It couldn't be. Slowly I turned around.

She was there. "It took you long enough." Gemma smiled at me and my eyes filled with tears.

"Daddy!"

My eyes shot toward the second voice and Liam ran up to me. I swept him up in my arms and lifted him into the air, my heart bursting with joy. "Liam!" I exclaimed, hugging him tight.

Gemma watched us, a smile on her lips and her expression radiant. I put our son down and gazed at her for a long, eternal moment before smothering her in my arms. Then I broke down and wept all the tears left in me.

"We've been waiting for you for so long."

I closed my eyes at the sound of her voice. "It's really you . . ." I murmured. I cupped her face in my hands and kissed her as desperation returned to torment me, telling me it wasn't true, it must be a dream or a mirage my mind had sought refuge in to cope with the pain. I held Gemma even tighter, touching her face, her skin, to make sure she was real. "I'm afraid that if I let you go you'll disappear again," I confessed, squeezing my eyes shut.

"I'm here," she reassured me. "I'm not going anywhere."

"But . . . how is this possible?" The mark of the Children of Eve had disappeared and I could see the other Souls around us.

"You had your expiation, Evan. Your curse is lifted."

"Did you do it?"

"It's not every day that a Witch renounces evil and chooses to die in the name of love. I kept my promise: I searched inside myself and there I found you."

I held her tight. "What's going to happen now?"

"Our souls will be immortal."

"You were here and I . . . I'm sorry I kept you waiting."

"I would have waited for you for eternity."

"Gem." I rested my forehead against hers and smiled, my eyes full of tears.

She took my hand, biting her lip. "There's someone else who's been waiting for you too."

I looked at her questioningly as a woman in a white dress appeared. My eyes went wide. "Mother!"

"Hello, Evan." My mother smiled and walked up to me. It seemed impossible that at last I could hug her again. I held her close and invited Gemma to join us as well. Liam grabbed hold of my leg and we all laughed. I had reunited with my family.

I was in Heaven. And this time it would be forever.

EPILOGUE

High atop our vast treehouse, I rested my hand on a small branch to help it grow as I watched Gemma playing with Liam at the edge of Red Lagoon where the Moon Maidens sang, warming us with their breath.

The house was almost ready. I'd fashioned a corner of Heaven just for us and soon it would become our hideaway. To build it I hadn't needed to chop down trees—just the opposite: I'd made their branches grow and intertwine over our heads, leaving ample spaces to watch the light displays in the sky. Inside, everything was made of woven branches, including a large bed I would cover with soft petals, a reading corner for Gemma and, most importantly, a large bookcase where she could keep the books I'd brought for her.

I leapt down and ran over to them at the water's edge. "Well? What do you think?" I asked Gemma, stealing a kiss.

"It's lovely." Flowers blossomed on the windowsill, filling it with colors. I lay on my stomach beside her and the water drenched me up to my waist. Gemma looked at me, a little smile on her lips. "Did you really have to take off your shirt to fix up our hideaway?"

I smiled. "Actually, no. That was for you. I was hoping to arouse sinful thoughts," I shot back, one eyebrow raised. "Did it work?"

She bit her lip and sought my mouth. "What do you think?"

"Daddy! Look what I can do!"

We both turned toward Liam, who disappeared under the water and attempted a handstand but failed. Gemma and I laughed, but the instant he emerged, bursting with enthusiasm, we grew serious again.

"That was really good, sweetheart. Keep trying," Gemma told him.

For a moment we watched him in silence. Liam was a bright, exuberant child. Not a day went by that he didn't learn new things or discover new places. He'd grown a year older in Eden—the same amount of time that had elapsed since his death, as though it had never happened. He wasn't a Soul like the others and none of us could understand why. Sometimes I imagined it was because his soul had been taken by one of the Màsala, but then I would convince myself it made no sense.

Days had passed since we'd found each other. We both missed Simon, Drake, and Ginevra, but our family was finally together for the first time, and that was what counted most. My brothers and sister had all made their own decisions and our paths had parted, but nothing—neither death nor destiny—could destroy certain bonds, and one day we would all find a way to be back together again.

On that now-distant April morning, my decision to save Gemma from the semi that was supposed to run her over had changed our fates and led us to that final agonizing battle. In Hell things had come to a head and it had seemed there was no longer any hope for us, but Gemma's ultimate sacrifice, made in the name of love, had put an end to it all. It had been rewarded with redemption: Gemma's and my own.

My fear had never been that Gemma would die, but the fact that once she passed on I would never see her again, since death would separate us due to my curse. As it turned out, the solution to the problem wasn't Gemma's immortality but my expiation.

She'd told me what actually happened during those terrible moments when I'd lost her. Just before she fell to her knees on the battlefield, her mind had flooded with memories: her shrieks of pain filling the forest, the wailing of newborn Liam. My voice calming her. The joy that filled her heart as Liam looked at her. She remembered that I'd been there to squeeze her hand.

When Sophìa hurled her deadly serpent at me, Gemma had sent a desperate cry for help to the Màsala. Time had stopped as they surrounded her. She asked that I be saved. The Màsala replied that it had all begun with her and that only she could put an end to it all. She could save me by choosing to renounce evil, sacrificing her life for mine. No Witch had ever done so before. Sophìa's poison had spawned her and in the same way only her venom could break the bond and free her from evil. Sophìa had been both her punishment and her atonement. When time began to advance again, Gemma hadn't hesitated to pit her serpent against the Empress's.

Kill a Dakor and his Witch dies with him. Her sacrifice had saved us both. At that moment, not even she knew that by asking to save me she would also be redeeming my soul.

"Liam, look who's come to visit you," Gemma called to him.

He emerged from the lagoon, cheeks bulging, and spat out a mouthful of water. "Grandma!"

"Welcome back, Danielle," Gemma told her. My mother came to see us often. Liam adored her and she'd stayed with him when I wasn't there.

"Hello, Mother."

She smiled at me and leaned over to kiss me on the head. "Liam, what do you say? Shall we go for a walk, you and I? I saw some red butterflies down in the valley."

Liam's eyes went wide with excitement and he ran to Gemma. "Can I go, Mommy?"

"Of course, sweetheart."

"Let's go! Let's go, Grandma!" he exclaimed, tugging on her arm.

My mother laughed at his enthusiasm. "I'll bring him back later." She and Gemma exchanged a strange look and my mother winked at her before disappearing with Liam.

"What's going on?" I asked suspiciously.

Gemma brushed it off. "What? I don't know what you're talking about."

"Oh, you don't?" I straddled her and tried to tickle a confession out of her.

She managed to break free and pin me beneath her instead. "Your mother is happy to see us together, that's all."

"Oh, now I get it," I whispered, moving closer to her mouth. "Keeping my shirt off worked. You wanted to be alone with me," I said to provoke her. "I'm warning you, our hideaway isn't ready yet. They might see us."

She ran her hands down my bare chest and her eyes sent me a sensual challenge. "Just because we're in Heaven doesn't mean we shouldn't break the rules any more."

I raised an eyebrow and pulled her against me. "Little witch," I murmured, craving her lips. She obliged me and our kiss grew hot and passionate. I rolled over on the sand and trapped her beneath my body. Her eyes pierced me whenever they rested on mine. Gemma wasn't a Witch any more, but I was still prey to her spell. My soul was hers.

"Kiss me, Evan," she whispered, and I obeyed. The hot water of the lagoon bathed our intertwined bodies as we made love, hidden in our little corner of Heaven, contemplating our eternal love.

The fire inside us eased into a sweet warmth as we held each other close, listening to the sound of the Moon Maidens. "I told you, Gem," I whispered, watching the shimmering particles drift through the air, "in the shade of that maple tree, when we pledged our love for the first time, I told you."

"What?"

"That we would find a world where we could be together. This is going to be our world." Gemma rubbed her head against my chest and began to hum a little tune. "What's that?" I asked, curious. Suddenly I remembered Eden was full of trees with trunks that looked like overlapping reeds and produced incredible music. I often stopped there to compose melodies using my power to control the air, and soon I would show them to Gemma.

"It's been in my head for a while—a song that's always made me think of us: *Uncover* by Zara Larsson."

"I'll show you an incredible place here in Heaven where everything is music."

"Is there really one? And can I listen to whatever I want?"

"Everything. Every form of art is a window to Heaven. We can go there now, if you like."

"No, let's stay here a little longer—just us."

I rested my chin on her head. "Sing it, then."

Gemma sighed and tenderly took my hand. *"Nobody sees, nobody knows. We are a secret, can't be exposed. That's how it is, that's how it goes. Far from the others, close to each other . . ."*

"You're right. It's perfect. Please, don't stop."

We were hidden in a dream that was all mine and Gemma's—a dream that would never end. No one could see us in that new world of ours. Gemma and I were a secret that couldn't be exposed. Far from everyone else, close to each other.

A butterfly with transparent wings alit on her hand and she contemplated it, fascinated. I closed my eyes and she began to sing softly again. I never wanted to stop listening to her voice. Being there with her was so wonderful it all seemed like a dream and I was afraid it might end at any moment.

But a whisper filled my mind, and I knew I had to go. Those were the hardest moments—when I received a mission and the fear of not finding Gemma upon my return came back to torment me. "Evan, can Souls return to Earth?" she asked me out of the blue. "Before you showed up here, I tried to."

"Souls can't cross over." Gemma grew sad. "Not on their own . . . but you have me. I can ferry Souls, remember? If you want, we can go back now and then."

Her face lit up. "Do you think Ginevra and Simon could also return once in a while?"

I laughed at her enthusiasm. "It was supposed to be a surprise, but at this point I guess I have to spill the beans. Ginevra and I have already talked about it. She misses you and wants to see you again. We'll be meeting secretly in our hideaway one day each month so we can be together again."

"When?"

"Soon. *And* . . . Drake will be there too. He's eager to meet Liam." I smiled. Earth, which had divided us, would now be our meeting place.

Gemma's eyes filled with tears. "How is that possible? What about Stella?"

"The Souls of the Damned aren't like Subterraneans. Simon and Drake can cross through the portal, thanks to Ginevra, but for Stella it would be too risky."

Gemma nodded. "Now you need to go," she said, sensing that I'd gotten a mission, though I hadn't said anything.

I stood up. "I'll be back soon. I promise."

She pressed her knees to her chest. "Don't worry, I'll be here waiting for you."

Smiling at her, I vanished. Though I was now free from the curse of the Subterraneans, orders had continued to appear in my head, and despite not being obligated to any more, I'd decided to continue my mission. No Soldier ever really stopped being a Soldier. I'd been to Hell, I'd seen the evil that corroded the world, I'd seen mortal Souls lose themselves to the darkness, but I could help them find the light again. I could save them. I'd been given a gift—

being able to find the person I loved when everything seemed lost forever. They all had the right to that same chance, and I helped them achieve it by helping them cross over.

I found myself on a desolate road, the same one where a few days earlier I'd come for a young man who'd been speeding on his motorcycle. The car I was waiting for came around the bend. Inside it was an elderly couple. I wouldn't take their lives—their time hadn't yet come. I was only there to make sure their fate took the right direction. I had to make them turn back in order to avoid the accident that later would claim the lives of others.

I carried out my mission and got the couple to make a U-turn. A car behind them stopped to give them room for the maneuver. I was about to leave when something made me freeze. Behind the wheel of the car was a young woman . . . *and she was looking at me.*

I frowned and stared into her eyes until she passed me by. She pulled over up ahead and looked behind her. Had she really seen me, then? I materialized beside her and studied her from close up. No, she couldn't see me. Her gaze was lost in the void, her expression focused, as though her mind were quickly processing information. She grabbed a tissue from the glove box, rifled through her purse, pulled out a pen, and began to jot something down. Soon she pulled out another tissue and another still.

One glimpse of the snippets she was writing made me start.

. . . *incredible gray eyes. What if only I could see him? And what if he had come for me?*

I studied the young woman again, but no, she couldn't see me, nor did she seem aware of my presence. Shaking my head, I laughed at myself. It must have been a coincidence. I turned around and focused on Gemma.

She welcomed me upside down, hanging from a branch by her knees, her head dangling in front of mine. "That was quick," she said.

I looked at her and grinned. "Get down from there, you little squirrel."

Gemma let herself fall, challenging me to catch her. "Well? Where were you this time?" she asked. Now that Death wasn't hunting her any more, Gemma had stopped fearing the darker side of me and always wanted me to tell her every detail.

"In a little town in Sicily."

"Sicily? Fascinating," she said enthusiastically.

"Yeah."

"What is it? You look shaken."

"Something weird happened," I admitted. She was all ears. "I was there to make sure an elderly couple made the right decision, but then a woman drove by and she . . . *saw me.*"

"What do you mean, she saw you?" Gemma asked, puzzled.

"I had the impression she looked me straight in the eye. She even pulled her car over to look back."

"Do you think it's happening again?"

"No, I don't think so. It wasn't like when it was you seeing me. It was different. It was like she saw me in her mind's eye . . . Like she'd only imagined me. I don't know how to describe it."

"And then what happened?"

"She took out a pen and started writing."

Gemma's eyes lit up. "What if she's a writer? Maybe her imagination pushed her mind beyond the confines of the mortal world!"

I sprawled out on the grass and chuckled. "You've got to stop reading those paranormal novels."

"Lots of writers don't know they *are* writers until they find the right story. Maybe you inspired her and she might become one," she continued, ignoring me. "Let's tell her our story, Evan! Let's whisper it in her mind. You know how much I love books. We could have one all our own."

I looked at Gemma dubiously. "Are you serious?" She didn't need to answer; her eyes spoke for her—*sparkled* for her. I smiled. "All right, let's do it. That way the whole world will know our story and will know true love exists."

Gemma smiled back at me and took my hand. "And that death isn't the end."

The room was illuminated by light from the window. Outside, birds chirped in the blossoming lemon trees. The young woman was there, her back to us, leaning over a blank sheet of paper.

"That's her," I told Gemma.

"I'm so excited!"

"Why are you whispering? She can't hear us," I teased her. It was true, but why, then, had the woman's pen stopped? She seemed to be listening.

"Look, she's writing about you. You were right. She saw you."

I moved closer and read what the woman was writing.

His eyes. They'd enchanted me like a dark spell, carrying me away to their fortress dungeon. As clear as crystal, as ardent as fire, they stirred up a whirlwind of uncontrollable emotion inside me. I watched them narrow, sharp as ice, as he stared at me in astonishment, but there was no trace of coldness in his gaze. It was warm, comforting. Like a mystical connection, it drew me to him and wouldn't let go.

I jumped. It really was bizarre. "You sure you want to do this?"

Gemma nodded, a light in her eyes. She peeked at the page and frowned. "She set their first encounter in an alley."

I laughed. "Gasp! We'd better roll up our sleeves, then!"

Gemma shot me a dirty look like she did whenever I teased her. She leaned in close to the young woman's ear and began to whisper to her heart. The woman's hand stopped on the page. She thought for a moment, then crossed out the word "alley" and above it wrote "woods."

Gemma continued with great joy and the woman followed her lead, racing her pen across the page to avoid missing a word. She seemed excited about our story. At times she laughed, at others a tear slid down her cheek. Whenever Gemma stopped she would appear to grow nervous, look at the page, gnaw on her pen, and await another whisper. Meanwhile, I looked through the woman's books and read a few of them. From time to time I would fill in for Gemma so the story could have my point of view as well.

"All right, that's enough for today," I told Gemma, who looked at me sadly. "It's already dark out. She's been writing nonstop for over six hours. She'll get cramps in her hand."

"Is it so late already? I was having loads of fun!" Gemma looked out the window. Night had fallen, shrouding everything, but neither she nor the woman had noticed.

"We'll come back tomorrow," I promised. "Right now there's someone else who can't wait to see you. Let's not keep them waiting." I squeezed Gemma's shoulders and we turned around, ready to leave, but Gemma stopped.

"Wait! We don't even know her name."

At my command, a breath of wind slipped in through the window, flipping over the pages of her notebook and closing it. The woman started and looked around as though she'd sensed our presence.

I squeezed Gemma's hand. It was time to go. I read the name written on the cover of the notebook and smiled before vanishing. *Until tomorrow, Elisa S. Amore.*

The air was cool, the bikes' roars filled the night, and Gemma was behind me, like in the old days. "You should ride with me instead," Ginevra told her. "It's a lot more fun to watch the others from the finish line."

"That's a lesson I taught you myself, little sister. Catch me if you can." My bike reared up and Gemma squeezed her arms around me.

"Man, have I missed you guys!" Drake exclaimed.

"We've missed you too, bro," Simon replied, jamming on the front brake to raise his rear wheel.

"I didn't mean you. I was talking about our bikes. Duh!"

Gemma shook her head. "I missed our nighttime races. You're lucky I don't have a bike of my own. I would cream you all!"

"I would never challenge a woman who's ridden a prehistoric horse," I joked.

"He's not a prehistoric horse!" Gemma laughed, thinking affectionately of Argas. "Okay, actually I guess you could call him that."

We looked at each other, our bikes lined up on the starting line. "First one across the Tri-Lakes region and back?" Simon challenged us.

"Lake Placid, Saranac Lake, and Tupper Lake. A joyride," I said.

"Prepare to eat my dust." Ginevra winked at me.

"I'm in." Drake gunned his engine, making the bike beneath him smolder. "Let the party begin."

The motorcycles roared, zooming off like missiles toward our new future. "*Hold on tight, Gem.*"

"I'm a Soul now. I can't die, remember?"

"*I wasn't saying it for you, but for me.*" Gemma held me tighter and I reared up.

We were ready to race: three Subterraneans, a Witch, and a redeemed Soul, separated by different worlds but united by the same emotion. Because bonds—be they of love or friendship—know no bounds.

Nobody sees, nobody knows.
We are a secret, can't be exposed.
That's how it is. That's how it goes.
Far from the others, close to each other.

Atyantam.

A few years later

"Liam! Where have you run off to?"

"Here I am!" he answered his mother.

Playing with the butterflies was Liam's favorite pastime. He would study them when they alit on his fingers, watch them flutter about, and spend hours lying in the fields letting them cover him.

"Liam!"

"Coming!"

Reluctantly, the boy let his red butterfly go, promising he would be back. He turned to leave, obeying his mother. From the rock where it rested, the butterfly watched him walk away. Something had happened after the boy touched it. The creature moved its big red wings as it transformed. At last it spread them and rose into the air, displaying to the world what it had become.

A magnificent black butterfly.

Hi! I'm Elisa S. Amore. Thank you for reading my series. I hope you enjoyed it, I can't wait to share my future books with you. Want to hear directly from me about my new releases?

Text AMORE to 77948 and I'll send you a message when my next book is out (US only).
If you prefer emails join my list of readers at:
www.ElisaSAmore.com/vip-list

And don't miss Drake and Stella's story: Dark Tournament!

***

If you enjoyed this book, consider supporting me by leaving a review wherever you purchased it. I'd love it!

THANK YOU.

ACKNOWLEDGEMENTS

Here we are at the end of this long—and, for me, unforgettable—journey. Gemma and Evan's love story has made me experience incredible emotions and touched my heart. As always, I hope you felt some of those emotions too. I'm grateful for the affection that all my readers and bloggers have lavished on these two star-crossed lovers, and it is most of all to you that I owe heartfelt THANKS for reading my story. Thank you for all the messages and emails, all the support and word-of-mouth publicity . . . Thank you for loving Evan and Gemma, for rejoicing and suffering along with them. Thank you for believing deep down in their true love. It means the world to me!

This journey wouldn't have been possible without the support of my husband Giuseppe. Thank you, my love, for your trust in me and your understanding during my intense writing sessions. And thanks most of all to my greatest treasure, my son Gabriel Santo. You're myreason for everything. I hope you learn from my experience to always pursue your dreams and fight with everything you have to achieve them, because no goal is ever too far away if you don't stop chasing after it.

I owe a debt of gratitude to my family for their support and unconditional love, and for all the chores they took over for me so I could work on my writing! Thank you,Mamma and Papa. I love you with all my heart!

Much-deserved thanks to the fantastic team at Editrice Nord publishers for the trust and enthusiasm they showed for Evan and Gemma's story right from the start. My dream was my passion, but thanks to you it also became my profession, and I couldn't be happier. In particular, I'm grateful to Cristina Prasso, who chose each title with great care and enthusiasm. It takes a great person to run a great publishing house, and I'm honored to have been chosen. Thanks most of all to my Italian editor Giorgia Di Tolle for being among the first people to experience Evan and Gemma's adventure at my side.

My final, heartfelt respects to the late Luigi Bernabò, who believed in me right from the start. I'll never forget his words when, after reading the first Italian draft of The Caress of Fate,he told me the text needed more work,but that my story had struck him because it had a voice. Thank you, Luigi, wherever you are.

I'm grateful to my American translator Leah Janeczko and my editor Annie Crawford, because thanks to them, Evan and Gemma's story crossed the border and won over thousands of American readers in a very short time. Okay, I admit it might have been partly because of Evan too!

Once again, my gratitude to Professor Saverio Sani for his translations into Sanskrit and Devanagari. And my appreciation to all the readers who got tattoos! If you got one too, or are thinking of doing so, please send me a picture!

An infinite THANK YOU to Alex McFaddin and Rhiannon Patterson, whose indispensable help allowed me to enrich the Touched saga with actual details about Lake Placid and its school, Lake Placid High. Thanks to the artists I mentioned in the books; I wanted Evan and Gemma to hear their songs because they gave me inspiration for many scenes. All my gratitude goes to Lana Del Rey, James Blunt, Hans Zimmer, Amy Lee,and Zara Larsson. Also, many thanks to the administrators of the saga's official page. You're FANTASTIC and your help is priceless to me!

I couldn't write these acknowledgements without thanking my pug Bam Bam—who inspired the character Irony—for keeping me company during my countless hours of writing, from the first to the last book—even though he slept the whole time!

I must admit I procrastinated in writing these acknowledgements—maybe because I didn't feel ready to write the last page of this great love story. But deep down, Gevan will live on in my mind and I hope in yours too. If you'd like to share your thoughts about them with me, write to me. You can find me on my Facebook page! I always read all the messages I receive, and I try to reply to most of them. And don't forget to stop by the saga's official site at www.touchedsaga.com, where you'll find quizzes, polls, and lots of exclusive content created just for you. Again, my thanks to all the bloggers who welcomed Evan and Gemma into their reading circles, and to all those who will welcome them in the future. Your support is truly precious!

And so here we are at the end. When I first imagined Evan and Gemma's love story and pulled over to the side of that road to jot down my ideas, I wasn't sure how it would end, but now I know there couldn't be a more fitting ending for them, because love—the true love we hold inside, the love we truly believe in, for which we're willing to fight against everyone and everything—that love always prevails.

Until the next adventure!

Affectionately,
Elisa

THE AUTHOR

Elisa S. Amore is the author of the paranormal romance saga *Touched.* She wrote the first book while working at her parents' diner, dreaming up the story between one order and the next. She lives in Italy with her husband, her son, and a pug that sleeps all day. She's wild about pizza and traveling, which is a source of constant inspiration for her. She dreamed up some of the novels' love scenes while strolling along the canals in Venice and visiting the home of Romeo's Juliet in romantic Verona. Her all-time favorite writer is Shakespeare, but she also loves Nicholas Sparks. She prefers to do her writing at night, when the rest of the world is asleep and she knows the stars above are keeping her company. She's now a full-time writer of romance and young adult fiction. In her free time she likes to read, swim, walk in the woods, and daydream. She collects books and animated movies, all jealously guarded under lock and key. Her family has nicknamed her "the bookworm." After its release, the first book of her saga quickly made its way up the charts, winning over thousands of readers. *Touched: The Caress of Fate* is her debut novel and the first in the four-book series originally published in Italy by one of the country's leading publishing houses. The book trailer was shown in Italian movie theaters during the premiere of the film *Twilight: Breaking Dawn—Part 2.*

Sign up for Elisa S. Amore's newsletter at: www.ElisaSamore.com/vip-list
Text AMORE to 77948 to get new release alerts

Find Elisa Amore online at www.touchedsaga.com and www.ElisaSAmore.com
On Facebook.com/eli.amore
On Twitter.com/ElisaSAmore
On Instagram/eli.amore
Add the book to your shelf on Goodreads!

Join the Official Group on FB to meet other fans addicted to the series:
Touched Saga Official Group

If you have any questions or comments, please write us at
touchedsaga@gmail.com

For Foreign and Film/TV rights queries, please send an email to
elisa.amore@touchedsaga.com

Citation credits:
Sanskrit text (Chapter 25) from the *Rig Veda*/Mandala 1/Hymn 89
The Honeysuckle and the Hazel Tree (Chapter 9), translated by Patricia Terry in *The Honeysuckle and the Hazel Tree: Medieval Stories of Men and Women.* Berkeley: University of California Press, 1995.
Credit lyrics:
Book 3: Dark Paradise by Lana Del Rey
Book 4: All of Me by John Legend
Book 4: Uncover by Zara Larsson

CPSIA information can be obtained
at www.ICGtesting.com
Printed in the USA
LVHW020147121220
674003LV00008B/263

9 781947 425088